DEAN KOONTZ

THREE COMPLETE NOVELS

DEAN KOONTZ

THREE COMPLETE NOVELS

◆ ◆ ◆

STRANGERS
THE VOICE OF THE NIGHT
THE MASK

G. P. PUTNAM'S SONS　　NEW YORK

G. P. Putnam's Sons
Publishers Since 1838
200 Madison Avenue
New York, NY 10016

Library of Congress Cataloging-in-Publication Data

Koontz, Dean R. (Dean Ray), date.
[Novels, Selections]
Three complete novels / Dean Koontz.
p.   cm.
Contents: Strangers—The voice of the night—The mask.
ISBN 0–399–13927–3
I. Title.
PS3561.O55A6   1994   93–26290   CIP
813'.54—dc20

Printed in the United States of America

1   2   3   4   5   6   7   8   9   10

CONTENTS

◆ ◆ ◆

STRANGERS

◆ ◆ ◆

To Bob Tanner
whose enthusiam at a crucial stage
was more important than he can know.

Definition for "fugue" on p. 26 taken from *Taber's Cyclopedic Medical Dictionary* Clayton L. Thomas, M.D., M.P.H., (Ed.), 12th Edition, p. F-44. Published in 1973 by F.A. Davis Company, Philadelphia.

PART ONE

◆ ◆ ◆

A TIME OF TROUBLE

A faithful friend is a strong defense.
A faithful friend is the medicine of life.
—APOCRYPHA

A terrible darkness has fallen upon us,
but we must not surrender to it. We shall
lift lamps of courage and find our way
through to the morning.
—ANONYMOUS MEMBER OF THE
FRENCH RESISTANCE (1943)

ONE

◆

November 7–December 2

1. Laguna Beach, California

Dominick Corvaisis went to sleep under a light wool blanket and a crisp white sheet, sprawled alone in his bed, but he woke elsewhere—in the darkness at the back of the large foyer closet, behind concealing coats and jackets. He was curled in the fetal position. His hands were squeezed into tight fists. The muscles in his neck and arms ached from the tension of a bad though unremembered dream.

He could not recall leaving the comfort of his mattress during the night, but he was not surprised to find that he had traveled in the dark hours. It had happened on two other occasions, and recently.

Somnambulism, a potentially dangerous practice commonly referred to as sleepwalking, has fascinated people throughout history. It fascinated Dom, too, from the moment he became a baffled victim of it. He had found references to sleepwalkers in writings that dated as far back as 1000 B.C. The ancient Persians believed that the wandering body of a sleepwalker was seeking his spirit, which had detached itself and drifted away during the night. Europeans of the grim medieval period favored demonic possession or lycanthropy as an explanation.

Dom Corvaisis did not worry about his affliction, though he was discomfited and somewhat embarrassed by it. As a novelist, he was intrigued by these new nocturnal ramblings, for he viewed all new experiences as material for his fiction.

Nevertheless, though he might eventually profit from creative use of his own somnambulism, it *was* an affliction. He crawled out of the closet, wincing as the pain in his neck spread up across his scalp and down into his shoulders. He had difficulty getting to his feet because his legs were cramped.

As always, he felt sheepish. He now knew that somnambulism was a condition to which adults were vulnerable, but he still considered it a childish problem. Like bed-wetting.

Wearing blue pajama bottoms, bare-chested, slipperless, he shuffled across the living room, down the short hall, into the master bedroom, and into the bath. In the mirror, he looked dissipated, a libertine surfacing from a week of shameless indulgence in a wide variety of sins.

In fact, he was a man of remarkably few vices. He did not smoke, overeat, or take drugs. He drank little. He liked women, but he was not promiscuous; he believed in commitment in a relationship. Indeed, he had not slept with anyone in—what was it now?—almost four months.

He only looked this bad—dissipated, wrung-out—when he woke and discovered that he had taken one of his unscheduled nocturnal trips to a makeshift bed. Each time he had been exhausted. Though asleep, he got no rest on the nights he walked.

He sat down on the edge of the bathtub, bent his leg up to look at the bottom of his left foot, then checked the bottom of his right foot. Neither was cut, scratched, or particularly dirty, so he had not left the house while sleepwalking. He had awakened in closets twice before, once last week and once twelve days prior to that, and he had not had dirty feet on those occasions, either. As before, he felt as if he had traveled miles while unconscious, but if he actually had gone that far, he had done it by making countless circuits of his own small house.

A long, hot shower soaked away a lot of his muscle discomfort. He was lean and fit, thirty-five years old, with recuperative powers commensurate with his age. By the time he finished breakfast, he felt almost human.

After lingering with a cup of coffee on the patio, studying the pleasant geography of Laguna Beach, which shelved down the hills toward the sea, he went to his study, sure that his work was the cause of his sleepwalking. Not the work itself so much as the amazing success of his first novel, *Twilight in Babylon,* which he had finished last February.

His agent put *Twilight* up for auction, and to Dom's astonishment a deal was made with Random House, which paid a remarkably large advance for a first novel. Within a month, movie rights were sold (providing the down-payment on his house), and the Literary Guild took *Twilight* as a main selection. He had spent seven laborious months of sixty-, seventy-, and eighty-hour weeks in the writing of that story, not to mention a decade getting himself *ready* to write it, but he still felt like an overnight success, up from genteel poverty in one great leap.

The once-poor Dominick Corvaisis occasionally caught a glimpse of the now-rich Dominick Corvaisis in a mirror or a sun-silvered window, saw himself unguarded, and wondered if he really deserved what had come his way. Sometimes he worried that he was heading for a great fall. With such triumph and acclaim came considerable tension.

When *Twilight* was published next February, would it be well received and justify Random House's investment, or would it fail and humiliate him? Could he do it again—or was *Twilight* a fluke?

Every hour of his waking day, these and other questions circled his mind with vulturine persistence, and he supposed the same damn questions still swooped through his mind while he slept. That was why he walked in his sleep: he was trying to escape those relentless concerns, seeking a secret place to rest, where his worries could not find him.

Now, at his desk, he switched on the IBM Displaywriter and called up chapter eighteen on the first disk of his new book, as yet untitled. He had stopped yesterday in the middle of the sixth page of the chapter, but when he summoned the document, intending to begin where he had left off, he saw a full page where there had been half. Unfamiliar green lines of text glowed on the word processor's video display.

For a moment he blinked stupidly at the neat letters of light, then shook his head in pointless denial of what lay before him.

The back of his neck was suddenly cool and damp.

The existence of those unremembered lines on page six was not what gave him the creeps; it was what the lines *said.* Furthermore, there should not have been a page seven in the chapter, for he had not yet created one, but it was there. He also found an eighth page.

As he scrolled through the material on the disk, his hands became clammy.

The startling addition to his work-in-progress was only a two-word sentence, repeated hundreds of times:

I'm scared. I'm scared. I'm scared. I'm scared.

Double-spacing, quadruple indentation, four sentences to a line, thirteen lines on page six, twenty-seven lines on page seven, another twenty-seven on page eight—that made 268 repetitions of the sentence. The machine had not created them by itself, for it was merely an obedient slave that did precisely what it was told. And it made no sense to speculate that someone had broken into the house during the night to tamper with his electronically stored manuscript. There were no signs of a break-in, and he could not think of anyone who would play such a prank. Clearly, he had come to the word processor while sleepwalking and had obsessively typed in this sentence 268 times, though he had absolutely no recollection of having done it.

I'm scared.

Scared of what—sleepwalking? It was a disorienting experience, at least on the morning end, but it was not an ordeal that would cause such terror as this.

He was frightened by the quickness of his literary ascent and by the possibility of an equally swift descent into oblivion. Yet he could not completely dismiss the nagging thought that this had nothing to do with his career, that the threat hanging over him was something else altogether, something strange, something his conscious mind did not yet see but which his subconscious perceived and which it had tried to convey to him by means of this message left while he was sleeping.

No. Nonsense. That was only the novelist's overactive imagination at work. Work. That was the best medicine for him.

Besides, from his research into the subject, he knew that most adult sleepwalkers made short careers of it. Few experienced more than half a dozen episodes, usually contained within a time span of six months or less. Chances were good that his sleep would never again be complicated by midnight ramblings and that he would never again wake huddled and tense in the back of a closet.

He deleted the unwanted words from the disk and went to work on chapter eighteen.

When he next looked at the clock, he was surprised to see that it was past one and that he had labored through the lunch hour.

Even for southern California, the day was warm for early November, so he ate lunch on the patio. The palm trees rustled in a mild breeze, and the air was scented with autumn flowers. With style and grace, Laguna sloped down to the shores of the Pacific. The ocean was spangled with sunlight.

Finishing his last sip of Coke, Dom suddenly tilted his head back, looked straight up into the brilliantly blue sky, and laughed. "You see—no falling safe. No plummeting piano. No sword of Damocles."

It was November 7.

2. Boston, Massachusetts

Dr. Ginger Marie Weiss never expected trouble in Bernstein's Delicatessen, but that was where it started, with the incident of the black gloves.

Usually, Ginger could deal with any problems that came her way. She relished every challenge life presented, thrived on trouble. She would have been bored if her path had been always easy, unobstructed. However, it had never occurred to her that she might eventually be confronted with trouble she could not handle.

As well as challenges, life provides lessons, and some are more welcome than others. Some lessons are easy, some difficult.

Some are devastating.

Ginger was intelligent, pretty, ambitious, hard-working, and an excellent cook, but her primary advantage in life was that no one took her seriously on first encounter. She was slender, a wisp, a graceful sprite who seemed as insubstantial as she was lovely. Most people underestimated her for weeks or months, only gradually realizing that she was a formidable competitor, colleague—or adversary.

The story of Ginger's mugging was legend at Columbia Presbyterian, in New York, where she had served her internship four years prior to the trouble at Bernstein's Delicatessen. Like all interns, she had often worked sixteen-hour shifts and longer, day after day, and had left the hospital with barely enough energy to drag herself home. One hot, humid Saturday night in July, after completing an especially grueling tour of duty, she headed for home shortly after ten o'clock— and was accosted by a hulking Neanderthal with hands as big as shovel blades, huge arms, no neck, and a sloping forehead.

"You scream," he said, launching himself at her with jack-in-the-box suddenness, "and I'll bust your goddamned teeth out." He seized her arm and twisted it behind her back. "You understand me, bitch?"

No other pedestrians were close, and the nearest cars were two blocks away, stopped at a traffic light. No help in sight.

He shoved her into a narrow night-mantled serviceway between two buildings, into a trash-strewn passage with only one dim light. She slammed into a garbage bin, hurting her knee and shoulder, stumbled but did not fall. Many-armed shadows embraced her.

With ineffectual whimpers and breathless protests, she made her assailant feel confident, because at first she thought he had a gun.

Humor a gunman, she thought. Don't resist. Resisters get shot.

"Move!" he said between clenched teeth, and he shoved her again.

When he pushed her into a recessed doorway three-quarters of the way along the passage, not far from the single faint bulb at the end, he started talking filthy, telling her what he was going to do with her after he took her money, and even in the poor light she could see he held no weapon. Suddenly she had hope. His vocabulary of obscenities was blood-curdling, but his sexual threats were so stupidly repetitive that they were almost funny. She realized he was just a big dumb loser who relied on his size to get what he wanted. Men of his type seldom carried guns. His muscles gave him a false sense of invulnerability, so he probably had no fighting skill, either.

While he was emptying the purse that she willingly relinquished, Ginger summoned all her courage and kicked him squarely in the crotch. He doubled over from the blow. She moved fast, seized one of his hands, and bent the index finger backward, savagely, until the pain must have been as excruciating as the throbbing in his bruised privates.

Radical, violent, backward extension of the index finger could quickly incapacitate any man, regardless of his size and strength. By this action she was straining the digital nerve on the front of his hand while simultaneously pinching the highly sensitive median and radial nerves on the back. The intense pain also traveled into the acromial nerves in his shoulder, into his neck.

He grabbed her hair with his free hand and pulled. That counterattack hurt, made her cry out, blurred her vision, but she gritted her teeth, endured the agony, and bent his captive finger even farther. Her relentless pressure quickly banished all thought of resistance from his mind. Involuntary tears burst from his eyes, and he dropped to his knees, squealing and cursing and helpless.

"Let go of me! Let go of me, you *bitch!*"

Blinking sweat out of her eyes, tasting the same salty effluence at the corners of her mouth, Ginger gripped his index finger with both hands. She shuffled cautiously backward and led him out of the passage in an awkward three-point crawl, as if dragging a dangerous dog on a tightened choke-chain.

Scuttling, scraping, hitching, and humping himself along on one hand and two knees, he glared up at her with eyes muddied by a murderous urge. His mean, lumpish face became less visible as they moved away from the light, but she could see that it was so contorted by pain and fury and humiliation that it did not seem human: a goblin face. And in a shrill goblin voice he squealed a chilling array of dire imprecations.

By the time they had clumsily negotiated fifteen yards of the serviceway, he was overwhelmed by the agony in his hand and by the sickening waves of pain rushing outward through his body from his injured testicles. He gagged, choked, and vomited on himself.

She still did not dare let go of him. Now, given the opportunity, he would not merely beat her senseless: he would kill her. Disgusted and terrified, she urged him along even faster than before.

Reaching the sidewalk with the befouled and chastened mugger in tow, she saw no pedestrians who could call the police for her, so she forced her humbled assailant into the middle of the street, where passing traffic came to a standstill at this unexpected spectacle.

When the cops finally arrived, Ginger's relief was exceeded by that of the thug who had attacked her.

In part, people underestimated Ginger because she was small: five-two, a hundred and two pounds, not physically imposing, certainly not intimidating. Likewise, she was shapely but not a blond bombshell. She *was* blond, however, and the particular silvery shade of her hair was what caught a man's eye, whether he was seeing her for the first time or the hundredth. Even in bright sunshine her hair recalled moonlight. That ethereally pale and radiant hair, her delicate features, blue eyes that were the very definition of gentleness, an Audrey Hepburn neck, slender shoulders, thin wrists, long-fingered hands, and her tiny waist—all contributed to a misleading impression of fragility. Furthermore, she was quiet and watchful by nature, two qualities that might be mistaken for timidity. Her voice was so soft and musical that anyone could easily fail to apprehend the self-assurance and underlying authority in those dulcet tones.

Ginger had inherited her silver-blond mane, cerulean eyes, beauty, and ambition from her mother, Anna, a five-foot-ten Swede.

"You're my golden girl," Anna said when Ginger graduated from sixth grade at the age of nine, two years ahead of schedule, after being promoted twice in advance of her peers.

Ginger had been the best student in her class and had received a gilt-edged scroll in honor of her academic excellence. Also, as one of three student performers who had provided entertainment before the graduation ceremony, she had played two pieces on the piano—Mozart, followed by a ragtime tune—and had brought the surprised audience to its feet.

"Golden girl," Anna said, hugging her all the way home in the car.

Jacob drove, blinking back tears of pride. Jacob was an emotional man, easily moved. Somewhat embarrassed by the frequency with which his eyes moistened, he usually tried to conceal the depth of his feelings by blaming his tears or reddened eyes on a never-specified allergy. "Must be unusual pollens in the air today," he said twice on the way home from graduation. "Irritating pollens."

Anna said, "It's all come together in you, *bubbeleh*. My best features and your father's best, and you're going places, by God, you just wait and see if you aren't. High school, then college, then maybe law school or medical school, anything you want to do. Anything."

The only people who *never* underestimated Ginger were her parents.

They reached home, turned into the driveway. Jacob stopped short of the garage and said, in surprise, "What are we doing? Our only child graduates from sixth grade, our child who—since she can do absolutely *anything*—will probably marry the King of Siam and ride a giraffe to the moon, our child wears her first cap and gown and we aren't celebrating? Should we drive into Manhattan, have maybe champagne at the Plaza? Dinner at the Waldorf? No. Something better. Only the best for our giraffe-riding astronaut. We'll go to the soda fountain at Walgreen's!"

"Yeah!" Ginger said.

At Walgreen's, they must have been as odd a family as the soda jerk had ever seen: the Jewish father, not much bigger than a jockey, with a Germanic name but a Sephardic complexion; the Swedish mother, blond and gloriously feminine, five inches taller than her husband; and the child, a wraith, an elf, petite though her mother was not, fair though her father was dark, with a beauty altogether different from her mother's—a more subtle beauty with a fey quality. Even as a child, Ginger knew that strangers, seeing her with her parents, must think she was adopted.

From her father, Ginger had inherited her slight stature, soft voice, intellect, and gentleness.

She loved them both so completely and intensely that, as a child, her vocabulary had been insufficient to convey her feelings. Even as an adult, she could not find the words to express what they had meant to her. They were both gone now, to early graves.

When Anna died in a traffic accident, shortly after Ginger's twelfth birthday, the common wisdom among Jacob's relatives was that both Ginger and her father would be adrift without the Swede, whom the Weiss clan had long ago ceased to regard as an interloping gentile and for whom they had developed both respect and love. Everyone knew how close the three had been, but, more important, everyone knew that Anna had been the engine powering the family's success. It was Anna who had taken the least ambitious of the Weiss brothers—Jacob the dreamer, Jacob the meek, Jacob with his nose always in a detective novel or a science fiction story—and made something of him. He had been an employee in a jewelry store when she married him, but by the time she died he owned two shops of his own.

After the funeral, the family gathered at Aunt Rachel's big house in Brooklyn Heights. As soon as she could slip away, Ginger sought solace in the dark solitude of the pantry. Sitting on a stool, with the aroma of many spices heavy in the air of that narrow place, praying to God to bring her mother back, she heard Aunt Francine talking to Rachel in the kitchen. Fran was bemoaning the grim future awaiting Jacob and his little girl in a world without Anna:

"He won't be able to keep the business going, you know he won't, not even once the grief has passed and he goes back to work. The poor *luftmensch.* Anna was his common sense and his motivation and his best adviser, and without her in five years he'll be lost."

They were underestimating Ginger.

To be fair, Ginger was only twelve, and even though she was already in tenth grade, she was still a child in most people's eyes. No one could have foreseen that she would fill Anna's shoes so quickly. She shared her mother's love of cooking, so in the weeks following the funeral she pored through cookbooks, and, with the amazing diligence and perseverance that were her trademarks, she acquired what culinary skills she had not already learned. The first time relatives came for dinner after Anna's death, they exclaimed over the food. Homemade potato rolls and cheese *kolacky.* Vegetable soup with plump cheese and beef *kreplach* floating in it. Schrafe fish as an appetizer. Braised veal paprika, *tzimmes* with prunes and potatoes, creamy macaroni patties fried in hot fat and served in tomato sauce. A choice of baked peach pudding or apple *schalet* for dessert. Francine and Rachel thought Jacob was hiding a marvelous new housekeeper in the kitchen. They were disbelieving when he pointed to his daughter. Ginger did not think she had done anything remarkable. A cook was needed, so she became a cook.

She had to take care of her father now, and she applied herself to that responsibility with vigor and enthusiasm. She cleaned house swiftly, efficiently, and with a thoroughness that defied her Aunt Francine's sub rosa inspections for dust and grime. Although she was only twelve, she learned to plan a budget, and before she was thirteen she was in charge of all the household accounts.

At fourteen, three years younger than her classmates, Ginger was the valedictorian of her high-school class. When it became known that she had been accepted by several universities but had chosen Barnard, everyone began to wonder whether, at the tender age of fourteen, she had finally taken too big a bite and would choke trying to swallow it.

Barnard *was* more difficult than high school. She no longer learned faster than the other kids, but she learned as well as the best of them, and her grade average was frequently 4.0, never less than 3.8—and *that* was the semester in her junior year when Jacob was sick with his first bout of pancreatitis, when she spent every evening at the hospital.

Jacob lived to see her get her first degree, was sallow and weak when she received her medical degree, even hung on tenaciously until she had served six months of her internship. But after three bouts of recurring pancreatitis, he developed pancreatic cancer, and he died before Ginger had finally made up her mind to go for a surgical residency at Boston Memorial instead of pursuing a career in research.

Because she had been given more years with Jacob than she had been given with her mother, her feelings for him were understandably more profound, and the loss of him was even more devastating than the loss of Anna had been. Yet she dealt with that time of trouble as she dealt with every challenge that came her way, and she finished her internship with excellent reports and superb recommendations.

She delayed her residency by going to California, to Stanford for a unique and arduous two-year program of additional study in cardiovascular pathology. Thereafter, following a one-month vacation (by far the longest rest she had ever taken), she moved East again, to Boston, acquired a mentor in Dr. George Hannaby (chief of surgery at Memorial and renowned for his pioneering achievements in various cardiovascular surgical procedures), and served the first three-quarters of her two-year residency without a hitch.

Then, on a Tuesday morning in November, she went into Bernstein's Deli to buy a few items, and terrible things began happening. The incident of the black gloves. That was the start of it.

Tuesday was her day off, and unless one of her patients had a life-threatening crisis, she was neither needed nor expected at the hospital. During her first two months at Memorial, with her usual enthusiasm and tireless drive, she had gone to work on most of her days off, for there was nothing else that she would rather do. But George Hannaby put an end to that habit as soon as he learned of it. George said that the practice of medicine was high-pressure work, and that every physician needed time off, even Ginger Weiss.

"If you drive yourself too hard, too fast, too relentlessly," he said, "it's not only you that suffers, but the patient as well."

So every Tuesday she slept an extra hour, showered, and had two cups of coffee while she read the morning paper at the kitchen table by the window that looked out on Mount Vernon Street. At ten o'clock she dressed, walked several blocks to Bernstein's on Charles Street, and bought pastrami, corned beef, home-made rolls or sweet pumpernickel, potato salad, blintzes, maybe some lox, maybe some smoked sturgeon, sometimes cottage cheese *vareniki* to be reheated at home. Then she walked home with her bag of goodies and ate shamelessly all day while she read Agatha Christie, Dick Francis, John D. MacDonald, Elmore Leonard, sometimes a Heinlein. While she had not yet begun to like relaxation half as much as she liked work, she gradually began to enjoy her time off, and Tuesday ceased to be the dreaded day it had been when she first began her reluctant observance of the six-day week.

That bad Tuesday in November started out fine—cold with a gray winter sky, brisk and invigorating rather than frigid—and her routine brought her to Bernstein's (crowded, as usual) at ten-twenty-one. Ginger drifted from one end of the long counter to the other, peering into cabinets full of baked goods, looking through the cold glass of the refrigerated display cases, choosing from the array of delicacies with gluttonous pleasure. The room was a stewpot of wonderful smells and happy sounds: hot dough, cinnamon; laughter; garlic, cloves; rapid conversations in which the English was spiced with everything from Yiddish to Boston accents to current rock-and-roll slang; roasted hazelnuts, sauerkraut; pickles; coffee; the *clink-clank* of silverware. When Ginger had everything she wanted, she paid for it, pulled on her blue knit gloves, and hefted the bag, going past the small tables at which a dozen people were having a late breakfast, then headed for the door.

She held the grocery bag in her left arm, and with her free hand she tried to put her wallet back in the purse that was slung over her right shoulder. She was looking down at the purse as she reached the door, and a man in a gray tweed topcoat and a black Russian hat entered the deli at that moment, his attention as distracted as hers; they collided. As cold air swept in from outside, she stumbled backward a step. He grabbed at her bag of groceries to keep it from falling, then steadied her with one hand on her arm.

"Sorry," he said. "That was stupid of me."

"My fault," she said.

"Daydreaming," he said.

"I wasn't looking where I was going," she said.

"You all right?"

"Fine. Really."

He held the bag of groceries toward her.

She thanked him, took the bag—and noticed his black gloves. They were obviously expensive, of high-grade genuine leather, so neatly and tightly stitched that the seams were hardly visible, but there was nothing about those gloves that could explain her instant and powerful reaction to them, nothing unusual, nothing strange, nothing threatening. Yet she *did* feel threatened. Not by the man. He was ordinary, pale, doughy-faced, with kind eyes behind thick tortoiseshell glasses. Inexplicably, unreasonably, the gloves themselves were what abruptly terrified her. Her breath caught in her throat, and her heart hammered.

The most bizarre thing was the way every object and all the people in the deli began to fade as if they were not real but merely figments of a dream that was dissolving as the dreamer woke. The customers having breakfast at the small tables, the shelves laden with canned and packaged food, the display cases, the wall clock with the Manischewitz logo, the pickle barrel, the tables and chairs all seemed to shimmer and slip away into a niveous haze, as if a fog was rising from some realm beneath the floor. Only the portentous gloves did not fade, and, in fact, as she stared at them they grew more detailed, strangely more vivid, more *real,* and increasingly threatening.

"Miss?" the doughy-faced man said, and his voice seemed to come from a great distance, from the far end of a long tunnel.

Although the shapes and colors of the delicatessen bleached toward white on all sides of Ginger, the sounds did not dwindle as well but, instead, grew louder, louder, until her ears filled with a roar of meaningless jabber and with the jarring clatter of silverware, until the clinking of dishes and the soft chatter of the electronic cash register were thunderous, unbearable.

She could not take her eyes off the gloves.

"Is something wrong?" the man asked, holding up one leather-clad hand, half-reaching toward her in an inquisitive gesture.

Black, tight, shiny . . . with a barely visible grain to the leather, neat little stitches along the fingers . . . taut across the knuckles . . .

Dizzy, disoriented, with a tremendous weight of indefinable fear pressing down on her, she suddenly knew that she must run or die. Run or die. She did not know why. She did not understand the danger. But she *knew* she must run or perish where she stood.

Her heartbeat, already fast, became frantic. The breath that was snagged in her throat now flew free with a feeble cry, and she lunged forward as if in pursuit of the pathetic sound that had escaped her. Amazed by her response to the gloves but unable to be objective about it, confused by her own behavior even as she acted, clutching the grocery bag to her breast, she shouldered past the man who had collided with her. She was only vaguely aware that she almost knocked him off his feet. She must have wrenched open the door, though she could not remember having done so, and then she was outside, in the crisp November air. The traffic on Charles Street—car horns, rumbling engines, the hiss-sigh-crunch of tires—was to her right, and the deli windows flashed past on her left as she ran.

Thereafter she was oblivious of everything, for the world around her faded completely away, and she was plunging through a featureless grayness, legs pumping hard, coattails flapping, as if fleeing across an amorphous dreamscape, struck dumb by fear. There must have been many other people on the sidewalk, people whom she dodged or shoved aside, but she was not cognizant of them. She was aware only of the need to escape. She ran deer-swift though no one pursued her, with her lips peeled back in a grimace of pure terror though she could not identify the danger from which she fled.

Running. Running like crazy.

Temporarily blind, deaf.

Lost.

Minutes later, when the mists cleared, she found herself on Mount Vernon Street, part of the way up the hill, leaning against a wrought-iron railing beside the front steps of a stately red-brick town house. She was gripping two of the iron balusters, with her hands curled so tightly around them that her knuckles ached, her forehead on the heavy metal balustrade as if she were a melancholy prisoner slumped against the door of her cell. She was sweating and gasping for breath. Her mouth was dry, sour. Her throat burned, and her chest ached. She was bewildered, unable to recall how she had arrived at this place, as if washed onto an alien shore by moon-timed tides and waves of amnesia.

Something had frightened her.

She could not remember what it had been.

Gradually the fear subsided, and her breathing regained an almost regular rhythm; her heartbeat slowed slightly.

She raised her head and blinked her eyes, looking around warily and in bafflement as her tear-blurred vision slowly cleared. She turned her face up until she saw the bare black branches of a linden and a low, ominous gray November sky beyond the skeletal tree. Antique iron gas lamps glowed softly, activated by solenoids that had mistaken the wintry morning for the onset of dusk. At the top of the hill stood the Massachusetts State House, and at the bottom the traffic was heavy where Mount Vernon intersected Charles Street.

Bernstein's Delicatessen. Yes, of course. It was Tuesday, and she had been at Bernstein's when . . . when something happened.

What? What had happened at Bernstein's?

And where was the deli bag?

She let go of the iron railing, raised her hands, and blotted her eyes on her blue knit gloves.

Gloves. Not hers, not *these* gloves. The myopic man in the Russian hat. His black leather gloves. That was what had frightened her.

But why had she been gripped by hysteria, overwhelmed by dread at the sight of them? What was so frightening about black gloves?

Across the street, an elderly couple watched her intently, and she wondered what she had done to draw their attention. Though she strained to remember, she could not summon the faintest recollection of her journey up the hill. The past three minutes—perhaps longer?—were utterly blank. She must have run up Mount Vernon Street in a panic. Evidently, judging by the expressions on the faces of those observing her, she had made quite a spectacle of herself.

Embarrassed, she turned away from them and started hesitantly down Mount Vernon Street, back the way she had come. At the bottom, just around the corner, she found her bag of groceries lying on its side on the pavement. She stood over it for long seconds, staring at the crumpled brown bundle, trying to recall the moment when she had dropped it. But where that moment should have been, her memory contained only grayness, nothingness.

What's wrong with me?

A few items had spilled from the fallen parcel, but none was torn open, so she put them back in the paper sack.

Unsettled by her baffling loss of control, weak in the knees, she headed home, her breath pluming in the frosty air. After a few steps she halted. Hesitated. Finally she turned back toward Bernstein's.

She stopped just outside the deli and had to wait only a minute or two before the man in the Russian hat and the tortoiseshell glasses came out with a grocery bag of his own.

"Oh." He blinked in surprise. "Uh . . . listen, did I say I'm sorry? The way you stormed out of there, I thought maybe I'd only *meant* to say it, you know—"

She stared at his leather-sheathed right hand where it gripped the brown paper bag. He gestured with his other hand as he spoke, and she followed it as it described a brief, small pattern in the chilly air. The gloves did not frighten her now. She could not imagine why the sight of them had thrown her into a panic.

"It's all right. I was here waiting to apologize. I was startled and . . . and it's been an unusual morning," she said, quickly turning away from him. Over her shoulder, she called out, "Have a nice day."

Although her apartment was not far away, the walk home seemed like an epic journey over vast expanses of gray pavement.

What's wrong with me?

She felt colder than the November day could explain.

She lived on Beacon Hill, on the second floor of a four-story house that had once been the home of a nineteenth-century banker. She'd chosen the place because she liked the carefully preserved period detail: elaborate ceiling moldings, medallions above the doorways, mahogany doors, bay windows with French panes, two fireplaces (living room, bedroom) with ornately carved and highly polished marble mantels. The rooms had a feeling of permanence, continuity, stability.

Ginger prized constancy and stability more than anything, perhaps as a reaction to having lost her mother when she was only twelve.

Still shivering even though the apartment was warm, she put away the groceries in the breadbox and refrigerator, then went into the bathroom to look closely at herself in the mirror. She was very pale. She did not like the hunted, haunted look in her eyes.

To her reflection, she said, "What happened out there, *shnook?* You were a real *meshuggene,* let me tell you. Totally *farfufket.* But why? Huh? You're the big-shot doctor, so tell me. *Why?*"

Listening to her voice as it echoed off the high ceiling of the bathroom, she knew she was in serious trouble. Jacob, her father, had been a Jew by virtue of his genes and heritage, and proud of it, but he had not been a Jew by virtue of his religious practices. He seldom went to synagogue and observed holidays in the same secular spirit with which many fallen-away Christians celebrated Easter and Christmas. And Ginger was one step farther removed from the faith than Jacob had been, for she called herself an agnostic. Furthermore, while Jacob's Jewishness was integral, evident in everything he did and said, that was not true of Ginger. If asked to define herself, she would have said, "Woman, physician, workaholic, political dropout," and other things before finally remembering to add, "Jew." The only time Yiddish peppered her speech was when she was in trouble, when she was deeply worried or scared, as if on a subconscious level she felt those words possessed talismanic value, charms against misfortune and catastrophe.

"Running through the streets, dropping your groceries, forgetting where you are, afraid when there's no reason to be afraid, acting like a regular *farmishteh*," she said disdainfully to her reflection. "People see you behaving like that, they'll think for sure you're a *shikker*, and people don't go to doctors who're drunkards. *Nu?*"

The talismanic power of the old words worked a little magic, not much but enough to bring color to her cheeks and soften the stark look in her eyes. She stopped shivering, but she still felt chilled.

She washed her face, brushed her silver-blond hair, and changed into pajamas and a robe, which was her usual ensemble for a typically self-indulgent Tuesday. She went into the small spare bedroom that she used as a home office, took the well-thumbed *Taber's Cyclopedic Medical Dictionary* from the bookshelf, and opened it to the F listings.

Fugue.

She knew what the word meant, though she did not know why she had come in here to consult the dictionary when it could tell her nothing new. Maybe the dictionary was another talisman. If she looked at the word in cold print, it would cease to have any power over her. Sure. Voodoo for the overeducated. Nevertheless, she read the entry:

> **fugue** (fyug) [L. *fuga,* flight]. Serious personality dissociation. Leaving home or surroundings on impulse. Upon recovering from the fugue state there usually is loss of memory for actions occurring while in the state.

She closed the dictionary and returned it to the shelf.

She had other reference volumes that could provide more detailed information about fugues, their causes and significance, but she decided not to pursue the matter. She simply could not believe her transient attack had been a symptom of a serious medical problem.

Maybe she was under too much stress, working too hard, and maybe the overload had led to that one, isolated, transient fugue. A two- or three-minute blank. A little warning. So she would continue taking off every Tuesday and would try to knock off work an hour earlier each day, and she would have no more problems.

She had worked very hard to be the doctor that her mother had hoped she would be, to make something special of herself and thereby honor her sweet father and the long-dead but well-remembered and desperately missed Swede. She had made many sacrifices to come this far. She had worked more weekends than not, had forgone vacations and most other pleasures. Now, in only six months, she would finish her residency and establish a practice of her own, and nothing would be allowed to interfere with her plans. Nothing was going to rob her of her dream.

Nothing.

It was November 12.

3. Elko County, Nevada

Ernie Block was afraid of the dark. Indoor darkness was bad, but the darkness of the outdoors, the vast blackness of night here in northern Nevada, was what most terrified Ernie. During the day he favored rooms with several lamps and lots of windows, but at night he preferred rooms with few windows or even no windows at all because sometimes it seemed to him that the night was pressing against the glass, as if it were a living creature that wanted to get in at him and gobble him up. He obtained no relief from drawing the drapes, for he still knew the night was out there, waiting for its chance.

He was deeply ashamed of himself. He did not know why he had recently become afraid of the dark. He just *was*.

Millions of people shared his phobia, of course, but nearly all of them were children. Ernie was fifty-two.

On Friday afternoon, the day after Thanksgiving, he worked alone in the motel office because Faye had flown to Wisconsin to visit Lucy, Frank, and the grand-kids. She would not be back until Tuesday. Come December, they intended to close up for a week and both go to Milwaukee for Christmas with the kids; but this time Faye had gone by herself.

Ernie missed her terribly. He missed her because she was his wife of thirty-one years *and* his best friend. He missed her because he loved her more now than he had on their wedding day. And because . . . without Faye, the nights alone seemed longer, deeper, darker than ever.

By two-thirty Friday afternoon he had cleaned all the rooms and changed the linens, and the Tranquility Motel was ready for its next wave of journeyers. It was the only lodging within twelve miles, perched on a knoll north of the su-perhighway, a neat little way station on a vast expanse of sagebrush-strewn plains that sloped up into grassy meadows. Elko lay over thirty miles to the east, Battle Mountain forty miles to the west. The town of Carlin and the tiny village of Beowawe were closer, though from the Tranquility Motel Ernie had not a glimpse of either settlement. In fact, from the parking lot, no other building was visible in any direction, and there was probably no motel in the world more aptly named than this one.

Ernie was now in the office, working with a can of wood stain, touching up a few scratches on the oak counter where guests signed in and checked out. The counter was not really in bad shape. He was just keeping busy until customers started pulling in from Interstate 80 in the late afternoon. If he did not keep his mind occupied, he would start thinking about how early dusk arrived in Novem-ber, and he would begin to worry about nightfall, and then by the time darkness actually came, he would be as jumpy as a cat with a can tied to its tail.

The motel office was a shrine to light. From the moment he had opened at six-thirty this morning, every lamp had been burning. A squat fluorescent lamp with a flexible neck stood on the oak desk in the work area behind the check-in counter, casting a pale rectangle on the green felt blotter. A brass floor lamp glowed in the corner by the file cabinets. On the public side of the counter was a carousel of postcards, a wall rack holding about forty paperbacks, another rack full of free travel brochures, a single slot machine by the door, and a beige sofa flanked by end tables and ginger-jar lamps equipped with three-way bulbs—75, 100, and 150 watts—which were turned up all the way. There was a frosted-glass ceiling fixture, too, with two bulbs, and of course most of the front wall of the office featured a large window. The motel faced south-southwest, so at this time of day the declining sun's honey-colored beams angled through the enormous pane, giv-ing an amber tint to the white wall behind the sofa, fracturing into hundreds of bright erratic lines in the crackled glaze of the ginger-jar lamps, and leaving blazing reflections in the brass medallions that ornamented the tables.

When Faye was here, Ernie left some of the lamps off because she was sure to remark on the waste of electricity and extinguish a few of them. Leaving a lamp unlit made him uneasy, but he endured the sight of dead bulbs in order to keep his secret. As far as he knew, Faye was not aware of the phobia that had been creeping up on him during the past four months, and he did not want her to know because he was ashamed of this sudden strangeness in himself and because he did not want to worry her. He did not know the cause of his irrational fear, but he knew he would conquer it, sooner or later, so there was no sense in humiliating himself and causing Faye unnecessary anxiety over a temporary condition.

He refused to believe that it was serious. He had been ill only rarely in his fifty-two years. He had only been laid up in the hospital once, after taking a bullet in the butt and another one in the back during his second tour of duty in Vietnam. There had never been mental illness in his family, and Ernest Eugene Block was absolutely sure-as-hell-and-without-a-doubt *not* going to be the first one of his clan to go crawling and whimpering to a psychiatrist's couch. You could bet your ass on that and never have to worry what you would sit on. He would tough this out, weird as it was, unsettling as it was.

It had begun in September, a vague uneasiness that built in him as nightfall approached and that remained until dawn. At first he was not troubled every night, but it got steadily worse, and by the middle of October, dusk always brought with it an inexplicable spiritual distress. By early November the distress became fear, and during the past two weeks his anxiety grew until now his days were measured—and almost totally defined—by this perplexing fear of the darkness to come. For the past ten days, he'd avoided going out after nightfall, and thus far Faye had not noticed, though she could not remain oblivious much longer.

Ernie Block was so big that it was ridiculous for him to be afraid of *anything*. He was six feet tall and so solidly and squarely built that his surname was equally suitable as a one-word description of him. His wiry gray hair was brush-cut, revealing slabs of skullbone, and his facial features were clean and appealing, though so squared-off that he looked as if he had been carved out of granite. His thick neck, massive shoulders, and barrel chest gave him a top-heavy appearance. When he had been a high-school football star, the other players called him "Bull," and during his twenty-eight-year career in the Marines, from which he had been retired for six years, most people called him "sir," even some who were of equal rank. They would be astonished to learn that, lately, Ernie Block's palms got sweaty every day when sunset drew near.

Now, intent upon keeping his thoughts far from sunset, he dawdled over the repairs to the counter and finally finished at three-forty-five. The quality of the daylight had changed. It was no longer honey-colored but amber-orange, and the sun was drawing down toward the west.

At four o'clock he got his first check-in, a couple his own age, Mr. and Mrs. Gilney, who were heading home to Salt Lake City after spending a week in Reno, visiting their son. He chatted with them and was disappointed when they took their key and left.

The sunlight was completely orange now, burnt orange, no yellow in it at all. The high, scattered clouds had been transformed from white sailing ships to gold and scarlet galleons gliding eastward above the Great Basin in which almost the entire state of Nevada lay.

Ten minutes later a cadaverous man, visiting the area on special assignment for the Bureau of Land Management, took a room for two days.

Alone again, Ernie tried not to look at his watch.

He tried not to look at the windows, either, for beyond the glass the day was bleeding away.

I'm not going to panic, he told himself. I've been to war, seen the worst a man can see, and by God I'm still *here,* still as big and ugly as ever, so I won't come unglued just because night is coming.

By four-fifty the sunlight was no longer orange but bloody red.

His heart was speeding up, and he began to feel as if his rib cage had become a vise that was squeezing his vital organs between its jaws.

He went to the desk, sat down in the chair, closed his eyes, and did some deep-breathing exercises to calm himself.

He turned on the radio. Sometimes music helped. Kenny Rogers was singing about loneliness.

The sun touched the horizon and slowly sank out of sight. The crimson afternoon faded to electric blue, then to a luminous purple that reminded Ernie of day's end in Singapore, where he had been stationed for two years as an embassy guard when he had been a young recruit.

It came. The twilight.

Then worse. Night.

The outside lights, including the blue and green neon sign that could be seen clearly from the freeway, had blinked on automatically as dusk crept in, but that had not made Ernie feel any better. Dawn was an eternity away. Night ruled.

With the dying of the light, the outside temperature fell below freezing. To cut the chill in the office, the oil furnace kicked in more frequently. In spite of the chill, Ernie Block was sweating.

At six o'clock, Sandy Sarver dashed over from the Tranquility Grille, which stood west of the motel. It was a small sandwich shop with a limited menu, serving only lunch and dinner to the guests and to hungry truckers who swung in from the highway for a bite. (Breakfast for guests was complimentary sweet rolls and coffee delivered to their rooms, if they asked for it the night before.) Sandy, thirty-two, and her husband, Ned, ran the restaurant for Ernie and Faye; Sandy waited tables, and Ned cooked. They lived in a trailer up near Beowawe and drove in every day in their battered Ford pickup.

Ernie winced when Sandy entered, for when she opened the door he had the irrational feeling that the darkness outside would spring, pantherlike, into the office.

"Brought supper," Sandy said, shivering in the gust of cold air that entered with her. She set a small, lidless, cardboard box on the counter. It held a cheeseburger, French fries, a plastic container of cole slaw, and a can of Coors. "Figured you'd need a Coors to sluice all this cholesterol out of your system."

"Thanks, Sandy."

Sandy Sarver was not much to look at, plain and washed out, even drab, though she had more potential than she realized. Her legs were too thin but not unattractive. She was underweight, but if she put on fifteen or even twenty pounds, she would have a reasonably good shape. She was flat-chested, though an appealing suppleness compensated for her lack of amplitude, and she had a charming feminine delicateness most apparent in her small bones, slender arms, and swanlike neck. Also, she possessed an infrequently seen but arresting gracefulness that was usually disguised by her habit of shuffling when she walked and slumping round-shouldered when she sat. Her brown hair was lusterless and limp, probably because she washed it with soap instead of shampoo. She never wore makeup, not even lipstick. Her nails were bitten and neglected. However, she was good-hearted, with a generous spirit, which was why Ernie and Faye wished she could look better and get more out of life.

Sometimes Ernie worried about her, the same way he used to worry about Lucy, his own daughter, before Lucy found and married Frank and became so obviously, perfectly happy. He sensed that something bad had happened to Sandy Sarver a long time ago, that she had taken a very hard blow which had not broken her but had taught her to keep a low profile, to keep her head tucked down, to harbor only meager expectations in order to protect herself from disappointment, pain, and human cruelty.

Relishing the aroma of the food, popping the tab on the Coors, Ernie said, "Ned makes the best darned cheeseburgers I've ever eaten."

Sandy smiled shyly. "It's a blessing having a man who cooks." Her voice was soft, meek. "Especially in my case 'cause I'm no good at it."

"Oh, I'll bet you're a fine cook, too," Ernie said.

"No, no, not me, not even a little bit. Never was, never will be."

He looked at her bare, goose-pimpled arms, exposed by her short-sleeved uniform. "You shouldn't come out on a night like this without a sweater. You'll catch your death."

"Not me," she said. "I . . . I got used to the cold a long time ago."

That seemed an odd thing to say, and the tone of voice in which she said it was even odder. But before Ernie could think of a way to draw her out and discover her meaning, she headed toward the door.

"See you later, Ernie."

"Uh . . . much business?"

"Some. And the truckers'll be pulling in for supper soon." She paused with the door open. "You sure keep it bright in here."

A bite of cheeseburger stuck in his throat when she opened the door. She was exposing him to the dangers of the darkness.

Cold air swept in.

"You could get a tan in here," she said.

"I . . . I like it bright. People come into a motel office that's dimly lit . . . well, the impression is it's dirty."

"Oh! I would've never thought of that. Guess that's why you're the boss. I was in charge, I'd never think of little things like that. I'm no good at details. Gotta scoot."

He held his breath while the door was open, sighed with relief when she pulled it shut behind her. He watched her scurry past the windows and out of sight. He could not remember ever hearing Sandy admit to a virtue. Likewise, she never hesitated to point out her faults and shortcomings, both real and imagined. The kid was sweet, but she was sometimes dreary company. Tonight, of course, even dreary company was welcome. He was sorry to see her go.

At the counter, eating while standing up, Ernie concentrated intently on his food, not once lifting his eyes from it until he was done, using it to take his mind off the irrational fear that made his scalp prickle and kept the cold sweat trickling down from his armpits.

By six-fifty, eight of the motel's twenty rooms were occupied. Because it was the second night of a four-day holiday weekend, with more than the usual number of travelers, he would rent out at least another eight units if he stayed open until nine o'clock.

He could not do it. He was a Marine—retired, but still a Marine—to whom the words "duty" and "courage" were sacred, and he had never failed to do his duty, not even in Vietnam, not even with bullets flying and bombs bursting and people dying on all sides, but he was incapable of the simple task of manning the motel desk until nine o'clock. There were no drapes at the big office windows, no blind over the glass door, no way to escape the sight of darkness. Each time the door opened, he was sick with dread because no barrier lay between him and the night.

He looked at his big strong hands. They were trembling. His sour stomach churned. He was so jumpy he could not keep still. He paced the small work area. He fiddled with this and that.

Finally, at a quarter past seven, surrendering to his irrational anxiety, he used a switch under the counter to turn on the NO VACANCY sign outside, and he locked the front door. He clicked off the lamps, one at a time, edging away from the shadows that rushed in where light had ruled, and he quickly retreated to the rear of the room. Steps led up to the owner's apartment on the second floor. He intended to climb them at an ordinary pace, telling himself that it was silly and stupid to be afraid, telling himself that nothing was coming after him from the dark corners of the office behind, nothing— such a *ridiculous* thought—nothing, absolutely nothing. But reassurances of that sort did him no good whatsoever, for it was not something *in* the dark that scared him; he was, instead, terrified by the darkness itself, by the mere absence of light. He started moving faster, grabbing at the handrail. To his chagrin, he quickly panicked and bounded up the steps two at a time. At the top, heart pounding, Ernie stumbled into the living room, fumbled for the wall switch, snapped off the last of the lights below, slammed the door so hard that the whole wall seemed to shake, locked it, and leaned with his broad back against it.

He could not stop gasping. He could not stop shaking, either. He could smell his own rank sweat.

Several lights had been burning in the apartment during the day, but a few were unlit. He hurried from room to room, clicking on every lamp and ceiling fixture. The drapes and shades were all drawn tight from his previous nocturnal ordeal, so he had not a single glimpse of the blackness beyond the windows.

When he had regained control of himself, he phoned the Tranquility Grille and told Sandy that he was not feeling well, that he had shut down early. He asked them to keep the day's receipts until tomorrow morning rather than bother him tonight when they closed the restaurant.

Sickened by his pungent perspiration odor—not so much by the smell itself as by the total loss of control that the smell represented—Ernie showered. After he had toweled himself dry, he put on fresh underwear, belted himself into a thick warm robe, and stepped into slippers.

Heretofore, in spite of his bewilderingly unfocused apprehension, he had been able to sleep in a dark room, though not without anxiety, and not without the aid of a couple of beers. Then, two nights ago, with Faye in Wisconsin, when he was alone, he was able to nod off only with the constant companionship of the nightstand lamp. He knew he would need that luminous comfort tonight, as well.

And when Faye returned on Tuesday? Would he be able to go back to sleeping without a light?

What if Faye turned off the lights . . . and he started screaming like a badly frightened child?

The thought of that impending humiliation made him grind his teeth with anger and drove him to the nearest window.

He put one beefy hand on the tightly drawn drapes. Hesitated. His heart did an imitation of muffled machine-gun fire.

He had always been strong for Faye, a rock on which she could depend. That was what a man was supposed to be: a rock. He must not let Faye down. He had to overcome this bizarre affliction before she returned from Wisconsin.

His mouth went dry and a chill returned when he thought about what lay beyond the now-concealed glass, but he knew the only way to beat this thing was to confront it. That was the lesson life had taught him: be bold, confront the enemy, engage in battle. That philosophy of action had always worked for him. It would work again. This window looked out from the back of the motel, across the vast meadows and hills of the uninhabited uplands, and the only light out there was what fell from the stars. He must pull the drapes aside, come face to face with that tenebrous landscape, stand fast, endure it. Confrontation would be a purgative, flushing the poison from his system.

Ernie pulled open the drapes. He peered out at the night and told himself that this perfect blackness was not so bad—deep and pure, vast and cold, but not malevolent, and in no way a personal threat.

However, as he watched, unmoving and unmovable, portions of the darkness seemed to . . . well, to shift, to *coalesce,* forming into not quite visible but nonetheless solid shapes, lumps of pulsing and denser blackness within the greater blackness, lurking phantoms that at any moment might launch themselves toward the fragile window.

He clenched his jaws, put his forehead against the ice-cold glass.

The Nevada barrens, a huge emptiness to begin with, now seemed to expand even farther. He could not see the night-cloaked mountains, but he sensed that they were magically receding, that the plains between him and the mountains were growing larger, extending outward hundreds of miles, thousands, expanding swiftly toward infinity, until suddenly he was at the center of a void so immense that it defied description. On all sides of him, there was emptiness and lightlessness beyond man's ability to measure, beyond the limits of his own feeble imagination, a terrible emptiness, to the left and right, front and back, above and below, and suddenly he could not *breathe*.

This was considerably worse than anything he had known before. A deeper-reaching fear. Profound. Shocking in its power. And it was in total control of him.

Abruptly he was aware of all the *weight* of that enormous darkness, and it seemed to be sliding inexorably in upon him, sliding and sliding, incalculably high walls of heavy darkness, collapsing, pressing down, squeezing the breath out of him—

He screamed and threw himself back from the window.

He fell to his knees as the drapes dropped into place with a soft rustle. The window was hidden again. The darkness was concealed. All around him was light, blessed light. He hung his head, shuddered, and took great gulps of air.

He crawled to the bed and hoisted himself onto the mattress, where he lay for a long time, listening to his heartbeat, which was like footfalls, sprinting then running then just walking fast inside him. Instead of solving his problem, bold confrontation had made it worse.

''What's happening here?'' he said aloud, staring at the ceiling. ''What's wrong with me? Dear God, what's *wrong* with me?''

It was November 22.

4. Laguna Beach, California

Saturday, in desperate reaction to yet another troubling episode of somnambulism, Dom Corvaisis thoroughly, methodically exhausted himself. By nightfall, he intended to be so wrung out that he'd sleep as still as a stone locked immemorially in the bosom of the earth. At seven o'clock in the morning, with the night's cool mist lingering in the canyons and bearding the trees, he performed half an hour of vigorous calisthenics on the patio overlooking the ocean, then put on his running shoes and did seven arduous miles on Laguna's sloped streets. He spent the next five hours doing heavy gardening. Then, because it was a warm day, he put on his swimsuit, put towels in his Firebird, and went to the beach. He sunbathed a little and swam a lot. After dinner at Picasso's, he walked for another hour along shop-lined streets sparsely populated by off-season tourists. At last he drove home.

Undressing in his bedroom, Dom felt as if he were in the land of Lilliput, where a thousand tiny people were pulling him down with grappling lines. He rarely drank, but now he tossed back a shot of Rémy Martin. In bed, he fell asleep even as he clicked off the lamp.

The incidents of somnambulism were growing more frequent, and the problem was now the central issue of his life. It was interfering with his work. The new book, which had been going well—it contained the best writing he had ever done—was stalled. In the past two weeks, he had awakened in a closet on nine occasions, four times in the last four nights. The affliction had ceased to be amusing and intriguing. He was afraid to go to sleep because, asleep, he was not in control of himself.

Yesterday, Friday, he had finally gone to his physician, Dr. Paul Cobletz, in Newport Beach. Haltingly, he told Cobletz all about his sleepwalking, but he found himself unwilling and unable to express the true depth and seriousness of his concern. Dom had always been a very private person, made so by a childhood spent in a dozen foster homes and under the care of surrogate parents, some of whom were indifferent or even hostile, all of whom were dismayingly temporary presences in his life. He was reluctant to share his most important and personal thoughts except through the mouths of imaginary characters in his fiction.

As a result, Cobletz was not unduly worried. After a full physical examination, he pronounced Dom exceptionally fit. He attributed the somnambulism to stress, to the upcoming publication of the novel.

"You don't think we should do any tests?" Dom asked.

Cobletz said, "You're a writer, so of course your imagination is running away with you. Brain tumor, you're thinking. Am I right?"

"Well . . . yes."

"Any headaches? Dizziness? Blurred vision?"

"No."

"I've examined your eyes. There's no change in your retinas, no indication of intracranial pressure. Any inexplicable vomiting?"

"No. Nothing like that."

"Giddy spells? Giggling or periods of euphoria without apparent reason? Anything of that nature?"

"No."

"Then I see no reason for tests at this stage."

"Do you think I need . . . psychotherapy?"

"Good heavens, no! I'm sure this will pass soon."

Finished dressing, Dom watched Cobletz close the file. He said, "I thought perhaps sleeping pills—"

"No, no," Cobletz said. "Not yet. I don't believe in drugs as a treatment of first resort. Here's what you do, Dom. Get away from the writing for a few weeks.

working on. A few days of that, and you'll be cured. I'm convinced of it.''

Saturday, Dom began the treatment Dr. Cobletz prescribed, devoting himself to physical activity, though with more single-mindedness and flagellant persistence than the doctor had suggested. Consequently, he plummeted into a deep sleep the moment he put his head upon the pillow, and in the morning he did not wake in a closet.

He did not wake in bed, either. This time, he was in the garage.

He regained consciousness in a breathless state of terror, gasping, his heart hammering so hard it seemed capable of shattering his ribs with its furious blows. His mouth was dry, his hands curled into fists. He was cramped and sore, partly from Saturday's excess of exercise, but partly from the unnatural and uncomfortable position in which he had been sleeping. During the night he evidently had taken two folded canvas dropcloths from a shelf above the workbench, and had squirreled into a narrow service space behind the furnace. That was where he lay now, concealed beneath the tarps.

"Concealed" was the right word. He had not dragged the tarpaulins over himself merely for warmth. He had taken refuge behind the furnace and beneath the canvas because he had been hiding from something.

From what?

Even now, as Dominick pushed the tarps aside and struggled to sit up, as sleep receded and as his bleary eyes adjusted to the shadow-filled garage, the intense anxiety that had accompanied him up from sleep still clung tenaciously. His pulse pounded.

Fear of what?

Dreaming. In his nightmare he must have been running and hiding from some monster. Yes. Of course. His peril in the nightmare caused him to sleepwalk, and when, in the dream, he sought a place to hide, he also hid in reality, creeping behind the furnace.

His white Firebird loomed ghostlike in the vague light from the wall vents and the single window above the workbench. Shuffling across the garage, he felt as if he were a revenant himself.

In the house, he went directly to his office. Morning light filled the room, making him squint. He sat at the desk in his filthy pajama bottoms, switched on the word processor, and studied the documents on the diskette that he had left in the machine. The diskette was as he had left it on Thursday; it contained no new material.

Dom had hoped that, in his sleep, he might have left a message that would help him understand the source of his anxiety. That knowledge was obviously held by his subconscious but thus far denied to his conscious mind. When sleepwalking, his subconscious was in control, and possibly it would try to explain things to his conscious mind by way of the Displaywriter. But as yet, it had not.

He switched off the machine. He sat for a long time, staring out the window, toward the ocean. Wondering . . .

Later, in the bedroom, as he was on his way to the master bath, he found something strange. Nails were scattered across the carpet, and he had to be careful where he walked. He stooped, picked up several of them. They were all alike: 1.5-inch steel finishing nails. At the far side of the room, he saw two objects that drew him there. Beneath the window, from which the drapes had been drawn aside, a box of nails lay on the floor by the baseboard; it was only half full because part of its contents had spilled from it. Beside the box was a hammer.

He lifted the hammer, hefted it, frowned.

What had he been doing in those lonely hours of the night?

He raised his eyes to the windowsill and saw three loose nails that he had laid there. They gleamed in the sunlight.

Judging from the evidence, he'd been preparing to nail the windows shut. Jesus. Something had so frightened him that he had intended to nail the windows shut and make a fortress of his house, but before he could set himself to the task, he had been suddenly *overwhelmed* by fear and had fled to the garage, where he had hidden behind the furnace.

He dropped the hammer, stood, looked out the window. Beyond lay only bloom-laden rose bushes, a small strip of lawn, and an ivy-covered slope that led up to another house. A lovely landscape. Peaceful. He could not believe that it had been any different last night, that something more threatening had been crouching out there in the darkness.

And yet . . .

For a while Dom Corvaisis watched the day grow brighter, watched the bees visit the roses, then began to pick up the nails.

It was November 24.

5. Boston, Massachusetts

After the incident of the black gloves, two weeks passed without another attack.

For a few days following the embarrassing scene at Bernstein's Delicatessen, Ginger Weiss remained on edge, expecting another seizure. She was unusually self-aware, acutely conscious of her physiological and psychological conditions, searching for subtle symptoms of serious disorder, alert for the slightest sign of another impending fugue, but she noticed nothing worrisome. She had no headaches, no attacks of nausea, no joint or muscle pain. Gradually, her confidence rose to its usual high level. She became convinced that her wild flight had been entirely stress-related, a never-to-be-repeated aberration.

Her days at Memorial were busier than ever. George Hannaby, chief of surgery—a tall burly bear of a man who talked slow, walked slow, and looked deceptively lazy—maintained a heavy schedule, and though Ginger was not the only resident working under him, she was the only one who currently worked *exclusively* with him. She assisted in many—perhaps in a majority—of his procedures: aortal grafts, amputations, popliteal bypasses, embolectomies, portocaval shunts, thoracotomies, arteriograms, the installation of temporary and permanent pacemakers, and more.

George observed her every move, was quick to note the slightest flaw in her skill and techniques. Although he looked like a friendly bear, he was a tough taskmaster and had no patience for laziness, ineptitude, or carelessness. He could be scathing in his critiques, and he made all the young doctors sweat. His scorn was not merely withering; it was dehydrating, searing, a nuclear heat.

Some residents considered George tyrannical, but Ginger enjoyed assisting him precisely because his standards were so high. She knew that his criticisms, though sometimes blisteringly delivered, were motivated solely by his concern for the patient, and she never took them personally. When she finally earned Hannaby's unqualified blessing . . . well, that would be almost as good as God's own seal of approval.

On the last Monday in November, thirteen days after her strange seizure, Ginger assisted in a triple-bypass heart operation on Johnny O'Day, a fifty-three-year-old Boston police officer who had been forced into early retirement by cardiovascular disease. Johnny was stocky, rubber-faced, tousle-haired, with merry blue eyes, unassuming, quick to laugh in spite of his troubles. Ginger was especially drawn to him because, although he looked nothing whatsoever like the late Jacob Weiss, he nevertheless reminded her of her father.

She was afraid Johnny O'Day was going to die—and that it was going to be, in part, her fault.

She had no reason to believe that he was more vulnerable than other cardiac patients. In fact, Johnny was in comparatively little danger. He was ten years younger than the average recipient of bypass surgery, with greater resources for recuperation. His cardiac ailment was not complicated by any other debilitating condition, such as phlebitis or excessively high blood pressure. His prospects were encouraging.

But Ginger could not twist free of the dread in which she found herself increasingly tangled. On Monday afternoon, as the hour of surgery drew near, she grew tense, and her stomach turned sour. For the first time since she had sat a lonely vigil beside her father's hospital bed and had helplessly watched him die, Ginger was filled with doubt.

Perhaps her apprehension grew from the unjustified but inescapable notion that if she somehow failed this patient she would in a sense be failing Jacob yet again. Or perhaps her fear was utterly unwarranted and would seem foolish and laughable in hindsight. Perhaps.

Nevertheless, entering the operating theater at George's side, she wondered if her hands would shake. A surgeon's hands must never shake.

The operating room was all white and aqua tile, filled with gleaming chrome-plated and stainless-steel equipment. Nurses and an anesthesiologist were preparing the patient.

Johnny O'Day lay on the cruciform operating table, arms extended, palms up and wrists exposed for the intravenous spikes.

Agatha Tandy, a private surgical technician who was employed by George rather than by the hospital, stretched thin latex gloves over her boss's freshly scrubbed hands, then over Ginger's hands as well.

The patient had been anesthetized. He was orange with iodine from the neck to the waist, swathed in neatly tucked and folded layers of green cloth from the hips down. His eyes were taped shut to keep them from drying out. His breathing was slow but regular.

A portable tape deck with stereo speakers was on a stool in one corner. George preferred to cut to the accompaniment of Bach, and that calming music now filled the room.

It may have calmed the others, but today it did not calm Ginger. A secret scurrying something spun a web of ice in her stomach.

Hannaby positioned himself at the table. Agatha stood at his right side with an elaborately ordered tray of instruments. The circulating nurse waited to fetch whatever might be required from the cabinets along one wall. An assisting nurse with large gray eyes noticed an errant flap of green sheeting and quickly tucked it into place around the patient's body. The anesthesiologist and his nurse were at the head of the table, monitoring the IV and the EKG. Ginger moved into position. The team was ready.

Ginger looked at her hands. They were not shaking.

Inside, though, she was all aquiver.

In spite of her sense of impending disaster, the surgery went smoothly. George Hannaby operated with quickness, sureness, dexterity, and skill that were even more impressive than usual. Twice, he stepped aside and requested that Ginger complete a part of the procedure.

Ginger surprised herself by functioning with her customary sureness and speed, her fear and tension revealed only by a tendency to perspire more than usual. However, the nurse was always there to blot her brow.

Afterward, at the scrub sink, George said, "Like clockwork."

Soaping her hands under the hot water, she said, "You always seem so relaxed, as if . . . as if you weren't a surgeon at all . . . as if you were just a tailor altering a suit of clothes."

"I may seem that way," he said, "but I'm always tense. That's why I play Bach." He finished washing up. "You were very tense today."

"Yes," she admitted.

"Exceptionally tense. It happens." Big as he was, he sometimes seemed to have the eyes of a sweet, gentle child. "The important thing is that it didn't affect your skill. You were as smooth as ever. First rate. That's the key. You've got to use tension to your advantage."

"I guess I'm learning."

He grinned. "As usual, you're being too hard on yourself. I'm proud of you, kid. For a while there, I thought maybe you'd have to give up medicine and earn your living as a meat cutter in a supermarket, but now I know you'll make it."

She grinned back at him, but the grin was counterfeit. She had been more than tense. She had been seized by a cold, black fear that might easily have overwhelmed her, and that was much different from a healthy tension. That fear was something she had never felt before, something that she knew George Hannaby had never felt in his life, not in an operating room. If it continued, if the fear became a constant companion during surgery and would not be dispelled . . . what then?

At ten-thirty that evening, when she was reading in bed, the phone rang. It was George Hannaby. If the call had come earlier, she'd have panicked and assumed that Johnny O'Day had taken a serious turn for the worse, but now she had regained her perspective. "So sorry. Missy Weiss not home. I no speak the English. Call back next April, please."

"If that's supposed to be a Spanish accent," George said, "it's atrocious. If it's supposed to be Oriental, it's merely terrible. Be thankful you chose medicine as a career instead of acting."

"You, on the other hand, would've done well as a drama critic."

"I do have the refined and sensitive perspective, the cool judgment and unerring insight of a first-rate critic, don't I? Now shut up and listen: I've got good news. I think you're ready, smart-ass."

"Ready? For what?"

"The big time. An aortal graft," he said.

"You mean . . . I wouldn't just assist you? Do it entirely myself?"

"Chief surgeon for the entire procedure."

"Aortal graft?"

"Sure. You didn't specialize in cardiovascular surgery just to perform appendectomies for the rest of your life."

She was sitting straight up in bed now. Her heart was beating faster, and she was flushed with excitement. "When?"

"Next week. There's a patient checking in this Thursday or Friday. Name's Fletcher. We'll go over her file together on Wednesday. If things proceed according to schedule, I would think we'd be ready to cut on Monday morning. Of course, you'll be responsible for scheduling all the final tests and making the decision to go ahead."

"Oh, God."

"You'll do fine."

"You'll be with me."

"I'll assist you . . . if you feel you need me for anything."

"And you'll take over if I start to screw up."

"Don't be silly. You won't screw up."

She thought about it a moment, then said, "No. I won't screw up."

"That's my Ginger. You can do whatever you set your mind to."

"Even ride a giraffe to the moon."

"What?"

"Private joke."

"Listen, I know you came close to panic this afternoon, but don't worry. All residents experience that. Most have to deal with it early, when they begin to assist in the surgery. They call it The Clutch. But you've been cool and collected from the start, and I'd finally decided you'd never clutch up like the rest of them. Today, at last you did. The Clutch just came later for you than for most. And though I imagine you're still worried about it, I think you should be glad it happened. The Clutch is a seasoning experience. The important thing is that you dealt with it superbly."

"Thanks, George. Even better than a drama critic, you'd have made a good baseball coach."

Minutes later, when they concluded their conversation and hung up, she fell back against the pillows again and hugged herself and felt so fine that she actually giggled. After a while she went to the closet and dug around in there until she located the Weiss family photograph album. She brought it back to bed and sat for a time, paging through the pictures of Jacob and Anna, for although she could not share her triumphs with them any more, she needed to feel that they were close.

Later still, in the dark bedroom, as she lay balanced on the thin edge of wakefulness, she finally understood why she had been frightened this afternoon. She had not been seized by The Clutch. Although she had not been able to admit it until now, she had been afraid that, in the midst of surgery, she would black out, plummet into a state of fugue, as she had done that Tuesday, two weeks ago. If an attack came while she held a scalpel, while she was doing delicate cutting, or while stitching in a vascular graft . . .

That thought brought her eyes wide open. The creeping form of sleep retreated like a thief caught in the middle of a burglary. For a long time she lay there, stiff, staring at the dark and newly ominous shapes of the bedroom furniture and at the window, where incompletely drawn draperies revealed a band of glass silvered by a fall of moonlight and by the rising beams of streetlamps below.

Could she accept the responsibility of chief surgeon on an aortal graft? Her seizure had surely been a one-time occurrence. It would never happen again. Surely not. But did she dare test that theory?

Sleep crept back again and claimed her, though not for hours.

* * *

Tuesday, after a successful trip to Bernstein's Delicatessen, much food, and several lazy hours in an easy chair with a good book, her self-confidence was knit up again, and she began to look forward to the challenge ahead, with only an ordinary degree and kind of apprehension.

On Wednesday, Johnny O'Day continued to recover from his triple bypass and was in high spirits. *This* was what made the years of study and hard work worthwhile: preserving life, relieving suffering, bringing hope and happiness to those who had known despair.

She assisted in a pacemaker implantation that went without a hitch, and she performed an aortagram, a dye test on a patient's circulation. She also sat in with George while he examined seven people who had been referred to him by other physicians.

When all the new patients had been seen, George and Ginger huddled for half an hour over the file of the candidate for the aortal graft—a fifty-eight-year-old woman, Viola Fletcher. After studying the file, Ginger decided she wanted Mrs. Fletcher admitted to Memorial on Thursday for testing and preparation. If there were no counterindications, surgery could take place first thing Monday morning. George agreed, and all the necessary arrangements were made.

Thus Wednesday progressed, always busy, never dull. By six-thirty she had put in a twelve-hour day, but she was not tired. In fact, although she had nothing to keep her at the hospital, she was reluctant to leave. George Hannaby was home already. But Ginger hung around, chatting with patients, double-checking charts, until at last she went to George's office, where she intended to look again at Viola Fletcher's file.

The professional offices were in the back wing of the building, separate from the hospital itself. At that hour the corridors were virtually deserted. Ginger's rubber-soled shoes squeaked on the highly polished tile floors. The air smelled of pine-scented disinfectant.

George Hannaby's waiting room, examining rooms, and private office were dark and quiet, and Ginger did not switch on all the lights as she moved through the outer rooms into the inner sanctum. There, she snapped on only the desk lamp as she passed it on her way to the file-room door, which was locked. George had given her keys to everything, and in a minute she had withdrawn Viola Fletcher's records from the cabinet and returned with them to George's desk.

She sat down in the big leather chair, opened the folder in the pool of light from the desk lamp—and only then noticed an object that riveted her attention and caused her breath to catch in her throat. It lay on the green blotter, along the curvature of light: a hand-held ophthalmoscope, an instrument used to examine the interior of the eye. There was nothing unusual—certainly nothing ominous—about the ophthalmoscope. Every doctor used such an instrument during a routine physical examination. Yet the sight of this one not only inhibited her breathing but filled her with a sudden sense of terrible danger.

She had broken out in a cold sweat.

Her heart was hammering so hard, so loud, that the sound of it seemed to come not from within but without, as if a parade drum was thumping in the street beyond the window.

She could not take her eyes off the ophthalmoscope. As with the black gloves in Bernstein's Delicatessen more than two weeks ago, all other objects in George's office began to fade, until the shining instrument was the only thing that she could see in any detail. She was aware of every tiny scratch and minute nick on its handle. Every humble feature of its design seemed abruptly and enormously important, as if this were not a doctor's ordinary tool but the linchpin of the universe, an arcane instrument with the potential for catastrophic destruction.

Disoriented, suddenly made claustrophobic by a heavy, insistent, pressing mantle of irrational fear that had descended over her like a great sodden cloak, she pushed the chair away from the desk and stood up. Gasping, whimpering, she felt suffocated yet chilled to the bone at the same time.

The shank of the ophthalmoscope glistened as if made of ice.

The lens shone like an iridescent and chillingly alien eye.

Her resolve to stand fast now swiftly melted, even as her heart seemed to freeze under the cold breath of terror.

Run or die, a voice said within her. *Run or die.*

A cry escaped her, and it sounded like the tortured appeal of a lost and frightened child.

She turned from the desk, stumbled around it, almost fell over a chair. She crossed the room, burst into the outer office, fled into the deserted corridor, keening shrilly, seeking safety, finding none. She wanted help, a friendly face, but she was the only person on the floor, and the danger was closing in. The unknown threat that was somehow embodied in the harmless ophthalmoscope was drawing nearer, so she ran as fast as she could, her footsteps booming along the hallway.

Run or die.

The mist descended.

Minutes later, when the mist cleared, when she was again aware of her surroundings, she found herself in the emergency stairwell at the end of the office wing, on a concrete landing between floors. She could not remember leaving the office corridor and taking to the stairs. She was sitting on the landing, squeezed into the corner, her back pressed to the cinderblock wall, staring out at the railing along the far side of the steps. A single bare bulb burned behind a wire basket overhead. To her left and right, flights of stairs led up and down into shadow before coming to other lighted landings. The air was musty and cool. If not for her ragged breathing, silence would have ruled.

It was a lonely place, especially when your life was coming apart at the seams and you needed the reassurance of bright lights and people. The gray walls, stark light, looming shadows, the metal railing . . . The place seemed like a reflection of her own despair.

Her wild flight and whatever other bizarre behavior she exhibited in her inexplicable fugue had evidently not been seen, or she would not now be alone. At least that was a blessing. At least no one knew.

She knew, however, and that was bad enough.

She shivered, not entirely from fear, for the mindless terror that had gripped her was gone. She shivered because she was cold, and she was cold because her clothes clung to her, damp, soaked with sweat.

She raised one hand, wiped her face.

She rose, looked up the stairwell, then down. She did not know whether she was above or below the floor on which George Hannaby had his office. After a moment she decided to go up.

Her footsteps echoed eerily.

For some reason, she thought of tombs.

"*Meshuggene,*" she said shakily.

It was November 27.

6. Chicago, Illinois

The first Sunday morning in December was cold, under a low gray sky that promised snow. By afternoon the first scattered flakes would begin to fall, and by early evening the city's grimy face and soiled skirts would be temporarily concealed beneath the white pancake makeup and pristine cloak of snow. This night, from the Gold Coast to the slum tenements, everywhere in the city, the number-one topic of conversation would be the storm. Everywhere, that is, but in the Roman Catholic homes throughout the parish of St. Bernadette's, where they would still be talking about the shocking thing Father Brendan Cronin had done during the early Mass that morning.

Father Cronin rose at five-thirty a.m., said prayers, showered, shaved, dressed in cassock and biretta, picked up his breviary, and left the parish house without bothering to put on a coat. He stood for a moment on the rear porch, breathing deeply of the crisp December air.

He was thirty years old, but with his direct green eyes and unruly auburn hair and freckled face, he looked younger than he was. He was fifty or sixty pounds overweight, though not particularly thick in the middle. On him, fat distributed evenly, filling him out equally in face, arms, torso, and legs. From childhood through college, until his second year at the seminary, his nickname had been "Pudge."

Regardless of his emotional state, Father Cronin nearly always looked happy. His face had a natural cherubic aspect, and the round lines of it were not designed for the clear and easy expression of anger, melancholy, or grief. This morning he looked mildly pleased with himself and with the world, though he was deeply troubled.

He followed a flagstone path across the yard, past denuded flower beds where the bare earth lay in frozen clumps. He unlocked the door of the sacristy and let himself in. Myrrh and spikenard blended with the scent of the lemon-oil furniture polish with which the old church's oak paneling, pews, and other wooden objects were anointed.

Without switching on the lights, with only the flickering ruby glow of the sacristy lamp to guide him, Father Cronin knelt at the *prie-dieu* and bowed his head. In silence, he petitioned the Divine Father to make him a worthy priest. In the past, this private devotion, before the arrival of the sexton and the altar boy, had sent his spirits soaring and had filled him with exultation at the prospect of celebrating Mass. But now, as on most other mornings during the last four months, joy eluded him. He felt only a leaden bleakness, an emptiness that made his heart ache dully and that induced a cold, sick trembling in his belly.

Clenching his jaws, gritting his teeth, as if he could *will* himself into a state of spiritual ecstasy, he repeated his petition, elaborated upon his initial prayers, but still he felt unmoved, hollow.

After washing his hands and murmuring, *"Da Domine,"* Father Cronin laid his biretta on the *prie-dieu* and went to the vesting bench to attire himself for the sacred celebration ahead. He was a sensitive man with an artist's soul, and in the great beauty of the ceremony he perceived a pleasing pattern of divine order, a subtle echo of God's grace. Usually, when placing the linen amice over his shoulders, when arranging the white alb so that it fell evenly to his ankles, a shiver of awe passed through him, awe that *he,* Brendan Cronin, should have achieved this sacred office.

Usually. But not today. And not for weeks of days before this.

Father Cronin put on his amice, passed the strings around his back, then tied them against his breast. He pulled on the alb with no more emotion than a welder getting dressed for work in a factory.

Four months ago, in early August, Father Brendan Cronin had begun to lose his faith. A small but relentless fire of doubt burned within him, unquenchable, gradually consuming all of his long-held beliefs.

For any priest, the loss of faith is a devastating process. But it was worse for Brendan Cronin than it would have been for most others. He had never even briefly entertained the thought of being anything *but* a priest. His parents were devout, and they fostered in him a devotion to the Church. However, he had not become a priest to please them. Simply, as trite as it might sound to others in this age of agnosticism, he had been *called* to the priesthood at a very young age. Now, though faith was gone, his holy office continued to be the essential part of his self-image; yet he knew he could not go on saying Mass and praying and comforting the afflicted when it was nothing but a charade to him.

Brendan Cronin placed the stole around his neck. As he pulled on the chasuble, the courtyard door to the sacristy was flung open, and a young boy burst into the room, switching on the electric lights that the priest had preferred to do without.

''Morning, Father!''

''Good morning, Kerry. How're you this fine morning?''

Except that his hair was much redder than Father Cronin's, Kerry McDevit might have been the priest's blood relative. He was slightly plump, freckled, with green eyes full of mischief. ''I'm fine, Father. But it's sure cold out there this morning. Cold as a witch's—''

''Oh, yes? Cold as a witch's what?''

''Refrigerator,'' the boy said, embarrassed. ''Cold as a witch's refrigerator, Father. And that's *cold.*''

If his mood had not been so bleak, Brendan would have been amused by the boy's narrow avoidance of an innocent obscenity, but in his current state of mind he could not summon even a shadow of a smile. Undoubtedly, his silence was interpreted as stern disapproval, for Kerry averted his eyes and went quickly to the closet, where he stowed his coat, scarf, and gloves, and took his cassock and surplice from a hanger.

Even as Brendan lifted the maniple, kissed the cross in its center, and placed it on his left forearm, he felt nothing. There was just that cold, throbbing, hollow ache where belief and joy had once existed. As his hands were occupied with that task, his mind drifted back to a melancholy recollection of the exuberance with which he had once approached every priestly duty.

Until last August, he never doubted the wisdom of his commitment to the Church. He had been such a bright and hard-working student of both mundane subjects and religion that he had been chosen to complete his Catholic education at the North American College in Rome. He loved the Holy City—the architecture, the history, and the friendly people. Upon ordination and acceptance into the Society of Jesus, he had spent two years at the Vatican, as an assistant to Monsignor Giuseppe Orbella, chief speechwriter and doctrinal adviser to His Holiness, the Pope. That honor could have been followed by a prized assignment to the staff of the Cardinal of the Chicago Archdiocese, but Father Cronin had requested, instead, a curacy at a small or medium-sized parish, like any young priest. Thus, after a visit to Bishop Santefiore in San Francisco (an old friend of

Monsignor Orbella's), and after a vacation during which he drove from San Francisco to Chicago, he had come to St. Bernadette's, where he'd taken great pleasure in even the most ordinary day-to-day chores of a curate's life. And with never a regret or doubt.

Now, as he watched his altar boy slip into a surplice, Father Cronin longed for the simple faith that had for so long comforted and sustained him. Was it gone only temporarily, or had he lost it forever?

When Kerry was dressed, he led the way through the inner sacristy door, into the sanctuary of the church. Several steps beyond the door, he evidently sensed that Father Cronin was not coming after him, for he glanced back, a puzzled look upon his face.

Brendan Cronin hesitated. Through the door he had a side-view of the towering crucifix on the back wall and the altar platform straight ahead. This holiest part of the church was dismayingly strange, as if he were seeing it objectively for the first time. And he could not imagine why he had ever thought of it as sacred territory. It was just a *place*. A place like any other. If he walked out there now, if he went through the familiar rituals and litanies, he would be a hypocrite. He would be defrauding everyone in the congregation.

The puzzlement on Kerry McDevit's face had turned to worry. The boy glanced out toward the pews that Brendan Cronin could not see, then looked again at his priest.

How can I say Mass when I no longer believe? Brendan wondered.

But there was nothing else to be done.

Holding the chalice in his left hand, with his right hand over the burse and veil, he kept the sacred vessel close to his breast and followed Kerry, at last, into the sanctuary, where the face of Christ upon the cross seemed, for a moment, to gaze at him accusingly.

As usual, less than a hundred people were in attendance for the early service. Their faces were unusually pale and radiant, as if God had not allowed real worshipers to attend this morning but had sent a deputation of judgmental angels to witness the sacrilege of a doubting priest who dared to offer Mass in spite of his fallen condition.

As the Mass progressed, Father Cronin's despair deepened. From the moment he spoke the *Introibo ad altare Dei,* each step of the ceremony compounded the priest's misery. By the time Kerry McDevit transferred the missal from the Epistle to the Gospel side of the altar, Father Cronin's despondency was so heavy that he felt crushed beneath it. His spiritual and emotional exhaustion were so profound that he could barely lift his arms, could hardly find strength to focus on the Gospel and mutter the lines from the sacred text. The faces of the worshipers blurred into featureless blobs. By the time he reached the Canon of the Mass, Father Cronin could barely whisper. He knew that Kerry was gaping at him openly now, and he was sure that the congregation was aware that something was wrong. He was sweating and shaking. The awful grayness in him grew darker now, swiftly turning to black, and he felt as if he were spiraling down into a frighteningly dark void.

Then, as he held the Host in his hands and elevated it, speaking the five words that signified the mystery of transubstantiation, he was suddenly angry with himself for being unable to believe, angry with the Church for failing to provide him with better armor against doubt, angry that his entire life seemed misdirected, wasted, expended in pursuit of idiotic myths. His anger churned, heated up, reached the boiling point, was transformed into a steam of fury, a blistering vapor of *rage*.

To his astonishment, a wretched cry burst from him, and he pitched the chalice across the sanctuary. With a loud *clank,* it struck the sanctuary wall, spraying wine, rebounded, bounced off a statue of the Blessed Virgin, and clattered to a stop against the foot of the podium at which he had not long ago read from the Gospels.

Kerry McDevit stumbled back in shock, and in the nave a hundred people gasped as one, but that response had no effect on Brendan Cronin. In a rage that was his only protection against suicidal despair, he flung one arm wide and swept a paten of communion wafers to the floor. With another wild cry, half anger and half grief, he thrust his hand under his chasuble, tore off the stole that lay around his neck and threw it down, turned from the altar, and raced into the sacristy. There, the anger departed as suddenly as it had come, and he stopped and stood there, swaying in confusion.

It was December 1.

7. Laguna Beach, California

That first Sunday in December, Dom Corvaisis had lunch with Parker Faine on the terrace at Las Brisas, in the shade of an umbrella-table overlooking the sun-dappled sea. The good weather was holding well this year. While the breeze brought them the cries of gulls, the tang of the sea, and the sweet scent of star jasmine that was growing nearby, Dominick told Parker every embarrassing and distressing detail of his escalating battle with somnambulism.

Parker Faine was his best friend, perhaps the only person in the world with whom he could open up like this, though on the surface they seemed to have little in common. Dom was a slender, lean-muscled man, but Parker Faine was squat, burly, beefy. Beardless, Dom went to the barber for a haircut every three weeks; but Parker's hair was shaggy, and his beard was shaggy, and his eyebrows bristled. He looked like a cross between a professional wrestler and a beatnik from the 1950s. Dom drank little and was easily intoxicated, while Parker's thirst was legendary and his capacity prodigious. Although Dom was solitary by nature and slow to make friends, Parker had the gift of seeming like an old acquaintance just an hour after you first met him. At fifty, Parker Faine was fifteen years older than Dom. He had been rich and famous for almost a quarter of a century, and he was comfortable with both his wealth and fame, utterly unable to understand Dom's uneasiness over the money and notoriety that was beginning to come his way because of *Twilight in Babylon.* Dom had come to lunch at Las Brisas in Bally loafers, dark brown slacks, and a lighter brown-checkered shirt with a button-down collar, but Parker had arrived in blue tennis shoes, heavily crinkled white cotton pants, and a white-and-blue flowered shirt worn over his belt, which made it seem as if they had dressed for entirely different engagements, had met outside the restaurant sheerly by chance, and had decided to have lunch together on a whim.

In spite of all the ways they differed from each other, they had become fast friends, because in several important ways they were alike. Both were artists, not by choice or inclination but by compulsion. Dom painted with words; Parker painted with paint; and they approached their different arts with identical high standards, commitment, craftsmanship. Furthermore, though Parker made friends more easily than Dom did, each placed enormous value on friendship and nurtured it.

They had met six years ago, when Parker had moved to Oregon for eighteen months, in search of new subject matter for a series of landscapes done in his unique style, which successfully married suprarealism with a surreal imagination. While there, he had signed to give one lecture a month at the University of Portland, where Dom held a position in the Department of English.

Now, while Parker hunched over the table, munching on nachos that were dripping with cheese and guacamole and sour cream, Dom sipped slowly at a bottle of Modelo Negra and recounted his unconscious nocturnal adventures. He spoke softly, though discretion was probably unnecessary; the other diners on the terrace were noisily involved in their own conversations. He did not touch the nachos. This morning, for the fourth time, he had awakened behind the furnace in the garage, in a state of undiluted terror, and his continued inability to get control of himself had left him dispirited and without an appetite. By the time he finished his tale, he had drunk only half the beer, for even that rich, dark Mexican brew tasted flat and stale today.

Parker, on the other hand, had poured down three double-shot margaritas and already ordered a fourth. However, the painter's attention was not dulled by the alcohol he consumed. "Jesus, buddy, why didn't you tell me about this sooner, *weeks* ago?"

"I felt sort of . . . foolish."

"Nonsense. Bullshit," the painter insisted, gesturing expansively with one huge hand, but keeping his voice low.

The Mexican waiter, a diminutive Wayne Newton look-alike, arrived with Parker's margarita and inquired if they wished to order lunch.

"No, no. Sunday lunch is an excuse to have too many margaritas, and I'm a long way from having too many. What a sad waste to order lunch after only four margaritas! That'd leave most of the afternoon unfilled, and we'd find ourselves on the street with nothing to occupy us, and then without doubt we'd get into trouble, attract the attention of the police. God knows what might happen. No, no. To avoid jail and protect our reputations, we must not order lunch sooner than three o'clock. In fact, bring me *another* margarita. And another order of these magnificent nachos, please. More salsa—hotter if you've got it. A dish of chopped onions, too, please. And another beer for my dismayingly restrained friend."

"No," Dom said. "I'm only half-finished with this one."

"That's what I meant by 'dismayingly restrained,' you hopeless Puritan. You've sucked at that one so long it must be warm."

Ordinarily, Dominick would have leaned back and enjoyed Parker Faine's energetic performance. The painter's ebullience, his unfailing enthusiasm for life, was invigorating and amusing. Today, however, Dom was so troubled that he was not amused.

As the waiter turned away, a small cloud passed over the sun, and Parker leaned in farther under the suddenly deeper shadow beneath the umbrella, returning his attention to Dominick, as if he had read his companion's mind. "All right, let's brainstorm. Let's find some sort of explanation and figure out what to do. You don't think the problem's just related to stress . . . the upcoming publication of your book?"

"I did. But not any more. I mean, if the problem was just a mild one, I might be able to accept that career worries lay behind it. But, Jesus, my concerns about *Twilight* just aren't great enough to generate behavior this unusual, this obsessive

. . . this *crazy*. I go walking almost every night now, and it's not just the walking that's weird. The depth of my trance is incredible. Few sleepwalkers are as utterly comatose as I am, and few of them engage in such elaborate tasks as I do. I mean, I was attempting to nail the windows shut! And you don't attempt to nail your windows shut just to keep out your worries about your career.''

"You may be more deeply worried about *Twilight* than you realize.''

"No. It doesn't make sense. In fact, when the new book continued to go well, my anxiety about *Twilight* started fading. You can't sit there and honestly tell me you think all this middle-of-the-night lunacy springs just from a few career worries.''

"No, I can't,'' Parker agreed.

"I crawl into the backs of those closets to *hide*. And when I wake up behind the furnace, when I'm still half-asleep, I have the feeling that something's stalking me, searching for me, something that'll kill me if it finds my hidey-hole. A couple of mornings I woke up trying to scream but unable to get it out. Yesterday, I woke up shouting, 'Stay away, stay away, stay away!' And this morning, the knife . . .''

"Knife?'' Parker said. "You didn't tell me about a knife.''

"Woke up behind the furnace, hiding again. Had a butcher's knife. I'd removed it from the rack in the kitchen while I was sleeping.''

"For protection? From what?''

"From whatever . . . from whoever's stalking me.''

"And who *is* stalking you?''

Dom shrugged. "Nobody that I'm aware of.''

"I don't like this. You could've cut yourself, maybe badly.''

"That's not what scares me the most.''

"So what scares you the most?''

Dom looked around at the other people on the terrace. Though some had followed Parker Faine's bit of theater with the waiter, no one was now paying the least attention to him or Dominick.

"What scares you the most?'' Parker repeated.

"That I might . . . might cut someone else.''

Incredulous, Faine said, "You mean take a butcher's knife and . . . go on a murdering rampage in your sleep? No chance.'' He gulped his margarita. "Good heavens, what a melodramatic notion! Thankfully, your fiction is not quite so sloppily imagined. Relax, my friend. You're not the homicidal type.''

"I didn't think I was the sleepwalking type, either.''

"Oh, bullshit. There's an explanation for this. You're not mad. Madmen never doubt their sanity.''

"I think I'm going to have to see a psychiatrist, a counselor of some kind. And have a few medical tests.''

"The medical tests, yes. But put a hold on the psychiatrist. That's a waste of time. You're no more neurotic than psychotic.''

The waiter returned with more nachos, salsa, a dish of chopped onions, a beer, and a fifth margarita.

Parker surrendered his empty glass, took the full one. He scooped up some of the corn chips with generous globs of guacamole and sour cream, spooned some onions on top, and ate with an appreciation only one step removed from manic glee.

"I wonder if this problem of yours is somehow related to the changes you underwent two summers ago.''

Puzzled, Dom said, "What changes?''

"You know what I'm talking about. When I first met you in Portland six years ago, you were a pale, retiring, unadventurous slug."

"Slug?"

"It's true, and you know it. You were bright, talented, but a slug nonetheless. You know why you were a slug? I'll tell you why. You had all those brains and all that talent, but you were afraid to use them. You were afraid of competition, failure, success, *life*. You just wanted to plod along, unnoticed. You dressed drably, spoke almost inaudibly, dreaded calling attention to yourself. You took refuge in the academic world because there was less competition there. God, man, you were a timid rabbit burrowing in the earth and curling up in its den."

"Oh, yeah? If I was all that disgusting, why on earth did you ever go out of your way to strike up a friendship with me?"

"Because, you thick-headed booby, I saw through your masquerade. I saw beyond the timidity, saw through the practiced dullness and the mask of insipidness. I sensed something special in you, saw glimpses and glimmers of it. That's what I *do*, you know. I see what other people can't. That's what any good artist does. He *sees* what most cannot."

"And *you* called *me* insipid?"

"It's true—about what an artist does and about you being a rabbit. Remember how long you knew me before you found enough confidence to admit being a writer? Three months!"

"Well, in those days, I wasn't really a writer."

"You had drawers full of stories! More than a hundred short stories, not *one* of which had ever been submitted to any publication anywhere! Not just because you were afraid of rejection. You were afraid of acceptance, too. Afraid of success. How many months did I have to hammer at you till you finally sent a couple to market?"

"I don't remember."

"*I* do. Six months! I wheedled and cajoled and demanded and pushed and nagged until you broke down and started submitting stories. I'm a persuasive character, but prying you out of your rabbit hole was almost beyond even my formidable talent for persuasion."

With an almost obscene enthusiasm, Parker scooped up dripping masses of nachos and stuffed himself. After slurping his margarita, he said, "Even when your short stories started selling, you wanted to stop. I had to push you constantly. And after I left Oregon and came back here, when I left you on your own again, you only continued to submit stories for a few months. Then you crawled back into your rabbit hole."

Dom did not argue because everything the painter said was true. After leaving Oregon and returning to his home in Laguna, Parker continued to encourage Dom through letters and phone calls, but long-distance encouragement was insufficient to motivate him. He'd convinced himself that, after all, he was not a writer worthy of publication, in spite of more than a score of sales he'd racked up in less than a year. He stopped sending his stories to magazines and quickly fabricated another shell to replace the one Parker had helped him break out of. Though he was still compelled to produce stories, he reverted to his previous habit of consigning them to his deepest desk drawer, with no thought of marketing them. Parker had continued to urge him to write a novel, but Dom had been certain that his talent was too humble and that he was too lacking in self-discipline to tackle such a large and complex project. He tucked his head down once more, spoke softly, walked softly, and tried to live a life that was largely beneath notice.

"But the summer before last, all of that changed," Parker said. "Suddenly you throw away your teaching career. You take the plunge and become a full-time writer. Almost overnight, you change from an accountant type to a risk-taker, a Bohemian. Why? You've never been clear about that. *Why?*''

Dominick frowned, considered the question for a moment, and was surprised that he had not thought about it much before this. "I don't know why. I really don't know."

At the University of Portland, he had been up for tenure, had felt that he would not be given it, and had grown panicky at the prospect of being cast loose from his sheltered moorings. Obsessed with keeping a low profile, he had faded *too* completely from the notice of the campus movers-and-shakers, and when the time arrived for the tenure board to consider him, they had begun to question whether he had embraced the University with sufficient enthusiasm to warrant a grant of lifetime employment. Dom was enough of a realist to see that, if the board refused tenure, he would find it difficult to obtain a position at another university, for the hiring committee would want to know why he had been turned down at Portland. In an uncharacteristic burst of self-promotion, hoping to slip out from under the university's ax before it fell, he applied for positions at institutions in several Western states, emphasizing his published stories because that was the *only* thing worth emphasizing.

Mountainview College in Utah, with a student body of only four thousand, had been so impressed by the list of magazines in which he had published that they flew him from Portland for an interview. Dom made a considerable effort to be more outgoing than he had ever been before. He was offered a contract to teach English and creative writing with guaranteed tenure. He had accepted, if not with enormous delight then at least with enormous relief.

Now, on the terrace of Las Brisas, as the California sun slid out from behind a band of white jeweled clouds, he took a sip of his beer, sighed, and said, "I left Portland late in June that year. I had a U-Haul trailer hooked to the car, just a small one, filled mostly with books and clothes. I was in a good mood. Didn't feel as if I'd failed at Portland. Not at all. I just felt . . . well, that I was getting a fresh start. I was really looking forward to life at Mountainview. In fact, I don't remember ever being happier than the day I hit the road."

Parker Faine nodded knowingly. "Of course you were happy! You had tenure in a hick school, where not much would be expected of you, where your introversion would be excused as an artist's temperament."

"A perfect rabbit hole, huh?"

"Exactly. So why didn't you wind up teaching in Mountainview?"

"I told you before . . . at the last minute, when I got there the second week in July, I just couldn't bear the idea of going on with the kind of life I'd had before. I was tired of being a mouse, a rabbit."

"Just like that, you were repelled by the low-key life. Why?"

"It wasn't very fulfilling."

"But why were you tired of it *all of a sudden?*"

"I don't know."

"You must have some idea. Haven't you thought about it a lot?"

"Surprisingly, I haven't," Dom said. He stared out to sea for a long moment, watching a dozen sailboats and a large yacht as they moved majestically along the coast. "I just now realized how amazingly *little* I've thought about it. Strange . . . I'm usually too self-analytical for my own good, but in this case I've never probed very deeply."

"Ah ha!" Parker exclaimed. "I knew I was on the right trail! The changes you went through *then* are somehow related to the problems you're having *now*. So go on. So you told the people at Mountainview that you didn't want their job any more?''

''They weren't happy.''

''And you took a tiny apartment in town.''

''One room, plus kitchen and bath. Not much of a place. Nice view of the mountains, though.''

''Decided to live on your savings while you wrote a novel?''

''There wasn't a *lot* in the bank, but I'd always been frugal.''

''Impulsive behavior. Risky. And not a damn bit *like* you,'' Parker said. ''So why did you do it? What changed you?''

''I guess it was building for a long time. By the time I got to Mountainview, my dissatisfaction was so great that I *had* to change.''

Parker leaned back in his chair. ''No good, my friend. There must be more to it than that. Listen, by your own admission, you were as happy as a pig in shit when you left Portland with your U-Haul. You had a job with a livable salary, guaranteed tenure, in a place where no one was ever going to demand too much of you. All you had to do was settle down in Mountainview and disappear. But by the time you got there, you couldn't wait to throw it all over, move into a garret, and risk eventual starvation, all for your art. What the hell happened to you during that long drive to Utah? Something must've given you a real jolt, something big enough to knock you out of your complacency.''

''Nope. It was an uneventful trip.''

''Not inside your head, it wasn't.''

Dominick shrugged. ''As far as I remember, I just relaxed, enjoyed the drive, took my time, looked at the scenery. . . .''

''*Amigo!*'' Parker roared, startling their waiter, who was passing by. ''*Uno* margarita! And another *cerveza* for my friend.''

''No, no,'' Dom said. ''I—''

''You haven't finished *that* beer,'' Parker said. ''I know, I know. But you are going to finish it and drink another, and gradually you're going to loosen up, and we're going to get to the bottom of this sleepwalking. I'm sure it's related to the changes you underwent the summer before last. You know why I'm so sure? I'll tell you why I'm so sure. Nobody undergoes *two* personality crises in two years for utterly unrelated reasons. The two have to be tied together somehow.''

Dom grimaced. ''I wouldn't exactly call this a personality *crisis.*''

''Oh, wouldn't you?'' Leaning forward, lowering his shaggy head, putting all the force of his powerful personality behind the question, Parker said, ''Wouldn't you really call it a crisis, my friend?''

Dom sighed. ''Well . . . yeah. I guess maybe I would. A crisis.''

They left Las Brisas late that afternoon, without arriving at any answers. That night, when he went to bed, he was filled with dread, wondering where he would find himself in the morning.

And in the morning, he virtually exploded out of sleep with a shrill scream and found himself in total, claustrophobic darkness. Something had hold of him, something cold and clammy and strange and *alive*. He struck out blindly, flailed and clawed, twisted and kicked, freed himself, scrambled away in panic, through the cloying blackness, on his hands and knees, until he collided with a wall. The lightless room reverberated with thunderous pounding and shouting, an unnerving cacophony, the source of which he could not identify. He scrambled along the baseboard until he came to a junction of walls, where he put his back into the corner and faced out upon the lightless chamber, certain that the clammy creature would leap on him from the gloom.

What was in the room with him?

The noise grew louder: shouting, hammering, a crash followed by a clatter-rattle of wood, more shouting, and another crash.

Still groggy from sleep, his senses distorted by hysteria and excess adrenaline, Dom was convinced that the thing from which he had been hiding had at last come for him. He had tried to fool it by sleeping in closets and behind the furnace. But tonight it would not be deceived: it meant to have him; he could hide no longer; the end had come.

From the darkness, someone or something shouted his name—*"Dom!"*—and he realized that someone had been calling to him for the last minute or two, maybe longer. *"Dominick, answer me!"*

Another shuddering crash. The brittle crack of splintering wood.

Huddling in the corner, Dom finally woke completely. The clammy creature had not been real. A figment of a dream. He recognized the voice calling to him as that of Parker Faine. Even as the residual hysteria of his nightmare subsided, another crash, the loudest of all, generated a chain-reaction of destruction, a crackling-sliding-scraping-toppling-crashing-booming-clattering-rattling that culminated with the opening of a door and the intrusion of light into the darkness.

Dom squinted against the glare and saw Parker silhouetted like some hulking troll in the bedroom door, the hall light behind him. The door had been locked, and Parker had forced it, had thrown himself against it until the lock disintegrated.

"Dominick, buddy, are you okay?"

The door had been barricaded as well, which had made entrance even more difficult. Dom saw that, in his sleep, he had evidently moved the dresser in front of the door, had stacked the two nightstands atop the dresser, and had put the bedroom armchair in front of it. Those overturned pieces of furniture now lay on the floor in a jumbled heap.

Parker stepped into the room. "Buddy? Are you all right? You were screaming. I could hear you clear out in the driveway."

"A dream."

"Must've been a lulu."

"I can't remember what it was," Dom said, remaining on the floor, in the corner, too exhausted and weak-kneed to get up. "You're a sight for sore eyes, Parker. But . . . what on earth are you doing here?"

Parker blinked. "Don't you know? You phoned me. Not more than ten minutes ago. You were shouting for help. You said *they* were here and were going to get you. Then you hung up."

Dom felt humiliation settle over him as if it were a painful burn.

"Ah, so you *did* make the call in your sleep," the painter said. "Thought as much. You sounded . . . not yourself. Maybe I should've called the police, but I suspected this sleepwalking thing. Knew you wouldn't want it brought into the open in front of strangers, a bunch of cops."

"I'm out of control, Parker. Something's . . . snapping inside me."

"That's enough of that crap. I won't listen to any more of it."

Dom felt like a helpless child. He was afraid he was going to cry. He bit his tongue, squeezed back the tears, cleared his throat, and said, "What time is it?"

"A few minutes after four. Middle of the night." Parker looked toward the window and frowned.

Following the other man's gaze, Dom saw that the draperies were drawn tight shut and that the highboy had been moved in front of the window, barring entrance by that route. He had been busy in his sleep.

"Oh, Christ," Parker said, moving to the bed, where he stopped, a vivid expression of shock on his broad face. "This is no good, my friend. This is no good at all."

Holding on to the wall, Dom rose shakily to his feet to see what Parker was talking about, but when he saw it, he wished he had remained on the floor. An arsenal was laid out on the bed: the .22 automatic that he usually kept in his nightstand; a butcher's knife; two other meat knives; a cleaver; a hammer; the ax he used for splitting firewood and which, the last he remembered, had been in the garage.

Parker said, "What were you expecting—a Soviet invasion? What frightens you so?"

"I don't know. Something in my nightmares."

"So what do you dream about?"

"I don't know."

"You can't remember any of it?"

"No." He shivered again, violently.

Parker came to him, put a hand on his shoulder. "You better take a shower, get dressed. I'll start rustling up some breakfast. Okay? Then I . . . I think we'd better pay a visit to that doctor of yours as soon as his office opens. I think he's got to take a second look at you."

Dominick nodded.

It was December 2.

TWO

◆

December 2–December 16

1. Boston, Massachusetts

Viola Fletcher, a fifty-eight-year-old elementary-school teacher, mother of two daughters, wife of a devoted husband, a wry and witty woman with an infectious laugh, was silent now and still, lying on the operating table, unconscious, her life in Dr. Ginger Weiss's hands.

Ginger's entire life had been a funnel, focusing on this moment: for the first time, she was assuming the senior surgeon's role in a major and complicated procedure. Years of arduous education, an immeasurable weight of hopes and dreams, lay behind her ascension to this moment. She had a prideful yet humbling sense of just how great a distance her journey had covered.

And she was half sick with dread.

Mrs. Fletcher had been anesthetized and draped in cool green sheets. None of the patient's body was visible except that portion of her torso on which surgery would be performed, a neat square of flesh painted with iodine and framed by lime-colored cloth. Even her face was out of sight beneath tented sheeting, as an added precaution against airborne contamination of the wound that would shortly be made in her abdomen. The effect was to depersonalize the patient, and perhaps that was in part the *intent* of the draping, as well, thereby sparing the surgeon the need to look upon the human face of agony and death if, God forbid, his skill and education should fail him.

On Ginger's right, Agatha Tandy, the surgical technician, stood ready with spreaders, rakes, hemostats, scalpels, and other instruments. On her left, a scrub nurse was prepared to assist. Another scrub nurse, the circulating nurse, the anesthesiologist, and his nurse also waited for the procedure to begin.

George Hannaby stood on the other side of the table, looking less like a doctor than like the former star fullback on a pro football team. His wife, Rita, had once talked him into playing Paul Bunyan in a comedy sketch for a hospital charity show, and he had appeared at home in woodsman's boots, jeans, and a red plaid shirt. He brought with him an aura of strength, calmness, and competency that was most reassuring.

Ginger held out her right hand.

Agatha put a scalpel in it.

A keen, thin, bright curve of light outlined the razor-sharp edge of the instrument.

Hand poised over the score lines on the patient's torso, Ginger hesitated and took a deep breath.

George's stereo tape deck stood on a small table in the corner, and familiar strains of Bach issued from the speakers.

She was remembering the ophthalmoscope, the shiny black gloves. . . .

However, as frightening as those incidents had been, they had not utterly destroyed her self-confidence. She had felt fine ever since the most recent attack: strong, alert, energetic. If she had noticed the slightest weariness or fuzzy-mindedness, she would have cancelled this procedure. On the other hand, she had not acquired her education, had not worked seven days a week all these years, only to throw away her future because of two aberrant moments of stress-related hysteria. Everything was going to be fine, just fine.

The wall clock said seven-forty-two. Time to get on with it.

She made the first cut. With hemostats and clamps and a faultless skill that always surprised her, she moved deeper, constructing a shaft through skin, fat, and muscle, into the center of the patient's belly. Soon the incision was large enough to accommodate both her hands and those of her assisting physician, George Hannaby, if his help should be required. The scrub nurses moved close to the table, one on each side, grasped the sculpted handles of the retractors, and pulled back gently on them, drawing apart the walls of the wound.

Agatha Tandy picked up a fluffy, absorbent cloth and quickly blotted Ginger's forehead, careful to avoid the jeweler's lenses that protruded from her operating glasses.

Above his mask, George's eyes squinted in a smile. *He* was not sweating. He seldom did.

Ginger swiftly tied off bleeders and removed clamps, and Agatha ordered new supplies from the circulating nurse.

In the brief blank spaces between Bach's concertos and in the silence at the end of the tape before it was turned over, the loudest sounds in the tile-walled room were the sibilant exhalations and groaning inhalations of the artificial lung machine that breathed for Viola Fletcher. The patient could not breathe for herself because she was paralyzed by a curare-derived muscle relaxant. Though entirely mechanical, those sounds possessed a haunting quality that made it impossible for Ginger to overcome her apprehension.

On other days, when George cut, there was more talk. He traded quips with the nurses and the assisting resident, using light banter to reduce the tension without also reducing concentration on the vital task at hand. Ginger was simply not up to that sort of dazzling performance, which seemed akin to playing basketball, chewing gum, and solving difficult mathematical problems at the same time.

Having completed the excursion into the belly, she ran the colon with both hands and determined that it was healthy. With damp gauze pads provided by Agatha, Ginger cradled the intestines, placed the hoe-like blades of the retractors against them, and turned them over to the scrub nurses, who held them out of the way, thus exposing the aorta, the main trunkline of the body's arterial system.

From the chest, the aorta entered the belly through the diaphragm, running parallel to the spine. Immediately above the groin, it split into two iliac arteries leading to the femoral arteries in the legs.

"There it is," Ginger said. "An aneurysm. Just like in the X rays." As if to confirm it, she glanced at the patient's X ray that was fixed on the light screen, on the wall at the foot of the operating table. "A dissecting aneurysm, just above the aortic saddle."

Agatha blotted Ginger's forehead.

The aneurysm, a weakness in the wall of the aorta, had permitted the artery to bulge outward on both sides, forming a dumbbell-shaped extrusion full of blood, which beat like a second heart. This condition caused difficulty in swallowing, extreme shortness of breath, severe coughing, and chest pains; and if the bulging vessel burst, death followed swiftly.

As Ginger stared at the pulsing aneurysm, an almost religious sense of mystery overcame her, a profound awe, as if she had stepped out of the real world into a mystic sphere, where the very meaning of life was soon to be revealed to her. Her feeling of power, of transcendence, rose from the realization that she could do battle with death—and win. Death was lurking there in the body of her patient right now, in the form of the throbbing aneurysm, a dark bud waiting to flower, but she had the skill and training to banish it.

From a sterile package, Agatha Tandy had taken a section of artificial aorta— a thick, ribbed tube that split into two smaller tubes, the iliac arteries. It was woven entirely of Dacron. Ginger positioned it over the wound, trimmed it to fit with a pair of small sharp scissors, and returned it to the technician. Agatha put the white graft in a shallow stainless-steel tray that already contained some of the patient's blood, and swished it back and forth to wet it thoroughly.

The graft would be allowed to soak until it had clotted a bit. Once it was installed in the patient, Ginger would run some blood through it, clamp it, allow that blood to clot a bit more, then flush it out before actually sewing it in place. The thin layer of clotted blood would help prevent seepage, and in time the steady flow of blood would form a neointima, a leak-proof new lining virtually indistinguishable from that in a real artery. The amazing thing was that the Dacron vessel was not merely an adequate substitute for the damaged section of aorta but was, in fact, actually superior to what nature had provided; five hundred years from now, when nothing remained of Viola Fletcher but dust and time-worn bones, the Dacron graft would be still intact, still flexible and strong.

Agatha blotted Ginger's forehead.

"How do you feel?" George asked.

"Fine," Ginger said.

"Tense?"

"Not really," she lied.

He said, "It's a genuine pleasure watching you work, Doctor."

"I'll second that," said one of the scrub nurses.

"Me, too," the other said.

"Thanks," Ginger said, surprised and pleased.

George said, "You have a certain grace in surgery, a lightness of touch, a splendid sensitivity of hand and eye that is, I'm sorry to say, not at all common in the profession."

Ginger knew that he never gave voice to an insincere compliment, but coming from such a stern taskmaster, this bordered on excessive flattery. By God, George Hannaby was *proud* of her! That realization flooded her with warm emotion. If she had been anywhere but in an operating room, tears would have come to her eyes, but here she kept a tighter rein on her feelings. However, the intensity of her reaction to his words made her aware of how completely he had filled the role of father-figure in her life; she took nearly as much satisfaction from his praise as she would have taken if it had come from Jacob Weiss himself.

Ginger proceeded with the operation in better spirits. The disturbing possibility of a seizure slowly receded from her thoughts, and greater confidence allowed her to work with even more grace than before. Nothing could go wrong now.

She set about methodically controlling the flow of blood through the aorta, carefully exposing and temporarily clamping all branching vessels, using thin elastic loops of extremely pliable plastic tubing to valve off the smaller vessels, placing mosquito clamps and bulldog clamps on the larger arteries, including the iliacs and the aorta itself. In little less than an hour, she had stopped all blood flow through the aorta to the patient's legs, and the throbbing aneurysm had ceased its mocking imitation of the heart.

With a small scalpel, she punctured the aneurysm, releasing a pool of blood; the aorta deflated. She sliced it open along its anterior wall. At that moment, the patient was without an aorta, more helpless and more dependent upon the surgeon than at any other time. There was no going back now. From this point on, the operation must be conducted not only with the greatest care but with the most prudent speed.

A hush had fallen on the surgical team. What little conversation there had been now ceased. The Bach tape had reached the end again, and no one moved to turn it over. Time was measured by the wheezing and sucking of the artificial lung machine and by the beeping of the EKG.

Ginger removed the Dacron graft from the steel tray, where it had been soaking up blood and clotting precisely as desired. She sewed the top of it into the aortal trunk, using an extremely fine thread. Then, with the top of the graft sewn in place and the unattached bottom clamped off, Ginger filled it with blood to let it clot again.

Throughout these steps of the operation, it had not been necessary for Ginger to have the sweat blotted from her forehead. She hoped that George noticed her new dryness—she was sure he did.

Without needing to be told that it was once again time for music, the circulating nurse reset the Bach tape.

Hours of work lay ahead of Ginger, but she pressed on without the least weariness. She moved down the draped body, folding back the green sheets, revealing both of the patient's thighs. With the help of the circulating nurse, Agatha had replenished the instrument tray and was ready now with everything that Ginger needed to make two more incisions, one in each of the patient's legs, below the inguineal creases, where the legs attached to the body trunk. Clamping and tying off vessels, Ginger eventually exposed and separated the femoral arteries. As with the aorta before, she used thin elastic tubing and a variety of clamps to valve off the blood flow through these vascular fields, then opened both arteries where the bifurcated legs of the graft would attach to them. A couple of times she caught herself humming along happily with the music, and the ease with which she worked made it seem almost as if she had been a surgeon in an earlier life, now reincarnated into the elite brotherhood of the caduceus, predestined for this labor.

But she should have remembered her father and his aphorisms, the bits of wisdom that he had collected and with which he had gently lectured or patiently admonished her on those rare occasions when she had been less than well behaved or when she had failed to do her very best in school. *Time waits for no man; God helps those who help themselves; a penny saved is a penny earned; resentment hurts only those who harbor it; judge not that ye be not judged. . . .* He had a thousand of them, but there was none he liked better and none he repeated more often than this one: *Pride goeth before a great fall.*

She should have remembered those six words. The operation was going so well, and she was so happy with her work, so *proud* of her performance in this first major solo flight, that she forgot about the inevitable great fall.

Returning to the opened abdomen, she unclamped the bottom of the Dacron graft, flushed it out, then tunneled the twin legs of it beneath the untouched flesh of the groin, beneath the inguineal creases, and into the incisions she had made in the femoral arteries. She stitched in both terminuses of the bifurcated graft, unclamped the restricted vascular network, and watched with delight as the pulse returned to the patched aorta. For twenty minutes, she searched for leaks and knitted them up with fine, strong thread. For another five minutes, she watched closely, in silence, as the graft throbbed like any normal, healthy arterial vessel, without any sign of chronic seepage.

At last she said, "Time to close up."

"Beautifully done," George said.

Ginger was glad she was wearing a surgical mask, for beneath it her face was stretched by a smile so broad that she must have looked like the proverbial grinning idiot.

She closed the incisions in the patient's legs. She took the intestines from the nurses, who were clearly exhausted and eager to relinquish the retractors. She replaced the guts in the body and gently ran them once again, searching for irregularities but finding none. The rest was easy: laying fat and muscle back in place, closing up, layer by layer, until the original incision was drawn shut with heavy black cord.

The anesthesiologist's nurse undraped Viola Fletcher's head.

The anesthesiologist untaped her eyes, turned off the anesthesia.

The circulating nurse cut Bach off in mid-passage.

Ginger looked at Mrs. Fletcher's face, pale now but not unusually drawn. The mask of the respirator was still on her face, but she was getting only an oxygen mixture.

The nurses backed away and skinned off their rubber gloves.

Viola Fletcher's eyelids fluttered, and she groaned.

"Mrs. Fletcher?" the anesthesiologist said loudly.

The patient did not respond.

"Viola?" Ginger said. "Can you hear me, Viola?"

The woman's eyes did not open, but though she was more asleep than awake, her lips moved, and in a fuzzy voice she said, "Yes, Doctor."

Ginger accepted congratulations from the team and left the room with George. As they stripped off their gloves, pulled off their masks, and removed their caps, she felt as if she were filled with helium, in danger of breaking loose of the bonds of gravity. But with each step toward the scrub sinks in the surgical hall, she became less buoyant. A tremendous exhaustion settled over her. Her neck and shoulders ached. Her back was sore. Her legs were stiff, and her feet were tired.

"My God," she said, "I'm pooped!"

"You should be," George said. "You started at seven-thirty, and it's past the lunch hour. An aortal graft is damned debilitating."

"*You* feel this way when you've done one?"

"Of course."

"But it hit me so suddenly. In there, I felt great. I felt I could go on for hours yet."

"In there," George said with evident affection and amusement, "you were godlike, dueling with death and winning, and no god ever grows weary. Godwork is too much fun to ever get weary of it."

At the sinks, they turned on the water, took off the surgical gowns they'd worn over their hospital greens, and broke open packets of soap.

As Ginger began to wash her hands, she leaned wearily against the sink and bent forward a bit, so she was looking straight down at the drain, at the water swirling around the stainless-steel basin, at the bubbles of soap whirling with the water, all of it funneling into the drain, around and around and down into the drain, around and down, down and down. . . . This time, the irrational fear struck and overwhelmed her with even less warning than at Bernstein's Deli or in George's office last Wednesday. In an instant her attention had become entirely focused upon the drain, which appeared to throb and grow wider as if it were suddenly possessed of malignant life.

She dropped the soap and, with a bleat of terror, jumped back from the sink, collided with Agatha Tandy, cried out again. She vaguely heard George calling her name. But he was fading away in the manner of an image on a motion picture screen, retreating into a mist, as if he were part of a scene that was dissolving to a full-lens shot of steam or clouds or fog, and he no longer seemed real. Agatha Tandy and the hallway and the doors to the surgery were fading, too. *Everything* was fading but the sink, which appeared to grow larger and more solid, super-real. A sense of mortal danger settled over her. But it was just an ordinary scrub sink, for God's sake, and she had to hold on to that truth, clutch at the cliff of reality and resist the forces pulling her over the edge. Just a sink. Just an ordinary drain. Just—

She ran. From every side, the mist closed around her, and she lost all conscious awareness of her actions.

The first thing she became aware of was the snow. Large white flakes sifted past her face, gently turning, lazily eddying toward the ground in the manner of fluffy airborne dandelion seeds, for there was no wind to drive them. She raised her head, looked up beyond the towering walls of the old high-rise buildings that shouldered in around her, and saw a rectangular patch of low gray sky, from which the snow descended. As she stared into the winter heavens, momentarily confused as to her whereabouts and condition, her hair and eyebrows grew white.

Flakes melted on her face, but she slowly realized that her cheeks were already wet with tears and that she was still weeping quietly.

Gradually, the cold impinged upon her. In spite of the absence of wind, the air was sharp-toothed; it bit her cheeks, nipped her chin, and her hands were numb from the cold venom of countless bites. The chill penetrated her hospital greens, and she was shivering uncontrollably.

Next she became aware of the freezing concrete beneath her and the ice-cold brick wall against her back. She was squeezed into a corner, facing out, knees drawn up to her chin, arms locked around her legs—a posture of defense and terror. Her body heat was being leached away through every contact point with pavement and masonry, but she did not have the strength or will to get to her feet and go inside.

She remembered fixating upon the drain of the scrub sink. With unmitigated despair, she recalled the mindless panic, her collision with Agatha Tandy, the startled look on George Hannaby's face as he had reacted to her screams. Although the rest was a blank, she supposed she had then taken flight from imaginary dangers, like some madwoman, to the shock of her colleagues—and to the certain destruction of her career.

She pressed harder against the brick wall, wishing that it would suck away her body heat even faster.

She was sitting at the end of a wide alley, a blind serviceway that led into the core of the hospital complex. To her left, double metal doors led into the furnace room, and beyond those was the exit from the emergency stairs.

Inevitably, she was reminded of her encounter with a mugger during her internship at Columbia Presbyterian in New York. That night, he had dragged her into an alleyway much like this. However, in the New York alleyway, she had been in command, victorious—while here she was a loser, descendant rather than ascendant, weak and lost. She perceived a bleak irony and a frightening symmetry in having been brought to the lowest point of her life in such a place as this.

Premed, medical school, the long hours and hardships of her intern year, all the work and sacrifices, all the hopes and dreams had been for nothing. At the last minute, with a surgical career almost within her grasp, she had failed George, Anna, Jacob, and herself. She could no longer deny the truth or ignore the obvious: Something was wrong with her, something so desperately wrong that it would surely preclude the resumption of a life in medicine. Psychosis? A brain tumor? Perhaps an aneurysm in the brain?

The door to the emergency stairs was flung open with a rattle and a screech of unoiled hinges, and George Hannaby came out into the snow, breathing hard. He took several quick steps into the alley, heedless of the risk posed by the quarter-inch skin of slippery new snow. The sight of her was sufficiently shocking to bring him to a lurching halt. A ghastly expression lined his face, and Ginger supposed he was regretting the extra time and attention and special guidance that he had given her. He had thought she was especially bright and good and worthy, but now she had proved him wrong. He had been so kind to her and so supportive that her betrayal of his trust, although beyond her control, filled her with self-loathing and brought more hot tears to her eyes.

"Ginger?" he said shakily. "Ginger, what's wrong?"

She was able to respond only with a wretched, involuntary sob.

Seen through her tears, he shimmered, blurred. She wished he'd go away and leave her to stew in humiliation. Didn't he know how much worse it was to have him staring at her while she was in this condition?

The snow was falling harder. Other people appeared in the doorway through which he had come, but she could not identify them.

"Ginger, please talk to me," George said as he drew near. "What's wrong? Tell me what's wrong. Tell me what I can do."

She bit her lip, tried to repress her tears, but instead she began to sob harder than ever. In a thin, blubbery voice that sickened her with proof of her own weakness, she said, "S-Something's wrong with me."

George stooped down in front of her. "What? What's wrong?"

"I don't know."

She had always been able to handle any trouble that came her way, unassisted. She was Ginger Weiss. She was different. She was a golden girl. She didn't know how to ask for help of this kind, of this degree.

Still stooping in front of her, George said, "Whatever it is, we can work it out. I know you're fiercely proud of your self-reliance. You listening, kid? I've always stepped carefully when I'm with you because I know you resent being helped along too much. You want to do it all yourself. But this time you simply can't handle it alone, and you don't have to. I'm here, and by God you're going to lean on me whether you like it or not. You hear?"

"I . . . I've ruined everything. I've d-disappointed you."

He found a small smile. "Not you, dear girl. Not ever. Rita and I have had all sons, but if we could've had a daughter, we would've hoped for one like you. Exactly like you. You're a special woman, Dr. Weiss, a dear and special woman. Disappoint me? Impossible. I would consider it an honor and a pleasure if you would lean on me now, just as if you *were* my daughter, and let me help you through this as if I were the father you've lost."

He held out a hand to her.

She grasped it and held on tightly.

It was Monday, December 2.

Many weeks would pass before she learned that other people in other places—all strangers to her—were living through eerie variations of her own nightmare.

2. Trenton, New Jersey

A few minutes before midnight, Jack Twist opened the door and left the warehouse, stepping into the wind and sleet, and some guy was just getting out of a gray Ford van at the foot of the nearest loading ramp. The van's arrival had been masked by the rumble of a passing freight train. The night was deep around the warehouse, except for four meager patches of murky yellow light from poorly maintained, grime-dimmed security lamps. Unfortunately, one of those lights was directly over the door through which Jack had exited, and its sickly glow reached precisely far enough to include the passenger's door of the van, out of which the unexpected visitor had appeared.

The guy had a face made for police mug books: heavy jaw, a mouth that was hardly more than a slash, a nose that had been broken a couple of times, and hard little pig eyes. He was one of those obedient but pitiless sadists that the mob employed as enforcers, a man who, in other times, might have been a rape and pillage specialist in the armies of Genghis Khan, a grinning Nazi thug, a torture master in one of Stalin's death camps, or a Morlock from the future as imagined by H. G. Wells in *The Time Machine*. To Jack, the guy looked like serious trouble.

They startled each other, and Jack did not immediately raise his .38 and put a bullet in the bastard, which is what he should have done.

"Who the hell are you?" the Morlock asked. Then he saw the canvas bag that Jack was dragging with his left hand and the lowered pistol in Jack's right hand. His eyebrows shot up, and he shouted, "Max!"

Max was probably the driver of the van, but Jack did not wait around for formal introductions. He did a quick reverse into the warehouse, slammed the door shut, and stepped to the side of it in case someone out there started using it for target practice.

The only light inside the warehouse came from the brightly lit office far at the back of the building and from an overhead bank of widely spaced, low-wattage bulbs set in tin shades, which were allowed to burn all night. But there was sufficient illumination for Jack to see the faces of his two companions—Mort Gersh and Tommy Sung—who had been following him. They did not look as happy as they had been only a couple of minutes ago.

They had been happy because they had successfully hit a major way station on the route of the mafia cash train, a collection point for narcotics money from half the state of New Jersey. Suitcases and flight bags and cardboard boxes and Styrofoam coolers full of cash arrived at the warehouse from a score of couriers, most of it on Sunday and Monday. Tuesdays, mob accountants in Pierre Cardin suits arrived to calculate the week's profits from the pharmaceutical division. Every Wednesday, suitcases full of tightly banded sacks of greenbacks went out to Miami, Vegas, Los Angeles, New York, and other centers of high finance, where investment advisers with Harvard or Columbia MBAs, on retainer to the mafia—or *fratellanza*, as the underworld referred to itself—wisely put it to work. Jack, Mort, and Tommy had simply stepped in between the accountants and the investment advisers, and had taken four heavy bags full of cash for themselves. "Just think of us as one more layer of middlemen," Jack had told the three glowering thugs who were, even now, tied up in the warehouse office, and Mort and Tommy had laughed.

Mort was not laughing now. He was fifty years old, pot-bellied, slump-shouldered, balding. He wore a dark suit, porkpie hat, and gray overcoat. He always wore a dark suit and porkpie hat, though not always the overcoat. Jack had never seen him in anything else. Tonight, Jack and Tommy were wearing jeans and quilted vinyl jackets, but there was Mort looking like one of the guys in the background of an old Edward G. Robinson movie. The snapbrim of his hat had lost its sharp edge and gone slightly soft, rather like Mort himself, and the suit was rumpled. His voice was weary and dour. He said, "Who's out there?" as Jack slammed the door and stepped hastily away from it.

"At least two guys in a Ford van," Jack said.

"Mob?"

"I only saw one of them," Jack said, "but he looked like one of Dr. Frankenstein's experiments that *didn't* work out."

"At least all the doors are locked."

"They'll have keys."

The three of them moved quickly away from the exit, back into the deep shadows in an aisle between piles of wooden crates and cardboard cartons that were stacked on pallets. The merchandise formed twenty-foot-high walls. The warehouse was immense, with a wide array of goods stored under its vaulted ceiling: hundreds of TV sets, microwave ovens, blenders, and toasters by the thousands, tractor parts, plumbing supplies, Cuisinarts, and more. It was a clean, well-run establishment, but as with any giant industrial building at night, the place was eerie when all the workers were gone. Strange, whispery echoes floated along the maze of aisles. Outside, the sleet fell harder than before, rustling and ticking and tapping and hissing on the slate roof, as if a multitude of unknown creatures moved through the rafters and inside the walls.

"I told you it was a mistake to hit the mob," Tommy Sung said. He was a Chinese-American, about thirty, which made him seven years younger than Jack. "Jewelry stores, armored cars, even banks, okay, but not the mob, for God's sake. It's stupid to hit the mob. Might as well walk into a bar full of Marines and spit on the flag."

"You're here," Jack said.

"Yeah, well," Tommy said, "I don't always show good judgment."

In a voice of doom and despair, Mort said, "A van shows up at this hour, it means one thing. They're delivering one kind of shit or another, probably coke or horse. Which means there won't be just the driver and the ape you saw. There'll be two other guys in the back of the van with the merchandise, carrying converted Uzis or worse."

Tommy said, "Why aren't they already shooting their way in?"

"As far as they know," Jack said, "there's ten of us, and we have bazookas. They'll move cautiously."

"A truck used on dope runs is sure to have radio communications," Mort said. "They'll have already called for backup."

Tommy said, "You telling me the mafia has a fleet of radio vans like the goddamned phone company or something?"

"These days, they're as organized as any business," Mort said.

They listened for sounds of purposeful human movement in farther reaches of the building, but all they heard was sleet hitting the roof.

The .38 in Jack's hand suddenly felt like a toy. Mort was carrying a Smith & Wesson M39 9mm pistol, and Tommy had a Smith & Wesson Model 19 Combat Magnum that he had tucked inside his insulated jacket after the men in the office had been securely tied up, when it had seemed that the dangerous part of the job had been completed. They were well armed, but they were not ready to face down Uzis. Jack remembered old documentaries of hopelessly outclassed Hungarians trying to turn back invading Russian tanks with rocks and sticks. In times of trouble, Jack Twist had a tendency to melodramatize his plight and, regardless of the situation, to cast himself in the role of the noble underdog battling the forces of evil. He was aware of this tendency, and he thought it was one of his most endearing qualities. At the moment, however, their position was so tenuous that there was no way to melodramatize it.

Mort's thoughts had led him to precisely the same consideration, for he said, "There's no use trying to get out by any of the back doors. They'll have split up by now—two in front, two in back."

The front and rear exits—both the regular doors and roll-up cargo bay doors— were the only ways out. There were no openings, not even windows or vents, on the sides of the enormous building, no basement and therefore no basement exit, no way to get onto the roof. In preparation for the robbery, the three of them had studied detailed plans of the building, and now they knew they were trapped.

Tommy said, "What are we going to do?"

The question was addressed to Jack Twist, not to Mort, because Jack organized any robbery he took part in. If unanticipated events required improvisation, Jack was expected to come up with the brilliant ideas.

"Hey," Tommy said, taking a stab at brilliance himself, "why don't we go out the same way we got in!"

They had entered the building with a variation on the Trojan Horse ploy, which was the only way to bypass the elaborate security systems that were in operation at night. The warehouse was a front for the illegal drug trade, but it was also a real, functioning, profitable warehouse that accepted regular shipments from legitimate businesses in need of temporary storage for excess inventory. Therefore, with the personal computer and modem in his apartment, Jack had tapped into the computers of both the warehouse and one of its reputable clients, and had created the file of electronic paperwork that would legitimize the delivery of a huge crate, which had arrived this morning and had been stored per instructions. He, Mort, and Tommy had been inside the crate, which had been designed and constructed with five concealed exits, so they could get out of it quietly even if it was blocked by other crates on four sides. A few minutes after eleven o'clock tonight, they had slipped out and had surprised the tough guys in the office, who had been quite confident that their multiple alarm systems and locked doors had transformed the warehouse into an inviolable fortress.

"We could get back in the crate," Tommy said, "and when they finally come in and don't find us, they'll go crazy trying to figure how we got away. By tomorrow night the heat'll be off. Then we can slip out and make our getaway."

"No good," Mort said sourly. "They'll figure it out. They'll search this place until they find us."

"No good, Tommy," Jack agreed. "Now, here's what I want you to do. . . ." He quickly improvised an escape plan, and they assented to it.

Tommy hurried to the master panel of light switches in the office, to kill every light in the warehouse.

Jack and Mort dragged the four heavy bags of money toward the south end of the long building, and the dry sound of canvas scraping along the concrete floor echoed and reechoed through the chilly air. At that far end of the building, instead of more stacks of merchandise, there were several trucks that had been parked in the interior staging area, where, first thing in the morning, they would be loaded. Jack and Mort were less than halfway through the maze, still half a city block from the semis, when the dim lights winked out and the warehouse was plunged into unrelieved darkness. They paused long enough for Jack to switch on his Eveready before continuing through the gloom.

Bearing his own flashlight, Tommy rejoined them and took one of the bags from Jack, one from Mort.

The clicking impact and susurrant slide of sleet upon the roof began to subside slightly as the storm entered a lull, and Jack thought he heard the screech of brakes outside. Could reinforcements have arrived so soon?

The warehouse's interior loading zone contained four eighteen-wheelers: a Peterbilt, a White, and two Mack trucks. Each of them faced out toward a loading-bay door.

Jack went to the nearest Mack, dropped his sack of money, stepped up on the running board, opened the door, and shone his flashlight inside, along the dashboard. The keys dangled from the ignition. He had expected as much. Confident of their multilayered security system, the warehouse employees did not believe there was any danger that one of these vehicles might be stolen during the night.

Jack and Mort went to the other three trucks, found keys in all of them, and started the engines.

In the cab of the first Mack, there was a sleeping berth behind the seat, where one member of a long-distance driving team could catch a nap while his partner took the wheel. Tommy Sung stowed the four bags of money in that recess.

Jack returned to the Mack just as Tommy finished with the sacks. He settled in behind the wheel and switched off his flashlight. Mort got in on the passenger's side. Jack started the engine but did not switch on the headlights.

All four trucks were idling noisily now.

Carrying his flashlight, Tommy ran to the farthest of the four big roll-down doors of the interior loading zone and touched the control that started it moving laboriously upward on its track. Jack watched him tensely from the high seat of the big rig. Tommy hurried back along that outer wall, his progress marked by the bobbling beam of his flash, slapping his right hand against the door controls as he came to each of them. Then, snapping off his flashlight, he bolted toward the Mack as the four doors slowly lumbered open with much grating and clattering.

Outside, the Morlocks would know the doors were going up, would hear the trucks' engines. But they'd be looking into a dark building, and until they could throw some light in here, they couldn't know which rig was the intended escape vehicle. They might spray *all* of the trucks with submachine-gun fire, but Jack was counting on gaining a few precious seconds before they opted for that violent course of action.

Tommy clambered up into the cab of the Mack, pulling the door shut behind him, sandwiching Mort between himself and Jack.

"Damn rollers move too slow," Mort said as the bay doors clattered toward the ceiling, gradually revealing the sleet-lashed night beyond.

"Drive through the sucker," Tommy urged.

Fastening his seatbelt, Jack said, "Can't risk getting hung up."

The door was one-third open.

Gripping the wheel with both hands again, Jack saw movement in the murky, wintry world beyond, where the few dim exterior security lights did little to push back the darkness. Two men hurried across the wet and icy blacktop, from the left, slipping and skidding, both of them armed, one of them with what appeared to be an Uzi. They were trying to stay low to make poor targets of themselves and trying to stay on their feet at the same time, squinting into the black warehouse under the rising bay doors, and as yet they had not thought of meeting the crisis with an indiscriminate spray of bullets.

The first door, the one in front of Jack, was halfway up.

Abruptly, angling in from the left, the same direction from which the two hoods had come, the gray Ford van appeared, its tires churning up silvery plumes of slush. It fishtailed to a stop between the second and third ramps, blocking those exits. Its front wheels were up on the lower edge of the third ramp, so its headlights speared into the fourth bay, revealing that the cab of that truck was untenanted.

In front of Jack, the door was two-thirds up.

"Keep your heads down," he said.

Mort and Tommy squeezed down as low as they could, and Jack hunched over the wheel. The heavy rolling panel was not all the way up, but he thought he could slip under it—with a little luck. In quick succession he released the brakes, popped the clutch, and hit the accelerator.

The instant he put the truck in gear, those outside knew that the break was being made from the first bay, and the night was shaken with the rattle of gunfire. Jack heard slugs slam into the truck as he reached the exit, drove through, and headed down the concrete ramp, but none penetrated the cab or shattered the windshield.

Below, another van, this one a Dodge, swept in at the foot of the incline, trying to block his path. Reinforcements had, indeed, arrived.

Instead of braking, Jack tramped down harder on the accelerator and grinned at the horrified expressions of the men in the Dodge as the massive grille of the Mack slammed into them. The rig rammed the van backward so hard that the smaller vehicle tipped over on its side and slid fifteen or twenty feet across the macadam.

The impact jolted Jack, but his safety belt held him in check. Mort and Tommy were thrown forward, against the lower part of the dash and into the cramped space below. They protested with cries of pain.

To execute that maneuver, Jack had been forced to descend the ramp faster than he should have done, and now as he tried to wheel the truck to the left, toward the lane leading away from the warehouse, the rig lurched, swayed, threatened either to tear itself out of his control or tip over as the Dodge had done. Cursing, he held on to it, brought it around with an effort that made his arms feel as if they were pulling out of his shoulders, and then he was headed straight into the lane.

Ahead of him, three men stood around a midnight-blue Buick, and at least two of them were armed. They opened fire as he bore down on them. One man aimed too low, and bullets snapped off the top of the Mack's grille, sparking brightly where they struck. The other guy aimed too high; Jack heard slugs ricocheting off the brow of the cab, above the windshield. One of the two overhead-mounted air-horns was hit and torn loose; it fell down along the side of the cab, thumped against Tommy's window, hanging from its wires.

Jack was almost on top of the Buick, and the gunmen realized he meant to hit it, so they stopped shooting and scattered. Handling the huge rig as if it were a tank, he broadsided the car, shoving it out of the way. He kept going, past the end of the warehouse, toward another warehouse, past that one, still accelerating.

Mort and Tommy pushed themselves back onto the seat, groaning. Both were battered. Mort had a bloody nose, and Tommy was bleeding from a small cut over his right eye, but neither of them was seriously hurt.

"Why does every job go sour?" Mort asked morosely, his voice more nasal than usual because of his injured nose.

"It hasn't gone sour," Jack said, switching on the windshield wipers to clear away the glimmering beads of sleet. "It's just turned out to be a little more exciting than we expected."

"I hate excitement," Mort said, putting a handkerchief to his nose.

Jack glanced in the side mirror, back toward the *fratellanza*'s warehouse, and he saw the Ford van turning around to follow him. He had put the Dodge and the Buick out of commission, and he only had the Ford to worry about. He had no hope of outrunning it. The roads were treacherously icy, and he had too little experience behind the wheel of a rig like this to risk pushing it to its limits in bad weather.

He was also worried about an unnerving chorus of small noises that had sprung up from the engine compartment following the ramming of the van and the Buick. Something rattled tinnily. Something else hissed. If the Mack broke down and left them stranded, they would very likely be killed in the ensuing shoot-out with the Morlocks.

They were in a vast industrial area of warehouses, packing plants, and factories, and the nearest major city street was more than a mile ahead of them. Though some of the factories had night shifts and were currently operating, the industrial park's main service road, along which they were speeding, was deserted.

Glancing at the mirror, Jack saw the Ford on their tail and gaining fast. He abruptly wheeled the rig to the right, into a branch road past a factory where a sign proclaimed HARKWRIGHT CUSTOM FOAM PACKAGING.

"Where the hell are you going?" Tommy asked.

"We can't outrun them," Jack said.

"We can't face them down, either," Mort said through his bloody handkerchief. "Not handguns against Uzis."

"Trust me," Jack said.

Harkwright Custom Foam Packaging did not operate a late shift. The building itself was dark, but the road around it and the big truck lot behind were lit by sodium-vapor lamps that colored the night yellow.

At the rear of the building, Jack turned left, into the truck lot, through drilling sleet that looked like molten gold under the big lamps. Two score of trailers, without cabs attached, stood in orderly ranks, like beheaded prehistoric beasts, all painted mustard by the fall of sodium light. He swung the rig in a wide circle, brought it in close to the back wall of the factory, doused the headlights, and drove parallel to the building, heading back toward the road that entered the lot and along which he had just come. He braked to a stop at the corner, close up against the factory wall, at a right angle to the branch road.

"Brace yourselves," he said.

Mort and Tommy already knew what was coming. Their feet were pressed flat up against the dashboard and their backs were jammed against the back of the seat, as protection against the impact.

No sooner had Jack braked at the corner of the building—the Mack poised like a crouching cat anticipating a mouse—than a glow appeared on the passing road. The light approached from the right, from the front of the factory: the most outreaching headlamp beams of the unseen but oncoming Ford van. The glow grew brighter, brighter still, and Jack tensed, trying to wait until the last best moment before pulling into the lane. Now the glow became two distinct parallel beams, lancing past the snout of the Mack, and the beams grew very bright. Finally Jack tramped hard on the accelerator, and the Mack lurched forward, but it was a big truck, not quick off the dime. The Ford, going faster than Jack had expected, shot past the corner, directly across the Mack's bow, and Jack surged forward in time to catch only the rear of it. But that was enough to send the small van into a spin. It whipped around 360 degrees, then again, on the icy surface of the parking lot, before crashing nose-first into one of the mustard-colored cargo trailers.

Jack was sure that none of the men in the Ford was in any condition to come out of the wreck shooting, but he did not dawdle. He swung the Mack around and headed back past the side of Harkwright Custom Foam Packaging. When he reached the main service road, he turned right, away from the distant *fratellanza* warehouse, toward the entrance to the industrial park and the network of city streets beyond.

They were not followed.

He drove three miles by a direct route to an abandoned Texaco service station that they had scouted days ago. He pulled past the useless pumps and parked alongside the dilapidated little building.

The moment Jack halted the rig, Tommy Sung threw open the door on his side, jumped out, and walked away into the darkness. He was heading for a lower-middle-class residential neighborhood three blocks away, where, on Monday, they had parked a dirty, rusted, battered Volkswagen Rabbit. The car was newer under the hood than it was outside—and fast. It would get them back to Manhattan, where they would dump it.

They had also stashed an untraceable Pontiac in the industrial park on Monday, within a two-minute walk of the mob warehouse. They intended to hump the bags of money to the Pontiac, then drive the Pontiac here for the switch to the Rabbit. But alternate transportation had become essential, and the Pontiac had been left to rot where they stashed it.

Jack and Mort heaved the sacks of money out of the Mack and stood them against the side wall of the shuttered service station, where the slanting sleet began to crust on the canvas. Mort climbed back in the cab and wiped down all the surfaces they might have touched.

Jack stood by the bags, looking at the street beyond the end of the rig, where an occasional car crept past on the glistening pavement. None of the motorists would be interested in a truck parked at a long-abandoned service station. But if a police car cruised by on patrol . . .

At last Tommy pulled in from the side street and parked between the rows of pumps. Mort grabbed two sacks, hustled them toward the car, slipped, fell, got right up, made for the Rabbit again. Dragging the other pair of bags, Jack followed with greater care. By the time Jack reached the Rabbit, Mort was already in the back seat. Jack threw the last bags in with Mort, slammed the door, and got in front with Tommy.

He said, "For God's sake, drive slow and careful."

"You can count on it," Tommy said.

The tires spun on the sleet-skinned blacktop as they pulled out from between the pumps, and when they left the lot and moved into the street, they slid sideways before the tread gripped.

"Why does every job turn sour?" Mort asked mournfully.

"It hasn't turned sour," Jack said.

The Rabbit hit a pothole and began to slide toward a parked car, but Tommy turned the wheel into the slide and got control. They continued at an even slower pace, found the expressway, and climbed a ramp under a sign that said NEW YORK CITY.

At the upper end of the ramp, as the tires slithered one last time before gripping and carrying them onto the expressway, Mort said, "Why'd it have to *sleet?*"

"They've got a lot of salt and cinders on these lanes," Tommy said. "It's going to be all right now, all the way into the city."

"We'll see," Mort said glumly. "What a bad night. Jesus."

"Bad?" Jack said. "Bad? Mort, they would never in a thousand years let you in the Optimist's Club. For God's sake, we're all of us millionaires. You're sitting on a fortune back there!"

Under his porkpie hat, which still dripped melting sleet, Mort blinked in surprise. "Well, uh, I guess that does take some of the sting out of it."

Tommy Sung laughed.

Jack laughed, and Mort, too, and Jack said, "The biggest score any of us ever made. And no taxes payable on it, either."

Suddenly, everything seemed uproariously funny. They settled in a hundred yards behind a highway maintenance truck with flashing yellow beacons, cruising at a safe and leisurely speed, while they gleefully recalled the highlights of their escape from the warehouse.

Later, when the tension was somewhat relieved, when their giddy laughter had subsided to pleased smiles, Tommy said, "Jack, I gotta tell you that was a first-rate piece of work. The way you used the computer to create paperwork for the crate . . . and that little electronic gizmo you used to open the safe so we didn't need to blow it . . . well, you are one hell of an organizer."

"Better than that," Mort said, "in a crisis you're just about the best knockover artist I've ever seen. You think fast. I tell you, Jack, if you ever decided to put your talents to work in the straight world, for a good cause, there's no telling what you could do."

"Good cause?" Jack said. "Isn't getting rich a good cause?"

"You know what I mean," Mort said.

"I'm no hero," Jack said. "I don't want any part of the straight world. They're all hypocrites out there. They talk about honesty, truth, justice, social conscience . . . but most of them are just looking out for number one. They won't admit it, and that's why I can't stand them. *I* admit it. I'm looking out for number one, and to hell with them." He heard the tone of his own voice changing from amusement to sullen resentment, but he could not help that. He scowled through the wet windshield, past the thumping wipers. "Good cause, huh? If you spend your life fighting for good causes, the so-called good people will sure as hell break your heart in the end. Fuck 'em."

"Didn't mean to touch a nerve," Mort said, clearly surprised.

Jack said nothing. He was lost in bitter memories. Two or three miles later, he said quietly, "I'm no damn hero."

In days to come, when he recalled those words, he would have occasion to wonder how he could have been so wrong about himself.

It was one-twelve a.m., Wednesday, December 4.

3. Chicago, Illinois

By eight-twenty, Thursday morning, December 5, Father Stefan Wycazik had celebrated the early Mass, had eaten breakfast, and had retreated to his rectory office for a final cup of coffee. Turning away from his desk, he faced the big French window that presented a view of the bare, snow-crusted trees in the courtyard, and he tried not to think about any parish problems. This was *his* time, and he valued it highly.

But his thoughts drifted inexorably to Father Brendan Cronin. The rogue curate. The chalice-hurler. Brendan Cronin, the talk of the parish. The Berserk Priest of St. Bernadette's. Brendan Cronin of all people. It just did not make sense. No sense at all.

Father Stefan Wycazik had been a priest for thirty-two years, the rector of the Church of St. Bernadette for nearly eighteen years, and throughout his life of service, he had never been tortured by doubt. The very concept baffled him.

Following ordination, he was assigned as a curate to St. Thomas's, a small parish in the Illinois farm country, where seventy-year-old Father Dan Tuleen was shepherd. Father Tuleen was the sweetest-tempered, kindest, most sentimental, and most lovable man Stefan Wycazik had ever known. Dan had also been troubled by arthritis and failing vision, too old for the job of running a parish. Any other priest would have been removed, gently forced into retirement. But Dan Tuleen had been permitted to remain at his post because he had been at St. Thomas's for forty years and was an integral part of the life of his flock. The

Cardinal, a great admirer of Father Tuleen, had looked around for a curate who could handle a good deal more responsibility than would usually be expected of a rookie, and he had finally settled on Stefan Wycazik. After only a day at St. Thomas's, Stefan had realized what was expected of him and had not been intimidated. He'd shouldered virtually all the work of the parish. Few young priests would have been equal to such a task. Father Wycazik never doubted he could handle it.

Three years later, when Father Tuleen died quietly in his sleep, a new priest was assigned to St. Thomas's, and the Cardinal sent Father Wycazik to another parish in suburban Chicago, where the rector, Father Orgill, was having troubles with alcohol. Father Orgill had not been a totally disgraced whiskey priest. He had been a man with the power to salvage himself, and he had been well worth salvaging. Father Wycazik's job had been to give Francis Orgill a shoulder to lean on and to guide him, subtly but firmly, toward an exit from his dilemma. Unhampered by doubt, he had provided what Francis Orgill had needed.

During the next three years, Stefan served at two more problem-plagued churches, and those who moved in the hierarchy of the archdiocese began to refer to him as "His Eminence's troubleshooter."

His most exotic assignment was to Our Lady of Mercy Orphanage and School in Saigon, Vietnam, where he was second in charge under Father Bill Nader for six nightmarish years. Our Lady of Mercy was funded by the Chicago Archdiocese and was one of the Cardinal's pet projects. Bill Nader had carried the scars of two bullet wounds, one in his left shoulder and one in his right calf, and had lost two Vietnamese priests and one previous American to Vietcong terrorists.

From the moment of Stefan's arrival, during his entire tour of duty in the war zone, he never doubted that he would survive or that his work in that hell-on-earth was worthwhile. When Saigon fell, Bill Nader, Stefan Wycazik, and thirteen nuns escaped the country with 126 children. Hundreds of thousands died in the subsequent bloodbath, but even in the face of mass slaughter, Stefan Wycazik never doubted that 126 lives were a *very* significant number, never allowed despair to grip him.

Back in the States, as a reward for his willingness to be the Cardinal's troubleshooter for a decade and a half, Stefan was offered a promotion to monsignor, which he modestly declined. Instead, he humbly requested—and was rewarded with—his own parish. At long last.

That was St. Bernadette's. It had not been a prosperous parish when it was put into Stefan Wycazik's able hands. St. Bernadette's was $125,000 in debt. The church was in desperate need of major repairs, including a new slate roof. The rectory was worse than decrepit; it threatened to come tumbling down in the next high wind. There was no parish school. Attendance at Sunday Masses had been on a steady decline for almost ten years. St. Bette's, as some of the altar boys referred to it, was precisely the kind of challenge that excited Father Wycazik.

He never doubted that he could rescue St. Bette's. In four years he raised the attendance at Mass by forty percent, retired the debt, and repaired the church. In five years he rebuilt the parish house. In seven years he doubled attendance and broke ground for a school. In recognition of Father Wycazik's unflagging service to Mother Church, the Cardinal, in his last week of life, had conferred the coveted honor of P.R.—permanent rector—on Stefan, guaranteeing him life tenure at the parish that he had single-handedly brought back from the edge of both spiritual and financial ruin.

The granite solidity of Father Wycazik's faith made it difficult for him to understand why, at the early Mass on the Sunday just past, Father Brendan Cronin's belief had dissolved so completely as to cause him to fling the sacred chalice across the chancel in despair and rage. In front of almost a hundred worshipers. Dear God. At least it had not happened at one of the three later Masses, which were better attended.

Initially, when Brendan Cronin had come to St. Bette's more than a year and a half ago, Father Wycazik had not wanted to like him.

For one thing, Cronin had been schooled at the North American College in Rome, reputedly the most splendid educational institution within the jurisdiction of the Church. But though it was an honor to be invited to attend that establishment, and though its graduates were considered the cream of the priesthood, they were often effete dainties, loath to get their hands dirty, with much too high an opinion of themselves. They felt that teaching catechism to children was beneath them, a waste of their complex minds. And visiting shut-ins was a task they found unspeakably distasteful after the glories that had been Rome.

In addition to the stigma of being trained in Rome, Father Cronin was fat. Well, not fat, really, but certainly plump, with a round soft face and liquid-green eyes that seemed, at first encounter, to betoken a lazy and perhaps easily corrupted soul. Father Wycazik, on the other hand, was a big-boned Pole whose family had not contained a single fat man. The Wycaziks were descended from Polish miners who had emigrated to the United States at the turn of the century, taking physically demanding jobs in steel mills, quarries, and the construction trades. They had produced big families that could be supported only through long hours of honest labor, so there wasn't time to get fat. Stefan had grown up with an instinctual sense that a *real* man was solid but lean, with a thick neck, big shoulders, and joints gnarled from hard work.

To Father Wycazik's surprise, Brendan Cronin had proved to be a hard worker. He had acquired no pretensions and no elitist opinions while in Rome. He was bright, good-natured, amusing, and he thrived on visiting shut-ins, teaching the children, and soliciting funds. He was the best curate Father Wycazik had been given in eighteen years.

That was why Brendan's outburst on Sunday—and the loss of faith that had inspired it—was so distressing to Stefan Wycazik. Of course, on another level, he looked forward to the challenge of bringing Brendan Cronin back into the fold. He had begun his career in the Church as a strong right arm for priests in trouble, and now he was being called upon to fill that role once more, which reminded him of his youth and engendered in him a buoyant feeling of vital purpose.

Now, as he took another sip of coffee, a knock came at the office door. He turned his gaze to the mantel clock. It was of ormolu and inlaid mahogany with a fine Swiss movement, a gift from a parishioner. That timepiece was the only elegant object in a room boasting strictly utilitarian—and mismatched—furniture and a threadbare imitation-Persian carpet. According to the clock, the time was eight-thirty, precisely, and Stefan turned to the door, saying, "Come in, Brendan."

As he came through the door, Father Brendan Conin looked no less distressed than he had on Sunday, Monday, Tuesday, and Wednesday, when they had met in this office to discuss his crisis of faith and to search for ways to reestablish his belief. He was so pale that his freckles burned like sparks on his skin, and by contrast his auburn hair looked more red than usual. The bounce had left his step.

"Sit down, Brendan. Coffee?"

"Thank you, no." Brendan bypassed the tattered Chesterfield and the Morris chair, slumping in the sag-bottomed wingback instead.

Did you eat a good breakfast? Stefan wanted to ask. Or did you just nibble at some toast and swill it down with coffee?

But he did not want to seem to be mothering his curate, who was thirty years old. So he said, "You've done the reading I suggested?"

"Yes."

Stefan had relieved Brendan of all parish duties and had given him books and essays that argued for the existence of God and against the folly of atheism from an intellectual point of view.

"And you've reflected on what you've read," Father Wycazik said. "So have you found anything so far that . . . helps you?"

Brendan sighed. Shook his head.

"You continue to pray for guidance?"

"Yes. I receive none."

"You continue to search for the roots of this doubt?"

"There don't seem to be any."

Stefan was increasingly frustrated by Father Cronin's taciturnity, which was utterly unlike the young priest. Usually, Brendan was open, voluble. But since Sunday he had turned inward, and he had begun to speak slowly, softly, and never at length, as if words were money and he a miser who begrudged the paying out of every penny.

"There must be roots to your doubt," Father Wycazik insisted. "There must be something from which doubts grow—a seed, a beginning."

"It's just there," Brendan muttered, barely audible. "Doubt. It's just there as if it's always been there."

"But it wasn't: you *did* believe. So when did doubt begin? Last August, you said. But what sparked it? There must've been a specific incident or incidents that led you to reevaluate your philosophy."

Brendan gave a softly exhaled "no."

Father Wycazik wanted to shout at him, shake him, shock him out of his numbing gloom. But he patiently said, "Countless good priests have suffered crises of faith. Even some saints wrestled angels. But they all had two things in common: Their loss of faith was a gradual process that continued many years before reaching a crisis; and they could all point to specific incidents and observations from which doubt arose. The unjust death of a child, for instance. Or a saintly mother stricken with cancer. Murder. Rape. Why does God allow evil in the world? Why war? The sources of doubt are innumerable if familiar, and though Church doctrine answers them, cold doctrine is sometimes little comfort. Brendan, doubt *always* springs from specific contradictions between the concept of God's mercy and the reality of human sorrow and suffering."

"Not in my case," Brendan said.

Gently but insistently, Father Wycazik continued. "And the only way to assuage that doubt is to focus on those contradictions that trouble you and discuss them with a spiritual guide."

"In my case, my faith just . . . collapsed under me . . . suddenly . . . like a floor that seemed perfectly solid but was rotten all along."

"You don't brood about unjust death, sickness, murder, war? Like a rotten floor, then? Just collapsed overnight?"

"That's right."

"*Bullshit!*" Stefan said, launching himself up from his chair.

The expletive and the sudden movement startled Father Cronin. His head snapped up, and his eyes widened with surprise.

"Bullshit," Father Wycazik repeated, matching the word with a scowl as he turned his back on his curate. In part he intended to shock the younger priest and force him out of his half-trance of self-pity, but in part he was also irritated by Cronin's uncommunicative funk and stubborn despair. Speaking to the curate but facing the window, where patterns of frost decorated the panes and where wind buffeted the glass, he said, "You didn't fall from committed priest in August to atheist in December. *Could* not. Not when you claim you've had no shattering experiences that might be responsible. There must be reasons for your change of heart, Father, even if you're hiding them from yourself, and until you're willing to admit them, face them, you'll remain in this wretched state."

A plumbless silence filled the room.

Then: the muffled ticking of the ormolu and mahogany clock.

At last, Brendan Cronin said, "Father, please don't be angry with me. I have such respect . . . and I value our relationship so highly that your anger . . . on top of everything else . . . is too much for me right now."

Pleased by even a thread-thin crack in Brendan's shell, delighted that his little stratagem had produced results, Father Wycazik turned from the window, moved quickly to the wingback chair, and put a hand on his curate's shoulder. "I'm not angry with you, Brendan. Worried. Concerned. Frustrated that you won't let me help you. But not angry."

The young priest looked up. "Father, believe me, I want nothing more than your help in finding a way out of this. But in truth, my doubt doesn't spring from any of the things you mentioned. I really don't know where it comes from. It remains . . . well, mysterious."

Stefan nodded, squeezed Brendan's shoulder, returned to his chair behind the desk, sat down, and closed his eyes for a moment, thinking.

"All right, Brendan, your inability to identify the cause of your collapsed faith indicates it's not an intellectual problem, so no amount of inspirational reading will help. If it's a psychological problem, the roots lie in your subconscious, awaiting revelation."

When he opened his eyes, Stefan saw that his curate was intrigued by the suggestion that his own inner mind was simply malfunctioning. Which meant God hadn't failed Brendan, after all: *Brendan* had failed *God*. Personal responsibility was far easier to deal with than the thought that God was unreal or had turned His back.

Stefan said, "As you may know, the Illinois Provincial of the Society of Jesus is Lee Kellog. But you may not know that he oversees two psychiatrists, both Jesuits themselves, who deal with the mental and emotional problems of priests within our order. I could arrange for you to begin analysis with one of those psychiatrists."

"Would you?" Brendan asked, leaning forward in his chair.

"Yes. Eventually. But not right away. If you begin analysis, the Provincial will refer your name to the province's Prefect of Discipline, who will begin to pick through your actions of the past year to see if you've violated any of your vows."

"But I never—"

"I *know* you never," Stefan said reassuringly. "But the Prefect of Discipline's job is to be suspicious. The worst thing is . . . even if your analysis leads to a cure, the Prefect will scrutinize you for years to come, to guard against a lapse into unpriestly conduct. Which would limit your prospects. And until your current problem, Father, you struck me as a priest who'd go far—monsignor, perhaps higher."

"Oh, no. Certainly not. Not me," Brendan said self-deprecatingly.

"Yes, you. And if you beat this problem, you could still go far. But once you're on the Prefect's danger list, you'll always be suspect. At best you'll wind up no better than me, a simple parish priest."

A smile flickered at the corners of Brendan's mouth. "It would be an honor— and a life well spent—to be, as you say, no better than you."

"But you can go farther and be of great service to the Church. And I'm determined you'll have that chance. So I want you to give me until Christmas to help you find a way out of this hole. No more pep talks. No debates about the nature of good and evil. Instead, I'll apply some of my own theories about psychological disorders. You'll get amateur treatment from me, but give it a chance. Just until Christmas. Then, if your distress is still as great, if we're no nearer an answer, I'll put you in the hands of a Jesuit psychiatrist. Deal?"

Brendan nodded. "Deal."

"Terrific!" Father Wycazik said, sitting up straight, rubbing his hands together briskly, as if about to chop wood or perform some other invigorating exercise. "That gives us more than three weeks. For the first week, you'll put away your ecclesiastical suits, dress in ordinary clothes, and report to Dr. James McMurtry at St. Joseph's Hospital for Children. He'll see that you're assigned to the hospital staff."

"As chaplain?"

"As an orderly—emptying bedpans, changing bedclothes, whatever is required. Only Dr. McMurtry will know you're a priest."

Brendan blinked. "But what's the point of this?"

"You'll figure it out before the week is up," Stefan said happily. "And when you understand why I sent you to the hospital, you'll have one important key to help you unlock your psyche, a key that'll open doors and give you a look inside yourself, and maybe then you'll see the cause of your loss of faith—and overcome it."

Brendan looked doubtful.

Father Wycazik said, "You promised me three weeks."

"All right." Brendan unconsciously fingered his Roman collar and seemed disturbed by the thought of removing it, which was a good sign.

"You'll move out of the rectory until Christmas. I'll give you funds to pay for meals and an inexpensive hotel room. You'll work and live in the real world, beyond the shelter of the ecclesiastic life. Now, change clothes, pack your suitcases, and report back to me. Meanwhile, I'll call Dr. McMurtry and make the necessary arrangements."

Brendan sighed, got up, went to the door. "There's one thing maybe supports the notion that my problem's psychological, not intellectual. I've been having these dreams . . . actually the same dream every time."

"A recurring dream. That's very Freudian."

"I've had it several times a month since August. But this week it's become a regular occurrence—three out of the last four nights. It's a bad one, too—a short dream that I have over and over again in one night. Short, but . . . intense. It's about these black gloves."

"Black gloves?"

Brendan grimaced. "I'm in a strange place. Don't know where. I'm lying in bed, I think. I seem to be . . . restrained. My arms are held down. And my legs. I want to move, run, get out of there, but I can't. The light is dim. Can't see much. Then these hands . . .'' He shuddered.

"Hands wearing black gloves?" Father Wycazik prompted.

"Yes. Shiny black gloves. Vinyl or rubber. Tightly fitted and shiny, not like ordinary gloves.'' Brendan let go of the doorknob, took two steps toward the middle of the room, and stood with his hands raised before his face, as if the sight of them would help him recollect the details of the menacing hands in his dream. "I can't see whose hands they are. Something wrong with my vision. I can see the hands . . . the gloves . . . but only up to the wrists. Beyond that, it's all . . . blurry.''

By the offhanded way that Brendan had mentioned the dream, almost as an afterthought, he obviously wanted to believe that it was of no consequence. However, his face was paler than before, and there was a vague but unmistakable flutter of fear in his voice.

A burst of winter wind rattled a loose window pane, and Stefan said, "The man with black gloves—does he say anything to you?''

"He never speaks.'' Another shudder. Brendan lowered his hands, thrust them in his pockets. "He touches me. The gloves are cold, slick.'' The curate looked as if he could feel those gloves even now.

Acutely interested, Father Wycazik leaned forward in his chair and said, "*Where* do these gloves touch you?''

The young priest's eyes glazed. "They touch . . . my face. Forehead. Cheeks, neck . . . chest. Cold. They touch me almost everywhere.''

"They don't hurt you?''

"No.''

"But you're afraid of these gloves, of the man wearing them?''

"Terrified. But I don't know why.''

"One can't help but see how Freudian a dream it is.''

"I suppose,'' the curate said.

"Dreams are a way for the subconscious mind to send messages to the conscious, and in this case it's easy to see Freudian symbolic meanings in these black gloves. The hands of the devil, reaching out to pull you down from grace. Or the hands of your own doubt. Or they could be symbols of temptations, of sins seeking your indulgence.''

Brendan seemed grimly amused by the possibilities. "Especially sins of the flesh. After all, the gloves *do* touch me all over.'' The curate returned to the door and put his hand on the knob, but paused again. "Listen, I'll tell you something odd. This dream . . . I'm half-sure it's not symbolic.'' Brendan let his gaze slide away from Stefan's, down to the worn rug. "I think those gloved hands represent nothing more than gloved hands. I think . . . somewhere, someplace, at some time or other, they were real.''

"You mean you were once in a situation like the one in your dream?''

Still looking at the rug, the curate said, "I don't know. Perhaps in my childhood. See, this might not have anything to do with my crisis of faith. The two things might be—probably are—unconnected.''

Stefan shook his head. "Two unusual and serious afflictions—a loss of faith and a recurring nightmare—troubling you at the same time, and you want me to think they've no relation? Too coincidental. There must be some connection. But tell me, at what point in your childhood would you've been menaced by this unseen, gloved figure?''

"Well, I had a couple of serious illnesses as a boy. Maybe during a fever I was examined by a doctor who was a little rough or scary-looking. And maybe the experience was so traumatic that I repressed it, and now it's coming back to me in a dream.''

"When doctors wear gloves for an examination, they use throwaway white latex. Not black. And not heavy rubber or vinyl gloves.''

The curate took a deep breath, blew it out. ''Yeah, you're right. But I just can't shake the feeling that the dream's not symbolic. It's crazy, I suppose. But I'm sure those black gloves are real, as real as that Morris chair, as real as those books on the shelf.''

On the mantel, the clock struck the hour.

The soughing of the wind in the eaves became a howl.

"Creepy,'' Stefan said, referring not to the wind or the hollow striking of the clock. He crossed the room and clapped the curate on the shoulder. ''But I assure you, you're wrong. The dream *is* symbolic, and it *is* related to your crisis of faith. The black hands of doubt. It's your subconscious warning you that you're in for a real battle. But it's a battle in which you're not alone. You've got me beside you.''

"Thank you, Father.''

"And God. He's beside you as well.''

Father Cronin nodded, but there was no conviction in his face or in the defeated hunching of his shoulders.

"Now go pack your suitcases,'' Father Wycazik said.

"I'm leaving you short-handed when I go.''

"I've got Father Gerrano and the sisters at the school. Now, off with you.'' When his curate had gone, Stefan returned to his desk.

Black gloves. It was only a dream, not particularly frightening in its essence, yet Father Cronin's voice had been so haunted when he spoke of it that Stefan was still affected by the image of shiny black rubber-clad fingers reaching out of a blur and prodding, poking. . . .

Black gloves.

Father Wycazik had a hunch that this was going to be one of the most difficult salvage jobs upon which he had ever embarked.

Outside, snow fell.

It was Thursday, December 5.

4. Boston, Massachusetts

On Friday, four days after the catastrophic fugue that followed the aortal graft on Viola Fletcher, Ginger Weiss was still a patient at Memorial Hospital, where she had been admitted after George Hannaby led her out of the snowy alleyway in which she had regained consciousness.

For three days, they had put her through exhaustive tests. An EEG study, cranial X rays, sonograms, pneumoventriculography, a lumbar puncture, an angiogram, and more, repeating the several procedures (though fortunately *not* the lumbar puncture) for cross-checked results. With the sophisticated tools and processes of modern medicine, they searched her brain tissue for neoplasms, cystic masses, abscesses, clots, aneurysms, and benign gummatous lumps. For a while they concentrated on the possibility of malignancies of the perineural nerves. They checked for chronic intracranial pressure. They analyzed the fluid from the spinal tap in search of abnormal protein, cerebral bleeding, a low sugar count that would indicate bacterial infection, or signs of a fungus infection. Because they were physicians who always gave their best to a patient, but especially because Ginger was one of their own colleagues, her doctors were diligent, determined, thoughtful, thorough, and firmly committed to pinpointing the cause of her problem.

At two o'clock Friday afternoon, George Hannaby came to her room with the results of the final battery of tests and with the reports of consultants who had given one last round of opinions. The fact that he had come himself, rather than let the oncologist or the brain specialist (who were in charge of her case) bring the news, most likely meant that it was bad, and for once Ginger was sorry to see him.

She was sitting in bed, dressed in blue pajamas that Rita Hannaby, George's wife, had been kind enough to fetch (along with a suitcase full of other necessities) from the Beacon Hill apartment. She was reading a paperback mystery, pretending to be confident that her seizures were the result of some easily corrected malady, but she was scared.

But what George had to tell her was so bad that she could no longer hold fast to her composure. In a way, it was worse than anything for which she had prepared herself.

They had found nothing.

No disease. No injury. No congenital defect. Nothing.

As George solemnly outlined the final results and made it clear that her wild flights, performed in a fugue, were without a discernible pathological cause, she finally lost control of her emotions for the first time since she had broken into tears in the alleyway. She wept, not noisily, not copiously, but quietly and with enormous anguish.

A physical ailment might have been correctable. And once cured, it would not have prevented her from returning to a career as a surgeon.

But the test results and the opinions of the specialists all conveyed the same unbearable message: Her problem was entirely in her mind, a psychological illness beyond the reach of surgery, antibiotics, or controlling drugs. When a patient suffered repeated incidents of fugue for which no physiological cause could be found, the only hope of ending the seizures was psychotherapy, though the finest psychiatrists could not boast of a high cure rate with patients thus afflicted. Indeed, a fugue was often an indication of incipient schizophrenia. Her chances of managing her condition and living a normal life were small; her chances of institutionalization were dismayingly high.

Within reach of her lifelong dream, within months of beginning her own surgical practice, her life had been shattered as thoroughly as a crystal goblet struck by a bullet. Even if her condition was not that extreme, even if psychotherapy gave her a chance to control her strange outbursts, she'd never be able to obtain a license to practice medicine.

George plucked several Kleenex from the box on the nightstand and gave them to her. He poured a glass of water. He got a Valium and made her take it, though at first she resisted. He held her hand, which seemed like that of a very small girl when clasped in his large mitt. He spoke softly, reassuringly. Gradually he calmed her.

When she could speak, she said, "But George, damn it, I wasn't raised in a psychologically destructive atmosphere. Our home was happy, at peace. And I certainly got more than my share of love and affection. I wasn't physically, mentally, or emotionally abused." She angrily snatched the box of tissues from the nightstand, tore Kleenex from it. "Why me? How could *I*, coming from my background, develop a psychosis? *How?* With my fantastic mother, my special papa, my damned-if-it-wasn't-happy childhood, how could *I* wind up seriously mentally disturbed? It isn't fair. It isn't right. It isn't even *believable.*"

He sat on the edge of her bed, and he was so tall that he still loomed over her. "First of all, Doctor, the consulting specialists tell me there's a whole school of thought that says many mental illnesses are the result of subtle chemical changes in the body, in the brain tissue, changes we're not yet advanced enough to detect or understand. So this doesn't have to mean that you're screwed up by your childhood. I don't think you've got to reevaluate your whole life because of this. Second, I'm not—I repeat, not—at all convinced that your condition is anything as serious as debilitating psychosis."

"Oh, George, please don't coddle—"

"Coddle a patient? *Me?*" he said, as if no one had ever suggested anything half as astonishing to him. "I'm not just trying to lift your spirits. I mean what I say. Sure, we didn't find a physical cause for this, but that doesn't mean there *isn't* a physical problem involved. You might have a condition that's not yet sufficiently advanced to be detectable. In a couple of weeks, or a month, or as soon as there's any worsening of the problem, any indication of deterioration, we'll run more tests; we'll take another look, and I'd bet everything I own that we'll eventually put our finger on the problem."

She allowed herself to hope. Discarding a wadded mass of tissues, she fumbled for the Kleenex box. "You really think it could be like that? A brain tumor or an abscess so small it doesn't show up yet?"

"Sure. I find that a hell of a lot easier to believe than that you're psychologically disturbed. You? You're one of the steadiest people I've ever known. And I can't accept that you could be psychotic or even psychoneurotic and not exhibit unusual behavior *between* these fugues. I mean, serious mental illness isn't expressed in neatly contained little bursts. It slops over into the patient's entire life."

She had not thought about that before. As she considered his point, she felt a little better, though not wildly hopeful and certainly not happy. On the one hand, it seemed weird to be *hoping* for a brain tumor, but a tumor could be excised, perhaps without gross damage to cerebral tissues. Madness, however, responded to no scalpel.

"The next few weeks or months are probably going to be the most difficult of your life," he said. "The waiting."

"I suppose I'm restricted from hospital work for the duration."

"Yes. But depending on how you come along, I don't see why you can't help me out at the office."

"And what if I . . . threw one of these fits?"

"I'd be there to keep you from hurting yourself until it passed."

"But what would your patients think? Wouldn't exactly help your practice any, would it? To have an assistant who suddenly turns into a *meshuggene* and runs shrieking through the office?"

He smiled. "Let me worry about what my patients think. Anyway, that's for the future. Right now, at least for a week or two, you've got to take it easy. No work at all. Relax. Rest. These last few days have been emotionally and physically exhausting."

"I've been in bed. Exhausting? Don't knock a teapot."

He blinked, confused. "Don't what?"

"Oh," she said, surprised to have heard those four words pop out of her, "it's something my father used to say. It's a Yiddish expression. *Hok nit kain tchynik:* don't knock a teapot. It means, don't talk nonsense. But don't ask me *why* it means that. It's just something I used to hear all the time when I was a kid.''

"Well, I'm not knocking a teapot," he said. "You may have been in bed all week, but it's been an exhausting experience nonetheless, and you need to take it easy for a while. I want you to move in with Rita and me for the next few weeks."

"What? Oh, I couldn't impose on you—"

"It's no imposition. We have a live-in maid, so you won't even have to make your bed in the morning. From the guest-room window, you'll have a nice view of the bay. Living around water is calming. In fact, it's quite literally what the doctor ordered."

"No. Really. Thank you, but I couldn't."

He frowned. "You don't understand. I'm not just your boss but your doctor, and I'm telling you this is what you're going to do."

"I'll be perfectly fine at the apartment—"

"No," he said firmly. "Think about it. Suppose one of these seizures struck while you were making dinner. Suppose you knocked over a pot on the stove. It could start a fire, and you might not even be aware of it until you came out of the fugue, by which time the whole apartment could be ablaze and you could be trapped. That's only one way you might hurt yourself. I can think of a hundred. So I have to insist that . . . for a while you must not live alone. If you don't want to stay with me and Rita, do you have relatives who'd take you in for a while?''

"Not in Boston. In New York, I've got aunts, uncles . . .''

But Ginger could not stay with any of her relatives. They would be happy to have her, of course—especially Aunt Francine or Aunt Rachel. However, she did not want them to see her in her current condition, and the thought of pitching a fit in front of them was intolerable. She could almost see Francine and Rachel huddling over a kitchen table, speaking in low voices, clucking their tongues: "Where did Jacob and Anna go wrong? Did they push her too hard? Anna always pushed her too hard. And after Anna died, Jacob relied on the girl too much. She had to take over the house at twelve. It was too much for her. Too much pressure too young." Ginger would receive considerable compassion, understanding, and love from them, but at the risk of sullying the memory of her parents, a memory she was determined to honor, always.

To George, who still sat upon the edge of the bed and awaited her response with an obvious concern that touched her deeply, she said, "I'll take the guest room with the view of the bay."

"Splendid!"

"Though I think it's a horrible imposition. And I warn you, if I really like it there, you might never get rid of me. You'll know you're in trouble if you come home some day, and I've hired people to repaint the walls and hang new drapes."

He grinned. "At the first mention of painters or draperies, we'll throw your butt out in the street." He kissed her lightly on the cheek, got up from the edge of the bed, and walked to the door. "I'm going to start the release procedures now, so you should be out of here in two hours. I'll call Rita and have her come pick you up. I'm sure you can beat this thing, Ginger, but you've got to keep thinking positive."

When he left the room and his footsteps faded down the hall, she stopped struggling to maintain her smile, and it collapsed instantly. She leaned back against her pillows and stared morosely at the age-yellowed acoustic tile on the ceiling.

After a while she got out of bed and went into the adjoining bathroom, where she approached the sink with trepidation. After a brief hesitation, she turned on the water and watched it whirling around and around and into the drain. On Monday, at the surgical scrub sink, after successfully performing the aortal graft on Viola Fletcher, Ginger had been panicked by the sight of water swirling into a drain, but she could not imagine why.

Damn it, *why?* She desperately wanted to understand.

Papa, she thought, I wish you were alive, here to listen, to help.

Life's nasty surprises had been the subject of one of Papa's little sayings that Ginger had once found amusing. When anyone fretted about the future, Jacob would shake his head and wink and say, "Why worry about tomorrow? Who knows what'll hit you *today?*"

How true. And how utterly *un*amusing now.

She felt like an invalid. She felt lost.

It was Friday, December 6.

5. Laguna Beach, California

When Dom went to the doctor's office on Monday morning, December 2, in the company of Parker Faine, Dr. Cobletz did not recommend immediate diagnostic procedures, for he had only recently given Dom a thorough examination and had seen no signs of physical disorder. He assured them there were other treatments to be tried before jumping to the conclusion that it was a brain disorder that sent the writer scurrying upon errands of fortification and self-defense in his sleep.

After Dom's previous visit, on November 23, the physician had, he said, become curious about somnambulism and had done some reading on the subject. With most adults the affliction was short-lived; however, in a few cases, there was a danger of it becoming habitual, and in its most serious forms it resembled the inflexible routines and pattern-obsessed behavior of worst-case neurotics. Once habitual, somnambulism was much harder to cure, and it could become the dominant factor in the patient's life, generating a fear of night and sleep, producing profound feelings of helplessness culminating in more serious emotional disorders.

Dom felt he was already in that danger zone. He thought of the barricade he had built across his bedroom door. The arsenal on the bed.

Cobletz, intrigued and concerned but not worried, had assured Dominick—and Parker—that in most instances of persistent somnambulism, the pattern of nocturnal rambling could be broken by the administration of a sedative before bed. Once a few untroubled nights had passed, the patient was usually cured. In chronic cases, the nightly sedative was augmented with a diazepam compound during the day when the patient was plagued by anxiety. Because the tasks that Dominick performed in his sleep were unnaturally strenuous for a somnambulist, Dr. Cobletz had prescribed both Valium during the day and a 15 mg. tablet of Dalmane, just before slipping under the covers each night.

On the drive back to Laguna Beach from Dr. Cobletz's offices in Newport, with the sea on the right and hills on the left, Parker Faine argued that, until the sleepwalking stopped, it was not wise for Dom to continue living alone. Hunched over the steering wheel of his Volvo, the bearded and shaggy-haired artist drove fast, aggressively but not recklessly. He seldom glanced away from the Pacific Coast Highway, yet he gave the impression, through the sheer force of his personality, that his eyes and attention were fixed constantly and entirely upon Dom.

"There's plenty of room at my place. I can keep an eye on you. I won't hover, mind you. I won't be a mother hen. But at least I'll *be* there. And we would have plenty of opportunity to talk about this, really get into it, just you and me, and try to figure how this sleepwalking is related to the changes you went through the summer before last, when you threw away that job at Mountainview College. I'm definitely the guy to help you. I swear, if I hadn't become a goddamned painter, I'd have become a goddamned psychiatrist. I have a knack for getting people to talk about themselves. How about it? Come stay with me for a while and let me play therapist."

Dom had refused. He wanted to stay at his own house, alone, for to do otherwise seemed to be a retreat into the same rabbit hole in which he had hidden from life for so many years. The change he had undergone during his trip to Mountainview, Utah, the summer before last, had been dramatic, inexplicable, but for the better. At thirty-three, he had finally seized the reins of life, had mounted it with a flourish, and had ridden into new territory. He liked the man he had become, and he feared nothing more than slipping back into his dreary former existence.

Perhaps his somnambulism was mysteriously related to the previous changes of attitude that he had undergone, as Parker insisted, but Dom had his doubts that the relationship was either mysterious or complex. More likely, the connection between the two personality crises was simple: The sleepwalking was an excuse to retreat from the challenges, excitement, and stress of his new life. Which could not be allowed. Therefore, Dom would stay in his own house, alone, take the Valium and Dalmane as Dr. Cobletz had prescribed them, and tough this thing out.

That was what he had decided in the Volvo, on Monday morning, and by Saturday, the seventh of December, it seemed that he had made the correct decision. Some days he needed a Valium and some days he did not. Every evening he took a Dalmane tablet with milk or hot chocolate. Somnambulism disturbed his nights less frequently. Before beginning drug therapy, he walked in his sleep every night, but in the past five nights he journeyed just twice, leaving his bed only in the predawn hours of Wednesday and Friday mornings.

Furthermore, his activities in his sleep were far less bizarre and less disturbing than they had been. He no longer gathered up weapons, built barricades, or tried to nail the windows shut. On both occasions, he merely left his Beautyrest for a makeshift bed in the back of the closet, where he woke stiff and sore and frightened by some unknown and nameless threat that had pursued him in dreams he could not recall.

Thank God, the worst seemed past.

By Thursday he had begun to write again. He worked on the new novel, picking up where he left off weeks ago.

On Friday, Tabitha Wycombe, his editor in New York, called with good news. Two prepublication reviews of *Twilight in Babylon* had just come in, and both were excellent. She read them to him, then revealed even better news: Bookseller excitement, aroused by industry publicity and by the distribution of several hundred advance reading copies, continued to grow, and the first printing, which had already been raised once, was now being raised again. They talked for almost half an hour, and when Dom hung up, he felt that his life was back on the rails.

But Saturday night brought a new development, which might have been either a turn for the better or the worse. Every night that he had gone walking in his sleep, he had been unable to recall even the smallest detail of the nightmares that drove him from his bed. Then, Saturday, he was plagued by an uncannily vivid, terrifying dream that sent him fleeing through the house in somnambulistic panic, but this time he remembered part of it when he woke, not most of it but at least the end.

In the last minute or two of the dream, he was standing in a half-glimpsed bathroom, everything blurred. An unseen man shoved him against a sink, and Dom bent over it, his face thrust down into the porcelain bowl. Someone had an arm around him and was holding him on his feet, for he was too weak to stand on his own. He felt rag-limp, and his knees were quivering, and his stomach was twisting and rolling. A second unseen person had two hands on his head, forcing his head into the sink. He could not speak. He could not draw breath. He knew he was dying. He had to get away from these people, out of this room, but he did not have the physical resources to take flight. Though his vision remained bleary, he could see the smooth porcelain and the chrome-plated rim of the drain in detail, for his face was only inches from the bottom of the sink. It was an old-fashioned drain without a mechanically operated stopper. The rubber plug had been removed and set aside, somewhere out of sight. The water was running, spewing out of a faucet, past his face, splattering against the bottom of the basin, whirling around and around, down into the drain, around and down. The two people forcing him into the sink were shouting, though he could not understand them. Around and down . . . around . . . Staring hypnotically into the miniature whirlpool, he grew terrified of the gaping drain, which was like a sucking orifice intent upon drawing him into its reeking depths. Suddenly he was aware they wanted to stuff him down into the drain, dispose of him. Might be a garbage disposal in there, something that would chop him to pieces and flush him away—

He woke, screaming. He was in his bathroom. He had walked in his sleep. He was at the sink, bent over, screaming into the drain. He leapt back from that gaping hole, stumbled, nearly fell over the edge of the bathtub. He grabbed a towel rack to steady himself.

Gasping for breath, shaking, he finally got up enough nerve to return to the sink and look into it. Glossy white porcelain. A brass drain rim and a dome-shaped brass stopper. Nothing else, nothing worse.

The room in his nightmare had not been this room.

Dominick washed his face and returned to the bedroom.

According to the clock on the nightstand, it was only two-twenty-five A.M.

Though it made no sense at all and seemed to have no symbolic or real connection with his life, the nightmare was profoundly disturbing. However, he had not nailed windows shut or gathered up weapons in his sleep, so it seemed that this was only a minor setback.

In fact, it might be a sign of improvement. If he remembered his dreams, not just pieces but all of them from beginning to end, he might discover the source of the anxiety that had made a night rambler of him. Then he would be better able to deal with it.

Nevertheless, he did not want to go back to bed and risk returning to that strange place in his dream. The bottle of Dalmane was in the top drawer of the nightstand. He was not supposed to take more than one tablet each evening, but surely one indulgence couldn't hurt.

He went out to the bar cabinet in the living room, poured some Chivas Regal. With a shaky hand, he popped the pill in his mouth, drank the Chivas, and returned to bed.

He was improving. Soon, the sleepwalking would stop. A week from now, he'd be back to normal. In a month, this would seem like a curious aberration, and he'd wonder how he'd allowed it to get the better of him.

Precariously prone upon the trembling wire of consciousness above the gulf of sleep, he began to lose his balance. It was a pleasant feeling, a soft slipping away. But as he floated down into sleep, he heard himself murmuring in the darkness of the bedroom, and what he heard himself saying was so strange it startled him and piqued his interest even as the Dalmane and whiskey inexorably had their way with him.

"The moon," he whispered thickly. "The moon, the moon." He wondered what he could possibly mean by that, and he tried to push sleep away at least long enough to ponder his own words. The moon? *"The moon,"* he whispered again, and then he was gone.

It was three-eleven A.M., Sunday, December 8.

6. New York, New York

Five days after stealing more than three million dollars from the *fratellanza,* Jack Twist went to see a dead woman who still breathed.

At one o'clock Sunday afternoon, in a respectable neighborhood on the East Side, he parked his Camaro in the underground garage beneath the private sanitarium and took the elevator up to the lobby. He signed in with the receptionist and was given a visitor's pass.

One would not think the place was a hospital. The public area was tastefully decorated in Art Deco style suited to the building's period. There were two small Erté originals, sofas, one armchair, tables with neatly arranged magazines, and all the furniture had a 1920s' look.

It was too damn luxurious. The Ertés were unnecessary. A hundred other economies were obvious. But the management felt that image was important in order to continue to attract upper-crust clientele and keep the annual profit around the hundred percent mark. The patients were of all types—middle-aged catatonic schizophrenics, autistic children, the long-term comatose both young and old—but they all had two things in common: Their conditions were all chronic rather than acute, and they were from well-to-do families who could afford the best care.

Thinking about the situation, Jack invariably became angry that no place in the city provided fine custodial care for the catastrophically brain-injured or mentally ill at a reasonable price. In spite of huge expenditures of tax money, New York's institutions, like public institutions everywhere, were a grim joke that the average citizen had to accept for a lack of alternatives.

If he had not been a skilled and highly successful thief, he would not have been able to pay the sanitarium's exorbitant monthly charges. Fortunately, he had a talent for larceny.

Carrying his visitor's pass, he went to another elevator and rode up to the fourth of six floors. The hallways in the upper levels were more reminiscent of a hospital than the lobby had been. Fluorescent lights. White walls. The clean, crisp, minty smell of disinfectant.

At the far end of the fourth-floor hall, in the last room on the right, lived the dead woman who still breathed. Jack hesitated with his hand on the push-plate of the heavy swinging door, swallowed hard, took a deep breath, and finally went inside.

The room was not as sumptuous as the lobby, and it was not Art Deco, either, but it was very nice, resembling a medium-priced room at the Plaza: a high ceiling and white molding; a fireplace with a white mantel; a deep hunter-green carpet; pale green drapes; a green leaf-patterned sofa and a pair of chairs. The theory was that a patient would be happier in a room like this than in a clinical room. Although many patients were oblivious of their surroundings, the cozier atmosphere at least made visiting friends and relatives feel less bleak.

The hospital bed was the only concession to utilitarian design, a dramatic contrast to everything else. But even that was dressed up with green-patterned designer sheets.

Only the patient spoiled the lovely mood of the chamber.

Jack lowered the safety railing on the bed, leaned over, and kissed his wife's cheek. She did not stir. He took one of her hands and held it in both of his. Her hand did not grip him in return, did not flex, remained slack, limp, senseless, but at least it was warm.

"Jenny? It's me, Jenny. How are you feeling today? Hmmmmm? You look good. You look lovely. You always look lovely."

In fact, for someone who had spent eight years in a coma, for someone who had not taken a single step and had not felt sunshine or fresh air upon her face in all that time, she looked quite good indeed. Perhaps only Jack could say that she was still lovely—and mean it. She was not the beauty she had once been, but she certainly did not look as if she had spent almost a decade in solemn flirtation with death.

Her hair was not glossy any more, though still thick and the same rich chestnut shade as when he had first seen her at her job, behind the men's cologne counter in Bloomingdale's, fourteen years ago. The attendants washed her hair twice a week here and brushed it every day.

He could have moved his hand under her hair, along the left side of her skull, to the unnatural depression, the sickening concavity. He could have touched it without disturbing her, for nothing disturbed her any more, but he did not. Because touching it would have disturbed *him*.

Her brow was uncreased, her face unlined even at the corners of her eyes, which were closed. She was gaunt though not shockingly so. Motionless upon those green designer sheets, she seemed ageless, as if she were an enchanted princess awaiting the kiss that would wake her from a century of slumber.

The only signs of life were the vague, rhythmic rise and fall of her breast as she breathed, and the soft movement of her throat as she occasionally swallowed saliva. The swallowing was an automatic, involuntary action and not a sign of awareness on any level whatsoever.

The brain damage was extensive and irreparable. The movements she made here and now were virtually the only movements she would ever make until, at last, she gave a dying shudder. There was no hope. He knew there was no hope, and he accepted the permanence of her condition.

She would have looked much worse if she had not received such conscientious care. A team of physical therapists came to her room every day and put her through passive exercise routines. Her muscle tone was not the best, but at least she *had* muscle tone.

Jack held her hand and stared down at her for a long time. For seven years, he had been coming to see her two nights a week and for five or six hours every

Sunday afternoon, sometimes on other afternoons as well. But in spite of the frequency of his visits and in spite of her unchanging condition, he never tired of looking at her.

He pulled up a chair and sat next to the bed, still holding her hand, staring at her face, and for more than an hour he talked to her. He told her about a movie that he had seen since his previous visit, about two books he had read. He spoke of the weather, described the force and bite of the winter wind. He painted colorful word pictures of the prettiest Christmas displays he had seen in shop windows.

She did not reward him with even a sigh or a twitch. She lay as always, unmoving and unmoved.

Nevertheless, he talked to her, for he worried that a fragment of awareness might survive, a gleam of comprehension down in the black well of the coma. Maybe she *could* hear and understand, in which case the worst thing for her was being trapped in an unresponsive body, desperate even for one-way communication, but receiving none because they thought she could not hear. The doctors assured him that these worries were groundless; she heard nothing, saw nothing, knew nothing, they said, except what images and fantasies might sputter across short-circuiting synapses of her shattered brain. But if they were wrong—if there was only one chance in a million that they were wrong—he could not leave her in that perfect and terrible isolation. So he talked to her as the winter day beyond the window changed from one shade of gray to another.

At five-fifteen, he went into the adjoining bathroom and washed his face. He dried off and blinked at his reflection in the mirror. As on countless other occasions, he wondered what Jenny had ever seen in him.

Not one feature or aspect of his face could be called handsome. His forehead was too broad, ears too big. Although he had 20–20 vision, his left eye had a leftward cast, and most people could not talk to him without nervously shifting their attention from one eye to the other, wondering which was looking at them when, in fact, *both* were. When he smiled he looked clownish, and when he frowned he looked sufficiently threatening to send Jack the Ripper scurrying for home and hearth.

But Jenny had seen something in him. She had wanted, needed, and loved him. In spite of her own good looks, she had not cared about appearances. That was one of the reasons he had loved her so much. One of the reasons he missed her so much. One of a thousand reasons.

He looked away from the mirror. If it was possible to be lonelier than he was now, he hoped to God that he never slipped down that far.

He returned to the other room, said goodbye to his unheeding wife, kissed her, smelled her hair once more, and got out of there at five-thirty.

In the street, behind the wheel of his Camaro, Jack looked at passing pedestrians and other motorists with loathing. His fellow men. The good, kind, gentle, righteous people of the straight world would regard him with disdain and possibly even disgust if they knew he was a professional thief, though it was what they had done to him and to Jenny that had driven him to crime.

He knew anger and bitterness solved nothing, changed nothing, and hurt no one but himself. Bitterness was corrosive. He did not want to be bitter, but there were times when he could not help it.

Later, after dinner alone at a Chinese restaurant, he returned to his apartment. He had a spacious one-bedroom co-op in a first-class building on Fifth Avenue, overlooking Central Park. Officially, it was owned by a Liechtenstein-based corporation, which had purchased it with a check written on a Swiss bank account, and each month the utilities and the association fees were paid by the Bank of America out of a trust account. Jack Twist lived there under the name ''Philippe Delon.'' To the doormen and other building employees, to the few neighbors with whom he spoke, he was known as the odd and slightly disreputable scion of a wealthy French family who had sent him to America ostensibly to scout investments but actually just to get him out of their hair. He spoke French fluently and could speak English with a convincing French accent for hours without slipping up and revealing his deception. Of course, there was no French family, and both the corporation in Liechtenstein and the Swiss bank account were his, and the only wealth he had to invest was that which he had stolen from others. He was not an *ordinary* thief.

In his apartment, he went directly to the walk-in closet in the bedroom and removed the false partition at the rear of it. He pulled two bags from the secret, three-foot-deep storage space and took them into the dark living room, not bothering to turn on lights. He piled the bags beside his favorite armchair, which stood by a large window.

He got a bottle of Beck's from the refrigerator, opened it, and returned to the living room. He sat in the darkness for a while, by the window, looking down on the park, where lights reflected off the snow-covered ground and made strange shadows in the bare-limbed trees.

He was stalling, and he knew it. Finally he switched on the reading lamp beside the chair. He pulled the smallest of the two bags in front of him, opened it, and began to scoop out the contents.

Jewels. Diamond pendants, diamond necklaces, glittering diamond chokers. A diamond and emerald bracelet. Three diamond and sapphire bracelets. Rings, brooches, barrettes, stickpins, jeweled hat pins.

These were the proceeds of a heist that he had pulled off single-handedly six weeks ago. It should have been a two-man job, but with extensive and imaginative planning, he had found a way to handle it himself, and it had gone smoothly.

The only problem was that he had gotten no kick whatsoever from that heist. When a job had been successfully concluded, Jack was usually in a grand mood for days after. From his point of view, these were not simply crimes but also acts of retribution against the straight world, payment for what it had done to him and to Jenny. Until the age of twenty-nine, he had given much to society, to his country, but as a reward he had wound up in a Central American hellhole, in a dictator's prison, where he had been left to rot. And Jenny . . . He could not bear to think about the condition in which he had found her when, at last, he had escaped and come home. Now, he no longer gave to society but *took* from it, and with intense pleasure. His greatest satisfaction was breaking the rules, taking what he wanted, getting away with it—until the jewelry heist six weeks ago. At the end of that operation, he had felt no triumph, no sense of retribution. That lack of excitement scared him. It was, after all, what he lived for.

Sitting in the armchair by the window, he piled the jewelry in his lap, held selected pieces up to the light, and tried once more to gain a feeling of accomplishment and revenge.

He should have disposed of the jewelry in the days immediately following the burglary. But he was reluctant to part with it until he had squeezed at least a small measure of satisfaction from it.

Troubled by his continued lack of feeling, he put the jewels back into the sack from which he had taken them.

The other sack contained his share of the proceeds from the robbery at the *fratellanza* warehouse five days ago. They had been able to open only one of the two safes, but that had contained over $3,100,000—more than a million apiece, in untraceable twenties, fifties, and hundreds.

By now he should have begun to convert the cash into cashier's checks and other negotiable instruments for deposit, by mail, in his Swiss accounts. However, he held on to it because, as with the jewelry, the possession of it had not yet given him a sense of triumph.

He removed thick stacks of tightly banded currency from the bag and held them, turned them over in his hands. He brought them to his face and smelled them. That singular scent of money was usually exciting in itself—but not this time. But he did not feel triumphant, clever, lawless, or in any way superior to the obedient mice who scurried through society's maze exactly as they were taught. He just felt empty.

If this change in him had occurred with the warehouse job, he would have attributed it to having stolen from other thieves, rather than from the straight world. But his reaction subsequent to the jewelry heist had been the same, and that victim had been a legitimate business. It was his ennui following the jewelry store action that caused him to move on to another job sooner than he should have. Usually he pulled off one job every three or four months, but only five weeks had elapsed between his most recent operations.

All right, so maybe the usual thrill eluded him on both these recent jobs because the money was no longer important to him. He had set aside enough to support himself in style for as long as he lived and to take care of Jenny even if she endured a normal lifespan in her coma, which was unlikely. Perhaps, all along, the most important thing about his work had not been the rebellion and defiance of it, as he had thought; perhaps, instead, he had done it all just for the money, and the rest of it had been merely cheap rationalization and self-delusion.

But he could not believe that. He knew what he had felt, and he knew how much he missed those feelings now.

Something was happening to him, an inner shifting, a sea-change. He felt empty, adrift, without purpose. He dared not lose his love of larceny. It was the only reason he had for living.

He put the money back into the bag. He turned out the light and sat in the darkness, sipping Beck's and staring down at Central Park.

In addition to his recent inability to find joy in his work, he had been plagued by a recurring nightmare more intense than any dream he had ever known. It had begun six weeks ago, before the jewelry store job, and he'd had it eight or ten times since. In the dream, he was fleeing from a man in a motorcycle helmet with a darkly tinted visor. At least he thought it was a motorcycle helmet, although he could not see many details of it or anything else of the man who wore it. The faceless stranger pursued him on foot through unknown rooms and along amorphous corridors and, most vividly, along a deserted highway that cut through an empty moon-washed landscape. On every occasion, Jack's panic built like steam pressure in a boiler, until it exploded and blew him awake.

The obvious interpretation was that the dream was a warning, that the man in the helmet was a cop, that Jack was going to get caught. But that was not the way the nightmare *felt*. In the dream, he never had the impression that the guy in the helmet was a cop. Something else.

He hoped to God he would not have the dream tonight. The day had been bad enough without that midnight terror.

He got another beer, returned to the chair by the window, and sat down in the darkness once more.

It was December 8, and Jack Twist—former officer in the elite United States Army Rangers, former POW in an undeclared war, a man who had helped save the lives of over a thousand Indians in Central America, a man who functioned under a burden of grief that might have broken some people, a daring thief whose reservoir of courage had always been bottomless—wondered if he had run out of the simple courage to go on living. If he could not regain the sense of purpose he had found in larceny, he needed to find a new purpose. Desperately.

7. Elko County, Nevada

Ernie Block broke all the speed limits on the drive back from Elko to the Tranquility Motel.

The last time he had driven so fast and recklessly had been on a gloomy Monday morning during his hitch with Marine Intelligence in Vietnam. He had been behind the wheel of a Jeep, passing through what should have been friendly territory, and had unexpectedly come under enemy fire. The incoming shells had spewed up geysers of dirt and chunks of macadam only feet away from his front and rear bumpers. By the time he had broken out of the fire zone, he had escaped more than twenty near-misses, had been hit by three small but painfully jagged pieces of mortar, had been rendered temporarily deaf from the thunderous explosions, and had found himself struggling to control a Jeep that was running on its wheel rims with four flat tires. Having survived, he figured he had known fear as profound as it could ever be.

But coming back from Elko, his fear was building toward a new peak. Nightfall was approaching. He had driven to the Elko freight office in the Dodge van to take delivery of a shipment of lighting fixtures for the motel. He had set out shortly after noon, leaving Faye in charge of the front desk, giving himself plenty of time to make the round-trip before twilight. But he had a flat tire and lost time changing it. Then, once he reached Elko, he wasted almost an hour having the tire repaired because he had not wanted to start home without a spare. With one thing or another, he had left Elko almost two hours later than expected, and the sun had westered to the far edge of the Great Basin.

He kept the accelerator most of the way to the floor, whipping around other traffic on the superhighway. He did not think he would be able to finish the drive home if he had to do it in full darkness. In the morning they would find him behind the wheel of the van, still parked along the roadside, stark raving mad from having spent long hours in horrified contemplation of the perfectly black landscape.

In the two and a half weeks since Thanksgiving, he had continued to conceal his irrational fear of darkness from Faye. After she returned from her visit to Wisconsin, Ernie found it more difficult to sleep without a lamp burning, having indulged himself with a night light while she was gone. Every morning he used Murine to clear his bloodshot eyes. Fortunately, she had not suggested going into Elko at night for a movie, so Ernie had not been required to make excuses. A few times, after sunset, he'd had to go from the office to the Tranquility Grille next door, and even though the walk was well-lighted by the motel's outdoor lamps and signs, he had been nearly overwhelmed by a sense of fragility, vulnerability. But he had kept his secret.

All his life, in the Marine Corps and out of it, to the best of his ability, Ernie Block had done what was required of him, all that could be expected. And now, by God, he was not going to fail his own wife.

Behind the wheel of the Dodge van, racing westward toward the Tranquility Motel under a smeary orange-purple sky, Ernie Block wondered if his problem was premature senility, Alzheimer's disease. Even though he was only fifty-two, it almost had to be something like Alzheimer's. Although it frightened him, at least he could understand it.

Understand it, yes, but he could not accept it. Faye depended on him. He could not become a mental invalid, a burden on her. The men in the Block family never let their womenfolk down. Never. Unthinkable.

The highway rounded a small hillock, and a mile ahead, north of the Interstate, lay the motel, the only building in that vast panorama. Its blue and green neon sign was already switched on, shining fiercely bright against the twilight sky. He'd never seen a more welcome sight.

Complete darkness was still ten minutes away, and he decided it was foolish to risk being stopped by a cop when he was this close to sanctuary. He eased up on the accelerator, and the speedometer needle swiftly dropped: *ninety . . . eighty-five . . . seventy-five . . . sixty . . .*

He was three-quarters of a mile from home when a curious thing happened: He glanced southward, away from the road, and his breath caught. He did not know what startled him. Something about the landscape. Something about the way the light and shadow played across those down-sloping fields. He was suddenly gripped by the odd idea that a particular piece of ground—a half-mile ahead, on the opposite side of the highway—was of supreme importance in understanding the bizarre changes that had been taking place in him during the past few months.

. . . fifty . . . forty-five . . . forty . . .

He could see nothing to make that piece of land different from the tens of thousands of acres around it. Besides, he had seen it countless times before and had been unimpressed by it. Nevertheless, in the slope of the terrain, in the gently folded contours of the earth, in the bisecting wound of an arroyo, in the configuration of sagebrush and grass, and in the scattered gnarled outcroppings of rock, something seemed to cry out for investigation.

He felt as if the land itself were saying, "Here, here, here is part of the answer to your problem, part of the explanation for your fear of the night. Here. Here . . ." But that was ridiculous.

To his surprise, he found himself pulling to the shoulder of the highway, stopping a quarter-mile from home, not far from the exit ramp to the county road that led past the motel. He squinted south across the highway, at the place that had mysteriously captured his attention.

He was gripped by the most amazing sense of impending epiphany, an overwhelming feeling that something of monumental importance was about to happen to him. The skin prickled along the back of his neck.

He got out of the van, leaving it idling behind him. In a state of tremulous expectation that he could not understand, he headed toward the far side of the interstate, where he could have a better look at the plot of ground that fascinated him. He traversed two lanes of blacktop, clambered into the twenty-foot-wide gulley that divided the halves of the interstate, and scrambled up the far slope. He waited for three huge trucks to roar past, then crossed the eastbound lanes in the windy wake of those rigs. His heart was pounding with an inexplicable excitement, and for the moment he had forgotten the advent of night.

He stopped on the far berm, at the crest of the highway's elevated bed, looking south and slightly west. He wore a bulky suede jacket with sheepskin lining, but his brush-cut gray hair provided little protection from the chilly wind, which scrubbed its cold knuckles across his skull.

He began to lose the feeling that something of immense importance was about to happen. Instead, he was seized by the even creepier notion that something had *already* happened to him on that patch of shadow-banded ground out there, something that accounted for his recent fear of the dark. Something he had assiduously banned from his memory.

But that made no sense. If important events had transpired here, they simply would not have slipped his mind. He was not forgetful. And he was not the kind of person who repressed unpleasant memories.

Still, the back of his neck continued to tingle. Out there, not far into those trackless Nevada plains, something had happened to him that he had forgotten but that now pricked him from his subconscious, where it was deeply embedded, much the way a needle, accidentally left in a quilt, might jab and startle a sleeper out of a dream.

With his legs spread wide and his feet planted firmly in the berm, with his blocky head hunched down on his blocky shoulders, Ernie seemed to be challenging the landscape to speak more clearly to him. He strained to resurrect the dead memory of this place—if, indeed, there was one—but the harder he tried to grasp the elusive revelation, the faster it receded from him. Then it was gone altogether.

The *déjà vu* deserted him as completely as the sense of impending epiphany had evaporated before it. The tingle left his scalp and neck. His frantically pounding heart settled slowly into a more normal pace.

Bewildered and somewhat dizzy, he studied the fast-fading scene before him—the angled land, the spines and teeth of rock, the brush and grass, the weathered convexities and concavities of the ancient earth—and now he could not imagine why it had seemed special to him. It was just a portion of the high plains virtually indistinguishable from a thousand other spots from here to Elko or from here to Battle Mountain.

Disoriented by the suddenness of his plunge from the brink of transcendent awareness, he looked back toward the van, which waited on the north side of the interstate. He felt conspicuous and foolish when he thought of the way he had dashed from there to here in the grip of a strange excitement. He hoped Faye had not seen him. If by chance she had been looking out a window in this direction, she could not have missed his performance, for the motel was only a quarter of a mile away, and the flashing emergency blinkers on the truck made it by far the most noticeable thing in the swiftly descending darkness.

Darkness.

Abruptly, the nearness of nightfall hit Ernie Block hard. For a while, the mysterious magnetism that had drawn him to this place had been stronger than his fear of the dark. But that changed in an instant when he realized that the eastern half of the sky was purple-black and that only minutes of vague light remained in the western realm.

With a cry of panic, he bolted across the eastbound lanes, in front of a motor home, oblivious of the danger. A horn blared at him. He did not care, did not pause, just ran pell-mell because he could feel the darkness clutching at him and pressing down on him. He reached the shallow gully that served as a lane divider, fell as he started down into it, rolled back onto his feet, terrified of the blackness that was welling up out of each depression in the land and from under every rock. He flung himself up the other side of the gully, fled into the westbound lanes. Fortunately there was no oncoming traffic, for he did not look to see if the way was clear. At the van, he fumbled with the door handle, acutely conscious of the perfect blackness *under* the truck. It was grappling at his feet. It wanted to pull him under the Dodge and devour him. He yanked the door open. Tore his feet loose of the hands of darkness. Clambered into the cab. Slammed the door. Locked it.

He felt better but far from safe, and if he had not been so close to home he would have frozen stiff. But he only had a quarter of a mile to go, and when he switched on his headlights, the gloom fell back, which encouraged him. He was shaking so violently that he did not trust himself to pull back into traffic, so he drove along the shoulder of the interstate until he came to the exit ramp. There were sodium-arc lamps along the ramp and at the base of it, and he was tempted to stop there at the bottom, in the yellow glare, but he gritted his teeth and turned onto the county road, out of the light. After driving only two hundred yards, Ernie reached the entrance to the Tranquility Motel. He swung through the parking area, slid the van into a slot in front of the office, switched off the headlights, and cut the engine.

Beyond the big windows of the office, he could see Faye at the front desk. He hurried inside, closing the door behind himself with too much force. He smiled at Faye when she glanced up, and he hoped the smile looked more convincing than it felt.

"I was beginning to worry, dear," she said, returning his smile.

"Had a flat tire," Ernie said, unzipping his jacket.

He felt somewhat relieved. Nightfall was easier to accept when he was not alone; Faye gave him strength, but he was still uneasy.

She said, "I missed you."

"I was only gone the afternoon."

"I guess I'm hooked, then. Seemed longer. Guess I've got to have my Ernie fix every couple of hours or go through withdrawal symptoms."

He leaned across the counter, and she leaned from her side, and they kissed. There was nothing half-hearted about their kiss. She put one hand to his head to hold him close. Most long-married couples, even if they remained in love, were perfunctory in their displays of affection, but that was not the case with Ernie and Faye Block. After thirty-one years of marriage, she could still make him feel young.

She said, "Where are the new lighting fixtures? They did come in, didn't they? The freight office didn't make a mistake?"

That question jolted him back to an acute awareness of the night outside. He glanced at the windows, then quickly away. "Uh, no. I'm tired. I don't really feel up to hauling them in here tonight."

"Just four crates—"

"Really, I'd rather do it in the morning," he said, striving to keep a tremor out of his voice. "The stuff will be all right in the truck. Nobody'll touch it. Hey, you put up the Christmas decorations!"

"You mean you *just* noticed?"

A huge wreath of pine cones and nuts hung on the wall above the sofa. A life-sized cardboard figure of Santa Claus stood in the corner beside the rack of postcards, and a small ceramic sleigh with ceramic reindeer was displayed at one end of the long counter. Red and gold Christmas-tree balls hung from the ceiling light fixture on lengths of transparent fishing line.

"You had to get up on a ladder for some of this," he said.

"Just the stepladder."

"But what if you'd fallen? You should've left this for me to do."

Faye shook her head. "Honey, I swear to God I'm not the fragile type. Now, hush up. You ex-Marines carry macho too far sometimes."

"Is that so?"

The outer door opened, and a trucker came in, asking about a room.

Ernie held his breath until the door closed.

The trucker was a lanky man in a cowboy hat, denim jacket, cowboy shirt, and jeans. Faye complimented him on the hat, which had an elaborately sculpted leather band brightened with chips of turquoise. In that easy way of hers, she made the stranger feel like an old friend as she shepherded him through the check-in process.

Leaving her to it, trying to forget his curious experience on the interstate, trying not to dwell on the night that had come, Ernie moved behind the counter, hung his coat on the brass rack in the corner by the file cabinets, and went to the oak desk, where mail was stacked on the blotter. Bills, of course. Advertisements. A charity solicitation. The first Christmas cards of the year. His military pension check.

Finally, there was a white envelope without a return address, which contained only a Polaroid color photograph that had been taken in front of the motel, beside the door to Room 9. It was of three people—man, woman, child. The man was in his late twenties, darkly tanned and good-looking. The woman was a couple of years younger, a pretty brunette. The little girl, five or six, was very cute. All three were smiling at the camera. Judging from their clothes—shorts and T-shirts—and the quality of sunlight in the picture, Ernie assumed that the snapshot had been taken in the middle of summer.

Puzzled, he turned the photo over, looking for a scribbled note of explanation. The back was blank. He checked the envelope again, but it was empty: no letter, no card, not even a business card to identify the sender. The postmark was Elko, December 7, last Saturday.

He looked again at the people in the picture, and although he did not remember them, he felt his skin prickle, just as it had done when he had been drawn to that place along the highway. His pulse accelerated. He quickly put the picture aside and looked away from it.

Faye was still chatting with the cowboy-trucker as she took a room key off the pegboard and passed it across the counter.

Ernie kept his eyes on her. She was a calming influence. She had been a lovely farmgirl when he'd met her, and had grown into a lovelier woman. Her blond hair might have begun to turn white, but it was hard to tell. Her blue eyes were clear and quick. Hers was an open, friendly Iowa face, slightly saucy but always wholesome, even beatific.

By the time the cowboy-trucker left, Ernie had stopped shaking. He took the Polaroid snapshot to Faye. "What do you make of this?"

"That's our Room Nine," she said. "They must've stayed with us." She frowned at the young couple and little girl in the photograph. "Can't say I remember them, though. Strangers to me."

"So why would they send us a photo without a note?"

"Well, obviously, they thought we *would* remember them."

"But the only reason they'd think that was if maybe they stayed for a few days and we got to know them. And I don't know them at all. I think I'd remember the tyke," Ernie said. He liked children, and they usually liked him. "She's cute enough to be in movies."

"I'd think you'd remember the *mother*. She's gorgeous."

"Postmarked Elko," Ernie said. "Why would anybody who lives in Elko come out here to stay?"

"Maybe they don't live in Elko. Maybe they were here last summer and always meant to send us a photo, and maybe they recently passed through and meant to stop and leave this off but didn't have time. So they mailed it from Elko."

"Without a note."

"It is odd," Faye agreed.

He took the picture from her. "Besides, this is a Polaroid. Developed a minute after it was taken. If they wanted us to have it, why didn't they leave it with us when they stayed here?"

The door opened, and a curly-haired guy with a bushy mustache came into the office, shivering. "Got any rooms left?" he asked.

While Faye dealt with the guest, Ernie took the Polaroid back to the oak desk. He meant to gather up the mail and go upstairs, but he stood by the desk, studying the faces of the people in the snapshot.

It was Tuesday evening, December 10.

8. Chicago, Illinois

When Brendan Cronin went to work as an orderly at St. Joseph's Hospital for Children, only Dr. Jim McMurtry knew that he was really a priest. Father Wycazik had obtained a guarantee of secrecy from the physician, as well as the solemn assurance that Brendan would be assigned as much work—and as much *unpleasant* work—as any orderly. Therefore, during his first day on the job, he emptied bedpans, changed urine-soaked bed linens, assisted a therapist with passive exercises for bed-ridden patients, spoon-fed an eight-year-old boy who was partially paralyzed, pushed wheelchairs, encouraged despondent patients, cleaned up the vomit of two young cancer victims nauseous from chemotherapy. No one pampered him, and no one called him "Father." The nurses, doctors, orderlies, candy-stripers, and patients called him Brendan, and he felt uncomfortable, like an impostor engaged in a masquerade.

That first day, overcome with pity and grief for St. Joseph's children, he twice slipped away to the staff men's room and locked himself in a stall, where he sat and wept. The twisted legs and swollen joints of those who suffered from rheumatoid arthritis, that mangler of the innocent young, was a sight almost too terrible to be borne. The wasted flesh of the muscular dystrophy victims, the suppurating wounds of the burn victims, the battered bodies of those whose parents had abused them: He wept for all of them.

He could not imagine why Father Wycazik thought this duty would help him regain his lost faith. If anything, the existence of so many pain-racked children only reinforced his doubt. If the merciful God of Catholicism really existed, if there *was* a Jesus, why would He allow the innocent to endure such atrocities? Of course, Brendan knew all the standard theological arguments on that point. Mankind had brought all forms of evil upon itself by choice, the Church said, by turning away from the grace of God. But theological arguments were inadequate when he came face to face with these smallest victims of fate.

By the second day, the staff was still calling him Brendan, but the children were calling him Pudge, a long-unused nickname which he divulged to them in the course of telling a funny story. They liked his stories, jokes, rhymes, and silly puns, and he found he could nearly always get a laugh or at least a smile out of them. That day, he went to the men's room and wept only once.

By the third day, both the children and staff called him Pudge. If he had another metier besides the priesthood, he had found it at St. Joseph's. In addition to performing the usual tasks expected of an orderly, he entertained the patients with comic patter, teased them, drew them out. Wherever he went, he was greeted with cries of *"Pudge!"* that were a better reward than money. And he did not cry until he was back in the hotel room that he had taken for the duration of Father Wycazik's unconventional therapy.

By Wednesday afternoon, the seventh day, he knew why Father Wycazik sent him to St. Joseph's. Understanding came while he was brushing the hair of a ten-year-old girl who'd been crippled by a rare bone disease.

Her name was Emmeline, and she was rightfully proud of her hair. It was thick, glossy, raven-black, and its healthy luster seemed to be a defiant response to the sickness that had wasted her body. She liked to brush her hair a hundred strokes every day, but often her knuckles and wrist-joints were so inflamed that she could not hold the brush.

On Wednesday, Brendan put her in a wheelchair and took her to the X-ray department, where they were monitoring a new drug's effects on her bone marrow, and when he brought her back to her room an hour later, he brushed her hair for her. Emmeline sat in the wheelchair, looking out a window, while Brendan pulled the soft bristles through her silken tresses, and she became enchanted with the winterscape beyond the glass.

With a gnarled hand more suited to the body of an eighty-year-old woman, she pointed down to the roof of another, lower wing of the hospital. "See that patch of snow, Pudge?" Rising heat within the building had caused most of the snow to loosen and slide off the pitched roof. But a large patch remained, outlined by dark slate shingles. "It looks like a ship," Emmy said. "The shape. You see? A beautiful old ship with three white sails, gliding across a slate-colored sea."

For a while Brendan could not see what she saw. But she continued to describe the imaginary vessel, and the fourth time that he looked up from her hair, he suddenly was able to see that the patch of snow did, indeed, bear a remarkable and delightful resemblance to a sailing ship.

To Brendan, the long icicles that hung in front of Emmy's window were transparent bars, the hospital a prison from which she might never be released. But to Emmy, those frozen stalactites were wondrous Christmas decorations that, she said, put her in the holiday mood.

"God likes winter as much as He likes spring," Emmy said. "The gift of the seasons is one of His ways of keeping us from getting bored with the world. That's what Sister Katherine told us, and right away I could see it must be true. When the sun hits those icicles just right, they cast rainbows across my bed. Ever-so-pretty rainbows, Pudge. The ice and snow are like . . . like jewels . . . and ermine cloaks that God uses to dress up the world in winter to make us ooh and ah. That's why He never makes two snowflakes alike: it's a way of reminding us that the world He made for us is a wonderful, wonderful world."

As if on cue, snowflakes spiraled down from the gray December sky.

In spite of her nearly useless legs and twisted hands, in spite of the pain she had endured, Emmy believed in God's goodness, and in the inspiring *rightness* of the world that He had created.

Strong faith was, in fact, a trait of nearly all the children in St. Joseph's Hospital. They remained convinced that a caring Father watched over them from His kingdom in the sky, and they were encouraged.

In his mind he could hear Father Wycazik saying: *If these innocents can suffer so much and not lose their faith, what sorry excuse do you have, Brendan? Perhaps, in their very innocence and naïveté, they know something that you have forgotten while chasing your sophisticated education in Rome. Perhaps there is something to be learned from this, Brendan. Do you think so? Just maybe? Something to be learned?*

But the lesson was not powerful enough to restore Brendan's faith. He continued to be deeply moved, not by the possibility that a caring and compassionate God might actually exist, but by the children's amazing courage in the face of such adversity.

He gave Emmy's hair a hundred strokes, then ten more, which pleased her, and then he lifted her from the wheelchair and put her into bed. As he pulled the covers over her pathetic bent-stick legs, he felt a surge of that same rage that had filled him during Mass at St. Bette's two Sundays ago, and if a sacred chalice had been close at hand, he would not have hesitated to hurl it at the wall once more.

Emmy gasped, and Brendan had the odd notion that she had read his blasphemous thoughts. But she said, "Oh, Pudge, did you hurt yourself?"

He blinked at her. "What do you mean?"

"Did you burn yourself? Your hands. When'd you hurt your hands?"

Bewildered by her question, he looked down at the backs of his hands, turned them over, and was surprised by the marks on his palms. In the center of each palm was a red ring of inflamed and swollen flesh. Each ring was two inches in diameter and sharply defined along all its edges. The circular band of irritated tissue which formed the ring was no more than half an inch wide, inscribing a perfect circle; the skin around and within the circle was quite normal. It almost looked as if the marks had been painted on his hands, but when he touched one of the rings with a fingertip, he could feel the bump it made in his palm.

"That's strange," he said.

Dr. Stan Heeton was the resident physician on duty in St. Joseph's emergency room. Standing at the examining table on which Brendan sat, peering with interest at the odd rings on Brendan's hands, he said, "Do they hurt?"

"No. Not at all."

"Itching? A burning sensation?"

"No. Neither."

"Do they at least tingle? No? You've never had these before?"

"Never."

"Do you have any allergies that you're aware of? No? Hmmmm. At first glance, it looks like a mild burn, but you'd have remembered leaning against something hot enough to cause this. There'd be pain. So we can rule that out. Same for acid contact. Did you say you'd taken a little girl to radiology?"

"Yes, but I didn't stay in the room while the X rays were taken."

"Doesn't really look like a radiation burn. Maybe dermatomycosis, a fungal infection, perhaps in the ringworm family, though the symptoms aren't sufficiently indicative of ringworm. No scaling, no itching. And the ring is much too clearly defined, not like the inflammation patterns you get with a Microsporum or Trichophyton infection."

"So what does all this boil down to?"

Heeton hesitated, then said, "I don't think it's anything serious. The best guess is a rash related to an unidentified allergy. If the problem persists, you'll have to take the standard patch tests and find the source of your problem." He let go of Brendan's hands, went to a chair at a corner desk, and began to fill out a prescription form.

Puzzled, Brendan stared at his hands a moment longer, then folded them in his lap.

At the corner desk, still writing, Heeton said, "I'll start with the simplest treatment, a cortisone lotion. If the rash doesn't disappear in a couple of days, come see me again." He returned to the examining table, holding out the prescription form.

Brendan took the paper from him. "Listen, is there any chance I might pass on an infection to the kids or anything like that?"

"Oh, no. If I thought there was the slightest chance, I'd have told you," Heeton said. "Now, let me have one last look."

Brendan turned his hands palms-up for examination.

"What the devil?" Dr. Heeton said, surprised.

The rings were gone.

That night, in his room at the Holiday Inn, Brendan again endured the by-now familiar nightmare about which he had spoken with Father Wycazik. It had disturbed his sleep twice before in the past week.

He dreamed he was lying in a strange place, with his arms and legs restrained by straps or braces. From out of a haze, a pair of hands reached for him. Hands encased in shiny black gloves.

He woke in knots of sweat-soaked sheets, sat up in bed, and leaned back against the headboard, letting the dream evaporate as sweat dried on his forehead. In the dark he brought his hands to his face to blot it—and went rigid when his palms touched his cheeks. He switched on the lamp. The swollen, inflamed rings had returned to his palms. But as he watched, they faded.

It was Thursday, December 12.

9. Laguna Beach, California

Dom Corvaisis thought he had slept Wednesday night straight through in peace. He woke in bed, in precisely the same position in which he had gone to sleep, as if he had not moved an inch during the night.

But when he went to work at his Displaywriter, he was dismayed to find proof of his somnambulistic wandering on the current work diskette. As on a few other occasions, he apparently had gone to the Displaywriter in his night trance and had repeatedly typed two words. Previously, he had typed, "I'm scared," but this time there were two different words:

The moon. The moon. The moon. The moon.
The moon. The moon. The moon. The moon.

There were hundreds of repetitions of those seven letters, and he was at once reminded that he had heard himself murmuring the same words in a state of drowsy disorientation, just as he had fallen asleep last Sunday. Dominick stared at the screen for a long time, chilled, but he had no idea what special meaning "the moon" held for him, if any.

The Valium and Dalmane therapy was working well. Until now, there had been no new episodes of sleepwalking and no dreams since last weekend, when he'd had that nasty nightmare about being forced face-down into a sink. He had seen Dr. Cobletz again, and the physician had been pleased by his swift progress.

Cobletz had said, "I'm going to extend your prescriptions, but be sure not to take the Valium more than once—or at most, twice—a day."

"I never do," Dom had lied.

"And only one Dalmane a night. I don't want you becoming drug-dependent. I'm sure we'll beat this thing by the first of the year."

Dom believed Cobletz was correct, which was why he did not want to worry the doctor by confessing that there were days when he only made it through with the aid of Valium and nights when he took two or even three Dalmane tablets, washing some of them down with beer or Scotch. But in a couple of weeks he could stop taking them without fear that the somnambulism would get a new grip on him. The treatment was working. That was the important thing. The treatment was, thank God, working.

Until now.

The moon.

Frustrated and angry, he deleted the words from the diskette, a hundred lines of them, four repetitions to the line.

He stared at the screen a long time, growing increasingly nervous.

Finally he took a Valium.

That morning Dom got no work done, and at eleven-thirty he and Parker Faine picked up Denny Ulmes and Nyugen Kao Tran, the two boys assigned to them by the Orange County chapter of Big Brothers of America. They had planned a lazy afternoon at the beach, dinner at Hamburger Hamlet, and a movie, and Dominick had been looking forward to the outing.

He had become involved in the Big Brothers program years earlier in Portland, Oregon. It had been his only community involvement, the only thing that had been able to bring him out of his rabbit hole.

He had spent his own childhood in a series of foster homes, lonely and increasingly withdrawn. Some day, when he finally got married, he hoped to adopt kids. In the meantime, when he spent time with these kids, he was not only helping them but was also comforting the lonely child within himself.

Nyugen Kao Tran preferred to be called "Duke," in imitation of John Wayne, whose movies he loved. Duke was thirteen, the youngest son of boat people who had fled the horrors of "peacetime" Vietnam. He was bright, quick-witted, as startlingly agile as he was thin. His father—after surviving a brutal war, a concentration camp, and two weeks in a flimsy boat on the open sea—had been killed three years ago in a holdup while working at his second job as a night-shift clerk at a Seven-Eleven store in sunny southern California.

Denny Ulmes, the twelve-year-old who was Parker's little brother, lost his father to cancer. He was more reticent than Duke, but the two got along famously, so Dom and Parker frequently combined their outings.

Parker became a Big Brother at Dom's insistence, with curmudgeonly reluctance. "Me? *Me?* I'm not father material—or surrogate father material," Parker had said. "Never was and never will be. I drink too much, womanize too much. It'd be downright criminal for any kid to turn to me for advice. I'm a procrastinator, a dreamer, and a self-centered egomaniac. And I *like* me that way! What in God's name would I have to offer a kid? I don't even like dogs. Kids like dogs, but I hate 'em. Damn dirty flea-bitten things. Me, a Big Brother? Friend, you have lost your marbles for sure.''

But Thursday afternoon at the beach, when the water proved too cold for swimming, Parker organized a volleyball game and surfside races. He got Dom and the boys involved in a complicated game of his own devising, involving two frisbees, a beach ball, and an empty soda can. Under his direction they also built a sandcastle complete with a menacing dragon.

Later, during an early dinner at Hamburger Hamlet in Costa Mesa, while the kids were in the bathroom, Parker said, "Dom, good buddy, this Big Brother thing was sure one of the best ideas I've ever had."

"*Your* idea?" Dominick said, shaking his head. "I had to drag you into it kicking and screaming."

"Nonsense," Parker said. "I've always had a way with kids. Every artist is a bit of a kid at heart. We have to stay young to create. I find kids invigorate me, keep my mind fresh."

"Next, you'll be getting a dog," Dom said.

Parker laughed. He finished his beer, leaned forward. "You okay? At times today, you seemed . . . distracted. A little out of it."

"Lot on my mind," Dom said. "But I'm fine. The sleepwalking's pretty much stopped. And the dreams. Cobletz knows what he's doing."

"Is the new book going well? Don't shit me, now."

"It's going well," Dom lied.

"At times you have that look," Parker said, watching him intently. "That . . . doped up. Following the prescribed dosage, I assume?"

The painter's perspicacity disconcerted Dom. "I'd have to be an idiot to snack on Valium as if it was candy. Of course, I follow the prescribed dosage."

Parker stared hard at him, then apparently decided not to push it.

The movie was good, but during the first thirty minutes Dom grew nervous without reason. When he felt the nervousness building toward an anxiety attack, he slipped out to the men's room. He'd brought another Valium for just such an emergency.

The important thing was that he was winning. He was getting well. The somnambulism was losing its grip on him. It really was.

Beneath a strong pine-scented disinfectant, there was an acrid stench from the urinals. Dom felt slightly nauseous. He swallowed the Valium without water.

That night, in spite of the pills, he had the dream again, and he remembered more of it than just the part where people were forcing his head into a sink.

In the nightmare, he was in a bed in an unknown room, where there seemed to be an oily saffron mist in the air. Or perhaps the amber fog was only in his eyes, for he could not see anything clearly. Furniture loomed beyond the bed, and at least two people were present. But those shapes rippled and writhed as if this were purely a realm of smoke and fluid, where nothing had a fixed appearance.

He almost felt as if he were underwater, very deep underneath the surface of some mysterious cold sea. The atmosphere in the dream-place had more weight than mere air. He could barely draw breath. Each inhalation and exhalation was agony. He sensed that he was dying.

The two blurred figures came close. They seemed concerned about his condition. They spoke urgently to each other. Although he knew they were speaking English, he could not understand them. A cold hand touched him. He heard the clink of glass. Somewhere a door shut.

With the flash-cut suddenness of a scene transition in a film, the dream shifted to a bathroom or kitchen. Someone was forcing his face down into the sink. Breathing became even more difficult. The air was like mud: with each inhalation it clogged his nostrils. He choked and gasped and tried to blow out the mud-thick air, and the two people with him were shouting at him, and as before he could not understand what they were saying, and they pressed his face down into the sink—

Dom woke and was still in bed. Last weekend he had been flung free of the dream only to discover that he had walked in his sleep and had been acting out the nightmare at his own bathroom sink. This time, he was relieved to find himself beneath the sheets.

I *am* getting better, he thought.

Trembling, he sat up and switched on the light.

No barricades. No signs of somnambulistic panic.

He looked at the digital clock: two-oh-nine A.M. A half-empty can of warm beer stood on the nightstand. He washed down another Dalmane tablet.

I am getting better.

It was Friday the thirteenth.

10. Elko County, Nevada

Friday night, three days after his weird experience on the I-80, Ernie Block couldn't sleep at all. As darkness embraced him, his nerves wound tighter, tighter, until he thought he would start screaming and be unable to stop.

Slipping out of bed as soundlessly as he could, pausing to make sure that Faye's slow and even breathing had not changed, he went into the bathroom, closed the door, turned on the light. Wonderful light. He reveled in the light. He put down the lid of the commode and sat for fifteen minutes in his underwear, just letting the brightness sear him, as mindlessly happy as a lizard on a sun-washed rock.

Finally he knew he must return to the bedroom. If Faye woke, and if he remained in here too long, she would begin to think something was wrong. He was determined to do nothing that would make her suspicious.

Although he had not used the toilet, he flushed it for cover, and went to the sink to wash his hands. He had just finished rinsing off the soap and had plucked the towel off the rack when his eyes were drawn to the only window in the room. It was above the bathtub, a rectangle about three feet wide and two feet high, which opened outward on an overhead piano hinge. Although the glass was frosted and provided no view of the night beyond, a shiver passed through Ernie as he stared at the opaque pane. More disturbing than the shiver was the sudden rush of peculiar, urgent thoughts that came with it:

The window's big enough to get through, I could get away, escape, and the roof of the utility room is under the window, so there's not a long drop, and I could be off, into the arroyo behind the motel, up into the hills, make my way east, get to a ranch somewhere and get help. . . .

Blinking furiously as that swift train of thoughts flashed through his mind and faded away, Ernie discovered that he had stepped from the sink to the bathtub. He did not remember moving.

He was bewildered by the urge to escape. From whom? From what? Why?
This was his own home. He had nothing to fear within these walls.

Yet he could not take his gaze from the milky window. A dreaminess had
come over him. He was aware of it but unable to cast it off.

*Got to get out, get away, there won't be another chance, not another chance
like this, now, go now, go, go. . . .*

Unwittingly, he had stepped into the tub and was directly in front of the window, which was set in the wall at face-level. The porcelain coating of the tub
was cold against his bare feet.

*Slide back the latch, push up the window, stand on the rim of the tub, pull
yourself up onto the sill, out and away, a three- or four-minute headstart before
you're missed, not much but enough. . . .*

Panic rose in him without reason. There was a fluttering in his guts, a tightness
in his chest.

Without knowing why he was doing it, yet unable to stop himself, he slid the
bolt from the latch on the bottom of the window. He pushed out. The window
swung up.

He was not alone.

Something was at the other side of the window, out there on the roof, something
with a dark, featureless, shiny face. Even as Ernie recoiled in surprise, he realized
it was a man in a white helmet with a tinted visor that came all the way down
over his face, so darkly tinted that it was virtually black.

A black-gloved hand reached through the window, as if to grab him, and Ernie
cried out and took a step backward and fell over the edge of the tub. Toppling
out of the tub, he grabbed wildly at the shower curtain, tore it loose from several
of its rings, but could not arrest his fall. He hit the bathroom floor with a crash.
Pain flashed through his right hip.

"*Ernie!*" Faye cried, and a moment later she pushed open the door. "Ernie,
my God, what's wrong, what happened?"

"Stay back." He got up painfully. "Someone's out there."

Cold night air poured through the open window, rustling the half-wrecked,
bunched-up shower curtain.

Faye shivered, for she slept in only a pajama shirt and panties.

Ernie shivered, too, though partly for different reasons. The moment the pain
had throbbed through his hip, the dreaminess had left him. In the sudden rush of
clear-mindedness, he wondered if the helmeted figure had been imaginary, a hallucination.

"On the roof?" Faye said. "At the window? Who?"

"I don't know," Ernie said, rubbing his sore hip as he stepped back into the
tub and peered out the window again. He saw no one this time.

"What'd he look like?" Faye asked.

"I couldn't tell. He was in motorcycle gear. Helmet, gloves," Ernie said, realizing how outlandish it sounded.

He levered himself up on the windowsill far enough to lean out and look across
the full length and breadth of the utility room's roof. Shadows were deep in
places, but nowhere deep enough to hide a man. The intruder was gone—if indeed
he had ever existed.

Abruptly Ernie became aware of the vast darkness behind the motel. It stretched
across the hills, off to the distant mountains, an immense blackness relieved only
by the stars. Instantly, a crippling weakness and vulnerability overwhelmed him.
Gasping, he dropped off the sill, back into the tub, and started to turn away from
the window.

"Close it up," Faye said.

Squeezing his eyes shut to guard against another glimpse of the night, he turned once more to the in-rushing cold air, fumbled blindly for the window, and pulled it shut so hard that he almost broke the pane. With unsteady hands he struggled to secure the latch bolt.

When he stepped out of the tub, he saw concern in Faye's eyes, which he expected. He saw surprise, which he also expected. But he saw a penetrating awareness for which he was unprepared. For a long moment they looked at each other, neither of them speaking.

Then she said, "Are you ready to tell me about it?"

"Like I said . . . I thought I saw a guy on the roof."

"That's not what I'm talking about, Ernie. I mean, are you ready to tell me what's wrong, what's been eating at you?" Her eyes did not waver from his. "For a couple of months now. Maybe longer."

He was stunned. He thought he had concealed it so well.

She said, "Honey, you've been worried. Worried like I've never seen you before. And scared."

"No. Not scared exactly."

"Yes. Scared," Faye said, but there was no scorn in her, just an Iowan's forthrightness and a desire to help. "I've only ever seen you scared once before, Ernie—back when Lucy was five and came down with that muscle fever, and they thought it might be muscular dystrophy."

"God, yes, I was scared shitless then."

"But not since."

"Oh, I was scared in Nam sometimes," he said, his admission echoing hollowly off the bathroom walls.

"But *I* never saw it." She hugged herself. "It's rare that I see you like this, Ernie, so when you're scared *I'm* scared. Can't help it. I'm even more scared because I don't know what's *wrong*. You understand? Being in the dark like I am . . . that's worse than any secret you're withholding from me."

Tears came to her eyes, and Ernie said, "Oh, hey, don't cry. It's going to be all right, Faye. Really it is."

"*Tell me!*" she said.

"Okay."

"Now. Everything."

He had woefully underestimated her, and he felt thick-headed. She was a Corps wife, after all, and a good one. She had followed him from Quantico to Singapore to Pendleton in California, even to Alaska, almost everywhere but Nam and, later, Beirut. She had made a home for them wherever the Corps allowed dependents to follow, had weathered the bad times with admirable aplomb, had never complained, and had never failed him. She was tough. He could not imagine how he had forgotten that.

"Everything," he agreed, relieved to be able to share the burden.

Faye made coffee, and they sat in their robes and slippers at the kitchen table while he told her everything. She could see that he was embarrassed. He was slow to reveal details, but she sipped her coffee, remained patient, and gave him a chance to tell it in his own way.

Ernie was about the best husband a woman could want, but now and then his Block-family stubbornness reared its head, and Faye wanted to shake some sense into him. Everyone in his family suffered from it, especially the men. Blocks did things *this* way, never *that* way, and you better never question why. Block men liked their undershirts ironed but never their underpants. Block women *always* wore a bra, even at home in the worst summer heat. Blocks, both men and women, always ate lunch at precisely twelve-thirty, always had dinner at six-thirty sharp, and God forbid if the food was put on the table two minutes late: The subsequent complaining would burst eardrums. Blocks drove only General Motors vehicles. Not because GM products were notably better than others, but because Blocks had *always* driven only General Motors vehicles.

Thank God, Ernie was not a tenth as bad as his father or brothers. He had been wise enough to get out of Pittsburgh, where the Block clan had lived for generations in the same neighborhood. Out in the real world, away from the Kingdom of the Blocks, Ernie had loosened up. In the Marine Corps he could not expect every meal at precisely the time that Block tradition demanded. And soon after their marriage, Faye had made it clear that she would make a first-rate home for him but would not be bound by senseless traditions. Ernie adapted, though not always easily, and now he was a black sheep among his people, guilty of such sins as driving a variety of vehicles not made by General Motors.

Actually, the only area where the Block family stubbornness still had a hold on Ernie was in some man-woman matters. He believed that a husband had to protect his wife from a variety of unpleasantnesses that she was just too fragile to handle. He believed that a husband should never allow his wife to see him in a moment of weakness. Although their marriage had never been conducted according to those rules, Ernie did not always seem to realize they had abandoned the Block traditions more than a quarter of a century ago.

For months, she had been aware something was seriously wrong. But Ernie continued to stonewall it, straining to prove he was a happy retired Marine blissfully launched on a second career in motels. She had watched an unknown fire consuming him from within, and her subtle and patient attempts to get him to open up had gone right over his head.

During the past few weeks, ever since returning from Wisconsin after Thanksgiving, she had been increasingly aware of his reluctance—even inability—to go out at night. He could not seem to make himself comfortable in a room where even one lamp was left unlit.

Now, as they sat in the kitchen with cups of steaming coffee, the blinds tightly closed and all the lights on, Faye listened intently to Ernie, interrupting only when he seemed to need a word of encouragement to keep him going, and nothing he told her was more than she could cope with. Indeed, her spirits rose, for she was increasingly certain that she knew what was wrong with him and how he might be helped.

He finished, his voice low and thin. "So . . . is that the reward for all the years of hard work and careful financial planning? Premature senility? Now, when we can really start enjoying what we've earned, am I going to wind up with my brains all scrambled, drooling, pissing my pants, useless to myself and a burden on you? Twenty years before my time? Christ, Faye, I've always realized that life isn't fair, but I never thought the deck was stacked against me *this* bad."

"It won't be like that." She reached across the table and took his hand. "Sure, Alzheimer's can strike people even younger than you, but this isn't Alzheimer's. From what I've read, from the way it was with my father, I don't think the onset of senility—premature or otherwise—is ever like this. What it sounds like is a simple phobia. Phobia. Some people have an irrational fear of flying or heights. For some reason, you've developed a fear of the dark. It can be overcome."

"But phobias just don't develop overnight, do they?"

Their right hands were still clasped. She squeezed his as she said, "Do you remember Helen Dorfman? Almost twenty-four years ago. Our landlady when you were first assigned to Camp Pendleton.''

''Oh, yeah! The building on Vine Street, lived in number one, first floor front. We lived in number six.'' He seemed to take heart from his ability to recall those details. ''She had a cat . . . Sable. Remember how the damn cat took a liking to us, left little gifts on our doorstep?''

''Dead mice.''

''Yeah. Right there beside the morning paper and the milk.'' He laughed, blinked, and said, ''Hey, I see what you mean by bringing up Helen Dorfman! She was afraid to go out of her apartment. Couldn't even walk out on her own lawn.''

''The poor woman had agoraphobia,'' Faye said. ''An irrational fear of open spaces. She was a prisoner in her own home. Outside, she was overwhelmed with fear. Doctors call it a 'panic attack,' I think.''

''Panic attack,'' Ernie said softly. ''Yeah, that's it, all right.''

''And Helen didn't develop her agoraphobia till she was *thirty-five,* after her husband died. Phobias *can* spring up suddenly, later in life.''

''Well, whatever the hell a phobia *is,* wherever it comes from . . . I guess it's a lot better than senility. But good God, I don't want to spend the rest of my life being afraid of the dark.''

''You won't have to,'' Faye said. ''Twenty-four years ago, nobody understood phobias. There hadn't been much study done. No effective treatments. But it's not like that now. I'm sure it's not.''

He was silent a moment. ''I'm not crazy, Faye.''

''I know that, you big jerk.''

He mulled over the word ''phobia,'' and he plainly wanted to believe her answer. In his blue eyes, she saw a rebirth of hope.

He said, ''But the weird experience I had on the interstate on Tuesday. . . . And the hallucination—I'm sure it must've been a hallucination—of the motor-cyclist on the roof. . . . How does stuff like that fit this explanation? How could that be a part of my phobia?''

''I don't know. But an expert in the field could explain it all and tie it together. I'm sure it's not as unusual as it seems, Ernie.''

He pondered for a moment, then nodded. ''Okay. But how do we begin? Where do we go for help? How do I *beat* this damn thing?''

''I already have it figured out,'' she said. ''No doctor in Elko is going to know how to treat a case like this. We need a specialist, someone who deals with phobic patients every day. Probably isn't anyone like that in Reno, either. We'll have to go to a bigger city. Now, I suspect Milwaukee's big enough to have a doctor with experience in these things, and we could stay with Lucy and Frank—''

''And at the same time get to see a lot of Frank, Jr., and Dorie,'' Ernie said, smiling at the thought of his grandchildren.

''Right. We'll go there for Christmas a week sooner than planned, this Sunday instead of next. Which is tomorrow, in fact. It's already Saturday. When we get to Milwaukee, we'll look up a doctor. If, by New Year's, it looks like we'll have to stay there awhile, then I'll fly back here, find a full-time couple to manage the place, and rejoin you. We were planning to hire somebody this spring, anyway.''

''If we close the motel a week early, Sandy and Ned will lose out on some money over at the Grille.''

''Ned will still get the truckers off the interstate. And if he doesn't do as well as usual, we'll make it up to him.''

Ernie shook his head and smiled. "You've got it all worked out. You're something, Faye. You sure are. You're an absolute wonder."

"Well, I will admit I can be dazzling sometimes."

"I thank God every day that I found you," he said.

"I don't have any regrets either, Ernie, and I know I never will."

"You know, I feel a thousand percent better than when we first sat down here. Why'd it take me so damn long to ask you for help?"

"Why? Because you're a Block," she said.

He grinned and finished the old joke: "Which is only one step removed from a blockhead."

They laughed. He grabbed her hand again and kissed it. "That's the first *real* laugh I've had in weeks. We're a terrific team, Faye. We can face anything together, can't we?"

"Anything," she agreed.

It was Saturday, December 14, near dawn, and Faye Block was sure they would come out on top of their current problem, just as they had always come out on top before when they worked together, side by side.

She, like Ernie, had already forgotten the unidentified Polaroid photograph that they had received in a plain envelope last Tuesday.

11. Boston, Massachusetts

On an intricately crocheted doily, on the highly polished maple dresser, lay black gloves and a stainless-steel ophthalmoscope.

Ginger Weiss stood at a window to the left of the dresser, looking out at the bay, where the gray water seemed to be a mirror image of the ashen mid-December sky. Farther shores were hidden by a lingering morning mist that shimmered with a pearly luminosity. At the end of the Hannaby property, at the bottom of a rocky slope, a private dock thrust out into the choppy bay. The dock was covered with snow, as was the long expanse of lawn leading back to the house.

It was a big house, built in the 1850s, with new rooms added in 1892, in 1905, and again in 1950. The brick driveway curved beneath an enormous front portico, and broad thick steps led up to massive doors. Pillars, pilasters, carved granite lintels above doors and windows, a multitude of gables and circular dormers, bay-facing second-story balconies at the back, and a large widow's walk on the roof contributed to an impression of majesty.

Even for a surgeon as successful as George, the house might have been too expensive, but he had not needed to buy it. He had inherited the place from his father, and his father had inherited it from George's grandfather, and *his* father had bought it in 1884. The house even had a name—Baywatch—like ancestral homes in British novels, and more than anything else, that inspired awe in Ginger. Houses in Brooklyn, where she came from, did not have their own names.

At Memorial, Ginger never felt uncomfortable around George. There, he was a figure of authority and respect, but he seemed to have his roots in common stock like everyone else. At Baywatch, however, Ginger was aware of the patrician heritage, and that made George different from her. He never never invoked a claim to privilege. That would not be like him. But the ghost of the New

England patriciate haunted the rooms and corridors of Baywatch, often making her feel out of place.

The corner guest suite—bedroom, reading alcove, and bath—in which Ginger had been settled for the past ten days, was simpler than many chambers in Baywatch, and there she was almost as comfortable as in her own apartment. Most of the pegged-oak floor was covered by a figured Serapi carpet in shades of blue and peach. The walls were peach, the ceiling white. The maple furniture, which consisted of various kinds of chests used as nightstands and tables and dressers, had all come off 19th-century sailing ships owned by George's great-grandfather. There were two upholstered armchairs covered in peach-colored silk from Brunschwig & Fils. On the nightstands, the bases of the lamps were actually Baccarat candlesticks, a reminder that the apparent simplicity of the room was built upon an elegant foundation.

Ginger went to the dresser and stared down at the black gloves that lay upon the doily. As she had done countless times during the past ten days, she put the gloves on, flexed her hands, waiting for a rush of fear. But they were only ordinary gloves that she had bought the day she had been discharged from the hospital, and they did not have the power to bring her to the trembling edge of a fugue. She took them off.

A knock sounded at the door, and Rita Hannaby said, "Ginger, dear, are you ready?"

"Coming," she said, snatching her purse from the bed and taking one last quick glance at herself in the dresser mirror.

She was wearing a lime-green knit suit with a creamy white blouse that had a simple lime-green bow at the throat. Her ensemble included a pair of green pumps that matched the suit, an eelskin purse that matched the pumps, a gold and malachite bracelet. The outfit perfectly complemented her complexion and golden hair. She thought she looked chic. Well, perhaps not chic, but at least stylish.

However, when she stepped into the hall and got a look at Rita Hannaby, Ginger felt at a disadvantage, a mere pretender to class.

Rita was as slim as Ginger, but at five-eight she was six inches taller, and everything about her was queenly. Her chestnut-brown hair swept back from her face in a perfectly feathered cut. If her facial bones had been more exquisitely chiseled, she would have looked severe. However, beauty and warmth were assured by her luminous gray eyes, translucent skin, and generous mouth. Rita was wearing a gray St. John's suit, pearls, pearl earrings, and a broad-brimmed black hat.

To Ginger, the amazing thing was that Rita's fashionable appearance did not seem planned. One had no sense that she had spent hours getting ready. Instead, she seemed to have been *born* with impeccable grooming and a fashionably tailored wardrobe; elegance was her natural condition.

"You look smashing!" Rita said.

"Next to you, I feel like a frump in blue jeans and a sweatshirt."

"Nonsense. Even if I were twenty years younger, I'd be no match for you, dear. Wait and see who the waiters pamper the most at lunch."

Ginger had no false modesty. She knew she was attractive. But her beauty was more that of a pixie, while Rita had the blueblood looks of one who could sit upon a throne and convince the world she belonged.

Rita did nothing to cause Ginger's newfound inferiority complex. The woman treated her not like a daughter but like a sister and an equal. Ginger's feelings of inadequacy were, she knew, a direct result of her pathetic condition. Until two weeks ago, she had not been dependent on anyone in ages. Now she was dependent again, not entirely able to look after herself, and her self-respect slipped a bit further every day. Rita Hannaby's good humor, carefully planned outings, woman-to-woman *shmoozing,* and unflagging encouragement were not enough to distract Ginger from the cruel fact that fate once more had cast her, at thirty, in the frustrating role of a child.

Together, they descended to the marble-floored foyer, where they got their coats from the closet, then went out the door and down the steps under the portico to the black Mercedes 500 SEL in the driveway. Herbert, who was sort of a cross between a butler and a Man Friday, had brought the car around five minutes ago and had left the engine running, so the interior was a toasty-warm haven from the frigid winter day.

Rita drove with her usual confidence, away from the old estates, out of quiet streets lined with bare-limbed elms and maples, through ever-busier thorough-fares, heading to Dr. Immanuel Gudhausen's office on bustling State Street. Ginger had an eleven-thirty appointment with Gudhausen, whom she had seen twice last week. She was scheduled to visit him every Monday, Wednesday, and Friday until they got to the bottom of her attacks of fugue. In her bleaker moments, Ginger was sure she'd still be lying on Gudhausen's couch thirty years from now.

Rita intended to do a bit of shopping while Ginger was with the doctor. Then they would go to lunch at some exquisite restaurant in which, no doubt, the decor would seem to have been planned to flatter Rita Hannaby and in which Ginger would feel like a schoolgirl foolishly trying to pass for a grownup.

"Have you given some thought to what I suggested last Friday?" Rita asked as she drove. "The Women's Auxiliary at the hospital?"

"I don't really think I'm up to it. I'd feel so awkward."

"It's important work," Rita said, expertly slipping the Mercedes out from behind a *Globe* newspaper truck, into a gap in traffic.

"I know. I've seen how much money you've raised for the hospital, the new equipment you've bought . . . but I think I've got to stay away from Memorial right now. It'd be too frustrating to be around the place, too constant a reminder that I can't do the work I've been trained for."

"I understand, dear. Don't give it another thought. But there's still the Symphony Committee, the Women's League for the Aged, and the Children's Advocacy Committee. We could use your help at any of those."

Rita was an indefatigable charity worker, ably chairing committees or serving on them, not only organizing beneficent societies but getting her hands dirty in the operation of them. "What about it?" she pressed. "I'm sure you'd find working with children especially rewarding."

"Rita, what if I had one of my attacks while I was with the children? It would frighten them, and I—"

"Oh, pish posh," Rita said. "Every time I've gotten you out of the house these last two weeks, you've used that same excuse to try to resist leaving your room. 'Oh, Rita,' you say, 'I'll have one of my awful fits and embarrass you.' But you haven't, and you won't. Even if you *did,* it wouldn't embarrass me. I don't embarrass easily, dear."

"I never thought for a moment you were a shrinking violet. But you haven't seen me in this fugue state. You don't know what I'm like or—"

"Oh, for goodness' sake, you make it sound as if you're a regular Dr. Jekyll and Mr. Hyde—or *Ms.* Hyde—which I'm sure you're not. You haven't beaten anyone to death with a cane yet, have you, Ms. Hyde?"

Ginger laughed and shook her head. "You're something else, Rita."

"Excellent. You'll bring so much to the organization."

Although Rita probably did not think of Ginger as another charity case, she had approached this recuperation and rehabilitation as a new cause. She rolled up her sleeves and *committed* herself to seeing Ginger through the current crisis, and nothing on earth was going to stop her. Ginger was touched by Rita's concern—and depressed by the need for it.

They stopped at a traffic light, third car from the intersection, with cars, trucks, buses, taxis, and delivery vans crowding them on all sides. In the Mercedes, the cacophony of the city was muffled but not silenced altogether, and when Ginger looked out the window at her side to search for the source of a particularly annoying engine roar, she saw a large motorcycle. The rider turned his head toward her at that moment, but she could not see his face. He was wearing a helmet with a tinted visor that came all the way down to his chin.

For the first time in ten days, the amnesic mist descended over Ginger. It happened much faster this time than it had with the black gloves, ophthalmoscope, or sink drain. She looked into the blank and shiny visor, and her heart stuttered, and her breath was pinched off, and she was instantly swept away by a massive wave of terror, gone.

First, Ginger became aware of horns. Car horns, bus horns, the air-horns of trucks. Some like the high squeals of animals, some low and ominous. Wailing, whooping, barking, shrieking, honking, bleating.

She opened her eyes. Her vision swam into focus. She was still in the car. The intersection was still in front of them, though evidently a couple of minutes had passed and the traffic ahead had moved. With the engine running but the gearshift in park, the Mercedes was ten feet closer to the crosswalk and angled slightly into the next lane, which was what was causing the horn blowing as other vehicles tried to get around.

Ginger heard herself whimpering.

Rita Hannaby was leaning across the console that separated the driver's and passenger's seats, very close, gripping both of Ginger's hands, holding them down and holding them very tightly. "Ginger? Are you there? Are you all right? Ginger?"

Blood. After the jarring blasts of the horns, after Rita's voice, Ginger became aware of the blood. Red spots marked her lime-green skirt. A dark smear stained the sleeve of her suit jacket. Her hands were gloved in blood, as were Rita's hands.

"Oh, my God," Ginger said.

"Ginger, are you with me? Are you back? Ginger?" One of Rita's manicured nails was torn off, with only a splintered stub sticking up jaggedly from the cuticle, and both her hands appeared to have been *gouged*. Scratches on the woman's fingers, on the backs of her hands, and on her palms were bleeding freely, and as far as Ginger could tell, all of the blood was Rita's, none of it her own. The cuffs of the gray St. John's suit were wet with blood. "Ginger, talk to me."

Horns continued to blare.

Ginger looked up and saw that Rita's perfectly coiffed hair was now in disarray. A two-inch-long scratch furrowed her left cheek, and blood tinted with makeup was trickling along her jaw to her chin.

"You're back," Rita said with obvious relief, letting go of Ginger's hands.

"What've I done?"

"Only scratches," Rita said. "It's all right. You had an attack, panicked, tried to leave the car. I couldn't let you go. You might've been hit in traffic."

A passing driver, maneuvering around the Mercedes, angrily shouted something unintelligible at them.

"I've hurt you," Ginger said. Sickness throbbed through her at the thought of the violence she had done.

Other drivers sounded their horns with increasing impatience, but Rita ignored them. She took Ginger's hands again, not to restrain her this time but to offer comfort and reassurance. "It's all right, dear. It's passed now, and a little iodine will patch me up just fine."

The motorcyclist. The dark visor.

Ginger looked out the side window; the cyclist was gone. He had, after all, been no threat to her, just a stranger passing in the street.

Black gloves, an ophthalmoscope, a sink drain, and now the dark visor of a motorcyclist's helmet. Why had those particular things set her off? What did they have in common, if anything?

As tears spilled down her face, Ginger said, "I'm so sorry."

"No need to be. Now, I better get us out of the way," Rita said. She pulled handsful of Kleenex from the box on the console and used them to grip the wheel and gearshift, to avoid spreading bloodstains.

Her own hands wet with Rita's blood, Ginger sagged back against her seat and closed her eyes and tried to stop the tears but could not.

Four psychotic episodes in five weeks.

She could no longer glide placidly through the gray winter days, defenseless, docile in the face of this vicious turn of fate, merely waiting for another attack or for a shrink to explain what was wrong.

It was Monday, December 16, and Ginger was suddenly determined to *do* something before she suffered a fifth fugue. She could not imagine what she possibly could do, but she was sure she'd think of something if she put her mind to it and stopped feeling sorry for herself. She had reached bottom now. Her humiliation, fear, and despair could not bring her to any greater depths. There was nowhere to go but up. She would claw her way back to the surface, damned if she wouldn't, up toward the light, out of the dark into which she had fallen.

THREE

◆

Christmas Eve–Christmas Day

1. Laguna Beach, California

At eight A.M., Tuesday, December 24, when Dom Corvaisis got out of bed, he went through his morning ablutions in a haze resulting from the lingering effects of yesterday's indulgence in Valium and Dalmane.

For the eleventh night in a row, he had been troubled by neither somnambulism nor the bad dream that involved the sink. The drug therapy was working, and he was willing to tolerate a period of pharmaceutically induced detachment to put an end to his unnerving midnight journeys.

He did not believe he was in danger of becoming physically addicted to—or even psychologically dependent on—Valium or Dalmane. He *had* been exceeding the prescribed dosage, but he was still not worried. He had almost run out of pills, and in order to get another prescription from Dr. Cobletz, he had fabricated a story about a break-in at his house, claiming that the drugs had been taken along with his stereo and TV set. Dom had *lied* to his doctor in order to obtain drugs, and sometimes he saw his action in exactly that harsh and unfavorable light; but most of the time, in the soft haze that accompanied continuous tranquilization, he was able to dress the shabby truth in self-delusion.

He dared not think about what would happen to him if the episodes of somnambulism returned in January, after the drugs were discontinued.

At ten o'clock, unable to concentrate enough to work, he put on a light corduroy jacket and left the house. The late-December morning was cool. Except for a few unseasonably warm days now and then, the beaches would not be busy again until April.

As Dom descended the hills in his Firebird, heading for the center of town, he noticed that Laguna looked dull under a somber gray sky. He wondered how much of the leaden gloom was real and how much resulted from the dulling effects of the drugs, but he quickly abandoned that disturbing line of thought. In acknowledgment of his somewhat fuzzy perceptions and impaired responsiveness, he drove with exaggerated care.

Dom received most mail at the post office. Because he subscribed to so many publications, he rented a large drawer rather than just a box, and that day before Christmas, the drawer was more than half full. He didn't look at the return addresses but carried everything back to the car with the intention of reading his mail at breakfast.

The Cottage, a popular restaurant for decades, was on the east side of Pacific Coast Highway, on the slope above the road. At that hour, the breakfast rush had passed, and the lunch crowd had not yet arrived. Dom was given a table by the window with the best view. He ordered two eggs, bacon, cottage fries, toast, and grapefruit juice.

As he ate, he went through the mail. In addition to magazines and bills, there was a letter from Lennart Sane, the wonderful Swedish agent who handled translation rights in Scandinavia and Holland, and a padded envelope from Random House. As soon as he saw the publisher's address on the label, he knew what he had. Finally, his mind began to clear, the fuzziness partially dispelled by excitement. He put down the toast he had been eating and tore open the large envelope, and an advance copy of his first novel slid out. No man can know what a woman feels when taking her newborn child in her arms for the first time, but a novelist who holds the first copy of his first book must experience a joy similar to that of the mother who looks upon the face of her baby for the first time and feels its warmth through the swaddling clothes.

Dom kept the book beside his plate and could barely look away from it. He had finished his meal and had ordered coffee by the time he was able to tear his attention from *Twilight* and examine what mail remained. Among other things, there was a plain white envelope with no return address, which contained a single page of white paper on which had been typewritten two sentences that rocked him:

The sleepwalker would be well-advised to search
the past for the source of his problem. That is
where the secret is buried.

He read the passage again, astonished. The sheet of paper rattled as a tremor passed through him. The back of his neck went cold.

2. Boston, Massachusetts

When Ginger got out of the cab, she was in front of a six-story, brick, Victorian Gothic building. A blustery wind slapped her, and the bare-limbed trees along Newbury Street rasped, clattered, and clicked: the sound of rattling bones. Huddling against the bitter wind, she scurried past a low iron fence and entered 127 Newbury, the former Hotel Agassiz, one of the city's finest historic landmarks, now converted into condominiums. She had come to see Pablo Jackson, about whom she knew only what she had read in yesterday's *Boston Globe*.

She had left Baywatch after George departed for the hospital and after Rita went off to do some last-minute Christmas shopping, for she had been afraid they would try to stop her. In fact, the maid, Lavinia, had pleaded with her not to go out alone. Ginger had left a note, explaining her whereabouts, and she hoped they would not be too upset.

When Pablo Jackson opened his door, Ginger was surprised. That he was a black man, that he was in his eighties—those things were not surprising, for she had learned as much about him from the article in the *Globe*. However, she was not prepared for such a vital and vigorous octogenarian. He was about five-eight, slight, but age had not bowed his legs, bent his back, or rounded his shoulders. He stood militarily erect, in white shirt and sharply creased black trousers, and there was a sprightliness and youthfulness in his smile and in the way he waved her into the apartment. His thick kinky hair had not receded, but it had gone so white that it seemed to glow with a spectral light, giving him a curiously mystical aura. He escorted Ginger into the living room, moving with the stride of a man forty or fifty years his junior.

The living room was a surprise, too, not what she expected either of a sedate old monument like the Hotel Agassiz or of Pablo Jackson, an elderly bachelor. The walls were cream-colored, and the contemporary sofas and chairs were upholstered in a matching fabric. An Edward Fields carpet of the same creamy shade provided relief from the dominant scheme by means of a deeply sculpted wave pattern. Color was provided by pastel accent pillows—yellow, peach, green, and blue—on the sofas, and from two large oil paintings, one a Picasso. The result was an airy, bright, warm, and modern decor.

Ginger settled into one of two armchairs that faced each other across a small table near a long, bay window. She declined coffee and said, "Mr. Jackson, I'm afraid I'm here under false pretenses."

"What an interesting beginning," he said, smiling, crossing his legs, resting his long-fingered black hands on the arms of his chair.

"No, really, I'm not a reporter."

"Not from *People?*" He studied her speculatively. "Well, that's all right. I knew you weren't a reporter when I let you in. These days, reporters have an oily smoothness about them, and they're an arrogant lot. Soon as I saw you standing at the door, I said to myself, 'Pablo, this bitty girl is no reporter. She's a *real* person.' "

"I need some help that only you can provide."

"A damsel in distress?" he said, amused. He seemed not at all angry or uneasy, which she had expected he would be.

She said, "I was afraid you wouldn't see me if I told you my real reasons for wanting to meet you. You see, I'm a doctor, a surgical resident at Memorial, and when I read the article about you in the *Globe,* I thought you might be able to help."

"I'd be delighted to see you even if you were selling magazines. An eighty-one-year-old man can't afford to turn anyone away . . . unless he prefers to spend his days talking to the walls."

Ginger appreciated his efforts to put her at ease, though she suspected that his social life was more interesting than her own.

He said, "Besides, not even a burnt-out old fossil like me would turn away such a lovely girl as you. But now tell me what this help is that only I can give you."

Ginger leaned forward in her chair. "First, I've got to know if the article in the newspaper was accurate."

He shrugged. "As accurate as newspaper articles ever are. My mother and father were expatriate Americans living in France, just as the newspaper said. She was a popular chanteuse, a cafe singer in Paris, before and after World War I. My father was a musician, as the *Globe* said. And it's true that my parents knew Picasso and recognized his genius early on. I was named after him. They bought two score of Picasso's pieces when his work was cheap, and he gave them several paintings as gifts. They had *bon goût.* They didn't own a hundred works, as the paper said, but fifty. Still, that collection was an embarrassment of riches. Sold gradually over the years, it cushioned their retirement and gave me something to fall back on as well."

"You *were* an accomplished stage magician?"

"For over fifty years," he said, raising both hands in a graceful and elegant expression of amazement at his own longevity. That gesture was marked by the rhythm and fluidity of prestidigitation, and Ginger half-expected him to pluck living white doves from thin air. "And I was famous, too. *Sans pareil,* even if I say so myself. Not famous over here so much, you understand, but all over Europe and in England."

"And your act involved hypnotizing a few members of the audience?"

He nodded. "That was the centerpiece. It always wowed them."

"And now you're helping the police by hypnotizing witnesses to crimes, so they can recall details they've forgotten."

"Well, it's not a full-time job," he said, waving one slender hand as if to dismiss any such thoughts she might have had. The gesture seemed likely to end with the magical appearance of a bouquet of flowers or deck of cards. "In fact, they've only come to me four times in the past two years. I'm usually their last resort."

"But what you've done has worked for them?"

"Oh, yes. Just as the newspaper said. For instance, a by-stander might see a murder take place and get a glimpse of the car in which the killer escaped, but not be able to recall the license number. Now, if he glanced at the license even for a split second, that number is buried in his subconscious mind, 'cause we never really forget anything we see. Never. So if a hypnotist puts the witness in a trance, regresses him in time—that is, takes him back in his memories to the shooting—and tells him to look at the car, then the license number can be obtained.''

''Always?''

''Not always. But we win more than we lose.''

''Why turn to you? Aren't the police department's psychiatrists capable of using hypnosis?''

''Certainly. But they're psychiatrists not hypnotists. Hypnosis is not what they *specialized* in. I've made it a lifelong study, developed my own techniques that often succeed where standard methods fail.''

''So when it comes to hypnotism, you're a *maven*.''

''An expert? Yes, that's true. Even a *maven's maven*. But why does any of this interest you, Doctor?''

Ginger had been sitting with her purse in her lap and her hands at rest upon it. But as she told Pablo Jackson about her attacks, she clutched the purse tighter, tighter, until her knuckles were white.

Jackson's relaxed demeanor changed to shocked interest and concern. ''You poor child. You poor, poor little thing. *De mal en pis—en pis!* From bad to worse—to worse! How horrible. You wait there. Don't you move.'' He popped up from the chair and hurried from the room.

When he returned, he was carrying two glasses of brandy. She tried to refuse hers. ''No thank you, Mr. Jackson. I don't drink much, and certainly not at this hour of the morning.''

''Call me Pablo. How much sleep did you get last night? Not much? You were up most of the night, woke up hours ago, so for *you* this isn't morning, it's the middle of the afternoon. And there's no reason a person can't have a drink in the afternoon, is there?''

He settled into his chair again, and for a moment they were silent as they sipped their brandies.

Then she said, ''Pablo, I want you to hypnotize me, regress me back to the morning of November twelfth, to Bernstein's Delicatessen. I want you to hold me at that point in time and question me relentlessly until I can explain *why* the sight of those black gloves terrified me.''

''Impossible!'' He shook his head. ''No, no.''

''I can pay whatever—''

''Money is not the issue. I don't need money.'' He frowned. ''I'm a magician, not a physician.''

''I'm already seeing a psychiatrist, and I've broached the subject with him, but he won't do it.''

''He must have his reasons.''

''He says it's too soon for hypnotic regression therapy. He admits the technique might help me discover the cause of my attacks, but he says that might be a mistake because I might not yet be ready to face up to the truth. He says premature confrontation with the source of my anxieties might contribute to . . . a breakdown.''

''You see? He knows best. I would be meddling.''

''He does *not* know best,'' Ginger insisted, angered by the vivid recollection of her recent conversation with the psychiatrist, in which he had been infuriatingly condescending. ''Maybe he knows what's best for most patients, but he doesn't know what's best for *me*. I can't go on like this. By the time Gudhausen's willing to resort to hypnosis, maybe in a year, I'll no longer be sane enough to benefit. I've got to get a grip on this problem, take control, *do* something.''

"But surely you see that I can't be responsible—"

"Wait," she interrupted, putting her brandy aside. "I anticipated your reluctance." She opened her purse, withdrew a folded sheet of typing paper, and held it out to him. "Here. Please take this."

He took the paper. Though Pablo was half a century older than she, his hands were far steadier than hers. "What is it?"

"A signed release making it clear that I came here in desperation, exonerating you in advance for anything that goes wrong."

He did not bother to read it. "You don't understand, dear lady. I'm not concerned about being sued. Considering my age and the snail's pace of the courts, I wouldn't live to see a judgment placed against me. But the mind is a delicate mechanism, and if something went wrong, if I led you into a breakdown, I would surely roast in Hell."

"If you don't help me, if I've got to spend long months in therapy, uncertain of the future, I'll have a breakdown anyway." Desperate, Ginger raised her voice, venting her frustration and anger. "If you send me away, leave me to the well-meaning mercy of friends, abandon me to Gudhausen, I'm finished. I swear, that'll be the end of me. *I can't go on like this!* If you refuse to help me, you'll still be responsible for my breakdown because you could've prevented it."

"I'm sorry," he said.

"Please."

"I can't."

"You cold, black bastard," Ginger said, startled by the epithet even as she spoke it. The hurt expression on his benign and gnomish face stung and shamed her. Now it was her turn to say, "I'm sorry. So sorry." She brought her hands to her face, bent forward in her chair, and wept.

He came to her, stooped down in front of her. "Dr. Weiss, please don't cry. Don't despair. It'll be all right."

"No. It never will," she said. "Not ever like it was."

He gently pried her hands away from her face. He put one of his hands under her chin, lifted her head until she was looking at him. He smiled, winked, and held a hand before her eyes to show her that it was empty. Then, to her surprise, he plucked a quarter from her right ear.

"Hush now," Pablo Jackson said, patting her shoulder. "You've made your point. And I certainly don't have an *âme de boue,* a soul of mud, an ungenerous spirit. A woman's tears can move the world. Against my better judgment, I'll do what I can."

Instead of putting an end to her crying, his offer of help renewed her weeping, though these were tears of gratitude.

". . . and now you are in a deep sleep, deep, very deep, utterly relaxed, and you will answer all my questions. Is that understood?"

"Yes."

"You cannot refuse to answer. Cannot refuse. Cannot."

Pablo had drawn the drapes over the three-bay window and had turned out all the lights except the lamp beside Ginger Weiss's chair. The amber beams fell over her, giving her hair the appearance of real gold filaments and emphasizing the unnatural paleness of her skin.

He stood before her, looking down at her face. She had a fragile beauty, an exquisite femininity, yet in her face there was also a great strength almost masculine in quality. *Le juste milieu:* perfect balance, the golden mean, was nowhere better defined than in her countenance, where character and beauty were given equal weight.

Her eyes were closed, and they moved very little beneath her lids, an indication that she was in a deep trance.

Pablo returned to his chair, which stood in shadow, beyond the amber light from the single lamp. He sat, crossed his legs. "Ginger, why were you frightened by the black gloves?"

"I don't know," she said softly.

"You cannot lie to me. Do you understand? You can withhold nothing from me. Why were you afraid of the black gloves?"

"I don't know."

"Why were you afraid of the ophthalmoscope?"

"I don't know."

"Why were you afraid of the sink drain?"

"I don't know."

"Did you know the man on the motorcycle on State Street?"

"No."

"Then why were you frightened of him?"

"I don't know."

Pablo sighed. "Very well. Ginger, we'll now do something amazing, something that might seem impossible but which I assure you is possible. In fact, it's easy. We're going to make time run backward, Ginger. Nothing to it. We're going to send you slowly but surely back in time. You are going to get younger. It's already happening. You can't resist it . . . time like a river . . . flowing backward . . . ever back . . . and now it's no longer December twenty-fourth. It's December twenty-third, Monday, and still the clock runs backward . . . a little faster . . . now it is the twenty-second . . . now the twentieth . . . the eighteenth. . . ." He continued in that manner until he had regressed Ginger to the twelfth of November. "You are in Bernstein's Delicatessen, waiting for your order to be filled. Can you smell the hot baked goods, the spices?" She nodded, and he said, "Tell me what you smell."

She drew a deep breath, and a pleased look overtook her face. Her voice became more animated: "Pastrami, garlic . . . honey cookies . . . cloves and cinnamon . . ." She remained in her chair, with her eyes closed, but she lifted her head and turned left and right, as if surveying the deli. "Chocolate. Just *smell* that cocoa pound cake!"

"It's wonderful," Pablo said. "Now, you pay for your order, turn from the counter . . . head toward the door, preoccupied with your purse."

"I can't get my wallet in," she said, scowling.

"You have the bag of groceries in one arm."

"Got to clean out this purse."

"*Bang!* You bump into the man in the Russian hat."

Ginger gasped and twitched in surprise.

"He grabs your grocery bag to keep it from falling," Pablo said.

"Oh!" she said.

"He tells you he's sorry."

"My fault," Ginger said. Pablo knew she was not talking to him but to the doughy-faced man in the Russian hat, who was now as real to her as he had been that Tuesday in the deli. Apologetically, she said, "I wasn't looking where I was going."

"He holds out your groceries, which you take from him." The aged magician watched her closely. "And you notice . . . his gloves."

Her transformation was instantaneous and electrifying. She sat straight up; her eyes popped open. "The gloves! Oh, God, the gloves!"

"Tell me about the gloves, Ginger."

"Black," she said in a small, quavering voice. "Shiny."

"What else?"

"*No!*" she cried, starting to get up from the chair.

"Sit down, please," Pablo said.

She froze, half out of her seat.

"Ginger, I am ordering you to sit down and relax."

She sat rigidly, her small hands fisted. Her radiant blue eyes were open wide, focused not on Pablo but on the gloves in her memory. She looked as if she would bolt again at the slightest provocation.

"You will relax now, Ginger. You will be calm . . . calm . . . very calm. Do you understand?"

"Yes. All right," she said. Her breath came less rapidly than it had done, and her shoulders slumped a bit, but she was still tense.

Ordinarily, when he put someone into a trance, he maintained total and instantaneous control of the subject. He was surprised and made uneasy by this woman's continued distress in spite of his admonitions to relax, but he could not calm her further. Finally he said, "Tell me about the gloves, Ginger."

"Oh, my God." Her face twisted in fear.

"Relax and tell me about the gloves. Why are you afraid of them?"

She shook. "D-Don't let them t-t-touch me."

"Why are you afraid of them?" he persisted.

She hugged herself and shrank back into her chair.

"Listen to me, Ginger. That moment in time is frozen. The clock is moving neither forward nor back. The gloves cannot touch you. I will never let them touch you. Time is suspended. I have the power to suspend time, and I have stopped it. You are safe. Do you hear me?"

"Yes," she said, but as she cringed against the back of her armchair, there were doubt and barely suppressed terror in her voice.

"You are perfectly safe." Pablo was distressed to see this sweet girl so oppressed by fear. "Time has been stopped, so you can study those black gloves without being afraid they'll get hold of you. You will study them and tell me why they frighten you."

She was silent, shaking.

"You must answer me, Ginger. Why are you afraid of the gloves?" She only whimpered, so he thought a moment, then said, "Is it really *this* pair of gloves that frighten you?"

"N-No. Not exactly."

"The gloves on this man in the deli . . . they remind you of a pair of other gloves, perhaps from some incident long ago? Is that it?"

"Oh, yes. Yes."

"When did this other incident take place? Ginger, what other gloves do these remind you of?"

"I don't know."

"Yes, you do." Pablo rose from his chair, moved to the draped windows, and observed her from those shadows. "All right . . . the hands of the clock are moving again. Time is moving backward again . . . back . . . back . . . all the way back to the time when you were *first* frightened by a pair of black gloves. You are drifting back . . . back . . . and now you are *there*. You are at the very time, at the very place, at the precise moment and spot where you were first frightened by black gloves.''

Ginger's eyes were fixed on a horror in a different time, not in this room or in Bernstein's Delicatessen, but in some other place.

Pablo watched her anxiously. ''Where are you, Ginger?'' When she remained silent, he said, ''You must tell me where you are.''

''The face,'' she said in a haunted voice that made Pablo shiver. ''The face. The blank face.''

''Explain yourself, Ginger. What face? Tell me what you see.''

''The black gloves . . . the dark glass face.''

''Do you mean . . . like the motorcyclist?''

''The gloves . . . the visor.'' A spasm of fear throbbed through her.

''Be calm, relax. You're safe. Safe. Now, wherever you are, do you see a man wearing a helmet and a visor? And black gloves?''

She began a monotonous chant of stark terror: ''Uh, uh, uh, uh . . .''

''Ginger, you must be calm. Be calm, relaxed, and at ease. Nothing can harm you. You're safe.'' Afraid that he was losing control of her and would have to bring her out of the trance soon, Pablo moved quickly to her chair, knelt at her side, put one hand on her arm, and stroked gently as he spoke to her. ''Where are you, Ginger? How far back in time have you gone, Ginger? Where are you? *When* are you?''

''Uh, uh, *uhhhhhhhh*.'' A pathetic cry escaped her, an echo out of time, the tortured response to a long-suppressed terror and despair.

He became very stern, switching from a soft to a hard voice. ''I am in command of you. You are deeply asleep and completely in my control, Ginger. I demand that you answer me, Ginger.''

A shudder, worse than any previous spasm, passed through her.

''I demand that you answer. Where are you, Ginger?''

''Nowhere.''

''Where are you?''

''No place.'' Abruptly, she stopped shaking. She sagged in the chair. The fear melted out of her face, and her features went soft, slack. In a thin and emotionless voice, she said, ''Dead.''

''What do you mean? You're not dead.''

''Dead,'' she insisted.

''Ginger, you must tell me where you are and how far back in time you've gone, and you must tell me about the black gloves, that *first* pair of black gloves, the ones you were reminded of when you saw the gloves on that man in the delicatessen. You absolutely must tell me.''

''*Dead.*''

Suddenly, because he was kneeling beside her chair and was close to her, Pablo realized her breathing was extremely shallow. He took her hand and was startled by how cold it was. He pressed two fingers to her wrist, feeling for her pulse. Weak. *Very* weak. Frantic, he put his fingertips to her throat and located a slow and weak heartbeat.

To avoid answering his questions, she seemed to be withdrawing into a sleep far deeper than her hypnotic trance, perhaps into a coma, into an oblivion where she could not hear his demanding voice. He had never encountered a reaction like this before, had never even read of such a thing. Was it possible for Ginger to *will* herself dead merely to escape his questions? Memory blocks erected around traumatic experiences were not uncommon; his reading in psychology journals sometimes turned up accounts of these psychological barricades to recollection, but they were barriers that could be dismantled without killing the subject. Surely no experience could be so horrendous that a person would rather die than remember it. Yet even as Pablo pressed his fingers to her throat, the throbbing of her pulse grew fainter and more irregular.

"Ginger, listen," he said urgently. "You don't have to answer me. No more questions. You can come back. I won't insist on answers."

She seemed suspended on a terrible brink, teetering.

"Ginger, listen to me! No more questions. I'm finished asking questions. I swear it." After a long and frightening hesitation, he detected a slight improvement in her pulse rate. "I'm no longer interested in the black gloves or anything else, Ginger. I just want to bring you back to the present and out of your trance. Do you hear me? Please hear me. *Please*. I've finished questioning you."

Her pulse stuttered shockingly, but then it throbbed more steadily. Respiration improved, too. As he talked to her in that reassuring manner, she quickly got better. Color returned to her lovely face.

In less than a minute, he returned her to December 24 and woke her.

She blinked. "It didn't work, huh? You couldn't put me under."

"You were under," he said shakily. "Too far under."

She said, "Pablo, you're trembling. Why're you trembling? What's wrong? What happened?"

This time, she went to the kitchen and poured the brandy.

Later, at the door of Pablo's apartment, as Ginger was leaving to meet the taxi that Pablo had summoned for her, she said, "I still can't think what it could be. Nothing so terrible has ever happened to me, certainly nothing so bad I'd rather die than reveal it."

"There's something very traumatic in your past," Pablo said. "An incident involving a man wearing black gloves, a man with what you said was a 'dark glass face.' Perhaps a motorcyclist like the one that panicked you on State Street. It's an incident you've buried very deep . . . and which you seem determined to keep buried at any cost. I really think you should tell Dr. Gudhausen what happened here today and let him proceed from there."

"Gudhausen is too traditional, too slow. I want *your* help."

"I won't risk putting you in a trance and questioning you again."

"Unless your research turns up a similar case."

"Not much chance of that. I've done a lot of reading in psychology and hypnosis for fifty years, and I've never heard of anything like it."

"But you're going to research it, aren't you? You promised."

"I'll see what I can find," he said.

"And if you discover that someone developed a workable technique for getting through a memory block like this, you'll use it on me."

Ginger was mystified, but she was also considerably less distraught than she had been when she first arrived at Pablo Jackson's apartment. At least they had gotten somewhere, even if they did not yet know where. They had found the problem, some mysterious traumatic experience in the past, and though they had not learned a single detail of it, they knew it was back there, a dark shape waiting to be explored. In time they would find a way to throw a light on it, and when it was revealed, she would know the cause of her fugues.

"Tell Dr. Gudhausen," Pablo said again.

"I'm pinning all my hopes on you."

"You're damn stubborn," the old magician said, shaking his head.

"No. Just persistent."

"Willful."

"Just determined."

"*Acharnée!*"

"When I get back to Baywatch I'll look up that word, and if it's an insult, you'll be sorry when I come back on Thursday," she teased.

"Not Thursday," he said. "The research is going to take time. I'm not going to hypnotize you again unless I can find a record of a similar case and can follow someone else's procedures, knowing they succeeded."

"Okay, but if you don't call by Friday or Saturday, I'll probably come back and bust my way in. Remember, you're my best hope."

"I am your best hope . . . only for want of anything better."

"You underrate yourself, Pablo Jackson." She kissed him on the cheek. "I'll be waiting for your call."

"*Au revoir.*"

"*Shalom.*"

Outside, as she got into the cab, she remembered one of her father's favorite aphorisms, and, like a lead weight, it counteracted her new buoyancy: *It's always brightest just before the dark.*

3. Chicago, Illinois

Winton Tolk—the tall, jovial, black patrolman riding shotgun—got out of the police cruiser to buy three hamburgers and Cokes at a corner sandwich shop, leaving his partner, Paul Armes, behind the wheel, and Father Brendan Cronin in the back seat. Brendan glanced at the shop, but he could not see inside, for the big front windows were painted with festive holiday images: Santa, reindeer, wreaths, angels. A light snow had just begun to fall, and the weather forecast called for eight inches by midnight, which meant tomorrow would be a white Christmas.

As Winton got out of the car, Brendan leaned forward and said to Paul Armes, "Yeah, well, nobody's knocking *Going My Way,* but what about *It's a Wonderful Life?* Now there was a terrific picture!"

"Jimmy Stewart and Donna Reed," Paul said.

"What a cast." They had been talking about great Christmas films, and now Brendan was sure he had hit upon the best of the best. "Lionel Barrymore played the skinflint. Gloria Grahame was in that, too."

"Thomas Mitchell," Paul Armes said as, outside, Winton reached the door of the sandwich shop. "Ward Bond. *God,* what a cast!" Winton had gone into the sandwich shop. "But you're forgetting another great one. *Miracle on 34th Street.*"

"That was terrific, sure, but I still think Capra's better—"

It seemed that the gunshots and the startling cascade of shattering glass came at the same instant, with not a fraction of a second between. Even with the car doors shut, the heater fan making noise, and the police-band radio crackling and chirruping, the shots were loud enough to halt Brendan in midsentence. As the explosions blew away the Christmas peace of the Uptown street, the sandwich shop's painted window tableau dissolved, erupted in a glittering spray. New shots overlaid the echo of old reports, and the blasts were accompanied by a brittle and atonal music of glass smashing on the roof, hood, and trunk of the cruiser.

"Oh, shit!" Paul Armes tore the dash-mounted riot gun free of its clasps, throwing open his door even as the glass was still raining. "Stay down," he shouted back at Brendan, and then he was out, crouching, moving around the car, and using it as a shield.

Stunned, Brendan looked through the window at his side, back toward the sandwich-shop entrance. Abruptly, that door was flung wide open, and two young men appeared, one black, one white. The black man wore a knit cap and a long navy peacoat—and carried a semiautomatic sawed-off shotgun. The white man, in a plaid hunting jacket, was armed with a revolver. They came out fast, half-crouched, and the black man swung the shotgun toward the patrol car. Brendan was looking directly into the muzzle. There was a flash, and he was sure he had been shot, but the rear passenger-side window in front of his face remained intact. Instead, the front window exploded inward, fragments of glass and lead pellets showering across the seat, rattling off the dashboard. The near-miss shocked Brendan out of his daze, and he rolled off his seat, to the floor, his heart hammering almost as loud as the gunfire.

Winton Tolk had had the bad luck to walk unsuspecting into the middle of an armed robbery. He was probably dead.

As Brendan pressed himself to the floor of the squad car, he heard Paul Armes shouting outside: "*Drop it!*"

Two shots cracked. Not a shotgun. Revolver fire. But who pulled the trigger? Paul Armes or the guy in the plaid hunting jacket?

Another shot. Someone screamed.

But who had been hit? Armes or one of the robbers?

Brendan wanted to look, but he did not dare show himself.

Thanks to an arrangement Father Wycazik had made with the local precinct captain, Brendan had been riding as an observer with Winton and Paul for five days. In an ordinary suit, tie, and topcoat, he was supposed to be a lay consultant employed by the Church to study the need for Catholic charity outreach programs, a cover story which everyone seemed to accept. Winton's and Paul's beat was Uptown, an area bordered by Foster Avenue on the North, Lake Shore Drive high-rises on the east, Irving Park Road on the south, and North Ashland Avenue on the west. It was Chicago's poorest and most crime-ridden neighborhood, home to blacks and Indians, but mostly to Appalachians and Hispanics. After five days with Winton and Paul, Brendan developed a strong liking for both men and a deep sympathy for all the honest souls who lived and worked in those decaying buildings and filthy streets—and who were prey to the packs of human jackals among them. He had learned to expect anything riding with these guys, but the sandwich-shop shootout was the worst incident yet.

Another shotgun blast slammed into the car, rocking it.

Brendan curled fetally on the floor and tried to pray, but no words came. God was still lost to him, and he cowered in terrible solitude.

Outside, Paul Armes shouted, "Give it up!"

The gunman said, "Fuck you!"

When he'd reported to Father Wycazik after a week at St. Joseph's, Brendan had been sent to another hospital, where he'd been given work on the terminal ward, a dreadful place with no children at all. There, as at St. Joseph's, Brendan quickly discovered the lesson that Stefan Wycazik expected him to learn. To most who were at the end of life, death was not to be feared but welcomed, a blessing for which they thanked God rather than cursing Him. And in dying, many who had never been believers became believers at last, and those who had fallen away from faith came back. There was frequently something noble and deeply moving in the suffering that accompanied a person's exit from this world, as if each shared, for a while, the mystical burden of the cross.

Yet, that lesson learned, Brendan remained unable to believe. Now, the fierce beating of his heart hammered the words of the prayer to dust before he could speak them, and his mouth was as dry as powder.

Outside, there was shouting, but he could not make sense of the words any more, maybe because the people shouting were incoherent and maybe because he was partially deaf from the gunfire.

He did not yet fully understand the lesson that Father Wycazik had hoped he would learn from this Uptown portion of his unconventional therapy. And now as he listened to the chaos outside, he knew that the lesson, regardless of its nature, would be insufficient to convince him that God was as real as bullets. Death was a bloody, stinking, foul reality, and in the face of it, the promise of a reward in the afterlife was not the least persuasive.

The shotgun discharged again, followed by the roar of the riot gun, then by shouting and the *slap-slap-slap* of running feet. It sounded like a war out there. Another blast from the riot gun. More shattering glass. Another scream, more horrible than the one that had rent the air before it. Yet another shot. Silence. Silence perfect and profound.

The driver's door was jerked open.

Brendan cried out in surprise and terror.

"Stay down!" Paul Armes said from the front seat, keeping a low profile himself. "Two dead, but there might be other shitheads inside."

"Where's Winton?" Brendan asked.

Paul did not answer. Instead, he grabbed the radio microphone up front and called Central. "Officer down. Officer down!" Armes gave his position, the address of the sandwich shop, and requested backup.

Lying on his side on the floor of the squad car, Brendan closed his eyes and saw, with heartbreaking clarity, the pictures that Winton Tolk carried in his wallet and that he proudly displayed when queried about his family—pictures of his wife, Raynella, and his three children.

"Those rotten fucking bastards," Paul Armes said, his voice shaking.

Brendan heard soft clicking and scraping sounds that puzzled him until he realized Armes was reloading. He said, "Winton's been shot?"

"Bet on it," Armes said.

"He might need help."

"It's on the way."

"But he may need help *now*," Brendan said.

"Can't go in there. Might be another one. Two more. Who knows? We gotta wait for backup."

"Winton might need a tourniquet . . . other first aid. He might be dead by the time help gets here."

"Don't you think I *know* that?" Paul Armes said bitterly, furiously. He finished reloading and slid out of the car to take up a position from which he could watch the shop.

The more Brendan thought about Winton Tolk sprawled on the floor in there, the angrier he became. If he had still believed in God, he might have quenched his anger in prayer. But now it fed on itself and grew into a hot rage. His heart pounded even harder than when the shotgun blasts were crashing into the car inches from him. The injustice of Winton's fate—the unfairness, the *wrongness*—was like an acid eating at Brendan.

He got out of the car and started across the sidewalk, through the falling snow, toward the entrance to the sandwich shop.

"Brendan!" Paul Armes shouted from the far side of the police cruiser. "Stop! For God's sake, don't!"

Brendan kept going, driven by his rage and by the thought that Winton Tolk might need immediate first aid to survive.

A dead man in a plaid hunting jacket was lying on his back on the sidewalk. A round from Armes's revolver had taken him in the chest, a second round in the throat. There was a stink of loosed bowels. In the snow beside the corpse lay a handgun, perhaps the very one with which Winton Tolk had been shot.

"Cronin!" Paul Armes yelled. "Get your ass back here, you idiot!"

Moving past the broken windows, Brendan could see into the shop, which was surprisingly dark. The lights had been shot out or a switch thrown, and the gray daylight penetrated only a couple of feet inside. He could not see anyone, but that did not mean it was safe to enter.

"Cronin!" Paul Armes shouted.

Brendan went to the entrance, where he found the black man in the peacoat. This one had been hit by a shotgun blast that also demolished the glass door; he was crumpled in a thousand bright fragments.

Stepping over the body, Brendan entered the sandwich shop. He did not have his Roman collar, which might have been something of a shield if he had been wearing it. On the other hand, degenerates like these would probably kill a priest as reflexively and as happily as they blew away police officers. In his suit and tie and topcoat, he was as ordinary and vulnerable as any man, but he did not care. He was *that* furious. Furious that God did not exist or, existing, did not care.

At the back of the small shop was a service counter. Behind the counter was a grill, other equipment. On this side were five very small tables and ten chairs, most of which had been toppled. On the floor were a couple of napkin dispensers, ketchup and mustard bottles, scattered one- and five-dollar bills, a lot of blood, and Winton Tolk.

Not bothering to study the overturned tables to see if a gunman was sheltering behind them, Brendan went to the officer, knelt beside him. Winton had been hit twice in the chest. Not with the shotgun. Probably the other thug's revolver. The wounds were sickening, far too traumatic to respond dramatically to a mere tourniquet or first-aid procedures. His breast was mantled with blood, and blood trickled from his mouth. The pool of blood in which he lay was so deep that he appeared to be floating on it. He was still, eyes closed, either unconscious or dead.

"Winton?" Brendan said.

The cop did not respond. His eyelids did not even flutter.

Filled with a rage akin to that which had caused him to heave the holy chalice against the wall during Mass, Brendan Cronin gently put both hands on Winton Tolk's neck, one on each side, feeling for the throbbing carotid arteries. He detected no life, and in his mind he saw the photographs of Raynella and the Tolk children again, and now he was *seething* with resentment at the indifference of the universe. "He can't die," Brendan said angrily. "He can't." Suddenly he thought he felt a thready pulse, so faint it was virtually nonexistent. He moved his hands, seeking confirmation that Tolk lived. He found it: a less feeble beat than that first phantom drumming, though no less irregular.

"Is he dead?"

Brendan looked up and saw a man coming around the side of the service counter, an Hispanic in a white apron, the owner or an employee. A woman, also in a white apron, had risen from behind the counter.

Outside, distant sirens were growing nearer.

Under Brendan's hands, the throbbing in Winton Tolk's neck seemed to be getting stronger and more regular, which was surely not the case. Winton had lost too much blood to stage even a limited spontaneous recovery. Until the paramedics arrived with life-support machines, his vital signs would deteriorate unavoidably, and even expert medical care might not stabilize his condition.

The sirens were no more than two blocks away.

Puffs of snow blew in through the shattered windows.

The sandwich-shop employees edged closer.

Numb with shock, in a haze of anger at fate's capricious brutality, Brendan trailed his hands from Winton's neck to the wounds in his chest. When he saw the blood oozing up between his fingers, his rage gave way to overwhelming helplessness and uselessness, and he began to cry.

Winton Tolk choked. Coughed. Opened his eyes. Breath rattled thinly and wetly in his throat, and a soft groan escaped him.

Amazed, Brendan felt for a pulse in the man's throat again. It was weak but definitely not as weak as before, and hardly irregular at all.

Raising his voice over the shrieking sirens, which were now so near that the air trembled, Brendan said, "Winton? Winton, do you hear me?"

The cop did not seem to recognize Brendan—or even to know where he was. He coughed again and choked more violently than before.

Brendan quickly lifted Tolk's head a few inches and turned it to one side, to let the blood and mucus drain more freely from his mouth. Immediately the wounded man's respiration improved, though it remained noisy, each inhalation hard-won. He was still in critical condition, in desperate need of medical attention, but he was alive.

Alive.

Incredible. All this blood, and he was still alive, hanging on.

Outside, three sirens died one after the other. Brendan shouted for Paul Armes. Excited by the hope that Winton could be saved, but also panicked by the possibility that medical attention would arrive seconds too late, he glanced at the sandwich-shop employees and shouted, "Go! Get them in here. Let them know it's safe. Paramedics, damn it!"

The man in the apron hesitated, then moved toward the door.

Winton Tolk expelled bloody mucus and finally drew an unobstructed breath. Brendan carefully lowered Winton's head to the floor again. The cop continued to breathe shallowly, with difficulty, but steadily.

Outside there were shouts and doors slamming and running feet coming toward the sandwich shop.

Brendan's hands were wet with Winton Tolk's blood. Unthinking, he blotted them on his coat—and it was then that he realized the rings had reappeared on his hands for the first time in nearly two weeks. One on each palm. Twin bands of raised and inflamed tissue.

Cops and paramedics burst through the front door, stepping over the dead man in the navy peacoat, and Brendan quickly moved out of their way. He backed up until he bumped against the service counter, where he leaned in sudden exhaustion, staring at his hands.

For a few days following the first appearance of the rings, he had used the cortisone prescribed by Dr. Heeton at St. Joseph's, but when the rings had not reappeared, he had soon stopped applying the lotion. He had almost forgotten about the marks. They had been a curiosity—baffling, but of little concern. Now, as he looked at the strange marks, he heard the voices of those around him, fuzzy and strange:

"Jesus, the blood!"

"Can't be alive . . . twice in the chest."

"Get the fuck out of my way!"

"Plasma!"

"Type his blood. No! Wait . . . do it in the ambulance."

Brendan finally looked at the crowd around Winton Tolk. He watched the paramedics as they worked to keep the wounded man alive, get him on a stretcher, and move him out of the sandwich shop.

He saw a cursing policeman dragging the dead man out of the doorway to make it easier for the paramedics to exit with Tolk.

He saw Paul Armes moving along beside the stretcher.

He saw that the blood in which Tolk had been lying was not merely a pool but a *lake*.

He looked at his hands again. The rings were gone.

4. Las Vegas, Nevada

The Texan in the yellow Day-Glo polyester pants would not have tried to get Jorja Monatella into bed if he had known she was in the mood to castrate someone.

Although it was the afternoon of December 24, Jorja was not yet in the Christmas spirit. Usually even-tempered and easygoing, she was in an exceedingly sour state of mind as she strode back and forth through the casino, from the bar to the blackjack tables and back to the bar again, delivering drinks to the gamblers.

For one thing, she hated her job. Being a cocktail waitress was bad enough in a regular bar or lounge, but in a hotel casino bigger than a football field, it was a killer. At the end of a shift, her feet ached, and often her ankles were swollen. The hours were irregular, too. How were you supposed to provide a stable home for a seven-year-old daughter when you did not have a job with normal hours?

She also hated the costume: a little red nothing, cut high in the crotch and hips, very low at the bustline, smaller than a bathing suit. An elastic corset was built in to minimize the waistline and emphasize the breasts. If you were already small-waisted, with generous breasts—as Jorja was—the getup made you look almost freakishly erotic.

And she hated the way the pit bosses and casino floormen were always hitting on her. Maybe they figured any girl who would strut her stuff in an outfit like that was an easy lay.

She was sure that her name had something to do with their attitude as well: Jorja. It was cute. Too cute. Her mother must have been drunk when she got creative with the spelling of Georgia. It was all right when people heard it, because they had no way of knowing she spelled it cute, but she had to wear a name tag on her costume—JORJA—and at least a dozen people a day commented on it. It was a frivolous name, misspelled like that, so it gave them the idea she was a frivolous person. She had considered going to court to have the proper spelling made legal, but that would hurt her mother. However, if guys at work kept hitting on her, she might even have it changed to Mother Teresa, which ought to cool off some of the horny bastards.

And fending off the bosses was not the worst of it. Every week, some high-roller—a bigshot from Detroit or L.A. or Dallas, dropping a bundle at the tables—would take a shine to Jorja and ask the pit boss to fix him up with her. A few cocktail waitresses *were* available—not many, but a few. But when the pit bosses approached Jorja, her answer was always the same: "To hell with him. I'm a waitress, not a hooker."

Her routine, cold refusal did not stop them from pressuring her to relent, which they had done an hour ago. A wart-faced, bug-eyed oilman from Houston—in phosphorescent yellow pants, a blue shirt, and a red string tie—one of the hotel's favored clients, had gotten the hots for her and had made inquiries. His breath stank of the burritos he had eaten for lunch.

Now the bosses were angry with her for refusing a highly valued customer, for being "too stuffy." Rainy Tarnell, the blackjack pit boss on the day shift, had the gall to put it just like that—"Honey, don't be so stuffy!"—as if falling on her back and spreading her legs for a stranger from Houston was merely the equivalent of a fashion gaucherie like wearing white shoes either before Memorial Day or after Labor Day.

Though she hated being a casino cocktail waitress, she could not afford to quit. No other job would pay her as well. She was a divorced mother raising a daughter without benefit of child-support payments, and in order to protect her credit rating, she was still paying off bills that Alan had run up in her name before walking out on her, so she was acutely aware of the value of a dollar. Her wages were low, but the tips were exceedingly good, especially on those occasions when one of her customers started winning big at cards or dice.

On this day before Christmas, the casino was two-thirds empty, and tips were bad. Vegas was always slow Thanksgiving and Christmas, and the crowds did not return until December 26. The whizzing-rattling-ringing of slot machines was muted. Many of the blackjack dealers stood idle and bored in front of empty tables.

No wonder I'm in a sour mood, Jorja thought. Sore feet, back pain, a horny creep who figures I ought to be as available as the drinks I serve, an argument with Rainy Tarnell, and no tips to show for it.

When her shift ended at four o'clock, she hurried to the changing room down-stairs, punched the time clock, slipped out of her costume and into street clothes, and was out the door into the employee parking lot with a speed that would have drawn praise from an Olympic runner.

The unpredictable desert weather did nothing to instill the Christmas spirit in her. A Las Vegas winter day could be cold, with bone-numbing wind, or it could be warm enough for shorts and halters. This year, the holiday was warm.

Her dusty, battered Chevette started on only the third try, which should have improved her mood. But listening to the starter grind and the engine cough, she was reminded of the shiny new Buick that Alan had taken with him fifteen months ago, when he had abandoned her and Marcie.

Alan Rykoff. More than her job, more than any of the other things that irritated her, Alan was the cause of Jorja's foul mood. She had shed his name when the marriage had been dissolved, reverting to her maiden name, Monatella, but she could not as easily shed the memories of the pain he had inflicted on her and Marcie.

As she drove out of the parking lot into the street behind the hotel, Jorja tried to banish Alan from her thoughts, but he remained at center stage. The bastard. With his current bedmate, an airhead blonde bearing the unlikely name "Pepper," he had flown off to Acapulco for a week, not even bothering to leave a Christmas gift for Marcie. What did you tell a seven-year-old girl when she asked why her daddy didn't buy her anything for Christmas—or even come to see her?

Although Alan left Jorja saddled with bills, she had willingly forgone alimony because, by then, she loathed him so much that she had not wanted to be dependent on him. However, she had gone after child support and had been shocked when he countered by insisting Marcie was not his child and, therefore, not his responsibility. Damn him. Jorja had married him when she was nineteen and he was twenty-four, and she'd never been unfaithful. Alan knew she hadn't cheated, but protecting his jazzy lifestyle—he needed every dollar for clothes, fast cars, and women—was more important to him than his wife's reputation or his daughter's happiness. To spare little Marcie humiliation and pain, Jorja had released Alan from responsibility before he could voice his sleazy accusations in the courtroom.

So she was finished with him. She could put him out of her mind.

But as she drove past the mall at the intersection of Maryland Parkway and Desert Inn Road, Jorja thought about how young she had been when she tied herself to Alan, too young for marriage and too naïve to see through his facade. When she was nineteen, she thought he was *très* sophisticated, charming. For more than a year, their union had seemed blissful, but gradually she began to see him for what he was: shallow, vain, lazy, a shockingly promiscuous womanizer.

The summer before last, when their relationship had been rocky, she had tried to salvage the marriage by coercing Alan into a carefully planned three-week vacation. She believed that part of their problem was that they spent too little time together. He was a baccarat dealer in one hotel, and she was employed in another, and they frequently worked different shifts, slept on different schedules. Just the two of them—and Marcie—embarked upon an adventurous three-week car trip seemed a good way to repair their damaged relationship.

Unfortunately but predictably, her scheme had not worked. After the vacation, upon their return to Vegas, Alan had been more promiscuous than before. He seemed determined—*driven*—to take a poke at anything in skirts. In fact, it was almost as if the car trip had somehow pushed him over the edge, for the number and intensity of his one-night stands developed a manic quality, a frightening desperation. Three months later, in October of that year, he walked out on her and Marcie.

The only good thing about the car trip had been the brief encounter with that young woman doctor who had been driving cross-country from Stanford to Boston on, she'd said, her first vacation ever. Jorja still remembered the woman's name: Ginger Weiss. Although they had met only once, and then for little more than an hour, Ginger Weiss had quite unwittingly changed Jorja's life. The doctor had been so very young—so slender, pretty, feminine—it had been difficult to accept that she was really a doctor, yet she'd been uncommonly self-assured and competent. Deeply impressed by Ginger Weiss during that encounter, Jorja was later motivated by the doctor's example. She'd always thought of herself as a born cocktail waitress, incapable of anything more challenging, but when Alan walked out, she had remembered Dr. Weiss and decided to make more of herself than she had previously thought possible.

During the past eleven months, Jorja had taken business management courses at UNLV, squeezing them into an already hectic schedule. When she finished paying the bills that Alan had left her, she would build a nest egg so she could eventually open her own business, a dress shop. She had worked out a very detailed plan, revising and honing it until it was realistic, and she knew she would stick with it.

It was a shame that she would never have a chance to thank Ginger Weiss. Of course, it was not any favor that Dr. Weiss had performed that so deeply affected Jorja; it was not so much what the doctor had done as what she *was*. Anyway, at twenty-seven Jorja's prospects were more exciting than they had been previously.

Now, she turned off Desert Inn Road onto Pawnee Drive, a street of comfortable homes behind the Boulevard Mall. She stopped in front of Kara Persaghian's house and got out of the car. The front door opened before she reached it, and Marcie rushed out, into her arms, shouting happily. "Mommy! Mommy!" And Jorja was at last able to forget about her job, the Texan, the argument with the pit boss, and the dilapidated condition of the Chevette. She squatted down and hugged her daughter. When all else failed to cheer her, she could count on Marcie for a lift.

"Mommy," the girl said, "did you have a great day?"

"Yes, honey, I did. You smell like peanut butter."

"Cookies! Aunt Kara made peanut-butter cookies! I had a great day, too. Mommy, do you know why elephants came . . . ummm, why they came all the way from Africa to live in this country?" Marcie giggled. " 'Cause we got orchestras here, and elephants just *love* to dance!" She giggled again. "Isn't that *silly.*"

Even allowing for maternal prejudice, Jorja knew that Marcie was an adorable child. The girl had her mother's hair, so dark brown that it was virtually black, and her mother's dusky complexion. Her eyes were a striking contrast to the rest of her, not brown like Jorja's but blue like her father's. She had an immensely appealing gamine quality.

Marcie's huge eyes opened wide. "Hey, know what day it is?"

"I sure do. Almost Christmas Eve."

"Will be soon as it's dark. Aunt Kara's giving us cookies to take home. You know, Santa's already left the North Pole, and he's started going down chimleys already, but in other parts of the world, of course, where it's dark, not chimleys here. Aunt Kara says I been so bad all year I'll only get a necklace made out of coal, but she's just teasing. Isn't she just teasing, Mommy?"

"Just teasing," Jorja confirmed.

"Oh, no, I'm not!" Kara Persaghian said. She came through the doorway, onto the front walk, a grandmotherly woman in a housedress and apron. "A coal necklace . . . and *maybe* a set of matching coal earrings."

Marcie giggled again.

Kara was not Marcie's aunt, merely her after-school babysitter. Marcie called her "Aunt Kara" from the second week she knew her, and the sitter was obviously delighted by that affectionately bestowed honorary title. Kara was carrying Marcie's jacket, a big coloring-book picture of Santa that they had been working on for a few days, and a plate of cookies. Jorja gave the picture and jacket to Marcie, accepted the cookies with expressions of gratitude and with some chatter about diets, and then Kara said, "Jorja, could I speak with you a moment—just the two of us?"

"Sure." Jorja sent Marcie to the car with the cookies and turned inquisitively to Kara. "It's about . . . Marcie. What's she done?"

"Oh, nothing bad. She's an angel, that one. Couldn't misbehave if she tried. But today . . . well, she was talking about how the thing she wants most for Christmas is that Little Ms. Doctor play kit—"

"It's the first time she's ever really *nagged* me about a toy," Jorja said. "I don't know why she's obsessed with it."

"She talks about it every day. You are getting it for her?"

Jorja glanced at the Chevette, confirming that Marcie was out of earshot, then smiled. "Yes, Santa definitely has it in his bag."

"Good. She'd be heartbroken if you didn't. But the oddest thing happened today, and it made me wonder if she'd ever been seriously ill."

"Serious illness? No. She's an exceptionally healthy kid."

"Never been in the hospital?"

"No. Why?"

Kara frowned. "Well, today she started talking about the Little Ms. Doctor kit, and she told me she wanted to be a doctor when she grew up because then she could treat herself when she got sick. She said she never wanted a doctor to touch her again because she was once hurt real bad by doctors. I asked her what she meant, and she got quiet for a while, and I thought she wasn't going to answer me. Then finally, in this *very* somber voice, she said some doctors had once strapped her down in a hospital bed so she couldn't get out, and then they stuck her full of needles and flashed lights in her face and did all sorts of horrible things to her. She said they hurt her real bad, so she was going to become her own doctor and treat herself from now on."

"Really? Well, it's not true," Jorja said. "I don't know why she'd make up such a story. That *is* odd."

"Oh, that's not the odd part. When she told me all this, I was concerned. I was surprised you'd never told me. I mean, if she'd been seriously ill, I ought to've been told in case there was a possibility of a recurrence. So I questioned her about it—just casually, the way you coax things out of a child—and suddenly the poor little thing just *burst* into tears. We were in the kitchen, making cookies, and she started to cry . . . and shake. Just shaking like a leaf. I tried to calm her, but that only made her cry harder. Then she pulled away from me and ran. I found her in the living room, in the corner behind the big green Lay-Z-Boy, huddled down as if she was hiding from someone."

"Good heavens," Jorja said.

Kara said, "Took me at least five minutes to get her to stop crying and another ten to coax her out of her hidey-hole behind that chair. She made me promise, if those doctors ever came for her again, that I'd let her hide behind the chair and not tell them where she was. I mean, Jorja, she was in a real *state*."

On the way home, Jorja said, "That was some story you told Kara."

"What story?" Marcie asked, looking straight ahead, barely able to see over the dashboard.

"That story about the doctors."

"Oh."

"Being strapped in bed. Why'd you make up a thing like that?"

"It's true," Marcie said.

"But it isn't."

"Yes, it is." The girl's voice was little more than a whisper.

"The only hospital you were ever in was the one where you were born, and I'm *sure* you don't remember that." Jorja sighed. "A few months ago we had a little talk about fibbing. Remember what happened to Danny Duck when he fibbed?"

"The Truth Fairy wouldn't let him go to the woodchuck's party."

"That's right."

"Fibbing's bad," Marcie said softly. "Nobody likes fibbers—'specially not woodchucks and squirrels."

Disarmed, Jorja had to bite back a laugh and struggle to keep a stern tone in her voice. "*Nobody* likes fibbers."

They stopped at a red traffic light, but Marcie still looked straight ahead, refusing to meet Jorja's eyes. The girl said, "It's 'specially bad to fib to your mommy or your daddy."

"Or to *anyone* who cares about you. And making up stories to scare Kara— that's the same as fibbing."

"Wasn't tryin' to scare her," Marcie said.

"Trying to get sympathy, then. You were never in a hospital."

"Was."

"Oh, yeah?" Marcie nodded vigorously, and Jorja said, "When?"

"Don't 'member when."

"You don't remember, huh?"

"Almost."

"Almost isn't good enough. Where was this hospital?"

"I'm not sure. Sometimes . . . I 'member it better than other times. Sometimes I can hardly 'member it at all, and sometimes I 'member it real good, and then I . . . I get scared."

"Right now you don't remember too well, huh?"

"Nope. But today I 'membered real good . . . and scared myself."

The traffic light changed, and Jorja drove in silence, wondering how best to handle the situation. She had no notion what to make of it. It was foolish ever to believe that you understood your child. Marcie had always been able to surprise Jorja with actions, statements, big ideas, musings, and questions that seemed not to have come from within herself but which it seemed she had carefully selected from some secret book of startling behavior that was known to all kids but not to adults, some cosmic volume perhaps titled *Keeping Mom and Dad Off-Balance*.

As if she had just dipped into that book again, Marcie said, "Why were all Santa Claus's kids deformed?"

"*What?*"

"Well, see, Santa and Mrs. Claus had a whole bunch of kids, but all of them was *elves*."

"The elves aren't their children. They work for Santa."

"Really? How much does he pay 'em?"

"He doesn't pay them anything, honey."

"How do they buy food, then?"

"They don't have to buy anything. Santa gives them all they need." This was certainly the last Christmas that Marcie would believe in Santa; nearly all of her classmates were already doubters. Recently, she had been asking these probing questions. Jorja would be sorry to see the fantasy disproved, the magic lost. "The elves are part of his family, honey, and they work with him simply for the love of it."

"You mean the elves are adopted? So Santa doesn't have real kids of his own? That's sad."

"No, 'cause he's got all the elves to love."

God, I love this kid, Jorja thought. Thank you, God. Thank you for this kid, even if I did have to get tied up with Alan Rykoff to get her. Dark clouds and silver linings.

She turned into the two-lane driveway that encircled Las Huevos Apartments and parked the Chevette in the fourth carport. Las Huevos. The Eggs. After five years in the place, she still couldn't understand why anyone would name an apartment complex The Eggs.

The instant the car stopped, Marcie was out of it with the poster from the coloring book and the plate of cookies, dashing up the walkway to their entrance. The girl had deftly changed the subject just long enough to finish the ride and escape from the confines of the car.

Jorja wondered if she should press the issue farther. It was Christmas Eve, and she had no desire to spoil the holiday. Marcie was a good kid, better than most, and this business about being hurt by doctors was an extremely rare instance of fabrication. Jorja had made the point that fibbing was not acceptable, and Marcie had understood (even if she had persisted a bit with her medical fantasy), and her sudden change of subject had probably been an admission of wrongdoing. So it was an aberration. Nothing would be gained by harping on it, especially not at the risk of ruining Christmas.

Jorja was confident she would hear no more about it.

5. Laguna Beach, California

During the afternoon, Dominick Corvaisis must have read the unsigned type-written note a hundred times:

> The sleepwalker would be well-advised to search
> the past for the source of his problem. That is
> where the secret is buried.

In addition to the letter's lack of signature and return address, the postmark on the plain white envelope was double-struck and badly smeared, so he could not determine whether it had been mailed in Laguna Beach or from another city.

After he paid for his breakfast and left The Cottage, he sat in his car, the copy of *Twilight in Babylon* forgotten on the seat beside him, and read the note half a dozen times. It made him so nervous that he withdrew a pair of Valiums from his jacket pocket and almost took one without water. But as he put the tablet to his lips, he hesitated. To explore all the ramifications of the note, he would need a clear mind. For the first time in weeks, he denied himself chemical escape from his anxieties; he returned the Valium to his pocket.

He drove to South Coast Plaza, a huge shopping mall in Costa Mesa, to buy some last-minute Christmas gifts. In each store he visited, while he waited for the clerks to gift-wrap his purchases, he took the curious message from his pocket and read it again and again.

For a while Dom had wondered if the note had come from Parker, if perhaps the artist had sent it to jolt him and intrigue him and propel him out of his drug-induced haze. Parker might be capable of such highly theatrical, amateur psycho-therapy. But finally Dom dismissed that idea. Machiavellian maneuvers were simply not aspects of the painter's personality. He was, in fact, almost excessively forthright.

Parker was not the author of the note, but he was certain to have some original speculations about who might be behind it. Together, they might be able to decide just how the arrival of this letter changed things and how they ought to proceed.

Later, back in Laguna, when Dom was within a block of Parker's house, he was suddenly shaken by a previously unconsidered, profoundly troubling possi-bility. This new idea was *so* disconcerting that he pulled the Firebird to the curb and stopped. He got the note from his pocket, read it again, fingered the paper. He felt cold inside. He looked into the reflection of his own eyes in the rearview mirror, and he did not like what he saw.

Could he have written the note himself?

He could have composed it on the Displaywriter while asleep. But it was out-landish to suppose he'd dressed, gone to the mailbox, deposited the note, returned home, and changed into pajamas again without waking up. Impossible. Wasn't it? If he had done such a thing, his mental imbalance was worse than he had thought.

His hands were clammy. He blotted them on his trousers.

Only three people in the world were aware of his sleepwalking: himself, Parker Faine, and Dr. Cobletz. He had already eliminated Parker. Dr. Cobletz had cer-tainly not sent the note. So if Dom himself had not sent it—who had?

When he pulled away from the curb at last, he did not continue to Parker's house but headed home instead.

Ten minutes later, in his study, he took the by-now rumpled note from his pocket. He typed those two sentences, which appeared on the Displaywriter's dark screen in glowing green letters. Then he switched on the printer and in-structed the computer to produce a hard copy of the document. He watched as it hammered out those twenty-three words.

The Displaywriter came with two printwheels in two typefaces. He had bought two more to provide options for different tasks. Now, Dom used the three addi-tional printwheels to produce a total of four copies of the note, and with a pencil he labeled each according to the style of type used for it: PRESTIGE ELITE, ARTISAN 10, COURIER 10, LETTER GOTHIC.

He smoothed out the original rumpled note and placed each of the copies beside it for comparison. He hoped to eliminate all four type styles that he possessed, disproving the theory that he had sent the note to himself. But the Courier 10 appeared to be a perfect match.

That did not conclusively prove he'd written the note. In offices and homes all over the country, there must be millions of printwheels and printer elements in the Courier face.

He compared the paper of the original note to that of the copy he had made. They were both twenty-pound, $8^1/_2$" $\times$ 11", standard products sold under a dozen labels in thousands of stores in all fifty states. Neither sheet was of sufficient quality to contain fibers. Dom held them up to the light and saw that neither page featured a mill seal or brand-name watermark, which might have proven that the original note had not been typed on paper from his own stock.

He thought: Parker, Dr. Cobletz, and me. Who else could know?

And what was the note trying to tell him, exactly? What secret was buried in his past? What suppressed trauma or forgotten event lay at the root of his somnambulism?

Sitting at his desk, staring at the night beyond the big window, straining blindly toward understanding, he grew tense. Again, he felt a need for Valium, almost a craving, but he resisted.

The note engaged his curiosity, logic, and reason. He was able to focus his intellect on the search for a solution and concentrate with an intensity of which he had not been capable recently, and thus he found the will power to forsake the solace of tranquilization.

He was beginning to feel good about himself for the first time in weeks. In spite of the helplessness in which he had been wallowing, he now realized that, after all, he still had the power to shape and direct the course of his own life. All he had needed was something like the note, something tangible on which he could focus.

He paced around the house, carrying the note, thinking. Eventually he came to a front window from which he could see his curbside mailbox—a brick column with a metal receptacle mortared into it—standing in the bluish fall of light from a mercury-vapor streetlamp.

Because he kept the post office drawer in town, the only mail he got at home was that addressed to "Occupant" and occasional cards or letters from friends who had both his mailing and street address but who sometimes forgot that all correspondence was to go to the former. Standing at the window, staring at the curbside receptacle, Dom realized that he had not picked up today's delivery.

He went outside, down the front walk to the street, and used a key to unlock the receptacle. Except for the breeze that rustled the trees, the night was quiet. The wind carried the scent of the sea, and the air was chilly. The overhead mercury-vapor lamp was sufficiently bright for Dom to identify the mail as he withdrew it from the box: six advertising flyers and catalogs, two Christmas cards . . . and a plain white business-size envelope with no return address.

Excited, fearful, he hurried back into the house, to his study, tearing open the white envelope and extracting a single sheet of paper as he went. At his desk, he unfolded the letter.

The moon.

No other words could have shocked him as badly as those. He felt as if he had fallen into the White Rabbit's hole and was tumbling down into a fantastic realm where logic and reason no longer applied.

The moon. This was *impossible*. No one knew he had awakened from bad dreams with those words on his lips, repeating them in panic: "The moon, moon. . . ." And no one knew that, while sleepwalking, he had typed those words on the Displaywriter. He'd told neither Parker nor Cobletz, because those incidents had transpired after he'd begun drug therapy and after the drugs seemed to be working, and he had not wanted to appear to be slipping backward. Besides, although those two words filled him with dread, he did not understand their significance. He did not know *why* they had the power to raise gooseflesh, and he instinctively felt that it was unwise to mention this development to anyone until he had gotten a better handle on it. He had been afraid Cobletz would conclude that the drugs were not helping him and would discontinue them in favor of psychotherapy—and Dom had *needed* the drugs.

The moon.

No one knew, damn it. No one but . . . Dom himself.

In the streetlamp's dim glow, he had not checked for a postmark. Now, he saw that its point of origin was not a mystery, as was the case with the letter that had come this morning. It was clearly stamped NEW YORK, N.Y., and dated December 18. Wednesday of last week.

He almost laughed out loud. He was not insane, after all. He was not sending these cryptic messages to himself—could not *possibly* be sending them—because he had been in Laguna last week. Three thousand miles separated him from the mailbox in which this—and undoubtedly the other—strange message had first been deposited.

But who had sent him the notes—and why? Who in New York could know that he was sleepwalking . . . or that he had repeatedly typed "the moon" on his word processor? A thousand questions crowded Dom Corvaisis' mind, and he had no answers to any of them. Worse, at the moment, he could see no way even to *seek* answers. The situation was so bizarre that there was no logical direction for his inquiries to take.

For two months, he had thought that his sleepwalking was the strangest and most frightening thing that had ever happened—or ever would happen—to him. But whatever lay behind the somnambulism must be even stranger and more frightening than the nightwalking itself.

He recalled the first message he had left for himself on the word processor: *I'm afraid.* What *had* he been hiding from in closets? When he had started to nail the windows shut while sound asleep, what had he hoped to keep out of his house?

Dom saw now that his sleepwalking had not been caused by stress. He was not suffering anxiety attacks because he feared the success or failure of his first novel. It was nothing as mundane as that.

Something else. Something very strange and terrible.

What did he know in his sleep that he did not know when awake?

6. New Haven County, Connecticut

The sky had cleared before nightfall, but the moon had not yet risen. The stars shed little light upon the cold earth.

With his back against a boulder, Jack Twist sat in the snow atop a knoll, at the edge of pines, waiting for the Guardmaster armored truck to appear. Only three weeks after personally netting more than a million dollars from the mafia warehouse job, he was already setting up another heist. He was wearing boots, gloves, and a white ski suit, with the hood over his head and tied securely under his chin. Three hundred yards behind him and to the southwest, beyond the small woods, the darkness was relieved by the light of a housing development; however, Jack waited in utter blackness, his breath steaming.

In front of him, two miles of night-clad fields lay northeast, barren but for a few widely spaced trees and some winter-stripped brush. In the distance beyond the emptiness, there were electronics plants, then shopping centers, then residential neighborhoods, none of which was visible from Jack's position, though their existence was indicated by the glow of electric lights on the horizon.

At the far edge of the fields, headlights appeared over a low rise. Raising a pair of night binoculars, Jack focused on the approaching vehicle, which was following the two-lane county road that bisected the fields. In spite of the leftward cast of his left eye, Jack had superb vision, and with the help of the night binoculars, he ascertained that the vehicle was not the Guardmaster truck, therefore of no consequence to him. He lowered the glasses.

In his solitude upon the snowy knoll, he thought back to another time and a warmer place, to a humid night in a Central American jungle, when he had studied a nocturnal landscape with binoculars just like these. Then, he had been searching anxiously for hostile troops that had been stalking and encircling him and his buddies. . . .

His platoon—twenty highly trained Rangers under the leadership of Lieutenant Rafe Eikhorn, with Jack as second in command—had crossed the border illegally and gone fifteen miles inside the enemy state without being detected. Their presence could have been construed as an act of war; therefore, they wore camouflage suits stripped of rank and service markings, and they carried no identification.

Their target was a nasty little ''re-education'' camp, cynically named the Institute of Brotherhood, where a thousand Miskito Indians were imprisoned by the People's Army. Two weeks earlier, courageous Catholic priests had led another fifteen hundred Indians through the jungles and out of the country before they could be imprisoned, too. Those clergymen had brought word that the Indians at the Institute would be murdered and buried in mass graves if not rescued within the month.

The Miskitos were a fiercely proud breed with a rich culture that they refused to forsake for the anti-ethnic, collectivist philosophy of the country's latest leaders. The Indians' continued loyalty to their own traditions would ensure their extermination, for the ruling council did not hesitate to call up the firing squads to solidify its power.

Nevertheless, twenty Rangers in mufti would not have been committed to such a dangerous raid merely to save Miskitos. Both left- and right-wing dictatorial regimes routinely slaughtered their citizenry in every corner of the world, and the United States did not—could not—prevent those state-sanctioned murders. But in addition to the Indians at the Institute, there were eleven others whose rescue, along with the Indians, made the risky operation worthwhile.

Those eleven were former revolutionaries who had fought the just war against the now-deposed right-wing dictator, but who had refused to remain silent when their revolution had been betrayed by totalitarians of the left. Undoubtedly, those eleven possessed valuable information. The opportunity to debrief them was more important than saving the lives of a thousand Indians—at least as far as Washington was concerned.

Undetected, Jack's platoon reached the Institute of Brotherhood in a farming district at the edge of the jungle. It was a concentration camp in all but name, a place of barbed-wire fences and guard towers. Two buildings stood outside the fenced perimeter of the camp: a two-story concrete-block structure from which the government administered the district, and a dilapidated wooden barracks housing sixty troops.

Shortly after midnight, the platoon of Rangers stealthily took up positions and launched a rocket attack on the barracks and the concrete building. The initial artillery barrages were followed by hand-to-hand combat. Half an hour after the last shot was fired, the Indians and other prisoners—as jubilant a group as Jack had ever seen—were formed into a column and moved out toward the border, fifteen miles away.

Two Rangers had been killed. Three were wounded.

As first in command of the platoon, Rafe Eikhorn led the exodus and oversaw security along the column's flanks, while Jack stayed behind with three men to be sure the last of the prisoners got out of the camp in orderly fashion. It was also his responsibility to gather up files relating to the interrogation, torture, and murder of Indians and district peasants. By the time he and his four men left the Institute of Brotherhood, they were two miles behind the last of the Miskitos.

Though Jack and his men made good time, they never caught up with their platoon and were still miles from the Honduran border when, at dawn, hostile army helicopters, like giant black wasps, came in low over the trees and began off-loading enemy troops wherever a clearing could be found. The other Rangers and all the Indians reached freedom, but Jack and his three men were captured and transported to a facility similar to the Institute of Brotherhood. However, the place was so much worse than the concentration camp that it had no official existence. The ruling council did not admit that such a hellhole existed in the new workers' paradise—or that monstrous inquisitions were conducted within its walls. In true Orwellian tradition, because the four-story complex of cells and torture chambers had no name, it did not exist.

Within those nameless walls, in cells without numbers, Jack Twist and the three other Rangers were subjected to psychological and physical torture, relentless humiliation and degradation, controlled starvation, and constant threats of death. One of the four died. One went mad. Only Jack and his closest friend, Oscar Weston, held on to both life and sanity during the eleven and a half months of their incarceration. . . .

Now, eight years later, leaning against a boulder atop a knoll in Connecticut, waiting for the Guardmaster truck, Jack heard sounds and detected odors which were not of this wind-swept winter night. The hard footfalls of jackboots on concrete corridors. The stench from the overflowing slops bucket, which was the cell's only toilet. The pathetic cry of some poor bastard being taken from his cell to another session with interrogators.

Jack took deep breaths of the clean, cold Connecticut air. He was seldom troubled by bad memories of that time and nameless place. He was more often haunted by what had happened to him *after* his escape—and by what had happened to his Jenny in his absence. It was not his suffering in Central America that turned him against society; rather, subsequent events were what had soured him.

He saw other headlights out on the black fields and raised his night binoculars. It was the Guardmaster armored transport.

He looked at his watch. Nine-thirty-eight. It was right on schedule, as it had been every night for a week. Even with the holiday tomorrow, the truck kept to its route. Guardmaster Security was nothing if not reliable.

On the ground beside Jack was an attaché case. He lifted the lid. The blue numerals of a digital scanner were locked on the Guardmaster's open radio link to the company dispatcher. Even with his state-of-the-art equipment, he had needed three nights to discover the truck's frequency. He turned the volume dial on his own receiver. Static crackled, hissed. Then he was rewarded by a routine exchange between the driver and the distant dispatcher.

''Three-oh-one,'' the dispatcher said.

''Reindeer,'' the driver said.

''Rudolph,'' the dispatcher said.

''Rooftop,'' the driver said.

The hiss and crackle of static settled in once more.

The dispatcher had opened the exchange with the truck's number, and the rest of it had been the day's code which served as confirmation that 301 was on schedule and in no trouble of any kind.

Jack switched off his receiver. The lighted dials went dark.

The armored transport passed less than two hundred feet from his position on the knoll, and he turned to watch its dwindling taillights.

He was confident of Guardmaster 301's schedule now, and he would not be returning to these fields until the night of the stickup, which was tentatively scheduled for Saturday, January 11. Meanwhile, there was a great deal more planning to be done.

Ordinarily, planning a job was nearly as exciting and satisfying as the actual commission of the crime. But as he left the knoll and headed toward the houses to the southwest, where he had parked his car on a quiet street, he felt no elation, no thrill. He was losing the ability to take delight in even the *contemplation* of a crime.

He was changing. And he did not know why.

As he drew near the first houses to the southwest of the knoll, he became aware that the night had grown brighter. He looked up. The moon swelled fat on the horizon, so huge it seemed to be crashing to earth, an illusion of enormousness created by the odd perspective of the early stages of the satellite's ascension. He stopped abruptly and stood with his head tilted back, staring up at the luminous lunar surface. A chill seized him, an inner iciness unrelated to the winter cold.

"The moon," he said softly.

Hearing himself speak those words aloud, Jack shuddered violently. Inexplicable fear welled in him. He was gripped by an irrational urge to run and hide from the moon, as if its luminescence were corrosive and would, like an acid, dissolve him as he stood bathed in it.

The compulsion to flee passed in a minute. He could not understand why the moon had so suddenly terrified him. It was only the ancient and familiar moon of love songs and romantic poetry. Strange.

He headed toward the car again. The looming lunar face still made him uneasy, and several times he glanced up at it, perplexed.

However, by the time he got in the car, drove into New Haven, and picked up Interstate 95, that curious incident had faded from his mind. He was once more preoccupied with thoughts of Jenny, his comatose wife, whose condition haunted him more than usual at Christmastime.

Later, in his apartment, as he stood by a big window, staring out at the great city, a bottle of Beck's in one hand, he was sure that from 261st Street to Park Row, from Bensonhurst to Little Neck, there could be no one in the Metropolis whose Christmas Eve was lonelier than his.

7. Christmas Day

ELKO COUNTY, NEVADA.

Sandy Sarver woke soon after dawn came to the high plains. The early sun glimmered vaguely at the bedroom windows of the house trailer. The world was so still that it seemed time must have stopped.

She could turn over and go back to sleep if she so desired, for she had eight more days of vacation ahead of her. Ernie and Faye Block had closed the Tranquility Motel and had gone to visit their grandchildren in Milwaukee. The adjacent Tranquility Grille, which Sandy operated with her husband, Ned, was also closed over the holidays.

But Sandy knew she could not get back to sleep, for she was wide awake— and horny. She stretched like a cat beneath the blankets. She wanted to wake Ned, smother him with kisses, and pull him atop her.

Ned was merely a shadowy form in the dark bedroom, breathing deeply, sound asleep. Although she wanted him badly, she did not wake him. There would be plenty of time for lovemaking later in the day.

She slipped quietly out of bed, into the bathroom, and showered. She made the end of it a *cold* shower.

For years she had been uninterested in sex, frigid. Not long ago, the sight of her own nude body had embarrassed her and filled her with shame. Although she did not know the reason for the new feelings that had risen in her lately, she definitely had changed. It had started the summer before last, when sex had suddenly seemed . . . well, appealing. That sounded silly now. *Of course* sex was appealing. But prior to that summer, lovemaking had always been a chore to be endured. Her late erotic blossoming was a delightful surprise and an inexplicable mystery.

Nude, she returned to the shadowy bedroom. She took a sweater and a pair of jeans from the closet, and dressed.

In the small kitchen, she started to pour orange juice but stopped when stricken by the urge to go for a drive. She left a note for Ned, put on a sheepskin-lined jacket, and went outside to the Ford pickup.

Sex and driving were the two new passions in her life, and the latter was almost as important to her as the former. That was another funny thing: until the summer before last, she hated going anywhere in the pickup except to work and back, and she seldom drove. She'd not only disliked highway travel but had dreaded it the way some people were afraid of airplanes. But now, other than sex, there was nothing she liked better than to get behind the wheel of the truck and take off, journeying on a whim, without a destination, speeding.

She had always understood why sex repelled her—that had been no mystery. She could blame her father, Horton Purney, for her frigidity. Though she had never known her mother, who had died giving birth, Sandy had known her father far too well. They had lived in a ramshackle house on the outskirts of Barstow, on the edge of the lonely California desert, just the two of them, and Sandy's earliest memories were of sexual abuse. Horton Purney had been a moody, brooding, mean, and dangerous man. Until Sandy escaped from home at fourteen, her father had used her as if she had been an erotic toy.

Only recently had she realized that her strong dislike for highway travel was also related to something else that her father had done to her. Horton Purney had run a motorcycle repair shop out of a sagging, sun-scorched, unpainted barn on the same property as his house, but he had never made much money from it. Therefore, twice a year, he put Sandy in the car and made the two-and-a-half-hour drive across the desert to Las Vegas, where he knew an enterprising pimp, Samson Cherrik. Cherrik had a list of perverts with a special interest in children, and he was always happy to see Sandy. After a few weeks in Vegas, Sandy's father packed, put Sandy in the car, and drove back to Barstow, his pockets bulging with cash. For Sandy, the long drive to Vegas was a nightmare journey, for she knew what awaited her at their destination. The trip back to Barstow was worse, for it was not an escape from Vegas but a return to the grim life in that ramshackle house and the dark, urgent, insatiable lust of Horton Purney. In either direction, the road had led to hell, and she had learned to loathe the rumble of the car's engine, the hum of tires on the pavement, and the unspooling highway ahead.

Therefore, the pleasure she now took from driving and sex seemed miraculous. She could not understand where she'd found the strength and will to overcome her horrible past. Since the summer before last, she simply . . . *changed*, was still changing. And, oh, it was glorious to feel the chains of self-loathing and the bonds of fear breaking apart, to feel self-respect for the first time in her life, to feel *free*.

Now, she got into the Ford pickup and started the engine. Their house trailer was set on an unlandscaped half-acre lot at the southern edge of the tiny—almost nonexistent—town of Beowawe, along Route 21, a two-lane blacktop. As Sandy drove away from the trailer, there seemed to be nothing but empty plains, rolling hills, scattered buttes, rocky outcroppings, grass, brush, and waterless arroyos for a thousand miles in every direction. The intensely blue morning sky was immense, and as she got the Ford up to speed, Sandy felt as if she might take flight.

If she headed north on 21, she would pass through Beowawe and soon come to Interstate 80, which led east toward Elko or west toward Battle Mountain. Instead, she went south, into a beautifully barren landscape. With skill and ease, she guided the four-wheel-drive pickup over the badly weathered county road at seventy miles an hour.

In fifteen minutes, Route 21 petered out into a gravel roadbed that led south through another eighty-three miles of uninhabited and desolate territory. She did not follow it, choosing instead to turn east on a one-lane dirt track flanked by wild grass and scrub.

Some snow lay on the ground this Christmas morning, though not much. In the distance, the mountains were white, but down here, the annual precipitation was less than fifteen inches a year, little of it in the form of snow. Here was an inch-deep skin of snow, there a small hillock against which a shallow drift had formed, and here a sparkling bush on which wind-driven snow had hardened into a lacy garment of ice, but by far the largest portion of the land was bare and dry and brown.

Sandy drove fast on the dirt, too, and behind her a cloud of dust plumed up. In time she left the track, headed overland—north, then west, coming at last to a familiar place, though she had not set out with this destination in mind. For reasons she did not understand, her subconscious often guided her to this spot during her solitary drives, seldom in a direct line but by wandering routes, so her arrival was usually a surprise to her. She stopped, set the brake. With the engine idling, she stared for a while through the dusty windshield.

She came here because it made her feel better, though she did not know why. The slopes, the spines and teeth of rock, the grass and brush, formed a pleasing picture, though the scene was no prettier and no different from thousands of other places nearby. Yet here she felt a sublime peacefulness that could not be attained anywhere else.

She switched off the engine and got out of the pickup, and for a while she strolled back and forth, hands jammed into the pockets of her sheepskin-lined jacket, oblivious of the stingingly cold air. Her drive through the wildlands had brought her back toward civilization, and Interstate 80 lay only a couple of hundred yards to the north. The occasional roar of a passing truck echoed like a distant dragon's growl, but the holiday traffic was light. Beyond the highway, on the uplands to the northwest, lay the Tranquility Motel and Grille, but Sandy glanced just once in that direction. She was more interested in the immediate terrain, which exerted a mysterious and powerful attraction for her, and which seemed to radiate peace the way a rock, in evening, radiated the heat of the sun that it had absorbed during the day.

She wasn't trying to analyze her affinity for this patch of ground. Evidently, there was some subtle harmony in the contours of the land, an interplay of line, form, and shadow that defied definition. Any attempt to decode its attraction would be as foolish as trying to analyze the beauty of a sunset or the appeal of a favorite flower.

That Christmas morning, Sandy did not yet know that Ernie Block had been drawn, as if possessed, to the same patch of ground on December 10, when he had been on his way home from the freight office in Elko. She did not know that it aroused in Ernie an electrifying sense of pending epiphany and more than a little fear—emotions quite unlike those that it stirred in her. Weeks would pass before she learned that her special retreat had a strong attraction for others besides herself—both friends and strangers.

CHICAGO, ILLINOIS.

For Father Stefan Wycazik—that stocky Polish dynamo, rector of St. Bernadette's, rescuer of troubled priests—it was the busiest Christmas morning he had ever known. And as the day wore on, it swiftly became the most meaningful Christmas of his life.

He celebrated the second Mass at St. Bernadette's, spent an hour greeting parishioners who stopped by the rectory with fruit baskets and boxes of homemade cookies and other gifts, then drove to University Hospital to pay a visit to Winton Tolk, the policeman who had been shot in an uptown sandwich shop yesterday afternoon. Following emergency surgery, Tolk had been in the intensive care unit yesterday afternoon and all through the night. Christmas morning he had been moved to a semiprivate room adjacent to the ICU, for although he was no longer in critical condition, he still needed to be monitored constantly.

When Father Wycazik arrived, Raynella Tolk, Winton's wife, was at her husband's bedside. She was quite attractive, with chocolate-brown skin and stylish close-cropped hair. "Mrs. Tolk? I'm Stefan Wycazik."

"But—"

He smiled. "Relax. I'm not here to give anyone the last rites."

"Good," Winton said, " 'cause I'm sure not planning on dying."

The wounded policeman was not only fully conscious but alert and apparently suffering no pain. His bed was raised to a sitting position. Although his broad chest was heavily bandaged, and although a cardiac telemetry device hung around his neck, and in spite of the IV line that was dripping glucose and antibiotics into the median basilic vein in his left arm, he looked remarkably well considering his recent misadventure.

Father Wycazik stood at the foot of the bed, his tension betrayed only by the way he kept turning his black fedora around and around in his strong hands. When he realized what he was doing, he quickly put the hat on a chair.

He said, "Mr. Tolk, if you feel up to it, I've come to ask you a few questions about what happened yesterday."

Both Tolk and his wife looked puzzled by Stefan's curiosity.

The priest gave a partial explanation for his interest—though only partial. "The fellow who cruised the Uptown district with you for the past week, Brendan Cronin, was in my employ," he said, maintaining Brendan's cover as a lay worker for the Church.

"Oh, I'd like to meet *him,*" Raynella said, her face brightening.

"He saved my life," Tolk said. "He did a *crazy*-brave thing, which he shouldn't have done in a million years, but I'm sure glad he did it."

Raynella said, "Mr. Cronin walked into that sandwich shop not knowing if all the gunmen were dead, not knowing if he might be shot."

"It's strictly against police procedure to walk into a situation like that," Winton said. "I'd have handled it by the book myself if I'd been one of those outside. I can't exactly applaud what Brendan did, Father, but I owe him my life for doing it."

"Amazing," Father Wycazik said, as if this were the first time he had heard of Brendan's bravery. In fact, yesterday he had spoken at length with Winton Tolk's precinct captain, an old friend, and had heard Brendan praised for courage and damned for foolishness. "I've always known Brendan's a dependable fellow. Did he also provide first aid?"

"He might have," Winton said. "Don't really know. I remember regaining consciousness . . . and there he was . . . sort of looming over me . . . calling my name . . . but I was still in a haze, you see."

"It's a miracle Win survived," Raynella said in a tremulous voice.

"Now, now, honey," Winton said softly. "I *did* make it, and that's all that counts." When he was sure his wife would be all right, he looked at Stefan and said, "Everyone's amazed that I could lose so much blood and pull through. From what I hear, I must've lost buckets."

"Did Brendan apply a tourniquet?"

Tolk frowned. "Don't know. Like I said, I was in a haze, a daze."

Father Wycazik hesitated, wondering how to find out what he needed to know without revealing the extraordinary possibility that motivated this visit. "I know you're not very clear about what happened but . . . did you notice anything peculiar about . . . Brendan's hands?"

"Peculiar? What do you mean?"

"He touched you, didn't he?"

"Sure. I guess he felt for a pulse . . . then checked around to see where the bleeding was coming from."

"Well, did you feel anything . . . anything unusual when he touched you . . . anything odd?" Stefan asked carefully, frustrated by the need to be vague.

"I don't seem to be following your line of thought, Father."

Stefan Wycazik shook his head. "Never mind. The important thing is that you're well." He glanced at his watch and, feigning surprise, said, "Good heavens, I'm late for an appointment." Before they could respond, he snatched his hat from the chair, wished them godspeed, and hurried out, no doubt leaving them astonished by his behavior.

When people saw Father Wycazik walking toward them, they were usually reminded of drill sergeants or football coaches. His solid body and the self-confident, aggressive way he used it were not what one expected of a priest. And when he was in a hurry, he was not so much like a drill sergeant or a football coach as he was like a *tank.*

From Tolk's room, Father Wycazik blitzed down the hall, shoved through a pair of heavy swinging doors, then through another pair, into the intensive care unit, where the wounded policeman had been until just an hour ago. He asked to speak to the physician on duty, Dr. Royce Albright. With the hope that God would forgive a few little white lies told in a good cause, Stefan identified himself as the Tolk family's priest and implied that Mrs. Tolk had sent him to get the full story of her husband's condition, about which she was not yet entirely clear.

Dr. Albright looked like Jerry Lewis and had a deep rumbling voice like Henry Kissinger, which was disconcerting, but he was willing to answer whatever questions Father Wycazik wished to pose. He was not Winton Tolk's personal physician, but he was interested in the case. "You can assure Mrs. Tolk that there's almost no danger of a setback. He's coming along marvelously. Shot twice in the chest, point-blank, with a .38. Until yesterday, no one here would've believed that anyone could take two shots in the chest from a large-caliber handgun *and be out of intensive care in twenty-four hours!* Mr. Tolk is incredibly lucky."

"The bullets missed the heart, then . . . and all vital organs?"

"Not only that," Albright said, "but neither round did major damage to any veins or arteries. A .38-caliber slug has lots of punch, Father. Ordinarily, it chews up the victim. In Tolk's case, one major artery and vein were nicked, but neither was severed. Very fortunate, indeed."

"Then I suppose the bullet was stopped by bone at some point."

"Deflected, yes, but not stopped. Both slugs were found in soft tissue. And that's another amazing thing—no shattered bones, not even a small fracture. A *very* lucky man."

Father Wycazik nodded. "When the two slugs were removed from his body, was there any indication they were underweight for .38-caliber ammunition? I mean, maybe the cartridges were faulty, with too little lead in the bullets. That would explain why, even though it was a .38 revolver, the shots did less damage than a pair of .22s."

Albright frowned. "Don't know. Could be. You'd have to ask the police . . . or Dr. Sonneford, the surgeon who took the slugs out of Tolk."

"I understand Officer Tolk lost a great deal of blood."

Grimacing, Albright said, "Must be a mistake about that on his chart. I haven't had a chance to talk to Dr. Sonneford today, it being Christmas, but according to the chart, Tolk received over four liters of whole blood in the operating room. Of course, that can't be correct."

"Why not?"

"Father, if Tolk actually lost four liters of blood before they got him to the hospital, there wouldn't be enough in him to maintain even minimal circulation. He'd have been dead. Stone cold dead."

LAS VEGAS, NEVADA.

Mary and Pete Monatella, Jorja's parents, arrived at her apartment at six on Christmas morning, bleary-eyed and grumpy from too little sleep, but determined to take up their rightful posts by the brightly trimmed tree before Marcie awoke. Mary, as tall as Jorja, had once been almost as shapely as her daughter too; now she was heavy, girdled. Pete was shorter than his wife, barrel-chested, a bantam rooster who seemed to strut when he walked but was one of the most self-effacing men Jorja had ever known. They came burdened with presents for their only grandchild.

They had a present for Jorja—plus the usual gifts they brought every time they visited: well-meant but annoying criticism, unwanted advice, guilt. Mary was hardly through the door before she announced that Jorja should clean the ventilation hood above the range, and she rummaged under the sink until she found a spray bottle of Windex and a rag, with which she performed the chore herself. She also observed that the tree looked underdecorated—"It needs more lights, Jorja!"—and when she saw how Marcie's presents were wrapped, she professed despair. "My God, Jorja, the wrapping papers aren't bright enough. The ribbons aren't big enough. Little girls like bright papers with Santa Claus on them and lots of ribbons."

For his part, her father was content to focus all of his discontent upon the huge tray of cookies on the kitchen counter. "These are all store-bought, Jorja. Didn't you make any homemade cookies this year?"

"Well, Dad, I've been working a little overtime lately, and then there're the classes I'm taking at UNLV, and—"

"I know it's hard being a single mother, baby," he said, "but we're talking fundamentals here. Homemade cookies are one of the best parts of Christmas. It's an absolute fundamental."

"Fundamental," Jorja's mother agreed.

The Christmas spirit had been late in coming to Jorja this year, and even now she had a tenuous grip on it. Subject to her parents' well-intentioned but infuriating nonstop commentary on her shortcomings, she might have lost the holiday mood altogether if Marcie had not put in a timely appearance at six-thirty, just after Jorja had slipped a fourteen-pound turkey into the oven for the big meal later in the day. The girl shuffled into the living room in her pajamas, as cute as any idealized child in a Norman Rockwell painting.

"Did Santa bring my Little Ms. Doctor kit?"

Pete said, "He brought you more than that, pumpkin. Look here! Just *look* at all Santa brought."

Marcie turned and saw the tree—which "Santa" had put up during the night—and the mountain of gifts. She gasped. "Wow!"

The child's excitement was transmitted to Jorja's parents, and for the time being they forgot about such things as dusty ventilation hoods and store-bought cookies. For a while the apartment was filled with joyous, busy sounds.

But by the time Marcie had opened half her gifts, the celebratory mood began to change, and in crept a little of the darkness that would reappear in a far more frightening form later in the day. In a whiny voice that was out of character, the girl grumped that Santa had not remembered the Little Ms. Doctor kit. She discarded a much-wanted doll without even taking it out of its box, moving to the next package in the hope that it contained Little Ms. Doctor, clawing at the wrappings. Something in the child's demeanor, a queerness in her eyes, disquieted Jorja. Soon Mary and Pete noticed it as well. They began urging Marcie to take more time with each present, to get more pleasure out of each before rushing on to the next, but their entreaties were not successful.

Jorja had not put the doctor play-kit under the tree; it was hidden in a closet as a final surprise. But with only three boxes left, Marcie was pale and trembling in anticipation of Little Ms. Doctor.

In God's name, what was so important about it? Many of the toys already unwrapped were more expensive and more interesting than the play-doctor's bag. Why was her attention so intently and unnaturally focused on that single item? Why was she so obsessed with it?

When the last of the gifts beneath the tree and the last of those from Mary and Pete were opened, Marcie let out a sob of purest misery. "Santa didn't bring it! He forgot! He forgot!"

Considering all the wondrous presents strewn across the room, the girl's despondency was shocking. Jorja was disconcerted and displeased by Marcie's rudeness, and she saw that her own parents were startled, dismayed, and impatient with this unexpected and unjustified tantrum.

Suddenly afraid that Christmas was collapsing into ruins around her, Jorja ran to the bedroom closet, plucked the crucial gift from behind the shoe boxes, and returned to the living room with it.

With frenzied desperation, Marcie snatched the box from her mother.

"What's gotten into the child?" Mary asked.

"Yeah," Pete said, "what's so important about this Little Doctor?"

Marcie tore frantically at the wrappings until she saw that the package contained the item she most desired. Immediately, she grew calm, stopped trembling. "Little Ms. Doctor. Santa didn't forget!"

"Honey, maybe it's not from Santa," Jorja said. She was relieved to see the child she loved emerging from that strange and unpleasant mood. "Not all your gifts came from Santa. Better look at the tag."

Marcie dutifully searched for the tag, read the few words on it, and looked up with an uncertain smile. "It's from . . . Daddy."

Jorja felt her parents' staring at her, but she did not meet their eyes. They knew that Alan had gone off to Acapulco with his latest bimbo, the airhead blonde named Pepper, and that he had not bothered to leave so much as a card for Marcie, and they no doubt disapproved of Jorja letting him off the hook like this.

Later, when Jorja was in the kitchen, squatting in front of the oven, checking on the turkey, her mother stooped down beside her and said softly, "Why'd you do it, Jorja? Why'd you put that louse's name on the gift she wanted most of all?"

Jorja slid the rack part way out of the oven, bringing the turkey into the light. With a ladle, she scooped the drippings from the pan and basted the roasting bird. Finally she said, "Marcie shouldn't have her Christmas ruined just because her father's a jackass."

"You shouldn't protect her from the truth," Mary said quietly.

"The truth's too ugly for a seven-year-old."

"The sooner she knows what a louse her father is, the better. You know what your dad heard about this woman Alan's living with?"

"I sure hope this bird's going to be done by noon."

Mary would not drop the subject. "She's on the call list of two casinos, Jorja. That's what Pete heard. You know what I mean? She's a call girl. Alan's living with a call girl. What's *wrong* with him?"

Jorja closed her eyes and took a deep breath.

Mary said, "Well, if he wants nothing to do with Marcie, that's fine. God knows what diseases he's picked up living with *that* woman."

Jorja pushed the turkey back into the oven, closed the door, and stood up. "Could we not talk about this any more?"

"I thought you'd want to know what the woman is."

"So now I know."

Their voices dropped lower, became more intense: "What if he comes around some day and says, 'Pepper and I want Marcie to go to Acapulco with us,' or Disneyland, or maybe just stay at their place for a while?"

Exasperated, Jorja said, "Mother, he doesn't want anything to do with Marcie because she reminds him of his responsibilities."

"But what if—"

"Mother, damn it!"

Although Jorja had not raised her voice, there was such anger in those three words that the effect on her mother was immediate. A hurt look crossed Mary's face. Stung, she turned away from Jorja. She went quickly to the refrigerator, opened it, and looked over the contents of the overloaded shelves. "Oh, you made gnocchi."

"Not store-bought," Jorja said shakily. "Homemade." She meant to be conciliatory, but she realized that her comment might be misconstrued as a snide reference to her father's dismay over store-bought cookies. She bit her lip, and fought back scalding tears.

Still looking into the refrigerator, a tremor still in her voice, Mary said, "You're going to have potatoes, too? And what's this—oh, you've already grated the cabbage for coleslaw. I thought you'd need help, but I guess you've thought of everything." She closed the refrigerator door and looked for something she could do to occupy her and get them through this awkward moment. Tears were visible in her eyes.

Jorja virtually flung herself away from the counter and threw her arms around her mother. Mary returned the hug, and for a while they clung to each other, finding speech both unnecessary and impossible.

Holding fast, Mary said, "I don't know why I'm like this. My mother was the same with me. I swore I'd never be like this with you."

"I love you just the way you are."

"Maybe it's because you're my only. If I'd been able to have a couple others, I wouldn't be so tough on you."

"It's partly my fault, Mom. I've been so touchy lately."

"And why shouldn't you be?" her mother said, holding her tight. "That louse walks out on you, you're supporting yourself and Marcie, going to school. . . . You got every *right* to be touchy. We're so proud of you, Jorja. It takes such courage to do what you're doing."

In the living room, Marcie began shrieking.

What now? Jorja wondered.

When she got to the living room archway, she saw her father trying to persuade Marcie to play with a doll. "Look here," Pete said, "dolly cries when you tilt her this way, giggles when you tilt her that way!"

"I don't want to play with the dumb doll," Marcie pouted. She was holding the make-believe plastic-and-rubber hypodermic syringe from the Little Ms. Doctor kit, and that unsettling intensity and urgency had taken possession of her again. "I want to give you another *shot*."

"But honey," Pete said, "you've already given me twenty shots."

"I've got to practice," Marcie said. "I'll never grow up to be my own doctor if I don't start practicing *now*."

Pete looked at Jorja with exasperation.

Mary said, "What *is* it with this Little Ms. Doctor thing?"

"I wish I knew," Jorja said.

Marcie grimaced as she pushed the plunger of the fake hypodermic. Perspiration glistened on her brow.

"I wish I knew," Jorja repeated uneasily.

BOSTON, MASSACHUSETTS.

It was the worst Christmas of Ginger Weiss's life.

Although Jewish, her beloved father had always celebrated Christmas in a secular spirit, because he liked the harmony and good will that the holiday promoted, and after his death, Ginger had continued to regard December 25 as a special day, a time of joy. Until today, Christmas had never depressed her.

George and Rita did all they could to make Ginger feel a part of their celebration, but she was acutely aware that she was an outsider. The Hannabys' three
sons had brought their families to Baywatch for several days, and the huge house
was filled with the silvery laughter of children. Everyone made an effort to include
Ginger in all the Hannaby traditions, from popcorn-stringing to neighborhood
caroling.

Christmas morning, she was there to watch the children attack the mountain
of gifts, and following the example of the other adults, she crawled around on
the floor with the kids, helping them assemble and play with their new toys. For
a couple of hours, her despair abated, and she was assimilated by the Hannaby
family in spite of herself.

However, at lunch—rich with holiday delicacies yet essentially a light meal,
just a hint of the extravagant dinner feast to come that evening—Ginger felt out
of place again. Much conversation involved reminiscences of previous holidays
of which she'd not been a part.

After lunch, she pleaded a headache and escaped to her room. The splendid
view of the bay calmed her but couldn't arrest her spiral into depression. She
desperately hoped Pablo Jackson would call tomorrow and say that he had studied
the problem of memory blocks and was ready to hypnotize her again.

Ginger's visit to Pablo had distressed George and Rita less than she had expected. They were upset that she had gone out alone, risking an amnesic seizure
with no friend to help her, and they made her promise she would allow either
Rita or one of the servants to drive her to and from Pablo's apartment in the
future, but they did not attempt to argue against the unconventional treatment she
had sought from the magician.

The bay view's capacity to calm Ginger was limited. She turned from the
window, got up, and went to the bed, where she was surprised to find two books
on the nightstand. One was a fantasy by Tim Powers, an author she had read
before, the other a copy of something called *Twilight in Babylon,* and she had no
idea where they had come from.

There were half a dozen other books in the room, borrowed from the library
downstairs, for during the past few weeks she had had little to do but read. But
this was the first time she'd seen Powers' book and *Twilight in Babylon.* The
former, a tale of time-traveling trolls fighting their own secret war against British
goblins during the American revolution, looked delightful, the type of exotic story
that her father had enjoyed. A slip of paper laid loosely in the front identified it
as a review copy. Rita had a friend who was a reviewer for the *Globe,* and who
sometimes passed along intriguing books before they were available in the stores.
Evidently, these had come within the last day or two, and Rita, aware of Ginger's
tastes in fiction, had put them in her room.

She set the Powers book aside for later delectation, and she took a closer look
at *Twilight in Babylon.* She had never heard of the author, Dominick Corvaisis,
but the brief summary of the story was intriguing, and when she had read the
first page, she was hooked. However, before continuing, she moved from the bed
to one of the comfortable chairs and, only then, glanced at the author's photograph
on the back of the jacket.

Her breath caught in her throat. Fear filled her.

For a moment she thought the photograph was going to be the kicker that
knocked her into another fugue. She tried to fling the book aside but could not,
tried to stand up but could not. She drew deep breaths, closed her eyes, and
waited for her pulse rate to sink toward normal.

When she opened her eyes and looked at the author's photograph again, it still disturbed her, though not as badly as it had at first. She knew that she had seen this man before, had met him somewhere, and not in the best of circumstances, though she could not remember where or when. His brief biography on the jacket flap informed her that he had lived in Portland, Oregon, and now resided in Laguna Beach, California. As she had never been in either of those places, she could not imagine when their paths might have crossed. Dominick Corvaisis, about thirty-five, was a striking man who reminded Ginger of Anthony Perkins when that actor had been younger. His looks were compelling enough that she could not imagine having forgotten where she had met him.

Her instant reaction to the photo was strange, and some might have dismissed it as a meaningless fillip of an overwrought mind. But during the past two months she had learned to respect strange developments and to look for meaning in them, no matter how meaningless they seemed.

She stared at Corvaisis' photograph, hoping to nudge her memory. Finally, with an almost clairvoyant sense that *Twilight in Babylon* would somehow change her life, she opened it and began to read.

CHICAGO, ILLINOIS.

From University Hospital, Father Stefan Wycazik drove across town to the laboratory operated by the Scientific Investigation Division of the Chicago Police Department. Though it was Christmas Day, municipal workers were still cleaning last night's snowfall from the streets.

Only a couple of men were on duty at the police lab, which was located in an aging government building, and the old rooms had the deserted feeling of an elaborate Egyptian tomb buried far beneath desert sands. Footsteps echoed resoundingly back and forth between the tile floors and the high ceilings.

Ordinarily, the lab did not share its information with anyone from outside the police and judicial systems. But half the police officers in Chicago were Catholics, which meant that Father Wycazik had more than a few friends on the force. Stefan had importuned some of those friends to make petitions in his name and to pave the way for him at the SID.

He was greeted by Dr. Murphy Aimes, a paunchy man with a perfectly bald head and walrus mustache. They'd spoken on the telephone earlier, before Stefan left the rectory for University Hospital, and now Murphy Aimes was ready for him. They settled on two stools at a laboratory bench. A tall opaque window loomed in front of them, decorated with dark streaks of pigeon dung. On the marble top of the bench, Aimes had laid out a file folder and several other items.

"I must say, Father, I'd never compromise case information like this if there were any possibility of a trial arising from the shootout at that sandwich shop. But I suppose, as both perpetrators are dead, there's no one to be put on trial."

"I appreciate that, Dr. Aimes. I really do. And I'm grateful for the time and energy you've expended on my behalf."

Curiosity ruled Murphy Aimes's face. He said, "I don't really understand the reason for your interest in the case."

"I'm not entirely sure of it myself," Stefan said cryptically.

He had not revealed his purpose to the higher authorities who had made him welcome at the lab, and he did not intend to enlighten Aimes, either. For one thing, if he told them what was on his mind, they would think he was dotty and would be less inclined to cooperate with him.

"Well," Aimes said, miffed at not being taken into Stefan's confidence, "you asked about the bullets." He opened a manila envelope of the type that ties shut with a string, and he emptied its contents into his palm: two gray lumps of lead. "The surgeon removed these from Winton Tolk. You said you were particularly interested in them."

"I certainly am," Stefan said, taking them in his own hand when Aimes offered them. "You've weighed these, I suppose. I understand that's standard procedure. And they weigh what .38 slugs should?"

"If you mean, did they fragment on impact—they did not. They're so misshapen they must've impacted bone, so it's surprising they didn't fragment a little—or a lot—but in fact they're both intact."

"Actually," Father Wycazik said, staring at the slugs in his hand, "I meant were they underweight for .38s? Malformed ammunition, factory mistakes? Or were they the right size?"

"Oh, the right size. No doubt of that."

"Big enough to do plenty of damage, terrible damage," Father Wycazik said thoughtfully. "The gun?"

From a larger envelope, Aimes produced the revolver with which Winton Tolk was shot. "A snubnose Smith and Wesson .38 Chief's Special."

"You've examined it, test-fired it?"

"Yes. Standard procedure."

"No indication that anything's wrong with it? Specifically, is the bore poorly machined or is there some other anomaly that'd result in the bullet leaving the muzzle at a much slower velocity than it should?"

"That's a peculiar question, Father. The answer is no. It's a fine Chief's Special, up to the usual high standards of Smith and Wesson."

Putting the two expended bullets back into the small envelope from which he had seen Aimes take them, Father Wycazik said, "What about the cartridges these bullets came from? Is there any chance they were filled with too little powder, that they carried an inadequate charge?"

The SID man blinked. "I gather one thing you're trying to find out is why two .38s in the chest didn't do more damage."

Stefan Wycazik nodded but offered no elaboration. "Were there any unexpended cartridges in the revolver?"

"A couple. Plus spare ammunition in one of the gunman's jacket pockets— another dozen."

"Did you cut open any of the unexpended shells to see if maybe they carried an inadequate charge?"

"No reason to," Murphy Aimes said.

"Would it be possible for you to check one of them now?"

"Possible. But why? Father, what in the world is this all about?"

Stefan sighed. "I know this is an imposition, Dr. Aimes, and it behooves me to repay your kindness with an explanation. But I can't. Not yet. Priests, like physicians and attorneys, must sometimes respect confidences, keep secrets. But if I'm ever at liberty to reveal what lies behind my curiosity, you'll be the first to know."

Aimes stared and Stefan met his eyes forthrightly. Finally the SID man opened another envelope. This contained the unexpended cartridges from the dead gunman's .38 Chief's Special. "Wait here."

In twenty minutes, Aimes returned with a white enamel lab tray in which were two dissected .38 Special cartridges. Using a pencil as a pointer, he commented on the disassembled elements. "This is the case head in which the primer assembly is seated. The firing pin strikes here. This opening on the other side of the case head is the flashhole that leads from the primer packet to the powder compartment. There's no problem with this, no manufacturing errors. At the other end of the cartridge, you've got a lead semiwadcutter bullet with a copper gas-check crimped onto its base to retard bore leading. The tiny cannelures around the bullet are packed with grease to ease its passage through the barrel. Nothing out of order here, either. And in between the case head and the bullet is the powder compartment—or it's sometimes called the combustion chamber—out of which I've taken this small pile of gray, flaky material. This is nitrocellulose, a highly combustible material; it's ignited by the spark that comes through the flashhole from the primer; it explodes, ejecting the bullet from the cartridge. As you can see, there's enough nitrocellulose to fill the powder chamber. Just to be sure, I opened another round.'' Aimes pointed the pencil at the second disassembled cartridge. ''There was nothing wrong with this, either. The gunman was using well-made, reliable, Remington ammunition. Officer Tolk was just a lucky man, Father, a very lucky man.''

NEW YORK, NEW YORK.

Jack Twist spent Christmas in the sanitarium room with Jenny, his wife of thirteen years. Being with her on holidays was especially grim. But being anywhere else, leaving her alone, would have been grimmer.

Although Jenny had spent almost two-thirds of their marriage in a coma, the years of lost communion had not diminished Jack's love for her. More than eight years had passed since she had smiled at him or spoken his name or been able to return his kisses, but in his heart, at least, time was stopped, and she was still the beautiful Jenny Mae Alexander, a fresh-faced young bride.

Incarcerated in that Central American prison, he had been sustained by the knowledge that Jenny waited at home for him, missed him, worried about him, and prayed each night for his safe return. Throughout his ordeal of torture and periodic starvation, he had clung to the hope that he would one day feel Jenny's arms around him and hear her marvelous laugh. That hope had kept him alive and sane.

Of the four captured Rangers, only Jack and his buddy Oscar Weston survived and came home, though their escape was a near thing. They had waited almost a year to be rescued, confident that their country would not leave them to rot. Sometimes they debated whether they would be freed by commandos or through diplomatic channels. After eleven months, they still believed their countrymen would bail them out, but they no longer dared to wait. They had lost weight and were dangerously thin, undernourished. They had also suffered unknown tropical fevers without treatment, which had further debilitated them.

Their only opportunity for escape was during one of their regular visits to the People's Center for Justice. Every four weeks, Jack and Oscar had been taken from their cells and driven to the People's Center—a clean, well-lighted, unwalled, unbarred institution in the heart of the capital—a model prison meant to impress foreign journalists with the current regime's humanitarianism. There, they were given showers, deloused, put in clean clothes, handcuffed to prevent gesturing, and seated before videotape cameras to be politely questioned. Usually, they answered questions with obscenities or wisecracks. Their answers did not matter because the tape was edited, and answers they had never made were dubbed in by linguists who could speak unaccented English.

Once the propaganda film had been made, they were interviewed over closed-circuit television by foreign reporters gathered in another room. The camera never provided closeups of them, and their answers were not heard by those who asked the questions; instead, once again, unseen intelligence men, stationed at another microphone outside the camera's range, answered for them.

At the start of their eleventh month in captivity, Jack and Oscar began making plans to escape the next time they were transported to that far less secure, less heavily guarded propaganda facility.

The once-formidable strength of their young bodies had been leached away, and their only weapons were shivs and needles made of rat bones, which they had painstakingly shaped and sharpened by rubbing them against the stone walls of the cells. Wickedly sharp, those instruments nevertheless made pathetic weapons; yet Jack and Oscar hoped to triumph over gun-toting guards.

Surprisingly, they *did* triumph. Once inside the People's Center, they were remanded into the custody of a single guard who escorted them to the showers on the second floor. The guard kept his gun holstered, probably because the facility was a detention center inside the larger detention center of the capital city itself. The guard was certain Jack and Oscar were demoralized, weak, and unarmed, so he was surprised when they suddenly turned on him and, with shocking savagery, stabbed him with the bone shivs they had concealed in their clothes. Pierced twice in the throat, his right eye skewered, he succumbed without producing a scream that might have drawn other police or soldiers.

Before their break was discovered, Jack and Oscar confiscated the dead guard's handgun and ammunition, then made bold use of the hallways, risking notice, alarm, and capture. But it was, after all, a minimum security "reeducation" center, and they were able to make their way to a stairwell and down to a dimly lighted basement, where they progressed swiftly and stealthily through a series of musty storage rooms. At the end of the building, they found the loading docks and a way out.

Seven or eight large boxes had just been off-loaded from a delivery truck, which was backed up to the nearest of the two big bays, and the driver was engaged in an argument with another man, both of whom were shaking clipboards at each other. Those two were the only men in sight, and as they turned and headed toward a glass-enclosed office, Jack and Oscar raced silently to the recently unloaded boxes and from there into the back of the delivery truck, where they made a nest for themselves behind the as-yet-undelivered packages. In a few minutes the driver returned, cursing, slammed the truck's cargo-bay door, and drove away into the city before the alarm sounded.

Ten minutes and many blocks from the People's Center, the truck stopped. The driver unbolted the rear doors, took out a single package without realizing Jack and Oscar were inches from him behind a wall of boxes, and went into the building before which he'd parked. Extricating themselves from their burrow, Jack and Oscar fled.

Within a few blocks they found themselves in a district of muddy streets and dilapidated shanties, where the poverty-stricken residents were no fonder of the new tyrants than they had been of the old and were willing to hide two Yankees on the lam. After nightfall, supplied with what little food the slum-dwellers could spare, they departed for the outskirts. When they came to open farmland, they broke into a barn and stole a sharp sickle, several withered apples, a leather blacksmith's apron and some burlap bags which could be used to fashion makeshift shoes when their shabby prison-issue eventually fell apart—and a horse. Before dawn, they had reached the edge of the true jungle, where they abandoned the horse and set out on foot once more.

Weak, poorly provisioned, armed only with the sickle—and the gun they had taken off the guard—without a compass and therefore required to plot a course by the sun and the stars, they headed north through the tropical forests toward the border, eighty miles away. Throughout that nightmare journey, Jack had one vital aid to survival: Jenny. He thought of her, dreamed of her, longed for her, and seven days later, when he and Oscar reached friendly territory, Jack knew that he had made it as much because of Jenny as because of his Ranger training.

At that point he thought the worst was behind him. He was wrong.

Now, sitting beside his wife's bed, with Christmas music on the tape deck, Jack Twist was suddenly overcome with grief. Christmas was a bad time because he could not help but remember how dreams of her had sustained him through his Christmas in prison—when in fact she had already been in a coma and lost to him.

Happy holidays.

CHICAGO, ILLINOIS.

As Father Stefan Wycazik moved through the halls and wards of St. Joseph's Hospital for Children, his spirits soared. That was no small thing, for he was already in a buoyant and elevated state.

The hospital was crowded with visitors, and Christmas music issued from the public address system. Mothers, fathers, brothers, sisters, grandparents, other relatives, and friends of the young patients were on hand with gifts, goodies, and good wishes, and there was more laughter in that usually grim place than one might ordinarily hear echoing through its chambers in an entire month. Even most of the seriously afflicted patients were smiling broadly and talking animatedly, their suffering forgotten for the time being.

Nowhere in the hospital was there more hope or laughter than among those people gathered around the bed of ten-year-old Emmeline Halbourg. When Father Wycazik introduced himself, he was greeted warmly by Emmy Halbourg's parents, two sisters, grandparents, one aunt, and one uncle, who assumed he was one of the hospital's chaplains.

Because of what he'd learned from Brendan Cronin yesterday, Stefan expected to find a happily mending little girl; but he was unprepared for Emmy's condition. She was positively *glowing*. Only two weeks ago, according to Brendan, she had been crippled and dying. But now her dark eyes were clear, and her former pallor was gone, replaced by a wholesome flush. Her knuckles and wrists were not swollen, and she seemed to be completely free of pain. She looked not like a sick child valiantly fighting her way back to health; rather, she seemed *already* cured.

Most startling of all, Emmy was not lying in bed but standing with the aid of crutches, moving among her delighted and admiring relatives. Her wheelchair was gone.

"Well," Stefan said, after a brief visit, "I must be going, Emmy. I only stopped by to wish you a merry Christmas from a friend of yours. Brendan Cronin."

"Pudge!" she said happily. "He's wonderful, isn't he? It was awful when he stopped working here. We miss him a lot."

Emmy's mother said, "I never met this Pudge, but from the way the kids talked about him, he must've been good medicine for them."

"He only worked here one week," Emmy said. "But he comes back—did you know? Every few days he comes back to visit. I was hoping he'd come today, so I could give him a big Christmas kiss."

"He wanted to stop by, but he's spending Christmas with his folks."

"Oh, that's good! That's what Christmas is for—isn't it, Father? Being together with your folks, having fun and loving each other."

"Yes, Emmy," Stefan Wycazik said, thinking that no theologian or philosopher could have put it better. "That's what Christmas is for."

If Stefan had been alone with the girl, he would have asked her about the afternoon of December 11. That was the day Brendan had been brushing her hair while she sat in her wheelchair before this very window. Stefan wanted to know about the rings on Brendan's hands, which had appeared for the first time that day, and which Emmeline had noticed before Brendan himself spotted them. He wanted to ask Emmy if she had felt anything unusual when Brendan had touched her. But there were too many adults around, and they would surely ask awkward questions. Stefan was not yet prepared to reveal the reasons for his curiosity.

LAS VEGAS, NEVADA.

After getting off to a rocky start, Christmas at the Monatella apartment improved dramatically. Mary and Pete stopped hammering Jorja with their well-meant but unwanted advice and criticism. They loosened up and involved themselves in Marcie's play the way grandparents should, and Jorja was reminded of just why she loved them so much. The holiday dinner was on the table at twelve-fifty, only twenty minutes late, and it was delicious. By the time Marcie sat down to eat, she had worked off her all-consuming interest in Little Ms. Doctor, and she did not rush through her meal. It was a leisurely dinner with much chit-chat and laughter, the Christmas tree twinkling in the background. Those were golden hours until, during dessert, the trouble started with surprising suddenness. With frightening speed, it escalated to total disaster.

Teasing Marcie, Pete said, "Where does a little bitty thing like you put so much food? You've eaten more than the rest of us combined!"

"Oh, Grandpa."

"It's true! You've been really shoveling it in. One more bite of that pumpkin pie, and you're going to *explode*."

Marcie lifted another forkful, held it up for all to see, and with great theatricality, she moved it toward her mouth.

"No, don't!" Pete said, putting his hands in front of his face as if to protect himself from the blast.

Marcie popped the morsel into her mouth, chewed, and swallowed. "See? I didn't explode."

"You will with the *next* bite," Pete said. "I was just one bite too soon. You'll explode . . . or else we'll have to rush you to the hospital."

Marcie frowned. "No hospital."

"Oh, yes," Pete said. "You'll be all swollen up, ready to burst, and we'll have to rush you to the hospital and have them deflate you."

"No hospital," Marcie repeated adamantly.

Jorja realized that her daughter's voice had changed, that the girl was no longer participating in the game but was, instead, genuinely if inexplicably . . . frightened. She was not scared of exploding, of course, but evidently the mere *thought* of a hospital had caused her to go pale.

"No hospital," Marcie repeated, a haunted look in her eyes.

"Oh, yes," Pete said, not yet aware of the change in the child.

Jorja tried to deflect him: "Dad, I think we—"

But Pete said, "Of course, they won't take you in an ambulance 'cause you'll be too big. We'll have to rent a truck to haul you."

The girl shook her head violently. "I won't go to a h-h-hospital in a million years. I won't ever let those doctors touch me."

"Honey," Jorja said, "Grandpa's only *teasing*. He doesn't really—"

Unplacated, the girl said, "Those hospital people will h-hurt me like they hurt me before. I won't let them hurt me again."

Mary looked at Jorja, baffled. "When was she in the hospital?"

"She wasn't," Jorja said. "I don't know why she—"

"I was, I was, I was! They t-tied me down in bed, stuck me full of n-needles, and I was scared, and I won't ever let them touch me again."

Remembering the strange tantrum that Kara Persaghian had reported yesterday, Jorja moved swiftly to forestall a similar scene. She put one hand on Marcie's shoulder and said, "Honey, you were never—"

"I *was!*" The girl's anger and fear burgeoned into rage and terror. She threw her fork, and Pete ducked to avoid being hit by it.

"Marcie!" Jorja cried.

The girl slipped off her chair and backed away from the table, white-faced. "I'm going to grow up and be my own doctor, so nobody else'll stick n-needles in me." Words gave way to a pitiful moaning.

Jorja went after Marcie, reaching for her. "Honey, don't."

Marcie held her hands out in front of her, as if warding off an attack, although it was not her mother that she feared. She was looking *through* Jorja, perhaps seeing some imaginary threat, though her terror was real. She was not merely pale but translucent, as if the very substance of her was evaporating in the tremendous heat of her terror.

"Marcie, what is it?"

The girl stumbled backward into a corner, shuddering.

Jorja gripped her daughter's defensively raised hands. "Marcie, talk to me." But even as Jorja spoke, a sudden stench of urine filled the air, and she saw a dark stain spreading from the crotch down both legs of Marcie's jeans. "Marcie!"

The girl was trying to scream, but could not.

"What's happening?" Mary asked. "What's wrong?"

"I don't know," Jorja said. "God help me, I don't know."

With her eyes still focused on some figure or object that remained visible only to her, Marcie began a wordless keening.

NEW YORK, NEW YORK.

The tape deck still played Christmas music, and Jenny Twist lay immobile and insensate, but Jack no longer engaged in the frustrating one-way communication with which he had filled the first few hours of his visit. Now he sat in silence, and inevitably his thoughts drifted back through the years to his homecoming from Central America. . . .

Upon returning to the States, he had discovered that the rescue of the prisoners at the Institute of Brotherhood had been misrepresented, in some quarters, as a terrorist act, a mass kidnapping, a provocation meant to spark a war. He and every Ranger involved were painted as criminals in uniform, and those taken prisoner were for some reason the special focus of the opposition's anger.

In a political panic, Congress had banned *all* covert activities in Central America, including a pending plan to rescue the four Rangers. Their release was to be arranged strictly through diplomatic channels.

That was why they had waited in vain for rescue. Their country had abandoned them. At first Jack had trouble believing it. When at last he believed, it was the second worst shock of his life.

Having won his freedom, home again, Jack was relentlessly pursued by hostile journalists and subpoenaed to appear before a Congressional committee to testify about his involvement in the raid. He expected to have a chance to set the record straight, but he quickly discovered that they weren't interested in his viewpoint, and that the televised hearing was merely an opportunity for politicians to do some grandstanding in the infamous tradition of Joe McCarthy.

In a few months, most people had forgotten him, and when he regained the pounds he had lost in prison, they ceased to recognize him as the alleged war criminal they had seen on television. But the pain and the sense of betrayal continued to burn fiercely in him.

If being abandoned by his country was the second worst shock of his life, the worst was what had happened to Jenny while he had been stuck in that Central American prison. A thug had accosted her in the hallway of her own apartment building as she was coming home from work. He put a gun to her head, hustled her into her apartment, sodomized and raped her, clubbed her brutally with his pistol, and left her for dead.

When Jack came home at last, he found Jenny in a state institution, comatose. The level of care she had been getting was abominable.

Norman Hazzurt, the rapist who attacked Jenny, had been tracked down through fingerprints and witnesses, but a clever defense attorney had managed to delay the trial. Undertaking an investigation of his own, Jack satisfied himself that Hazzurt, with a history of violent sex offenses, was the guilty man. He also became convinced that Hazzurt would be acquitted on a technicality.

Throughout his ordeal with the press and politicians, Jack made plans for the future. There were two primary tasks ahead of him: First, he would kill Norman Hazzurt in such a way as to avoid any suspicion falling upon himself; second, he would get enough money to move Jenny to a private sanitarium, though the only way to obtain so much cash in a hurry was to steal it. As an elite Ranger, he was trained in most weapons, explosives, martial arts, and survival techniques. His society had failed him, but it had also provided him with the knowledge and the means by which he could extract his revenge, and it had taught him how to break whatever laws stood in his way without punishment.

Norman Hazzurt died in an "accidental" gas explosion two months after Jack returned to the States. And two weeks later, Jenny's transference to a private sanitarium was financed by the proceeds from an ingenious bank robbery executed with military precision.

The murder of Hazzurt did not satisfy Jack. In fact, it depressed him. Killing in a war was different from killing in civilian life. He did not have the detachment to kill except in self-defense.

Robbery, however, was enormously appealing. After the successful bank job, he'd been excited, exalted, exhilarated. Daring robbery had a medicinal quality. Crime gave him a reason to live. Until recently.

Now, sitting at Jenny's bedside, Jack Twist wondered what would keep him going, day after day, if not grand larceny. The only other thing he had was Jenny. However, he no longer needed to provide for her; he had already piled up more than enough money for that. So his only reason for living was to come here several times a week, look upon her serene face, hold her hand—and pray for a miracle.

It was ironic that a man like him—a hard-headed, self-reliant individualist—should have no hope but mysticism.

As he brooded on that, he heard Jenny make a soft gurgling sound. She took two quick, deep breaths and produced a long, rattling sigh. For one crazy moment as he rose from his chair, Jack half-expected to find her eyes open, filled with awareness for the first time in more than eight years, the miracle having come to pass even as he had been day-dreaming of it. But her eyes were closed, and her face was slack. He put a hand against her face, then moved it to her throat. He felt for her pulse. What had happened was not, in fact, miraculous but *anti-miraculous*, mundane, and inevitable: Jenny Twist had died.

CHICAGO, ILLINOIS.

Few physicians were on duty at St. Joseph's that Christmas, but a resident named Jarvil and an intern named Klinet were eager to talk to Father Wycazik about Emmeline Halbourg's amazing recovery.

Klinet, an intense wiry-haired young man, escorted Stefan to a consultation room to review Emmy's file and X rays. "Five weeks ago, she was started on namiloxiprine—a new drug, just approved by the FDA."

Dr. Jarvil, the resident, was soft-spoken, with heavy-lidded eyes, but when he joined them in the consultation room, he too was visibly excited by Emmeline Halbourg's dramatic turn for the better.

"Namiloxiprine has several effects in bone diseases like Emmy's," Jarvil said. "In many instances it puts a stop to the destruction of the periosteum, promotes the growth of healthy osteocytes, and somewhat induces the accumulation of intercellular calcium. And in a case like Emmy's, where the bone marrow is the primary target of the disease, namiloxiprine creates an unusual chemical environment in the marrow cavity and in the haversian canals, an environment that's extremely hostile to microorganisms but actually *encourages* the growth of marrow cells, the production of blood cells, and hemoglobin formation."

"But it's not supposed to work *this* fast," Klinet said.

"And it's basically a stop-loss drug," Jarvil said. "It can arrest the progress of a disease, put a stop to bone deterioration. But it doesn't make regeneration possible. Sure, it's supposed to promote *some* reconstruction, but not the kind of rebuilding we're seeing in Emmy."

"*Fast* rebuilding," Klinet said, smacking his forehead with the heel of his hand, as if to knock this amazing fact into his unwilling brain.

They showed Stefan a series of X rays taken over the past six weeks, in which the changes in Emmy's bones and joints were obvious.

Klinet said, "She'd been on namiloxiprine for three weeks without noticeable effect, and then suddenly, two weeks ago, her body not only went into a state of remission but began rebuilding damaged tissues."

The timing of the girl's turnaround coincided perfectly with the first appearance of the strange rings on Brendan Cronin's hands. However, Stefan Wycazik made no mention of that coincidence.

Jarvil produced more X rays and tests that showed a remarkable improvement in the child's haversian canals, the elaborate network that carried small blood vessels and lymphatics throughout the bone for the purpose of maintenance and repair. Many of these had been clogged with a plaquelike substance that pinched off the vessels passing through them. In the past two weeks, however, the plaque almost disappeared, allowing the full circulation required for healing and regeneration.

"No one even knew that namiloxiprine could clean out the canals this way," Jarvil said. "No record of it. Oh, yes, minor unclogging, but only as a consequence of getting the disease itself under control. Nothing like this. Amazing."

"If regeneration continues at this rate," Klinet said, "Emmy could be a normal, healthy girl in three months. Really phenomenal."

Jarvil said, "She could be well again."

They grinned at Father Wycazik, and he did not have the heart to suggest that neither their hard work nor the wonder drug was responsible for Emmeline Halbourg's cure. They were euphoric, so Stefan kept to himself the possibility that Emmy's cure had been effected by some power far more mysterious than modern medicine.

MILWAUKEE, WISCONSIN.

Christmas Day with Lucy, Frank, and the grandchildren was fun and therapeutic for Ernie and Faye Block. By the time they went out for a walk (just the two of them) toward the end of the afternoon, they were feeling better than they had in months.

The weather was perfect for walking: cold, crisp, but without wind. The most recent snowfall was four days old, so the sidewalks were clear. As twilight approached, the air shimmered with a purple radiance.

Bundled in heavy coats and scarves, Faye and Ernie strolled arm in arm, talking animatedly about the day's events, enjoying the Christmas displays that Lucy's and Frank's neighbors had erected on their front lawns. The years slipped away, and Faye felt as if she and Ernie were still newlyweds, young and full of dreams.

From the moment they had arrived in Milwaukee on December 15, ten days ago, Faye had reason to hope that everything was going to work out all right. Ernie had seemed better—a new bounciness in his step, more genuine good humor in his smile. Evidently, just basking in the love of his daughter, son-in-law, and grandchildren was sufficient to burn away some of the crippling fear that had become the central fact of his life.

The therapy sessions with Dr. Fontelaine, six so far, had also been remarkably beneficial. Ernie was still afraid of the dark but far less terrified than when they left Nevada. Phobias, according to the doctor, were easy to treat compared to many other psychiatric disorders. In recent years therapists had discovered that, in most cases, the symptoms *were* the disease rather than merely shadows cast by unresolved conflicts in the patient's subconscious. It was no longer considered necessary—or even possible or desirable—to seek the psychological causes of the condition in order to treat it. Long courses of therapy had been abandoned in favor of teaching the patient desensitization techniques that could eradicate the symptoms in months or even weeks.

Approximately a third of all phobics could not be helped by these methods and, instead, required long-term treatment and even panic-blocking drugs like alprazolam. But Ernie had improved at a pace that even Dr. Fontelaine, an optimist by nature, found astonishing.

Faye had been reading extensively about phobias and had discovered she could help Ernie by digging up amusing, curious facts that allowed him to view his condition from a different—less fearsome—perspective. He was especially fond of hearing about bizarre phobias that made his terror of the dark seem reasonable by comparison. For example, knowing there were pteronophobics out there, people who lived in constant and unreasonable fear of feathers, made his abhorrence of nightfall seem not only bearable but almost ordinary and logical, as well. Ichthyophobes were horrified by the prospect of encountering a fish, and pediophobes ran screaming at the sight of a doll. And Ernie's nyctophobia was certainly preferable to coitophobia (the fear of sexual intercourse), and not a fraction as debilitating as autophobia (the fear of oneself).

Now, walking through the twilight, Faye tried to keep Ernie's mind off the descending darkness by telling him about the late author, John Cheever, winner of the National Book Award, who'd been gephyrophobic. Cheever had suffered from a crippling fear of crossing high bridges.

Ernie listened with fascination, but he was no less aware of the onset of night-fall. As the shadows lengthened across the snow, his hand steadily tightened on her arm until it would have been painful if she had not been wearing a thick sweater and heavy coat.

By the time they had gone seven blocks, they were too far from the house to have any hope of returning to it before full darkness settled on the land. Two-thirds of the sky was black already, and the other third was deep purple. The shadows had spread like spilt ink.

The streetlamps had come on. Faye halted Ernie in a cone of light, giving him a brief reprieve. His eyes had a wild look, and his steaming exhalations rushed from him at a rate that indicated incipient panic.

"Remember to control your breathing," Faye said.

He nodded and began at once to take deeper, slower breaths.

When all the light in the sky had been extinguished, she said, "Ready to go back?"

"Ready," he said hollowly.

They stepped out of the glow of the streetlamp, into darkness, heading back toward the house, and Ernie hissed between clenched teeth.

What they were engaged upon, for the third time, was a dramatic therapeutic technique called "flooding," in which the phobic was encouraged to confront the thing he feared and to endure it long enough to break its hold on him. Flooding is based on the fact that panic attacks are self-limiting. The human body cannot sustain a very high level of panic indefinitely, cannot produce endless adrenaline, so the mind must adapt to, and make peace—or at least a truce—with what it fears. Unmodified flooding can be a cruel, barbaric method of cracking a phobia, for it puts the patient at risk of a breakdown. Dr. Fontelaine preferred a modified version of the technique involving three stages of confrontation with the source of fear.

The first stage, in Ernie's case, was to put himself in darkness for fifteen minutes, but with Faye at his side for support and with lighted areas easily accessible. Now, each time they arrived at the lighted sidewalk beneath a streetlamp, they paused to let him gather his courage, then went on into the next patch of darkness.

The second stage, which they would try in another week or two, after more sessions with the doctor, would involve driving to a place where there were no streetlamps, no easily reached lighted areas. There, they would walk together arm in arm across an unrelieved vista of darkness until Ernie could tolerate no more, at which time Faye would switch on a flashlight and give him a moment's respite.

In the third stage of treatment, Ernie would go for a stroll alone in a completely dark area. After a few outings like that, he would almost certainly be cured.

But he was not cured yet, and by the time they covered six blocks of the seven-block return journey to the house, Ernie was breathing like a well-run racehorse, and he bolted for the safety of the light inside. Not bad, though—six blocks. Better than before. At this rate, he would be cured in no time.

As Faye followed him into the house, where Lucy was already helping him out of his coat, she tried to feel good about his progress to date. If this pace held, he would complete the third and final stage weeks—maybe even a couple of months—ahead of schedule. That was what worried Faye. His rapid improvement was amazing; it seemed too rapid and too amazing to be real. She wanted to believe the nightmare would be put behind them quickly, but the pace of his recuperation made her wonder if it was lasting. Striving always to think positive, Faye Block was nevertheless plagued by the instinctive and unnerving feeling that something was wrong. Very wrong.

BOSTON, MASSACHUSETTS.

Inevitably, given his exotic background as a godson of Picasso and a once-famous European stage performer, Pablo Jackson was a star in Boston social circles. Furthermore, during World War II, he had been a liaison between British Intelligence and the French Resistance forces, and his recent work as a hypnotist with police agencies had only added to his mystique. He never lacked invitations.

On the evening of Christmas Day, Pablo attended a black-tie dinner party for twenty-two at the home of Mr. and Mrs. Ira Hergensheimer in Brookline. The house was a splendid brick Georgian Colonial, as elegant and warmly welcoming as the Hergensheimers themselves, who had made their money in real estate during the 1950s. A bartender was on duty in the library, and white-jacketed waiters circulated through the enormous drawing room with champagne and canapés, and in the foyer a string quartet played just loudly enough to provide pleasant background music.

Among that engaging company, the man of most interest to Pablo was Alexander Christophson, former Ambassador to the Court of St. James's, one-term United States Senator from Massachusetts, later Director of the Central Intelligence Agency, now retired almost a decade, whom Pablo had known half a century. Now seventy-six, Christophson was the second eldest guest, but old age had been nearly as kind to him as to Pablo. He was tall, distinguished, with remarkably few lines in his classic Bostonian face. His mind was as sharp as ever. The true length of his journey on the earth was betrayed only by a mild trace of Parkinson's disease which, in spite of medication, left him with a tremor in his right hand.

Half an hour before dinner, Pablo eased Alex away from the other guests and led him to Ira Hergensheimer's oak-paneled study, adjacent to the library, for a private conversation. The old magician closed the door behind them, and they carried their glasses of champagne to a pair of leather wingback chairs by the window. "Alex, I need your advice."

"Well, as you know," Alex said, "men our age find it especially satisfying to give advice. It compensates for no longer being able to set a bad example ourselves. But I can't imagine what advice I could give on any problem that you wouldn't already have thought of yourself."

"Yesterday," Pablo said, "a young woman came to see me. She's an exceedingly lovely, charming, and intelligent woman who's accustomed to solving her own problems, but now she's bumped up against something very strange. She desperately needs help."

Alex raised his eyebrows. "Beautiful young women still come to you for help at eighty-one? I am impressed, humbled, and envious, Pablo."

"This is not a *coup de foudre,* you filthy-minded old lizard. Passion isn't involved." Without mentioning Ginger Weiss's name or occupation, Pablo discussed her problem—the bizarre and inexplicable fugues—and recounted the session of hypnotic regression that had ended with her frightening withdrawal. "She actually seemed to retreat into a deep self-induced coma, perhaps even into death, to avoid my questions. Naturally, I refused to put her in a trance again and risk another withdrawal of that severity. But I promised to do some research to see if any similar case was on record. I found myself poring through books most of last evening and this morning, searching for references to memory blocks with self-destruction built into them. At last I found it . . . in one of your books. Of course, you were writing about an *imposed* psychological condition as a result of brainwashing, and this woman's block is of her own creation; but the similarity is there.''

Drawing on his experiences in the intelligence services during World War II and the subsequent cold war, Alex Christophson had written several books, including two that dealt with brainwashing. In one, Alex had described a technique he called the Azrael Block (naming it for one of the angels of death) that seemed uncannily like the barrier that surrounded Ginger Weiss's memory of some traumatic event in her past.

As distant string music came to them muffled by the closed study door, Alex put down his champagne glass because his hands trembled too violently. He said, ''I don't suppose you'd drop this matter and forget all about it? Because I'm telling you that's the wisest course.''

''Well,'' Pablo said, a bit surprised by the ominous tone of his friend's voice, ''I've promised her I'll try to help.''

''I've been retired eight years, and my instincts aren't what they once were. But I have a very bad feeling about this. Drop it, Pablo. Don't see her again. Don't try to help her any more.''

''But, Alex, I've promised her.''

''I was afraid that'd be your position.'' Alex folded his tremulous hands. ''Okay. The Azrael Block . . . It's not something that Western intelligence services use often, but the Soviets find it invaluable. For example, let's imagine a topnotch Russian agent named Ivan, an operative with thirty years' service in the KGB. In Ivan's memory there'll be an incredible amount of highly sensitive information that, were it to fall into Western hands, would devastate Russian espionage networks. Ivan's superiors constantly worry that, on some foreign assignment, he'll be identified and interrogated.''

''As I understand it, with current drugs and hypnotic techniques, no one can withhold information from a determined interrogator.''

''Exactly. No matter how tough he is, Ivan will spill all he knows without being tortured. For that reason, his superiors would prefer to send younger agents who, if caught, would have less valuable information to reveal. But many situations require a seasoned man like Ivan, so the possibility of all his knowledge falling into enemy hands is a nightmare with which his superiors must live, whether they like it or not.''

''The risk of doing business.''

''Exactly. However, let's imagine that, among all the sensitive knowledge in his head, Ivan knows two or three things that're *especially* sensitive, so explosive that their revelation could destroy his country. These particular memories, less than one percent of his knowledge about KGB operations, could be suppressed without affecting his performance in the field. We're talking here about the suppression of a very tiny portion of his memories. Then, if he fell into enemy hands, he'd still give up a great deal of valuable stuff during interrogation—but at least he would not be able to reveal those few most crucial memories.''

''And this is where the Azrael Block comes in,'' Pablo said. ''Ivan's own people use drugs and hypnosis to seal off certain parts of his past before sending him overseas on his next assignment.''

Alex nodded. ''For example . . . say that years ago Ivan was one of the agents involved in the attempted assassination of Pope John Paul II. With a memory block in place, his awareness of that involvement could be locked in his subconscious, beyond the reach of potential interrogators, without affecting his work on new assignments. But not just any block will do. If Ivan's interrogators discover a standard memory block, they'll work diligently to unlock it, because they'll know that what lies behind it is of enormous importance. So the barrier must be one that cannot be tampered with. The Azrael Block is perfect. When the subject is questioned about the forbidden topic, he's programmed to retreat into a deep coma where he cannot hear the inquisitioner's voice—and even into death. In fact, it should more accurately be called the Azrael Trigger, because if the interrogator probes into the blocked memories, he pulls that trigger, shooting Ivan into a coma, and if he continues to pull the trigger he may eventually kill the subject.''

Fascinated, Pablo said, ''But isn't the survival instinct strong enough to overcome the block? When it comes to the point that Ivan must either remember and reveal what he has forgotten or die . . . well, surely the repressed memory would surface.''

''No.'' Even in the warm amber light of the floorlamp beside his chair, Alex's face appeared to have gone gray. ''Not with the drugs and hypnotic techniques we have these days. Mind control is a frighteningly advanced science. The survival instinct is the strongest we've got, but even that can be overridden. Ivan can be programmed to self-destruct.''

Pablo found his champagne glass empty. ''My young lady-friend seems to have invented a sort of Azrael Block of her own to hide from herself some extraordinarily distressing event in her past.''

''No,'' Alex said, ''she didn't form the block herself.''

''She must have. She's in a bad state, Alex. She just . . . slips away when I try to question her. So, as you know this field, I thought you might have a few ideas about how I can deal with it.''

''You still don't understand why I warned you to drop this whole thing,'' Alex said. He pushed up from his chair, moved to the nearby window, shoved his trembling hands in his pockets, and stared out at the snow-covered lawn. ''A self-imposed, naturally generated Azrael Block? Such a thing isn't possible. The human mind will not, of its own volition, put itself at risk of death merely to conceal something from itself. An Azrael Block is *always* an externally applied control. If you've encountered such a barrier, then someone planted it in her mind.''

''You're saying she's been brainwashed? Ridiculous. She's no spy.''

''I'm sure she's not.''

''She's no Russian. So why would she've been brainwashed? Ordinary citizens don't become targets for that sort of thing.''

Alex turned from the window and faced Pablo. ''This is just an educated guess . . . but perhaps she accidentally saw something she was not supposed to see. Something extremely important, secret. Subsequently, she was subjected to a sophisticated process of memory repression, to make sure she never told anyone about it.''

Pablo stared at him, astonished. ''But what could she possibly have seen to've made such extreme measures necessary?''

Alex shrugged.

''And who could've tampered with her mind?''

Alex said, ''The Russians, the CIA, the Israeli Mossad, Britain's MI6—any organization with the knowledge of how such things are done.''

''I don't think she's traveled outside the U.S., which leaves CIA.''

''Not necessarily. All the others operate in this country for their own purposes. Besides, intelligence organizations are not the only groups who're familiar with mind-control techniques. So are some crackpot religious cults, fanatical political fringe groups . . . others. Knowledge spreads fast, and evil knowledge spreads faster. If people like that want her to forget something, you sure don't want to help her remember. It wouldn't be healthy for either you or her, Pablo.''

"I can't believe—''

"Believe,'' Alex said somberly.

"But these fugues, these sudden fears of black gloves and helmets . . . these would seem to indicate that her memory block is cracking. Yet the people you've mentioned wouldn't have done a half-baked job, would they? If they'd implanted a block, it would be perfect.''

Alex returned to his chair, sat, leaned forward, fixing Pablo with an intense gaze, obviously striving to impress him with the gravity of the situation. "That's what worries me most, old friend. Ordinarily, such a firmly implanted mental barrier would never weaken on its own. The people capable of doing this to your lady-friend are absolutely expert at it. They wouldn't screw up. So her recent problems, her deteriorating psychological condition, can mean only one thing.''

"Yes?''

"The forbidden memories, the secrets buried behind this Azrael Block, are apparently so explosive, so frightening, so traumatic, that not even an expertly engineered barrier can contain them. Buried in this woman is a shocking memory of immense power, and it's straining to break out of its prison in her subconscious, into her conscious mind. These objects that trigger her blackouts—the gloves, the sink drain—are very likely elements of those repressed memories. When she fixates on one of these things, she's close to a breakthrough, trembling on the edge of remembrance. Then her program kicks in, and she blacks out.''

Pablo's heart quickened with excitement. "Then, after all, it might be possible to use hypnotic regression to probe at this Azrael Block, widen the cracks already in it, without driving her into a coma. One would have to be extremely cautious, of course, but with—''

"You're not listening to me!'' Alex said, bolting up again. He stood between their chairs, looming over Pablo, pointing one trembling finger at him. "This is incredibly dangerous. You've stumbled into something much too big for you to handle. If you help her to remember, you're going to make powerful enemies somewhere.''

"She's a sweet girl, and her life is in ruins because of this.''

"You can't help her. You're too old, and you're just one man.''

"Listen, maybe you don't understand enough of the situation. I haven't told you her name or profession, but I'll tell you now that—''

"I don't want to know who she is!'' Alex said, his eyes widening.

"She's a physician,'' Pablo persisted. "Or almost. She's spent the past fourteen years training herself for medical practice, and now she's losing everything. It's tragic.''

"Think about this, damn it: she's almost certain to discover that knowing the truth is even worse than not knowing. If the repressed memories are breaking through like this, then they must be so traumatic that they could destroy her psychologically.''

"Maybe,'' Pablo acknowledged. "But shouldn't *she* be the one to decide whether or not to keep digging for the truth?''

Alex was adamant. "If the memory itself doesn't destroy her, then she'll probably be killed by whoever implanted the block. I'm surprised they didn't kill her straightaway. If it *is* an intelligence agency behind this, ours or theirs, then you've got to remember that to them civilians are entirely expendable. She got a rare and amazing reprieve when they used brainwashing instead of a bullet. A bullet's quicker and cheaper. They won't give her a second reprieve. If they discover that the Azrael Block has crumbled, if they learn that she's uncovered the secret they've hidden from her, they'll blow her brains out."

"You can't be sure," Pablo said. "Besides, she's a real go-getter, Alex, an achiever, a mover and shaker. So from her point of view, her current situation is almost as bad as having her brains blown out."

Making no effort to conceal his frustration with the old magician, Alex said, "You help her, and they'll blow your brains out as well. Doesn't that give you pause?"

"At eighty-one," Pablo said, "not much of interest happens. You can't afford to turn your back on that rare bit of excitement when it comes along. *Vogue la galère*—I must chance it."

"You're making a mistake."

"Maybe I am, my friend. Maybe. But . . . then why do I feel so good?"

CHICAGO, ILLINOIS.

Dr. Bennet Sonneford, who had operated on Winton Tolk yesterday subsequent to the shooting at the sandwich shop, ushered Father Wycazik into a spacious den, where the walls were covered with mounted fish: marlin, an immense albacore, bass, trout. More than thirty glass eyes stared sightlessly down upon the two men. A trophy case was filled with silver and gold cups, bowls, medallions. The doctor sat at a pine desk in the shadow of a forever-swimming, open-mouthed marlin of startling proportions, and Stefan sat beside the desk in a comfortable chair.

Although the hospital had provided only Dr. Sonneford's office number, Father Wycazik had been able to track down the surgeon's home address with the aid of friends at the telephone company and police department. He had arrived at Sonneford's doorstep at seven-thirty Christmas night, effusively apologetic about interrupting holiday celebrations.

Now, Stefan said, "Brendan works with me at St. Bernadette's, and I think very highly of him, so I don't want to see him in trouble."

Sonneford, who looked a bit like a fish—pale, slightly protuberant eyes, a naturally puckered mouth—said, "Trouble?" He opened a kit of small tools, choosing a miniature screwdriver, and turned his attention to a fly-casting reel that lay on the blotter. "What trouble?"

"Interfering with officers in the performance of their duties."

"Ridiculous." Sonneford carefully removed tiny screws from the reel housing. "If he hadn't tended to Tolk, the man would be dead now. We gave him four and a half liters."

"Really? That isn't a mistake on the patient's chart."

"No mistake." Sonneford removed the metal case from the automatic reel, peered intently into its mechanical guts. "An adult has seventy milliliters of blood per kilogram of body weight. Tolk is a big man—one hundred kilos. He'd normally contain seven liters. So when I first ordered blood in the ER, he'd lost over sixty percent of his own." He put down the screwdriver and picked up an equally small wrench. "And they gave him another liter in the ambulance before I saw him."

"You mean he'd actually lost over seventy-five percent of his blood by the time they got him out of that sandwich shop? But . . . can a man lose so much blood and survive?"

"No," Sonneford said quietly.

A pleasant shiver passed through Stefan. "And both bullets lodged in soft tissue but damaged no organs. Deflected by ribs, other bones?"

Sonneford was still squinting at the reel but had stopped tinkering with it. "If those .38s had hit bone, the impact would've resulted in chipping, splintering. I found nothing like that. On the other hand, if they were *not* deflected by bone, they should've passed through him, leaving massive exit wounds. But I found them lodged in muscle tissue."

Stefan stared at the surgeon's bent head. "Why do I have the feeling there's something more you want to tell me, but that it's something you're afraid to talk about?"

At last Sonneford glanced up. "And why do I get the feeling that you've not told the truth about your reasons for coming here, Father?"

"Touché," Stefan said.

Sonneford sighed and put the tools away in the kit. "All right. The entry wounds make it clear that one bullet hit Tolk in the chest, impacted with the lower portion of the sternum, which should've snapped off or fractured; splinters like shrapnel should've pierced organs, vital blood vessels. Apparently, none of that happened."

"Why do you say 'apparently'? Either it happened, or it didn't."

"From the entry wound in the flesh, I *know* that bullet hit the sternum, Father, and I found it lodged harmlessly in tissue on the other side of the sternum; therefore . . . somehow . . . it passed *through* that bone without damaging it. Impossible, of course. Yet I found just an entry wound over the sternum, the undamaged bone directly under the wound—and then the bullet lodged inside behind the sternum, with no indication how it had gotten from one place to the other. Furthermore, the entry wound of the second slug was over the base of the fourth rib, right side, but that rib was undamaged as well. The bullet should have shattered it."

"Maybe you're wrong," Stefan said, playing devil's advocate. "Maybe the bullet entered just slightly off the rib, between ribs."

"No." Sonneford raised his head but did not look at Stefan. The physician's uneasiness still seemed peculiar and was not explained by what he had said thus far. "I don't make diagnostic errors. Besides, inside the patient, those bullets were lodged where you'd expect them to be if they *had* hit bone, had punched through, and had had the last of their energy absorbed by the muscle. But there were no damaged tissues *between* the point of entry and the expended slugs. Which is impossible. Bullets can't pass through a man's chest and leave no trail at all!"

"Almost seems as if we have a minor miracle."

"More than minor. Seems like a pretty damn *major* miracle to me."

"If only one artery and vein were injured, and if both were only nicked, how did Tolk lose so much blood? Were those nicks big enough to account for it?"

"No. He couldn't have hemorrhaged so massively from those traumas."

The surgeon said nothing more. He seemed gripped in the talons of some dark fear that Stefan could not understand. What had he to fear? If he believed that he had witnessed a miracle, should he not be joyous?

"Doctor, I know it's difficult for a man of science and medicine to admit he's seen something that his education can't explain, something that in fact is in opposition to everything he had believed to be true. But I beg you to tell me everything you saw. What are you holding back? How did Winton Tolk lose so much blood if his injuries were so small?"

Sonneford slumped back in his chair. "In surgery, after beginning transfusions, I located the bullets on the X rays and made the necessary incisions to remove them. In the process, I found a tiny hole in the superior mesenteric artery and another small tear in one of the superior intercostal veins. I was certain there must be other severed vessels, but I couldn't locate them immediately, so I clamped off both the superior mesenteric and the intercostal for repair, figuring to search further when those were attended to. It only took a few minutes, an easy task. I sewed the artery first, of course, because the bleeding was in spurts and was more serious. Then . . ."

"Then?" Father Wycazik urged gently.

"Then, when I had quickly finished stitching the artery, I turned to the torn intercostal vein . . . and the tear was gone."

"Gone," Stefan said. A quiver of awe passed through him, for this was the thing he had expected—yet it was also a revelation of such astounding importance that it seemed too much to have hoped for.

"Gone," Sonneford repeated, and at last he met Stefan's gaze. In the surgeon's watery gray eyes, a shadow moved like the half-perceived passage of a leviathan through the depths of a murky sea, the shadow of fear, and Stefan confirmed that for some inexplicable reason the miracle occasioned dread in the doctor. "The torn vein healed itself, Father. I *know* the tear had been there. Clamped it off myself. My technician saw it. My nurse saw it. But when I was ready to sew it up, the rent was gone. Healed. I removed the clamps, and the blood flowed again through the vein, and there was no leakage. And later . . . when I excised the bullets, the muscle tissue appeared to . . . knit up before my eyes."

"Appeared to?"

"No, that's an evasion," Sonneford admitted. "It *did* knit before my eyes. Incredible, but I saw it. Can't prove it, Father, but I know those two slugs *did* smash Tolk's sternum and shatter his rib. They *did* send bone fragments through him like shrapnel. Major, mortal damage *was* done, had to have been. But by the time he was on the table in surgery, his body had almost entirely healed itself. The shattered bones had . . . reformed. The superior mesenteric artery and the intercostal vein were severed to begin with, which is why he lost blood so fast, but by the time I opened him, both vessels had knitted up except for a small tear in each. Sounds crazy, but if I hadn't moved to repair the artery, I'm sure it would've finished closing on its own . . . just as the vein did."

"What did your nurse and other assistants think of this?"

"Funny thing is . . . we didn't talk much about it. I can't account for how little we discussed it. Maybe we didn't talk about it because . . . we're living in a rational age when the miraculous is unacceptable."

"How sad if true," Stefan said.

With the shadow of dread still shimmering anemonelike in the depths of his eyes, Sonneford said, "Father, if there is a God—and I'm not admitting there is—why would He save this particular cop?"

"He's a good man," Father Wycazik said.

"So? I've seen hundreds of good men die. Why should this one be saved and none of the others?"

Father Wycazik pulled a chair around from the side of the desk in order to be able to sit near the surgeon. "You've been frank with me, Doctor, so I'll be upfront with you. I sense a force behind these events that's more than human. A Presence. And that Presence isn't primarily concerned with Winton Tolk but with Brendan, the man . . . the *priest* who first reached Officer Tolk in that sandwich shop."

Bennet Sonneford blinked in surprise. "Oh. But you wouldn't have gotten such a notion unless . . ."

"Unless Brendan was linked to at least one other miraculous event," Stefan said. Without using Emmy Halbourg's name, he told Sonneford about the girl's mending limbs that had once been crippled by disease.

Instead of taking hope from what Stefan told him, Bennet Sonneford shriveled farther in the heat of his strange despair.

Frustrated by the physician's relentless gloominess, Father Wycazik said, "Doctor, maybe I'm missing something, but it seems to me you've got every reason to be joyous. You were privileged to witness what—I personally believe— was the hand of God at work." He held one hand out to Sonneford and was not surprised when the doctor gripped it tightly. "Bennet, why're you so despondent?"

Sonneford cleared his throat and said, "I was born and raised a Lutheran, but for twenty-five years I've been an atheist. And now . . ."

"Ah," Stefan said, "I see. . . ."

Happily, Stefan began angling for Bennet Sonneford's soul in the fish-lined den. He had no suspicion that, before the day was done, his current euphoria would be dispelled and that he would experience a bitter disappointment.

RENO, NEVADA.

Zeb Lomack had never imagined that his life would end in bloody suicide on Christmas, but by that night he had sunk so low that he longed to end his existence. He loaded his shotgun, put it on the filthy kitchen table, and promised himself that he would use it if he was unable to get rid of all the goddamned moon stuff before midnight.

His bizarre fascination with the moon had begun the summer before last, though at first it had seemed innocent enough. Toward the end of August that year, he had taken to going out on the back porch of his cozy little house and watching the moon and stars while sipping Coors. In mid-September, he purchased a Tasco 10VR refracting telescope and bought a couple of books on amateur astronomy.

Zebediah was surprised by his own sudden interest in star-gazing. For most of his fifty years, Zeb Lomack, a professional gambler, had shown little interest in anything but cards. He worked Reno, Lake Tahoe, Vegas, occasionally one of the smaller gambling towns like Elko or Bullhead City, playing poker with the tourists and local would-be poker champs. He was not only good at card games: He *loved* cards more than he loved women, booze, food. Even the money was not important to Zeb; it was just a handy by-product of playing cards. The important thing was staying in the game.

Until he got the telescope and went crazy.

For a couple of months he used the scope on a casual basis, and he bought a few more books on astronomy, and it was just a hobby. But by last Christmas he began to focus his attention less on the stars than on the moon, and thereafter something strange happened to him. The new hobby soon became as interesting as card games, and he found himself canceling planned excursions to the casinos in order to study the lunar surface. By February, he was glued to the eyepiece of the Tasco every night that the moon was visible. By April he built a collection of books about the moon that numbered more than one hundred, and he went out to play cards only two or three nights a week. By the end of June, his book collection had grown to five hundred titles, and he had begun to paper the bedroom walls and ceiling with pictures of the moon clipped from old magazines and newspapers. He no longer played cards, but began living off his savings, and thereafter his interest in things lunar ceased to bear any resemblance to a hobby and became a mad obsession.

By September, his book collection had grown to more than fifteen hundred volumes stacked throughout his small house. During the day, he read about the moon or, more often, sat for hours staring intently at photographs of it, unable either to understand or to resist its allure, until its craters and ridges and plains became as familiar to him as the five rooms of his own house. On those nights when the moon was visible, he studied it through the telescope until he could no longer stay awake, until his eyes were bloodshot and sore.

Before this obsession took control of him, Zeb Lomack had been a ruggedly hewn and relatively fit man. But as his preoccupation with things lunar tightened its grip, he stopped exercising and began eating junk food—cake, ice cream, TV dinners, bologna sandwiches—because he no longer had time to prepare good meals. Furthermore, the moon not only fascinated him but also made him uneasy, filled him not only with wonder but with dread, so he was always nervous; and he tranquilized himself with food. He became softer, flabbier, though he was only minimally aware of the physical changes he was undergoing.

By early October, he thought about the moon every hour of every day, dreamed of it, and could go nowhere in his house without seeing hundreds of images of the lunar face. He had not stopped repapering the walls when he had finished his bedroom in June, but had carried that project throughout. The full-color and black-and-white moon pictures came from astronomy journals, magazines, books, and newspapers. On one of his infrequent ventures out of the house, he had seen a three-by-five-foot poster of the moon, a color photograph taken by astronauts, and he had bought fifty copies, enough to paper the ceiling and every wall in the living room; he had even taped the poster over the windows, so every square inch of the room was decorated with that repeating image, except for doorways. He moved the furniture out, transforming the empty chamber into a planetarium where the show never changed. Sometimes he'd lie on his back on the floor and stare up and around at those fifty moons, transported by an exhilarating sense of wonder and an inexplicable terror, neither of which he could understand.

Christmas night, as Zeb was sprawled on the floor with half a hundred bloated moons hanging over him, bearing down on him, he suddenly noticed writing on one of them, a single word scrawled across the lunar image with a felt-tip pen, where there had never been a word before. The picture had been defaced with a name: *Dominick*. He recognized his own handwriting, but he could not remember having scrawled that name across the moon. Then his eye was caught by another name written on another poster: *Ginger*. And then a third name on a third poster: *Faye*. And a fourth: *Ernie*. Suddenly anxious, Zeb stumbled around the room, checking the other posters, but he found no more names.

In addition to being unable to recall writing those words, he could not think of anyone he knew named Dominick, Ginger, or Faye. He knew a couple of Ernies, though neither was a close friend, and the appearance of that name on one of the moons was no less mysterious than the three others. Staring at the names, he grew increasingly uneasy, for he had the odd feeling that he *did* know them, that they had played a terribly important role in his life, and that his very sanity and survival depended on remembering who they were.

Some long-forgotten memory swelled in him like a steadily inflating balloon, and intuitively he knew that when the balloon popped he would recollect everything, not only the identities of these four people, but also the origins of his fevered fascination with—and underlying fear of—the moon. But as the memory balloon swelled within him, his fear grew as well, and he began to sweat and then to shake uncontrollably.

He turned from the posters, suddenly terrified of remembering, and lurched out to the kitchen, driven by that gnawing hunger that was always occasioned by thoughts that made him nervous. He wrenched open the refrigerator door and was startled to discover that the shelves were bare. They held dirty bowls and empty plastic containers in which food had been kept, two empty milk cartons, an egg carton with one broken and dried egg. He looked in the freezer, found only frost.

Zeb tried to remember when he had last been to the supermarket. It might have been days or weeks since his most recent shopping expedition. He could not remember because, in his moon-filled world, time no longer had any meaning. And how much time had passed since his last meal? He vaguely remembered having some canned pudding, but he was not clear whether that had been earlier today or yesterday or even two days ago.

Zebediah Lomack was so shocked by this development that his mind cleared for the first time in weeks, and when he looked around the kitchen, he made a strangled sound of disgust and fear. For the first time he saw—*really* saw—the mess in which he'd been living, a situation previously masked by his all-encompassing fascination with the moon. Garbage covered the floor: discarded cans sticky with fruit juice, slimy with traces of rancid gravy; empty cereal boxes and a score of drained milk cartons; dozens of wadded-up and discarded potato-chip bags and candy wrappers. And roaches. They squirmed, scuttled, and jigged through the garbage, raced across the floor, climbed walls, crouched on counters, and lurked in the sink.

"My God," Zeb said in a voice that was hardly more than a croak, "what's happened to me? What've I been doing? What's *wrong* with me?"

He put one hand to his face and twitched with surprise when he felt a beard. He had always been clean-shaven, and he had thought he shaved just this morning. The wiry hair on his face sent him in a panic to the bathroom, where he could look in the mirror. He saw a stranger: filthy, matted hair hanging in tangled clumps; pale, soft, sickly-looking skin; a two-week beard crusted with food and dirt; wild eyes. He became aware of his body odor: His stink was so rank that he gagged on his own aroma. Apparently, he had not bathed in days, weeks.

He needed help. He was sick. Confused and sick. He could not understand what had happened to him, but he knew that he must go to the telephone and call for help.

But he did not go immediately to the phone because he was afraid they'd say he was hopelessly insane and would lock him away forever. Like they had locked away his father. When Zebediah was eight, his father pitched a terrible fit, ranting and raving about lizard-things that were crawling out of the walls, and the doctors took him to the hospital to dry him out. But that time, unlike before, the DTs had not gone away, and Zeb's dad had been institutionalized for the rest of his life. Ever after, Zeb had been afraid his own mind might be flawed, too. Staring at his pale face in the mirror, he knew he could not call for help until he made himself presentable and straightened up the house; otherwise, they would lock him up and throw away the key.

He could not bear to look at his reflection long enough to shave, so he decided to deal with the house first. Keeping his head down to avoid seeing the moons, which exerted a tidal force on him as real as the true moon's effect on the seas, he scurried into the bedroom, opened the closet, shoved the clothes aside, located his Remington .12-gauge and a box of shells. Head bowed, fighting the urge to look up, he made his way to the kitchen, where he loaded the shotgun and put it on the garbage-strewn table. Speaking aloud, he made a bargain with himself:

"You get rid of the moon books, tear down the pictures so this place don't look so crazy, clean the kitchen, shave, bathe. Then maybe you'll get your head clear enough to figure what the hell's wrong with you. Then you can get help— just not while things are like this."

The shotgun was the unspoken part of the bargain. He had been fortunate to rise briefly out of the moon-dream in which he had been living, shocked to his senses by the lack of food in the refrigerator, but if he drifted back into that nightmare, he could not count on being jolted awake again. Therefore, if he could not resist the siren song of the moons on the walls, he would quickly return to the kitchen, pick up the shotgun, put it in his mouth, and pull the trigger.

Death was better than this.

And death was better than being locked up forever like his father.

Now, in the living room once more, keeping his eyes on the floor, he began to gather up the books. Some had once boasted jackets with photos of the moon, but he had clipped those pictures. He hefted an armload of them and went outside to the snow-covered back yard, where there was a barbecue pit lined with concrete blocks. Shivering in the crisp winter air, he dumped the books into the pit and headed back to the house for more, not daring to look at the night sky for fear of the great luminous body suspended in it.

As he worked, the urge to return to the study of the moon was as intense and demanding as the hideous need that forced a heroin addict to return again and again to the needle, but Zeb fought it.

Likewise, as he made trip after trip to the barbecue pit, he felt that memory of some long-forgotten event continuing to swell within him: *Dominick, Ginger, Faye, Ernie.* . . . Instinctively, he knew that he would understand the cause of his fascination with the moon if only he could recall who those four people were. He concentrated on the names, trying to use them to block out the alluring summons of the moon, and it seemed to work because soon he had disposed of two or three hundred volumes in the barbecue pit and was ready to set them ablaze.

But when he struck a match and leaned down to light the pages of a book, he discovered the pit was empty. He stared in shock and horror. Dropping the matches, he raced back to the house, threw open the kitchen door, stumbled inside, and saw what he had been most afraid of seeing. The books were piled there, damp with snow, smeared with wet ashes from the pit. He had indeed disposed of them, but then the lunacy had taken him again; under its spell and without knowing what he was doing, he had carried every volume back into the house.

He began to cry, but he was still determined he would not wind up in a padded room. He picked up a score of books and headed back toward the barbecue pit, feeling as if he were in hell and condemned, for eternity, to the performance of this frantic ritual.

When he figured he had filled the pit again, he suddenly realized he was not carrying books *to* the place of burning but away from it. Again, he had drifted off into his moon-dream and, instead of destroying the objects of his obsession, he was re-collecting them.

As he headed back toward the house, he noticed how the crust of snow glimmered with a scintillant, reflected light. Against his will, his head came up. He looked into the deep and nearly cloudless sky.

He said, "The moon."

He knew then that he was a dead man.

LAGUNA BEACH, CALIFORNIA.

For Dominick Corvaisis, Christmas was usually not much different from other days. He had no wife or children to make it special. Raised in foster homes, he had no relatives with whom he could share a turkey and mincemeat pie. A couple of friends, including Parker Faine, always invited him to join in their festivities, but he declined, for he knew he would feel like the proverbial fifth wheel. However, Christmas was not sad or lonely. He was never bored by his own company, and his home overflowed with good books that could fill the day with delight.

But this Christmas Dom could not concentrate to read, for he was preoccupied by the mysterious mail he had received the previous day and by the need to resist the urge to pop a Valium. Though he had been afraid that he would dream and walk in his sleep, he had taken no Valium yesterday and no Dalmane last night. He was determined to avoid any further reliance on chemicals, though he continued to crave them.

In fact, the craving became so bad that he emptied the pills into the toilet and flushed them away, because he did not trust himself. As the day wore on, his anxiety rose to the level he had experienced before he had begun drug therapy.

At seven o'clock Christmas night, Dom arrived at Parker's rambling hillside contemporary and accepted a glass of homemade eggnog with a cinnamon stick in it. The burly painter's beard, usually bushy and untamed, was neatly trimmed, and his mane of hair was newly cut and combed in honor of the holiday. Though he was more conservatively groomed and more subdued in dress than was his habit, he was every bit as ebullient as one expected him to be. "What a Christmas! Peace and love reigned in this house today, I tell you! My cherished brother made only forty or fifty nasty and envious remarks about my success, which is not half as many as he lets loose with on a less blessed occasion. My sainted half-sister, Carla, only *once* called her sister-in-law Doreen a bitch, and even that might be considered justified in light of the fact that Doreen started it by calling Carla a 'brainless New Age crackpot full of psychobabble.' Ah, truly a day of fellowship and caring! Not one punch thrown this year, if you can believe it. And Carla's husband, though he got plastered as usual, did not throw up or fall down a flight of stairs, as in past years, though he did insist on doing his Bette Midler imitation at least a dozen times."

As they moved toward a grouping of chairs by the window-wall overlooking the sea, Dom said, "I'm going on a trip, a long drive. I'll fly to Portland and rent a car up there. Then I'll retrace the journey I took the summer before last, from Portland down to Reno, across Nevada and half of Utah on Interstate 80, then to Mountainview."

Dom sat down as he spoke, but Parker remained on his feet, very still. The announcement pleasantly electrified him. "What's happened? That's no vacation. That's not a route you'd take for pleasure. Are you sleepwalking again? Must be. And something's happened to convince you this is related to the changes you underwent that summer."

"I haven't begun sleepwalking again, but I'm sure I will, probably tonight, because I've thrown the damn drugs away. They weren't curing me. I lied. I was getting hooked, Parker. I didn't care because it seemed that being hooked was better than enduring the things I did while sleepwalking. But now all that's changed because of these." He held up the two notes from his unknown correspondent. "The problem's not just within me, not just psychological. There's something stranger at work here." He gave the first note to Parker. His fearful state of mind was betrayed by the sheet of paper, which shook in his hand.

When the painter read it, he looked baffled.

Dom said, "It came in the mail yesterday at the post office. No return address. There was another note delivered to the house." He explained about having typed the words "the moon" on his word processor hundreds of times in his sleep and about waking from a dream with those same words on his lips, then passed the second note to Parker.

"But if I'm the first one you've told about this moon thing, how could anyone have known enough to send such a note?"

"Whoever he is," Dom said, "he knows about my sleepwalking, maybe because I've gone to a doctor about it—"

"You're saying you're being watched?"

"Apparently, to a degree. Periodically monitored if not constantly watched. But while the monitor knows about my sleepwalking, he probably doesn't know about my typing those words on the Displaywriter, or that I woke up repeating them in the night. Not unless he was standing beside my bed, which he wasn't. However, he indisputably *does* know that I'll react to 'the moon,' that those words'll frighten me. So he must know what lies behind this whole crazy mess."

At last Parker sat down on the edge of a chair. "Find him, and you'll know what's going on."

"New York is a big place," Dom said. "I have no starting point there. But when I got this first note—this business about the answer to my sleepwalking lying in the past—I realized you must be right about *this* personality crisis being tied to the previous one. The dramatic change I went through on the trip from Portland to Mountainview is somehow connected. If I make that trip again, stop at the same motels, eat in the same roadside restaurants, try to recreate it as exactly as I can . . . something might turn up. My memory might be jogged."

"But how could you have forgotten something so major?"

"Maybe I didn't forget it. Maybe the memory was *taken* from me."

Leaving that possibility for later exploration, Parker said, "Whoever the hell this guy is—what reasons would he have for sending these notes? I mean, you've imagined a situation where it's you against Them, some unknown *Them,* and so this guy is on their side, not yours."

"Maybe he doesn't agree with everything that's been done to me—whatever it is that I've forgotten was done to me."

"Done to you? What're we talking about here?"

Dom nervously turned his glass of eggnog around and around in his hands. "I don't know. But this correspondent . . . he obviously wants me to know my problem's not psychological, that there's something more behind it. I think maybe he wants to help me find the truth."

"So why doesn't he just call you up and tell you the truth?"

"The only thing I can figure is that he doesn't dare *risk* telling me. He must be part of some conspiracy, God knows what, but part of some group that doesn't want the truth to come out. If he approaches me directly, the others will know, and he'll be in deep shit."

As if it helped him think, Parker ran one hand through his hair several times, mussing it badly. "You make this sound like some all-knowing secret society is on your ass—like the Illuminatus Society, Rosicrucians, CIA, and the Fraternal Order of Masons all rolled into one! You actually think you've been brainwashed?"

"If you want to call it that. Whatever traumatic episode I've forgotten, I didn't forget it without assistance. Whatever I saw or experienced was apparently so shocking, so traumatic, that it's still festering in my subconscious, trying to reach me through sleepwalking and through the messages I leave on the Displaywriter. It was so damned big that even brainwashing hasn't been able to wipe it out, so big that one of the conspirators is risking his own neck to send me hints.''

After reading them one more time, Parker returned the two notes to Dom, chugged down his own eggnog. ''Shit. I think you've got to be right, which upsets me. I don't want to believe it. It sounds too much as if you've let your novelistic imagination run wild, as if you're trying out the plot of a new book on me, something a bit more colorful than you should write. But crazy as the whole thing sounds, I can't think of any other answer.''

Dom realized he was squeezing the eggnog glass so tightly that he was in danger of shattering it. He put it on a small table and blotted his hands on his slacks. ''Me neither. There's nothing else that explains both the crazy damn sleepwalking, *and* my personality change between Portland and Mountainview, *and* those two notes.''

His face lined with worry, Parker said, ''What could it have been, Dom? What did you stumble into when you were out there on the road?''

''I don't have the foggiest.''

''Have you considered that it might be something so bad . . . so damn dangerous that you'd be better off not knowing?''

Dom nodded. ''But if I don't learn the truth, I won't be able to stop the sleepwalking for good. In my sleep I'm running from the memory of whatever happened to me out there on the road, the summer before last, and to stop running I've got to find out what it was, face up to it. 'Cause if I don't stop the sleepwalking, it'll eventually drive me mad. That might sound a bit melodramatic, too, but it's true. If I don't learn the truth, then the thing I fear in my dreams is going to start haunting the waking hours as well, and I'm not going to have a moment's peace, waking or sleeping, and eventually the only solution will be to put a gun in my mouth and pull the trigger.''

''Jesus.''

''I mean it.''

''I know you do. God help you, my friend, I know you do.''

RENO, NEVADA.

A cloud saved Zeb Lomack. It drifted across the moon before the grip of the lunar obsession had completely reclaimed him. With the empyreal lantern briefly dimmed, Zebediah abruptly became aware that he was standing coatless in the freezing December night, gaping up at the sky, mesmerized by moonbeams. If the cloud had not broken the trance, he might have stood there until the object of his grim fascination had descended past the horizon. Then, having sunk back into his lunacy, he might have returned to one of the rooms papered with the ancient god-face that the Greeks called Cynthia, that the Romans called Diana, there to lie in a stupor until, days hence, he had starved to death.

Reprieved, he let out a wretched cry and ran to the house. He slipped and fell in the snow, fell again on the porch steps, but immediately scrambled up, desperately seeking the safety of the indoors, where the face of the moon could not work its charms on him. But of course there was no safety inside, either. Though he closed his eyes and began at once to tear blindly at the moon pictures, ripping them from the kitchen walls and casting them on the garbage-covered floor, he began to succumb to his obsession yet again. Eyes tightly shut, he could not see the cratered images, but he could *feel* them. He could feel the pale light of a hundred moons upon his face, and he could feel the roundness of the moons in his hands as he tore them off the wall, which was crazy because they were only pictures that could not produce light or warmth and could not convey by touch the roundness of the lunar globe, yet he nevertheless felt those things strongly. He opened his eyes and was instantly captured by the familiar celestial body.

Just like my dad. Asylum-bound.

Like a distant crackle of lightning, that thought flickered through Zeb Lomack's rapidly dimming mind. It jolted him and allowed him to recover just long enough to turn away from the living room door and fling himself toward the kitchen table, where the loaded shotgun waited.

CHICAGO, ILLINOIS.

Father Stefan Wycazik, descendant of strong-willed Poles, rescuer of troubled priests, was not accustomed to failure, and he did not handle it well. "But after everything I've told you, how can you still not believe?" he demanded.

Brendan Cronin said, "Father Stefan, I'm sorry. But I simply don't feel any stronger about the existence of God than I did yesterday."

They were in a bedroom on the second floor of Brendan's parents' gingersnap brick house in the Irish neighborhood called Bridgeport, where the young priest was spending the holiday according to Father Wycazik's orders, issued yesterday after the Uptown shootout. Brendan, dressed in gray slacks and a white shirt, was sitting on the edge of a double bed that was covered by a worn, yellow chenille spread. Stefan, choosing to feel needled by his curate's stubbornness, moved constantly around the room from dresser to highboy to window to bed to dresser again, as if trying to avoid the prickling pain of his failure.

"Tonight," Father Wycazik said, "I met an atheist who was half-converted by Tolk's incredible recovery. But you're unimpressed."

"I'm happy for Dr. Sonneford," Brendan said mildly, "but his renewed belief doesn't rekindle my own."

The curate's refusal to be properly impressed by recent miraculous events was not the only thing that irritated Father Wycazik. The young priest's pacific demeanor was also bothersome. If he could not find the will to believe in God again, then it seemed he should at least be disheartened and downcast by his continued lack of faith. Instead, Brendan appeared untroubled by his miserable spiritual condition, which was quite different from his attitude when Father Wycazik had seen him last. He had changed dramatically; for reasons that were not at all clear, a great peace seemed to have settled over Brendan.

Still determinedly pressing his argument, Stefan said, "It was *you,* Brendan, who cured Emmy Halbourg and healed Winton Tolk. It was you, through the power of those stigmata on your hands. Stigmata that God visited upon you as a sign."

Brendan looked at his palms, now unmarked. "I believe . . . somehow I did heal Emmy and Winton. But it wasn't God acting through me."

"Who else but God could've granted you such curing power?"

"I don't know," Brendan said. "Wish I did. But it wasn't God. I felt no divine presence, Father."

"Good grief, how much more strongly do you expect Him to make His presence felt? Do you expect Him to thump you on the head with His great Staff of Justice, tip His diadem to you, and introduce Himself? You've got to meet Him halfway, Brendan."

The curate smiled and shrugged. "Father, I know these amazing events seem to have no explanation other than a religious one. But I feel very strongly that something other than God lies behind it.''

''Like what?'' Stefan challenged.

''I don't know. Something tremendously important, something really wonderful and magnificent . . . but not God. Look, you've said that the rings were stigmata. But if that's what they were, why wouldn't they have been in a form that had some Christian significance? Why rings—which seem to have no relation to the message of Christ?''

When Brendan began Stefan's unconventional course of psychological therapy at St. Joseph's Hospital for Children three weeks ago, the young priest had been so troubled by his loss of faith that he'd been growing rapidly thinner. Now he had stopped losing weight. He was still thirty pounds lighter than usual, but he was no longer as wan and haggard as he had been following his shocking outburst during Mass on the first of December. In spite of his spiritual fall, there was a glow to his skin and a light in his eyes that was almost . . . beatific.

''You feel splendid, don't you?'' Stefan asked.

''Yes, though I'm not sure why.''

''Your soul's no longer troubled.''

''No.''

''Even though you've still not found your way back to God.''

''Even though,'' Brendan agreed. ''Maybe it has something to do with the dream I had last night.''

''The black gloves again?''

''No. Haven't had that one in a while,'' Brendan said. ''Last night I dreamed that I was walking in a place of pure golden light, beautiful light, so bright I could see nothing around me, and yet it didn't hurt my eyes.'' A peculiar note, perhaps of reverence, entered the curate's voice. ''In the dream, I keep walking and walking, not knowing where I am or where I'm going, but with the sense that I'm approaching a thing or a place of monumental importance and unbearable beauty. Not just approaching but . . . being called to it. Not an audible call but a summons that just . . . reverberates in me. My heart is pounding, and I'm a little afraid. But it isn't a bad fear, Father, what I feel in that bright place, not bad at all. So I just keep walking through the light, toward something magnificent that I can't see but that I *know* is there.''

Drawn by Brendan's hushed voice as if by a magnet, Father Wycazik moved to the bed and sat upon the corner of it. ''But surely this is a spiritual dream, the call of God coming to you in sleep. He's calling you back to your faith, back to the duties of your office.''

Brendan shook his head. ''No. There was no religious quality to the dream, no sense of a divine presence. It was a different kind of awe that filled me, a joy unlike the joy I knew in Christ. I woke up four times during the night, and each time I woke, the rings were on my hands. And each time that I fell back to sleep, I dropped into the same dream again. Something very strange and important is happening, Father, and I'm a part of it; but whatever it is, it's not anything that my education, experiences, or previous beliefs have prepared me for.''

Father Wycazik wondered if the call that had come to Brendan in the dream had been from Satan instead of God. Perhaps the devil, aware that a priest's soul was in jeopardy, had dressed his hateful form in this deceptively attractive golden light, the better to lead the curate from the righteous path.

Still firmly determined to bring his curate back into the fold, but temporarily out of winning strategies, Stefan Wycazik decided to call a truce. He said, ''So . . . what now? You aren't ready to put on your Roman collar and resume your duties, as I thought you'd be by now. Do you want me to contact Lee Kellog, the Illinois Provincial, and ask him to authorize psychiatric counseling?''

Brendan smiled. ''No. That doesn't appeal to me any more. I don't believe it'd do any good. What I'd like to do—if it's all right with you, Father—is move back into my room in the rectory and wait this out, see what happens. Of course, as I remain a fallen-away priest, I can't hear confessions or say Mass. But while I'm waiting to see what happens, I could do some cooking, help you catch up on the filing.''

Father Wycazik was relieved. He had expected Brendan to express the intention of returning to a secular life. ''You're welcome, of course. There's much you can do. I'll keep you busy; no need to worry about that. But tell me, Brendan . . . you *do* think there's a possibility that you'll find your way back?''

The curate nodded. ''I don't feel *alienated* from God any more. Just empty of Him. As this situation develops, perhaps it'll lead me back to the Church, as you're convinced it will. I just don't know.''

Still frustrated and disappointed by Brendan's refusal to see the miraculous presence of God in the healing of Emmy and Winton, Father Wycazik was nonetheless glad that he would have the curate close and be provided the opportunity to continue guiding him back to salvation.

Brendan went downstairs with Father Wycazik, and at the front door the two men embraced in such a way that a stranger, without any knowledge of their occupation, would have thought them father and son.

Accompanying Father Wycazik as far as the front stoop, where a blustery wind gave a howl more suited to Halloween than to Christmas, Brendan said, ''I don't know why or how, Father Stefan, but I feel we're about to embark upon an amazing adventure.''

''The discovery—or rediscovery—of faith is always an amazing adventure, Brendan,'' Father Wycazik said. Then, having gotten in the last clean jab, as a good fighter for souls should always do, he left.

RENO, NEVADA.

Whimpering, gasping for breath, struggling valiantly against the narcotizing effect of his lunar obsession, Zeb Lomack clambered through the garbage and squirming roaches that carpeted the kitchen, grabbed the shotgun that lay upon the table, jammed the barrel between his teeth—and suddenly realized that his arms were not long enough to reach the trigger. The urge to look up at the bewitching moons on the walls was so overpowering that he felt as if someone had hold of him by the hair and was pulling his head back to force his gaze up from the floor. And when he closed his eyes defensively, it seemed as if some invisible adversary began to pry insistently at his eyelids. In his horror of being committed to a madhouse like his father, he found the strength to resist the mesmeric moon-call. Eyes still closed, he collapsed into a chair, kicked off one shoe, stripped away the sock, braced the shotgun with both hands, put the barrel in his mouth, raised his unshod foot, and touched one bare toe to the cold trigger. Imagined moonlight on his skin and imagined lunar tides in his blood (no less forceful for being imaginary) demanded his attention with such sudden power that he opened his eyes, saw the many moons on the walls, and cried ''no!'' into the barrel of the gun. Even as the spellbinding moon-call pulled him back toward a trance, even as he pressed his foot down upon the trigger, the swelling memory balloon at last burst in his mind, and he remembered everything that had been taken away from him: *the summer before last, Dominick, Ginger, Faye, Ernie, the young priest, the others, Interstate 80, the Tranquility Motel, oh, God, the motel, and oh, God, the moon!*

Perhaps Zebediah Lomack was unable to check the downward motion of his bare foot or perhaps, instead, the suddenly revealed memory was so terrible that it encouraged suicide. Whichever the case, the .12-gauge went off with a roar, and the back of his head blew out, and for him (though for no one else) the terror ended.

BOSTON, MASSACHUSETTS.

All Christmas afternoon, Ginger Weiss read *Twilight in Babylon,* and at seven o'clock that evening, when it was time to go downstairs for drinks and dinner with the Hannaby family, she resented the interruption and did not want to put the book aside. She was a willing captive of the engrossing story, but she was more captivated by the photo of the author. Dominick Corvaisis' commanding eyes and dark good looks continued to arouse in her an uneasiness bordering on fear, and she could not overcome the peculiar feeling that she knew him.

Dinner with her hosts, their children and grandchildren, might have been pleasurable if Dominick Corvaisis had not exerted a mysteriously powerful claim on her attention. At ten o'clock, when she could at last gracefully withdraw without offending anyone, she cast out and gathered in a final series of Christmas wishes for happiness and health, then returned to her room.

She began reading where she had left off, and with a minimum of interruptions to scrutinize the author's photograph again, she finished the book at three-forty-five A.M. In the deep post-midnight silence that had settled over Baywatch, Ginger sat with the book in her lap, the jacket photo turned up, her eyes fixed on Dominick Corvaisis' hauntingly familiar face. Minute by minute, as she sat in her strange, silent, one-sided communion with the writer's image, Ginger became increasingly convinced that she had met the man somewhere and that he was, in some unimaginable fashion, part of her recent troubles. Although her steadily growing conviction was tempered by the realization that this intuition might be part of the same mental disturbance that generated her fugues, and might therefore be unreliable, her agitation and excitement increased until, shaky and distraught, she was finally driven to action.

Leaving her room with exaggerated stealth, she went downstairs, through the dark and untenanted rooms of the great slumbering house, into the kitchen. She switched on the light and used the wall phone to call information in Laguna Beach. It was one o'clock in the morning in California, too rude an hour to wake Corvaisis. But if she could get a number for him, she would sleep better, knowing that she could get in touch with him in the morning. To her dismay though not to her surprise, his number was unlisted.

Switching off the kitchen light and creeping quietly back to her room, Ginger made up her mind to write Corvaisis in the morning, care of his publisher. She would dispatch the message by express mail, with an urgent plea to the publisher to forward the letter immediately.

Perhaps attempting to contact him was precipitate and irrational. Perhaps she had never met him, and perhaps he had nothing to do with her bizarre affliction. Perhaps he'd think she was a crackpot. But if this million-to-one shot proved a good bet, the payoff might be her very salvation, which was sufficient reward to risk making a fool of herself.

LAGUNA BEACH, CALIFORNIA.

As yet unaware that an advance review copy of his book had made a vital link between himself and a deeply troubled woman in Boston, Dom remained at Parker Faine's house until midnight, discussing the possible nature of the conspiracy that he had theorized. Neither he nor Parker had enough information to put together a detailed or even slightly useful picture of the conspirators, but the very process of sharing and exploring the mystery with a friend made it less frightening.

They agreed that Dom should not fly to Portland and begin his odyssey until he saw how bad his sleepwalking became now that he had thrown away the Valium and Dalmane. Maybe somnambulism would not recur, as he expected it would, in which case he could travel without fear of losing control of himself in a distant place. But if he resumed his night rambling, he would need a couple weeks to decide on the best way of restraining himself during sleep, before heading to Portland.

Besides, by waiting awhile, he might receive additional letters from his unknown correspondent. Those clues might make the trek from Portland to Mountainview unnecessary or might target a specific area along that route as the place where Dom would encounter some sight or experience that would free his imprisoned memories.

By midnight, when Dom rose to leave Parker's hillside house, the artist had become so intrigued by the situation that he looked as if he would be up for hours yet, his mind spinning. "You're sure it's wise to be alone tonight?" he asked at the front door.

Dom stepped outside onto a walkway patterned with spikey geometric forms of darkness and wedge-shaped slices of yellow light, which were formed by the beams of a decorative iron lantern half obscured by shadow-casting palm fronds. Looking back at his friend, he said, "We've been through this before. It might not be wise, but it's the only way."

"You'll call if you need help?"

"I'll call," Dom said.

"And take those precautions we talked about."

Dom attended to those precautions a short while later at home. He removed the pistol from his nightstand, locked it in a drawer of his office desk, and buried the desk key under a package of ice cream in the freezer. Better to be unprepared for a burglar than to risk firing the gun while sound asleep. Next, from a coil of rope in the garage, he cut a ten-foot length. After brushing his teeth and undressing, he knotted one end of the line securely around his right wrist in such a way that he could escape only by untying four difficult knots. He secured the other end of the rope to one post of the headboard, taking care to fasten it tightly. With one foot of the line's length used for the knots, he was left with nine feet of play, enough to assure his comfort while keeping him tethered within a safe distance of the bed.

In previous somnambulistic episodes, he had performed complex tasks that had required some concentration, though nothing quite so tedious as the unraveling of well-made knots, which were often a challenge to him when he was *awake*. In his sleep, he would surely lack the coordination and mental focus to free himself and the effort to do so would be frustrating enough to wake him.

Being thus hampered involved some danger. If a fire broke out in the night or if the house were damaged in an earthquake, he might be so delayed by the need to untie himself that he would perish in the smoke or beneath a collapsing wall. He had to risk it.

When he turned out the bedside light and slipped under the blanket, trailing the rope from one arm, the glowing red numerals of the digital clock read twelve-fifty-eight. Staring at the dark ceiling, wondering what in the name of God he had become involved in out there on the road the summer before last, he waited for sleep to creep upon him.

On the nightstand, the telephone was silent. If his number had not been unlisted, he might have received, at that moment, a long-distance call from a lonely and frightened young woman in Boston, a call that would have radically changed the course of the next few weeks and might have saved lives.

MILWAUKEE, WISCONSIN.

In the guest room of her only daughter's house, where a nightlight burned in consideration of Ernie's phobia, Faye Block listened to her husband as, asleep and dreaming, he mumbled into his pillow. A few minutes ago, she had been awakened when he had let out a soft cry and had thrashed for a moment in the sheets. Now she raised herself on one elbow, cocked her head, and listened intently, trying to decipher his muffled speech. He was saying the same thing again and again into the pillow. The almost panicky urgency in his voice made Faye nervous. She leaned closer to him, straining to understand.

Suddenly he shifted his head just enough to turn his mouth from the pillow, and his words became clear though no less mysterious than when they had been muffled: "The moon, the moon, the moon, the moon . . ."

LAS VEGAS, NEVADA.

Jorja took Marcie into her own bed that night, because it did not seem like a good idea to leave the girl alone after the disturbing events of the day. She did not get much rest because all night Marcie seemed to phase in and out of nightmares, frequently kicking at the sheets, squirming vigorously as if to free herself from restraining hands, and talking in her sleep about doctors and needles. Jorja wondered how long this had been going on. Their bedrooms were separated by back-to-back closets insulated by hanging clothes, and the child's sleep-talk was very soft, so it was possible that she had passed a lot of nights in unconscious terror without Jorja being aware of it. Her voice raised gooseflesh on Jorja's arms.

In the morning, she would take Marcie to the doctor. Given her unexplained dread of all physicians, the girl might cause a hell of a scene. But as much as Marcie feared going to a doctor, Jorja feared *not* going. If it had not been so hard to locate the right physician on Christmas Day, Jorja would have gone for help already. She was scared.

Following Marcie's outburst, when her grandfather's teasing about taking her to a hospital had driven her away from the table in a mad panic, the day had gone downhill. The girl was so overcome by fear that she peed her pants, and for ten or fifteen hideously embarrassing and terrifying minutes, she resisted all Jorja's efforts to get her cleaned up. She screamed, scratched, and kicked. The tantrum passed at last, and she submitted to a bath. But she was like a little zombie, slack-faced and empty-eyed, as if the terror, in passing out of her, had taken with it all her strength and her mind as well.

That quasicatatonic state lasted almost an hour while Jorja made a dozen telephone calls in an attempt to track down Dr. Besancourt, the pediatrician who treated Marcie on those rare occasions when she was sick. As Mary and Pete tried unsuccessfully to get a smile or at least a word of response from the stricken girl, and as Marcie continued to act as if she were deaf and mute, Jorja's mind was increasingly filled with half-remembered magazine articles about autistic children. She couldn't recall whether autism was a condition that began in infancy or whether it was possible for a perfectly normal little girl of seven to suddenly withdraw into a private place and close out the rest of the world forever. Not being able to remember made her a little crazy.

Gradually, however, Marcie came out of her daze. She began to answer Mary and Pete, though in one-word replies delivered in a flat, emotionless voice nearly as unsettling as her screams had been earlier. Sucking on her thumb as she had not done in at least two years, she went into the living room to play with her new toys. Most of the afternoon, she played without any visible pleasure, a faint scowl having taken unchallenged possession of her small face. Jorja was no less worried because of this change, but she was relieved to see that Marcie showed no further interest in the Little Ms. Doctor kit.

By four-thirty, the girl's scowl had faded, and she had become sociable once more. In a good mood again, she was such a natural charmer that she almost made it seem as if her outburst at the table had been no worse than any child's temper tantrum.

In fact, on the outside stairs of the apartment complex, beyond Marcie's hearing, Jorja's mother paused on the way down to the car and said, "She's just trying to let us know that she's hurt and confused. She doesn't understand why her father left, and right now she needs a lot of special attention, Jorja, a lot of love. That's all."

Jorja knew the problem was worse than that. She had no doubt that Marcie was still disturbed by her father's behavior, deeply hurt by his abandonment, and full of unresolved conflicts. But something else was eating the girl, something that seemed disturbingly irrational, and Jorja was scared of it.

Not long after Pete and Mary left, the girl began playing Little Ms. Doctor with the same unnerving intensity she had exhibited earlier, and when bedtime came she wanted to take the kit with her. Now, some of the Little Ms. Doctor things lay on the floor at Marcie's side of the bed, some on the nightstand. And in the dark bedroom the child dreamed and whimpered about doctors, nurses, needles.

Jorja would have been unable to sleep even if Marcie had been perfectly still and quiet. Worry induced insomnia even more effectively than a dozen cups of coffee. Since she was awake anyway, she listened attentively to her daughter's every dreamy utterance, hoping that she would hear something that would help her understand or that would assist the doctor in arriving at his diagnosis. It was after two o'clock in the morning when Marcie mumbled something different from what she had mumbled before, something that had nothing to do with doctors and nurses and big sharp needles. With a flurry of violent kicks, the girl flopped from her stomach onto her back, gasped, and went rigid, perfectly still. "The moon, moon, the moon," she said, in a voice that was filled with both amazement and fear, "the moon," a voice of such chilling whispery urgency that Jorja knew it was not just meaningless sleeptalk. "The moon, moon, *mooooooonnn . . .*"

CHICAGO, ILLINOIS.

Brendan Cronin, priest on probation, slept warmly under a blanket and patchwork quilt, smiling at something in a dream. The winter wind sighed through the giant pine tree outside, fluted and soughed in the eaves, and moaned at his window, exerting itself in evenly spaced gusts as if nature were ventilating the night with a huge mechanical bellows that faithfully produced eight exhalations to the minute. Even lost in his dream, Brendan must have been aware of the wind's slow pulse, for when he began to talk in his sleep, the words issued from him in a sympathetic rhythm: "The moon . . . the moon . . . the moon . . . the moon . . ."

LAGUNA BEACH, CALIFORNIA.

"The moon! The moon!"

Dominick Corvaisis was awakened by his own fearful shouting and by a burning pain in his right wrist. He was on his hands and knees in the darkness beside his bed, wrenching frantically at something that had a grip on his arm. He continued to struggle for a few seconds until the mists of sleep cleared, whereupon he realized that he was being held by nothing more sinister than the rope with which he had tethered himself.

Breathing raggedly, heart pounding, he fumbled for the lamp switch and winced as the sudden light stung his eyes. A quick look at the restraining rope showed that in his sleep (and in the dark) he had completely untied one of the four tightly drawn knots and partially unraveled a second before losing patience for the task. Then, in the panic that always accompanied his sleepwalking, he evidently had begun to pull and tug and twist against the belaying line as if he were a dumb animal protesting a leash, painfully abrading his right wrist.

Dom got off the floor and, pushing aside the tangled blankets, sat on the edge of the bed.

He knew he had been dreaming, though he could not recall anything about the dream. However, he was pretty sure that it was not the nightmare he had endured on other occasions during the past month, for that one had had nothing to do with the moon. This was another dream, equally terrifying but in a different way.

His shouts, which had been partly responsible for waking him, had been so importunate, so haunted, so fright-filled that he could even now summon them in memory as clearly as he had first heard them: *"The moon! The moon!"* He shuddered and raised his hands to his throbbing head.

The moon. What did it mean?

BOSTON, MASSACHUSETTS.

Ginger sat straight up in bed with a shrill cry.

Lavinia, the Hannabys' housekeeper, said, "Oh, I'm sorry, Dr. Weiss. Didn't mean to scare you. You were having a nightmare."

"Nightmare?" Ginger had no recollection of a dream.

"Oh, yes," Lavinia said, "and a really bad one from the sound of it. I was passing in the hall when I heard you crying out. I almost came in right away, until I realized you must be dreaming. I hesitated then, but you went on and on, shouting it over and over again, until I thought I'd better wake you."

Blinking, Ginger said, "Shouting? What was I shouting?"

"Over and over again," the housekeeper said. " 'The moon, the moon, the moon.' You sounded so frightened."

"I don't remember."

" 'The moon,' " Lavinia assured her, " 'the moon,' over and over again, in such a voice that I half-thought someone was killing you."

PART TWO

◆ ◆ ◆

DAYS OF DISCOVERY

Courage is resistance to fear, mastery
of fear—not absence of fear.
—MARK TWAIN

Is there some meaning to this life?
What purpose lies behind the strife?
Whence do we come, where are we bound?
These cold questions echo and resound
through each day, each lonely night.
We long to find the splendid light
that will cast a revelatory beam
upon the meaning of the human dream.
—THE BOOK OF COUNTED SORROWS

A friend may well be reckoned the
masterpiece of Nature.
—RALPH WALDO EMERSON

FOUR

◆

December 26–January 11

1. Boston, Massachusetts

Between December 27 and January 5, Dr. Ginger Weiss went to Pablo Jackson's Back Bay apartment six times. On six of those visits he used hypnotic therapy to probe cautiously and patiently at the Azrael Block that sealed off a portion of her memory.

To the old magician, she grew more beautiful each time she arrived at his door—more intelligent, charming, and appealingly tough-minded, too. Pablo saw in her the kind of woman he would have wanted as a daughter. Ginger had stirred in him protective fatherly feelings that he had never known before.

He told her nearly everything he had learned from Alexander Christophson at the Hergensheimers' Christmas party. She resisted the idea that her memory block had not developed naturally but had been implanted by persons unknown. "Too bizarre. Things like that don't happen to ordinary people like me. I'm just a *farmishteh* from Brooklyn, not someone who gets involved in international intrigue."

The only thing about his conversation with Alex Christophson that he did not tell her was that the retired espionage officer had warned against becoming involved with her. If Ginger knew Alex had been deeply disturbed, she might decide that the situation was too dangerous to justify Pablo's involvement. Out of concern for her and out of a selfish desire to be part of her life, he withheld that information.

At their first meeting on December 27, prior to the session of hypnosis, he prepared a lunch of quiche and salad. As they ate, Ginger said, "But, I've never been around a sensitive military installation, never been involved in any defense research, never associated with anyone who could conceivably be part of a spy ring. It's ludicrous!"

"If you stumbled on some dangerous bit of knowledge, it wasn't in a high security area. It was someplace you had every right to be ... except you just happened to be there at the wrong time."

"But listen, Pablo, if they brainwashed me, that would've taken time. They'd have had to hold me in custody somewhere. Right?"

"I imagine it would take a few days."

"So you can't be right," she said. "Of course, I realize that while they were forcing me to forget the thing I'd accidentally seen, they'd also repress the memory of the place where they held me for the brainwashing. But there'd be a blank spot in my past somewhere, an empty time when I couldn't remember where I'd been or what I'd done.''

"Not at all. They'd implant a set of false recollections to cover the missing days, and you'd never know the difference.''

"*Good God!* Really? They could do that?''

"One thing I hope to do is locate those false memories,'' Pablo explained as he finished his quiche. "It'll take a long time, slowly regressing you back through your life week by week, but when I find the phony memories, I'll recognize them *tout de suite* because they won't have the detail, the substance, of genuine memories. Mere stage sets, you see. If we find two or three days of tissue-thin memories, we'll have pinpointed the origin of your problem because those will be the dates when you were in the hands of these people . . . whoever they may be.''

"Yes, yes, I see,'' she said, suddenly excited. "The first day of the mushy memories will be the day that I saw something I shouldn't have seen. And the last day will be the day they finished brainwashing me. It's terribly difficult to believe. . . . But if someone really did *implant* this memory block, and if all my symptoms—the fugues—are a result of those repressed memories struggling to the surface, then my problem isn't really psychological. There's a chance I could practice medicine again. All I've got to do is dig out the memories, bring them into the light, and then the pressure will be relieved.''

Pablo took her hand and gave it a squeeze. "Yes, I believe there's real hope. But it's not going to be easy. Every time I probe at the block, I risk plunging you into a coma . . . or worse. I intend to be oh-so-careful, but the risk remains.''

The first two sessions of deep hypnosis were conducted in armchairs by the huge bay window, one on December 27, one on Sunday the 29th, each lasting four hours. Pablo regressed her day by day through the previous nine months but found no obviously artificial memories.

Also on Sunday, Ginger suggested he question her about Dominick Corvaisis, the novelist whose picture affected her in such a peculiar manner. When Pablo hypnotized her and established that he was speaking to the inner Ginger, to her deep subconscious self, he asked if she had ever met Corvaisis, and after a brief hesitation she said, "Yes.'' Pablo pursued the point cautiously and diligently, but he could get almost nothing more out of her. At last a thin vapor of memory escaped her: "He threw salt in my face.''

"Corvaisis threw salt on you?'' Puzzled, Pablo asked, "Why?''

"Can't . . . quite . . . remember.''

"Where did this happen?''

Her frown deepened, and when he continued to pursue the subject, she withdrew, sinking into that frightening comatose state. He quickly retreated before she had spiraled down as deep as she had done before. He assured her that he would ask no further questions about Corvaisis if only she would return, and gradually she responded to that promise.

Clearly, Ginger had at one time met Corvaisis. And her encounter with him was associated with the memories of which she had been robbed.

In the next two sessions—Monday the 30th and Wednesday, first day of the New Year—Pablo regressed Ginger yet another eight months, to the end of July, two summers ago, without discovering any tissue-thin memories that would indicate the work of mind-control specialists.

Then on Thursday, January 2, Ginger asked him to question her about her previous night's unremembered dream. For the fourth time since Christmas, she had cried out in her sleep—"The moon!"—with such insistence that she woke others in Baywatch. "I think the dream's about the place and time that's been stolen from me. Put me in a trance, and maybe we'll learn something."

But when hypnotized and returned to last night's dream, she refused to answer questions and drifted into a deeper sleep than a mere hypnotic trance. He had pulled the Azrael Trigger once more, which was proof positive that her dreams involved those forbidden memories.

On Friday they did not meet. Pablo needed the day to read further about memory blocks of all kinds and to think about how best to proceed.

In addition, he had recorded all five post-Christmas sessions, so he sat at the reproduction Sheraton desk in his book-lined study and listened to portions of those tapes for hours. He was searching for a single word or a change in Ginger's voice that might make a particular answer seem more important on rehearing than it had seemed at the time.

He found nothing startling, though he noticed that, during hypnotic regression, a subtle note of anxiety had entered her voice when their backward journey through time had reached August 31 of the year before last. It was nothing dramatic that would have caught his attention at the time the recordings were made. But by telescoping all the sessions into one afternoon, using the fast-forward control to skip from day to day, he saw the pattern of steadily building anxiety, and he suspected they were getting close to the event now hidden behind the Azrael Block.

Therefore, during their sixth post-Christmas session on Saturday, January 4, Pablo was not surprised when the breakthrough came. As usual, Ginger was sitting in one of the armchairs by the bay window, beyond which a fine snow was falling. Her silver-blond hair glowed with spectral light. As he regressed her back through July of the previous year, her brows knitted, and her voice became whispery and tense, and Pablo knew she was drawing closer to the moment of her forgotten ordeal.

Since they were going backward in time, he had already taken her through her busy months as a surgical resident at Memorial Hospital, back to the moment when she first reported to George Hannaby for duty on Monday, July 30, more than seventeen months ago. Her memories remained sharp and richly detailed as Pablo conveyed her into Sunday, July 29, when she still had been settling into her new apartment. July 28, 27, 26, 25, 24 . . . through those days she had been unpacking and shopping for furniture . . . all the way back to July 21, 20, 19. . . . On July 18, the moving van arrived with her household goods, which she had shipped from Palo Alto, California, where she had lived the previous two years while taking an advanced course of study in vascular surgery. Farther back . . .

On July 17, she arrived in Boston by car and booked a room overnight at the Holiday Inn Government Center, as close to Beacon Hill as possible, not yet able to stay at her new apartment because she had no bed there.

"By car? You drove cross-country from Stanford?"

"It was the first vacation I ever really had. I like to drive, and it was a chance to see a little of the country," Ginger said, but in such an ominous voice that she might have been talking about a journey through hell rather than a transcontinental holiday.

So Pablo began to regress her through the days of her journey, back across the midwestern heartland, around the northernmost horn of the Rocky Mountains, through Utah, into Nevada, until they came to Tuesday morning, July 10. She had stayed the previous night at a motel, and when he asked for the name of it, a shudder passed through her.

"T-Tranquility."

"Tranquility Motel? Where is this place? Describe it, too."

On the arms of her chair, her hands curled into fists. "Thirty miles west of Elko, on Interstate 80." Haltingly, reluctantly, she described the twenty-unit Tranquility Motel and Grille. Something about the place terrified her. Every muscle in her body went rigid.

Pablo said, "So you stayed the night of July ninth at the motel. That was a Monday. All right, so now it's Monday, July ninth. You're just arriving at the motel. You haven't stayed there yet; you're just driving up to it. . . . What time of the day is it?"

She did not answer, and her tremors grew more pronounced, and when he asked again, she said, "I didn't arrive on Monday. F-Friday."

Startled, Pablo said, "The previous Friday? You stayed at the Tranquility Motel from Friday, July sixth, through Monday, July ninth? Four nights at this small motel in the middle of nowhere?" He leaned forward in his chair, sensing that they had found the time when her mind had been tampered with. "Why would you want to stay so long?"

In a slightly wooden voice, she said, "Because it was peaceful. I was on vacation, after all. Her strangely stilted voice became more flat and devoid of nuance with each word she spoke. "I needed to relax, you see, and this was a perfect place to relax."

The old magician looked away from her, watched the faintly luminous snow slanting down through the dreary gray afternoon beyond the window, and carefully considered his next question. "You said this motel has no swimming pool. And the rooms you've described aren't luxurious. Not resort-style rooms for long-term visits. What on earth did you do for four days out there in the middle of nowhere, Ginger?"

"Like I said, I relaxed. Just relaxed. Napped. Read a couple of books. Watched some TV. They have good TV even way out there on the plains because they've got their own little satellite receiver dish on the roof." Her manner of speech was now entirely altered, and she sounded as if she were reading from a script. "After two intense years at Stanford, I needed a few days of doing absolutely nothing."

"What books did you read while at the motel?"

"I . . . I don't remember." Her hands were still fisted, and she was still rigid. Fine pearly beads of sweat popped out along her hairline.

"Ginger, you're there now, in the motel room, reading. Understand? You are reading whatever you were reading then. Now look at the title of the book and tell me what it is."

"I . . . no . . . no title."

"Every book has a title."

"No title."

"Because there really is no book—is there?" he said.

"Yes. I just relaxed. Napped. Read a couple of books. Watched some TV," she said in a soft, dead, emotionless voice. "They have good TV even way out there on the plains because they've got their own little satellite receiver dish on the roof."

"What TV shows did you watch?" Pablo asked.

"News. Movies."

"What movies?"

She flinched. "I . . . don't remember."

Pablo was quite sure that the reason she did not remember these things was precisely because she had never done them. She had been at that motel, all right, because she could describe it in minute detail, but she could not recall the books and the TV programs because she had never passed any of that time in those pursuits. Through clever post-hypnotic suggestions, she had been instructed to say that she had done those things, and she had actually been made to remember vaguely having done them, but they were merely artificial memories designed to cover what had really transpired at that motel. A specialist in brainwashing could insert false memories in a subject's mind, but even if he worked very hard at it and built an intricate web of interlocking details, he could not make the phony memories as convincing as real ones.

Pablo said, "Where did you eat dinner each night?"

"The Tranquility Grille. It's a small place, and it doesn't have much of a menu, but the food is reasonably good." That response was, once again, delivered in a flat and hollow voice.

Pablo said, "What did you eat at the Tranquility Grille?"

She hesitated. "I . . . I don't remember."

"But you told me the food was good. How could you make that judgment if you don't remember what you ate?"

"Uhhh . . . it's a small place, and it doesn't have much of a menu."

The more insistently he pressed for details, the more tense she became. Her voice remained emotionless as she spewed out her programmed responses, but her face twisted and hardened with anxiety.

Pablo could have told her that her apparent memories of those four days at the Tranquility Motel were false. He could have ordered her to blow them out of her mind the way one might blow dust from an old book, and she would have done it. Then he could have told her that her true memories were locked behind an Azrael Block, and that she must hammer it into more dust. But if he had done so, she would have plunged, as programmed, into a coma—or worse. He would have to spend many days, possibly weeks, looking for tiny cracks to exploit cautiously.

For today, he contented himself with identifying the precise number of hours of her life that had been stolen from her. He took her back to Friday, July 6 of the summer before last, and asked exactly when she signed the register at the Tranquility Motel.

"A little after eight o'clock." She no longer spoke in a wooden voice because these were real memories. "It was still an hour before sunset, but I was exhausted. All I wanted was dinner, a shower, and bed." She described the man and woman behind the check-in counter in detail. She even recalled their names: Faye and Ernie.

Pablo said, "Once you had checked in, you ate at the Tranquility Grille next to the motel. So describe the place."

She did so, and in convincing detail. But when he jumped her ahead to the moment at which she left the restaurant, her recollections were phony again, thin and without color. Clearly, her memories had been altered from some point after she had gone into the Tranquility Grille on that Friday evening until she had left the motel and had headed toward Utah the following Tuesday morning.

Pablo backtracked, returning Ginger to the small restaurant once more, searching for the exact moment at which the genuine memories ended and the false began. "Tell me about your dinner from the moment you went into Tranquility Grille that Friday evening. Minute by minute."

Ginger sat up straight in her chair. Her eyes were still closed, but under the shuttered lids, they moved visibly, as if she were looking left and right upon entering the Tranquility Grille. She unfisted her hands and got up, much to Pablo's surprise. She walked away from her chair, toward the center of the room. He walked beside her to prevent her from bumping into furniture. She did not know she was in his apartment but imagined herself to be making her way between the tables in the restaurant. As she moved, the tension and fear left her, for now she was wholly in that time, prior to all her trouble, when she had had nothing about which to be tense or afraid.

In a quiet, anxiety-free voice she said, "Took me a while to freshen up and get over here, so it's almost twilight. Outside, the plains are orange in the late sunlight, and the inside of the diner is full of that glow. I think I'll take that booth over in the corner by the window."

Pablo went with her, guiding her past the Picasso painting toward one of the sofas that was decorated with colorful pastel accent pillows.

She said, "Mmmm. Smells good. Onions . . . spices . . . French fries . . ."

"How many people in the diner, Ginger?"

She paused and turned her head, surveying the room with closed eyes. "The cook behind the counter and a waitress. Three men . . . truck drivers, I guess . . . on stools at the counter. And . . . three at that table . . . and the chubby priest . . . another guy over at that booth . . ." Ginger continued pointing and counting. "Oh, eleven in all, plus me."

"All right," Pablo said, "let's go to that booth by the windows."

She began walking again, smiled vaguely at someone, sidestepped an obstacle that only she could see, then suddenly twitched in surprise, jerked one hand to her face. "Oh!" She stopped.

"What is it?" Pablo asked. "What's happened?"

She blinked furiously for a moment, smiled, and spoke to someone in the Tranquility Grille back there on July 6 of last year. "No, no, I'm all right. It's nothing. I've already brushed it off." She wiped her face with one hand. "See?" She had been looking down, as if the other person was seated, and now she raised her eyes as he got up.

Pablo waited for her to continue the conversation.

She said, "Well, when you spill salt you'd *better* throw some over your shoulder, or God knows what'll happen. My father used to throw it three times, so if you'd been him, you'd have buried me in the stuff."

She started walking again, and Pablo said, "Stop. Wait, Ginger. The man who threw salt over his shoulder—tell me what he looks like."

"Young," she said. "Thirty-two or thirty-three. About five-ten. Lean. Dark hair. Dark eyes. Sort of handsome. Seems shy, sweet."

Dominick Corvaisis. No doubt about it.

She began to move again. Pablo stayed at her side until, realizing she was about to sit in the restaurant booth, he guided her gently to the sofa. She sat back on it and looked out a window, smiling at her private panorama of Nevada plains washed in the light of a dying sun.

Pablo watched and listened while Ginger exchanged pleasantries with the waitress and ordered a bottle of Coors. The beer was served, and Ginger pantomimed sipping it while she watched the sun fade. Seconds ticked past, but Pablo didn't speed her through the scene because he knew they were approaching the crucial moment when her real memories gave way to phony ones. The event—the thing that she saw and should not have seen—had transpired around this time, and Pablo wanted to learn everything he could about the minutes leading up to it.

Twilight arrived back there in the past.

When the waitress returned, Ginger ordered a bowl of the homemade vegetable soup and a cheeseburger with all the trimmings.

Night fell out there in Nevada.

Abruptly, before her food had been served, Ginger frowned and said, "What's that?" She looked out the imagined window, scowling.

"What do you see?" Pablo asked, chained to his inconvenient vantage point in present-day Boston.

A worried look came over her face, and she stood up. "What the devil *is* that noise?" She looked toward other people in the restaurant with a puzzled expression, and she spoke to them: "I don't know. I don't know what it is." She suddenly tottered sideways and nearly fell. *"Gevalt!"* She reached out as if supporting herself against the side of a booth or table. "Shaking. Why's everything shaking?" She jumped in surprise. "It's knocked over my beer glass. Is it an earthquake? What's happening? What *is* that sound?" She stumbled again. Now she was frightened. "The door!" She started to run across the living room, though in her mind she was heading toward the exit from the restaurant that, in reality, she had long ago departed. "The door," she cried again, but then she stopped abruptly, swaying, gasping, shuddering.

When Pablo caught up with her, she dropped to her knees and hung her head. "What's happening, Ginger?"

"Nothing." She had changed in an instant.

"What's that noise?"

"What noise?" The robot voice again.

"Ginger, damn it, what's happening in the Tranquility Grille?"

Horror was on her face, but she merely said, "I'm having dinner."

"That's a false memory."

"Having dinner."

He tried to make her continue with the crucial memory of the frightening thing that had been about to happen. But at last he had to accept that the Azrael Block, behind which her memories were repressed, took form when she had been running for the restaurant door, and it did not end until the following Tuesday morning, when she drove east toward Salt Lake City. In time, he might be able to chip it down to smaller dimensions, but enough had been accomplished for one day.

At last they were making real headway. They knew that on the night of Friday, July 6, the year before last, Ginger had seen something she had not been meant to see. Having seen it, she had almost certainly been detained in a room at the Tranquility Motel, where someone had used sophisticated brainwashing techniques to conceal the memory of that event from her and thereby prevent her from carrying word of it to the world. They had worked on her for three days— Saturday, Sunday, and Monday—releasing her, with sanitized recollections, on Tuesday.

But, in God's name, who were these omnipotent strangers? And what had she seen?

2. Portland, Oregon

Sunday, January 5, Dominick Corvaisis flew to Portland and took a hotel room near the apartment house in which he had once lived. Rain was falling hard, and the air was cold.

Except for dinner in the hotel restaurant, he spent the remaining hours of Sunday afternoon and evening at a table by the window of his room, alternately staring out at the rain-lashed city and studying the roadmaps. Again and again, he mentally reviewed the trip he had taken the summer before last (and would take again starting tomorrow).

As he had told Parker Faine on Christmas, he was convinced that he had stumbled into a dangerous situation out there on the road, and that (paranoid as it sounded) the memory of it had been wiped from his mind. The mail from his unknown correspondent pointed to no other conclusion.

Two days ago, he had received a third envelope without a return address, postmarked New York. Now, when Dom tired of looking at the maps and staring thoughtfully out at the Oregon rain, he picked up that envelope, shook out the contents, and studied them. This time there had been no note, just two Polaroid photographs.

The first picture had the least effect on him, although it made him tense—unaccountably tense, considering that it was a photograph of someone who, as far as he knew, was a stranger to him. A young, pudgy priest with unruly auburn hair, freckles, and green eyes. He was facing the camera, sitting in a chair near a small writing desk, a suitcase at his side. He was very erect, head up and shoulders squared off, hands limp in his lap, knees together. The picture disturbed Dom because the expression on the priest's face was only one step removed from the lifeless, sightless stare of a corpse. The man was alive; that much was evident from his rigid posture, yet his eyes were chillingly empty.

The second photograph hit Dom much harder than the first, and its powerful effect did not diminish with familiarity. A young woman was the subject of this snapshot, and she was no stranger. Although Dom could not recall where they had met, he knew they were acquainted. The sight of her made his heart quicken with a fear similar to that which filled him when he woke from one of his episodes of sleepwalking. She was in her late twenties. Blue eyes. Silver-blond hair. Exquisitely proportioned face. She would have been exceptionally beautiful if her expression had not been precisely that of the priest: slack, dead, empty-eyed. She had been photographed from the waist up, lying in a narrow bed, sheets pulled up chastely to her neck. Restraining straps held her down. One arm was partially bared to allow clearance for an IV needle in her wrist vein. She looked small, helpless, oppressed.

The photograph instantly brought to mind his own nightmare in which unseen men were shouting at him and forcing his face into a sink. A couple of times, that bad dream had not begun at the sink itself but in a bed in a strange room, where his vision was blurred by a saffron mist. Looking at the young woman, Dom was convinced that somewhere there was a Polaroid shot of him in similar circumstances: strapped to a bed, an IV needle in his arm, his face without expression.

When he had shown the two photographs to Parker Faine on Friday, the day they came in the mail, the artist jumped to similar conclusions. "If I'm wrong, roast me in hell and make sandwiches for the devil, but I swear this is a snapshot of a woman in a trance or drug-induced stupor, undergoing the brainwashing that you evidently underwent. Christ, this situation gets more bizarre and fascinating day by day! It's something you ought to be able to go to the cops about—but you can't, because who's to say which side *they'd* be on? It may have been a branch of our own government you ran afoul of out there on the road. Anyway, you weren't the only one who got in trouble, good buddy. This priest and this woman also stumbled into it. Whoever went to this much trouble is hiding something damned big, a lot bigger than I thought before.''

Now, sitting at the table by his hotel room window, Dom held one picture in each hand, side by side, and let his gaze travel back and forth from the priest to the woman. ''Who are you?'' he asked aloud. ''What're your names? What happened to us out there?''

Outside, lightning cracked whiplike in the night over Portland, as if a cosmic coachman were urging the rain to fall faster. Like the drumming hooves of a thousand harried horses, fat, hard-driven raindrops hammered against the wall of the hotel and galloped down the window.

Later, Dom fastened himself to the bed with a tether that he had improved considerably since Christmas. First he wrapped a length of surgical gauze around his right wrist and secured it with adhesive tape, a barrier between rope and flesh to prevent abrasion. He was no longer using an ordinary all-purpose line but a hawser-laid nylon rope, only a quarter-inch in diameter but with a breaking strength of twenty-six hundred pounds. It was expressly made for rock- and mountain-climbing.

He had switched to the sturdier rope because, on the night of December 28, he had slipped his previous tether by chewing all the way through it while asleep. The mountaineering rope was fray-resistant and nearly as impervious to teeth as copper cable would have been.

That night in Portland, he woke three times, wrestling furiously with the tether, perspiring, panting, his racing heart's accelerator floored beneath a heavy weight of fear. ''The moon! The moon!''

3. Las Vegas, Nevada

The day after Christmas, Jorja Monatella took Marcie to Dr. Louis Besancourt, and the examination turned into an ordeal that frustrated the physician, frightened Jorja, and embarrassed them both. From the moment Jorja took her into the doctor's waiting room, the girl screamed, screeched, wailed, and wept. ''No doctors! They'll hurt me!''

On those rare occasions when Marcie misbehaved (and they were rare, indeed), one hard slap on the bottom was usually all that was required to restore her senses and induce contrition. But when Jorja tried that now, it had the opposite effect of what she intended. Marcie screamed louder, wailed more shrilly, and wept more copiously than before.

The assistance of an understanding nurse was required to convey the shrieking child from the waiting area into an examination room, by which time Jorja was not only mortified but worried sick by Marcie's complete irrationality. Dr. Besancourt's good humor and bedside manner were not enough to quiet the girl, and in fact she became more frightened and violent the moment he appeared. Marcie pulled away from him when he tried to touch her, screamed, struck him, kicked him, until it became necessary for Jorja and a nurse to hold her down. When the doctor used an ophthalmoscope to examine her eyes, her terror reached a crescendo indicated by a sudden loosening of her bladder that was dismayingly reminiscent of the fiasco on Christmas Day.

Her uncontrolled urination marked an abrupt change in her demeanor. She became sullen, silent, just as she had for a while on Christmas. She was shockingly pale, and she shivered constantly. She had that eerie detachment that made Jorja think of autism.

Lou Besancourt had no simple diagnosis with which to comfort Jorja. He spoke of neurological and brain disorders, and psychological illness. He wanted Marcie to check into Sunrise Hospital for a few days of tests.

The ugly scene at Besancourt's office was just a warmup for a series of fits Marcie threw at the hospital. The mere sight of doctors and nurses catapulted her into panic, and invariably the panic became outright hysteria that escalated until, exhausted, the child fell into that semicatatonic trance from which she needed hours to recover.

Jorja took a week of sick-leave from the casino and virtually lived at Sunrise for four days, sleeping on a rollaway bed in Marcie's room. She didn't get much rest. Even in a drugged sleep, Marcie twitched, kicked, whimpered, and cried out in her dreams: "The moon, the moon . . ." By the fourth night, Sunday, December 29, worried and weary, Jorja almost needed medical attention for herself.

Miraculously, on Monday morning, Marcie's irrational terror simply went away. She still did not like being hospitalized, and she pleaded aggressively to go home. But she no longer appeared to feel that the walls were going to close in and crush her. She remained uneasy in the company of doctors and nurses, but she did not shrink from them in horror or strike them when they touched her. She was still pale, nervous, and watchful. But for the first time in days, her appetite was normal, and she ate everything on her breakfast tray.

Later in the day, after the final testing had been completed, while Marcie was sitting in bed eating lunch, Dr. Besancourt spoke with Jorja in the hall. He was a hound-faced man with a bulbous nose and moist, kind eyes. "Negative, Jorja. Every test, negative. No brain tumors, no cerebral lesions, no neurological dysfunction."

Jorja almost burst into tears. "Thank God."

"I'm going to refer Marcie to another doctor," Besancourt said. "Ted Coverly. He's a child psychologist, and a good one. I'm sure he'll ferret out the cause of this. Funny thing is . . . I have a hunch we *may* have cured Marcie without realizing we were doing it."

Jorja blinked. "Cured her? What do you mean?"

"In retrospect I can see that her behavior had all the earmarks of a phobia. Irrational fear, panic attacks . . . I suspect she'd begun to develop a severe phobic aversion to all things medical. And there's a treatment called 'flooding,' wherein the phobic patient is purposefully, even ruthlessly exposed to the thing he fears for such a long time—hours and hours—that the power of the phobia is shattered. Which is what we might've inadvertently done to Marcie when we forced her into the hospital."

"Why would she have developed such a phobia?" Jorja asked. "Where would it've come from? She's never had a bad experience with doctors or hospitals. She's never been seriously ill."

Besancourt shrugged, sidled out of the way of some nurses pushing a patient on a gurney. "We don't know what causes phobias. You don't have to crash in a plane in order to be afraid of flying. Phobias just . . . spring up. Even if we accidentally cured her, there'll be a residual apprehension that Ted Coverly can identify. He'll root out any remaining traces of phobic anxiety. Don't worry, Jorja."

That afternoon, Monday, December 30, Marcie was released from the hospital. In the car on the way home, she was almost her old self, happily pointing out animal shapes in the clouds. At home, she dashed into the living room and settled down immediately among the piles of new Christmas toys which she had not yet had much opportunity to enjoy. She still played with the Little Ms. Doctor kit, though not exclusively or with that disturbing intensity that she had exhibited on Christmas Day.

Jorja's parents raced over to the apartment. Jorja had kept them away from the hospital by arguing that they might disturb Marcie's delicate condition. Marcie remained in a splendid mood at dinner, sweet and amusing, leaving Jorja's parents disarmed.

For the next three nights, Marcie slept in Jorja's bed in case she suffered an anxiety attack, but none materialized. The nightmares came with less frequency and less power than before, and Marcie's sleeptalk awakened Jorja only twice in three nights. "The moon, moon, the moon!" But now it was a soft and almost forlorn call rather than a shout.

In the morning, at breakfast, she asked Marcie about the dream, but the girl could not remember it. "The moon?" she said, frowning into her bowl of Trix. "Didn't dream about the moon. Dreamed about horses. Can I have a horse someday?"

"Maybe, when we don't live in an apartment any more."

Marcie giggled. "I *know* that. You can't keep a horse in an apartment. The neighbors would complain."

Thursday, Marcie saw Dr. Coverly for the first time. She liked him. If she still had an abnormal fear of doctors, she hid it well.

That night Marcie slept in her own bed, with only the company of a teddy bear named Murphy. Jorja got up three times between midnight and dawn to look in on her daughter. Once she heard the now-familiar chant—"moon, moon, moon"—in a whisper that, because it was an eerie blend of fear and delight, made the hair prickle on her scalp.

And on Friday, with three days of school vacation still ahead for Marcie, Jorja put her in Kara Persaghian's care once more and returned to work. It was almost a relief to get back to the noise and smoke of the casino. Cigarettes, stale beer, and the occasional blast of halitosis were infinitely more pleasing than the antiseptic stink of the hospital.

She picked up Marcie at Kara's place, and on the way home the girl excitedly showed her the product of a day spent drawing on butcher's paper: scores of pictures of the moon in every imaginable hue.

On Sunday morning, January 5, when Jorja got out of bed and went to brew coffee, she found Marcie at the dining room table, engaged in a curious task. The girl, still in her pajamas, was taking all the photographs out of their picture album and making neat stacks of them.

"I'm putting the pictures in a shoebox, because I need the . . . ablum," the girl said, frowning over the hard word. "I need it for my moon collection." She held up a picture of the moon clipped from a magazine. "I'm going to make a *big* collection."

"Why? Baby, why're you so interested in the moon?"

"It's pretty," Marcie said. She put the picture on a blank page of the photo album and stared at it. In her fixed gaze, in the intensity of her fascination with the photograph, there was an echo of the single-mindedness with which she had played Little Ms. Doctor.

With a quiver of apprehension, Jorja thought, This is how the damn doctor phobia started. Quietly. Innocently. Has Marcie merely traded one phobia for another?

She had the urge to run to the telephone and somehow get hold of Dr. Coverly, even if it was Sunday and his day off.

But as she stood by the table, studying her daughter, Jorja decided she was overreacting. Marcie certainly had not traded one phobia for another. After all, the girl wasn't *afraid* of the moon. Just . . . well, strangely fascinated by it. A temporary enthusiasm. Any parent of a bright seven-year-old was accustomed to these short-lived but fiercely burning fascinations and infatuations.

Nevertheless, Jorja decided she would tell Dr. Coverly about it when she took Marcie to his office for a second session on Tuesday.

At twelve-twenty A.M. Monday, before she turned in for the night, Jorja looked in on Marcie to see if she was sleeping soundly. The girl was not in bed. In her dark room, she had drawn a chair up to the window and was sitting there, staring out.

"Honey? What's wrong?"

"Nothing's wrong. Come see," Marcie said softly, dreamily.

Heading toward the girl, Jorja said, "What is it, Peanut?"

"The moon," Marcie said, her eyes fixed on the silvery crescent high in the black vault of the sky. "The moon."

4. Boston, Massachusetts

On Monday, January 6, the wind from the Atlantic was bitterly cold and unrelenting, and all of Boston was humbled by it. On the blustery streets, heavily bundled and bescarfed people hurried toward sanctuary with their shoulders drawn up and heads tucked down. In the hard gray winter light, the modern glass office towers appeared to be constructed of ice, while the older buildings of historic Boston huddled together, presenting a drab and miserable face utterly unlike their charm and stateliness in better weather. Last night, sleet had fallen. The barren trees were jacketed in glittering ice, bare black branches poking through the white crust like the marrow core revealed beneath the outer layers of shattered bones.

Herbert, the efficient major domo who kept the Hannaby household functioning smoothly, drove Ginger Weiss to her seventh post-Christmas meeting with Pablo Jackson. The wind and the previous night's ice-storm had brought down power lines and disrupted the traffic lights at more than half the intersections. They finally reached Newbury Street at eleven-oh-five A.M., just five minutes past Ginger's eleven o'clock appointment.

After the breakthrough during Saturday's session, Ginger had wanted to contact the people at the Tranquility Motel in Nevada and broach the subject of the unremembered event that had transpired there on the night of July 6, the summer before last. Either the owners of that motel were accomplices of those who had tampered with Ginger's memory, or they were victims like her. If they had been subjected to brainwashing, perhaps they also were experiencing anxiety attacks of one sort or another.

Pablo was firmly opposed to immediate confrontation. He felt the risks were too great. If the owners of the motel were not victims but associates of the victimizers, Ginger might be putting herself in grave danger. "You've got to be patient. Before approaching them, you must have as much information as you can possibly obtain."

She had suggested they go to the police, seeking protection and an investigation, but Pablo had convinced her that the police would not be interested. She had no proof that she had been the victim of a mental mugging. Besides, the local constabulary could not unravel a crime across state lines. She'd have to go to the federal authorities or local Nevada police, and in either case she might be unwittingly seeking help from the very people responsible for what had been done to her.

Frustrated but unable to find a hole in Pablo's arguments, Ginger had agreed to continue following his program of treatment. He had wanted Sunday to himself, so he could review the crucial tape of Saturday's session, and he had said he was not available Monday morning because he intended to see a friend in the hospital. "But you come back at, say, one o'clock Monday afternoon, and we'll begin chipping away at the edges of that memory block—*en pantoufles,* 'in slippers' as they say, in a relaxed manner."

This morning he had called her from the hospital to say that his friend was being discharged sooner than expected, and that he, Pablo, would be home by eleven o'clock if she would like to come earlier than planned. "You can help me make lunch."

Now, disembarking from the elevator and stepping quickly along the short hall to Pablo's apartment, Ginger decided that she would make every effort to control her natural impatience and to settle for making progress *en pantoufles,* as the magician was determined they would.

The front door was ajar. Assuming he had left it open for her, she stepped into the foyer. Closing the door, she said, "Pablo?"

In another room, someone grunted. Something clattered softly. Something thudded to the floor.

"Pablo?" He did not answer. Moving into the living room, she called out louder than before. "Pablo?"

Silence.

One of the library's double doors was open, and a light was on. Ginger entered—and saw Pablo lying face-down on the floor near the Sheraton desk. He had evidently just returned from his visit to his hospitalized friend, for he was still wearing galoshes and an overcoat.

As she rushed to him and knelt at his side, grim possibilities occurred to her— cerebral hemorrhage, thrombosis, or embolism; massive heart attack—but she was not prepared for what she found when she eased him onto his back. Pablo had been shot high in the chest, and bright red arterial blood welled from the bullet hole.

His eyes fluttered open, and although they looked unfocused, he seemed to know who she was. Blood bubbled over his lower lip. He got out a single word in an urgent whisper: *"Run."*

Her instinctive reaction upon seeing him prone before the desk had been that of a friend and physician: Anguished, she had gone immediately to his aid. But until Pablo said, "Run," Ginger did not understand that her own life might be in jeopardy. Suddenly she realized that she had heard no gunfire, which meant a silencer-equipped pistol. The assailant was no ordinary burglar. Someone infinitely more dangerous. All those considerations flashed through her mind in an instant.

Her heart pounding, she rose and turned toward the door. The gunman—tall and broad-shouldered, wearing a leather topcoat belted tightly at the waist—came out from behind the door, holding the silencer-equipped pistol. He was big, but surprisingly less threatening in appearance than she had expected. He was her age, clean-cut, with innocent blue eyes and a face unsuited for menace.

When he spoke, the disparity between his unremarkable appearance and his murderous actions was even greater, for his first words were a tremulous apology of sorts. "Shouldn't have happened. Didn't have to happen, for Christ's sake. I just . . . I was duping those tapes on a high-speed recorder. That's all I wanted—dupes of the tapes."

He was pointing to the desk, and for the first time Ginger noticed an open attaché case in which was nestled a compact piece of electronic equipment. Tape cassettes were scattered across the top of the desk, and she knew at once what tapes they were.

"Let's call an ambulance," she said. She edged toward the phone, but he stopped her by gesturing pointedly and angrily with the gun.

"High-speed duplication," he said, torn between rage and tears. "I could've made copies of all six of your sessions and been out of here. He wasn't supposed to be home for another fucking hour at least!"

Ginger grabbed a chair cushion and used it to prop up Pablo's head, so he would not choke on the blood and phlegm in his throat.

Obviously stunned by what had happened, the gunman said, "He just comes in so quiet, gliding in here like a goddamned ghost."

Ginger remembered how gracefully and elegantly the magician carried himself, as if each movement was prelude to an act of prestidigitation.

Pablo coughed, closed his eyes. Ginger wanted to do more for him, but the only remedy was heroic surgery. At the moment, she could only keep a hand on his shoulder in a feeble attempt to reassure him.

She looked up entreatingly, but the gunman only said, "And what the hell's he doing packing a gun? A fucking eighty-year-old man, a gun in his fist, as if he knows how to handle something like this."

Until now, Ginger had not noticed the pistol on the carpet, a few feet from Pablo's out-flung hand. When she saw it, a cripplingly sharp pang of horror went through her, and she nearly passed out, for in that instant she knew Pablo had been aware all along that it was dangerous to help her. She had not suspected that the mere attempt to probe at the memory block would quickly draw the unwanted attentions of men like this one in the leather topcoat. Because this meant she was being watched. Maybe not hour by hour or even every day. But *they* were keeping tabs on her. The moment she first called Pablo, she unwittingly endangered his life. And somehow he had known, for he had been packing a gun. Now, Ginger felt the weight of guilt.

"If he hadn't pulled that stupid .22," the gunman said miserably, "and if he hadn't insisted on calling the cops, I'd have walked away without laying a hand on him. I didn't want to hurt him. Shit."

"For God's sake," Ginger said beseechingly, "let me call an ambulance. If you didn't mean to hurt him, then let's get help."

The gunman shook his head, and his gaze moved to the crumpled magician. "Too late anyway. He's dead."

Those last two words, like a pair of hard punches, knocked the breath out of her and drew the shadowy curtain of unconsciousness to the edges of her vision. One glance at the old man's glassy eyes was enough to confirm what the gunman had said, yet she resisted the truth. She lifted his left hand and put her fingertips to his thin black wrist, feeling for a pulse. Finding none, she searched along the carotid artery in his throat, but in spite of the remaining warmth of the flesh, there was only an awful stillness where once had been the throb of life. "No," she said. "Oh, no." She touched Pablo's dark brow, not with the diagnostic intent of a physician but tenderly, lovingly. Her heart was so painfully constricted with grief that it was difficult to believe she had known the magician only two weeks. Like her father, she was quick to give her heart, and because Pablo was the man he was, the gift of affection and love was even more easily bestowed than usual.

"I'm sorry," the killer said shakily. "I'm really sorry. If he hadn't tried to stop me, I'd have walked right out of here. Now, I've killed someone, haven't I? And . . . you've seen my face."

Blinking back her tears, suddenly aware that she could not afford to grieve right now, Ginger rose slowly to her feet and faced him.

As if thinking aloud, the gunman said, "You've got to be dealt with now, too. I'll have to ransack the place, empty out drawers, take a few things of value, and make it look like you two walked in on a burglar." He chewed worriedly on his lower lip. "Yeah, it'll work. Instead of copying the tapes, I'll just take them, so they won't be here to raise suspicions." He looked at Ginger and winced. "I'm sorry. Jesus, I really am, but that's the way it'll have to be. I wish it didn't. It's partly my fault. Should've heard the old bastard coming in. Shouldn't have let him surprise me." He moved toward her. "Should I maybe rape you, too? I mean, would a burglar just shoot a good-looking girl like you? Wouldn't he rape you first? Wouldn't that make this look more real?" He came closer, and she began to back away. "God, I don't know if I can do it. I mean, how can I get a hard-on and do it to you when I know I've got to kill you afterward?" He kept coming toward her, and she backed up against the bookshelves. "I don't like this. Believe me, I don't. This shouldn't have to happen. I really *hate* this."

His apparently genuine pity, repeated apologies, and sorrowful self-recriminations gave Ginger the creeps. He would have been less frightening if he had been pitiless and bloodthirsty. The fact that he had scruples but could set them aside long enough to commit one rape and two murders . . . that made him more of a monster.

He stopped six feet from her and said, "Please take off your coat."

It was useless to beg, but she hoped to make him overconfident. "I won't give a good description of you. I swear. Please let me go."

"Wish I could." His face defined remorse. "Take off your coat."

Buying time while she arrived at a course of action, Ginger slowly unbuttoned the coat. Her hands were shaking, but she exaggerated those genuine tremors and fumbled with the buttons. At last she shrugged out of the coat and let it drop to the floor.

He stepped closer. The pistol was only inches from her chest. He was more relaxed, holding the gun less rigidly than before, thrusting it forward less aggressively, though he was by no means lax with it.

"Please don't hurt me." She continued to beg because, if he thought she was nearly paralyzed with abject fear, he might slip up and give her an opportunity for escape.

"I don't *want* to hurt you," he said, as if deeply offended by the implication that he had any choice in the matter. "Didn't want to hurt him, either. That old fool was responsible for this. Not me. Listen, I'll make it as painless as I can. I promise you that."

Still holding the gun in his right hand, he used his left hand to touch her breasts through her sweater. She endured his fondling because he might become careless as he grew aroused. In spite of his claims that his empathy would render him impotent, Ginger was certain he'd have no difficulty raping her. Beneath his regret and sympathy, beneath the sensitivity he wished to project more for his own benefit than for hers, he was taking an unconscious savage pleasure in what he had done and would do. In spite of his gentle voice, violence burned in every word he spoke; he stank of violence.

He said, "Very pretty. Petite yet so nicely built." He slipped his hand under her sweater, gripped her bra, gave it a hard yank that broke it. As elastic snapped, the bra straps dug painfully into her shoulders; the metal clasp at her back bit the skin. He grimaced as if her pain was transmitted to him. "I'm sorry. Did I hurt you? I didn't mean it. I'll be more careful." He pushed aside the ruined brassiere and put his cool, clammy hand on her bare breasts.

Filled equally with terror and revulsion, Ginger pressed back even harder against the bookshelves, which jabbed painfully into her back. The gunman was less than an arm's length away from her now, but he kept the pistol between them. The muzzle was pressed coldly against her bare midriff, leaving her no room to maneuver. If she tried to twist free of him, she would be gut-shot for her temerity.

Fondling her, he continued to speak softly and to express great sadness at the necessity of raping and killing her, as though she simply *must* understand, as though it would be unthinkably cruel of her not to bestow upon him full absolution for the sin of taking her life.

With nowhere to run, with his monotonous self-justifications washing over her in numbing waves of words, subjected to his groping hand, Ginger was gripped by a claustrophobia so intense she felt the urge to claw at him and force him to pull the trigger, just to end it. His Certs-scented breath had a cloying minty aroma that, by its pervasiveness, gave her the feeling she was closed up in a bell-jar with him. She whimpered, pleaded with wordless sounds, turned her head from side to side as if trying to deny the reality of the assault. The picture of demoralizaion and terror that she presented could not have been more convincing if she'd had days to practice, but there was unfortunately little calculation in it.

Further inflamed by her distress, he pawed at her more roughly than before. "I think I can do it, baby. I think I can do it to you. Feel me, baby. Just feel me." He pressed his body to hers and ground his pelvis against her. Incredibly, he seemed to think that, under such stressful and tragic circumstances, his rampant tumescence was a tribute to her erotic appeal and that somehow she ought to be flattered.

Her reaction could only have been a disappointment for him.

When he pressed and rubbed himself against her, he was obliged to stop jamming the gun into her belly. Swept away by his own excitement, convinced that Ginger was weak and helpless, he did not even keep the weapon pointed at her but held it to one side with the muzzle aimed at the floor. Ginger's terror was exceeded by her loathing and anger, and the moment the pistol swung away from her, she translated those pent-up emotions into action. Turning her head to the side, she slumped against him as if about to faint in fear or in a swoon of reluctant passion, an action that brought her mouth to his throat. In swift succession, she bit him hard in the Adam's apple, slammed one knee into his crotch, and clawed at his gun hand to keep the pistol away from her.

He partially blocked the knee, limiting the damage to his privates, but he was unprepared for the bite. Shocked, horrified, and reeling from the devastating pain in his throat, the gunman pushed away from her and stumbled backward two steps.

She had bitten deep, and now she gagged on the taste of his blood, though she did not permit her revulsion to delay her counterattack. She grabbed his gun hand, brought it to her mouth, and bit his wrist.

A sharp cry of pain and astonishment burst from him. Because she was delicate, waiflike, he had not taken her seriously.

As she bit him again, he dropped the gun, but simultaneously he made a fist of his other hand and with tremendous force slammed it into her back. She was driven to her knees and thought for a moment that he had broken her spine. Pain as bright and scintillant as an electric current shot up her back into her neck, flashed through her skull.

Stunned, her vision briefly blurred, Ginger almost did not see him bending to retrieve the gun. Just as his fingers touched the butt, she frantically threw herself at his legs. Seeing her coming and hoping to jump out of her reach, he whipped upright as if he were a lashed-down sapling suddenly cut loose. When she hit him a fraction of a second later, he windmilled his arms in a brief attempt to keep his balance. Falling backward, he crashed into one of the library's chairs, knocked over a small table and a lamp, and rolled onto Pablo Jackson's corpse.

Equally breathless, staring warily at each other, they were both petrified for a moment. They were on their sides on the floor, curled fetally in reaction to their pains, gasping for breath.

To Ginger, the gunman's eyes seemed as wide and round as clock faces, proof that he was filled with fevered thoughts of his own mortality ticking close. The bite would not kill him. She had not bitten through the jugular vein or the carotid artery, had merely pierced the thyroid cartilage, mangling tissue, severing a few small vessels. However, it was easy to understand why he might be convinced it was a mortal wound; the pain must be excruciating. He put his unbitten hand to his damaged throat, then pulled it away and stared aghast at his own gore dripping off his fingers. The killer thought he was dying, and that might make him either less or more dangerous.

Simultaneously, they saw that his pistol had been kicked halfway across the library during their tussle. It was closer to him than to Ginger. Bleeding from throat and wrist, making a strange wheezing-gurgling noise, he scrambled across the floor toward the weapon, and Ginger had no option but to get up and run.

She fled from the library into the living room, hobbling more than running, slowed by the pain in her back, which pulsed through her in diminishing but still debilitating waves. She intended to leave the apartment by the front door, but then she realized there was no escape in that direction because the only exits from the public corridor were the elevator and the stairs. She could not wait for the elevator, and in the stairwell she could easily be trapped.

Instead, hunched because of her aching back, she scurried crablike across the living room, down a long hall, into the kitchen, where the swinging door softly swished shut behind her. She went directly to the utensils rack on the wall by the stove and took down a butcher's knife.

She became aware that a shrill, eerie keening was issuing from her. She held her breath, cut off the sound, and got a grip on herself.

The gunman did not immediately burst into the kitchen, as Ginger expected. After a few seconds she realized that she was lucky he had not yet appeared, because the butcher's knife was of no use against a pistol at a distance of ten feet. Silently cursing herself for almost having made a fatal error, she quickly and light-footedly returned to the door and took up a position to one side of it. Her back still ached, but the sharpest pain was gone. Now she was able to stand straight and flat against the wall. Her heart was pounding so loud that it seemed as if the wall against which she leaned was a drumhead, responding to her heartbeat, amplifying it until the hollow booming of atrium and ventricle must be echoing throughout the entire apartment.

She held the knife low, ready to swing it up and into him in a deadly arc. However, that desperate scenario depended on his slamming through the kitchen door in a fit of hysteria and rage, reckless, crazed by the conviction that he was dying from his throat wound, bent on blind revenge. If instead he came slowly, cautiously, nudging the swinging door open inch by inch with the barrel of the gun, Ginger would be in trouble. But every second that passed without his appearance made it less likely that he would play the drama out in the way she hoped.

Unless the throat wound was far worse than she had realized. In that case, he might be still in the library, bleeding to death on the Chinese carpet. She prayed that was what had happened to him.

But she knew better. He was alive. And he was coming.

She could scream and perhaps alert a neighbor who would call the police, but the gunman would not be driven off in time. He would not run until he killed her. Screaming was a waste of energy.

She pressed harder against the wall, as if trying to melt into it. The swinging door, just inches from her face, riveted her as a blacksnake might command the full attention of a fieldmouse. She was tense, poised to react to the first sign of movement, but the door remained still, maddeningly still.

Where the hell was he?

Five seconds passed. Ten. Twenty.

What was he doing?

The taste of blood in her mouth became more rather than less acrid as the seconds ticked past, and nausea worked its greasy fingers in her. As she had more time to consider what she'd done to him in the library, she grew acutely aware of the bestiality of her actions, and she was shaken by her own potential for savagery. She had time, as well, to think about what she still intended to do to him. She had a mental image of the wide blade of the butcher's knife spearing deep into his body, and a shudder of revulsion shook her. She was not a killer. She was a healer, not merely by education but by nature as well. She tried to stop thinking about stabbing him. It was dangerous to think too much about it, dangerous and confusing and enervating.

Where *was* he?

She could not wait any longer. Afraid that her inaction was damping the animal cunning and savage ferocity that she needed if she were to survive, uneasily certain that each passing second was somehow giving him a greater advantage, she eased to the doorway and put one hand on the edge of the door. But as she was about to pull it open a crack and peer out at the hallway and into the living room, she was chilled by the sudden feeling that he was there, inches away, on the other side of the portal, waiting for her to make the first move.

Ginger hesitated, held her breath, listened.

Silence.

She brought her ear to the door, still could not hear anything.

The handle of the knife had grown slippery in her sweaty hand.

At last, she took hold of the edge of the door and cautiously pulled it inward, until a half-inch gap opened. No shots rang out, so she put one eye to the crack. The gunman was not right in front of her, as she had feared, but at the far end of the hall where it met the foyer; he was just reentering the apartment from the public corridor, pistol in hand. Evidently, he had first looked for her at the elevator and on the stairs. Not finding her, he had returned. Now, by the way he closed the door, locked it, and engaged the chain to delay her exit, it was clear that he had decided she was still in the apartment.

He held his bitten hand to his bitten throat. Even at a distance she could hear his wheezy breathing. However, he was clearly no longer panicked. Having survived this long, he was gaining confidence by the second. He had begun to realize that he would live.

Moving to the edge of the foyer, he looked left toward the living room and right toward the bedroom. Then he looked straight back the long shadowy hall, and Ginger's heart stumbled through a flurry of irregular beats as, for a moment, he seemed to be staring directly at her. But he was too far away to see that the door was being held half an inch ajar. Instead of coming straight toward her, he went into the bedroom. He moved with a quiet purposefulness that was disheartening.

She let the kitchen door go shut, unhappily aware that her plan would no longer work. He was a professional, accustomed to violence, and although he was initially thrown off balance by the unexpected ferocity of her attack, he was rapidly regaining his equilibrium. By the time he searched the bedrooms and the closets in there, he would be completely cool and calculating once more. He would not come charging into the kitchen and make an easy target of himself.

She had to get out of the apartment. Fast.

She had no hope of reaching the front door. He might already be finished in the bedrooms and on his way back into the hall.

Ginger put the knife down. She reached under her sweater, pulled off her ruined bra, and dropped it on the floor. She stepped silently around the kitchen table, pulled the curtains away from the window, and looked out at the fire-escape landing in front of her. Quietly, she twisted the latch. She slid up the lower sash, which unfortunately was *not* quiet. The wooden frame, swollen by the winter dampness, moved with a squeak and squeal and scrape. When it abruptly loosened and slid all the way up with a solid thump and a rattle of glass, she knew she had alerted the gunman. She heard him coming at a run along the hallway.

She climbed hastily out of the window, onto the iron fire escape, and started down. The bitter wind lashed her, and the piercing subzero cold penetrated to her bones. The metal steps were crusted with ice from last night's storm, and icicles hung from the handrails. In spite of the treacherous condition of those switchback stairs, she had to descend quickly or risk a bullet in the back of her head. Repeatedly, her feet almost slipped out from under her. She could not get a secure grip on the icy railing with her ungloved hands, but it was even worse when she took hold of the bare metal, for she stuck to the frigid iron, pulling loose only by sacrificing the top layer of skin.

When she was still four steps from the next landing, she heard someone curse above her, and she glanced back. Pablo Jackson's killer was coming out of the kitchen window in frantic pursuit of her.

Ginger took the next step too fast, and the ice did its work. Her feet flew out from under her, and she fell over the final three steps onto the landing, crashing down on her side, reigniting the pain in her back. Her fall shattered the ice that coated the metal grid, and chunks fell through lower levels of the fire escape, making brittle music, disintegrating as they struck the steps below.

In the wind's maniacal howling, the whisper of the silenced pistol was lost altogether, but Ginger saw sparks leap off the iron inches from her face, and she knew a shot had narrowly missed her. She looked up in time to see the gunman taking aim—and to see him slip and stumble down several treads. He pitched forward, and she thought he was going to fall atop her. He grabbed at the railing three times before he was able to halt his uncontrolled descent.

He was sprawled on his back across several risers, clutching a step with one hand, one leg shot out into space between two of the narrow iron balusters. His other arm was hooked around a baluster, which was how he had arrested his fall; that was the hand holding the pistol, which was why he could not immediately take another shot at her.

Ginger scrambled to her feet, intent upon making as rapid a descent as possible. But when she cast one last quick look at the gunman, she was arrested by the sight of the buttons on his topcoat, which were the only colorful objects in that wintry gloom. Bright brass buttons, each decorated with the raised image of a lion passant, the familiar cadence mark from English heraldry. She had seen nothing special about the buttons before; they were similar to those on many sports jackets, sweaters, coats. But now her eyes fixed on them, and everything else faded away, as if only the buttons were real. Even the gabbling-hooting wind, which filled the day and blustered coldly in every corner of it, could not keep a grip on her awareness. The buttons. Only the buttons held her attention, and they generated in her a terror far more powerful than her fear of the gunman.

"No," she said, uselessly denying what was happening to her. *The buttons.* "Oh, no." *The buttons.* This was the worst possible time and place to lose control of herself. *The buttons.*

She could not forestall the attack. For the first time in three weeks, Ginger was overwhelmed by a crushing, irrational terror. It made her feel small, doomed. It plunged her into a strange and lightless interior landscape through which she was compelled to run blindly.

Turning from the buttons, she fled down the fire escape, and as total blackness claimed her, she knew that her reckless flight would terminate in a broken leg or fractured spine. Then, while she lay paralyzed, the killer would come to her, put the gun to her head, and blow her brains out.

Darkness.

Cold.

When the world returned to Ginger—or she to the world—she was huddled in dead leaves and snow and shadows at the foot of a set of exterior cellar steps behind a townhouse, an unguessable distance along Newbury Street from Pablo's building. A dull pain throbbed the length of her back. Her entire right side ached. The badly abraded palm of her left hand burned. But the severe cold was the worst discomfort. A chill lanced up through her from the snow and ice in which she sat. A frost passed into her by osmosis from the concrete retaining wall against which she leaned. The raw wind rushed down the single flight of ten steep steps, snuffling and growling like a living creature.

She did not know how long she had been cowering there, but she ought to get moving or risk pneumonia. However, the gunman might be nearby, searching for her, and if she revealed herself, the chase would be on again, so she decided to wait a minute or two.

She was astonished that she had clambered all the way down the ice-sheathed fire escape and had fled, by whatever roundabout route, to this hiding place without breaking her neck. Evidently, in her fugue, reduced to the miserable condition of a frightened and mindless animal, there was at least the compensation of an animal-like fleetness and sure-footedness.

Like a pair of industrious morticians, the wind and cold continued to drain the warmth from her. The narrow, gray concrete stairwell increasingly resembled an unlidded sarcophagus. Ginger decided it was time to go. She rose slowly. The small backyard was deserted, as were the yards of houses on both sides. Ice-crusted snow. A few bare trees. Nothing threatening. Shivering, sniffing, blinking away tears, Ginger climbed the stairs and followed a brick walkway that linked the rear of the house to the gate at the end of the small property.

She intended to find her way back to Newbury Street, locate a telephone, and call the police, but as she reached the gate, that plan was abruptly forgotten. On each of the two gateposts was a wrought-iron carriage lamp with amber panes of glass. Either they'd been left burning by accident or were activated by a solenoid that had mistaken the dreary winter morning for twilight. They were electric lamps but had those flickering bulbs that imitated gas flames, so the lantern-glass was alive with shimmering, dancing amber light. That throbbing, yellowish luminosity made Ginger's breath catch, and she was once more pitched into a state of unreasoning panic.

No! Not again.

But, yes. Yes. The mist. Nothingness. Gone.

Colder.

Her feet and hands were going numb.

She was apparently on Newbury Street again. She had crawled under a parked truck. Lying in the gloom under the oil pan, she peered out from beneath her sanctuary, getting a wheel-level view of the vehicles parked on the other side of the street.

Hiding. Every time she recovered from a fugue, she was hiding from something unspeakably terrifying. Today, of course, she was hiding from Pablo's killer. But what about other days? What had she been hiding from then? Even now, she was hiding not only from the gunman but from something else that hovered tantalizingly at the edge of remembrance. Something she had seen out in Nevada. Something.

"Miss? Hey, miss?"

Ginger blinked and turned stiffly toward the voice, which came from the back of the truck. She saw a man on his hands and knees, looking under the tailgate. For a moment she thought it was the gunman.

"Miss? What's wrong?"

Not the gunman. Evidently, he had given up when he couldn't find her quickly and had fled. This was someone she had never seen before, and this was one occasion when a stranger's face was welcome.

He said, "What the hell are you doing under there?"

Ginger was filled with self-pity. She realized how she had looked, running crazily through the neighborhood like some demented freak. All dignity had been stolen from her.

She squirmed toward the man who had spoken to her, grasped the gloved hand he offered, and allowed him to help her slide out from beneath the truck, which proved to be a Mayflower Moving Company van. The rear doors were open. She glanced inside and saw boxes, furniture. The guy who had pulled her out was young, brawny, and dressed in quilted thermal coveralls with the Mayflower logo stitched across the chest.

"What's going on?" he asked. "Who're you hiding from, lady?"

As the Mayflower man spoke, Ginger noticed a policeman standing in the middle of the intersection half a block away, directing traffic, where a signal light had failed. She ran toward him.

The Mayflower man called after her.

She was surprised she could run at all. She felt as if she were a creature constructed of nothing but aches and pains and chills. Yet she ran with a dreamy effortlessness into the shrieking wind. The gutters were full of icy slush, but the street itself was relatively dry and calcimine-streaked with deicing compounds. Dodging out of the way of a couple of oncoming cars, she even found the strength to call out to the cop as she drew near him. "There's been a man killed! Murder! You've got to come! Murder!" Then, when he started toward her with a look of concern on his broad Irish face, she saw the shiny brass buttons on his heavy, winter-weight uniform coat, and all was lost again. They were not exactly like the buttons on the leather topcoat the killer had been wearing; they were not decorated with a lion passant, but with some other raised figure. But one glimpse sent her thoughts flashing toward remembrance of buttons she had seen *then*, during the mysterious events at the Tranquility Motel. Some forbidden recollection began to surface, and that pulled the Azrael Trigger.

As she lost control and ran off into her private darkness, the last thing she heard was her own pathetic cry of despair.

Coldest.

That morning, at least for Ginger Weiss, Boston was the coldest place on earth. Bitter, polar, piercing, marrow-freezing, the January day induced a glaciation of the spirit as well as the flesh. When the fugue receded, she was sitting on the ground in ice and snow. Her hands and feet were numb, stiff. Her lips were chapped and cracked.

This time she had taken refuge in the narrow space between a row of well-manicured bushes and a brick building, in a shadowy corner where the angled wall of a bay-windowed tower met a flat portion of the main facade. The former Hotel Agassiz. Where Pablo had his apartment. Where he had been killed. She had come nearly full circle.

She heard someone approaching. Between the hoary branches of the snow-dressed and ice-laced shrubs, she saw someone climbing over the low wrought-iron fence that separated the front lawn from the sidewalk. She did not see the person himself, merely his booted feet, legs clad in blue trousers, and the flaps of a long, heavy, navy-blue coat. But as he came across the narrow strip of lawn toward the shrubbery, she knew who he was: the traffic cop from whom she had turned and run.

Fearing yet another seizure at the sight of his coat buttons, Ginger closed her eyes.

Perhaps irreversible psychological damage was a side-effect of the brainwashing she had undergone, an inevitable result of the tremendous and constant stress generated by the artificially repressed memories struggling mightily to make themselves known. Even if she could find another hypnotist to do for her what Pablo had done, perhaps there was no way the block could be broken or the pressure relieved, in which case she was destined to deteriorate further. If she was stricken by three fugues in one morning, what was to prevent three more in the next hour?

The policeman's boots crunched noisily through the sleet-skinned snow. He stopped in front of her. She heard him pressing against the low bushes and parting them to look into her hiding place. "Miss? Hey, what's wrong? What were you shouting about murder? Miss?"

Maybe she would fall into a fugue and *remain* there forever.

"Oh, now, what're you crying about?" the cop said sympathetically. "Darlin', I can't help if you won't tell me what's wrong."

She would not be the daughter of Jacob Weiss if she failed to respond warmly and eagerly to the slightest sign of kindness in others, and the policeman's concern finally affected her. She opened her eyes and looked up at the topmost brass button on his coat. The sight of it did not bring the hateful darkness upon her. But that meant nothing, for the ophthalmoscope, black gloves, and other triggering items had not affected her later, when she had forced herself to confront them again.

In a crackle of ice, the cop pushed between the bushes.

She said, "They've killed Pablo. They murdered Pablo."

And as she spoke those words, her distress over her condition was made worse by a rush of guilt. The 6th of January would forever be a black day in her life. Pablo was dead. Because he tried to help her.

Such a very cold day.

5. On the Road

Monday morning, the 6th of January, Dom Corvaisis cruised his old Portland neighborhood in a rented Chevrolet, trying to recapture the mood he had been in when he had left Oregon for Mountainview, Utah, more than eighteen months ago. The rain, as heavy as any he had ever seen, had stopped near dawn. Now the sky, though still cloudy from horizon to horizon, was a particularly powdery, dry-looking shade of gray, like a burnt field, as if there had been a fire behind the clouds that had forced out all that precipitation. He drove through the university campus, stopping repeatedly to let the familiar scenes stir feelings and attitudes of times past. He parked across the street from the apartment where he'd lived, and as he stared up at the windows, he tried to recall the man he had been then.

He was surprised at how difficult it was to recollect the timidity with which that other Dom Corvaisis had viewed life. Though he could bring to mind the way he had been, there was no intimacy or poignancy to those memories. He could see those old days again, but he could not *feel* them, which seemed to indicate that he could never be that old Dom again, regardless of how much he feared the possibility.

He was convinced that he had seen something terrible on the road the summer before last, and that something monstrous had been done to him. But that conviction generated both a mystery and a contradiction. The mystery was that the event had wrought in him an undeniably positive change. How could an experience fraught with pain and terror effect a beneficial change in his outlook? The contradiction was that, in spite of the beneficial effect on his personality, the event filled his dreams with horror. How could his ordeal have been both terrifying and positive, both horrible and uplifting at the same time?

The answer, if it could be found, was not here in Portland but out on the highway. He started the engine, put the Chevy in gear, pulled away from his old apartment building, and went looking for trouble.

The most direct route from Portland to Mountainview began with Interstate 80 north. But as he had done nineteen months ago, Dom took a more roundabout trail, heading south on Interstate 5. That special summer, he had scheduled a layover in Reno for a few days to do some research for a series of short stories about gambling, so the less direct route had been necessary.

Now in his rented Chevy, he followed the familiar highway, keeping his speed down to fifty, even as low as forty on the steeper hills, for he had been pulling a U-Haul trailer that last day in June, and he had not made good time. And, as before, he stopped for lunch in Eugene.

Hoping to spot something that would goose his memory and provide a link with the mysterious events of the previous trip, Dom looked over the small towns that he passed. However, he saw nothing that made him uneasy, and nothing bad happened all the way to Grants Pass, where he arrived shortly before six o'clock that evening, right on schedule.

He stayed in the motel where he had been a guest eighteen months ago. He remembered the number of the room—ten—because it was near the soft drink and ice machines, which had been the source of irritating noises half the night. It was unoccupied, and he took it, vaguely explaining to the clerk that it had sentimental associations for him.

He ate at the same restaurant, across the road from the motel.

He was seeking *satori,* which was a Zen word meaning "sudden enlightenment," a profound revelation. But enlightenment eluded him.

All day he had used the rearview mirror, hoping to spot a tail. During dinner, he surreptitiously watched the other customers. But if he was being followed, his tail was masterful, invisible.

At nine o'clock, rather than use the telephone in his room, he walked to a nearby service station pay phone. With his credit card, he placed a call to the number of another pay phone in Laguna Beach. By prearrangement, Parker Faine was waiting there with a report on the mail that he had collected for Dom earlier in the day. There was little chance that either of their phones was tapped; however, after receiving those two disturbing Polaroid snapshots, Dom had decided (and Parker had agreed) that in this case prudence and paranoia were synonymous.

"Bills," Parker said, "advertisements. No more strange messages, and no more Polaroids. How's it going at your end?"

"Nothing so far," Dom said, leaning wearily against the Plexiglas and aluminum wall of the phone booth. "Didn't sleep well last night."

"But you didn't go for a walk?"

"Didn't even get one knot untied. Had a nightmare, though. The moon again. Anybody follow you to that pay phone?"

"Not unless he was as thin as a dime and a master of camouflage," Parker said. "So you can call me here again tomorrow night and not have to worry that they've tapped the line."

"We sound like two madmen," Dom said.

"I'm kind of having fun," Parker said. "Cops and robbers, hide and seek, spies—I was always good at games like that when I was a kid. You just hang in there, my friend. And if you need help, I'll come fast.''

"I know," Dom said.

He walked back to the motel through a cold damp wind. As in the hotel in Portland, he woke three times before dawn, always surfacing from an unremembered nightmare, always shouting about the moon.

Tuesday, January 7, Dom rose early and drove to Sacramento, then took Interstate 80 east toward Reno. Rain fell, silvery and cold, for most of the drive, and by the time he reached the foothills of the Sierras, it was snowing. He stopped at an Arco station, bought tire chains, and put them on before heading into the mountains.

The summer before last, he had taken more than ten hours to get from Grants Pass to Reno, and this time the drive took even longer. When he finally checked in at Harrah's Hotel where he had stayed before, called Parker Faine from a pay phone, and had a bite of dinner in the coffee shop, he was too tired to do anything but pick up a copy of the Reno newspaper and return to his room. So at eight-thirty that evening, sitting in bed in his underwear, he saw the story about Zebediah Lomack.

MOON MAN'S ESTATE
WORTH HALF A MILLION DOLLARS

RENO—Zebediah Harold Lomack, 50, whose suicide on Christmas Day led to the discovery of his bizarre obsession with the moon, left an estate valued at more than $500,000. According to documents filed with the probate court by Eleanor Wolsey, sister of the deceased and executrix of Lomack's will, most of the funds are in accounts at various savings and loan associations and in treasury bills. The modest house in which Lomack lived at 1420 Wass Valley Road, has an appraised value of only $35,000.

Lomack, a professional gambler, is said to have amassed his wealth primarily from the game of poker. "He was one of the best players I ever knew," said Sidney "Sierra Sid" Garfork of Reno, another professional gambler and winner of last year's World Championship of Poker at Binion's Horseshoe Casino in Las Vegas. "He took to cards when he was just a kid the way some others might have a natural knack for baseball or math or physics." According to Garfork and other friends of Lomack, the gambler's estate would have been even larger if he had not had a weakness for dice games. "He lost back more than half his winnings at the craps tables, and the IRS took a big chunk, of course," Garfork said.

On Christmas night, responding to a neighbor's report of shotgun fire, Reno police officers found Lomack's body in the garbage-strewn kitchen of his home. Upon further investigation, they found thousands of photographs of the moon decorating walls, ceilings, and furniture.

There was more to the story, which had apparently been a local sensation for the past two weeks. Dom read with growing fascination and uneasiness. Most likely, Zebediah Lomack's mad obsession with the moon had nothing to do with Dom's own problems. Coincidence. Yet . . . he felt a stirring of precisely that fear—part terror, part horror, and part awe—that filled him when he woke from his nightmares, that also overwhelmed him when he went sleepwalking and tried to nail windows shut.

He pored over the article several times, and at nine-fifteen, in spite of his weariness, he decided that he had to get a look in the Lomack house. He dressed, retrieved his rented car from the hotel's valet parking, and got directions to Wass

Valley Road from the attendant. Reno was below the snowline, so the night was dry and the roads clean. Dom stopped at an all-night Sav-On drugstore to buy a flashlight. He arrived at 1420 Wass Valley Road shortly after ten o'clock and parked across the street.

The house was actually a bungalow with large porches, every bit as modest as the news account had indicated. It sat on a half-acre lot. From previous storms, snow lay in patches on the roof, covered the lawn, weighted the branches of several large pines. The windows were dark.

According to the article in the Reno newspaper, Eleanor Wolsey, Zebediah Lomack's sister, had flown in from Florida three days after his death, on December 28. She arranged the funeral services, which had been conducted on the thirtieth, and was staying over until the estate was settled. However, she was at a hotel rather than in her brother's house, because the bungalow was too depressing.

Dom was a law-abiding citizen; the prospect of breaking into the house gave him no thrill. But it had to be done because there was no way he could see it except by forced entry. He saw no point in trying to persuade Eleanor Wolsey to allow a visit tomorrow, for she had been quoted in the newspaper as saying that she was sick and tired of gawkers and that she was repulsed by the perverse curiosity of strangers.

Five minutes later, on the back porch of the Lomack bungalow, Dom discovered that the door was equipped with a deadbolt in addition to its regular lock. He tried the windows that faced onto the porch. The one above the kitchen sink was unlatched. He slid it open and clambered inside.

Hooding the flashlight with one hand to avoid drawing the notice of anyone outside, he swept the narrowed beam around the kitchen, which was no longer in the disgusting condition in which Reno policemen had found it on Christmas. According to the newspaper, just two days ago Lomack's sister began cleaning the house and preparing it for sale. Evidently she had started here. The garbage was gone. The counters were clean, and the floor was spotless. The air was filled with the stink of new paint and Spectracide. A single startled roach scurried along the baseboard and disappeared behind the refrigerator, but there was no longer a gross infestation. And there were no pictures of the moon.

Dom was suddenly worried that Eleanor Wolsey and her helpers might have made too much progress. Perhaps all traces of Zebediah Lomack's obsession had been stripped down, scrubbed out, and thrown away.

But that concern was quickly put to rest when Dom followed the pale probing beam of the flashlight into the living room, where the walls and ceiling and windows were still papered with big posters of the moon. It seemed as if he were hanging in deep space, in some crowded realm where half a hundred cratered worlds orbited impossibly close to one another. The effect was disorienting. He felt dizzy, and his mouth went dry.

He moved slowly out of the living room into a hallway, where hundreds of pictures of the moon—some color and some black-and-white, some large and some small, some overlapping others—had been fixed to every inch of the walls with glue, Scotch tape, masking tape, and staples. The same decorations had been applied in both bedrooms as well, so the omnipresent moons seemed almost like a fungus that had spored and spread throughout the house, creeping into every corner.

The newspaper report had said that no one but Lomack had been in the house for more than a year prior to his suicide. Dom believed it, for if visitors had seen the work of this lunatic cut-and-paste Michelangelo, they would have contacted the mental health authorities at once. The neighbors told of the gambler's rapid metamorphosis from a hail-fellow to a recluse. Apparently his fascination with the moon had begun the summer before last.

The summer before last . . . The timing uncannily paralleled the changes in Dom's own life.

Second by second, Dom grew more uneasy. He could not understand the insane behavior that had created this eerie display, could not put himself inside the fevered mind of Lomack, but he *could* empathize with the gambler's terror. Just moving through the moon-crowded house, shining his flashlight on the lunar faces, Dom felt a tingling along the back of his neck. The moons did not mesmerize him as they had evidently mesmerized Lomack, but as he stared at them he sensed instinctively that the impulse that had driven Lomack to paper his house with moon images was the same impulse that drove Dom himself to dream of them.

He and Lomack had shared some experience in which the moon had figured or of which it was an apt and powerful symbol. The summer before last they had been in the same place at the same time. The wrong place at the wrong time. Lomack had been driven mad by the stress of repressed memories.

Will I be driven mad, too? Dom wondered as he stood in the master bedroom, turning slowly in a circle.

A new and grim thought struck him. Suppose Lomack had not killed himself out of despair over his unshakable obsession but had, instead, been compelled to shove the shotgun barrel into his mouth *because he had finally remembered what had happened to him the summer before last.* Maybe the memory was far worse than the mystery. Maybe, if the truth were revealed, sleepwalking and nightmares would seem less terrifying than what had happened during that drive from Portland to Mountainview.

Moons . . . The oppressiveness of those pendulant forms drastically increased. The claustrophobic mural made breathing difficult. The moons seemed to portend some unreadable but manifestly evil fate that awaited him, and he stumbled out of the room, suddenly eager to flee from them.

Among a herd of leaping and prancing shadows whipped up by the bobbling beam of the flashlight, he ran down the short hall, into the living room, tripped over a stack of books, and fell with a jarring crash. For a moment he lay stunned. But his senses swiftly cleared, and he was jolted to find himself staring at the word "Dominick," which was scrawled in felt-tip pen across the luminous moon-face in one of the dozens of identical big posters. He had not noticed it when he had come through from the kitchen earlier, but now he had fallen so that the flash in his right hand was aimed just right.

A chill rippled through Dom. He had read nothing about this in the newspaper, but the handwriting surely belonged to Lomack. To the best of his knowledge, he had not known the gambler. Yet to pretend that this was *another* Dominick would be to embrace an outrageous coincidence.

He got up from the floor and took a couple of steps toward the poster that bore his name, stopping six feet from it. In the penumbra of the flashlight beam, he saw writing on an adjacent poster. His own name was only one of four that Lomack had scribbled across four lunar images: DOMINICK, GINGER, FAYE, ERNIE. If his name was here because he had shared a forgotten nightmarish experience with Lomack, then the other three must have been fellow sufferers as well, though Dom could remember nothing whatsoever about them.

He thought of the priest in the Polaroid snapshot. Was that Ernie?

And the blond strapped to the bed. Was she Ginger? Or Faye?

As he moved the light from one name to the other and back again, some dark and awesome memory did indeed stir in him. But it remained far down in his subconscious, an amorphous blur like a giant ocean creature swimming past just below the mottled surface of a murky sea, its existence revealed only by the rippled wake of its passage and by the flicker of shadow and light in the water. He tried to reach out for the memory and seize it, but it dove deep and vanished.

From the moment he had come into the Lomack place, Dom had been in the hands of fear, but now frustration took an even tighter grip on him. He shouted in the empty house, and his voice echoed coldly off the moon-papered walls. "Why can't I remember?" He knew why, of course: Someone had mucked with his mind, scrubbing out certain memories. But still he shouted—fearful, furious. "Why can't I remember? I've got to *remember!*" He held his left hand toward the poster that featured his name, as if to wrench from its substance the memory that had been in Lomack's mind when he had scrawled "Dominick." His heart thumped. He roared with hot anger: "Goddamn it, goddamn you whoever you are, I will remember. I will remember you sons of bitches. You bastards! I *will.*"

Suddenly, impossibly, even though he was not touching it, though his hand was still a few feet from it, the poster bearing his name tore loose from the wall. It was fixed in place with four strips of masking tape angled across its corners, but the tape peeled up with the sound of zippers opening, and the poster *leapt* off the wall as if a wind had blown straight through the lathe and plaster behind it. With a rattle and rustle of paper wings, it swooped at him, and he staggered back across the living room in surprise, nearly falling over the books again.

In his unsteady hand, his flashlight revealed that the poster had stopped a few feet from him. It hung at eye-level, unsupported in thin air, undulating slightly from top to bottom, first bulging out at him and then bending away when the direction of undulation reversed itself. As the pocked surface of that moon rippled, his own handwritten name fluttered and writhed as if it were the legend on a wind-stirred banner.

Hallucination, he thought desperately.

But he knew it was really happening.

He could not breathe, as if the cold air were so syrup-thick with miraculous power that it could not be inhaled.

The poster floated closer.

His hands shook. The flashlight jiggled. Sharp glints of light lanced off the undulant surface of the glossy paper.

After a timeless moment in which the only sound was the crackle of the animated poster, other noise abruptly arose from every part of the room: the zipper-sound of masking tape being pulled loose. On the ceiling, walls, and windows, the other posters simultaneously disengaged themselves. With a brittle clatter-rattle-whoosh, half a hundred moon images exploded toward Dom from every direction, and he cried out in surprise and fear.

The loosed cry was like a blockage expelled from his windpipe, for he was suddenly able to breathe.

The last of the tape pulled loose. Fifty posters hung unmoving in mid-air, not even rippling, as if pasted firmly to nothing whatsoever. The silence in the dead gambler's house was as profound as in a temple devoid of worshipers, a cold and penetrating silence that seemed to pierce to the core of Dom, seeking to replace even the soft liquid susurration of his blood's movement through his arteries and veins.

Then as if they were fifty parts of a single mechanism brought to life with the flick of a switch, the three-by-five-foot lunar images shivered, rustled, flapped. Although there was not the slightest breeze to propel them, they began to whirl around the room in the orderly manner of horses on a carousel. Dom stood in the middle of that eerie merry-go-round, and the moons circled him; they capered and twirled, curled and uncurled, flexed and flapped, here seen as half-moons and here as crescents and here full-face, and they waxed and waned, ascended and descended, faster, faster, faster still. In the flashlight glow, it seemed like a procession set in motion by the sorcerer's apprentice who, in the old story, had magically imparted life to a bunch of broomsticks.

Dom's fear receded, making room for wonder. At the moment there seemed no threat in the phenomenon. In fact a wild delight burgeoned in him. He could think of no explanation for what he was witnessing, but stood in dumb astonishment, puzzled and amazed. Usually nothing was so terrifying as the unknown, but perhaps he sensed a benign power at work. Wonderstruck, he turned slowly in a circle, watching the moons parade around him, and at last a tremulous laugh escaped him.

In an instant, the mood changed dramatically. In a cacophony of imitation wings, the posters flew at Dom as if they were fifty enormous and furious bats. They swooped and darted over his head, slapped his face, beat against his back. Though they were not alive, he attributed malevolent intent to their assault. He put one arm across his face and flailed at the moons with the hand that held the flashlight, but they did not fall back. The noise grew louder and more frantic as the paper wings beat on the chilly air and on one another.

His previous delight forgotten, Dom stumbled across the room in a panic, searching for the way out. But he could see nothing but zooming, soaring, spinning moons. No doors. No windows. He staggered one way, then another, disoriented.

The noise grew still worse as, in the hallways and other rooms of the bungalow, a thousand moons began to tear free of their petrified orbits upon the walls. Tape pulled loose, and staples popped out of plaster, and glue suddenly lost its adhesiveness. A thousand cratered moonforms—and then a thousand more—detached themselves and rose into suspension with ten thousand rustles, spun and swooped toward the living room with a hundred thousand clicks and crackles and hisses, swinging into orbit around Dom with a steadily swelling roar that sounded as if he were immersed in raging flames. The glossy full-color pictures torn from magazines and books now flashed and sparkled and shimmered as they darted through the flashlight beam, contributing to the scintillant illusion of fire, and the black-and-white pictures cascaded down and spiraled up like bits of ash caught in thermal currents.

Gasping for breath, he sucked in slick-paper and newsprint moons and had to spit them out. Thousands of small paper worlds seethed around him in layer upon layer, and when he hysterically parted one curtain composed of false planetoids, there was only another behind it.

Intuitively, he perceived that this impossible display was meant to help him break through to a full recollection of his unremembered nightmares. He had no idea who or what lay behind the phenomenon, but he sensed the purpose. If he immersed himself in the storm of moons and let them sweep him away, he'd understand his dreams, understand the frightening cause of them, and know what had happened to him on the road eighteen months ago. But he was too scared to let go and be drawn into a trance by the mesmerizing weave-and-bobble of the pale spheres. He longed for that revelation but was terrified of it. He said, "No. No." He pressed his hands over his ears and squeezed his eyes shut. "Stop it!

Stop it!'' His heart hammered two beats to each exclamation. ''Stop it!'' His throat cracked as his cries broke loose: *''Stop it!''*

He was astonished when the tumult was cut off with the suddenness of a symphony orchestra terminating a thunderous crescendo on one last bone-shaking note. He did not expect his shouted commands to be obeyed, and he still did not think his words had done the trick.

He took his hands away from his ears. He opened his eyes.

A galaxy full of moons hung around him.

With a trembling hand, he plucked one of the pictures from its unsupported perch upon the air. Wonderingly, he turned it over in his hand. Tested its substance between two fingers. There was nothing special about the picture, yet it had been suspended magically before him, just as thousands more were still suspended, motionless.

''How?'' he said shakily, as if the moons, being able to levitate, ought also to be able to speak. ''How? *Why?*''

The moons fell as one. As by the breaking of some spell, the thousands of pieces of paper dropped straight to the floor, where they lay in uneven heaps, in a drift over Dom's winter boots, with no lingering trace of the mysterious life-force that had possessed them.

Bewildered and half in shock, Dom shuffled toward the doorway that led to the hall. The moons crunched and rustled like dry autumn leaves. At the door he stopped and played his flashlight beam slowly over the short corridor, where not a single lunar image remained moored by staples, tape, or glue. The walls had been stripped bare.

Turning, he took a couple of steps into the center of the living room once more, then knelt among the debris. He put down the glowing flashlight and sifted paper moons through his trembling hands, trying to understand what he had seen.

Within him, fear fought delighted amazement and terror battled awe. But in truth he could not decide how he ought to feel, because there was no precedent for what he had experienced. One moment a giddy laugh began to build, but then joy was frozen by a breath of cold horror. Now he felt he'd been in the presence of something unspeakably evil, but *now* he was just as convinced it had been something good and pure. Evil. Good. Perhaps both . . . or neither. Just . . . well *something.* Some mysterious thing beyond the descriptive, definitive power of words.

He knew one thing only: Whatever had happened to him the summer before last was far stranger than he had realized heretofore.

Still sifting paper moons through his fingers, he noticed something unusual on his hands. He brought them palms-up into the direct beam of the flashlight. Rings. On each palm blazed a ring of swollen red skin, each as perfect as if the inflamed tissues had conformed to a pattern drawn with a draftsman's compass.

Even as he watched, the stigmata faded, vanished.

It was Tuesday, January 7.

6. Chicago, Illinois

In his bedroom on the second floor of St. Bernadette's rectory, Father Stefan Wycazik woke to the thump of a drum. The beat had the deep boom of a bass drum and the hollow reverberation of tympani. It sounded like the pounding of an enormous heart, although it embellished the simple two-stroke rhythm of the heart with an extra beat: *LUB-DUB-dub . . . LUB-DUB-dub . . . LUB-DUB-dub . . .*

Bewildered and still half asleep, Stefan switched on the lamp, squinted in the blaze of light, and looked at his alarm clock. It was two-oh-seven, Thursday morning, certainly not a reasonable hour for a parade.

LUB-DUB-dub . . . LUB-DUB-dub . . .

After each triad of thumps, there was a three-second pause, then a set of beats identical to all the others, then another three-second pause. The precise timing and unfaltering repetition of the noise began to seem less like the work of a drummer and more like the laborious piston-stroke of an enormous machine.

Father Wycazik threw back the covers and padded barefoot to the window that looked out on the courtyard between the rectory and the church. He saw only snow and bare-limbed trees in the backwash of the carriage lamp above the sacristy door.

The beats grew louder, and the pause between the groups shortened to about two seconds. He took his robe from the back of a chair and slipped it on over his pajamas. The sonorous pounding was so loud now that it was no longer merely an annoyance and puzzlement. It had begun to frighten Stefan. Each burst of sound rattled the windowpanes and shook the door in its frame.

He hurried into the upstairs hall. He fumbled in the dark for the wall switch and finally turned on the overhead light.

Farther along the short hall, on the right, another door opened, and Father Michael Gerrano, Stefan's other curate, dashed out of his room, struggling into his own robe. "What is that?"

"Don't know," Stefan said.

The next triple-thud was twice as loud as the group preceding it, and the entire house reverberated as if it had been struck by three gigantic hammers. It was not a hard sharp sound, but muffled in spite of its loudness—as if the hammers were thinly padded yet swung with tremendous force. The lights flickered. Now the thumps were separated by no more than a second of silence, not long enough for the echo of the previous fulminations to fade away. And with each powerful hammering, the lights flickered again and the floor under Stefan trembled.

In the same instant, Father Wycazik and Father Gerrano perceived the locus of the noise: Brendan Cronin's room. They moved swiftly to that door, which was directly across the hall from Father Gerrano.

Incredibly, Brendan was fast asleep. In spite of the thunderous explosions that made Father Wycazik flash back to the mortar fire of Vietnam, Brendan dreamed on, untroubled. In fact, in the pulsing light, there seemed to be a vague smile tugging at the young priest's lips.

The windows rattled. Drapery hooks clicked against the rods to which they were attached. On the dresser, a hairbrush bounced up and down, and several coins clinked together, and Brendan's breviary slid first to the left and then to the right. On the wall above the bed, a crucifix jiggled wildly under the picture hook from which it was hung.

Father Gerrano shouted, but Stefan could not hear what the curate said, for now there were no pauses between muffled detonations. With each tripartite beat, Father Wycazik retreated further from his initial mental image of a huge drum and became increasingly convinced that what he was hearing was the throbbing of some enormous and immeasurably powerful machine. But it seemed as if the sound came from all sides, as if the machinery was hidden within the walls of the house itself, laboring at some mysterious and unknowable task.

As the breviary finally slid off the dresser and the coins began to spill to the floor, Father Gerrano backed to the doorway and stood there wide-eyed, as if he might flee.

But Stefan went to the bed, bent over the dozing priest, and shouted his name. When that had no effect, he grabbed Brendan by the shoulders and shook him.

The auburn-haired curate blinked and opened his eyes.

The hammering stopped abruptly.

The sudden cessation of thunderous noise jolted Father Wycazik as badly as the first boom that had shattered his sleep. He let go of Brendan and looked around the room, disbelieving.

"I was so close," Brendan said dreamily. "I wish you hadn't wakened me. I was so close."

Stefan pulled aside the covers, took hold of the curate's hands, and turned them palms-up. There was an angry red ring in each palm. Stefan stared at them in fascination, for this was the first time that he had seen the stigmata.

What in God's name is this all about? he wondered.

Breathing hard, Father Gerrano approached the bed. Staring at the rings, he said, "What're those from?"

Ignoring the question, Father Wycazik spoke to Brendan: "What was that sound? Where did it come from?"

"Calling," Brendan said in a voice still thick with sleep—and with a soft, excited pleasure. "Calling me back."

"What was calling you?" Stefan demanded.

Brendan blinked, sat up, and leaned against the headboard. His eyes had been out of focus. Now his gaze cleared, and he really looked at Father Wycazik for the first time. "What happened? You heard it, too?"

"Somehow, yes," Stefan said. "It shook the whole house. Amazing. What was it, Brendan?"

"A call. It was calling me, and I was following the call."

"But what was calling you?"

"I . . . I don't know. Something. Calling me back . . ."

"Back where?"

Brendan frowned. "Back into the light. The golden light of the dream I told you about."

"What's this all about?" Father Gerrano persisted. His voice was shaky, for he was not as accustomed to the miraculous as were his rector and his fellow curate. "Will somebody clue me in?"

The other priests continued to ignore him.

To Brendan, Stefan said, "This golden light . . . what is it? Could it have been God calling you back to His fold?"

"No," Brendan said. "Just . . . something. Calling me back. Next time, maybe I'll get a better look at it."

Father Wycazik sat on the edge of the bed. "You think this will happen again? You think it'll keep calling to you?"

"Yes," Brendan said. "Oh, yes."

It was Thursday, January 9.

7. Las Vegas, Nevada

Friday afternoon, Jorja Monatella was at the casino, working, when she learned that her ex-husband, Alan Rykoff, had killed himself.

The news came by way of an emergency telephone call from Pepper Carrafield, the hooker with whom Alan had been living. Jorja took the call on one of the phones in the blackjack pit, cupping a hand over one ear to block out the roar of voices, the click and snap of cards being dealt and shuffled, the ringing of slot machines. When she heard that Alan was dead, she was shocked and sickened, but she felt no grief. By his own selfish and cruel behavior, Alan had ensured she would have no reason to grieve for him. Pity was the only emotion she could summon.

"He shot himself this morning, two hours ago," Pepper elaborated. "The police are here now. You've got to come."

"The police want to see me?" Jorja said. "But why?"

"No, no. The police don't want to see you. You got to come and clean his stuff out. I want his stuff out of here as soon as possible."

"But I don't want his things," Jorja said.

"It's still your job, whether you want them or not."

"Miss Carrafield, it was a bitter divorce. I neither want nor—"

"He had a will drawn up last week. He named you executor, so you got to come. I want his stuff out of here *now*. It's your job."

Alan had lived with Pepper Carrafield in a high-rise condominium, a ritzy place called The Pinnacle, on Flamingo Road, where the call-girl owned an apartment. It was a fifteen-story white concrete monolith with bronze windows. Surrounded by undeveloped desert land, it appeared to be even taller than it was. And because it stood alone, it looked oddly like a monument, the world's largest, swankiest tombstone. The grounds were lushly planted with sprinkler-tended lawns and flowerbeds, but a few dry tumbleweeds had blown in from the bordering plots of sand and scrub. The chill and desolate wind which stirred the tumbleweeds also fluted hollowly under the condominium's portico.

Two police cars and a morgue wagon stood in front of the building, but no cops were in the lobby: just a young woman on a mauve sofa near the elevators, forty feet away; and at a desk near the entrance, a man in gray slacks and blue blazer, who was security guard and doorman. The travertine marble floor, crystal chandeliers, oriental carpet, Henredon sofas and chairs, and brass elevator doors contributed to a decor that strained too hard to convey class—but conveyed it nonetheless.

As Jorja asked the doorman to announce her, the young woman on the sofa rose and said, "Mrs. Rykoff, I'm Pepper Carrafield. Er . . . I think you use your maiden name now."

"Monatella," Jorja said.

Like the building in which she lived, Pepper strained for Fifth Avenue class, but her efforts were less successful than those of the interior designers who had worked on The Pinnacle. Her blond hair had been cut in an excessively shaggy carefree style that hookers preferred, perhaps because when you spent your workday in a series of beds, shaggy hair required less grooming. She wore a purple silk blouse that might have been a Halston, but she'd left too many buttons open, revealing a daring amount of cleavage. Her gray slacks were well tailored but too tight. She wore a Cartier watch encrusted with diamonds, but the elegant effect of the watch was spoiled by her indulgence in flashy diamond rings: She wore four of them.

"I couldn't bear to stay upstairs in the apartment," Pepper said, motioning for Jorja to join her on the sofa. "I'm not going back up there until they've taken the body away." She shivered. "We can talk right here, just so we keep our voices low." She nodded toward the doorman at the desk. "But if there's going to be a scene, I'll just get up and walk away. You understand? People here don't know what I do for a living. I intend to keep it that way. I never do business out of my home. I'm strictly out-call." Her gray-green eyes were flat.

Jorja stared coldly at her. "If you think I'm a scorned, suffering wife, you can relax, Miss Carrafield. Anything I ever felt for Alan is gone now. Even knowing he's dead, I feel nothing. Nothing much. I'm not proud of it. I was in love with him once, and we created a lovely child together. I should feel *something,* and I'm ashamed that I don't. But I'm definitely not going to cause a scene."

"Great," Pepper said, genuinely pleased, so involved with herself and her own concerns that she was oblivious of the domestic tragedy Jorja had just described. "There're a lot of high-class people live here, you know. When they hear my boyfriend killed himself, they're going to be standoffish for a long time. These kind of people don't like messy scenes. And if they found out what I do for a living . . . well, there'd be no way I'd ever fit in here again. You know? I'd have to move, and I sure don't want to. No way, honey. I like it here a lot."

Jorja looked at Pepper's ostentatiously diamond-encumbered hands, looked at her plunging neckline, looked into her avaricious eyes, and said, "What do you suppose they think you are—an heiress?"

Astonishingly, missing the sarcasm, Pepper said, "Yeah. How'd you know? I paid for the condo with hundred-dollar bills, so no credit check was necessary, and I've let them all think my family has money."

Jorja did not bother to explain that heiresses did not pay for condominiums with bundles of hundred-dollar bills. She simply said, "Could we talk about Alan? What happened? What went wrong? I would never have thought Alan was the type to . . . to kill himself."

Glancing at the doorman to make sure he had not left his post and drifted nearer, Pepper said, "Me neither, honey. I'd never have pegged him as the type. He was so . . . macho. That's why I wanted him to move in and take care of me, manage me. He was strong, tough. Of course, a few months ago he started acting a little weird, and lately he was downright creepy. Weird and creepy enough that I was thinking about maybe finding someone else to look after me. But I didn't expect he'd screw things up for me by killing himself. Christ, you just never know, do you?"

"Some people have no consideration," Jorja said. She saw Pepper's eyes narrow, but before the hooker could say anything, Jorja said, "Am I to understand that Alan was pimping for you?"

Pepper scowled. "Listen, I don't need a pimp. Whores need pimps. I'm no whore. Whores give fifty-dollar blow-jobs, screw eight or ten johns a day for whatever they can get, spend half their lives with the clap, and wind up broke. That's not *me,* sister. I'm an escort for gentlemen of means. I'm on the approved escort lists of the finest hotels, and last year I made two hundred thousand bucks. What do you think of that? I got investments. Whores don't have investments, honey. Alan wasn't my pimp. He was my *manager.* In fact, he managed a couple of my girlfriends, too. I fixed him up with them because, at first, before he started getting strange, he was the best.''

Dazzled by the woman's self-delusion, Jorja said, ''And Alan took a managerial fee for handling your career—and theirs?''

Her scowl fading, somewhat placated by Jorja's willingness to use euphemisms, Pepper said, ''No. That was one of the best things about our arrangement with him. He was still a blackjack dealer, see; that's where he made his money. He had all the contacts needed to manage us, but all he wanted for his trouble was free trade. I never knew a man who needed so much pussy. He couldn't get enough. In fact, the last couple of months, he seemed obsessed with pussy. Was he like that with you, honey?'' Repulsed by this sudden intimacy, Jorja tried to stop the woman, but Pepper would not be quiet. ''In fact, the last few weeks he was so horny all the time that I started to think maybe I should dump him. I mean, there was something a little crazy about it. He'd do it and do it and do it until he just couldn't get his pecker up to do it any more, and then he'd want to watch X-rated videotapes.''

Jorja was suddenly angry that Alan had made her executor, forcing her to witness the moral squalor in which he had passed the last year of his life. And she was angry because she would have to find a way to explain his death to Marcie, who was already treading a psychological tightrope. But she was not really angry with Pepper Carrafield; not angry but appalled, yes, because even Alan deserved a little mourning and respect from his live-in lover, more than this shark could ever give him. But there was no point in blaming the shark for *being* a shark.

One of the elevators opened, disgorging uniformed policemen, morgue employees, and a gurney bearing a corpse in an opaque plastic body bag.

Jorja and Pepper rose from the sofa.

Even as the stretcher was being rolled out of the first elevator, the doors of the second opened, and four more cops appeared, two in uniform plus a team of plainclothes detectives. A detective came to Pepper Carrafield and asked a few final questions.

No one asked any questions of Jorja. She stood rigid and suddenly numb, staring at the body bag that contained her ex-husband.

They rolled the gurney across the travertine. The wheels squeaked.

Jorja watched it moving away.

Two cops held the lobby doors while the morgue attendants pushed the gurney outside. It moved past the lobby windows. Jorja turned to observe its progress. She still felt no grief, but she was swept by a powerful wave of melancholy, a profound sadness at what might have been.

From the nearest of the elevators, where she was holding a door open, Pepper said, ''Let's go up to my place.''

Outside, they closed the doors of the coroner's van.

In the elevator on the way up, and in a discreet whisper in the fourteenth-floor hallway, then continuing in a normal tone of voice as they entered her big living room, Pepper insisted on describing Alan's peculiar sexual hunger. He had always had the carnal appetite of a gourmand, but apparently sex had become a sick obsession with him as his life had wound down through its last couple months.

Jorja did not want to hear about it, but stopping the hooker seemed more difficult than simply enduring her chatter.

In recent weeks, Alan's days had been devoted to erotic pursuits, though it all sounded feverish and desperate rather than pleasurable. He had used sick leave and vacation time to spend long—often frantic—hours in bed with Pepper or others whose "careers" he managed, and there was no variation or perversion that he failed to explore to excess. The hooker chattered on: Alan had developed a fascination with lascivious substances, devices, appliances, and clothing—dildos, penis rings, spike-heeled shoes, vibrators, cocaine ointment, handcuffs. . . .

Jorja, already weak-kneed and dizzy since seeing the body bag, grew queasy. "Please stop. What's the point? He's dead, for God's sake."

Pepper shrugged. "I thought you'd want to know. He threw away a lot of his money on this . . . this sex binge. Since you're the executor of the estate, I thought you'd want to know."

The last will and testament of Alan Arthur Rykoff, which he had left with Pepper for safekeeping, was a simple preprinted one-page form of the type obtainable at any business supply store.

Jorja sat on a cobalt-blue Ultrasuede chair beside a lacquered black Tavola table, quickly scanning the will in the light from a high-tech, burnished-steel, cone-shaped lamp. The most surprising thing was not that Alan had named Jorja as executor, but that he had left what he owned to Marcie, whose fatherhood he had been prepared to deny.

Pepper sat on a black lacquered chair with white upholstery, near a wall of windows. "I don't figure it's much of an estate. He spent money pretty freely. But there's his car, some jewelry."

Jorja noticed that Alan's will had been notarized just four days ago, and she shivered. "He must've been considering suicide when he had this notarized; otherwise, he wouldn't have felt the need for it."

Pepper shrugged. "I guess."

"But didn't you see the danger? Didn't you see he was troubled?"

"Like I told you, honey, he'd been weird for a couple months."

"Yes, but there must've been a noticeable change in him during the last few days, something different from that other strangeness. When he told you he'd made out a will and asked you to put it in that lockbox of yours, didn't you wonder? Wasn't there anything about him—his manner, his look, his state of mind—that worried you?"

Pepper stood up impatiently. "I'm no psychologist, honey. His stuff's in the bedroom. If you want to give his clothes to Goodwill, I'll call them. But his other stuff—jewelry, personal things—you can get them out of here right now. I'll show you where everything is."

Jorja was sickened by the moral squalor into which Alan had sunk, but she also felt a measure of guilt for his death. Could she have done something to save him? By leaving his few possessions to Marcie and by naming Jorja executor of his will, he seemed to have reached out to them in his last days, and although that gesture was pathetic and inadequate, it touched Jorja. She tried to remember how he had sounded on the telephone before Christmas, when she had last spoken with him. She remembered his coldness, arrogance, and selfishness, but perhaps there had been other more subtle things that she should have heard beneath the surface cruelty and bravado: distress, confusion, loneliness, fear.

Brooding on that, she followed Pepper toward the bedroom. She loathed this task, pawing through Alan's things, but it had to be done.

Halfway down a long hall, Pepper stopped at a door, pushed it inward. "Oh, shit. I can't believe the damned cops left it like this."

Jorja looked in the open door before she realized that this was the bathroom in which Alan had killed himself. Blood was all over the beige tile floor. More blood was spattered over the glass door of the shower stall, sink, towels, wastecan, and toilet. The wall behind the toilet was stained with dried blood in a macabre pattern resembling a Rorschach blot, as if Alan's psychological condition and the meaning of his death were there to be read by anyone with sufficient insight.

"Shot himself twice," Pepper said, supplying details Jorja did not want to hear. "First in the crotch. Is that queer or what? Then he put the gun in his mouth and pulled the trigger."

Jorja could smell the vague coppery scent of blood.

"The damned cops should've cleaned up the worst of it," Pepper said, as if she thought policemen ought to be armed not only with guns but with scrub brushes and soap. "My housekeeper doesn't come until Monday. And she's not going to want to deal with this disgusting mess."

Jorja broke the bloody bathroom's hypnotic hold on her and stumbled blindly a few steps along the hall.

"Hey," Pepper Carrafield said, "you okay?"

Jorja gagged, clenched her teeth, moved quickly along the hall, and leaned against the jamb of another doorway.

"Hey, honey, you *were* still carrying a torch for him, weren't you?"

"No," Jorja said softly.

Pepper moved closer, too close, putting an unwanted consoling hand upon her shoulder. "Sure, you were. Jesus, I'm sorry." Pepper oozed unctuous sympathy, and Jorja wondered if the woman was capable of any genuine emotion that did not have its roots in self-interest. "You said you were burnt out on him, but I should've seen."

Jorja wanted to shout: *You stupid bitch, I'm not carrying a torch for him, but he was still a human being, for Christ's sake. How can you be so callous? What's wrong with you? Is something missing in you?*

But she only said, "I'm all right. I'm all right. Where are his things? I want to sort through them and get out of here."

Pepper ushered Jorja through the doorway in which she had been leaning, into a bedroom. "He had the bottom drawers of the highboy, plus the left side of the dresser, and that half of the closet. I'll help." She pulled out the lowest drawer of the highboy.

For Jorja, the room suddenly was as eerie and unreal as a place in a dream. Her heart began to pound, and she moved around the bed toward the first of three things that had filled her with fear. Books. Half a dozen books were stacked on the nightstand. She had seen the word "moon" on the spines of two of them. With trembling hands, she sorted through them and found that all six dealt with the same subject.

"Something wrong?" Pepper asked.

Jorja moved to the dresser, on which stood a globe the size of a basketball. A cord trailed from it. She clicked a switch on the cord and found the globe was opaque with a light inside. It was not a globe of the earth but of the moon, with geological features—craters, ridges, plains—clearly named. She gave the glowing sphere a spin.

The third thing that frightened her was a telescope on a tripod beside the dresser, in front of a window. Nothing about the instrument was different from other amateur telescopes, but to Jorja it seemed ominous, even dangerous, with dark and unknowable associations.

"Those're Alan's things," Pepper said.

"He was interested in astronomy? Since when?"

"For the past couple months," Pepper said.

The similarities between Alan's and Marcie's conditions troubled Jorja. Marcie's irrational fear of doctors. Alan's compulsive sex drive. Those were different psychological problems—obsessive fear in one case, obsessive attraction in the other—but they shared the element of obsession. Apparently, Marcie had been cured of her phobia. Alan was not as fortunate. He'd had no one to help him, and he had snapped, shooting off the genitals that had come to control him, putting a bullet in his brain. Jorja shuddered. It was too coincidental that father and daughter had been stricken by psychological problems simultaneously, but what made it more than coincidence was the *other* strangeness they shared: their interest in the moon. Alan had not seen Marcie in six months, and their most recent phone conversation had been in September, weeks before either had become fascinated by the moon. There had been no contact by which either could have transmitted that fascination to the other; it appeared to have sprung up spontaneously in each of them.

Remembering Marcie's moon-troubled sleep, Jorja said, "Do you know if he was having unusual dreams? About the moon?"

"Yeah. How'd you figure that? He was having them, but he could never remember any details when he woke up. They started . . . back in late October, I think it was. Why? What's it matter?"

"These dreams—were they nightmares?"

Pepper shook her head. "Not exactly. I'd hear him talking in his sleep. Sometimes he sounded afraid, but lots of times he'd smile, too."

Jorja felt as if ice had formed in her marrow.

She turned to look at the lighted globe of the moon.

What in the hell is going on? she wondered. A shared dream? Is that possible? How? Why?

Behind her, Pepper said, "Are you okay?"

Something had driven Alan to suicide.

What might happen to Marcie?

8. Saturday, January 11

BOSTON, MASSACHUSETTS.

The memorial service for Pablo Jackson was held at eleven o'clock Saturday morning, January 11, in a nondenominational chapel on the grounds of the cemetery where he was to be buried. The coroner and police pathologists had not been finished with the body until Thursday, so five days had passed between Pablo's murder and his funeral.

When the last eulogy was delivered, the mourners adjourned to the grave, where the casket waited. Snow had been cleared around Pablo's plot, but the space was insufficient. Scores of people stood outside the prepared area, some in snow deeper than their boots. Others remained on the sidewalks that crisscrossed the memorial park, watching from a distance. Three hundred had come to pay their last respects to the old magician. The chilly air steamed with the breath of the rich and the poor, the famous and the unknown, Boston socialites, magicians.

Ginger Weiss and Rita Hannaby stood in the first circle around the gravesite.

Since Monday, Ginger had not had much of an appetite and had gotten little sleep. She was pale, nervous, and very tired.

Both Rita and George had argued against Ginger's attendance at the services. They were concerned that such a wrenchingly emotional experience would trigger a fugue. But the police had encouraged her, hoping she might see Pablo's killer at the services. In self-defense she'd hidden the truth from the cops, leading them to believe that the killer was an ordinary burglar, and sometimes burglars were driven by such sick compulsions. But she knew that he was no mere burglar and that he would not risk arrest by coming to the cemetery.

Ginger wept during the eulogies, and by the time she walked from the chapel to the grave, her grief was a vise squeezing her heart. But she did not lose control. She was determined not to make a circus of this solemn occasion, determined to pay her respects with dignity.

Besides, she had come with a second purpose that could not be fulfilled if she spiraled down into a fugue or suffered an emotional collapse. She was sure that Alexander Christophson—former Ambassador to Great Britain, former United States Senator, and former Director of the CIA—would be at the funeral of his old friend, and she wanted very much to speak with him. It was to Christophson, on Christmas Day, that Pablo had turned for advice about Ginger's problems. And it was Alex Christophson who had told him about the Azrael Block. She had an important question to ask Christophson, though she dreaded the answer.

She had seen him in the chapel, recognized him from his days in public life, when he had been on television and in newspapers. He was a striking figure, tall, thin, white-haired, unmistakable. Now, they stood on opposite sides of the grave, the draped casket between them. He had glanced at her a couple times, though without recognition.

The minister said a brief final prayer. After a moment, some of the mourners greeted one another, formed small groups to talk. Others, including Christophson, moved away through a forest of headstones, past snow-laden pines and winter-stripped maples, toward the parking lot.

"I've got to talk to that man," Ginger told Rita. "Be right back."

Startled, Rita called after her, but Ginger did not pause or offer further explanation. She caught up with Christophson in the jagged shadows cast by the skeletal branches of an immense oak that was all black bark and crusted snow. She called his name, and he turned. He had piercing gray eyes, which widened when she told him who she was.

"I can't help you," he said, and began to turn away from her.

"Please," she said, putting a hand on his arm. "If you blame me for what happened to Pablo—"

"Why should you care what I think, Doctor?"

She held fast to his arm. "Wait. Please, for God's sake."

Christophson surveyed the slowly dispersing crowd in the cemetery, and Ginger knew that he was afraid the wrong people—dangerous people—might see him with her and assume he was helping her as Pablo had done. His head twitched slightly, and Ginger thought it was an indication of his nervousness, but then she realized it was the faint tremor of Parkinson's disease. He said, "Dr. Weiss, if you're seeking some form of absolution, then by all means let me provide it. Pablo knew the risks, and he accepted them. He was the captain of his own fate."

"*Did* he understand the risks? That's what I've got to know."

Christophson seemed surprised. "I warned him myself."

"Warned him about who? About what?"

"I don't know who or what. But considering the enormous effort expended to

tamper with your memory, you must've seen something of tremendous importance. I warned Pablo that whoever had brainwashed you was no amateur and
that if they realized the two of you were trying to break through the Azrael Block,
they might come after not just you but him as well.'' Christophson's gray eyes
searched her eyes for a moment, and then he sighed. ''He *did* tell you about his
conversation with me?''

''He told me everything—except about your warning.'' Her eyes filled with
tears again. ''He didn't breathe a word of that.''

He withdrew one elegant but palsied hand from his pocket and gripped her arm
reassuringly. ''Doctor, now that you've told me this, I can't possibly lay any of
the blame at your doorstep.''

''But *I* blame me,'' Ginger said in a voice thin with misery.

''No. You can't blame yourself for any of it.'' Looking around again to make
sure they were not under surveillance, Christophson opened the top two buttons
of his overcoat, reached inside, plucked the display handkerchief from the breast
pocket of his suit jacket, and gave it to Ginger. ''Please stop punishing yourself.
Our friend lived a full and fortunate life, Doctor. His death might've been violent,
but it was relatively quick, which can be a blessing.''

Drying her eyes on the swatch of pale blue silk that he had given her, Ginger
said, ''He was a dear man.''

''He was,'' Christophson agreed. ''And I'm beginning to understand why he
took the risks he did for you. He said *you* were a very dear woman, and I see
his judgment was as accurate and reliable as usual.''

She finished blotting her eyes. Her heart still felt pinched in a vise, but she
began to believe there was a chance that guilt and grief would eventually give
way to grief alone. ''Thank you.'' As much to herself as to him, Ginger said,
''What now? Where do I go from here?''

''I'm in no position to help you,'' he said at once. ''I've been out of the
intelligence business for almost a decade, and I've no contacts any more. I've no
idea who might be behind your memory block or why.''

''I wouldn't ask you to help me. I'm not risking any more innocent lives. I
just thought you might have some idea how I can help myself.''

''Go to the police. It's their *job* to help.''

Ginger shook her head. ''No. The police are slow, too slow. Most of them are
overworked, and the rest are just bureaucrats in uniforms. My problem's too
urgent to wait for them to solve it. Besides, I don't trust them. Suddenly I don't
trust authorities of any kind. The tapes Pablo made of our sessions were gone
when I took the police back to his apartment, so I didn't mention them. I spooked.
I didn't tell the cops about my fugues or about how Pablo had been helping me.
I just said we'd been friends, that I'd stopped by to have lunch and walked in on
the killer. I let them think it was an ordinary burglary. Sheer paranoia. Didn't
trust them. Still don't. So the cops are out.''

''Then find another hypnotist to regress you—''

''No. I'm not risking any more innocent lives,'' she repeated.

''I understand. But those are the only suggestions I have.'' He shoved both
hands into the deep pockets of his overcoat. ''I'm sorry.''

''No need to be,'' she said.

He started to turn away, hesitated, sighed. ''Doctor, I want you to understand
me. I served in the war, the big war, with some distinction. Later, I was a good
ambassador. As head of the CIA and as a senator, I made many difficult decisions,
some that put me in personal danger. I never backed away from risk. But I'm an

old man now. Seventy-six, and I feel older. Parkinson's. A bad heart. High blood pressure. I have a wife I love very much, and if anything happens to me, she'll be alone. I don't know how well she'd deal with being alone, Dr. Weiss.''

"Please, there's no need to justify yourself," Ginger said. She realized how completely and quickly their roles had reversed. In the beginning, he had been the one full of reassurances and absolution; now she was returning the favor. Jacob, her father, had often said that the capacity for mercy was humankind's greatest virtue, and that the giving and receiving of mercy formed a bond unbreakable. Ginger remembered Jacob's words now because, in allowing Alex Christophson to allay her guilt and in trying to allay his, she felt that bond.

Apparently, he felt it, too, for although he did not stop trying to explain himself, his explanations became more intimate and were offered now in a tone of voice that was less defensive and more conspiratorial. "Quite frankly, Doctor, my reluctance to get involved is not so much because I find life infinitely precious but because I am increasingly afraid of death." As he spoke, he reached into an inside pocket and withdrew a notepad and pen. "In my life I've done some things of which I'm not proud." Holding the pen in his palsied right hand, he began to print. "True, most of those sins were committed in the line of duty. Government and espionage are both necessary, but neither is a clean business. In those days, I didn't believe in God or an afterlife. Now I wonder. . . . And wondering, I'm sometimes afraid." He tore the top page from the pad. "Afraid of what might await me after death, you see. That's why I want to hold on to life as long as I can, Doctor. That's why, God help me, I've become a coward in my old age."

As Christophson folded and passed to her the slip of paper on which he had been printing, Ginger realized that he had managed to put his back to all of the remaining mourners before he had removed the notepad and pen from his coat. No one could have seen what he had done.

He said, "I've just given you the phone number of an antique store in Greenwich, Connecticut. My younger brother, Philip, owns the place. You can't call me direct because the wrong people may have seen us talking; my telephone might be tapped. I won't risk associating with you, Dr. Weiss, and I won't pursue any investigation of your problem. However, I have many years of broad experience in these matters, and there may be times when that experience will be of help to you. You may encounter something you don't understand, a situation you don't know how to deal with, and I may be able to offer advice. Just call Philip and leave your number with him. He'll immediately call me at home and use a prearranged codeword. Then I'll go out to a pay phone, return his call, get the number you left with him, and contact you as quickly as possible. Experience, my peculiar kind of malevolent experience, is all I'm willing to offer you, Dr. Weiss."

"It's more than enough. You're not obligated to help me at all."

"Good luck." He turned abruptly and walked away, his boots crunching in the frozen snow.

Ginger returned to the grave, where Rita, the mortician, and two laborers were the only people remaining. The velvet curtain around the grave had been collapsed and removed. A plastic tarpaulin had been pulled off a waiting mound of earth.

"What was that all about?" Rita asked.

"Tell you later," Ginger said, bending down to pick up a rose from the pile of flowers beside Pablo Jackson's final resting place. She leaned forward and tossed the bloom into the hole, on top of the casket. *"Alav ha-sholem.* May this sleep be only a little dream between this world and something better. *Baruch ha-Shem.*"

As she and Rita walked away, Ginger heard the laborers begin to shovel dirt onto the casket.

ELKO COUNTY, NEVADA.

On Thursday, Dr. Fontelaine was satisfied that Ernie Block was cured of his disabling nyctophobia. "Fastest cure I've ever seen," he said. "I guess you Marines are tougher than ordinary mortals."

On Saturday, January 11, after only four weeks in Milwaukee, Ernie and Faye went home. They flew into Reno on United, then caught a ten-seat commuter flight to Elko, arriving at eleven-twenty-seven in the morning.

Sandy Sarver met them at the airport in Elko, though Ernie did not immediately recognize her. She was standing by the small terminal, in the crystalline winter sunshine, waving as Ernie and Faye disembarked. Gone was the pale-faced mouse, the familiar slump-shouldered frump. For the first time since Ernie had known her, Sandy was wearing a little makeup, eye shadow, and lipstick. Her nails were no longer bitten. Her hair, always limp and dull and neglected in the past, was now full, glossy. She had gained ten pounds. She had always looked older than she was. Now she looked years younger.

She blushed when Ernie and Faye raved about her makeover. She pretended the changes were of little consequence, but she was clearly pleased by their praise, approval, and delight.

She had changed in other ways, as well. For one thing, she was usually reticent and shy, but as they walked to the parking lot and put the baggage in the back of her red pickup, she asked lots of questions about Lucy, Frank, and the grandchildren. She did not ask about Ernie's phobia because she knew nothing of it; they had kept his condition secret and had explained the extension of their Wisconsin visit by saying they wanted to spend more time with the grandchildren. In the truck, as Sandy drove through Elko and onto the interstate, she was downright garrulous as she spoke of the Christmas just past and of business at the Tranquility Grille.

As much as anything, Sandy's driving surprised Ernie. He knew she had an aversion to four-wheel travel. But now she drove fast, with an ease and skill Ernie had never seen in her before.

Faye, sitting between Ernie and Sandy, was aware of this change, too, for she gave Ernie meaningful looks when Sandy maneuvered the pickup with special fluidity and audacity.

Then a bad thing happened.

Less than a mile from the motel, Ernie's interest in Sandy's metamorphosis was suddenly displaced by the queer feeling that had first seized him on December 10, when he'd been coming home from Elko with the new lighting fixtures: the feeling that a particular piece of ground, half a mile ahead, south of the highway, was *calling* him. The feeling that something strange had happened to him out there. As before, it was simultaneously an absurd and gripping feeling, characterized by the eerie attraction of a talismanic place in a dream.

This was an unsettling development because Ernie had supposed that the peculiar magnetism of that place had been, somehow, a part of the same mental disturbance that resulted in his crippling dread of the dark. His nyctophobia cured, he had assumed that all other symptoms of his temporary psychological imbalance would disappear along with his fear of the night. So this seemed like a bad sign. He did not want to consider what it might indicate about the permanency of his cure.

Faye was telling Sandy about Christmas morning with the grandkids, and Sandy was laughing, but to Ernie the laughter and conversation faded. As they drew nearer the plot of ground that exerted a mesmeric attraction on him, Ernie squinted through the sun-streaked windshield, possessed by a sense of impending epiphany. Something of monumental importance seemed about to happen, and he was filled with fear and awe.

Then, as they were passing that beguiling place, Ernie became aware that their speed had dropped. Sandy had slowed to under forty miles an hour, half the speed she had maintained since Elko. Even as Ernie realized the truck had slowed, it accelerated again. He looked at Sandy too late to be certain that she also had been temporarily spellbound by that same portion of the landscape, for now she was listening to Faye and watching the road ahead and bringing the pickup back to speed. But it seemed to him there was a strange look on her face, and he stared at her in bewilderment, wondering how she could share his mysterious and irrational fascination with that piece of quite ordinary land.

"It's good to be home," Faye said as Sandy switched on the right-turn signal and steered the truck toward the exit lane.

Ernie watched Sandy for an indication that she had slowed the truck in answer to the same eerie call that he felt, but he saw none of the fear that the call engendered in him. She was smiling. He must have been wrong. She had slowed the truck for some other reason.

A chill had taken residence in his bones, and now as they drove up the sloped county road and turned into the motel lot, he felt a cold damp dew of sweat on his palms, on his scalp.

He looked at his watch. Not because he needed to know the time. But because he wanted to know how long until sundown. About five hours.

What if it wasn't darkness in general that he feared? What if it was a *specific* darkness? Perhaps he had quickly overcome his phobia in Milwaukee because he was only mildly frightened by the night out there. Perhaps his real fear, his deep fear, was of the darkness of the Nevada plains. Could a phobia be that narrowly focused, that localized?

Surely not. Yet he looked at his watch.

Sandy parked in front of the motel office, and when they got out of the truck and went around to the tailgate to get the luggage, she hugged both Faye and Ernie. "I'm glad you're back. I missed you both. Now I'd better get over to the diner and help Ned. Lunch hour's started."

Ernie and Faye watched Sandy as she hurried away, and Faye said, "What on earth do you suppose happened to her?"

"Damned if I know," Ernie said.

Her breath steaming in the cold air, Faye said, "At first, I thought she must've learned she's pregnant. But now I don't think so. If she was pregnant and over-joyed about it, she'd have told us. She'd have been *bursting* with the news. I think it's something . . . else."

Ernie pulled two of the four suitcases out of the back of the truck and stood them on the ground, surreptitiously glancing at his watch as he put the bags down. Sundown was five minutes closer.

Faye sighed. "Well, whatever the cause, I'm sure happy for her."

"Me, too," Ernie said, lifting the other two bags out of the truck.

" 'Me, too,' " Faye said, affectionately mimicking him as she picked up the two lightest suitcases. "Don't play cool with me, you big softy. I know you've worried about her almost like you used to worry about our own Lucy. When you first saw the change in Sandy back at the airport, I was watching you, and I thought your heart was going to melt."

He followed her with the two heavier bags. "Do they have a medical term for a calamity like that, for a melting heart?"

"Sure. Cardio-liquefaction."

He laughed in spite of the tension that knotted his stomach. Faye was always able to make him laugh—usually when he needed it most. When they got inside, he would put his arms around her, kiss her, and convey her straight upstairs and into bed. Nothing else would be as certain to chase away the fear that had popped up in him like a jack-in-the-box. Time spent with Faye was always the best medicine.

She put her two bags down by the office door and fished her keys out of her purse.

When it had become clear, early on, that Ernie was likely to have an exceptionally swift recovery and that they would not need to stay in Milwaukee for months, Faye had decided against flying home to search for a motel manager. They simply kept the place closed. Now they needed to unlock, turn up the thermostat, clean away the accumulated dust.

A lot of work to be done . . . but still enough time for a little horizontal dancing first, Ernie thought with a grin.

He was standing behind Faye as she put the key in the office door, so fortunately she did not see him twitch and jump in surprise when the bright day was suddenly claimed by shadows. They were not actually plunged into darkness; a large cloud merely moved across the sun; the level of light dropped by no more than twenty percent. Yet even that was sufficient to startle and unnerve him.

He looked at his watch.

He looked toward the east, from whence the night would come.

I'll be all right, he thought. I'm cured.

ON THE ROAD: RENO TO ELKO COUNTY.

Following the paranormal experience in Lomack's house on Tuesday, when countless paper moons took orbit around him, Dominick Corvaisis spent a few days in Reno. On his previous journey from Portland to Mountainview, he had stayed over to research a series of short stories about gambling. Re-creating that trip, he passed Wednesday, Thursday, and Friday in "The Biggest Little City in the World."

Dom wandered from casino to casino, watching gamblers. There were young couples, retirees, pretty young women, middle-aged women in stretch pants and cardigans, leather-faced cowboys fresh from the range and soft-faced rich men on junkets from far cities, secretaries, truckers, executives, doctors, ex-cons and off-duty cops, hustlers and dreamers, escapees from every social background, drawn together by the hope and thrill of organized games of chance, surely the most democratizing industry on earth.

As during his previous visit, Dom gambled only enough to be part of the scene, for his primary purpose was to observe. After the storm of paper moons, he had reason to believe that Reno was the place where his life had been changed forever and where he would find the key to unlock his imprisoned memories. Those around him laughed, chattered, grumbled about the unkindness of cards, shouted to encourage the rolling dice, but Dom remained cool and alert, among them yet distanced from them, the better to spot any clue to the unremembered events in his past.

No clue was revealed.

Each night he contacted Parker Faine in Laguna Beach, hoping that the unknown correspondent had sent an additional message.

No message was received.

Each night before sleep came, he tried to understand the impossible dance of paper moons. And he sought an explanation of the circular, swollen, red rings in his hands, which he had watched fade as he knelt in a drift of moons in Lomack's living room. No understanding came.

Day by day, his craving for Valium and Dalmane diminished, but his unremembered nightmares—*the moon*—grew worse. Each night, he fought fiercely against the tether with which he moored himself to his bed.

By Saturday, Dom still suspected that the answer to his night fear and somnambulism lay in Reno. But he decided that he must not change his plans, must go on to Mountainview. If he concluded the journey without achieving *satori,* he could return to Reno at that time.

The summer before last, he departed Harrah's at ten-thirty a.m. Friday, July 6, after an early lunch. On Saturday, January 11, he therefore followed that timetable, driving onto I-80 at ten-forty, heading northeast across the Nevada wasteland toward distant Winnemucca, where Butch Cassidy and the Sundance Kid had robbed a bank in another age.

The immense unpopulated expanses of land were little different from the way they had been a thousand years ago. The highway and power lines, often the only signs of civilization, followed the route that had been called the Humboldt Trail in the days of wagon trains. Dom drove over barren plains and hills bearded with scrub, through an uninviting yet starkly beautiful primeval world of sagebrush, sand, alkaline flats, dry lakes, solidified lava beds with columnar crystallizations, distant mountains. Sheered bluffs and veined monoliths showed traces of borax, sulfur, alum, and salt. Isolated rocky buttes were splendidly painted in ocher, amber, umber, and gray. North of the trackless Humboldt Sink, where the Humboldt River simply vanished into the thirsty earth, were more streams, as well as the Humboldt itself, and here the forbidding land featured some contrastingly fertile valleys with lush grasses and trees—cottonwoods, willows, though not in profusion. Adequate water meant communities and agriculture, but even in the hospitable valleys, the settlements were small, the grip of civilization tenuous.

As always, Dom was humbled by the vastness of the West. But the landscape also aroused new feelings this time: a sense of mystery and an unsettling awareness of limitless—and eerie—possibilities. Hurtling through this lonely realm, it was easy to believe something frightening had happened to him here.

At two-forty-five he stopped for gasoline and a sandwich in Winnemucca, a town of only five thousand souls yet by far the largest in a county of sixteen thousand square miles. Then I-80 turned eastward. The land rose gradually toward the rim of the Great Basin. More mountains peaked on every horizon, with snow far down their slopes, and more bunch-grass appeared midst the sagebrush, and there were genuine meadows in some places, though the desert was by no means left entirely behind.

At sunset, Dom pulled off the interstate at the Tranquility Motel, parked near the office, got out of the car, and was surprised by a cold wind. Having driven so long through deserts, he was psychologically prepared for heat, though he knew it was winter on the high plains. He reached into the car, grabbed a fleece-lined suede jacket, and put it on. He started toward the motel . . . then stopped, suddenly apprehensive.

This was the place.

He did not know *how* he knew. But he knew.

Here, something strange had happened.

He had stopped here on Friday evening, July 6, the summer before last. He had found the curious isolation of the place and the majesty of the land enormously appealing and inspiring. Indeed, he had become convinced that this territory was good material for fiction, and he had decided to stay a couple of days to familiarize himself with it and to brood about story ideas suitable to the background. He had not left for Mountainview, Utah, until Tuesday morning, the 10th of July.

Now, he turned slowly, studying the scene in the fast-fading light, hoping to prick his memory. As he turned, he became convinced that what had happened to him here was more important than anything that would ever happen to him, anywhere, as long as he lived.

The diner, with its big windows and blue neon sign, was at the western end of the complex, detached from the motel, surrounded by a large parking lot to accommodate long-haul trucks, of which three were in attendance. The entire length of the single-story white motel was served by a breezeway sheltered under an aluminum awning that glistened darkly with a well-kept coat of forest-green enamel. The west wing had ten rooms with glossy green doors. It was separated from the east wing by a two-story section that housed the office on the first floor and, no doubt, the owner's quarters on the second. Unlike the west wing, the east wing was L-shaped, with six rooms in the first section, four in the shorter arm. Dom kept turning and saw the dark sky in the east, the interstate dwindling into that gloom, then the immense and uninhabited panorama of shadowed land to the south. More plains and mountains lay in the west, where the sky above was streaked crimson by the sunset.

Moment by moment, Dom's apprehension grew, until he had turned in a complete circle and was looking once more at the Tranquility Grille. As if in a dream, he moved toward the diner. By the time he reached the door, his heart was hammering. He had the urge to flee.

Steeling himself, he opened the door and went inside.

It was a clean well-lighted place, cozy and warm. Delicious odors filled the air: french fries, onions, fresh hamburger sizzling on the griddle, frying ham.

In dreamlike fear, he crossed to an empty table. A ketchup bottle, a squeeze-bottle of mustard, a sugar bowl, salt and pepper shakers, and an ashtray were clustered in the center. He picked up the salt shaker.

For a moment he did not know why he had picked it up, but then he remembered sitting at this very table the summer before last, his first night at the Tranquility Motel. He had spilled a bit of salt and had reflexively cast a pinch of it over his shoulder, inadvertently throwing it in the face of a young woman approaching behind him.

He sensed that the incident was important, but he did not know why. Because of the woman? Who had she been? A stranger. What had she looked like? He tried to recall her face but could not.

His heart raced without apparent reason. He felt as if he were on the brink of some devastating revelation.

He strove to recall additional details, but they eluded him.

He put the salt shaker down. Still moving dreamily, shivering with unfocused anxiety, he crossed to the corner booth by the front windows. It was unoccupied, but Dom was sure that the young woman, having blinked the salt out of her eyelashes, had come here that *other* night.

"Can I help you?"

Dom was aware that a waitress in a yellow sweater was standing beside him and had spoken to him, but he remained spellbound by the tantalizing ascension of some terrible memory. It had not swum into view yet, but it was rising, rising. The woman out of his past, whose face remained a blank to him, had sat in this booth, radiantly beautiful in the orange light of the sunset.

"Mister? Is something wrong?"

The young woman had ordered dinner, and Dom had gone on with his meal, and the sunset had faded, and night had fallen, and— *No!*

The memory swam out of the deeps, almost broke through the murky surface into light, into his consciousness, but at the last moment he recoiled from it in panic, as if he had seen the horrible face of some monstrously evil leviathan streaking toward him. Abruptly not wanting to remember, refusing, Dom loosed a wordless cry, stumbled back, turned away from the startled waitress, and ran. He was aware of people staring, aware that he was making a scene, but he did not give a damn. All he cared about was getting out. He hit the door, flung it open, and rushed out under a post-sunset, black, purple, and scarlet sky.

He was afraid. Afraid of the past. Afraid of the future. But afraid mostly because he did not know *why* he was afraid.

CHICAGO, ILLINOIS.

Brendan Cronin was saving his announcement for after dinner, when Father Wycazik, with a full belly and a glass of brandy in hand, would be in his best mood of the day. Meanwhile, in the company of Fathers Wycazik and Gerrano, he ate a hearty dinner: double portions of potatoes and beans and ham, disposing of a third of a loaf of homemade bread.

Though he had regained his appetite, he had not regained his faith. When his belief in God had collapsed, it had left in him a terrible dark emptiness and despair, but now the despair was gone, and the emptiness, though not entirely filled, was shrinking. He was beginning to perceive that one day he might lead a meaningful life *that had nothing to do with the Church.* For Brendan—for whom no temporal pleasures had been as enticing as the spiritual joy of the Mass—the mere contemplation of a secular life was a revolutionary development.

Perhaps his despair had lifted because, since Christmas, he had at least journeyed along from atheism to a qualified agnosticism. Recent events had conspired to make him consider the existence of a Power that, though not necessarily God, was nevertheless above nature.

After dinner, Father Gerrano went upstairs to spend a few hours with the latest novel by James Blaylock, the fantasist whom Brendan, too, found interesting, but whose colorful tales of bizarre fantasy creatures and even more bizarre human beings were too imaginative for a hard-nosed realist like Father Wycazik. Adjourning to the study with Brendan, the rector said, "He writes well, but when I'm finished with one of his stories, I get the peculiar feeling that nothing's what it seems to be, and I don't like that feeling."

"Maybe nothing *is* what it seems to be," Brendan said.

The rector shook his head, and his gray hair caught the light in such a way that it looked like steel wire. "No, when I read for entertainment, I prefer it in big, solid, heavy blocks that let you grapple with the *reality* of life."

Grinning broadly, Brendan said, "If there's a heaven, Father, and if I somehow manage to get there with you, I hope I'll have a chance to arrange a meeting between you and Walt Disney. I'd love to see you convince him that he should've spent his time animating the collected works of Dostoevsky instead of the adventures of Mickey Mouse."

Laughing at himself, the rector poured their drinks, and they settled into armchairs, the fallen priest with a glass of schnapps, his superior with a small brandy.

Deciding there would be no better time for his news, Brendan said, "If it's all right with you, I'll be going away for a while, Father. I'd like to leave on Monday, if I can. I need to go to Nevada."

"Nevada?" Father Wycazik made it sound as if his curate had just said Bangkok or Timbuktu. "Why Nevada?"

With the taste of peppermint schnapps on his tongue and the scent burning his sinuses, Brendan said, "That's where I'm being called. Last night, in the dream, though I still saw nothing but a brilliant light, I suddenly knew where I was. Elko County, Nevada. And I knew I must go back there in order to find an explanation for Emmy's cure and Winton's resurrection."

"Back there? You've been there before?"

"The summer before last. Just before I came to St. Bernadette's."

Upon leaving his post with Monsignor Orbella in Rome, Brendan had flown directly to San Francisco to carry out a final assignment from his Vatican mentor. He stayed two weeks with Bishop John Santefiore, an old friend of Orbella. The bishop was writing a book on the history of papal selection, and Brendan came laden with research material provided by the monsignor in Rome. It was his job to answer any questions about those documents. John Santefiore was a charming man with a sly dry wit, and the days flashed past.

His task concluded, Brendan was left with two weeks to himself before he was required to report to his superiors in Chicago, his hometown, where he would be assigned as curate to some parish in that archdiocese. He spent a few days in Carmel, on the Monterey Peninsula. Then, making up his mind to see some of the country that he had never seen before, Brendan set out on a long drive eastward in a rental car.

Now, Father Wycazik leaned forward, brandy snifter clasped in both hands. "I remembered about Bishop Santefiore, but I'd forgotten you drove from there to here. And you passed through Elko County, Nevada?"

"Stayed there, at a motel in the middle of nowhere. Tranquility Motel. I stopped for the night, but it was so peaceful, the countryside so beautiful, that I stayed a few days. Now I've got to go back."

"Why? What happened to you out there?"

Brendan shrugged. "Nothing. I just relaxed. Napped. Read a couple books. Watched TV. They have good TV reception even way out there because they've got their own little receiver dish on the roof."

Father Wycazik cocked his head. "What's wrong? There for a moment you sounded . . . odd. Wooden . . . as if repeating something you'd memorized."

"I was just telling you what it was like."

"So if nothing happened to you there, why is the place so special? What will happen when you go back there?"

"I'm not sure. But it's going to be something . . . incredible."

Finally revealing his frustration with his curate's obtuseness, Father Wycazik put the question bluntly: "Is it *God* calling you?"

"I don't think so. But maybe. A slim maybe. Father, I want your permission to go. But if I can't have your blessing, I'll go anyway."

Father Wycazik took a larger swallow of brandy than was his habit. "I think you should go, but I don't think you should go alone."

Brendan was surprised. "You want to come with me?"

"Not me. I've got St. Bette's to run. But you should be in the company of a qualified witness. A priest familiar with these things, one who can verify any miracle or miraculous visitation—"

"You mean some cleric who has the Cardinal's imprimatur to investigate every hysterical report of weeping statues of the Holy Mother, bleeding crucifixes, and divine manifestations of all kinds."

Father Wycazik nodded. "That's right. Someone who knows the process of authentication. I had in mind Monsignor Janney of the archdiocese's office of publications. He's had a lot of practice."

Reluctant to disappoint his rector but determined to proceed in his own fashion, Brendan interrupted: "There's no visitation involved here, so there's no need for Monsignor Janney. None of this has an obvious Christian significance or source."

"And who ever said God isn't permitted to be subtle?" Father Wycazik asked. His grin made it clear he expected to win this argument.

"These things could all be merely psychic phenomena."

"Bah! Claptrap. Psychic phenomena are just the nonbeliever's pathetic explanation for glimpses of the divine hand at work. Examine these events closely, Brendan; open your heart to the meaning of them, and you'll see the truth. God's calling you back to His bosom. And I believe a divine visitation is what this may be building toward."

"But if this is building to a divine manifestation, why couldn't it happen right here? Why's it necessary to go all the way to Nevada?"

"Perhaps it's a test of your obedience to the will of God, a test of your underlying desire to believe again. If your desire's strong enough, you'll discomfit yourself by taking this long journey, and as reward you'll be shown something to make you believe again."

"But why Nevada? Why not Florida or Texas—or Istanbul?"

"Only God knows."

"And why would God go to all this trouble to recapture the heart of one fallen priest?"

"To Him who made the earth and stars, this is no trouble at all. And one heart is as important to Him as a million hearts."

"Then why did He let me lose my faith in the first place?"

"Perhaps losing and regaining it is a tempering process. You may have been put through it because God needs you to be stronger."

Brendan smiled and shook his head in admiration. "You're never caught without an answer, are you, Father?"

Looking self-satisfied, Stefan Wycazik settled back in his chair. "God blessed me with a quick tongue."

Brendan was aware of Father Wycazik's reputation as a savior of troubled priests, and he knew the rector would not give up easily—or at all. But Brendan was determined not to go to Nevada with Monsignor Janney in tow.

From the other armchair, over the rim of his brandy snifter, Father Wycazik watched Brendan with evident affection and iron determination, waiting eagerly for another argument that he could swiftly refute, for another thrust that he could parry with his unfailing Jesuitical aplomb.

Brendan sighed. It was going to be a long evening.

ELKO COUNTY, NEVADA.

After hurrying out of the Tranquility Grille in fear and confusion, into the last fading scarlet and purple light of dusk, Dom Corvaisis went directly to the motel office. There, he walked into the middle of a scene that initially appeared to be a domestic quarrel, though he quickly saw that it was something stranger than that.

A squarely built man in tan slacks and a brown sweater stood in the center of the room, this side of the counter. He was only two inches taller than Dom, but in other dimensions he was considerably larger. He seemed to have been hewn from massive slabs of oak. The gray of his brush-cut hair, the weathered lines of his face, indicated he was in his fifties, although his bull-strong body had a younger presence and power.

The big man was shaking, as if enraged. A woman stood beside him, staring up at him with an odd and urgent expression. She was a blonde with vivid blue eyes, younger than him, though it was difficult to judge her age. The man's pale face was shiny with sweat. As Dom stepped across the threshold, he realized that his flash impression was wrong: This guy was not enraged but terrified.

"Relax," the woman said. "Try to control your breathing."

The big man was gasping. He stood with his thick neck bent, head lowered, shoulders hunched, staring at the floor, inhalation following exhalation in an arhythmic pattern that betrayed a growing panic.

"Take deep slow breaths," the woman said. "Remember what Dr. Fontelaine taught you. When you're calm, we'll go outside for a walk."

"No!" the big man said, shaking his head violently.

"Yes, we will," the woman said, putting a reassuring hand on his arm. "We'll go outside for a walk, Ernie, and you'll see that this darkness is no different from the darkness in Milwaukee."

Ernie. The name chilled Dom and immediately brought to mind those four posters of the moon on which names had been scrawled in Zebediah Lomack's living room, in Reno.

The woman glanced at Dom, and he said, "I need a room."

"We're full," she said.

"The vacancy sign is lit."

"Okay," she said. "Okay, but not now. Please. Not now. Go over to the diner or something. Come back in half an hour. *Please.*"

Until that exchange, Ernie had seemed unaware of Dom's intrusion. Now, he looked up from the floor, and a moan of fear and despair escaped him. "The door. Close it before the darkness comes in!"

"No, no, no," the woman told him, her voice firm yet full of compassion. "It's not coming in. Darkness can't hurt you, Ernie."

"It's coming in," he insisted miserably.

Dom realized that the room was unnaturally bright. Table lamps, a floor lamp, a desk lamp, and the ceiling fixtures blazed.

The woman turned to Dom again. "For God's sake, close the door."

He stepped in, rather than out, and shut the door behind him.

"I meant, close it as you leave," the woman said pointedly.

The expression on Ernie's face was part terror, part embarrassment. His eyes shifted from Dom to the window. "It's right there at the glass. All the darkness . . . pressing, pressing." He looked sheepishly at Dom, then lowered his head again, shut his eyes tight.

Dom stood transfixed. Ernie's irrational fear was horribly like the terror which drove Dom to walk in his sleep and to hide in closets.

Using anger to repress her tears, the woman turned to Dom. "Why won't you go? He's nyctophobic. He's afraid of the dark sometimes, and when he has one of these attacks, we have to work it out together."

Dom remembered the other names scrawled on the posters in Lomack's house—Ginger, Faye—and he chose one by instinct. "It's all right, Faye. I think I understand a little of what you're going through."

She blinked in surprise when he used her name. "Do I know you?"

"Do you? I'm Dominick Corvaisis."

"Means nothing to me," she said, staying with the big man as he turned and, eyes still closed, shuffled toward the back of the office.

Ernie moved blindly toward the gate in the counter. "Got to get upstairs, where I can pull the drapes, keep the dark out."

Faye said, "No, Ernie, wait. Don't run from it."

Stepping in front of Ernie, putting a hand on the man's chest to halt him, Dom said, "You have nightmares. When you wake up, you can't remember what they were, except they had something to do with the moon."

Faye gasped.

Ernie opened his eyes in surprise. "How'd you know that?"

"I've had nightmares for over a month," Dom said. "Every night. And I know a man who suffered from them so bad he killed himself."

They stared at him in astonishment.

"In October," Dom said, "I started walking in my sleep. I'd creep out of bed, hide in closets, or gather weapons to protect myself. Once, I tried to nail the windows shut to keep something out. Don't you see, Ernie, I'm afraid of something in the dark. I'll bet that's what you're afraid of, too. Not just the dark itself but something else, something specific that happened to you"—he gestured toward the windows—"out there in the darkness on that same weekend, the summer before last."

Still baffled by this turn of events, Ernie glanced at the night beyond the windows, then immediately looked away. "I don't understand."

"Let's go upstairs, where you can draw the drapes," Dom said. "I'll tell you what I know. The important thing is you aren't alone in this. You're not alone any more. And, thank God, neither am I."

NEW HAVEN COUNTY, CONNECTICUT.

Clockwork. Jack Twist's heists always ticked along like clockwork mechanisms. The armored-car job was no exception.

The night was solidly roofed with clouds. No stars, no moon. No snow was falling, but a cold moist wind swept up from the southwest.

The Guardmaster truck rumbled past empty fields, coming from the northeast toward the knoll from which Jack had watched it Christmas Eve. Its headlights bored through thin ragged sheets of patchy winter fog. In the snow-wrapped fields, the county lane resembled a strip of black satin ribbon.

Dressed in a white ski suit with hood, Jack lay half buried in snow, south of the roadway, across from the knoll. On the other side of the road, at the foot of the knoll, the second member of the team, Chad Zepp, also in white camouflage, sprawled in another drift.

The third member of the team, Branch Pollard, was halfway down the knoll with a Heckler and Koch HK91 heavy assault rifle.

The truck was two hundred yards away. Refracting the headlights, fog formations drifted across the road, into the lightless fields.

Suddenly the muzzle of the HK91 flashed up on the hillside. A shot cracked above the sound of the grinding engine.

The HK91, perhaps the finest combat rifle made, could fire hundreds of rounds without jamming. Extremely accurate, effective at a thousand yards, the HK91 could put a 7.62 NATO round through a tree or concrete wall, with sufficient punch left to kill someone on the other side.

Tonight, however, they did not intend to kill anyone. Aided by an infra-red telescopic sight, Pollard put the first shot where he wanted it, blowing out the right front tire of the Guardmaster transport.

The truck swerved wildly. Encountering ice, it began to slide.

Even while the armored transport was sliding, its fate unsettled, Jack was up and running. He leaped a ditch and dashed onto the road in front of the vehicle, which loomed like a tank. At the last moment, when it seemed bound inexorably for the ditch, the driver regained control and brought the truck to a jerky halt thirty feet from Jack.

He saw one of the Guardmaster crewmen talking excitedly into a radio handset. That call for help was futile. The moment Pollard had fired from the knoll, Chad Zepp, still concealed in the snow north of the road, had switched on a battery-powered transmitter, jamming the transport's radio frequency with shrill electronic static.

As the rising wind harried fog-ghosts past Jack, he stood in the middle of the road, feeling naked in the blazing headlights, taking time to aim the tear-gas rifle at the truck's grille. The gun was of British manufacture, designed for anti-terrorist squads. Other tear-gas weapons fired grenades that spewed disabling fumes on impact, requiring the marksman to aim at windows. But upon seizing an embassy, terrorists usually boarded up the windows. The new British gun, which Jack had acquired from a black-market arms dealer in Miami, had a two-inch bore and fired a high-velocity, steel-jacketed tear-gas *shell* that could penetrate most wooden doors or punch through a boarded window. When Jack fired, the shell smashed through the truck's grille into the engine compartment. A noxious yellow vapor began roiling into the cab by way of its ventilation system.

The guards had been trained to remain in their secure roost in a crisis, for the cab had steel doors and bulletproof glass. But when they switched off the heater and closed the vents too late, they found themselves choking in the gas-filled cabin. They opened their locked doors, spilled out into the cold winter night, wheezing, coughing.

In spite of the blinding, suffocating gas, the driver had drawn his revolver. Dropping to his knees, gagging, he squinted his copiously watering eyes in search of a target.

But Jack kicked the gun out of his hand, grabbed him by the coat, and dragged him to the front of the truck, where he handcuffed him to a support strut on the bumper.

After firing the shot that disabled the truck, Branch Pollard had sprinted down the knoll. Now, at the other end of the front bumper, he handcuffed the other protesting guard to another strut.

Both guards were blinking furiously, trying to clear their gas-blurred vision to get a look at their attackers' faces, but that was wasted effort because Jack, Pollard, and Zepp were wearing ski masks.

Leaving the securely shackled men, Jack and Pollard ran to the back of the truck, moving fast, though not because they feared being seen by other traffic on that lonely road. No traffic would pass until they were gone. The moment the

Guardmaster unit had entered the flats, the last two members of the robbery team, Hart and Dodd, had sealed off both ends of the road with stolen vans that had been repainted and equipped with Department of Highway signs. Against an impressive backdrop of emergency beacons flashing on the roofs of their vans and on sawhorses they had set out on the pavement, Dodd and Hart would turn back everyone who wanted through, spinning a tale of a tanker-truck accident.

Clockwork.

When Jack and Pollard got to the rear of the truck, Chad Zepp was already there. In the glow of a battery-powered light that he had fixed to the truck with a magnet, Zepp was unscrewing the faceplate that covered the lock mechanism on the doors to the cargo hold.

They had brought explosives, but when trying to peel a truck as well-constructed as the Guardmaster, there was a risk that explosives would fuse the lock pins, sealing the honeypot even tighter. They had to try going in through the lock, leaving explosives as a last resort.

Some older armored cars had locks that operated with a key or pair of keys, and some had combination dials, but this was a new vehicle with state-of-the-art equipment. This lock was engaged and disengaged by pressing a sequence of code numbers on a ten-digit keyboard that was the size and appearance of the "dial" on a touch-tone telephone. To activate the lock, the guard closed the doors and simply punched in the middle number of the three-number code. To deactivate it, he pressed all three numbers in the correct order. The code was changed every morning, and of the two men crewing the truck, only the driver knew it.

There were one thousand possible three-number sequences in ten digits. Because it would take between four and five seconds to key in each sequence and wait for it to be accepted or rejected, they would have to delay at least an hour and a quarter to try every combination. That was far too risky.

Chad Zepp removed the faceplate from the lock. The ten numbered buttons remained, but now it was possible to see a bit of the mechanism between and behind them.

Hung on a strap from Zepp's shoulder was a battery-powered, attaché-sized computer, which could assess and control the circuitry of electronic locks and alarms. It was SLICKS, an acronym for Security Lock Intervention and Circumvention Knowledge System. Intended solely for military or intelligence-agency personnel with security clearance, SLICKS was unavailable to the public. Unauthorized possession was a criminal violation of the Defense Security Act. To obtain a SLICKS, Jack had gone to Mexico City and had paid twenty-five thousand dollars to a black-market arms dealer who had a contact inside the firm that manufactured the device.

Zepp unslung the computer and held it so he and Jack and Pollard could see the four-inch-square video display, which was dark. Three retractable probes were slotted in the SLICKS, and Jack withdrew the first of these from its niche: It looked like a copper-tipped steel thermometer on a two-foot wire umbilical. Jack looked closely at the partially exposed guts of the electronic lock and carefully inserted the slender probe between the first two buttons, touching it to the contact point at the base of the button marked "1." The display screen remained dark. He moved the probe to button number 2, then 3. Nothing. But when he touched number 4, a pale green word—CURRENT—appeared on the screen, plus numbers that measured trace-electricity in the contact.

This meant that the middle number of the three-digit lock-code was 4. After loading sacks of money and checks into the cargo-hold at the last stop on the route, the driver had pushed 4 to activate the lock. The contact point of that button would remain closed until the entire code was punched in, thereby unlocking the door.

With three unknown numbers, the possible combinations had been one thousand. But now that they needed to find only the first and last numbers, the search was reduced to one hundred combinations.

Ignoring the howling wind, Jack withdrew another instrument from the SLICKS. This was also on a two-foot cord but resembled a watercolor brush though with a single bristle. The bristle glowed with light and was thicker than a sixty-pound fishing line, stiff yet flexible. Jack inserted it into a crack at the base of the 1 button on the lock keyboard, glanced at the computer video display, but was not rewarded. He moved the bristle-probe from number to number. The display screen blinked, then showed a partial diagram of a circuit board.

The bristle that he had thrust inside the mechanism was actually the end filament of an optical laser, a more sophisticated cousin of the similar device which, in supermarket cash registers, read the bar codes on grocery items. The SLICKS was not programmed to read bar codes but to recognize circuitry patterns and render models of them on the display screen. The screen would register nothing whatsoever until the bristle-probe was aimed directly at a circuit or portion thereof, but then it would faithfully reproduce the hidden pattern that it saw.

Jack had to move the probe three times, insert it into the lock mechanism at three different points, before the computer was able to piece together a picture of the entire circuitry from partial views. The diagram glowed in bright green lines and symbols on the miniature video display. After three seconds of consideration, the computer drew boxes around two small portions of the diagram to indicate those points at which a tap could easily be applied to the circuitry. Then it superimposed an image of the ten-digit keyboard over the diagram, to show where those two weak points were in relation to that portion of the lock mechanism that was visible to Jack.

"There's a good tap-in spot below the number four button," Jack said.

"You need me to drill?" Pollard asked.

"I don't think so."

Jack returned the optical probe to its slot and withdrew a third slender instrument with a spongy mesh tip of some material he could not identify, which the designer of SLICKS had labeled the "tap-wand." He inserted it through the tiny gap in the lock mechanism at the base of the 4 button, slowly moved it up and down, left and right, until the computer beeped and flashed INTERVENTION on the miniature video display.

While Jack held the tap-wand in place and Chad Zepp held the SLICKS upright, Pollard used the computer's small programming board to quickly type instructions. INTERVENTION disappeared, and onto the screen came other words: SYSTEM CONTROL ESTABLISHED. The computer could now feed commands directly to the microchip that processed the lock codes and that directed the sliding steel bolts to either close or open.

Pollard hit two more keys, and the SLICKS began to send sequences of three numbers to the microchip, one combination every six-hundredths of a second, all of which used the already known 4 as the middle digit of the code. SLICKS hit the right code—545—in only nine seconds.

With four simultaneous thumps, the lock bolts retracted as one.

Jack returned the tap-wand to its niche, switched off the computer. Only four minutes had passed since the rifle-shot that had blown out the truck's right front tire.

Clockwork.

As Zepp slung the SLICKS over his shoulder again, Pollard opened the rear doors of the armored car. The money was theirs for the taking.

Zepp laughed with delight. With a gleeful whoop, Pollard clambered into the truck and began to push out bulging canvas bags.

But Jack still felt empty and cold inside.

A few snow flurries suddenly appeared in the wind.

The unexplained change in Jack, which had begun weeks ago, had now reached completion. He no longer cared about getting even with society. He felt purposeless, as adrift as the wind-borne flakes of snow.

ELKO COUNTY, NEVADA.

Faye Block had turned on the no vacancy notice to ensure that they would not be disturbed.

Sitting around the table in the cheery kitchen of their apartment above the motel office, with the blinds shut against the night, the Blocks sipped coffee and listened spellbound as Dom told his story.

The only point at which they registered disbelief was when he told them of the impossible dance of paper moons in Zebediah Lomack's house in Reno. But he was able to describe that startling event in such sharp detail that he felt goose-flesh pimpling his arms, and he saw that his own awe and fear were being transmitted to Faye and Ernie.

They appeared most impressed by the two Polaroid photographs that had arrived in the mail from the unknown correspondent two days before Dom had flown to Portland. They studied the picture in which the zombie-faced priest was sitting at a writing desk, and they were certain it had been taken in one of their motel rooms. The photo of the blond in bed with an IV line in her arm was a closeup that showed nothing of the room, but they recognized the floral-patterned bedspread visible in one corner of the shot; it was the kind that had been in use in some units until ten months ago.

To Dom's surprise, they had been sent a similar photograph. Ernie remembered receiving it in a plain envelope on December 10, five days before they had flown to Milwaukee. Faye got it from the center drawer of the desk in the downstairs office, and they hunched conspiratorially over the kitchen table, studying the print. It was a shot of three people—man, woman, child—standing in sunshine by the door to Room 9. All three were dressed in shorts, T-shirts, and sandals.

"Do you recognize them?" Dom asked.

"No," Faye said.

"But I feel like I *ought* to remember them," Ernie said.

Dom said, "Sunshine . . . summer clothes . . . so we can almost certainly conclude it was taken the summer before last, *that* weekend, between Friday the sixth of July and the following Tuesday. These three people were part of whatever happened. Maybe innocent victims like us. And our unknown correspondent wants us to think about them, remember them."

Ernie said, "Whoever sent the pictures would've been one of the people who erased our memories. So why would he want to stir us up like this after so much trouble was taken to make us forget?"

Dom shrugged. "Maybe he never believed it was right—what was done to us. Maybe he only went along with it because he had to, and maybe it's been on his conscience ever since. Whoever he is, he's afraid to come right out with what he knows. He's got to do it indirectly."

Abruptly, Faye pushed her chair back from the table. "Five weeks of mail piled up while we were away. Might be something more in it."

As the sound of Faye's descending footsteps echoed up from the stairs, Ernie said, "Sandy—that's our waitress at the Grille—sorted through the mail and paid the bills as they arrived. But the rest of the mail she just dropped in a paper sack. Since we came back this morning, we've been so busy getting the place open, we didn't bother looking to see what the postman brought."

Faye returned with two plain white envelopes. In a state of high excitement, they opened the first. It contained a Polaroid of a man lying on his back in bed, an intravenous needle in his arm. He was in his fifties. Dark hair, balding. In ordinary circumstances, he probably had a jovial look, for he resembled W. C. Fields. But he was staring blankly toward the camera, face bleak. Zombie eyes. . . .

"My God, it's Calvin!" Faye said.

"Yeah," Ernie said. "Cal Sharkle. He's a long-haul trucker movin' freight between Chicago and San Francisco."

"He stops at the Grille most every trip," Faye said. "Sometimes, when he's beat, he stays overnight. Calvin's such a nice man."

"What company's he drive for?" Dom asked.

"He's independent," Ernie said. "Owns his own rig."

"Would you know how to get in touch with him?"

"Well," Ernie said, "he signs the registry every time he checks in, so we'll have his address . . . around Chicago somewhere, I think."

"We'll check later. First, let's look in that other envelope."

Faye opened it and produced another Polaroid. Again, it was a shot of a man lying in one of the Tranquility Motel's beds, an IV line in one arm. Like all the others, he had no expression whatsoever, and soulless eyes that reminded Dom of horror movies about the living dead.

But this time, they all recognized the man in the bed. It was Dom.

LAS VEGAS, NEVADA.

When Marcie's bedtime came, she was sitting at the little desk in the corner of her room, occupied with her collection of moons.

Jorja stood in the doorway, watching. The girl was so thoroughly engaged by the task that she remained unaware she was being observed.

A box of crayons lay beside the album full of moons. Marcie was hunched over the work surface, carefully coloring one of the lunar faces. This was a new development, and Jorja wondered what it meant.

In the week since Marcie had begun her collection with magazine clippings, she had filled the album. She had few sources for photos, so she drew hundreds of pictures to add to the monotonous gallery. Using templets as varied as coins, jar lids, vases, drinking glasses, cans, and thimbles, she traced lunar forms of all sizes on tablet paper, construction paper, paper bags, envelopes, and wrapping paper. She did not spend most of her time with the album, but each day she devoted a bit more time to it than she had the day before.

Dr. Ted Coverly, the psychologist treating Marcie, believed the anxiety that had generated the girl's irrational fear of doctors had not been relieved. Now, the child was expressing that anxiety through her lunar preoccupation. When Jorja noted that Marcie did not seem to be particularly frightened of the moon, Coverly said, "Well, her anxiety doesn't have to seek expression in another *phobia*. It can show itself in other ways . . . such as an obsession." Jorja could not understand where her daughter's extraordinary anxiety came from. Coverly said, "That's why the therapy—to seek understanding. Don't worry, Miss Monatella."

But Jorja *was* worried.

She was worried because Alan had killed himself only yesterday. Jorja had not yet told Marcie of her father's death. On leaving Pepper Carrafield's apartment, she had called Coverly to ask his advice. He was astonished to learn that Alan, too, had been dreaming of the moon and had independently developed an intense lunar fascination of his own. *That* one would take time to ponder. Meanwhile, Coverly thought it wise to withhold the bad news from Marcie until Monday. "Come with her to the appointment. We'll tell her together." Jorja was afraid that, in spite of Alan's inattention, Marcie would be devastated by his death.

As she stood in the bedroom doorway, watching Marcie diligently applying a crayon to one of the moons, Jorja was stricken by an acute awareness of the girl's fragility. Although she was seven years old and in second grade, the three-quarter-scale chair was still too big for her, and only the toes of her sneakers touched the floor. Even for a macho man armored with muscles, life was tenuous, and every additional day of existence was against the odds. But for a child as petite as Marcie, continued life seemed downright miraculous. Jorja realized how easily her precious daughter could be taken from her, and her heart swelled and ached with love.

When at last Jorja said, "Honey, better put your pajamas on and brush your teeth," she could not keep a tremor out of her voice.

The girl looked bewildered, as if she were not quite sure where she was or who Jorja was. Then her eyes cleared, and she gave her mother a smile that could melt butter. "Hi, Mommy. I been coloring moons."

"Well, now it's time to get ready for bed," Jorja said.

"In a little while, okay?" The girl appeared to be relaxed, yet she was gripping a crayon so tightly that her knuckles were white. "I want to color some more moons."

Jorja wanted to destroy the hateful album. But Dr. Coverly had warned that arguing with the child about the moons and forbidding her to collect them would only strengthen her obsession. Jorja was not sure he was right, but she stifled the urge to destroy the album.

"Tomorrow, you'll have lots of time to color, Peanut."

Reluctantly, Marcie closed the album, put away her crayons, and went to the bathroom to brush her teeth.

Alone beside the child's desk, Jorja was overcome by weariness. In addition to working a full shift, she'd arranged a mortician for Alan's body, ordered flowers, and settled details with the cemetery for Monday's funeral. She had also called Alan's estranged father in Miami to break the bad news. She was drained. Wearily, she opened the album.

Red. The girl was coloring all the moons red, both those she had drawn and those clipped from newspapers and magazines. She had already painted more than fifty lunar images. The obsessive quality of the girl's work was evident in the great care she had taken to keep the crayon from slipping past the outline of each moon. The crayon had been applied more heavily picture by picture, until some moons were coated with so much scarlet wax that they had a glisteningly wet look.

The use of red—and red alone—profoundly disturbed Jorja. It almost seemed as if Marcie had glimpsed an augury of some onrushing terror, a premonition of blood.

ELKO COUNTY, NEVADA.

Faye Block had gone downstairs to the file cabinets, from which she had extracted the motel registry that had been in use the summer before last. Upon her return, she put the book on the kitchen table, in front of Dom, open to the guest lists of Friday and Saturday, July 6 and 7.

"There, just like Ernie and I remembered. That Friday was the night they closed the interstate because of a toxic spill. A truckload of dangerous chemicals headed out to Shenkfield. That's a military installation about eighteen miles southwest of here. We had to close the motel until Tuesday, until they got the situation under control."

Ernie said, "Shenkfield's an isolated testing ground for chemical and biological weapons, so the crap in that truck was damned nasty."

Faye continued, a new wooden note in her voice, as if reciting carefully memorized lines. "They erected roadblocks and ordered us to evacuate the danger zone. Our guests left in their own cars." Her face remained expressionless. "Ned and Sandy Sarver were allowed to go up to their trailer near Beowawe because it was outside the quarantine area."

Astonished and confused, Dom said, "Impossible. I don't remember any evacuation. I was *here*. I remember reading, researching the geography for a series of short stories . . . but those memories are so thin I suspect they aren't real. No substance to them. Still, I was here and nowhere else, and something weird was done to me." He indicated the Polaroid snapshot of himself. "There's the proof."

When Faye spoke, she sounded stiffer than before, and Dom saw a strangeness in her eyes, a slightly glazed look. "Until the all-clear was given, Ernie and I stayed with friends who have a small ranch in the mountains ten miles northeast of here—Elroy and Nancy Jamison. It was a difficult spill to clean up. The Army needed more than three days to do the job. They wouldn't let us back here until Tuesday morning."

"What's wrong with you, Faye?" Dom asked.

She blinked. "Huh? What do you mean?"

"You sound as if you'd been . . . programmed with that little speech."

She seemed genuinely baffled. "What're you talking about?"

Frowning, Ernie said, "Faye, your voice went . . . flat."

"Well, I was only explaining what happened." She leaned over and put one finger on Friday's page of the registry. "See, we'd rented out eleven rooms by the time they closed the interstate that night. But nobody paid for the rooms because nobody stayed. They were evacuated."

"There's your name, seventh on the list," Ernie said.

Dom stared at his signature and at the Mountainview, Utah, address to which he had been moving at the time. He could remember checking in, but he sure as hell could not remember climbing back into his car and driving out the same night in response to an evacuation order. He said, "Did you actually see the accident, the tanker truck?"

Ernie shook his head. "No, the truck overturned a couple miles from here." He spoke in that by-rote tone that had marked Faye's speech. "The Army experts from Shenkfield were concerned the chemicals would be dispersed by the wind, so the quarantine zone was very large."

Chilled by the unconscious artificiality in Ernie's voice, Dom looked at Faye and saw that she too had noticed her husband's unnatural tone. He said, "That's what *you* sounded like a moment ago, Faye." He looked at Ernie. "You two have been programmed with the same script."

Faye frowned. "Are you saying the spill never happened?"

"It happened, all right," Ernie told Dom. "For a while we saved a bunch of newspaper clippings about it from the Elko *Sentinel*. But I think we eventually threw them out. Anyway, people around these parts still wonder what might've happened if we'd gotten big winds and been contaminated with that top-secret stuff before the evacuation order was even given. No, it's not just some delusion of Faye's and mine."

"You can ask Elroy and Nancy Jamison," Faye said. "They were here that night, visiting. When we had to evacuate, they offered to take us back to their place and put us up for the duration."

Dom smiled sourly. "I wouldn't put much credence in their recall of events. If they were here, then they saw what the rest of us saw, and it was scrubbed from their minds. They remember taking you back to their place because that's what they were *told* to remember. In fact they were probably right here, being brainwashed with the rest of us."

"My head's swimming," Faye said. "This is positively Byzantine."

"But, damn it, the toxic spill and evacuation happened," Ernie said. "It was in the newspapers."

Dom thought of a disturbing explanation that made his scalp crawl. "What if everyone here at the motel that night *was* contaminated with some chemical or biological weapon headed for Shenkfield? And what if the Army and the government covered it up to avoid bad press, millions of dollars in lawsuits, and the disclosure of top-secret information? Maybe they closed the highway and announced that everyone was safely evacuated, when in fact we had *not* been gotten out in time. Then they used the motel as a clinic, decontaminated us as much as they could, scrubbed the memory of the incident out of our minds, and reprogrammed us with false memories, so we'd never know what had happened to us."

They stared at one another in shocked silence for a moment. Not because the scenario sounded entirely right, which it did not. But because it was the first scenario they'd come up with that made sense of the psychological problems they had been having and explained the drugged people in those Polaroid snapshots.

Then Ernie and Faye began to think of objections. Ernie voiced the first: "In that case, the logical thing for them to've done was to make our false memories tie in closely with their cover story about the toxic spill and evacuation. That's exactly what they did with Faye and me, with the Jamisons, Ned and Sandy Sarver. So why didn't they do the same with you? Why'd they program you with different memories that didn't have anything to do with the evacuation? That was irrational and risky. I mean, the radical differences between our memories is virtually proof that you or we—or all of us—were brainwashed."

"Don't know," Dom said. "That's just one more mystery to unravel."

"And here's another flaw in that theory," Ernie said. "If we'd been contaminated by a biological weapon, they wouldn't have let us go in just three days. They'd have been afraid of contagion, epidemic."

Dom said, "All right. So it was a *chemical* agent, not a virus or bacterium. Something they could wash off or flush out of our systems."

"That doesn't make sense, either," Faye said. "Because the things they test at Shenkfield are meant to be deadly. Poison gas. Nerve gas. Hideous damn stuff. If we'd got caught in a cloud like that, we'd have been dead on the spot or brain-damaged or crippled."

"Maybe it was a slow-acting agent," Dom said. "Something that generates tumors, leukemia, or other conditions that only begin to show up two or three or five years from the date of contamination.''

That thought also shocked them into silence. They listened to the ticking of the kitchen clock, to the mournful fluting of the wind at the windows, wondering if malignancies were even now sprouting within them.

Finally, Ernie said, ''Maybe we were contaminated, and maybe we're all slowly rotting inside, but I don't think so. After all, they test potential *weapons* at Shenkfield. And what use would a weapon be that didn't kill the enemy for years and years?''

''Virtually no use at all,'' Dom acknowledged.

''And,'' Ernie said, ''how could chemical contamination explain that bizarre experience you had in Lomack's house in Reno?''

''I've no idea,'' Dom said. ''But now that we know they cordoned off this whole area using the excuse of a toxic spill—whether it was a real spill or not—my theory that we were brainwashed is a lot more credible. Because, see, before this I wasn't able to explain how someone could've rounded us up at will and held us long enough to make us forget the thing we saw. But the quarantine gave them the time they needed, and it also kept away prying eyes. So . . . at least now we have a good idea who we're up against. The United States Army, maybe acting in collusion with the government, maybe acting alone, has been trying to hide something that happened here, something it did but shouldn't have done. I don't know about you, but the thought of being up against an enemy that big and that potentially ruthless scares the hell out of me.''

''An old Leatherneck like me is bound to be scornful of the Army,'' Ernie said. ''But they're not devils, you know. We can't leap to the conclusion we're victims of a wicked right-wing conspiracy. That crackpot stuff makes millions for paranoid novelists and for Hollywood, but in the real world, evil is more subtle, less identifiable. If Army and government officials are behind what happened to us, they don't necessarily have immoral motives. They probably think they did the only wise thing they could've done in the circumstances.''

''But whether or not it's wise,'' Faye said, ''we've got to dig into this situation. If we don't, Ernie's nyctophobia will surely get worse. And your sleepwalking will also get worse, Dom. And what then?''

They all knew ''what then.'' ''What then'' was a shotgun barrel jammed in the mouth, the route to peace that Zebediah Lomack had taken.

Dom looked down at the motel registry on the table before him. Four spaces above his own name, he saw another entry that electrified him. Dr. Ginger Weiss. Her address was in Boston.

''Ginger,'' he said. ''The fourth name on those moon posters.''

Furthermore, Cal Sharkle, the Blocks' trucker-friend from Chicago, the zombie-eyed subject of one of the Polaroid snapshots, had checked into the motel just before Dr. Weiss. The first guests to sign in that day were Mr. and Mrs. Alan Rykoff and daughter, of Las Vegas. Dom was willing to bet that they were the young family photographed in front of the door to Room 9. Zebediah Lomack's name was not in the registry, so he had probably just been unlucky enough to stop at the Grille for dinner that night, on his way between Reno and Elko. One of the other names might have been that of the young priest in the other Polaroid, but if so, he had signed without appending his title.

''We'll have to talk to all these people,'' Dom said excitedly. ''We can start calling them first thing tomorrow and see what *they* remember about those days in July.''

CHICAGO, ILLINOIS.

By allowing no slightest hairline crack to appear in his resolve, by showing no equivocation whatsoever, Brendan managed to obtain Father Wycazik's permission to go to Nevada alone on Monday, without Monsignor Janney trailing him in expectation of miracles.

By ten-ten, he was in bed with the lights out, lying on his side in blackness, staring at the window, where the palest light glistered softly in the frost that skinned the pane. The window looked out upon the courtyard, where no lights burned at this hour, so Brendan knew that he was seeing indirect moonglow refracted by the thin layer of ice that had welded itself to the glass. It had to be indirect light because the moon was traversing the sky on a course that had made it visible from the study windows earlier in the evening, and the study was on the other side of the rectory; the moon could not now be over the courtyard unless it had made a sudden ninety-degree turn in the path it had previously been following, which was not possible. As he patiently lay waiting for sleep, he became increasingly intrigued by the subtle patterns made by the second-hand moonbeams that had been trapped in the frost; light splintered at every point where one ice crystal interfaced with another, each beam shattering into a hundred beams, a hundred more.

"The moon," he whispered, surprised by his voice. "The moon."

Gradually, Brendan realized that something uncanny was happening.

At first he was merely fascinated by the harmonious interaction of frost and moonlight, but soon fascination evolved into a more intense attraction. He could not look away from the pearly window. It offered an indefinable promise, and he was drawn as a sailor by a siren's song. Before he knew what he intended, he had slipped one arm out from beneath the blankets and was reaching toward the window, though it was ten feet away and could not be touched from where he lay. The black silhouette of his spread-fingered hand was clearly defined against the niveous pane of glass that glowed softly beyond, and his futile straining was the essence of yearning. Brendan longed to be within the light, not the light that lived in the frost but that *other* golden light of his dreams.

"The moon," he whispered, again surprised that he had spoken.

His heartbeat accelerated. He began to tremble.

Suddenly, upon the glass, the sugary-looking frost underwent an inexplicable change. As Brendan watched, the thin rime melted away from the edges of the pane, toward the center. In a few seconds, when the melting stopped, there remained only a perfect circle of ice, about ten inches in diameter, glowing eerily in the middle of an otherwise clear, dry, dark rectangle of glass.

The moon.

Brendan knew it was a sign, though he did not know from whom or what or where it came, nor did he understand it.

On Christmas night, when he had stayed at his parents' house in Bridgeport, Brendan had apparently had a dream featuring the moon, for he had awakened his mother and father with his loud and panicky cries. But he could remember nothing of the dream. Since then, as far as he knew, none of his dreams had involved the moon, but were concerned exclusively with that mysterious place full of dazzling golden light, where he felt himself called toward some incredible revelation.

Now, as he still reached with one hand toward the glimmering frost on the window, the vaguely phosphorescent rime grew brighter, as if some peculiar chemical reaction was at work within the ice crystals. The moon-image changed from a milky hue to the crisper white of sun-dappled snow, then grew even brighter, until it was a scintillant circle of silver blazing on the glass.

Heart pounding furiously, certain he was teetering on the edge of some astounding epiphany, Brendan continued to hold his hand toward the window, and he gasped in shock as a shaft of light leapt out from the frost-moon and fell across the bed. It was like the beam of a spotlight and every bit as brilliant. As he squinted into the glare, trying to see how such fierce incandescence could possibly originate from ordinary hoarfrost and glass, the light changed to pale red, to darker red, to crimson, to scarlet. Around him, the rumpled blankets shone like molten steel, and his outstretched hand appeared to be wet with blood.

He was gripped by *déjà vu,* absolutely convinced that he had once really stood under a scarlet moon, bathed in its bloody glow.

Although he wanted to understand how this strange red light related to the wondrous golden light of his dreams, although he still felt himself being called by something unknown that waited in that radiance, he was suddenly afraid. As the scarlet beams intensified, as his room became a caldron of heatless red fire and red shadows, his fear grew into terror of such power that it made him shake and sweat.

He pulled his hand back, and the scarlet light rapidly faded to silver, and the silver dimmed as well, until the circle of frost on the window shone with only a natural reflection of the January moon.

As darkness laid claim to his room once more, Brendan sat up and hastily switched on the lamp. Damp with sweat, as full of the night-shakes as any child frightened by fantasies of carnivorous goblins, he went to the window. The icy circle was still there, a moon image in the center of the otherwise unfrosted pane of glass.

He had wondered if the light had been but a dream or hallucination. In a way, he almost wished it had been only that. But the frost-moon was still there, proof that what he had seen was real, not a delusion.

Hesitantly, he touched the glass. He felt nothing unusual. Just the bitter cold of winter pressing against the other side of the pane.

With a start, he realized that he felt the swollen rings in his palms. He turned his hands over and watched as the stigmata faded.

He returned to bed. For a long while he sat with his back against the headboard, with his eyes open and the light on, waiting for the courage to lie down in darkness.

ELKO COUNTY, NEVADA.

Ernie stood by the tub in the bathroom, trying to recall precisely what he had thought and felt in the early hours of Saturday, December 14, when he had been driven by some strange impulse to open the window and had suffered that frightening hallucination. The writer, Dominick Corvaisis, stood by the sink, and Faye watched from the doorway.

Reflections of the ceiling light and the light above the mirror imparted a warmth to the ceramic-tile floor, glimmered in the chrome faucets and shower rod, gave a bright flat sheen to the plastic shower curtain, and gradually illuminated the memories that Ernie sought.

"Light. I came in here for the light. My fear of the dark was at a peak then, and I was trying to hide it from Faye. Couldn't sleep, so I slipped out of bed, came here, closed the door, and just . . . just sort of *reveled* in the light." He told how his gaze was drawn to the window above the tub and how he was overcome by an irrational and urgent need to escape. "It's hard to explain. But suddenly crazy thoughts ... *whirled* into my head. For some reason, I panicked. I thought, This is my one chance to escape, so I'd better take it, go through that window, head up into the hills ... get to a ranch, get help."

"Help for what?" Corvaisis asked. "Why did you need help? Why did you feel you needed to escape from your own home?"

Ernie frowned. "Don't have the foggiest notion." He remembered the way he had felt that night—the eeriness, urgency strangely mixed with dreaminess. He pointed to the window. "I actually slid back the bolt. Opened it. Might've crawled out, too, except I saw someone outside. On the roof of the utility room."

"Who?" Corvaisis asked.

"Sounds silly. It was a guy in motorcycle gear. White crash helmet. Dark visor over his face. Black gloves. In fact, he reached one hand through the window, as if making a grab for me, and I stepped backward, fell over the edge of the tub."

"That's when I came running," Faye said.

"I got off the floor," Ernie said, "went back to the window, looked out on the roof. No one there. It'd been just ... hallucination."

Faye said, "In extreme cases of phobia, when the sufferer is in almost constant anxiety, hallucinations sometimes occur."

The writer stared at the opaque window above the tub, as if hoping to find some vital secret revealed in the uneven milky texture of the glass. At last he said, "It wasn't exactly a hallucination. I have a hunch that what you saw, Ernie, was a ... well, call it a memory-flash. From the summer before last. From the lost days. For a moment, back on December fourteenth, your repressed memories surged toward the surface. You had a flashback to a time when you really *were* a prisoner in your own home, when you really did try to escape."

"And I was stopped by that guy on the roof of the utility room? But what was he doing there in a motorcycle helmet? Strange, isn't it?"

Dom said, "A man in a decontamination suit, sent to deal with a spill of chemicals or biological toxins, would wear an airtight helmet."

"Decontamination," Ernie said. "But if they were actually here in suits like that, then there must've really been a spill."

"Maybe," Dom said. "We still don't know enough to decide."

Faye said, "But listen, if we all went through this experience, like you think we did, then how come only you and Ernie and that Mr. Lomack are suffering repercussions? How come *I'm* not having bad dreams and psychological problems?"

The writer's gaze drifted back to the window. "I don't know. But those are some of the questions we've got to answer if we've any hope of relieving the subconscious anxiety that this experience left in us, if we've any hope of getting on with normal lives."

CONNECTICUT TO NEW YORK CITY.

After the money had been removed from the armored car, Jack and his men drove only nine miles and parked the two phony Department of Highway vans in a four-stall rented garage leased with fake IDs, where they had left their cars. The garage was one of a long row that faced both sides of a litter-strewn alley in a shabby neighborhood, where relaxed zoning laws permitted intermingling of commercial and industrial facilities with residences. The area was characterized by peeling paint, grime, broken streetlamps, empty storefronts, and mean-looking mongrel dogs on the loose.

They emptied the contents of the canvas bags on the oily concrete floor of the garage and did a hasty count of the cash. They split it quickly into five shares of approximately three hundred fifty thousand dollars each, all in used bills that could never be traced.

Jack felt no triumph, no thrill. Nothing.

In five minutes, the gang had dispersed like dandelion fluff on a brisk wind. Clockwork.

As Jack headed home to Manhattan, spits of snow fell in brief squalls, though not enough to dust the highway or interfere with travel.

During the drive from Connecticut, in a strange mood, he underwent a change he could not have anticipated. Minute by minute and mile by mile, the grayness in him began at last to be colored by emotion; his ennui gave way to feelings that surprised him. He would not have been surprised by a new welling-up of grief or loneliness, for Jenny had been dead only seventeen days. But the emotion that steadily tightened its grip on him was *guilt*. The stolen money in the trunk of the car began to weigh on his conscience as heavily as if it were the first ill-gotten goods ever to fall into his hands.

Through eight busy years of meticulously planned and triumphantly executed larcenies, several on an even grander scale than the armored car, he had never experienced the mildest quiver of guilt. Until now. He had seen himself as a just avenger. Until now.

Cruising to Manhattan through the blustery winter night, he began to see himself as little more than a common thief. Guilt wrapped him like flypaper. He tried repeatedly to shake it off. It clung.

Sudden as it seemed, the guilt had actually been building for a long time; that was where his growing dissatisfaction had been leading for months. Disillusionment had set in noticeably with the jewelry-store job last October, and he'd thought the changes had begun then. But now, forced into self-analysis, he realized he had stopped getting a full measure of pleasure from his work long ago. As he scrolled backward in his memory, seeking the most recent job that had left him fulfilled, he was startled to discover it was the McAllister burglary in Marin County, north of San Francisco, the summer before last.

Ordinarily, he worked only in the East near Jenny, but Branch Pollard—with whom he had pulled off the just-completed Guardmaster heist—had settled in California for a while, and during that Pacific sojourn he had spotted Avril McAllister, a sheep waiting to be sheared. McAllister, an industrialist worth two hundred million, lived on an eight-acre estate in Marin County, protected by stone walls, a complex electronic security system, and guard dogs. With information developed from a half-dozen sources, Branch had determined that McAllister was a collector of rare stamps and coins, two eminently fenceable commodities. Besides, the industrialist was a gambler who went to Vegas three times a year, usually dropping a quarter of a million each visit, but sometimes winning big; he always took his winnings in cash to avoid the taxman, and some of that cash was surely in the mansion. Branch needed Jack's sense of strategy and expertise in electronics, and Jack needed a change of scenery, so they pulled it off with the help of a third man.

After considerable planning, getting onto the estate and into the house went smoothly. They were prepared with an electronic listening device that could detect the soft tick of a safe's tumblers and amplify them, which made deducing the combination mere child's play, but as insurance they also took a full set of safe-cracking tools *and* a plastic explosive. The problem was that Avril McAllister had no mere safe. He had a damn *vault*. The industrialist was so certain of the vault door's inviolability that he'd made no effort to conceal it with a sliding partition or tapestry; it was in one wall of the immense game room, a massive stainless-steel portal as big as anything in a first-class bank. The listening device Jack had brought was not sensitive enough to detect the movement of tumblers through twenty inches of stainless steel. The plastic explosive would have peeled any safe, but the vault was blastproof. The set of safecracker's tools was a joke.

They left the estate with no stamps or coins, but with sterling silver, a complete collection of Raymond Chandler and Dashiell Hammett first editions, a few jewels that Mrs. McAllister carelessly left out of the vault, and a handful of other items, which they fenced for only sixty thousand dollars, split three ways. The take was by no means a pittance, but it was far less than anticipated, insufficient to cover their expenses and to make their time, planning, and risks worthwhile.

In spite of this debacle, Jack had gotten a kick out of the job. Once they had safely fled the McAllister estate, he and Branch had seen the humor in the catastrophe and had been able to laugh about it. They spent two days relaxing in the California sun; then, on a whim, Jack took his twenty thousand to Reno to see if he could do better at craps and blackjack than he had done at burglary. Twenty-four hours after checking into Harrah's, he checked out, the twenty thousand having grown to an amazing $107,455. The exquisite symmetry of bad-luck money bringing good luck was enormously appealing. Deciding to extend his vacation, he rented a car and drove back to New York, all the way across the country, in a splendid mood, eager to see Jenny.

Now, more than eighteen months later, as he entered Manhattan on his return trip from Connecticut, Jack realized that, curiously, the fiasco at the McAllister estate had been the last enterprise to provide untainted satisfaction. At that point he had begun a long journey from dead-end amorality all the way across the moral spectrum until he had become, once more, capable of guilt.

But *why?* What had initiated the change in him? What continued to power it? He had no answers.

All he knew was that he was no longer able to think of himself as a melancholy and romantic bandit with a just mission to redress the wrongs done to him and to his beloved wife. He was merely a thief. For eight years he had been deluding himself. Now he saw himself for what he really was, and the sudden insight was devastating.

He had not merely become a man without purpose. Worse, without realizing it, he had been lacking a worthwhile purpose *for eight years.*

He drove aimlessly through the streets of Manhattan, going nowhere in particular, unwilling to return straightaway to the apartment.

He soon found himself on Fifth Avenue, approaching St. Patrick's, and on impulse he pulled to the curb, parked illegally before the main doors of the immense cathedral. He got out of the car, went around to the trunk, opened it, and pulled half a dozen banded stacks of twenty-dollar bills from the plastic garbage bag.

It was foolhardy to leave the car illegally parked in so prominent a location when its trunk contained more than a third of a million dollars in stolen money, an illegally obtained device like SLICKS, and guns. If a cop stopped to give him a ticket and became suspicious and demanded to search the car, Jack would be finished. But he had ceased to care. In some ways, he was a dead man who still walked, just as Jenny had been a dead woman who still breathed.

Though not a Catholic, he pulled open one of the sculpted bronze doors of St. Patrick's, went inside, into the nave, where a handful of people knelt in the front pews, praying or saying the rosary, and where an old man was lighting a votive candle even at this hour. Jack stood for a moment looking up at the elegant baldachin above the main altar. Then he located the poor-boxes, removed the bundles of twenty-dollar bills from inside his winter jacket, broke the paper bands that bound them, and stuffed the money into the containers as if he were jamming garbage into trash receptacles.

Outside again, as he was descending the granite steps, he stopped abruptly and blinked at the night-draped cityscape, for something was different about Fifth Avenue. As a few huge snowflakes spiraled lazily through the glow of streetlamps and through the lights of cars moving along the thoroughfare, Jack gradually realized the city had reacquired a fraction of the glitter, glamour, and mystery that it always had for him before he'd gone to Central America but which it had not possessed in ages. It seemed *cleaner* now than it had been in a long time, and the air was crisper, less polluted.

Staring around in amazement, he slowly understood that the city had not undergone a metamorphosis during the past few minutes. It was the same city that it had been an hour ago—and yesterday. But when he had come back from Central America, he had been a different man from the one who had gone away, and on returning he had been unable to see anything good in the metropolis or in any other works of the society he hated. Much of the Big Apple's dreariness and degeneration had been merely a reflection of his own blasted, burnt-out, corrupted inner landscape.

Jack returned to the Camaro, went west to Sixth Avenue, north to Central Park, made a right turn, then another right onto Fifth Avenue again, heading south, not sure where he was going until he reached the Fifth Avenue Presbyterian Church. Once more, he parked illegally, took cash from the trunk, and went into the church.

There was no poor-box as in St. Patrick's, but Jack found a young assistant minister in the process of closing the place for the night. From various pockets, Jack produced bundles of ten- and twenty-dollar bills wrapped with rubber bands, and handed them to the startled cleric, claiming to have won a fortune in the casinos of Atlantic City.

In two stops, he had given away thirty thousand dollars. But that was not even one-tenth of what he had brought back from Connecticut, and those dispensations did not allay his guilt. In fact, his newfound shame was growing stronger by the minute. The bag of money in the trunk was, to him, like the telltale heart buried under the floorboards in the story by Poe, a throbbing annunciator of his guilt, and he was as anxious to be rid of it as Poe's narrator had been anxious to silence the incriminating heartbeat of his dismembered victim.

Three hundred thirty thousand dollars remained. For some New Yorkers, Christmas was about to come two and a half weeks late.

ELKO COUNTY, NEVADA.

The summer before last, Dom had stayed in Room 20. He remembered it well because it was the last unit in the motel's L-shaped east wing.

Ernie Block's curiosity was more compelling than his nyctophobia, so he decided to accompany Faye and Dom to Room 20, where it was hoped that Dom's memories would be stirred by the sight of the familiar walls and furnishings. Ernie walked between Faye and Dom, who held his arms. During the trip along the breezeway, the frigid night wind made Dom glad for his fleece-lined jacket. More concerned about the black night than the chill, Ernie kept his eyes shut for the entire journey.

Faye went in first, snapping on the lights, closing drapes. Dom followed with Ernie, who opened his eyes only when Faye shut the door.

Upon entering the room, Dom was filled with apprehension. He walked to the queen-sized bed, stared down at it. He tried to remember lying here, drugged and helpless.

Faye said, "The bedspread's not the same, of course."

The Polaroid had shown the corner of a floral-patterned spread. The current model was brown- and blue-striped.

"The bed itself is the same, and all the furniture," Ernie said.

The padded headboard was upholstered with a coarse brown fabric, slightly snagged and worn. The nightstands were plain two-drawer chests with laminated walnut veneer. The bases of the lamps resembled large hurricane lanterns, black metal with two panes of smoky amber glass in each side; the cloth shades were the same amber hue as the glass in the base. Each lamp had two bulbs: The main one, under the shade, provided most of the light; the second bulb, inside the base, was shaped like a candle flame and gave off a dim flickering glow that imitated a real flame and was used only for its decorative effect, to enhance the illusion of hurricane lanterns.

Dom remembered every detail of the place now that he was standing in it, and he had the impression that a multitude of ghosts flitted teasingly through the room, staying just at the periphery of his vision. The ghosts were actually bad memories rather than spirits, and they haunted not the room but the shadowy corners of his own mind.

"Remember anything?" Ernie asked. "Is it coming back to you?"

"I want to have a look at the john," Dom said.

It was small and strictly functional, with a shower stall but no bathtub, a speckled tile floor, and durable Formica counter tops.

Dom was interested in the sink, for it was surely the one in his recurring nightmare. But when he looked into the bowl, he was surprised to see a mechanical stopper. And an inch below the rim of the bowl, the overflow drain consisted of three round holes, a more modern design than the six slanted lozenge-shaped outlets in the sink of his dreams.

"This isn't the same," he said. "The sink was old, with a rubber stopper attached to a bead-chain and hung from the cold-water faucet."

"We're always upgrading the place," Ernie said from the doorway.

"We took that sink out eight or nine months ago," Faye said. "We replaced the Formica then, too, although it's the same color as before."

Dom was disappointed because he had been convinced that at least some memories from those lost days would begin to return to him when he touched the sink. After all, judging from the stark terror of the nightmare, something particularly frightening had happened to him at that very spot; therefore, it seemed likely that the sink might act as a lightning rod upon the supercharged memories that drifted in the darkness of his subconscious, drawing them back in a sudden crackling blaze of recollection. He put his hands on the new sink, but he felt only cold porcelain.

"Anything?" Ernie asked again.

"No," Dom said. "No memories . . . but bad vibrations. If I give it time, I think the room might break down the barriers. I'll sleep here tonight, give it a chance to work on me . . . if that's all right."

"No problem," Faye said. "The room's yours."

Dom said, "I have a hunch the nightmare will be worse here than it's ever been before."

LAGUNA BEACH, CALIFORNIA.

Although Parker Faine was one of the most respected of living American artists, although his canvases were assiduously collected by major museums, although he had been commissioned to create works for the President of the United States and other luminaries, he was not too old and certainly not too dignified to get a thrill from the intrigue upon which he was engaged in Dominick Corvaisis' behalf. To be a successful artist, one needed maturity, an adult's perception and sensitivity and dedication to craftsmanship, but one also had to hold on to a child's curiosity, wonder, innocence, and sense of fun. Parker held tighter to those things than most artists did; therefore, he fulfilled his role in Dom's plans with a spirit of adventure.

Each day, when he picked up Dom's mail, Parker pretended to go about his business without the slightest suspicion that he might be under surveillance, but in fact he searched surreptitiously, diligently for the watchers—spies, cops, or whatever they might be. He never saw anyone observing him, and he never detected a tail.

And each night, when he left his house and went to a different pay phone to await Dom's prearranged call, he drove miles out of his way, turned back on his own route, made sudden turns calculated to throw off a tail, until he was sure that he was not being followed.

A few minutes before nine o'clock, Saturday night, he arrived by his usual devious means at a telephone booth beside a Union 76 station. A hard rain fell, sluicing down the Plexiglas walls, distorting the world beyond and screening Parker from prying eyes.

He was wearing a trenchcoat and a rainproof khaki hat with the rim turned down all the way around to let the rain run off. He felt as if he belonged in a John le Carré tale. He loved it.

Promptly at nine o'clock, the phone rang. It was Dom. "I'm on schedule, at the Tranquility Motel. This is the place, Parker."

Dom had a lot to tell: a disturbing experience in the Tranquility Grille, Ernie Block's nyctophobia. . . . And by indirection, he managed to convey that the Blocks had received strange Polaroid snapshots, too.

Discretion was essential; if the Tranquility Motel was, indeed, the center of the unremembered events of the summer before last, the Blocks' phones might be tapped. If the listeners heard about the photographs, they would know they had a traitor in their midst, and they would surely find him, and there would be no more notes or photos forthcoming.

"I've got news, too," Parker said. "Ms. Wycombe, your editor, left a message on your answering machine. *Twilight in Babylon* had another printing, and there are now a hundred thousand copies in the stores."

"Good God, I'd forgotten the book! Since Lomack's house four days ago, I haven't thought about anything but this crazy situation."

"Ms. Wycombe has more good news she wants to share, so you're to call her as soon as you get a chance."

"I'll do that. Meanwhile . . . seen any interesting pictures?" Dom asked, indirectly inquiring if any more Polaroids had been received.

"Nope. No amusing notes, either." When the headlights of passing cars swept across the booth, the thin skin of flowing water on the transparent walls flared briefly with a rippling-shimmering brilliance. Parker said, "But something came in the mail that'll knock your socks off, buddy. You've identified three of the names on those moon posters at Lomack's. So how'd you like to hear who the fourth one is?''

"Ginger? I forgot to tell you. I think her name's on the motel registry. Dr. Ginger Weiss of Boston. I intend to call her tomorrow.''

"You've stolen some of my thunder. But you'll be surprised to hear you got a letter today from Dr. Weiss. She sent it to Random House on December twenty-sixth, but it got caught in their bureaucracy. Anyway, she's at the end of her rope, see, and then she gets hold of a copy of your book, gloms your photo, and she gets this feeling she's met you before, and that *you* are a part of what's been happening to her.''

"Do you have the letter with you?'' Dom asked excitedly.

Parker had it in his hand, waiting. He read it, glancing now and then at the night beyond the booth.

"I've got to call her right away,'' Dom said when Parker finished the letter. "Can't wait till morning now. I'll talk to you again tomorrow night. Nine o'clock.''

"If you'll be calling from the motel, where the phones are likely to be tapped, there's no point in my running out to a phone booth.''

"You're right. I'll call you at home. Take care,'' Dom said.

"You, too.'' With mixed feelings, Parker put the receiver on the hook, relieved that these inconvenient nightly journeys to a pay phone were at an end, but also certain that he would miss the intrigue.

He stepped out of the phone booth, into the rain, and he was almost disappointed when no one took a shot at him.

BOSTON, MASSACHUSETTS.

Pablo Jackson had been buried that morning, but he was with Ginger Weiss throughout the afternoon and evening. Like a ghost, his memory haunted her, a smiling revenant in the chambers of her mind.

Keeping to herself in the guestroom at Baywatch, she tried to read, could not concentrate. When not preoccupied with memories of the old magician, she was eaten up by worry, wondering what would become of her.

She got into bed at a quarter past midnight and was reaching for the switch to turn off the lamp when Rita Hannaby came to tell her that Dominick Corvaisis was on the phone and that she could take the call in George's study, down the hall, adjacent to the master bedroom. Excited and trepidatious, Ginger put on a robe over her pajamas.

The study was warm and shadowy with dark oak paneling. The Chinese carpet was beige and forest-green, and the stained-glass lamp on the desk was either a genuine Tiffany or a superb reproduction.

George's puffy eyes made it clear that the call woke him. He began surgery early most mornings and was usually in bed by nine-thirty.

"I'm sorry,'' Ginger told him.

"No need,'' George said. "Isn't this what we've been hoping for?''

"Maybe,'' she said, unwilling to raise her hopes.

Rita said, "We'll give you privacy.''

"No,'' Ginger said. "Stay. Please.'' She went to the desk, sat down, picked up the uncradled handset. "Hello? Mr. Corvaisis?''

"Dr. Weiss?'' His voice was strong yet melodic. "Writing to me was the best thing you could've done. I don't think you're nuts. Because you're not alone, Doctor. There are more of us with strange problems.''

Ginger tried to respond, but her voice cracked. She cleared her throat. "I . . . I'm sorry . . . I'm not . . . I don't . . . don't usually cry."

Corvaisis said, "Don't try to talk until you're ready. I'll tell you about *my* problem: sleepwalking. And my dreams . . . about the moon."

A thrill, half cold fear and half exultation, throbbed through her. "The moon," she agreed. "I never remember the dreams, but they must involve the moon because that's what I wake up screaming about."

He told her about a man named Lomack in Reno, dead by his own hand, driven to suicide by an obsession with the moon.

Ginger sensed some vast gulf beneath her, a fearful unknown.

"We've been brainwashed," she blurted. "All these problems we're having are the result of repressed memories trying to surface."

For a moment there was a stunned silence on the line. Then the writer said, "That's been my theory, but you sound sure of it."

"I am. I underwent hypnotic regression therapy after I wrote to you, and we turned up evidence of systematic memory repression."

"Something happened to us the summer before last," he said.

"Yes! The summer before last. The Tranquility Motel in Nevada."

"That's where I'm calling from."

Startled, she said, "You're there *now?*"

"Yes. And if possible, you ought to come. A lot has happened that I can't risk talking about on the phone."

"Who *are* they?" she asked in frustration. "What are they hiding?"

"We'll have a better chance finding out if we all work together."

"I'll come. Tomorrow, if I can book a flight that quickly."

Rita started to protest that Ginger was in no condition to travel. In the many-colored light of the Tiffany lamp, George's scowl deepened.

To Corvaisis, Ginger said, "I'll let you know how and when I'll arrive."

When Ginger hung up, George said, "You can't possibly go all that way in your condition."

Rita said, "What if you black out on the airplane, become violent?"

"I'll be all right."

"Dear, you had *three* seizures last Monday, one after the other."

Ginger sighed and slumped back in the green leather chair. "Rita, George, you've been wonderful to me, and I can never adequately repay you. I love you, I really do. But I've been living with you for five weeks, five helpless weeks during which I've been more like a dependent child than an adult, and I'm just not capable of going on that way. I've got to go to Nevada. I've no other option. I've got to."

NEW YORK, NEW YORK.

A couple of blocks farther down Fifth Avenue from the Presbyterian Church, Jack stopped again, in front of St. Thomas's Episcopal Church. In the nave, he stared in fascination at the huge reredos of Dunville stone behind the altar. He met the strangely portentous gazes of the statues in the shadowy niches along the walls—Saints, Apostles, the Blessed Virgin, Christ—and he realized that the primary purpose of religion was the expiation of guilt, to provide people with forgiveness for being less than they were meant to be. The human species seemed incapable of living up to its potential, and some would be driven mad by guilt if they did not believe that a god—be it Jesus, Yahweh, Mohammed, Marx, or some other—looked on them with favor in spite of themselves. But Jack found no comfort in St. Thomas's, no expiation of his sins, not even when he left twenty thousand dollars in the charity box.

In the Camaro again, he set out to dispose of the rest of the cash from the Guardmaster heist, not because giving it away would salve his guilt; it would not, for redistribution of the funds was not the moral equivalent of repayment. He had too much to atone for to expect to shrive himself of all his transgressions in one night. But he did not need or want the money any more, could not simply throw it in the trash, so giving the damn stuff away was his only possible course of action.

He stopped at more churches and temples. Some were open, some locked. Where he could gain entrance, he left money.

He drove down to the Bowery and left forty thousand dollars with the startled night attendant at the Salvation Army Mission.

On Bayard Street in nearby Chinatown, Jack saw a sign in a second-floor window that proclaimed, in both Chinese characters and in English: THE ALLIANCE AGAINST OPPRESSION OF CHINESE MINORITIES. The place was above a quaint apothecary that specialized in the herbs and powdered roots of traditional Chinese medicines. The apothecary was closed, but a light shone in a window of the Alliance offices. Jack rang the bell at the street-level door, rang it and rang it until an elderly and wizened Chinese man came down the stairs and spoke to him through a small grille. When Jack ascertained that the Alliance's current major project was the rescue of brutalized Chinese families from Vietnam (and resettlement in the States), he passed twenty thousand in cash through the grille. The Chinese gentleman reverted to his native language in surprise and came out into the cold winter wind, insistent upon shaking hands. "Friend," the elderly mandarin said. "You can't know what suffering this gift will relieve." Jack echoed the old man, "Friend." In that single word, and in the warm grasp of the venerable Oriental's callused hand, Jack found something he thought he had lost forever: a sense of belonging, a feeling of community, fellowship.

In his car again, he drove up Bayard to Mott Street, turned right, and had to pull to the curb. A flood of tears blurred his vision.

He could not remember ever having been more confused than he was now. He wept in part because the stain of guilt, for the moment at least, seemed an ineradicable mark upon his soul. Yet some of the tears were tears of joy, for he was abruptly brimming over with brotherhood. For the better part of a decade, he had been outside society, distanced in mind and spirit if not in body. But now, for the first time since Central America, Jack Twist had the need, desire, *and* ability to reach out to the society around him, to make friends.

Bitterness was a dead-end. Hatred hurt no one more than he who harbored it. The wine of alienation was loneliness.

During the past eight years, he had often wept for Jenny, and he had sometimes wept in fits of self-pity. But *these* tears were different from all others he had let previously, for they were cleansing tears, purging tears, washing all the rage and resentment out of him.

He still did not understand the cause of these radical and rapid changes taking place in him. However, he sensed that his evolution—from outcast and criminal to law-abiding citizen—was not finished and would generate several more surprises before it reached a conclusion. He wondered where he was bound and by what route he would arrive there.

That night in Chinatown, hope swept back into his world like a summer breeze stirring music from a cluster of wind chimes.

ELKO COUNTY, NEVADA.

Ned and Sandy Sarver were able to run the diner by themselves because they were hard workers by nature, but also because their menu was simple and because Ned had learned efficient food service as a cook in the U.S. Army. A hundred tricks were employed to make the Tranquility Grille function smoothly with as little effort as possible.

Nevertheless, at the end of work, Ned was always glad that Ernie and Faye provided the motel's guests with a free continental breakfast in their rooms, so it was not necessary to open the diner before noon.

Saturday evening, while he grilled hamburgers and made french fries and served chili-dogs, Ned Sarver glanced frequently at Sandy as she worked. He still could not get used to the change in her, the sudden flowering. She had added ten pounds, and her figure had acquired an appealing female roundness it never possessed before. And she no longer shuffled slump-shouldered through the diner, but moved with a fluid grace and a jaunty good humor that Ned found enormously appealing.

He was not the only man who had eyes for the new Sandy. Some of the truckers watched the roll of her hips and the flex of her buttocks as she crossed the room with plates of food or bottles of cold beer.

Until recently, although Sandy had been unfailingly polite to the customers, she had not been chatty. That changed, too. She was still somewhat shy, but she responded to the truckers' teasing and even teased them in return, and came up with some damn good quips.

For the first time in eight years of marriage, Ned Sarver feared losing Sandy. He knew she loved him, and he told himself that these changes in her appearance and personality would not also change the nature of their relationship. But that was precisely what he feared.

This morning, when Sandy went to Elko to meet Ernie and Faye at the airport, Ned had worried that she would not come back. Maybe she would just keep going until she found a place she liked better than Nevada, until she met a man who was handsomer, richer, and smarter than Ned. He knew that he was being unfair to Sandy by harboring such suspicions, that she was incapable of infidelity or cruelty. Maybe his fear lay in the fact that he'd always thought Sandy deserved better than him.

At nine-thirty, when the dinner crowd thinned to seven customers, Faye and Ernie came into the Grille with that dark, good-looking guy who had caused a scene earlier in the evening when he had wandered through the door as if in a dream and then had turned and run out as though hell hounds were at his heels. Ned wondered who the guy was, how he knew Faye and Ernie, and whether *they* knew their friend was a little weird.

Ernie looked pale and shaky, and to Ned it seemed as if his boss was taking considerable care to keep his back to the windows. When he raised a hand in greeting to Ned, there was a visible tremor in it.

Faye and the stranger sat facing each other across the table, and from the looks they gave Ernie, you could see they were concerned about him. They didn't look so good themselves.

Something peculiar was going on. Intrigued by Ernie's condition, Ned was briefly distracted from thoughts of Sandy leaving him.

But when Sandy stopped at their table, she was so long taking their order that Ned's concern rose again. From his post behind the counter, with a hamburger and a pair of eggs sizzling noisily on the griddle, he could not hear what they were saying over there, but he had the crazy notion that the stranger was taking undue interest in Sandy and that she was responding to his slick patter. Jealous nonsense, of course. Yet the guy was handsome, and he was younger than Ned, closer Sandy's age, and apparently successful, just the kind of guy she *ought* to run off with because he would be better for her than Ned could ever be.

In his own view, Ned Sarver was not much to brag about. He was not ugly, but certainly not handsome. His brown hair had receded from his forehead in a deep widow's peak; unless you were Jack Nicholson, such a hairline was not sexy. He had pale-gray eyes that perhaps had been startling and magnetic when he was a young man, but with the passing years, they merely made him appear tired and washed-out. He was neither rich nor destined to be rich. And at forty-two, ten years older than Sandy, Ned Sarver was not likely to be gripped suddenly by the driving need to make something of himself.

All of this dismaying self-criticism roiled through his mind as he watched Sandy finally leave the stranger's table and come to the counter. With an odd and troubled expression, she handed the order slip to him and said, "What time we closing? Ten or ten-thirty?"

"Ten." Indicating the few customers, Ned added: "No profit hanging around tonight."

She nodded and went back to Faye, Ernie—and the stranger.

Her brusqueness and her speedy return to the stranger aggravated Ned's worries. As far as he could see, he had only three qualities that gave Sandy any reason to stay with him. First, he could always make a decent living as a short-order cook because he was good. Second, he had a talent for fixing things, both inanimate objects and living creatures. If a toaster, blender, or radio went on the blink, Ned set to work with a tool kit and soon had the appliance back in operation. Likewise, if he found a panicky bird with a broken wing he stroked it until it grew calm, took it home, nursed it back to health, then sent it on its way. Having the talent to fix things seemed important, and Ned was proud of it. Third, he loved Sandy with all his body, mind, and heart.

Preparing the order for Faye, Ernie, and the stranger, Ned glanced repeatedly at Sandy, and he was surprised when she and Faye started moving around the room, lowering the Levolor blinds over the windows.

Something unusual was going on. Returning to Ernie's table, Sandy leaned forward in earnest conversation with the good-looking stranger.

It was ironic that he was worried about losing Sandy, for it had been his talent for fixing things that contributed to her transformation from duckling to swan. When Ned first met her at a diner in Tucson, where they worked, Sandy was not just bashful and self-conscious but painfully shy, fearful. She was a hard worker, always willing to lend a hand to other waitresses when they got behind in their orders, but she was incapable of interacting with anyone on a personal level. A pale, scuttling girl (twenty-three, but still more girl than woman), she was reluctant to open the door on friendship, for fear she would put her trust in someone who might hurt her. She had been drab, mousy, meek, beaten by life—and the instant Ned had seen her, he had felt the need to *fix* things for her. With enormous patience, he began work on her, so subtly that, at first, she was not aware that he was interested in her.

They were married nine months later, although his repair work on her was far from finished. She was more badly broken than any creature he'd encountered before, and there were times when, in frustration, he felt that, even with his talent, he would be unable to fix her and would spend the rest of his life tinkering endlessly without much effect.

During their first six years of marriage, however, he *had* witnessed a slow healing in her, maddeningly gradual. Sandy had an indisputably bright mind, but she was retarded emotionally; she learned to take and give affection only with tremendous effort, much as a dim-witted child struggles mightily to learn to count to ten.

The first indication Ned had had that *major* changes were taking place in Sandy was the sudden marked improvement in her sexual appetite. The turnaround had come in late August, two summers ago.

She'd never been a hesitant lover. She exhibited extensive carnal knowledge, but she made love more like a machine than a woman, with a joyless expertise. He had never known a woman as silent in bed as Sandy had been. He suspected something in her childhood had stunted her, the same thing that had broken her spirit. He tried to get her to talk about it, but she was adamant about letting the past stay buried, and his persistence was the one thing that might have caused her to leave him; so he asked about it no more, though it was difficult to fix something when you could not get at the part of it that was broken.

Then, in August of the summer before last, she came to the conjugal bed with a noticeably different attitude. Nothing dramatic at first. No sudden release of long-imprisoned passions. Initially, the change involved only a subtle new relax- ation during the act of love. Sometimes she smiled or murmured his name as he made love to her.

Slowly, slowly, she blossomed. By that Christmas, four months after the change began, she no longer lay upon the bed as if she were made of metal. She strove to find and match his rhythm, searching for the fulfillment that still eluded her.

Slowly, slowly, she freed the erotic power chained within her. Finally, on April 7, last year, a night Ned would never forget, Sandy had an orgasm for the first time. It was a climax of such power that for a moment it frightened Ned. After- ward, she wept with happiness and clung to him with such gratitude, love, and trust that he wept as well.

He thought her orgasmic breakthrough would finally enable her to speak of the source of her long-hidden pain. But when he cautiously inquired, she rebuffed him: "The past is past, Ned. Won't help to dwell on it. If I talk about it . . . that might just give it a new hold on me."

Through last spring, summer, and early autumn, Sandy gradually achieved sat- isfaction more often until, by September, their love-making nearly always brought her fulfillment. And by Christmas Day, less than three weeks ago, it was clear that her sexual maturation was not the only change in her but was accompanied by a new pride and self-respect.

Concomitant with her sexual development, Sandy learned to enjoy driving, an activity she had once found even less pleasurable than sex. Initially, she expressed the modest intention of driving to work from their trailer out near Beowawe. Before long she was lighting out in the truck on solo spins. Sometimes Ned stood at a window and watched his uncaged bird soar off, and he viewed each flight with delight but also with an uneasiness he could not explain.

By New Year's Day, just past, the uneasiness became dread and was with him twenty-four hours a day, and by then he understood it. He was afraid Sandy would fly away from him.

Maybe with the stranger who'd come in with Ernie and Faye.

I'm probably overreacting, Ned thought as he put three hamburger patties on the griddle. Fact is, I know damn well I'm overreacting.

But he worried.

By the time Ned prepared cheeseburgers with all the fixings for the Blocks and their friend, the other customers were gone. As Sandy served the loaded plates, Faye locked the door and switched on the CLOSED sign that was visible from I-80, though it was shy of ten o'clock.

Ned joined them for a closer look at the stranger, and to insinuate himself between the guy and Sandy. When he got to their table, he was surprised to see that Sandy had a bottle of beer and had opened one for him, too. He did not drink much; Sandy drank less.

"You'll need it when you hear what they have to tell us," Sandy said. "In fact, you might even need a couple more bottles."

The guy's name was Dominick Corvaisis, and he had an amazing tale that drove all worries of infidelity from Ned's mind. When Corvaisis was finished, Ernie and Faye had an incredible story of their own, and that was when Ned first learned about the ex-Marine's fear of the dark.

"But I remember we were evacuated," Ned said. "We couldn't have been here at the motel those three days, 'cause I remember we had a sort of mini-vacation at home—watching TV, reading Louis L'Amour."

"I believe that's what you were *told* to remember," Corvaisis said. "Did any-one visit you at the trailer during that time? Any neighbors drop by? Anyone who could confirm that you were actually there?"

"We're outside Beowawe, where we don't really have neighbors. Far as I remember, we didn't see anybody who could swear we was there."

Sandy said, "Ned, they wondered if anything strange has been happening to either of us."

Ned met his wife's eyes. Without words, he let her know it was up to her whether she told them about the changes she had been undergoing.

Corvaisis said, "The two of you were here the night it happened. Whatever it was, it started while I was having dinner. So you must have been a part of it. But the memory was stolen from you."

The thought of strangers messing with his mind gave Ned the creeps. Uneasy, he studied the five Polaroid snapshots that Faye had fanned out on the table, especially the picture of Corvaisis staring empty-eyed.

To Sandy, Faye said, "Honey, Ernie and I would have to've been blind not to've noticed the changes in you recently. I don't mean to embarrass you, and I don't want to pry, but if those changes might be related to whatever happened to us, then we ought to know about it."

Sandy reached for Ned's hand, held it. Her love for him was so evident that he was ashamed of himself for the ridiculous thoughts of betrayal that had pre-occupied him earlier.

Staring intently at her beer, she said, "Most all my life, I've had the lowest opinion of myself. I'll tell you why, because you've got to know how bad it was for me when I was a kid if you want to understand how miraculous it is that I ever found any self-respect. It was Ned who first lifted me up, believed in me, gave me a chance to be somebody." Her hand tightened on his. "Almost nine years ago, he started courting me, and he was the first person ever treated me like a lady. He married me knowing that inside I was tied up in tangled knots, and he's spent eight years doing his best to untie and untangle them. He thinks I don't know how hard he's tried to help me, but I know all right."

Her voice cracked with emotion. She paused for a swallow of beer.

Ned was unable to speak.

Sandy said, "The thing is . . . I want everyone to know that maybe what happened the summer before last, the thing none of us remembers . . . maybe it *did* have a powerful effect on me. But if Ned hadn't taken me under his wing all those years ago, I never would've had a chance.''

Love enwrapped Ned as if it were bands of iron, closing his throat, constricting his chest, applying a pleasant pressure to his heart.

She glanced at him, returned her gaze to the bottle of beer, and recounted a childhood in hell. She did not describe her father's violations of her in explicit detail, and she spoke demurely—almost primly—of her periodic exploitation as a child prostitute under the management of a Vegas pimp. Her account of this monstrous abuse was all the more shocking and moving because she related it without drama. Everyone at the table listened in a silence resulting not merely from shock but from respect for her suffering and from a certain reverence for her ultimate triumph.

When Sandy finished, Ned embraced her, held her close. He was amazed by her strength. He had always known she was special, and the things she told them tonight only strengthened his love and admiration.

Though he was deeply saddened by what had been done to Sandy, he was delighted that she was at last able to talk about it. Surely this meant that the past had lost its hold on her.

Faye and Ernie commiserated with her in the awkward manner of friends who want to help but who know they can offer only words.

Everyone needed another beer. Ned got five bottles of Dos Equis out of the cooler and brought them to the table.

Corvaisis, who no longer seemed like the enemy to Ned, shook his head and blinked as if Sandy's story had left him in a daze of horror. ''This turns things upside down. I mean, if our unremembered experience had one basic effect on the rest of us, it was *terror*. Oh, I benefited because I was brought out of my shell; I share that with Sandy. But Ernie, Dr. Weiss, Lomack, and me . . . we were for the most part left with a residue of fear. Now Sandy tells us the effect on her was strictly beneficial, not frightening in the least. How could it affect us so differently? You really have no fear, Sandy?''

''None,'' Sandy said.

Ever since Ernie pulled a chair up to the table, he'd been sitting with his shoulders hunched and his head lowered, as if protecting his neck from attack. Now, with one hand clamped around a bottle of Dos Equis, he leaned back and relaxed, though not much. ''Yeah, fear's the core of it. But you remember that place along the interstate I told you about, little more than a quarter-mile from here? I'm sure something weird happened there, something that relates to the brainwashing. But when I'm standing at that place, I feel more than just fear. My heart starts to race . . . and I get excited . . . but it's not entirely a *bad* excitement. Fear's a part of it, yeah, maybe the biggest part of it, but there's a stew of other emotions, as well.''

Sandy said, ''I think the place Ernie's talking about is where I often wind up when I take the truck out for a ride. I'm . . . *drawn* there.''

Ernie leaned forward, excited. ''I knew it! Coming back from the airport this morning, as we were passing that place, you let the truck slow way down. And I said to myself, 'Sandy feels it, too.' ''

Faye said, ''Sandy, what exactly do *you* feel when you're drawn to that piece of ground?''

With a smile so warm that Ned could almost feel the heat of it, Sandy said, ''Peace. I feel at peace there. It's hard to explain . . . but it's as if the rocks, dirt, and trees all radiate harmony, tranquility.''

"I don't feel peaceful there," Ernie said. "Fear, yes. A queer excitement. An eerie sense that something . . . shattering will happen. Something that I'm eager for, even though it scares the hell out of me."

"And I feel none of what you feel," Sandy said.

"We ought to go there," Ned suggested. "See if the place affects the rest of us."

"In the morning," Corvaisis said. "When it's light."

Faye said, "I can see this might've had a different effect on each of us. But why has it changed Dom's and Sandy's and Ernie's lives—and the lives of that Mr. Lomack in Reno and Dr. Weiss in Boston—yet done nothing to Ned and me. Why aren't we having problems, too?"

Dom said, "Maybe the brainwashers did a better job on you and Ned."

That thought gave Ned the heebie-jeebies again.

For a while they discussed their situation, and then Ned suggested that Corvaisis try to re-create his actions on that Friday night, July 6, up to the point where his memories were erased. "You recollect the early part of the evening better than we do. And when you came in the first time tonight, you were close to remembering something important."

"Close," Corvaisis agreed, "but at the last moment, when I felt the memory within grasp, it scared the crap out of me . . . and the next thing I knew, I was running for the door. Made quite a spectacle of myself. I was totally freaked out. It was such a visceral thing, instinctual, so utterly uncontrollable, that I think it would probably happen again if I made a second attempt to force the memories."

"Still, it's worth a try," Ned said.

"And you've got us for moral support this time," Faye said.

Corvaisis needed coaxing, which Ned interpreted as meaning that the experience earlier this evening had been considerably more unnerving than words could express. But at last the writer got up and, carrying his glass of beer, went to the front door of the diner. He stood with his back to the exit, chugged a long swallow of Dos Equis. He looked around the room, trying hard to see the people of that other time.

He said, "There were three or four men sitting at the counter. Maybe a dozen customers altogether. I can't remember their faces." Moving away from the door, he walked past Ned and the others, to the next table, where he pulled out a chair and sat with his back turned partly toward them. "This is where I sat. Sandy waited on me. I took a bottle of Coors while I looked at the menu. Ordered the ham-and-egg sandwich. French fries, coleslaw. As I was salting the fries, the shaker slipped out of my hand. Salt spilled on the table. I threw a pinch over my shoulder. Silly gesture. Threw it too hard. Dr. Weiss! Ginger Weiss was the woman I threw the salt on. I didn't remember that before, but I can see her clearly now. The blonde in the photo."

Faye tapped the Polaroid snapshot of Dr. Weiss that was on the table in front of Ned.

Still sitting alone at the other table, Corvaisis said, "Quite a beautiful woman. Pixie-cute yet also sophisticated-looking, a really interesting mix. Could hardly take my eyes off her."

Ned looked more closely at the photo of Ginger Weiss. He supposed she might, indeed, be unusually attractive when her face was not so pale and slack, when her eyes were not so cold, empty, dead.

In a voice that had grown odd, as if he were actually speaking to them from out of the past, Corvaisis said, "She sits in the corner booth by the window, facing this way. Sunset is near. The sun's out there on the horizon, balanced like a big red ball, and the diner's filled with orange light slanting in through the windows. Almost like firelight. Ginger Weiss looks especially lovely in that light. I can hardly keep from staring openly at her. . . . Twilight now. I've got a second beer.'' He sipped some Dos Equis. When he continued, his voice was softer: ''The plains are all purple . . . then black . . . night . . .''

Like Ernie and Faye and Sandy, Ned was spellbound by the writer's struggle to remember, for it stirred in him, at last, faint and shapeless—but compelling— memories of his own. He began to recall that particular evening out of the many he'd spent in the Tranquility Grille. The young priest had been here, the one in the Polaroid snapshot now lying on the table. And the young couple with their little girl.

''Not long after nightfall . . . nursing my second beer mainly so I can stare at Ginger Weiss a little longer.'' Corvaisis looked left, right, raised his right hand to his ear. ''An unusual sound of some kind. I remember that much. A distant rumble . . . getting louder.'' He was silent for a while. ''Can't remember what happened next. Something . . . something . . . but it just won't come.''

As the writer spoke of the rumbling, Ned Sarver experienced the vaguest possible memory of that frightening, swelling sound, but he could not clearly call it to mind. He felt as if Corvaisis had brought him to the edge of a dark chasm into which he was desperately afraid to look but into which he *must* look, and now they were turning away without shining a light down in those black depths. Heart racing, he said, ''Concentrate on remembering the sound, the *exact* sound, and maybe that'll bring the rest of it back to you.''

Corvaisis pushed his chair back from the table, got up. ''Rumbling . . . like thunder, very distant thunder . . . but growing closer.'' He stood beside the table, seeking the direction from which the sound had come, looking left, right, up, down at the floor.

Suddenly Ned heard the noise, not in memory but in reality, not back there in the past but *now*. The hollow roll of far-away thunder. But it came in one endless peal, not a series of rising and falling crashes, and it was growing louder, louder. . . .

Ned looked at the others. They heard it, too.

Louder. Louder. Now he could feel the vibrations in his bones.

He could not remember what had happened that night, but he knew the astonishing events they had endured had started with this sound.

He pushed back his chair and got up. He was awash in a rising tide of fear, and he had to fight against the urge to run.

Sandy stood, and there was fear in her face, as well. Though the unknown events seemed to have had an entirely positive effect on her, she was frightened now. She put one hand on Ned's arm for reassurance.

Ernie and Faye were frowning, looking around for the source of the noise, but they did not yet appear frightened. Their memory of the sound was apparently more thoroughly scrubbed away, so they could not as easily connect it with the events of that Friday night in July.

Another sound arose, underlying the thunderlike rumble: a queer, ululating whistle. That, too, was unpleasantly familiar to Ned.

It was happening again. Whatever had taken place that night more than eighteen months ago was somehow being repeated. Jesus, happening all over again, and Ned heard himself saying. ''No, no. *No!*''

Corvaisis backed a couple of steps away from his table, cast a glance at Ned and the others. He was white-faced.

The growing roar began to resonate in the window glass, behind the closed blinds. A loose pane, unseen, started rattling in its frame.

The Levolor blinds were vibrating now, adding a jangly chorus.

Sandy's hold on Ned became a panicky clutch.

Ernie and Faye were on their feet, and they were no longer merely bewildered but as afraid as everyone else.

The ululant whistle had grown in volume with the thunder. Now it became piercingly shrill, an oscillating electronic shriek.

"What *is* it?" Sandy cried, and the continuous fulminations attained such volume and power that the walls of the Tranquility Grille shook.

On the table at which Corvaisis had been sitting, the beer glass fell on its side, cracking, spilling what Dos Equis remained in it.

Ned looked at the table beside him and saw the objects on it—ketchup bottle, mustard dispenser, salt and pepper shakers, ashtray, glasses, plates, and silverware—bouncing, clinking against one another, moving back and forth across the surface. A beer glass toppled, and another, and the ketchup bottle.

Wide-eyed, Ned and the others turned this way and that, as if in anticipation of the imminent materialization of a demonic entity.

Throughout the room, objects fell off tables. The clock with the Coors logo leapt from the hook on which it hung, crashed to the floor.

This very thing had happened that night in July—Ned remembered as much. But he could not remember what had come next.

"Stop it!" Ernie shouted with the conviction and authority of a Marine officer accustomed to obedience—but without effect.

Earthquake? Ned wondered. A quake did not explain the electronic shriek that accompanied the thunder.

The chairs jittered across the floor, bumping against one another. One of them slid into Corvaisis, and the writer jumped in surprise.

Ned could feel the floor shaking.

The thunderlike rumble and the accompanying oscillatory shriek rose to an ear-splitting peak, and with the hard flat crash of a bomb blast, the big front windows imploded. Faye screamed and threw her arms up in front of her face, and Ernie stumbled backward and nearly fell over a chair. Sandy buried her face against Ned's chest.

They might have been badly cut by flying glass if the closed blinds had not imposed a barrier between them and the shattering panes. Even so, the force of the implosion flung the blinds up as a strong wind might blow curtains at an open window, and some glittering shards fell onto the booths, rained over Ned, and smashed on the floor around him.

Silence. The implosion of the windows was followed by a profound silence disturbed only by a few last, loose, little pieces of glass falling out of window frames, one at a time.

On that Friday night in July, the summer before last, much more than this had happened, though Ned could not remember what. Tonight, however, the mysterious drama apparently was not going to progress as far as it had gone then. For now, it was over.

Dom Corvaisis was bleeding lightly from a nick in his cheek, hardly worse than a shaving cut. Ernie's forehead and the back of his right hand had been slightly scratched by splinters of glass.

When he had determined that Sandy was unhurt, Ned reluctantly left her and rushed to the front door. He went out into the night in search of the cause of the weird noise and destruction, but he found only the deep, dark, solemn silence of the plains. No smoke or blackened rubble marked the source of an explosion. At the bottom of the hill on which the Tranquility Motel and Grille stood, widely separated cars and trucks moved on the interstate. Over at the motel, drawn by the commotion, a few guests had come outside in their nightclothes. The sky above was full of stars. The air was numbingly cold, but there was no wind, only a soft breeze, like the frigid sigh of Death. Nothing in sight could have caused the thunder, shaking, or implosion of the windows.

Dom Corvaisis came out of the Grille, bewildered. "What the hell?"

"I was hoping *you'd* know," Ned responded.

"It's what happened the summer before last."

"I know."

"But just the start of it. Damn it, I can't remember what happened that night *after* the windows blew in."

"Me neither," Ned replied.

Corvaisis turned his hands palms-up, held them out for inspection. In the blue neon light from the sign on the diner's roof, Ned saw rings of swollen flesh in the writer's palms. Because the light was blue, he could not ascertain the true color of the marks. But from what Corvaisis had told them earlier, Ned knew the rings were an angry red.

"What the hell?" Corvaisis said again.

Sandy was standing in the open door of the diner, backlit by the fluorescent glow from inside, and Ned went to her, embraced her. He felt one shudder after another passing through her. But he did not realize how badly *he* was trembling until she said, "You're shaking like a leaf."

Ned Sarver was scared sick. With an almost clairvoyant vividness, he sensed that they were involved in something of monumental importance, something unimaginably dangerous, and that it was likely to end in death for some or all of them. He was a natural-born fixer of both inanimate objects and people, a damned good repairman. But this time he was up against a force with which he did not know how to tinker. What if Sandy were killed? He took pride in his talents, but even the best fixer in the whole damned world could not undo the wreckage wrought by Death.

For the first time since meeting her in Tucson, Ned felt powerless to protect his wife.

At the horizon, the moon had begun to rise.

FIVE

◆

January 12–January 14

1. Sunday, January 12

Air as dense as molten iron.

In the nightmare, Dom could not draw breath. A tremendous pressure bore down on him. He was choking violently. He was dying.

He could not see much; his vision was clouded. Then two men came close, both wearing white vinyl decontamination suits with dark-visored helmets similar to those of astronauts. One man was at Dom's right, frantically disconnecting the IV line, withdrawing the intravenous spike from his arm. The other man, on the left, was cursing the cardiological data on the video readout of the EKG machine. One of them unbuckled the straps and tore off the electrodes connecting Dom to the EKG, and the other lifted him into a sitting position. They pressed a glass to his lips, but he could not drink, so they tipped his head back and forced his mouth open and poured some noxious stuff down his throat.

The men communicated with each other via radios built into their helmets, but they were leaning so close to Dom that he could hear their voices clearly even through the muffling Plexiglas of their dark visors. One of them said, "How many detainees were poisoned?" And the other said, "Nobody's sure yet. Looks like at least a dozen." The first said, "But who'd want to poison them?" And the second said, "One guess." The first said, "Colonel Falkirk. Colonel fucking Falkirk." The second man said, "But we'll never prove it, never nail the bastard."

Flash-cut. The motel bathroom. The men were holding Dom on his feet, forcing his face down into the sink. This time, he understood what they were saying to him. With growing urgency, they were insisting that he vomit. Colonel fucking Falkirk had somehow had him poisoned, and these guys had made him drink a foul-tasting emetic, and now he was supposed to purge himself of the poison that was killing him. But even as sick as he was, he still could not puke. He gagged, retched; his stomach roiled; sweat poured off him like melting fat off a broiling chicken; but he could not rid himself of the poison. The first man said, "We need a stomach pump." And the second said, "We don't *have* a stomach pump." They pressed Dom's face deeper into the porcelain bowl. The crushing pressure grew worse, and Dom could hardly breathe at all now, and hot greasy waves of nausea washed through him, and sweat *gushed* from him, but he could not puke, could not, could not. And then he did.

Flash-cut. In bed again. Weak, kitten-weak. But able to breathe, thank God. The men in the decontamination suits had cleaned him up and strapped him to the mattress once more. The one on the right prepared a hypodermic and administered an injection of something apparently meant to counteract the remaining effects of the poison. The one on the left reconnected him to the intravenous drip from which he was receiving drugs, not nourishment. Dom was woozy, holding on to consciousness only with considerable effort. They hooked him to the EKG again, and as they worked, they talked. "Falkirk's an idiot. We can keep a lid on this, given half a chance." "He's afraid the memory block will wear off. He's afraid that some of them will eventually remember what they saw." "Well, he may be right. But if the asshole kills them all, how's he going to explain the bodies? *That's* going to draw reporters like raw meat draws jackals, and then there'll be no way to keep the lid on. A nice memory wipe—that's the only sensible answer." "You don't have to convince me. Go burn Falkirk's ear about it."

The dream-figures faded away, as did their voices, and Dom passed into a different nightmare country. He no longer felt weak, no longer sick, but his fear exploded into stark terror, and he began to run with that maddening slow-motion panic indigenous to nightmares. He did not know what he was running from, but he was certain that something was pursuing him, something threatening and inhuman, he could sense it right behind him, closer, reaching for him, closer, and finally he knew he could not outrun it, knew he must face it, so he stopped and turned and looked up and cried out in surprise: *"The moon!"*

Dom was awakened by his own cry. He was in Room 20, on the floor beside the bed, kicking, flailing. He got up and sat on the bed.

He looked at his travel clock. Three-oh-seven A.M.

Shivering, he blotted his damp palms on the sheets.

Room 20 was having precisely the effect on him that he had thought it would. The bad vibrations of the place stimulated his memory, made his nightmares more vivid and more detailed than ever.

These dreams were radically different from all others he had ever known, for they were not fantasies but glimpses of a past reality seen through a distorting lens. They were not dreams as much as they were memories, forbidden recollections that had been weighted and dropped into the black sea of his subconscious, like dead bodies encumbered with cement shoes and thrown from a bridge into the deeps. Finally, the memories had slipped out of the cement and were surging to the surface.

He really *had* been imprisoned here, drugged, brainwashed. And during that ordeal, someone named Colonel Falkirk had actually poisoned him to prevent him from talking about whatever he had seen.

Falkirk was right, Dom thought. Eventually, we'll overcome the brainwashing and remember the truth. He *should* have killed us all.

Sunday morning, Ernie purchased panels of plyboard from a friend in Elko who owned a building supply. With his portable tablesaw, he cut the panels to fit the busted-out diner windows. Ned and Dom helped nail the plyboard in place, and by noon they had completed the job.

Ernie did not want to call a glazier and have the windows replaced because last night's phenomena might recur. Until they knew what had caused the thunderous noise and shaking, installing new glass seemed foolhardy. In the interim, the Tranquility Grille would not be open.

The Tranquility Motel also would be closed. Ernie did not want business to distract him from helping Dom and the others probe into the mystery of the "toxic spill." When the last of yesterday's check-ins departed later today, the motel would house only Ernie, Faye, Dom, and any other victims who, when contacted, might decide to journey to Elko County to participate in the investigation. He did not know how many rooms he might need for those fellow-sufferers, so he decided to reserve all twenty. For the time being, the Tranquility was less a motel than a barracks, where the troops would be quartered until this war with an unknown enemy was finally brought to a conclusion.

When the diner was boarded up, they all got into the motel's Dodge van, and Faye drove them down to the interstate and just over a quarter of a mile east, where she parked on the shoulder of the highway near the place that had a special attraction for Ernie and Sandy. The five of them stood along the guardrail, staring south, seeking a communion with the landscape that might illuminate the past. The winter solstice was three weeks behind them, so the sunlight was almost as hard and flat and cold as fluorescent light. In the grip of January, the scrub- and grass-covered plains, rugged hills, arroyos and gnarled rock formations were basically trichromatic, rendered in browns and grays and deep reds, with only an occasional patch of white sand, snow, or vein of borax. The scene was stark and dreary under a sky that grew more clouded and gray by the hour, but it also possessed an undeniable austere grandeur.

Faye wanted very much to feel something special about this place, for if she felt nothing, that would mean the people who brainwashed her had totally controlled her, totally *violated* her. She allowed no room in her self-image for the concept of absolute submission. She was a proud, capable woman. But she felt nothing other than the winter wind.

Ned and Dom appeared to be no more moved than Faye was, but she could see that Ernie and Sandy were receiving some cryptic message from the vista before them. Sandy was smiling beatifically. But Ernie had that look he got when night fell: pale, drawn, with haunted eyes.

"Let's go closer," Sandy said. "Let's go right down there."

All five climbed over the guardrail and plunged down the steep embankment of the elevated road. They moved across the plain—fifty yards, a hundred—carefully avoiding the cold-weather prickly pear which grew in profusion near the foot of the interstate but soon disappeared in favor of sagebrush and bunchgrass, which in turn gave way to another kind of grass which was also brown but thicker, silkier. Portions of the plain were rocky and sandy and in the grip of worthless bristly scrub, while other portions were almost like small lush meadows, for this was a land in transition from the semidesert of the south to the rich mountain pastures of the north. More than two hundred yards from the interstate, they stopped on a patch of ground not appreciably different from surrounding territory.

"Here," Ernie said with a shudder, jamming his hands in his pockets and pulling his neck down into the rolled sheepskin collar of his coat.

Sandy smiled and said, "Yes. Here."

They spread out and moved back and forth across the ground. Here and there, in one shadowed niche or another, meager patches of snow lay hidden from the evaporating effect of the dry wind and from the cold winter sun. Those traces of winter, plus the lack of green grass and scattered late-blooming wildflowers, were the only things that made the landscape different from the way it had looked two summers ago. After a minute or two, Ned announced that he did, indeed, feel an inexplicable connection with the place, though it did not bring him peace as it did his wife. His fear became so acute that, expressing surprise and embarrassment at his reaction, he turned and walked away. As Sandy hurried after Ned, Dom Corvaisis admitted that he was strangely affected by the place, too. However, he was not merely frightened, like Ned; Dom's fear, like Ernie's, was spiced by an unexplained awe and a sense of impending epiphany. Only Faye remained unaffected, unmoved.

Standing in the middle of the area in question, Dom turned slowly in a circle. "What was it? What the hell happened here?"

The sky had turned to gray slate.

The blunt wind became sharp. Faye shivered.

She remained unable to feel what Ernie and the others felt, and that inability increased her sense of violation. She hoped she would one day meet the people who had messed with her mind. She wanted to look in their eyes and ask them how they could have so little respect for the personal integrity of another human being. Now that she knew she had been manipulated, she would never again feel entirely secure.

Stirred by the wind, the dry sagebrush made a scraping-rustling noise. Ice-crusted twigs clicked against one another with a sound that, fancifully, made Faye think of small, scurrying skeletons of little animals long-dead but somehow reanimated.

Back at the motel, in the Blocks' apartment, Ernie and Sandy and Ned sat at the kitchen table, while Faye made coffee and hot chocolate.

Dom perched on a stool by the wall phone. On the counter in front of him lay the Tranquility Motel's registration book that had been in use the year before last. Referring to the page for Friday, July 6, he began to call those who must have shared the unremembered but important experiences of that far-away summer night.

In addition to his own name and that of Ginger Weiss, there were eight on the list. One of them, Gerald Salcoe of Monterey, California, had rented two rooms for himself, his wife, and two daughters. He had entered an address but no telephone. When Dom tried to get it from the Area Code 408 Information Operator, he was told the number was unlisted.

Disappointed, he moved on to Cal Sharkle, the long-haul trucker, a repeat customer known to Faye and Ernie. Sharkle lived in Evanston, Illinois, a suburb of Chicago. He had included his telephone number in the motel registry. Dom dialed it but discovered that the telephone had been disconnected and that no new number was listed.

"We can check his more recent entries on the current registry," Ernie said. "Maybe he's moved to another town. Maybe we have his new address somewhere."

Faye put a cup of coffee on the counter where Dom could reach it, then joined the others at the table.

Dom had better luck on his third attempt, when he dialed Alan Rykoff in Las Vegas. A woman answered, and he said, "Mrs. Rykoff?"

She hesitated. "I was Mrs. Rykoff. My name's Monatella now, since the divorce."

"Oh. I see. Well, my name's Dominick Corvaisis. I'm calling from the Tranquility Motel up here in Elko County. You, your former husband, and your daughter stayed here for a few days in July, two summers ago?"

"Uh . . . yes, we did."

"Miss Monatella, are either you or your daughter or your ex-husband having . . . difficulties—frightening and extraordinary problems?"

This time her hesitation was pregnant with meaning. "Is this some sick joke? Obviously, you know what happened to Alan."

"Please, Miss Monatella, believe me: I don't know what happened to your ex-husband. But I do know there's a good chance that you or him or your daughter— or all of you—are suffering from inexplicable psychological problems, that you're having frightening and repetitive nightmares you can't remember, and that some of these nightmares involve the moon."

She gasped twice in surprise as Dom was speaking, and when she tried to respond she had difficulty talking.

When he realized she was on the verge of tears, he interrupted. "Miss Monatella, I don't know what's happened to you and your family, but the worst is past. The worst is past. Because whatever might still be to come . . . at least you're not alone any more."

Over twenty-four hundred miles east of Elko County, in Manhattan, Jack Twist spent Sunday afternoon giving away more money.

On returning from the Guardmaster heist in Connecticut the previous night, he had driven through the city, looking for those who were both in need and deserving, and he had not rid himself of all the cash until five o'clock in the morning. On the edge of physical and emotional collapse, he'd returned to his Fifth Avenue apartment, gone immediately to bed and instantly to sleep.

He dreamed again of the deserted highway in an empty moon-washed landscape, and of the stranger in the dark-visored helmet who pursued him on foot. As the moonlight suddenly turned blood-red, he woke from the dream in panic at one o'clock Sunday afternoon, flailing at his pillow. A blood-red moon? He wondered what that meant, if anything.

He showered, shaved, dressed, and took time for only a quick breakfast consisting of an orange and a half-stale croissant.

In the large walk-in closet that served the master bedroom, he removed the cleverly concealed false panel and inventoried the contents of the three-foot-deep secret storage space. The jewelry from the job in October was finally gone, successfully fenced, and most of the money from the *fratellanza* warehouse in early December had been converted to scores of cashiers' checks and mailed to Jack's accounts at three Swiss banks. Only a hundred twenty-five thousand remained, his emergency getaway fund.

He transferred most of the cash to a briefcase: nine banded packets of hundred-dollar bills, a hundred bills in each, and five packets of twenty-dollar bills, a hundred in each. That left twenty-five thousand still in his cache, which seemed more than enough now that he was no longer involved in criminal activity and would not be putting himself in situations that might necessitate a swift exit from the state or country.

Although Jack intended to dispose of a considerable portion of his ill-gotten wealth, he certainly did not plan to give away all of it and leave himself penniless. That might be good for his soul, but it would be bad for his future and undeniably foolish. However, he had eleven safe-deposit boxes in eleven of the city's banks— additional emergency caches in case he needed to escape but could not reach the money behind the false partition in his bedroom closet—and those caches contained more than another quarter of a million. His Swiss accounts were worth in excess of four million. It was far more than he needed. He was looking forward to shedding half of that fortune during the next couple of weeks, at which point he would pause to decide what he wanted to do with his future. Eventually, he might give away even more.

At three-thirty Sunday afternoon, he carried his money-filled briefcase out into the city. All the strangers' faces, which for eight years had seemed fiercely hostile, every one, now seemed like animated portraits of promise and dazzling possibilities, every one.

The Block kitchen smelled of coffee and hot chocolate, then of cinnamon and pastry dough when Faye took a package of breakfast rolls from the freezer and popped them in the oven.

While the others sat at the table, listening, Dom continued to call the people who had registered at the motel on that special Friday night.

He reached Jim Gestron, who turned out to be a photographer from L.A. Gestron had driven throughout the West that summer, shooting on assignment for *Sunset* and other magazines. Initially, he was friendly, but as he heard more of Dom's story, he cooled off. If Gestron had been brainwashed, the mind-control experts had been as successful with him as with Faye Block. The photographer was having no dreams, no problems. Dom's tale of brainwashing, somnambulism, nyctophobia, obsessions with the moon, suicides, and paranormal experiences struck Gestron as the babbling of a seriously disturbed person. He said as much and hung up in the middle of the conversation.

Next, Dom called Harriet Bellot in Sacramento, who was no more troubled than Gestron. She was, she said, a fifty-year-old unmarried schoolteacher who had developed an interest in the Old West when, as a young WAC, she was stationed in Arizona. Every summer, she traveled old wagon-train routes and visited the sites of the forts and Indian settlements of another age, usually sleeping in her little camper but sometimes splurging on a motel room. She sounded like one of those likable, dedicated, but stern teachers who brooked no nonsense from her pupils, and she brooked none from Dom. When he started talking about fanciful stuff like poltergeist phenomena, she hung up, too.

"Does that make you feel better, Faye?" Ernie asked. "You're not the only one whose memories were so thoroughly scrubbed away."

"Doesn't make me feel one damn bit better," Faye said. "I'd rather be suffering problems like you or Dom than feel nothing. I feel as if a piece of me was cut out and thrown away."

Perhaps she's right, Dom thought. Perhaps nightmares, phobias, and terrors of one kind or another *are* better than having a little pocket of absolute emptiness inside, cold and dark, which would be like carrying a fragment of death around within her for the rest of her life.

When Dominick Corvaisis telephoned St. Bernadette's rectory at 4:26 Sunday afternoon, seeking Brendan Cronin, Father Wycazik was in the study with officers of the Knights of Columbus, concluding the first of many planning sessions for the annual St. Bernadette's Spring Carnival.

At four-thirty, Father Michael Gerrano interrupted with the news that the call he had just taken on the kitchen phone was from Father Wycazik's "cousin" in Elko, Nevada. Only a few hours ago, one day ahead of schedule, Brendan Cronin had boarded a United flight to Reno, taking advantage of cancellations that had opened up some seats, and intending to use a small commuter airline from Reno to Elko on Monday. At the moment, Brendan was still in the air with United, not yet even as far as Reno and in no position to be calling anyone, so Michael's message intrigued Father Wycazik and instantly pried him loose of the planning session without alerting the visitors that something extraordinary was happening in the lives of their parish clergy.

Leaving the young priest to conclude matters with the Knights, the rector hurried to the kitchen phone and took the call meant for Brendan. Dominick Corvaisis, with a writer's appreciation for the fantastic, and Stefan, with a priest's appreciation for mystery and mysticism, became increasingly excited and voluble as they spoke to each other. Stefan swapped his knowledge of Brendan's problems and adventures—lost faith, miraculous cures, strange dreams—for Corvaisis' stories of poltergeist phenomena, somnambulism, nyctophobia, lunar obsessions, and suicides.

Finally, Stefan could not resist asking, "Mr. Corvaisis, do you see any reason for an old unregenerate religious like me to hold out the hope that what is happening to Brendan is somehow divine in nature?"

"Quite frankly, Father, in spite of the miraculous cures of that police officer and the little girl you mentioned, I don't see the hand of God in this. There are too many indications of human connivery in this to support the interpretation you'd like to put on it."

Stefan sighed. "I suppose that's true. But I'll still cling to the hope that what Brendan's being called to witness there in Nevada is something meant to bring him back into the hands of Christ. I won't give up on the possibility."

The writer laughed softly. "Father, just from what I've learned of you during this conversation, I suspect you'd *never* give up on the possibility of redeeming any soul, anywhere, any time. I'd guess you don't save souls quite the way other priests do—by finesse, by gentle and genteel encouragement. You strike me more as . . . well, as a blacksmith of the soul, hammering out the salvation of others by the sweat of your brow and the application of plenty of muscle. Please understand: I mean this as a compliment."

Stefan laughed, too. "How else could I possibly take it? I firmly believe that nothing easy is worth doing. A blacksmith bent over a glowing forge? Yes, I do rather like the image."

"I'll look forward to Father Cronin's arrival here tomorrow. If he's anything like you, Father, we'll be glad to have him on our side."

"I'm on your side as well," Father Wycazik said, "and if there's anything I can do to help with your investigation, please call on me. If there's the slightest chance these strange events involve the manifest presence of God, then I do not intend to sit on the sidelines and miss all the action."

The next entry on the guest list was for Bruce and Janet Cable of Philadelphia. Neither of them was having trouble of the sort that plagued Dom, Ernie, and the others. However, they were more willing to hear Dom out than Jim Gestron and Harriet Bellot had been, but in the end they were no more swayed by his story.

The final name on the list was Thornton Wainwright, who had given a New York City address and telephone number. When Dom dialed it, he reached a Mrs. Neil Karpoly, who said the number had been hers for more than fourteen years and that she had never heard of Wainwright. When Dom read the Lexington Avenue address from the registry and inquired if that was where Mrs. Karpoly lived, she asked him to repeat it, then laughed. "No, sir, that's not where I live. And your Mr. Wainwright's not a trustworthy sort if he told you that's *his* address. Nobody lives there, although I'm sure there are thousands who might enjoy it. I know I enjoyed working there. That's the address of Bloomingdale's.''

Sandy was astonished when Dom reported this news: ''Phony name and address? What's that mean? Was he really a guest that night? Or did someone add the name to the registry just to confuse us? Or . . . what?''

Jack Twist possessed complete sets of sophisticated false IDs—driver's licenses, birth certificates, Social Security cards, credit cards, passports, even library cards—in eight names, including ''Thornton Bains Wainwright,'' and he always employed an alias when planning and executing a heist. But he worked anonymously that Sunday afternoon, portioning out another hundred thousand dollars to startled recipients all over Manhattan. The largest gift was fifteen thousand to a young sailor and his bride of one day, whose battered old Plymouth had broken down on Central Park South, near the statue of Simón Bolívar. ''Get a new car,'' Jack told them as he stuffed money into their hands and playfully stuck a wad of bills under the sailor's hat. ''And if you're wise, you won't tell anyone about this, especially not the newspapers. That'll just bring the IRS down on you. No, you don't need to know my name, and there's no need to thank me. Just be kind to each other, all right? Always be kind to each other, because we never know how much time we have on this world.''

In less than an hour, Jack gave away the entire hundred thousand that he had taken from the secret compartment in the back of his bedroom closet. With plenty of time on his hands, he bought a bouquet of coral-red roses and drove out to Westchester County, an hour from the city, to the memorial park in which Jenny had been buried over two weeks ago.

Jack had not wanted to put her to rest in one of the city's crowded and grim cemeteries. Although he knew he was being sentimental, he felt that the only suitable resting place for his Jenny was in open country, where there would be expansive green grassy slopes and shade trees in the summer and peaceful vistas of snow in the winter.

He arrived at the memorial park shortly before twilight. Although the uniform headstones were set flush with the earth, with no features to distinguish one from another, and although most of them were covered with snow, Jack went directly to Jenny's plot, the location of which was branded on his heart.

While the dreary day faded into a drearier dusk, in a world colorless except for the blazing roses, Jack sat in the snow, oblivious of the dampness and cold, and spoke to Jenny as he had spoken to her during her years in a coma. He told her about the Guardmaster heist yesterday, about giving away all the money. As the curtain of twilight pulled down the heavier drape of night, the memorial park's security guard began driving slowly around the grounds, warning the few late visitors that the gates would soon close. Finally Jack stood and took one last look at Jenny's name cast in bronze letters on the headstone plaque, now illuminated by the vaguely bluish light of one of the streetlamps that lined the park's main drive. ''I'm changing, Jenny, and I'm still not sure why. It feels good, right . . . but also sort of strange.'' What he said next surprised him: ''Something big is going to happen, Jenny. I don't know what, but something big is going to happen to me.'' He suddenly sensed that his newfound guilt and subsequent peace with society were only the beginning steps of a great journey that would take him places he could not yet imagine. ''Something big is going to happen,'' he repeated, ''and I sure wish you were here with me, Jenny.''

* * *

The blue Nevada sky had been armoring itself with dark storm clouds ever since Ernie, Ned, and Dom had begun boarding up the diner's broken windows. Hours later, when Dom drove his rental car to the Elko airport to pick up Ginger Weiss, the world turned under a gloomy light, girdled in battlefield gray. He was too restless to wait inside the small terminal. He stood on the windswept tarmac, huddled in his heavy winter jacket, so he heard the twin engines of the ten-seat commuter craft even before he saw it descend through the low clouds. The roar of the engines contributed to the mood of impending warfare, and Dom realized uneasily that, in a sense, they were assembling their army; war against their unknown enemy loomed nearer day by day.

The plane taxied within eighty feet of the terminal, and Dr. Weiss was the fourth passenger to disembark. Even in a bulky, thoroughly unattractive carcoat, she looked petite and beautiful. The wind made a streaming banner of her silky silver-blond hair.

Dom hurried toward her; she stopped and put down her bags. They hesitated, staring at each other in silence, with a peculiar mixture of amazement, excitement, pleasure, and apprehension. Then with an impulsiveness that obviously surprised her as much as it did him, they virtually threw themselves at each other, embracing as if they were old and dear friends too long apart. Dom held her close, and she held him tightly, and he felt her heart pounding as hard and as fast as his.

What the hell is happening here? he wondered.

But he was in too much turmoil to analyze the situation. For the moment, he could *feel* but not think.

Neither of them wanted to let go, and when they finally separated, neither could speak. She tried to say something, but her voice cracked with emotion, and Dom was incoherent. So she picked up one of her bags, and he picked up the other, and they went out to the parking lot.

In the car, with the engine running and the heater blowing warm air in their faces, Ginger said, "What was *that* all about?"

Still shaken, but curiously not embarrassed by the bold greeting he had given her, Dom cleared his throat. "Don't really know. But I think maybe, together, you and I went through something so shattering that the experience created a special bond between us, a powerful bond we weren't entirely aware of until we saw each other in the flesh."

"When I first came across your picture on the book jacket, it had a very odd effect on me, but nothing like this. Stepping off the plane, seeing you there . . . it was as if we'd known each other all our lives. No, not exactly that. More precisely . . . it was as if we'd known each other far better, more completely, than we'd ever known anyone else, as if we shared some tremendous secret that all the world might want to know but that only we possessed. Does that sound crazy?"

He shook his head. "No. Not at all. You've put into words what I was feeling . . . as nearly as words can explain it."

"You've met some of the others," Ginger said. "Was it like this when you first encountered them?"

"No. I instantly felt . . . a certain warmth toward them, a strong sense of community, but nothing a fraction as powerful as what I felt when you got off that plane. All of us went through something unusual that linked our lives, our futures, but evidently you and I shared an experience even stranger and more affecting than anything we shared with them. Damn. It's as layered as an onion, one strangeness on another.''

For half an hour they sat in the car, in the airport parking lot, talking. Outside, cars and pickups came and went around them, and the January wind buffeted the Chevy and moaned at the windows; however, they were seldom aware of anything but each other.

She told him about her fugues, the hypnotic regression sessions with Pablo Jackson, and the mind-control technique known as the Azrael Block. She told him about Pablo's murder and her own narrow escape.

Although, clearly, Ginger sought neither sympathy for her suffering nor praise for the way she had handled herself in trying circumstances, Dom's respect and admiration for her grew by the minute. She was only five-two, a hundred pounds, but somehow she had a physical presence more imposing than many men twice her size.

Dom recounted the events of the past twenty-four hours, and when Ginger heard about his dream of the previous night and about the new memories that surfaced in it, she appeared immensely relieved. In Dom's dream, there was proof of Pablo Jackson's theory: Her fugues were not caused by mental aberration; they were, instead, always triggered by objects associated with her imprisonment at the motel two summers ago. The black gloves and dark-visored helmet had terrified her because they made a direct connection with the repressed memories of the people in decontamination suits who tended her while she underwent brainwashing. The drain in the hospital scrub sink threw the panic switch because she probably had been one of those ''detainees'' poisoned by Colonel Falkirk (whoever the hell he was), then forced to vomit up the deadly substance, just as Dom had been. While strapped in the motel bed, she must have undergone many eye examinations to determine the depth of her drug-induced trance, which was why an ophthalmoscope had sent her reeling away in a dark terror that night in George Hannaby's office. Dom saw a relaxation of the tension at this irrefutable evidence that her blackouts were not a sign of madness and were, in fact, a desperate but entirely rational method of avoiding the repressed memories that the mind-control experts had forbidden her to recall.

She said, ''But what about the brass buttons on the coat of the man who killed Pablo? And on the policeman's uniform? Why did they terrify me and throw me into a fugue?''

''We know the military is involved in this cover-up,'' Dom said, turning up the heater to counteract the cold air pouring off the car's wind-buffeted windows, ''and officers' uniforms have brass buttons like that, though not a lion passant. Most likely . . . raised images of eagles. The buttons on the killer's and cop's coats were probably similar to the buttons on the uniforms of those who imprisoned us in the motel.''

''Okay, but you said they wore decontamination suits, not uniforms.''

''Maybe they didn't wear the decon suits for the entire three and a half days. At some point they decided it was safe to take them off.''

She nodded. ''I'm sure that's right. Which leaves only one thing. Those carriage lamps behind the house on Newbury Street, the day Pablo was murdered. I told you about them: black iron with pebbled amber panes of glass. They had those bulbs that flickered like a gas flame. Perfectly innocent lamps. But they kicked me into another blackout.''

''The bases of the lamps in the rooms at the Tranquility Motel are designed like hurricane lamps, with little windows of amber glass.''

"I'll be damned. So every blackout was triggered by an object that reminded me of something from those days when I was being brainwashed."

Dom hesitated, then reached inside his sweater and withdrew the Polaroid photograph from his shirt pocket and handed it to her.

She paled and shuddered when she saw herself staring up with vacant eyes at the camera. *"Gevalt!"* She looked away from the picture.

Dom gave her time to recover from the shock of the snapshot.

Outside, in the fading dirty-gray light, a score of vehicles waited silently like dark, dumb, brooding beasts. The wind harried collections of litter, dead leaves, and miscellaneous debris across the macadam.

"It's *meshugge,*" she said, lowering her troubled gaze to the photo again. "It's crazy. What could possibly have happened to us that would justify this elaborate, risky conspiracy? What could we have seen that was so dreadfully goddamned important?"

"We'll find out," he promised.

"Will we? Will they let us? They killed Pablo. Won't they do whatever's necessary to keep us from uncovering the truth?"

Adjusting the heater again, Dom said, "Well, I figure there're two factions among the conspirators. There are the hard-asses represented by Colonel Falkirk and his people, and the better guys—can't call them *good* guys exactly—represented by the fella who sent us these snapshots and by the two men in decontamination suits in my dream last night. The hard-asses wanted to kill all of us right at the start, so there'd never be any doubt that the cover-up would be permanent. But the better guys wanted to scrub our memories, use mind-control techniques instead of violence, so we could go on living, and the better guys must be the stronger of the two factions because they got their way."

"The gunman who killed Pablo was most likely one of the hard-asses."

"Yeah. Working for Falkirk. The colonel's evidently *still* willing to kill anyone who jeopardizes the cover-up, which means none of us is safe. But there's the other faction that doesn't believe in Falkirk's ultimate solution, and they're still trying to protect us, I think. So we have a chance. Anyway, we can't walk away. We can't go home and try to get on with our lives just because the enemy looks formidable."

"No," Ginger agreed, "we can't. Because until we find out what happened, we don't really *have* lives to get on with." The wind blew withered leaves against the windshield, over the roof. Ginger swept the parking lot with her gaze. "They must know we're gathering at the motel, that things are falling apart. Do you think they're watching us now?"

"Very likely they've got the motel under surveillance," Dom said. "But no one followed me to the airport. I watched for a tail."

"They wouldn't need to tail you here," she said grimly. "They knew where you were going. They knew who you were picking up."

"Are we laboring under a delusion of free will? Are we only bugs on a giant's palm, and can the giant crush us whenever he wants?"

"Maybe," Ginger Weiss said. "But by God, we can at least give him a couple of nasty bites before he smashes us."

She spoke with a fierce determination that was convincing but also amusing in the context of a metaphor as basically comic as a giant and a bunch of bugs. Though he was pleased by her fierce resolution in the face of such overwhelmingly poor odds, Dom could not help laughing.

Blinking at him in surprise, she laughed too. "Hey, am I spunky, or what?

Might be smashed by a giant, but I feel triumphant 'cause I'll be able to bite him just before he reduces me to a bloody smear.''

"Spunky should be your middle name," Dom agreed, laughing harder.

As he watched Ginger laughing at her own expense, Dom was again stricken by her beauty. His response to her, on seeing her disembark from the plane, had been instant and powerful because of unremembered experiences they shared. But even if they had been complete strangers whose lives had never crossed, he would have felt something more at the sight of her than he felt when he saw other beautiful women. Under any circumstances, she would have turned his head. She was special.

He drew a deep breath. "Shall I take you to meet the others?"

"Oh, yes," she said, dabbing her slender fingers at the corners of her eyes to wipe away tears that her graveyard laughter had occasioned. "Yes, I'm eager to meet them. The other bugs on the giant's hand."

Less than half an hour before nightfall, the shadows on the high plains were long, and the muddy gray light of the overcast dusk lent an air of mystery even to such ordinary objects as clumps of sagebrush, rock formations, and twisted mounds of dead brown bunch-grass.

Before taking her to the motel, Dom Corvaisis had brought Ginger to what he called "the special place," more than two hundred yards south of Interstate 80. The wind rustled half-seen vegetation. The ice on the grass and sagebrush, when glimpsed at all, looked black, shiny black.

The writer stood away from her, hands jammed in his jacket pockets, silent. He had told her that he did not want to influence her reaction to the place or color her first feelings with a description of his own.

Ginger wandered slowly back and forth, feeling slightly foolish, as if taking part in a half-baked experiment in psychic perception, seeking clairvoyant vibrations. But she quickly stopped feeling foolish when the vibrations actually began to shake her. A queer uneasiness arose, and she found herself staying away from the deeper pockets of shadows, as if something hostile lurked in them. Her heart pounded. Uneasiness became fear, and she heard the tempo of her breathing change.

"It's inside me. It's inside me."

She whirled toward that voice. It was Dom's voice, but it had not come from him. The words had been spoken behind her. But no one was there: only dry sagebrush and a thin patch of snow glowing softly, luminously within a nest of shadows.

"What's the matter?" Dom asked, moving toward her.

She was wrong. Dom's other voice, the ghostly-sounding voice, had not come from behind her. It had come from within her. She heard that other Dom again, and she realized she was hearing a fragment of memory, an echo from the past, something he had said to her that Friday night, July 6, perhaps when they had both stood in this same place. The scrap of memory came with no visual or olfactory element because it was part of the events locked behind the Azrael Block. There were just those three urgent words repeated twice: *"It's inside me. It's inside me."*

Abruptly, her simmering fear flashed bright. The landscape around her seemed to embody a nameless but monstrous threat. She started back toward the highway, walking fast, and Dom asked what was wrong, and she walked even faster, unable to answer because fear was like a paste in her mouth and throat. He called her name, and she began to run. Every object in sight seemed to have been wounded on its eastern flank, for black blood-shadows spilled in that direction.

She was not able to speak until they were back in the Chevy, with the doors locked, the engine running, and the heater blowing warm air on her chilled face. Shakily, she told him about the nameless threat she had felt on that ordinary-looking piece of ground, and about the memory of his urgent voice and the three-word sentence.

" 'It's inside me,' " he said thoughtfully. "You're sure it's really something I said to you that night?"

"Yes." She shivered.

"It's inside me. What in the world did I mean by that?"

"I don't know," Ginger said. "But it gives me the creeps."

He was silent a moment. Then he said, "Yeah. Me, too."

That evening, at the motel, Ginger Weiss felt almost as if she was with her family on a holiday gathering like Thanksgiving. In spite of the difficulties in which they found themselves, their spirits were high; for in the manner of a real family, they drew strength from one another. The six of them crowded into the kitchen and prepared dinner together, and through that domestic labor, Ginger got to know the others better and felt a strengthening of the ties that bound her to them.

Ned Sarver, being a professional cook, prepared the main dish—chicken breasts baked in a spicy green tomatillo sauce with sour cream. Initially, Ginger mistakenly thought Ned was a brooding, unfriendly sort, but she soon changed her opinion. Taciturnity sometimes could be a sign of a healthy ego that did not require constant gratification, which was the case with Ned. Besides, Ginger could not help but like a man who loved his wife as deeply as Ned loved Sandy, a love apparent in every word he spoke to her, in every glance he cast her way.

Sandy, the only one of them to be affected *only* positively by their mysterious ordeal, was so sweet-tempered, so delighted with the recent changes in herself, that she was especially good company. Together, she and Ginger prepared the dinner salad and vegetables, and as they worked, an almost sisterly affection developed between them.

Faye Block made the dessert, a refrigerator pie with a chocolate crust and banana-cream filling. Ginger liked Faye, who reminded her of Rita Hannaby. That cultured society woman was different from Faye in many ways, but in fundamental respects they were alike: efficient, take-charge types, tough of mind, tender of spirit.

Ernie Block and Dom Corvaisis put the extra leaf in the table and arranged six place settings. Ernie had seemed gruff and intimidating at first, but now she saw he was a sweetheart. He inspired much affection because of his fear of darkness, which made him seem boyish in spite of his size and age.

Of the five people among whom Ginger found herself, only Dominick Corvaisis stirred emotions that she could not understand. For him, she felt the same friendship that she felt for the others, and she was aware of a special bond between them related to an unremembered experience just the two of them had shared. But she was also sexually attracted to him. That surprised her because she never felt desire for a man until she knew him for several weeks, at least, and knew him well. Wary of her romantic yearnings, Ginger kept a tight rein on her emotions, and she tried hard to convince herself that Dom did not feel a similar attraction for her, which he so patently did.

Through dinner, the six of them continued to discuss their strange predicament and search for clues that might have been overlooked.

Like Dom, Ginger had no recollection of the toxic spill two years ago, though the Blocks and Sarvers recalled it clearly. I-80 had really been closed, and an environmental emergency had been declared; there was no doubt about that much. Last night, however, Dom convinced the Blocks that their memories of evacuating to Elroy and Nancy Jamison's mountain ranch were phony and that both they *and* the Jamisons had almost surely been kept at the motel. (According to Faye and Ernie, the Jamisons had not mentioned having any nightmares or odd problems lately, so their brainwashing must have been effective, though it would be necesary to talk to them soon.) Likewise, Ned and Sandy had reluctantly concluded that their own recollections of sitting out the crisis at their trailer were too shallow to be real and that they had been strapped into motel beds, drugged, and brainwashed like everyone else in those Polaroids.

"But," Faye wondered, "why wouldn't they give us all approximately the same false memories?"

Ginger said, "Maybe all you locals have had the toxic spill and the highway closure woven into your false memories. That'd be necessary because, later, people would be asking you where you went during the emergency, and you'd have to know what they were talking about. But Dom and I are from distant places, unlikely ever to return, unlikely to run into anyone who would know that we'd been within the quarantine zone, so they didn't bother including that bit of reality in the set of fake memories they gave us."

Sandy paused with a morsel of chicken on her fork. "But wouldn't it be safer and easier to make your memories fit the toxic spill, too?"

"Ever since Pablo Jackson helped me discover that my mind had been tampered with," Ginger said, "I've been reading about brainwashing, and I think maybe it's a lot less difficult to implant recollections that are *entirely* false than it is to weave in threads of reality such as the environmental emergency and the road closure. It probably takes a lot longer to construct fake memories that have some reality to them, and maybe they simply didn't have time to do that with all of us. So they gave the super-deluxe brainwashing job only to you locals."

"That feels like the truth," Ernie said, and everyone agreed.

Faye said, "But did the toxic spill really happen, or was it just a cover story that gave them an excuse to close I-80 and bottle us up, a way of preventing us from talking about what we'd seen Friday night?"

"I suspect there *was* contamination of some sort," Ginger said. "In Dom's nightmare, which we know is really more memory than dream, those men were wearing decontamination suits. Now, when they came into the quarantine zone, maybe they'd wear costumes like that for the benefit of newsmen or other onlookers. But once here, where only we could see them, they wouldn't keep the suits on unless they absolutely had to."

Glancing uneasily at the blind-covered window nearest the table, as if he thought he had seen a trickle of darkness dribbling in from the night beyond, Ernie cleared his throat and said, "Yeah, uh . . . well, which was it, do you think? You're the doctor. Does it sound like chemical or biological contamination? The story they gave the media was that it involved chemicals being delivered to Shenkfield's testing facilities."

Ginger had been thinking about this question for some time, long before Ernie asked it. Chemical or biological contamination? She had arrived at an answer that deeply disturbed her. "Generally speaking, the suits required for a chemical spill don't have to be air-tight. They just have to cover the worker from head to toe in order to prevent any caustic or toxic substance from coming into contact with his skin, and they have to include a respirator, rather like a scuba diver's tank and mask, so he won't breathe deadly fumes. They're usually made of lightweight nonporous cloth, and the headgear consists of a simple cloth hood with a plastic visor. But Dom described heavy-looking suits with an outer level of thick vinyl, with gloves that were of one piece with the sleeves, and a hard helmet that locked into an airtight seal at the collar. That is unquestionably gear that's been designed to prevent exposure to a dangerous *biological* agent, microbes."

For a while no one said a word, pondering this disquieting news.

Then Ned took a long swallow of his Heineken for fortification and said, "So we must've been infected with something."

Faye said, "Some virus they developed for biological warfare."

"If it was headed for Shenkfield, that's the only kind of bug it could've been," Ernie said. "Something mean."

"Yet we lived," Sandy said.

"Because they were immediately able to quarantine us and treat us," Ginger said. "Surely they wouldn't be intending to test a genetically engineered virus, some new and deadly organism that could be used as a weapon, unless they had simultaneously developed an effective cure for it. So they had a supply of a new antibiotic or serum to guard against just such an accident. If they contaminated us, they also cured us."

Ernie said, "It sounds right, doesn't it? Maybe it's all starting to fall together, piece by piece."

Dom disagreed. "It still doesn't explain what happened on that Friday night, what we saw that they didn't want us to see. It doesn't explain what made the whole damned diner shake or what blew out the windows—either on that first night or again last night."

"And it doesn't explain the other weird stuff," Faye said. "Like all those paper moons whirling around Dom in Lomack's house. Or Father Wycazik's claim that this young priest's been performing miracle cures."

They looked at one another, waiting in silence for someone to put forth an explanation that would tie biological contamination with those paranormal events, but no one had an answer.

Less than three hundred miles west of the Tranquility Motel, in another motel in Reno, Brendan Cronin had gone to bed and turned out the lights. Although it was only a few minutes after nine o'clock, he was still functioning on Chicago time, so for him it was after eleven.

However, sleep eluded him. After checking into the motel and having dinner at a nearby Bob's Big Boy, he had telephoned St. Bette's rectory and had spoken with Father Wycazik, who had told him of the call from Dominick Corvaisis. Brendan was electrified by the news that he was not the only one caught up in this mystery. He considered calling the Tranquility, but they already knew he was on his way, and whatever they could say on the phone could be said better in person, tomorrow. Thoughts of tomorrow and speculations about what might happen were what kept sleep at bay.

He had lain awake less than an hour and his thoughts had drifted to the eerie luminescence that had filled his rectory bedroom two nights ago, when suddenly that phenomenon appeared once more. This time, there was no visible source of light, not even one so unlikely as the frost-moon upon the window from which the uncanny radiance had sprung last Friday night. Now, the glow appeared above him and on all sides, as if the very molecules of the air had acquired the ability to produce light. It was a lunar-pale, milky shimmer at first, growing brighter by the second, until it seemed as if he must be lying in an open field, under the looming countenance of a full moon.

This was different from the peaceful golden light that was featured in his recurring dream, and as it had done two nights ago, it filled him with conflicting emotions—horror and rapture, fear and wild excitement.

As in his rectory bedroom, the lactescent light changed color, darkening to scarlet. He seemed suspended in a radiant bubble of blood.

It's inside me, he thought, wondering what that meant. *Inside me.* The thought reverberated in his mind. Suddenly he was cold with fear.

His thundering heart seemed about to explode. He lay rigid. In his hands, the rings appeared. Throbbing.

2. Monday, January 13

When they gathered in Ernie and Faye's kitchen for breakfast the next morning, Dom was excited to learn that the previous night had been an ordeal for most of them. "It's unraveling the way I hoped it might," he said. "By gathering together here, by re-creating the group that was gathered here *that* night, and by working together to get at the truth, we're putting constant pressure on the memory blocks that've been implanted in us. And now, that barrier is crumbling a bit faster."

Last night, Dom, Ginger, Ernie, and Ned experienced exceptionally vivid nightmares of such similarity that they were surely fragments of forbidden memories. In every case they had involved being strapped to motel beds and tended by men in decontamination suits. Sandy had a pleasant dream, although it lacked the clarity and detail of the others' nightmares. Faye was the only one who did not dream at all.

Ned had been so disturbed by his nightmare that on Monday morning, when he and Sandy arrived from Beowawe for breakfast, he announced they were moving into a room at the motel for the duration. "During the night, after the dream woke me, I couldn't get back to sleep. And while I was laying there, I got to thinking how lonely it is at our trailer, empty plains all around. . . . Maybe this Colonel Falkirk will decide to kill us like he wanted to do in the first place. And if he comes for us, I don't want me and Sandy to be alone out there at the trailer."

Dom sympathized with Ned because these dark and vivid dreams were new to the cook. Over recent weeks, Dom, Ginger, and Ernie had learned a little about coping with the frighteningly powerful nightmares, but Ned had developed no armor, so he was badly shaken.

And, of course, Ned was well advised to fear Falkirk. The closer they came to exposing the conspiracy and learning the truth, the more likely they were to become targets of a preemptive strike. Dom did not think Falkirk would make a move until Brendan Cronin, Jorja Monatella, and perhaps other victims had gathered at the Tranquility. But once they were in one place, they would need to be prepared for trouble.

Now, in the Blocks' kitchen, Ned Sarver picked at his breakfast without appetite as he spoke of the images that had disturbed his sleep. At first he had dreamed of being held prisoner by men in decontamination suits, but later they had worn either lab coats or military uniforms, an indication that the biological danger had passed. One of the uniformed men had been Colonel Falkirk, and Ned described that officer in detail: about fifty years old, black hair graying at the temples, gray eyes like circles of polished steel, a beakish nose, thin lips.

Ernie was able to confirm the word-portrait that Ned painted, for Falkirk had also been in his nightmare. The amazing coincidence of the same man appearing in both Ned's and Ernie's dreams made it clear that his face was not merely a figment of imagination but a memory of a real face that both Ernie and Ned had seen two summers ago.

"And in my nightmare," Ernie said, "another Army officer referred to Falkirk by his first name. Leland. Colonel Leland Falkirk."

"He's probably stationed at Shenkfield," Ginger said.

"We'll try to find out later," Dom said.

The barriers to memory were definitely crumbling. That prospect boosted Dom's spirits higher than they had been in months.

In Ginger's nightmare, which she recounted for them, she had not been the only person being brainwashed in Room 5, the room she had occupied that summer and which she now occupied again. "There was a rollaway bed in one corner, and the redhead in it was someone I'd never seen before. She was about forty years old. They had her connected to her own IV drip and EKG machine. She had that . . . vacant stare."

Just as Ernie and Ned had shared a new development—the appearance of Colonel Falkirk—in their nightmares, Dom and Ginger had shared this other discovery. In Dom's dream, there had been a rollaway bed, flanked by an IV stand and an EKG monitor, and in the bed had been a young man in his twenties with a pale face, bushy mustache, and zombie eyes.

"What does it mean?" Faye Block asked. "Did they have so many subjects for brainwashing that they more than filled all twenty rooms?"

"But," Sandy said, "the registry showed only eleven rooms rented."

Ginger said, "There must've been people on the interstate, in transit, who saw what we saw. The Army managed to stop them and bring them here. None of their names would appear on the registry."

"How many?" Faye wondered.

"We'll probably never know for sure," Dom said. "We never actually met them; we only shared rooms with them while we were drugged. We might eventually remember the faces of those we saw, but we can't possibly remember names and addresses we never knew in the first place."

But at least those reprogrammed memories, those tissues of lies, were dissolving, allowing the truth to show through. Dom was grateful for that much. In time, they would uncover the entire story—if Colonel Falkirk did not first come after them with heavy artillery.

Monday morning, while the group at the Tranquility ate breakfast, Jack Twist was being escorted to a safe-deposit box in a vault of a Fifth Avenue branch of Citibank, in New York. The attending bank employee, an attractive young woman, kept calling him "Mr. Farnham," for that was the false identity under which he had acquired the box.

After they used their separate keys to remove the box from the wall of the vault, when he was alone with it in a cubicle, he opened the lid and stared in shock at the contents. The rectangular metal container held something that he had not put there, which was an impossibility since only he knew about the box and possessed the only master key.

It should have contained five white envelopes, each filled with five thousand dollars in hundred-dollar and twenty-dollar bills, and indeed that money appeared to be untouched. This was one of eleven emergency caches he kept in safe-deposit boxes all over the city. He had set out this morning to remove fifteen thousand dollars from each, a total of $165,000, which he intended to give away. He opened each of the five envelopes and counted the contents with trembling hands. Not a single bill was missing.

Jack was not even slightly relieved. Though his money was still there, the presence of the other object proved that his false identity had been penetrated, his privacy violated, and his freedom jeopardized. Someone knew who "Gregory Farnham" really was, and the item that had been left in the box was a bold notification that his elaborately constructed cover had been penetrated.

It was a postcard. There was no writing on the back, no message; the presence of the card itself was message enough. On the front was a photograph of the Tranquility Motel.

The summer before last, after he and Branch Pollard and a third man had burglarized the Avril McAllister estate in Marin County, north of San Francisco, and after Jack paid a profitable visit to Reno, he rented a car and drove east, stopping the first night at the Tranquility Motel along Interstate 80. He had not thought about the place since, but he recognized it the instant he saw the photograph.

Who could possibly know he had stayed at that motel? Not Branch Pollard. He'd never told Branch about Reno or about his decision to drive back to New York. And not the third man on the McAllister job, a guy named Sal Finrow from Los Angeles; Jack had never seen him again after they had split the take from that sour job.

Then Jack realized that at least *three* of his phony IDs had been penetrated. He rented this safe-deposit box as "Farnham" but he stayed at the Tranquility Motel as "Thornton Wainwright." Both *noms de guerre* were now blown, and the only way anyone could have linked them was by connecting Jack with his "Phillipe Delon" identity, under which he resided at his Fifth Avenue apartment, so that name was blown as well.

Jesus.

He sat in the bank cubicle, stunned but thinking furiously, trying to decide who his enemy might be. It could not be the police or the FBI or any other legitimate authority, for they would simply have arrested him once they had accumulated this much evidence; they would not play games. Nor could it be any of the men with whom he ever worked on a heist, for he took great care to keep his acquaintances in the criminal underworld well out of his life on Fifth Avenue. None of them knew where he really lived; in the event they scouted a job requiring his planning skills and special knowledge, they could reach him only through a series of mail drops or through a chain of pseudonymously listed phone numbers backed up by answering machines. He was confident of the effectiveness of those precautions. Besides, if some hoodlum had gotten into this box, he would not have left the twenty-five thousand bucks untouched; he would have taken every dollar of it.

So who's on to me? Jack wondered.

He focused on the *fratellanza* warehouse robbery that he and Mort and Tommy

Sung had pulled off December 3. Was the mafia after him? When they wanted to find someone, those boys had more contacts, sources, determination, and sheer perseverance than the FBI. And the *fratellanza* would most likely not have taken the twenty-five thousand, leaving it as an ominous notice that they wanted more than the money he had stolen from them. It was also in character for the *fratellanza* to leave a teaser like the postcard, because those guys enjoyed making a target sweat a lot before they finally pulled the trigger.

On the other hand, even if the mob tracked him down, then somehow searched back through his criminal career to see who else he had hit, they would not have gone to the trouble of acquiring cards from the Tranquility Motel just to put the fear of God in him. If they had wanted to leave an upsetting teaser in the safe-deposit box, they would have left a photo of the warehouse that he had robbed in New Jersey.

So it was not the mafia. Then who? Damn it, who?

The tiny cubicle began to seem even smaller than it was. Jack felt claustrophobic and vulnerable. As long as he was in the bank, there was nowhere to run, nowhere to hide. He stuffed the twenty-five thousand into his overcoat pockets, no longer intending to give away any of it; suddenly, it had become his escape money. He put the postcard in his wallet, closed the empty box, and rang the buzzer for the attendant.

Two minutes later, he was outside, drawing deep breaths of the freezing January air, studying the people on Fifth Avenue for one who might be tailing him. He saw no one suspicious.

For a moment he stood rocklike in the river of people that flowed around him. He wanted to get out of the city and the state as quickly as possible, flee to an unlikely destination, where they would not look for him. Whoever *they* were. Yet he was not entirely sure that flight was necessary. In Ranger training, he had been taught never to act until he understood why he was acting and until he knew what he hoped to achieve by his actions. Besides, fear of his faceless enemy was outweighed by curiosity; he needed to know who he was up against, how they had broken his various covers, and what they wanted from him.

Outside the Citibank Building, Jack hailed a cab and went to the corner of Wall Street and William Street, in the heart of the financial district, where he had six safe-deposit boxes in six banks. He went to five of them, from each of which he collected twenty-five thousand dollars and a postcard of the Tranquility Motel.

He decided to stop after the fifth, because his coat pockets were already bulging with $125,000, a sufficiently dangerous sum to be carrying, and because, by now, he knew beyond a doubt that his other six phony identities and clandestine safe-deposit boxes had been found out as well. He had enough money with which to travel, and he was not particularly worried about leaving the remaining $150,000 in the other six boxes. For one thing, Jack had four million in his Swiss accounts; and for another thing, the distributor of the postcards would already have taken the available money if that had been his intention.

By now, he'd had time to think about that motel out in Nevada, and he had begun to realize something was strange about the time that he had spent at the place. He had remained there for three days, relaxing, enjoying the quiet and the scenery. But now, for the first time, it seemed to him that he would have done no such thing. Not with so much cash in the trunk of his rental car. Not when he had already been away from New York (and Jenny) for two weeks. He would have driven straight home from Reno. Now that he was forced to contemplate it, the three-day stay at the Tranquility Motel did not make much sense.

Another taxi conveyed him to his Fifth Avenue apartment building, where he arrived shortly before eleven. He promptly telephoned Elite Flights, a company that chartered small jets, with whom he had dealt previously, and he was relieved to discover that, fortuitously, they had an unbooked Lear available for departure at his convenience.

He took the twenty-five thousand from the secret compartment in the back of his bedroom closet. With the funds he had removed from the safe-deposit boxes, he now had $150,000 in immediate operating capital, enough to deal with virtually any contingency that might arise.

He hurriedly packed three suitcases, distributing a few clothes in each, but leaving most of the space for other items. He stowed away two handguns: a Smith & Wesson Model 19 Combat Magnum, chambered for the .357 Magnum cartridge but also capable of firing .38 Special cartridges with considerably less kick; and a .32 Beretta Model 70, its stubby barrel grooved to accept a screw-on, pipe-type silencer, of which Jack included two. He also took an Uzi submachine gun, which he'd illegally modified for full automatic fire, plus plenty of ammunition.

Jack's newly acquired guilt had substantially transformed him during the past forty-eight hours, but it had not overwhelmed him to such an extent that he was incapable of dealing violently with those who might deal violently with him. His determination to be an honest and upstanding citizen did not interfere with his instinct for self-preservation. And considering his background, no one was better prepared to preserve himself than Jack Twist.

Besides, after eight years of alienation and loneliness, he had begun to rejoin society, had begun to hope for a normal life. He would not let anyone destroy what might be his last chance for happiness.

He also packed the portable SLICKS computer, which he had used to get through the armored transport's sophisticated electronic lock the night before last in Connecticut. In addition, he decided he might need a Police Lock Release Gun, a tool that could instantly open any type of pin-tumbler lock—mushroom, spool, or regular—without damaging the mechanism, and which was sold only to law-enforcement agencies. And a Star Tron MK 202A, a compact, hand-held "night vision" device that could also be rifle-mounted. And a few other things.

Although he distributed the heaviest weapons and equipment equally among the three large suitcases, none of the bags was light when he finally closed and locked them. Anyone who helped him with his luggage might wonder about the contents, but no one would ask embarrassing questions or raise an alarm. That was the advantage of leasing a Lear jet for the journey: He would not be required to pass through airport security, and no one would inspect his baggage.

From his apartment, he taxied to La Guardia.

The waiting Lear would take him to Salt Lake City, Utah, the nearest major airport to Elko, a shade closer than Reno International, and a lot closer if you considered the necessity of overflying to Reno and then doubling back in a conventional-engine commuter plane to Elko. Elite Flights had told him that Reno was anticipating a major snowstorm that might close them down later in the day, and the same was true of the two smaller fields in southern Idaho that were capable of handling Lear-size jets. But the weather forecast for Salt Lake City was good throughout the day. At Jack's request, Elite was already arranging the lease of a conventional-engine plane from a Utah company to carry him from Salt Lake to the little county airport in Elko. Although it was in the easternmost fourth of Nevada, Elko was still within the Pacific time zone, so he would benefit from a gain of three hours, though he did not think he would arrive in Elko much before nightfall.

That was all right. He'd need darkness for what he was planning.

To Jack, the taunting postcards, retrieved from his safe-deposit boxes, implied there were people in Nevada who had learned everything worth knowing about his criminal life. The cards seemed to be saying that he could reach those people through the Tranquility Motel or perhaps find them in residence there. The postcard was an invitation. Or a summons. Either way, he could ignore it only at his peril.

He did not know if he was being followed to La Guardia; he did not bother looking for a tail. If his apartment phone was tapped, they knew he was coming the moment he called Elite Flights. He wanted them to see him approaching openly, for then they might be off-guard when, on arrival in Elko, he suddenly shook loose of them and went underground.

Monday morning, after breakfast, Dom and Ginger went into Elko, to the offices of the *Sentinel,* the county's only newspaper. The biggest town in the county, Elko boasted a population of less than ten thousand, so its newspaper's offices were not housed in a gleaming glass highrise but in a humble one-story concrete-block building on a quiet street.

Like most papers, the *Sentinel* provided access to its back-issue files to anyone with legitimate research needs, though permission for the use of the files was granted judiciously.

In spite of the financial success of his first novel, Dom still had difficulty identifying himself as a writer. To his own ears, he sounded pretentious and phony, though he realized his uneasiness was a holdover from his days as an excessively self-effacing Milquetoast.

The receptionist, Brenda Hennerling, did not recognize his name, but when he mentioned the title of his novel that Random House had just shipped to the stores, she said, ''It's the book-club selection this month! You wrote it? Really?'' She had ordered it a month ago from the Literary Guild, and it had just arrived in the mail. She was (she said) an avid reader, two books a week, and it was truly a thrill to meet a genuine novelist. Her enthusiasm only added to Dom's embarrassment. He was of a mind with Robert Louis Stevenson, who had said, ''The important thing is the tale, the well-told tale, not he who tells it.''

The *Sentinel's* back-issue files were kept in a narrow, windowless chamber. There were two desks with typewriters, a microfilm reader, a file of microfilm spools, and six tall filing cabinets with oversize drawers containing those editions of the newspaper that had not yet been transferred to film. The exposed concrete-block walls were painted pale gray, and the acoustic-tile ceiling was gray, too, and the fluorescent lights shed a cold glare. Dom had the odd sensation that they were in a submarine, far beneath the surface of the sea.

After Brenda Hennerling explained the filing system to them and left them alone to do their work, Ginger said, ''I'm so caught up in our problems that I keep forgetting you're a famous author.''

''So do I,'' Dom said, reading the labels on the filing cabinets that held issues of past *Sentinels.* ''But of course, I'm not famous.''

''Soon will be. It's a shame: With all that's happening to us, you're getting no chance to savour the publication of your first novel.''

He shrugged. ''This isn't a picnic for any of us. You've had to put an entire medical career on hold.''

''Yes, but now I know I'll be able to go back to medicine once we've dug to the bottom of this,'' Ginger said, as if there was no doubt they would triumph over their enemies. By now, Dom knew that conviction and determination were as much a part of her as the blueness of her eyes. "But this is your *first* book."

Dom had not yet recovered from his embarrassment at being treated like a celebrity by the receptionist. Now Ginger's kind comments kept a blush on his cheeks. However, this was not the mark of embarrassment; it was an indication of the intense pleasure he took in being the object of her concern. No woman had ever affected him as this one did.

Together, they went through the file drawers and removed the pertinent back issues of the *Sentinel*. They would not need to use the microfilm reader, for the newspaper was running two years behind in the transferral to film. They withdrew a full week's editions, beginning with Saturday, July 7, of the summer before last, and took them to one of the desks, where they both pulled up chairs.

Although the unremembered event that they had witnessed, and the possible contamination, and the closure of I-80 had happened on Friday night, July 6, the Saturday paper carried no report of the toxic spill. The *Sentinel* was primarily a source of local and state news and, though it included some national and international material, was not interested in fast-breaking stories. Its halls would never ring with that dramatic cry, "Stop press!" There would be no last-minute recomposition of the front page. The pace of life in Elko County was rural, relaxed, sensible, and no one felt a burning need to be breathlessly up-to-the-minute on anything. The *Sentinel* was put to bed late in the evening, for distribution in the morning; therefore, since no Sunday edition was published, the story of the toxic spill and the closure of I-80 did not appear until the edition of Monday, July 9.

But Monday's and Tuesday's editions were emblazoned with urgent headlines: TOXIC SPILL CLOSES I-80, and ARMY ESTABLISHES QUARANTINE ZONE, and NERVE GAS LEAKING FROM DAMAGED TRUCK?, and ARMY SAYS EVERYONE EVACUATED FROM DANGER ZONE, and WHERE ARE EVACUEES?, and SHENKFIELD ARMY TESTING GROUNDS: WHAT REALLY GOES ON THERE?, and I-80 CLOSURE ENTERS FOURTH DAY, and CLEAN-UP ALMOST FINISHED; HIGHWAY OPEN BY NOON.

For both Dom and Ginger, it was eerie to read about these events that had transpired during days when they remembered nothing more than relaxing quietly at the Tranquility Motel. As Dom read about the crisis, he became convinced Ginger's theory was correct; it seemed obvious that the mind-control technicians would have needed an extra week or two in order to have incorporated this elaborate toxic-spill cover story into the phony memories of both Elko County locals *and* passers-through, and there was no way they could have kept the highway closed and the area sealed tight for that long.

The edition of Wednesday, July 11, continued the saga: I-80 OPENS!, and QUARANTINE REMOVED: NO LONG-TERM CONTAMINATION, and FIRST EVACUEES LOCATED: THEY SAW NOTHING.

Editions of the *Sentinel,* distinctly a small-town paper, averaged between sixteen and thirty-two pages. During those days in July, most of its news space was given to reports of the toxic crisis, for this event had drawn reporters from all over the country, and the low-key *Sentinel* found itself at the center of a big story. Poring over that wealth of material, Dom and Ginger discovered a lot that was pertinent to their quest and that would help them plan their next move.

For one thing, the degree of security imposed by the United States Army was soberly instructive of the lengths to which they would go to keep the lid on the truth. Although it was not strictly within their authority to do so, Army units attached to Shenkfield had established roadblocks and closed a ten-mile stretch of I-80 immediately after the accident; they had not even informed the Elko County Sheriff or the Nevada State Police of the crisis until they had secured the quarantine zone. That was a startling breach of standard procedure. Throughout the emergency, the sheriff and state police complained with increasing vehemence that the Army was freezing them out of every aspect of crisis management and usurping civilian authority; state and local police were neither included in the maintenance of the quarantine line nor consulted on essential contingency planning for the possibility that increased winds or other factors might spread the nerve gas beyond the initial area of danger. Clearly, the military trusted only its own people to keep the secret of what was actually happening in the quarantine zone.

Following two days of frustration, Foster Hanks, the Elko County Sheriff, had complained to a *Sentinel* reporter that: "This here's *my* bailiwick, by God, and the people elected *me* to keep peace. This is no military dictatorship. If I don't get some cooperation from the Army, I'll see a judge first thing tomorrow and get a court order to make them respect the legal jurisdictions in this matter." The Tuesday *Sentinel* reported that Hanks had, indeed, gone before a judge, but before a determination could be made, the crisis was drawing to an end and the argument about jurisdiction was moot.

Huddling over the newspaper with Dom, Ginger said, "So we don't have to worry that *all* authorities are aligned against us in this. The state and local police weren't part of it. Our only adversary is—"

"The United States Army," Dom finished, laughing at the unconscious element of graveyard humor in her assessment of the enemy.

She also laughed sourly. "Us against the Army. Even with state and local police out of the battle, it's hardly a fair match, is it?"

According to the *Sentinel,* the Army kept sole and iron control of the roadblocks on I-80, the only east-west artery through forbidden territory, and also closed eight miles of the north-south county road. Civilian air traffic was restricted from passing over the contaminated area, necessitating the rerouting of flights, while the Army maintained continuous helicopter patrols of the perimeter of the proscribed land. Obviously, substantial manpower was required to secure eighty square miles, but regardless of expense and difficulty, they were determined to stop anyone entering the danger zone on foot, on horseback, or in four-wheel-drive vehicles. The choppers flew in daylight and after dark, as well, sweeping the night with searchlights. Rumors circulated that teams of soldiers, equipped with infrared surveillance gear, were also patrolling the perimeter at night, looking for interlopers who might have slipped past the big choppers' searchlights.

"Nerve gases rate among the deadliest substances known to man," Ginger said as Dom turned a page of the newspaper they were currently perusing. "But even so, this much security seems excessive. Besides, though I'm no expert on chemical warfare, I can't believe *any* nerve gas would pose a threat at such a distance from a single point of release. I mean, according to the Army, it was only one cylinder of gas, not an enormous quantity, not a whole tanker truck as Ernie and Faye remembered it. And it's the nature of gas to disperse, to expand upon release. So by the time the stuff spread a couple of miles, it would've been diluted to such a degree that surely the air would've contained no more of it than a few parts per billion. In three miles . . . not even one part per billion. Not enough to endanger anyone."

"This supports your idea that it was biological contamination."

"Possibly," Ginger said. "It's too early to say. But it was certainly more serious than the nerve-gas story they put out."

By Saturday, July 7, less than one day after the interstate was closed, an alert wire-service reporter had noted that the uniforms of many of the soldiers in the quarantine operation bore—in addition to rank and standard insignia—an unusual company patch: a black circle with an emerald-green star in the center. This was different from the markings on the uniforms of the men from Shenkfield Testing Grounds. Among those wearing the green star, the ratio of officers to enlisted men was high. When questioned, the Army identified the green-star soldiers as a little-known, super-elite company of Special Forces troops. "We call them DERO, which stands for Domestic Emergency Response Organization," an Army spokesman was quoted by the *Sentinel*. "The men of DERO are superbly trained, and they've all had extensive field experience in combat situations, *and* all of them carry top-security clearances, as well, which is essential because they may find themselves operating in highly classified areas, witness to sensitive sights."

Dom translated that to mean DERO men were chosen, in part, for their ability and willingness to keep their goddamn mouths shut.

The *Sentinel* quoted the Army spokesman further: "They're the cream of our young career soldiers, so naturally many have attained the rank of at least sergeant by the time they qualify for DERO. Our intention is to create a superbly trained force to deal with extraordinary crises, such as terrorist attacks on domestic military installations, nuclear emergencies on bases housing atomic weapons, and other unusual problems. Not that there's any aspect of terrorism involved in this case. And there's no nuclear emergency here, either. But several DERO companies are stationed around the country, and since one was near when this nerve-gas situation arose, it seemed prudent to bring in the best we had to insure public safety." He refused to tell reporters where this DERO company had been stationed, how far they had been flown, or how many were involved. "That's classified information." Not one of the DERO men would speak with any member of the press.

Ginger grimaced and said, *"Shmontses!"*

Dom blinked. "Huh?"

"Their whole story," she said, leaning back in her chair and rolling her head from side to side to work out a cramp in her lovely neck. "It's all just *shmontses.*"

"But what's *shmontses?*"

"Oh. Sorry. Yiddish word, adapted from German, I guess. One of my father's favorites. It means something of no value, something foolish, absurd, nonsense, worthy of contempt or scorn. This stuff the Army put out is just *shmontses.*" She stopped rolling her head, leaned forward in her chair, and stabbed one finger at the newspaper. "So this DERO team just happened to be hanging around here in the middle of nowhere precisely when this crisis arose, huh? Too damned neat."

Dom frowned. "But, Ginger, according to these stories, although the roadblocks on I-80 were set up by men from Shenkfield, the DERO team took over little more than an hour later. So if they didn't just happen to be nearby, the only way they could've gotten here so quickly was if they were airborne and on their way *before the accident ever happened.*"

"Exactly."

"You're saying they knew in advance there'd be a toxic spill?"

She sighed. "At most, I'm willing to accept a DERO team might've been at one of the nearest military bases . . . in western Utah or maybe up in southern Idaho. But even that's not near enough to make the Army's scenario work. Even if they dropped everything and flew in here the moment they heard about the spill, they couldn't have been manning those roadblocks within an hour. No way. So, yeah, it sure looks to me as if they had a little advance warning that something was going to happen out at the western end of Elko County. Not much warning, mind you. Not days. But maybe a one- or two-hour advance notice."

"Which means the toxic spill couldn't have been an accident. In fact, probably wasn't a spill at all, neither chemical nor biological. So why in hell were they wearing decontamination suits when they were treating us?" Dom was frustrated by the elaborate maze of this mystery, which twisted and turned inward but not toward a solution, toward nothing but twistier and more complex pathways that led into ever deeper puzzlement. He had the irrational urge to tear the newspapers to shreds, as if, by ripping them to pieces, he would also be ripping apart the Army's lies and would somehow find the truth revealed, at last, in the resultant confetti.

With a note of frustration that matched his own, Ginger said, "The only reason the Army called in a DERO company to enforce the quarantine was because the men patrolling the zone would have a view of something highly classified, something absolutely top-secret. The Army felt they couldn't trust ordinary soldiers who didn't have the very highest security clearance. That's the sole reason the DERO team was used."

"Because they could be trusted to keep their mouths shut."

"Yes. And if it'd been nothing more than a toxic spill out there on I-80, the DERO men wouldn't have been required for the job. I mean, if it was just a spill, what would there've been to see except maybe an overturned truck and a damaged, leaking cannister of gas or liquid?"

Turning their attention once more to the newspapers spread before them, they found additional evidence indicating the Army had had at least some warning that unusual and spectacular trouble would erupt in western Elko County that hot July night. Both Dom and Ginger distinctly remembered that the Tranquility Grille had been filled with a strange sound and shaken by earthquake-like tremors about half an hour after full darkness had settled on the land; and because sunset came later during the summer (even at 41 degrees North Latitude), the trouble must have started approximately at eight-ten. Their memory blocks began at the same time, which further pinpointed The Event. Yet Dom spotted a line in one of the *Sentinel*'s stories stating that the roadblocks on I-80 had been erected almost at eight o'clock on the dot.

Ginger said, "You mean the Army had the highway closed off five or ten minutes before the 'accidental' toxic spill even happened?"

"Yeah. Unless we're wrong about the time of the sunset."

They checked the weather column in the July 6 edition of the *Sentinel*. It painted a more than adequate portrait of that fateful day. The high temperature had been expected to hit ninety degrees, with an overnight low of sixty-four. Humidity between twenty and twenty-five percent. Clear skies. Light to variable winds. And sunset at seven-thirty-one.

"Twilight's short out here," Dom said. "Fifteen minutes, tops. Figure full darkness at seven-forty-five. Now, even if we're wrong to think it was half an hour after nightfall that trouble hit, even if it came just fifteen minutes after dark, the Army *still* had its roadblocks up first."

"So they knew what was coming," Ginger said.

"But they couldn't stop it from happening."

"Which means it must've been some process, some series of events, that they initiated and then were unable to control."

"Maybe," Dom said. "But maybe not. Maybe they weren't really at fault. Until we know more, we're just speculating. No point to it."

Ginger turned the page of the *Sentinel's* edition for Wednesday, July 11, which they were currently examining, and her gasp of surprise directed Dom's attention to a head-and-shoulders photograph of a man in an Army officer's uniform and cap. Although Colonel Leland Falkirk had appeared in neither Dom's nor Ginger's dreams last night, they both recognized him at once because of the description that Ernie and Ned had supplied from their nightmares: dark hair graying at the temples, eyes with an eerie translucency, a beakish nose, thin lips, a face of flat hard planes and sharp angles.

Dom read the caption under the picture: *Colonel Leland Falkirk, commanding officer of the company of DERO troops manning the quarantine line, has been an elusive target for reporters. This first photograph was obtained by* Sentinel *photographer, Greg Lunde. Caught by surprise, Falkirk was angry about being photographed. His answers to the few questions asked of him were even shorter than the standard "no comment."*

Dom might have smiled at the quiet humor in the last sentence of the caption, but Falkirk's stony visage chilled him. He instantly recognized the face not only because of Ernie's and Ned's description, but because he had seen it before, the summer before last. Furthermore, there was a ferocity in that hawklike countenance and in those predatory eyes that was dismaying; this man routinely got what he wanted. To be at his mercy was a frightening prospect.

Staring at the photograph of Falkirk, Ginger softly said, *"Kayn aynhoreh."* Aware of Dom's puzzlement, she said, "That's Yiddish, too. *Kayn aynhoreh.* It's an expression that's used to . . . to ward off the evil eye. Somehow, it seemed appropriate."

Dom studied the photograph, half mesmerized by it.

After a moment, he said, "Yes. Quite appropriate."

Colonel Falkirk's sharply chiseled face and cold pale eyes were so striking that it seemed as if he were alive within this photograph, as if he were returning their scrutiny.

While Dom and Ginger were examining the back-issue files at the Elko *Sentinel,* Ernie and Faye Block were working in the office of the Tranquility Motel, trying to contact the people whose names were on the guest list for July 6, two summers ago, but who had thus far been unreachable. They were behind the check-in counter, sitting opposite each other at the oak desk, which had kneeholes on both sides. A pot of coffee stood within reach on an electric warming-plate.

Ernie composed a telegram to Gerald Salcoe, the man who had rented two rooms for his family on July 6, the summer before last, and who was unreachable by phone because his number in Monterey, California, was unlisted. Meanwhile, Faye went back through last year's guest book, day by day, looking for the most recent entry for Cal Sharkle, the trucker who had stayed with them on that July 6. Yesterday, Dom had tried the telephone number Cal had printed in the guest registry that night, but it had been disconnected. The hope was that a more recent entry would provide his new address and phone number.

As they performed their separate tasks, Ernie was reminded of countless other times throughout their thirty-one years of marriage when they had sat facing each other at a desk or, more often, at a kitchen table. In one apartment or another, in one house or another, at one end of the world or another, from Quantico to Pendleton to Singapore, nearly everywhere the Marines sent him, the two of them had spent long evenings at a kitchen table, working or dreaming or worrying or happily planning together, often late into the night. Ernie was suddenly filled with poignant echoes of those thousands of huddled conferences and shared labors. How very fortunate he had been to find and marry Faye. Their lives were so inextricably linked that they might as well have been a single creature. If Colonel Falkirk or others resorted to murder to terminate this investigation, if anything happened to Faye, then Ernie hoped he would die, too, simultaneously.

He finished composing the telegram to Gerald Salcoe, called it in to Western Union, and requested immediate delivery—all the while warmed by a love that was strong enough to make their dangerous situation seem less threatening than it really was.

Faye found five occasions during the past year when Cal Sharkle had stayed overnight, and in every case he had listed the same Evanston, Illinois, address and phone number that he had entered in the registry for July 6 of the previous year. Apparently, he had not moved, after all. Yet, when they dialed this number, they obtained the recording that Dom had gotten yesterday, informing them that the telephone had been disconnected and that no new Evanston listing existed.

On the chance that Cal had moved out of Evanston into the "Windy City" itself, Faye dialed Area Code 312 Information and asked if there was a number for Calvin Sharkle in Chicago. There was not. Using a map of Illinois, she and Ernie placed calls to Information in the Chicago suburbs: Whiting, Hammond, Calumet City, Markham, Downer's Grove, Oak Park, Oakbrook, Elmhurst, Des Plaines, Rolling Meadows, Arlington Heights, Skokie, Wilmette, Glencoe. . . . No luck. Either Cal Sharkle had moved out of the Chicago area, or had dropped off the face of the earth.

While Faye and Ernie worked in the first-floor office, Ned and Sandy Sarver were already preparing dinner in the kitchen upstairs. This evening, after Brendan Cronin arrived from Chicago, after Jorja Monatella and her little girl flew in from Vegas, there would be nine for dinner, and Ned did not want to leave preparations until the last minute. Yesterday, when all six of them joined forces to prepare and serve the evening meal, Ginger Weiss had observed that the occasion was almost like a family holiday gathering; and indeed, they felt an extraordinary closeness though they hardly knew one another. With the idea that reinforcement of their special affection and camaraderie might give them strength to face whatever lay ahead of them, Ned and Sandy had decided that tonight's meal ought to be like a Thanksgiving feast. Therefore, they were preparing a sixteen-pound turkey, pecan stuffing, scalloped potatoes, baked corn, carrots with tarragon, pepper slaw, pumpkin pie, and made-from-scratch crescent rolls.

As they chopped celery, diced onions, cubed bread, and grated cabbage, Ned occasionally wondered if what they were cooking was not only a family feast but also the last hearty meal of the condemned. Each time that morbid thought rose, he chased it away by pausing to watch Sandy as she worked. She smiled almost constantly, and sometimes softly hummed a song. Surely, an event that had induced this radical and wonderful change in Sandy could not ultimately culminate in their deaths. Surely, they had nothing to worry about. Surely.

* * *

After three hours at the Elko *Sentinel,* Ginger and Dom ate a light lunch—chef's salads—at a restaurant on Idaho Street, then returned to the Tranquility Motel at two-thirty. Faye and Ernie were still in the office, which was filled with appetizing aromas drifting down from the apartment upstairs: pumpkin, cinnamon, nutmeg, onions fried lightly in butter, the yeasty odor of baking bread dough.

"And you can't smell the turkey yet," Faye said. "Ned just put that in the oven half an hour ago."

"He says dinner's at eight," Ernie told them, "but I suspect the odors'll drive us mad and force us to storm the kitchen before then."

Faye said, "Learn anything at the *Sentinel?*"

Before Ginger could tell them what she and Dom had uncovered, the front door of the motel office opened, and a slightly pudgy man entered in a burst of cold whirling wind. He had hurried from his car without bothering to put on a topcoat; although he wore gray slacks, a dark blue blazer, a light blue sweater, and an ordinary white shirt, rather than a black suit and Roman collar, his identity was not for a moment in doubt. He was the auburn-haired, green-eyed, round-faced young priest in the Polaroid snapshot that the unknown correspondent had sent to Dom.

"Father Cronin," Ginger said.

She was as immediately and powerfully drawn to him as she'd been to Dominick Corvaisis. With the priest as with Dom, Ginger sensed a shared experience even more shattering than the one which she had shared with the Blocks and Sarvers. Within The Event that they had all witnessed that Friday in July, there had been a Second Event experienced by only some of them. Although it was a frightfully improper way to greet a man who was a virtual stranger *and* a priest, Ginger rushed to Father Cronin and threw her arms around him.

But apologies were not required, for Father Cronin evidently sensed the same thing she did. Without hesitation, he returned her hug, and for a moment they clung to each other, not as if they were strangers but brother and sister greeting each other after a long separation.

Then Ginger stepped back as Dom said, "Father Cronin," and came forward to embrace the priest.

"There's no need to call me 'Father.' At the moment I neither want nor deserve to be considered a priest. Please just call me Brendan."

Ernie shouted upstairs to Ned and Sandy, then followed Faye out from behind the check-in counter. Brendan shook Ernie's hand and embraced Faye, obviously feeling great affection for them, though not a closeness as powerful and inexplicable as the tremendous emotional magnetism that pulled him toward Dom and Ginger. When Ned and Sandy came downstairs, he greeted them the same as he had Ernie and Faye.

Just as Ginger had done last night, Brendan said, "I have a truly wonderful sense of . . . being among family. You all feel it, don't you? As if we've shared the most important moments of our lives . . . went through something that'll always make us different from everyone else."

In spite of his insistence that he did not deserve the deference accorded a priest, Brendan Cronin had a profoundly spiritual air about him. His somewhat pudgy face, sparkling eyes, and broad warm smile conveyed joy; and he moved among them, touched them, and spoke with an ebullience that was infectious and that somehow lifted Ginger's soul.

Brendan said, "What I feel in this room only reassures me that I've made the right decision in coming. I'm *meant* to be with you. Something will happen here that'll transform us, that's already begun to transform us. Do you feel it? Do you *feel* it?''

The priest's soft voice sent a pleasant shiver up Ginger's spine, filled her with an indescribable sense of wonder reminiscent of what she'd felt the first time that, as a medical student, she had stood in an operating room and had seen a patient's thorax held open by surgical retractors to reveal the pulsing, mysterious complexity of the human heart in all its crimson grandeur.

''Called,'' Brendan said. The softly spoken word echoed eerily around the room. ''All of us. Called back to this place.''

''Look,'' Dom said, packing a paragraph of amazement into that one syllable, raising his arms and holding his hands out to show them the red rings of swollen flesh that had appeared in his palms.

Surprised, Brendan raised his hands, which were also branded by the strange stigmata. As the men faced each other, the air thickened with unknown power. Yesterday, on the telephone, Father Wycazik had told Dom that Brendan was relatively certain no religious element was involved in the miraculous cures and other events that had recently transformed the young priest's life. Yet the motel office seemed, to Ginger, to be filled with a force that, if not supernatural, was certainly beyond the ken of any man or woman.

''Called,'' Brendan said again.

Ginger was gripped by breathless expectancy. She looked at Ernie, who stood behind Faye with his hands on her shoulders, and both their faces were full of tremulous suspense. Ned and Sandy, who were by the rack of postcards, holding hands, were wide-eyed.

Ginger felt the flesh prickling on the back of her neck. She thought, *Something's going to happen,* and even as the thought took form, something did.

Every lamp in the motel office was aglow in deference to Ernie's uneasiness in the presence of deep shadows, but abruptly the place was even brighter than it had been. A milky-white light filled the room, springing magically from molecules of air. It shimmered on all sides but rained mostly from overhead, a silvery mist of luminosity. She realized this was the same light that featured in her unremembered lunar dreams. She turned in a circle, looking around and up through spangled curtains of brilliant yet soft radiance, not in search of the source but with the hope of remembering her dreams and, ultimately, the events of that long-lost summer night that had inspired the dreams.

Ginger saw Sandy reach into the glowing air with one hand, as if to grasp a fistful of the miraculous light. A tentative smile pulled at Ned's mouth. Faye smiled, too, and Ernie's expression of childlike wonder was almost laughably out of place on his ruggedly hewn face.

''The moon,'' Ernie said.

''The moon,'' Dom echoed, the stigmata still blazing on his hands.

For one thrilling moment, Ginger Weiss was poised on the brink of complete understanding. The black, blank membrane of her memory block trembled; revelation pressed strenuously against the far side, and that membrane seemed certain to split and spill forth everything that had been dammed beyond it.

Then the light changed from moon-white to blood-red, and with it the mood changed from wonder and growing delight to fear. She no longer sought revelation but dreaded it, no longer welcomed understanding but withdrew from it in terror and revulsion.

Ginger stumbled back through the bloody glow, bumped against the front door. Across the room, beyond Dom and Brendan, Sandy Sarver had ceased reaching up to seize a handful of light; she was holding tightly to Ned, whose smile had become a rictus of repulsion. Faye and Ernie were pressing back against the check-in counter.

As scarlet incandescence welled like fluid into the room and filled it from corner to corner, the stunning visual phenomena were augmented by sound. Ginger jumped in surprise as a loud three-part crash shook the sanguineous air, jumped once more as it repeated, then flinched but did not jump when it came again. It had a cardiac quality, like the thunderous beating of a great heart, though it featured one more stroke than a usual heartbeat: *LUB-DUB-dub, LUB-DUB-dub, LUB-DUB-dub.* . . . She knew at once that it was the apparitional noise of which Father Wycazik had spoken in his telephone conversation with Dom, the noise that had arisen in Brendan Cronin's bedroom and had shaken St. Bernadette's.

But she also knew that she had heard this very thing before. This entire display—the moonlike light, the blood-red radiance, the noise—was part of something that had happened the summer before last.

LUB-DUB-dub . . . LUB-DUB-dub . . .

The window frames rattled. The walls shook. The bloody light and the lamplight began to pulse in time with the pounding.

LUB-DUB-dub . . . LUB-DUB-dub . . .

Again, Ginger was approaching a shocking recollection. With each crash of sound and throb of light, long-buried memories surged nearer.

However, her inhibiting fear grew; a towering black wave of terror bore down on her. The Azrael Block was doing what it was designed to do; rather than let remembrance have its way with her, she would plunge into a fugue state, as she had not done since the day Pablo Jackson had been killed, one week ago. The familiar signs of oncoming blackout were present: She was having difficulty breathing; she trembled with a sense of mortal danger so strong it was palpable; the world around her began to fade; an oily darkness seeped in at the edges of her vision.

Run or die.

Ginger turned her back on the phenomenal events transpiring in the office. With both hands, she gripped the frame of the front door, as if to anchor herself to consciousness and thwart the black wave that sought to sweep her away. In desperation, she looked through the glass at the vast Nevada landscape, at the somber winter sky, trying to block out the stimuli—the impossible light and sound—that pushed her toward a dark fugue. Terror and mindless panic grew so unbearable that escape into a hateful fugue seemed almost preferable, yet she somehow held fast to the door-frame, held tight, held on, shaking and gasping, held on, terrified not so much by the strange events occurring behind her but by the unremembered events of *that* summer of which these phenomena were only dim echoes, and still she held on, held on . . . until the three-stroke thunder faded, until the red light paled, until the room was silent, and until the only light was that coming through the windows or from ordinary lighting fixtures.

She was all right now. She was not going to black out.

For the first time, she had successfully resisted a seizure. Maybe her ordeal of the past few months had toughened her. Maybe just *being* here, within reach of all the answers to the mystery, had given her the heart to resist. Or maybe she had drawn strength from her new "family." Whatever the reason, she was confident that, having once fended off a fugue, she would find it easier to deal with future attacks. Her memory blocks were crumbling. And her fear of facing up to what had happened that July 6 was now far outweighed by the fear of never knowing.

Shaky, Ginger turned toward the others again.

Brendan Cronin tottered to the sofa and sat, trembling visibly. The rings were no longer visible in either his hands or Dom's.

To the priest, Ernie said, "Did I understand you? That same light sometimes fills your room at night?"

"Yes," Brendan acknowledged. "Twice before."

"But you told us it was a *lovely* light," Faye said.

"Yeah," Ned agreed. "You made it sound . . . wonderful."

"It is," Brendan said. "Partly, it is. But when it turns red . . . well, then it scares the hell out of me. But when it first starts . . . oh, it uplifts me and fills me with the strangest joy."

The ominous scarlet light and the frightening three-part hammering had generated such terror in Ginger that she had temporarily forgotten the exhilarating moon-white glow that had preceded it and that had filled her with wonder.

Wiping his palms on his shirt, as if the vanished rings had left an unwanted residue upon his hands, Dom said, "There was both a good and evil aspect to the events of that night. We long to relive a part of what happened to us, yet at the same time it scares us . . . scares us . . . "

"Scares us shitless," Ernie said.

Ginger noticed that even Sandy Sarver, who heretofore had perceived only a benign shape to the mystery, was frowning.

When Jorja Monatella buried her ex-husband, Alan Rykoff, at eleven o'clock Monday morning, the Las Vegas sun beamed down between scattered iron-gray clouds. A hundred shafts of golden sunshine, some half a mile across, some only a few yards wide, like cosmic spotlights, left many buildings in winter shadows while highlighting others. Several shafts of sunshine moved across the cemetery, harried by the rushing clouds, sweeping eastward across the barren floor of the desert. As the portly funeral director concluded a nondenominational prayer, as the casket was lowered into the waiting grave, a particularly bright beam illuminated the scene, and color *burst* from the flowers.

In addition to Jorja and Paul Rykoff—Alan's father, who had flown in from Florida—only five people had shown up. Even Jorja's parents had not come. By his selfishness, Alan had assured an exit from life accompanied by a minimum of grieving. Paul Rykoff, too like his son in some respects, blamed Jorja for everything. He had been barely civil since his arrival yesterday. Now that his only child was in the ground, he turned from Jorja, stone-faced, and she knew she would meet him again only if his stubbornness and anger eventually were outweighed by a desire to see his grandchild.

She drove only a mile before she pulled to the side of the road, stopped, and finally wept. She wept neither for Alan's suffering nor for the loss of him, but for the final destruction of all the hope with which their relationship had begun, the burnt-out hopes for love, family, friendship, mutual goals, and shared lives. She had not wished Alan dead. But now that he *was* dead, she knew it would be easier to make the new beginning toward which she had been planning and working, and that realization made her feel neither guilty nor cruel; it was just sad.

Last night, Jorja told Marcie her father was dead, though not that he'd committed suicide. Initially, Jorja had not intended to tell her until this afternoon, in the presence of Dr. Coverly, the psychologist. But the appointment with Coverly had to be canceled because, later today, Jorja and Marcie were flying to Elko to join Dominick Corvaisis, Ginger Weiss, and the others. Marcie took the news of Alan's death surprisingly well. She cried, but not hard or long. At seven, she was old enough to understand death, but still too young to grasp the cruel finality of it. Besides, by his abandonment of Marcie, Alan unwittingly had done the girl a favor; in a sense, for her, he had died more than a year ago, and her mourning had already been done.

One other thing had helped Marcie overcome her grief: her obsession with the collection of moon pictures. Only an hour after she learned of her father's death, the child was sitting at the dining room table, eyes dry, small pink tongue poked between her teeth in total concentration, a crayon stub in one hand. She'd begun the moon-coloring project on Friday evening and pursued it through the weekend. By breakfast this morning, every one of the photographs and all but fifty of the hundreds of hand-drawn moons had been transformed into fiery globes.

Marcie's obsession would have disturbed Jorja even if she had not known others shared it and that two had killed themselves. The moon was not yet the focus of the girl's every waking hour. However, Jorja required little imagination to see that, if the obsession progressed, Marcie might travel irretrievably into the land of madness.

Her anxiety about Marcie was so acute that she quickly overcame the tears that had forced her to pull to the side of the road. She put the Chevette in gear and drove to her parents' house, where Marcie waited.

The girl was at the kitchen table with the ubiquitous album of moons, applying a scarlet crayon. She glanced up when Jorja arrived, smiled weakly, and returned at once to the task before her.

Pete, Jorja's father, was also at the table, frowning at Marcie. Occasionally, he thought of a stratagem to interest her in some activity less bizarre and more wholesome than the endless coloring of moons, but all his attempts to lure her away from the album failed.

In her parents' bedroom, Jorja changed from her dress into jeans and a sweater for the trip north, while Mary Monatella badgered her. "When will you take that book away from Marcie? Or let *me* take it away?"

"Mother, I told you before: Dr. Coverly believes taking the book from her right now would only reinforce her obsession."

"That doesn't make any sense to me," Jorja's mother said.

"Dr. Coverly says if we make an issue of the moon collection at this early stage, we'll be emphasizing its importance and—"

"Nonsense. Does this Coverly have kids of his own?"

"I don't know, Mom."

"I'll bet he doesn't have kids of his own. If he did, he wouldn't be giving you such dumb advice."

Having put her dress on a hanger, having stripped down to bra and panties, Jorja felt naked and vulnerable, for this situation reminded her of when her mother used to watch her dress for dates with boys who did not meet approval. No boy ever met Mary's approval. In fact, Jorja married Alan in part because Mary disapproved of him. Matrimony as rebellion. Stupid, but she had done it and paid dearly. Mary had driven her to it—Mary's suffocating and authoritarian brand of love. Now, Jorja grabbed the jeans that were laid out on the bed and slipped into them, dressing fast.

Mary said, "She won't even say why she's collecting those things."

"Because she doesn't know why. It's a compulsion. An irrational obsession, and if there's a reason for it, the reason is buried down in her subconscious, where even she can't get a look at it.''

Mary said, "That book should be taken away from her."

"Eventually," Jorja said. "One step at a time, Mom."

"If it was up to me, I'd do it right now."

Jorja had packed two big suitcases and had left them here earlier. Now, when it was time to go to the airport, Pete drove, and Mary went along for the opportunity to engage in more nagging.

Jorja and Marcie shared the back seat. On the way to the airport, the girl paged continuously, silently back and forth through her album.

Between Jorja and Mary, the subject of conversation had changed from the best way to deal with Marcie's obsession to the imminent trip to Elko. Mary had doubts about this expedition and did not hesitate to express them. Was the plane just a twelve-seater? Wasn't it dangerous to go up in a bucket of bolts owned by a small-time outfit that was probably short of cash and skimped on maintenance? What was the purpose of going, anyway? Even if some people in Elko were having problems like Marcie's, how could it possibly have anything to do with the fact that they'd all stayed at the same motel?

"This Corvaisis guy bothers me," Pete said as he braked for a red traffic light. "I don't like you getting involved with his kind."

"What do you mean? You don't even know him."

"I know enough," Pete said. "He's a writer, and you know what they're like. I read once where that Norman Mailer hung his wife out a high window by her heels. And isn't it Hemingway who's always getting in fist-fights?''

Jorja said, "Daddy, Hemingway's dead."

"*See?* Always getting in fights, drunk, using drugs. Writers are a flaky bunch. I don't like you being involved with writers."

"This trip is a big mistake," Mary said flatly.

It never ended.

At the airport, when she kissed them goodbye, they told her they loved her, and she told them the same, and the strange thing was that they were all telling the truth. Though they continuously sniped at her and though she had been deeply wounded by their sniping, they loved one another. Without love, they would have stopped speaking long ago. The parent-child relationship was sometimes even more perplexing than the mystery of what had happened at the Tranquility Motel two summers ago.

The feeder line's bucket of bolts was more comfortable than Mary would have believed, with six well-padded seats on each side of a narrow aisle, free headphones providing bland but mellowing Muzak tapes, and a pilot who handled his craft as gently as a new mother carried her baby.

Thirty minutes out of Las Vegas, Marcie closed the album and, in spite of the daylight streaming through the portholes, she drifted off to sleep, lulled by the loud but hypnotic droning of the engines.

During the flight, Jorja thought about her future: the business degree toward which she was working, her hope of owning a dress shop, the hard work ahead—and loneliness, which was already a problem for her. She wanted a man. Not sexually. Although *that* would be welcome too! She had dated a few times since the divorce but had been to bed with no one. She was no female eunuch. Sex was important to her, and she missed it. But sex was not the main reason she wanted a man, one special man, a mate. She needed someone to share her dreams, triumphs, and failures. She had Marcie, but that was not the same. The human species seemed genetically compelled to make life's journey two-by-two, and the need was particularly strong in Jorja.

As the plane droned north-northeast, Jorja listened to Mantovani on the headphones and indulged in a bit of uncharacteristic, girlish fantasizing. At the Tranquility Motel, perhaps she would meet a special man with whom she could share this new beginning. She recalled Dominick Corvaisis' gentle but confident voice, and included him in her fantasy. If Corvaisis was the one for her, imagine what her father would say when he learned she was marrying one of those flaky, drunken writers who held their wives by the heels and dangled them out high windows!

She scrapped that particular fantasy soon after the plane landed, for she quickly perceived that Corvaisis' heart was already claimed.

At four-thirty in Elko, half an hour before sunset, the sky was plated with dark clouds, and the Ruby Mountains were purple-black on the horizon. A penetratingly cold wind, sweeping in from the west, was ample proof that they had come four hundred miles north from Las Vegas.

Corvaisis and Dr. Ginger Weiss were waiting on the tarmac beside the small terminal, and the moment that Jorja saw them, she had the odd but reassuring feeling that she was among family. That sensation was something of which Corvaisis had spoken on the phone, but Jorja had not understood what he meant until she experienced it. And it was quite separate from the feelings she had for Ginger as her roadside savior.

Even Marcie—bundled in coat and scarf, her eyes still puffy from the nap on the plane, the album clutched to her chest—was stirred from her moody trancelike state by the sight of the writer and the physician. She smiled and answered their questions with more enthusiasm than had marked her speech in days. She offered to show them her album, and she submitted with a giggle when Corvaisis scooped her up in his arms to carry her to the parking lot.

We were right to come, Jorja thought. Thank God we did.

Carrying Marcie, Corvaisis led the way to the car, while Jorja and Ginger followed with the suitcases. As they walked, Jorja said, "Maybe you don't remember, but you provided emergency treatment for Marcie that Friday evening in July, even before we checked into the Tranquility."

The physician blinked. "In fact, I hadn't remembered. Was that you and your late husband? Was that Marcie? But of course it was!"

"We had parked along I-80, five miles west of the motel," Jorja recalled. "The view to the south was so spectacular, such a wonderful panorama, that we wanted to use it as a backdrop for some snapshots."

Ginger nodded. "And I was driving east in your wake. I saw you up ahead, parked along the shoulder. You were focusing the camera. Your husband and Marcie had stepped over the guardrail and were standing a few feet farther out, posing at the edge of the highway embankment."

"I didn't want them standing so close to the brink. But Alan insisted it was the best position for the best picture, and when Alan insisted on something, there was no use arguing with him."

However, before Jorja had been able to click the shutter, Marcie had slipped and fallen backward, over the edge, tumbling down the thirty- or forty-foot embankment. Jorja screamed—"Marcie!"—flung the camera aside, vaulted the guardrail, and started down toward her daughter. Fast as she was, however, Jorja had just reached Marcie when she heard someone shouting: "Don't move her! I'm a doctor!" That had been Ginger Weiss, and she had descended the slope so rapidly that she had arrived at Marcie's side simultaneously with Alan, who had started down before her. Marcie was still and silent but not unconscious, only stunned, and Ginger quickly determined that the girl had not sustained a head injury. Marcie began to cry, and because her left leg was tucked under her at a somewhat odd angle, Jorja was certain it was broken. Ginger was able to allay that fear, too. In the end, because the slope was rock-free and cushioned by bunchgrass, Marcie came through with only minor injuries—a few scrapes and bruises.

"I was so impressed by you," Jorja said.

"Me?" Ginger looked surprised. She waited for an incoming single-engine plane to pass overhead. Then: "I did nothing special, you know. I only examined Marcie. She didn't need heroic care, just Band-Aids."

As they put the suitcases in the trunk of Dom's car, Jorja said, "Well, I was impressed. You were young, pretty, feminine, yet you were a doctor—efficient, quick-thinking. I'd always thought of myself as a born cocktail waitress, nothing more, but that encounter with you started a fire in me. Later, when Alan walked out on us, I didn't fall apart. I remembered you, and I decided to make more of myself than I'd ever thought I could. In a way, you changed my life."

Closing the trunk lid, locking it, handing the keys to Dom (who had already put Marcie in the car), Ginger said, "Jorja, I'm flattered. But you're giving me much too much credit. You changed your own life."

"It wasn't what you did that day," Jorja said. "It's what you *were*. You were exactly the role model I needed."

Embarrassed, the physician said, "Good God! No one's ever called me a role model before! Oh, honey, you're definitely unbalanced!"

"Ignore her," Dom told Jorja. "She's the best role model I've ever seen. Her humble mutterings are pure *shmontses*."

Ginger Weiss whirled on him, laughing. *"Shmontses?"*

Dom grinned. "I'm a writer, so it's my job to listen and absorb. I hear a good expression, I use it. Can't fault me for doing my job."

"Shmontses, huh?" Ginger Weiss said, pretending anger.

Still grinning, the writer said, "If the Yiddish fits, wear it."

That was the moment when Jorja knew Dominick Corvaisis' heart was already claimed and that she would have to exclude him from any romantic fantasies she might cook up in the future. The spark of desire and glimmer of deep affection shone brightly in his eyes when he looked at Ginger Weiss. The same heat warmed the physician's gaze. The funny thing was, neither Dom nor Ginger appeared quite to realize the true power of their feelings for each other. Not quite yet, but soon.

They drove out of Elko, toward the Tranquility, thirty miles to the west. As twilight faded toward night in the east, Dom and Ginger told Jorja what had happened prior to her and Marcie's arrival. Jorja found it increasingly difficult to hold the good mood she'd been in since stepping off the plane. As they sped through the gloom-mantled barrens, with craggy and threatening black mountains thrusting up at the horizon under a blood-dark sky, Jorja wondered if this place was, as she had thought, the threshold of a new beginning . . . or a doorway to the grave.

After the Lear landed in Salt Lake City, Utah, Jack Twist quickly transferred to a chartered Cessna Turbo Skylane RG piloted by a polite but tight-lipped man with a huge handlebar mustache. They arrived in Elko, Nevada, at four-fifty-three, in the last light of day.

The airport was too small to have Hertz and Avis counters, but a local entrepreneur operated a modest little taxi company. Jack had the cab take him—and his three big suitcases—to a local Jeep dealership, where they were getting ready to close, and where he startled the salesman by paying cash for a four-wheel-drive Cherokee wagon.

To this point, Jack took no evasive action to shake off a tail or even to determine if he had one. His adversaries clearly possessed great power and resources, and regardless of how frantically he tried to elude them, they would have sufficient manpower to keep tabs on a lone target trying to escape on foot or by taxi in a town as small as Elko.

Once the Cherokee was his, Jack drove away from the dealership, and for the first time he looked for a tail. He glanced repeatedly at the rearview and side mirrors, but he spotted no suspicious vehicles.

He went directly to an Arco Mini-Mart that he had noticed during the taxi ride from the airport. He parked at the dark end of the lot, beyond the reach of the arc lamps, got out of the wagon, and surveyed the shadowy street behind for an indication of a pursuer.

He saw no one.

That didn't mean they weren't out there.

In the Mini-Mart, the blindingly excessive fluorescent lighting and chrome display fixtures made him long for the good old days of quaint corner groceries operated by immigrant couples who spoke with appealing accents, where the air would have been redolent of Mama's homemade baked goods and Papa's made-to-order deli sandwiches. Here, the only aromas were a vague trace of disinfectant and the thin odor of ozone coming off the motors of refrigerated display cases. Squinting in the glare, Jack bought a map of the county, a flashlight, a quart of milk, two packages of dried beef, a little box of small chocolate doughnuts—and, on a morbid impulse, something called a "Hamwich," which was "a guaranteed delicious one-piece sandwich of pulverized, blended, remolded ham paste, bread, and spices," and which was claimed to be especially "convenient for hikers, campers, and sportsmen." Ham paste? At the bottom of the airtight plastic package was this legend: REAL MEAT.

Jack laughed. They had to tell you it was "real meat" because, even though it was wrapped in clear plastic, you couldn't tell what the hell it was by looking at it. Yes, sir—oh, yes—ham paste and real meat: *That* was why he had gone to Central America to fight for his country.

He wished Jenny were alive and here with him. Real meat. As opposed to fake, polyester meat. She'd have gotten a kick out of that.

When he walked out of the Mini-Mart, he paused to study the street again, but again he saw no one suspicious.

He returned to the Cherokee at the dark end of the lot and put up the tailgate. He opened one of his suitcases, withdrew an empty nylon rucksack, the Beretta, a loaded clip, a box of .32 ammunition, and one of the pipe-type silencers. As his breath steamed from him in the cold air, he transferred the groceries from the paper bag to the rucksack. He screwed the silencer onto the gun, slammed the loaded clip into the butt. When he had distributed all the loose ammunition among the many pockets of his heavily insulated leather jacket, he closed the tailgate.

Behind the wheel of the Cherokee once more, Jack put the Beretta on the seat beside him and set the rucksack on top of it for concealment. Using the new flashlight, he passed a few minutes studying the map of Elko County. When he switched the flashlight off and put the map away, he was ready to engage the enemy.

For the next five minutes, he drove through Elko, using every trick he knew to reveal a tail, staying on quiet residential streets where traffic was light and where a surveillance team would be as obvious as a festering cold sore, no matter how good they were. Nothing.

He parked at the end of a cul-de-sac and got an anti-surveillance broadband receiver from one of the suitcases. This device, the size of two packs of cigarettes, with a short antenna that telescoped out of the top, received all possible radio bands from 30 to 120, including FM from 88 to 108. If a transmitter had been fixed to the Jeep while he was in the market, enabling a tail to follow at a distance, his broadband receiver would pick up the signals; a feedback loop would cause the receiver to emit an ear-piercing squeal. He pointed the antenna at the Jeep and slowly circled the vehicle.

The Cherokee had not been bugged.

He put the broadband receiver away and got behind the wheel of the wagon again, where he sat for a minute in thought. He was under neither visual nor electronic surveillance. Did that make sense? When his adversaries put those Tranquility Motel postcards in his safe-deposit boxes, they must have known he would come to Nevada at once. Surely they also knew that he was a potentially dangerous man, and surely they would not allow him to plot against them on their own turf unobserved. Yet that seemed to be precisely what they were doing.

Frowning, Jack twisted the key in the ignition. The engine roared.

On the Lear from New York, he had pondered the situation at length and had arrived at several theories (most of them half-baked) as to the identity and intentions of his adversaries. Now he decided that nothing he dreamed up was half as strange as whatever was actually happening.

No one was watching. That spooked him.

The inexplicable *always* spooked him.

When you couldn't understand a situation, that usually meant you were missing something important. If you were missing something important, that meant you had a blind side. If you had a blind side, you could get your ass shot off when you were least expecting it.

Alert, cautious, Jack Twist drove north from Elko on State Route 51. After a while, he turned west, following a series of gravel and dirt tracks, sneaking behind the Tranquility Motel instead of making an open approach on I-80. Eventually he was reduced to traveling overland on sometimes dangerous terrain, from an elevation as high as four thousand feet, down across sloping foothills toward the plains. When the clouds parted, revealing a three-quarter moon, he switched off the headlights and continued, guided only by the glow of the lunar lamp, and his eyes soon adjusted to the night.

Jack topped a rise and saw the Tranquility Motel, a lonely group of lights in a vast dark emptiness, a mile and a half below and southwest of him, this side of I-80. There were not as many lights as there ought to have been; either the place had little business or it was not open. He did not want to advertise his arrival, so he would proceed on foot.

He left the Beretta in the Jeep and took the Uzi submachine gun. Actually, he did not expect trouble. Not yet. His adversaries, whoever the hell they were, had not teased him into coming all this way merely to kill him. They could have killed him in New York if that was all they wanted. Nevertheless, he was prepared for violence.

In addition to the Uzi—and a spare magazine—he took the rucksack of groceries, a battery-powered directional microphone, and the Star Tron night-vision device. He pulled on gloves and a toboggan cap.

Jack found the hike invigorating. The night was cold, and when the wind gusted, it stung but not unpleasantly.

Because he'd expected to go to ground immediately upon arrival in Nevada, he had dressed suitably when he left New York. He wore high-topped hiking shoes with hard rubber soles and heavy tread, longjohns and jeans, a sweater, and a leather jacket with a thick quilted lining. The crew of the chartered Lear was surprised by his appearance, but they treated him as if he were in tuxedo and top hat; even an ugly man with one cast eye, dressed like an ordinary laborer, elicited respect when he could afford to lease a private jet rather than fly commercial airlines.

Now Jack walked. Ragged tears in the clouds disrobed the moon, and the few widely scattered patches of snow shone brightly, as if they were shards of bone glimpsed in the darker carcass of the hump-backed hills; the bare earth, rock formations, sagebrush, and plentiful dry grass accepted the caress of moonlight and were limned in a vague milky-blond hue. But when the moon slipped behind the clouds, deep rich darkness flooded forth.

At last he reached a suitable observation point on the southern slope of a hill, only a quarter of a mile behind the Tranquility Motel. He sat down, putting the Uzi and his rucksack aside.

The Star Tron night-vision device took available light—starlight, moonlight, the natural phosphorescence of snow and of certain plants, meager electric light if any—and amplified it eighty-five thousand times. With the gadget's single lens, Jack could transform all but the very blackest nights into gray daylight or better.

He propped his elbows on his knees, held the Star Tron in both hands, and focused on the Tranquility. The rear of the structure popped into view with sufficient clarity for him to determine that no lookouts were posted in any shadowed niches. None of the motel units had windows along the back wall, so no guards could be watching from those rooms. The center third of the motel had a second floor, probably the owner's apartment, and light shone at most of those windows. However, he could not see into the apartment because the drapes and blinds were drawn.

He put the Star Tron in the rucksack and picked up the battery-powered, hand-held, directional microphone, which resembled a futuristic gun. Only a few years ago, "rifle mikes" were effective to a distance of only two hundred yards. But these days, a good power-amplified unit could suck in a conversation up to a quarter of a mile, much farther if conditions were ideal. The device included a pair of compact earphones, which he put on. He aimed the mike at a window shielded by drapes, and at once heard animated voices. However, he got only scraps of their conversation because he was trying to pull their voices out of a closed room *and* through a quarter-mile of blustery wind.

With great caution, he grabbed the Uzi and other gear, and moved closer, choosing a second observation point less than a hundred yards from the building. When he aimed the mike at the window again, he picked up every word spoken beyond the glass, in spite of the muffling draperies. He heard six voices, maybe more. They were eating dinner and complimenting the cook (someone named Ned) and his helper (Sandy) on the turkey, the pecan stuffing, and other dishes.

They're not just eating dinner, Jack thought enviously, they're having a damned banquet in there.

He'd eaten a light lunch on the Lear but had taken nothing since. He was still on Eastern Standard Time, so for him it was almost eleven o'clock. He would probably be eavesdropping for hours, piecing together these people's identities, gradually determining if they were his adversaries. He was too hungry to wait that long for his own dinner, such as it was. With a few rocks, he made a brace for the microphone to keep it angled toward the window. He unwrapped the

Hamwich and bit into that "pulverized, blended, and remolded" treat. It tasted like sawdust soaked in rancid bacon fat. He spat out the gummy mouthful and settled down to a meager meal of dried beef and doughnuts, which would have been more satisfying if he had not had to listen to those strangers indulging in a modern version of a harvest feast.

Soon, Jack had heard enough of the conversation in the apartment to know these people were not his enemies. Strangely, one way or another, they had been drawn or summoned here, as he'd been. Monitoring them, he began to think their voices were curiously familiar, and he was overcome with the feeling that he belonged among them as a brother among family.

A woman named Ginger and a man—either Don or Dom—began to tell the others about research they'd done earlier in the offices of the Elko *Sentinel*. Listening to talk of toxic spills, roadblocks, and highly trained DERO troops, Jack felt his appetite fading. DERO! Shit, he'd heard about the DERO companies, though they'd been formed after he'd left the service. They were gung-ho types who'd happily accept an order to go into a pit against a grizzly bear, armed only with a meat grinder; and they were tough enough to make sausages out of the bear. Forced to choose between a quick, painless suicide and hand-to-hand combat with a DERO, the ordinary man would be well-advised to blow his own brains out and save himself pain. Jack realized he was involved in something far bigger and more dangerous than *fratellanza* revenge or any of the other things he had hypothesized during his flight from New York.

Although the picture he got from eavesdropping was full of holes, he began to grasp that these people had come together to discover what had happened to them the summer before last, the same weekend Jack had stayed here. They'd made considerable headway in their investigation, and Jack winced as they openly discussed their progress. They were so naïve that they thought closed doors and covered windows ensured privacy. He wanted to shout: *Hey, for God's sake, shut up already! If I can hear you,* they *can hear you.*

DERO. That bit of news made him even sicker than the Hamwich.

In the motel they continued to chatter, revealing their strategy to the enemy even as they worked it out, and at last Jack tore off the earphones, frantically grabbed his guns and equipment, and hurried down through the darkness toward the Tranquility Motel.

The apartment had no dining room, just the alcove in the kitchen, but that area was too small to seat nine. In the living room, they moved the furniture against the walls, brought in the kitchen table, and used both extra leaves to extend it, accommodating everyone. To Dom, the impromptu arrangements contributed to the feeling of a family gathering and to the mood of cautious festivity.

Rather than have to repeat themselves, Dom and Ginger had waited until dinner, when the group was gathered, to report on their research at the newspaper in Elko. Now, over the clinking of silverware, they revealed that the Army had blockaded I-80 minutes *before* the toxic spill that Friday night. Which meant that choppers full of soldiers had been dispatched from distant Shenkfield at least half an hour earlier, and that the Army knew in advance the "accident" was going to happen.

Tearing a crescent roll, Dom said, "If Falkirk and a DERO company flew in and took over security on the quarantine line so soon after the crisis hit . . . well, it means the Army must've had advance warning."

"But then why didn't they stop it from happening?" Jorja Monatella asked as she cut her daughter's serving of turkey into bite-size pieces.

"Apparently, they *couldn't* stop it," Dom said.

"Maybe there was a terrorist attack on the truck, and maybe Army Intelligence only got wind of it just before it went down," Ernie said.

"Maybe," Dom said doubtfully. "But they would've gone public with that kind of story if it happened. So it must've been something else. Something involving top-secret data of such importance that only DERO troops could be trusted to keep quiet about it."

Brendan Cronin had a heartier appetite than anyone at the table, but his temporal appetite did not diminish the spiritual air that had surrounded him. He swallowed some baked corn and said, "This explains why there weren't hundreds of people on those ten miles of interstate when the thing happened, as there should've been at that hour. If the Army sealed it off ahead of the event, they had time to get most traffic out of the danger zone before anything actually happened."

Dom said, "Some didn't get out, saw too much, and were held and brainwashed with the rest of us who were already here at the motel."

For a while everyone joined in the discussion and arrived at all the same theories and unanswerable questions that had occurred to Dom and Ginger at the newspaper offices earlier in the day.

Finally, Dom told them about the important discovery he and Ginger had made when, as an afterthought, they had looked through issues of the *Sentinel* published during the weeks *following* the toxic spill. When they had finished poring through editions for the week of the crisis, Ginger had suggested that clues to the secret of what really happened on the closed highway that night might be hidden in other news, in unusual stories that appeared to have nothing to do with the crisis but were, in fact, related to it. They pulled more issues from the files, and by studying every story from a paranoid perspective, they soon found what they hoped for. One place in particular figured in the news in such a way that it seemed linked to the closure of I-80.

"Thunder Hill," Dom said. "We believe that's where our trouble came from. Shenkfield was just a ruse, a clever misdirection to focus attention away from the *real* source of the crisis. Thunder Hill."

Faye and Ernie looked up from their plates in surprise, and Faye said, "Thunder Hill's ten or twelve miles north-northeast of here, in the mountains. The Army has an installation up there, too—the Thunder Hill Depository. There're natural limestone caves in those hills, where they store copies of service records and a lot of other important files, so they won't lose all copies if military bases in other parts of the country are wiped out in a disaster ... nuclear war, like that."

Ernie said, "The Depository was here before Faye and me. Twenty years or more. Rumors have it that files and records aren't the only things in storage there. Some believe there's also huge supplies of food, medicines, weapons, ammunition. Which makes sense. In case a big war breaks out, the Army wouldn't want all its weapons and supplies on ordinary military bases because those would be the first nuked. They've surely got fallback caches, and I guess Thunder Hill is one of those."

"Then *anything* might be up there," Jorja Monatella said uneasily.

"Anything," Ned Sarver said.

"Is it possible the place isn't just a storage dump?" Sandy asked. "Could they also maybe be doing some kind of experiments up there?"

"What kind of experiments?" Brendan asked, leaning over to look past Ned, beside whom he was seated.

Sandy shrugged. "Any kind."

"It's possible," Dom said. The same thought had occurred to him.

"But if there wasn't a toxic spill on I-80, if it was something at Thunder Hill that went wrong," Ginger said, "how could it have affected us, more than ten miles to the south?"

No one could think of an answer.

Marcie, who had been preoccupied with her moon collection for most of the evening and who had said nothing during dinner, put down her fork and piped up with a question of her own: "Why's it called Thunder Hill?"

"Sweetie," Faye said, "that's one I *can* answer. Thunder Hill's really one of four huge, connecting mountain meadows, a long sloping piece of high pasture-land. It's surrounded by a great many high peaks, and during a storm, the place acts like a sort of . . . well, a sort of funnel for sound. The Indians named it Thunder Hill hundreds of years ago because thunder echoes between those peaks and rolls down the mountainsides, and it all pours in on that one particular meadow in a most peculiar way, so that it seems as if the roar isn't coming out of the sky, but as if it's coming right up out of the ground around you."

"Wow," Marcie said softly. "I'd probably pee my pants."

"Marcie!" Jorja said as everyone broke into laughter.

"Well, gee, I probably would," the child replied. "You 'member when Grandma and Grandpa came over to dinner at our place, and there was a big storm, really big, and some lightning struck the tree in our yard, and there was this *boom!* and I peed my pants?" Looking around the table at her new extended family, she said, "I was *soooo* embarrassed."

Everyone laughed again, and Jorja said, "That was more than two years ago. You're a bigger girl now."

To Dom, Ernie said, "You haven't told us yet why Thunder Hill is the place, rather than Shenkfield. What'd you find in the newspaper?"

In the *Sentinel* for Friday, July 13, exactly one week after the closure of I-80 and three days after its reopening, there was a report of two county ranchers—Norvil Brust and Jake Dirkson—who were having trouble with the Federal Bureau of Land Management. A disagreement between ranchers and the BLM was not unusual. The government owned half of Nevada, not merely deserts but a lot of the best grazing land, some of which it leased to cattlemen for their herds. Ranchers were always complaining that the BLM kept too much good land out of use, that the government ought to sell off part of its holdings to private inter-ests, and that leases were too expensive. But Brust and Dirkson had a new com-plaint. For years they leased BLM land surrounding a three-hundred-acre Army installation, the Thunder Hill Depository. Brust held eight hundred acres to the west and south, and Dirkson was using over seven hundred acres on the east side of Thunder Hill. Suddenly, on Saturday morning, July 7, though four years re-mained on Brust's and Dirkson's leases, the BLM took five hundred acres from Brust, three hundred from Dirkson; and at the request of the Army, those eight hundred acres were incorporated into the boundaries of the Thunder Hill Depos-itory.

"Which just happens to be the very morning after the toxic spill and the closure of I-80," Faye observed.

"Brust and Dirkson showed up Saturday morning to inspect their herds, per their usual routine," Dom said, "and both discovered that their livestock had been driven off most of the leased pasture. A temporary barbed-wire fence was being thrown into place along the new perimeter of the Thunder Hill Depository."

Having finished dinner, Ginger pushed her plate aside and said, "The BLM simply told Brust and Dirkson it was unilaterally abrogating their leases, without compensation. But they didn't receive an official written notice till the following Wednesday, which is extremely unusual. Ordinarily, a notice of termination comes sixty days in advance.''

''Was that kind of treatment legal?'' Brendan Cronin asked.

''Right there's the problem of doing business with the government,'' Ernie told the priest. ''You're dealing with the very people who decide what's legal and what isn't. It's like playing poker with God.''

Faye said, ''The BLM's despised around these parts. No bunch of bureaucrats is more high-handed.''

''That's what we gathered from reading the *Sentinel*,'' Dom said. ''Now, Ginger and I might've figured the Thunder Hill business was just coincidental, that the BLM just happened to go after that land the same time as the crisis on I-80. But the way the government dealt with Brust and Dirkson *after* the land was seized was so extraordinary it made us suspicious. When the ranchers hired attorneys, when stories about the cancellation of their leases began appearing in the *Sentinel*, the BLM did a sudden about-face and offered compensation, after all.''

''That's not a bit like the BLM!'' Ernie said. ''They'll always make you drag them into court, hoping litigation will wear you down.''

''How much were they willing to pay Brust and Dirkson?'' Faye asked.

''The figure wasn't revealed,'' Ginger said. ''But it was evidently darned good, because Brust and Dirkson accepted it overnight.''

''So the BLM bought their silence,'' Jorja said.

''I think it was the Army working secretly through the BLM,'' Dom said. ''They realized the longer the story was in the news, the more chance there was of someone wondering about a link between the crisis on I-80 that Friday night and the unorthodox seizure of land the very next morning, even if the two events were ten or twelve miles apart.''

''Surprises me somebody *didn't* make the connection,'' Jorja said. ''If you and Ginger could spot it this long after the fact, why didn't anyone think of it then?''

''For one thing,'' Ginger said, ''Dom and I had the enormous benefit of hindsight. We know there was a lot more going on during the days of the crisis than anyone suspected at the time. So we were specifically *looking* for connections. But that July, all the hoopla about a toxic spill diverted attention from Thunder Hill. Furthermore, there was nothing extraordinary about ranchers fighting the BLM, so nothing in the situation linked it in anyone's mind with the I-80 quarantine. In fact, when the BLM made that totally out-of-character offer to Brust and Dirkson, a *Sentinel* editorial praised the repentant attitude of the government and prophesied a new age of reason.''

''But from what you've told us,'' Dom said to Faye and Ernie, ''and from what else we've read, that was the first and last time the Bureau of Land Management dealt reasonably with ranchers. So it wasn't a new policy—just a one-time response to a crisis. And it's too coincidental to believe that the crisis evolving at Thunder Hill was unrelated to the crisis simultaneously under way here along the interstate.''

''Besides,'' Ginger said, ''once our suspicion was aroused, we got to thinking that if the trouble that night *had* been related to Shenkfield, there'd have been no need for the Army to use DERO troops for security. Because the soldiers stationed at Shenkfield would already have full security clearance in all matters related to that base, and there would've been nothing about a Shenkfield crisis too sensitive for them to see. The only reason DERO would've been called in is if the crisis was utterly unrelated to Shenkfield, involving something the soldiers at that base were not cleared for.''

"So if there're answers to our problems," Brendan said, "we'll most likely find them at the Thunder Hill Depository."

"We already suspected the story about a spill was less than half true," Dom said. "Maybe there was no truth to it at all. Maybe the crisis had nothing to do with Shenkfield. If the real source was Thunder Hill, the rest was just smoke they blew in the public's eyes."

"It sure feels right," Ernie said. He had finished dinner, too. His silverware was neatly arranged on the plate, which was almost as clean as before dinner, evidence that his military discipline and order had not departed him. "You know, part of my service career was in Marine Intelligence, so I'm speaking with some experience when I say this Shenkfield stuff truly does smack of an elaborate cover-story."

Ned's frown exaggerated his pronounced widow's peak. "There're a couple of things I don't understand. The quarantine didn't extend from Thunder Hill all the way down here. There were miles of territory in between that weren't sealed off. So how did the effects of an accident on Thunder Hill leap-frog over all that distance and come down on *our* heads, without causing trouble between there and here?"

"You're not dull-witted," Dom said. "I can't explain it, either."

Still frowning, Ned said, "Another thing: The Depository doesn't need a lot of land, does it? From what I've heard, it's underground. They've got a couple of big blast-doors in the side of the hill, a road leading up to the doors, maybe a guard post, and that's it. The three hundred acres you mentioned—the area around the entrance—is plenty big enough for a security zone. So why the land-grab?"

Dom shrugged. "Beats me. But whatever the hell happened up there on July sixth, it prompted two emergency actions on the part of the Army: first, a temporary quarantine down here, ten or twelve miles away, until we witnesses could be dealt with; second, an immediate enlargement of the security zone around the Depository, up there in the mountains; a secondary quarantine that's still in effect. I have a hunch . . . if we're ever going to find out what happened to us—what's *still* happening—we're going to have to dig into the activities up on Thunder Hill."

They were all silent. Though everyone was finished with dinner, no one was ready for dessert. Marcie was using her spoon to draw circles in the greasy residue of turkey gravy on her plate, creating fluid and temporary moon-forms. No one moved to clear away the dirty dishes, for at this point in the discussion, no one wanted to miss a word. They were at the crux of their dilemma: How were they to move against enemies as mighty as the U.S. Government and Army? How were they to penetrate an iron wall of secrecy that had been forged in the name of national security, with the full power of the state and the law behind it?

"We've put together enough to go public," Jorja Monatella said. "The deaths of Zebediah Lomack and Alan, the murder of Pablo Jackson. The similar nightmares that many of you have shared. The Polaroids. It's the kind of sensational stuff the media thrives on. If we let the world know what we think happened to us, we'll have the power of the press and public opinion on our side. We won't be alone."

"No good," Ernie said. "That kind of pressure'll just make the military stonewall like hell. They'll construct an even more confusing and impenetrable cover-up. They don't crack under pressure the way politicians do. On the other hand, as long as they see us stumbling around on our own, fumbling for explanations, they'll be confident—which might give us time to probe for their weak spots."

"And don't forget," Ginger warned, "apparently Colonel Falkirk advocated killing us instead of just blocking our memories, and we've no reason to believe he's mellowed since then. He was obviously overruled, but if we tried to go public, he might be able to persuade his superiors that a final solution is required, after all."

"But even if it's dangerous, maybe we've got to go public," Sandy said. "Maybe Jorja's right. I mean, there's no way we can get inside the Thunder Hill Depository to see what's going on. They've got lots of security and a pair of blast-doors built to take a nuclear hit."

Dom said, "Well, it's like Ernie told us . . . we'll have to just stay loose and search for their weaknesses until we find a way."

"But it looks like they don't *have* any weaknesses," Sandy said.

"Their cover-up has been falling apart ever since they brainwashed us and let us go," Ginger said. "Each time one of us remembers another detail, that's another gaping hole in their cover-up."

"Yeah," Ned said, "but seems to me they're in a better position to keep patching the holes than we are to keep poking new ones."

"Let's can the goddamn negative thinking," Ernie said gruffly.

Smiling beatifically, Brendan Cronin said, "He's right. We must not be negative. We *need* not be negative because we're meant to win." His voice was again infused with the eerie serenity and certitude which arose from his belief that the revelation of their special fate was inevitable. At moments like this, however, the priest's tone and manner did not comfort Dom, as they were meant to but, for some odd reason, stirred up a sediment of fear and muddled his emotions with anxiety.

"How many men are stationed at Thunder Hill?" Jorja asked.

Before Dom or Ginger could respond with information they'd gleaned from the *Sentinel*, a stranger appeared in the doorway at the head of the stairs that led up from the motel office. He was in his late thirties, lean and tough-looking, dark-haired, dark-complexioned, with a crooked left eye that was not coordinated with his right. Though the downstairs door was locked, and although the linoleum on the stairs did nothing to quiet ascending footsteps, the intruder appeared with magical silence, as if he were not a real man but an ectoplasmic visitation.

"For God's sake, shut up," he said, sounding every bit as real as anyone else in the room. "If you think you can plot in privacy here, you're badly mistaken."

Eighteen miles southwest of the Tranquility Motel, at Shenkfield Army Testing Grounds, all the buildings—laboratories, administration offices, security command center, cafeteria, recreation lounge, and living quarters—were underground. In the blazing summers on the edge of the high desert and in the occasionally bitter winters, it was easier and more economical to maintain a comfortable temperature and humidity level in underground rooms than in structures erected on the less-than-hospitable Nevada barrens. But a more important consideration was the frequent open-air testing of chemical—and occasionally even biological—weapons. The tests were conducted to study the effects of sunlight, wind, and other natural forces on the distribution patterns and potency of those deadly gases, powders, and superdiffusible mists. If the buildings were aboveground, any unexpected shift in the wind would contaminate them, making unwilling guinea pigs of base personnel.

No matter how involved they became in work or leisure, the staff of Shenkfield never forgot they were beneath the earth, for they had two constant reminders of their condition: the lack of windows; plus the susurration of the piped-in air coming through the wall vents, and the echoing hum of the motors that fanned the air along the pipes.

Sitting alone at a metal desk in the office to which he had been temporarily assigned, waiting impatiently and worriedly for the phone to ring, Colonel Leland Falkirk thought: *God, I hate this place!*

The never-ending whine and hiss of the air-supply system gave him a headache. Since his arrival on Saturday, Falkirk had been eating aspirin as though they were candy. Now he tipped two more out of a small bottle. He poured a glass of ice-water from the metal carafe that stood on the desk, but he did not use it to wash down the pills. Instead, he popped the dry aspirin into his mouth and chewed them.

The taste was bitter, disgusting, and he almost gagged.

But he did not reach for the water.

He did not spit out the aspirin, either.

He persevered.

A lonely, miserable childhood filled with uncertainty and pain, followed by an even worse adolescence, had taught Leland Falkirk that life was hard, cruel, and utterly unjust, that only fools believed in hope or salvation, and that only the tough survived. From an early age, he had forced himself to do things that were emotionally, mentally, and physically painful, for he had decided that self-inflicted pain would toughen him and make him less vulnerable. He tempered the steel of his will with challenges that ranged from chewing dry aspirin to major tests like the outings that he called "desperation survival treks." Those expeditions lasted two weeks or longer, and they put him face-to-face with death. He parachuted into a forest or jungle wilderness, far from the nearest outpost, without supplies, with only the clothes on his back. He carried no compass or matches. His only weapons were his bare hands and what he could fashion with them. The goal: reach civilization alive. He spent many vacations in that self-imposed suffering, which he judged worthwhile because he came back a harder and more self-reliant man than he'd been at the start of each adventure.

Now he crunched dry aspirin. The tablets were reduced to powder, and the powder turned his saliva to an acidic paste.

"Ring, damn you," he said to the telephone on the desk. He was hoping for news that would get him out of this hole in the ground.

In DERO, the Domestic Emergency Response Organization, a colonel was less a desk-jockey and more a field officer than in any other branch of the Army. Falkirk's home base was in Grand Junction, Colorado, not Shenkfield, but even in Colorado, he spent little time in his office. He thrived on the physical demands of the job, so the low-ceilinged, windowless rooms of Shenkfield felt like a many-chambered coffin.

If he had been engaged upon any mission but this one, he might have established temporary unit headquarters up at Thunder Hill Depository. That place was also underground but its caves were huge, high-ceilinged, not like these tomb-sized rooms.

But there were two reasons he had to keep his men away from Thunder Hill. First, he dared not draw attention to the place because of the secret it harbored. Several ranchers lived in the highlands along the road leading to the gated Thunder Hill turnoff. If they spotted a fully equipped DERO company moving into the Depository, they'd speculate about it. Locals must not start wondering about Thunder Hill. Two summers ago, he'd used Shenkfield as a red herring to divert attention from the Depository. Now, with another crisis building, he would stay here at Shenkfield again, so he would be in position to spread the same kind of disinformation to the press and public that he'd spread before. The second reason he set up HQ at Shenkfield was because he had certain dark suspicions about everyone in the Depository: He trusted none of them, would not feel safe among them. They might be . . . changed.

The residue of crushed aspirin had been in his mouth so long that he had adjusted to the bitter taste. He was no longer sickened, no longer had to struggle against the gag reflex, so it was all right to drink the water now. He drained the glass in four swallows.

Leland Falkirk suddenly wondered if he had crossed the line that separated the constructive use of pain from the enjoyment of it. Even as he asked the question, he knew the answer: Yes, to some degree, he had become a masochist. Years ago. He was a very well-disciplined masochist, one who benefited from the pain he inflicted on himself, one who controlled the pain instead of letting it control him, but a masochist nonetheless. At first he subjected himself to pain strictly to make himself tough. But along the way, he began to enjoy it, too. That insight left him blinking in surprise at the empty water-glass.

An outrageous image formed in his mind: himself more than a decade from now, a sixty-year-old pervert sticking bamboo shoots under his fingernails every morning for the thrill and to get his heart running. That grotesque picture was grim. It was also funny, and he laughed.

As recently as a year ago, Leland would not have been capable of self-critical insights of this nature. He had never been much of a laugher, either. Until recently. Lately, he was not merely noticing—and being amused by—traits in himself that he had never noticed before, but he was also becoming aware that he could and should change some of his attitudes and habits. He saw that he could become a better and more satisfied person, without losing the toughness he prized. This was a strange state of mind for him, but he knew the cause of it. After what had happened to him two summers ago, after all the things that he had seen, and considering what was happening right now up at Thunder Hill, he could not possibly go on with his life exactly as before.

The telephone rang. He grabbed it, hoping it was news about the situation in Chicago. But it was Henderson from Monterey, California, reporting that the operation at the Salcoe house was going smoothly.

The summer before last, Gerald Salcoe, with his wife and two daughters, rented a pair of rooms at the Tranquility Motel. On the wrong night. Recently, all of the Salcoes had experienced marked deterioration of their memory blocks.

The CIA's experts in brainwashing, who were usually used only in covert foreign operations, had been borrowed for the Tranquility job that July and had promised to repress witnesses' memories without fail; now they were embarrassed by the number of subjects whose conditioning was breaking down. The experience these people had undergone was too profound and shattering to be easily repressed; the forbidden memories possessed mythopoeic power and exerted relentless pressure on the memory blocks. The mind-control experts now claimed that *another* three-day session with the subjects would guarantee their eternal silence.

In fact, the FBI and CIA, working in conjunction, were illegally holding the Salcoe family incommunicado in Monterey at this very moment, putting them through another intricate program of memory repression and alteration. Although Cory Henderson, the FBI agent on the phone, claimed it was going well, Leland decided it was a lost cause. This was one secret that could not be kept.

Besides, too many agencies were involved: FBI, CIA, one entire DERO company, others. Which made too many chiefs and not enough Indians.

But Leland was a good soldier. In charge of the military side of the operation, he'd carry out his assignment even if it was hopeless.

In Monterey, Henderson said, "When are you moving in on the other witnesses at the motel?"

That was the word they used for everyone who had been brainwashed that July—witnesses. Leland thought it was apt, for in addition to its obvious meaning, it also embodied mystical and religious overtones. He remembered, as a child, being taken to tent revivals at which scores of Holy Rollers writhed upon the floor while the raving minister screamed at them to "be a witness to the miraculous, be a heartfelt witness for the Lord!" Well, what the witnesses at the Tranquility Motel had seen was every bit as paralyzing, amazing, humbling, and terrifying as the face of God that those spasming Pentecostals had longed to see.

To Henderson, Leland said, "We're standing by, ready to seal off the motel with half an hour's notice. But I'm not giving the go-ahead until someone straightens out the mess in Chicago with Calvin Sharkle. Not until I know for sure what's going on out in Illinois."

"What a screwup! Why was the situation with Sharkle allowed to deteriorate so far? He should've been grabbed, put into a new memory-repression program days ago, like we've done with the Salcoes here."

"Wasn't my screwup," Leland said. "Your Bureau is in charge of monitoring the witnesses. I only come in and mop up after you."

Henderson sighed. "I wasn't trying to shift the blame to your men, Colonel. And hell, you can't blame us, either. The trouble is, even though we're only doing visual surveillance of each witness four days a month and listening to only about half the tapes of their phone calls, we need twenty-five agents. But we only have twenty. Besides, the damn case is so highly classified that only three of the twenty know why the witnesses have to be watched. A good agent doesn't like being kept in the dark like that. Makes him feel he's not trusted. Makes him sloppy. So you get a situation like this Sharkle: The witness starts breaking through his memory block, and nobody notices until it's at crisis stage. Why'd we ever think we could maintain such an elaborate deception for an unlimited length of time? Nuts. I'll tell you what our problem was: We believed the CIA's brain-scrubbers. We believed those motherfuckers could do what they said they could do. That was our mistake, Colonel."

"I always said there was a simpler solution," Leland reminded him.

"Kill them all? Kill thirty-one of our own citizens just because they were in the wrong place at the wrong time?"

"I wasn't proposing it seriously. My point was that, short of barbarism, we couldn't contain the secret and shouldn't have tried."

Henderson's silence made it clear he did not believe Leland's disclaimer. Finally: "You *will* move on the motel tonight?"

"If the Chicago situation clears up, if I can figure what's going on there, we'll move tonight. But there're questions need answered. These strange . . . psychic phenomena. What's it mean? We both have ideas, don't we? And we're scared puke-sick. No, sir, I'm not moving against the motel and jeopardizing my men until I understand the situation."

Leland hung up.

Thunder Hill. He wanted to believe that what was happening up in the mountains would lead to a better future than mankind deserved. But in his heart he was afraid it was, instead, the end of the world.

* * *

When Jack stepped into the living room—which they had converted to a dining room—and spoke to the group, some gasped in surprise and started to rise, bumping the table in their eagerness to turn around, sending up a clatter of dishes and flatware. Others flinched in their chairs as if they thought he had been sent to kill them. He'd left the Uzi downstairs to avoid causing just such a panic, but his unexpected arrival still scared them. Good. They needed a nasty shock to make them more cautious. Only the little girl, playing in her gravy-smeared plate with a spoon, did not react to his arrival.

"All right, okay, be calm. Sit down, sit," Jack said, gesturing impatiently. "I'm one of you. That night, I registered at the motel as Thornton Wainwright. Which is how you've probably been looking for me. But that's not my real name. We'll get into that later. For now—"

Suddenly, everyone was excitedly pitching questions at him.

"Where did you—"

"—scared the bejesus—"

"How did you—"

"—tell us if—"

Raising his voice enough to silence them, Jack said, "This isn't the place to discuss these things. You can be heard here, for God's sake. I've been eavesdropping for nearly an hour. And if I can listen in on everything you say, then so can the people you're pitted against."

They stared dumbly at him, startled by his assertion that their privacy was an illusion. Then a big, blocky man with gray brush-cut hair said, "Are you telling us these rooms are bugged? 'Cause I find that hard to believe. I mean, I've searched, you know; I've checked, found nothing. And I've had some experience in these matters."

"You must be Ernie," Jack said, speaking in a sharp cold tone of voice meant to keep them on edge and get his message through to them. They had to understand, right away, that their conversations must be far better guarded, and the lesson had to be driven into them so hard and deep that they would not forget it. "I heard you mention your years in Marine Intelligence, Ernie. Christ, how long ago was that? Better part of a decade, I'll bet. Things have changed since then, man. Haven't you heard about the high-tech revolution? Shit, they don't need to come in here and physically plant listening devices. Rifle mikes are a hell of a lot better than they used to be. Or they can just hook up an infinity transmitter to their phone and dial your number." Jack pushed rudely past Ernie and stepped to the living room extension, which stood on a table by the sofa. He put his hand on the phone. "You know what an infinity transmitter is, Ernie? When they dial your number here, an electric tone oscillator deactivates the bell while it simultaneously opens the microphone in your telephone handset. There's no ringing for you to hear; you've no way of knowing you've been called, that your line's wide open. But they can monitor you in any room where you've got an extension." He plucked up the handset and held it toward them with a calculated look of scorn. "Here's your bug. You had it installed yourself." He slammed the handset back into the cradle. "You can bet your ass they've been tuning in on you a lot lately. Probably listened all through dinner. You people keep this up, you might as well just cut your own throats and save everybody a lot of trouble."

Jack's caustic performance had been effective. They were stunned. He said, "Now, is there a room without windows, big enough to hold a war council? Doesn't matter if there's a phone; we'll just unplug it."

An attractive middle-aged woman, apparently Ernie's wife, whom Jack vaguely remembered from checking into the motel two summers ago, thought for a moment and said, "There's the restaurant, the diner, next door."

"Your restaurant doesn't have any windows?" Jack asked.

"They were . . . broken," Ernie said. "Right now they're boarded up."

"Then let's go," Jack said. "Let's work out our strategy in privacy, then come back here for some of that pumpkin pie I heard you talking about. I had a *lousy* dinner while you people were in here eating yourselves into a stupor."

Jack went quickly down the stairs, confident they would follow.

Ernie loathed the crooked-eyed bastard for five minutes. But slowly, the hatred turned to grudging respect.

For one thing, Ernie admired the caution and stealth with which the guy had answered his own call to the Tranquility Motel. He had not just walked in like the others. He'd even brought a submachine gun.

But as he watched "Thornton Wainwright" slip the carrying-strap of the Uzi over one shoulder and head out the front door of the motel office, Ernie was still stung by the criticism he had endured. In fact, his rage was so great he did not pause to grab a coat, as most of the others did, but plunged after the stranger, through the door and across the macadam toward the diner, keeping pace with him in order to chew him out. "Listen, what the hell's the point of being a wiseass? You could've made your point without being so goddamn snide."

The stranger said, "Yeah, but I couldn't have made it as fast."

Ernie was about to reply when he abruptly realized he was outside, vulnerable, at night, in the *dark*. Halfway between the office and the diner. His lungs seemed to collapse; he could not draw the slightest wisp of breath. He made a disgustingly pitiful mewling sound.

To Ernie's surprise, the newcomer immediately grasped his arm, providing support, with no trace of the scorn he'd shown before. "Come on, Ernie. You're halfway there. Lean on me, and you'll make it."

Furious with himself for letting this bastard see him disabled and weak with childish fear, furious with the guy, too, for playing the Samaritan, humiliated, Ernie jerked his arm away from the helping hand.

"Listen," the newcomer said, "while I was eavesdropping, I heard about your problem, Ernie. I don't pity you, and I don't find your condition amusing. Okay? If your fear of the dark has something to do with this situation we all find ourselves in, it's not your fault. It's those bastards who messed with us. We need one another if we're going to get through this thing. Lean on me. Let me help you over to the diner, where we can turn on some lights. Lean on me."

When the newcomer began to talk, Ernie was unable to breathe, but by the time the guy finished his spiel, Ernie had the opposite problem; he was hyperventilating. As though pulled by a magnetic force, he turned from the diner and looked southeast, out into the terrifyingly immense darkness of the barrens. And suddenly he *knew* the darkness itself was not what he feared, but something that had been out there on the night of July 6, that bad summer. He was looking toward that special place along the highway, where they had gone yesterday to commune with the land in search of clues. That strange place.

Faye had arrived, and Ernie had not shaken loose of her when she had taken hold of him. But now the crooked-eyed man tried to take his arm again, and he was still angry enough to reject *that* assistance.

"Okay, okay," the guy said. "You're a bull-headed old Leatherneck bastard, and it's going to take your hurt pride a while to heal. If you want to be a thick-skulled mule, go ahead, stay pissed at me. It was only your blind anger that got you this far into the dark, wasn't it? Sure as hell wasn't Marine backbone. Just dumb blind anger. So if you stay pissed at me, maybe you'll be able to get to the diner.''

Ernie knew the crooked-eyed man was cleverly taunting him into completing the trip to the Tranquility Grille, that he was not really being cruel. *Hate me enough,* the guy was saying, *and you'll fear the darkness less. Focus on me, Ernie, and take one step at a time.* This was not much different than taking the guy's arm and leaning on it, and if Ernie had not been scared half to death by the surging night on all sides of him, he would have been amused at being conned this way. But he held fast to his anger, fanned the flames of it, and used it to light his way to the diner. He stepped through the door after the newcomer, and sighed with relief when the lights came on.

"It's freezing in here," Faye said. She went directly to the thermostat to switch on the oil furnace.

Sitting in a chair in the center of the room, his back to the door, Ernie recuperated from his ordeal as the others entered behind him. He watched the crooked-eyed newcomer moving from window to window, checking the plyboard slabs that had been nailed up to replace the shattered glass. And that was when, to Ernie's surprise, he realized he no longer loathed the guy, merely harbored an extreme dislike for him.

The newcomer examined the payphone near the door. Being a coin-operated unit, it did not unplug, so he lifted the receiver, tore the cord free of the wall-mounted box, and threw the useless handset aside.

"There's a private phone back of the counter," Ned said.

The newcomer told him to unplug it, and Ned obliged.

Then he told Brendan and Ginger to push three tables together and pull up chairs to accommodate everyone, and they did as they were told.

Ernie watched the crooked-eyed man with keen interest.

The newcomer was concerned about the diner's front door, which had not shattered during the weird phenomena on Saturday night because it was made of much thicker glass than the windows had been. It was not boarded up, so it offered a weak point to anyone trying to monitor them with a directional microphone. He wanted to know if any plywood was left from the window job, and Dom told him there was, and he sent Ned and Dom to bring back a suitable piece from the stack in the maintenance room behind the motel. They soon returned with a section of wood that was slightly larger than the door, and the newcomer stood it in front of the glass portal, bracing it in place with a table. "Not perfect," he said, "but good enough to defeat a rifle mike, I think." Then he headed toward the back of the restaurant to "have a look in the storeroom," and on his way he told Sandy to plug in the jukebox, switch it to free-play, and punch in some songs. "Some background noise makes eavesdropping more difficult." Even before he explained why he wanted music, Sandy jumped up and headed for the jukebox, quick to obey him.

Abruptly, Ernie realized why the crooked-eyed man fascinated him. The guy's quick thinking, precision movements, and ability to command indicated that he was—or had once been—a career soldier, an officer, a damn good one. He could tune an intimidatingly hard edge into his voice one moment, and the next moment tune it out in favor of cajolery.

Hell, Ernie thought, he's fascinating because he reminds me of me!

That was also why the newcomer had been able to needle Ernie so effectively back in the apartment. The guy knew just where to stick the sharp points because he and Ernie were, in some ways, two of a kind.

Ernie laughed softly. Sometimes, he thought, I can be such a perfect jackass.

The crooked-eyed man returned from the storeroom and smiled with satisfaction when he saw everyone seated at the long table which he had told Brendan and Ginger to put together from three smaller ones. He came to Ernie and said, "No hard feelings?"

"Hell, no," Ernie said. "And thanks . . . thanks a lot."

The newcomer went to the head of the table, where a chair had been left for him. With Kenny Rogers crooning on the jukebox, the guy said, "My name's Jack Twist, and I don't know any more than you what in hell's happening, probably less than you know. The whole thing gives me the heebie-jeebies, but I also have to tell you this is the first time in eight years that I've really and truly felt like I'm on the right side of an issue, the first time I've felt like one of the good guys—and dear God in Heaven, you can't know how much I've needed to feel *that!*"

Lieutenant Tom Horner, Colonel Falkirk's aide-de-camp, had enormous hands. The small tape recorder was totally concealed in his right hand when he carried it into the windowless office. His fingers were so large that he seemed certain to have trouble using the little control buttons. But he was remarkably dextrous. He produced the recorder, placed it on the desk, switched it on, and set it in the playback mode.

The tape had been duplicated from the reel-to-reel machine on which all phone-monitored conversations were recorded. It was a portion of an exchange that had taken place between several people at the Tranquility only minutes ago. The first part of the tape concerned the witnesses' discovery that the source of their trouble was not Shenkfield but Thunder Hill. Leland listened with dismay. He had not anticipated that their quest would take the right trail so soon. Their cleverness worried and angered him.

On the tape: *"For God's sake, shut up. If you think you can plot in privacy here, you're badly mistaken."*

"That's Twist," Lieutenant Horner said. He had a big voice, too, which was as well controlled as his enormous hands: a soft rumble. He stopped the tape. "We knew he was coming here. And we know he's dangerous. We figured he'd be more cautious than the others, sure, but we didn't expect him to act as if he was at war from the get-go."

As far as they knew, Jack Twist's memory block had not seriously deteriorated. He was not suffering fugues, sleepwalking, phobias, or obsessions. Therefore, only one thing might have motivated him to suddenly lease a plane and fly to Elko County: mail from the same traitor who had sent Polaroids to Corvaisis and to the Blocks.

Leland Falkirk was furious that someone involved in the cover-up, probably someone at Thunder Hill, was sabotaging the entire operation. He had made this discovery only last Saturday night, when Dominick Corvaisis and the Blocks had sat at the kitchen table and discussed the strange snapshots they'd been sent. Leland had ordered an immediate investigation and intense screening of everyone at the Depository, but that was going a lot slower than he had anticipated.

"There's worse," Horner said. He switched on the tape again.

Leland listened to Twist tell the others about rifle microphones and infinity transmitters. Shocked, they adjourned to the diner, where they could discuss their strategy without being overheard.

"They're in the diner now," Horner said, shutting off the recorder. "Ripped out the phones. I've spoken by radio with the observers we have stationed south of I-80. They watched the witnesses move to the Grille, but they haven't had any luck tuning in with a rifle mike."

"And won't," Leland said sourly. "Twist knows what he's doing."

"Now that they're aware of Thunder Hill, we've got to move on them as soon as possible."

"I'm waiting to hear from Chicago."

"Sharkle's still barricaded in his house?"

"Last I heard, yes," Leland said. "I've got to know if his memory block has completely crumbled. If it has, and if he gets a chance to tell anyone what he saw that summer, then the operation's blown, anyway, and it'd be a mistake to move against the witnesses at the motel. We'll have to fall back to another plan."

Under the diner's wagonwheel lights, safe in her mother's lap, Marcie dozed off even as Jack Twist introduced himself. In spite of the nap the girl had taken on the plane, sooty rings of weariness encircled her eyes, and a tracery of blue veins marked her porcelain-pale skin.

Jorja was tired, too, but Twist's dramatic arrival was an effective antidote to the narcotizing effects of the dinner. She was wide awake and eager to hear what he had to tell them of his own tribulations.

He began by briefly mentioning his imprisonment in Central America, with which his military career had ended. He made the experience sound more boring and frustrating than frightening, but Jorja sensed that he had endured grueling hardship. From his matter-of-fact tone, she had the impression that he was a man so secure in his self-image, so certain of his emotional and physical and intellectual strengths, that he never needed to boast or to hear the praise of others.

When he spoke of Jenny, his late wife, he was less able to maintain an air of detachment. Jorja heard the cadences of lingering grief in this part of his story; a river of love and longing flowed beneath his feigned placidity. The intimacy of mind and spirit between Jack Twist and Jenny, prior to her coma, had surely been extraordinary, for only a special and magical relationship would have ensured his unflagging devotion through the woman's long deathlike sleep. Jorja tried to imagine what a marriage of that sort might be like, then realized that, regardless of how magical their marriage had been, Jack would not have committed himself so totally to his afflicted wife if he'd been any less than the man he was. Their relationship had been special, yes, but even more special was this man himself. That realization increased Jorja's already strong interest in Twist and his story.

He was vague in describing the enterprises by which he had financed Jenny's long stay at a sanitarium. He made it clear only that what he had done was illegal, that he was not proud of it, and that his lawless days were over. "At least I never killed any innocent bystanders, thank God. Otherwise, I think it's best if you don't know any details that might somehow make you accessories-after-the-fact."

Their mutual unremembered ordeal had affected Jack Twist. But as with Sandy, the mysterious events of that July night had wrought only beneficial changes in him.

Ernie Block said, "I think what you've indirectly told us is that you were a professional thief." When Jack Twist said nothing, Ernie continued: "It occurs to me that you were almost certainly forced to reveal your criminal life to the people who brainwashed us. In fact, from what little you've said, I figure those safe-deposit boxes in which the postcards turned up were kept under the identities

STRANGERS   ◆   309

you also used when committing robberies; therefore, since that July, the Army
and government must've known about your illegal activities.''

Jack's silence was confirmation that he had, indeed, been a thief.

Ernie said, ''Yet, once they'd blocked your memories of what really happened
here that summer, they turned you loose and let you continue with what you'd
been doing. Why in the hell would they do that? I can understand the Army and
government bending—even breaking—the law to hide whatever happened at
Thunder Hill if it involves national security. But otherwise, you'd expect them
to uphold the law, wouldn't you? So why wouldn't they at least anonymously
inform the New York police or arrange for you to be caught in the middle of a
crime?''

Jorja said, ''Because from the start they've not been certain that our memory
blocks would hold up. They've been monitoring us, at least checking in on us
once in awhile, to be sure we don't need a refresher course in forgetfulness. What
happened to Ginger and Pablo Jackson seems to prove they're watching, all right.
And if they decided it was necessary to grab Jack—or any of us—and put him
through another session with the mind-control doctors, they'd want him where
they could reach him without too much trouble. It'd be a lot easier to snatch Jack
out of his apartment or from his car than to spirit him out of prison.''

''Good grief,'' Jack said, smiling at her, ''I think you've hit on it. Absolutely.''
Although Jorja had been slightly chilled by his smile the first time she'd seen it,
she perceived it differently now; it was a warmer smile than it had seemed initially.

Marcie murmured wordlessly in her sleep. Suddenly and curiously shy about
meeting Jack Twist's eyes, Jorja used her daughter's dreamy mutterings as an
excuse to look away from him.

Jack said, ''Whatever secret they're protecting is so important they had to let
me carry on with whatever crimes I chose to commit.''

Ginger Weiss shook her head. ''Maybe not. Maybe they engineered this guilt.
Maybe they planted the seed, so you'd change.''

''No,'' Jack said. ''If they didn't have time to weave the story of the toxic
spill into everyone's false memories, they sure wouldn't have had time to finesse
me toward the straight-and-narrow path. Besides . . . this is difficult to explain
. . . but, since coming here tonight, I feel in my heart that I relearned guilt and
found my way back into society because something so important happened to us
two summers ago that it put my own suffering in perspective and made me see
that none of my bad experiences was *so* bad as to justify the warping of my
entire life.''

''Yes!'' Sandy said. ''I feel that, too. All the hell I went through as a child
. . . none of it matters after what happened that July.''

They were silent, trying to imagine what experience could have been so shattering as to make even the most painful of life's tricks seem of little consequence.
But none of them could puzzle it out.

After he selected more songs on the jukebox, Jack asked a lot of questions of
the others, filling the gaps in his knowledge of their various ordeals and putting
together a complete picture of their discoveries to date. That done, he guided
them through a discussion of strategy, formulating a set of tasks for tomorrow.

Jorja was again intrigued by Jack's leadership skills. By the time the group
discussed what steps should be taken next and settled on an agenda, they had
agreed to undertake precisely the tasks Jack thought ought to be accomplished,
though there was never a sense that he had commanded or manipulated them.

When he'd first appeared in the Blocks' apartment, he'd proved he could take control of a situation and, by sheer force of personality, make people obey him. But now he chose indirection, and the speed with which everyone came around to his purposes was proof this was the right tactic.

Jorja realized that he impressed her for many of the same reasons that Ginger Weiss had impressed her. She saw in him the kind of person she had been struggling to become since her divorce—and the kind of man that Alan could never have been.

The final problem the group dealt with was the danger of an attack by Falkirk's men. Now that there was a real chance their memory blocks would substantially decay—or crumble completely—in the near future, they posed a greater threat to their enemy than at any time since July, the summer before last. Tomorrow, they would be separated most of the day as they carried out their various tasks and researches, but tonight they were in danger if they all stayed at the motel, making one easy target. Therefore, they agreed that most of them would go to bed now, while two or three drove into Elko and spent part of the night circling through town, always on the move, alert. Assuming that the Tranquility was under observation, the enemy would at once realize they could no longer seize everyone in a clean sweep. At four o'clock in the morning, a second group of outriders could rendezvous with the first team in Elko and relieve them, so they could come back here and get some sleep.

"I'll volunteer for the first team," Jack said. "I just have to fetch my Cherokee from the hills, where I left it. Who'll go with me?"

"I will," Jorja said at once, then became aware of the weight of her daughter on her lap. "Uh, that is, if someone'll let Marcie sleep in their room tonight."

"No problem," Faye said. "She can stay with Ernie and me."

Jack said they ought to divide their numbers further, and Brendan Cronin volunteered to join him and Jorja on the first team. The priest's response triggered a peculiar feeling in Jorja, a pang she would not identify as disappointment until much later.

Because everyone else had errands to run early tomorrow, the second team was composed of only Ned and Sandy. A rendezvous between the teams was set for four o'clock in the morning at the Arco Mini-Mart.

"If you get there first," Jack said, "for God's sake don't buy a Hamwich. Okay, I guess that's it. We should get moving."

"Not quite yet," Ginger said. The physician folded her hands and looked down at her interlaced fingers, collecting her thoughts. "Since this afternoon, when Brendan first arrived, when the rings appeared on his and Dom's hands, when the motel office was filled with that strange noise and the light . . . I've been chewing over everything we've been able to learn, trying to make those bizarre phenomena fit in somehow. I've hit on an explanation for some of it; not all, but some of it."

Everyone expressed an eagerness to hear the theory, half-formed though it might be.

Ginger said, "As different as our dreams are, one element links all of them: the moon. Okay. Our other dreams—decon suits, IV needles, beds with restraining straps—proved to be based on real experiences, real threats. In fact, they weren't dreams but memories surfacing in the form of dreams. So it seems reasonable to suppose the moon also featured prominently in whatever happened to us, that the moon, too, is a memory trying to surface in our dreams. Agreed?"

"Agreed," Dom said, and everyone else nodded.

"We've seen how Marcie's lunar obsession changed to a fascination with a *scarlet* moon,'' Ginger continued. ''And Jack's told us that, a couple nights ago, the ordinary moonlight in his own nightmare turned into a bloody glow. None of the rest of us has dreamed of a red moon yet, but I submit that the appearance of this scarlet image in Marcie's and Jack's dreams is proof that it's also a memory. In other words, on the night of July 6, we saw something that made the moon turn red. And the apparitional light, which sometimes fills Brendan's bedroom, which some of us witnessed today in the motel office, is a strange sort of reenactment of what happened to the real moon on the night in July. The apparitional light is a message meant to nudge our memories.''

''Message,'' Jack said. ''All right. But who the devil's *sending* the message? Where's the light come from? How is it generated?''

''I've got an idea about that,'' Ginger said. ''But let me take this one step at a time. First, let's consider what might've happened to make the moon turn red that night.''

Jorja listened, as did the others, with interest at first and then with growing uneasiness, while Ginger got up from her chair and, pacing, outlined an unnerving explanation.

Ginger Weiss wholeheartedly embraced the scientific worldview. To her, the universe unfailingly operated by the rules of logic and reason, and no mystery could long endure once attacked in a logical fashion. But unlike some in the scientific community—and *many* in the medical community—she did not believe that a vivid imagination was necessarily a hindrance to logic and reason. Otherwise, she might not have devised the theory she now conveyed to the others in the Tranquility Grille.

It was a pretty strange theory, and she was nervous about how the others would receive it. So she paced to the jukebox, over to the service counter, back to the table, moving constantly as she talked:

''The men who dealt with us in the first day or two of imprisonment were wearing decontamination suits designed to handle biological risks. They must've been worried we were infected with something. So perhaps part of what we saw was a scarlet cloud of biological contaminant. When it passed overhead, it turned the moon red.''

''And we were all infected with some strange disease,'' Jorja said.

Ginger said, ''That may be why, yesterday at the special place along the highway, I had the memory-flash of Dom shouting, 'It's inside me. It's inside me.' That would have been a logical thing for him to shout if, that night, he had found himself caught up in a red cloud of some contaminant and realized he was breathing it in. And Brendan's told us that the same words—'It's inside me'— came spontaneously to his lips last night in Reno, when the red apparitional light filled his room.''

''Bacteria? Disease? Then why didn't we get sick?'' Brendan said.

''Because they treated us immediately,'' Dom said. ''We've already worked that one out, Brendan—yesterday, before you got here. But, Ginger, the light that filled the office this afternoon was too bright to represent moonlight filtered through a red cloud.''

''I know,'' Ginger said, pacing. ''Underdeveloped as it is, my idea doesn't explain everything—like the rings on your hands. So maybe it's not the right idea. On the other hand, it does explain some things, and maybe if we think about it long enough, we'll see how it explains these other puzzles, as well. And as a theory, it has one big plus.''

''What's that?'' Ned asked.

"It could explain why Brendan was involved in two miracle cures in Chicago. It could explain the whirling paper moons in Zebediah Lomack's house. And the destruction here at the diner on Saturday night, when Dom was trying to recall what had happened the summer before last. It could explain the source of the apparitional light.''

On the jukebox, the last of a series of songs had faded to its end as Ginger began to speak. But no one got up to choose more music, for they were riveted by her promise to explain the inexplicable.

"To this point,'' Ginger said, "the theory's pretty mundane. A red cloud of contaminant. Nothing hard to accept in that. But now . . . you've got to take a big leap of imagination with me. We've been assuming that the miraculous healing and certainly the poltergeist phenomena have some mysterious external source. Father Wycazik, Brendan's rector, thinks that external source is God. The rest of us don't feel it's exactly divine. We don't know what the hell it is, but we all assume that it's an external power, something out there somewhere that's taunting us or trying to reach us with a message or threatening us. But what if these wonders have an *internal* source. Suppose Brendan and Dom really possess some power, and suppose that they possess it *because of what happened during the night of the red moon.* Suppose they have telekinesis—which is the power to move objects without touching them, which would explain the whirling paper moons and the destruction in the diner.''

Everyone looked at Dom and Brendan in amazement, but no one was more startled than those two men, who gaped at Ginger, shocked.

Dom said, "But that's ridiculous! I'm no psychic, no sorcerer.''

"Me neither,'' Brendan said.

Ginger shook her head. "Not consciously, no. I'm saying maybe the power is in you, and you're just not aware of it. Bear with me. Think about it. The first time the rings appeared on Brendan's hands, the first time he exercised his healing power, was when he was combing the hair of the little girl in the hospital. He's said he was overwhelmed with pity for her and filled with frustration and anger that he couldn't help her. Maybe it was his intense frustration and anger that freed the power in him, even though he wasn't aware of it. He *couldn't* be aware of it because the acquisition of this power is part of what he's been made to forget. Okay, the second time, with the wounded policeman, Brendan found himself in an extreme crisis, which might trigger these powers.'' She began pacing and talking more rapidly to prevent debate until she'd finished. "Now think about Dom's experiences. The first one, in Reno, at Lomack's house. The way you told it to us, Dom . . . as you wandered through the house, you became so frustrated by the ever-deepening nature of the mystery that you wanted to rush through those rooms *and tear those paper moons off the walls*. Those were your very words. And, of course, that's what happened: You pulled those moons off the walls, not with your hands but with this power. And remember, the pictures only fell to the floor when you shouted, 'Stop it, stop it!' When it did stop, you thought something had heard you and obeyed or relented, but in fact you stopped it yourself.''

Brendan, Dom, and a couple of the others still looked skeptical.

But Ginger had captured Sandy Sarver's imagination. "It makes sense! It makes even more sense if you think about what happened here on Saturday night, right in this very room. Dom was trying to remember back to that Friday in July, trying to remember what happened right up to the second where his memory block took effect. And while he was struggling to remember . . . all of a sudden this strange noise, this thunder, started to rumble through the diner, and everything started to shake. He could've been unconsciously using this power of his to re-create the *effects* of whatever happened back then.''

''Good!'' Ginger said encouragingly. ''See? The more you think about it, the more it hangs together.''

''But the strange light,'' Dom said. ''You're saying Brendan and I somehow manufactured that?''

''Yes, possibly,'' Ginger said, returning to the table, leaning on her empty chair. ''Pyrokinesis. The ability to spontaneously generate heat or fire with the power of the mind alone.''

''This wasn't fire,'' Dom said. ''It was light.''

''So . . . call it 'photokinesis,' '' Ginger said. ''But I think when you and Bren-dan met, you subconsciously recognized the power in each other. On a deep level, you were both reminded of what happened to you that July night, the thing you've been forced to forget. And both of you wanted to blast those memories into view. So unwittingly you generated that weird light, which was a re-creation of the way the moon changed from white to red on the night of July 6. It was your subcon-scious trying to jolt the memory through the block.''

Ginger could see that their minds were spinning with all these odd ideas, and she wanted to keep them unsettled a while longer, because when they were un-settled they were more likely to absorb what she was saying. Given time for quiet reflection, the heavy armor of skepticism would fall back into place, and her ideas would bounce off.

Ernie Block shook his head. ''Wait a minute. You're losing me now. You started all this by suggesting that what turned the moon red was a scarlet cloud of some biological contaminant. Then you jumped way the hell to one side and started talking about how the thing that happened to us was responsible for Dom and Brendan developing these supposed powers. Where's the connection? What does biological contamination have to do with all this psychic stuff, anyway?''

Ginger took a deep breath because they had come to the core of her theory, the wildest part of it. ''What if . . . *what if* we were contaminated by some virus or bacterium that, as a side-effect, causes profound chemical or genetic or hor-monal changes in its host, changes in the host's brain? And what if those changes leave the host with something very like psychic powers, even once the infection is gone?''

They stared at her with a variety of expressions, though not as if they thought her mad, and not as if she was too imaginative for her own good. Rather, they seemed impressed by the complex chain of logic which she had forged and by the inevitability of the final link.

''Good God,'' Dom said, ''I doubt that it's the right answer, but it's sure the prettiest, most neatly constructed theory I ever expect to hear. What a concept for a novel! A genetically engineered virus that, as a surprise side-effect, causes a sort of forced evolution of the human brain, resulting in psychic powers. For the first time in weeks, I have a terrific urge to rush to a typewriter. Ginger, if we get out of this alive, I'll have to give you a piece of the royalties on the book that's sure to grow out of that idea.''

Gently rocking her slumbering daughter, Jorja Monatella said, ''But why *couldn't* it be the right answer? Why does it just have to be a terrific concept for a novel?''

''For one thing,'' Jack Twist said, ''if it were true, if we'd been contaminated with a virus like that, we'd all have developed psychic powers. Right?''

''Well,'' Ginger said, ''maybe we weren't all contaminated. Or maybe we were contaminated, but the virus didn't get a foothold in all of us.''

Faye said, "Or maybe this special side-effect isn't manifested in everyone who's infected by the bug."

"Good thought," Ginger said. She began to pace again: this time, not because she was nervous but because she was excited.

Ned Sarver pushed one hand through his receding hair and said, "Are you saying the Army knew about this side-effect of the virus, knew that it might cause these changes in some of us?"

"I don't know," Ginger said. "Maybe they knew. Maybe not."

"I think not," Ernie said. "Definitely not. From what you found in the *Sentinel,* we know they closed the interstate shortly before the 'accident' happened, which means it was no accident. So . . . first of all, I find it hard to believe our own military would intentionally subject us to contamination with a biological-warfare microorganism in a hare-brained scheme to test its effectiveness in the field. But even if such an atrocity was possible, they wouldn't expose us to a virus that could transform us in the way Ginger has suggested. Because, my friends, people with strong psychic powers would be a new species, a *superior* breed of humanity. Formidable psychic power would translate directly into military, economic, and political power. So if the government *knew* it had a virus that conferred these powers, it would not expose a group of ordinary people like us. Not in a million years. That blessing would be reserved for those already in positions of high authority, for the elite. I agree with Dom: I find the red-cloud-of-virus theory quite fascinating . . . though unlikely. However, if we *were* contaminated by such a thing, the side-effect was unknown to the government."

In light of what Ernie had said, everyone was looking at Brendan and Dom with a new appreciation composed equally of awe, uneasiness, wonder, respect, and fear. Ginger saw both the priest and the writer squirm with the exhilarating yet frightening realization that they might have within them the potential for superhuman power, a potential that, if fulfilled, would forever separate them from the rest of mankind.

"No," Dom said, starting to get up in protest, then sitting back down as if he did not think his legs would support him. "No, no. You're not right, Ginger. I'm no superman, no wizard, no damn . . . freak. If you were right, I'd feel it. I'd *know* it, Ginger."

Brendan Cronin, equally shaken, said, "I've thought that somehow I've been the *vehicle* for the healing of Emmy and Winton. I've thought that something— not God, perhaps, but something—is working through me. I never thought of *myself* as the actual healer. Listen, I was under the impression we'd already decided the toxic-spill story was entirely a fake, a cover, that what happened to us wasn't an accident of any kind, neither chemical nor biological, but something altogether different."

Jack and Jorja and Faye and Ned started talking at the same time. The noise level rose so loud that little Marcie frowned in her sleep, and Ginger said, "Wait, wait, wait a minute. There's no point discussing it because we can't prove there was such a virus any more than we can prove there wasn't one. Not yet. But maybe we can prove the other part."

"What do you mean?" Sandy Sarver asked.

Ginger said, "Maybe we can prove Dom and Brendan have the power. Not how they got it, but just that they have it."

Dom was incredulous. "How?"

"We'll set up a test," Ginger said.

* * *

Dom was absolutely certain that it would not work, that they were wasting time, that the whole idea was foolish.

Yet he was also scared that it *would* work, and that the proof of his power would condemn him to the condition of a freak or at least to a life forever closed to ordinary human relationships. If he possessed godlike power, no one would ever regard him without wonder and fear. In even the most relaxed or intimate moments with friends or lovers, their awareness of his extraordinary gifts would intrude, either overtly or in an unspoken subtext. Others, perhaps most, would envy or hate him.

The unfairness of his predicament grated on him. For most of his thirty-five years, he had been shy and ineffectual, condemned to a drab existence by his timidity. Then he had changed, and for fifteen months, until his sleepwalking began last October, he'd been outgoing. Now, that brief, wonderful season of normality might be passing. If the test that Ginger outlined were to prove Dom had somehow acquired psychic powers, he would be isolated again, not by his own sense of inferiority, as before, but by everyone else's uneasy awareness of his superiority.

The test. Dom hoped to God he failed.

He and Brendan Cronin were sitting by themselves at the long table, one at each end. Jorja Monatella had put her slumbering daughter in a booth, and the girl had not awakened. The adults—all seven, including Jorja—stood in a semicircle around the table, back a couple of paces, giving Dom and Brendan space to concentrate free of distraction.

A salt shaker stood on the table in front of Dom. Ginger's test required that he concentrate on moving the object without touching it. "Just an inch," she had said. "If you can evoke just the slightest perceptible motion in the shaker, we'll know you've got the power."

At the far end of the three joined tables, a pepper shaker stood in front of Brendan Cronin. The priest was staring at the small glass cylinder as intently as Dom was staring at his own shaker, and his round freckled face was filled with a foreboding only marginally less grim than Dom's. Although Brendan had denied that the hand of God lay behind the miraculous cures and apparitional lights, it was clear to Dom that the priest secretly and deeply hoped to discover that, in fact, a divine Presence was at work. He wanted to be drawn back into his faith, into the bosom of the Church. If the miracles proved to be his own work, accomplished by the exertion of heretofore unrecognized psychic powers, and if those powers proved to have been conferred by a mere *germ,* as Ginger's crazy-but-canny theory would have it, Brendan's yearning for spiritual elevation and holy guidance would be unfulfilled.

The salt shaker.

Dom fixed his eyes on it and tried to clear every thought from his mind except the determined intention to move the shaker. Although he did not want to discover that he had these strange talents, he had to make a sincere attempt to employ them. He had to know if it was true.

If the power existed, neither Ginger nor any of the others could suggest techniques for tapping it. "But," Ginger had said, "if it can explode spontaneously and spectacularly in moments of stress, surely you can learn to call upon it and control it whenever and however you desire . . . just as a musician can apply his *musical* talent any time he pleases. Or just as you apply your writing talent to the blank page."

The salt shaker remained motionless, unaffected.

Dom strove to narrow his attention until that humble glass cylinder—with its perforated stainless-steel cap and grainy white contents—was the only thing in his universe. He brought all his mind to bear upon it, every speck of his will, and tried to push it along the table, strained until he realized he was gritting his teeth, fisting his hands.

Nothing.

He changed tack. Instead of mentally assaulting the shaker as if he were blasting away with a cannon at the mighty walls of a fortress, he relaxed and studied the object to get an intimate sense of its size, shape, and texture. Perhaps the key was to develop an empathy for the shaker. "Empathy" was the word that seemed right to him, though he was relating to an inanimate and inorganic object; instead of battling it, perhaps he could empathize and somehow . . . induce it to cooperate in a short telekinetic journey. Only an inch. He leaned forward slightly to better examine the functional simplicity of its design: five beveled facets to make it easy to grip and hold; a thick glass bottom to provide balance and reduce the frequency of spills; a shiny metal cap. . . .

Nothing. Standing unaffected on the table before him, the shaker seemed like the mythical immovable object, heavy beyond weighing, welded forever to this spot in space and time.

But of course, like all forms of matter in the universe, it was not immovable, and in some ways it was *always* moving, never still. After all, it was composed of billions of ceaselessly moving atoms, the outer parts of which orbited, planet-like, around the billions of sunlike nuclei. The salt shaker was engaged in uninterrupted motion on a subatomic level, frantically moving *within* its structure, so it should not be difficult to induce it to make one additional movement, one little jaunt on the macrocosmic level of human perception, just one little hop and skip, just one—

Dom felt a sudden buoyancy, almost as if he himself were going to be moved by some arcane force, but instead—and at last—the salt shaker moved. He had become so deeply involved with that homely object that he had actually forgotten Ginger and the others; he was reminded of their presence when, as one, they gasped and exclaimed softly. The shaker did not simply slide one inch along the table—or two or ten or twenty. It rose into the air instead, as if gravity had ceased to have a claim on it. Like a tiny glass balloon, it floated upward: one foot, two, three, and stopped four feet above the surface on which, only seconds ago, it had appeared immovable. It remained suspended several inches above the eye-level of those who were standing, and they stared up at it in awe.

At the far end of the table, Brendan's pepper shaker rose, too. Mouth open, eyes wide, Brendan stared at the rising cylinder. When it stopped at precisely the same height as the salt shaker, Brendan finally dared to take his eyes from it. He looked at Dom, glanced nervously at the pepper shaker again, as if certain it would crash down the moment he shifted his gaze, then looked at Dom once more when he realized that eye-contact was not required to maintain levitation. Several sentiments were apparent in the priest's eyes: wonder, amazement, puzzlement, fear, and an emotional acknowledgment of the profound brotherhood that existed between him and Dom by virtue of the strange power they shared.

Dom was intrigued that he did not need to strain to keep the salt shaker aloft. In fact, it seemed hard to believe that he was actually responsible for its magical performance. He was not conscious of either possessing or exerting control of the object. He felt no power surging in him. Evidently, his telekinetic ability functioned automatically, in a fashion similar to respiration and heartbeat.

Brendan raised his hands. The red rings had reappeared on them.

Dom looked at his own hands and saw the same inscrutable stigmata burning brightly.

What did they mean?

Looming overhead, the salt and pepper shakers generated a sense of expectancy in Dom even greater than he had felt at the beginning of this test. Apparently, the others felt it as well, for they began to urge Dom and Brendan to perform additional feats.

"Incredible," Ginger said breathlessly. "You've shown us vertical movement, levitation. Can you also move them horizontally?"

"Can you lift something heavier?" Sandy Sarver asked.

"The light," Ernie said. "Can you generate the red light?"

Seeking first to accomplish a more modest task than any they had proposed, Dom thought about giving the salt shaker a slight spin, and immediately it began to twirl in midair, eliciting another gasp from the onlookers. A moment later, Brendan's pepper shaker began to spin, too. Reflections of the overhead lights glimmered liquidly across the shiny metal caps of the spinning dispensers, flashed off the facets of the glass, traveled scintillatingly along the edges where one facet met another, so the shakers looked like glittery Christmas-tree ornaments.

Simultaneously, the two small dispensers began drifting toward one another, the horizontal movement Ginger had requested, though Dom was not aware of consciously directing the salt shaker on this course. He supposed Ginger's suggestion was accepted by his subconscious, which now employed psychic energy to accomplish the task, without waiting for him to make a conscious effort. It was eerie—the way he controlled the shaker yet was unaware of how that control was exerted.

Above the centermost point of the three joined tables, the salt and pepper shakers stopped moving horizontally when they were about ten inches apart. They hung side by side, spinning a bit faster than before, throwing off spangles of reflected light. Then they began to revolve around each other in perfectly circular synchronized orbits. But that lasted only a few seconds. Suddenly, the shakers were spinning faster than before, and swinging around each other much faster as well, and in much more complex, parabolic counterorbits.

Captivated and delighted, the onlookers laughed, applauded. Dom looked at Ginger. Her radiant face shone with an expression of pure, spiritual uplift that made her more beautiful than ever. She lowered her gaze from the salt and pepper shakers to Dom, grinning with wild excitement, and gave him a thumbs-up sign. Ernie Block and Jack Twist watched the aerobatics with open-mouthed wonder that made them look not like hard-bitten ex-soldiers but like two small boys seeing fireworks for the first time in their lives. Laughing, Faye stood with her hands raised toward the shakers, as if she were trying to feel the miraculous field of power in which they were suspended. Ned Sarver was laughing, too, but Sandy was crying, a sight that startled Dom until he realized she was also smiling and that the tears on her cheeks were tears of joy.

"Oh," Sandy said, turning to Dom as if she had sensed that he was looking at her, "isn't it wonderful? Whatever it means, isn't it just wonderful? The freedom . . . the freedom of it . . . the breaking away of all the bonds . . . the rising up and above and away . . . "

Dom knew precisely what she was feeling and trying to say, because he felt it too. For the moment, he forgot that possession of these abilities would forever alienate him from people who were without the talent, and he was filled with a rapturous sense of transcendence, with an appreciation for what it might mean to take a giant leap up the ladder of evolution, breaking away from the chains of human limitations. In the Tranquility Grille tonight, there was a sense of history being made, a sense that nothing in the world would ever be the same again.

"Do something else," Ginger said.

"Yes!" Sandy said. "Show us more. Show us more."

In other parts of the room, other salt shakers flew up from the tables on which they had been standing: six, eight, ten in all. They hung motionless for a moment, then began to spin like the first shaker.

Instantly, an equal number of pepper shakers took flight and began spinning as well.

Dom still did not know how he was doing these things; he made no effort to perform each new trick; the thought merely became fact, as if wishes could come true. He suspected that Brendan was equally baffled.

The jukebox had been silent. Now it began to play a Dolly Parton tune, though no one had punched the programming buttons.

Did I do that, Dom wondered, or was it Brendan?

Ginger said, "My God, I'm so excited I'm going to *plotz!*"

Laughing, Dom said, "*Plotz?* What's *that* one mean?"

"Bust, explode," Ginger said. "I'm so excited I'm going to bust!"

Every salt and pepper shaker spun, and the halves of every pair orbited each other, and now all eleven sets began moving around the room in a train, faster, faster, making a soft *whoosh* as they cut the air, casting off sparks of reflected light.

Abruptly, a dozen chairs rose off the floor, not in the controlled and playful manner in which the salt and pepper shakers had risen from the tables, but with such violence and momentum that they shot instantly to the ceiling, smashing against that barrier with a deafening clatter. One of the wagon-wheel lighting fixtures was struck by two chairs; its lightbulbs burst, and the room was only three-quarters as brightly illuminated as it had been. That wagon wheel broke loose of its anchor brackets and wires, crashing to the floor a few feet behind Dom. The chairs remained against the ceiling, vibrating as if they were a flock of enormous bats hovering on dark wings. Most of the salt and pepper shakers were still whirling maniacally around the room above everyone's head, though a few had been brought down by the upflung chairs. Now, a few more stopped spinning, swung erratically out of their orbits, out of the train as well, wobbled, and shot to the floor. One of them struck Ernie's shoulder, and he cried out in pain.

Dom and Brendan had lost control. And because they had never known exactly how they had established control in the first place, they did not know how to regain it.

In a blink, the celebratory mood changed to panic. The onlookers scrambled for shelter under the tables, acutely aware that the levitated chairs—rattling ominously against the ceiling—were potentially far more dangerous missiles than the salt and pepper shakers. The noise awakened Marcie. She sat up in the booth where she had been sleeping, crying now and calling for her mother. Jorja pulled the girl off the booth and scrambled under one of the tables with her, hugging her close, and everyone was out of the line of fire except Brendan and Dom.

Dom felt as if this psychic power was a live grenade that had been wired irremovably to his hand.

Overhead, three or four more shakers lost momentum and came down like bullets. The dozen levitated chairs began to bounce against the ceiling more aggressively, shedding small pieces of themselves.

Dom didn't know if he should dive for cover or attempt to regain control. He looked at Brendan, who was equally paralyzed.

Overhead, the three remaining wagon-wheel lights swayed wildly on their chains, causing goblin shadows to leap across the room.

The battering chairs gouged out small chunks of the ceiling.

A salt shaker dropped in front of Dom, impacting like a tiny meteorite against the table. The glass was too thick to shatter, but the small jar cracked into three or four pieces, flinging up what salt it still contained, and Dom flinched from the white spray.

Remembering the spinning carousel of paper moons in Lomack's house six days ago, Dom raised both hands toward the rattling chairs and whirling shakers. Clenching his hands into fists, shutting the red-ring stigmata out of sight, he said, "Stop it. Stop it now. *Stop it*!"

Overhead, the chairs ceased vibrating. The salt and pepper shakers halted in midwhirl and hung motionless in the air.

For a second or two, the diner was preternaturally silent.

Then the twelve chairs and the last of the shakers dropped straight down, bouncing off tables and other chairs that had never taken flight. When everything at last came to rest in tangled rubble, Dom and Brendan were as unscathed as those who had taken refuge under the tables. Dom blinked at the priest, and around them all was graveyard-still. This moment of silence was longer than the first. It seemed as if time had stopped, until Marcie's thin whimpering and her mother's murmured assurances started the engines of reality purring again, drawing the others from their places of shelter.

Ernie was still massaging his shoulder, where he had been hit by a salt shaker, but he was not seriously hurt. No one else was injured, though everyone was shaken.

Dom saw the way they were looking at him and Brendan. Warily. Just as he had figured they would look at him if he proved to have the power. Just the way he had dreaded being looked at. Damn.

Ginger seemed to be the only one who was not put off by his new status. She enthusiastically embraced Dom and said, "What matters is that you've got it. You've got it, and eventually you can learn to use it, and that's wonderful."

"I'm not so sure," Dom said, looking at the broken chairs, fallen lighting fixtures. Jack Twist was brushing salt and drywall dust off his clothes. Jorja was still comforting her frightened child. Faye and Sandy were picking splinters and other bits of debris out of their hair, and Ned was pondering the danger of the live wires dangling from the ceiling where the chandelier had torn loose. Dom said, "Ginger, even when I was using the power, I didn't know how I was doing it. And when it ran wild . . . I didn't know how to stop it."

"But you did stop it," she said. She kept one arm around his waist as if she knew—God bless her—that he needed the reassurance of human contact. "You *did* stop it, Dom."

"Maybe next time I won't be able." He realized he was shivering. "Look at this mess. My God, Ginger, someone could've been badly hurt."

"No one was."

"Someone could have been killed. Next time—"

"It'll be better," she said.

Brendan Cronin came around the long table. "He'll change his mind, Ginger. Give him time. I know *I'm* going to try again. Alone, next time. In a couple of days, when I've had time to think it through, I'll go out somewhere in an open field, away from people, where no one can be hurt except me, and I'll give it another try. I think it's going to be difficult to control the . . . energy. It's going to take a lot of time, a lot of work, maybe years. But I'll explore, practice. And so will Dom. He'll realize as much when he's had a couple of minutes to think about it.''

Dom shook his head. "I don't want this. I don't want to be so different from other people."

"But now you are," Brendan said. "We both are."

"That's damn fatalistic."

Brendan smiled. "Though I'm having a crisis of faith, I'm still a priest, so I believe in predestination, fate. That's an article of faith. But we priests are a clever bunch, so we can be fatalistic and believe in free will at the same time! *Both* are articles of faith." For the priest, the psychological effects of these events were far different from the fear raised in Dom. As he talked, he repeatedly rose onto his toes as if he were nearly buoyant enough to float away.

At a loss to understand the priest's good humor, Dom changed the subject. "Well, Ginger, if we've proved half of your crazy theory, at least we've disproved the other half."

She frowned. "What do you mean?"

"In the midst of all that . . . uproar," Dom said, gesturing toward the battered ceiling, "when I saw the rings appear on my hands again, I decided the psychic power wasn't a side-effect of my strange viral infection. I know the source of it is something else, something even stranger, though I don't know what it may be."

"Oh? Well, which is the case?" she asked. "Have you merely decided, or do you really know?"

"I know," Dom said. "Deep inside, I know."

"Oh, yes, me too," Brendan said happily, as Ernie and Faye and the others gathered around. "You were correct, Ginger, when you suggested the power was in Dom and me. And it's been in us since that July night, like you said. However, you're not right about the method by which we acquired the gift. Like Dom said . . . in the middle of all the chaos, I sensed that biological contamination wasn't the right explanation. I haven't the foggiest notion what the answer is, but we can rule out that part of your theory."

Now Dom understood why Brendan was in such good spirits in spite of the frightening exhibition in which they'd just participated. Though he professed to see no religious aspect to recent events, in his heart of hearts, the priest had retained hope that the miraculous cures and apparitional lights were of divine origin. He had been depressed by the dismayingly secular thought that the gift could have been bestowed on him not by his Lord but simply as the chance side-effect of an exotic infection, by the unwitting office of a mindless virus—and a *man-made* virus, as well. He was relieved to be able to dismiss that possibility. His high spirits and good humor, even amidst the destruction of the diner, arose from the fact that a divine Presence was once again, for Brendan, at least a viable—if still unlikely—explanation.

Dom wished he, too, could find courage and strength in the notion that their troubles were part of a divine scheme. But at the moment, he believed only in danger and death, twin juggernauts that he sensed bearing down on him. The personality changes that had occurred in him during his move from Portland to Mountainview were laughably minor in comparison to the changes that had begun working in him tonight, with the discovery of this unwanted power. He almost felt as if the power was *alive* in him, a parasite that in time would eat away everything that had been Dominick Corvaisis and, having assumed his identity, would stalk the world in his body, masquerading as human.

Crazy.

Nevertheless, he was worried and scared.

He looked at each of the others who were gathered around him. Some met his eyes for a moment, then quickly looked away, just as one might hesitate to meet the gaze of a dangerous—or intimidating—man. Others—most notably Jack Twist, Ernie, and Jorja—met his eyes forthrightly, but were incapable of concealing the uneasiness and even apprehension with which they now regarded him. Only Ginger and Brendan seemed to have suffered no change in their attitude toward him.

"Well," Jack said, breaking the spell, "we should call it a night, I guess. We've got a lot to do tomorrow."

"Tomorrow," Ginger said, "we'll have cleared up even more of these mysteries. We're making progress every day."

"Tomorrow," Brendan said softly, happily, "will be a day of great revelation. I feel it somehow."

Tomorrow, Dom thought, we might all be dead. Or wish we were.

Colonel Leland Falkirk still had a splitting headache. With his new talent for introspection—acquired gradually since his involvement in the emotionally and intellectually shattering events of two summers ago—he was able to see that, on one level, he was actually glad that the aspirin had been ineffective. He thrived on the headache in the same way he thrived on other kinds of pain, drawing a perverse strength and energy from the relentless throbbing in his brow and temples.

Lieutenant Horner had gone. Leland was alone once more in his temporary, windowless office beneath the testing grounds of Shenkfield, but he was no longer waiting for the call from Chicago. It had come soon after Horner departed, and the news had been all bad.

The siege at Calvin Sharkle's house in Evanston, which had begun earlier today, was still under way, and that volatile situation would probably not be brought to an end within the next twelve hours. If possible, the colonel did not want to commit his men to another closure of I-80 and another quarantine of the Tranquility Motel until he could be certain the operation would not be compromised by revelations that Sharkle might make either to Illinois authorities or to the news media. Delay made Leland nervous, especially now that the witnesses at the motel were focused on Thunder Hill and were planning their moves beyond the reach of rifle microphones and infinity transmitters. He figured he could afford to wait, at most, one more day. However, if the dangerous standoff in Illinois was still under way by sunset tomorrow, he would give the order to move on the Tranquility in spite of the risks.

The other news from Chicago was that operatives had discreetly investigated Emmeline Halbourg and Winton Tolk and had found reasons to believe their amazing recoveries could not be adequately explained by current medical knowledge. And a reconstruction of Father Stefan Wycazik's activities on Christmas Day—including visits to Halbourg and Tolk, and a stop at the Metropolitan Police Laboratory to consult a ballistics expert—confirmed that the priest had been convinced that his curate, Brendan Cronin, had been responsible for those miraculous cures.

Leland had first become aware of Cronin's healing powers just yesterday, Sunday, when he had monitored a telephone call between Dominick Corvaisis at the

Tranquility and Father Wycazik in Chicago. That conversation would have been a real shocker if the events of Saturday night had not prepared him for the unexpected.

Saturday night, when Corvaisis had arrived at the Tranquility, Leland Falkirk and his surveillance experts had monitored the first conversations between the Blocks and the writer with growing disbelief. The outlandish tale of moon photographs animated by a poltergeist in Lomack's Reno house had sounded like the product of a fevered mind no longer able to distinguish between fiction and reality.

Later, however, after Corvaisis and the Blocks had eaten dinner at the Grille, the writer had attempted to relive the minutes just before the trouble had started on the night of July 6. What happened then was astonishing, confirmed both by the hidden surveillance team watching the Tranquility from a point south of the interstate and by the infinity transmitter tap on the diner's payphone. Everything in the Grille had begun to shake, and a strange rumble had filled the place, then an eerie electronic ululation, culminating in the implosion of all the windows.

These phenomena came as a total—and nasty—surprise to Leland and to everyone involved in the cover-up, especially the scientists, who were electrified. The following day's discovery of Cronin's healing power added voltage to the excitement. At first, these developments seemed inexplicable. But after only a little thought, Leland arrived at an explanation that made his blood cold. The scientists had come to similar conclusions. Some of them were as scared as Leland was.

Suddenly, no one knew what to expect. Anything might happen now.

We believed we were in control of the situation that night in July, Leland thought somberly, but perhaps it had escalated beyond our control even before we arrived on the scene.

The single consolation was that, thus far, only Corvaisis and the priest appeared to be . . . infected. Maybe "infected" wasn't exactly the right word. Maybe "possessed" was better. Or maybe there wasn't a word for what had happened to them, because what had happened to them had never happened to anyone else in history, so a specific word for it had not heretofore been required.

Even if the siege at Sharkle's house ended tomorrow, even if that possibility of media exposure was eliminated, Leland would not be able to strike at the group at the motel with full confidence. Corvaisis and Cronin—and perhaps the others—might be more difficult to apprehend and incarcerate than they'd been two summers ago. If Corvaisis and Cronin weren't entirely themselves any more, if they were now someone else—or some*thing* else—dealing with them might prove downright impossible.

Leland's headache was worse.

Feed on it, he told himself, getting up from the desk. Feed on the pain. You've been doing that for years, you dumb son of a bitch, so you can feed on it for another day or two, until you've dealt with this mess or until you're dead, whichever comes first.

He left the windowless office, crossed a windowless outer chamber, walked a windowless hall, and entered the windowless communications center, where Lieutenant Horner and Sergeant Fixx sat at a table in one corner. "Tell the men they can hit the sack," Leland said. "It's off for tonight. I'll risk another day to see if the situation at Sharkle's house gets resolved."

"I was just coming to you," Horner said. "There's a development at the motel. They finally left the diner. After they came out, Twist brought a Jeep Cherokee in from the hills behind the motel. He, Jorja Monatella, and the priest piled in it and drove off toward Elko.''

''Where the hell are they going at this time of night?'' Leland asked, uncomfortably aware that those three might have slipped through his fingers if he *had* ordered his men to move against the motel tonight, for he'd been certain the witnesses were settled down until morning.

Horner pointed to Fixx, who was wearing headphones and listening to the Tranquility. ''From what we've heard, the others are going to bed. Twist, Monatella, and Cronin have gone off as . . . as sort of insurance against us getting our hands on all the witnesses in one quick clean sweep. This had to be Twist's idea.''

''Damn.'' Massaging his throbbing temples with his fingertips, Leland sighed. ''All right. We aren't going after them tonight, anyway.''

''But what about tomorrow? What if they split up all day tomorrow?''

''In the morning,'' Leland said, ''we'll put tails on all of them.'' To this point, he had seen no need to tail the witnesses everywhere they went, for he had known that, in the end, they would all wind up at the same place—the motel—making it easier for him to deal with them. But now, if they were going to be spread out when the time came to take them into custody, he would need to know where they were at all times.

Horner said, ''Depending on where they go tomorrow, they're likely to spot any tails we put on them. In this kind of open country, it's not easy to be discreet.''

''I know,'' Leland said. ''So let them see us. I've wanted to stay out of sight, but we're at the end of that approach. Maybe seeing us will throw them off balance until it's too late. Maybe, scared, they'll even get back together for protection and make our job easier again.''

''If we have to take some of them at a place other than the motel, say in Elko, it'll be difficult,'' Horner said worriedly.

''If they can't be taken, they've got to be killed.'' Leland pulled up a chair, sat down. ''Let's work out surveillance details now and have the tails in position before dawn.''

3. Tuesday, January 14

At seven-thirty Tuesday morning, in response to a telephone call from Brendan Cronin very late the previous night, Father Stefan Wycazik prepared to set out on a drive to Evanston, to the last known address of Calvin Sharkle, the trucker who had been at the Tranquility Motel that summer but whose telephone was now disconnected. In light of the enormity of last evening's developments in Nevada, everyone was agreed that every possible effort must be made to contact the other victims who had thus far been unreachable. Standing in the warm rectory kitchen, Stefan buttoned his topcoat and put on his fedora.

Father Michael Gerrano, who was just sitting down to oatmeal and toast after celebrating sunrise Mass, said, ''Perhaps I should know more about this whole situation, about what on earth's wrong with Brendan, in case . . . well, in case something happens to you.''

"Nothing's going to happen to me," Father Wycazik said firmly. "God hasn't let me spend five decades learning how the world works just to have me killed now that I'm able to do my best work for the Church."

Michael shook his head. "You're always so . . ."

"Certain in my faith? Of course I am. Rely on God, and He will never fail you, Michael."

"Actually," Michael said, smiling, "I was going to say: You're always so bullheaded."

"Such impudence from a curate!" Stefan said, winding a thick white scarf around his neck. "Attend thee, Father: What is wanted of a curate is humility, self-effacement, the strong back of a mule, the stamina of a plow horse—and an unfailingly adoring attitude toward his rector."

Michael grinned. "Oh, yes, I suppose if the rector is a pious old geezer grown vain from the praise of his parishioners—"

The telephone rang.

"If it's for me, I'm gone," Stefan said.

Stefan pulled on a pair of gloves but was not quite able to make it to the back door before Michael held the receiver toward him.

"It's Winton Tolk," Michael said. "The cop whose life Brendan saved. He sounds almost hysterical, and he wants to talk to Brendan."

Stefan took the phone and identified himself.

The policeman's voice was haunted and full of urgency. "Father, I've got to talk to Brendan Cronin right away, it can't wait."

"I'm afraid he's away," Stefan said, "out at the other end of the country. What's the matter? Can I be of assistance?"

"Cronin," Tolk said shakily. "Something . . . something's happened, and I don't understand, it's strange, Jesus, it's the strangest craziest thing, but I knew right away it was somehow related to Brendan."

"I'm sure I can help. Where are you, Winton?"

"On duty, end of the shift, graveyard shift, Uptown. There's been a knifing, a shooting. Horrible. And then . . . Listen, I want Cronin to come up here, he's got to explain this, he's got to, right away."

Father Wycazik elicited an address from Tolk, left the rectory at a run, and drove too fast. Less than half an hour later, he arrived in a block of identical, shabby, six-story, brick tenements in the Uptown district. He was unable to park in front of the address he had been given and settled for a spot near the corner, for the prime space was occupied by police vehicles—marked and unmarked cars, an SID wagon—whose radios filled the cold air with a metallic chorus of dispatchers' codes and jargon. Two officers were watching over the vehicles to prevent vandalism. In answer to Stefan's question, they told him the action was on the third floor, in 3-B, the Mendozas' apartment.

The glass in the front door was cracked across one corner, and the temporary repair with electrician's tape looked as if it had become a permanent solution. The door opened on a grim foyer. Some floor tiles were missing and others were hidden by grime. The paint was peeling.

As he climbed the stairs, Stefan encountered two beautiful children playing "dead doll" with a battered Raggedy Ann and an old shoebox.

When he walked through the open door and into the Mendozas' third-floor apartment, Father Wycazik saw a beige sofa liberally stained with still-wet blood, so much that in some places the cushions were almost black. Hundreds of drops had sprayed across the pale-yellow wall behind the sofa, a pattern that evidently had resulted when someone in front of the wall had been hit by large-caliber slugs that passed through him. Four bullet holes marred the plaster. Blood was spattered over a lampshade, coffee table, bookshelf, and part of the carpet.

The gore was even more disgusting than it might ordinarily have been because the apartment was otherwise extremely well-kept, which made the areas of bloody chaos more shocking by comparison. The Mendozas could afford to live only in a slum tenement, but like some other poor people, they refused to surrender to— or become part of—the Uptown squalor. The filth of the streets, the grime of public hallways and staircases, stopped at their door, as if their apartment was a fortress against dirt, a shrine to cleanliness and order. Everything gleamed.

Removing his fedora, Stefan took only two steps into the living room—which flowed without interruption into a small dining area, which itself was separated from a half-size kitchen by a serving counter. The place was crowded with detectives, uniformed officers, lab technicians—maybe a dozen men altogether. Most of them were not acting like cops. Their demeanor puzzled Stefan. Apparently, the lab men had completed their work and the others had nothing to do, yet no one was leaving. They were standing in groups of two or three, talking in the subdued manner of people at a funeral parlor—or in church.

Only one detective was working. He was sitting at the dinette table with a Madonna-faced Latino woman of about forty, asking questions of her (Father Wycazik heard him call her Mrs. Mendoza), and recording her answers on legal-looking forms. She was trying to cooperate but was distracted as she glanced repeatedly at a man her own age, probably her husband, who was pacing back and forth with a child in his arms. The child was a cute boy of about six. Mr. Mendoza held the child in one burly arm, talking constantly to him, patting him, ruffling his thick hair. Obviously, this man had almost lost his son in whatever violence had occurred here, and he needed to touch and hold the child to convince himself that the worst had not actually happened.

One of the patrolmen noticed Stefan and said, "Father Wycazik?"

The officer's voice was soft, but at the mention of Stefan's name, the entire group fell silent. Stefan could not remember ever seeing expressions quite like those that came over the faces of the people in the Mendozas' small apartment: as if he were expected to deliver unto them a single sentence that would shed light upon all the mysteries of existence and succinctly convey the meaning of life.

What in the world is going on here? Stefan wondered uneasily.

"This way, Father," said a uniformed officer.

Pulling off his gloves, Stefan followed the officer across the room. The hush prevailed, and everyone made way for the priest and his guide. They went into a pin-neat bedroom, where Winton Tolk and another officer were sitting on the edge of the bed. "Father Wycazik's here," Stefan's guide said, then retreated to the living room.

Tolk was sitting bent forward, his elbows on his knees, his face hidden in his hands. He did not look up.

The other officer rose from the edge of the bed and introduced himself as Paul Armes, Winton's partner. "I . . . I think you'd better get it directly from Win," Armes said. "I'll give you some privacy." He left, closing the door behind him.

The bedroom was small, with space for only the bed, one nightstand, a half-size dresser, one chair. Father Wycazik pulled the chair around to face the foot of the bed and sat down, so he could look directly at Winton Tolk. Their knees were almost touching.

Removing his scarf, Father Wycazik said, "Winton, what's happened?"

Tolk looked up, and Stefan was startled by the man's expression. He had thought Tolk was upset by whatever had happened in the living room. But his face revealed that he was exhilarated, filled with an excitement he could barely contain. Simultaneously, he seemed fearful—not terrified, not quaking with fear, but troubled by something that prevented him from giving in completely, happily, to his excitement.

"Father, who is Brendan Cronin?" The tremor in the big man's voice was of an odd character that might have betrayed either incipient joy or terror. "*What* is Brendan Cronin."

Stefan hesitated, decided on the full truth. "He's a priest."

Winton shook his head. "But that's not what we were told."

Stefan sighed, nodded. He explained about Brendan's loss of faith and about the unconventional therapy that had included a week in a police patrol car. "You and Officer Armes weren't told he was a priest because you might've treated him differently . . . and because I wished to spare him embarrassment."

"A fallen priest," Winton said, looking baffled.

"Not fallen," Father Wycazik said confidently. "Merely faltering. He'll regain his faith in time."

The room's inadequate light came from a dim lamp on the nightstand and from a single narrow window, leaving the dark policeman in velvet gloom. The whites of his eyes were twin lamps, very bright by contrast with the darknesses of shadows and genetic heritage. "How did Brendan heal me when I was shot? How did he perform that . . . miracle? *How?*"

"Why have you decided it was a miracle?"

"I was shot twice in the chest, point-blank. Three days later I left the hospital. Three days! In ten days, I was ready to go back to work, but they made me stay home two weeks. Doctors kept talking about my hardy physical condition, the extraordinary healing that's possible if a body's in tip-top shape. I started thinking they were trying to explain my recovery not to me but to themselves. But I still figured I was just really lucky. I came back to work a week ago, and then . . . something else happened." Winton unbuttoned his shirt, pulled it open, and lifted his undershirt to reveal his bare chest. "The scars."

Father Wycazik shivered. Though he was close to Winton, he leaned closer, staring in amazement. The man's chest was unmarked. Well, not entirely unmarked, but the entry wounds had already healed until they were just discolored spots as big as dimes. The surgeon's incisions had almost vanished—thin lines visible now only on close inspection. This soon after major trauma, some swelling and inflammation should have been evident, but there was none. The minimal scar tissue was pale pink-brown against dark-brown skin, neither lumpy nor puckered.

"I've seen other guys with old bullet wounds," Winton said, his excitement still restrained by a rope of fear. "Lots of them. Gnarly, thick. Ugly. You don't take two .38s in the chest, undergo major surgery, and look like *this* three weeks later—or ever."

"When's the last time you visited your doctor? Has he seen this?"

Winton rebuttoned his shirt with trembling hands. "I saw Dr. Sonneford a week ago. The sutures hadn't been removed long before, and my chest was still a mess. It's only been the past four days that the scars melted away. I swear, Father, if I stand at a mirror long enough, I can *see* them fading."

Finishing with his shirt buttons, Winton said, "Lately, I've been thinking about your visit to the hospital Christmas Day. The more I've gone over it in my mind, the more it seems your behavior was peculiar. I remember some of what you said, some of the questions you asked about Brendan, and I start wondering. . . . One thing I wonder about—one thing I've got to know—is whether Brendan Cronin ever healed anyone else.''

"Yes. Nothing as dramatic as your case. But there's another. I'm . . . not at liberty to reveal who,'' Stefan said. "But this isn't why you called the rectory, Winton. Not to show Brendan how well you've healed. Your voice was so full of urgency, even panic. And what about all these policemen with the Mendozas . . . ? What's happened here, Winton?''

A mercurial smile appeared on—and quickly faded from—the man's broad face, followed by a transient glimmer of fear. Emotional turmoil was also evident in his voice. "We're cruising. Me and Paul. We get a call. This address. We get here, find a sixteen-year-old kid high on PCP. You know what they're like on PCP sometimes? Crazy. Animals. Damn stuff eats brain cells. Later, after it's over, we find out his name's Ernesto, son of Mrs. Mendoza's sister. He came to live here a week ago because his mother can't control him any more. The Mendozas . . . they're good people. You see how they keep this place?''

Father Wycazik nodded.

Winton said, "The kind of people take in a nephew when he's gone wrong, try to set him straight. But you can't set a kid like that straight. You break your heart trying, Father. This Ernesto, he's been in trouble since he was in fifth grade. Juvenile arrest record. Six offenses. Two of them pretty serious. We get here, he's naked as a jaybird, screaming his head off, eyes bugged out like the pressure in his head's going to blow his skull apart.''

Winton's gaze unfocused, as if he were seeing back into time and had as clear a view of that scene as when he had first encountered it.

"Ernesto's got Hector, the little boy you probably saw when you came in, he's got him down on the sofa, holding him, and he's got a goddamn six-inch switchblade at Hector's throat. Mr. Mendoza . . . well, he's going crazy, wanting to rush Ernesto and take the knife, but scared Ernesto will slash Hector. Ernesto's screaming, he was blissed on angel dust. He's PCP-crazy, and you can't talk sense to him. We drew our guns because you don't just walk up to some doped-out freak with a knife and shake hands. But we didn't want to try to shoot him because he had the knife at Hector's throat, Hector was crying, and Ernesto could've killed the kid if we made the wrong move. So we tried to talk him down, talk him away from Hector, and we seemed to make headway, 'cause he started to take the knife off the boy. But then all of a sudden, Jesus, he slashed quick, cut Hector's throat almost from ear to ear, deep''—Winton shuddered—"deep. Then he raised the knife over his head, so we shot him, I'm not sure how many times, blew him away, and he fell dead on top of Hector. We pulled him off, and there was little Hector, one hand trying to close up the hole in his throat, blood spurting between his fingers, eyes already glazing over. . . . ''

The cop took a deep breath and shuddered again. His eyes came back into focus, as if he needed to retreat from the horror of the past. He looked toward the window, beyond which the gray winter daylight sifted like soot over the gray Uptown street.

Stefan's heart had begun to pound, not because of the bloody horror that Winton had described but because he could see where the cop's story had to be leading, and he was eager to hear the miracle described.

Looking at the window, Winton continued. His voice grew shakier as he spoke:

"There's no first aid for that kind of wound, Father. Severed arteries, veins. Big arteries in the neck. Blood pumps out like water from a hose, and you can't use a tourniquet, not on a neck, and direct pressure won't seal up a carotid artery. Shit, no. I knelt on the floor beside the sofa, and I saw Hector was dying fast. He looked so little, Father, so little. That kind of wound, they're gone in two minutes, sometimes a lot less, and he was so little. I knew it was useless, but I put my hands on Hector's neck, like somehow I could hold the blood in him, hold the life in him. I was sick, angry, scared, and it just wasn't right that a boy so little should die that way, that hard, not right he should die at all, not right, and then . . . then . . . ''

"And then he healed," Father Wycazik said softly.

Winton Tolk finally looked away from the gray light at the window and met Stefan's eyes. "Yes, Father. He healed. He was soaked in his own blood, seconds away from death, but he healed. I didn't even know what was happening, didn't feel it happening, nothing special in my hands. Wouldn't you think I'd feel something special in my hands? But the first I realized that something incredible was happening was when the blood stopped spurting against my fingers, and the boy shut his eyes at the same time, which was when I thought he was dead for sure, and I just . . . I shouted, 'No! God, no!' And I started to take my hands away from Hector's throat, to look at it, and that's when I saw the wound was . . . the wound was closed up. It still had a raw, ugly look to it, an awful line where the knife cut deep, but the flesh was knit together into a bright red scar, a healing scar."

The big man stopped speaking because shimmery lenses of tears had formed over his eyes. He was overcome once more. If he'd been racked by grief, he probably would have suppressed it, but this was something even more powerful: joy. Pure wild disbelieving joy. He could not contain several explosive, wrenching sobs.

With hot tears in his own eyes, Father Wycazik held out both hands.

Winton took them, squeezed them tight, and did not let go as he continued: "Paul, my partner, saw it happen. So did the Mendozas. And two other uniforms arrived just as we shot Ernesto: They saw it, too. And when I looked at that red line across his throat, somehow I knew what I had to do. I put my hands on the boy again, covered up the wound again, and I thought about him being alive, sort of wished him alive. My mind was in high gear, and I made the connection with Brendan and me, the sandwich shop. I thought about how the scars on my chest had been disappearing the last few days, and I knew somehow it's connected. So I kept my hands on his throat, and in a minute or so he opened his eyes, he smiled at me, you should've *seen* that smile, Father, so I took my hands away again, and the scar was there but lighter. The boy sat up and asked for his mother, and that's . . . that's when I went to pieces." Winton paused and gulped some air. "Mrs. Mendoza took Hector into the bathroom, stripped him out of his bloody clothes, bathed him, and all the time more people from the department kept showing up. Word was getting around. Thank God, the reporters haven't cottoned to it yet."

For a while the two men sat facing each other in silence, gripping hands. Then Stefan said, "Did you try to bring Ernesto back?"

"Yes. In spite of what he'd done, I put my hands on his wounds. But it didn't work with him, Father. Maybe because he was already dead. Hector was only dying, not yet gone, but Ernesto was dead."

"Did you notice odd marks in your hands, on your palms? Red rings of swollen flesh?"

"Nothing like that. What would it've meant if there'd been rings?"

"I don't know," Father Wycazik said. "But they appear in Brendan's hands when . . . when these things happen."

They were silent again, and then Winton said, "Is Brendan . . . is Father Cronin some kind of saint?"

Father Wycazik smiled. "He's a good man. But he's no saint."

"Then how did he heal me?"

"I don't know precisely. But surely it's a manifestation of the power of God. Somehow. For some reason."

"But how did Brendan pass along this power to heal?"

"I don't know, Winton. If he *did* pass it along. Maybe the power isn't yours. Maybe it's just God acting through you, first through Brendan and then through you."

At last Winton let go of Father Wycazik's hands. He turned his palms up and stared at them. "No, the power's still here, still in me. I know that. Somehow. I feel it. And not just . . . not just the power to heal. There's more."

Father Wycazik raised his eyebrows. "More? What else?"

Winton frowned. "I don't know yet. It's all so new. So strange. But I feel . . . more. It'll take time for it to develop." He looked up from the pale palms of his callused black hands, awe-stricken and fearful. "What is Father Cronin, and what has he made of me?"

"Winton, get rid of the notion there's anything evil or dangerous about this. It's entirely a wondrous thing. Think of Hector, the child you saved. Remember what it was like to feel life regaining its hold in his small body. We're players in a divine mystery, Winton. We can't understand the meaning of it until God allows us to understand."

Father Wycazik said he wanted to have a look at the boy, Hector Mendoza, and Winton said, "I'm not ready to go out there and face that crowd, even though they're mostly my people. I'll stay here a while. You'll come back?"

"I've got other rather urgent business this morning, Winton. I have to get on with it soon. But I'll be in touch with you. Oh, you can be sure of that! And if you need me, just call St. Bette's."

When Stefan left the bedroom, the waiting crowd of policemen and lab technicians fell silent as before. They parted in his path as he crossed to the dinette table, where little Hector was now perched on his mother's lap, nibbling happily at a Hershey bar with almonds.

The boy was small, even for a six-year-old, with delicate facial bones. His eyes were bright and full of intelligence, proof that he'd suffered no brain damage in spite of losing most of his blood. But even more astonishing was the fact that his lost blood had evidently been *replaced,* without need of transfusions, which made the boy's recovery even more miraculous than Tolk's. The power in Winton's hands seemed greater than it had been in Brendan's.

When Father Wycazik stooped down to be at eye-level with Hector, the child grinned at him. "How are you feeling, Hector?"

"Okay," the boy said shyly.

"Do you remember what happened to you, Hector?"

The child licked chocolate from his lips and shook his head: no.

"Is that a good candy bar?"

The boy nodded and offered Father Wycazik a bite.

The priest smiled. "Thank you, Hector, but that's all yours."

"Mama might give you one," Hector said. "But don't drop any on the carpet. That's big trouble."

Stefan looked up at Mrs. Mendoza. "He really doesn't remember . . . ?"

"No," she said. "God lifted the memory from him, Father."

"You're Catholic, Mrs. Mendoza?"

"Yes, Father," she said, crossing herself with her free hand.

"Do you attend Our Lady of Sorrow? Yes, well, that's Father Nilo's parish. Have you called him?"

"No, Father. I didn't know if . . . "

Father Wycazik looked up at Mr. Mendoza, who stood on the other side of his wife's chair. "Call Father Nilo. Tell him what's happened, ask him to come. Explain that I'll be gone when he gets here but that I'll talk to him later. Explain that I've much to tell him, that what he sees here isn't the whole story."

Mr. Mendoza hurried to the telephone.

Looking up at one of the detectives who had come close, Stefan said, "Have you taken pictures of the boy's throat wound?"

The detective nodded. "Yeah. Standard procedure." He laughed nervously. "What am I saying? There's nothing standard about this."

"Just so you have photographs to prove this happened," Father Wycazik said. "Because I think soon there will be little or no scar."

He turned to the boy again. "Now, Hector, if it's okay, I'd like to touch your throat. I'd like to feel that mark."

The boy lowered the candy bar.

Father Wycazik's fingers were trembling when they touched the fiery scar tissue and moved slowly around the boy's neck from one end of the wound to the other. A strong pulse beat in the carotid arteries on each side of the slender young throat, and Stefan's heart leapt when he felt the miracle of life. Death had been defeated here, and Stefan believed he had been privileged to witness a fulfillment of the promise which was at the root of the Church's existence: "Death shall not last; unto you shall be given life everlasting." Tears rose in the priest's eyes.

When at last Stefan reluctantly took his hand away from the boy and stood, one of the policemen said, "What's it mean, Father? I heard you tell Mr. Mendoza this wasn't the whole story. What's happening?"

Stefan turned to look upon the assembly, which now numbered twenty. In their faces, he saw a longing to believe, not particularly in the truths of Catholicism or Christianity, for not all were Catholics or Christians, but a deep-seated longing to believe in *something* greater and better and cleaner than humankind, an intense yearning for spiritual transcendence.

"What's it mean, Father?" one of them asked again.

"Something's happening," he told them. "Here, elsewhere. A great and wonderful something. This child is part of it. I can't tell you for sure what it means or that we've seen the hand of God here, though I believe we have. Look at Hector on his mother's lap, eating candy, and remember God's promise: 'There shall be no more death, neither sorrow nor crying, neither shall there be any more pain: for the former things are passed away.' In my heart of hearts, I feel that the former things are about to pass away. Now I must go. I've urgent business."

Somewhat to his surprise, even though his explanation had been vague, they parted to make way for him and did not detain him further, perhaps because the miracle of Hector Mendoza had *not* been vague—had in fact been emphatically specific—and had already given them more answers than they could handle. But as Stefan went, some reached out to touch him, to squeeze his hand or shoulder, not with religious fervor but with an emotional camaraderie. Stefan was overcome by the need to touch them as well, to share a profound sense of the community of humankind, which had filled everyone in the room, to share the conviction that they were being swept toward some great destiny.

In Boston, at ten o'clock, Alexander Christophson, former United States Senator and Ambassador to Great Britain, former Director of the CIA, now retired for a decade, was reading the morning newspaper when he received a telephone call from his brother, Philip, the antiques dealer in Greenwich, Connecticut. They spoke for five minutes about nothing important, just two brothers keeping in touch, but the conversation had a secret purpose. At the end Philip said, "Oh, by the way, I spoke with Diana just this morning. Do you remember her?"

"I certainly do," Alex said. "How's she doing?"

"Oh, she has her troubles," Philip said. "Too boring to discuss. But she says hello." Then he changed the subject, recommending two new books that Alex might enjoy, as if Diana were of no real importance.

Diana was the code word that meant Ginger Weiss had phoned Philip and needed to speak with Alex. The moment he had seen Ginger at Pablo's funeral, her silver-blond hair a-shimmer as if with a light of its own, she had made him think of Diana, goddess of the moon.

After he said goodbye to Philip, he told his wife, Elena, that he intended to drive to the mall. "I want to stop at the bookstore and pick up a couple of novels that Philip recommended."

He actually went to the mall, but before he bought the books, he found a public phone booth and, using his AT&T credit card, called Philip to get the number that Ginger Weiss had left.

"She says it's a pay phone in Elko, Nevada," Philip told him.

When Alex put the Nevada call through, Ginger Weiss did not answer until the fifth ring. "Sorry," she said. "I was in the car, parked beside the booth. It was just too cold to stand here and wait."

"What are you doing in Nevada?" Alex asked.

"If I understood you correctly at Pablo's funeral, you really don't want me to answer questions like that."

"Right. Less I know, the better. What did you want to ask me?"

She explained, with a minimum of detail, that she had found others suffering from memory blocks similar to hers, some with different false memories covering the same time span. Since Alex was the expert on brainwashing, Ginger wanted to know if implanting fake memories that included threads of reality was more difficult than implanting entirely false recollections, and he was able to assure her that, indeed, it was.

"That's what we figured," Ginger said. "But it's good to hear you confirm it. Shows we're on the right track. Now, one more thing: I want you to get some information for us. We need to know whatever you can learn about a Colonel Leland Falkirk, an officer in one of the Army's elite DERO companies. I also need—"

"Wait, wait," Alex said, looking nervously through the glass door of the booth at shoppers walking past in the mall, as if he were already under observation or even targeted for removal. "At the cemetery, I said I'd provide advice or background on mind-control techniques. But I warned you I wouldn't dig up information. I *explained* my position."

"Well, even though you've been retired for years, you must still know people in many of the right places—"

"Didn't you hear me, Doctor? I will not get actively involved in your problems. I simply can't afford to. I've got too much to lose."

"Now, don't worry about digging up anything exotic or highly classified. We don't expect that," she said, as if she had not heard him. "Just the bare details of Falkirk's service record might help us understand him and form an idea of what to expect from him."

"Please, I—"

But she was indefatigable: "I also need to know about the Thunder Hill Depository, an Army facility here in Elko County."

"No."

"It's supposed to be an underground storage facility, and maybe that's all it was for a long time, or maybe it's always been something else, but I know it's not just an underground warehouse these days."

"Doctor, I won't do this for you."

"Colonel Leland Falkirk and Thunder Hill Depository. It's not so much to ask: no deep snooping, just what details you can glean. Talk to your old friends who're still in the game. Then report to either Dr. George Hannaby there in Boston or to Father Stefan Wycazik, a priest in Chicago." She gave him phone numbers. "I can get in touch with them, and they won't mention your name when they tell me what you've reported. That way you don't have to call me direct, and you stay in the clear."

He tried and failed to control the palsied shaking of his hands. "Doctor, I'm sorry I volunteered even limited assistance. I'm an old man who's afraid to die."

"You're also worried about sins you might've committed in the name of duty," she said, repeating what he'd told her at the cemetery. "And you'd probably like to do something to atone for some of those sins, real or imagined. This would be atonement of a sort, Mr. Christophson." She repeated the telephone numbers for Hannaby and Wycazik.

"No. If you're interrogated, remember I said no, emphatically no."

With maddening good cheer, she said, "Oh, and it would help if you had something for me within the next six or eight hours. I know that's a tall order. But then again, I'm only asking for basic information, whatever's in the unclassified files."

"Goodbye, Doctor," he said pointedly.

"I'll look forward to hearing from you."

"You will *not* hear from me."

"Toodle-oo," she said, and hung up on him first.

"Christ!" he said, slamming the receiver down.

She was an attractive woman, personable, intelligent, appealing in so many ways. But her absolute conviction that she would always get what she wanted—this was a trait he sometimes admired in a man, seldom or never in a woman. Well, she'd be disappointed this time. This time, she'd not get what she wanted. Damned if she would.

Yet . . . with his Cross pen, he had made note of the telephone numbers for Hannaby and Wycazik, which she had given him.

Dom and Ernie set out early Tuesday morning to reconnoiter at least part of the perimeter of Thunder Hill Depository. They went in Jack Twist's new Jeep Cherokee. Jack himself was sleeping back at the motel, having gone to bed only a few hours ago, after spending half the night driving around Elko, staying on the move with Brendan Cronin and Jorja Monatella. Both the Cherokee and the mo-

tel's Dodge van had four-wheel drive, but the Jeep was tougher, more maneu-
verable. The foothill and mountain roads up toward Thunder Hill might be icy
in spots, and as the day promised new snow, they wanted the most reliable transportation.

Dom did not like the look of the sky. Thick dark clouds hung low over the
high plains, lower over the foothills, and obscured the tops of the mountains. The
weather forecast called for the first big storm of the year (later than usual this
season), as much as fourteen inches of snow in the higher elevations. Not a single
flake had fallen yet.

The raised and threatening lash of winter did not induce a pensive mood in
Dom or Ernie; they were in high spirits upon setting out from the motel. They
were finally *doing* something, acting not just reacting. In addition, there was the
pleasant fellowship that exists when men who like each other set out on an adventure together—a fishing trip or an expedition to a ballpark. Or a scouting trip
to explore the perimeter defenses of a military installation.

In no little measure, their excellent mood grew from the unexpected peacefulness of the night just past. For the first time in weeks, Dom's sleep hadn't been
disturbed by nightmares or sleepwalking. He'd dreamed only of an undetailed
chamber filled with golden light, evidently the same place that featured in Brendan's dreams. Likewise, instead of lying awake in fear of the shadows beyond
the glow of the bedside lamp, Ernie had drifted off to sleep at once. The others
also said it was the most restful night in recent memory. Ginger's theory, put
forth over a quick cup of coffee this morning, was that their worst dreams had
been related not to the mysterious events they'd witnessed on the night of July
6, but to the subsequent brainwashing. Therefore, now that they had an idea of
what they'd endured at the hands of the mind-control experts, the subconscious
pressure related to those experiences was relieved, eliminating the source of those
particular bad dreams.

And Dom had a reason of his own to feel good about the day. This morning,
no one had looked warily at him or treated him with deference because of his
telekinetic power. At first he was baffled by their quick adjustment to his new
status. Then he realized what must be going through their minds: Since they had
shared his experiences of the summer before last, it was logical that they would
also share his strange power sooner or later. They must believe their own development of paranormal abilities was merely lagging behind his. Eventually, if they
did not acquire the power, they might build the emotional, intellectual, and psychological walls between them and him that would isolate him, as he feared. But
for the moment, anyway, they were acting as if no gulf separated them from him,
and he was grateful.

Now, humming softly, Ernie drove north on the two-lane county road, leaving
the motel and the interstate behind them. They climbed some of the same rugged
hills down which Jack Twist had come last night when making his clandestine
approach to the Tranquility (although Jack had traveled overland), and Dom studied the changing terrain with interest. The rising land seemed leaner the higher
it rose, revealing less flesh and more rocky bones that poked up everywhere in
clavicles and scapulae and sternums of limestone, in fibulae and femurs of crumbling shale, in occasional ribs and spines of formidable granite. As if in awareness
of the colder air of higher altitudes, the land wore more clothes: thicker petticoats
of grass; more lavish skirts of sage and other bushes; then trees, trees, more
trees—mountain mahogany, tall pines, cedar, quaking-aspen, and on eastern
slopes, an occasional spruce or fir.

They'd gone only three miles when they reached the snow line. A thin mantle flanked the road at first, but in the next two miles it deepened to eight inches. Although a winter drought had held sway from September until early December, and although no major storm had swept the area yet this season, a few light snows had put down a respectable ground-cover, also frosting the bristled boughs of the evergreens.

But for a few small scattered patches of ice, the county road was cleared for easy travel. "They always keep it clean as far as Thunder Hill, even in killing weather," Ernie explained. "But up beyond the Depository, the road crews don't do as thorough a job."

In no time they had gone ten miles, always following the crest of the valley that fell away on the east, and always with rising mountains on the west. They passed several dirt and gravel lanes leading to isolated homes and ranches in the eastward-sloping lands to their right, and at the ten-mile point they reached the guarded entrance road to Thunder Hill Depository, also on the right.

Ernie slowed the Cherokee but did not turn into the entranceway. "Haven't been this far up here in a long time. They've made changes since I saw the place last. Didn't used to look this formidable."

A sign announced the Depository. Beside the sign another paved road branched off the county lane, leading away between towering pines of such a dark-green hue they seemed nearly black in the somber prestorm light. Fifteen feet in from the turnoff, the lane was blocked by long metal spikes that speared up from the pavement, precisely angled to puncture the tires of any vehicle that tried to proceed farther, but also large enough to catch on the axle of a hurtling truck or car and instantly arrest its progress. Twenty feet beyond the spikes, there was a massive steel gate, crowned with spears, painted red. A concrete-block guardhouse—twenty feet by ten—stood inside the gate, and its black metal door looked capable of withstanding a bazooka barrage.

Ernie pulled to the edge of the main road and slowed almost to a full stop as they eased past the entrance to Thunder Hill. He pointed to a yard-square post at the verge of the entrance lane, just this side of the wicked spikes. "Looks like an intercom to the guardhouse. Not just a voice link, either. One of those systems like they have in drive-in banks, with a video monitor so they can see you in your car. The man in the guardhouse approves a visitor before the road spikes lower and the gate opens. Even then, I'll bet there're permanently emplaced machine guns to take you out if the guard decides he's been duped after he's already opened the gates."

From each end of the gate, an eight-foot-high chainlink fence with a barbed-wire overhang disappeared into the trees, and Dom noted a white sign with red lettering that warned DANGER—ELECTRIFIED. Although the perimeter fence led into the forest, no trees overhung it; from the small sections that he could see flanking the main gate, there appeared to be a twenty-foot-wide no-man's-land on each side.

Dom's good mood faded. He'd thought that the security along the perimeter of the facility would be minimal. After all, once you got onto the grounds, the actual entrance to Thunder Hill was through eight- or ten-foot-thick blast doors set in the hillside. That barrier was so impregnable that it seemed wasteful to install maximum security around the entire outer edge of the property. Yet that was what they had done. Which meant the secret they were guarding was so important that they did not even trust nuclearproof doors and subterranean limestone vaults to keep it safe.

"The spikes in the road are new," Ernie said. "And the gate they had a couple of years ago was pretty flimsy by comparison. The fence was always here, but it wasn't electrified before."

"We've no hope at all of getting a look inside."

Although no one had said as much (for fear of sounding foolish), they all hoped they might get as far as the blast doors of the facility, have a look around the newly expanded grounds that had been taken from ranchers Brust and Dirkson, and be fortunate enough to stumble across another piece of the puzzle they were committed to solve. Dom had never imagined they would actually get *inside* the underground rooms of Thunder Hill. That was an improbable scenario. But from the comfort of the Tranquility Motel, getting onto the grounds and snooping around had not seemed like an impossible dream. Until now.

Dom wondered if his newly discovered telekinetic powers might be used to circumvent the Depository's fortifications, but he dismissed that thought as quickly as it occurred to thim. Until he could control the gift, it was of little use. It scared him. He sensed that the power was sufficient to cause tremendous destruction and death if he lost control of it, and he would not take the chance again—except under very tightly controlled conditions.

"Well," Ernie said, "it was never our intention to try waltzing through the front gate. Let's have a look along some of the perimeter fence." He touched his foot lightly on the accelerator. Looking in the rearview mirror, he said, "Oh, and by the way, we're being followed."

Startled, Dom turned and looked through the rear window of the Cherokee. Less than a hundred yards behind was a pickup truck, an all-terrain job, loftily perched on tires twice as wide and more than twice as high as ordinary tires. Spotlights, currently unlit, were mounted on the roof, and a snowplow, currently raised off the road, was fitted to the front. Although Dom was certain that private citizens living in the mountains might own similar trucks, this one had the look of a military vehicle. The windshield was tinted, the driver unrevealed.

He said, "You sure they're following us? When did they show up?"

Piloting the Cherokee up the county road, Ernie said, "I noticed them about half a mile after we left the motel. When we slow down, they slow down, too. When we speed up, so do they."

"You think there's going to be trouble?"

"There will be if they ask for it. They're probably only Army pussies," Ernie said. He grinned.

Dom laughed. "Don't get me in a war just to prove Leathernecks are tougher than GIs. I'll happily accept your word for it."

The road became steeper. The somber ashen sky grew lower. The dark trees drew closer on both sides. The pickup stayed behind them.

Mrs. Halbourg, Emmy's mother, answered the door, letting a puff of warm air out of the house into the frigid Chicago morning.

Father Wycazik said, "Sorry to come unannounced like this, but the most extraordinary thing is happening, and I had to find out if Emmy—"

He stopped in midsentence when he realized that Mrs. Halbourg was in terrible distress. Her eyes were wide with shock—with fear, too.

Before he could ask what was wrong, she said, "My God, it's you, Father. From the hospital, I remember. But how did you know to come? We haven't called anyone yet. How'd you know to come?"

"What's happened?"

Rather than answer, she took him by the arm, ushered him inside, slammed the door, and hurried him upstairs. "This way. Quickly."

Coming directly from the Mendozas' apartment Uptown, he expected to find something odd at the Halbourg place, but not this state of crisis. When they reached the second-floor hallway, Mr. Halbourg was there with one of Emmy's older sisters. They were standing halfway down the hall at an open door, staring into a room at something that seemed equally to attract and repel them. In the room, something thumped, rattled, then thumped twice again, followed by a musical burst of girlish laughter.

Mr. Halbourg turned, a ghastly expression on his face, and blinked in surprise at Stefan. "Father, thank God you're here, we didn't know what to do, didn't want to make complete fools of ourselves by calling for help and then maybe nothing's happening when help gets here, you know. But now you've come, so it's settled, and I'm relieved."

Stefan looked warily through the open doorway and saw the usual accouterments of a bedroom occupied by a girl of ten-going-on-eleven, the changeling age between childhood and adolescence: half a dozen teddy bears; big posters of the current teenage idols, boys utterly unknown to Stefan; a wooden hat rack hung with a collection of exotic chapeaux probably purchased from thrift shops; roller skates; a tape deck; a flute lying in an open case. Emmy's other sister—in a white sweater, tartan-plaid skirt, and kneesocks—was standing a few feet inside the room, pale and half-paralyzed. Emmy was standing up in bed, pajama-clad, looking even healthier than on Christmas Day. She was hugging a pillow, grinning at the same astonishing performance—a poltergeist at play—that riveted her sister and frightened the rest of her family.

As Father Wycazik stepped into the room, Emmy laughed delightedly at the antics of two small teddy bears waltzing in midair. Their movements were nearly as precise and formal as those of real dancers.

But the bears were not the only inanimate objects infused with magical life. The roller skates were not standing still in a corner but were moving about on separate courses, this one past the foot of the bed and then to the closet door, that one to the desk, this one to the window, moving fast, then slow. The hats jiggled on the rack. A Care Bear on a bookshelf bounced up and down.

Stefan went to the foot of the bed, careful to avoid the roller skates, and looked up at Emmy, who still stood on the mattress. "Emmy?"

The girl glanced down at him. "Pudge's friend! Hello, Father. Isn't it terrific? Isn't it wild?"

"Emmy, is this you?" he asked, gesturing at the capering objects.

"Me?" she said, genuinely surprised. "No. Not me."

But he noticed that the flying-waltzing bears faltered when she turned her attention away from them. They did not drop to the floor, but bobbled and turned and bumped against one another in a clumsy and aimless manner quite different from their previous measured grace.

He also saw indications that the previous phenomena had not all been this harmless. A ceramic lamp had been knocked to the floor and broken. One of the posters was torn. The dresser mirror was cracked.

Seeing the direction of his gaze, Emmy said, "It was scary at first. But it calmed down, and now it's just . . . fun. Isn't it *fun?*"

As she was speaking, the flute rose out of the open carrying case, up and up, until it was about seven feet off the floor, only a few feet to the left of the floating teddy bears. Out of the corner of her eye, the girl caught a glimpse of the rising instrument. When she turned to look directly at the flute, sweet music began to issue from it, not just random notes but a well-executed tune. Emmy jumped up and down on the bed excitedly. "That's *'Annie's Song'*! I used to play that."

"You're playing it now," Stefan said.

"Oh, no," she said, still staring at the flute. "My hands got so bad, my knuckle joints, that I had to give up the flute a year ago. I'm cured now, but my hands still aren't good enough to play."

Stefan said, "But you aren't using your hands to play it, Emmy."

His meaning finally penetrated. She looked down at him. "Me?"

Deprived of her focused attention, the flute produced only a few more poorly executed notes and fell silent. It still hung in the air, but now it bobbled and dipped erratically. Emmy returned her attention to the instrument. It steadied in the air and began to play again.

"Me," she said wonderingly. She turned to her sister, who was still paralyzed by fear and amazement. "Me," Emmy said, then looked at her parents, who were standing in the doorway. *"Me!"*

Stefan appreciated what the child must be feeling, and his throat was pinched so tightly with emotion that he had difficulty swallowing. A month ago, she'd been a cripple, unable to dress herself, with nothing to look forward to except further deterioration, pain, and death. Now she was not only cured and her damaged bones reknit, but she was also in possession of this spectacular gift.

Father Wycazik wanted to tell her that somehow this gift had been given to her unwittingly by Brendan Cronin, her Pudge, but then he would have to explain where Brendan had gotten *his* gift, and he could not do that. Besides, he hadn't time even to tell them what he did know. It was nine-fifteen. He should have been in Evanston by now. Time was of the essence, for Stefan was beginning to suspect that he would be catching a flight for Nevada before the day ended. Whatever was happening in Elko County was bound to be even more incredible than what was happening here, and he was determined to be a part of it.

Emmy looked at the floating bears, and they resumed their formal dance once more. She giggled.

Stefan thought about what Winton Tolk had said only a short while ago in the Mendozas' Uptown apartment: *The power's still here, still in me. I know . . . I feel it. And not just . . . not just the power to heal. There's more.* Winton had not known what powers he might possess in addition to the healing touch, but Stefan suspected that the policeman was in for some surprises similar to those that had thrown the Halbourg household into turmoil.

"Father, will you do it yourself?" Mr. Halbourg asked from the doorway, where he stood with his wife, his voice sharp with anxiety.

Mrs. Halbourg said, "Please, we want it to be done as soon as possible. Immediately. Can't you begin at once?"

Baffled, Stefan said, "I'm sorry . . . but what is it you want done?"

Mr. Halbourg said, "An exorcism, of course!"

Stefan stared at them incredulously, only now fully realizing why they had been in such distress when he had arrived and why they had greeted him with such relief. He laughed. "There won't be any need for an exorcism. This isn't Satan at work. Oh, no. My heavens, no!"

From the corner of his eye, Stefan saw movement on the floor. He looked down at a two-foot-high teddy bear that was tottering past him on stiff little stuffed legs.

Winton Tolk had said that he sensed he would need a long time to learn what his powers were and to be able to control them. Either he was wrong or the task was far easier for Emmy than for him. That might be the case. Children were much more adaptable than adults.

Emmy's parents and her other sister edged into the room, fascinated but wary.

Stefan understood their wariness. All *seemed* well, the power benign. But the situation was so awesome, so profoundly affecting on a primitive level, that even an unfaltering optimist like Stefan Wycazik felt a tingle of fear.

After using a pay phone at a Shell service station in Elko to get in touch with Alexander Christophson in Boston, Ginger accompanied Faye to Elroy and Nancy Jamison's ranch in the Lemoille Valley, twenty miles from Elko. The Jamisons were the Blocks' friends who had been visiting on the evening of July 6, the summer before last. They had surely been caught up in the unknown events of that night and had been detained at the motel for brainwashing with everyone else, though they remembered differently, of course. According to their program of false memories, they had been allowed to evacuate the danger zone, taking Ernie and Faye with them. They believed they had returned to their small ranch, where they and the Blocks had passed the next few days. That was also what Faye and Ernie had believed—until recently.

Ginger and Faye were paying a visit to the Jamisons not to inform them of what had actually happened but to determine, as indirectly as possible, if the Jamisons were having troubles of the kind afflicting Ginger, Ernie, Dom, and some of the others. If they were suffering, they would be brought into the mutually supportive community at the motel—the members of which had come to think of themselves as the "Tranquility family"—and would join the search for answers.

But if the brainwashing had been effective, the Jamisons would not be told anything. To tell the Jamisons would be to endanger them.

Besides, given the urgent strategy developed last night with Jack Twist, if the Jamisons were not already suffering, there was no point wasting a lot of time convincing them that they'd been brainwashed. Time was precious, and every passing hour carried the Tranquility family deeper into danger. Jack believed—and convinced Ginger—that their enemies would soon move against them.

The drive from Elko in the motel's van was quick and scenic. The picturesque Lemoille Valley—fifteen miles long, four miles wide—began at the foot of the Ruby Mountains. Wheat, barley, and potato farms occupied the lowlands, though the fields were unplanted now, slumbering under scattered patches of snow.

Between the valley floor and the mountains, the higher lands and foothills offered lush pasturage, and that was where the Jamisons had their ranch. At one time, they owned hundreds of acres on which they raised cattle, but eventually they sold off much of their property, which had risen substantially in value, and got out of the livestock business. Now, in their early sixties and retired, they owned about fifty acres in the foothills, employed no ranch hands, and kept only three horses and a few chickens.

As Faye turned off the main valley road onto a lane leading into the highlands, she said, "I think someone's following us."

The back doors of the van had no windows, so Ginger looked at the side-mounted mirror. A nondescript sedan was about a hundred feet behind them. "How do you know?"

"Same car's been back there since the Union 76 in town."

"Maybe it's coincidence," Ginger said.

When they had followed the lane over halfway up the valley wall, they reached the long narrow driveway to the Jamisons' ranch, which led half a mile back through deep shadows thrown by flanking rows of big piñons. Faye pulled into the driveway and slowed to see what the other car would do. Instead of going past, farther up into the hills, it pulled to a stop and parked along the outer lane, directly across from the entrance to the Jamisons' property.

In the sideview mirror, Ginger could see that the car was a late-model Plymouth, painted a flat ugly brown-green.

"Obviously a government heap," Faye said.

"Pretty bold, aren't they?"

"Well, if they've been eavesdropping on us the way Jack says, through our own telephones, then they know we're on to them, so maybe they figure there's no point in playing coy with us." Faye took her foot off the brake and headed up the driveway.

Watching the unmarked Plymouth dwindle in the side mirror, Ginger said, "Or maybe they're getting in position to take us into custody. Maybe they've put tails on all of us, and maybe they're just waiting for the order to snatch us all at the same time."

On the narrow, gravel driveway, the interlacing shadows of the overarching piñons wove a darkness nearly as deep as night.

As they drove up the two-lane road through the broad snow-covered meadow toward the massive blast doors, Colonel Falkirk sat in the front passenger's seat of the Wagoneer, thinking about the catastrophe that would ensue from the revelation of Thunder Hill's secret.

From a political perspective, this would make the Watergate mess look like a tea party. An unprecedented number of competing government institutions were involved in the cover-up, organizations that often operated in jealous opposition to one another—the FBI, CIA, National Security Agency, the United States Army, the Air Force, and others. It was a testament to the degree of potential danger that these groups could work together with nary a hitch and without a single leak in more than eighteen months. But if the cover-up were uncovered, the scandal would extend throughout so much of the government that the faith of the American people in their leaders would be severely shaken. Of course, very few in any of those organizations knew what had happened, no more than six in the FBI, fewer in the CIA; most of their men involved in the cover-up didn't know *what* they were covering up, which was why there had been no leaks. But the *número uno* of each organization—the Director of the FBI, the Director of the CIA, the Chief of Staff of the Army—was completely in the know. Not to mention the Chairman of the Joint Chiefs of Staff. And the Secretary of State. And the President, his closest advisers, the Vice-President. A lot of prominent men might fall from grace if this affair was not kept under lock and key.

The political destruction wrought by the release of the secret would be only a small part of the devastation. The CISG—a think-tank of physicists, biologists, anthropologists, sociologists, theologists, economists, educators, and other learned people—had pondered precisely this crisis at great length and depth, years before it had arisen here in Nevada. The CISG had issued a 1220-page top-secret report on its conclusions, a document that offered some disturbing reading. Leland knew that report by heart, for he was the military representative to the CISG and had helped write several position papers included in the final text. Within the CISG, the opinion was unanimous that the world would never be the same if such an event were to occur. All societies, all cultures would be radically changed forever. Projected deaths over the first two years ranged in the millions.

Lieutenant Horner, who was driving the Wagoneer, braked twenty feet in front of the giant blast doors that were set in the sudden steep upper slope of the meadow. He didn't wait for the huge barriers to open, for he was not driving directly into Thunder Hill. Horner turned right, into a small parking lot, where three minibuses, four Jeep wagons, a Land Rover, and several other vehicles stood side by side.

The twin blast doors, each thirty feet high and twenty feet wide, were so thick they could be opened only at a ponderous pace, producing a rumble that could be heard a mile away and *felt* in the air and in the ground at least half as far. When a truck—loaded with ammunition, weapons, or supplies—pulled up in front of the drive-in entrance, the doors required five minutes to roll apart. Opening those hangar-sized portals every time a lone man needed to walk in or out was unthinkably inefficient, so a second, man-sized door—nearly as formidable—was set in the hillside thirty feet to the right of the main entrance.

There was no better vault than Thunder Hill in which to keep the secret of July 6. It was an impregnable fortress.

Leland and Lieutenant Horner hurried through the bitter air to the walk-in entrance. The small steel door, almost as blastproof as the massive versions to the left, had an electronic lock that could be disengaged only by tapping the proper four numbers on a keyboard. The code changed every two weeks, and those entrusted with it were required to commit it to memory. Leland punched in the code, and the fourteen-inch-thick, lead-core door slid aside with a sudden pneumatic *whoosh*.

They stepped into a twelve-foot-long concrete tunnel about nine feet in diameter and brightly lit. It angled to the left. At the end was another door identical to the first, but it could not be opened until the outer door was closed. Leland touched a heat-sensitive switch just inside the tunnel entrance, and the outer door hissed shut behind him and Lieutenant Horner.

Immediately, a pair of video cameras, mounted on the ceiling at opposite ends of the chamber, clicked on. The cameras tracked the two men as they walked to the inner door.

No human eyes were watching the colonel and lieutenant on any video display, for the system was operated entirely by VIGILANT, the security computer, as a precaution against the possibility that a traitor within Thunder Hill's own guard unit might open the facility to hostile forces. VIGILANT was not linked to the installation's main computer or to the outside world; therefore, it was invulnerable to saboteurs seeking to take control of it by means of a modem or other electronic tap.

The guard at the perimeter fence had notified VIGILANT that Colonel Leland Falkirk and Lieutenant Thomas Horner would be arriving. Now, as they approached the inner door under the gazes of video cameras, the computer compared their appearance to stored holographic images of them, rapidly matching forty-two points of facial resemblance. It was impossible to deceive VIGILANT either with makeup or with a look-alike for an approved visitor. If Leland or Horner had been an imposter or unauthorized visitor, VIGILANT would have sounded an alarm, simultaneously filling the entrance tunnel with a sedative gas.

The lock on the inner door had no keyboard; no code would open it. Instead, a one-foot-square panel of glass was set in the wall beside the door. Leland almost pressed his right hand palm-down against the panel, hesitated, then used his left, and the glass lit, and a faint humming arose. VIGILANT scanned his palmprint and fingerprints, comparing them to the prints in its files.

Lieutenant Horner said, "Almost as hard to get in here as into heaven."

"Harder," Leland said.

The light behind the milky glass winked out, and Leland took his hand away. The inner door opened.

They stepped into a huge natural tunnel that had been improved by human hands. The domed rock overhead was lost in darkness because the lighting fixtures were suspended from black metal scaffolding, creating the illusion of a ceiling perhaps twenty or thirty feet below the true ceiling. The tunnel was sixty feet across and led into the mountain about a hundred and twenty yards. In some places the rock walls had natural contours, but in other places they carried the imprints of dynamite blasts and jackhammers and other tools that had been used to widen the narrow portions of the passageway. Incoming trucks could drive along the concrete floor to unloading bays beside immense cargo elevators that went down into deeper regions of the facility.

A guard sat at a table beyond the door by which Leland and Horner entered. Considering the remoteness of Thunder Hill, the extent of sophisticated defenses, and the thoroughness with which VIGILANT examined all visitors, a lone sentry seemed superfluous to Leland.

Evidently, the sentry was of that same opinion, for he was not prepared for trouble. His revolver was holstered. He was eating a candy bar. Reluctantly, he looked up from an old novel by Jack Finney.

He wore a coat because the open areas of the Depository were never heated; only the enclosed living quarters and work areas were kept warm. An enormous power supply was provided by a mini hydroelectric plant that harnessed an underground river, plus backup diesel generators, but there was not enough to warm the mammoth caverns. The subterranean temperature was a stable fifty-five degrees, quite bearable if one dressed for long work periods in the chilly air, as the guard had done.

He saluted. "Colonel Falkirk, Lieutenant Horner, you're cleared to see Dr. Bennell. You know how to find him, of course."

"Of course," Falkirk said.

Ten feet to the left, the burnished steel surface of the giant blast doors glimmered softly in the fluorescent light, looking rather like the sheer face of a great glacier. Leland and Lieutenant Horner turned right, away from the big doors, and walked deeper into the mountain, toward the elevators.

Thunder Hill Depository was equipped with hydraulic lifts of three sizes, the largest of which rivaled the enormous elevators on aircraft carriers. A carrier's lifts were used to bring planes from the ship's hold onto the flight deck, and Thunder Hill's also lowered and raised planes, among other things. In addition to 2.4 billion dollars of equipment and materiel—freeze-dried food, medicine, portable field hospitals, clothing, blankets, tents, handguns, rifles, mortars, field artillery, ammunition, light military vehicles such as Jeeps and armored personnel carriers, and twenty backpack nukes—the vast storage dump contained a variety of useful aircraft. First, the helicopters: thirty Sikorsky S-67 Blackhawk antitank gunships; twenty Bell Kingcobras; eight Anglo-French Westland Pumas, general purpose transports; and three big Medevac choppers. No conventional aircraft were stored at Thunder Hill, but there were twelve vertical takeoff jets of the type manufactured in England by Hawker Siddeley and known there as Harriers, but which were called AV-8As when in U.S. service. Because the Harriers were equipped with powerful vectored-thrust engines, the craft could land and take off vertically, without need of a runway. In a grave crisis—for example, subsequent to a limited nuclear strike and a land invasion by enemy troops—the aircraft of Thunder Hill, both choppers and Harriers, could be lifted to the top level, rolled out through the massive blast doors, and sent hurtling into the sky.

However, the current crisis did not involve war or require the unleashing of the Depository's aircraft, so Leland and the lieutenant bypassed the two immense elevators. They also passed the two smaller but still oversize cargo elevators, their footsteps echoing off the stone walls, and took one of the three smallest cabs— about the size of a standard lift in a hotel—down into the bowels of Thunder Hill.

Medical supplies, food, guns, and all ammunition were stored on the third level, the bottom floor of the complex, in a network of chambers which had been caulked, equipped with pressure-release bores, and fitted with doors for the purpose of blast containment. On the second—the middle—level, all the vehicles and aircraft were kept in other huge caverns, and it was there, too, that the staff lived and worked.

Leland and Lieutenant Horner got off the lift at the second level. They stepped into a lighted, circular, rock-wall chamber three hundred feet in diameter. It served as a hub—in fact, personnel called it The Hub—from which four other caverns opened; and still more rooms lay beyond those four. The larger of those deep vaults contained—among other things—the aircraft, Jeeps, and armored personnel carriers.

There were no doors on three of the four caverns which led off The Hub, for there was no serious danger of fire or explosion on that level. But the fourth chamber did, indeed, have doors, for it contained the secret of July 6, which Leland and many others had conspired to conceal. He stopped now, a few steps out of the elevator, to study those portals, which were twenty-six feet high and sixty-four feet wide. They were made of cross-braced two-by-fours rather than steel, because they had been jerry-built to meet an emergency situation; there had been no time to order a fabricated metal door to close off the cavern. They reminded the colonel of the enormous wooden doors in the wall that had protected the frightened natives from the beast on the other half of their island in the original *King Kong*. Considering what lay behind these doors, that horror-movie image did not inspire confidence. Leland shuddered.

Lieutenant Horner said, "Still gives you the creeps, huh?"

"You mean you're comfortable with it now?"

"Hell, no, sir. Hell, no."

Inset in the bottom of one of those huge wooden barriers was a much smaller, man-sized door through which researchers entered and exited the room beyond. An armed guard was positioned there to allow entrance only to those with the proper pass. The activities in that forbidden chamber had nothing to do with the other—primary—functions of the Depository, and ninety percent of the personnel were not permitted access to the area. Indeed, ninety percent did not know what was in that cavern.

Around the circumference of The Hub, between the openings to other caverns, buildings had been erected along the walls and anchored to the rock. The structures dated to the first year of the Depository's construction, back in the early 1960s. Then, they had served as offices for engineers, superintendents, and the Army's project officers. Over the years, an entire subterranean town had been erected in other caverns—sleeping quarters, cafeteria, recreation rooms, laboratories, machine shops, vehicle service center, computer rooms, even a PX, among other things. They were now occupied by the military and government personnel who were doing one- and two-year tours of duty at Thunder Hill. In the buildings, there was heat, better lighting, inside and outside telephone lines, kitchens, bathrooms, and all the myriad comforts of home. They were constructed of metal panels coated with baked blue or white or gray enamel, with only small windows and narrow metal doors. Though they had no wheels, they somewhat resembled motor homes or house trailers drawn in a circle, as if they were the property of a modern-day encampment of gypsies who had found their way to this snug haven, 240 feet below the winter snows.

Now, turning from the forbidden chamber with the wooden doors, Leland walked across The Hub toward a white metal structure—Dr. Miles Bennell's offices. Lieutenant Horner fell in dutifully at his side.

The summer before last, Miles Bennell (whom Leland Falkirk loathed) had moved into Thunder Hill to head all scientific inquiry into the events of that fateful July night. He'd only been out of the Depository on three occasions since then, never for longer than two weeks. He was obsessed with his assignment. Or something worse than obsessed.

A dozen officers, enlisted men, and civilians were in sight within The Hub, some crossing from one adjoining cavern to another, some just standing in conversation with one another. Leland looked them over as he passed them, unable to understand what kind of person would volunteer to work underground for weeks and months at a stretch. They were paid a thirty percent hardship bonus, but to Leland's way of thinking, that was inadequate compensation. The Depository was less oppressive than Shenkfield's small, windowless warrens, but not by much.

Leland supposed he was slightly claustrophobic. Being underground made him feel as if he were buried alive. As an admitted masochist, he should have relished his discomfort, but this was one kind of pain he did not seek or enjoy.

Dr. Miles Bennell looked ill. Like nearly everyone in Thunder Hill, he was pasty-faced from being too long beyond the reach of sunlight. His curly black hair and beard only made his pallor more pronounced. In the fluorescent glare of his office, he looked almost like a ghost. He greeted Leland and Lieutenant Horner curtly, and he did not offer to shake hands with either of them.

That suited the colonel fine. He was no friend of Bennell's. A handshake would have been sheer hypocrisy. Besides, Leland was half-afraid that Miles Bennell had been compromised, that the scientist was no longer who or what he appeared to be . . . was no longer entirely human. And if that crazy, paranoid possibility was in fact true, he wanted no physical contact with Bennell, not even a quick handshake.

"Dr. Bennell," Leland said coldly, using the hard tone of voice and icy demeanor that always elicited quaverous obedience, "your handling of this security breach has been either criminally inept, or *you're* the traitor we're looking for. Now, hear me loud and clear: this time, we're going to find the bastard who sent those Polaroid snapshots—no more broken lie detectors, no more botched interrogations—and we're going to find out if he's the one who teased Jack Twist into returning, and we're going to come down on him so hard he'll wish he'd been born a fly and spent his life in a stable sucking up horseshit."

Utterly unruffled, Miles Bennell smiled and said, "Colonel, that was the best Richard Jaeckel impression I've ever seen, but entirely unnecessary. I'm as anxious as you to find the leak and plug it."

Leland wanted to punch the son of a bitch. This was one reason he loathed Miles Bennell: The bastard could not be intimidated.

Calvin Sharkle lived on O'Bannon Lane in a pleasant middle-class residential neighborhood in Evanston. Father Wycazik had to stop twice at service stations to ask directions. When he got to the corner of O'Bannon and Scott Avenue, only two blocks from Sharkle's address, he was turned back by policemen manning an emergency barricade formed by two black-and-white cruisers and one paramedic van. There were also television crews running around with minicams.

He also knew at once that the trouble on O'Bannon Lane was not merely coincidental. Something was happening at the Sharkle house.

In spite of temperatures in the mid-twenties and wind gusting to thirty miles an hour, a crowd of about a hundred had gathered outside the police barricade— on the sidewalks and on the lawns of the corner houses. Passing traffic on Scott Avenue was slowed by gawkers, and Stefan had to drive almost two blocks at a frustratingly slow pace before he found a parking space.

When he walked back to the crowd and became part of it, seeking information from the well-bundled onlookers, Father Wycazik found that they were for the most part a friendly and strangely excited group. But creepy, too. Not blatantly weird. In fact, they were ordinary people—except for their totally insensitive fascination with the tragedy unfolding before them, as if it were as legitimate a source of thrills as a football game.

It was definitely a tragedy, and one of a particularly horrible nature, which Father Wycazik discovered a minute after he joined the crowd and began to ask questions. A florid-faced, mustachioed man in a plaid hunting jacket and toboggan hat said, ''Jesus, man, don't you watch the goddamned TV?'' He was not the least restrained because he did not know he was talking to a priest; Stefan's topcoat and scarf concealed all evidence of his holy office. ''Christ, fella, that's Sharkle down there. Sharkle the Shark, man. That's what they're callin' him. Guy's a dangerous loony. Been sealed up in his house there since yesterday, man. He shot him two of his neighbors and one cop already, and he's got him two goddamn hostages who, if you ask me, got about as much chance as a fuckin' cat at a Doberman convention.''

Tuesday morning, via Pacific Southwest Airlines, Parker Faine flew into San Francisco from Orange County, then caught a connecting West Air flight to Monterey. It was an hour's trip up the California coast on PSA, a one-hour layover in San Francisco, and then only thirty-five minutes to Monterey. The journey seemed shorter because one of the other travelers, a pretty young woman, recognized his name, liked his paintings, and was in the mood to be enthralled by his burly charms.

In Monterey, at the small airport rental agency, he hired a vomit-green Ford Tempo. It was an offense to his refined sense of color.

The Tempo's tempo was satisfyingly allegro on flat roads but a bit adagio on the hills. Nevertheless, he required less than half an hour to find the address Dom had given him for Gerald Salcoe, the man who had stayed at the Tranquility Motel with his wife and two daughters on the night of July 6, and who had thus far been unreachable by both phone and Western Union. It was a big Southern Colonial manor house, hideously out of place on the California coast, set on a prime half-acre, in the shade of massive pines, with enough elaborately tended shrubbery to employ a gardener one full day a week, including beds of impatiens that blazed with red and purple flowers even now, in January.

Parker swung the Tempo into the majestic circular driveway and parked in front of broad, flower-bordered steps that led up to a deep pillared veranda. In the shadows of the trees, there was sufficient gloom to require lights indoors, but he saw none at the front windows. All of the drapes were tightly shut, and the house had a vacant look.

He got out of the Tempo, hurried up the steps, and crossed the wide veranda, voicing his objection to the chilly air as he went: "Brrrrrrr." The area's usual morning fog had cleared from the airport, permitting landings, but it was still clinging to this part of the peninsula, bearding the pines, weaving tendrils between their trunks, muting the impatiens' brilliant blooms. Winter in northern California was a more bracing season than in Laguna Beach, and with the added damp chill of fog, it was not at all to Parker's taste. He had come dressed for it, however, in heavy corduroy slacks, a green-plaid flannel shirt, a green pullover that mocked Izod-Lacoste by featuring a goofy-looking appliquéd armadillo on the breast instead of an alligator, and a three-quarter-length navy peacoat with sergeant's stripes on one sleeve: quite an outfit, especially when accented by Day-Glo-orange running shoes. As he rang the doorbell, Parker looked down at himself and decided that maybe sometimes he dressed too eccentrically, even for an artist.

He rang the doorbell six times, waiting half a minute between each ring, but no one came.

Last night, when a man named Jack Twist had called him at eleven o'clock from a pay phone in Elko, claiming to have a message from Dom, and had asked him to go to a specific pay phone in Laguna for a callback in twenty minutes, Parker had still been working on a new and exciting painting that he had begun at three o'clock that afternoon. Nevertheless, deeply involved as he was with the work, he had hastened to the booth as directed. And he had agreed to the trip to Monterey without hesitation. The fact was that he had plunged into work as a means of taking his mind off Dom and the unfolding events in Elko County, for that was where he really wanted to be, neck-deep in the mystery. When Twist told him about Dom's and the priest's psychic demonstration—floating salt and pepper shakers, levitating chairs!—nothing short of World War III could have prevented Parker from going to Monterey. And now he was not going to be defeated by an empty house. Wherever the Salcoes were, he would find them, and the best place to start was with the neighbors.

Because of the half-acre lots and walls of intervening shrubbery, he could not easily walk next door. Back in the Tempo, as he put the car in gear, he glanced at the house again, and at first he thought he saw movement at one of the downstairs windows: a slightly parted drape falling back into place. He sat for a moment, staring, then decided the movement had been a trick of fog and shadows. He popped the handbrake and drove around the second half of the circular driveway, out to the street, delighted to be playing spy again.

Ernie and Dom parked the Jeep Cherokee at the end of the county road, and the pickup with the tinted windshield halted two hundred yards behind them. Perched on its high all-terrain tires, with goggle-eyed spotlights on its roof, it looked (Dom thought) like a big insect poised alertly on the down-sloping lane, ready to skitter toward a hidey-hole if it saw someone with a giant economy-size can of Raid. The driver did not get out, nor did the passenger, if there was one.

"Think there's going to be trouble here?" Dom asked, getting out of the Cherokee and joining Ernie at the side of the road.

"If they'd meant trouble, they'd already have made it," Ernie said. His breath steamed in the frigid air. "If they want to tag along and watch, that's all right by me. To hell with them."

They got two hunting rifles—a Winchester Model 94 carbine loaded with .32 special cartridges, and a .30/06 Springfield—from the back of the Jeep Cherokee, handling the weapons conspicuously in the hope that the men in the pickup would be encouraged to remain peaceable by the realization that their quarry could fight back.

The mountain still rose on the western side of the lane, and forest still clothed those slopes. But the land that fell away to the east had become a broad treeless field, the northern end of the series of meadows that lay along the valley wall.

Although snow had not yet begun to fall, the wind was picking up. Dom was thankful for the winter clothes he had purchased in Reno, but he wished he had an insulated ski suit like Ernie was wearing. And a pair of those rugged lace-up boots instead of the flimsy zippered pair he now wore. Later today, Ginger and Faye would stop at a sporting-goods store in Elko with a list of gear needed for tonight's operation, including suitable clothes for Dom and everyone else who did not already have them. At the moment, however, the insistent wind found entrance at Dom's coat collar and at the unelasticized cuffs of his sleeves.

Leaving the Cherokee, he and Ernie went over the side of the road, down into the sloping meadow, continuing their inspection of the Thunder Hill perimeter on foot. The high, electrified chainlink fence with the barbed-wire overhang led out of the trees farther back; it ceased to parallel the northward course of the county road, turning east and down toward the valley floor. The snow in the meadow was ten inches deep, but still below the tops of their boots. They slogged two hundred yards to a point along the fence from which they could see, in the distance, the enormous steel blast doors set in the side of the valley wall.

Dom saw no signs of human or canine guards. The snow on the other side of the fence was not marked by footprints or pawprints, which meant no one walked the perimeter on a regular schedule.

"A place like this, they're not going to be sloppy," Ernie said. "So if there aren't any foot patrols, there must be one hell of a lot of electronic security on the other side of this fence."

Dom had been glancing toward the top of the meadow, a little worried that the men in the all-terrain truck might be up to something with the Cherokee. This time, when he looked back, he saw a man in dark clothes, starkly silhouetted against the snow. The guy wasn't around the Cherokee and seemed to have no interest in it, but he had come down from the edge of the county road, descending a few yards into the inclined meadow. He was standing up there, unmoving, maybe a hundred and eighty yards above Dom and Ernie, watching them.

Ernie noticed the observer, too. He tucked his Winchester under his right arm and lifted the binoculars he had been carrying on a strap around his neck. "He's Army. At least that looks like a regulation Army greatcoat he's wearing. Just watching us."

"You'd think they'd be more discreet."

"Can't follow anyone discreetly, not in these wide-open spaces. Might as well be forthright. Besides, he wants us to see what he's carrying, so we'll know our rifles don't worry him."

"What do you mean?" Dom asked. "What's he carrying?"

"A Belgian FN submachine gun. Damn fine weapon. It can fire up to six hundred rounds a minute."

* * *

If Father Wycazik had watched television news, he would have heard about Cal-vin Sharkle last night, for the man had been a hot story for twenty-four hours. However, he'd stopped watching TV news years ago, for he'd decided that its relentless simplification of every story into stark black and white issues was in-tellectually corrupt and that its gleeful concentration on violence, sex, gloom, and despair was morally repellent. He also might have read about the tragedy on O'Bannon Lane on the front pages of this morning's *Tribune* and *Sun-Times,* but he had left the rectory in such a hurry that he'd had no time for newspapers. Now he pieced the story together from information provided by those in the crowd behind the police barricades.

For months, Cal Sharkle had been acting . . . odd. Ordinarily cheerful and pleas-ant, a bachelor who lived alone and was well-liked by everyone on O'Bannon Lane, he'd become a brooder, dour and even grim. He told neighbors he had "a bad feeling about things," and believed something "important and terrible is going to happen." He read survivalist books and magazines, and talked about Armageddon. And he was plagued by vivid nightmares.

December first, he quit trucking, sold his rig, and told neighbors and relatives the end was imminent. He wanted to sell his house, buy remote property in the mountains, and build a retreat like those he had seen in the survivalist magazines. "But there isn't time," he told his sister, Nan Gilchrist. "So I'll just prepare this house for a siege." He didn't know what was going to happen, did not understand the source of his own fear, though he said he was not concerned about nuclear war, Russian invasion, economic collapse, or anything else that alarmed most survivalists. "I don't know what . . . but something strange and horrible is going to happen," he told his sister.

Mrs. Gilchrist made him see a doctor, who found him fit, suffering only from job-related stress. But after Christmas, Calvin's previously garrulous nature gave way to a closed-mouth suspicion. During the first week of January, he had his phone disconnected, cryptically explaining: "Who knows how they'll get at us when they come? Maybe they can do it over the phone." He was unable or unwilling to identify "they."

No one considered Cal really dangerous. He had been a peaceful, kind-hearted man all his life. In spite of his new eccentric behavior, there was no reason to think he would turn violent.

Then, yesterday morning at eight-thirty, Cal visited the Wilkersons, the family across the street, with whom he had once been close but from whom he had recently kept his distance. Edward Wilkerson told reporters that Cal said, "Listen, I can't be selfish about this. I'm all prepared, and here you are defenseless. So when they come for us, Ed, it'll be okay if you and your family hide out at my place." When Wilkerson asked who "they" were, Cal said, "Well, I don't know what they'll look like, or what they'll call themselves. But they're going to do something bad to us, maybe turn us into zombies." Cal Sharkle assured Wilkerson that he had plenty of guns and ammunition in his house and had taken steps to make a fortress of the place.

Alarmed by talk of weapons and shootouts, Wilkerson had humored Cal and, as soon as the man left, had called his sister. Nan Gilchrist had arrived at half-past-ten with her husband and had told a worried Wilkerson that she would handle it, that she was sure she could persuade Cal to enter the hospital for observation. But after she and Mr. Gilchrist went into the house, Ed Wilkerson decided they might need some backup, so he and another neighbor, Frank Krelky, went to the Sharkle house to provide what assistance they could.

Wilkerson expected Mr. or Mrs. Gilchrist to answer the bell, but Cal himself came to the door. He was distraught, nearly hysterical—and armed with a 20-gauge semiautomatic shotgun. He accused his neighbors of being zombies already. "You've been *changed*," he shouted at Wilkerson and Krelky. "Oh God, I should've seen it. I should've known. When did it happen, when'd you stop being human? My God, now you've come to get us all in one swoop." Then, with a wail of terror, he opened fire with the shotgun. The first blast took Krelky in the throat at such close range that it decapitated him. Wilkerson ran, was hit in the legs as he reached the end of Sharkle's front walk, fell, rolled, and played dead, a ruse that saved his life.

Now Krelky was in the morgue, and Wilkerson was in the hospital in good enough condition to talk to reporters.

And Father Wycazik was at the entrance to O'Bannon Lane, where a young man in the crowd behind the police line was eager to fill in the last of it for him. The man's name was Roger Hasterwick, a "temporarily unemployed beverage concoctionist," which Stefan suspected was an out-of-work bartender. He had a disturbing gleam in his eyes that might have been a sign of intoxication, drug use, lack of sleep, psychopathy, or all four, but his information was detailed and apparently accurate:

"So, see, the cops close the block, evacuate the people out their houses, then they try to talk with this Sharkle the Shark. But he don't have a phone, see, and when they use a bullhorn, he won't answer them. The cops figure his sister and brother-in-law are in there alive, hostages, so nobody wants to do nothin' rash."

"Wise," Father Wycazik said bleakly, feeling even colder than the winter day in which he stood.

"Wise, wise, wise," Roger Hasterwick said impatiently, making it clear he preferred not to be interrupted. "So finally, with a half-hour daylight left, they decide they'll send in the SWAT guys to dig him out, maybe save the sister and brother-in-law. So they lob tear gas in there, see, and the SWAT guys rush the place, but when they get in they hit trouble. Sharkle must've been workin' on the house for weeks, settin' traps. The cops start fallin' over these thin wires he's strung everywhere, and one gets brained by a deadfall, which don't kill him but sure does some damage. Then, Christ, Sharkle opens fire on 'em because he's wearin' a gas mask same as they are and just waitin' like a cat. The dude was *prepared*. So he blows one cop away, utterly, and wounds one, then he heads down into the cellar and pulls the door shut, and nobody can get in after him 'cause it's not any regular cellar door but a *steel* door he's put in special. Not only that, but the outside cellar door, around back, is steel, too, and what he's done is he's put heavy sheet-metal shutters over the insides of the cellar windows, so it's your typical stalemate, see."

By Stefan's calculations, two people were dead, three wounded.

Hasterwick said, "So the cops they pulled in their horns real fast and figured to wait him out through the night. This mornin', Sharkle the Shark slides open one of them sheet-metal shutters on a basement window, see, and he shouts a bunch of stuff, really crazy stuff, and they figure somethin' more is gonna go down, but then he closes the shutter again, and since then—nothin'. I sure hope he does somethin' soon, 'cause it's cold and I'm beginnin' to get bored."

"What did he shout?" Stefan asked.

"Huh?"

"This morning, what crazy stuff did he yell from the basement?"

"Oh, well, see, what he says . . ." Roger Hasterwick stopped when he realized that a piece of news, passing in from the edge of the crowd, had electrified everyone. People hurried away from the barricade, some walking fast and some running south on Scott Avenue. Appalled by the prospect of missing new bloodshed, Hasterwick grabbed frantically at a blotchy-faced man in a deerstalker cap, the flaps of which were down but flopping loose. "What is it? What's happenin'?"

Trying to pull away from Hasterwick, the man in the deerstalker cap said, "Guy down here has a van with his own police-band radio. He's tuned in on the cops, the SWAT team, they're getting ready to wipe that fuckin' Sharkle off the map!" He wrenched loose of Hasterwick and rushed away, and Hasterwick hurried after him.

Father Wycazik stared after the departing throng for a moment. Then he glanced around at the ten or twelve onlookers who had remained, at the officers manning the barricade, past the barricade. More death, murder. He could sense it coming. He should do something to stop it. But he could not think. He was numb with dread. Until now, he had seen—and been *able* to see—only a positive side to the unfolding mystery. The miraculous cures and other phenomena had engendered only joy and an expectation of divine revelations to come. But now he was seeing the dark side of the mystery, and he was badly shaken by it.

Finally, hoping he would not be mistaken for just another ghoul in the bloodthirsty crowd, Stefan hurried after Roger Hasterwick and the others. They had gathered almost a block south of O'Bannon Lane, around a recreational van, a metallic-blue Chevrolet with a California-beach mural on the side. The owner, a huge and hugely bearded man sitting behind the wheel, had opened both doors and turned up the volume on the police-band radio, so everyone could hear the cops in action.

In a minute or two, the essentials of their attack plan were clear. The SWAT team was already moving into place, back into the first floor of Sharkle's house. They would use a small, precisely shaped charge of plastic explosives to blow the steel cellar door off its pins, not enough to send shrapnel cutting through the basement. Simultaneously, another group of officers would blow off the exterior cellar door with a similar carefully gauged charge. Even as the smoke was clearing, the two groups would storm into the basement and catch Cal Sharkle in a pincer attack. That strategy was terribly dangerous for the officers and the hostages, though the authorities had decided that they would be in far greater danger if action was delayed any further.

Listening to the radio-relayed voices crackle in the cold January air, Father Wycazik suddenly knew he must stop the attack. If it was carried out, the slaughter would be worse than anyone imagined. He had to be allowed to go past the barricade, to the house, and talk to Cal Sharkle. Now. Right away. *Now*. He turned from the Chevy van and raced back toward the entrance to O'Bannon Lane, a block away. He was not sure what he would say to Sharkle to get through his paranoia. Perhaps, "You are not alone, Calvin." He'd think of something.

His abrupt departure from the van apparently gave the crowd the idea that he had heard or seen something happening up at the barricade. He was less than halfway back to the entrance to O'Bannon Lane when younger and fleeter onlookers began to pass him, shouting excitedly, plunging off the sidewalk and out into the street, bringing a complete halt to the already crawling traffic on Scott Avenue. Brakes barked. Horns blew. There was the thud of one bumper hitting another. Stefan was jostled by runners and struck so hard that he fell to his hands and knees on the pavement. No one stopped to help him. Stefan got up and ran on. The air seemed to have thickened with animal madness and bloodlust. Stefan was horrified at the behavior of his fellow men, and his heart was pounding, and he thought, *This is what it might be like in Hell, running forever in the midst of a frantic and gibbering mob.*

By the time Stefan reached the police blockade, more than half the frenzied crowd had returned ahead of him. They were jammed against the sawhorses and police cars, craning to see into the forbidden block of O'Bannon Lane. He pushed in among them, desperate to get to the head of the mob, so he could speak to the police. He was pushed, shoved, but he shoved back, telling them he was a priest, but no one was listening, and he felt his fedora knocked off his head, but he persisted, and then at last he was through to the front of the surging multitudes.

The policemen angrily ordered the mob to move back, threatened arrest, drew batons, lowered the visors on their riot helmets. Father Wycazik was prepared to lie, to tell the police anything that might get them to postpone the imminent attack on the house, tell them that he was not just a priest but Sharkle's own priest, that he knew what was wrong, knew how to get Sharkle to surrender. Of course, he didn't really know how to obtain Sharkle's surrender, but if he could buy time and talk to Sharkle, he might think of something. He caught the attention of an officer who ordered him to step back. He identified himself as a priest. The cop wasn't listening, so Stefan tore open his topcoat and pulled off his white scarf to reveal his Roman collar. "I'm a priest!" But the crowd surged forward, pushing Stefan against a sawhorse, and the barrier fell over, and the cop shoved back angrily, in no mood to listen.

An instant later, two small explosions shook the air, one a split-second after the other, low and flat but hard. The hundred voices of the crowd gasped as one, and everybody froze, for they knew what they had heard: the SWAT team blowing the steel doors off the cellar. A third explosion followed the first two, an immense and devastating blast that shook the pavement, that hurt the ears, that vibrated in bones and teeth, that shot slabs and splinters of Sharkle's house into the wintry sky, that seemed to shatter the day itself and cast it down in a billion broken pieces. Again with a single voice, the crowd cried out. Instead of pressing toward the blockade this time, they scrambled back in fear, suddenly realizing that death could be not just an interesting spectator sport but a participatory activity.

"He had a bomb!" one of the barricade cops said. "My God, my God, Sharkle had a bomb in there!" He turned to the emergency medical van in which two paramedics were waiting, and he shouted, "Go! *Go!*"

The red beacons flashed atop the paramedic's wagon. It pulled out of the barricade, speeding toward the middle of the block.

Shaking with horror, Father Wycazik tried to follow on foot. But one of the cops grabbed him and said, "Hey, get the hell back there."

"I'm a priest. Someone may need comforting, last rites."

"Father, I wouldn't care if you were the pope himself. We don't know for sure that Sharkle's dead."

Numbly, Father Wycazik obeyed, though the tremendous power of the explosion left no doubt in his mind that Cal Sharkle was dead. Sharkle *and* his sister. And his brother-in-law. And most members of the SWAT team. How many altogether? Maybe five? Six? Ten?

Moving aimlessly back through the crowd, absentmindedly tucking his scarf in place and buttoning his coat, partially in a state of shock, murmuring a *Pater Noster* he saw Roger Hasterwick, the unemployed bartender with the queerly gleaming eyes. He put a hand on Hasterwick's shoulder, and said, "What did he shout to the police this morning?"

Hasterwick blinked. "Huh? What?"

"Before we got separated, you told me Calvin Sharkle slid open the metal shutter on one of the cellar windows and shouted a lot of weird stuff this morning, and you thought something was going to happen, but then nothing did. What exactly did he say?"

Hasterwick's face brightened with the memory. "Oh, yeah, yeah. It was real weird, see, straight-out crazy stuff." He scrunched up his face, striving to recall the madman's exact words. When he had them, he grinned, rolled his mouth as if savoring the revelation, then repeated Sharkle's ravings for Stefan's enjoyment.

Stefan not only failed to enjoy the performance, but second by dreadful second, he became increasingly convinced that Calvin Sharkle had not been insane. Confused, yes, baffled and afraid because of the tremendous stress generated by his brainwashing and by the collapse of his memory blocks, badly confused but not insane. Roger Hasterwick and everyone else thought Sharkle's shouted accusations and declarations and imprecations, flung at the world through the shielded window of a jerry-built fortress, were obviously the lunatic fantasies of a demented mind. But Father Wycazik had an advantage over everyone else: He saw Sharkle's statements in the context of events at the Tranquility Motel, in the context of miracle cures and telekinetic phenomena, and he wondered if there might be some truth in the claims and accusations that the poor frightened man had shouted through the basement window. And wondering, he felt the fine hairs rise on the back of his neck. He shivered.

Seeing that reaction, Hasterwick said, "Hey, ain't no point takin' it serious, for Christ's sake. You don't think what he said was true? Hell, the guy was a nut. He blowed himself up, didn't he?"

Father Wycazik ran north along Scott Avenue to the parish car.

Even before he had arrived in Evanston and discovered the unfolding tragedy at Calvin Sharkle's house, Stefan Wycazik had half-expected to be on a flight to Nevada before the day was through. The events at the Mendozas' apartment and at the Halbourgs' place had set a fire of wonder and curiosity burning in him, and the blaze would not be quenched unless he plunged into the activities of the troubled group in Elko County.

Now, because of what he had just learned from Hasterwick, the urge to go to Nevada had become a burning need. If only half of what Sharkle had shouted through the basement window was true, Stefan *had* to go to Nevada, not only to witness a miracle but to do what he could to protect those who had gathered at the Tranquility. All his life, he had been a rescuer of troubled priests, a shepherd bringing lost souls back into the fold. This time, however, he might be called upon to save minds and lives as well. The threat of which Calvin Sharkle had spoken was one that might put body and brain in as much jeopardy as the spirit.

He slipped the car in gear again. He drove out of Evanston.

He decided not to return to the rectory to pack. There was no time. He would head straight to O'Hare International Airport and take the first available seat on the first available flight west.

Dear God, he thought, what have You sent us? Is it the greatest gift for which we could have asked? Or a plague to make all Biblical plagues pale by comparison?

Father Stefan Wycazik put the pedal to the metal and drove south and then west toward O'Hare like . . . well, like a bat out of Hell.

* * *

Ginger and Faye spent the larger part of the morning with Elroy and Nancy Jamison under the pretense that Ginger, supposedly the daughter of an old friend of Faye's, was moving west for unspecified health reasons and was interested in learning about Elko County. The Jamisons were local-history buffs, eager to talk about the county, especially about the beauty of the Lemoille Valley.

Actually, indirectly and directly, Ginger and Faye were seeking indications that Elroy and Nancy were suffering from the effects of collapsing memory blocks. They found none. The Jamisons were happy, untroubled. Their brainwashing had been as successful as Faye's; their false memories were firmly rooted. Bringing them into the Tranquility family would put them in jeopardy while serving no great purpose.

In the motel van, as they pulled away from the Jamison house (with Elroy and Nancy waving from the front porch), Ginger said, "Good people. Really nice people."

"Yes," Faye said. "Reliable. Wish they were standing beside us in this thing. On the other hand, I'm happy they're well out of it."

Both women were quiet then, and Ginger figured Faye's thoughts were the same as her own: They were wondering if the government car was still parked along the county road, near the entrance to the Jamisons' place, and if the men in it would still be content merely to follow them. Ernie and Dom had armed themselves for their expedition into the mountains around Thunder Hill Depository. However, considering the unprovocative nature of Faye's and Ginger's errands, no one had thought that they might be in special danger, too. Ginger, like many attractive women living alone in a city, knew how to use a handgun, and Faye, a good Marine wife, was something of an expert, but their knowledge and expertise were of no use when they were not armed.

Having driven only a quarter-mile along the Jamisons' half-mile driveway, Faye stopped the van in one of the deepest pools of shadows cast by the over-hanging piñons. "I'm probably being melodramatic," she said. She slipped open a few buttons on her coat and reached under her sweater. "And these won't be much good if they point guns at our heads." Grimacing, she withdrew two steak knives and put them on the seat between her and Ginger.

Surprised, Ginger said, "Where'd you get these?"

"This is why I insisted on drying the breakfast dishes while Nancy washed them. Putting away the silverware, I swiped these. Didn't want to ask straight-out for a weapon; that would've meant bringing Nancy and Elroy into it, which it was clear we weren't going to have to do. I can return them later, when this is over." She picked up one of the knives. "The end's nicely pointed. The blade's sharp and serrated. Like I said, not much help if they've got a gun at your head. But if they were to run us off the road and try to force us into their car, you keep the knife a secret until you get your opening, then stab the bastard."

"Got it," Ginger said. She grinned and shook her head. "Someday, I hope you'll get a chance to meet Rita Hannaby."

"Your friend in Boston."

"Yes. You and Rita are a lot alike, I think."

"Me and a high-society lady?" Faye said doubtfully. "Can't imagine what we'd have in common."

"Well, for one thing, you both have such equanimity, such serenity, regardless of what's happening."

Putting the knife back on the seat, Faye said, "When you're a service wife, you either learn to go with the flow, or you go crazy."

"And both you and Rita look so feminine, soft and dependent on the outside—but inside, each of you is, in your own way, tough as nails."

Faye smiled. "Honey, you got a bit of that yourself."

They drove the last quarter-mile of the piñon-shaded driveway, out of the shadows and into the midday gloom of the pending storm.

The brown-green, stripped-down government car was still parked along the county road. Two men were in it. They looked impassively at Ginger. Impulsively, she waved at them. They did not wave back.

Faye drove down toward the floor of the Lemoille Valley.

The car followed.

Miles Bennell slumped in the big chair behind his gray metal desk and looked bored, and Miles Bennell ambled around his office while answering questions in a tone of voice that was sometimes indifferent and sometimes amusedly ironic, but Miles Bennell never fidgeted, groveled, looked frightened, or became angry, as almost any other man would have done in the same situation.

Colonel Leland Falkirk hated him.

Sitting at a scarred table in one corner of the room, Leland worked slowly through a stack of personnel files, one for each of the civilian scientists who were conducting studies and experiments in the cavern with the immense wooden doors, where the secret of July 6 was contained. He was hoping to narrow the field of possible traitors by determining which men and women could have been in New York City during the time the two notes and Polaroid snapshots had been mailed to Dominick Corvaisis in Laguna Beach. He had told Thunder Hill's military security staff to do this work on Sunday, and they professed to have completed the inquiries and to have found nothing to pinpoint the leak. But in light of the screwups in their investigation thus far—including *two* sabotaged lie detectors—he no longer trusted them any more than he trusted Bennell or the other scientists. He had to do it himself.

But right away Leland ran into problems. For one thing, during the past eighteen months, two damn many civilians had been brought into the conspiracy. Thirty-seven men and women, representing a broad spectrum of scientific disciplines, had possessed both high-security clearances and specialized knowledge essential to the research program Bennell had devised. Thirty-eight civilians, counting Bennell. It was a miracle that thirty-eight eggheads, utterly lacking in military discipline, could have kept any secret so long, let alone this one.

Worse, only Bennell and seven others were engaged in the research full-time, to the exclusion of all other professional pursuits and to the extent that they actually lived in Thunder Hill. The other thirty had families and university positions they could not leave for long periods of time, so they came and went as their schedules permitted, sometimes staying a few days, maybe a few weeks, rarely as long as a few months. Therefore, it would be a long and arduous job to investigate each and determine if and when he—or she—had been in New York.

Worse still, of the eight members of the full-time investigatory team, three had been in New York in December, including Dr. Miles Bennell himself. In short, the list of suspects currently numbered at least thirty-three among the scientific research staff alone.

Leland was also suspicious of the entire Depository security staff, though Major Fugata and Lieutenant Helms, the head of security and his right-hand man, were supposedly the only security personnel who knew what was happening in the forbidden cavern. On Sunday, soon after Fugata began questioning the full-time research staff and those part-time researchers currently in residence, he discovered that the polygraph was damaged and could not produce reliable results. Yesterday, when a new machine was sent up from Shenkfield, it also proved defective. Fugata said that the second machine was already damaged when it arrived from Shenkfield, but that was bullshit.

Someone involved in the project had seen reports that the witnesses' memory blocks were breaking down. Deciding to exploit that opportunity, he egged some of them along with cryptic notes and Polaroids stolen from the files. The bastard had nearly gotten away with it, and now that the heat was coming down on him, he had sabotaged the lie detectors.

Pausing in his perusal of the personnel files, Leland looked at Miles Bennell, who was standing in the small window. "Doctor, give me the benefit of your insight into the scientific mind."

Turning away from the window, Bennell said, "Certainly, Colonel."

"Everyone working with you knows about the classified CISG report that was done seven years ago. They know the terrible consequences that might result if we went public with our discoveries. So why would any of them be so irresponsible as to undermine project security?"

Dr. Bennell assumed a tone of earnest helpfulness, but Leland heard the acid-sharp disdain beneath the surface: "Some disagree with CISG's conclusions. Some think going public with these discoveries wouldn't result in a catastrophe, that the CISG was fundamentally wrong, too elitist in its viewpoint."

"Well, I believe the CISG was correct. And you, Lieutenant Horner?"

Horner was sitting near the door. "I agree with you, Colonel. If the news is broken to the public, they'll have to be prepared slowly, over maybe ten years. And even then . . ."

Leland nodded. To Bennell, he said, "I have a low but realistic opinion of my fellow men, Doctor, and I know how poorly most would cope with the new world that would follow the release of these discoveries. Chaos. Political and social upheaval. Just like the CISG report said."

Bennell shrugged. "You're entitled to your view." But his tone said: *Even if your view is ignorant and arrogant and narrow-minded.*

Leaning forward in his chair, Leland said, "How about you, Doctor? Do you believe the CISG was right?"

Evasively, Bennell said, "I'm not your man, Colonel. I didn't send those notes and Polaroids to Corvaisis and the Blocks."

"Okay, Doctor, then will you support my effort to have everyone in the project interrogated with the assistance of drugs? Even if we get the polygraph fixed, the answers we obtain will be less reliable than those we'd get with sodium pentothal and certain other substances."

Bennell frowned. "Well, there are some who'd object strenuously. These are people of superior intellect, Colonel. Intellectual life is their *primary* life, and they won't risk subjecting themselves to drugs that might, as a side-effect, have even the slightest permanent detrimental effect on their mental function."

"These drugs don't have that effect. They're safe."

"They're safe *most* of the time, maybe. But some of my people will have moral objections to using drugs for *any* reason—even safe drugs, even for a worthwhile purpose."

"Doctor, I'm going to push for drug-assisted interrogation of everyone in Thunder Hill, those who know the secret and those who don't. I'm going to demand General Alvarado approve." Alvarado was commanding officer of the

Thunder Hill Depository, a pencil-pushing desk-jockey who had spent his career on his backside. Leland liked Alvarado no more than he liked Bennell. "If the general approves drug-assisted interrogation, and if any of your people then refuse, I'll come down hard on them, hard enough to break them. That includes you, if you refuse. You understand me?"

"Oh, perfectly," Bennell said, still unruffled.

Disgusted, the colonel pushed the remaining personnel files aside. "This is too damn slow. I need the traitor quickly, not a month from now. We'd better repair the polygraph." He started to get up, then sat down as if he'd just thought of what he was about to ask, though it had been on his mind since he entered the Depository. "Doctor, what do *you* think of this development with Cronin and Corvaisis? These miraculous cures, the other bizarre phenomena. What do you make of it?"

Finally Bennell showed strong, genuine emotion. He unfolded his hands from behind his head and leaned forward in his chair. "I'm sure it scares the hell out of you, Colonel. But there could be another, less cataclysmic explanation than the one on which you've fixated. Fear is *your* only reaction, while I think it might be the greatest moment in the history of the human race. But whatever the case— we've absolutely got to talk with Cronin and Corvaisis. Tell them everything and seek their cooperation to discover exactly how they obtained these wonderful powers. We can't simply eliminate them or put them through another memory-wipe without knowing all the answers."

"If we bring everyone at the Tranquility into this, tell them the secret, and then don't wipe their memories again, the cover-up can't be maintained."

"Possibly not," Bennell said. "And if that's the case . . . then the public will just have to be told. Damn it, Colonel, because of these recent developments, studying Cronin and Corvaisis takes precedence over *everything* else, including the cover-up. Not only studying them . . . but letting them have a chance to develop whatever strange talents they may have. In fact, when will you take them into custody?"

"This afternoon, at the latest."

"Then we can expect you to bring them to us sometime tonight?"

"Yes." Leland rose from his chair again. He picked up his coat and walked to the office door, where Lieutenant Horner was waiting. He paused. "Doctor, how will you know if Cronin and Corvaisis are changed or not? You think there's no real chance of . . . possession. But if you're wrong, if they're not entirely human any more, and if they don't want you to know the truth, how would you possibly discover it? Obviously, they could defeat a lie detector or any truth serums we have."

"That's a puzzler, all right." Miles Bennell stood up, jammed his hands into the pockets of his lab coat, and began to pace energetically. "My God, it's a real challenge, isn't it? We've been working on the problem ever since we learned about their new powers from you on Sunday. We've been through ups and downs, despair, but now we think we can deal with it. We've devised medical tests, psychological tests, some tricky damn stuff, and we think that all of it taken together will accurately determine whether or not they're infected, whether or not they're . . . human any more. I think your fears are utterly unfounded. We thought infection . . . *possession* was a danger at first, but it's been more than a year since we learned we were wrong. I think they can be entirely human and still have these powers. *Are* entirely human."

"I don't agree. My fears are well founded. And if Corvaisis and Cronin and the others have changed, and if you believe you can get the truth out of them, you're kidding yourself. If they've changed, they're so superior to you that deceiving you would be child's play.''

"You haven't even heard what we've—''

"And something else, Doctor. Something you haven't thought of but which *I* must consider. Maybe this will help you appreciate my position, with which you've thus far had little sympathy. Don't you realize I have to be suspicious and scared of more than just the people at the Tranquility? Ever since we've learned of these recent developments, these paranormal powers, I've been scared of *you,* as well.''

Bennell was thunderstruck. *"Me?''*

"You've been working here with it, Doctor. You're in that cavern nearly every day, doing lab work every day, probing, testing every damn day for eighteen months, with only three brief vacations. If Corvaisis and Cronin were changed in a few hours of contact, why shouldn't I suspect you've been changed after eighteen months?''

For a moment Bennell was too shocked to speak. Then he said, ''But this isn't the same at all. My studies here were after the fact. I'm essentially a . . . well, a fire marshal, a guy who came in after the blaze to sift through the ashes and figure out what happened. The potential for possession or infection—if it ever existed—was at the beginning, in the first hours, not later.''

"How can I be sure of that?'' Leland asked, staring at him coldly.

"But under these lab conditions, with safety precautions—''

"We're dealing with the unknown, Doctor. We can't foresee every problem that might arise. That's the very nature of the unknown. And you can't take precautions against something you can't foresee.''

Bennell shook his head violently in denial of the very possibility. ''No, no, no. Oh, no.''

"If you think I'm exaggerating my concern just to irritate you,'' Leland said, "then you might ask yourself why Lieutenant Horner sat in that chair so alertly during our long conversation. After all, as you know, he's an expert in polygraphs, and he could have gone and repaired yours while you and I talked. But I didn't want to be in a room with you alone, Doctor Bennell. Not alone. No way.''

Blinking, Bennell said, ''You mean, because I might've somehow . . . ''

Leland nodded. ''Because if you *have* been changed, then you might have been able to change me, too, by some process I can't even begin to imagine. Alone, you might have used the opportunity to attack me, infect me, arrange for me to be possessed, pour the human spirit out of me and pour something else in.'' Leland shuddered. ''Hell, I don't know how to put it best, but we both know what I mean.''

"We even wondered if two of us were enough to insure our safety,'' Lieutenant Horner said, his voice rumbling through the low-ceilinged room and vibrating vaguely in the metal walls. ''I kept a close eye on you, Doctor. You didn't notice my hand was always near my revolver.''

Bennell was too astonished to speak.

Leland said, ''Doctor, you may think I'm a suspicious bastard who's too quick on the trigger, an unregenerate xenophobic fascist. But I've been put in charge of this not merely to keep the truth from the public but also to protect them, and it's part of my job to think of the worst and then to act as if it will inevitably happen.''

"Jesus H. Christ!'' Bennell said. ''You're total, off-the-wall paranoids, both of you!''

"I'd expect you to react that way," Leland told him, "whether or not you're still a full-fledged member of the human race." To Horner he said, "Let's go. You have a polygraph to repair."

Horner went out into The Hub, and Leland started after him.

Bennell said, "Wait, wait. Please."

Leland looked back at the pale, black-bearded man.

"All right, Colonel. Okay. Maybe I can see why you've got to be suspicious, why it's just part of your job. It's crazy nonetheless. There's no chance that I or any of my people could've been . . . inhabited by something else. No chance. But if you were ready to kill me if I aroused your suspicion, would you also kill everyone working under me if you decided they'd all been taken over?"

"Without hesitation," Leland said bluntly.

"But if I and my people could've been changed, if that much was possible— and it *isn't* possible—then don't you realize that the entire staff in Thunder Hill could've been changed, too? Not just the people who know what's in that cavern, but everyone, military as well as civilians, all the way up to and including General Alvarado."

"Well, sure," Leland said. "I realize that."

"And you'd be willing to kill everyone in the facility?"

"Yes."

"*Jesus!*"

"If you've decided to split," Leland said, "you can forget about leaving for the duration. Eighteen months ago, looking ahead to this possibility, I secretly had a special program entered into VIGILANT, the security system. At my direction, VIGILANT can institute a new policy that makes it impossible for anyone to leave Thunder Hill without a special code. I'm the only one with the code, of course."

Bennell's posture was the essence of indignation and righteous outrage. "You mean, you'd *imprison* us out of some misguided . . ." He fell silent as the truth hit him. Then: "My God, you wouldn't have told me this if you hadn't already activated VIGILANT's new program."

"That's right," Leland said. "When I came in, I identified myself with my left hand on the ID plate, instead of my right. That was the signal to VIGILANT to institute the new order. No one but Lieutenant Horner and I can get out of Thunder Hill until I decide it's safe."

Leland Falkirk left the office, walked out into The Hub, as pleased with himself as was possible under these disturbing conditions. It had taken eighteen months, but he had at last shattered Miles Bennell's infuriating composure.

If he had chosen to make one more revelation, he could have brought the scientist all the way to his knees. But there was one secret the colonel had to keep to himself. He had already devised a plan to kill everyone and everything in Thunder Hill in the event that he decided they were infected and only masquerading as human. He had the means to reduce the installation to molten slag and stop the plague right here. The hitch was that he would have to kill himself along with everyone else. But he was prepared for that sacrifice.

After sleeping only five and a half hours, Jorja showered, dressed, and went to the Blocks' apartment, where she found Marcie sitting at the kitchen table with Jack Twist. She stopped at the end of the living room, just outside the kitchen doorway, and watched them for a moment, while they remained unaware they were being observed.

Last night, at four-forty a.m., after Jorja and Jack and Brendan had rendez-voused at the Mini-Mart with the second team of outriders and had returned from

Elko, Jack had slept on the floor in the Blocks' living room, so Marcie would not be alone in the morning after Faye and Ernie had gone off on their respective tasks. Jorja had wanted to move the girl to their own room, but Jack had insisted that he did not mind doing a little babysitting after Marcie woke. "Look," he said, "she's sleeping with Faye and Ernie in their bed. If we try to move her now, we'll wake all of them, and everyone needs whatever sleep he can get tonight." Jorja said, "But Marcie's been sleeping for hours, so she'll be up and around before you are in the morning. She'll wake you." And he said, "Better me than you. Really, I don't need much sleep. Never have." And she said, "You're a nice guy, Jack Twist." He said self-mockingly, "Oh, I'm a saint!" And she said with great seriousness, "You may be the nicest guy I've ever met."

She had firmly settled on that opinion during the hours they had cruised through the night-clad streets of Elko in his Cherokee. He was smart, witty, perceptive, gentle, and the best listener she'd ever encountered. At one-thirty in the morning, Brendan pleaded exhaustion and curled up in the back of the Cherokee, instantly falling asleep. Jorja, dismayed that the priest had come with them, had not really understood her dismay until Father Cronin went to sleep; then she realized that her feelings had nothing to do with the priest, but resulted from her desire to have Jack Twist to herself. With Brendan out of the way, she got what she unconsciously wanted, and she fell entirely under Jack's spell, telling him more about herself than she had told anyone since her all-time closest friend had moved away when they were both sixteen. In almost seven years of marriage, she had never had a conversation with Alan that was half as profound as that she had with Jack Twist, a man she'd known less than twelve hours.

Now, as she stood just outside the kitchen doorway in the Blocks' apartment and watched Jack with Marcie, Jorja saw another good side of him. He could talk comfortably with a child, without the slightest note of condescension or boredom, something few adults could manage. He joked with Marcie, questioned her about her favorite songs, foods, and movies, helped her color one of the last untinted moons in her album. But Marcie was in a deeper and even more frightening trance than she had been yesterday. She did not answer Jack; she rewarded his attention with nothing more than an occasional blank or puzzled look, but he was not discouraged. Jorja realized that he had spent eight years talking to a comatose wife who had never responded, so he would not lose patience with Marcie anytime soon. Jorja stood in the shadows just beyond the doorway for several minutes, unannounced, torn between the pleasure of watching Jack be Jack and the agony of watching her daughter descend even farther into a state increasingly similar to some of the behavior of an autistic child.

"Good morning!" Jack said, looking up from the book of red moons, spotting Jorja. "Sleep well? How long have you been standing there?"

"Not long," she said, entering the kitchen.

"Marcie, say good morning to your mother," Jack told the girl.

But Marcie did not look up from the moon that she was coloring.

Jorja met Jack's eyes and saw sympathy and concern in them. She said, "Well, it's not really morning any more. Almost noon."

She went to Marcie, put a hand under her chin, lifted her head. The child's gaze focused on her mother's eyes, but only for a moment, then turned inward. It was a terrible and empty look. When Jorja let go, Marcie turned immediately to the image of the moon before her and began to scrub hard at the paper with her last red crayon.

Jack pushed his chair back, got up, and went to the refrigerator. "Hungry, Jorja? I'm starved. Marcie ate earlier, but I've been waiting breakfast on you."

He pulled open the refrigerator door. "Eggs and bacon and toast? Or I could whip up an omelet with some cheese, herbs, just a touch of onion, a few slivers of green peppers."

"You cook, too," Jorja said.

"I'll never win any prizes," he said. "But it's usually edible, and at least half the time you can even tell what it is when I put it on your plate." He pulled open the freezer door. "They have frozen waffles. I could toast a few of those to go along with the omelet."

"Whatever you're having." She was unable to look away from Marcie, and as she watched her stricken daughter, her appetite faded.

Jack loaded his arms with a carton of milk, another of eggs, a package of cheese, a green pepper, and a small onion, and carried the fixings to the cutting board beside the sink.

When Jack began cracking eggs into a bowl, Jorja joined him at the counter. Although she did not think Marcie would hear her even if she shouted, she spoke *sotto voce* to Jack: "Did she really eat breakfast?"

He whispered too: "Sure. Some cereal. A piece of toast with jelly and peanut butter. I had to help her a little, that's all."

Jorja tried not to think about what Dom had told her of Zebediah Lomack, or about how Lomack tied in with what had happened to Alan. But if two grown men had been unable to cope with the sick obsessions that had evolved from what they'd seen on July 6 and from the subsequent brainwashing, what chance did Marcie have of coping, living?

"Hey, hey," Jack said softly, "don't cry, Jorja. Crying won't help anything." He took her in his arms. "She'll be all right. I promise you. Listen, just this morning, the others were saying they had a terrific night last night, no dreams for a change, and Dom didn't sleepwalk, and Ernie wasn't half as afraid of the dark as usual. Know why? Because just being here, pulling together like a family—it's already making the memory blocks crumble, relieving the pressure. All right, yes, Marcie's a bit worse this morning, but that doesn't mean it's all downhill for her. She'll improve. I know she will."

Jorja was not expecting the embrace, but she welcomed it. God, how she welcomed it! She leaned against him and allowed herself to be held, and instead of feeling weak and foolish, she felt a new strength flowing into her. She was tall for a woman, and he was *not* tall for a man, so they were almost the same height, yet she had the atavistic feeling of being protected, guarded. She was reminded of what she'd been thinking yesterday, on the flight north from Las Vegas: Human beings were not meant for solitude, lonely struggles; the very essence of the species was its need to give and receive friendship, affection, love. Right now, she needed to receive, and Jack needed to give, and the confluence of their needs gave new purpose and determination to both of them.

"An omelet with cheese, herbs, a little bit of chopped onion, and slivers of green pepper," he said softly, his lips against her ear, as if sensing that she had regained her footing and was ready to go on. "Does that sound all right?"

"Sounds delicious," she said, reluctantly letting go of him.

"And one other ingredient," he said. "I warned you I wouldn't win any cooking prizes. I always get one little chip of eggshell in every omelet, no matter how careful I am."

"Oh, that's the secret of a good omelet," she said. "One bit of eggshell for texture. The finest restaurants make omelets that way."

"Yeah? Do they also leave one bone in every fish?"

"And a bit of hoof in every order of beef Bourguignon," she said.

"One antler in every chocolate mousse?"

"And one shoemaker's nail in every apple cobbler."

"One old maid in every apple pandowdy?"

"Oh, God, I hate puns."

"Me too," he said. "Truce?"

"Truce. I'll grate the cheddar for the omelet."

Together they made breakfast.

At the kitchen table, Marcie colored moons. And colored moons. And murmured that one word in monotonous, mesmeric, rhythmic chains.

In Monterey, California, Parker Faine had almost fallen into the lair of a trap-door spider. He counted himself fortunate to have gotten out alive. A trap-door spider—that was how he thought of the Salcoes' neighbor, a woman named Essie Craw. The trap-door spider constructed a tubular nest in the ground and fixed a cleverly concealed hinged lid at the top. When other hapless insects, innocent and unsuspecting, crossed the perfectly camouflaged lid, it opened and dropped them down to the rapacious arachnoid beast below. Essie Craw's tubular nest was a lovely large Spanish home far more suited to the California coast than the Salcoes' Southern Colonial manse, with graceful arches and leaded-glass windows and flowers blooming in large terra cotta pots on the portico. One look at the place, and Parker was prepared to encounter charming and exquisitely gracious people, but when Essie Craw answered the door he knew he was in deep trouble. When she discovered that he was seeking information about the Salcoes, she virtually seized him by his sleeve and dragged him inside and slammed the lid of her tubular nest behind him, for those who sought information often had information to give in return, and Essie Craw fed on gossip as surely as the trap-door spider fed on careless beetles, centipedes, and pillbugs.

Essie did not look like a spider but rather like a bird. Not a scrawny, thin-necked, meager-breasted sparrow. More like a well-fed sea gull. She had a quick birdlike walk, and she held her head slightly to the side in the manner of a bird, and she had beady little avian eyes.

After leading him to a seat in the living room, she offered coffee, but he declined, and she insisted, but he protested that he did not want to be a bother. She brought coffee anyway, plus butter cookies, which she produced with such alacrity that he suspected she was as perpetually prepared for drop-in guests as was the trap-door spider.

Essie was disappointed to hear that Parker knew nothing about the Salcoe family and had no gossip. But since he was not their friend, either, he offered a fresh pair of ears for her observations, tales, slanders, and mean-spirited suppositions. He did not even have to ask questions in order to learn more than he wanted to know. Donna Salcoe, Gerald's wife, was (Essie said) a brassy sort, too blond, too flashy, phony-sweet. Donna was so thin she was surely a problem drinker who survived on a liquid diet—or maybe she was anorexic. Gerald was Donna's second husband, and although they had been married eighteen years, Essie did not think it would last. Essie made the sixteen-year-old twin girls sound so wild, so unrestrained, so nubile and licentious, that Parker pictured packs of young men sniffing around the Salcoe house like dogs seeking bitches in heat. Gerald Salcoe owned three thriving shops—an antiques store, two art galleries— in nearby Carmel, though Essie could not understand how any of these enterprises showed a profit when Salcoe was a hard-drinking libertine and a thick-headed boob with no business sense.

Parker drank only two sips of his coffee and didn't even nibble at the butter cookies, because Essie Craw's enthusiasm for malicious gossip went beyond the limits of ordinary behavior into a realm of weirdness that made him uncomfortable and unwilling to turn his back on her—or consume much of what she provided.

But he learned a few useful things, as well. The Salcoes had taken an impromptu vacation—one week in the wine country, Napa and Sonoma—and had been so desperate to escape the pressures of their various enterprises that they had not wanted to reveal the name of the hotel where they could be reached, lest it get back to the very business associates from whom they needed a rest.

"*He* called me Sunday to tell me they were off and wouldn't be back until Monday, the twentieth," Essie said. "Asked me to keep a watch over the place, as usual. They're terrible gadabouts, and it's such a bother to be expected to look out for burglars and God knows what. I have my own life to live, which of course concerns them not at all."

"You didn't speak with any of them face to face?"

"I guess they were in a hurry to be off."

"Did you see them leave?"

"No, though I . . . well . . . I looked out a couple of times, but I must've missed them."

"The twins went with them?" Parker asked. "Isn't school in?"

"It's a progressive school—too progressive, I say—and travel is thought to be as broadening as classroom work. Did you ever hear such—"

"How did Mr. Salcoe sound when you spoke with him on the phone?"

Impatiently, Essie said, "Well . . . he sounded . . . like he always sounds. What do you mean?"

"Not at all strained? Nervous?"

She pursed her tight little mouth, cocked her head, and her bird-bright eyes glittered at the prospect of potential scandal. "Well, now that you mention it, he *was* a bit odd. Stumbled over his words a few times, but until now I didn't realize he'd probably been drinking. Do you think . . . oh, that he's had to go off to some clinic to dry out or—"

Parker had heard enough. He rose to leave, but Essie got between him and the doorway, trying to delay him by making him feel guilty that he had not finished his coffee or even tasted a cookie. She suggested tea instead of coffee, some strudel, or "perhaps an almond croissant." By dint of the same indomitable will that had made him a great painter, he managed to get to the front door, through it, and onto the portico.

She followed him all the way to the rental car in her driveway. The little vomit-green Tempo looked, for that one moment, as beautiful as a Rolls-Royce, for it offered escape from Essie Craw. As he sped away, he quoted Coleridge aloud, an apt passage.

> Like one that on a lonesome road
> Doth walk in fear and dread,
> And having once turned round walks on,
> And turns no more his head;
> Because he knows a frightful fiend
> Doth close behind him tread.

He drove around for half an hour, working up the courage to do what must be done. Finally, upon his return to the Salcoe house, he parked boldly at the head of the circular driveway, in the shadows of the massive pines. He went to the front door again, insistently pressed the bell for three minutes. If anyone was home and merely unwilling to see visitors, he would have answered that unrelenting ring out of sheer desperation. But no one responded.

Parker walked along the veranda, studying the front windows, being nonchalant, acting as if he belonged there, though the property was so shrouded by trees and lush landscaping that he could not be spotted easily from the street—or from Essie Craw's windows. The drapes were shut, preventing a glimpse of the interior. He expected to see the telltale electricity-conducting tape of an alarm system on the glass. But there was no tape and no other indication of electronic security.

He stepped off the end of the veranda and went around the western side of the house, where the morning sun had not shrunk the long, deep shadows of the pines. He tried two windows there. They were locked.

In back of the house were more shrubs, flowers, and a large brick patio with a lattice cover, outdoor wet-bar, expensive lawn furniture.

He used his coat-protected elbow to smash in a small pane on one of the French doors. He unlocked the door and went inside, pushing through the drapes into a tile-floored family room.

He stood very still, listening. The house was silent.

It would have been uncomfortably dark if the family room had not opened onto a breakfast area and the breakfast area onto the kitchen, where light entered through the glass in that uncurtained door to the patio. Parker moved past a fireplace, billiards table—and froze when he spotted the motion-detection alarm unit on the wall. He recognized it from when he had investigated security systems for his Laguna house. He was about to flee when he recalled that a small red light should have been visible on the unit if it was in operation. The bulb was there—but dark. Apparently the system had not been activated when the Salcoes had left.

The kitchen was roomy, with the best appliances. Beyond that was a serving pantry, then the dining room. The light from the kitchen did not reach that far, so he decided to risk turning on lights as he went.

In the living room, he stood very still again, listening.

Nothing. The silence was deep and heavy, as in a tomb.

When Brendan Cronin entered the Blocks' kitchen after rising late and taking a long hot shower, he found little Marcie coloring moons and murmuring eerily to herself. He thought of how he had mended Emmeline Halbourg with his hands, and he wondered if he could cure Marcie's psychological obsession by the application of that same psychic power. But he dared not try. Not until he learned to control his wild talent, for he might do irreparable harm to the girl's mind.

Jack and Jorja were finishing omelets and toast, and they greeted him warmly. Jorja wanted to make breakfast for Brendan, too, but he declined. He only wanted a cup of coffee, black and strong.

As Jack ate, he examined four handguns that were lying on the table beside his plate. Two of them were Ernie's. Jack had brought the other two with him from the East. Neither Brendan nor anyone else referred to the firearms, for they knew their enemy might be listening right now. No point revealing the size of their arsenal.

The guns made Brendan nervous. Maybe because he had a prescient feeling that the weapons would be used repeatedly before day's end.

His characteristic optimism had left him, largely because he had not dreamed last night. He'd had his first uninterrupted sleep in weeks, but for him that was no improvement. Unlike the others, Brendan had been having a *good* dream every night, and it had given him hope. Now the dream was gone, and the loss made him edgy.

"I thought it would be snowing by now," he said as he sat down at the table with a cup of coffee.

"Soon," Jack said.

The sky looked like a great slab of dark-gray granite.

Ned and Sandy Sarver, serving as the second team of outriders, had driven into Elko to rendezvous with Jack, Jorja, and Brendan at the Arco Mini-Mart at four in the morning, then had cruised around town until seven-thirty, by which time some of those back at the Tranquility would have set out on their tasks for the day. They returned to the motel at eight o'clock, ate a quick breakfast, and went back to bed to get a few more hours of rest in order to cope with the busy day ahead.

Ned woke after little more than two hours, but he did not get out of bed. He lay in the dimness of the motel room for a while, watching Sandy sleep. The love he felt for her was deep and smooth and flowing like a great river that could bear them both away to better places and times beyond all the worries of the world.

Ned wished he was as good a talker as he was a fixer. Sometimes he worried that he had never been able to tell her exactly how he felt about her. But when he tried to put his sentiments into words, he either became tongue-tied or heard himself expressing his emotions in hopelessly inarticulate sentences and leaden images. It was good to be a fixer, with the talent to repair everything from broken toasters to broken cars to broken people. Yet sometimes, Ned would have traded all his mending skills for the ability to compose and speak one perfect sentence which would convey his deepest feelings for her.

Now, watching her, he realized that she was no longer sleeping. "Playing possum?" he asked.

She opened her eyes and smiled. "I was scared, the way you were watching me, that I was going to get eaten alive, so I played possum."

"You look good enough to eat; that's for sure."

She threw aside the covers and, naked, opened her arms to him. They fell at once into the familiar silken rhythms of love-making at which they had become so sensuously adept during the past year of her sexual awakening.

In the afterglow, as they lay side by side, holding hands, Sandy said, "Oh, Ned, I must be the happiest woman on earth. Since I met you down in Arizona all those years ago, since you took me under your wing, you've made me very happy, Ned. In fact, I'm so crazy-happy now that if God struck me dead this minute, I wouldn't complain."

"Don't say that," he told her sharply. Rising up on one elbow, leaning over her, looking down at her, he said, "I don't like you saying that. It makes me . . . superstitious. All this trouble we're in—it's possible some of us will die. So I don't want you tempting fate. I don't want you saying things like that."

"Ned, you're about the least superstitious man I know."

"Yeah, well, I feel different about this. I don't want you saying you're so happy you wouldn't mind dying, nothing like that. Understand? I don't want you even *thinking* it."

He slipped his arms around her again, pulling her very tightly against him, needing to feel the throb of life within her. He held her so close that after a while he could no longer detect the strong and regular stroking of her heart, which was only because it had become synchronized with—and lost in—his own beat.

* * *

In the Salcoe family's Monterey house, Parker Faine was looking primarily for two things, either of which would fulfill his obligation to Dom. First, he hoped to find something to prove they had actually gone to Napa-Sonoma: If he found a brochure for a hotel, he could call and confirm that the Salcoes had checked in safely; or if they went to the wine country regularly, perhaps an address book would contain the telephone number of the place where they stayed. But he half-expected to find the other thing instead: overturned furniture, bloodstains, or other evidence that the Salcoes had been taken against their will.

Of course, Dom had only asked him to come talk with these people. He would be appalled to know that Parker had gone to these illegal lengths when the Salcoes had been unlocatable. But Parker never did anything by halves, and he was enjoying himself even though his heart had begun to pound and his throat had clutched up a bit.

Beyond the living room was a library. Beyond that, a small music room contained a piano, music stands, chairs, two clarinet cases, and a ballet exercise bar. Evidently, the twins liked music and dance.

Parker found nothing amiss on the first floor, so he slowly climbed the stairs, staying in the runner of plush carpet between oak inlays. The light from the first floor reached just to the top step. Above, the second-floor hallway was dark.

He stopped on the landing.

Stillness.

His hands were clammy.

He did not understand why he was clutching up. Maybe instinct. It might be wise to pay attention to his more primitive senses. But if anyone had wanted to ambush him, there had been plenty of places on the first floor ideal for the purpose, yet the rooms had been deserted.

He continued upward, and when he reached the second-floor hallway, he finally heard something. It was a cross between a *beep*-sound and a *blip*-sound, and it came from rooms on both ends of the hall. For a moment he thought the alarm system was about to go off, after all, but an alarm would have been a thousand times louder than these *beep-blips*. The sounds came in counterpointed, rhythmic patterns.

He found a switch at the head of the stairs and snapped on the overhead lights in the hall. Standing motionless once more, he listened for noises other than the curious *beep-blips*. He heard none. There was something familiar about the sound, but it eluded him.

His curiosity was greater than his fear. He had always been compelled by a chronic curiosity, with frequent acute attacks of same, and if he had not allowed it to drive him in the past, he'd never have become a successful painter. Curiosity was the heart of creativity. Therefore, he looked both ways along the hall, then turned right and walked cautiously toward one source of the *beep-blips*.

At the end of the hallway, there were two distinct sets of beeping sounds, each with a slightly different rhythm, both coming from a dark room where the door was three-quarters shut. Poised to flee, he pushed the door all the way open. Nothing leaped at him out of the darkness. The beeping became louder, but only because the door was out of the way now. He saw that the room was not entirely dark. On the far wall, thin ribbons of pale gray light outlined drapes that were drawn across a very large window or perhaps a pair of balcony doors; the Salcoes' Southern Colonial had lots of balconies. In addition, around the corner from the doorway, out of sight, were two sources of eerie soft green light that did little to dispel the gloom.

Parker eased forward, clicked the light switch, entered the room, saw the Salcoe twins, and thought for an instant that they were dead. They were lying on their backs in a queen-sized bed, covers drawn up to their shoulders, unmoving, eyes open. Then Parker realized that the beeping and the green light came from EEG and EKG monitors to which both girls were connected, and he saw the IV racks trailing lines to spikes inserted in their arms, so he knew they were not dead but merely in the process of being brainwashed. The chamber had none of the quality of a teenaged girl's room; from the lack of personal mementos or any stamp of individuality, he assumed it was a guest room and that the girls had been put here in a single bed simply to make it easier to monitor them.

But where were their captors and tormentors? Were the mind-control experts so certain of the effectiveness of their drugs and other devices that they could leave the family alone and dash out for a Big Mac and fries at McDonald's? Was there no risk at all that one of the Salcoes, in a moment of lucidity, might tear out his IV line, rise up, and flee?

Parker went to the nearest girl, looked into her blank eyes. For a few seconds she peered up unblinking, then suddenly blinked furiously—ten, twenty, thirty times—then stared unblinking again. She did not see Parker. He waved a hand across her eyes and got no reaction.

He saw that she was wearing a pair of earphones connected to a tape recorder that lay on the pillow beside her head. He leaned close to her, lifted one earphone an inch, and listened to a soft, melodic, and very soothing voice, a woman's voice: *"On Monday morning, I slept in late. It's a wonderful hotel for sleeping late because the staff is so quiet, so respectful. It's actually a country club as well as a hotel, so it's not like other places, where maids make a racket in the halls as soon as the sun rises. Oh, don't you just love the wine country! I'd like to live there someday. Anyway, after we finally got up, Chrissie and I took a long walk around the grounds, sort of hoping we'd run into some neat boys, but we couldn't find any. . . ."* The hypnotic rhythms of the woman's voice spooked Parker. He put the earphones back in place.

Evidently, one or more of the Salcoes had remembered what they had experienced at the Tranquility Motel the summer before last. So those memories had again been repressed. Now to cover the time span of this current brainwashing session, new false memories were being implanted, a process that included the repeated playing of a tape recording that undoubtedly had subliminal as well as audible messages to impart.

Dom had explained some of it to Parker on the telephone, Saturday and Sunday nights. But Parker had not fully appreciated the hideousness of the conspiracy until he heard that insidious whisper in the Salcoe girl's ear.

He moved to the foot of the bed and studied the other twin, whose eyes also alternated between blinkless stares and abrupt, machine-gun bursts of blinks. He wondered if he would do any physical or mental harm to them if he pulled out their IV lines, disconnected them from the machines, and moved them out of the house before their captors returned. Better to find a phone, call the police—

How long they were watching him he did not know, but suddenly he was aware that he and the twins were not alone. He jumped and whirled toward the door, where two men had entered the room. They were wearing dark slacks, white shirts with the sleeves rolled up and the collars unbuttoned, neckties loosened and askew. At the doorway behind them was another man, bespectacled and in a suit with his tie in place. They had to be government agents, for no one else would bother to wear business clothes while engaged upon activities of such a dubious nature.

One of them said, "And who the fuck are you?"

Parker did not attempt to jive them, did not foolishly claim his rights as a U.S. citizen, did not bother to say anything at all. He just took three running steps toward the drawn drapes, praying that a big window or sliding-glass balcony door lay beyond them, that it would shatter on impact, that the drapes would protect him from serious cuts, and that he would be outside and gone before they knew what happened. If the drapes were a lot wider than the window, covering more blank wall than glass, he was in big trouble. Behind him, the men shouted in surprise just as he hit the drapes, for they'd obviously believed they'd trapped him. He went through the material with the unstoppable power of a locomotive. The impact was tremendous, sending a devastating shock across his shoulder and through his chest, but something gave way with a crack and a screech and a crash of glass, and he was through into daylight, vaguely aware that the doors had been French rather than sliding panels and that he had been lucky the lock was flimsy.

He found himself on a second-floor balcony with a pair of redwood lounge chairs and a glass-topped table, over which he fell. Even as he was going down on top of chairs, banging knees and barking shins, he was already coming up again, up and over the balcony rail, leaping out into space, praying he would not land in a particularly woody shrub and be castrated by a sharp, sturdy branch. He fell only twelve feet onto bare lawn, jarring his other shoulder and his back but breaking no bones. He rolled, scrambled to his feet, and ran.

Suddenly, in front of his eyes, foliage snapped-fluttered-shredded, and he didn't know what was happening, and then as he continued to run, pieces of bark exploded off a tree, and he realized they were shooting at him. He heard no gunfire. Silencer-equipped weapons. He zigzagged toward the perimeter of the property, fell in an azalea bed, scrambled up, ran on, reached a hedge, threw himself over it, and kept on running.

They had been ready to kill him to stop him from spreading the news of what he had seen in the Salcoe house. Right now, they were probably hastily moving— or killing—the Salcoes. If he found a phone and called the police, and if the killers were agents of the U.S. government, whose side would the police be on? And who would they believe? One eccentric and rather curiously dressed artist with a woolly beard and flyaway hair? Or three neatly attired FBI men claiming they were in the Salcoe house on a legitimate stakeout of some kind, and that Parker Faine was, in fact, the felon they had attempted to arrest. If they demanded custody of him, would the police cooperate?

Jesus.

He ran. Abandoning the Tempo, he sprinted down the sloped wall of a shallow glen, along the rocky course of a narrow brook, between trees, through underbrush, up another wall of the same glen, into someone's back yard, across that lawn and into another yard, alongside a house, out into a street, from that street to another. He slowed to a fast walk to avoid drawing attention to himself, but he continued to follow a twisty route away from the Salcoe house.

He knew what he had to do. The horror he had just seen had made the extremity of Dom's plight clearer than ever. Parker had known his friend was in danger, deep in a conspiracy of monumental proportions, but knowing it in his mind was not the same as knowing it in his *guts*. There was nothing for him to do but go to Elko County. Dom Corvaisis was his friend, perhaps his best friend, and this was what friends did for each other: shared their trouble, fought back the darkness together. He could walk away, go back to Laguna Beach to continue work on the painting that he had begun yesterday. But if he chose that course, he would never like himself very much again—which would be an intolerable circumstance, for he had always liked himself immensely!

He had to find a ride back to the Monterey Airport, catch a flight to San Francisco International, and head east from there toward Nevada. He was not concerned that the men in the Salcoes' house would be looking for him at the airport. The only words any of them had spoken in his presence were: "And who the fuck are you?" If they did not know who he was, they would most likely figure he was a local. The keys to the Tempo had a rental-company tag on them, but they were in his pocket. In an hour or two, of course, the bad guys would trace the car to the airport, but by then he should have taken off for San Francisco.

He kept walking. On a quiet residential street he saw a young man, about nineteen or twenty, in the driveway of a more modest house than the Salcoes', carefully scrubbing the whitewalls on the tires of a meticulously restored, banana-yellow, 1958 Plymouth Fury, one of those long jobs with a plenitude of grille and big sharky fins. The kid had a slicked-back ducktail haircut to match the era of his vehicle. Parker went up to him and said, "Listen, my car broke down, and I've got to get to the airport. I'm in a big hurry, so would you drive me out there for fifty bucks?"

The kid knew how to hurry. If he had not been a superb driver, he would have fishtailed out of control and spun them off the road into trees or ditches on a half-dozen tight turns, for he got all possible speed out of the big Fury. After they came through the third sharp turn alive, Parker knew he was in good hands, and he finally relaxed a bit.

At the airport, he bought a ticket for one of two remaining seats on a West Air flight leaving for San Francisco in ten minutes. He boarded the plane, half-expecting it to be halted by federal agents before it could take off. But soon they were airborne, and he could worry about something else: getting another flight from San Francisco to Reno before they tracked him that far.

Jack Twist went through the Blocks' apartment from north- to west- to south- to east-facing windows, surveying the vast landscape for signs of the enemy's observation post—or posts. At least one surveillance team would be watching the motel and diner, and no matter how well concealed they were, he had a device that would pinpoint their location.

He'd brought it from New York with the other gear—an instrument the armed forces called the HS101 Heat Analyzer. It was shaped like a sleek futuristic raygun from the movies, with a single two-inch-diameter lens instead of a barrel. You held it by the butt and looked through the eyepiece as if peering into a telescope. Moving the viewfinder across the landscape, you saw two things: an ordinary magnified image of the terrain, and an overlaid representation of heat sources within that terrain. Plants, animals, and sun-baked rocks radiated heat, but thanks to microchip technology, the HS101's computer could differentiate among types of thermal radiation and screen out most natural background sources. The device would show only heat from living sources larger than fifty pounds: animals bigger than house-dogs and human beings. Even if they were out there in insulated ski suits that trapped a lot of body heat, enough would escape their garments to give him a fix on them.

Jack spent a considerable length of time studying the land north of the motel, through which he had approached the place last night, but finally he decided no one was watching from that direction, and he moved to the west-facing windows in other rooms. The west also looked clear, so he went next to the windows on the south side of the apartment.

Marcie had colored the last moon in her album, and when Jack set out with the HS101 to look for surveillance teams, she came with him, staying close by his side. Maybe she had taken a liking to him because he'd spent hours talking to her in spite of her failure to respond. Or maybe she was scared of something and felt safer in his presence. Or another reason too strange to imagine. He could do nothing for her except keep talking softly to her as she accompanied him.

Jorja followed along as well, and though she did not interrupt with questions, she was considerably more distracting than her daughter. She was a strikingly beautiful woman, but more importantly he *liked* her a lot. He thought she liked him, too, although he didn't suppose she was attracted to him, not in the man-woman sense. After all, what would a woman like her see in a guy like him? He was an admitted criminal, and he had a face like an old battered shoe, not to mention one cast eye. But they could be friends, at least, and that was nice.

At the living room windows, he finally spotted what he was seeking: points of body heat out there in the cold barrens. Across the top of the image that filled the lens—Nevada plains and overlaid heat patterns—came a digital readout of data that told him there were two sources of heat, that they were due south of his position, and that they were approximately four-tenths of a mile away. That information was followed by numerals that represented an estimation of the size of each source's radiant surface, which told him he had found two men. He switched off the HS101's heat-analysis function and turned up the magnification, using the device as a simple telescope, zeroing in on the area in which the heat had been detected. He had to search for a couple of minutes, for they were wearing camouflage suits.

"Bingo," he said at last.

Jorja did not ask what he saw, for she had learned well the lesson he had taught them last night: Everything spoken in the apartment was sucked directly into the enemy's electronic ears.

Out there on the barrens, the two observers were prone on the cold ground. Jack saw that one man had a pair of binoculars. But the guy was not using the glasses at the moment, so he was not aware of Jack watching him from the window.

He moved to the east windows and surveyed that landscape, as well, but it was uninhabited. They were being watched only from the south, which the enemy figured was sufficient because the front of the motel and the only road leading to it could be seen from that single post.

They were underestimating Jack. They knew his background, knew that he was good, but they didn't realize *how* good.

At one-forty, the first snowflakes fell. For a while they came down only as scattered flurries, with no particular force.

At two o'clock, when Dom and Ernie returned from their scouting trip around the perimeter of the Thunder Hill Depository, Jack said, "You know, Ernie, when the storm really hits later, there might be some people on the interstate who'll see our wheels out front and pull in here, looking for shelter, even if we leave the sign and other lights off. Better move my Cherokee, the Sarvers' truck, and the cars around back. We don't want a lot of people rapping at your door wanting to know why you're giving rooms to some people and not to them."

Actually, certain that the enemy was even now listening to them, Jack was using the specter of weary snow-bound motorists as a plausible excuse to move the pickup truck and the Cherokee, the two four-wheel-drive vehicles, out of sight of the observers south of I-80. Later, when heavier snow and the early darkness of the storm settled in, the entire Tranquility family would surreptitiously leave the motel from the rear, heading overland in the truck and the Cherokee.

Ernie sensed Jack's real purpose; equally aware of eavesdroppers, he played along. He and Dom went outside again to move all the vehicles around back.

In the kitchen, Ned and Sandy had nearly finished preparing and packaging the sandwiches that everyone would be issued for dinner.

Now they had only to wait for Faye and Ginger.

The snow flurries intermittently surrendered to furious but short-lived squalls. The day dimmed. By two-forty, the squalls turned to steady snow that, in spite of a complete cessation of wind, reduced visibility to a few hundred feet. Out on the barrens, the camouflaged observers were probably picking up their gear and moving closer to the motel.

Jack checked his watch more frequently. He knew time was running out. But he had no way of knowing how *fast* it might be running out.

While Lieutenant Horner repaired the sabotaged polygraph in the security office, Falkirk lectured the Depository's chief of security and his assistant—Major Fugata and Lieutenant Helms—letting them know they were on his list of possible traitors. He made two enemies, but that didn't matter. He did not want them to like him—only to respect and fear him.

He had not yet finished chewing out Fugata and Helms when General Alvarado arrived. The general was a lardass with a pot gut, fingers like sausages, and jowls. He stormed into the security office in a red-faced outrage, having just heard the bad news from Dr. Miles Bennell: "Is it true, Colonel Falkirk? By God, is it true? Have you actually taken control of VIGILANT and made prisoners of us all?"

Sternly but in a tone that could not be construed as disrespectful, Leland informed Alvarado that he had the authority to include the secret program in the security computer and to activate it at his discretion. Alvarado demanded to know whose authority, and Leland said, "General Maxwell D. Riddenhour, Chief of Staff of the Army and Chairman of the Joint Chiefs." Alvarado said he knew perfectly well who Riddenhour was, but he did not believe that the colonel's mentor in this matter was the Chief of Staff himself. "Sir, why don't you call him and ask?" Leland suggested. He took a card out of his wallet and gave it to Alvarado. "That's General Riddenhour's number."

"I have the Staff HQ number," Alvarado said scornfully.

"Sir, that's not Staff HQ. That's General Riddenhour's unlisted home line. If he's not in his office, he'd want you to contact him on the unlisted phone. After all, this is a deadly serious matter, sir."

Burning a brighter red, Alvarado stalked out, the card pinched between thumb and forefinger and held away from his side as if it were an offensive object. He was back in fifteen minutes, no longer flushed but pale. "All right, Colonel, you have the authority you claim. So . . . I guess you're in command of Thunder Hill for the time being."

"Not at all, sir," Leland said. "You're still the CO."

"But if I'm a prisoner—"

Leland interrupted. "Sir, your orders take precedence as long as they don't directly conflict with my authority to guarantee that no dangerous persons—no dangerous creatures—escape from Thunder Hill."

Alvarado shook his head in amazement. "According to Miles Bennell, you have this crazy idea that we're all . . . some kind of monsters." The general had used the most melodramatic word he could think of, with the intent of belittling Leland's position.

"Sir, as you know, one or more people in this facility attempted, by indirection, to bring some of the witnesses back to the Tranquility, evidently with the hope that the witnesses will remember what they've been made to forget and will create a media circus that'll force us to reveal what we've hidden. Now, these traitors are probably just well-intentioned men, most likely members of Bennell's staff, who simply believe the public should be informed. But the possibility also exists that they've got other and darker motives."

"Monsters," Alvarado repeated sourly.

When the polygraph was repaired, Leland charged Major Fugata and Lieutenant Helms with interrogating everyone in Thunder Hill who had knowledge of the special secret harbored there for more than eighteen months. "If you screw up again," Leland warned them, "I'll have your heads." If they failed again to find the man who'd sent the Polaroids to the witnesses, he would view their failure as one more bit of evidence that rot had spread widely through the Thunder Hill staff, and that it was not ordinary human corruption but the result of an extraordinary and terrifying infection. Their failure would cost them their lives.

At one-forty-five, Leland and Lieutenant Horner returned to Shenkfield, leaving the Depository's entire staff locked deep in the bosom of the earth. Upon his return to his windowless office in that other underground facility, the colonel received several doses of bad news, all courtesy of Foster Polnichev, the head of the Chicago office of the FBI.

First, Sharkle was dead out in Evanston, Illinois, which should have been good news, but he had taken his sister, brother-in-law, and an entire SWAT team with him. The siege of Sharkle's house had become national news due to the extreme violence of its conclusion. The blood-hungry media would be focused on O'Bannon Lane until endless rehashing of the story drained it of thrills. Worse, among Sharkle's mad ravings, there had been enough truth to lead a perceptive and aggressive reporter to Nevada, to the Tranquility, and perhaps all the way to Thunder Hill.

Worst of all, Foster Polnichev reported that "something almost . . . well . . . supernatural is happening here." A stabbing and shooting in an Uptown apartment, involving a family named Mendoza, had caused such a sensation within the city's police department that newspaper reporters and television crews had virtually set siege to the tenement house hours ago. Evidently, Winton Tolk, the officer whose life had been saved by Brendan Cronin, had brought a stabbed child back from near-death.

Incredibly, Brendan Cronin had passed his own amazing talents to Tolk. But what *else* had he passed on to the black policeman? There might be only a wondrous new power in Winton Tolk . . . or something dark and dangerous, alive and inhuman, living within the cop.

The worst possible scenario was, after all, unfolding. Leland was half-sick with apprehension as he listened to Polnichev.

According to the FBI agent, Tolk was giving no interviews to the press and was, in fact, now in seclusion in his own house, where another mob of reporters had gathered. Sooner or later, however, Tolk would agree to speak with the press, and he would mention Brendan Cronin, and from there they would eventually find the link to the Halbourg girl.

The Halbourg girl. That was another nightmare. Upon receiving this morning's news of Tolk's unexpected healing powers, Polnichev had gone to the Halbourgs' home to determine if Emmy had acquired unusual powers subsequent to her own miraculous recovery. What he found there beggared description, and he immediately isolated the entire Halbourg family from the press and public before their secret was discovered. Now all five Halbourgs were in an FBI safe-house, under the watchful eyes of six agents who'd been informed only that the family was as much to be feared as protected and that no agent was to be alone with any member of the family at any time. If the Halbourgs made threatening or unusual moves, they would all be killed instantly.

"But I think it's all pointless now," Polnichev said on the phone from Chicago. "I think we've lost control of it. It's spread, and we've no hope of containing it again. So we might as well call an end to the cover-up, go public."

"Are you mad?" Leland demanded.

"If it's come to the point where we have to kill people, lots of people, like the Halbourgs and the Tolks and all the witnesses there in Nevada, in order just to keep the story contained, then the cost of containment has gotten too damn high."

Leland Falkirk was furious. "You've lost sight of what's at stake here. My God, man, we're no longer merely trying to keep the news from the public. That's almost immaterial now. Now, we're trying to protect our entire species from obliteration. If we go public, and if then we decide to use violence to contain the infection, every goddamn politician and bleeding-heart will be second-guessing us, interfering, and before you know it, we'll have lost the war!"

"But I think what's being proven here is that the danger isn't that great," Polnichev said. "Sure, I've told the men guarding the Halbourgs to regard them as a threat, but I don't really believe they're a danger to us. That little Emmy . . . she's a darling, not a monster. I don't know how the power got in Cronin or how he conveyed it to the girl, but I'm almost willing to bet my life that the power is the *only* thing inside the child. The only thing inside any of them. If you could meet Emmy and watch her, Colonel! She's a delight. All evidence points to the fact that we should regard what's happening as the greatest event in the history of mankind."

"Of course," Leland said coldly, "that's what an enemy like this would want us to believe. If we can be convinced that accommodation and surrender are a great blessing, we'll be conquered without a fight."

"But Colonel, if Cronin and Corvaisis and Tolk and Emmy *have* been infected, if they're no longer human, or at least no longer like you and me, they wouldn't advertise by performing miraculous cures and feats of telekinesis. They'd keep their amazing abilities secret in order to spread their infection to more people without detection."

Leland was unmoved by that argument. "We don't know exactly how this thing works. Maybe a person, once infected, surrenders control to the parasite, becomes a slave. Or to answer the point you've just made, maybe the relationship between the host and parasite is benign, mutually supportive—and maybe the host doesn't even know the parasite is inside him, which would explain why the Halbourg girl and the others don't know where their power comes from. But in *either* case, that person is no longer strictly human. And in my estimation, Polnichev, that person can no longer be trusted. Not an inch. Now, for God's sake, you've got to take the entire Tolk family into custody, too. Isolate them at once."

"As I told you, Colonel, journalists surround the Tolk house. If I go in there with agents and take the Tolks into custody in front of a score of reporters, our cover-up is blown. And although I no longer believe in the cover-up, I'm not going to sabotage it. I know my duty."

"You've at least got agents watching the house?"

"Yes."

"What about the Mendozas? If Tolk infected the boy the way Cronin apparently infected *him* . . . ' '

"We're watching the Mendozas," Polnichev said. "Again, we can't make a bold move because of the reporters."

The other problem was Father Stefan Wycazik. The priest had been to the Mendozas' apartment and then to the Halbourg house before Foster Polnichev had known what was going on at either location. Later, an FBI agent had seen Wycazik at barricades near the Sharkle house in Evanston, at the very moment when Sharkle had detonated his bomb. But no one knew where he had gone; no one had seen him in almost six hours. "Obviously he's putting it together, piece by piece. One more reason to call off the cover-up and go public, before we're all caught in the act anyway."

Leland Falkirk suddenly felt that everything was flying apart, out of control, and he had trouble breathing, for he had dedicated his life to the philosophy and principles of control, unremitting iron control in all things. Control was what mattered more than anything else. First came self-control. You had to learn to exert unfaltering control over your desires and ignoble impulses, or otherwise you risked destruction by one vice or another: alcohol, drugs, sex. He had learned that much from his ultra-religious parents, who had begun drumming the lesson into him before he was even old enough to understand what they were saying. And you also had to control your intellectual processes; you had to force yourself to rely always on logic and reason, for it was human nature to drift into superstition, into patterns of behavior based on irrational assumptions. That was a lesson he had learned *in spite of* his parents, from attending Pentecostal services with them and watching in shock and fear as they fell to the floor of the church or revival tent, where they screamed and thrashed in wild abandon, transported by what they claimed was the spirit of God—though it was actually just hysterical Holy Rollerism. You had to control your fear, too, or you could not hold on to sanity for long. He had taught himself to conquer his fear of his parents, who had routinely beat and punished him while claiming it was for his own good because the devil was in him and must be driven out. One way of learning to control fear was by subjecting yourself to pain and thereby increasing your tolerance for it, because you couldn't be afraid of anything if you were sure you could bear the pain it might cause you. Control. Leland Falkirk controlled himself, his life, his men, and any assignment that he was given, but now he felt control of this situation slipping quickly out of his grasp, and he was closer to panic than he had been in more than forty years.

"Polnichev," he said, "I'm going to hang up, but you stand by your phone. My man will set up a scrambled conference call between me, you, your director, Riddenhour in Washington, and our White House contact. We're going to agree on a tough policy and the best way of implementing it. Damned if I'll let you gutless wonders fall apart on this. We'll keep control. We're going to eradicate the infected people if that's necessary, even if some of them are cute little girls and priests, and we're going to save our asses. By God, I'm going to make sure we do!"

When Faye and Ginger returned from Elko at two-forty-five in the motel van, the green-brown car followed them down the exit ramp from I-80. Ginger was half-convinced it would swing into the motel lot and park beside them, but it stopped along the county road, a hundred feet short of the Tranquility, and waited in the slanting snowfall.

Faye parked in front of the motel office door, and Dom and Ernie came out to help them unload the purchases they had made in Elko: ski suits, ski masks, boots, and insulated gloves for those who didn't already have them, based on sizes everyone had provided last night; two new semiautomatic .20-gauge shotguns; ammunition for those weapons and the others; backpacks, flashlights, two compasses, a small acetylene torch with two bottles of gas, and a number of other items.

Ernie embraced Faye, and Dom embraced Ginger. Simultaneously, both men said, "I was worried about you." And Ginger heard herself saying, "I was worried about you, too," even as Faye said it. Ernie and Faye kissed. With snowflakes frosting his eyebrows and melting into jeweled beads of water on his lashes, Dom lowered his face to Ginger's, and they kissed, too—a sweet, warm, lingering kiss. Somehow, it was as right for her and Dom to greet each other in such a fashion as it was for Faye and Ernie, husband and wife. That rightness was part of everything Ginger had felt for him since arriving in Elko two days ago.

When everything had been unloaded from the van and stashed in the Blocks' apartment, all ten members of the Tranquility family adjourned to the diner. Jack, Ernie, Dom, Ned, and Faye brought guns.

As she pulled some chairs up to the table where Brendan and Dom had tested their powers last night, Ginger noticed that the priest regarded the weapons with a mixture of displeasure and fear, that he seemed far less optimistic than yesterday, when his discovery of his amazing gift had sent his spirit soaring. "No dream last night," he explained when she asked the reason for his grim mood. "No golden light, no voice calling to me. You know, Ginger, I told myself all along that I didn't believe I was being called here by God. But deep down that *is* what I believed. Father Wycazik was right: There was always a core of faith in me. Recently, I've been edging back to an acceptance of God. Not only acceptance: I *need* Him again. But now . . . no dream, no golden light . . . as if God's abandoned me."

"No, you're wrong," Ginger said, taking his hand as if she could absorb his distress by osmosis and leave him feeling better. "If you believe in God, He never abandons you. Right? You can abandon God, but never the other way around. He always forgives, always loves. Isn't that what you tell a parishioner?"

Brendan smiled wanly. "Sounds like *you* went to seminary."

She said, "The dream was probably just a memory surging against the block that's holding it down in your subconscious. But if it was really God summoning you here . . . well, the reason you no longer have the dream is because you've arrived. You've come as He wanted, so there's no need for Him to send you the dream any more. See?"

The priest's face brightened a little.

They took up seats around the table.

With dismay, Ginger saw that Marcie's condition had worsened since last night. The girl sat with her head bent, face half-hidden by her thick black hair, staring at her tiny hands, which lay limply in her lap. She mumbled: "Moon, moon, the moon, moon. . . . " She was in all-out pursuit of those memories of July 6, which remained teasingly on the edge of her awareness and which, by their tantalizing inaccessibility, had drawn her into obsessive contemplation of their half-glimpsed forms.

"She'll come out of it," Ginger told Jorja, knowing how empty and foolish the statement was, yet unable to think of anything else to say.

"Yes," Jorja said, apparently not finding it empty or foolish but reassuring. "She has to come out of it. She has to."

Jack and Ned stood the plywood panel against the door and braced it with a table again, assuring freedom from eavesdroppers.

Quickly, Faye and Ginger told of their visit to the Jamisons' ranch and of being followed by the two men in the Plymouth. Ernie and Dom had been followed, too.

This news made Jack edgy. "If they're coming out in the open to keep tabs on us, that means they're almost ready to grab us again."

Ned Sarver said, "Maybe I'd just better stand watch, make sure nobody's moving in on us already." Jack agreed, and Ned went to the door and put one eye against the narrow crack between the plywood and the door frame, looking out at the snow-swept parking lot.

At Jack's request, Dom and Ernie explained what they had found on their tour of the Thunder Hill Depository's perimeter fence.

Jack listened carefully, asking a number of questions for which Ginger could not always discern the purpose. Were any thin bare wires woven through the chainlink fence? What were the fenceposts like? Finally, he asked, "No guard dogs or men on patrol?"

Dom said, "No. There'd have been prints in the snow along the fence. Must be heavy electronic security. I'd hoped we'd be able to get on the grounds—but not after I got a close-up view of the place."

"Oh, we'll get on the grounds all right," Jack said. "The tricky part will be getting inside the Depository itself."

Dom and Ernie looked at him with such astonishment that Ginger knew Thunder Hill must have looked formidable, indeed.

"Get *inside?*" Dom said.

"No can do," Ernie said.

"If they rely on multiple electronic systems for the perimeter security," Jack said, "they'll very likely also rely on electronics at the main entrance. That's the way it is these days. Everyone's dazzled by high-tech. Oh, sure, Thunder Hill will have a guard at the front gate, but he'll be so used to depending on computers, video cameras, and other gadgets that he'll be lax. So we might be able to surprise him, get by him. Once inside, though, I don't know how far we can go or what we might be able to get a peek at before we're nailed."

Ginger said, "But how can you be so sure—"

"For eight years," Jack reminded her, "getting into and back out of difficult places was my line of work. And it was the government that originally trained me, so I know their routines and tricks." He winked his misaligned eye. "I have some tricks of my own."

Jorja spoke up, obviously more than a little distressed: "But you've as much as said you'll be caught in there."

"Oh, yes," Jack said.

"But then what's the point of going in?" Jorja asked.

He had it all planned out, and Ginger listened at first in utter bafflement and then with growing admiration for his sense of strategy.

Jack laid out the details of his plan as if it were a foregone conclusion that the other nine members of the group would agree to do precisely what he told them, regardless of the risks involved. He employed every trick of coercion and leadership that he knew, not because he was unwilling to consider alternatives to his strategy or modifications of it, but because there simply was no time to explore other courses of action. His intellect and his instinct had the same message for him: *Time is running out.* So he explained to the rest of the Tranquility family that:

Within the next hour, everyone—except Dom, Ned, and Jack himself—would pile in the Cherokee, leave overland from the rear of the motel, and drive into Elko by a roundabout route, thereby slipping the waiting tails. In Elko the group would split up. Ernie, Faye, and Ginger would drive the Cherokee north to Twin Falls, Idaho, then to Pocatello. From there they would arrange to fly to Boston, where they would stay with Ginger's friends, the Hannabys. They should get to Boston late Thursday or early Friday. Immediately upon their arrival, they would tell the Hannabys every detail of what they had discovered. Then, within an hour or two, Ginger would call together as many of her colleagues at Boston Memorial as possible, and she and the Blocks would tell those physicians what had been done to a lot of innocent people in Nevada two summers ago. Meanwhile, George and Rita Hannaby would contact influential friends and arrange meetings at which Ginger and the Blocks could spread their tale. Only then would Ginger, Faye, and Ernie go to the press. And only after they had gone to the press would they go to the police with a statement contesting the heretofore accepted wisdom that Pablo Jackson had been murdered by an ordinary burglar eight days ago.

"The trick," Jack said, "is to get your story into wide circulation among some important people, so if you have an 'accident' before you've convinced the press to take up your cause, there will be a whole lot of powerful folks demanding to know who killed you and why. That's the special value you have for us now, Ginger—your associations with a spectrum of important people in one of the country's most influential cities. If you can electrify those people with your story, you'll be creating an imposing group of advocates. Just remember, when you get back there, you're going to have to move *fast,* before the conspirators discover you've gone home and decide to grab you or blow you away."

Outside, the wind suddenly rose, keening at the plywood-covered windows. Good. If the storm worsened, cutting visibility farther, they would have a better chance of slipping away from the motel unobserved.

"After Ginger, Faye, and Ernie leave Elko in the Cherokee, heading up toward Pocatello," Jack said, using a tone of voice that implied these steps were not suggestions but immutable necessities, "you other four—Brendan, Sandy, Jorja, and Marcie—will go to the local Jeep dealership and buy another four-wheel-drive vehicle with cash that I'll give you before you leave the Tranquility. Immediately after signing the papers, you'll head out of Elko in a different direction from Ginger and the Blocks—east toward Salt Lake City, Utah. The snow will slow you down, of course, but you should be able to reach Salt Lake, get a flight out as soon as the storm subsides, and be in Chicago by Thursday afternoon or evening." He turned to the priest. "Brendan, when you touch down at O'Hare, you'll contact your rector, this Father Wycazik you've told us about. He must use his pull to arrange an immediate emergency meeting with whoever's head of the Chicago Archdiocese."

"Richard Cardinal O'Callahan," Brendan said. "But I don't know if even Father Wycazik could arrange an *immediate* meeting with him."

"He has to," Jack said firmly. "Brendan, you've got to move fast, just as Ginger will be moving fast in Boston. We've got to assume our enemies will be quick about spotting you when you turn up in Chicago. Anyway, at the meeting with Cardinal O'Callahan, you and Jorja and Sandy will explain what's happened in Elko County—and Brendan, you'll give a demonstration of your newly discovered telekinetic ability. Pull out all the stops, okay? Do cardinals wear pants under their robes?"

Brendan blinked in surprise. "*What?* Of course, they wear pants."

"Then I want you to scare the pants off your Cardinal O'Callahan. Give him a show that'll let him know he's part of the biggest story since they found the stone rolled away from the mouth of that tomb two thousand years ago. And I don't mean to be blasphemous, Brendan. I really think it *is* the biggest story since."

"So do I," Brendan said. Though he had been glum all morning, he seemed to take heart from Jack's tone of authority and quiet excitement.

Now, the wild wind was vibrating the sheets of plywood at the windows, filling the restaurant with a low and ominous thrumming.

Ernie Block cocked his gray-bristled head, listening, and said, "With winds like this already, so soon after the snow hits, it's going to be a roof-raiser later on."

Jack didn't want the weather to deteriorate *too* rapidly, for if the enemy was going to strike within the next few hours, as he anticipated, they might accelerate their schedule to avoid the messy complications of conducting the round-up in a full-scale blizzard.

"Okay, Brendan," Jack said, "convince Cardinal O'Callahan and get him to arrange quick meetings with the mayor, city councilmen, social and financial leaders. You might have as much as twenty-four hours to spread your story before your life is in danger. The farther you spread it, the less danger you're in. But in any case, you shouldn't risk spending more than twelve hours putting together a network of powerful advocates before you ask them to arrange a press conference. Just picture it: the city's most prominent citizens forming a backdrop for you, reporters wondering what the hell is about to happen—and then you display your telekinetic ability by levitating a chair and sending it on a nice slow trip around the room!"

Brendan grinned broadly. "That'll put an end to their cover-up for sure. No way they can continue it after that."

"Let's hope so," Jack said. "Because while the rest of you are off on your various missions, Dom and Ned and I will be inside Thunder Hill, perhaps under military arrest, and our only chance of getting out in the same condition we went in is if you blow this wide open."

Jorja said, "I don't like that part of it—the three of you going into the mountain. Why's it necessary? I asked you that same question fifteen minutes ago, and you still haven't answered me, Jack. If we can slip out of here, back to Boston and Chicago, use Ginger's and Brendan's connections to blast this story wide open, then there's no need to go poking around in the Depository. Once we've set the wheels of the press in motion, the Army and whatever government agencies are involved will eventually have to come clean. They'll have to tell us what happened that summer and what they've been doing in Thunder Hill."

Jack took a deep breath, for this was the part at which they might balk—especially Ned and Dom. "Sorry, Jorja. But that's naïve. If we *all* split and tell our stories, there'll be enormous pressure on the military and government to reveal the truth, yes, but they'll delay. They'll drag their feet and spread contradictory stories for weeks, months. That'll give them time to devise a convincing lie to explain everything, yet reveal nothing. Our only hope of exposing the truth is to make them open up fast. And to speed things along, the rest of you have to be able to tell the world that three of your friends—Dom, Ned, and me—are being held against our will inside the mountain. Hostages. The element of a hostage drama, with agencies of our own government in the role of terrorists, will be the final ingredient that might make it impossible for the Army to stonewall more than a day or two.''

He could see that this revelation startled everyone. Ernie and Faye regarded him with a mixture of shock and sadness, as if he were already dead—or mind-wiped.

Fear had risen like a dark moon in Jorja's face. She said, ''But you can't. No, no. You simply can't sacrifice yourselves—''

''If the rest of you do your jobs properly,'' Jack said quickly, ''we won't be sacrificing ourselves. You'll pry us out of Thunder Hill with the lever of public protest that you create. That's why it's so important we all do exactly what we're supposed to.''

''But,'' Jorja said, ''what if, by some chance, you get inside the mountain and manage to see something that explains what happened to us that July. And what if you could snap a few pictures of it and get back out alive. Surely, in that case, you'd try to escape. You're not saying that the hostage drama *has* to be a part of it—are you?''

Jack said, ''No, of course not.''

He was lying. Though there was at least a small chance of getting deep into the Depository, Jack knew there was little hope of getting all the way back out again undetected. As for finding something in there that would immediately explain what they had seen the summer before last—there was no hope whatsoever. For one thing, they had no idea what they were looking for. It was possible—even probable—that they would pass right by the thing they were after without knowing what they had seen. Furthermore, if dangerous experiments had been taking place in Thunder Hill, and if one of those experiments had gotten out of hand that July night, the answer to the mystery was likely to lie in paper or microfilm files or in lab reports; even if they could gain access to the labs, he and Dom and Ned would not have time to pore leisurely through tons of paperwork looking for the few pertinent ounces that would shed light upon their experience. He did not say any of this to Jorja or the others. He could not permit the meeting to degenerate into debate about potential risks and other options.

Outside, the wind howled.

Jorja said, ''And if you absolutely insist on going in there, why couldn't the rest of us stay as near to you as possible? I mean, the seven of us could just go into Elko, to the offices of the *Sentinel,* and Brendan could demonstrate his power to the local press. We could start exposing the conspiracy here instead of in Chicago and Boston.''

''No.'' Jack was moved but also frustrated by her concern for him. (The hands on his wristwatch seemed to be *spinning,* for God's sake.) ''The national media wouldn't pay quick enough attention to a small-town newspaper's report that it had turned up a man with psychic powers and a major government conspiracy. It would be viewed as just another jerkwater story in the same league as reports of abominable snowmen and UFOs. Our enemies would find you and squash you—squash any local reporters you spoke with—long before the national media would bother sending anyone to check it out. You've got to go, Jorja. The way I've outlined it—that's our best hope.''

She slumped in her chair with a defeated look.

''Dom,'' Jack said, ''are you with me?''

''Yeah, I guess I am,'' the writer said, as Jack had known he would. Corvaisis was one of those stand-up types you could rely on, though he probably didn't see himself that way. He smiled ironically and said, ''But, Jack, mind telling me why the honor fell on my shoulders?''

"Sure. Ernie's still not entirely over his nyctophobia, so it's hard enough on him just to ride all night to Pocatello. He isn't up to making a night-assault on the Depository. Which leaves you and Ned. And frankly, Dom, it won't hurt our case if one of the hostages in Thunder Hill is a novelist, a celebrity of sorts. That adds one more bit of the kind of sensationalism the press thrives on."

Ginger Weiss had been frowning as Jack outlined his plan. Now she spoke: "You're a great strategist, Jack, but you're also chauvinistic. You're only considering men for the expedition into Thunder Hill. I think the three who go should be you, Dom, and me."

"But—"

"Hear me out," she said, getting up, moving around to the far end of the table, drawing everyone's attention from Jack to her. Jack was aware of how she focused her intellect, will, and beauty upon him, for her techniques were similar to his own methods of compelling everyone to accept his plans without argument. "Ned and Sandy could go to Chicago, which would still give Brendan two adults to back up his story. Jorja and Marcie could go with Faye and Ernie to the Hannabys in Boston, with a note from me. George and Rita will take them seriously, get them an audience. My note alone will assure they're welcome and listened to. But their reception is doubly assured because in ten minutes Rita will recognize herself in Faye, and they'll be like sisters, and Rita will go to the mat for her. My presence is not essential there. I'm needed more here. For one thing, the infiltration of the Depository will be a dangerous undertaking. Either of you— Dom, Jack—might be hurt and need emergency medical attention. We don't know for sure that Dom has the same healing power as Brendan, and even if he has it, he might not be able to control it. So a doctor might come in handy, huh? Second, if it'll help having a famous author—all right, Dom, *moderately* famous—as a hostage, then we'll get even more press attention if a woman's held in Thunder Hill. God damn it, you really *need* me, Jack!"

"You're right," he said, startling her by his quick agreement. But what she said made sense, and there was no point wasting time debating it. "Ned, you'll go with Sandy and Brendan to Chicago."

"I don't mind going to the Depository with you, if that's what you think's best," Ned told him.

"I know," Jack said. "I did think it was best, but now I don't. Jorja, you and Marcie will go to Boston with Ernie and Faye. Now, if we don't get the hell out of here soon, the whole question of who goes where won't matter anyway, because we'll be back in the hands of the people who had us drugged senseless the summer before last."

Ned pulled the table away from the door. Ernie removed the panel of plywood standing there, and beyond the glass the world was a whirling white wall of wind and snow.

"Terrific," Jack said. "Good cover."

As they stepped out into the driving snow, they could see only as far as the place where the green-brown, government Plymouth had been parked out by the county road. It was gone. That made Jack uneasy. He preferred the watchers out in the open—where *he* could also watch *them*.

The conference call did not progress as Colonel Leland Falkirk had foreseen. He intended to seek agreement that the witnesses at the motel must be rounded up at once and conveyed to the Thunder Hill Depository. He expected that he and General Riddenhour would be able to convince the others that the threat of a spreading infection was both real and acute, and that he should be permitted to destroy everyone in the Tranquility group as well as the entire staff of Thunder Hill the moment he put his hands on proof that those individuals were no longer human, proof he fully expected to obtain. But from the moment he picked up the phone, nothing went his way. The situation deteriorated.

Emil Foxworth, the Director of the Federal Bureau of Investigation, had news of yet another disastrous development. The team making new memory modifications in the Salcoe family in Monterey, California, had been visited by a persistent intruder. They had thought they'd cornered him—a burly, bearded man— but he had made a spectacular escape. The four Salcoes were quickly transferred to a medical van and moved to a safe-house for continuation of memory modifications. A registration check on the bearded intruder's abandoned car identified it as a rental from the local airport agency, and the lessee was not merely a burglar but Parker Faine, Corvaisis' friend. "Subsequently," the Director said, "we traced Faine on a flight out of Monterey to San Francisco, but there we've lost him. We have no idea where he's been or what he's been up to since his West Air flight landed at SFX."

Foster Polnichev, in the FBI's Chicago office, was already of the view that maintaining the cover-up was impossible, and news of Faine's escape confirmed that opinion. The two political appointees—Foxworth of the FBI, and James Herton, National Security Adviser to the President—were in agreement with him.

Furthermore, with oily skill, Foster Polnichev argued that every development— the miraculous cures effected by Cronin and Tolk; the wondrous telekinetic powers of Corvaisis and Emmy Halbourg—indicated that the ultimate effects of the events of July 6 were going to be beneficial to mankind, not detrimental. "And we know that Doctor Bennell and most of the people working with him are of the opinion that there is no threat whatsoever and never was. They've been convinced of it for many months now. Their arguments are quite persuasive."

Leland tried to make them see that Bennell and his people might be infected and unreliable. No one inside Thunder Hill could be trusted any more. But he was a military leader, not a debater, and in a contest with Foster Polnichev, Leland knew he sounded like a raving paranoid.

Leland did not even get much support from the one source on which he had counted most: General Maxwell Riddenhour. The Chairman of the Joint Chiefs was noncommittal at first, listening carefully to every point of view, playing the role of mediator, for his position put him somewhere between a political appointee and a career soldier. But it soon became clear that he agreed more with Polnichev, Foxworth, and Herton than he did with Leland Falkirk.

"I understand your instincts in this situation, Colonel, and I admire them," General Riddenhour said. "But I believe the matter has gone beyond the scope of our authority. It requires the input not just of soldiers but of neuropathologists, biologists, philosophers, and others before precipitous action can be taken. Upon disclosure of any evidence of an imminent threat, I will of course change my mind; I'll favor the roundup of the witnesses at the motel, order the quarantine on Thunder Hill continued indefinitely, and take most of the other strong measures you now favor. But for the moment, in the absence of a grave and obvious threat, I believe we should move a bit more cautiously and leave open the possibility that the cover-up will have to be undone."

"With all due respect," Leland said, barely able to control his fury, "the threat seems both grave and obvious to me. I don't believe there's *time* for neuropathologists or philosophers. And certainly not for the spineless equivocating of a bunch of gutless politicians."

That honest appraisal brought a stormy reaction from Foxworth and Herton, the mealy spawn of politicians. When they shouted at Leland, he lost his usual reserve and shouted back at them. In an instant the conference call degenerated into a noisy verbal brawl that ended only when Riddenhour exerted control. He forced a quick agreement that no moves would be made against the witnesses or any steps taken to further cement the cover-up, while at the same time no steps would be taken to *weaken* the cover-up, either. "I'll seek an emergency meeting with the President the instant I end this call," Riddenhour said. "In twenty-four hours, forty-eight at the latest, we'll try to have a plan that satisfies everyone from the Commander-in-Chief to Bennell and his boys out there in Thunder Hill."

That, Leland thought sourly, is impossible.

When Leland hung up, the ill-fated conference call having concluded in un-anticipated humiliation, he stood for at least a minute at his desk in the window-less room at Shenkfield, seething with such pure anger that he did not trust himself to summon Lieutenant Horner. He did not want Horner to know that the tide had gone against him, did not want Horner to have any reason to suspect that the operation he was about to launch was in absolute contradiction of General Rid-denhour's orders.

His duty was clear. Grim, terrible—but clear.

He would order the closure of I-80 under the pretense of a toxic spill, in order to isolate the Tranquility Motel. He would then take the witnesses into custody and transport them directly to the Thunder Hill Depository. When they were all underground with Dr. Miles Bennell and the other suspect workers staffing the Depository, trapped behind massive blast doors, Leland would take them—and himself—out with a pair of the five-megaton backpack nukes that were stored among the munitions in the subterranean facility. A couple of five-megatoners would incinerate everyone and everything inside the mountain, reduce them all to ash and bone fragments. That would eliminate the primary source of this hid-eous contamination, the home nest of the enemy. Of course, other potential sources of contamination would remain: the Tolk family, the Halbourg family, all remaining witnesses whose brainwashing had not developed holes and who had not returned to Nevada, others. . . . But Leland was confident that, once he had taken the courageous action required to eliminate the largest and primary source of contamination, Riddenhour would be shamed by his example of self-sacrifice and would find the backbone to do what was necessary to finish the work and scrub every trace of contagion from the face of the earth.

Leland Falkirk was trembling. Not with fear. It was pride that made him trem-ble. He was enormously proud to have been chosen to fight and win the greatest battle of all time, thus saving not just one nation but all the world from a menace with no equal in history. He knew he was capable of the sacrifice required. He had no fear. As he wondered what he would feel in the split-second it took him to die in a nuclear blast, a thrill coursed through him at the prospect of pitting himself against the most intense pain of which the human mind could conceive. Oh, it would be cruelly intense and yet so short in duration that there was no doubt he'd prove capable of enduring it as stout-heartedly as he had endured all other pain to which he had subjected himself.

He was calm now. Perfectly calm. Serene.

Leland savored the sweet anticipation of the blistering pain to come. That brief atomic agony would be of such exquisite purity that the endurance of it would ensure the reward of heaven, which his Pentecostal parents, seeing the devil in every aspect of him, had always sworn he would not attain.

* * *

Stepping out of the Tranquility Grille behind Ginger, Dom Corvaisis looked up into the maelstrom of driving-whirling-spinning snow, and for an instant he saw and heard and felt what was not there:

Behind him rang out the atonal musical clatter of demolished glass still falling from the explosion of the windows, and ahead lay the glow of the parking-lot lights and the hot summer darkness beyond, and all around the thunder-roar and earthquake-shudder of mysterious source; his heart pounding; his breath like taffy that had stuck in his throat; and as he ran out of the Grille he looked around and then up....

"What's wrong?" Ginger asked.

Dom realized that he had staggered across the snowy pavement, skidding not on that surface but on the slippery recollection that had escaped his memory block. He looked around at the others, all of whom had come out of the diner. "I saw . . . like I was there again . . . that July night. . . . " Two nights ago, in the diner, when he'd come close to remembering, he had unconsciously re-created the thunder and shaking of July 6. This time, there was no such manifestations, maybe because the memory was no longer repressed and was breaking through and needed no help. Now, unable to adequately convey the intensity of the memory, he turned away from the others and peered up into the falling snow, and—

The roar was so loud that it hurt his ears, and the vibrations so strong that he felt them in his bones and in his teeth the way thunder sometimes reverberated in window glass, and he stumbled out across the macadam, looking up into the night sky and—there!—an aircraft flying only a few hundred feet above the earth, red and white running lights flashing across darkness, so low that the glow from within the cockpit was visible, a jet judging by the speed with which it rocketed past, a fighter jet judging by the powerful scream of its engines, and—there!— another one, sweeping past and wheeling up across the field of stars that filled the clear black sky in a panoramic speckle-splash; but the roar and the shaking that had shattered the diner's windows and had set small objects adance on the tables now grew worse instead of better, even though he would have expected it to subside once the jets were past, so he turned, sensing the source behind him, and he cried out in terror when a third jet shot over the Grille at an altitude of no more than forty feet, so low that he could see the markings—serial numbers and an American flag—on the bottom of one wing, illuminated by the parking-lot light bouncing up from the macadam; Jesus, it was so low that he fell flat on the ground in panic, certain that the jet was crashing, that debris would be raining over him in a second, perhaps even a shower of burning jet fuel. . . .

"Dom!"

He found himself lying face-down in the snow, clutching the ground in a reenactment of the terror he had felt on the night of July 6, when he'd thought the jet was crashing on top of him.

"Dom, what's wrong?" Sandy Sarver asked. She was kneeling beside him, a hand on his shoulder.

Ginger was kneeling at his other side. "Dom, are you all right?"

With their support, he got up from the snow. "The memory block is going, crumbling." He turned his face up toward the sky again, hoping that the white snowy day would flash away, as before, and be replaced by a dark summer night, hoping that the recollections would continue to pour forth. Nothing. Wind gusted. Snow lashed his face. The others were watching him. He said, "I remembered jets, military fighter craft . . . two at first, swooping by a couple of hundred feet above . . . and then a third one so low that it almost took the roof off the diner."

"Jets!" Marcie said.

Everyone looked at her in surprise, even Dom, for it was the first word— other than "moon"—that she had spoken since dinner the previous night. She was in her mother's arms, bundled against the weather. She had turned her small face to the sky. In response to what Dom had said, she seemed to be searching the stormy heavens for some sign of the long-departed jets of a summer lost.

"Jets," Ernie said, looking up as well. "I don't . . . recall."

"Jets! Jets!" Marcie reached up with one hand toward the heavens.

Dom realized that he was doing the same thing, although with both hands, as if he could reach up beyond the blinding snow of time-present, into the hot clear night of time-past, and pull the memory down into view. But he could not bring it back, no matter how hard he strained.

The others were not able to recall what he described, and in a moment their tremulous expectation turned to frustration again.

Marcie lowered her face. She put a thumb in her mouth and sucked earnestly on it. Her gaze had turned inward again.

"Come on," Jack said. "We've got to get the hell out of here."

They hurried toward the motel, to dress and arm themselves for the journeys and battles ahead of them. Reluctantly, with the smell of July heat still in his nose, with the roar of jet engines still echoing in his bones, Dom Corvaisis followed.

PART THREE

◆ ◆ ◆

NIGHT ON THUNDER HILL

By strangers honored, and by strangers
Courage, love, friendship,
compassion, and empathy
lift us above the simple beasts
and define humanity.
—THE BOOK OF COUNTED SORROWS

By foreign hands thy humble grave adorned;
By strangers honored, and by strangers mourned.
—ALEXANDER POPE

SIX

◆

Tuesday Night, January 14

1. Strife

Father Stefan Wycazik flew Delta from Chicago to Salt Lake City, then caught a feeder flight into the Elko County Airport. He landed after snow had begun to fall but before the rapidly dropping visibility and the oncoming false dusk of the storm had curtailed air traffic.

In the small terminal, he went to a public phone, looked up the number of the Tranquility Motel, and dialed it. He got nothing, not even a ring. The line hissed emptily. He tried again with no success.

When he sought help from an operator, she was also unable to ring the number. "I'm sorry, sir, there seems to be trouble with the line."

Taking that as very bad news, Father Wycazik said, "Trouble? What trouble? What's wrong?"

"Well, sir, I suppose the storm. We're getting really gusty wind."

But Stefan was not as certain as she was. The storm had hardly begun. He could not believe telephone lines had already succumbed to the first tentative gusts, which he had experienced on his way into the terminal. The isolation of the Tranquility was an ominous development, more likely to be the handiwork of men than of the impending blizzard.

He placed a call to St. Bette's rectory in Chicago, and Father Gerrano answered on the second ring. "Michael, I've arrived safely in Elko. But I haven't gotten Brendan. Their phone isn't working."

"Yes," Michael Gerrano said, "I know."

"You know? How could you possibly know?"

"Just minutes ago," Michael said, "I received a call from a man who refused to identify himself but who said he was a friend of this Ginger Weiss, one of those people out there with Brendan. He said she called him this morning and asked him to dig up some information for her. He found what she wanted, but he couldn't get through to the Tranquility. She'd apparently foreseen that problem, so she'd given him our number and the number of friends of hers in Boston, told him to tell us what he'd found, and she'd call us at her convenience."

"Refused to give his name?" Father Wycazik said, puzzled. "And you say she asked him to dig up information?"

"Yes," Michael said. "About two things. First, this place called the Thunder Hill Depository. He says to tell her that, as far as he could determine, the Depository is what it's always been: an elaborate blastproof storage depot, one of eight virtually identical underground facilities situated across the country, and not the largest one. She also asked him to get her some background on an army officer, Colonel Leland Falkirk, who's with something called the Domestic Emergency Response Organization. . . .''

As he stared at one glimmering and bejeweled moment of the storm framed in the terminal window, Father Wycazik listened to Michael rattle off a service biography of the colonel. Just as Stefan was beginning to sweat with the strain of remembering all the details, his curate told him none of that was important. Michael said, ''Mr. X seemed to feel that only one part of Colonel Falkirk's background might have a bearing on what's happened to the people at the Tranquility Motel.''

''Mr. X?'' Father Wycazik said.

''Since he wouldn't give me his name, X will have to do.''

''Go on,'' Father Wycazik said.

''Well, Mr. X believes the key fact here is that Colonel Falkirk was the military's representative to a government committee, the CISG, that undertook some important think-tank-type research starting about nine years ago. The reason Mr. X thinks the key is CISG is because, while poking around, he discovered two odd things. First, many of the same scientists who served on that committee are now—or have recently been—on long and unusual vacations, leaves of absence, or unexplained furloughs. Second, a new level of security restrictions was put on the CISG files on July eighth, two summers ago, exactly two days after Brendan and the others had trouble out there in Nevada.''

''What does CISG stand for? What was that committee studying?''

Michael Gerrano told him.

Father Wycazik said, ''My God, I thought that might be it!''

''You did? Father, you're hard to surprise. But *this!* Surely you can't have foreseen this was what lay behind Brendan's problems. And . . . you mean . . . that's really . . . really what might've happened out there?''

''Could still *be* happening, but I must admit I can't claim to have deduced it sheerly by the application of my gigantic intellect. This is part of what Calvin Sharkle was shouting at the police just this morning, before he blew himself to smithereens.''

Michael said, ''Dear God.''

Father Wycazik said, ''We may be teetering on the brink of a whole new world, Michael. Are you ready for it?''

''I . . . I don't know,'' Michael said. ''Are you ready, Father?''

''Oh, yes!'' Stefan said. ''Oh, yes, very ready. But the way to it might be filled with danger.''

Ginger was aware of Jack Twist's growing agitation as the minutes passed. He was operating on a hunch that told him the last few grains of sand were dribbling through the neck of the hourglass. As Jack assisted with the tasks required for their departure, he kept glancing at windows and doors, as if he expected to see hostile faces.

They needed almost half an hour to suit up for the bitter winter night ahead, load all the guns and spare ammunition clips, and transfer the gear to the Sarvers' pickup and to Jack's Cherokee behind the motel. They did not work in silence, for that might have given warning of their imminent departure to the eavesdroppers. Instead, they chatted about inconsequential things as they hurried through their preparations.

Finally, at four-ten, turning on a radio very loud, hoping to cover their absence for a while, they left by the rear door of the maintenance room. They milled around in the wind and snow, hugging one another and saying, "goodbye," and "take care of yourself," and "I'll pray for you," and "it's going to be all right," and "we'll beat the bastards." Ginger noticed that Jack and Jorja spent an especially long time together, embracing, and when he kissed Marcie and hugged her goodbye, it was as if she were his own child. It was worse than the end of a family reunion, for in spite of protestations to the contrary, the members of this family were more than half-convinced that some of them would not survive to attend another gathering.

Squeezing back her tears, Ginger said, "All right, enough already, let's get the hell out of here."

With Ned driving, the seven who would go to Chicago and Boston left first, crammed in the Cherokee. The fine snow was falling so fast and heavy that the Cherokee was half-lost to sight within a hundred feet and became only a ghostly form within a hundred and fifty. Nevertheless, it did not head straight up the hills, for fear of being spotted by the observers Jack had located with his heat-reading device. Instead, the Cherokee entered the sloping folds of land by way of a narrow glen. Ned would stay in glens, vails, and gulleys as long as he could. The sound of the engine was swallowed up in the greater howl of the wind even before the Jeep began to vanish in the snow.

Ginger, Dom, and Jack climbed into the cab of the Sarvers' pickup and followed in the tracks of the Cherokee. But with its headstart, the Jeep soon disappeared into the white turmoil that claimed the land. As they thumped, jolted, tilted, and rocked upward through the glen, Ginger sat between Jack and Dom, looking through the windshield and past the beating wipers, wondering if she would ever see those in the Jeep again. In a few days, Ginger had come to love them all. She was afraid for them.

We care. That is what differentiates us from the beasts of the field. That's what Jacob had always said. Intellect, courage, love, friendship, compassion, and empathy—each of those qualities was as important to the human species as all the others, Jacob had said. Some people thought only intellect counted: knowing how to solve problems, knowing how to get by, knowing how to identify an advantage and seize it. All were important factors that had contributed to the ascendancy and supremacy of humankind, yes, but the many functions of intellect were insufficient without courage, love, friendship, compassion, and empathy. We care. It is our curse. It is our blessing.

At first Parker Faine was afraid that the pilot of the ten-seat feeder flight would not descend through the storm front and attempt a landing but would instead divert to another airfield farther south in Nevada. When, after all, the plane descended through the leading edge of the storm, Parker almost wished they had diverted. The buffeting wind and blinding snow seemed too hazardous even for a veteran pilot accustomed to instrument landings. Then they were safely on the ground, one of the last planes in before the Elko County Airport shut down.

The small airport provided no covered ramp for debarkation. Parker hurried across the snow-patched macadam toward the door of the small terminal, wincing as his bare face was stung by wind-driven snow like thousands of tiny cold needles.

After his Air West flight from Monterey had landed in San Francisco earlier today, he bought scissors and an electric razor at an airport gift shop and hastily shaved off his beard in the men's room. He had not seen his own unadorned visage in a decade. It was much prettier than he had expected. He trimmed his hair, too. When he was in the midst of this transformation, another guy in the men's room, washing his hands at the next sink, said jokingly, "On the run from the cops, huh?" And Parker said, "No, from my wife." And the guy said, "Yeah, me, too," as if he meant it.

To avoid leaving a credit-card trail, he paid cash for a ticket on an Air Cal jet to Reno. After a forty-five-minute trip over the Sierra Nevada to the Biggest Little City in the World, he had the good fortune to find a feeder line with a single empty seat on a flight departing for Elko in twelve minutes. He paid cash again, leaving only twenty-one dollars in his wallet. For two hours and fifteen minutes, he endured a frequently turbulent journey east across the Great Basin, toward the higher country of northeastern Nevada, where he sensed his friend was in desperate trouble.

By the time he pushed through the doors into the humble but clean little building that served as the Elko County Airport's offices and public terminal, Parker should have felt wrung-out both because of the horrible experience in Monterey and because of his hectic travels. Strangely, however, he felt vital, energetic, brimming with purpose and overflowing with determination. He saw himself as a bull, storming into a field to deal with a fox that had been frightening the herd.

He found the two public telephones, only one of which was in use. He looked up the number of the Tranquility, tried to call Dom, but the motel's phones were out of service. He supposed the storm might have something to do with it, but he was suspicious and worried. He had to get out there where he was needed, and fast.

In two minutes flat, he discovered there were no rental cars and that the town's taxi company, equipped with only three vehicles, was so busy because of the storm that he would have to wait ninety minutes to get a cab. So he looked around the terminal at a couple of stragglers from his own flight and at a few others who evidently had landed in private craft just as the airport was closing down, and he accosted them one by one, seeking a ride without success. Turning from one of them, Parker literally collided with a distinguished gray-haired man. The guy looked as frantic as Parker felt. He had pulled his coat open to reveal a Roman collar. To Parker, he said, "Excuse me, please, I'm a priest with urgent business, a matter of life or death, and I'm desperately in need of a ride to the Tranquility Motel. Do you have a car?"

Dom Corvaisis sat tensely in the Sarvers' pickup truck, with the passenger-side door on his right and Ginger Weiss on his left, squinting ahead into a snowfall so heavy that it seemed as if they were driving through countless barriers of gauzy white curtains. He peered forward as though an incredible revelation lay just beyond the next curtain. But when each parted without resistance, it revealed only an infinite array of additional curtains blowing-rippling-fluttering beyond.

After a while he realized what he was so tensely anticipating: a recurrence of the memory-flash that had stricken him when he had walked out of the Tranquility Grille. Jets . . . What had happened after the third jet swooped over, driving him to the pavement in terror?

Although the streaming snowflakes made the winter day appear to be a tapestry of millions of randomly arranged white threads, they did not help illuminate the glen. The false twilight of the storm brought a deep-gray gloom to the land three-quarters of an hour ahead of the real twilight. Gnarled, toothy rock formations and an occasional cottonwood loomed suddenly out of the murkiness like prehistoric beasts out of a primeval mist, never failing to startle. However, Dom knew that Jack dared not risk turning on the headlights yet. Though the truck itself was hidden by the snow and by the steep walls of the hollow in which they were sheltered, the lights would reflect up through the falling mega-trillion bits of ice crystals, and the glow would certainly be visible to the observers below.

They came to a place where the fading tire tracks of the Cherokee, like the trails of huge twin serpents, turned east into a branching glen that led off the main hollow. Jack did not follow Ned Sarver and the others, for the plan required them to head in a different direction. Instead, he pressed the pickup steadily north, relying on Dom's reading of a compass for guidance.

In another hundred yards, they reached the head of the glen, where it narrowed to—and finally terminated in—a steep upward slope. Dom thought they would have to turn back and follow Ned, after all, but Jack shifted gears, accelerated, and the four-wheel-drive pickup started to climb. The slope was rocky and rutted. The pickup progressed with many a jounce and sway and lurch that repeatedly threw Ginger Weiss against Dom in a series of collisions that were not without a pleasant aspect.

In the dreary gray storm light of the waning day, and in the dull and well-worn interior of the pickup, Ginger looked, by contrast, more beautiful than ever. Compared to her lustrous silver-blond hair, the white snow appeared soiled.

With a leap and a crash that bumped Dom's head against the roof, the truck crested the long hill. They drove down a brief incline, then across a level strip of land. As they started up another slope, Jack suddenly slammed on the brakes and cried, ''Jets!''

Dom gasped, looked up into the seething snowstorm, expecting to see an aircraft plummeting at them, then realized that Jack was speaking of jets from the past. He had remembered the same thing that had come back to Dom less than an hour ago. Judging by Jack's sure-handed control of the pickup, however, he had not *seen* the memory as vividly as Dom had seen it, but had merely recalled it.

''Jets,'' Jack said again, keeping one foot on the brake and one on the clutch, gripping the steering wheel hard with both hands, staring out at the snow but trying to look back into time. ''One, two, roaring high up, the way you said, Dom. And then another, low over the diner, and right after that one . . . a fourth. . . .''

''I didn't remember a fourth,'' Dom said excitedly.

Hunching over the wheel, Jack said, ''The fourth jet came just as I rushed out of the motel. I wasn't over there in the diner with you. There was this tremendous shaking and roaring, and I rushed out of my room in time to see the third fighter— an F-16, I think. It virtually exploded out of nowhere, out of the darkness, over the roof of the diner. You're right: Its altitude couldn't have been more than forty or fifty feet. And while I was still taking that in, a fourth came straight over the motel, from behind the place, and it was even lower. Maybe ten feet lower than the other one, and the window behind me burst when it passed. . . .''

''And then?'' Ginger asked in a whisper, as if a louder tone would shake the emerging memory back down into Jack's subconscious.

Jack said, ''The third and fourth fighters, the low ones, roared down toward the interstate, about twenty feet above the goddamn power lines, you could see right into the red-hot intakes of their engines, and they went screaming out over the plains beyond I-80, one of them peeling up and out to the east, the other to the west, both swinging around and coming back . . . and I started running toward you . . . toward the group of you who'd come out of the diner over there . . . 'cause I thought maybe you'd know what was going on. . . .''

Snow tapped on the windshield.

The wind whispered susurrant secrets at the tightly shut windows. At last Jack Twist said, ''That's all. I can't remember any more.''

''You will,'' Dom said. ''We all will. The blocks are crumbling.''

Jack slipped the pickup into gear again and started up the next slope, continuing their roundabout trek to Thunder Hill.

* * *

Colonel Leland Falkirk and Lieutenant Horner, accompanied by two heavily armed DERO corporals, took one of Shenkfield's Jeep Wagoneers to the road-block at the western end of the quarantine zone. Two large Army transports had been parked across the wide eastbound lanes of I-80, effectively blocking them. (The westbound lanes were blocked on the other side of the Tranquility, ten miles from this point.) Emergency beacons mounted on sawhorses flashed in profusion. Half a dozen DERO men were in sight, dressed in Arctic-issue. Three of them were leaning down to the open windows of halted automobiles, talking to motorists, courteously explaining the situation.

Telling Horner and the two corporals to wait in the car, Leland got out and walked to the center of the blockade, to have a brief word with Sergeant Vince Bidakian, who was in charge of this aspect of the operation. "How's it going so far?" Leland asked.

"Good, sir," Bidakian said, raising his voice slightly to compete with the wind. "Not too many people on the road. The storm hit to the west of here earlier, so most motorists with any common sense at all stopped earlier at Battle Mountain or even back at Winnemucca, until things clear. And it looks like virtually all the truckers decided to hole up rather than try to make it through to Elko. It'll take us an hour, I bet, before we've got even two hundred vehicles in line."

They were not turning the motorists back to Battle Mountain. They were telling everyone that the closure was expected to last only an hour and that the wait would not be insufferable.

A longer closure would have meant a massive backup even with the reduction in traffic brought by the storm. To deal with that larger number of inconvenienced travelers and to enforce a longer quarantine, Leland would have had to alert the Nevada State Police and the county sheriff by now. But he did not want to bring the police into it until that was unavoidable, for they would quickly seek confirmation of his authority from higher Army officials—and would soon learn that he had gone rogue. If the cops could be kept in the dark about the closure for just half an hour, and if they could be stalled for another few minutes once they did find out about it, no one would discover Leland's perfidy until it was too late. He needed only an hour to scoop up the witnesses at the motel and convey them into the deep vaults of Thunder Hill.

To Bidakian, Leland said, "Sergeant, make sure all the motorists have sufficient gasoline, and if any of them are running on low tanks, pump them ten gallons from that emergency supply you've brought."

"Yes, sir. That was my understanding, sir."

"No sign of any cops or snow plows?"

"Not yet, sir," Bidakian said, glancing beyond the short line of cars, where two new pairs of headlights appeared in the distant snow-swaddled dusk. "But we'll see one or the other within ten minutes."

"You know the story to give them?"

"Yes, sir. Truck bound for Shenkfield sprung a small leak. It's carrying harmless *and* toxic fluids, so we don't—"

"Colonel!" Lieutenant Horner was hurrying from the Wagoneer. He was wearing so many bulky clothes he looked half-again as large as usual. "Message from Sergeant Fixx at Shenkfield, sir. Something's wrong at the motel. He hasn't heard a voice in fifteen minutes. Just a radio, playing real loud. He doesn't think anyone's there."

"They go back into the damn diner?"

"No, sir. Fixx thinks they're just—gone, sir."

"Gone? Gone where?" Leland demanded, neither expecting an answer nor waiting for one. Heart pounding, he ran back to the Wagoneer.

Her name was Talia Ervy, and she looked like Marie Dressler, who'd played Tugboat Annie in those wonderful old movies with Wallace Beery. Talia was even larger than Dressler, who'd been far from petite: big bones, broad face, wide mouth, strong chin. But she was the prettiest woman Parker Faine had seen in days, for she not only offered him and Father Wycazik a ride from the airport to the Tranquility, but refused to take any money for it. "Hell, I don't mind," she said, sounding a little like Marie Dressler, too. "I wasn't going anywheres much special anyway. Just home to cook dinner for myself. I'm a flat-out horrible cook, so this'll just put off the punishment for a bit. Fact is, when I think of my meatloaf, I figure maybe you're doing me a big favor."

Talia had a ten-year-old Cadillac, a big boat of a car, with winter-tread tires and snow chains. She claimed it would take her anywhere she wanted to go, regardless of the weather, and she called it "Old Paint." Parker sat up front with her, and Father Wycazik sat in back.

They had gone less than a mile when they heard the emergency radio bulletin about the purported toxic spill and the closure of I-80 west of Elko. "Those muddle-headed, fumble-fingered damn goofballs!" Talia said, turning the volume louder but raising her voice to talk over it. "Dangerous stuff like that, you'd think they'd treat it like a load of babies in glass cradles, but this here's twice in two years."

Neither Parker nor Father Wycazik was capable of commenting. They both knew that their worst fears for their friends were now coming true.

Talia Ervy said, "Well, gentlemen, what do we do now?"

Parker said, "Is there anyplace that rents cars? Four-wheel-drive is what we'll need. A Jeep, something like that."

"There's a Jeep dealer," Talia said.

"Can you take us there?" Parker asked.

"Me and Old Paint can take you anywheres, even if it starts putting down snowflakes big as dogs."

The salesman at the Jeep dealership, Felix Schellenhof, was far less colorful than Talia Ervy. Schellenhof wore a gray suit, gray tie, and pale-gray shirt, and spoke in a gray voice. No, he told Parker, they didn't rent vehicles by the day. Yes, they had many for sale. No, they couldn't complete a deal in just twenty minutes. The salesman said if Parker intended to finance, that would take until tomorrow. Even a check would not clinch the deal quickly because Parker was from out of state. "No checks," Parker said. Schellenhof raised gray eyebrows at the prospect of cash. Parker said, "I'll put it on my American Express Gold Card," and Schellenhof looked grayly amused. They took American Express, he said, but in payment for accessories, repairs; no one had ever bought an entire *vehicle* with plastic. Parker said, "There's no purchase limit on the card. Listen, I was in Paris, saw a gorgeous Dali oil in a gallery, *thirty thousand bucks,* and they took my American Express!" With deliberate, plodding diplomacy, Schellenhof began to turn them away.

"For the love of God, man, *move* your tired butt!" Father Wycazik roared, slamming one fist into the top of Schellenhof's desk. He was flushed from his hairline to his backwards collar. "This is a matter of life or death for us. Call American Express." He raised his hand high, and the salesman's shocked gray eyes followed its swift upward arc. "Find out if they'll authorize the purchase. For the love of God, hurry!" the priest shouted, slamming his fist down again.

The sight of such fury in a clergyman put some speed into the salesman at last. He took Parker's card and nearly sprinted out of his small office, across the showroom to the manager's glass-walled domain.

"Good grief, Father," Parker said, "if you were a Protestant, you'd be a famous fire-and-brimstone evangelist by now."

"Oh, Catholic or not, I've made a few sinners quake in my time."

"I don't doubt it," Parker assured him.

American Express approved the purchase. With hasty repentance, Schellenhof produced a sheaf of forms and showed Parker where to sign. "Quite a week!" the salesman said, though he was still drab and gray in spite of his new enthusiasm. "Late Monday a fella walks in, buys a new Cherokee with cash—bundles of twenty-dollar bills. Must've hit it big in a casino. Now this. And the week's hardly started. Something, eh?"

"Fascinating," Parker said.

Using the telephone on Schellenhof's desk, Father Wycazik placed a collect call to Michael Gerrano in Chicago and told him about Parker and about the closing of I-80. Then, when Schellenhof popped out of the room again, Wycazik said something that startled Parker: "Michael, maybe something'll happen to us, so you call Simon Zoderman at the *Tribune* the minute I hang up. Tell him everything. Blow it wide open. Tell Simon how Brendan ties in with Winton Tolk, the Halbourg girl, Calvin Sharkle, all of it. Tell him what happened out here in Nevada two summers ago, *what they saw.* If he finds it hard to believe, you tell him I believe it. He knows what a hard-headed customer I am."

When Father Wycazik hung up, Parker said, "Did I understand you right? My God, you know what happened to them on that July night?"

"I'm almost certain I do, yes," Father Wycazik said.

Before the priest could say more, Schellenhof returned in a gray blur of polyester. Now that his commission seemed real to him, he was obviously determined not to exceed Parker's time limit.

"You've got to tell me," Parker said to the priest.

"As soon as we're on our way," Father Wycazik promised.

Ned drove Jack's Cherokee eastward across the snowswept slopes, moving at a crawl. Sandy and Faye rode up front with him, leaning forward, peering anxiously through the windshield, helping Ned spot the obstacles in the chaotic whiteness ahead of them.

Riding in back—crowded in with Brendan and Jorja, with Marcie on her mother's lap—Ernie tried to convince himself that he would not succumb to panic when the last light of the storm-dimmed dusk gave way to darkness. Last night, when he'd snuggled under the covers in bed, staring at the shadows beyond the reach of the lamp's glow, his anxiety had been only a fraction of what he'd come to expect. He was improving.

Ernie also took hope from Dom's resurrected memory of jets buzzing the diner. If Dom could remember, so could Ernie. And when the memory block crumbled away, when at last he recalled what he'd seen that July night, he would stop being afraid of darkness.

"County road," Faye said as the Jeep came to a stop.

They had indeed reached the first county road, the same one that ran past the Tranquility and under I-80. The motel lay about two miles south, and Thunder Hill lay eight miles north along that ribbon of blacktop. It had been plowed already, and recently, because the federal government paid the county to keep the approach to the Depository open at all times.

"Quickly," Sandy urged Ned.

Ernie knew what she was thinking: Someone going from or to Thunder Hill might appear and accidentally discover them.

Gunning the engine, Ned drove hurriedly across the empty road, into the foothills on the other side, traversing a series of ruts with such haste that Brendan and Jorja were thrown repeatedly against Ernie, who sat between them. Once more, they took cover in the snow which fell like a storm of ashes from a coldly burning sky. Another north-south county artery—Vista Valley Road—lay six miles east, and that was where they were headed. Once there, they would turn south and go to a third county road that paralleled I-80 and that would carry them into Elko.

Ernie suddenly realized twilight was falling to the shadow armies of the night. Darkness had nearly stolen up on them. It was standing just a little way off, not in distance but in time, only a few minutes away, but he could see it watching them from billions of peepholes between billions of whirling snowflakes, creeping closer each time he blinked, soon to leap through the curtains of snow and seize him. . . .

No. There were too many other things worth fearing to waste energy on a nonsensical phobia. Even with a compass, they could get lost at night in this shrieking maelstrom. With visibility reduced to a few yards, they might drive off the edge of a ridge crest or into a rocky chasm, unaware of the hole until it swallowed them. Driving blindly to their own destruction was such a real threat that Ned could make no speed but could only nurse the Cherokee forward at a cautious crawl.

I fear what's worth fearing, Ernie told himself adamantly. I don't fear you, Darkness.

Faye looked over her shoulder from the front seat. He smiled and made an OK sign—only slightly shaky—with thumb and forefinger.

Faye started to give him an OK sign of her own, and that was when little Marcie screamed.

In his office along the wall of The Hub, deep inside Thunder Hill, Dr. Miles Bennell sat in darkness, thinking, worrying. The only light was the wan glow at two windows that faced into the central cavern of the Depository's second level, illumination insufficient to reveal any details of the room.

On the desk in front of him lay six sheets of paper. He'd read them twenty or thirty times during the past fifteen months; he did not need to read them again tonight to recall, word for word, what was typed on them. It was an illegally obtained printout of Leland Falkirk's psychological profile, stolen from the computer-stored personnel records of the elite Domestic Emergency Response Organization.

Miles Bennell—Ph.D. in biology and chemistry, dabbler in physics and anthropology, musician proficient on the guitar and piano, author of books as diverse as a text on neurohistology and a scholarly study of the works of John D. MacDonald, connoisseur of fine wine, aficionado of Clint Eastwood movies, the nearest thing to a late-twentieth-century Renaissance man—was among other things a computer hacker of formidable skill. He had begun adventuring through the complex worldwide network of electronic information systems when he had been a college student. Eighteen months ago, when his work on the Thunder Hill project threw him into frequent contact with Leland Falkirk, Miles Bennell had decided that the colonel was a psychologically disturbed individual who would have been declared unfit for military service even as a private—but for one thing: He was apparently one of those rare paranoids who had learned how to *use* his special brand of insanity to mold himself into a smoothly functioning machine-man who looked and acted normal enough. Miles had wanted to know more. What made Falkirk tick? What stimulus might make him explode unexpectedly?

The answers were to be found only at DERO headquarters. So sixteen months ago, Miles began using his personal terminal and modem to seek a route into DERO files in Washington.

The first time he'd read the profile, Miles had been frightened, though he had developed a thousand rationalizations for staying on the job even if it meant working with a dangerous and violent man like the colonel. There was less chance of trouble if Miles treated Falkirk with the coolness and grudging respect that a controlled paranoid would understand. You dared not be buddy-buddy with such a man—or flatter him—for he would assume you were hiding something. Polite disdain was the best attitude.

But now Miles was totally in Falkirk's power, sealed beneath the earth, to be judged and sentenced according to the colonel's warped view of guilt and innocence. He was scared sick.

The Army psychologist who'd written the profile was neither very well educated as psychologists went nor too perceptive. Nevertheless, though he had proclaimed the colonel more than fit enough for the elite DERO companies, he had noted peculiarities of the man's personality that made his report disturbing reading for Miles, who could read not only what was on the paper but what lay hidden between the lines.

First: Leland Falkirk feared and despised all religion. Because love of God and country were prized in career military men, Falkirk tried to conceal his antireligious sentiments. Evidently, these attitudes sprang from a difficult childhood in a family of fanatics.

Miles Bennell decided that this fault in Falkirk was especially troublesome because the current undertaking, in which he and the colonel were involved, had a multiplicity of mystical connotations. Aspects of it had undeniable religious overtones and associations that were certain to trigger intense negative reactions in the colonel.

Second: Leland Falkirk was obsessed with control. He *needed* to dominate every aspect of his environment and everyone he encountered. This urgent need to control the external world was a reflection of his constant internal struggle to control his own rages and paranoid fears.

Miles Bennell shuddered when he thought of the terrible strain this current assignment had put on the colonel, for the thing being hidden here in Thunder Hill could not be controlled forever. Which was a realization that might lead Falkirk to a harmless breakdown—or to an explosion of psychotic anger.

Third: Leland Falkirk suffered a mild but persistent claustrophobia that was strongest in subterranean places. This fear might have arisen in his childhood as a result of his parents' unrelenting assertion that he would one day wind up in Hell.

Falkirk, uncomfortable when underground, would be automatically suspicious of everyone in a place like Thunder Hill. In retrospect, it was frighteningly obvious that the colonel's growing paranoid suspicion of everyone on the project had been inevitable from the first day.

Fourth and worst: Leland Falkirk was a controlled masochist. He subjected himself to tests of physical stamina and resistance to pain, pretending these ordeals were necessary to maintain the high level of fitness and superb reflexes required of a DERO officer. His dirty little secret, hidden even from himself, was that he enjoyed the suffering.

Miles Bennell was more disturbed by that aspect of Falkirk's character than by anything else in the profile. Because the colonel liked pain, he would not mind suffering along with everyone in Thunder Hill if he decided their suffering was necessary to cleanse the world. He might actually *enjoy* the prospect of death.

Miles Bennell sat in darkness, troubled and bleak.

But it was not even his death or the deaths of his colleagues that most frightened him. What made his gut clench was the fear that, while destroying everyone on the project, Falkirk would also destroy the project itself. If he did, he would be denying mankind the greatest news in history. And he'd also be denying the species its best—perhaps only—chance for peace, immortality, endless plenty, and transcendence.

Leland Falkirk stood in the Blocks' kitchen, looking down at the album that lay on the table. When he opened it, he saw photographs and drawings of the moon, all colored red.

Outside, searching the property end to end, a dozen DERO troops shouted to one another, voices garbled and muffled by the raging wind.

Doing deep breathing exercises that were supposed to expel a little of his tension with each exhalation, Leland turned a page of the album and saw more scarlet moons: the child's weird collection.

The sound of engines rose to the kitchen window from behind the motel as the men drove at least two vehicles around from the front. Leland recognized the souped-up, all-terrain pickup's distinctive snarl.

The colonel continued to page through the album, remaining calm, totally in control in spite of the series of setbacks that continued to plague him. He was proud of his control. Nothing could faze him.

Lieutenant Horner's quick heavy footsteps sounded on the stairs leading up from the office. A moment later he thumped across the living room, into the kitchen. "Sir, we've checked all the motel rooms. No one's there. They left by the back, overland. Two *very* vague sets of tire tracks in the snow. Can't have gone far. Not in this weather, not already."

"Have you sent the men to follow them?"

"No, sir. But I had them pull the pickup and a Wagoneer around back. They're ready to go."

"Move them out," Leland said in a soft, measured tone.

"Don't worry, sir, we'll get our hands on them."

"I'm sure we will," Leland said, totally in control of himself, showing a firm and steady sense of command to his lieutenant. Horner turned and started to leave, and Leland said, "As soon as you've sent the men off, meet me downstairs with a county map. They'll intend to connect with a county or state road somewhere. We'll anticipate their next move and be waiting for them."

"Yes, sir," Horner said.

Alone, Leland calmly turned a page of the album. Red moons.

Horner's crashing footsteps reached the bottom of the stairs; then the front door slammed shut behind him, reverberating through the walls.

Calmly, so calmly, Leland turned a page in the album, and another.

Outside, Horner was shouting orders to the men.

Leland turned a page, another, another. Red moons.

Outside, engines revved. Eight men, in two parties of four, moved out on the trail of the escaped witnesses.

Leland calmly turned two, three, six pages, saw red moons and more red moons, and calmly picked up the album and threw it across the room. The book slammed into cupboards, bounced off the refrigerator, fell. A score of scarlet moons flew free and fluttered briefly. On a counter, Leland saw a ceramic jar: a smiling bear sitting with forepaws clasped over his tummy. He scooped it up, threw it to the floor, where it exploded in a hundred fragments. Broken chocolate-chip cookies landed atop the album and crumbled across the scattered red moons. He swept a radio off the counter, onto the floor. A canister of sugar. Flour. He pitched a breadbox against the wall and threw a Mr. Coffee machine at the oven.

He stood for a moment, breathing deeply, evenly. Then he turned and walked calmly out of the kitchen, went calmly down the stairs to the office, to calmly study the county map and calmly assess the situation with his lieutenant.

"The moon!" Marcie cried, then screamed shrilly again. "Mommy, look, look, the moon! Why, Mommy, why? Look, the *moon!*"

The girl suddenly tried to pull loose of her mother, wrenched and flailed. Jorja strove to hold on to her but was unsuccessful.

Startled by the screams, Ned had halted the Jeep.

Screaming again, Marcie tore loose of her mother, scrambled across Ernie, with no particular destination as far as Ernie could determine, with no intention but to escape from whatever she had seen in memory. She was apparently not aware that she was in the Cherokee but believed herself to be in another place altogether, a scary place.

Ernie grabbed her before she could scrabble and kick her way into Brendan's lap. He held the small child tightly in his big arms, held her against his chest, and as she continued to scream, he cooed soothingly to her.

Gradually, Marcie's terror subsided. She stopped struggling and went limp in his arms. She stopped screaming, too, and merely chanted softly: "Moon, the moon, moon. . . ." And quietly, but with terrible dread: "Don't let it get me, don't let it, don't let it."

"Be still, honey," Ernie said, patting her, stroking her hair, "be still, you're safe, I won't let it get you."

"She remembered something," Brendan said as Ned drove forward again. "A crack opened for just a moment."

"What did you see, baby?" Jorja asked her daughter.

The girl had slipped back into her deep catatonic glaze, unhearing, unheeding . . . except that, after a while, Ernie felt her arms tighten around him in a hug. He hugged her in return. She said nothing. She was still not really with them, adrift on a dark inner sea. Evidently, however, she felt safe in Ernie's bearish embrace, and she held fast to him as the Cherokee rocked and lurched through the snowy night.

After months of living in fear of every shadow, after regarding each oncoming twilight with despair and horror, Ernie felt indescribably good, delighted that someone needed *his* strength. It was profoundly satisfying. And as he held her and murmured to her and stroked her thick black hair, he was oblivious of the fact that night now surrounded the Cherokee and pressed its face to the windows.

Eventually, Jack turned the pickup east and finally connected with the county road to Thunder Hill at a point approximately one mile north of the place where Ned should have already crossed the same lane in the Cherokee. He turned right and headed up toward the Depository, the route that Dom and Ernie had covered this morning.

He had never seen a storm this bad back East. The higher he went into the mountains, the harder and faster the snow came down. It was as dense as a heavy rainfall.

"The entrance to the Depository is about a mile ahead," Dom said.

Jack cut the headlights and proceeded at a slower pace. Until his eyes adjusted to the loss of light, the world seemed composed only of whirling white specks and darkness.

He could not always tell if he was in his own lane. He expected another vehicle to hurtle out of the night and ram him head-on.

Evidently Ginger had the same thought, for she shrank down in her seat as if for protection in a crash. She nervously bit her lower lip.

"Those lights ahead," Dom said. "The entrance to the Depository."

Two mercury-vapor lamps blazed on poles flanking the electric gate. A warmer amber glow shone in the two narrow windows of the guardhouse.

Even with those lights, Jack could see only a vague outline of the small building on the far side of the fence, for the falling snow masked all details. He felt confident that, with no headlights, the pickup would be invisible to any guard who might happen to look out a window as the truck drifted past on the county lane. Their engine noise would be swallowed by the wind.

They rolled slowly up the steep slope, deeper into the night and mountains. The windshield wipers were doing a poorer job by the moment, for snow had clogged the blades and turned to ice.

When they had gone a mile past the entrance to Thunder Hill, Ginger said, "Maybe we could turn the lights on now."

Hunching over the wheel, squinting into the gloom ahead, Jack said, "No. We'll go in darkness all the way."

In the motel office, Leland Falkirk and Lieutenant Horner unfolded the county map on the check-in counter. They were still studying it when the men who had gone after the escaping witnesses returned in defeat, only minutes after departing. The search party had followed the tire tracks a couple of hundred yards through a glen running north into the hills, at which point the snow and wind erased the trail. However, there was some evidence that at least one vehicle had turned into another hollow leading east, and since there seemed no reason for the witnesses to split up, it was assumed both the Sarvers' pickup and the Cherokee were now headed in that general direction.

Returning his attention to the map, Leland said, "It makes sense. They wouldn't go west. Nothing's out there until Battle Mountain, forty miles away, then Winnemucca over fifty miles farther. Neither town's big enough to hide in for long. And neither's exactly a transportation hub; aren't many ways out. So they'll go east, into Elko."

Lieutenant Horner put a cigar-sized finger on the map. "Here's the road that runs past the motel and up to Thunder Hill. They'll have crossed that by now and still be heading east."

"What's the next southbound road they'll come to?"

Lieutenant Horner bent down to read the small print on the map. "Vista Valley. Looks to be about six miles east of the road to Thunder Hill."

A knock sounded, and Miles Bennell said, "Come in."

General Robert Alvarado, CO of Thunder Hill, opened the door and entered the dark office in a swath of silvery light that came with him from The Hub and coated a portion of the room in an imitation of frost. He said, "Sitting alone in the dark, huh? Just imagine how suspicious that would seem to Colonel Falkirk."

"He's a madman, Bob."

"Not long ago," Bob Alvarado said, "I'd have argued that he was a fairly good officer, though a bit too by-the-book and much too gung-ho. But tonight, I have to agree with you. The man's only got one oar in the water. Maybe no oars.

I just got a request from him a few minutes ago, by telephone. Supposed to be a request, but it was phrased like an order. He wants the entire staff, all military men and all civilians, to report to their quarters and stay there until further notice. You'll hear my order on the public address system in a couple minutes."

"But why's he want that?" Miles asked.

Alvarado sat in a chair near the open door, the frosty swath of light falling across his feet and up to the middle of his chest, leaving his face in darkness. "Falkirk's bringing in the witnesses and doesn't want them to be seen by any of our people who don't already know about them. Or that's what he claims is behind the request."

Astonished, Miles said, "But if the time's come to put them through another memory-scrub, it's better to keep them at the motel. Though as far as I know, he's not called in the damn brain-fuckers."

"He hasn't," Bob Alvarado confirmed. "He says the cover-up might not be continued. He wants you to study the witnesses, especially Cronin and Corvaisis. He says maybe he's right, maybe they're not human any more. But he says he's been thinking over his conversation with you, wondering if maybe *you* could be right and maybe he's too paranoid about this. He says if you decide they're fully human, if you determine that their gifts are not evidence of an inhuman presence within them, he'll accept your word; he'll spare them. Then, so he says, he might decide against another brainwashing session and even recommend to his superiors that the whole story be revealed to the public."

Miles was silent a moment. Then he shifted in his chair, more uneasy than ever. "It sounds as if he's finally got some common sense. Why do I find that so hard to believe? Do you think it's true?"

Alvarado reached out from his chair, pushed the door shut, plunging the room into darkness. Sensing Miles reaching for the lamp switch, he said, "Let's keep it this way, huh? Maybe it's a little easier to be frank with each other when we can't see faces." Miles settled back in his chair, leaving the lamp unlit, and Alvarado said, "Tell me, Miles, was it you who sent the photographs to Corvaisis and the Blocks?"

Miles said nothing.

"We're friends, you and I," Alvarado said. "At least I've felt we are. I never met another guy I could enjoy playing *both* chess and poker with. So I'll tell you . . . I'm the one who got Jack Twist back here."

Startled, Miles said, "How? Why?"

"Well, like you, I knew some of the witnesses were slowly shedding their memory blocks and having psychological problems in the process. So before anyone could decide to wipe them again one by one, I figured to do something to focus their attention on the motel. I hoped to stir up enough trouble to make it impossible to continue the cover-up."

"Why?" Miles repeated.

"Because I'd finally decided the cover-up was wrong."

"But why sabotage it by such a back-door approach?" Miles asked.

"Because if I'd gone public, I'd have been disobeying orders. I'd have been throwing my career away, maybe my pension. And besides . . . I thought Falkirk might kill me."

Miles had worried about the same thing.

Alvarado said, "I started with Twist because I thought his Ranger background and his inclination to challenge authority would make him a good candidate for organizing the other witnesses. From the information turned up during his memory-wipe session that summer, I knew about his safe-deposit boxes. So I searched the file on him, got the names of the banks, the passwords. The file also contained copies of all the keys to his boxes; Falkirk had them made in case it was ever necessary to turn up criminal evidence against Twist to use as blackmail or to put him out of the way in prison. I made copies of the copies. Then, when I was on leave for ten days in late December, I went to New York with a bunch of postcards of the Tranquility Motel, and I put one in each of his boxes. He didn't go to those banks often, just a few times a year, and they've all got thousands of safe-deposit customers, so nobody remembered what Twist looked like or suspected that I wasn't him. It was easy.''

"And ingenious," Miles said, staring with admiration and fondness at the bulky, shadowy form of his friend. "Finding those cards would've electrified Twist. And if Falkirk had gotten wind of it, he'd have no way of knowing who'd done it."

"Especially since I always handled the postcards with gloves," Alvarado said. "Didn't even leave a fingerprint. I planned to come back here, give Twist time to find them. Then I was going to go into Elko and, from a pay phone, make a couple of anonymous calls to other witnesses, give them Twist's unlisted number, tell them he had answers to their various mental problems. That would've set the ball rolling pretty well. But before it got that far, someone else had sent notes and Polaroids to Corvaisis, more Polaroids to the Blocks, and a new crisis was already underway. Like Falkirk, I know whoever sent those pictures has to be here in Thunder Hill. You going to fess up, or am I the only one in a confessional mood?''

Miles hesitated. His glance fell upon the vague grayness of the report on his desk: Falkirk's psychological profile. He shuddered and said, "Yeah, Bob, I sent the pictures. Great minds think alike, huh?''

From his own pocket of darkness, Alvarado said, "I told you why I picked Twist. And I can figure why you'd want to stir up the Blocks, since they're local and sort of at the center of everything. But why'd you pick Corvaisis instead of one of the others?''

"He's a writer, which means a vivid imagination. Anonymous notes and odd pictures in the mail would probably grab his interest a little faster and tighter than anyone else's. And his first novel has had tremendous prepublication publicity, so if he dug up some of the truth, reporters might be more likely to listen to him than to the others.''

"We're a clever pair.''

"Too clever for our own good," Miles said. "Looks like sabotaging the cover-up was too slow. We should've just violated our secrecy oaths and gone public with the news, even if it meant risking Falkirk's anger and government prosecution.''

They were silent a moment, and then Alvarado said, "Why do you think I've come here and opened up to you like this, Miles?''

"You need an ally against the colonel. Because you don't think he meant a word of what he told you on the phone. You don't think he's suddenly gotten reasonable. You don't think he's bringing the witnesses back here to let us study them.''

"He's going to kill them, I think," Alvarado said. "And us, too. All of us.''

"Because he thinks we've all been taken over. The damn fool.''

The public address system crackled, whistled. A speaker was set in the wall of Miles's office, as in every room within the Depository. The announcement followed the whistle: All personnel, military and civilian, were to report first to the armory to be issued handguns, then to their quarters to await further instructions.

Getting up from his chair, Alvarado said, "When they're all in their quarters, I'll tell them it was Falkirk's idea to put them there but my idea to arm them. I'll warn them that, for reasons that'll be clear to some and a mystery to others, we're all in danger from Falkirk and his DEROs. Later, if the colonel sends some of his men to round up the staff and shoot them all, my people will be able to shoot back. I hope we can stop him before it goes that far.''

"Do I get a handgun, too?"

Alvarado moved to the door but did not open it. Standing in the dark, he said, "You especially. Wear a lab coat with the gun under it, so Falkirk won't see you're armed. I intend to wear my uniform coat unbuttoned, with a small pistol tucked into the back of my waistband, so he won't realize I'm armed, either. If it seems he's about to order our destruction, I'll pull the gun and kill him. But I'll alert you first, with a code word, so you can turn on Horner and kill him, too. It's no good unless we get both, because if Horner has a chance, he'll kill me when I open fire on Falkirk. And it's imperative I survive, not just because I'm inordinately fond of my own hide, which I am, but because I'm a *general,* and I ought to be able to make Falkirk's men obey me once their CO's dead. Can you do that? Can you kill a man, Miles?"

"Yes. I'll be able to pull the trigger if it means stopping Horner. I consider *you* a good friend, too, Bob. Not just because of the poker and chess, either. There's also the fact that you've actually read all of T. S. Eliot."

" 'I think we are in rats' alley, Where the dead men lost their bones,' " Bob Alvarado quoted. Laughing softly, he pulled the door open and stood revealed in the argentine glow of the cavern lights. "How ironic. Ages ago, my daddy used to worry that my interest in poetry was a sign I'd grow up to be a skirt-wearing sissy. Instead, I became a one-star general, and in the hour of my greatest need, it's poetry that persuades you to kill for me and save my ass. Coming to the armory, Dr. Bennell?"

Miles rose from his chair and joined the general in the spill of frosty light in the doorway. He said, "You realize that Falkirk is, in essence, acting in the name of the Army Chief of Staff himself and even higher authorities. So after you've killed him, you'll have General Riddenhour and maybe even the President coming down hard on your neck."

"Fuck Riddenhour," Bob Alvarado said, clapping a hand on Miles's shoulder. "Fuck all the politicians and their toadying generals like Riddenhour. Even though Falkirk will take the security computer's new codes with him when we kill him, we'll get out of here in a few days, even if we have to dismantle the damn exit. And then . . . do you realize, when we take the news to the world, we're going to be two of the most famous men on this sorry planet? Maybe two of the most famous men in history. Fact is, I can't think of anyone in history who had quite such important news to spread . . . except Mary Magdalene on Easter Morning.''

Father Stefan Wycazik drove the Cherokee because he had experience with four-wheel-drive vehicles from his service with Father Bill Nader in Vietnam. Of course, those adventures had been laid in swamp and jungle, not in a blizzard. But he discovered the Jeep handled about the same in either condition. And though his daredevil experiences were long ago in time, they seemed recent in his heart and mind, and he controlled the wheel with the same reckless disregard for danger and sure-handed expertise that he'd shown in his younger days, under fire. As he and Parker Faine headed away from the lights of Elko into the snow-blasted night, Father Wycazik knew that God had called him to the priesthood precisely because, at times, the Church required a man who carried a thick splinter of an adventurer's soul lodged in his own.

Because I-80 was closed, they went north on State Route 51. They switched to a series of westward-leading county roads—macadam, gravel, dirt, all under a mantle of snow. The roads were marked by cat's-eye-yellow reflectors on widely spaced posts along the berm, and the luster of those periodic guideposts, casting back the headlight beams, was frequently the only thing that kept Stefan from going astray. Sometimes, he had to drive overland to get from one lane to another. Fortunately, they had bought a dash-mounted compass and a county map. Although their route was winding and rough, they made steady progress in the general direction of the Tranquility Motel.

On the way, Stefan told Parker about the CISG, about which he had learned from Michael Gerrano, after Michael had gotten the news from Mr. X, Ginger Weiss's friend. "Colonel Falkirk was the only military member. The CISG looks like a typical waste of tax dollars: a study group funded to do a think-tank-type assessment of a social problem that would most likely never arise. The committee consisted of biologists, physicists, cultural anthropologists, medical doctors, sociologists, psychologists. The acronym CISG stands for Contact Impact Study Group, which means they tried to determine the positive and negative impact on human society of first contact with an intelligent species not of this world."

Keeping his eyes on the snowy road, Stefan paused to let his meaning sink in, smiled slightly when he heard the artist take a sudden sharp breath. Parker said, "You don't mean . . . you couldn't mean . . ."

"Yes," Stefan said.

"Something came . . . you mean that . . . something . . ." For the first time in Stefan Wycazik's acquaintance, Parker Faine was speechless.

"Yes," Stefan said. Although this amazing development was no longer news to him, he still shivered at the thought of it, and he appreciated what Parker was feeling. "Something came down that night. Something came down from the sky on July sixth."

"Jesus!" Parker exclaimed. "Uh, sorry, Father. Didn't mean to be blasphemous. Came down. Holy shit. Sorry. Really. But . . . *Jesus!*"

Following cat's-eye reflectors along an especially twisty gravel road that hugged the lower contours of folded and refolded hills, Father Wycazik said, "Under the circumstances, I don't think God's grading you on verbal restraint. The CISG's primary purpose was to arrive at a consensus of how human cultures—and human beings themselves—would be affected by face-to-face contact with extraterrestrials."

"But that's an easy question to answer. What a joyous, wondrous thing to discover we're not alone!" Parker said. "You and I know how people would react. Look how they've been fascinated by movies about other worlds and aliens for decades now!"

"Yes," Stefan said, "but there's a difference how they react to fictional contact and how they might react to the reality. At least that's the opinion of many scientists, especially in the soft sciences like sociology and psychology. And anthropologists tell us that when an advanced culture interacts with one less advanced, the less advanced culture suffers a loss of confidence in—and often a complete collapse of—its traditions, institutions. The primitive culture loses respect for its religions and systems of government. Its sexual practices, social values, and family structures deteriorate. Look what happened to the Eskimos following their encounter with Western civilization: soaring alcoholism, family-destroying generational conflict, a high rate of suicide. . . . It's not that Western culture is dangerous or evil. It isn't. But our culture was far more sophisticated and richly textured than the Eskimo culture, and contact led to a serious loss of self-esteem among the Eskimos that they've never regained and never will."

Stefan had to pause in his elaboration of the issue, for they came to the end of the gravel track on which they had been traveling.

Parker studied the map in the dim glow of the glove-compartment light. Then he checked the dash-mounted compass. "That way," he said, pointing left. "We go three miles due west, all of it overland. Then we'll come to a north-south county route called . . . Vista Valley Road. We cross Vista Valley, and from there it looks about eight or nine miles, overland again, until we might come up behind the Tranquility."

"You keep checking the compass, make sure I stay pointed west." Stefan drove the Cherokee into the snow-shrouded nightscape ahead.

Parker said, "This stuff about the Eskimos, all this detail about what the CISG's point of view is like—Mr. X didn't pass all these fine points along to Father Gerrano in one telephone call."

"Some of it; not all of it."

"So I gather you've thought about the subject before."

"Not about extraterrestrial contact, no," Father Wycazik said. "But part of Jesuit education involves a hard look at both the good and bad results of the Church's efforts to spread the faith to backward cultures throughout history. The general feeling is we did a disturbing amount of damage even as we brought enlightenment. Anyway, we study a lot of anthropology, so I can understand the concern of the CISG."

"You're drifting north. Angle left as soon as the land will let you," Parker said, checking the compass. "Listen, I'm still not sure *I* understand the CISG's concern."

"Consider the American Indian. Ultimately, the white man's guns didn't destroy them; the clash of cultures did them in; the influx of new ideas forced the Indians to view their comparatively primitive societies from a different perspective, resulting in a loss of esteem, a loss of cultural validity and direction. According to what Mr. X told Father Gerrano, the CISG believed contact between mankind and *very* advanced extraterrestrials could have those same effects on us: the destruction of religious faith, a loss of faith in all governments and other secular belief-systems, a rising feeling of inferiority, suicide."

Parker Faine made a harsh scoffing sound in the back of his throat. "Father, would your faith collapse because of this?"

"No. Just the opposite," Stefan said excitedly. "If this enormous universe didn't contain any other life, if the trillions of stars and billions of planets were all barren of life—*that* might make me think there was no God, that our species' evolution was just happenstance. Because if there's a God, He loves life, cherishes life and all the creatures He created, and He'd never leave the universe so empty."

"A lot of people—most people—would feel the same," Parker said.

"And even if the species we encounter is frighteningly different from us in physical appearance, that wouldn't shake me. When God told us He created us in His image, He didn't mean our physical appearance was like His. He meant our souls, minds, our capacity for reason and compassion, love, friendship: *Those* are the aspects of humanity that are in His image. Which is the message I'm taking to Brendan. I believe Brendan's crisis of faith was related to a memory of an encounter with a race vastly different from us—and so shatteringly superior to us—that he subconsciously believed it put the lie to what the Church teaches us about mankind being in God's image. I want to tell him that it's not what they look like that matters or whether they're far more advanced than us. What indicates the divine hand in them is their capacity to love, to care—and to use their God-given intelligence to triumph over the challenges of the universe that He gave them."

"Which they've had to do in order to come so far," Parker said.

"Exactly!" Father Wycazik said. "I'm sure when the brainwashing loses its hold on Brendan, when he remembers what happened and has time to think about it, he'll come to the same conclusion. But just in case, I want to be there beside him, to help him, guide him."

"You love him very much," Parker said.

For several seconds, Father Wycazik squinted into the tumultuous white world ahead, progressing more slowly and cautiously than when he'd been following the reflectors along a known road. At last he said, in a soft voice: "Sometimes I've regretted entering the priesthood. God help me, it's true. Because sometimes I think about the family I might have had: a wife whose life I could share, who'd share mine, and children to watch grow. . . . The family that might have been— that's what I miss. Nothing else. The thing about Brendan is . . . well, he's the son I never had and never will. I love him more than I can say."

After a while, Parker sighed and said, "Personally, I think the CISG was full of crap. First contact wouldn't destroy us."

"I agree," Stefan said. "Their fallacy lies in comparing this situation to our contact with primitive cultures. The difference is that *we* aren't primitive. This will be the contact between one very advanced culture and another *super*-advanced culture. The CISG believed if there ever was contact it'd have to be concealed, if at all possible, and that news of it would have to be broken to the public over ten or even twenty years. But that's wrong, dead wrong, Parker. We can handle the shock. Because we're ready for them to come. Oh, dear God, but we are so desperately and longingly ready for them!"

"So ready," Parker agreed in a whisper.

For perhaps another minute they bumped and rocked along in silence, unable to speak, unable to put in words exactly what it felt like to know that mankind did not stand alone in creation.

Finally, Parker cleared his throat, checked the compass, and said, "You're right on course, Stefan. Ought to be less than a mile to Vista Valley Road. This man in Chicago that you mentioned a while ago . . . Cal Sharkle. What was it he yelled to the cops this morning?"

"He insisted he'd seen aliens land and that they were hostile. He was afraid they were taking us over, that most of his neighbors had been possessed. He said the aliens tried to take control of him by strapping him in a bed and dripping themselves into his veins. Initially, I was afraid maybe he was right, that what had come down here in Nevada was a threat. But on the trip from Chicago, I had time to think about it. He was confusing his incarceration and brainwashing with the landing of the starship he'd seen. He thought it was aliens in pressurized space suits who'd kept him captive and stuck him full of needles. He witnessed the descent of a starship, and then these government men in decontamination suits came, and by the time they'd rammed all that stuff into his subconscious and weighted it down with a memory block, he was completely mixed up. No aliens apprehended him. It was his fellow men who mistreated him."

"You're saying government agents would've worn decontamination suits until it was clear whether or not the alien contact carried a risk of bacteriological contamination."

"Exactly," Stefan said. "Some guests at the Tranquility must've approached the ship openly, so they had to be considered contaminated until evidence to the contrary was turned up. And we know some at the motel have distinctly remembered *men* inside decontamination suits: a few soldiers, brainwashing specialists. So poor Calvin was driven insane by a misconception arising from his inability to remember clearly."

"Must be less than half a mile to Vista Valley Road," Parker said, studying the map in the light from the open glove-compartment door.

Snow drove relentlessly through the yellow cones of the headlights. Now and then, when the wind faltered or briefly changed the angle of its assault, short-lived forms of snow capered in arabesque dances, this way and that, but always dispersing and vanishing like ghostly performers the moment that the wind recovered its momentum and purpose.

As they started up a steep slope, Parker said softly, "Something came down. . . . And if the government knew enough to close I-80 ahead of the event, they must've been tracking the craft a long time. But I still don't see how they could know where it would come down. I mean, the crew of the ship might've changed its course at any time."

"Unless it was crashing," Father Wycazik said. "Maybe it was picked up by satellite observation far out in space, monitored for days or weeks. If it approached on an undeviating course that would indicate it wasn't traveling under control, there'd have been time to calculate its point of impact."

"Oh, no. No. I don't want to think it crashed," Parker said.

"Nor do I."

"I want to think they got here alive . . . all that way."

When the Jeep Cherokee was halfway up the slope, the tires spun on an especially icy patch of ground, then caught hold and propelled them forward again with a jolt.

Parker said, "I want to believe Dom and the others didn't just see a ship . . . but encountered whoever came in it. Imagine. Just imagine . . ."

Father Wycazik said, "Whatever happened to them that night in July was very strange indeed, a whole lot stranger than just seeing a ship from another world."

"You mean . . . because of Brendan's and Dom's powers?"

"Yes. Something more happened, more than just contact."

They topped the crest of the hill and started down the other side. Even through shifting curtains of the storm, Stefan saw the headlights of four vehicles on Vista Valley Road below. All four were stopped and angled every which way, and their blazing beams crisscrossed like gleaming sabers in the snow-bleeding darkness.

As he drove down toward the gathering, he quickly realized that he was heading into trouble.

"Machine guns!" Parker said.

Stefan saw that two of the men below were holding submachine guns on a group of seven people—six adults and one child—who were lined up against the side of a Cherokee that was different only in color from the one Parker had just bought. Eight or ten other men were standing around, a substantial force, obviously military because they were all dressed in the same Arctic-issue uniforms. Stefan had no doubt that these were some of the same forces involved in the closure of I-80 both tonight and eighteen months ago.

They had turned toward him and were staring uphill, surprised at being interrupted.

He wanted to swing the Jeep around, gun the engine, and flee, but although he slowed down, he knew there was no point in running. They would come after him.

Abruptly, he recognized a familiar Irish face among those lined up against the Cherokee. "That's him, Parker! That's Brendan on the end of the lineup."

"The others must be from the motel," Parker said, leaning forward to peer anxiously through the windshield. "But I don't see Dom."

Now that he had spotted Brendan, Father Wycazik could not have turned back even if God had opened the mountains for him and provided a highway clear to

Canada, as He had parted the Red Sea for Moses. On the other hand, Stefan was unarmed. And as a priest, he would have had little use for a gun even if he had possessed one. Having neither the means nor desire to attack, yet unable to run, he let the Cherokee roll slowly down the hill as he frantically wracked his mind for some course of action that would turn the tables on the soldiers below.

The same concern had gripped Parker, for he said, "What in the devil are we going to do?"

Their dilemma was resolved by the soldiers below. To Stefan's astonishment, one of the men with a machine gun opened fire on them.

Dom watched as Jack Twist directed the flashlight beam over the chainlink fence, then up to the barbed-wire overhang that thrust out above their heads. They were at that long length of Thunder Hill's perimeter that ran through an open meadow, down toward the floor of the valley. Windblown snow had stuck to large sections of the thick, interlocking steel loops of the fence, but other areas were bare, and those uncrusted links were what Jack studied most closely.

"The fence itself isn't electrified," Jack said above the shrieking wind. "There aren't conducting wires woven through it, and the current can't be carried by the links. No way. There'd be just too damn much resistance because they're too thick and because the ends of some of them don't make tight contact with each other."

Ginger said, "Then why the warning signs?"

"Partly to spook away amateurs," Jack said. He put the beam of the flash on the overhang again. "However, there *are* conducting wires strung carefully through the center of that barbed-wire roll, so you'd get fried if you went over the top. We'll cut through the bottom."

Ginger held the flashlight while Dom dug into one of the canvas rucksacks, found the acetylene torch, and passed it to Jack.

After he had slipped on a pair of tinted ski goggles, Jack lit the torch and began to cut an entrance through the chainlink barrier. The fierce hissing of the burning gas was audible even above the keening, moaning wind. The intense blue-white acetylene flame cast an eerie light that struck a thousand jewel-bright glints in the snow.

They were not at a position where they risked being seen from the main entrance of the Depository, which lay over the brow of a hill that sloped up from the other side of the fence. However, Dom was sure the weird acetylene light reached high enough into the night to be spotted from the other side of that rise. If seen, it would draw guards this way. But if Jack was right, if the Depository's security was largely electronic, there would not be guards prowling the grounds tonight; and in this weather, surveillance by video cameras was pretty much ruled out, too, for their lenses would be iced-over or packed with snow.

Of course, though they wanted to get inside the Depository and have a quick look around, it would not be a tragedy if they were apprehended here. After all, being taken into custody was part of Jack's plan for focusing attention on Thunder Hill.

Dom, Ginger, and Jack were not armed. All the weapons had been for the others, in the Cherokee, because their escape was essential. If they were stopped, all was lost. Dom hoped they wouldn't need their guns, and that they were already safely in Elko.

As Jack cut a crawl-through opening in the fence, the eldritch light of the acetylene torch increasingly captivated Dom and, suddenly, made a connection with the past, hurtling him back once more in memory:

The third jet roared over the roof of the diner, so low that he threw himself flat on the parking lot, certain the airplane was crashing on top of him, but it swooped past, leaving shattered air and a blast of engine heat in its wake; he started to get

*up, and a fourth jet boomed over the roof of the motel, a huge half-glimpsed shad-
owy shape, its running lights carving white and red wounds through the night as it
thundered south and angled east, out across the barrens beyond I-80, where the
third jet had gone, and now the first two craft, which had passed over at a greater
altitude, were far out there, swinging back, one to the east and one to the west; yet
still the earth shook and the night was filled with a great rumble like an ongoing and
never-ending explosion, and he thought there must be more jets coming, even
though the queer electronic oscillation that had throbbed under the roar was now
getting louder and shriller and stranger and was unlike anything jets would produce; he shoved up onto his feet and turned, and there was Ginger Weiss and Jorja
and Marcie, and there was Jack running over from the motel, and Ernie and Faye
coming out from the office, and others, all the others, Ned and Sandy; the rumble
was now like the crash of Niagara Falls combined with the base-throb pounding of
a thousand timpani; the ululant electronic whistle made him feel as if the top of his
head was going to be sliced off by a bandsaw; there was frost-silver light of a peculiar kind; he looked up, away from the jets that had gone past, over the roof of the
diner, looked up toward the light; he pointed and said, ''The moon! The moon!''
Others looked where he pointed; he was filled with a sudden terror, and he cried,
''The moon! The moon!'' and staggered back several steps in surprise and fear;
someone screamed. . . .*

"The moon!" he gasped.

He was down in the snow, driven to his knees by the shock of the memory-
flash, and Ginger was kneeling in front of him, holding him by the shoulders.
"Dom? Dom, are you okay?"

"Remembered," he said numbly as the wind rushed between their faces and
tore their smoking breath out of their mouths. "Something . . . the moon . . . but
I didn't quite get enough."

Beyond them, having cut a crawl-through in the chainlink fence, Jack switched off
the acetylene torch. The darkness folded around them again like the wings of a great
bat.

"Come on," Jack said, turning to Dom and Ginger. "Let's go in. Quickly now."

"Can you make it?" Ginger asked Dom.

"Yeah," he said, though there was an icy cramping in his guts and a tightness
in his chest. "But all of a sudden . . . I'm scared."

"We're all scared," she said.

"I don't mean scared of getting caught. No. It's something else. Something I
almost remembered just then. And I'm . . . shaking like a leaf, for God's sake."

Brendan gasped in disbelief when Colonel Falkirk ordered one of his men to open
fire on the Jeep that was approaching Vista Valley Road from the hillside above.
The madman didn't know who was in the vehicle. The soldier given the order
also thought it was out of line, for he did not immediately raise his weapon. But
Falkirk took a menacing step toward him and shouted: "I told you to open fire,
Corporal! This is an urgent national security matter. Whoever's in that vehicle is
no friend of yours, mine, or our country. You think any innocent civilians would
be driving overland, sneaking around the roadblock, in a goddamn blizzard like
this? Fire! Waste them!"

This time, the corporal obeyed. The clatter of automatic gunfire hammered the
night, briefly overpowering the voice of the raging wind. Up on the hillside, the
headlights of the oncoming Jeep blew out. The two hundred hard cracks of two
hundred bullets erupting in a murderous stream from the muzzle of the machine
gun were augmented by the sound of slugs tearing through sheet metal and smack-

ing onto more solid barriers. The windshield imploded under raining lead, and the Jeep, which had braked immediately after topping the crest of the hill and had been descending slowly, abruptly gained speed and rushed down at them, then angled left when its wheels jolted over a lateral hump that extended across most of the slope. Obviously no longer under anyone's control, it started to slow again, hit another bump, slid sideways, almost tipped over, almost rolled, but finally came to rest just forty feet away in the already drifting snow.

Five minutes ago, when Ned had driven over the hill on the *other* side of Vista Valley Road and had turned south, only to encounter the colonel and his men waiting less than a half-mile south, it had been instantly clear that all the shotguns and handguns—and even the Uzi that Jack had provided—would be of no help. Considering that their lives depended on their escape from Elko County, they would have made a stand against a smaller force. But Falkirk was accompanied by too many men, all heavily armed. Resistance would have been purest folly.

And Brendan had been filled with frustration because he had not dared use his special power to ensure their freedom. He felt he ought to be able to apply his telekinetic talent to the situation. If he concentrated hard enough, perhaps he could cause the guns to fly out of the soldiers' hands. He sensed he had that much— and more—power in him, but he did not know how to bring it to bear effectively. He could not forget how the experiment in the diner had gotten entirely out of hand last night; they had been fortunate that none of them had been hurt by the careening salt and pepper shakers, and the violently levitating chairs. If he used his power to wrench the weapons from the soldiers, he might not be able to disarm all of them simultaneously, in which case the ones still in possession of their weapons might open fire in self-defense. Or at his instigation, the guns might tear free of the soldiers' hands and go whirling through the air, out of control— firing until their magazines had emptied, pumping bullets into everything and everyone in sight. Sure, he might be able to heal the wounded. But what if he was shot? Could he heal himself? Probably. But if he was shot *dead?* He would not be able to bring himself back to life. And if anyone else was shot dead, he was not sure he would be able to bring them back, either. It was no good being gifted with the power of a god if no clear instructions came with the blessing.

Now, watching scores of bullets slam into the Jeep, watching it rush like a crazed and blinded beast down the hillside, seeing it come to a shuddering stop in the headlight beams of one of the vehicles on Vista Valley Road, Brendan felt his frustration ballooning beyond containment. The occupants of the Jeep had been hit. He could help them. He knew he could help them, and it was his duty to do so, not merely the duty of a priest but the minimal duty of a human being. He did not understand his healing power, either, but there was no greater danger in trying to use it than there was in attempting to employ telekinesis. So he thrust away from the Cherokee against which he had been standing, dashed through the group of soldiers whose attention had been distracted by the drama on the hillside, and ran toward the blasted Jeep even as it came to a stop.

There were shouts behind him. He distinctly heard Falkirk warning him that he would be shot.

Brendan ran anyway, slipping on the snowy pavement. He stepped into a ditch, fell, scrambled up, ran on to the bullet-riddled Jeep.

No one fired, but he sensed people sprinting after him.

The passenger's side of the Jeep was nearest, bathed in a beam of light from one of the military vehicles, so he pulled open that door first. A stocky man of about fifty, wearing a navy peacoat, was slumped against the door and fell out into Brendan's arms. Brendan saw blood, but not a lot. The stranger was conscious, though on the precarious edge of a faint; his eyes were unfocused. Brendan pulled him all the way out of the Jeep and lowered him gently onto his back on the snow-covered ground.

A pursuing soldier put a hand on Brendan's shoulder, and Brendan whirled on him, screamed in his face: "Get away from me, you rotten-crazy son of a bitch! I'll heal him! I'll *heal* him!" Then he vented an oath of such a vicious, ferocious, and filthy nature that he was astounded to hear it pass his lips. He hadn't known he could use such obscene language. The soldier, thrown into an instantaneous fury, swung his machine gun high, intending to slam the butt into Brendan's face.

"Wait!" Falkirk shouted, stepping in and grabbing his man's arm to halt the blow. The colonel turned to Brendan and regarded him with eyes like polished flint. "Go ahead. I want to see this. I want to see you incriminate yourself right in front of me."

"Incriminate?" Brendan said. "What're you talking about?"

"Go ahead," the colonel said.

Brendan waited for no more encouragement but knelt at once beside the wounded man and threw the flaps of his peacoat wide open. Blood was soaking through the sweater in two places: just below the left shoulder; and low on the right side, a couple of inches above the beltline. He rolled up the victim's sweater, tore open the shirt beneath. Brendan put his hands on the abdominal wound first, for that appeared the worse of the two. He didn't know what to do next. He could not recall what he'd thought or felt when he had healed Emmy and Winton. What triggered the healing power? He knelt in the snow, feeling the stranger's blood oozing between his fingers, acutely sensitive to the life throbbing out of the man, yet unable to concentrate the miraculous power he *knew* was in him. Frustration filled him again, turned to anger, and the anger turned to rage at his own impotence and stupidity, at the injustice of death, this death specifically and all death in general—

A tingle. In each palm.

He knew the red circles had appeared again, but he did not lift his hands from the victim to look at those stigmata.

Please, he thought desperately, please let it happen, let the healing happen, please.

Amazingly, for the first time Brendan actually felt the mysterious energy flowing from him into the wounded man. It took shape in him and raveled out of him as if he were a spinning wheel and as if the wondrous power were the thread that he created. He *whirled* it into existence in the same manner by which the formless mass on the distaff was drawn into a strong filament of thread by the action of a spinning wheel, and the wounded man was the spindle onto which this power wound itself. But Brendan was not merely a single machine producing one meager thread; he felt, within himself, a thousand-million wheels flashing round and round so fast they whistled and hissed as they spewed out a thousand-million insubstantial and invisible—yet binding, strongly binding—filaments.

He was a loom, as well, for somehow he used the countless threads of godlike power to weave a cloth of health. Unlike his experiences with Emmy Halbourg and Winton Tolk, during which he had been unaware of the cures he was performing, Brendan was acutely aware of knitting up the rent tissues of this gunshot stranger. He could almost hear the clatter of the pumping treadles, the thumping of the batten beating the threads into place, the reeds forcing the weft to the web, the heddles guiding the warp, the shuttle working, working, working.

Not only had he begun to acquire a conscious appreciation of his power, but he sensed that the magical force he harbored was increasing, that he was ten times the healer he had been when he saved Winton—and would be twice as good tomorrow. Indeed, beneath him, the stranger's eyes swam into focus within seconds, blinked. And when Brendan lifted his hands from the wound, he was rewarded with a sight that took his breath away and gladdened his heart: The bleeding had already stopped. He was even more amazed to see the bullet rise out of the man's body as if being expelled by some inner pressure; it squeezed backwards from the entrance wound and popped free of the flesh with a sucking sound. Even as the spent slug, wet and dully gleaming, rolled out onto the victim's belly, the ragged hole began to close as if Brendan were not watching the healing of a real wound but a time-lapse film of the healing.

He quickly touched the lesser wound in the man's shoulder. At once he felt the second bullet, not as deeply buried as the first, nudging out of the torn flesh. It pushed and squirmed against his palm.

A thrill of triumph raced through Brendan. He had an urge to throw his head back and laugh into the chaotic fury of the storm, into the night, for the ultimate chaos and darkness of death had been defeated.

The victim's eyes cleared entirely, and he looked up at Brendan with bewilderment at first, then with recognition, then with horror. "Stefan," he said. "Father Wycazik."

That familiar and beloved name, coming from the lips of this complete stranger, startled Brendan and filled him with inexplicable fear for his rector and mentor. "What? What about Father Wycazik?"

"He must need your help more than I do. Quickly!"

For an instant, Brendan did not understand what the man was telling him. Then with sudden dread he realized that the driver of the machine-gunned Jeep must be his rector. But that wasn't possible. How had he gotten here? When? Why? For what possible purpose would he have come?

"Quickly," the stranger repeated.

Brendan leaped up, whirled toward the onlooking soldier and Colonel Falkirk, pushed between them, slipped in the snow, stumbled against the front bumper of the Jeep. Holding on to the vehicle with one hand, he clambered as fast as he could around the front to the driver's door on the other side. It wouldn't open. Seemed to be locked. Or damaged by gunfire. He wrenched in panic, but it would not budge. He pulled harder. Still nothing. Then he *willed* it open, and it came with a grinding and squealing of broken bits of metal, fell wide on twisted hinges. A body, slumped against the steering wheel, began to tip slowly out through the open door.

Brendan grabbed Father Wycazik, dragged him out of the driver's seat, and laid him on the cold blanket of snow. This side of the Jeep was touched by less light than the other. In spite of the darkness, he saw his rector's eyes, and as if his tortured voice were coming from a great distance, Brendan heard himself say, "Dear God, no. Oh, no." The shepherd of St. Bette's had flat, sightless, unmoving eyes that gazed at nothing in this world but at something far beyond the veil. "Please, no." Brendan saw, too, the furrow of a bullet that had dug its way along the skull, from the corner of the right eye to a spot just past the ear. That was not a mortal wound, but the other was: a devastating hole in the base of the throat, gaping horribly, filled with shattered flesh and stilled blood.

Brendan placed his trembling hands upon Stefan Wycazik's ravaged throat. From within himself he felt the threads of power spinning out again, a thousand-million filaments in a multitude of colors and tensile strengths, all invisible yet sufficient to provide the weft and warp of a strong and flexible fabric, the very fabric of life. Then, reaching psychically within the cooling body of this man he so deeply loved and respected, Brendan tried with all his mysterious skill to weave those threads upon the loom, to repair the torn cloth of life.

However, he soon became aware that the miraculous healing process required an empathy between the healer and the healed. He realized that he had previously misunderstood the process, that he was not *both* the spinning wheel, providing the threads of power, *and* the loom which wove them into the cloth of life. Instead, the patient had to provide the loom to use the threads of life-giving power that Brendan provided. In some strange way, the healing was a bilateral process. And no loom of life remained in Stefan Wycazik; he had died within seconds, had been dead before Brendan reached the Jeep. Therefore, the multiple threads of healing power only tangled and knotted uselessly, unable to sew the damaged flesh together. Brendan could heal the wounded and cure the sick, but he could not do what had been done for Lazarus.

A great, thick sob of grief shuddered from him, and another. But he refused to surrender to despair. He shook his head violently in stubborn denial of his loss, choked back another sob, and redoubled his efforts, determined to raise the dead even though he knew he could not.

He was dimly aware that he was talking, but it was a minute or two before he realized that he was praying as he had prayed so many times in the past, though not recently: "Mary, Mother of God, pray for us; Mother most pure, pray for us; Mother most chaste, pray for us. . . ."

He was praying not by reflex, not unconsciously, but ardently, with the deep, sweet conviction that the Mother of God heard his desperate cries and that, by the combination of his new power and the Virgin's intercession, Father Wycazik would be raised up again. If he had ever lost his faith, he regained it in that dark moment. With all his heart and mind, he *believed*. If Father Wycazik had been taken wrongly, before his appointed time, and if the Virgin handed these pleas, wet with her own tears, to Him who can never refuse His Mother anything she asks in the name of love, then the ruined flesh would be made whole and the rector would be restored to this world to complete his mission.

Keeping his hands upon the wet and awful wound, kneeling, wearing no priestly raiments other than those the pure falling snow painted on his humbled shoulders, Brendan chanted the Litany of the Blessed Virgin. He beseeched Mary—Queen of Angels, Queen of Apostles, Queen of Martyrs. But still his cherished rector lay motionless on the bosom of the earth. He pleaded for the Virgin's mercy, she who was the Mystical Rose, the Morning Star, the Tower of Ivory, Health of the Sick, Comforter of the Afflicted. But the dead eyes, once so full of warmth and intelligence and affection, stared unblinking as flakes of snow spiraled into them. "Mirror of Justice, pray for us; Cause of our joy, pray for us. . . ."

At last, Brendan admitted that it was the will of God that Father Wycazik move on from this place.

He softly concluded the litany in a voice that grew shakier by the word. He removed his hands from the monstrous wound. Instead, he took one of Stefan Wycazik's limp dead hands in both his own and held fast to it like a lost child. His heart was a deep vessel of grief.

Colonel Leland Falkirk loomed over him. "So you've got limits to your power, do you? Good. That's good to know. All right, then, come on. Get back there with the others."

Brendan looked up into the sharp face and polished-flint eyes, and he felt none of the fear that the colonel previously aroused in him. He said quietly, "He died without an opportunity to make a last confession. I am a priest, and I will stay here and do what a priest must do, and when I'm finished I will rejoin the others. The only way you'll move me now is if you kill me and drag me away. If you can't wait, then you'll have to shoot me in the back." He turned away from the colonel. Face wet with tears and melting snow, he took a deep breath and found that the Latin phrases came to his tongue without hesitation.

The crawl-through that Jack had cut in the chainlink fence was small, but none of them—Jack, Dom, or Ginger—was a large person, so they all squeezed onto the grounds of Thunder Hill without difficulty, having pushed the rucksacks full of equipment ahead of them.

At Jack's direction, Dom and Ginger stayed close to the fence until he had a chance to study the immediate landscape through the Star Tron night-vision device. He was searching for posts on which surveillance cameras and photoelectric-cell alarm systems might be rigged. Though blowing snow made the inspection more difficult than it would have been in better weather, he located two poles on which were mounted cameras that covered this portion of the Thunder Hill perimeter from different angles. He believed the lenses of both cameras were filmed with snow, though due to the storm he could not be certain. He saw no evidence of photoelectric systems to detect movement across this part of the meadow.

Next, from a zippered pocket, he withdrew a wallet-size device—an extremely sophisticated variation of a voltameter. It could detect the passage of electric current through a line without making contact with that line, although it could not measure the strength of the current.

He turned toward the open meadow, putting his back to the fence. Crouching, he held the object out at arm's length, about two feet above the ground, and moved slowly forward. The voltage detector would register a current from lines buried as deep as eighteen inches underground, unless they were sheathed in pipes. The kind of lines he was looking for were neither that deep nor sheathed. Even the foot of new and old snow would not measurably affect the device's performance. He edged forward only about three yards before the detector began beeping softly and flashing its amber light.

He halted immediately, stepped back a couple of feet, and called Dom and Ginger to his side. They huddled together, and Jack said, "There's a pressure-sensitive alarm grid buried an inch or two under the ground. It starts about ten feet inside the fence, and I'm sure it runs parallel to the fence all around the facility. It's a web of wires—sealed in thin plastic—that carry a low-voltage current. It's designed so the connections of some of the wires will be broken and the current interrupted if anything above a certain weight—oh, say fifty pounds—steps on them. The weight of the snow doesn't affect it because that's evenly distributed. It reacts to localized pressure—like a footstep."

"Even *I* weigh more than fifty pounds," Ginger said. "How wide's this alarm grid?"

"At least eight or ten feet," Jack said. "They want to be sure that if someone immensely clever like me should come along and detect the system, it'll be impossible just to jump across it."

"I don't know about you," Dom said, "but I can't *fly* across."

"I'm not so sure you can't," Jack said. "I mean, if you had time to explore that power of yours. . . . If you can levitate chairs, why couldn't you levitate yourself?" He saw this suggestion had startled Dom. "But you haven't time to learn to control your power, so we'll have to rely on what's gotten us this far."

"What's that?" Ginger asked.

"My genius," Jack said with a grin. "Here's what we'll do. We'll walk along the perimeter, staying in the safe ground between the fence and the alarm grid, until we find a place where there's a big sturdy tree standing twenty or thirty feet deeper in the meadow, well beyond the width of the grid."

"Then?" Dom asked.

"You'll see."

"What if we don't find a tree?" Ginger asked.

"Doc," Jack said, "I had you pegged as a go-getting optimist. If I say we need a tree, I'd expect you to tell me we'll find a forest and have a thousand to choose from."

They found the tree only three hundred yards down the slope toward the valley floor. It was a huge pine of such age and character that it offered the thick and widely separated limbs that Jack required. It towered eighty feet or higher, a snow-dusted monolith looming out of the storm, and it was thirty or thirty-five feet back from the fence, well beyond the farther edge of the alarm grid.

Using the Star Tron again, Jack studied the massive pine until he found exactly the right branch. It had to be sturdy, yet not much higher than the fence, with which it would form the opposing stanchions of a rope bridge. He put the Star Tron away again.

From one of the rucksacks, he removed the four-pronged grappling hook that had been one of the many items on Ginger's and Faye's shopping list when they had visited Elko earlier in the day. Tied to the hook was a hundred-foot length of hawser-laid nylon rope, five-sixteenths of an inch in diameter, the kind made for serious climbers and capable not only of holding one of them but of supporting all their weight at the same time.

He tested the knot where the line tied to the hook, though he had tested it a dozen times before. He arranged the coil of rope at his feet, stepping on the loose end to prevent the entire length from being carried away when he pitched the grappling hook, but leaving most of it free to pay out. "Stand aside," he said. Dangling the hook from his right hand on two feet of line, he began to swing it around and around, faster, faster, until the *whoosh* of it cutting the air was even louder than the storm wind. When he felt the velocity was right, he let go with his right hand, and the rope slipped loosely through his left hand, trailing after the grapple. The hook arced up and out into the storm. Though it had sufficient mass and momentum to be unbothered by the wind, it fell short of its target by about three feet.

Jack reeled it back through the snow, churning the virgin mantle. He had to jerk on it a few times and then patiently finesse it when it got caught on something. He was not concerned about dragging it across the buried pressure-sensitive grid, for it was not nearly heavy enough to trigger that alarm. In a minute or two he had it in hand again. Without having been told what to do, Dom had knelt and coiled the rope once more as it came in. Now Jack was ready to try again.

His second pitch landed just where he wanted it. The hook firmly snared the target branch.

With the grapple securely planted, he took the other end of the rope to the nearest fence post. He slipped it through the chainlink about seven feet off the ground, wrapped it around the post, threaded it through the chainlink on the other side, and all the way around the post again. He pulled on it with all his strength, until the line between the post and the distant tree was taut. Then he enlisted Dom's and Ginger's help to keep it taut while he knotted it tightly to the post.

As a result, they had a rope bridge that was seven feet off the ground where it began at the fence, angling up to a height of about nine feet at the tree. That slight incline, even over a mere thirty-five feet, would make the crossing more difficult, but it was as near to level as Jack could make it.

He jumped high, grabbed the line with both hands, swung his body back and forth a few times to get momentum, then kicked up and threw his legs over the rope, crossing his ankles atop it. Like a playful koala bear clinging to the underside of a horizontal branch, he hung with his face turned skyward and his back parallel to the ground. By extending his arms behind him and pulling himself on the line and by alternately scrunching his legs up and extending them while keeping his ankles locked, he could inchworm along with no danger of touching the ground. He demonstrated the technique for Dom and Ginger. Before he reached the danger zone defined by the pressure-sensitive alarm grid, he let go first with his feet, then with his hands, and dropped to the ground.

Dom tried getting onto the line. He attained a handgrip with his first jump. But he needed a full minute to swing his legs up and over, though he did it, then dropped back to the ground.

Ginger, only five-two, had to be given a boost to get a proper handgrip. But to Jack's surprise she required no assistance to kick up and wrap her legs over the line without delay.

"You're in pretty good shape," Jack told her.

"Yes, well," she said, swinging back to the ground, "that's because every Tuesday, on my day off, I eat buckets of *vareniki,* several pounds of graham cracker cake, and enough blintzes to sink a ship. Diet, Jack. That's the key to fitness."

Shrugging his arms through the straps on one of the rucksacks and buckling it in place on his back, Jack said, "Okay, now, I'll cross the rope bridge first with the two heaviest bags, which leaves one sack for each of you. Ginger, you'll come second. Dom, you'll bring up the rear. When you come across, the rope will sag more the closer you get to the center of the span, even as taut as we've made it, but don't worry. It won't droop far enough to put you in contact with the ground and set off the alarm. Keep your feet locked around the line, and for God's sake don't accidentally let go with both hands at the same time as you're pulling yourself along. Try to make it all the way to the tree, just to be safe. But if your arms and legs give out, you can come down ten or twelve feet this side of the pine if you must, which'll probably be past the other end of the alarm grid."

"We'll make it all the way," Ginger said confidently. "It's only thirty or thirty-five feet."

"In just ten feet," Jack said, fastening the second rucksack to his chest, "you'll feel as if your arms are coming out of their sockets. In fifteen feet, you'll feel as if they *have* come out of their sockets."

Something about Brendan Cronin's reaction to his rector's death had jolted Leland Falkirk. When the young priest demanded to be given time and privacy to deliver the last rites to Stefan Wycazik, there had been a fierce fire of indignation in his eyes and such hot grief in his voice that his humanity could not be in doubt.

Leland's fear of alien possession was voracious, eating him alive. He had seen— and others had discovered—strange things inside that starship, enough to justify his fear if not his total paranoia. But even he found it difficult to believe that Cronin's anguish was the clever play-acting of an inhuman intelligence in disguise.

Yet Cronin, with his bizarre powers, was one of two prime suspects, one of the two witnesses most likely to have been taken over, the other being Dominick Corvaisis. Where did the healing and telekinesis come from if not from an alien puppet-master living within the man's body?

Leland was confused.

With powdery snow pluming up around his feet, he walked away from the kneeling priest, then stopped and shook his head and tried to clear his thoughts. He saw the other six witnesses by Jack Twist's Cherokee still under guard. He saw his soldiers caught between the need to do their duty as they were told and a confusion worse than Leland's own. He saw the stranger who had been with Wycazik—now up and moving around, miraculously whole. That healing seemed wonderful, an event calling for celebration, not fear; a blessing, not a curse. *But Leland knew what lay inside Thunder Hill.* That dark knowledge put things in a different perspective. The healing was a ruse, clever misdirection to make him think the benefits of co-operation with the enemy were too great to justify resistance. They were offering an end to pain. And perhaps an end to all death other than that too sudden to be avoided. But Leland knew the very essence of life was pain. It was dangerous to believe escape from suffering was possible. Dangerous, because such hopes were routinely destroyed. And the pain following in the wake of shattered hopes was far worse than it would have been if you had just faced it and endured it in the first place. Leland believed that pain—physical, mental, emotional—was the core of the human condition, that survival and sanity depended upon embracing pain rather than resisting it or dreaming of escape. You had to thrive on pain to avoid being defeated by it, and anyone who came along with an offer of transcendence must be greeted with disbelief, contempt, and deep distrust.

Leland was no longer confused.

The big Army truck—Jorja supposed it was a troop transport—had hard metal benches along both sides and also against the forward wall that separated the driver's compartment from the rear. Dangling leather loops, riveted to the walls at regular intervals, provided those on the benches with something to hang on to when the ride got rough or steep. Father Wycazik's corpse had been laid on the forward bench and secured with lines that tied under the seat and then to the wall straps, forming a rope basket to restrain the body's movement. Everyone else— Jorja, Marcie, Brendan, Ernie, Faye, Sandy, Ned, and Parker—sat on the side benches. Usually, the rear doors were held shut only by the interior latch, allowing soldiers to get out quickly in case of an accident or other emergency. But this time Colonel Falkirk himself slid the bolt into place on the outside. The sound of it made Jorja think of prison cells and dungeons, and filled her with despair. A fluorescent light was set in the ceiling, but Falkirk did not order it lit; they were forced to ride in darkness.

Although Ernie Block had endured the night remarkably well thus far, everyone had expected him to come apart when he was locked in the pitch-black bay of the truck. But he sat beside Faye, holding her hand, and coped. He had periodic bouts of anxiety marked only by spells of hyperventilation, which he quickly overcame. "I'm beginning to remember the jets Dom spoke of," Ernie said soon after they got in the truck, before it started to move. "There were at least four, swooping low, two *very* low . . . and then something else happened I can't recall. . . but after that, I remember getting in the motel van and driving like hell down toward I-80 . . . out toward the special place along the highway that means so much to Sandy, too. That's all so far. But the more I remember . . . the less afraid I am of the dark."

The colonel put no guards in with them. He seemed to think it would be dangerous for even two or three heavily armed soldiers to ride in their company.

Before herding them into the truck, the colonel had seemed on the brink of ordering their execution, right there along Vista Valley Road. Jorja's stomach had knotted painfully with fear. Finally Falkirk calmed down, though Jorja was not convinced he would let them live once they arrived wherever they were going.

He had demanded to know where Ginger, Dom, and Jack had gone. At first, no one would respond, which infuriated him. He placed his hand on Marcie's head and quietly told them what pain he would put the child through if they continued to be difficult. Ernie had spoken at once, cursing Falkirk as a disgrace to his uniform—and reluctantly revealing that Ginger, Dom, and Jack had gone west from the Tranquility, heading for Battle Mountain, Winnemucca, and ultimately Reno. "We were afraid all the routes to Elko would be watched," Ernie said. "We didn't want to put all our eggs in one basket." It was a lie, of course. For a moment Jorja wanted to scream at Ernie not to jeopardize her daughter's life with transparent lies, but she realized Falkirk had no way of knowing for sure that it was a phony story. The colonel was suspicious. But Ernie provided more details of the route Jack was supposedly following, and at last Falkirk sent four of his men to check it out.

Now, as the truck rumbled and jolted through the windy night toward a destination Falkirk had not shared with them, Jorja hung on to a strap with one hand and held Marcie with her free arm. The girl made things easier by clinging fiercely to Jorja. Her semicatatonic limpness had given way to a strong need for affection and contact, though she was still by no means connected with reality. But her sudden need to hug and be hugged seemed, to Jorja, a hopeful sign that she would find her way back from the dark domain into which she had retreated.

Jorja would not have believed that anything could distract her entirely from her intense concern about her daughter. But a couple of minutes after the truck started to move, Parker Faine began to tell them why he and Father Wycazik had been making that risky cross-country trek through the snowswept night. The news he related was so momentous that it pushed everything else from Jorja's mind and held her, rapt. He told them about Calvin Sharkle, about how Brendan had passed on his power to Emmy Halbourg and Winton Tolk. "And now . . . perhaps . . . to *me*," Parker said with such wonder in his voice that it was communicated instantly to Jorja and caused gooseflesh to break out all over her. Parker spoke of the CISG. And he told them what they must have seen on that long-lost summer night in July: Something had come down. Something had come down from the sky, and the world would never be the same again.

Something had come down.

As that amazing news was revealed, the darkness in the truck was filled with an excited babble of voices. Reactions from Faye's initial stunned disbelief to Sandy's instant and enthusiastic acceptance.

Not only did Sandy accept, but she abruptly remembered large pieces of the forbidden night, as if Parker's revelation had been a sledge that had struck a wrecking blow upon her memory block. "The jets came over, and the fourth one blew across the roof of the motel, so low it almost took the top off the building, and by that time we were all out of the diner, people were coming over from the motel, but the shaking was still going on. The ground vibrating just like in a quake. The air vibrating too." Her tone of voice was a peculiar mix of delight and trepidation, both joyful and haunted. In the darkness everyone fell silent to hear what she had to say. "Then Dom . . . I didn't know his name then, but it was Dom, all right . . . he turned away from the jets and looked up and back across the roof of the diner, and he shouted: 'The moon! The moon!' We all turned . . . and there was a moon, brighter than usual, creepy-bright, and for a moment it seemed to be falling on us. Oh, don't you remember? Don't you remember what it felt like to look up and see the moon falling on us?"

"Yes," Ernie said softly, almost reverently. "I remember."

"I remember," Brendan said.

And Jorja had a glimmer of memory: the recollected image of a lambent moon, eerily bright, rushing toward them. . . .

Sandy said, "Some people screamed, and some started to run, we were so scared, all of us. And the powerful shaking and roaring got louder, you could feel it in your bones, a sound like kettledrums and shotgun blasts all mixed up with the greatest wind you ever heard, though there was no wind. But there was the other sound, too, the queer whistling, warbling, fluty sort of sound under the thunder, getting louder by the second. . . . The moon got *very* bright all of a sudden. These beams came down from it, lit up the parking lot with a frosty sort of glow . . . and then *changed*. The moon turned red, blood-red! Then we all knew it wasn't the moon, not the moon, but something else.''

Jorja saw, in memory, the lunar form turning from frost-white to scarlet. With that recollection, barriers implanted by the mind-control specialists began to crumble like sand castles under the assault of a high tide. She wondered how she could have looked so often at Marcie's album of moons and not have been nudged toward understanding. Now understanding came in a flood, and she began to tremble with fear of the unknown and with an indescribable exultation.

''Then it came over the diner,'' Sandy said, with such awe in her voice that she might have been seeing the starship descend right now, not in memory but in reality and for the first time. ''It came in as low as the jet that had gone before it, but it wasn't moving nearly as fast as the jet . . . slow . . . slow . . . hardly faster than the Goodyear blimp. Which seemed impossible because you could tell it was *heavy*, not like a blimp. Ever-so-heavy. Yet it drifted across us so slow, so beautiful and slow, and in that instant we all knew what it was, what it had to be, because it was nothing that had ever been made on this world. . . .''

Jorja's tremors grew as the memory returned with greater vividness. She recalled standing in the parking lot of the Tranquility Grille, with Marcie in her arms, looking up at the craft. It glided through the warm July night above and would have looked almost serene except for the thunderous sounds and base vibrations that accompanied it. As Sandy had said—once the misapprehension of a falling moon was dispelled, they knew instantly what they were seeing. Yet the ship looked nothing like the flying saucers and rockets seen in a thousand movies and television shows. There was nothing dazzling about it—other than the very fact of its existence!—no coruscating bands of multicolored lights, no weirdly extruding spines and nodules, no inexplicable excrescences in its design, no unearthly sheen of unknown metal or peculiarly positioned viewports or blazing exhausts or strange wicked-looking armaments. The enveloping scarlet glow was apparently an energy field by which it remained aloft and propelled itself. Otherwise, it was quite plain: a cylinder of considerable size, though not even as large as, say, the fuselage of an old DC-3, perhaps only fifty feet long and twelve or fifteen feet in diameter; it was rounded at each end, rather like two well-worn tubes of lipstick welded together at their bases; through the shining energy field, a hull was visible, though it was singularly unimpressive, with few features and none of them dramatic, somewhat mottled as if by time and great tribulation. In memory, Jorja watched it descend again, across the diner, toward I-80, while the jet escorts wheeled and barrel-rolled and swooped and zoomed in the sky above and to the east and west. Now, as on that wondrous night, her breath caught, her heart pounded, her breast swelled with turbulently mixed emotions, and she felt as if she were standing before a door beyond which lay the meaning of life, a door to which she had suddenly been given the key.

Sandy said, ''It came down in the barrens beyond I-80, at that place some of us knew was special, though we didn't know why. The jets were buzzing it. Everyone at the motel and diner just had to get down there, couldn't hold us back, my God, nothing could've held us back! So we piled in cars and trucks and took off—''

''Faye and I went in the motel van,'' Ernie said out of the darkness in the troop transport, no longer breathing hard, his nyctophobia burned away in the heat of memory. ''Dom and Ginger went with us. That pro gambler, too. Lomack.

Zebediah Lomack from Reno. That's why he wrote our names on the moon posters in his house, the ones Dom told us about. Some dim but urgent memory of riding with us in the van, down to the ship, must have almost busted through his memory block.''

"And Jorja," Sandy said, "you and your husband and Marcie and a couple other people rode in the back of our pickup. Brendan, Jack, and others went in cars, strangers piling in with strangers, but in some way none of us were strangers any more. When we got there we parked on the berm, and a couple of other cars pulled up coming west from Elko, people were running across the divider, cars driving in from the west just stopped right on the highway, and we all gathered on the shoulder of the road for a minute, looking out there at the ship. The glow around it had faded, though there was still a . . . a luminous quality to it, amber now instead of red. It set some clumps of sagebrush and bunch-grass on fire when it first touched down, but those burnt out almost entirely by the time we got there. It was funny . . . how we all gathered along the edge of the road, not shouting or talking or noisy in any way, you know, but quiet, all of us so quiet at first. Hesitating. Knowing we were standing on . . . a cliff, but that jumping off the cliff wasn't going to be a fall, it was going to be like . . . like jumping off and *up*. I can't explain that feeling too well, but you know. You know.''

Jorja knew. She felt it now, as she had then, the almost-too-wonderful-to-bear feeling that humankind had been living in a dark box and that the lid had just been torn off at last. The feeling that the night would never again seem as dark and foreboding or the future as frightening as it had been in the past.

"And as I stood there," Sandy said, "looking out at that luminous ship, so beautiful, so impossible there on the plains, everything that had happened to me when I was a little girl, all the abuse and pain and terror . . . didn't matter as much any more. Just like that—" She snapped her fingers in the dark. "Just like *that* my father didn't terrify me any more.'' Her voice cracked with emotion. "I mean, I hadn't seen him since I was fourteen, more than a decade, but I still lived with the fear that some day he'd walk in again, you know, and he'd *take* me again, make me go with him. That was . . . that was silly . . . but I still lived with the fear, 'cause life was a nightmare for me, and in bad dreams those things happen. But as I stood there watching the ship, with everyone silent and the night so big, the jets overhead, I knew my father could never scare me again even if he did show up some day. Because he's nothing, nothing, just a sick little man, a speck, one tiny grain of sand on the biggest beach you can ever imagine. . . .''

Yes, Jorja thought, filled with the joy of Sandy's discovery. Yes, that was what this ship from beyond meant—freedom from our worst and most inhibiting fears. Although the vessel's occupants might bring no answers to the problems that beset humanity, their mere presence was in a way an answer in itself.

Her voice thickening even further with emotion, beginning to cry now, not with sadness but with happiness, Sandy said, "And looking at the ship out there, I felt all of a sudden as if I could put all the pain behind me forever . . . and as if I *was* somebody. All my life, see, I'd felt I was nothing, less than nothing, filthy and worthless, just a *thing* that had its uses maybe, but nothing with . . . dignity. And then I realized we're *all* just grains of sand on that beach, none of us so very much more important than any of the rest of us, but more than that . . .'' She gave a small cry of frustration. "Oh, I wish I had words, I wish I had *words* and knew how to use them better.''

"You're doing all right," Faye said quietly. "By God, girl, you're doing all right.''

And Sandy said, "But even though we're just grains of sand, we're also . . .

also part of a race that might some day go up there, out there into all that darkness, out where the creatures in that ship came from, so even as grains of sand we have a place and purpose. Do you see? We just got to be kind to one another and keep going. And one day all of us—all the billions of us who were and are— we'll be out there with those who'll come after us . . . out there *on top of all the darkness,* and anything we ever endured will have been worth it, somehow, because it'll have been a part of our getting there. All of that hit me in a flash while we stood there along the interstate. And suddenly that night, right there, I started crying and laughing both. . . .''

"I remember!'' Ned said from his part of the darkness. "Oh, God, now I remember, I do, it's all coming back. We were standing there on the side of the road, and you grabbed hold of me and hugged me. It was the first time you ever told me you loved me, the first time, though I'd known you did. You hugged me, you told me you loved me, it was crazy, right there with a *spaceship* come down! And you know what? For a few minutes, you holding me and telling me you loved me . . . the spaceship didn't matter. All that mattered was you telling me, telling me after so long.'' His voice filled with emotion, too, and Jorja sensed that he was putting his arms around Sandy, in the gloom on the other side of the truck. "And they took that away from me,'' he said. "They came with their damn drugs and their mind control, and they took away from me the first time you told me you loved me. But I got it back now, Sandy, and they're never taking it away from me again. Never again.''

Faye said plaintively, "I still can't remember anything. I want to remember, too. I want to be a *part* of it.''

Everyone was silent as the transport rumbled through the night.

Jorja knew the others must be pondering some of the same thoughts that were rushing through her mind. The mere existence of another—and superior—intelligence put human strife in a different context. Mankind's endless, violent struggles to dominate and enslave, to impress one philosophy or another upon the entire race at any cost in blood and pain—that seemed so hopelessly petty and fruitless now. All narrow, power-centered philosophies would surely collapse. Religions that preached the oneness of all men would probably thrive, but those that encouraged violent conversion would not. In some way impossible to explain but easy to *feel,* just as Sandy had felt it, Jorja was aware that extraterrestrial contact had the potential to make one nation of all mankind, one vast family; for the first time in history, every individual could have the respect that only a good, loving family—no king, no government—could bestow.

Something had come down from the sky.

And all humankind could be lifted up.

"Moon,'' Marcie murmured against Jorja's neck. "Moon, moon.''

Jorja wanted to say: Everything'll be fine, honey; we'll help you remember now that we know what it is you've forgotten, and when you do recall it, you'll realize it's nothing to be scared about; you'll realize it's wonderful, honey, and you'll laugh. But she did not say any of that, for she did not know what Falkirk intended to do with them. As long as they were in the colonel's custody, she did not hold out much prospect for a happy ending.

Brendan Cronin said, "I remember more. I remember descending the embankment from the interstate. Moving out toward the ship. It lay like shimmering amber quartz. I walked slowly toward it with the jets swooping overhead, other people coming with me . . . including you, Faye . . . and you, Ernie . . . and Dom and Ginger. But only Dom and Ginger came all the way to the ship with me, and when we got there we found a door . . . a round portal . . . open. . . .''

Jorja remembered standing on the shoulder of I-80, afraid to go closer to the ship and blaming her reluctance on the need to keep Marcie safe. Wanting to call out a warning and at the same time wanting to urge them on, she had watched Brendan, Dom, and Ginger approach the golden craft. The three had begun to move out of sight along the side of the ship, and everyone still on the shoulder of the highway had rushed eastward a hundred feet or so to keep them in view. Jorja had seen the portal, too, a round circle of blazing light on the side of the glimmering hull.

"The three of us gathered in front of the door." Brendan spoke softly, yet his voice carried above the rumble of the truck. "Dom and Ginger and me. We thought . . . something would come out. But nothing did. Instead, there was a quality about the light inside . . . the wonderful golden light I've seen in my dreams . . . a comforting and compelling warmth that *drew* us somehow. We were scared, dear God, we were scared! But we heard helicopters coming, and we sensed government people would take over the second they arrived on the scene, take over and push us back, and we were determined to be part of it. And that *light!* So . . ."

"So you went inside," Jorja said.

"Yes," Brendan said.

"I remember," Sandy said. "Yes. You went inside. All three of you went inside."

The immensity of the memory was overwhelming. The moment when the first representatives of the human race had set foot for the first time into a place built neither by nature nor by human hands. The moment that forever divided history into Before and After. Remembering, their memory blocks having entirely crumbled, no one could speak for a while.

The truck rumbled toward its unguessable destination.

The darkness within the vehicle seemed vast. Yet the eight of them were as close as any people had ever been since the dawn of time.

At last Parker said, "What happened, Brendan? What happened to the three of you when you went inside?"

Using the rope bridge, they crossed the pressure-sensitive alarm grid. Pausing several times to employ other clever devices in Jack's bag of tricks, they passed through the finely woven web of electronic security that guarded the grounds of Thunder Hill, coming at last to the main entrance.

Ginger looked up at the immense blast doors. The blowing snow had stuck and frozen to the burnished steel in cryptic patterns that looked as if they ought to have some meaning.

A two-lane blacktop led away from the doors. Heating coils were evidently embedded in it, for not a speck of snow lay on the pavement, and steam rose from its surface. The road curved down and west across the meadow, into the forest, where the lights of the main gate glowed softly in the distance. She could not see the guardhouse past which they had crept in the pickup, but she knew it was out there.

If visitors were admitted during the next few minutes, or if the guards changed shifts and returned to the Depository, the jig was up. She and Dom and Jack could scurry off, lie in the snow, hide. However, obviously little traffic passed through here, for the snow around the smaller door was smooth and undisturbed when they arrived; therefore, the fresh tracks they left would guarantee apprehension as surely as a tripped alarm. They had to get inside quickly—if they had any hope of getting inside at all.

The smaller single door to the right of the blast doors looked no less formidable than those giant portals, but Jack was unperturbed. He had brought along an attaché-sized computer called SLICKS, and although Ginger had forgotten exactly what the acronym stood for, she knew from Jack that it was a device for pene-trating electronic locks of various types and that it was not for sale to members of the general public. She did not ask where he had gotten it.

They worked in silence. Ginger kept a lookout for incoming headlights from the main gate and surveyed the snowy expanse of the meadow for a foot patrol, though they were confident no guards were on prowl. Dom held a flashlight on the ten-digit codeboard that was the equivalent of a keyhole in an ordinary door, while Jack employed the probes of the SLICKS in search of the sequence of numbers that would gain entrance.

Crouching on one knee in the snow, alert for trouble, Ginger felt exposed—and much farther than twenty-four hundred miles from her life in Boston. The wind stung her face. The snow melted in her lashes and trickled into her eyes. What a cockamamy situation. *Meshugge.* That an innocent person could be driven to such a state as they'd been. Who did this damn Colonel Falkirk think he was? The people who gave him his orders—who did they think they were? Not true Americans. Real *momzers*—that's what they were, all of them. She remembered the picture of Falkirk in the newspaper: She had known at once that he was a *treyfnyak,* a person not to be trusted, not an inch, never. And she knew something else, too: Whenever she began to pepper her thoughts or her speech with this much Yiddish, she must be in deep trouble or very much afraid.

Less than four minutes after Jack set to work, Ginger was startled by a *whoosh* of compressed air behind her. She turned and saw the door had already slid into its recess. Dom stumbled back in surprise. Jack fell on his butt. When Ginger went to help him up, he showed her that the door had slid open so suddenly and with such force that he had not had time to withdraw the SLICKS probe from the mechanism; it had torn the probe right out of the computer.

But the door was open, and no alarms were ringing. Beyond was a twelve-foot-long concrete tunnel, about eight or nine feet in diameter. It was lit by fluorescent bulbs. It angled to the left, where it ended at another steel door.

"Stay here," Jack said, stepping into the tunnel to look around.

Ginger stood at Dom's side, and though she knew part of the plan was to give them-selves up as hostages, she also knew that, on instinct, she would bolt and run at the first sign of trouble. Dom apparently sensed her thoughts, for he put an arm around her as much to restrain her as to reassure her that she was not alone.

After a minute or so, when still no alarm bells or sirens had split the night, Jack stepped back out into the storm and joined them where they stood six or eight feet from the door. "Two surveillance cameras on the ceiling of the tunnel—"

"They saw you?" Dom asked.

"I don't believe so, no. Because they didn't track my movements. I suspect you have to close the outer door before there's any hope of getting the inner door open, and as soon as you *do* close the outer door, the cameras are activated. I also noticed some gas jets concealed along the lighting fixtures. Way I see it—you close the outer door, and the cameras look you over, and if they don't like what they see, they can hit you with either a knockout gas or something deadly."

Dom said, "We're ready to be captured, but not gassed like moles."

"We aren't going to close the outer door unless we've already got the inner one open," Jack said.

"But you told us that wasn't—"

"There may be a way," Jack said, winking his cast eye.

The first step was to pile their rucksacks out of the way and cover them with snow. Jack did not think they would have any further need of his high-tech devices and would only be slowed down by the weight. The second step, after they entered the tunnel, was for Dom to lift Ginger so, instructed by Jack, she could use a knife to saw through the wires on the surveillance cameras, putting them out of commission. Again, she expected an alarm to go off, but none did.

Leaving the outer door open, Jack led them to the inner barrier. "This one has no keyboard to disengage the lock, so it doesn't matter that the SLICKS was damaged."

"Should we be talking in here?" Ginger asked nervously. "Aren't there liable to be microphones?"

"Yes, but I doubt anyone's monitoring until that outer door closes, because that's probably what engages the computer's attention and starts the clearance program for anyone trying to enter. And even if there's a guard beyond this door, he's not going to hear our voices through all this steel. Not even if we shout," Jack said, though he spoke barely above a whisper. He pointed to a panel of glass set in the tunnel wall to the right of the door. "That's the only way to unlock it. They were just starting to install locks like this in high-security installations when I left the service eight years ago. You put your palm against the glass, the security computer scans your prints, and if you're authorized to enter, the door opens."

"And if you're not authorized to enter?" Dom asked in a whisper.

"The gas jets."

"So how can you open it?" Ginger asked.

"I can't," Jack said.

"But you said—"

"I said there might be a way," Jack told her. "And there might." He looked at Dom and smiled. "*You* can probably open it."

Dom stared at Jack as if the ex-thief had lost his mind. "Me? You serious? What would I know about sophisticated security systems?"

"Nothing," Jack said. "But you have the power to peel thousands of paper moons off walls and send them dancing through the air all at once, and you can levitate a score of chairs and perform other nifty tricks, so I don't see why you can't . . . reach into the mechanism of that door and cause it to slide open."

"But I can't. I don't know how."

"Think about it, concentrate, do whatever you did to move the salt shaker last night."

Dom shook his head vigorously. "I can't control the power. You saw how it got out of hand. What if it runs wild here? I could hurt you or Ginger. I might inadvertently activate the gas jets and kill us all. No, no. Too risky."

They stood in silence for a moment, with the wind huffing and whistling eerily at the open outer door.

Jack said, "Dom, if you don't try, then the only way we'll get inside is as captives."

Dom remained adamant.

Jack walked back to the outer door. Ginger started to follow him because she thought he was leaving. But he stopped just inside the mouth of the tunnel and raised his hand over a button on the wall. He said, "This is a heat-sensitive switch, Dom. If you won't try to open that inner door, then I'll touch this switch and close the outer door, trapping us here. That'll start the computer's entry-clearance program, and when the computer discovers the surveillance cameras have been put out of commission, it'll sound an alarm that'll alert the security men."

"One of the reasons we came here was to be caught," Dom said.

"We came to have a look around and *then* get caught, if possible."

"Well," Dom said, "we'll have to settle for just getting caught."

The tunnel's heat had escaped into the night. Their breath plumed from them again. Those smoking exhalations heightened the impression that the two men were engaged in a battle, though it was a battle of wills rather than one of physical strength.

Standing between them, Ginger had no doubt who would win. She liked and admired Dom Corvaisis more than any man she had met in a long time, partly because he seemed to embody both the drive and determination of Anna Weiss and the modest shyness of Jacob. He was good-hearted and, in his own way, wise. She would have trusted him with her life. In fact, she had already trusted him with it. But she knew Jack Twist would win, for he was *used* to winning, while Dom, by his own admission, had been a winner only since the summer before last.

Jack said, "If they can't see us, they'll gas us for sure. Maybe they'll just sedate us. But maybe, to be safe, they'll use cyanide gas or some deadly nerve gas that'll penetrate our clothes because, after all, they can't be sure we're not wearing gas masks."

"You're bluffing," Dom said.

"Am I?" Jack said.

"You wouldn't kill us."

"You're dealing with a professional criminal, remember?"

"You were. No more."

"Still got a black heart," Jack said, grinning, and this time there was a disconcertingly maniacal note to his humor and a cold glint in his misaligned eye that made Ginger wonder if he actually might risk killing them all if he didn't get his way.

"Our dying isn't part of the plan," Dom said. "It'll screw up everything."

"And your refusal to help—that's not part of the plan, either," Jack said. "For God's sake, Dom, do it!"

Dom hesitated. He glanced at Ginger. "Step as far out of the way as you can."

She moved back beside Jack Twist.

"Dom, if it does come open," Jack said, still keeping one hand raised over the heat-sensitive switch that would close the outer door, "go through fast. There's a guard in there somewhere. He'll be real surprised when the door opens because the entry-clearance program hasn't been run. If you can knock him down quickly, I'll be right behind you to silence him. That'll improve our chances of getting deeper into the installation and seeing what's to see before they nail our asses."

Dom nodded, faced the inner door again. He looked over the frame, put one hand to the steel, moved his fingertips back and forth in the manner of an old-time safecracker feeling for the telltale vibration of falling tumblers. Then he turned to study the glass panel that read palmprints and fingerprints.

Jack lowered his hand from the switch that he'd threatened to hit, and glanced at the stormy night beyond the outer door. He whispered so softly to Ginger that Dom, at the far end of the tunnel, could not have heard: "I get a creepy feeling that, any minute now, the giant's going to come down the beanstalk and stomp us all flat."

She knew then that he would not have risked their destruction, that he would probably just have led them out to the guardhouse at the main gate and asked to be arrested. But with his murderous glower, he had been thoroughly convincing.

Abruptly, the inner door *whooshed* open. Even though Dom was the agent of its movement, he was so startled that he jumped back a step instead of rushing through immediately, as Jack had told him to do. He realized his error as he made it, and he leapt across the threshold, into the subterranean world beyond.

Jack hit the button to close the outer door even before Dom was across the inner threshold, then ran after the writer.

Ginger followed. She expected the sounds of struggle or gunfire, but heard neither. When she stepped out of the concrete tunnel, she found herself in another, huge tunnel with natural rock walls, where lights were suspended from scaffolding overhead. The passage was about sixty feet across, at least a hundred yards long, beginning inside the massive steel blast doors, and ending far away at what appeared to be banks of elevators. Three yards in from the door, a guard's table was cemented to the concrete floor. A watchman's log was chained to the table. A few issues of recent magazines were stacked beside the log. There was a computer terminal as well. But no guards were in sight.

In fact, the entire tunnel was deserted. The place was as still and silent as a mausoleum. Not even the drip of water from a stalactite or the rustle of batwings in the vault above. But Ginger supposed that a multibillion-dollar facility designed to weather World War III would not be plagued by either condensation or flying rodents.

"Should be guards," Jack murmured. His voice echoed sibilantly off the rock walls.

"What now?" Dom asked shakily. Clearly, he had been surprised by his ability to focus his power so soon after the near-catastrophe in the diner last night.

"Something's wrong," Jack said. "I don't know what. But no guard . . . something's wrong." He skinned back the hood of his ski suit and pulled the zipper down a few inches, and the others did the same. Jack said softly, "This is just the cargo-receiving area. Trucks come in and unload. The main part of the installation must be below us. So . . . I don't like this emptiness . . . but I guess we go down."

"If we've got to go, then let's stop *shmoozing* and get a move on," Ginger said, heading toward the far end of the tunnel.

She heard the inner door swish as Jack closed it.

They went farther into Thunder Hill.

2. Fear

They made hardly more noise than three mice easing past a dozing cat, yet their footsteps echoed in the rock-walled vault. Not loudly. The echoes did not sound like footsteps but rather like the whispers and murmurs of conspirators hidden within the shadowed niches on all sides.

Dom's uneasiness grew.

They crept past a couple of enormous elevators. Each of them was seventy feet wide and nearly as deep, open platforms that were raised and lowered by synchronized hydraulic shafts at each corner, more than big enough to move fighter aircraft in and out of the bowels of the mountain. They passed smaller cargo lifts, too, and finally came to a pair of standard-size elevators.

Before Jack could press the call button for the lift, Dom was hit by another flash of memory. As before, it was sufficiently vivid to displace current reality. This time, he recalled the crucial event of July 6: the white-to-scarlet metamorphosis of the moon, which suddenly proved not to be the moon at all but a head-on view of the rounded bow of a descending ship. It was a plain cylinder with few features, none remarkable, almost *homely* in a way, yet he sensed immediately that its journey, ending here, had not begun anywhere on this world.

When the initial power of the memory faded enough to allow reality to impinge upon him once more, Dom found himself leaning against the closed doors of the lift with both hands, his head hanging down between his arms. He felt a hand on his shoulder, turned, and saw Ginger. Jack was standing behind her.

She said, "What's wrong?"

"I remembered . . . more."

"What?" Jack asked.

Dom told them.

He didn't need to convince them that contact with an extraterrestrial craft had been made that summer night. The moment he reminded them of what they'd seen, their own memory blocks crumbled as quickly as his. In their faces, he saw the singularly unique blend of awe, terror, joy, and hope that the event aroused.

"We went inside," Ginger said wonderingly.

"Yes," Jack said. "You, Dom, and Brendan."

"But," Ginger said, "I can't . . . can't quite remember what happened to us in there."

"Me neither," Dom said. "That part hasn't come back to me yet. I recall everything up to the minute we went through the hatch, into that golden light . . . then nothing."

For a moment they were oblivious of their perilous surroundings.

Ginger's lovely, delicate face was bone-white. Partly, it was the bloodless look of fear. But not fear alone.

Dom now understood, as Ginger did, why they had responded to each other so powerfully the instant that she had gotten off the plane at the Elko County Airport on Sunday. That summer night, they went into the ship together and shared something that had forever bonded them.

"The ship's here, inside Thunder Hill," she said. "It must be."

Dom agreed. "That's why the government took the land away from those ranchers. They enlarged the grounds of the Depository to make it more difficult for anyone to spot the truck that brought the ship in."

Jack said, "It would've been a hell of a big load."

"Like those huge trucks they haul the space shuttle on," Dom said.

Jack said, "Yeah, but why would they hide what happened?"

"I don't know," Dom said. He tapped the button that would summon the elevator. "But maybe we can find out."

The elevator arrived with a quiet hum, and they rode down to the second level. Judging from the length of the ride, the top two floors of the installation were separated by several stories of solid rock.

The doors opened at last, and they stepped into an immense circular cavern three hundred feet in diameter. From far above, the scaffolded lights shed wintry beams on an odd collection of sheet-metal buildings that hugged the walls most of the way around the chamber. Warmer light shone at small windows in two of those structures; otherwise, they were dark and appeared untenanted. Dom thought it looked a little like a film crew on location, a bunch of dressing-room trailers. Four large caverns branched from the main chamber, one of which was closed off by huge wooden doors that were curiously primitive for an otherwise highly modern facility. In the three adjacent open caverns, lights glowed, and Dom saw stored equipment—Jeeps, troop carriers, trucks, helicopters, and even jet aircraft—in addition to other trailer-like buildings with more lights at the windows than those in the main chamber. Thunder Hill was an enormous arsenal and a self-sustaining subterranean city, which Dom had known, but he had not guessed at the immensity of it.

More mystifying than the Depository's many wonders was its air of abandonment. The second level was as deserted and silent as the first. No guards, no busy personnel, no voices or sounds of labor. True, the caverns were slightly cool; and at this time of the evening, most of the staff would probably keep to the heated living quarters. But a few should have been in sight. And if most were off duty, there should have been music, TV, voluble poker-game conversations, and other muted recreational sounds wafting from the farther reaches of the facility.

In a whisper so thin it was little more than a subvocalization, Ginger said, "Are they all dead?"

"I told you," Jack said in an equally quiet voice, "something's wrong. . . ."

Dom felt drawn toward the huge wooden doors—almost three stories high, at least sixty feet wide—that sealed the entrance to the fourth cavern, so he allowed his feelings to guide him. Followed by Ginger and Jack, he walked as quietly as he could toward a smaller, man-sized door set in the bottom of one of those giant wooden portals. It was ajar, and a wedge of light, brighter than that in the main cavern, fell out onto the stone floor. He put one hand upon the door to pull it open, then stopped when he heard low voices inside. He listened until he ascertained there were only two of them, both men. They were speaking too softly for him to follow their conversation. Dom considered turning back, but he had a hunch that if he had an opportunity to look into any one room before being apprehended, he could do no better than this one. He pulled open the small door in the huge door and walked through.

The ship was there.

Ginger stood with one hand on her breast, as if to restrain her heart from hammering loose.

The cavern beyond the wooden doors was enormous, fully two hundred feet long and varying between eighty and a hundred-twenty feet in width, with a high domed ceiling. The rock floor had been chiseled, planed, and abraded to form a level surface from wall to wall; all the deep holes and crevices had been filled with concrete. Judging from scattered oil and grease stains, and from recessed ringbolts in the floor, the chamber had once been used for storing or servicing vehicles. To the right of the entrance, along the wall, were more trailer-like buildings with small windows and metal doors, a dozen stretching almost to the end of the chamber. Though probably used as offices or living quarters at one time, they'd been converted to research facilities. Hand-lettered signs were fixed to some doors: CHEM LAB, CHEM LIBRARY, PATHOLOGY, BIO LAB, BIO LIBRARY, PHYSICS 1, PHYSICS 2, ANTHROPOLOGY, and others too far away to read. In addition, work tables and large machines—a conventional X-ray unit, a large sound spectrograph of exactly the kind in use at Boston Memorial Hospital, and many other pieces of equipment Ginger did not recognize—stood in rows or clusters in the open area immediately in front of the metal buildings, as if someone were conducting a sidewalk sale of high-tech laboratory equipment. The amount of research to be done had outstripped the available quarters, which was no surprise, considering the object of the inquiry.

The ship from another world lay to the left of the entrance. It looked exactly as Ginger had recollected minutes ago, when the forbidden memory had at last pushed through the block and returned to her: a cylinder between fifty and sixty feet long, fifteen feet in diameter, rounded at both ends. It had been set upon a series of five-foot-high steel trestles to keep it off the floor, rather like a submarine in dry dock for repairs. The only thing different from its appearance on the night of July 6 was the absence of the eerie glow that had changed from moon-white to scarlet to amber. It possessed no visible propulsion system, no rockets. The hull was nearly as featureless as she recalled: here, a ten-foot-long row of shallow depressions in the metal, each big enough for her to insert her fist, but without evident purpose; there, four protruding hemispheres like halves of cantaloupes, also without apparent function; here and there, half a dozen circular elevations, some as large as the lid of a trash can, some no bigger than the mouth of a mayonnaise jar, none higher than three inches, all quite mysterious. Otherwise, but for the marks of wear and age, the long curving hull was smooth over ninety-eight percent of its surface. Yet its unspectacular design did not prevent it from being by far the most spectacular thing Ginger had ever seen. She was simultaneously terrified and joyous, overcome with a dread of the unknown yet exultant.

Two men were sitting at a table at the foot of portable stairs that led up to an open hatch in the flank of the elevated spacecraft. The more imposing was a lanky man in his forties, with curly black hair and beard, wearing dark trousers, dark shirt, and white lab coat. The other was in an Army uniform with the jacket unbuttoned, a somewhat portly man ten years older than his bearded companion. Now, seeing their three visitors, they fell silent, rose from their chairs, but did not shout for guards or rush to trip an alarm switch. The two merely watched Dom, Jack, and Ginger with interest, gauging their first reactions to the trestled craft that loomed over them.

They were expecting us, Ginger thought.

That realization should have concerned her, but it did not. She had no interest in anything but the ship.

With Dom close by her right side and Jack on her left, she moved with them in silence to the nearest end of the cylindrical vessel. Although her heart had begun beating hard and fast the moment she had entered the chamber and seen the ship, its previous pounding was mild compared to its current furious hammering. They stopped within an arm's length of the hull and studied it with an attitude of wonder bordering on veneration.

Random swirling patterns of fine-grain abrasion swept across the entire curving bulk of it, as if it had persevered through clouds of cosmic dust or particles of a type and origin as yet unknown to man. Random nicks and small dents were scattered across the surface, clearly not part of the design but inflicted by elements far more hostile than the winds and storms that battered the ships of earth's seas and skies. The hull was mottled gray-black-amber-brown as if bathed in a hundred different acids and scorched in a thousand fires.

Aside from its intrinsic and powerful alienness, the strongest impression Ginger got from the ship was a sense of great age. For all she knew, it could have been built only a few years ago and could have journeyed to Elko County at faster-than-light speeds, arriving on the night of July 6, just a few months or a year after being launched. But she did not think that was the case. She could not ascertain the source of her conviction—call it intuition—but she was certain that she was standing in the shadow of an *ancient* vessel. And when she reached out and touched the cool metal, letting her fingertips move lightly over its scarred and finely abraded surface, she felt even more strongly that she was in the presence of a venerable relic.

They had come such a long way. Such a very long way.

Following her lead, Dom and Jack had touched the hull, too. Dom took a deep quaverous breath. His, "Ahhhhhhh," was more eloquent than any words could have been.

"Oh, how I wish my father could have lived for this," Ginger said, remembering dear Jacob the dreamer, Jacob the *luftmentsch,* who had always loved tales of other worlds and distant times.

Jack said, "I wish Jenny'd lived longer . . . just a little longer. . . . "

Ginger suddenly realized that Jack did not mean the same thing she meant, that he was not saying he wished his Jenny had lived to see this vessel. He was wishing she had lived through these events because, as a result of this extraterrestrial contact, Brendan and Dom had acquired the power to heal her. If she had not succumbed on Christmas Day, they might have been able to go back to her—assuming they got out of Thunder Hill alive—and might have knit up her damaged brain, bringing her out of her coma, returning her to the arms of her devoted husband. *That* jolting moment of comprehension made Ginger aware that she had hardly begun to grasp the implications of this incredible event.

The portly man in the military uniform and the bearded man in the lab coat had walked over from the table near the ship's portal. The civilian put his hand to the hull, which Ginger and Dom and Jack were still exploring. He said, "An alloy of some kind. Harder than any steel produced on this world. Harder than diamond, yet extremely light and with surprising flexibility. You're Dom Corvaisis."

"Yes," Dom said, offering his hand to the stranger, a courtesy that would have surprised Ginger if she had not also sensed that this mild-spoken scientist and the military man with him were not their enemies.

"I'm Miles Bennell, director of the team studying this . . . wonderful event. And this is General Alvarado, commanding officer of Thunder Hill. I can't tell you how deeply I regret what's been done to you. This shouldn't be a secret possessed by a few. It belongs to the world. And if I had my way, the world would hear about it tomorrow."

Bennell shook Jack's and Ginger's hands, too.

Ginger said, "We have questions. . . . "

"And you deserve answers," Bennell said. "I'll tell you everything we've been able to learn. But we might as well wait until everyone's assembled. Where are the others?"

"What others?" Dom asked.

And Ginger said, "You mean from the motel? They're not with us."

Bennell blinked in surprise. "You mean most of them managed to slip through Colonel Falkirk's hands?"

"Falkirk?" Jack said. "Do you think *he* brought us here?"

Bennell said, "If not Falkirk—who?"

"We came in ourselves," Dom said.

Ginger saw the shock of that news register with both Bennell and General Alvarado. They looked at each other in surprise, and then a light of hope lit both their faces.

Alvarado said, "You're not telling us you found a way through the Depository's security? But that's not possible!"

"Have you read the file on Jack?" Bennell asked his friend. "Yes? Well, just remember his Ranger training and what he's been doing for a living these past eight years or so."

Jack shook his head. "I can't take all the credit. Yeah, I got us through the perimeter, across the grounds, and past the first door, but it was Dom who actually got us inside."

"Dom?" Bennell said, turning in surprise to the writer. "But what do you know about security systems? Unless . . . of course! This strange damn power of yours! Since that experience in Lomack's house and since the light you generated when Cronin first arrived at the Tranquility, you must've discovered the power wasn't external. You must know now that it's actually in *you*."

Ginger realized that Bennell's statement had revealed that their conversations at the Tranquility had, indeed, been monitored. But it also revealed that their discussions and strategy sessions in the diner, after Jack's arrival, had *not* been penetrated. Otherwise Bennell would have known about the experiment last night in which both Dom and Brendan had learned that their apparently mystical experiences were, in fact, events of their own creation.

"Yes," Dom said. "We know the power's in us—me and Brendan. But where does it come from, Doctor Bennell?"

"You don't know?"

"I think it has something to do with what happened to us when we went in the ship, but I can't remember. Can't you tell me?"

"No," Miles Bennell said. "Not really. It was known that three of you went into the vessel, but we didn't know that anything . . . peculiar had happened to you in there. You'd come out just as the helicopters with DERO troops and scientific observers began to arrive on the site, and no one figured you'd been in there more than a couple minutes. When you were taken into custody, you didn't tell anyone that something important had happened while you'd been aboard. I believe you said you'd just looked around. And for ease of handling, you were all sedated immediately after being arrested and conveyed back to the Tranquility. So even if you'd changed your mind and decided to tell us what happened, you didn't have a chance." Excited, the lanky scientist absentmindedly began to comb his long fingers through his curly black beard as he talked. "When the decision was made to put a lid on the event, to brainwash every civilian who'd seen it, there wasn't time for a thorough debriefing of all the witnesses. In fact, you were never brought out of sedation; you were moved directly onto the drug program that was part of your memory-wipe. That's one reason I was opposed to the cover-up. I felt that by brainwashing you without giving us plenty of time to debrief . . . well, it was not only unfair and cruel to you but a really stupid waste of potential sources of data."

Ginger looked toward the open portal farther along the flank of the vessel, at the top of the portable stairs. "If we go back inside now, maybe the last of the memory block will crumble."

"That might help," Bennell agreed.

Looking up at the starship again, Jack said, "How'd you know it was coming down out there along I-80?"

"Yeah," Dom said. "And why'd they think it *should* be covered up?"

"And the creatures who came in it," Jack said.

"God, yes," Ginger said, "where are they? What's happened to them?"

Interrupting, General Alvarado said, "Like Miles said, you'll get the answers because you deserve them. But first, there's more urgent business." He turned to Dom. "I suppose if you can levitate things and create light out of thin air, there's no problem getting through an electronic security system. And if you can get in, you ought to be able to use your power to keep other people out. You think you could? Keep both the blast doors and the smaller entrance from opening until we're ready to open them?"

Dom was clearly as baffled by these questions as Ginger was. He said, "Well, maybe. I don't know."

Bennell looked at the general. "Bob, if you keep the colonel out, that'll be like lighting the fuse. He knows no one can control VIGILANT but him. If he can't get in . . . it'll look like voodoo to him. He'll be *sure* we're all infected."

"Infected?" Ginger said uneasily.

Alvarado said, "The colonel is convinced that we—you, me, Miles, all of us—have been somehow *possessed* by alien beings, taken over like a bunch of puppets, and that we're not human any more."

"That's insane," Jack said.

But with greater uneasiness, Ginger said, "Of course, we know we haven't been. But is there reason to believe it could've happened?"

"Initially, yes, some small reason," Miles Bennell said, "but it didn't happen. It's not true. And we understand now that it was never a possibility. Just typical black-minded human nature . . . putting the worst interpretation on everything. I'll explain later."

Ginger was about to demand an immediate explanation, but General Alvarado said, "Please, hold the questions. We don't have much time. Right now, we believe Falkirk is returning here, having taken your friends into custody—"

"No," Dom said, "they got away before we did. They're gone."

"Never underestimate the colonel," Alvarado said. "But see, the thing is—if Dom could use his power to shut down the entrances and keep Falkirk out, maybe we'd have the time to find a way to blow this whole story wide open. Because if he gets in here . . . I'm afraid there's going to be bloodshed one way or another."

Movement at the front of the chamber caught Ginger's attention, and she gasped in dismay when she saw Jorja, Marcie, Brendan, and then all the others coming in through the small door in the big door.

"Too late," Miles Bennell said. "Too late."

At the entrance to Thunder Hill Depository, the seven witnesses and Parker Faine were taken out of the transport and grouped in the snow in front of the smaller steel door. Lieutenant Horner's machine gun discouraged flight and resistance.

Leland ordered the other DERO men back to Shenkfield, where they were to bury Stefan Wycazik in an unmarked grave and await further orders. But no orders would be forthcoming from Leland, for he would not be alive to give them. It was not necessary to sacrifice the entire company, for just he and one other man could control the prisoners and destroy the entire Depository, and it was Lieutenant Horner's bad luck to be second-in-command and have that responsibility fall upon his shoulders.

In the entrance tunnel, Leland was alarmed to see that the video cameras were not working. But then he realized that the new emergency program under which VIGILANT was operating did not require visual ID for admittance, for it would respond only to one key: the prints of the palm and all the fingers on Leland's left hand. When he put his palm to the glass panel beside the inner door, VIGILANT admitted him at once.

He and Horner took the eight prisoners down to the second level and across The Hub to the cavern where Alvarado and Bennell waited. As Leland stood back and watched them file through the man-sized door in the huge wooden wall, he looked beyond them and saw the other witnesses—Corvaisis, Weiss, and Twist—and although he did not know how they had gotten here, he was exhilarated by the realization that, contrary to expectations, he had the whole group exactly where he wanted them.

He left Horner to follow the prisoners, while he hurried back to the elevators. He could never trust poor Tom again, not now that the lieutenant had been alone with people who might be contaminated.

Carrying his submachine gun at the ready, Leland took a smaller elevator down to the third level. He intended to kill anyone who moved toward him. And if they rushed him in great numbers, he would turn the gun on himself. He wouldn't let himself be *changed*. Through childhood and adolescence, his parents had striven to change him into one of them: a shouter-and-wailer-in-churches, a self-flagellator, a God-terrorized speaker of tongues. He had resisted the changes his parents would have wrought in him, and he would not be changed now. *They* had been after him all his life, in one guise or another, and they would not get him after he had come this far with his identity and dignity intact.

The bottom level of Thunder Hill Depository was given over entirely to the storage of supplies, munitions, and explosives. Staff members all lived on the second level and most worked there as well. However, at any hour of the day, a few workers and a guard were usually on duty on the third and lowest floor. When Leland stepped out of the elevator, into the central cavern off which other chambers opened—an arrangement much like that on the second floor—he was pleased to see the basement was deserted tonight. General Alvarado had obeyed Leland's orders and had sent all of his people to their quarters.

Alvarado probably thought that, by cooperating, he could convince Leland that he and all his people were unquestionably human. But Leland was not naïve enough to be taken in by such a ruse. His own parents had been capable of behaving like normal human beings, too—oh, yes, smiles and plenty of sweet-talk, oaths of love and affection—and just when you started to think they actually cared about you and wanted the best for you, they'd suddenly reveal themselves for what they really were. They would get out the leather strap or the Ping-Pong paddle in which the old man had drilled holes, and the beatings would be administered in the name of God. Leland Falkirk couldn't be easily deceived by a masquerade of humanity, for at an early age he had learned to look for—in fact, to *expect*—an inhuman presence below the skin of normality.

Crossing the main cavern to the massive steel blast door that sealed off the munitions room, Leland looked nervously left and right and up into the darkness between the lights. One of his punishments, as a child, had been long imprisonments in a windowless coal cellar.

Leland pressed his left hand to the glass panel beside the door, which rolled open. Banks of lights flickered on automatically down the length of a room piled twenty feet high with anchored crates and drums and racks that contained live ammunition, mortar shells, grenades, mines, and other instruments of destruction.

At the end of the long chamber was a twenty-foot-square vault that also required a palm ID to be opened. The weapons within were of such deadly magnitude that only eight people out of the hundreds in Thunder Hill were authorized to enter, and no *one* of them alone could open the vault. The system required three of the eight to apply their palms to the glass panel, one after another, within one minute, before access would be granted. But this also was overseen by Vigilant, and the computer's new program, designed by Leland, made him the sole keeper of the Depository's tactical nuclear arsenal. He put his palm to the cool glass, and fifteen seconds later the many-layered, steel MacGruder vault door swung slowly open with a hum of electric motors.

To the right of the vault door, twenty backpack nukes hung on wall pegs, missing only their primary detonators and their binary packages of explosive material. The detonators were stored in drawers along the back wall. To the left of the door, in lead-lined cabinets, the binary packages lay waiting for Armageddon.

DERO training included familiarization with a variety of nuclear devices that terrorists might conceivably plant in American cities, so Leland knew how to assemble, arm, and disarm The Bomb in virtually all of its design permutations. He got the components from the cabinets, took two backpack-bomb frames down from the wall pegs, and put together both weapons in only eight minutes, glancing nervously at the door as he worked. He breathed easier only when he had set the timers on both detonators for fifteen minutes and had started the clocks.

He slung his submachine gun over his shoulder, slipped each arm into the straps of a backpack nuke. Each device weighed sixty-nine pounds. He heaved both off the floor and lurched out of the vault, bent like a hunchback and grunting under that apocalyptic weight.

Another man might have had to stop two or three times during the journey back through the immense munitions room. *Any* other man might have been forced to pause, put the bombs down, catch his breath, and stretch his muscles before going on. But not Leland Falkirk. That dead weight wrenched his back and pulled at his shoulders and made his arms ache, but he grew happier as the pain intensified.

In the main cavern into which the elevators opened, he put one of the backpack nukes on the center of the floor. He looked around at the solid rock walls and up at the granite ceiling with a feeling of satisfaction. If there were any faults at all in the rock strata—and surely there were—the place would cave in, bringing everything above down with it. But even if the mighty stone chambers could contain and withstand the blast, no one who tried to take refuge on this level would survive. Not even an alien lifeform of great adaptability could reconstitute itself after being vaporized in a nuclear heat and reduced to random atoms.

Nuclear pain.

He would not be able to survive it, but he would prove that he had the nerve to contemplate and endure it. Only a fraction of a second of blinding agony. Not bad, actually. In fact, not as bad as vigorous and drawn-out beatings with a leather strap or with a Ping-Pong paddle that had been drilled full of holes to increase the sting.

Still holding the second nuke by its straps, Leland smiled down at the changing numbers on the first bomb's digital-display clock, which was already counting toward Ragnarok. The nicest thing about backpack nukes was that, once armed, they could not be *dis*armed. He did not have to worry that someone could undo his work.

He entered the elevator and rode up to the second level.

Carrying Marcie, Jorja crossed directly to Jack Twist and stood beside him, looking up at the ship cradled on trestles. Although the collapse of her memory block and the inrushing recollections had more or less prepared her for this sight, she was overcome with an awe as powerful as that which had seized her in the troop transport, when the astounding truth had first been revealed. She reached out to touch the mottled hull, and a shiver—part fear, part wonder, part delight—coursed through her when her fingertips made contact with the scorched and abraded metal.

Whether following her mother's lead or acting on an impulse of her own, Marcie reached forward, too. When her small tentative hand pressed against the hull, she said, "The moon. The moon."

"Yes," Jorja said immediately. "Yes, honey. This is what you saw come down. Remember? It wasn't the moon falling. It was this, glowing white like the moon, then red, then amber."

"Moon," the child said softly, sliding her tiny hand back and forth across the flank of the vessel, as if she were trying to clean off the mottled film of age and tribulation and, thereby, also clean off the clouded surface of her own memory. "Moon fell down."

"Not the moon, honey. A ship. A very special ship. A spaceship like in the movies, baby."

Marcie turned and looked at Jorja, actually *looked* at her, with eyes that were no longer out of focus or turned inward. "Like Captain Kirk and Mr. Spock?"

Jorja smiled and hugged her tighter. "Yes, honey, like Captain Kirk and Mr. Spock."

"Like Luke Skywalker," Jack said, leaning forward and pushing a lock of hair out of the girl's eyes.

"Luke," Marcie said.

"And Han Solo," Jack said.

The child's eyes blurred out of focus. She had returned to her private place to contemplate the news she had just received.

Jack smiled at Jorja and said, "She's going to be all right. It may take time, but she'll be all right because her whole obsession was a struggle to remember. Now, she's begun to remember, and she doesn't need to struggle any more."

As usual, Jorja was reassured merely by his presence, by his aura of calm competence. "She'll be all right—*if* we can get out of here alive and with our memories intact."

"We will," Jack said. "Somehow."

A rush of warm emotion filled Dom when he saw Parker. He embraced the stocky artist and said, "How in God's name did you wind up here, my friend?"

"It's a long story," Parker said. A sorrow in his face and eyes said, better than words, that at least part of the story was bleak.

"I didn't mean to get you so deep in this trouble," Dom said.

Looking up at the starship, Parker said, "I wouldn't have missed it for the world."

"What happened to your beard?"

"When *this* kind of company's coming," Parker said, gesturing at the ship, "they're worth shaving for."

Ernie moved along the side of the starship, staring, touching.

Faye stayed with Brendan, for she was concerned about him. Months ago, he had lost his faith—or had thought he'd lost it, which was just as bad for him. And tonight he had lost Father Wycazik, a blow that had left him hollow-eyed and shaky.

"Faye," he said, looking up at the ship, "it's truly wonderful, isn't it?"

"Yes," she said. "I never was one for stories about other worlds, never gave much thought to what it would mean. . . . But it's the end of everything and the start of something new. Wonderful and new."

"But it's not God," he said, "and in my heart, that's what I'd hoped it would be."

She took his hand. "Remember the message that Parker brought you from Father Wycazik? What he told you in the truck? Father Wycazik knew what had happened, what had come down that night, and for him it was a reaffirmation of his faith."

Brendan smiled forlornly. "For him, *everything* was a reaffirmation of his faith."

"Then it'll also be a reaffirmation for you," she told him. "You just need time, a little time to think about it. Then you'll see it the same way Father Wycazik did because, though you aren't aware of it, you are a lot like him."

He looked at her, surprised. "Not me. You didn't know him. I'm not half the priest . . . not half the man that he was."

Faye smiled and pinched his cheek affectionately. "Brendan, when you told us all about your rector, it was clear how much you admired him. And within one day, it was *also* clear that you were more like him than you realized. You're young, Brendan. You've still got things to learn. But when you're Father Wycazik's age, you're going to be the man *and* the priest that he was. And every day of your life is going to be a living testament to him.''

A fragile hopefulness replaced his despair. His mouth trembled and his voice cracked. ''You . . . you really think so?''

''I know it,'' Faye said.

He put his arms around her, and she hugged him.

Ned and Sandy stood with their arms around each other's waists, looking up at the ship. Neither spoke because nothing more needed to be said. At least, that's the way it seemed to him.

Then Sandy said something that *did* need to be said. ''Ned, if we get out of this alive . . . I want to go see a doctor. You know—one of those fertility experts. I want to do whatever I can to bring a baby into the world.''

''But . . . you've always . . . you never . . . ''

''I never liked the world enough before,'' she said softly. ''But now . . . I want a part of us to be there when our kind go out to ride on top of all the darkness, to other worlds, maybe to meet the strangers—the wonderful strangers—who came in this. I'll be a real good mother, Ned.''

''I know you will.''

When Miles Bennell saw the last of the witnesses and Parker Faine filing into the chamber, he gave up hope of employing Dom Corvaisis' new powers to freeze Falkirk out of Thunder Hill. He would have to rely, instead, on the .357 Magnum that was tucked into his belt. It pressed hard against his stomach, hidden beneath his loose white lab coat.

Miles thought Leland would come with at least twenty men, probably twice that number. He expected the colonel, Horner, and half a dozen soldiers to enter the chamber behind the last of the witnesses. But only Horner appeared, toting a submachine gun and prepared to use it.

As the Blocks, the Sarvers, Brendan Cronin, and the others were drawn instantly and irresistibly to the starship, Horner said, ''General Alvarado, Dr. Bennell—Colonel Falkirk will be along in a moment.''

''How dare you come in here with an automatic weapon at the ready,'' Bob said with an aplomb Miles admired. ''Good God, man! Don't you realize if your finger slipped and you let off a burst, the slugs would keep ricocheting off these rock walls, killing all of us—you included!''

''My finger never slips, sir,'' Horner said in such a way that he was virtually challenging Bob to make an issue of it.

Instead, Bob said sharply, ''Where's Falkirk?''

''Sir, the colonel had some things to attend to,'' Horner said. ''He apologizes for keeping you waiting. He'll join us shortly.''

''What things?'' Bob Alvarado asked.

''Sir, the colonel doesn't always consult me about his every move.''

Miles was half-afraid Falkirk had already taken squads of DERO troops to liquidate the staff. But that grim possibility seemed less likely with every second that passed unmarred by the rattle of gunfire.

He was a heavily armed man looking for a chance to turn the tables on his enemies, but he did not want to appear that way to Horner, so Miles decided the most natural thing to do would be to talk with the witnesses and begin to answer some of the many questions they had. He discovered that most of them had already heard about the CISG, so he quickly summarized the findings of that committee for the others, by way of explaining why the cover-up had initially been ordered.

The ship before them, Miles explained, had first been spotted by deeply positioned defense satellites orbiting the earth at a distance of more than 22,000 miles. They had seen it coming in past the moon. (The Soviets, whose defense satellites were cruder, did not spot the visitor until much later—and never accurately identified it.)

Initially, observers thought the alien craft was a large meteorite or small asteroid on a collision course with Earth. If it was a soft, porous material, it might burn up during descent. And even if Earth were unlucky, if the incoming debris was made of more solid stuff, it still might fragment into a host of small and relatively harmless meteorites. However, if Earth were *very* unlucky, if the wandering rock had a high nickel-iron content, which might eliminate the possibility of extensive fragmentation, it was definitely a menace. Of course, it was almost certain to hit water, since oceans covered seventy percent of the planet's surface. Water impact would result in little damage, unless it hit close enough to shore for its tsunami to devastate a port. The worst-case possibility was a land strike in a heavily populated area.

"Imagine a lump of nickel and iron the size of a bus hurtling into the heart of Manhattan at a couple of thousand miles an hour," Miles told them. "That picture was horrifying enough to make us consider measures to destroy or deflect it."

Less than six months earlier, the first satellites in the nation's Strategic Defense Shield had been placed secretly in orbit. They had comprised less than ten percent of the system as it would be ultimately constituted, and on their own they could not have done much to prevent nuclear war. But thanks to several forward-thinking designers, every satellite had been given high maneuverability that would allow it to turn its armaments outward and double as a planetary defense against just such a threat as that hurtling piece of space junk. Recent theory proposed that impacting comets or asteroids had wiped out the dinosaurs, and prudent planners had decided it might be wise to use the Strategic Defense Shield to knock down not only Soviet missiles but the fate-flung missiles of the universe itself. Therefore, one of the satellites was repositioned while the meteorite streaked nearer Earth, and plans were laid to fire all of its antimissile missiles at the intruder. Although none of those projectiles was nuclear, their explosive warheads, in combination, were believed sufficient to fragment the meteorite into enough pieces to ensure that none would be large enough to reach the surface of Earth with destructive potential.

"Then," Miles said, "hours before the scheduled attack on the intruder, an analysis of the latest photographs indicated a shockingly symmetrical shape. And spectrographic readings, forwarded by the satellite, began to confirm that it might be something stranger than a meteorite. Its analysis did not match any of the standard profiles for meteorites." He had walked among the witnesses as he talked, and now he put one hand upon the flank of the ship, still capable of being awed by it even after eighteen months. "New photos were ordered every ten minutes. During the following hour, the approaching shape grew ever more distinct, until the likelihood of it being a ship was so great that no one would risk ordering its destruction. We hadn't informed the Soviets of the object or of our intention to destroy it, for that would have given them information about our defense satellite capabilities. Now, we purposefully began random jamming of Soviet high-atmosphere radar, dropping bogeys and electronic shadows on them, to cover the ship's advance and thus keep the secret of its visit. At first, we thought it would take up orbit around Earth. But very late in the game, we realized it was going to come straight in, following the very path an unpowered meteorite would have followed, though in a controlled fashion. Defense computers were able to give a thirty-eight-minute warning that point of impact would be here in Elko County."

"Just enough time to close I-80," Ernie Block said, "and call Falkirk and his DERO men in from wherever they were."

"Idaho," Miles said. "They were on training maneuvers in southern Idaho, fortunately quite close. Or unfortunately, depending on your point of view."

"Of course, Dr. Bennell, I know *your* point of view," said Leland Falkirk from the door where he had, at last, appeared.

The .357 Magnum felt as big as a cannon against Miles Bennell's belly, but suddenly it seemed as useless as a pea-shooter.

Upon seeing Leland Falkirk for the first time, Ginger realized how little justice the newspaper photograph had done him. He was handsomer, more imposing—and more frightening—than he'd appeared in the *Sentinel*. He didn't carry his submachine gun in the stern attitude of readiness that Horner affected, nonchalantly dangling it in one hand. However, his apparent laxity was more threatening than Horner's posturing. Ginger had the feeling that, by seeming to be careless, he was taunting them to try something. As Falkirk drew nearer the group, Ginger thought that he brought with him a palpable aura—and almost a stench—of hatred and madness.

Dr. Bennell said, "Where are all your men, Colonel?"

"No men," Falkirk said mildly. "Just Lieutenant Horner and me. No need for a display of force, really. I'm quite sure that when we've had time to discuss the situation rationally, we'll reach a solution to the problem that will satisfy everyone."

Ginger had an even stronger feeling that the colonel was taunting them. He had the air of a child who, in possession of a secret, not only takes enormous pleasure in his special knowledge but is especially tickled by the ignorance of others. She saw that Dr. Bennell seemed baffled by Falkirk's behavior and wary of him.

"Go on with your discussion," the colonel said, checking his watch. "For heaven's sake, don't let me interrupt. You must have a thousand questions you'd like Doctor Bennell to answer."

"I have one," Sandy said. "Doctor, where are the . . . the people who came in this ship?"

"Dead," Bennell said. "There were eight of them, but they were all dead before they got here."

A pang of regret pierced Ginger's heart, and from their expressions she saw that the others were equally shocked and disappointed. Parker and Jorja even groaned softly, as if they had just been given news of a friend's death.

"How did they die?" Ned asked. "Of what?"

Glancing repeatedly at Colonel Falkirk, Bennell said, "Well, first, you've got to know a little about them, about why they came in the first place. In their ship, we found a virtual encyclopedia of their species—a crash course in their culture, biology, psychology—recorded on something like our own videodisks. We required a couple of weeks to even identify the player and a month to learn how to operate it. But once we figured it out, we found the machine still operable, astonishing when you consider . . . well, better not jump ahead. Suffice to say we're still going through the trove of material on those disks. It's superbly visual, explaining so much in spite of the language barrier—though it also slowly teaches their language. Those of us on the project almost feel . . . a brotherhood with the people who built this ship."

Colonel Falkirk laughed sourly. Mockingly, he said, "Brotherhood."

Dr. Bennell glared at him, then continued: "I'd need weeks to tell you what we know of them now. Suffice to say they're an unimaginably ancient spacegoing species which had, at the time this ship departed its home port, searched out and located five other intelligent species in other solar systems than their own.''

''Five!'' Ginger said in amazement. ''But—even if the galaxy is positively packed with life, that's incredible. Considering the vast distances to be traveled, the endless places to search.''

Dr. Bennell nodded. ''But you see, from the time they achieved the means of traveling from star to star, they apparently decided it was their sacred duty to seek out other intelligences. In fact, it seems to have become a religion to them.'' He shook his head and sighed. ''It's difficult to be sure we understand this, because even their excellent visual encyclopedia more readily describes physical things than it does philosophies. But we think they see themselves as servants of some supreme force that created the universe—''

''God?'' Brendan interrupted. ''Are you saying they see themselves as servants of God?''

''Something like that,'' Bennell said. ''However, they aren't spreading any religious message. They simply feel they have a sacred obligation to help intelligent species find one another, to bind intelligences across the vast emptiness of space.''

''Bind,'' Falkirk said ominously, and he looked at his watch.

General Alvarado had been moving slowly to his right, putting himself at the periphery of the colonel's vision. He took another step.

Ginger was increasingly uneasy about the undercurrent of antagonism between Falkirk and Bennell and Alvarado, which she did not entirely understand. She moved closer to Dom and put an arm around him.

''And they bring another gift,'' Bennell said, frowning toward the colonel. ''They're such an ancient species that they've evolved certain abilities we think of as psychic. The ability to heal. Telekinesis. Other things. Not only have they evolved those talents, but they've learned to . . . to infuse the same abilities in other intelligent species that lack them.''

''Infuse?'' Dom said. ''How?''

''We don't entirely understand,'' Bennell said. ''But they can pass these powers along. That is evidently what was done with you, and now you have the ability to pass the power to others.''

''Pass the power?'' Jack said, astonished. ''You mean Dom and Brendan could give us . . . or anyone . . . what they have?''

''I've already given it,'' Brendan said. ''Ginger, Dom, Jack—you didn't hear the news Parker brought from Father Wycazik. Those two I healed in Chicago— Emmy and Winton—they've both got the power now.''

''New sources of infection,'' Falkirk said somberly.

''And evidently,'' Parker said, ''since Brendan healed me, I'll have it too, sooner or later.''

''Although I don't think it's passed *only* in healing,'' Brendan said. ''It's just that the healing is such an intimate contact. Along with knitting up the tissues of the person you're healing, you somehow pass the power to them.''

Ginger's mind reeled. This news was every bit as earth-shaking as the existence of the starship. ''You mean . . . my God . . . you mean they came to help us evolve to a new level as a species? And that evolution is now already under way?''

''It would seem to be, yes,'' Bennell said.

Looking at his wristwatch again, Leland Falkirk said, ''Please, this masquerade is getting boring.''

''What masquerade?'' Faye Block asked. ''What are you talking about, Colonel? We were told you believe we've all been somehow possessed, some nonsense like that. How can you have gotten such a crazy idea?''

"Spare me this charade," Falkirk said sharply. "You all pretend to know nothing. In reality, you know everything. Not one of you is human any longer. You're all . . . possessed, and this innocence is play-acting to convince me to spare you. But it won't work. It's too late."

Repelled by Falkirk's air of madness, Ginger turned again to Bennell. "What *is* all this stuff about infection and possession?"

"A mistake," Bennell said, moving a few steps to his left.

Ginger realized he was trying to pull the colonel's attention in that direction, away from General Alvarado, in order to give the general a better chance of slipping entirely out of Falkirk's notice.

"A mistake," Bennell repeated. "Or rather . . . an example of the human race's typical xenophobia—hatred and suspicion of strangers, of anyone that's different. When we first viewed some of the videodisks I mentioned, when we first learned about the extraterrestrials' desire to pass these powers to other species, we apparently misinterpreted what we were seeing. Initially, we thought they were taking possession of those they changed, inserting an alien consciousness into a host body. I guess it's an understandable paranoia, after all the horror novels and movies. We thought perhaps we had a parasitical race on our hands. But that misapprehension was quickly dispelled when we'd seen more of their disks and had time to puzzle out some of the finer points. Now we know we were wrong."

"*I* don't know it," Falkirk said. "I think you were all infected and then, under the control of these creatures, you began to downplay the danger. Or . . . or the disks are merely propaganda. Lies."

"No," Bennell said. "For one thing, I don't think these creatures would be capable of lying. Besides, if they could so easily take us over, they wouldn't require propaganda. And they sure as hell wouldn't bring us this encyclopedia that *tells* us they're going to change us."

Ginger had noticed Brendan Cronin following the discussion even more avidly than everyone else, and now he said, "I know the religious metaphor may not be entirely appropriate here. But if they feel they come to us as the servants of God . . . and if they come to hand down to us these miraculous gifts, then you could almost say they were angels, archangels bestowing special blessings."

Falkirk laughed harshly. "Oh, that's rich, Cronin! Do you really think you can get to me from a religious angle? *Me?* Even if I were a religious fanatic, like my dead and rotting parents, I wouldn't buy these creatures as angels. Angels with faces like buckets of worms?"

"Worms? What's he talking about?" Brendan asked Bennell.

The scientist said, "They look very different from us. Bipeds with forearms rather like us, yes. Six digits instead of five. But that's about all we have in common in the way of looks. Initially, they seem repulsive. In fact, repulsive is a mild word. But in time . . . you begin to see they have a certain beauty of their own."

"Beauty of their own," Falkirk said scornfully. "Monsters is what they are, and they'd only have beauty in the eyes of other monsters, so you've just proven my point, Bennell."

Ginger's anger with Falkirk drove her to take a couple of steps toward him in spite of his submachine gun. "You damn fool," she said. "What does it matter what they look like? The important thing is what they *are*. And evidently they're creatures with a deep sense of purpose, noble purpose. No matter how different they look, the things we have in common with them are greater than our differences. My father always said that, as much as intelligence, the things that separated us from the beasts were courage, love, friendship, compassion, and empathy. Do you realize what courage it took for them to set out on this journey across God knows how many thousands of millions of miles? So that's one big thing we share with them—courage. And love, friendship? They must have those too. Otherwise how would they have built a civilization that could reach to the stars? You need love and friendship to have a *reason* to build. Compassion? They've got a mission to bring other intelligent species to a higher rung on the evolutionary ladder. Surely, that takes compassion. And empathy? Isn't that obvious? They empathize with our fear and loneliness, with our dread that we're adrift in a meaningless universe. They empathize so much that they commit themselves to these incredible journeys on the mere *hope* of encountering us and bringing us the news that we are not alone.'' Suddenly she knew her anger wasn't directed so much at Falkirk as at this horrid blindness in the human species that led it frequently into spirals of self-destruction. ''Look at me,'' she told the colonel. ''I'm a Jew. And there are those who'd say I'm not the same as they are, not as good, even dangerous. Stories of Jews drinking the blood of gentile babies—there are the ignorant who believe that garbage. Is there any difference between that sick antisemitism and your stubborn insistence, in spite of all evidence to the contrary, that these creatures come to drink *our* blood? Let us go, for God's sake. Stop the endless hatred here. Stop it now. We have a destiny that leaves no room for hatred.''

''Bravo,'' Falkirk said acidly. ''A very nice speech.'' Even as he spoke, the colonel swung his machine gun toward General Alvarado and said, ''Don't go for your gun, General. I assume you're carrying one. I won't be shot. I want to die in the glorious fire.''

''Fire?'' Bennell said.

Falkirk grinned. ''That's right, Doctor. The glorious fire that will consume us all and save the world from this infection.''

''Christ!'' Bennell said. ''That's why you didn't bring more men with you. You didn't want to sacrifice more than necessary.'' He turned to Alvarado. ''Bob, the crazy bastard's gotten into the tactical nukes.''

Ginger knew that Alvarado was feeling precisely what she felt at this news, for his face twisted and went instantly gray.

''Two backpack nukes,'' Falkirk said. ''One right outside that door. The other in the main chamber downstairs.'' He checked his watch. ''Less than three minutes, and we'll all be vapor. Not even time left for you to *change* me, I'll bet. How long does it take to change one of us to one of you? Longer than three minutes, I suppose.''

Abruptly, the machine gun tore out of Falkirk's hands as if it had acquired life and taken flight, wrenching loose of his grasp with such force that it cut his fingers and tore off a couple of his nails. At the same instant, Lieutenant Horner screamed as his machine gun erupted from his grasp with equal suddenness and force. Ginger saw both weapons spin through the air and drop with a clatter, one at the feet of Ernie Block and the other at Jack Twist's side, both of whom jubilantly took up the guns and covered Falkirk and Horner.

''You?'' Ginger said wonderingly, turning to Dom.

''Me, yeah, I think,'' he said breathlessly. ''I . . . I didn't know I could do it until I *had* to. Sort of the way Brendan heals people.''

Stunned, Dr. Bennell said, ''But it doesn't matter. Falkirk said three minutes.''

''Two,'' Falkirk said, cradling one bleeding hand in the other and grinning happily. ''Two minutes now.''

''And backpack nukes can't be disarmed,'' Alvarado said.

Running, Dom shouted: ''Brendan, you take the one outside this door. I'll get the one downstairs.''

''They can't be disarmed!'' Alvarado repeated.

* * *

Brendan knelt beside the nuclear device and winced when he saw the time remaining on the clock. One minute, thirty-three seconds.

He didn't know what to do. He had healed three people, yes, and he had caused some pepper shakers to whirl through the air, and he had even generated light out of nothingness. But he remembered how the pepper shakers had gotten out of control and how the chairs had leapt off the diner floor and smashed against the ceiling. And he knew if he made one false move with the detonator in this bomb, he would not be saved by all his superhuman power.

One minute, twenty-six seconds.

The others had come out of the cavern where the ship rested and had gathered around. Even Falkirk and Horner remained under guard, though there was no reason for them to try to get their guns. They trusted in the efficacy of the bomb.

One minute, eleven seconds.

"If I smash the detonator," Brendan said to Alvarado, "pulverize it, would that—"

"No," the general said. "Once armed, the detonator will trigger the bomb automatically if you try to wreck it."

One-oh-three.

Faye knelt beside him. "Just make it pop right up out of the damn bomb, Brendan. The way Dom tore those guns out of their hands."

Brendan stared at the rapidly changing numerals on the detonator's clock and tried to imagine that entire device popping free of the rest of the bomb.

Nothing happened.

Fifty-four seconds.

Cursing the slowness of the elevator, Dom virtually flew out of the doors when they opened, with Ginger close behind him, and dashed to the backpack nuke standing in the center of the main cavern on the bottom level of Thunder Hill. Heart pounding even faster than his stomach was churning, he crouched beside the bomb and said, "Jesus," when he saw the digital clock.

Fifty seconds.

"You can do it," Ginger said, stooping at the other side of the hateful device. "You've got a destiny."

"Here goes."

"Love you," she said.

"Love you," he said, as surprised as she was by that statement.

Forty-two seconds.

He raised his hands over the nuclear device, and he felt the rings appearing immediately in his palms.

Forty seconds.

Brendan had broken out in a sweat.

Thirty-nine seconds.

He strained, trying to work the magic that he knew was in him. But though the stigmata burned on his palms, and in spite of the fact that he could feel the power surging in him, he could not focus on the urgent task. He kept thinking about what could go wrong, and that in some way he would be responsible if it did go wrong, and the more he thought the less he could direct the miraculous energy within him.

Thirty-four seconds.

Parker Faine pushed between two onlookers and dropped to his knees beside

Brendan. "No offense, Father, but maybe the problem is that you, being a Jesuit, are just too damn prone to intellectualize. Maybe this requires going with your gut. Maybe what this needs is the wild-ass, go-for-it, try-anything, gonzo, berserker commitment of an artist." He thrust his own large hands toward the detonator and shouted: "Come out of there you fucker!"

With a snap of wires, the detonator leapt out of its niche in the bomb package and straight into Parker's hands.

There were cries of relief and congratulations, but Brendan said, "The clock's still counting down.

Eleven seconds.

"Yeah, but it's not connected to the bomb any more," Parker said, grinning broadly.

Alvarado said, "But there's a conventional explosive charge in the damn detonator."

The detonator erupted out of the bomb, into Dom's hands. He saw the clock still counting, and he sensed it had to be stopped even though there was no longer a chance of a nuclear explosion. So he simply *willed* it to stop, and the lighted numerals froze at 0:03.

0:03.

Parker, unaccustomed to the role of magician, panicked at this secondary crisis. Certain his power was depleted, he chose a course of action perfectly in character. With a war cry to rival John Wayne in one of the Duke's old movies, Parker turned and threw the detonator toward the far wall of the cavern, as if lobbing a grenade. He knew he could not cast it clear to the other side of the chamber, but he hoped he could pitch it far enough. Even as it left his hand, he flung himself to the floor, as the others had already done.

Dom was kissing Ginger when the explosion sounded overhead, and they both jumped. For an instant he thought Brendan had failed to disarm the other device, then realized a nuclear explosion would have brought the ceiling down on them.

"The detonator," she said.

"Come on," he said. "Let's see if anyone's hurt."

The lift crawled upward. When they arrived at the second level, the main chamber was filled with scores of Depository staff members, all carrying guns and responding to the sound of battle.

Holding Ginger's hand, Dom pushed through the crowd, toward the place where he had left Brendan with the first backpack nuke. He saw Faye, Sandy, and Ned. Then Brendan—alive, unhurt. Jorja, Marcie.

Parker loomed on his right and gave both him and Ginger a bear hug. "You shoulda seen me, kids. If they'd had *both* me and Audie Murphy, World War II would've been over in about six months."

"I'm beginning to see why Dom admires you so," Ginger said.

Parker raised his eyebrows. "But of course, my dear! To know me is to love me."

A sudden cry of alarm rose, which jolted Dom because he thought all danger was past,. When he turned, he saw that Falkirk had dodged away from Jack and Ernie in the turmoil and had wrenched a revolver from one of the Thunder Hill staff. Everyone fell back from him.

"For Christ's sake," Jack shouted, "it's over, Colonel. It's over, damn you."

But Falkirk had no intention of resuming his private war. His gray translucent eyes shone with madness. "Yes," he said. "It's over, and I won't be changed like the rest of you. You won't get *me*." Before anyone could reach him, or before anyone could think to tear the weapon from his hands with telekinetic power, he thrust the barrel of the revolver into his mouth and pulled the trigger.

With a cry of horror, Ginger looked away from the falling corpse, and Dom turned his head, too. It was not the bloody death itself that repelled but the stupid, pointless waste when, at last, humankind had within its grasp the secret of immortality.

3. Transcendence

As the staff of Thunder Hill filled the cavern, milling around the ship that most had never seen before, Ginger and Dom and the other witnesses followed Miles Bennell into the vessel.

The interior was not dramatic, but as plain as the exterior, with none of the complex and powerful machinery that one expected in a craft capable of such a journey. Miles Bennell explained that the builders had advanced beyond machinery as humankind understood it, perhaps even beyond physics as humankind understood it. There was one long chamber within, and it was for the most part gray, drab, featureless. The warm golden luminosity which had filled the vessel on the night of July 6—and which Brendan had remembered in his dreams—was not visible now. There was only a line of ordinary work lights that the scientists had strung for their convenience.

In spite of its plainness, the chamber had a warmth, appeal, and magic that, strangely enough, reminded Ginger of her father's private office at the back of his first jewelry store in Brooklyn, the one he always used as his headquarters. The walls of that sanctum sanctorum had been decorated only with a calendar, and the furniture had been inexpensive, old, and well used. Plain. Even drab. But for Ginger, it had been a fine and magical room, because Jacob had seldom worked there but had squirreled away with one book or another, from which he'd often read to her. Sometimes it would be a mystery, or a fantasy about gnomes and witches, a story of other worlds, or a thriller about spies. And when Jacob read, his voice acquired a resonant and mesmerizing timbre. The reality of the gray little office faded, and for hours Ginger could believe herself to be investigating with Sherlock Holmes upon the misty moors, celebrating with the Hobbit Mr. Bilbo Baggins inside the Hill at Bag End, or with Jim and Will as they explored the terrible carnival in Mr. Bradbury's lovely book. Jacob's office hadn't been only what it seemed to be. And although this ship bore no physical resemblance to Jacob's office, it was similar in that it was more than it appeared; under its drab skin, it harbored wondrous things, great mysteries.

Spaced along each long wall were four coffinlike containers of a semitransparent, milky-blue substance that looked like carved quartz. These were, Miles Bennell explained, the beds in which the travelers had passed their long journey in a state of near-suspended animation, aging only the equivalent of one earth-year for every fifty that passed. As they dreamed, the fully automated ship proceeded through the void, reaching ahead with an array of sensors and probes for indications of life in the hundreds of thousands of solar systems that it passed.

It did not escape Ginger's notice that the top of each container was marked by two raised rings precisely the size of those that had appeared in Dom's and Brendan's hands.

"You told us they were dead when they got here," Ned reminded Bennell. "But you never answered my question. What did they die from?"

"Time," Bennell said. "Although the ship and all its devices continued to function well right through the descent and the landing there along I-80, the occupants had perished of old age long before they ever got here."

Faye said, "But . . . you've told us they aged one year for every fifty that passed."

"Yes," Bennell said. "And from what we've learned about them, they're long-lived by our standards. Five hundred years seems to be their average life-span."

Standing with Marcie in his arms, Jack Twist said, "But, my God, at one year for fifty, they'd have to've been traveling twenty-five thousand years to have died of old age!"

"Longer," Bennell said. "In spite of their vast knowledge and technology, they never found a way to exceed the speed of light—186,000 miles per second. In fact, their ship cruises at ninety-eight percent of that, something like 182,000 miles per second. Fast, yes, but not fast enough when you consider the distances involved. Our own galaxy—in which they're our neighbors—has a diameter of 80,000 lightyears, or about 240,000 *trillion* miles. They tried to pinpoint the location of their home world for us through tridimensional galactic diagrams. We believe they come from a place more than 31,000 lightyears around the perimeter of the galaxy from us. And since they travel at just under the speed of light, that means they left home a little less than 32,000 years ago. Even with their lives extended by suspended animation, they must have perished nearly 10,000 years ago."

Ginger found herself shaking again, as she had shaken upon first turning her gaze upon the ancient ship. She touched the nearest of the milky-blue containers, which seemed to her to be a powerful testimony to compassion and empathy beyond human understanding, the embodiment of a sacrifice that staggered the mind and humbled the heart. To have willingly given up the comforts of home, to have left their world and all their kind to travel such distances on the mere *hope* of being able to help a struggling species at the far, far end. . . .

Bennell's voice had grown lower as he spoke, and now it was as soft as if he had been speaking in a church. "They died twenty-five thousand lightyears from home. They were already dead when humankind still lived in caves and was just beginning to learn the basics of agriculture. When these . . . incredible journeyers died, the entire population of our world was only about five million, fewer people than now live in Manhattan alone. During the past ten thousand years, while we've struggled out of the dirt and broken our backs to build a shaky civilization always teetering on the edge of destruction, those eight dead seekers were coming steadily toward us across the vastness of the galactic rim."

Ginger saw Brendan touch the other corner of the coffin on which she'd rested her own hands. Tears glistened in his eyes. She knew what he was thinking. As a priest, he had taken vows of poverty and celibacy and had forsworn many of the pleasures of secular life as an offering to God. He knew the meaning of sacrifice, but none of his sacrifices compared to what these beings had given up in the name of *their* cause.

Parker said, "But to have found five other intelligent species when the distances are so great and the odds so small, they must send out a great many of these ships."

"We think they dispatch hundreds a year, maybe even thousands—and had been doing so for longer than 100,000 years before this vessel left port. As I said, it's their religion and their racial purpose combined. All the other five species they discovered were within 15,000 lightyears from their world. And remember, even when they locate an intelligence at *that* distance, they don't know of it until 15,000 years after the discovery, for it takes that long for the message of the contact to reach home again. Are you beginning to grasp the depth and scale of their commitment?''

''Most ships,'' Ernie said, ''must go out and never come back—and never meet with any success. Most of them just cruise on and on into endless space while the crew perishes, as this crew perished.''

''Yes,'' Bennell said.

''And yet they keep going,'' Dom said.

''And yet they keep going,'' Bennell said.

''We may never meet others of them face-to-face,'' Ned said.

''Give humanity a hundred years to learn to apply all the knowledge and technology they brought us,'' Bennell said. ''Then give us another . . . oh, at least one thousand years more to mature to the point where we're capable of making that same commitment. Then a ship will be launched, manned by a human crew in suspended animation. And possibly we'll find a way to improve the process, so that they don't age at all or age far more slowly. None of us will be alive to watch it take off, but it will go. I know in my heart it will. Then . . . 32,000 years after *that,* our distant descendants will be there, returning the call, remaking the contact these creatures don't even know they've established.''

They stood in stunned silence, trying to grasp the immensity of what Bennell envisioned.

Ginger felt a chill of the most delicious and indescribable nature.

Brendan said, ''It's God's scale. We're talking about . . . thinking, planning, and *doing* on God's scale rather than mankind's.''

Parker said, ''Sort of makes it a whole lot less important who's going to win this year's World Series, doesn't it?''

Dom put his hands upon the rings that were featured on the top of that particular suspended-animation chamber around which everyone was gathered. He said, ''I believe only six of the crew were dead, *fully dead* that night in July, Dr. Bennell. I'm beginning to recall what happened when we entered this ship, and I feel as if we were called to two of these containers by something that still lived within them. *Barely* lived but was not yet entirely dead.''

''Yes,'' Brendan said, tears weaving down his cheeks now. ''In fact, I remember the golden light was coming from two of these boxes and that it exerted not only an obvious but subliminal attraction. I was compelled to come and put my hands upon the rings. And when I put them here . . . somehow I knew that, beneath the lid, something was desperately clinging to life, not for its own sake but for the sake of passing on some gift. And by putting its own hands against the inner surface of those conductive rings . . . it gave me what it had come so far to give. Then it died at last. I didn't know what was in me then, exactly. I suppose it would have taken some time to understand, to learn how to use the power. But before I ever had a chance, we were taken into custody.''

''Alive,'' Bennell said—shocked, fascinated. ''Well, the condition of the eight bodies . . . two were virtually turned to dust . . . two more were badly decomposed . . . apparently because their suspended-animation boxes had shut down once they died. Four were in much better condition, and two seemed perfectly preserved. But we never dared imagine . . .''

''Yes,'' Dom said, clearly recalling more. ''Just barely alive, but holding on to pass the gift. Of course, I expected to be interrogated, to have a chance to tell what had happened to me in the ship. But the government was so eager to protect society from the shock of contact, and then so afraid of the unknown . . . I never had the chance to tell.''

''Soon,'' Bennell said, ''we can tell the world.''

''And change the world,'' Brendan said.

Ginger looked at the faces of the Tranquility family, at Parker and Bennell, and sensed the bond that would soon exist between all men and women, an incredible closeness that would arise from their sudden shared leap up the evolutionary ladder toward a better world. No more would people be strangers, one to another, not anywhere on earth. All prior human history had been lived in the dark, and now they stood at the gates of a new dawn. She looked at her two small hands, a surgeon's hands, and she thought of the decade-long studies to which she had diligently applied herself with the hope of saving lives. Now, perhaps all that training would be for nothing. She didn't care. She was filled with joy at the prospect of a world that did not *need* medicine or surgery. Soon, when Dom had passed the gift to her, as she would ask him to, she'd be able to heal with her touch. More important, with only her touch, she would be able to pass unto others the power to heal themselves. The human life-span would increase dramatically overnight—three hundred, four hundred, even five hundred years. Except for accidents, the specter of death would be banished to a distant horizon. No more would the Annas and Jacobs be wrenched away from the children who loved them. No more would husbands have to sit in mourning at the deathbeds of young wives. No more, *Baruch ha-Shem,* no more.

THE VOICE
OF THE NIGHT

◆ ◆ ◆

To old friends—
Harry and Diane Record
Andy and Ann Wickstrom
—who, like wine, get better
year by year

*A faint cold fear
thrills through my veins.*
—SHAKESPEARE

PART ONE

◆ ◆ ◆

ONE

◆

"You ever killed anything?" Roy asked.

Colin frowned. "Like what?"

The two boys were on a high hill at the north end of town. The ocean lay beyond.

"Anything," Roy said. "You ever killed anything at all?"

"I don't know what you mean," Colin said.

Far out on the sun-dappled water, a large ship moved northward, toward distant San Francisco. Nearer shore stood an oil-drilling platform. On the deserted beach a flock of birds relentlessly worked the damp sand for their lunch.

"You must've killed something," Roy said impatiently. "What about bugs?"

Colin shrugged. "Sure. Mosquitoes. Ants. Flies. So what?"

"How'd you like it?"

"Like what?"

"Killing 'em."

Colin stared at him, finally shook his head. "Roy, sometimes you're pretty weird."

Roy grinned.

"You like killing bugs?" Colin asked uneasily.

"Sometimes."

"Why?"

"It's a real popper."

Anything that Roy thought was fun, anything that thrilled him, he called a "popper."

"What's to like?" Colin asked.

"The way they squish."

"Yech."

"Ever pull the legs off a praying mantis and watch it try to walk?" Roy asked.

"Weird. Really weird."

Roy turned to the insistently crashing sea and stood defiantly with his hands on his hips, as if he were challenging the incoming tide. It was a natural pose for him; he was a born fighter.

Colin was fourteen years old, the same age as Roy, and he never challenged anything or anyone. He rolled with life, floated where it took him, offering no resistance. Long ago he had learned that resistance caused pain.

Colin sat on the crown of the hill, in the spare dry grass. He looked up admiringly at Roy.

Without turning from the sea, Roy said, "Ever kill anything bigger than bugs?"

"No."

"I did."

"Yeah?"

"Lots of times."

"What'd you kill?" Colin asked.

"Mice."

"Hey," Colin said, suddenly remembering, "my dad killed a bat once."

Roy looked down at him. "When was that?"

"Couple of years ago, down in Los Angeles. My mom and dad were still together then. We had a house in Westwood."

"That where he killed the bat?"

"Yeah. Must've been some of them living in the attic. One of them got into my folks' bedroom. It happened at night. I woke up and heard my mom screaming."

"She was really scared, huh?"

"Terrified."

"I sure wish I'd seen that."

"I ran down the hall to see what was wrong, and this bat was swooping around their room."

"Was she naked?"

Colin blinked. "Who?"

"Your mother."

"Of course not."

"I thought maybe she slept naked and you saw her."

"No," Colin said. He could feel his face turning red.

"She wearing a negligee?" Roy asked.

"I don't know."

"You don't *know?*"

"I don't remember," Colin said uneasily.

"If I was the one who saw her," Roy said, "I'd sure as hell remember."

"Well, I guess she was wearing a negligee," Colin said. "Yeah. I remember now."

Actually, he couldn't recall whether she had been wearing pajamas or a fur coat, and he didn't understand why it mattered to Roy.

"Could you see through it?" Roy asked.

"See through what?"

"For Christ's sake, Colin! Could you see through her negligee?"

"Why would I want to?"

"Are you a *moron?*"

"Why would I want to stand around gaping at my own mom?"

"She's built, that's why."

"You gotta be kidding!"

"Nice tits."

"Roy, don't be ridiculous."

"Terrific legs."

"How would you know?"

"Saw her in a swimsuit," Roy said. "She's foxy."

"She's what?"

"Sexy."

"She's my *mother!*"

"So what?"

"Sometimes I wonder about you, Roy."

"You're hopeless."

"*Me?* Jeez."

"Hopeless."

"I thought we were talking about the bat."

"So what happened to the bat?"

"My dad got a broom and knocked it out of the air. He kept hitting it until it stopped squealing. Boy, you should have heard it squeal." Colin shuddered. "It was awful."

"Blood?"

"Huh?"

"Was there a lot of blood?"

"No."

Roy looked at the sea again. He didn't seem impressed by the story about the bat.

The warm breeze stirred Roy's hair. He had the kind of thick golden hair and the wholesome freckled face that you saw in television commercials. He was a sturdy boy, strong for his age, a good athlete.

Colin wished he looked like Roy.

Someday, when I'm rich, Colin thought, I'll walk into a plastic surgeon's office with maybe a million bucks in cash and a picture of Roy. I'll get myself totally remade. Totally transformed. The surgeon will change my brown hair to corn yellow. He'll say, *Don't want this thin, pale face any more, do you? Can't blame you. Who would want it? Let's make it handsome.* He'll take care of my ears, too. They won't be so big when he's done. And he'll fix these damned eyes. I won't have to wear thick glasses any more. And he'll say, *Want me to add a bunch of muscles to your chest and arms and legs? No problem. Easy as cake.* And then I won't just look like Roy; I'll *be* as strong as Roy, too, and I'll be able to run as fast as Roy, and I won't be afraid of anything, not anything in the world. Yeah. But I better go into that office with *two* million.

Still studying the progress of the ship on the sea, Roy said, "Killed bigger things, too."

"Bigger than mice?"

"Sure."

"Like what?"

"A cat."

"You killed a cat?"

"That's what I said, didn't I?"

"Why'd you do that?"

"I was bored."

"That's no reason."

"It was something to do."

"Jeez."

Roy turned away from the sea.

"What a crock," Colin said.

Roy hunkered in front of Colin, locked eyes with him. "It was a popper, a really terrific popper."

"A popper? Fun? Why would killing a cat be fun?"

"Why *wouldn't* it be fun?" Roy asked.

Colin was skeptical. "How'd you kill it?"

"First I put it in a cage."

"What kind of cage?"

"A big old birdcage, about three feet square."

"Where'd you get a thing like that?"

"It was in our basement. A long time ago my mother owned a parrot. When it died she didn't get a new bird, but she didn't throw away the cage either."

"Was it your cat?"

"Nah. Belonged to some people down the street."

"What was its name?"

Roy shrugged.

"If there'd really been a cat, you'd remember its name," Colin said.

"Fluffy. Its name was Fluffy."

"Sounds likely."

"It's true. I put it in the cage and worked on it with my mother's knitting needles."

"Worked on it?"

"I poked at it through the bars. Christ, you should have heard it!"

"No thanks."

"That was one damned mad cat. It spat and screamed and tried to claw me."

"So you killed it with the knitting needles."

"Nah. The needles just made it angry."

"Can't imagine why."

"Later I got a long, two-pronged meat fork from the kitchen and killed it with that."

"Where were your folks during all this?"

"Both of them at work. I buried the cat and cleaned up all the blood before they got home."

Colin shook his head and sighed. "What a great big load of bull."

"You don't believe me?"

"You never killed any cat."

"Why would I make up a story like that?"

"You're trying to see if you can gross me out. You're trying to make me sick."

Roy grinned. "Are you sick?"

"Of course not."

"You look kinda pale."

"You can't make me sick because I know it didn't happen. There wasn't any cat."

Roy's eyes were sharp and demanding. Colin imagined he could feel them probing like the points of that meat fork.

"How long have you known me?" Roy asked.

"Since the day after Mom and I moved here."

"How long's that?"

"You know. Since the first of June. A month."

"In all that time, have I ever lied to you? No. Because you're my friend. I wouldn't lie to a friend."

"You're not lying exactly. Just sort of playing a game."

"I don't like games," Roy said.

"But you like to joke around a lot."

"I'm not joking now."

"Sure you are. You're setting me up. As soon as I say I believe about the cat, you'll laugh at me. I won't fall for it."

"Well," Roy said, "I tried."

"Hah! You *were* setting me up!"

"If that's what you want to think, it's okay with me."

Roy walked away. He stopped twenty feet from Colin and faced the sea again. He stared at the hazy horizon as if he were in a trance. To Colin, who was a science-fiction buff, Roy appeared to be in telepathic communication with something that hid far out in the deep, dark, rolling water.

"Roy? You *were* joking about the cat, weren't you?"

Roy turned, stared at him coolly for a moment, then grinned.

Colin grinned too. "Yeah. I knew it. You were trying to make a fool out of me."

TWO

◆

Colin stretched out on his back, closed his eyes and roasted for a while in the sun.

He couldn't stop thinking about the cat. He tried to conjure up pleasant images, but each of them faded and was replaced by a vision of a bloody cat in a birdcage. Its eyes were open, dead yet watchful eyes. He was certain the cat was waiting for him to get too close, waiting for a chance to strike out with razor-sharp claws.

Something bumped his foot.

He sat up, startled.

Roy stared down at him. "What time is it?"

Colin blinked, looked at his wristwatch. "Almost one o'clock."

"Come on. Get up."

"Where we going?"

"The old lady works afternoons at the gift shop," Roy said. "We've got my house to ourselves."

"What's to do at your place?"

"There's something I want to show you."

Colin stood and brushed sandy soil from his jeans. "Gonna show me where you buried the cat?"

"I thought you didn't believe in the cat."

"I don't."

"Then forget it. I want to show you the trains."

"What trains?"

"You'll see. It's a real popper."

"Race into town?" Colin asked.

"Sure."

"Go!" Colin shouted.

As usual, Roy reached his bicycle first. He was fifty yards away, racing into the wind, before Colin touched foot to pedal.

Cars, vans, campers, and lumbering motor homes jostled for position on the two-lane blacktop. Colin and Roy rode on the oiled berm.

Most of the year, Seaview Road carried very little traffic. Everyone except local residents used the interstate that bypassed Santa Leona.

During the tourist season the town was crowded, teeming with vacationers who drove too fast and recklessly. They seemed to be pursued by demons. They were all so frantic, in a great hurry to relax, relax, relax.

Colin coasted down the last hill, into the outskirts of Santa Leona. The wind buffeted his face, ruffled his hair, and blew the automobile exhaust fumes away from him.

He couldn't suppress a grin. His spirits were higher than they had been in a long, long time.

He had a lot to be happy about. Two more months of bright California summer lay ahead of him, two months of freedom before school began. And with his father gone, he no longer dreaded going home each day.

His parents' divorce still disturbed him. But a broken marriage was better than the loud and bitter arguments that for several years had been a nightly ritual.

Sometimes, in his dreams, Colin could still hear the shouted accusations, the uncharacteristically foul language that his mother used in the heat of a fight, the inevitable sound of his father striking her, and then the weeping. No matter how warm his bedroom, he was always freezing when he woke from these nightmares—cold, shivering, yet drenched with sweat.

He did not feel close to his mother, but life with her was far more enjoyable than life with his father would have been. His mother didn't share or even understand his interests—science fiction, horror comics, werewolf and vampire stories, monster movies—but she never forbade him to pursue them, which his father had tried to do.

However, the most important change in recent months, the thing that made him happiest, had nothing to do with his parents. It was Roy Borden. For the first time in his life, Colin had a friend.

He was too shy to make friends easily. He waited for other kids to come to him, even though he realized they weren't likely to be interested in a thin, awkward, myopic, bookish boy who didn't mix well or enjoy sports or watch a lot of television.

Roy Borden was self-confident, outgoing, and popular. Colin admired and envied him. Nearly any boy in town would have been proud to be Roy's best friend. For reasons that Colin could not grasp, Roy had chosen him. Going places with someone like Roy, confiding in someone like Roy, having someone like Roy confide in him—these were new experiences for Colin. He felt as if he were a pitiful pauper who had miraculously fallen into favor with a great prince.

Colin was afraid that it would end as abruptly as it had begun.

That thought made his heart race. In an instant his mouth went dry.

Before he'd met Roy, loneliness was all he had ever known; therefore, it had been endurable. Now that he had experienced comradeship, however, a return to loneliness would be painful, devastating.

Colin reached the bottom of the long hill.

One block ahead, Roy turned right at the corner.

Suddenly Colin thought the other boy might duck out on him, disappear down an alleyway, and hide from him forever. It was a crazy thought, but he couldn't shake it.

He leaned forward, into the handlebars. *Wait for me, Roy. Please wait!* He pedaled frantically, trying to catch up.

When he rounded the corner, he was relieved to see that his friend had not vanished. In fact, Roy had slowed down; he glanced back. Colin waved. They were only thirty yards apart. They weren't really racing any more because they both knew who would win.

Roy turned left, into a narrow residential street that was flanked by date trees. Colin followed through the feathery shadows that were cast by the wind-stirred palm fronds.

The conversation he'd had with Roy on the hill now echoed through Colin's mind:

You killed a cat?

That's what I said, didn't I?

Why'd you do that?

I was bored.

At least a dozen times during the past week, Colin had sensed that Roy was testing him. He felt certain the gruesome story about the cat was just the latest test, but he couldn't imagine what Roy had wanted him to say or do. Had he passed or failed?

Although he didn't know what answers were expected of him, he knew instinctively *why* he was being tested. Roy possessed a wonderful—or perhaps terrible—secret that he was eager to share, but he wanted to be certain that Colin was worthy of it.

Roy had never spoken of a secret, not one word, but it was in his eyes. Colin could see it, the vague shape of it, but not the details, and he wondered what it might be.

THREE

◆

Two blocks from his home, Roy Borden turned left, into another street, away from the Borden house, and for a moment Colin again felt that the other boy was trying to lose him. But Roy pulled into a driveway in the middle of the block and parked his bike. Colin stopped beside him.

The house was neat and white with dark blue shutters. A two-year-old Honda Accord was parked in the open garage, facing out, and a man was leaning under the raised hood, repairing something. He was thirty feet away from Colin and Roy, and he was not immediately aware that he had company.

"What're we doing here?" Colin asked.

"I want you to meet Coach Molinoff," Roy said.

"Who?"

"He coaches the junior-varsity football team," Roy said. "I want you to meet him."

"Why?"

"You'll see."

Roy walked toward the man who was working under the hood of the Honda. Reluctantly, Colin followed. He was not much good at meeting people. He never knew what to say or how to act. He was sure that he always made a terrible first impression, and he dreaded scenes like this one.

Coach Molinoff looked up from the Honda's engine as he heard the boys approaching. He was a tall, broad-shouldered, sandy-haired man with gray-blue eyes. He grinned when he saw Roy.

"Hey, what's up, Roy?"

"Coach, this is Colin Jacobs. He's new in town. Moved up from L.A. He'll be going to school at Central in the fall. Same grade as me."

Molinoff held out one big calloused hand. "Really glad to meet you."

Colin accepted the greeting awkwardly, his own hand disappearing in Molinoff's bearish grip. The coach's fingers were slightly greasy.

To Roy, Molinoff said, "So how's the summer treating you, my man?"

"It's been okay so far," Roy said. "But I'm mainly just killing time, waiting for preseason practice to start the end of August."

"We're going to have a terrific year," the coach said.

"I know it," Roy said.

"You handle yourself as well as you did last year," said Molinoff, "and Coach Penneman might just give you some fourth-quarter time in varsity games later in the season."

"You really think so?" Roy asked.

"Don't give me that wide-eyed look," Molinoff said. "You're the best player on the junior-varsity team, and you know it. There's no virtue in false modesty, my man."

Roy and the coach began to discuss football strategy, and Colin just listened, unable to contribute anything to the conversation. He never had shown much interest in sports. If asked about athletics of any kind, he always said that sports bored him and that he preferred the excitement of stimulating books and movies. In truth, while novels and films gave him endless pleasure, he sometimes wished he also could share the special camaraderie that athletes seemed to enjoy among themselves. For a boy like him, on the outside looking in, the world of sports was intriguing and glamorous; however, he did not waste a lot of time daydreaming about it, for he was fully aware that nature had given him less than the necessary equipment for a successful career in sports. With his myopic vision, his skinny legs, and his thin arms, he would never be more involved in sports than he was at that moment—a listener, a watcher, never a participant.

Molinoff and Roy talked football for a few minutes, and then Roy said, "Coach, what about the team managers?"

"What about them?" Molinoff asked.

"Well, last year you had Bob Freemont and Jim Safinelli. But Jim's folks moved to Seattle, and Bob is going to be one of the varsity team's managers next season. So you need a couple of new guys."

"You have somebody in mind?" Molinoff asked.

"Yeah," Roy said. "How about giving Colin a chance?"

Colin blinked in surprise.

The coach stared at him appraisingly. "You know what's involved, Colin?"

"You get a team jacket of your own," Roy told Colin. "You sit with the players on the bench at every game. And you get to travel on the team bus with us to all the out-of-town games."

"Roy's painting only the rosy part of the picture," the coach said. "Those are just the benefits of being a manager. You'll have duties, too. Like collecting and bundling the uniforms for the laundry. And taking care of the towel supply. You'll have to learn how to give the players good neck and shoulder massages. You'll run errands for me. A lot of other things. You'll be taking on a good bit of responsibility. Think you can handle it?''

Suddenly, for the first time in his life, Colin was able to picture himself on the inside instead of the outside, moving in the right circles, mingling with some of the most popular kids in school. Deep down, he knew that a team manager was a glorified messenger boy, but he pushed all the negative thoughts out of his mind. The important thing—the *incredible* thing—was that he would be a part of a world that previously had been completely beyond his reach. He would be accepted by the players; at least to some extent, he would be one of the guys. One of the guys! His mental image of life as a team manager was dazzling, enormously appealing, for he had been an outcast all of his life. He couldn't quite believe this was really happening to him.

"Well?" Coach Molinoff asked. "Do you think you'd make a good team manager?"

"He'd be perfect," Roy said.

"I'd sure like to try," Colin said. His mouth was dry.

Molinoff stared at Colin, his blue-gray eyes calculating, weighing, judging. Then he glanced at Roy and said, "I guess you wouldn't recommend anybody who was a complete washout."

"Colin's right for the job," Roy said. "Very dependable."

Molinoff looked at Colin again, finally nodded. "Okay. You're a team manager, son. Come with Roy to the first practice. That's August twentieth. And be ready to work hard!"

"Yes, sir. Thank you, sir."

As he walked with Roy to the bicycles at the end of the driveway, Colin felt taller and stronger than he had felt only a few minutes ago. He was grinning.

"You'll like traveling on the team bus," Roy said. "We'll have a lot of laughs."

As Colin got on his bike, he said, "Roy, I . . . well . . . I think you're just about the best friend a guy could ask for."

"Hey, I did it as much for me as for you," Roy said. "Those trips to out-of-town games can be boring sometimes. But with you and me together on the bus, there won't be a dull minute. Now come on. Let's go to my place. I want to show you those trains." He pedaled away.

Following Roy along the tree-shaded, sun-speckled pavement, elated and somewhat dazed, Colin wondered if the team manager's job was the thing for which Roy had been testing him. Was it the secret that Roy had been harboring for the past week? Colin thought about that for a while, but by the time he reached the Borden house, he decided there was something else that Roy was concealing, something so important that Colin had still not proved himself worthy to hear it.

FOUR

◆

They entered the Borden house through the kitchen door.

"Mom?" Roy called. "Dad?"

"I thought you said they weren't home."

"Just checking. I better be sure. If they caught us. . ."

"Caught us doing what?"

"I'm not supposed to mess around with the trains."

"Roy, I don't want to get in trouble with your folks."

"We won't. Wait here." Roy hurried into the living room. "Anyone home?"

Colin had been here on only two other occasions, and as before he was amazed at how spotless everything was. The kitchen gleamed. The floor was freshly scrubbed and waxed. The counters shone almost like mirrors. No dirty dishes waited to be washed; no overlooked crumbs marred the table; and there was not even a single vague stain in the sink. The utensils were not hung on wall racks; all pots and pans and spoons and ladles were secreted away in drawers and dust-free cupboards. Mrs. Borden apparently did not appreciate knickknacks, for there was not a single decorative plate or plaque or piece of needlepoint wisdom on the walls, no spice rack, no calendar, no clutter at all—and no sense that this was a place where real people cooked real food. The house looked as if Mrs. Borden spent all of her time performing an elaborate series of cleaning operations—first scraping, then scouring, then scrubbing, then washing, rinsing, polishing, buffing—much the same way that a cabinetmaker sanded a piece of wood, beginning with coarse sandpaper and working up gradually to the finest grain.

Colin's own mother didn't keep a *dirty* kitchen. Far from it. They had a cleaning woman. She came in twice a week to help keep things neat. But their place didn't look like this.

According to Roy, Mrs. Borden refused to consider a cleaning woman. She didn't think anyone else in the world would have standards as high as hers. She wasn't satisfied with a neat house; she wanted it to be sterile.

Roy returned to the kitchen. "No one's here. Let's play with the trains awhile."

"Where are they?"

"In the garage."

"Whose are they?"

"The old man's."

"And you're not supposed to touch them?"

"Screw him. He'll never know."

"I don't want your folks mad at me."

"For Christ's sake, Colin, how are they ever going to find out?"

"Is this the secret?"

Roy had started to turn away. Now he looked back. "What secret?"

"You've got one. You're almost ready to explode with it."

"How do you know?"

"I can see . . . the way you act. You've been testing me to see if you can trust me with a secret."

Roy shook his head. "You're pretty smart."

Colin shrugged, embarrassed.

"No, you really are. You've just about been reading my mind."

"So you *have* been testing me."

"Yeah."

"That dumb stuff about the cat—"

"—was true."

"Oh sure."

"Better believe it."

"You're still testing me."

"Maybe."

"So there *is* a secret?"

"A big one."

"The trains?"

"Nah. That's just a tiny part of it."

"So what's the rest of it?"

Roy grinned.

Something in that grin, something strange in those bright blue eyes made Colin want to step back from the other boy. But he didn't flinch.

"I'll tell you all about it," Roy said. "But only when I'm ready."

"When will that be?"

"Soon."

"You can trust me."

"Only when I'm ready. Now come on. You'll like the trains."

Colin followed him across the kitchen and through a white door. Beyond, there were two short steps and then the garage—and the model railroad.

"*Wow!*"

"Isn't it a popper?"

"Where's your dad park the car?"

"Always in the driveway. No room in here."

"When did he get all this stuff?"

"Started collecting when he was a kid," Roy said. "He added to it every year. It's worth more than fifteen thousand dollars."

"Fifteen thousand! Who'd pay that much money for a bunch of toy trains?"

"People who should have lived in better times."

Colin blinked. "Huh?"

"That's what my old man says. He says people who like model railroads are people who were meant to live in a better, cleaner, nicer, more organized world than the one we've got today."

"What's that supposed to mean?"

"I'll be damned if I know. But that's what he says. He can ramble on for an hour about how much better the world was back when there were trains but not airplanes. He can bore your ass off."

The train set was on a waist-high platform that nearly filled the three-car garage. On three sides there was just enough room to walk. On the fourth side, which featured the master-control console, there were two stools, a narrow workbench, and a tool cabinet.

A brilliantly conceived, incredibly detailed miniature world had been constructed upon that platform. There were mountains and valleys, streams and rivers and lakes, meadows dotted with minuscule wildflowers, forests where timid deer peered out of the shadows between the trees, picture-postcard villages, farms, outposts, realistic little people engaged in a hundred chores, scale-model cars, trucks, buses, motorcycles, bicycles, neat houses with picket fences, four exquisitely rendered train stations—one Victorian-style, one Swiss, one Italian, one Spanish—and shops and churches and schools. Narrow-gauge railroad tracks ran everywhere—alongside the rivers, through the towns, across the valleys, around the sides of the mountains, across trestles and drawbridges, into and out of the stations, up and down and back and forth in graceful loops and straightaways and sharp turns and horseshoes and switchbacks.

Colin slowly circled the display, studying it with unconcealed awe. The illusion was not shattered by a close inspection. Even from a distance of only one inch the pine forests looked *real*; each tree was superbly crafted. The houses were complete in every detail, even down to rain spouting, workable windows in some of them, walkways made from individual stones, and television antennae secured by fine guy wires. The automobiles were not merely toy cars. They were carefully crafted, tiny but otherwise exact, replicas of full-size vehicles; and except for those that were parked along the streets and in the driveways, they all boasted a driver, sometimes passengers as well, and occasionally a family dog or cat on the back seat.

"How much of this did your dad build himself?" Colin asked.

"Everything but the trains and a few of the model cars."

"It's fantastic."

"It takes a whole week to make just one of those little houses, sometimes longer if it's really something special. He spent months and months on each of those train stations."

"How long ago did he finish it?"

"It isn't finished," Roy said. "It'll never be finished—until he's dead."

"But it can't possibly get bigger," Colin said. "There isn't any more room for it."

"Not bigger, just better," Roy said. His voice held a new note, a hardness, an iciness; his teeth were very nearly clenched tight, but he still smiled. "The old man keeps improving the layout. All he does when he comes home from work is tinker with this damned thing. I don't think he even takes time to screw the old lady any more."

That kind of talk embarrassed Colin, and he didn't respond to it. He saw himself as being considerably less sophisticated than Roy, and he tried hard to change himself for the better in every way he was able; however, he simply could not learn to be comfortable with strong curse words and sex talk. The hot blush and the sudden thickness of tongue and throat were uncontrollable. He felt childish and stupid.

"He squirrels himself away in here every damn night," Roy said, still using that new, cold voice. "He even eats supper in here sometimes. He's a nut case just like she is."

Colin had read a great deal about many things but only a little about psychology. Nevertheless, as he continued to marvel at the miniatures, he realized that the uncompromising attention to detail was an expression of the same fanatical insistence on neatness and order that was so evident in Mrs. Borden's endless battle to keep the house as clean as a hospital operating room.

He wondered if Roy's parents really were nut cases. Of course, they weren't a couple of raving lunatics; they weren't certifiable. They weren't so far gone that they sat in corners talking to themselves and eating flies. Maybe just a little bit crazy. Just a tiny bit nuts. Perhaps they'd get a lot worse as time went on, gradually crazier and crazier, until ten or fifteen years from now they *would* be eating flies. It sure was something to think about.

Colin decided that if he and Roy became lifelong friends, he would hang around Roy's house only for another ten years. After that he'd maintain his friendship with Roy but avoid Mr. and Mrs. Borden, so that when they finally went completely insane they wouldn't be able to get their hands on him and force him to eat flies or, worse yet, chop him up with an ax.

He knew all about lunatic killers. He'd seen the movies about them. *Psycho. Straitjacket. Whatever Happened to Baby Jane?* A couple dozen others, too. Maybe a hundred. One thing he learned from those films was that crazy people favored messy killing. They used knives and scythes and hatchets and axes. You'd never catch one of them resorting to something bloodless like poison or gas or a smothering pillow.

Roy sat on one of the stools in front of the control console. "Over here, Colin. You'll be able to see more of it from here than anywhere else."

"I don't think we should mess around with this if your dad doesn't want us to."

"Will you relax, for Christ's sake?"

With an odd mixture of reluctance and pleasant anticipation, Colin sat on the second stool.

Roy carefully turned a dial on the board in front of him. It was connected to a rheostat, and the overhead garage lights slowly dimmed.

"It's like a theater," Colin said.

"No," Roy said. "It's more like . . . I'm God."

Colin laughed. "Yeah. Because you can make it day or night any time you want."

"And a whole lot more than that."

"Show me."

"In a minute. I won't make it completely dark. Not full night. Too hard to see. I'll make it early evening. Twilight."

Next, Roy flipped four switches, and all over the miniature world, lights came on. In every village, street lamps threw down opalescent pools on the pavement beneath them. In most of the houses, a yellow, warm, and welcoming glow brought life to the windows. Some houses even had porch lights and little lampposts at the ends of their walks, as if guests were expected. Churches cast colorful stained-glass patterns on the ground around them. At a few major intersections traffic lights changed gradually from red to green to amber to green again. In one hamlet a movie marquee pulsed with a score of tiny lights.

"Fantastic!" Colin said.

As he stared at the layout, Roy's expression and posture were peculiar. His eyes were narrow slits; his lips were pressed tightly together. His shoulders were drawn up, and he was clearly tense.

"Eventually," Roy said, "the old man's going to put working headlights in the automobiles. And he's designing a pump and drainage system that'll let water flow through the rivers. There'll even be a waterfall."

"Your dad sounds like an interesting guy."

Roy didn't respond. He stared at the small world in front of him.

At the far left corner of the platform, four trains waited for orders on the sidings in the railroad yard. Two were freight trains, and two were for passengers only.

Roy threw another switch, and one of the trains came to life. It buzzed softly; lights flickered in the cars.

Colin leaned forward in anticipation.

Roy manipulated switches, and the train chugged out of the yard. As it moved toward the nearest town, red warning lights flashed where a street intersected the tracks; black-and-white-striped crossing barriers lowered over the roadway. The train gathered speed, whistled noisily as it passed through the village, climbed a slight incline, vanished into a tunnel, reappeared around the far side of the mountain, accelerated, crossed a trestle, picked up more speed, entered a straightaway, really moving now, rounded a wide curve with a violent clatter, wheels whizzing, took a sharper curve with a dangerous tilt, and moved faster, faster, faster.

"For God's sake, don't wreck it," Colin said nervously.

"That's exactly what I'm going to do."

"Then your dad will know we've been here."

"Nah. Don't worry about it."

The train flashed through the Swiss station without slowing down, rocked wildly on the edge of disaster as it negotiated a switchback, roared through a tunnel, and entered a straightaway, picking up speed by the second.

"But if the train's broken, your dad—"

"I won't break it. Relax."

A drawbridge began to go up directly in the path of the train.

Colin gritted his teeth.

The train reached the river, swept beneath the raised bridge, and plunged off the track. The miniature locomotive and two cars wound up in the channel, and all the other cars fell off the rails in a brief splash of sparks.

"Jeez," Colin said.

Roy slid off his stool and went to the scene of the accident. He bent down and peered closely at the wreck.

Colin joined him. "Is it ruined?"

Roy didn't answer. He squinted through the tiny windows in the train.

"What are you looking for?" Colin asked.

"Bodies."

"What?"

"Dead people."

Colin squinted into one of the fallen cars. There were no people in it—that is, there were no figurines. He looked at Roy. "I don't understand."

Roy didn't look up from the train. "Understand what?"

"I don't see any 'dead people.' "

Moving slowly from car to car, staring into each of them, almost entranced, Roy said, "If this was a *real* train full of people that went off the tracks, the passengers would have been thrown out of their seats. They'd have cracked their heads against the windows and against the handrails. They'd have ended up in a big tangled pile on the floor. There'd be broken arms, broken legs, smashed teeth, slashed faces, eyes punched out, blood over everything. . . . You'd be able to hear them screaming a mile away. Some of them would be dead, too."

"So?"

"So I'm trying to imagine what it would look like in there if this was real."

"Why?"

"It interests me."

"What does?"

"The idea."

"The idea of a real train wreck?"

"Yeah."

"Isn't that kind of sick?"

Roy looked up at last. His eyes were flat and cold. "Did you say 'sick'?"

"Well," Colin said uneasily, "I mean . . . finding enjoyment in other people's pain. . ."

"You think that's unusual?"

Colin shrugged. He didn't want to argue.

"In other parts of the world," Roy said, "people go to bullfights, and deep down inside most of them hope they'll see a matador get gored. They *always* get to see the bull in pain. They love it. And a hell of a lot of people go to the auto races just to see the bad crackups."

"That's different," Colin said.

Roy grinned. "Oh, is it? How?"

Colin thought hard about it, trying to find words to express what he knew intuitively to be true. "Well . . . for one thing, the matador knows when he goes into the arena that he might get hurt. But people riding home on a train . . . not expecting anything . . . not asking for trouble . . . and then it happens. . . . That's a tragedy."

Roy laughed. "You know what 'hypocrite' means?"

"Sure."

"Well, Colin, I hate to say this 'cause you're my good friend, my *real* good friend. I like you a lot. But as far as this thing goes, you're a hypocrite. You think I'm sick because the idea of a train wreck interests me, but then you spend most of your spare time going to horror movies or watching them on television or reading books about zombies and werewolves and vampires and other monsters."

"What's that got to do with anything?"

"Those stories are *filled* with murders!" Roy said. "Death. Killing. That's practically all they're about. People get bitten and clawed and torn apart and chopped up with axes in those stories. And you love 'em!"

Colin winced at the mention of axes.

Roy leaned close. His breath carried the scent of Juicy Fruit chewing gum.

"That's why I like you, Colin. We're two of a kind. We got things in common. That's why I wanted to get you the job of team manager. So we could knock around together during football season. We're both smarter than other people. We both get straight-A averages in school without half trying. Each of us has been given IQ tests, and each of us has been told he's a genius or the next thing to it. We see deeper into things than most kids do and even deeper than a hell of a lot of grown-ups. We're special. Very special people."

Roy put a hand on Colin's shoulder and locked eyes with him, seemed to be looking not just at him but also deep into him and ultimately through him. Colin could not look away.

"We're both interested in the things that count," Roy said. "Pain and death. That's what intrigues you and me. Most people think death is the end of life, but we know different, don't we? Death isn't the end. It's the center. It's the center of life. Everything else revolves around it. Death is the most important thing in life, the most interesting, the most mysterious, the most *exciting* thing in life."

Colin cleared his throat nervously. "I'm not sure I know what you're talking about."

"If you aren't afraid of death," Roy said, "then you can't be afraid of anything. When you learn to conquer the biggest fear, you conquer all the smaller fears at the same time, isn't that right?''

"I . . . I guess so.''

Roy spoke in a stage whisper for emphasis, spoke with amazing intensity, fervently. "If I'm not afraid of death, then no one can do anything to hurt me. Nobody. Not my old man or the old woman. No one. Not ever again as long as I live.''

Colin didn't know what to say.

"Are you afraid of death?'' Roy asked.

"Yes.''

"You've got to learn not to be.''

Colin nodded. His mouth went dry. His heart was racing and he felt slightly dizzy.

"You know the first thing you've got to do to get over your fear of dying?'' Roy asked.

"No.''

"Become familiar with death.''

"How?''

"By killing things,'' Roy said.

"I can't do that.''

"Of course you can.''

"I'm a peaceable kid.''

"Deep down everyone's a killer.''

"Not me.''

"Shit.''

"Same to you.''

"I know myself,'' Roy said. "And I know you.''

"You know me better than *I* know me?''

"Yeah.'' Roy grinned.

They stared at each other.

The garage was as quiet as an undisturbed Egyptian tomb.

At last Colin said, "You mean . . . like we'd kill a cat?''

"For starters,'' Roy said.

"For starters? Then what?''

Roy's hand tightened on Colin's shoulder. "Then we'd move on to something bigger.''

Suddenly Colin realized what was happening and he relaxed. "You almost had me going again.''

"Almost?''

"I know what you're trying to do.''

"Do you?''

"You're testing me again.''

"Am I?''

"You're setting me up,'' Colin said. "You want to see if I'll make a fool of myself.''

"Wrong.''

"If I'd agreed to kill a cat to prove something to you, you'd have busted out laughing.''

"Try me.''

"No way. I know your game.''

Roy let go of his shoulder. "It's not a game.''

"You don't have to test me. You can trust me.''

"To some extent," Roy said.

"You can trust me completely," Colin said earnestly. "Jeez, you're the best friend I ever had. I wouldn't disappoint you. I'll do a good job as team manager. You won't be sorry you recommended me to the coach. You can trust me with that. You can trust me with anything. So what's the big secret?"

"Not yet," Roy said.

"When?"

"When you're ready."

"When will that be?"

"When I say you are."

"Jeez."

FIVE

◆

Colin's mother came home from work at five-thirty.

He was waiting in the cool living room. The furniture was all shades of brown, and the walls were papered in burlap. Wooden shades covered the windows. The lighting was indirect, soft and easy on the eyes. It was a restful room. He was on the big sofa, reading the latest issue of his favorite comic book, *The Incredible Hulk.*

She smiled at him, ruffled his hair, and said, "What kind of a day have you had, Skipper?"

"It was okay," Colin said, aware that she didn't really want the details and would gently cut him off when he was halfway through the story. "What about your day?" he asked.

"I'm pooped. Will you be a love and mix me a vodka martini the way I like?"

"Sure."

"Twist of lemon."

"I wouldn't forget it."

"Of course you wouldn't."

He got up and went into the family room, where there was a well-stocked wet bar. He couldn't stand the taste of hard liquor, but he mixed her drink quickly, with professional skill; he had done it hundreds of times.

When he returned to the living room, she was sitting in a large chocolate-brown chair, her legs tucked under her, head laid back, eyes closed. She didn't hear him coming, so he stopped just inside the doorway and studied her for a moment.

Her name was Louise, but everyone called her Weezy, which was sort of a kid's name but which suited her because she looked like a college girl. She was wearing jeans and a short-sleeve blue sweater. Her bare arms were tan and slender. Her hair was long, dark, shiny; and it framed a face that Colin suddenly thought was pretty, really quite beautiful, although some people might say the mouth was too wide. As he looked at her, he began to realize that thirty-three was not really old, as he'd always thought.

For the first time in his life, Colin was consciously aware of her body: full breasts, narrow waist, round hips, long legs. Roy was right; she had a terrific figure.

Why didn't I ever notice it before?

He answered himself at once: Because she's my own *mother*, for God's sake!

Heat blossomed in his face. He wondered if he was turning into some sort of pervert, and he forced himself to stop looking at her well-filled sweater.

He cleared his throat and went to her.

She opened her eyes, lifted her head, took the martini, and sipped it. "Mmmmm. Perfect. You're a sweetheart."

He sat on the sofa.

After a while she said, "When I got into this thing with Paula, I didn't realize that the owner of a business has to work harder than the employees."

"Was the gallery busy today?" Colin asked.

"We had more people in and out of there than you'd find in a bus station. This time of year you expect a lot of browsers, tourists who don't really intend to buy anything. They figure that because they're vacationing in Santa Leona they're entitled to a few free hours of each shopkeeper's time."

"Sell many paintings?" Colin asked.

"Surprisingly, we sold quite a few. In fact, it's the best day on record."

"That's great."

"Of course, it's just one day. Considering what Paula and I paid for the gallery, we have to have a lot more days like this if we're going to keep our heads above water."

Colin couldn't think of anything more to say.

She sipped her martini. Her throat rippled slightly when she swallowed. She looked so dainty and graceful.

"Skipper, can you make your own supper this evening?"

"Aren't you eating at home?" he asked.

"The shop's still very busy. I can't leave Paula alone this evening. I just came home to freshen up. Much as I dread the thought of it, I'll be going back to the grind in twenty minutes."

"You've only been home for supper once in the past week," he said.

"I know, Skipper, and I'm sorry about that. But I'm trying hard to build a future for us, for me *and* you. You understand that, don't you?"

"I guess so."

"It's a tough world, baby."

"I'm not hungry anyway," Colin said. "I can wait until you get home after the gallery closes."

"Well, baby, I won't be coming straight home. Mark Thornberg asked me to share a late dinner with him."

"Who's Mark Thornberg?"

"An artist," she said. "We opened a show of his work yesterday. In fact, about a third of what we're selling is his stuff. I want to persuade him to let us be his sole representatives."

"Where's he taking you to dinner?"

"We're going to Little Italy, I think."

"Boy, that's a neat place!" Colin said, leaning forward on the sofa. "Can I come? I won't be any bother. You wouldn't even have to stop back here to pick me up. I can ride my bike and meet you there."

She frowned and avoided his eyes. "Sorry, Skipper. This is strictly for grown-ups. We'll be talking a lot of business."

"I won't mind."

"Perhaps not, but we would. Listen, why don't you go to Charlie's Cafe and have one of those big cheeseburgers you like so much? And one of those extra-thick milkshakes that you have to eat with a spoon."

He settled back against the sofa as if he were a balloon that had rapidly deflated.

"Don't pout," she said. "It doesn't become you. Pouting's for little babies."

"I'm not pouting," he said. "It's okay."

"Charlie's Cafe?" she prompted.

"I guess so. Sure."

She finished her martini and picked up her handbag. "I'll give you some money."

"I've got money."

"So I'll give you some more. I'm now a successful businesswoman. I can afford it."

She brought him a five-dollar bill, and he said, "It's too much."

"Blow the rest of it on comic books."

She bent down, kissed his forehead, and left to freshen up and change clothes.

For several minutes he sat in silence, staring at the five-dollar bill. At last he sighed and stood and took out his wallet and put the money away.

SIX

◆

Mr. and Mrs. Borden gave Roy permission to have supper with Colin. The boys ate at the counter at Charlie's Cafe, basking in the incomparably wonderful aroma of bubbling grease and onions. Colin paid the check.

From the diner they went to the Pinball Pit, an amusement arcade that was one of the chief gathering places for young people in Santa Leona. It was a Friday night, and the Pit was crowded with kids feeding coins to pinball machines and a wide variety of electronic games.

Half the customers knew Roy. They called to him, and he called back. "Ho, Roy!" "Ho, Pete!" "Hi there, Roy!" "What ya say, Walt?" "Roy!" "Roy!" "Here, Roy!" They wanted to challenge him to games or tell him jokes or just talk. He stopped here and there for a minute or two at a time, but he didn't want to play with anyone but Colin.

They competed in a two-player pinball game that was decorated with paintings of big-breasted, long-legged girls in skimpy bikinis. Roy chose that machine rather than one with pirates, monsters, or spacemen; and Colin tried not to blush.

Colin usually disliked cheap thrill palaces like the Pit and avoided them. The few times he'd ever ventured into one, he'd found the din unbearable. The sounds of computer scorekeepers and robot adversaries—*beep-beep-beep, pong-pong-*

pong, bomp-bompada-bomp, whoop-whoop-whoooooooooop—mixed with laughter and girls' happy screams and half-shouted conversations. Assaulted by continuous, thunderous noise, he became claustrophobic. He always felt like an alien, a being from a distant world, trapped on a primitive planet, caught in a mob of hostile, screeching, gibbering, barbaric, loathsome natives.

But he didn't feel that way tonight. He was enjoying every minute and he knew why. Because of Roy, he was no longer a frightened visitor from space; he was now one of the natives.

With his thick yellow hair, blue eyes, muscles, and quiet self-confidence, Roy drew the girls. Three of them—Kathy, Laurie, and Janet—gathered around to watch the game. They were all better than average-looking: taut, tan, vital teenage girls in halter tops and shorts, with shiny hair and California complexions and budding breasts and slender legs.

Roy clearly favored Laurie, while Kathy and Janet showed more than passing interest in Colin. He didn't think they were attracted to him for himself. In fact, he was certain they were not. He had no illusions. Before girls like them swooned over boys like him, the sun would rise in the west, tiny babies would grow beards, and an honest man would be elected President. They were flirting with him because he was Roy's friend, or because they were jealous of Laurie and wanted to make Roy jealous of them. Whatever their reasons, they were concentrating on Colin, asking questions, drawing him out, laughing at his jokes, cheering when he won a game. Until now, girls had never wasted time with him. He really didn't care what their motives were; he just reveled in all the attention and prayed it would never end. He knew he was blushing brightly, but the arcade's odd orange lighting provided him with cover.

Forty minutes after entering the Pit, they left to a chorus of good-byes: "So long, Roy; take it easy, Roy; see ya around, Roy." Roy seemed to want to be rid of all of them, including Kathy, Laurie, and Janet. Colin went reluctantly.

Outside, the evening air was mild. A light breeze carried the faint scent of the sea.

Complete darkness had not yet descended. Santa Leona lay in a smoky yellow twilight similar to that which Roy had created earlier in the day for the miniature world in the Borden garage.

Their bicycles were chained to a rack in the parking lot behind the Pit.

As he bent and unlocked his bike, Roy said, "You like the Pit?"

"Yeah."

"I thought you would."

"You spend much time there?" Colin asked.

"Nah. Not much."

"I thought you were a regular."

Roy stood and pulled his bike from between the pipes. "I hardly ever go."

"Everybody knew you."

"I know the kids who *are* regulars. But not me. I'm not a fan of games. At least not games as easy as the ones in the Pit."

Colin finished unchaining his bicycle. "If you don't like it, why'd we come?"

"I knew you'd enjoy it," Roy said.

Colin frowned. "But I don't want to do things that bore you."

"I wasn't bored," Roy said. "I didn't mind playing a game or three. And I sure didn't mind having a chance to look at Laurie. She has a terrific little body, doesn't she?"

"I guess so."

"You *guess!*"

"Well, sure . . . she has a nice body."

"I'd like to settle down between her pretty legs for a few months."

"You seemed anxious to get away from her."

"After about fifteen minutes I get sick of talking to her," Roy said.

"Then how could you stand her for a few months?"

"We wouldn't talk," Roy said, grinning wickedly.

"Oh."

"Kathy, Janet, Laurie . . . all those girls are just teasers."

"What do you mean?"

"They never put out."

"Put out what?"

"Ass, for Christ's sake! They never put out any ass, not ever, not for anyone."

"Oh."

"Laurie shakes it at me, but if I actually put a hand on her tits, she'd scream so loud the roof would fall in."

Colin was blushing and sweating. "Well, after all, she's only fourteen, isn't she?"

"Plenty old enough."

Colin wasn't pleased with the direction the conversation had taken. He tried to get back on course. "Anyway, what I wanted to say was, from now on let's not do anything that bores you."

Roy put a hand on his shoulder and squeezed gently. "Listen, Colin, am I your friend or not?"

"Sure you are."

"A good friend should be willing to keep you company even when you're doing things that you enjoy but maybe he doesn't care so much about. I mean, I can't expect to always do exactly what *I* like, and I can't expect that you and I will always want to do the same things."

"We like the same things," Colin said. "We have the same interests." He was afraid Roy would suddenly realize how different they were and would walk away, never to be seen again.

"You love horror films," Roy said. "I don't have any interest in that stuff."

"Well, aside from that one thing—"

"We've got other differences. But the point is, if you're my buddy, you'll do things with me that *I* want to do but that *you* don't like at all. So it works both ways."

"No, it doesn't," Colin said, "because I happen to like doing everything you suggest."

"So far," Roy said. "But there'll come a time when you won't want to do something that's important to me, but you *will* do it because we're friends."

"I can't imagine what," Colin said.

"Just wait," Roy said. "You'll see. Sooner or later, good buddy, the time will come."

The scarlet light of the Pit's neon sign was refracted in Roy's eyes, giving them a strange and somewhat frightening aspect. Colin thought they resembled a movie vampire's eyes: glassy, red, violent, two windows on a soul that had been corrupted by the repeated satisfaction of unnatural desires. (But then again, Colin thought the same thing every time he saw Mr. Arkin's eyes, and Mr. Arkin was just the man who owned the corner grocery store; the closest thing Mr. Arkin had to an unnatural desire was a taste for liquor, and his red eyes were nothing more than the most obvious sign of a nearly continuous hangover.)

"Just the same," Colin said to Roy, "I hate the idea that I'm boring you with—"

"I wasn't bored! Will you relax? I don't mind going to the Pit if that's what you want. Just remember what I said about those girls. They'll hang on you a little bit. Now and then they'll 'accidentally' rub their tight little asses against you or maybe 'accidentally' brush their boobs against your arm. But you'll never have any real fun with them. Their idea of a big, big night is to sneak out to the parking lot, hide in the shadows, and steal kisses."

That was also Colin's idea of a big, big night. In fact, it was his idea of heaven on earth, but he didn't tell Roy.

They walked their bicycles across the lot to the alley.

Before Roy could climb on his bike and pedal away, Colin got up the nerve to say: "Why me?"

"Huh?"

"Why do you want to be friends with me?"

"Why shouldn't I be friends with you?"

"I mean with a nobody like me."

"Who said you're a nobody?"

"I did."

"What kind of a thing is that to say about yourself?"

"Anyway, I've been wondering for a month."

"Wondering what? You aren't making sense."

"I've been wondering why you want to be friends with someone like me."

"What do you mean? What makes you different? You got leprosy or something?"

Colin wished he had never brought up the subject, but now that he had done so, he stumbled ahead with it. "Well, you know, someone who's not normally very popular and, you know, not good at sports, you know, not really good at much of anything and . . . well, you know."

"Stop saying, 'you know,' " Roy said. "I hate that. One of the reasons I want to be friends with you is that you can *talk*. Most kids around here chatter away all day and never use more than twenty words. Two of which are 'you know.' But you actually have a decent vocabulary. It's refreshing."

Colin blinked. "You want to be friends because of my vocabulary?"

"I want to be friends because you're as smart as I am. Most kids bore me."

"But you could pal around with any guy in town, any guy your age, even some a year or two older than you. Most of those guys in the Pit—"

"They're assholes."

"Be serious. They're some of the most popular guys in town."

"Assholes, I tell you."

"Not all of them."

"Believe me, Colin, *all* of them. Half of them can't figure any way to have a good time except to smoke dope or pop pills or get stinking drunk and vomit all over themselves. The rest of them want to be either John Travolta or Donny Osmond. *Yech!*"

"But they like you."

"Everyone likes me," Roy said. "I make sure of that."

"I sure wish I knew how to make everyone like *me*."

"It's easy. You just have to know how to manipulate them."

"Okay. How?"

"Stick around me long enough, and you'll learn."

Instead of riding away from the Pit, they walked down the alley, side by side, pushing their bikes. They both knew there was more to be said.

They passed an oleander hedge. The flowers looked slightly phosphorescent in the growing gloom, and Colin took a deep whiff of them.

Oleander berries contained one of the deadliest substances known to man. Colin had seen an old movie in which a lunatic had murdered a dozen people with a poison extracted from the plant. He couldn't remember the title. It had been a really dumb film, even worse than *Godzilla Versus King Kong,* which meant it was one of the all-time most terrible works in cinematic history.

After they had gone nearly a block, Colin said, "You ever used dope?"

"Once," Roy said.

"What was it?"

"Hash. Through a waterpipe."

"You like it?"

"Once was enough. What about you?"

"No," Colin said. "Drugs scare me."

"You know why?"

"You can get killed."

"Dying doesn't scare you."

"It doesn't?"

"Not much."

"Dying scares me a lot."

"No," Roy insisted. "You're like me, exactly like me. Drugs scare you because if you used them you wouldn't be in control. You can't bear the idea of losing control of yourself."

"Well, sure, that's part of it."

Roy lowered his voice, as if he were afraid someone would overhear, and he spoke rapidly, running the words together in his eagerness to get them out. "You've got to stay sharp, on your toes, alert. Always look over your shoulder. Always protect yourself. Don't let your guard down for even a second. There are people who will take advantage of you the moment they see you're not in complete control. The world's filled with people like that. Nearly everyone you meet is like that. We're animals in a jungle, and we've got to be prepared to fight if we want to survive."

Roy walked his bike with his head thrust forward, shoulders hunched, muscles corded in his neck, as if he expected someone to strike him hard on the back of the head. Even in the fast-dwindling, purple-amber light of late evening, the sudden sprinkle of sweat on his forehead and upper lip was visible; darkly glistening jewels. "You can't trust hardly anyone, hardly anyone at all. Even people who're supposed to like you can turn on you faster than you think. Even friends. People who say they love you are the worst, the most dangerous, the most untrustworthy of all." He was breathing harder, talking faster by the moment. "People who say they love you will pounce when they get the chance. You gotta always remember that they're just waiting for the opportunity to get you. Love's a trick. A cover. A way to catch you off guard. Never let down your guard. Never." He glanced at Colin, and his eyes were wild.

"Do you think I'd turn on you, tell lies about you, snitch on you to your parents, things like that?"

"Would you?" Roy asked.

"Of course not."

"Not even if your own neck was in the wringer, too, and the only way you could save yourself was to snitch on me?"

"Not even then."

"What if I broke some law, some really serious law, and the cops were after me and came to you with a lot of questions?"

"I wouldn't snitch on you."

"I hope you wouldn't."

"You can trust me."

"I hope so. I really hope so."

"You don't have to hope. You should *know*."

"I gotta be careful."

"Should I be careful of you?"

Roy said nothing.

"Should I be careful of you?" Colin asked again.

"Maybe. Yeah, maybe you should. When I said we were all just animals, just a bunch of selfish animals, I meant me, too."

There was such a haunted look in Roy's eyes, such a knowledge of pain that Colin had to look away.

He didn't know what had sparked Roy's diatribe, but he didn't want to pursue the subject. He was worried that it would lead to an argument and that Roy would never want to see him again; and he desperately wanted to be friends with Roy for the rest of their lives. If he blew apart this relationship, he would never get another chance to be best buddies with anyone as terrific as Roy. He was positive of that. If he spoiled this, he would have to go back to being a loner; and now that he had experienced acceptance, companionship, and involvement, he didn't think he *could* go back.

For a while they walked in silence. They crossed a busy side street under a canopy of oak trees and entered another block of the alleyway.

Gradually the extraordinary tension that had given Roy the appearance of an angry snake began to seep out of him, much to Colin's relief. Roy lifted his head and let his shoulders down and stopped breathing like a horse at the end of an eight-furlong race.

Colin knew a bit about race horses. His father had taken him to the track half a dozen times, expecting him to be impressed with the amount of money wagered and with the sweaty manliness of the sport. Instead, Colin had been delighted by the grace of the horses and had spoken of them as if they were dancers. His father hadn't liked that and had thereafter gone to the races alone.

He and Roy reached another corner, turned left, out of the alley, and pushed their bicycles along an ivy-framed sidewalk.

Look-alike stucco houses lay on both sides of the street, sheltering under a variety of palm trees, skirted by oleander and jade plants and dracaena and schefflera and roses and cacti and holly and ferns and poinsettia bushes—ugly houses made elegant by California's lush natural beauty.

Finally Roy spoke. "Colin, you remember what I said about how a guy sometimes has to do things his buddy wants to do even if he himself maybe really doesn't like it?"

"I remember."

"That's one of the true tests of friendship. Don't you agree?"

"I guess so."

"For Christ's sake, can't you at least once in a while have a firm opinion about something? You never say a flat yes or no. You're always 'guessing.' "

Stung, Colin said, "All right. I think it's a true test of friendship. I agree with you."

"Well, what if I said I wanted to kill something just for fun and I wanted you to help me."

"You mean like a cat?"

"I've already killed a cat."

"Yeah. It was in all the newspapers."

"I *did*. In a cage. Like I said."

"I just can't believe it."

"Why would I lie?"

"Okay, okay," Colin said. "Let's not go through the whole argument again. Let's pretend I swallowed your story—hook, line, and sinker. You killed a cat in a birdcage. So what next—a dog?"

"If I wanted to kill a dog, would you help?"

"Why would you want to?"

"It might be a popper."

"Jeez."

"Would you help kill it?"

"Where would you get the dog? You think the humane society gives them out to people who want to torture them?"

"I'd just steal the first pooch I saw," Roy said.

"Someone's pet?"

"Sure."

"How would you kill it?"

"Shoot it. Blow its head off."

"And the neighbors wouldn't hear?"

"We'd take it out in the hills first."

"You expect it to just pose and smile while we plug it?"

"We'd tie it up and shoot it a dozen times."

"Where do you expect to get the gun?"

"What about your mother?" Roy asked.

"You think my mother sells illegal guns out of the kitchen or something?"

"Doesn't she have a gun of her own?"

"Sure. A million of 'em. And a tank and a bazooka and a nuclear missile."

"Just answer the question."

"Why would she have a gun?"

"A sexy woman living alone usually has a gun for protection."

"But she doesn't live alone," Colin said. "Did you forget about me?"

"If some crazy rapist wanted to get his hands on your mom, he'd walk right over you."

"I'm tougher than I look."

"Be serious. Does your mother have a gun?"

Colin didn't want to admit there was a gun in the house. He had a hunch that he would save himself a lot of trouble if he lied. But at last he said, "Yeah. She has a pistol."

"You're sure?"

"Yeah. But I don't think she keeps it loaded. She could never shoot anyone. My father loves guns: *ergo,* my mother hates them. And so do I. I'm not going to borrow her gun to do something crazy like shoot your neighbor's dog."

"Well, we could kill it some other way."

"What would we do—bite it?"

A night bird sang in the branches above them.

The sea breeze was cooler than it had been ten minutes ago.

Colin was tired of pushing the bike, but he sensed that Roy still had a lot to say and wanted to say it quietly, which he couldn't do if they were riding.

Roy said, "We could tie the dog up and kill it with a pitchfork."

"Jeez."

"*That* would be a popper!"

"You're making me sick."

"Would you help me?"

"You don't need my help."

"But it would prove you're not just a fair-weather friend."

After a long while Colin said, "I suppose if it was really important to you, if you just had to do it or die, I could be there when you did it."

"What do you mean by 'be there'?"

"I mean . . . I guess I could watch."

"What if I wanted you to do more than watch?"

"Like what?"

"What if I wanted you to take the pitchfork and stab the dog a few times yourself?"

"Sometimes you can be really weird, Roy."

"Could you stab it?" Roy persisted.

"No."

"I'll bet you could."

"I couldn't ever kill anything."

"But you could watch?"

"Well, if it would prove to you once and for all that I'm your friend and that I can be trusted. . . ."

They entered the circle of light under a street lamp, and Roy stopped. He was grinning. "You're getting better every day."

"Oh?"

"You're developing nicely," Roy said.

"Am I?"

"Yesterday, you'd have said you couldn't even watch a dog being killed. Today, you say you could watch but you couldn't participate. Tomorrow or the day after tomorrow, you'll tell me you could find it within yourself to pick up that pitchfork and make mincemeat of that damned dog."

"No. Never."

"And a week from now, you'll finally admit that you'd *enjoy* killing something."

"No. You're wrong. This is stupid."

"I'm right. You're just like me."

"And you're no killer."

"I am."

"Not in a million years."

"You don't know me."

"You're Roy Borden."

"I mean what's inside me. You don't know, but you'll learn."

"There's no cat-and-dog killer inside you."

"I've killed things bigger than a cat."

"Like what?"

"Like people."

"And then I suppose you moved on to even bigger things—like elephants."

"No elephants. Just people."

"I guess with an elephant there's problems disposing of the corpse."

"Just people."

Another night bird cried hollowly from its perch in a nearby tree, and in the distance two lonely dogs howled to each other.

"This is ridiculous," Colin said.

"No, it's true."

"You're trying to tell me you've *killed* people?"

"Twice."

"Why not a hundred times?"

"Because it was only twice."

"Next you'll be saying you're really an eight-legged, six-eyed creature from Mars disguised as a human being."

"I was born in Santa Leona," Roy said soberly. "We've always lived here, all my life. I've never been to Mars."

"Roy, this is getting boring."

"Oh, it'll be anything *but* boring. Before the summer's through, you and me together, we're going to kill someone."

Colin pretended to think about it. "The President of the United States maybe?"

"Just someone here in Santa Leona. It'll be a real popper."

"Roy, you might as well give up. I don't believe a word of this, and I'm never going to believe it."

"You will. Eventually you will."

"No. It's just a fairy tale, a game, a test of some sort that you're putting me through. And I wish you'd tell me what I'm being tested *for*."

Roy said nothing.

"Well, so far as I can see," Colin said, "I've passed the test, whatever it is. I've proven to you that I can't be fooled. I won't fall for this dumb story of yours. You understand?"

Roy smiled and nodded. He glanced at his watch. "Hey, what do you want to do now? Want to go out to the Fairmont and see a movie?"

Colin was disconcerted by the sudden change of subject and Roy's abruptly transformed attitude. "What's the Fairmont?"

"The Fairmont Drive-in, of course. If we ride way the hell out on Ranch Road and then double back through the hills, we'll come out on the slope above the Fairmont. We can sit up there and watch the movie for nothing."

"But can you hear it?"

"No, but you don't need to hear the kind of movies they play at the Fairmont."

"What the hell do they play—silent films?"

Roy was amazed. "You mean you've lived here a whole month and you don't know what the Fairmont is?"

"You're making me feel retarded."

"You really don't *know?*"

"You said it was a drive-in."

"It's more than that," Roy said. "Boy, are you in for a surprise!"

"I don't like surprises."

"Come on. Let's go."

Roy climbed onto his bike and pedaled away. Colin followed, off the sidewalk and into the street, from lamppost to lamppost, through alternating patches of shadow and light, pumping his legs hard to keep up.

When they reached Ranch Road and headed southeast, away from town, there were no more street lamps, and they switched on their headlights. The last traces of the sun had disappeared from the westward edges of the high-flying clouds: Night had arrived. Chains of gentle, treeless, pitch-black hills rose on both sides, silhouetted against a gray-black sky. Now and then a car passed them, but most of the time they had the road to themselves.

Colin was not on good terms with darkness. He had never lost his childish fear of being alone at night, a weakness that sometimes dismayed his mother and never failed to infuriate his father. He always slept with a light on. And right now he stayed close to Roy, genuinely afraid that if he fell behind he would be in extreme danger; something hideous, something unhuman, something hiding in the impenetrable shadows of the roadside would reach out for him, seize him in ghastly claws as big as sickles, tear him from his seat, and devour him alive with a noisy crunching of bones and splattering of blood. Or worse. He was a devoted fan of horror movies and novels, not because they dealt with colorful myths and were crammed full of movement and excitement, but because, to his way of thinking, they explored a sobering reality that most adults refused to take seriously. Werewolves, vampires, zombies, decaying corpses that would not rest peacefully in their coffins, and a hundred other hellish creatures *did* exist. Intellectually he could dismiss them as mere beasts of fantasy, denizens of the imagination, but in his heart he knew the truth. They were out there. The undead. Lurking. Waiting. Concealed. Hungry. The night was a vast, dank cellar, home to that which crept and crawled and slithered. The night had ears and eyes. It had a horrible, scratchy old voice. If you listened closely, tuning out your doubt and keeping an open mind, you could hear the dreadful voice of the night. It whispered about graves and rotting flesh and demons and ghosts and swamp monsters. It spoke of unspeakable things.

I have absolutely got to stop this, he told himself. Why do I do this to myself all the time? Jeez.

He rose slightly from the bicycle seat to gain better leverage and jammed his thin legs down hard on the pedals, determined to stay close to Roy.

His arms had broken out in gooseflesh.

SEVEN

◆

From Ranch Road they turned onto a dirt track that was barely visible in the moonlight. Roy led the way. Over the crown of the first hill, the track became a narrow footpath. A quarter of a mile farther on, the footpath turned north, and they continued west, pushing their bicycles through coarse grass and sandy soil.

Less than a minute after they left the path, Roy's bike light went out.

Colin stopped at once, heart leaping wildly like a startled rabbit in a cage. "Roy? Where are you? What's wrong? What's happened, Roy?"

Roy walked out of the darkness, into the pale fan of light that spread in front of Colin's bicycle. "We've got two more hills to cross before we reach the drive-in. No sense struggling with the bikes any further than this. We'll leave them here and pick them up on the way back."

"What if somebody steals them?"

"Who?"

"How should I know? But what if somebody does?"

"An international ring of bicycle thieves with undercover operatives in every town?" Roy shook his head, making no effort to conceal his exasperation. "You worry about more goddamned things than anyone I've ever known."

"If somebody stole them, we'd have to walk all the way home—five or six miles, maybe more."

"For Christ's sake, Colin, no one even knows the bikes are here! No one's going to see them, let alone steal them."

"Well, what if we come back and can't find them in the dark?" Colin asked.

Roy grimaced, and he looked not just disgusted but demonic. It was a trick of light; the headlamp's glow illuminated only the sharp edges of his features, leaving most of his face in darkness, so that he looked distorted, less than human.

"I know this place," Roy said impatiently. "I come here all the time. Trust me. Now will you come on? We're missing the movie."

He turned and walked away.

Colin hesitated until he realized that if he didn't leave the bike, Roy would leave him. He didn't want to be alone in the middle of nowhere. He put the bike on its side and switched off the lamp.

The darkness enfolded him. He was suddenly acutely aware of a thousand eerie songs: the incessant croaking of toads. Just toads? Perhaps something much more dangerous than that. The many strange voices of the night rose in a screeching chorus.

Fear washed through him like bile spreading from a pierced gut. The muscles in his throat grew tight. He had difficulty swallowing. If Roy had spoken to him, he could not have replied. In spite of the cool breeze, he began to sweat.

You're no longer a child, he told himself. Don't act like a baby.

He desperately wanted to bend down and switch on the bike light again, but he didn't want Roy to discover that he was afraid of the dark. He wanted to be like Roy, and Roy wasn't afraid of anything.

Fortunately Colin was not entirely blind. The bike light was not terribly powerful, and his eyes adapted quickly to a world without it. Milky moonlight spilled across the rolling land. He could see Roy loping swiftly up the hillside ahead.

Colin tried to move; he couldn't. His legs seemed to weigh a thousand pounds each.

Something hissed.

Colin tilted his head. Listened.

The hissing again. Louder. Closer.

Something rustled through the grass a few inches from his foot, and Colin bolted. It might have been only a harmless toad, but it gave him the motivation he needed to get moving.

He caught up with Roy, and a few minutes later they reached the slope behind and above the Fairmont. They descended halfway down the hill and sat on the ground, side by side in the dark.

Below them, the parked cars in the bowl of the drive-in pointed westward. The movie screen faced them, and beyond lay the main highway to Santa Leona.

On the giant screen a man and a woman were walking on the beach at sunset. Although there was no speaker on the hillside and therefore no sound, Colin could see from the close-ups that the actors were talking animatedly, and he wished he could read lips.

After a while Colin said, "I'm beginning to think this was a dumb idea—coming all the way out here to see a movie we can't even hear."

"You don't need to hear this one," Roy said.

"If we can't hear it, how can we follow the plot?"

"People don't go to the Fairmont for plot. All they want to see here is tits and ass."

Colin gaped at Roy. "What are you talking about?"

"The Fairmont's got a good location. No houses nearby. You can't see the screen from the highway. So they play soft-core porn."

"They play what?" Colin asked.

"Soft-core porn. Don't you know what that is?"

"No."

"You got a lot to learn, good buddy. Fortunately, you have a good teacher. Namely, me. It's pornography. Dirty movies."

"Y-you mean we're going to see people . . . *doing it?*"

Roy grinned. His teeth and eyes caught the moonlight. "That's what we'd see if this was hard-core," Roy said. "But it's only soft stuff."

"Oh," Colin said. He didn't have the slightest idea what Roy meant.

"So all we get to see," Roy explained, "is naked people *pretending* to do it."

"They're . . . really naked?"

"Sure."

"Not completely naked."

"Completely."

"Not the girls."

"Especially the girls," Roy said. "Pay attention to the movie, dummy."

Colin looked at the screen, afraid of what he might see.

The couple on the beach was kissing. Then the man stepped back, and the woman smiled, and she caressed herself, teasing him, and then she reached behind her back and unhooked the bikini top she was wearing and let it slide slowly down her arms, and suddenly her bare breasts bobbled into view, large and firm and upswept, jiggling deliciously, and the man touched them—

"Yeah, get her. Get her good," Roy said.

—and the man stroked the breasts, squeezed them, and the woman closed her eyes and seemed to be sighing, and the man gently thumbed the swollen nipples.

Colin had never been so embarrassed in his life.

"What a set she's got," Roy said enthusiastically.

Colin wished he were somewhere else. Anywhere else. Even back with the bicycles, in the dark, alone.

"Doesn't she have a terrific set?"

Colin wanted to crawl into a hole and hide.

"You like that set?"

Colin couldn't speak.

"Like to suck on those?"

He wished Roy would shut up.

On the screen, the man bent down and sucked on the woman's breasts.

"Like to smother yourself in those?"

Although the movie both shocked and embarrassed Colin, he couldn't look away from it.

"Colin? Hey, Colin!"

"Huh?"

"What do you think?"

"Of what?"

"Her set."

On the screen the man and the woman were running up the beach toward a grassy spot where they could lie down. Her breasts bounced and swung.

"Colin? You forget how to talk?"

"Why do you want to talk about it?"

"It's more fun if we do. We don't have any sound up here, so we can't hear *them* talking about it."

The couple had stretched out on the grass, and the man was kissing her breasts again.

"You like her knockers?"

"Jesus, Roy."

"Do you?"

"I guess."

"You *guess?*"

"Well, sure. They're nice."

"What kind of guy wouldn't like that set?"

Colin didn't respond.

"Maybe a queer wouldn't like them," Roy said.

"I like them," Colin said thinly.

"What do you like?"

"Did you forget what we're talking about?"

"I want to hear you say it."

"I said it already. I like them."

"What do you like?" Roy persisted.

On the screen: erect nipples.

"What's wrong with you?" Colin said.

"Nothing's wrong with *me*."

"You're weird, Roy."

"*You're* the one who's afraid to say it."

"Say what?"

"What do you call them?"

"Jeez."

"What do you call them?"

"Okay, okay. If it'll make you shut up, I'll say it."

"So say it."

"I like her set," Colin said. "There. Happy now?"

Colin was blushing like crazy. He was glad it was dark.

"Give me another word," Roy said.

"Huh?"

"Something besides 'set.' "

"Will you buzz off?"

On the screen: breasts wet with saliva.

Roy put a hand on his arm and squeezed, hurting him a little. "Another word."

"*You* say it. You seem to know all the words."

"And you've got to learn them."

"What's such a big deal about talking dirty?"

"Is little Colin afraid his mommy will hear him and wash out his mouth with soap?"

"Don't be absurd," Colin said, struggling to hold on to his dignity.

"So if you aren't afraid of Mommy, give me another word. Look up there at that screen and tell me what you see that you like."

Colin nervously cleared his throat. "Well . . . I like her breasts."

"Breasts? Jesus, Colin! Breasts are what you find on a chicken!"

"Well, a woman's are called that, too," Colin said defensively.

"By doctors maybe."

"By everyone."

Roy tightened his grip on Colin's arm, dug his sharp fingernails into the flesh.

"Dammit, let go!" Colin said. "You're hurting me."

He tried to pull away but couldn't free himself. Roy was very strong.

Roy's face was only partly visible in the frosty moonlight, but Colin didn't like what little he was able to see. The eyes were wide, piercing, fevered; Colin imagined he could feel heat radiating from them. Roy's lips were drawn back in a mirthless grin, as if he were going to snarl like an attack dog.

Because of something extraordinary in those eyes, something eerie and powerful but indefinable, and because of the intensity with which the other boy spoke, Colin realized that this bizarre conversation held tremendous importance for Roy. He was not just teasing Colin; he was challenging him. This was a battle of wills, and in some way that Colin could not grasp, the outcome would determine their future together. He also sensed, without truly understanding why, that if he didn't win this contest he would live to regret it with all his heart.

Roy squeezed harder.

Colin said, "Ahhhh, Jeez. Please let go."

"Give me another word."

"What's the point?"

"Give me another word."

"Roy, you're hurting me."

"Give me another word and I'll let go."

"I thought you were my friend."

"I'm the best friend you'll ever have."

"If you were my friend you wouldn't hurt me," Colin said between clenched teeth.

"If you were *my* friend, you'd say the word. What the hell does it cost you to say it?"

"And what does it cost you if I don't say it?"

"I thought you said I could trust you, that you'd do anything I wanted, like a friend should do. Now you won't even talk with me about this lousy movie."

"Okay, okay," Colin said. And he actually felt a little guilty because it *was* such a small thing that Roy wanted from him.

"Say 'tits' for me."

"Tits," Colin said thickly.

"Say 'knockers' for me."

"Knockers."

"Say 'boobs.' "

"Boobs."

"Tell me you like her tits."

"I like her tits."

Roy let go. "Was that so difficult?"

Colin gingerly massaged his arm.

"Hey," Roy said, "wouldn't you like to wear her tits for earmuffs?"

"You're gross."

Roy laughed. "Thank you."

"I think you drew blood."

"Don't be a baby. I just squeezed a little. Wow! Look at the screen!"

The man had pulled off the bottom half of the girl's bikini. He was caressing her bare buttocks, which were very white against her tan back and thighs, so white that they looked like the plump halves of a pale nut surrounded by soft brown shell.

"I could eat ten pounds of that ass for breakfast," Roy said.

The man on the screen was naked, too. He stretched out on his back, and the girl straddled him.

"They won't show us the good part," Roy said. "Not at the Fairmont. They won't show her getting it."

The camera concentrated on her bouncing breasts and on her gorgeous face, which was contorted with feigned ecstasy.

"Does that make you stiff?" Roy asked.

"Huh?"

"Does it give you a hard-on?"

"You're weird."

"You afraid of that word, too?"

"I'm not afraid of any words."

"So say it."

"Jeez."

"Say it."

"Hard-on."

"You got one?"

Colin was almost sick with embarrassment.

"You got a hard-on, good buddy?"

"Yeah."

"Know what it's called?"

"Marvin."

Roy laughed. "That's funny. Real quick. I like that."

The other boy's approval was a palliative. Colin's fear subsided just a bit.

"Do you really know what it's called?" Roy asked.

"A penis."

"That's as bad as 'breast.'"

Colin said nothing.

"Say 'cock' for me."

Colin said it.

"Very good," Roy said. "Excellent. Before this movie's over, you'll know all the words, and you'll feel comfortable with them, just like I do. Stick with me, kid, and I'll bring you up right. Hey, look! Look what he's doing to her now! Look, Colin! What a popper! Look!"

Colin felt as if he were on a skateboard, rocketing down a long, steep hill, totally out of control. But he looked.

EIGHT

◆

They got back to Santa Leona at ten forty-five and stopped at a service station on Broadway. The place was closed for the night; the only light was in the soft-drink machine.

Roy fished in his pocket for change. "What do you want? I'm buying."

"I have some money," Colin said.

"You bought supper."

"Well . . . okay. I'll have grape."

They were silent for a while, chugging their drinks.

Finally Roy said, "This is a great night, isn't it?"

"Yeah."

"You having fun?"

"Sure."

"I'm having one hell of a good time, and you know why?"

"Why?"

"Because you're here," Roy said.

"Yeah," Colin said, heavy on the self-deprecation, "I'm always the life of the party."

"I mean it," Roy said. "A guy couldn't ask for a better friend than you."

This time, the cause of Colin's blush was as much pride as embarrassment.

"In fact," Roy said, "you're the only friend I have, and the only friend I need."

"You've got hundreds of friends."

"They're just acquaintances. There's a big difference between friends and acquaintances. Until you moved to town, I'd been a long time between friends."

Colin didn't know if Roy was telling the truth or making fun of him. He had no experience by which to judge, for no one else had ever talked to him as Roy had just done.

Roy put down his half-finished bottle of cola and took a penknife out of his pocket. "I think it's time for this."

"For what?"

Standing in the soft light from the soda machine, Roy opened the knife, put the sharp point against the meaty part of his palm, and pressed hard enough to draw blood: a single thick drop like a crimson pearl. He squeezed the tiny wound until more blood oozed from it and trickled down his hand.

Colin was aghast. "Why'd you do that?"

"Hold out your hand."

"Are you crazy?"

"We'll do it just like the Indians."

"Do what?"

"We'll be blood brothers."

"We're already friends."

"Being blood brothers is a whole lot better."

"Oh yeah? Why?"

"When our blood has mingled, we'll be like one person. In the future, any friends I make will automatically become your friends. And your friends will be mine. We'll always stand together, never apart. The enemies of one will be the enemies of the other, so we'll be twice as strong and twice as smart as anyone else. We'll never fight alone. It'll be you and me against the whole damned world. And the world better look out."

"All of that just because of a bloody handshake?" Colin asked.

"The important thing is what the handshake symbolizes. It stands for friendship and love and trust."

Colin was unable to take his eyes from the scarlet thread that crossed Roy's palm and wrist.

"Give me your hand," Roy said.

Colin was excited about being blood brothers with Roy, but he was also squeamish. "That knife doesn't look clean."

"It is."

"You can get blood poisoning from a dirty cut."

"If there was any chance of that, would I have cut myself first?"

Colin hesitated.

"For Christ's sake," Roy said, "the hole won't be any bigger than a pinprick. Now give me your hand."

Reluctantly Colin held out his right hand, palm up. He was trembling.

Roy grasped him firmly and put the point of the blade to his skin.

"It'll just sting for a second," Roy assured him.

Colin didn't dare speak for fear his voice would quaver badly.

The pain was sudden, sharp, but not long-lasting. Colin bit his lip, determined not to cry out.

Roy folded the knife and put it away.

With shaky fingers Colin pressed the wound until it was bleeding freely.

Roy slipped his bloody hand into Colin's. His grip was firm.

Colin squeezed back with all his strength. Their wet flesh made a barely audible squishing sound as they shook hands.

They stood in front of the deserted service station, in cool night air scented with gasoline, staring into each other's eyes, breathing each other's breath, feeling strong and special and wild.

"My brother," Roy said.

"My brother."

"Forever," Roy said.

"Forever."

Colin concentrated hard on the pinprick in his hand, trying to sense that moment when Roy's blood first began to creep into his own veins.

NINE

◆

After the impromptu ceremony, Roy wiped his sticky hand on his jeans and picked up his unfinished Pepsi. "What do you want to do next?"

"It's after eleven," Colin said.

"An hour from now, do you turn into a pumpkin?"

"I'd better go home."

"It's early."

"If my mother gets back and I'm not there, she'll worry."

"From what you've told me, she doesn't sound like the kind of mother who'd worry about a kid too much."

"I don't want to get in trouble."

"I thought she went to dinner with this Thornberg guy."

"That was around nine o'clock," Colin said. "She might be getting home soon."

"Boy, are you naïve."

Colin looked at him warily. "What's that supposed to mean?"

"She won't be home for hours."

"How do you know?"

"About now," Roy said, "they've had dinner and brandy, and old Thornberg's just getting her into bed at his place."

"You don't know what you're talking about," Colin said uneasily. But he remembered how his mother had looked when she'd gone out: fresh, crisp, and beautiful in a clinging, low-cut dress.

Roy leered at him, winked. "You think your mother's a virgin?"

"Of course not."

"So did she suddenly become a nun or something?"

"Jeez."

"Face it, good buddy, your mother screws around like everyone else."

"I don't want to talk about it."

"*I'd* sure as hell like to screw her."

"Stop it!"

"Touchy, touchy."

"Are we blood brothers or not?" Colin asked.

Roy swallowed the last of his soft drink. "What's that got to do with it?"

"If you're my blood brother, you've got to show some respect for my mother, just as if she were your mother."

Roy put his empty bottle in the rack beside the soda machine. He cleared his throat and spat on the pavement. "Hell, I don't even respect my own mother. The bitch. She's a real bitch. And why should I treat your old lady like some sort of goddess when *you* don't have any respect for her?"

"Who says I don't?"

"*I* say you don't."

"You think you can read minds or something?"

"Didn't you tell me that your old lady always spent more time with her girl-friends than she did with you? Was she ever around when you needed her?"

"Everyone has friends," Colin said weakly.

"Did you have friends before you met me?"

Colin shrugged. "I've always had my hobbies."

"And didn't you tell me that when she was married to your old man, she left him once a month—"

"Not that often."

"—just walked out for a few days at a time, even for a week or more?"

"That was because he beat her," Colin said.

"Did she take you with her when she left?"

Colin finished his grape soda.

"Did she take you with her?" Roy asked again.

"Not usually."

"She left you there with *him*."

"He's my father, after all."

"He sounds dangerous to me," Roy said.

"He never touched me. Just her."

"But he might have hurt you."

"But he didn't."

"She couldn't know for sure what he'd do when she left you with him."

"It worked out okay. That's all that matters."

"And now all her time's taken up with this art gallery," Roy said. "She works every day and most evenings."

"She's building a future for herself and for me."

Roy made a sour face. "Is that her excuse? Is that what she tells you?"

"It's true, I guess."

"How touching. Building a future. Poor, hard-working Weezy Jacobs. It breaks my heart, Colin. It really does. Shit. More nights than not, she's out with someone like Thornberg—"

"That's business."

"—and she *still* doesn't have time for you."

"So what?"

"So you should stop worrying about getting home," Roy said. "Nobody gives a damn if you're home or not. Nobody cares. So let's have some fun."

Colin put his empty bottle in the rack. "What'll we do?"

"Let's see . . . I know. The Kingman place. You'll like the Kingman place. You been there yet?"

"What's the Kingman place?" Colin asked.

"It's one of the oldest houses in town."

"I'm not much interested in landmarks."

"It's that big house at the end of Hawk Drive."

"The spooky old place on top of the hill?"

"Yeah. Nobody's lived there for twenty years."

"What's so interesting about an abandoned house?"

Roy leaned close and cackled like a fiend, twisted his face grotesquely, rolled his eyes, and whispered dramatically: "*It's haunted!*"

"What's the joke?"

"No joke. They say it's haunted."

"Who says?"

"Everyone." Roy rolled his eyes again and tried to imitate Boris Karloff. "People have seen exceedingly strange things at the Kingman place."

"Such as?"

"Not now," Roy said, dropping the Karloff voice. "I'll tell you all about it when we get there."

As Roy lifted his bicycle away from the wall, Colin said, "Wait a minute. I think you're serious. You mean this house is really haunted?"

"I guess it depends on whether or not you believe in that sort of thing."

"People have seen ghosts there?"

"People say they've seen and heard all kinds of crazy things at that house ever since the Kingman family died up there."

"Died?"

"They were killed."

"The whole family?"

"All seven of them."

"When was this?"

"Twenty years ago."

"Who did it?"

"The father."

"Mr. Kingman?"

"He went crazy one night and chopped up everyone while they were sleeping."

Colin swallowed hard. "Chopped them up?"

"With an ax."

Axes again! Colin thought.

For a moment his stomach seemed to be not a part of him but a separate entity alive within him, for it slipped and slid and twisted wetly back and forth, as if trying to crawl out of him.

"I'll tell you all about it when we get there," Roy said. "Come on."

"Wait a minute," Colin said nervously, stalling for time. "My glasses are dirty."

He took off his glasses, pulled a handkerchief from his pocket, and carefully polished the thick lenses. He could still see Roy fairly well, but everything farther than five feet was blurry.

"Hurry up, Colin."

"Maybe we should wait for tomorrow."

"Is it going to take you that long to clean your goddamned glasses?"

"I mean, in daylight we'll be able to see more of the Kingman place."

"Seems to me it's more fun to look at a haunted house at night."

"But you can't see much at night."

Roy regarded him silently for a few seconds. Then: "Are you scared?"

"Of what?"

"Ghosts."

"Of course not."

"Sounds like it."

"Well . . . it *does* seem kind of foolish to go poking around a place like that in the dark, in the dead of night, you know."

"No. I don't know."

"I'm not talking about ghosts. I mean, one of us is bound to get hurt if we mess around in an old broken-down house in the middle of the night."

"You *are* scared."

"Like hell."

"Prove you're not."

"Why should I prove anything?"

"Want your blood brother to think you're a coward?"

Colin was silent. He fidgeted.

"Come *on!*" Roy said.

Roy mounted his bike and pedaled out of the deserted service station, heading north on Broadway. He did not glance back.

Colin stood at the soda machine. Alone. He didn't like being alone. Especially at night.

Roy was a block away and still moving.

"Damn!" Colin said. He shouted, "Wait for me," and clambered onto his bicycle.

TEN
◆

They walked the bikes up the last steep block toward the dilapidated house that crouched above them. With each step, Colin's trepidation grew.

It sure *looks* haunted, he thought.

The Kingman place was well within the Santa Leona city limits, yet it was separated from the rest of the town, as if everyone were afraid to build nearby. It stood on top of a hill and held dominion over five or six acres. At least half of that land had once been well-tended, formal gardens, but long ago it had gone badly to seed. The north leg of Hawk Drive dead-ended in a wide turnaround in front of the Kingman property; and the lampposts did not go all the way to the end of the street, so that the old mansion and its weed-choked grounds were shrouded in blackest shadows, highlighted only by the moon. On the lower two thirds of the hill, on both sides of the road, modern California-style ranch houses clung precariously to the slopes, waiting with amazing patience for a mudslide or the next shock wave from the San Andreas Fault. Only the Kingman place occupied the upper third of the hill, and it appeared to be waiting for something far more terrifying, something a great deal more malevolent than an earthquake.

The house faced the center of town, which lay below it, and the sea, which was not visible at night, except in the negative as a vast expanse of lightlessness. The house was a huge, rambling wreck, ersatz Victorian, with too many fancy chimneys and too many gables, and with twice as much gingerbread around the eaves and windows and railing as true Victorian demanded. Storms had ripped shingles from the roof. Some of the ornate trim was broken, and in a few spots it had fallen down altogether. Where shutters still survived, they often hung at a slant, by a single mounting. The white paint had been weathered away. The boards were silver-gray, bleached by the sun and the constant sea wind, waterstained. The front-porch steps sagged, and there were gaps in the railing. Half of the windows were haphazardly boarded shut, but the others were without protection, thus shattered; moonlight revealed jagged shards of glass like transparent teeth biting at the empty blackness where stones had been pitched through. In spite of its shabby condition, however, the Kingman place did not have the air of a ruin; it did not give rise to sadness in the hearts of those who looked upon it, as did many once-noble but now decrepit buildings; somehow it seemed vital, alive ... even frighteningly alive. If a house could be said to have a human attitude, an emotional aspect, then this house was angry, very angry. *Furious.*

They parked their bicycles by the front gate. It was a big rusted iron grill with a sunburst design in the center.

"Some place, huh?" Roy said.

"Yeah."

"Let's go."

"Inside?"

"Sure."

"We don't have a flashlight."

"Well, at least let's go up on the porch."

"Why?" Colin asked shakily.

"We can look in the windows."

Roy walked through the open gate and started up the broken flagstone walk, through the tangled weeds, toward the house.

Colin followed him for a few steps, then stopped and said, "Wait. Roy, wait a sec."

Roy turned back. "What is it?"

"You been here before?"

"Of course."

"You been inside?"

"Once."

"Did you see any ghosts?"

"Nah. I don't believe in 'em."

"But you said people see things here."

"Other people. Not me."

"You said it was haunted."

"I told you other people said it was haunted. I think they're full of shit. But I knew you'd enjoy the place, what with you being such a big horror-movie fan and everything."

Roy began to walk along the path again.

After several more steps, Colin said, "Wait."

Roy looked back and grinned. "Scared?"

"No."

"Ha!"

"I just have some questions."

"So hurry up and ask them."

"You said a lot of people were killed here."

"Seven," Roy said. "Six murders, one suicide."

"Tell me about it."

During the past twenty years, the very real tragedy of the Kingman murders had evolved into a highly embellished tale, a grisly Santa Leona legend, recalled most often at Halloween, composed of myth and truth, perhaps more of the former than the latter, depending on who was telling it. But the basic facts of the case were simple, and Roy stuck close to them when he told the story.

The Kingmans had been wealthy. Robert Kingman was the only child of Judith and Big Jim Kingman; but Robert's mother died of massive hemorrhaging while delivering him. Big Jim was even then a rich man, and he grew continually richer over the years. He made millions from California real estate, farming, oil, and water rights. He was a tall, barrel-chested man, as was his son, and Big Jim liked to boast that there was no one west of the Mississippi who could eat more steak, drink more whiskey, or make more money than he could. Shortly before Robert's twenty-second birthday, he inherited the entire estate when Big Jim, having drunk too much whiskey, choked to death on a large, inadequately chewed chunk of filet mignon. He lost that eating contest to a man who had yet to make a million dollars in plumbing supplies, but who could at least boast of having lived through the feast. Robert had not developed his father's competitive attitude toward food and beverage, but he had acquired the old man's business sense, and although he was quite young, he made even more money with the funds that had been left to him.

When he was twenty-five, Robert married a woman named Alana Lee, built the Victorian house on Hawk Hill, just for her, and began fathering a new generation of Kingmans. Alana was not from a wealthy family, but she was said to be the most beautiful girl in the county, with the sweetest temper in the state. The children came fast, five of them in eight years—Three boys and two girls. Theirs was the most respected family in town, envied, but also liked and admired. The Kingmans were churchgoers, friendly, graced with the common touch in spite of their high station, charitable, involved in their community. Robert obviously loved Alana, and everyone could see that she adored him; and the children returned the affection their parents lavished upon them.

On a night in August, a few days before the Kingmans' twelfth wedding anniversary, Robert secretly ground up two dozen sleeping tablets that a physician had prescribed for Alana's periodic insomnia, and sprinkled the powder in drink and food that his family shared for a bedtime snack, as well as in various items consumed by the live-in maid, cook, and butler. He neither ate nor drank anything he had contaminated. When his wife, children, and servants were soundly asleep, he went out to the garage and fetched an ax that was used to chop wood for the mansion's nine fireplaces. He spared the maid, cook, and butler, but no one else. He killed Alana first, then his two young daughters, then his three sons. Every member of the family was dispatched in the same hideously brutal, gory fashion: with two sharp and powerful blows of the ax blade, one vertical and one horizontal, in the form of a cross, either on the back or on the chest, depending on the position in which each was sleeping when attacked. That done, Robert visited his victims a second time and crudely decapitated all of them. He carried their dripping heads downstairs and lined them up on the long mantel above the fireplace in the drawing room. It was a shockingly gruesome tableau: six lifeless, blood-splashed faces observing him as if they were a jury or judges in the court of Hell. With his beloved dead watching him, Robert Kingman wrote a brief note to those who would find him and his maniacal handiwork the following morning: "My father always said that I entered the world in a river of blood, my dying mother's blood. And now I will shortly leave on another such river." When he had written that curious good-bye, he loaded a .38-caliber Colt revolver, put the barrel in his mouth, turned toward the death-shocked faces of his family, and blew his brains out.

As Roy finished the story, Colin grew cold all the way through to his bones. He hugged himself and shivered violently.

"The cook was the first to wake up," Roy said. "She found blood all over the hallway and stairs, followed the trail to the drawing room, and saw the heads on the mantel. She ran out of the house, down the hill, screaming at the top of her lungs. Went almost a mile before anyone stopped her. They say she nearly lost her mind over it.''

The night seemed darker than it had been when Roy had begun the story. The moon appeared to be smaller, farther away than it had been earlier.

On a distant highway a big truck shifted gears and accelerated. It sounded like the cry of a prehistoric animal.

Colin's mouth was as dry as ashes. He worked up enough saliva to speak, but his voice was thin. ''For God's sake, *why? * Why did he kill them?''

Roy shrugged. ''No reason.''

''There *had* to be a reason.''

''If there was, nobody ever figured it out.''

''Maybe he made some bad investments and lost all of his money.''

''Nah. He left a fortune.''

''Maybe his wife was going to leave him.''

''All of her friends said she was very happy with her marriage.''

A dog barking.

A train whistling.

Wind whispering in the trees.

The stealthy movement of unseen things.

The night was speaking all around him.

''A brain tumor,'' Colin said.

''A lot of people thought the same thing.''

''I'll bet that's it. I'll bet Kingman had a brain tumor, something like that, something that made him act crazy.''

''At the time it was the most popular theory. But the autopsy didn't turn up any signs of a brain disease.''

Colin frowned. ''You seem to have filed away every single fact about the case.''

''I know it almost as well as if it had happened to me.''

''But how do you know what the autopsy uncovered?''

''I read about it.''

''Where?''

''The library has all the back issues of the Santa Leona *News Register* on microfilm,'' Roy said.

''You researched the case?''

''Yeah. It's exactly the kind of thing that interests me. Remember? Death. I'm fascinated by death. As soon as I heard the Kingman story, I wanted to know more. A whole lot more. I wanted to know every last bit and piece of it. You understand? I mean, wouldn't it have been terrific to be in that house on that night, the night it happened, just sort of observing, just hiding in a corner, on *that* night, hiding and watching him do it, watching him do it to all of them and then to himself? Think of it! Blood everywhere. You've never seen so much goddamned blood in your life! Blood on the walls, soaked and clotted in the bedclothes, slick puddles of blood on the floor, blood on the stairs, and blood splashed over the furniture. . . . And those six heads on the mantel! Jesus, what a popper! What a terrific popper!''

''You're being weird again,'' Colin said.

''Would you like to have been there?''

''No thanks. And neither would you.''

''I sure as hell would!''

''If you saw all that blood, you'd puke.''

''Not me.''

"You're just trying to gross me out."

"Wrong again."

Roy started toward the house.

"Wait a minute," Colin said.

Roy didn't turn back this time. He climbed the sagging steps and walked onto the porch.

Rather than stand alone, Colin joined him. "Tell me about the ghosts."

"Some nights there are strange lights in the house. And people who live farther down the hill say that sometimes they hear the Kingman children screaming in terror and crying for help."

"They hear the *dead kids?*"

"Moaning and carrying on something fierce."

Colin suddenly realized he had his back to one of the broken first-floor windows. He shifted away from it.

Roy continued somberly: "Some people say they've seen spirits that glow in the dark, crazy things, headless children who come out on this porch and run back and forth as if they're being chased by someone . . . or something."

"*Wow!*"

Roy laughed. "What they've probably seen is a bunch of kids trying to hoax everybody."

"Maybe not."

"What else?"

"Maybe they've seen just what they say they have."

"You really *do* believe in ghosts."

"I keep an open mind," Colin said.

"Yeah? Well, you better be more careful about what kind of junk falls into it, or you'll wind up with an open sewer."

"Aren't you clever."

"Everyone says so."

"And modest."

"Everyone says that, too."

"Jeez."

Roy went to the shattered window and peered inside.

"What do you see?" Colin asked.

"Come look."

Colin moved beside him and stared into the house.

A stale, extremely unpleasant odor wafted through the broken window.

"It's the drawing room," Roy said.

"I can't see anything."

"It's the room where he lined up their heads on the mantel."

"What mantel? It's pitch dark in there."

"In a couple of minutes our eyes will adjust."

In the drawing room something moved. There was a soft rustling, a sudden clatter, and the sound of something rushing toward the window.

Colin leaped back. He stumbled over his own feet and fell with a crash.

Roy looked at him and burst out laughing.

"Roy, there's something in there!"

"Rats."

"Huh?"

"Just rats."

"The house has rats?"

"Of course it does, a rotten old place like this. Or maybe we heard a stray cat.

Probably both—a cat chasing a rat. One thing I guarantee: It wasn't any ghoul or ghost. Will you relax, for God's sake?''

Roy faced the window again, leaned into it, head cocked, listening, watching.

Having sustained much greater injury to his pride than to his flesh, Colin got up quickly and nimbly, but he didn't return to the window. He stood at the rickety railing and looked west toward town, then south along Hawk Drive.

After a while he said, ''Why haven't they torn this place down? Why haven't they built new houses up here? This must be valuable land.''

Without looking away from the window, Roy said, ''The entire Kingman fortune, including the land, went to the state.''

''Why?''

''There weren't any living relatives on either side of the family, nobody to inherit.''

''What's the state going to do with the place?''

''In twenty years they've managed to do absolutely zilch, nothing at all, big zero,'' Roy said. ''For a while there was talk of selling the land and the house at public auction. Then they said they were going to make a pocket park out of it. You still hear the park rumor every once in a while, but nothing ever gets done. Now will you please shut up for a minute? I think my eyes are finally beginning to adjust. I have to concentrate on this.''

''Why? What's so important in there?''

''I'm trying to see the mantel.''

''You've been here before,'' Colin said. ''You've already seen it.''

''I'm trying to pretend it's *that* night. The night Kingman went berserk. I'm trying to imagine what it must have been like. The sound of the ax . . . I can almost hear it . . . *whooooosh-chunk, whooooosh-chunk* . . . and maybe a couple of short screams . . . his footsteps coming down the stairs . . . heavy footsteps . . . the blood . . . all that blood. . . ''

Roy's voice gradually trailed away as if he had mesmerized himself.

Colin walked to the far end of the porch. The boards squeaked underfoot. He leaned against the shaky railing and craned his neck so that he could look around the side of the house. He could see only the overgrown garden in shades of gray and black and moonlight-silver: knee-high grass; shaggy hedges; orange and lemon trees pulled to the ground by the weight of their own untrimmed boughs; sprawling rose bushes, some with pale flowers, white or yellow, that looked like puffs of smoke in the darkness; and a hundred other plants that were woven into a single, tangled entity by the loom of the night.

He had the feeling something was watching him from the depths of the garden. Something less than human.

Don't be childish, he thought. There's nothing out there. This isn't a horror movie. This is *life*.

He tried to stand his ground, but the possibility that he was being observed became a certainty, at least in his own mind. He knew that if he stood there much longer, he would surely be seized by a creature with huge claws and dragged into the dense shrubbery, there to be gnawed upon at the beast's leisure. He turned away from the garden and went back to Roy.

''You ready to go?'' Colin asked.

''I can see the whole room.''

''In the dark?''

''I can see a lot of it.''

''Yeah?''

''I can see the mantel.''

"Yeah?"

"Where he lined up the heads."

As if he were drawn by a magnet stronger than his will, Colin stepped up beside Roy and bent forward and peered into the Kingman house. It was extremely dark in there, but he could see a bit more than he had seen a while ago: strange shapes, perhaps piles of broken furniture and other rubble; shadows that seemed to be moving but, of course, were not; and the white-marble mantel above the enormous fireplace, the sacrificial altar upon which Robert Kingman had offered up his family.

Suddenly Colin felt that this was a place he must get away from at once, a place he must stay away from forever. He knew it instinctively, on a deep animal level; and as if he were an animal, the hairs rose on the back of his neck, and he hissed softly, involuntarily, through bared teeth.

Roy said, *"Whooooosh-chunk!"*

ELEVEN

◆

Midnight.

They cycled down Hawk Drive to Broadway and followed Broadway until it ended at Palisades Lane. They stopped at the head of the wooden steps that led down to the public beach. On the other side of the narrow street, elegant old Spanish houses faced the sea. The night was still. There was no traffic. The only sound was the steady pounding of the surf fifty feet below them. From here they would go separate ways: Roy's house was several blocks north, and Colin's lay to the south.

"What time will we get together?" Roy asked.

"We won't. I mean, we can't," Colin said unhappily. "My dad's coming up from L.A. to take me fishing with a bunch of his friends."

"You like to fish?"

"Hate it."

"Can't you get out of it?"

"No way. He spends two Saturdays a month with me, and he makes a big production out of it every time. I don't know why, but I guess it's important to him. If I tried to back out, he'd raise hell."

"When you lived with him, did he even spend two days a month with you?"

"No."

"So tell him to take his fishing pole and shove it up his ass. Tell him you won't go."

Colin shook his head. "No. It's not possible, Roy. I just can't. He'd think my mom put me up to it, and then there'd be real trouble between them."

"What do you care?"

"I'm in the middle."

"So let's get together tomorrow evening."

"That's out, too. I won't be home until ten o'clock."

"I really think you should tell him to shove it."

"We'll get together Sunday," Colin said. "Come over about eleven. We'll swim for an hour before lunch."

"Okay."

"Then we can do whatever you want."

"Sounds good."

"Well . . . see ya then."

"Wait a minute."

"Huh?"

"Someday soon, if I can arrange it for us, you want to get a piece?"

"A piece of what?"

"A piece of *ass.*"

"Oh."

"Do you?"

Colin was embarrassed. "Where? I mean, who?"

"You remember those girls we saw tonight?"

"At the Pinball Pit?"

"Nah. They're just kids. Teasers. I told you that. I'm talking about *real* girls, the ones in that movie."

"What about them?"

"I think I know where I can get something that good for us, a girl just like one of those."

"You been drinking?"

"I'm serious."

"I'm Colin."

"She's got a beautiful face."

"Who?"

"The girl I think we can get."

"Jeez."

"And really big boobs."

"Really big?"

"Really."

"Big as Raquel Welch?"

"Bigger."

"Big as weather balloons?"

"I'm serious. And she has a pair of *gorgeous* legs."

"Good," Colin said. "One-legged girls never turn me on."

"Will you stop it? I told you I'm serious. She's hot stuff."

"I'll bet."

"She really is."

"How old is she?"

"Twenty-five or twenty-six."

"First of all," Colin said, "you'll have to put on a false mustache. Then you can stand on my shoulders, and we can dress up in one suit, just one suit to cover us both, so she won't realize we're only a couple of kids. She'll think we're a tall, dark, handsome man."

Roy scowled. "I'm serious."

"You keep saying that, but you sure don't sound very serious to me."

"Her name's Sarah."

"A beautiful, twenty-five-year-old girl won't be interested in you and me."

"Maybe not at first."

"Not in a million years."

"She'll just need some persuading."

"Persuading?"

"You and me together should be able to handle her."

Colin gaped at him.

"You willing to try?" Roy asked.

"Are you talking about—*rape?*"

"What if I am?"

"You want to wind up in prison?"

"She's hot stuff. She's worth taking the chance."

"Nobody's worth going to prison for."

"You haven't seen her."

"Besides, it's wrong."

"You sound like a preacher."

"It's a terrible thing to do."

"Not if it feels good."

"It won't feel good to *her*."

"She'll love me by the time I'm done with her."

Blushing fiercely, Colin said, "You're weird."

"Wait'll you see Sarah."

"I don't want to see her."

"You'll want her when you see her."

"This is all jive."

"Think about it."

A cream-colored van went by on Palisades Lane. A desert scene, framed in grinning skulls, was painted on the side of it.

They heard loud rock music and the high, sweet laughter of a girl.

"Think about it," Roy said again.

"I don't need to think about it."

"Beautiful big boobs."

"Jeez."

"Think about it."

"This is just like that story about the cat," Colin said. "You wouldn't ever kill a cat, and you wouldn't rape anyone, either."

"If I knew I could get away with it, I'd sure as hell get me a piece or two of that Sarah, and you'd better believe it, good buddy."

"I don't."

"Two of us working together *could* get away with it. Easy. Real easy. Will you at least think about it for a couple of days?"

"Give up, Roy. I know you're putting me on."

"I'm serious."

Colin sighed, shook his head, glanced at his watch. "I can't waste time listening to this baloney. It's late."

"Think about it."

"Jeez!"

Roy smiled. The odd, metallic light played a trick on him, transformed his teeth into fangs; the cold glow of the mercury-vapor street lamp tinted his teeth blue-white, darkened and emphasized the narrow spaces between them, made them look ragged and pointy. At least to Colin's eyes, Roy appeared to be wearing a set of costume-party teeth, the ugly wax dentures you could buy in a novelty shop.

"I've got to get home," Colin said. "See you Sunday at eleven?"

"Sure."

"Don't forget to bring your swimsuit."

"Have fun on your fishing trip."

"Fat chance."

Colin rose on his bike, jammed his feet on the pedals, and pumped south on Palisades Lane. As the wind *shushed* over him, as the relentless crash of the surf echoed off to his right, and as his fear of being alone at night returned, he heard Roy shouting behind him:

"Think about it!"

TWELVE

◆

When Colin arrived home at twelve-thirty, his mother had not yet returned from her date with Mark Thornberg. Her car was not in the garage. The house was dark and forbidding.

He did not want to go inside by himself. He stared at the blank windows, at the pulsing darkness beyond the glass, and he suspected that something was waiting for him in there, some nightmare creature that intended to chew him up alive.

Stop it, stop it, stop it! he told himself angrily. There's nothing waiting for you in there. Nothing. Don't be so damned silly. Grow up! You want to be like Roy, so do exactly what Roy would do if he were here. Waltz right into the house, just like Roy would. Do it. Now. Go!

He fished the key out of a redwood planter that stood beside the walk. His hands shook. He thrust the key into the lock, hesitated, then found sufficient strength to open the door. He reached inside and switched on the light but didn't step across the threshold.

The front room was deserted.

No monsters.

He went to the corner of the house, stepped behind a screen of bushes, and urinated. He didn't want to have to use the bathroom when he got in the house. Something might be waiting there for him, waiting behind the door, behind the shower curtain, perhaps even in the clothes hamper, something dark and fast with wild eyes and lots of teeth and razor-sharp claws.

Got to stop thinking like this! he told himself. It's crazy. Got to stop it. Grown-ups aren't afraid of the dark. If I don't get over this fear soon, I'm going to wind up in an asylum. Jeez.

He replaced the key in the planter and entered the house. He tried to swagger as Roy would have done; however, as if he were a giant marionette, he needed ropes of courage to hold him in a hero's stance, but all that he could find within himself was one thin thread of bravery. He closed the door and put his back against it. He stood quite still, holding his breath, listening.

Ticking. An antique mantel clock.

Moaning. Wind pressing the windows.

Nothing else.

He locked the door behind him.

Paused.

Listened.

Silence.

Suddenly he dashed across the living room, dodging furniture, burst into the downstairs hallway, slapped the light switch there, saw nothing out of the ordinary, thundered up the stairs, turned on the second-floor hall lights, ran into his bedroom, hit the lights there, too, felt a tiny bit better when he saw he was still alone, jerked open the closet door, found no werewolves or vampires lurking among the clothes, shut the bedroom door, locked it, braced it with a straight-backed chair, drew the drapes over both windows so that nothing could look in at him, and collapsed onto the mattress, gasping. He didn't have to look under the bed: It was a platform job, built right on the floor.

He would be safe until morning—unless, of course, something broke down the door in spite of the chair that was wedged under the knob.

Stop it!

He got up, undressed, put on a pair of blue pajamas, set the clock for six-thirty so he'd be ready when his dad arrived, slipped under the sheet, and fluffed his pillow. When he took off his glasses, the room turned fuzzy at the edges, but he had secured the territory and didn't have to be 100 percent watchful. He stretched out on his back, and for a long time he lay listening to the house.

Click! Creeeeeaaak . . . A soft groan, a brief rattle, a barely audible squeak. Just the normal sounds of a house. Settling noises. Nothing more than that.

Even when his mother was home, Colin slept with a night light. But tonight, unless she returned before he fell asleep, he would leave *all* the lamps burning. The room was as bright as an operating theater that had been prepared for surgery.

The sight of his possessions provided him with a little comfort. Five hundred paperbacks filled two tall shelves. The walls were decorated with posters: Bela Lugosi in *Dracula*; Christopher Lee in *The Horror of Dracula*; the monster in *The Creature from the Black Lagoon*; Lon Chaney, Jr., as the Wolfman; the monster from Ridley Scott's *Alien*; and the spooky night-highway poster from *Close Encounters of the Third Kind*. His monster models, which he had built himself from kits, were arranged on a table beside his desk. A plastic ghoul lurched forever through a hand-painted graveyard. Frankenstein's creation stood with plastic arms outstretched, face frozen in a snarl of pure hatred. There were a dozen models in all. The many hours he had spent building them had been hours during which he'd been able to suppress his fear of the night and his awareness of its sinister voice; for so long as he had held those plastic symbols of evil in his hands, he had felt in control of them, master of them, and, curiously, he had felt superior to the very real monsters they represented.

Click!

Creeeeeaaak . . .

After a while he became accustomed to the noises made by the house and almost ceased to hear them. He heard, instead, the voice of the night, the voice that no one else seemed able to hear. It was there from sundown to sunrise, a constant evil presence, a supernatural phenomenon, the voice of the dead who wanted to come back from their graves, the voice of the Devil. It jabbered insanely, cackled, chuckled, wheezed, hissed, murmured about blood and death. In sepulchral tones, it spoke of the dank and airless crypt, of the dead who still walked, of flesh riddled with worms. To most of the world, it was a subliminal voice and spoke only to the subconscious mind; but Colin was *very* aware of it. A steady whisper. Sometimes a shout. Sometimes even a loud scream.

One o'clock.

Where in the hell was his mother?

Tap-tap-tap!

Something at the window.

Tap. Tap-tap. Tap-tap-tap-tap. Tap.

Just a big moth bumping against the glass. That was it. That *had* to be it. Just a moth.

One-thirty.

He had been spending nearly every night alone. He didn't mind eating supper by himself. She had to work a lot, and she had every right to date men now that she was single again. But did she have to leave him alone every night at bedtime?

Tap-tap.

The moth again.

Tap-tap-tap.

He tried to tune out the moth and think about Roy. What a guy Roy was. What a great friend. What a truly terrific buddy. Blood brothers. He could still feel the shallow puncture in the palm of his hand; it throbbed faintly. Roy was on his side, there to help, now and forever, always and always, or at least until one of them died. That's what it meant to be blood brothers. Roy would protect him.

He thought about his best friend, papered over the visions of monsters with images of Roy Borden, blocked out the voice of the night with memories of Roy's voice, and shortly before two o'clock he drifted into sleep. But there were nightmares.

THIRTEEN

◆

The alarm clock woke him at six-thirty.

He got out of bed and pulled open the drapes. For a minute or two he basked in the wan early-morning sunshine, which had no voice and presented no threat.

Twenty minutes later he was showered and dressed.

He walked down the hall to his mother's room and found the door ajar. He rapped lightly, but there was no response. He pushed the door open a few inches and saw her. She was out cold, lying on her belly, her face turned toward him; the knuckles of her left hand were pressed against her slack mouth. Her eyelids fluttered as if she was dreaming; she breathed shallowly and rhythmically. The sheet had pulled halfway down her body during the night. She appeared to be nude beneath the flimsy covers. Her back was bare, and he could see just a hint of her left breast, an exciting suggestion of fullness where it was squashed against the mattress. He stared at the smooth flesh, hoping she would roll over in her sleep and reveal the entire, soft, white globe.

—She's your own *mother!*

But she's built.

—Close the door.

Maybe she'll roll over.

—You don't want to see.

Like hell I don't. Roll over!

—Close the door.

I want to see her breasts.

—This is disgusting.

Her tits.

—Jeez.

I'd sure like to touch them.

—Are you crazy?

Sneak in and touch 'em without waking her.

—You're turning into a pervert. A regular goddamned pervert. You ought to be ashamed.

Blushing, he quietly closed the door. His hands were cold and damp with sweat.

He went downstairs and ate breakfast: two cookies and a glass of orange juice.

Although he tried to clear his mind of it, he could think of nothing except Weezy's bare back and the plump outline of her breast.

"What's happening to me?" he said aloud.

FOURTEEN

◆

His father arrived in a white Cadillac at 7:05, and Colin was waiting for him at the curb in front of the house.

The old man slapped him on the shoulder and said, "How ya doin', Junior?"

"Okay," Colin said.

"Ready to catch some big ones?"

"I guess."

"They're going to be biting today."

"They are?"

"That's the word."

"From who?"

"From those who know."

"The fish?"

His father glanced at him. "What?"

"Who are those who know?"

"Charlie and Irv."

"Who're they?"

"The guys who run the charter service."

"Oh."

Sometimes Colin had difficulty believing that Frank Jacobs was really his father. They were not at all alike. Frank was a big, rangy, rugged man, six-foot-two, a hundred and eighty pounds, with long arms and large, leathery hands. He was an excellent fisherman, a hunter with many trophies, and a highly skilled archer. He was a poker player, a partygoer, a hard drinker but not a drunk, an extrovert, a man's man. Colin admired some of his father's qualities; however, there was a great deal that he merely tolerated, and a few things that aroused anger, fear, and even hatred. For one thing, Frank routinely refused to admit to his mistakes, even when proof of them was before his eyes. On those rare occasions when he realized he could not avoid an owning up, he sulked like a spoiled child, as if it were grossly unfair for him to be held responsible for the results of his own errors. He never read books or any magazines other than those published for sportsmen, yet he had an unshakable opinion about everything from the Arab-Israeli situation to the American ballet; and he stubbornly, vociferously defended his uninformed views without ever realizing that he was making a fool of himself. Worst of all, he lost his temper at the slightest provocation but regained his composure only with enormous effort. When he was very angry he behaved like a raging madman: shouting paranoid accusations, screaming, punching, breaking things. He had been in more than a few fist fights. And he was a wife beater.

He also drove too fast and recklessly. During the forty-minute ride south to Ventura, Colin sat straight and stiff, hands fisted at his sides, afraid to look at the road but also afraid *not* to look. He was amazed when they made it to the marina alive.

The boat was the *Erica Lynn*. She was large and white and well maintained, but there was an unpleasant odor about her that only Colin seemed to notice—a blend of gasoline fumes and the stench of dead fish.

The charter group was composed of Colin, his father, and nine of his father's friends. They were all tall, tan, rugged-looking men, just as Frank was, with names like Jack and Rex and Pete and Mike.

As the *Erica Lynn* cast off, maneuvered out of the harbor, and motored toward the open sea, a breakfast of sorts was served on the deck aft of the pilot's cabin. They had several thermos bottles filled with bloody Marys, two kinds of smoked fish, chopped green onions, slices of melon, and soft rolls.

Colin ate nothing because, as usual, mild seasickness took hold of him the moment the boat moved away from the dock. From experience he knew that he would be all right in an hour or so, but until he got his sea legs, he wasn't taking any chances with food. He even regretted having eaten the two cookies and orange juice, although that had been an hour ago.

At noon the men ate sausage and chugged beer. Colin nibbled at a roll, drank a Pepsi, and tried to stay out of everyone's way.

By then it was clear to all of them that Charlie and Irv had been wrong. The fish were not biting.

They had begun the day in pursuit of shallow-water game only a couple of miles from shore, but the shoals had seemed deserted, as if every aquatic citizen in the neighborhood had gone away on vacation. At ten-thirty they had moved farther out, into deeper water, where they rigged for bigger game. But the fish were having none of it.

The combination of high energy, boredom, frustration, and too much liquor created an explosive mood. Colin sensed trouble coming long before the men decided to play their dangerous, violent, and bloody games.

After lunch they trolled in a zigzag pattern—northwest, south, northwest, south—starting ten miles off shore, moving steadily farther out. They cursed the fish that weren't there and the heat that was. They stripped out of their shirts and trousers, put on swimsuits they'd brought along; the sun darkened their already brown bodies. They told dirty jokes and talked about women as if they were discussing the relative merits of sports cars. Gradually they began to spend more time drinking than watching their lines, chasing shots of whiskey with cold cans of Coors.

The cobalt-blue ocean was unusually calm. The swells seemed to have been tamed with oil; they rolled smoothly, almost sluggishly, beneath the *Erica Lynn*.

The boat's engine produced a monotonous noise—*chuga-chuga-chuga-chuga-chuga*—that you could eventually *feel* as well as hear.

The cloudless summer sky was as blue as a gas flame.

Whiskey and beer. Whiskey and beer.

Colin smiled a lot, spoke when spoken to, but mostly just tried to be invisible.

At five o'clock the sharks showed up, and the day got ugly after that.

Ten minutes earlier, Irv had started chumming again, dumping bucketsful of stinking, chopped bait into their wake, trying to attract big fish. He had done the same thing half a dozen times before, always without effect; but even under the gimlet-eyed stares of his disillusioned clients, he continued to express confidence in his methods.

Charlie was the first to spot the action from his place on the bridge. He called to them through the loudspeaker: "Sharks off the stern, gentlemen. Approximately one hundred and fifty yards."

The men crowded along the railing. Colin found a spot between his father and Mike, wedged himself into it.

"One hundred yards out," Charlie said.

Colin squinted, concentrated hard on the fluid landscape, but he could not find the sharks. The sun shimmered on the water. There appeared to be millions upon millions of living things wriggling across the surface of the sea, but most of them were only slivers of light dancing from point to point on the waves.

"Eighty yards!"

A shout went up as several of the men spotted the sharks at the same instant. A moment later Colin saw a fin. Then another. Two more. At least a dozen.

Suddenly line sang out of one of the reels.

"A bite!" Pete said.

Rex jumped into the deck-mounted chair behind the bent and jerking rod. As Irv strapped him down, Rex slipped the deep-sea rig out of the steel brace that had been holding it.

"Hell, sharks are just junk fish," Jack said disdainfully.

"You're not going to get a trophy for a shark, no matter how damned big it is," Pete said.

"I know," Rex said. "And I'm not about to eat the damned thing either. But I sure as hell won't let the bastard get away!"

Something took the bait on the second line and ran with it. Mike claimed that chair.

At the start it was one of the most exciting things Colin had ever seen. Although this wasn't his first time on a charter boat, he watched in awe as the men battled their catches. They shouted and swore, and the others urged them on. Muscles bulged in their thick arms. Veins popped out in their necks and at their temples.

They groaned and thrashed and held on, pulling and reeling, pulling and reeling. Perspiration streamed from them, and Irv patted their faces with a white rag to keep the sweat from getting in their eyes.

"Keep the line taut!"

"Don't let him throw the hook!"

"Run him some more."

"Tire him out."

"He's already tired out."

"Be careful they don't tangle the lines."

"It's been fifteen minutes."

"Jesus, Mike, a little old lady would've landed him by now."

"My *mother* would've landed him by now."

"Your mother's built like Arnold Schwarzenegger."

"He's breaking water!"

"You got him now, Rex!"

"Big! Six foot or more!"

"And the other one. There!"

"Keep fighting!"

"What the hell will we do with two sharks?"

"Have to cut 'em loose."

"Kill 'em first," Colin's father said. "You never let a shark go back alive. Isn't that right, Irv?"

"Right, Frank."

Colin's father said, "Irv, you better get the gun."

Irv nodded and hurried away.

"What gun?" Colin asked uneasily. He was uncomfortable around firearms.

"They keep a .38 revolver aboard just for killing sharks," his father said.

Irv returned with the gun. "It's loaded."

Frank took it and stood by the railing.

Colin wanted to put his fingers in his ears, but he didn't dare. The men would laugh at him, and his father would be angry.

"Can't see either of the critters yet," Frank said.

The fishermen's hard bodies glistened with sweat.

Each rod appeared to be bent far beyond its breaking point, as if it were held together by nothing more than the indomitable will of the man who controlled it.

Suddenly Frank said, "You've almost got yours, Rex! I can see him."

"He's an ugly son-of-a-bitch," Pete said.

Someone else said, "He looks like Pete."

"He's right on the surface," Frank said. "He doesn't have enough line to run deep again. He looks beat."

"So am I," Rex said. "So will you for God's sake shoot the bastard?"

"Bring him a bit closer."

"What the hell do you want? You want me to make him stand up against a wall and wear a blindfold?"

Everyone laughed.

Colin saw the slick, gray, torpedolike creature only twenty or thirty feet from the stern. It was riding just under the waves, dark fin protruding into the air. For a moment it was very still; then it began to pitch and toss and twist wildly, trying to free itself from the hook.

"Jesus!" Rex said. "It'll tear my arms right out of their sockets."

As the fish was drawn nearer in spite of its violent struggle, it rolled from side to side, writhing on the hook, willing to tear its own mouth to shreds in hope of getting loose, but succeeding only in setting the barbed hook even deeper. Its flat, malevolent head rose from the sea as it rolled, and for an instant Colin was staring into a bright and very alien eye that shone with a fierce inner light and seemed to radiate pure fury.

Frank Jacobs fired the .38 revolver.

Colin saw the hole open a few inches behind the shark's head. Blood and flesh sprayed across the water.

Everyone cheered.

Frank fired again. The second shot entered a couple of inches back of the first. The shark should have been dead, but instead it seemed to take a new life from the bullets.

"Look at the bastard kick!"

"He doesn't like that lead."

"Shoot him again, Frank."

"Get him square in the head."

"Shoot him in the head."

"You got to get a shark in the head."

"Between the eyes, Frank!"

"Kill it, Frank!"

"Kill it!"

The foam that sloshed around the fish had once been white. Now it was pink.

Colin's father squeezed the trigger twice. The big gun bucked in his hands. One shot missed, but the other took the prey squarely in the head.

The shark leaped convulsively, as if trying to heave itself aboard the boat, and everyone on the *Erica Lynn* cried out in surprise; but then it fell back into the water and was absolutely still.

A second later Mike brought his catch to the surface, within striking distance, and Frank fired at it. This time his aim was perfect, and he finished the shark with the first shot.

The sea foam was crimson.

Irv rushed forward with a tackle knife and severed both lines.

Rex and Mike collapsed in their chairs, relieved and surely aching from head to foot.

Colin watched the dead fish drifting belly-up on the waves.

Without warning the sea began to boil as if a great flame had been applied beneath it. Fins appeared everywhere, converging on a small area immediately aft of the *Erica Lynn*: a dozen . . . two dozen . . . fifty sharks or more. They slashed viciously at their dead comrades, ripped and tore at meat like their very own meat, smashed into one another, fought over every morsel, soaring and diving and striking in a mindless, savage feeding frenzy.

Frank emptied the revolver into the turmoil. He must have hit at least one of the monsters, for the commotion grew considerably worse than it had been.

Colin wished he could look away from the slaughter. But he couldn't. Something held him.

"They're cannibals," one of the men said.

"Sharks will eat anything."

"They're worse than goats."

"Fishermen have found some pretty strange things in sharks' stomachs."

"Yeah. I know a guy who found a wristwatch."

"I heard of someone finding a wedding ring."

"A cigar case full of water-logged stogies."

"False teeth."

"A rare coin worth a small fortune."

"Anything indigestible that the victim was wearing or carrying, it stays right there in the shark's gut."

"Why don't we haul in one of these mothers and see what it's keeping in its belly?"

"Hey, that might be interesting."

"Cut it open right here on the deck."

"Might find a rare coin and get rich."

"Probably just find a lot of freshly eaten shark meat."

"Maybe, maybe not."

"At least it's something to do."

"You're right. It's been one hell of a day."

"Irv, better rig one of those rods again."

They started drinking whiskey and beer again.

Colin watched.

Jack took the chair, and two minutes later he had a bite. By the time he'd brought the shark alongside, the feeding frenzy had ended; the pack had moved away. But the frenzy aboard the *Erica Lynn* had just begun.

Colin's father reloaded the .38. He leaned over the railing and pumped two bullets into the huge fish.

"Right in the head."

"Scrambled his fuckin' brains a little."

"Shark's got a brain like a pea."

"Same as yours?"

"That thing dead?"

"Ain't movin'."

"Bring it up."

"Let's have a look inside."

"Find that rare coin."

"Or the false teeth."

Whiskey and beer.

Jack reeled in as much line as he could. The dead shark was bumping against the side of the boat.

"Damn thing's ten feet long."

"Nobody's going to haul that baby up with just a gaff."

"They have a winch."

"It's going to be a messy job."

"Might be worth it if we find that rare coin."

"We're more likely to find a coin in *your* stomach."

With five men, two ropes, three gaffs, and a power winch, they managed to hoist the shark out of the sea and over the stern railing, and then lost control of it a second before it was down, so that it crashed onto the deck, whereupon it came back to life unexpectedly, or half life anyway, for the bullets had hurt it and stunned it, but they had not killed it, and the beast thrashed on the deck, and everyone jumped back, and Pete grabbed a gaff and swung and slammed the hook into the shark's head, spraying blood on several people, and the mighty jaws snapped, trying to get at Pete, and another man rushed forward with another gaff and embedded the long point in one of the shark's eyes, and a third gaff found its way into one of the bullet wounds, and there was blood everywhere, so that Colin thought of the Kingman killings, and all the men in their swimsuits were spotted and streaked with blood, and Colin's father yelled for everyone to stand back, and although Irv told him not to fire toward the deck, Colin's father put one more round in the shark's brain, and finally it stopped moving, and everyone was *very* excited, talking and shouting at once, and they got down in the blood and rolled the shark over and tore at its belly with the gutting knife, and the white flesh resisted for a moment but then gave, and out of the long rent spilled a putrid, slimy mass of guts and half-digested fish, and those still standing cheered while those on their knees pawed through the disgusting muck, looking for the mythical rare coin, the wedding ring, the cigar case, or the false teeth, laughing and joking, even tossing handfuls of gore at one another.

Suddenly Colin found the strength to move. He bolted toward the front of the boat, slipped in blood, stumbled, almost fell, regained his balance. When he had gone as far from the revelers and as far forward as he could, he leaned through the railing and vomited over the side.

By the time Colin finished, his father was there, towering over him, the very image of savagery, skin painted with blood, hair matted with blood, eyes wild. His voice was soft but intense. "What's wrong with you?"

"I was sick," Colin said weakly. "Just sick. It's over now."

"What the hell is *wrong* with you?"

"I'm okay now."

"Do you *try* to embarrass me?"

"Huh?"

"In front of my friends like this?"

Colin stared, unable to comprehend.

"They're making jokes about you."

"Well. . ."

"They're making fun of you."

Colin was dizzy.

"Sometimes I wonder about you," his father said.

"I couldn't help it. I threw up. There wasn't anything I could do to stop it."

"Sometimes I wonder if you *are* my son."

"I am. Of course I am."

His father leaned close and studied him, as if searching for the telltale features of an old friend or milkman. His breath was foul.

Whiskey and beer.

And blood.

"Sometimes you don't act like a boy at all. Sometimes you don't look like you'll ever make a man," his father said quietly but urgently.

"I'm trying."

"Are you?"

"I really am," Colin said despairingly.

"Sometimes you act like a pansy."

"I'm sorry."

"Sometimes you act like a goddamned queer."

"I didn't mean to embarrass you."

"Do you want to pull yourself together?"

"Yeah."

"*Can* you pull yourself together?"

"Yeah."

"Can you?"

"Sure I can."

"Will you?"

"Sure."

"Do it."

"I need a couple of minutes—"

"Now! Do it now!"

"Okay."

"Pull yourself together."

"Okay. I'm okay."

"You're shaking."

"No I'm not."

"You going to come back with me?"

"All right."

"Show those guys whose son you are."

"I'm your son."

"You've got to prove it, Junior."

"I will."

"You've got to show me proof."

"Can I have a beer?"

"What?"

"I think maybe it would help."

"Help what?"

"It might make me feel better."

"You want a beer?"

"Yeah."

"Now, that's more like it!"

Frank Jacobs grinned and mussed his son's hair with one bloody hand.

FIFTEEN

◆

Colin sat on a bench by the cabin wall, sipped his cold beer, and wondered what would happen next.

Having found nothing of interest in the shark's stomach, they heaved the dead beast over the side. It floated for a moment, then suddenly sank or was dragged under by something with a big appetite.

The blood-drenched men lined up along the starboard rail while Irv hosed them down with sea water. They stripped out of their swimsuits, which had to be thrown away, and they lathered up with bars of grainy, yellow soap, all the while making jokes about one another's genitalia. Each received one bucket of fresh water with which to rinse. While they went below to dry off and change into their street clothes, Irv sluiced the deck, washing the last traces of blood into the scuppers.

Later, the men did some skeet shooting. Charlie and Irv always carried two shotguns and a target launcher aboard the *Erica Lynn,* to entertain customers when the fish weren't biting. The men drank whiskey and beer, blasted away at the whirling discs, and forgot all about fishing.

At first Colin winced each time the guns boomed, but after a while the explosions didn't bother him.

Later still, when the men became bored with shooting clay pigeons, they opened up on the sea gulls that were diving for small fish not far from the *Erica Lynn*. The birds did not react to the roar of the shotguns; they continued to feed and to issue their strange shrill cries, apparently unaware that they were being cut down one by one.

The slaughter did not sicken Colin, as it once would have done, nor did it appeal to him. He felt nothing at all as he watched the birds being blown away, and he wondered about his inability to respond. He felt cool and perfectly still inside.

The guns fired, and the gulls burst apart in the sky. Thousands of tiny droplets of blood sprayed up like beads of molten copper in the golden air.

At seven-thirty they said good-bye to Charlie and Irv, and they went to a harbor restaurant for a steak-and-lobster dinner. Colin was starved. He greedily devoured everything on his plate, without a thought about the disemboweled shark or the gulls.

Well after the late, summer sunset, his father took him home. As always, Frank drove too fast and with no regard at all for other motorists.

Ten minutes from Santa Leona, Frank Jacobs turned the conversation away from the events of the day to more personal matters. "Are you happy living with your mother?"

The question put Colin on the spot. He didn't want to spark an argument. He shrugged and said, "I guess."

"That's no answer."

"I mean, I guess I'm happy."

"You don't know?"

"I'm happy enough."

"Is she taking good care of you?"

"Sure."

"Are you eating well?"

"Yeah."

"You're still so skinny."

"I eat real well."

"She's not much of a cook."

"She does okay."

"Does she give you enough spending money?"

"Oh yeah."

"I could send you something every week."

"I don't need it."

"How about if I sent ten dollars every week?"

"You don't have to do that. I have plenty. I'd just waste it."

"You like Santa Leona."

"It's okay."

"Just okay?"

"It's really nice."

"You miss your friends from Westwood?"

"I didn't have any friends there."

"Of course you did. I saw them once. That red-headed boy and—"

"Those were just guys from school. Acquaintances."

"You don't have to keep a stiff upper lip for me."

"I'm not."

"Know you miss them."

"I really don't."

They swerved left, passed a truck that was already exceeding the speed limit, and pulled back into the right lane much too quickly.

Behind them the trucker angrily blew his horn.

"What the hell's eating him? I left plenty of room, didn't I?"

Colin said nothing.

Frank let up on the accelerator. The car slowed from sixty-five to fifty-five miles an hour.

The truck tooted again.

Frank pounded hard on the Cadillac's horn, trumpeted for at least a minute to show the other driver that he wasn't intimidated.

Colin glanced back anxiously. The big truck was no more than four feet from their bumper. Its headlights flashed.

"Bastard," Frank said. "Who the hell does he think he is?" He slowed down to forty miles an hour.

The truck swung into the passing lane.

Frank whipped the Cadillac to the left, in front of the truck, blocking it and holding it at forty.

"Hah! That'll piss the son-of-a-bitch! That'll burn his ass, won't it?"

The trucker used his horn again.

Colin was sweating.

His father was hunched forward, hands like talons on the wheel. His teeth were bared; his eyes were wide as they moved rapidly back and forth from the road to the mirror. He was breathing heavily, almost snorting.

The truck shifted to the right-hand lane.

Frank quickly cut it off again.

At last the trucker seemed to realize that he was dealing with either a drunk or a nut, and that extreme caution was the best course of action. He slowed to about thirty and fell steadily behind.

"That'll teach the asshole. Did he think he owned the goddamned road?"

Having won the battle, Frank put the Cadillac back up to seventy, and they rocketed away into the night.

Colin closed his eyes.

They rode in silence for a few miles, and then Frank said, "What with your friends all down there in Westwood, how'd you like to come back and live with me?"

"You mean all the time?"

"Why not?"

"Well . . . I guess that would be okay," Colin said, only because he knew it was impossible.

"I'll see what I can do, Junior."

Colin glanced at him with alarm. "But the judge gave Mom custody. You've just got visiting rights."

"Maybe we can change that."

"How?"

"There's several things we'd have to do, and a couple of them wouldn't be exactly pleasant."

"Like what?"

"For one thing, you'd have to be willing to stand up in court and say you're not happy living with her."

"I'd have to do that before they'd make a change?"

"I'm pretty sure you would."

"I suppose you're right," Colin said noncommittally. He relaxed a little because he didn't intend to tell the court any such thing.

"You've got the guts to do it, don't you?"

"Oh sure," Colin said. Because it might help to know the enemy's strategy, he said, "What else would we have to do?"

"Well, we'd have to show that she's an unfit mother."

"But she's not."

"Oh, I don't know. I have a hunch we could prove a loose-morals charge to the satisfaction of any judge."

"Huh?"

"That art crowd," Frank said sullenly. "Those people she hangs around with."

"What about them?"

"Those artists have different values from most people. They pride themselves on it."

"I don't understand."

"Well . . . weird politics, atheism, drugs . . . orgies. They sleep around a lot."

"You think Mom—"

"I hate to say it."

"Then don't."

"For your sake, I've got to consider the possibility."

"She doesn't . . . live like that," Colin said, although he wasn't sure if she did or not.

"You've got to face the facts of life, Junior."

"She doesn't."

"She's human. She might surprise you. She's sure as hell no saint."

"I can't believe we're talking about this."

"It's worth considering, worth looking into if it'll get you back with me. A boy needs to have his father around when he's growing up. He needs a man there to show him how to become a man himself."

"But how would you ever prove that she . . . did things like that?"

"Private detectives."

"You'd really hire a bunch of private eyes to snoop on her everywhere she goes?"

"I don't want to have to do that. But it might be necessary. It would be the quickest and easiest way to find out about her."

"Don't do it."

"I'd only be doing it for you."

"Then don't."

"I want you to be happy."

"I am."

"You'd be happier in Westwood."

"Please, Dad, I wouldn't be happy if you put a pack of dogs on her."

His father scowled. "Dogs? Who's talking about dogs? Look, these detectives are professionals. They aren't goons. They wouldn't hurt her. She wouldn't even know they were watching."

"Please, don't do it."

All his father would say was, "I hope it isn't necessary."

Colin thought about going back to Westwood, about living with his father, and it was like having a nightmare without being asleep.

SIXTEEN

◆

At eleven o'clock Sunday morning, Roy arrived with his swimsuit wrapped in a towel. "Where's your mother?"

"She's at the gallery."

"On Sunday?"

"Seven days a week."

"I thought I'd get to see her in a bikini."

" 'Fraid not."

The house was what the real-estate people called "prime lease property." Among other things, it had a sunken living room with a huge stone fireplace, three large bathrooms, a gourmet kitchen, and a forty-foot pool. Since they'd moved in, they'd used the living room less than two hours a week, for they'd had no company; they hadn't entertained overnight guests and had no reason to use the third bath; and of all the fancy equipment in the kitchen, they'd used nothing but the refrigerator and two burners on the stove. Only the pool was worth the rent.

Colin and Roy raced the length of the pool, played with inner tubes and inflated plastic rafts, made a game of retrieving coins from the bottom, splashed, splattered, and finally dragged themselves out onto the concrete apron to bake in the sun.

It was the first time Colin had been swimming with Roy, the first time he had gotten a look at him without a shirt—and the first time that he had seen the horrible marks that disfigured Roy's back. Jagged bands of scar tissue slanted from the boy's right shoulder to his left hip. Colin tried to count them—six, seven, eight, perhaps as many as ten. It was difficult to be sure, for they melted together at a couple of points. Where there was healthy skin between the ugly lines, it was well tanned, but the raised scars did not take the sun; they were pale and shiny-smooth in some places, pale and puckered in others.

"What happened to you?" Colin asked.

"Huh?"

"What happened to your back?"

"Nothing."

"What about those scars?"

"It's nothing."

"You weren't *born* that way."

"Just an accident."

"What kind of accident?"

"It was a long time ago."

"Were you in a car wreck or something?"

"I don't want to talk about it."

"Why not?"

Roy glared at him. "I said I don't want to fucking talk about the fucking scars!"

"Okay. Sure. Forget it."

"I don't have to give you any reason either."

"I didn't mean to pry."

"Well, you did."

"I'm sorry."

"Yeah." Roy sighed. "So am I."

Roy got up and walked to the far end of the pool. He stood there for a while, his back to Colin, staring at the ground.

Feeling stupid and awkward, Colin quickly slid into the pool, as if he wanted to hide in the cool water. He swam hard, trying to work off a sudden overcharge of nervous energy.

Five minutes later, when Colin climbed out of the pool again, Roy was still at the corner of the concrete apron, but now he was hunkered down. He was poking at something in the grass.

"What'd you find?" Colin asked.

Roy was so intent on whatever he was doing that he did not hear the question. Colin went to him and squatted beside him.

"Ants," Roy said.

At the edge of the concrete lay a teacup-size mound of powdery earth. Tiny red ants were scurrying around and over it.

Grinning broadly, Roy mashed the insects into the concrete. A dozen. Two dozen. As he killed them other ants came out of the hill and raced into his shadow, as if they had abruptly realized that their destiny was not mindless labor in the hive but sacrificial death under the hands of a monster god a million times their size.

Roy paused now and then to look at the greasy, rust-colored remains that stained his fingers. "No bones," he said. "They squash into nothing, into just a little drop of juice, 'cause they don't have any bones."

Colin watched.

SEVENTEEN

◆

After Roy had smashed a great many ants and had kicked apart their hill, he and Colin played water polo with a blue-and-green beach ball. Roy won.

By three o'clock they were tired of the pool. They changed out of their swimsuits and sat in the kitchen, eating chocolate-chip cookies and drinking lemonade.

Colin drained his glass, chewed on a sliver of ice, and said, "Do you trust me?"

"Sure."

"Did I pass the test?"

"We're blood brothers, aren't we?"

"Then tell me."

"Tell you what?"

"You know. The big secret."

"I already told you," Roy said.

"You did?"

"I told you Friday night, after we left the Pit, before we went out to the Fairmont to see that porno flick."

Colin shook his head. "If you told me, I didn't hear."

"You heard, but you didn't want to."

"What kind of double-talk is that?"

Roy shrugged. He rattled the ice in his glass.

"Tell me again," Colin said. "This time I want to hear."

"I kill people."

"Jeez. That's *really* your big secret?"

"Seemed like a hell of a secret to me."

"But it's not true."

"Am I your blood brother?"

"Yeah."

"Do blood brothers lie to each other?"

"They're not supposed to," Colin admitted. "Okay. If you killed people, they must have had names. What were their names?"

"Stephen Rose and Philip Pacino."

"Who were they?"

"Just two kids."

"Friends?"

"They could have been if they'd wanted."

"Why'd you kill 'em?"

"They refused to be blood brothers with me. After that I couldn't trust them."

"You mean you'd have killed me if I hadn't wanted to be blood brothers?"

"Maybe."

"Bullshit."

"If it makes you happy to think so."

"Where'd you kill them?"

"Right here in Santa Leona."

"When?"

"I got Phil last summer, the first day of August, the day after his birthday, and I nailed Steve Rose the summer before that."

"How?"

Roy smiled dreamily and closed his eyes, as if he were reliving it in his mind. "I pushed Steve off the cliff at Sandman's Cove. He hit the rocks at the bottom. You should have seen him bounce. When they brought him up the next day, he was such a mess that even his old man couldn't make a positive ID."

"What about the other one—Phil Pacino?"

"We were at his house, building a model airplane," Roy said. "His parents weren't home. He didn't have any brothers or sisters. Nobody knew I'd gone there. It was a perfect opportunity, so I squirted lighter fluid on his head and lit him."

"Jeez."

"As soon as I could see for sure that he was dead, I got the hell out of there.

The whole house burned down. It was a real popper. A couple of days later, the fire marshal decided that Phil had started it by playing with matches.''

"You sure tell a good story," Colin said.

Roy opened his eyes but didn't speak.

Colin took their plates and glasses to the sink, washed them, and stacked them in the rack. As he worked he said, "You know, Roy, with your imagination, maybe you ought to write horror stories when you grow up. You'd make a bundle at it.''

Roy made no move to help with the clean-up. "You mean you still think I'm playing some sort of game with you?"

"Well, you make up a couple of names—"

"Steve Rose and Phil Pacino were real people. You can check on that easy enough. Just go to the library and look through the back issues of the *News Register*. You can read all about how they died.''

"Maybe I'll do that.''

"Maybe you should.''

"But even if this Steve Rose did fall off the cliff at Sandman's Cove, and even if Phil Pacino burned to death in his own home—it wouldn't prove anything. Not a thing. Both of them could have been accidents.''

"Then why would I try to take credit for them?''

"To make your story about being a killer seem more realistic. To make me believe it. To set me up for some kind of joke.''

"You sure can be stubborn," Roy said.

"So can you.''

"What will it take to make you face the truth?''

"I already know the truth," Colin said. He finished the dishes and dried his hands on a red-and-white-checked dish towel.

Roy got up and went to the window. He stared at the sun-dappled swimming pool. "I guess the only way I'm ever going to convince you is to kill someone.''

"Yeah," Colin said. "Why don't you do that?''

"You think I won't.''

"I *know* you won't.''

Roy turned to him. Sunlight streamed through the window, painted one side of Roy's face, left one side in shadow, and made one of his eyes even more fiercely blue than the other. "Are you daring me to kill someone?''

"Yeah.''

"Then if I do it," Roy said, "half the responsibility will be yours.''

"Okay.''

"Just like that?''

"Just like that.''

"Doesn't it bother you that you might wind up in jail?'' Roy asked.

"No. Because you won't do it.''

"Is there anyone special you'd like me to take care of, anyone you'd like to see dead?''

Colin grinned because he was now certain that it was just a game. "Nobody particular. Anyone you want. Why don't you pick a name out of the phone book?''

Roy turned to the window again.

Colin leaned against the counter and waited.

After a while Roy looked at his watch and said, "I've got to be getting home. My parents are going to dinner at my Uncle Marlon's place. He's a genuine asshole. But I have to go with them.''

"Wait a minute, wait a minute!" Colin said. "You can't change the subject that easily. You can't slip out of it. We were talking about who you're going to kill."

"I wasn't trying to slip out of it."

"Well?"

"I've got to think about it for a while."

"Yeah," Colin said. "Like for fifty years."

"No. By tomorrow I'll tell you who it'll be."

"I won't let you forget."

Roy nodded somberly. "And once I'm rolling, I won't let you stop me."

EIGHTEEN

◆

Weezy Jacobs had an important dinner engagement Sunday evening. She gave Colin money to eat at Charlie's Cafe, and she also gave him a short lecture about the importance of ordering something more nutritious than a greasy cheeseburger and french fries.

On his way to dinner, Colin stopped at Rhinehart's, a big drugstore one block from the cafe. Rhinehart's had a large paperback-book section. Colin browsed through the titles in the wire pockets, searching for interesting science fiction and novels about the supernatural.

After a while he realized that a pretty girl, about his own age, had walked up to the racks a few feet away. There were two shelves of books above the wire pockets, and those titles were shelved sideways instead of with their covers showing; she was looking at these, her head tilted to one side so that she could read the spines. She was wearing shorts, and for a moment he stared at her lovely slender legs. She had a graceful neck. Her hair was golden.

She became aware that he was staring at her, and she looked up, smiled. "Hi."

He smiled, too. "Hi."

"You're a friend of Roy Borden's, aren't you?"

"How'd you know that?"

She cocked her head to one side again, as if he were another book on the shelf and she were reading his title. She said, "The two of you are almost like Siamese twins. I hardly ever see one without the other."

"You see me now," he said.

"You're new in town."

"Yeah. Since the first of June."

"What's your name?"

"Colin Jacobs. What's yours?"

"Heather."

"That's pretty."

"Thank you."

"Heather what?"

"Promise you won't laugh."

"Huh?"

"Promise you won't laugh at my name."

"Why would I laugh at your name?"

"It's Heather Lipshitz."

"No," he said.

"Yes. It would be bad enough if it were Zelda Lipshitz. Or Sadie Lipshitz. But Heather Lipshitz is worse because the two don't go together, and the first name just calls attention to the last. You didn't laugh."

"Of course not."

"Most kids do."

"Most kids are stupid."

"You like to read?" Heather asked.

"Yeah."

"What do you read?"

"Science fiction. You?"

"I'll read almost anything. I've read some science fiction. *Stranger in a Strange Land.*"

"That's a great book."

"You see *Star Wars?*" she asked.

"Four times. And *Close Encounters* six times."

"Have you seen *Alien?*"

"Yeah. You enjoy stuff like that?"

"Sure. When there's an old Christopher Lee movie on TV, you can't pull me away from the set," she said.

He was amazed. "You actually like horror movies?"

"The scarier the better." She looked at her wristwatch. "Well, I've got to get home for dinner. It's been real nice talking to you, Colin."

As she started to turn away, he said, "Uh . . . wait a sec." She looked back at him, and he shifted awkwardly from one foot to the other. "Uh . . . there's a new horror flick coming to the Baronet this week."

"I saw the previews."

"Did it look good to you?"

"Might be," she said.

"Would you . . . well . . . I mean . . . do you think. . . ."

She smiled. "I'd like to."

"You would?"

"Sure."

"Well . . . should I call you or what?"

"Call me."

"What's your number?"

"It's in the book. Believe it or not, we're the only Lipshitz family in town."

He grinned. "I'll call you tomorrow."

"Okay."

"If that's all right."

"That's fine."

"Bye."

"Good-bye, Colin."

He watched her walk out of the store. His heart was racing.

Jeez.

Something strange was happening to him. For sure, for sure. He never before had been able to talk like that with a girl—or with a girl like that. He usually got tongue-tied right at the start, and the whole conversation went into the toilet. But not this time. He'd been smooth. For God's sake, he'd even made a date with her! His first date. Something sure was happening to him.

But what?

And why?

Several hours later, as he lay in bed, listening to a Los Angeles radio station, unable to sleep, Colin thought about all of the wonderful new developments in his life. With a terrific friend like Roy, with an important position like team manager, and with a girl as pretty and nice as Heather—what more could he possibly ask?

He had never been so content.

Roy was the most important part of his new life, of course. Without Roy, he would never have been brought to the attention of Coach Molinoff and would never have gotten the job as junior-varsity team manager. And without Roy's liberating influence, he would very likely never have had the nerve to ask Heather for a date. More than that—she probably wouldn't even have said hello to him if he hadn't been Roy's friend. Wasn't that the first thing she had said to him? *You're a friend of Roy Borden's, aren't you?* If he hadn't been a friend of Roy's, she probably wouldn't even have looked at him twice.

But she *had* looked twice.

And she had agreed to date him.

Life was good.

He thought about Roy's strange stories. The cat in the birdcage. The boy burned with lighter fluid. He knew those were just tall tales. Tests. Roy was testing him for something. He put the cat and the burned boy out of his mind. He wasn't going to let those silly stories destroy his lovely mood.

He closed his eyes and pictured himself dancing with Heather in a magnificent ballroom. He was wearing a tuxedo. She was in a red gown. There was a crystal chandelier. They danced so well together that they seemed to be floating.

NINETEEN

◆

Early Monday afternoon, Colin was at the worktable in his bedroom, putting together a plastic model of Lon Chaney as the Phantom of the Opera. When the telephone rang, he had to run into his mother's room to answer it, for he had no extension of his own.

It was Roy. "Colin, you've got to come right away."

"Come where?"

"My house."

Colin looked at the digital read-out clock on the nightstand: 1:05. He said, "We were supposed to meet at two o'clock."

"I know. But you've got to come now."

"Why?"

"My folks aren't home, and there's something here that you absolutely have to see. I can't talk about it on the phone. You've got to come now, right away, just as quick as you can. Hurry!"

Roy hung up.

The game continues, Colin thought.

Ten minutes later, Colin rang the bell at the Borden house.

Roy answered the door. He was flushed and excited.

"What's up?" Colin asked.

Roy pulled him inside and slammed the door. They stood in the foyer. The immaculate living room lay beyond; the emerald-green drapes filtered the sun and filled the place with cold light that gave Colin the feeling they were deep beneath the sea.

"I want you to get a good look at Sarah," Roy said.

"Who?"

"I told you about her Friday night, when we were at the beach steps on the palisades, just before we split up. She's the girl, the one who looks good enough to be in a porn movie, the one I think we can find a way to screw."

Colin blinked. "You've got her *here?*"

"Not exactly. Come on upstairs. You'll see."

Colin had never been in Roy's bedroom before, and it surprised him. It didn't look like a kid's room; in fact, it didn't look like a place where anyone, either child or adult, really lived. The nap on the carpet stood up as if it had been vacuumed only minutes ago. The dark pine furniture was highly polished; Colin couldn't see a nick or a scratch in it, but he could see his reflection. No dust. No grime. No fingerprints around the light switch. The bed was neatly made, the lines as straight and the corners as tightly tucked as those on a bunk in an Army barracks. In addition to the furniture, there was a big red dictionary and the uniform volumes of an encyclopedia. But nothing else. Nothing else at all. There were no knickknacks, no model airplanes, no comic books, no sports equipment, nothing to show that Roy had any hobbies or even any normal human interests. Quite clearly, the room was a mirror of Mrs. Borden's personality and not her son's.

To Colin's eyes, the oddest thing about the place was the total absence of decoration on the walls. No paintings. No photographs. No posters. In the downstairs foyer, in the living room, and on the wall along the stairs, there were a couple of oils, a watercolor, and a few inexpensive prints, but here the walls were bare and white. Colin felt as if he were in a monk's cell.

Roy led him to a window.

Not more than fifty feet away, in the backyard of the house next door, a woman was sunbathing. She was wearing a white bikini and was lying on a red beach towel that was draped across a cot. Small cotton pads shielded her eyes from the sun.

"She's really a terrific piece of ass," Roy said.

Her arms were at her sides, palms turned up as if in supplication. She was tan and lean and shapely.

"That's Sarah?" Colin asked.

"Sarah Callahan. She lives next door." Roy picked up a pair of binoculars that had been on the floor beneath the window. "Here. Take a closer look."

"What if she sees me?"

"She won't."

He put the glasses to his eyes, focused them, and found the woman. If she actually had been as close as she suddenly appeared to be, she would have felt his breath on her skin.

Sarah was beautiful. Even in repose, her features held great sensual promise. Her lips were full, ripe; she licked them once while he watched.

A peculiar sense of power overcame Colin. In his mind he touched and caressed Sarah Callahan, but in reality she was unaware of it. The binoculars were his lips and tongue and fingers, feeling and tasting her, exploring her, surreptitiously violating the sanctity of her body. He experienced mild synesthesia: Magically, his eyes seemed to possess senses other than sight. With his eyes he smelled her fresh, thick, yellow hair. With his eyes he felt the texture of her skin, the pliancy of her flesh, the soft roundness of her breasts, and the moist warmth in the musky junction of her thighs. With his eyes he kissed her concave belly and tasted the salty beads of perspiration that ringed her like a jeweled belt. For a moment Colin felt that he could do anything to her that he wished; he had complete immunity. He was the invisible man.

"How'd you like to get in her pants?" Roy asked.

Finally Colin lowered the binoculars.

"You want her?" Roy asked.

"Who wouldn't?"

"We can have her."

"You're living in a dream."

"Her husband's at work all day."

"So?"

"She's pretty much alone over there."

"What do you mean—'pretty much'?"

"She has a five-year-old kid."

"Then she's not alone at all."

"The kid won't give us any trouble."

Colin knew that Roy was playing the game again, but this time he decided to play along. "What's your plan?"

"We just go over and knock on the door. She knows me. She'll open up."

"And then?"

"You and me can handle her. We'll push inside, knock her down. I'll put a knife at her throat."

"She'll scream."

"Not with a knife at her throat."

"She'll think you're bluffing."

"If she does," Roy said, "I'll cut her a little to show we mean business."

"What about the kid?"

"I'll have Sarah under control, so you'll be free to catch the brat and tie him up."

"What'll I tie him with?"

"We'll take along some clothesline."

"After I've gotten him out of the way, what happens?"

Roy grinned. "Then we'll strip her, tie her to the bed, and use her."

"And you think she's not going to tell anybody what we've done?"

"Oh, of course, when we're finished with her, we'll have to kill her."

"And the kid, too?" Colin asked.

"He's a rotten little brat. I'd like to snuff him most of all."

"It's a bad idea. Forget it."

"Yesterday, you dared me to kill someone," Roy said. "And now the idea scares you."

"Look who's talking."

"What do you mean?"

Colin sighed. "You've protected yourself by coming up with a plan that can't possibly work. You figured I'd shoot it down, and then you could say, 'Well, I wanted to prove I could kill someone, but Colin chickened out on me.'"

"What's wrong with my plan?" Roy demanded.

"First of all, you live next door to her."

"So what?"

"The cops would suspect you right off."

"Me? I'm just a fourteen-year-old kid."

"Old enough to be a suspect."

"You really think so?"

"Sure."

"Well . . . you could give me an alibi. You could swear I was at your house when she was murdered."

"Then they'd suspect both of us."

For a long time Roy stared down at Sarah Callahan. Finally he turned away from the window and began to pace. "What we'd have to do is leave clues that pointed away from us. We'd have to mislead them."

"You realize the kind of lab equipment they've got? They can trace you by a single hair, a thread, almost anything."

"But if we could snuff her in such a way that they'd never in a million years think it was just kids that did it. . . ."

"How?"

Roy continued to pace. "We'd make it look like some raving lunatic killed her, some sex maniac. We'd stab her a hundred times. We'd cut off her ears. We'd slice up the brat pretty good, too, and we'd use blood to write a lot of crazy things on the walls."

"You're really gross."

Roy stopped pacing and stared hard at him. "What's the matter? Are you a sissy about blood?"

Colin felt queasy but tried not to show it. "Even if you could mislead the cops that way, there's too many other things wrong with your plan."

"Like what?"

"Someone will see us going into the Callahan place."

"Who?"

"Maybe somebody taking out the garbage. Or somebody washing windows. Or just somebody going by in a car."

"So we'll use the Callahans' back door."

Colin glanced out the window. "Looks to me like that wall goes all around the property. We'd have to enter by the front walk and go around the house to get to the back door."

"Nah. We could climb over the wall in a minute."

"If anyone saw us, they'd be sure to remember. Besides, what about fingerprints when we get into the house?"

"We'll wear gloves, of course."

"You mean we'll walk up to the door wearing gloves in ninety-degree heat, carrying a lot of rope and a knife—and she'll let us in without a second thought?"

Roy was becoming impatient. "When she opens the door, we'll move so fast she won't have time to realize anything's wrong."

"What if she does? What if she's faster than we are?"

"She won't be."

"We've at least got to consider the possibility," Colin insisted.

"Okay. I've considered it, and I've decided it's nothing to worry about."

"Another thing. What if she opens the inner door but not the storm door?"

"Then we'll open the storm door," Roy said. "What's the problem?"

"What if it's locked?"

"Christ!"

"Well, we have to expect the worst."

"Okay, okay. It's a bad idea."

"That's what I said."

"But I'm not giving up."

"I don't want you to give up," Colin said. "I'm enjoying the game."

"Sooner or later, I'll find the right setup. I'll find someone for us to kill. You better believe it."

For a while they took turns watching Sarah Callahan through the binoculars.

Earlier, Colin had been eager to tell Roy about Heather. But now, for reasons he couldn't quite define, he felt the time wasn't right. For the moment Heather would be his little secret.

When Sarah Callahan finished sunning herself, Colin and Roy went down to the garage and passed Monday afternoon with the trains. Roy engineered elaborate wrecks and laughed excitedly each time the cars plunged off the tracks.

That night Colin telephoned Heather, and she accepted a movie date for Wednesday. They talked almost fifteen minutes. When Colin finally hung up, he felt that his happiness was a visible light, that it was radiating from him in a golden nimbus; he was glowing.

TWENTY

◆

Colin and Roy spent part of Tuesday at the beach, getting tanned and watching the girls. Roy seemed to have lost interest in his macabre game; he didn't say a single word about killing anyone.

At two-thirty Roy stood up and brushed sand from his bare legs and his cut-off jeans. He had decided it was time to go back into town. "I want to stop by your mother's gallery."

Colin blinked. "What for?"

"To look at the paintings, of course."

"Why?"

"'Cause I'm interested in paintings, dummy."

"Since when?"

"Since always."

"You never mentioned it before."

"You never asked," Roy said.

They rode their bicycles back to town and parked on the sidewalk in front of the gallery.

A few browsers were in the shop. They moved slowly from painting to painting.

Weezy's business partner, Paula, was sitting at the big antique desk in the far right corner of the room, where sales were written. She was a wispy, freckled woman with lustrous auburn hair and large glasses.

Weezy was circulating among the browsers, offering to answer any questions they might have about the paintings. When she saw Colin and Roy, she headed straight for them, smiling stiffly. It was clear to Colin that she thought a pair of sandy, sweaty, bare-chested boys in cut-off jeans were definitely not conducive to business.

Before Weezy could ask them what they wanted, Roy pointed to a large painting by Mark Thornberg and said, "Mrs. Jacobs, this artist is terrific. He really is. His work has a lot more depth than the two-dimensional stuff that most current painters are turning out. The detail is really something. Wow. I mean, it almost looks like he's trying to adapt the style of the old Flemish masters to a more modern sort of viewpoint."

Weezy was surprised by Roy's observations.

Colin was surprised, too. More than surprised. Stunned. Depth? Two-dimensional? Flemish masters? He gaped at Roy, amazed.

"Are you interested in art?" Weezy asked.

"Oh yes," Roy said. "I'm thinking of majoring in art when I go to college. But that's still a few years away."

"Do you paint?"

"A little. Mostly watercolors. I'm not really very good."

"I'll bet you're being modest," Weezy said. "After all, you apparently have quite an understanding of art—and a very good eye. You went right to the heart of what Mark Thornberg is trying to achieve."

"I did?"

"Yes. That's astounding. Especially for someone your age. Mark *is* attempting to take the meticulous detail and the three-dimensional techniques of the Flemish masters and combine those qualities with a modern sensibility and modern subject matter."

Roy looked at other Thornberg canvases on the same wall as the first, and he said, "I think I detect a trace of . . . Jacob DeWitt."

"Exactly!" Weezy said, astonished. "Mark is a great admirer of DeWitt. You really *do* have a knowledge of art. You're quite remarkable."

Roy and Weezy moved from one Thornberg painting to another, spending a few minutes in front of each, discussing the artist's merits. Colin tagged along behind them, left out, embarrassed by his ignorance—and baffled by Roy's unexpected expertise and brilliant perception.

The very first time that Weezy had met Roy, she had been favorably impressed by him. She had told Colin as much, and she had suggested that a fine boy like Roy Borden was a much better influence than the few bookworms and social rejects with whom he had previously established tenuous relationships. She had seemed unaware that he, too, was a bookworm and a social reject and that her words stung him. Now she was intrigued by Roy's interest in fine arts. Colin could see the delight in her eyes. Roy knew how to be charming without ever seeming phony, insincere. He could win the approval of virtually any adult—even those he secretly despised.

In a flash of jealousy, Colin thought: *She approves of him more than she does of me. The way she's looking at him! Has she ever looked at me like that? Hell, no. The bitch!*

The intensity of his sudden anger surprised and disconcerted him. As Weezy and Roy looked at the last of the Thornberg paintings, Colin struggled to regain control of himself.

A few minutes later, outside the gallery, as he and Roy were climbing on their bicycles, Colin said, "Why didn't you ever tell me you were interested in art?"

Roy grinned. "Because I'm *not* interested in art. It's a bunch of crap. It's too damned boring."

"But all that stuff you said in there—"

"I knew your old lady was dating this Thornberg and handling his paintings at the gallery. I went to the library to see if I could find out anything about him. They subscribe to several art magazines at the library. *California Artist* ran an article about Thornberg almost a year ago. I just read it for background."

"Why?" Colin asked, perplexed.

"To impress your mother."

"Why?"

"'Cause I want her to like me."

"You went to all that trouble just to make my mother like you? It's that important to you?"

"Sure," Roy said. "We don't want her getting the idea I'm a bad influence on you. She might forbid you to see me any more."

"Why would she think you're a bad influence?"

"Grown-ups can get funny ideas sometimes," Roy said.

"Well, she'd never tell me not to hang around with you. She thinks you're a *good* influence."

"Yeah?"

"Yeah."

"Well then, my little act was just more insurance."

Roy pedaled away fast.

Colin hesitated, then followed him. He was certain there was more behind Roy's "little act" than the boy was willing to talk about. But what? What had Roy really been up to?

TWENTY-ONE

◆

Weezy couldn't come home Tuesday evening; she had dinner with a business associate. She gave Colin money to eat at Charlie's Cafe again, and Colin took Roy with him.

After cheeseburgers and milkshakes, Colin said, "Want to see a movie?"

"Where?"

"There's a good one on television."

"What is it?"

"*The Shadow of Dracula.*"

"Why do you want to see junk like that?"

"It's not junk. It's gotten good reviews."

"There's no such thing as vampires," Roy said.

"Maybe. Maybe not."

"No maybes. Positively not. Vampires . . . that's bunk."

"But they make for scary movies."

"Boring," Roy said.

"Why don't you give it a chance?"

Roy sighed and shook his head. "How can you be scared of something that doesn't exist?"

"You just have to use your imagination a little."

"Why should I *imagine* scary things when there are so many *real* things to be afraid of?"

Colin shrugged. "Okay. So you don't want to see the movie."

"Besides, I have something planned for later."

"What?" Colin asked.

Roy gave him a sly look. "You'll see."

"Don't be mysterious. Tell me."

"In good time."

"When?"

"Oh . . . eight o'clock," Roy said.

"What'll we do till then?"

They rode down Central Avenue to the small craft harbor, chained their bicycles in a parking lot, and explored the maze of waterfront shops and amusements. They strolled through swarms of buzzing tourists, looking for pretty girls in shorts or bikinis.

Over the bay, sea gulls soared and swooped. With piercing, melancholy cries, they darted up and down, back and forth, sewing together the sky, the earth, and the water.

Colin thought the harbor was beautiful. The westering sun streamed between scattered white clouds and appeared to lay in shimmering bronze puddles on the water. Seven small boats were sailing in formation, snaking across the sheltered water toward the open sea. The evening was drenched in that peculiar California light that is perfectly clear but that seems at the same time to have considerable substance, as if you were looking at the world through countless sheets of expensive, highly polished crystal.

At that moment the harbor seemed to be the safest and most welcoming place on earth, but Colin was cursed with the ability to see how it would change for the worse in just an hour or two. In his mind he could picture it at night—The crowds gone, the shops closed, and no light but that from a few wharf lamps. In the late hours the only sound would be the voice of the night: the continuous lapping of the sea at the dark pilings, the creaking of moored boats, the sinister rustling of wings as the gulls settled down to sleep, and that ever-present undercurrent of demonic whispers that most people could not hear. He knew that evil would creep in with the dying of the light. In the lonely shadows, something hideous would rise out of the water and snatch away the unwary passerby; something slimy and scaly; something with awful, insatiable hungers; something with razor teeth and powerful jaws that could tear a man apart.

Unable to shake that horror-movie image, Colin suddenly found that he could no longer enjoy the beauty around him. It was as if he were looking at a pretty girl and, against his will, seeing within her the rotting corpse that she would eventually become.

Sometimes he wondered if he were crazy.

Sometimes he hated himself.

"It's eight o'clock," Roy said.

"Where we going?"

"Just follow me."

With Roy in the lead, they cycled all the way to the eastern end of Central Avenue, then continued east on Santa Leona Road. In the hills beyond town, they turned onto a narrow dirt lane, followed it down one flank of a shallow glen and up the other. On both sides of the dusty track, wildflowers shone like blue and red flames in the tall, dry grass.

Sunset was nearly upon them; and this close to the sea, the twilight hour was more like fifteen minutes. Night would swiftly lay claim to the land. Wherever they were going, they would have to come back in the dark. And Colin didn't like that.

On high ground again, they rounded a curve that lay in shadows cast by several eucalyptus trees. The land ended fifty yards beyond the curve, in the middle of an automobile graveyard.

"Hermit Hobson's place," Roy said.

"Who's he?"

"Used to live here."

A one-story clapboard building, more shack than house, overlooked two hundred or more decaying automobiles that were strewn across a few acres of the grassy hilltop.

They parked their bicycles in front of the shack.

"Why's he called 'Hermit'?" Colin asked.

"Because that's what he was. He lived all alone out here, and he didn't like people."

A four-inch, blue-green lizard slithered onto a sagging porch step and halfway across the breadth of it, then froze, rolling one milky eye at the boys.

"What're all these cars for?" Colin asked.

"When he first moved in, that's how he supported himself. He bought up cars that had been in real bad accidents and sold spare parts."

"You can make a living that way?"

"Well, he didn't want much."

"I can see that."

The lizard came off the step, onto a patch of hard, dry earth. It was still watchful.

"Later on," Roy said, "old Hermit Hobson inherited some money."

"He was rich?"

"No. He got just enough so he could keep on living here without the spare-parts business. After that he saw other people just once a month, when he came to town for supplies."

The lizard skittered back toward the step, froze again, this time facing away from them.

Roy moved fast. The lizard's eyes looked backward as well as sideways and forward, so it saw him coming. Nevertheless, he caught it by the tail, held it, and brought his foot down hard on its head.

Colin turned away in disgust. "Why the hell did you have to do that?"

"Did you hear it crunch?"

"What was the point?"

"It was a popper."

"Jeez."

Roy wiped his shoe in the grass.

Colin cleared his throat and said, "Where's Hermit Hobson now?"

"Dead."

Colin looked suspiciously at Roy. "I guess you're going to try to make me believe you killed him, too."

"Nope. Natural causes. Four months ago."

"Then why're we here?"

"For the train wreck."

"Huh?"

"Come see what I've done."

Roy walked toward the rusting automobiles.

After a moment, Colin followed him. "It'll be dark before long."

"That's good. It'll cover our escape."

"Escape from what?"

"The scene of the crime."

"What crime?"

"I told you. The train wreck."

"What're you talking about?"

Roy didn't answer.

They walked through knee-high grass. Close to the abandoned junkers, where a mower couldn't reach and where Hermit Hobson had never trimmed, the grass was much higher and thicker than it was elsewhere.

The hilltop ended in a rounded point somewhat like the prow of a ship.

Roy stood on the edge of the slope and looked down. "That's where it'll happen."

Eighty feet below, railroad tracks curved around the prow of the hill.

"We'll derail it on the curve," Roy said. He pointed to two parallel ribbons of heavy corrugated sheet metal that led from the tracks, up the slope, and over the brow of the hill. "Hobson was a real packrat. I found fifty of those six-foot long sheets in big piles of junk behind his shack. That was a hell of a piece of luck. Without them, I wouldn't have been able to set this up."

"What're they for?" Colin asked.

"The truck."

"What truck?"

"Over there."

A four-year-old, battered Ford pickup stood about thirty feet back from the slope. The corrugated strips led to it, then under it. The Ford had no tires; its rust-filmed wheels rested on the sheet metal.

Colin hunkered down beside the truck. "How'd you get the corrugated panels under there?"

"I lifted one wheel at a time with a jack I found in one of these wrecks."

"Why go to all that trouble?"

"Because we can't just push the truck across bare ground," Roy said. "The wheels would dig into the earth and stop it."

Colin looked from the truck to the brow of the hill. "Let me get this straight. Let me see if I understand. You want to push the truck along this track you've made, let it roll down the slope, into the side of the train."

"Yeah."

Colin sighed.

"What's wrong?" Roy asked.

"Another damned game."

"No game."

"I guess I'm supposed to do what I did with the Sarah Callahan scheme. You want me to show you the holes in it so you'll have an excuse to chicken out."

"What holes?" Roy challenged.

"For one thing, a train is too damned big and heavy to be derailed by a little truck like this."

"Not if we do it right," Roy said. "If it's perfectly timed, if the truck's coming down the slope just as the train's rounding the bend, the engineer will hit the brakes. When he tries to stop the train on a sharp curve like that, it'll start rocking like crazy. And then when the truck hits it, it'll roll right off the tracks."

"I don't think so."

"You're wrong," Roy said. "There's a pretty good chance it'll happen just like I say."

"No."

"It's worth a try. Even if it doesn't derail the train, it'll scare the hell out of them. Either way, it'll be a popper."

"There's something else you haven't thought of. This truck's been sitting out here for a couple of years. The wheels are rusted. No matter how hard we push, they aren't going to turn."

"You're wrong again," Roy said happily. "I thought of that. There hasn't been that much rain the past few years. They weren't rusted really bad. I had to spend a few days working on the truck, but now the wheels will turn for us."

For the first time, Colin noticed dark, oily stains on the wheel beside him. He reached behind it and found that it had been freshly, excessively lubricated. His hand came away with gobs of grease on it.

Roy grinned. "You see any other flaws in the plan?"

Colin wiped his hand in the grass and stood up.

Roy stood, too. "Well?"

The sun had just set. The western sky was golden.

"When do you figure to do it?" Colin asked.

Roy looked at his wristwatch. "About six or seven minutes from now."

"There'll be a train then?"

"Six nights a week at this time, a passenger train comes through here. I've done some checking. It starts in San Diego, stops in L.A., goes on to San Francisco and then Seattle before starting back. I've sat on the hill and watched it a lot of nights. It really moves. It's an express."

"You said the timing has to be perfect."

"It will be. Or near enough."

"But no matter how carefully you've planned it, you can't expect the railroad to cooperate. I mean, trains don't always run on time."

"This one usually does," Roy said confidently. "Besides, that's not too important. All we have to do is push the truck closer to the edge, then wait until the train is almost here. When we see the locomotive coming, we'll give the truck a little shove, tip it over the brink, and away it'll go."

Colin bit his lip, frowned. "I know you set this up so it can't be done."

"Wrong. I want to do it."

"It's a game. There's a big hole in the plan, and you expect me to find it."

"No holes."

"I must be missing something."

"You haven't missed anything."

Each of the ruined pickup's front wheels was jammed against a wooden chock. Roy removed these braces and threw them aside.

"What's the joke?" Colin asked.

"We've got to get moving."

"There must be a joke."

"We don't have much time."

Both of the truck's doors had been removed, either by the collision or by Hermit Hobson. Roy went to the open driver's side, reached in, and put his right hand on the steering wheel. He put his left hand on the door frame, ready to push.

"Roy, why don't you give up? I *know* there's got to be a catch."

"Get around on the other side and help."

Still trying to find the hole, still wondering what he had overlooked, still certain that Roy was playing an elaborate trick on him, Colin walked around the truck and stationed himself at the open passenger side.

Roy looked through the truck at him. "Put both hands on the front of the door frame and push."

Colin did as he was told, and Roy pushed from the other side.

The truck didn't move.

What's the joke?

"It's been sitting here awhile," Roy said. "It's made a sort of depression for itself."

"Ahhh," Colin said. "And of course we're not strong enough to push it out."

"Sure we are," Roy said. "Put your back into it."

Colin strained.

"Harder!" Roy said.

It won't come up out of its little depression, Colin thought. He knows it. That's the way he planned it.

"Push!"

The land was not flat. It graded down toward the edge of the hill.

"Harder!"

The firm, sun-baked earth helped them, and the corrugated metal tracks helped them.

"Harder!"

The recent grease job helped them.

"Harder!"

But most of all, the gently sloping land and gravity helped them.

The truck moved.

TWENTY-TWO

◆

When he felt the pickup moving, Colin jumped back, astonished.

The truck stopped with a sharp squeak.

"What'd you do that for?" Roy demanded. "We had it going, for Christ's sake! Why'd you stop?"

Colin looked at him through the open cab of the truck. "Okay. Tell me. What's the joke?"

Roy was angry. His voice was hard and cold, and he emphasized each word. "Get . . . it . . . through . . . your . . . head. There . . . is . . . no . . . joke!"

They stared at each other in the fast-fading, smoky light of dusk.

"Are you my blood brother?" Roy asked.

"Sure."

"Isn't it you and me against the world?"

"Yeah."

"Won't blood brothers do anything for each other?"

"Almost anything."

"Anything! It has to be anything! No ifs, ands, or buts. Not with blood brothers. Are you my blood brother?"

"I said I was, didn't I?"

"Then push, damnit!"

"Roy, this has gone far enough."

"It won't have gone far enough until it's gone over the edge of the hill."

"Fooling around like this could be dangerous."

"Have you got concrete for brains?"

"We might accidentally wreck the train."

"It won't be an accident. Push!"

"You win. I give up. I won't push the truck or you any further. You win the game, Roy."

"What the hell are you doing to me?"

"I just want to get out of here."

Roy's voice was strained now, almost hysterical. His eyes were wild. He glared at Colin through the truck. "Are you turning your back on me?"

"Of course not."

"Betraying me?"

"Look, I—"

"Are you a phony, too? Are you just like all the other goddamned cheats and back-stabbers and liars?"

"Roy—"

"Didn't you mean one word you said to me?"

In the distance a train whistle pierced the twilight. "That's it!" Roy said frantically. "The engineer always blows the whistle when he crosses Ranch Road. We've only got three minutes. Help me."

Even in the dimming, orange-purple light, Colin could clearly see the rage in Roy's face, the madness in his blue, blue eyes. Colin was shocked. He took another step back, away from the truck.

"Bastard!" Roy said.

He tried to push the Ford by himself.

Colin remembered how Roy acted in the garage when they played with Mr. Borden's trains. How he wrecked them with such fierce glee. How he peered through the windows of the derailed toy cars. How he imagined that he was seeing real bodies, real blood, real tragedy—and somehow found pleasure in those sick fantasies.

This was not a game.

It had never been a game.

Pushing, then relaxing, pushing, then relaxing, keeping a hard, fast rhythm, Roy rocked the truck until suddenly he overcame inertia. The pickup moved.

"No!" Colin said.

Gravity helped again. The truck's wheels turned slowly, reluctantly. They squealed and squeaked. The metal rims ground harshly against the heavy corrugated tracks. But they *turned.*

Colin raced around the pickup, grabbed Roy, and pulled him away from the truck.

"You little creep!"

"Roy, you can't!"

"Let me alone!"

Roy wrenched loose, shoved Colin backward, and returned to the truck.

The pickup had ceased all movement the instant Roy had been dragged from it. The slope was not steep enough to encourage the Ford to run away.

Roy rocked it again.

"You can't kill all those people."

"Just watch me."

The truck needed considerably less coaxing this time than it had the last. Or perhaps Roy had found even greater strength in his madness. In a few seconds the Ford began to roll.

Colin leaped at him and wrestled him away from the truck.

Furious, cursing, Roy turned and punched him twice in the stomach.

Colin collapsed around the blows. He let go of Roy, gagged, bent forward, caved in, staggered back, and fell. The pain was terrible. He felt as if Roy's fists had gone all the way through him leaving two big holes. He couldn't get his breath.

His glasses had been knocked off. He could see only blurry outlines of the junkyard. Coughing, gagging, still struggling to breathe, he felt the grass around him, anxious to regain his sight.

Roy grunted and mumbled to himself as he tried to move the pickup.

Suddenly Colin was aware of another sound: a steady *chuka-chuka-chuka-chuka-chuka-chuka.*

The train.

In the distance. But not too far.

Coming closer.

Colin found his glasses and put them on. Through tears, he saw that the truck was still more than twenty feet from the brink, and that Roy had only just begun to get it moving again.

Colin attempted to stand. He got as far as his knees when a wave of excruciating pain washed through his guts, immobilizing him.

The truck was no more than twenty feet from the edge of the hill, gaining inches slowly, slowly but relentlessly.

By the sound of it, the train had reached the curve in the glen below.

The truck was eighteen feet from the brink.

Sixteen.

Fourteen.

Twelve.

Then it ran off the corrugated track; its wheels bit into the dry earth; and it would not move. If they had been pushing from both sides, if the force had been applied evenly, the truck would not have deviated from the twin ribbons of metal. But because all the effort was being exerted on the left side, the Ford turned inexorably to the right, and Roy didn't use the steering wheel fast enough to correct the truck's course.

Colin clutched the door handle of a dilapidated Dodge beside him and drew himself to his feet. His legs were shaky.

The thunderous clatter of the rails filled the night: a cacophonous roar like an orchestra of machinery tuning itself.

Roy ran to the edge of the hill. He looked down at the train that Colin couldn't see.

In less than a minute, the sound of the passenger express diminished. The last car was around the curve; it was speeding away, toward San Francisco.

The small noises of the oncoming night crept back across the hilltop. For a while, Colin was too stunned to hear anything at all. Gradually, he began once more to perceive the crickets, the toads, the breeze in the trees, and the pounding of his own heart.

Roy screamed. He looked down at the tracks that were now empty, and he raised his fists toward the sky, and he cried out like an animal in agony. He turned and started toward Colin.

Only thirty feet of open ground separated them.

"Roy, I had to do it."

"I hate you."

"You don't really."

"You're like all the rest."

"Roy, you'd have gone to jail."

"I'll kill you."

"But Roy—"

"You fucking traitor!"

Colin ran.

TWENTY-THREE

◆

As Colin ran for his life, he was acutely aware that he had never won a race. His legs were thin; Roy's legs were muscular. His reserves of strength were pathetically shallow; Roy's energy and power were awesome. Colin did not dare look back.

The automobile graveyard was an elaborate maze. He ran in a crouch through the twisting, crisscrossing passages, taking full advantage of the cover provided by the junkers. He turned right, between the gutted shells of two Buicks. He ran past huge stacks of tires, past bent and rusted Plymouths, past smashed and corroded Fords, Dodges, Toyotas, Oldsmobiles, and Volkswagens. He jumped over a disconnected transmission, did broken-field running through scattered tires, darted east toward Hermit Hobson's shack, which lay impossibly far away, at least six hundred feet, and then he swung sharply south through a narrow alley dotted with mufflers and headlamp assemblies that were like land mines in the tall grass. Ten yards farther along, he turned west, expecting to be tackled from behind at any second, but nevertheless determined to put walls of wreckage between himself and Roy.

After what seemed like an hour but was probably no more than two minutes, Colin realized that he could not keep running forever, and that he might quickly become confused about directions and dash headlong into Roy at a turn or an intersection. In fact, Colin was no longer certain whether he was rushing toward or away from the point at which the chase had begun. He risked a glance over his shoulder and saw that he was miraculously alone. He stopped at a crumpled Cadillac and huddled in the darkness along its ruined flank.

The last few minutes of murky copper-colored sunlight did little to illuminate the open spaces between the cars. Purple-black velvet shadows lay everywhere; and as he watched they grew with incredible speed, like a nightmare fungus intent upon blanketing the entire planet. Colin was terrified of being trapped in the dark with Roy. But he was equally frightened of the threatening creatures that might lurk in the junkyard at night: strange beasts; monsters; blood-sucking things; perhaps even the ghosts of people who had died in those broken cars.

Stop it! he thought angrily. That's stupid. It's childish.

He had to concentrate on the danger he *knew* was out there. Roy. He had to save himself from Roy. *Then* he could worry about the other things.

Think, damnit!

He became aware of his noisy breathing. His panting would carry quite a distance in the crisp night air, and Roy would be able to home in on it. In view of his precarious position, Colin could not be calm, but with a bit of effort he managed to breathe quietly.

He listened for Roy.

Nothing.

Colin began to notice the minutiae of the little world in which he cowered. The Cadillac was hard and warm against his back. The grass was dry and stiff and smelled like hay. Heat radiated upward as the earth gave off its stored sun to the cooler night. As the final light seeped out of the sky, the shadows on the land appeared to sway and shiver like dark masses of kelp at the bottom of the sea. There were noises, too: the shrill cry of a bird; the furtive scampering of a field mouse; the omnipresent toads; and the wind soughing through the eucalyptus trees that lined three sides of the property.

But Roy didn't make a sound.

Was he still out there?

Had he gone home in a rage?

Too nervous to keep still for long, Colin rose up far enough to look through the Cadillac's dirty windows, at the wreckage-strewn field beyond. There was not much to be seen. The cars were fading rapidly into the spreading stain of night.

Suddenly his attention was diverted as he sensed rather than heard movement behind him. He whirled, heart pounding. Roy loomed over him, grinning, demonic. He was holding a tire iron as if it were a baseball bat.

For a moment neither of them moved. They were totally immobilized by a web of memories, by pleasant recollections that were like countless strands of spider silk. They had been friends, but now they were enemies. The change had been too abrupt, the motivation too bizarre for either of them to puzzle out the meaning of it. At least that's what Colin felt. And as they stared at each other, he began to hope Roy would see how crazy this was and would regain his senses.

"I'm your blood brother," Colin said softly.

Roy swung the tire iron. Colin fell to avoid the blow, and the iron smashed through the side of the Cadillac.

In one swift graceful movement, screaming all the while like a banshee, Roy pulled the tire iron out of the window, raised it high, as if he were chopping wood, and brought it down with all his strength. Colin rolled away from the Cadillac, tumbled over and over, through the crackling grass, as the club descended. He heard it strike the earth with incredible force where he had been just a second ago, and he knew it would have shattered his skull if he had not gotten out from under it.

"Son-of-a-bitch!" Roy said.

Colin rolled five or six yards and scrambled to his feet. As he got up, Roy rushed him and struck with the tire iron again. It cut the air—*whoosh!*—and missed him by only a few inches. Gasping, Colin stumbled backward, trying to stay out of Roy's reach, and he came up against another car.

"Trapped," Roy said. "Got you trapped, you little bastard."

Roy swung the club so fast that Colin almost didn't see it coming. He ducked at the last possible instant, and the iron bar whistled over his head; it rang off the automobile behind him. The loud, sharp sound was like a rifle shot striking a huge unmelodious bell, and it echoed through the junkyard. The iron hit the car so hard that it leaped from Roy's grasp, spun up into the night, and fell back to the grass a few yards from him.

Roy cried out in agony. The shock of the impact had been transmitted through the tire iron, into his flesh. He gripped one stinging hand with the other and swore at the top of his voice.

Colin took advantage of Roy's brief incapacitation and got the hell out of there.

TWENTY-FOUR

◆

The interior of the Chevrolet stank. There were quite a few distinctly different, unpleasant odors, and Colin was able to imagine the source of some of them, although not all. Old grease alive with mold. Damp upholstery laced with mildew. Rotting carpet. But one of the smells that he could not identify was the strongest of them all: an odd fragrance like cooking ham, sweet one moment but rancid the next. It made him wonder if there was a dead animal in the car, a decaying squirrel or mouse or rat, festooned with writhing maggots, just inches away in the impenetrable dark. At times the image of an oozing corpse became so vivid in his mind that he gagged with revulsion, even though he knew the noise he made, small as it was, might draw Roy's attention.

Colin was stretched out on the Chevrolet's musty back seat, on his right side, facing front, knees drawn up a bit, arms against his chest, fetal, afraid, sweating yet shivering, seeking safety in the deep shadows but uncomfortably aware that there was no real security to be found in this place. The car's rear window and two rear side windows were intact, but all the glass in front was gone. Now and again, a breeze eddied into the car, but it didn't freshen the air; it only stirred the odors until they became thicker, even more pungent than they had been. He listened intently for any sound of Roy that the breeze might bring, but for a long time the junkyard was silent.

Night had come at last. On the western horizon, every trace of the sun had been blacked over. A fragment of the moon hung low in the east, but its light did not penetrate the interior of the automobile.

Lying in the darkness, Colin had nothing to do but think, and he could think of nothing but Roy. Colin could no longer resist the truth. This was not a game: Roy was really a killer. Roy would have pushed the truck down the hill. No doubt about it. He would have wrecked the train. He would have raped and killed Sarah Callahan if Colin hadn't found holes in his plan. And, Colin thought, he would have cracked my head open with that tire iron if I hadn't gotten away from him. There was not the slightest doubt about that either. The blood-brother oath no longer meant anything. Perhaps it never had. He supposed it was even possible that Roy had killed those two boys, just as he claimed he had: one pushed off the cliff at Sandman's Cove, the other drenched with lighter fluid and set afire.

But why?

The truth was clear, but its origins were not. The truth made no sense to him, and that was frightening. The facts were all in plain sight; but the facts were the end product of a long manufacturing process, and the machinery that had made them could not be seen.

Questions tumbled through Colin's mind. Why does Roy want to kill people? Does he get pleasure from it? What kind of pleasure, for God's sake? Is he a lunatic? Why doesn't he look like a lunatic if that's what he is? Why does he look so normal? He asked himself those questions and a hundred others, but he had no answers.

Colin expected the world to be simple and straightforward. He liked to be able to divide it into two camps: forces for good and forces for evil. In that way every event and a problem and solution clearly had a black side and a white side, and you always knew exactly where you stood. He pretty much believed that the real world was like the land in *The Lord of the Rings,* with the blessed and the damned marshaled into two distinct armies. But no matter how hard he probed at it, regardless of the angle from which he considered it, Roy's behavior over the past month could be labeled neither saintly nor entirely wicked. Roy had many qualities that Colin envied, admired, and wished to acquire; but Roy was also a cold-blooded murderer. Roy was not black. He was not white. He wasn't even gray. He was a hundred, no, a *thousand* shades of gray, all whirling and blending and shifting together like a thousand columns of smoke. Colin could not reconcile his view of life with the sudden discovery of a creature like Roy. The endless ramifications of Roy's quicksilver morality were frightening. It meant that Colin would have to reconsider everything in his cozy philosophy. All the people in his life would have to be taken out of the pigeonholes into which he had stuffed them. He would have to judge each of them again, more carefully than he had done before, and then he would have to put them . . . Put them where? If there was no black-and-white system, there were no pigeonholes either. If there was not always a clear division between right and wrong, people could not safely be labeled, slotted, and forgotten; and life would be unbearably difficult to manage.

Of course, Roy might be possessed.

As soon as that thought crossed Colin's mind, he knew it was the answer, and he eagerly seized it. If Roy was possessed by an evil spirit, he was not responsible for the monstrous acts he committed. Roy himself was good, but the demon within him was evil. Yes! That was it! That explained the apparent contradiction. Possessed. Like the girl in *The Exorcist*. Or the little boy in *The Omen*. Or perhaps Roy was possessed by an alien, a thing from another planet, an entity that had traveled to earth from the far stars. Sure. That must be it. That was a better, more scientific, less superstitious explanation than the first. Not a demon, but an evil, alien being. Maybe it was similar to the villains in the old Don Siegel movie, *Invasion of the Body Snatchers*. Or even more likely, maybe the thing that had Roy under its power was a parasite from another galaxy like in that great Heinlein novel, *The Puppet Masters*. If that were the case, there were steps he must take at once, without a moment's delay, while there was still a chance, however slim, to save the world. First of all, he had to find irrefutable proof of the invasion. Then he had to use that proof to convince other people that there was a clear and present danger. And finally he had to—

"Colin!"

He jerked, sat up, terrified, shaking. For a moment he was too shocked to get his breath.

"Hey, Colin!"

The sound of Roy calling his name snapped him back to reality.

"Colin, can you hear me?"

Roy was not close. At least a hundred yards away. Shouting.

Colin leaned toward the front seat, peered through the empty windshield frame, but he could not see anything. "Colin, I made a mistake."

Colin waited.

"Do you hear me?" Roy said.

Colin didn't respond.

"I did a very stupid thing," Roy said.

Colin shook his head. He knew what was coming, and he was amazed that Roy would try anything so obvious.

"I carried the game too far," Roy said.

It won't work, Colin thought. You won't convince me. Not now. Not any more.

"I guess I scared you more than I meant to," Roy said. "I'm sorry. I really am."

"Jeez," Colin said softly, to himself.

"I didn't really want to wreck the train."

Colin stretched out on the seat once more, on his side, knees drawn up, down in the shadows that smelled of decay.

For a few minutes, Roy went through other verses of his siren song, but eventually he realized that Colin was not going to be entranced by it. Roy was unable to conceal his frustration. With each patently insincere exhortation, his voice grew increasingly strained. Finally he exploded: "You rotten little creep! I'll find you. I'll get my hands on you. I'm going to beat your fuckin' head in, you little son-of-a-bitch! You traitor!"

Then silence.

The wind, of course.

And crickets, toads.

But not a peep from Roy.

The quiet was unnerving. Colin would have preferred to hear Roy cursing, bellowing, and crashing about the junkyard in search of him, for then he would have known where the enemy was.

As he listened for Roy, the sometimes sweet and sometimes rancid hamlike odor grew stronger than ever, and he developed a macabre explanation for it. The Chevy had been in a terrible accident; the front end was squashed and twisted; the windshield was gone; both front doors were buckled—one in, one out; the steering wheel was broken in half, a semicircle that ended in jagged points. Perhaps (Colin theorized) the driver had lost a hand in the crash. Perhaps the severed hand had fallen to the floor. Perhaps it had somehow gotten under the seat, into a recess where it could not be reached or even seen. Perhaps the ambulance crew had looked for the amputated member but had been unable to find it. The car had been towed to Hermit Hobson's place, and the hand had begun to wither and rot. And then . . . then . . . Oh God, and then it was just like that O'Henry story in which a blood-spotted rag had fallen behind a radiator and, due to unique chemical and temperature conditions, had acquired a life of its own. Colin shuddered. That's what had happened to the hand. He felt it. He knew it. The hand had started to decompose, but then a combination of intense summer heat and the chemical composition of the dirt under the seat had caused an incredible, evil change in the dead flesh. The process of decay had been arrested, though not reversed, and the hand had been infused with an eerie sort of life, a malevolent half life. And now, right this minute, he was in the car, in the dark, alone with the damned thing. It knew he was here. It could not see or hear or smell, but it *knew*. Mottled brown and green and black, slimy, riddled with weeping pustules, the hand must even now be dragging itself out from beneath the front seat and across the floorboards. If he reached down to the floor, he would find it, and it would seize him. Its cold fingers would grip like steel pincers, and it would—

No, no, no! I've got to stop this, Colin told himself. What the hell's the matter with me?

Roy was out there, hunting him. He had to listen for Roy and be prepared. He had to concentrate. Roy was the real danger, not some imaginary disembodied hand.

As if to confirm the advice that Colin had given himself, Roy began to make noise again. A car door slammed not far away. A moment later there was the sound of another rusted door being wrenched open; it screeched as the seal that time had put upon it was broken. After a few seconds, that door, too, slammed shut.

Roy was searching the cars.

Colin sat up, cocked his head.

Another corroded door opened with noisy protest.

Colin could not see anything important through the missing windshield.

He felt caged.

Trapped.

The third door slammed.

Panicky, Colin slid to the left, got off the back seat, leaned over the front seat as far as he could, and stuck his head out the front driver's side window. The fresh air that hit his face was cool and smelled of the sea even this far inland. His eyes had adjusted to the night, and the partial moon cast just enough light for him to see eighty or a hundred feet into the junkyard.

Roy was a shadow among shadows, barely visible, four cars in front of the Chevrolet in which Colin was hiding. Roy opened the door of another junker, leaned into it, came out a moment later, and threw the door shut. He moved toward the next car, closer to the Chevy.

Colin returned to the rear seat and slid quickly over to the door on the right. He had come in on the left side, but that's where Roy was now.

Another door crashed shut: *ka-chunk!*

Roy was only two cars away.

Colin took hold of the handle, then realized that he didn't know if the right-hand door worked. He had used only the one on the left. What if this one was jammed and made a lot of noise but wouldn't open? Roy would come on the double and trap him in here.

Colin hesitated, licked his lips.

He felt as if he had to pee.

He clamped his legs together.

The sensation was still there, and in fact it was getting worse: a warm pain in his loins.

Please, God, he thought, don't make me have to pee. Not here. Not now. It's the wrong damned place for that!

Ka-chunk!

Roy was one car away.

There was no time to worry whether the right-hand door would work or not. He had no choice but to try it and take his chances. He tugged on the handle. It moved. He took a deep breath, nearly choked on the rank air, and pushed the door all the way open with one violent shove. He winced at the loud scraping sound it made but thanked God that it functioned at all.

Frantically, gracelessly, he clambered out of the Chevy, making no effort to be quiet now that the door had betrayed him. He took two steps, tripped over a muffler, dropped to his knees, popped up again as if he were on springs, and bolted into the darkness.

"Hey!" Roy said from the far side of the car. The sudden explosive movement had caught him by surprise. "Hey, wait a minute."

TWENTY-FIVE

◆

Running at his top speed, Colin saw the tire a split second before it would have tripped him. He jumped over it, side-stepped a pile of fenders, and ran on through the high grass. He turned left and rounded a battered Dodge delivery van that was up on blocks. After a brief hesitation and a quick glance behind him, he sank to the ground and wriggled under the truck.

As Colin slipped out of sight, Roy came around the front of the van and stopped, looked both ways. When he saw that that avenue of the maze was deserted, he spat on the ground. "Damn."

The night was very dark, but from his hiding place beneath the Dodge, Colin could see Roy's white sneakers. Colin was lying on his belly, his head turned to the left, right cheek pressed against the earth; and Roy was standing no more than a yard away. He could have grabbed the other boy's ankle and toppled him. But then what?

After a moment of indecision, Roy opened the door on the driver's side of the van. When he saw that no one was in there, he slammed the door and stalked to the rear of the Dodge.

Colin drew shallow breaths through his mouth and wished he could soften the pounding beat of his heart. If he made any sound at all that Roy could hear, he would die for it.

At the back of the delivery van, Roy opened one of the double doors. When he peered into the rear compartment, he apparently could not see every corner of it to his satisfaction, for he opened the second door as well, then climbed into the cargo hold.

Colin listened to him poking at the shadows in the metal box overhead. He considered squeezing out from under the truck and creeping swiftly to another shelter, but he didn't think he would have sufficient time to get away undetected.

Even as Colin was assessing his chances, Roy came out of the truck and closed the doors. The opportunity, if there had ever been one, was lost.

Colin twisted around a bit and looked over his shoulder. He saw the white tennis shoes, and he prayed that Roy wouldn't think to investigate the narrow space beneath the Dodge.

Incredibly, his prayers were answered. Roy stepped to the front of the truck, paused, seemed to be looking at the junkyard on all sides, and said, "Where the hell . . . ?" He stood there for a while, drumming his fingers on the van, and then he walked northward until Colin could no longer see his shoes or hear his footsteps.

For a long time Colin lay motionless. He found the courage to breathe normally once more, but he still thought it wise to be as silent as possible.

His situation had improved in at least one respect: The air circulating under the van was not as stale and disgusting as that in the Chevrolet had been. He could smell wildflowers, the teasing scent of goldenrod, and the dusty aroma of the parched grass.

His nose itched. Tickled.

To his horror, he realized he was going to sneeze. He clamped one hand to his face, pinched his nose, but found he couldn't stop the inevitable. He muffled the noise as best he could and waited with dread to be discovered.

But Roy didn't come. He evidently hadn't been close enough to hear.

Colin passed another couple of minutes under the truck, just to be safe, then slithered out. Roy was not in sight, but he could be hunkered down in any of a thousand pockets of darkness, waiting to strike.

Cautiously, Colin stole eastward through the cemetery of dead machinery. He ran in a crouch across the open spaces, lingered in the wreckage between until he was fairly certain that the next unprotected patch of ground was safe, then dashed on. When he was fifty or sixty yards from the delivery van where he had last seen Roy, he turned north, toward Hermit Hobson's shack.

If only he could get to the bicycles while Roy was searching for him elsewhere, he would be able to escape. He would damage Roy's bike—bend a wheel or something—and then leave on his own, confident that there could be no effective pursuit.

He reached the edge of the junkyard and huddled next to a demolished station wagon while he surveyed the deep pools of blackness that lay around Hobson's shack. He saw the bicycles at the foot of the sagging porch steps, lying side by side where the grass was stunted and still a bit green, but he didn't go straight to them. Roy might expect him to come back to this place; he might be concealed already in those shadows, tense, waiting to pounce. Colin stared hard at each trouble spot, looking for movement or the glint of an errant moonbeam on a shape that did not belong there. In time he was able to see through most of the dark pockets and to determine that they were uninhabited. But in a few small areas the night seemed to back up like river sludge; and in those puddles it was far too thick for the eye to penetrate it.

At last Colin decided that the possibility of escape outweighed the risk of going to the bicycles and making a target of himself. He stood, wiped sweat from his brow, and walked into the twenty-yard-wide band of open ground between the junkyard and the shack. Nothing moved in the darkness. He advanced slowly at first, then more boldly, and finally sprinted the last ten yards.

Roy had locked their bikes together. He had used his security parking chain and padlock to bind one wheel of his bicycle to one wheel of Colin's.

Colin pulled on the chain and tugged angrily at the gate of the lock, but his efforts were wasted; the device was heavy and sturdy. He could see no way to get the bikes apart without the combination to Roy's lock. And he certainly couldn't use them in tandem, even if the chain had been loose enough to permit them to be stood on their wheels and moved simultaneously—which it was not.

Crestfallen, he scurried back to the station wagon to consider his options. He really had only two. He could try to get home on foot—or he could continue to play cat-and-mouse with Roy in the endless passageways of the junkyard.

He preferred to stick where he was. The chief recommendation for it was that he had survived thus far. If he held out long enough, his mother would report him missing. She might not get home until one or two o'clock in the morning, but it must be past midnight now. He pushed the button on his digital watch and was stunned to see how early it was: a quarter till ten. He could have sworn that he had been playing this dangerous game of hide-and-seek for at least three or four hours. Well, maybe Weezy would get home early. And if he wasn't in by midnight, she'd call Roy's folks and find out Roy wasn't home either. By one o'clock at the very latest, they would call the cops. The police would start looking for them at once and— Yeah, but *where* would they begin the search? Not out here in the junkyard. In town. And down at the beach. Then in the nearby hills. It would be late afternoon tomorrow, maybe even Thursday or Friday, before they came all the way out to Hermit Hobson's. As much as he wanted to stay near the myriad bolt-holes of the rubble-covered hilltop, he knew he could not keep out of Roy's grasp for forty-eight or thirty-six or even twenty-four hours. He'd be damned lucky to make it through to daylight.

He would have to walk home. Of course, he couldn't go back the way they had come, for if Roy suspected he'd left the junkyard and came looking for him, there was too great a danger that they would meet on a lonely stretch of road. A bicycle made little or no noise on a paved surface, and Colin was afraid he would not hear Roy coming in time to hide. He would have to trek overland, down the hill to the railroad tracks, along the tracks to the dry creekbed near Ranch Road, then into Santa Leona. That route would be more arduous than the other, especially in the dark, but it might also cut the distance from eight miles to seven or even six.

Colin was painfully aware that his planning was guided by one overriding consideration: cowardice. Hide. Run. Hide. Run. He seemed incapable of entertaining any alternative to those weak courses of action, and he felt miserably inadequate.

—So stay here. Turn the tables on Roy.

Fat chance.

—Don't run. Attack.

That's a pleasant fantasy, but it's impossible.

—It isn't. Become the aggressor. Surprise him.

He's faster and stronger than me.
—Then be devious. Set a trap.
He's too clever to fall for any trap I could set.
—How can you know if you don't try?
I know.
—How?
Because I'm me. And he's Roy.

Colin put a quick end to the interior dialogue because it was a waste of time.
He understood himself all too well. He simply did not have within him the power
or the will to transform himself. Before he tried to become the cat, he would have
to be convinced that there was absolutely no percentage whatsoever in continuing
to be the mouse.

This was one of those bleak and too-frequent moments in which he despised
himself.

Pausing every few yards to reconnoiter the way ahead before pressing on, Colin
crept from one car to another. He moved steadily toward the hill where Roy had
attempted to push the Ford pickup into the train, for it was there that he most
easily could get down to the railroad tracks. The night was much too still. Every
rustle of his shoes in the brittle grass sounded like thunder and seemed certain to
bring Roy down on him. Eventually, however, he came undiscovered to the far
end of the junkyard.

In front of him, the open space between the last of the cars and the brow of
the hill was approximately forty feet wide. At the moment it looked like a mile.
The moon was shining unhindered, and that stretch of grass was bathed in far
too much milky light to make a crossing feasible. If this area were being watched,
he would be spotted before he had covered a quarter of the distance. Fortunately,
scattered but solid masses of clouds had rolled in from the ocean during the past
hour. Each time that a cluster of them shrouded the moon, the resultant darkness
offered excellent cover. He waited for one of these brief eclipses. When the broad
belt of grass fell under a shadow, he ran as silently as he could manage, up on
his toes, holding his breath, to the brink, and then over.

The hillside was steep, but not so precipitous as to be unnegotiable. He went
down fast because there was no other way to go; the pull of gravity was irresistible. He bounded wildly from one foot to the other, out of control, taking big,
ungainly steps, and halfway to the bottom he found that he suddenly was dancing
on a landslide. The dry, sandy soil collapsed under him. For an instant he rode
it as if he were a surfer on a wave, but then he lost his footing, fell, and rolled
the last twenty feet. He came to a stop in a cloud of dust, flat on his back, on
the railroad right-of-way, one arm across the tracks.

Stupid. Stupid and clumsy. Stupid, clumsy idiot.

Jeez.

He lay still for several seconds, a bit winded, but surprised that nothing hurt.
His pride was injured, of course, but not anything else.

The dust began to settle.

As he started to sit up, Roy called to him: "Blood brother?"

Colin shook his head in disbelief and looked left, right, then up.

"Blood brother, is that you?"

The moon sailed out from behind the clouds.

In the wash of pale light, Colin saw Roy standing at the top of the eighty-foot
slope, silhouetted against the sky, staring down.

He can't see me, Colin told himself. At least he can't see me as clearly as I
see him. He's there with the sky behind him; I'm here in the shadows.

"It *is* you," Roy said.

He charged down the hillside.

Colin got up, stumbled over the railroad tracks, and hurried into the wasteland beyond.

TWENTY-SIX

◆

Colin felt terribly vulnerable as he raced across the field. As far as the moonlight revealed, there was no cover, no place for him to hide. He had the crazy thought that a giant shoe was going to come down on him at any second, squashing him as if he were a bug scurrying across a vast kitchen floor.

In the stormy season, rain saturated the hillsides, then gushed off the slopes into natural drainage channels that cut through the flat land west of the railroad tracks. At least once every winter, the gullies overflowed, and the plain became a lake, part of the water-retention system created by the county flood-control project. Because the earth was underwater an average of two months every winter, it boasted very little vegetation even in the summer. There were patches of grass that had a tenuous hold on the silt, beds of the wildflowers that thrived nearly everywhere in California, and prickly tumbleweed; but there were no trees, no dense undergrowth, and no bushes in which Colin could conceal himself.

He got off the bare land as quickly as he could by jumping down into a small arroyo. The gulch was fifteen to twenty feet in width and more than seven feet deep, with almost vertical walls. During a winter storm, it was a surging river, wild and muddy and dangerous, but now it held not one drop of water. He sprinted along a straightaway, pain stabbing through his calves and side, lungs burning. As he came to a broad curve in the arroyo, he glanced back for the first time since he'd crossed the railroad tracks. So far as he could see, Roy had not yet come down into the big ditch in pursuit of him. He was surprised that he had such an encouraging lead, and he wondered if it were possible that Roy had not seen where he'd gone.

Beyond the bend, seeking shelter, he turned into a secondary watercourse that branched off the main channel. This was about ten feet wide at its mouth, but the walls rapidly drew nearer to each other as he progressed to the source. The floor rose steadily until the depth of the gully decreased from seven to five feet. When he had gone no more than a hundred yards, the passageway had narrowed to six feet. If he stood erect, his head would be above ground level. At that point the channel split into a pair of short, dead-end corridors that cut no more than four feet below the surface of the field. He moved into one of these cul-de-sacs, wedged himself into it, each shoulder pressed firmly against a sandy embankment. He sat down, drew his knees up to his chin, clamped his arms around his legs, and tried to be invisible.

—Rattlesnakes.
Oh, Jeez.
—Better think about it.
No.
—This is rattlesnake country.
Just shut up.
—Well, it is.
They don't come out at night.
—The worst things always come out at night.
Not rattlesnakes.
—How do you know?
I read it in a book.
—What book?
Can't remember the title.
—There wasn't any book.
Just shut up.
—Rattlesnakes all over the place.
Jeez!

He hunched down in the dirt, listening for rattlesnakes, waiting for Roy; and a long time passed during which he was not bothered by either nemesis. Every few minutes he checked his digital watch, and when he had been in the ditch for half an hour, he decided it was time to leave. If Roy had been searching the network of drainage canals all this time, he would have come close enough for Colin to be aware of him, or at least he would have made a noise in the distance; but he had not. Evidently he had abandoned the pursuit, perhaps because he'd lost track of Colin in the dark, hadn't seen in which direction he had gone, and had no clear idea where to look for him. If true, it was a tremendous piece of luck. But Colin felt that he would be pushing Fate too hard if he stayed where he was, in this den of vipers, expecting to be safe forever from rattlesnakes.

He crawled out of the trench, stood, and studied the scarred, moonlit landscape. Within his limited circle of vision, there was no sign of Roy.

With extreme caution, stopping again and again to listen to the night, Colin headed southeast. Repeatedly, at the corners of his vision, there was movement; but it always proved to be a clump of tumbleweed rolling in front of the wind. Eventually he recrossed the flat land and reached the railroad tracks once more. He was at least a quarter of a mile south of the junkyard, and he quickly began to put even more distance between himself and Hermit Hobson's place.

An hour later, when he reached the intersection of the tracks and Santa Leona Road, he was weary to his bones. His mouth was dry. His back ached. Every muscle in his legs was knotted and throbbing.

He considered following the highway into town. It was tempting: fairly straight and direct, with no holes or ditches or obstacles hidden in its shadows. He already had shortened the trek as much as he possibly could by going overland. From this point on, continued avoidance of the roads would only prolong the journey.

He took a few steps on the blacktop but realized again that he did not dare pursue the easy route. He almost surely would be attacked before he reached the edge of town, where people and lights would make murder more difficult than it would be in the lonely countryside.

—Hitchhike.
There's no traffic at this hour.
—Someone will come along.

Yeah. Maybe Roy.

He left Santa Leona Road. He veered southwest from the railway line, striking out through more scrubland where only he and the tumbleweeds moved.

Within half a mile, he came to the dry creekbed that paralleled Ranch Road. It had been widened and deepened for flood-control purposes, and the walls of it were not earth but concrete. He descended on one of the regularly spaced service ladders, and when he stood on the floor of the creek, the rim was twenty feet above him.

Two miles farther, in the heart of town, he climbed up another ladder and through a safety railing. He was on the sidewalk along Broadway.

Although 1 A.M. was fast approaching, there were still people on the streets: several in passing cars; a few in an all-night diner; an attendant at a filling station. An elderly man walked arm-in-arm with a pixie-faced, white-haired woman, and a young couple strolled past the closed stores, window-shopping in spite of the hour.

Colin had an urge to rush up to the nearest of them and blurt out the secret, the story of Roy's madness. But he knew they would think he was a lunatic. They didn't know him, and they didn't know Roy. None of it would make sense to strangers. He wasn't even sure it made sense to him. And even if they did comprehend and believe, they couldn't help him.

His first ally would have to be his mother. When she heard the facts, she would call the police, and they would respond to her much more quickly and seriously than they would to a fourteen-year-old boy. He had to get home and tell Weezy all about it.

He hurried along Broadway toward Adams Avenue, but after only a few steps he stopped because he suddenly realized that he would have to undertake the last part of his journey with the same caution that had marked it thus far. Roy might intend to ambush him within a few feet of his front door. In fact, now that he thought about it, he was positive that's what would happen. Roy would most likely lie in wait directly across the way from the Jacobs's house; half that block was a pocket park with many hiding places from which he could observe the entire street. The instant he saw Colin approaching the house, he would move; he would move real fast. For just a moment, as if briefly cursed with a clairvoyant's vision, Colin could see himself being clubbed to the ground, being stabbed, being left there in blood and pain to die within inches of safety, on the threshold of sanctuary.

He stood in the middle of the sidewalk, trembling. He stood there for quite a while.

—Got to move, kid.

Where?

—Call Weezy. Ask her to come get you.

She'll tell me to walk. It's only a few blocks.

—So tell her why you can't walk.

Not on the phone.

—Tell her Roy's out there, waiting to kill you.

I can't make it sound right on the phone.

—Sure you can.

No. I've got to be there when I tell her. Otherwise, it won't sound right, and she'll think it's a joke. She'll be mad.

—You've got to try to do it on the phone so she'll come get you. Then you'll get home safely.

I can't do it on the phone.

—What's the alternative?

Finally he walked back to the service station near the dry creekbed. A telephone booth stood on one corner of the property. He dialed the number and listened to it ring a dozen times.

She wasn't home yet.

Colin slammed down the receiver and left the booth without recovering his dime.

He stood on the sidewalk, hands fisted at his sides, shoulders hunched. He wanted to punch something.

—The bitch.

She's your mother.

—Where the hell is she?

It's business.

—What's she doing?

It's business.

—Who's she with?

It's just business.

—I'll bet.

The service-station attendant started closing for the night. The banks of fluorescent lights above the pumps blinked out.

Colin walked west on Broadway, through the shopping district, just passing time. He looked in store windows, but he didn't see anything.

At ten minutes past one, he went back to the telephone booth. He dialed his home number, let it ring fifteen times, then hung up.

—Business my ass.

She works hard.

—At what?

He stood there for several minutes, one hand on the receiver, as if he were expecting a call.

—She's out screwing around.

It's business. A business dinner.

—This late?

A long, late business dinner.

He tried the number again.

No answer.

He sat down on the floor of the booth, in the darkness, and hugged himself.

—She's out screwing around when I need her.

You don't know for sure.

—I know.

You can't.

—Face it. She screws like everyone else.

Now you sound like Roy.

—Sometimes Roy makes sense.

He's crazy.

—Maybe not about everything.

At one-thirty he stood up, popped a dime into the phone, and called home again. It rang twenty-two times before he hung up.

It might be safe to walk home now. Wasn't it too late for Roy to keep a vigil? He was a killer, but he was also a fourteen-year-old boy; he couldn't stay out all night. His folks would wonder where he was. They might even call the cops. Roy would be in terrible trouble if he stayed out all night, wouldn't he?

Maybe. And maybe not.

Colin wasn't sure that the Bordens really cared what Roy did or what happened to him. So far as Colin knew, they had never set down rules for their son, other than the one about staying away from his father's trains. Roy did pretty much what he wanted, when he wanted.

Something was wrong with the Borden family. The relationships were curious, indefinable. Theirs was not a traditional parent-child arrangement. Colin had met Mr. and Mrs. Borden only twice; but both times he had sensed the strangeness in them, in their attitudes toward each other, and in their treatment of Roy. Mother, father, and son seemed like strangers. There was a peculiar stiffness in the way they talked among themselves, as if they were reciting lines from a script they hadn't learned very well. They were so *formal*. They almost seemed . . . afraid of one another. Colin had been aware of a coldness in the center of the family, but he had never spent much time wondering about it. Now that he gave it some thought, however, he realized that the Bordens were like people living in a rooming house; they smiled and nodded when they passed in the hall; they said hello when they met in the kitchen; but otherwise they led separate, distant lives. He didn't know why that was true. Something had happened to turn them away from one another. He couldn't imagine what it might have been. But he was certain that Mr. and Mrs. Borden wouldn't care very much if Roy stayed out until daybreak or even disappeared forever.

Therefore it wasn't safe for him to walk home. Roy would be waiting.

Colin dialed the number again, and he was surprised when his mother answered on the second ring.

"Mom, you've got to come get me."

"Skipper?"

"I'll wait for you at—"

"I thought you were upstairs, asleep."

"No. I'm over at—"

"I just got in. I thought you were home. What are you doing out at this hour?"

"It's not my fault. I was—"

"Oh, my God, have you been hurt?"

"No, no. I just—"

"You're hurt."

"No, just a few scrapes and bruises. I need—"

"What happened? What's happened to you?"

"If you'd shut up and listen, you'd find out," Colin said impatiently.

She was stunned. "Don't you snap at me. Don't you dare."

"I need help!"

"What?"

"You've got to help me."

"Are you in trouble?"

"Real bad trouble."

"What the hell have you done?"

"It's not what *I've* done. It's—"

"Where are you?"

"I'm over here at—"

"Have you been arrested?"

"What?"

"Is it *that* kind of trouble?"

"No, no. I'm—"

"Are you at the police station?"

"Nothing like that. I'm—"

"Where are you?"

"Near the Broadway Diner."

"What trouble have you caused at the diner?"

"That's not it. I—"

"Let me talk to someone there."

"Who? What do you mean?"

"Let me talk to a waitress or someone."

"I'm not *in* the diner."

"Where the hell are you?"

"In a phone booth."

"Colin, what's the matter with you?"

"I'm waiting for you to come get me."

"You're only a few blocks from home."

"I can't walk. He's waiting for me along the way."

"Who?"

"He wants to kill me."

A pause.

"Colin, you come straight home."

"I can't."

"This minute. I mean it."

"I can't."

"I'm getting angry, young man."

"Roy tried to kill me tonight. He's still out there, waiting for me."

"This isn't funny."

"I'm not joking!"

Another pause.

"Colin, did you take something?"

"Huh?"

"Did you take a pill or something?"

"Drugs?"

"Did you?"

"Jeez."

"Did you?"

"Where would I get drugs?"

"I know you kids can get them. It's as easy as buying aspirins."

"Jeez."

"It's a big problem these days. Is that it? Are you high and having trouble getting down?"

"Me? You really think that's a problem with *me*?"

"If you've been popping pills—"

"If that's what you really think—"

"—or if you've been drinking—"

"—then you don't know me at all."

"—mixing booze and pills—"

"If you want to hear about it," Colin said sharply, "you'll have to bring the car and pick me up."

"Don't use that tone with me."

"If you don't come," he said, "then I guess I'll just rot here."

He banged the receiver into the cradle and left the telephone booth.

"Shit!"

He kicked an empty soda can that was lying beside the walkway. It spun and rattled across the street.

He went to the Broadway Diner and stood at the curb, looking east, where Weezy would turn the corner if she bothered to come for him.

He was shaking uncontrollably with anger and fear.

He felt something else, too, something dark and devastating, something far more disturbing than anger, far more debilitating than fear, something uglier, like a terrible loneliness, but much worse than loneliness. It was a suspicion—no, a conviction—That he had been abandoned, forgotten, and that no one in the whole world cared or would ever care enough about him to really find out what he was like and what his dreams were. He was an outcast, a creature somehow vastly different from all other people, an object of scorn and derision, an outsider, secretly loathed and ridiculed by everyone who met him, even by those few who professed to love him.

He felt as if he would vomit.

Five minutes later she drew alongside him in the blue Cadillac. She leaned across the front seat and opened the door on the passenger's side.

When he saw her, he lost the grip that he'd had on himself ever since the nightmare at Hermit Hobson's place. Tears streamed down his face. By the time he got into the car and closed the door, he was sobbing like a baby.

TWENTY-SEVEN

◆

She didn't believe him. She refused to call the cops, and she wouldn't disturb the Bordens with a call at that hour.

At nine-thirty the following morning, she talked to Roy on the phone. Then she talked to his mother. She insisted on privacy, so Colin didn't even hear her side of the conversation.

After she had spoken with the Bordens, she tried to make Colin recant his story. When he wouldn't she became furious.

At eleven o'clock, after an extended argument, she and Colin went to the junkyard. Neither of them spoke during the drive.

She parked at the end of the dirt lane, near the shack. They got out of the car.

Colin was uneasy. Echoes of last night's terror still reverberated in his mind.

His bicycle was lying near the front porch steps. Roy's bike was gone, of course.

"You see," he said. "I was here."

She didn't respond. She wheeled the bike around to the back of the car.

Colin followed her. "It happened exactly the way I said it did."

She unlocked the trunk. "Help me."

They lifted the bicycle into the back of the car, but it wouldn't fit well enough to allow the compartment to be closed and locked. She found a spool of wire in the tool kit and used a length of that to tie down the trunk lid.

"Doesn't the bicycle prove anything?" Colin demanded.

She turned on him. "It proves you were here."

"Like I said."

"But not with Roy."

"He tried to kill me!"

"He tells me he was home last night from nine-thirty on."

"Well, of course that's what he'd tell you! But—"

"That's also what his mother tells me."

"It's not true."

"Are you calling Mrs. Borden a liar?"

"Well, she probably doesn't know she's lying."

"What's that supposed to mean?"

"Roy probably told her he was home, in his room, and she believed him."

"She knows he was home, not just because he told her so, but because she was home last night, too."

"But did she actually talk to him?"

"What?"

"Last night? Did she talk to him? Or did she just assume he was up in his room?"

"I didn't grill her in detail about—"

"Did she actually see him last night?"

"Colin—"

"If she didn't actually see him," Colin said excitedly, "she can't know for sure that he was up there in his room."

"That's ridiculous."

"No. It isn't. They don't talk to each other much in that house. They don't pay attention to each other. They don't go looking for each other to strike up a conversation."

"She'd know he was there when she looked in to say good night."

"But that's just what I'm trying to tell you. She'd never do that. She'd never go out of her way to say good night to him. I know it. I'd bet on it. They don't act like other people. There's something really strange about them. There's something wrong in that house."

"What do you think it is?" she asked angrily. "Are they invaders from another planet?"

"Of course not."

"Like in one of those crazy goddamned books you're always reading?"

"No."

"Should we call Buck Rogers to save us?"

"I just . . . I was only trying to say that they don't seem to love Roy."

"That's an awful thing to say."

"I'm pretty sure it's true."

She shook her head, amazed. "Did it ever occur to you that you might be too young to fully understand an emotion as complex as love, let alone all the forms it can take? My God, you're an inexperienced fourteen-year-old boy! Who are you to judge the Bordens on something like that?"

"But if you could see the way they act. If you could hear the way they talk to each other. And they never do anything together. Even we do more things together than the Bordens do."

"'Even we'? What do you mean by that?"

"Well, we don't do many things together, do we? I mean as a family."

There were things in her eyes that he didn't want to see. He looked away.

"In case you've forgotten," she said, "I'm divorced from your father. And also in case it somehow slipped your mind, it was a bitter divorce. The pits. So what the hell do you expect? Do you think the three of us should go on picnics now and then?''

Colin shuffled his feet in the grass. ''I mean even just you and me. The two of us. We don't see much of each other, and the Bordens see even less of Roy.''

''When do I have time, for God's sake?''

He shrugged.

''I work hard,'' she said.

''I know.''

''Do you think I like working as hard as I do?''

''You seem to.''

''Well, I don't.''

''Then why—''

''I'm trying to build a future for us. Can you understand? I want to be sure we never have to worry about money. I want security. Big security. But you don't appreciate it.''

''I do. I know you work hard.''

''If you appreciated what I'm doing for us, for you, then you wouldn't have tried to upset me with this bullshit story about Roy trying to kill you and—''

''It's not bullshit.''

''Don't use that word.''

''What word?''

''You know what I mean.''

''Bullshit?''

She slapped his face.

Shocked, he put a hand to his cheek.

''Don't smirk at me,'' she said.

''I wasn't.''

She turned away from him. She walked a few steps into the grass and stared at the junkyard for a while.

He almost cried. But he didn't want her to see him crying, so he bit his lip and held the tears back. After a while, the hurt and humiliation were replaced by anger, and then he didn't have to bite his lip any more.

When she gathered her composure, she came back to him. ''I'm sorry.''

''It's okay.''

''I lost my temper, and that's a bad example to set.''

''It didn't hurt.''

''You upset me so much.''

''I didn't want to.''

''You upset me because I know what's going on.'' He waited.

''You came out here last night on your bike,'' she said. ''But not with Roy. I know who you came with.''

He said nothing.

''Oh,'' she said, ''I don't know their names, but I know what kind of kids they are.''

He blinked. ''Who're you talking about?''

''You know who I'm talking about. I'm talking about these other friends of yours, these smart-ass kids you see standing on street corners these days, the punks on those skateboards who try to run you off in the gutter when you walk by them.''

''You think kids like that would want anything to do with me? I'm one of the people they'd run into the gutter.''

"You're being evasive."

"I'm telling the truth. Roy was the only friend I had."

"Nonsense."

"I don't make friends easily."

"Don't lie to me."

He was silent.

"Since we moved to Santa Leona," she said, "you've gotten mixed up with the wrong kids."

"No."

"And last night you came out here with some of them because this is probably a popular place—in fact, it's just an ideal place—to sneak away and smoke some dope and do . . . all sorts of other things."

"No."

"Last night you came here with them, popped a few pills—God knows what they were—and then you tripped out."

"No."

"Admit it."

"It's not true."

"Colin, I know you're basically a good boy. You've never been in any trouble before. Now you've made a mistake. You've let some other kids lead you astray."

"No."

"If you'll just admit it, if you'll face up to it, I won't be mad at you. I'll respect you for accepting your medicine. I'll help you, Colin, if you'll just give me a chance."

"Give *me* a chance."

"You popped a couple of pills—"

"No."

"—and for a few hours you were really gone, really out of it."

"No."

"When you finally came around, you realized you'd wandered away, back toward town, without your bike."

"Jeez."

"You weren't sure how to get back here and find your bike. Your clothes were torn, filthy, and it was one o'clock in the morning. You panicked. You didn't know how you were going to explain all that, so you made up this foolish story about Roy Borden."

"Will you listen?" He was barely able to keep from screaming at her.

"I'm listening."

"Roy Borden *is* a killer. He—"

"You disappoint me."

"Look at what I am, for Christ's sake!"

"Don't talk like that."

"Can't you see me?"

"Don't shout at me."

"Can't you see what I am?"

"You're a boy in trouble and getting deeper."

Colin was furious with her because she was forcing him to reveal himself in a way he never had done before. "Do I look like one of those kids? Do I look like the kind of guy they'd even bother to say hello to? They wouldn't even take time to spit on me. To them, I'm just a skinny, bashful, near-sighted creep." Tears shimmered in the corners of his eyes. He hated himself for being unable to hold them back. "Roy was the best friend I had. He was the *only* friend. Why would I make up a crazy story just to get him in trouble?"

"You were confused and desperate." She stared at him as if her gaze would crack him and reveal the truth as she imagined it to be. "And according to Roy, you were mad at him because he wouldn't come out here with you and the others."

Colin gaped at her. "You mean you got this whole theory from Roy? This whole dumb thing about me taking drugs—it comes from *Roy*?"

"I suspected it last night. When I mentioned it to Roy, he said I was right. He told me you were very upset with him because he wouldn't come to the party—"

"He tried to kill me!"

"—and because he wouldn't contribute any money to buy the pills."

"There weren't any pills."

"Roy says there were, and it explains a lot."

"Did he name even one of these wild dopers I'm supposed to be hanging out with?"

"They're none of my concern. It's you I'm worried about."

"Jeez."

"I *am* worried about you."

"But for the wrong reason."

"Playing with drugs is stupid and dangerous."

"I didn't do anything."

"If you want to be treated like an adult, you've got to start acting like one," she said in a lecturing tone that galled him.

"An adult admits his mistakes. An adult always accepts the consequences of his acts."

"Not most of the adults I see."

"If you persist in this bullheaded attempt to—"

"How can you believe him instead of me?"

"He's a very nice boy. He—"

"You've only talked to him a couple of times!"

"Often enough to know he's a well-rounded boy and very mature for his age."

"He's not! He's not like that at all. He's lying!"

"His story certainly rings truer than yours," Weezy said. "And he strikes me as a sensible boy."

"You think I'm not sensible?"

"Colin, how many nights have you gotten me out of bed because you were convinced something was crawling around in the attic?"

"Not that often," he mumbled.

"Yes. That often. Quite often. And was there ever anything there when we looked?"

He sighed.

"Was there?" she insisted.

"No."

"How many nights have you been absolutely certain that something was lurking outside the house, trying to get in through your window?"

He didn't answer.

She pressed her advantage. "And do level-headed boys spend all of their time building plastic models of movie monsters?"

"Is that why you don't believe me? Because I watch a lot of horror movies? Because I read science fiction?"

"Stop that. Don't try to make me sound simple-minded," she said.

"Shit."

"You're also picking up bad language from this crowd you're running around with, and I won't allow it."

He walked away from her, into the junkyard.

"Where are you going?"

As he walked away, he said, "I can show you proof."

"We're leaving," she said.

"Go ahead."

"I should have been at the gallery an hour ago."

"I can show you proof, if you'll bother to look at it."

He walked through the junkyard, toward the point at which the hill dropped down to the railroad tracks. He didn't know for sure if she was following him, but he tried to act as if he had no doubt about it. He believed that looking back would be a sign of weakness, and he felt that he had been a weakling for too damned long.

Last night Hermit Hobson's collection of wrecks had been a sinister labyrinth. Now, in the bright daylight, it was only sad, a very sad and lonely place. By squinting slightly, you could look through the dead and pitted surface, through the sorry present, and see the past glowing in all of it. Once, the cars had been shiny and beautiful. People had invested work and money and dreams in these machines, and all that had come to this: rust.

When he reached the western end of the junkyard, he had trouble believing what he could plainly see. The proof he had intended to show Weezy was gone.

The dilapidated pickup still stood ten feet from the brink, where Roy had been forced to abandon it, but the corrugated metal runners were not there any more. Although the truck had stopped with its angled front wheels in the dirt, the rear wheels had remained squarely on the tracks. Colin clearly remembered that. But now all four wheels rested upon bare earth.

Colin realized what had happened and knew that he should have expected it. Last night, when he had hidden successfully from Roy in the arroyo west of the railway line, Roy had not rushed immediately into town to wait for him at the house, but had finally given up the chase and had come back here to erase all traces of his plan to wreck the train. He had carted away every loose section of the make-shift track that he'd constructed for the truck. Then he had even jacked up the rear wheels of the Ford to retrieve the last two incriminating sheets of metal that were pinned under them.

The grass behind the truck, which surely must have been smashed flat when the Ford passed over it, now stood nearly as tall and undisturbed as the grass on all other sides of the junker; it swayed gently in the breeze. Roy had taken time to rake it, thereby removing the twin impressions of the pickup's wake. On closer inspection, Colin saw that the resilient blades of grass had sustained minor damage. A few were broken. A few more were bent. Some were pinched. But those subtle signs would not be proof enough to convince Weezy that his story was true.

Although it was twenty feet closer to the brow of the hill than any of the other wrecks, the Ford looked as if it had been in that same spot, undisturbed, for years and years.

Colin knelt beside the pickup and reached behind one of the rusty wheels. He brought out a gob of grease.

"What are you doing?" Weezy asked.

He turned to her and held up his greasy hand. ''This is all I can show you. He took away everything else, all the other proof.''

''What's that?''

''Grease.''

''So?''

It was hopeless.

PART TWO

◆ ◆ ◆

PART TWO

TWENTY-EIGHT

♦

For seven days Colin remained in the house.

Restriction to quarters was one part of his punishment. His mother made certain that he endured the confinement; she called home six or eight times every day, checking on him. Sometimes two or three hours would pass between the calls, and sometimes she would ring him three times in thirty minutes. He did not dare sneak out.

Actually, he didn't want to go anywhere. He was well accustomed to loneliness, comfortable and satisfied with just his own company. For most of his life, his room had been the largest part of his world, and for a while at least it would serve admirably as his entire universe. He had his books, horror comics, monster models, and radio; he could entertain himself for a week or a month or even longer. And he was afraid that if he set foot outside the door, Roy Borden would get him.

Weezy had also made it clear that when he had served his one-week sentence he would be on probation for a long time. For the remainder of the summer he would have to be home before dark. He didn't tell her how he felt about that when she laid down the rule, but in fact he didn't think of it as punishment. He had no intention of going anywhere at night. As long as Roy was running around loose, Colin would view every sunset with dread, as if he were a character in Bram Stoker's *Dracula*.

In addition to imposing a curfew, Weezy took away his allowance for one month. He wasn't bothered by that either. He had a big metal bank in the shape of a flying saucer, and it was full of coins and dollar bills that he had saved over the past two years.

He was distressed only by the fact that the restrictions would interfere with his courtship of Heather Lipshitz. He'd never had a girlfriend. No girl had ever been interested in him before. Not even a little bit. Now that he finally had a chance with a girl, he didn't want to spoil it.

He called Heather and explained that he had been grounded and could not keep their movie date. He didn't tell her the truth about why he had been restricted to the house; he didn't mention that Roy had attempted to kill him. She didn't know him well enough yet to accept such a wild story. And of all the people in Colin's life, Heather was the one whose opinion mattered the most right now; he didn't want her to think he was a nut case. When he explained his situation, she was very understanding, and they rescheduled their date for the following Wednesday, when he would be allowed out of the house again. She didn't even mind that they would have to go to the early show and that he would have to be home by dark to satisfy the curfew his mother had imposed. For twenty minutes they chatted about movies and books, and she was easier to talk to than any girl he had ever known.

When he hung up he felt better than he had before he'd telephoned her. For a third of an hour, at least, he had been able to push thoughts of Roy Borden to the back of his mind.

He called Heather every day during the week that he was grounded, and they were never at a loss for words. He learned a great many things about her, and the more he learned the more he liked her. He hoped he was making an equally good impression on her, and he was impatient to see her again.

He expected Roy to show up at the door some afternoon, or at least to call and make a lot of threats; but the days passed uneventfully. He considered taking the initiative, just to see what would happen. Once or twice each day, he picked up the telephone, but he never got farther than dialing the first three digits of the Borden number. Then the shakes always took him, and he hung up.

He read half a dozen new paperbacks: science fiction, sword and sorcery, occult stories, stuff that was filled with monstrous villains, the sort of thing he liked the most. But there must have been something wrong with the plots or with the writers' prose styles, because he didn't get that familiar cold thrill from them.

He reread a few pieces that he had found hair-raising when he'd first encountered them a couple of years ago. He discovered that he still could appreciate the color and suspense of Heinlein's *The Puppet Masters,* but the terror that it had communicated to him so forcefully when he had first read it was no longer there. John Campbell's *Who Goes There?* and Theodore Sturgeon's scariest stories—*It* and *The Professor's Teddy-Bear* among others—still pulsed with a rich vision of evil, but they no longer made him look over his shoulder while he turned the pages.

He had trouble sleeping. If he closed his eyes for more than a minute, he heard strange sounds: the furtive but insistent noises someone might make if he were trying to get into the bedroom through the locked door or window. Colin heard something in the attic, too, something heavy that kept dragging itself back and forth, as if it were looking for a weak spot in his bedroom ceiling. He thought about the things his mother had said with such scorn, and he told himself there was nothing in the attic; told himself that it was just his overactive imagination, but he continued to hear it nonetheless. After two bad nights, he surrendered to the fear and stayed up reading until dawn; then in the early light, he was able to sleep.

TWENTY-NINE

◆

Wednesday morning, eight days after the events at Hermit Hobson's junkyard, Colin was no longer restricted to quarters. He was reluctant to leave the house. He studied the surrounding grounds through all the first-floor windows; and although he could detect nothing out of the ordinary, his own front lawn seemed to him far more dangerous than any battlefield in any war there'd ever been, in spite of the lack of bursting bombs and whistling bullets.

—Roy wouldn't try anything in broad daylight.

He's crazy. How can you know what he'll do?

—Go. Go on. Get out and do what you have to do.

If he's waiting. . .

—You can't hide here for the rest of your life.

He went to the library. As he cycled along the sunny streets, he looked repeatedly behind. He was fairly sure that Roy was not following him.

Though Colin slept only three hours the night before, he was waiting at the front doors of the library when Mrs. Larkin, the librarian, opened for business. He'd gone to the library twice a week since they'd moved to town, and Mrs. Larkin had quickly learned what he liked. When she saw him standing on the steps, she said, "We received the new Arthur C. Clarke novel last Friday."

"That's swell."

"Well, I didn't put it out on the shelf right away because I thought you'd be in the same day or Saturday at the latest."

He followed her into the big, cool, stucco building, into the main room where their footsteps were smothered by the mammoth stacks of books, and where the air smelled of glue and yellowing paper.

"When you hadn't showed up by Monday afternoon," Mrs. Larkin said, "I felt I couldn't hold the book any longer. And now, wouldn't you just know it, someone checked it out a few minutes till five yesterday afternoon."

"That's all right," Colin said. "Thanks a lot for thinking about me."

Mrs. Larkin was a sweet-tempered, red-haired woman with too little brow, too much chin, too little bosom, and too much behind. Her glasses were as thick as Colin's. She loved books and bookish people, and Colin liked her.

"I mainly came to use one of the microfilm readers," he said.

"Oh, I'm sorry, but we don't have any science fiction on microfilm."

"I'm not interested in science fiction today. What I'd like to see is back issues of the Santa Leona *News Register*."

"Whatever for?" She made a face, as if she'd bitten into a lemon. "Perhaps I'm being a traitor to my own hometown when I say this, but the *News Register* is just about the dullest reading you can find. Lots of stories about bake sales and church socials, and reports of City Council meetings where silly politicians argue for hours about whether or not they should fill the potholes on Broadway."

"Well . . . I'm sort of looking ahead to starting school in September," Colin said, wondering if that sounded as ridiculous to her as it did to him. "English composition always gives me a little bit of trouble, so I like to think ahead."

"I can't believe that anything in school gives you trouble," Mrs. Larkin said.

"Anyway . . . I have this idea for an essay about summer in Santa Leona, not my summer but summer in general, and summer historically. I want to do some research."

She smiled approvingly. "You're an ambitious young man, aren't you?"

He shrugged. "Not really."

She shook her head. "In all the years I've worked here, you're the first boy who's come in during summer vacation to prepare for next fall's school assignments. I'd call that ambitious. I surely would. And it's refreshing, too. You keep that attitude, and you'll go a long way in this world."

Colin was embarrassed because he did not deserve the praise and because he had lied to her. He felt his face turn red, and he suddenly realized that this was the first time he had blushed in a week, maybe longer than that, which was some kind of record for him.

He went to the microfilm alcove, and Mrs. Larkin brought spools of film that contained every page of the *News Register* for June, July, and August of last year, and for the same three months of the year before that. She showed him how to use the machine, watched over his shoulder until she was certain that he had no questions, then left him to his work.

Rose.

Something Rose.

Jim Rose?

Arthur Rose?

Michael Rose?

He remembered the last name by associating it with the flower, but he couldn't quite recall what the boy's first name had been.

Phil Pacino.

He remembered that one because it was like Al Pacino, the movie actor.

He decided to start with Phil. He lined up the spools of last summer's newspapers.

He assumed both deaths would be front-page news, so he skimmed, looking for bold headlines.

He couldn't remember the date Roy had given. He started with June and worked all the way through to the first of August before he found the story.

LOCAL BOY DIES IN FIRE

He was reading the last paragraph of the article when he sensed a change in the air and knew that Roy was behind him. He whirled, bolting up from the swivel chair as he turned—but Roy wasn't there. No one was there. No one was at the worktables. No one was browsing through the stacks. Mrs. Larkin wasn't at her desk. He had imagined it.

He sat down and read the article again. It was exactly as Roy said. The Pacino house had burned to the ground, a total loss. In the rubble, firemen had found the blackened body of Philip Pacino, age fourteen.

Colin felt beads of sweat pop out on his forehead. He wiped his face with one hand and dried his hands on his jeans.

He went through the papers for the next week with special care, looking for follow-up stories. There were three.

FIRE MARSHAL'S REPORT
PLAYING WITH MATCHES

According to the final, official statement, Philip Pacino had caused the blaze. He had been playing with matches near a workbench on which he constructed model airplanes. Apparently there had been a number of highly flammable items on the bench, including several tubes and pots of glue, a can of lighter fluid, and an open bottle of paint remover.

The second follow-up was a page-two report of the boy's funeral. The story contained tributes from Philip's teachers, teary remembrances from his friends, and excerpts from the eulogy. A photograph of the grieving parents headed the three-column piece.

Colin read it twice with great interest because one of Philip Pacino's friends quoted in the story was Roy Borden.

Two days later there was a long editorial that was hard-hitting by the *News Register*'s standards.

PREVENTING TRAGEDY
WHO'S RESPONSIBLE?

In none of the four pieces was there the slightest indication that the police or the fire department suspected murder and arson. From the beginning they had assumed it was an accident, the result of carelessness or adolescent foolishness.

But I know the truth, Colin thought.

He was weary. He had been at the microfilm reader for almost two hours. He switched off the machine, stood up, and stretched.

He didn't have the library to himself any more. A woman in a red dress was looking through the magazine racks. At one of the tables in the center of the room, a chubby, balding priest was reading an enormous book and assiduously taking notes.

Colin walked to one of the two, big, mullioned windows at the east end of the room and sat sideways on the two-foot-deep sill. He stared through the dusty glass, thinking. Beyond the window lay a Roman Catholic cemetery, and at the far end of the graveyard, Our Lady of Sorrows Church watched over the remains of its ascended parishioners.

"Hi there."

Colin looked up, surprised. It was Heather.

"Oh hi," he said. He started to get up.

"Don't move on my account," she said in a soft, library voice. "I can't stay long. I have some errands to run for my mother. I just stopped in to pick up a book, and I saw you sitting here."

She was wearing a maroon T-shirt and white shorts.

"You look terrific," Colin said, keeping his voice as low as hers.

She smiled. "Thank you."

"I really mean it."

"Thank you."

"Absolutely terrific."

"You're embarrassing me."

"Why? 'Cause I said you look terrific?"

"Well . . . in a way, yeah."

"You mean you'd feel better if I said you looked awful?"

She laughed self-consciously. "No. Of course not. It's just that . . . no one ever told me I looked terrific before."

"You've got to be kidding."

"No."

"No guy ever told you that? What are they—all blind or something?"

She was blushing. "Well, I know I'm not really all that terrific."

"Sure you are."

"My mouth's too big," she said.

"No, it's not."

"Yes, it is. I've got a wide mouth."

"I like it."

"And my teeth aren't the greatest."

"They're very white."

"And a couple of them are kind of crooked."

"Not so that anyone would notice," Colin said.

"I hate my hands," she said.

"Huh? Why?"

"My fingers are so stubby. My mother has long, elegant fingers. But mine look like little sausages."

"That's silly. You have nice fingers."

"And my knees are knobby," she said.

"Your knees are perfect," he said.

"Just listen to me," she said nervously. "A boy finally says I look nice, and I try to make him change his mind."

Colin was amazed to discover that even a pretty girl like Heather could have doubts about herself. He always had thought that those kids he admired—those golden, blue-eyed, strong-limbed California boys and girls—were a race above all others, superior creatures who glided through life with perfect self-confidence, with an unshakable sense of worth and purpose. He was both pleased and displeased to discover this crack in the myth. He suddenly realized that those special, radiant kids were not really very different from him, that they were not so superior as he had thought they were, and this discovery buoyed him. On the other hand, he felt as if he had lost something important—a pleasant illusion that, at times, had warmed him.

"Are you waiting for Roy?" Heather asked.

He shifted uneasily on his windowsill seat. "Uh . . . no. I'm just doing some . . . research."

"I thought you were looking out the window for Roy."

"Just resting. Taking a break."

"I think it's nice how he shows up every day," she said.

"Who?"

"Roy."

"Shows up where?"

"There," she said, gesturing toward something beyond the window.

Colin looked through the glass, then back at the girl. "You mean he goes to church every day?"

"No. The graveyard. Don't you know about it?"

"Tell me."

"Well . . . I live in the house across the street. The white one with the blue trim. See it?"

"Yeah."

"Most times when he comes, I see him."

"What's he do there?"

"He visits his sister."

"He has a sister?"

"Had. She's dead."

"He never said a word."

Heather nodded. "I don't think he likes to talk about it."

"Not a word."

"One time I told him it was really nice, you know, how he stopped at her grave so faithfully. He got mad at me."

"He did?"

"Mad as hell."

"Why?"

"I don't know," Heather said. "At first I thought maybe he still felt the pain of her death. I thought maybe it still hurt him so much he didn't want to talk about it. But then later it seemed like he was mad because I'd caught him doing something wrong. But he wasn't doing anything wrong. It's kind of weird."

Colin thought about this news for a moment. He stared at the sunny graveyard. "How'd she die?"

"I don't know. It happened before my time. I mean, we didn't move to Santa Leona until three years ago. She was dead long before that."

A sister.

A dead sister.

Somehow, that was the key.

"Well," Heather said, unaware of the importance of the information she had given him, "I've got to be going. My mother gave me a shopping list. She expects me back with everything in an hour or so. She doesn't like people who are late. She says tardiness is a sign of a sloppy, selfish person. I'll see you at six o'clock."

"I'm sorry we have to go to the early show," Colin said.

"That's all right," she said. "It's the same movie no matter what time it's shown."

"And like I said, I've got to be home by nine o'clock or so, before it gets completely dark. That's a real drag."

"No," she said. "That's okay, too. You're not going to be punished forever. The curfew's only for a month, right? Don't worry about it. We'll have fun. See you later."

"Later," he said.

He watched her walk across the quiet library. When she was gone, he turned his gaze to the graveyard once more.

A dead sister.

THIRTY

◆

Colin had no trouble finding the tombstone; it was like a beacon. It was bigger and shinier and fancier than any other rock in the graveyard. Mr. and Mrs. Borden had spared no expense in the matter. It was a very elaborate stone, done in sections, constructed both of granite and marble, joined together almost seamlessly. Every aspect of it was artfully shaped and highly polished. Wide, beveled letters were cut deep into the richly veined, mirror surface of the marble.

BELINDA JANE BORDEN

According to the date on the marker, she had died more than six years ago, on the last day of April. The monument at the head of the grave was surely several times the size of the body that it memorialized, for Belinda Jane was only five years old when they put her in the ground.

Colin returned to the library and asked Mrs. Larkin for the spool of microfilm that contained the six-year-old, April 30 edition of the *News Register*.

The story was on page one.

Roy had killed his baby sister.

Not murder.

Just an accident. A horrible accident.

Nothing anyone could have done to prevent it.

An eight-year-old boy finds his father's car keys on the kitchen counter. He gets it in his head to take a ride around the block. That'll prove he's bigger and better than anyone gives him credit for. It'll prove he's even big enough to play with Dad's trains, or at least big enough to sit at Dad's side and just watch the trains, which is something he's not permitted to do but which he wants to do very badly. The car is parked in the driveway. The boy puts a pillow on the seat so that he can see over the steering wheel. But then he discovers that he can't quite reach the brake or the accelerator. He searches for a tool, and beside the garage he finds a piece of lumber, a three-foot length of two-by-two white pine that is just about exactly what he needs. He figures he can use the lumber to push the pedals that his feet won't reach. One hand to hold the two-by-two, and one hand for steering. In the car he starts the engine and fumbles with the gearshift. His mother hears. Comes out of the house. She's in time to see her little girl walk behind the car. She shouts at both the boy and the girl, and each of them waves at her. The boy finally throws the car into reverse as the mother rushes toward him, and at the same instant he thumps the accelerator with the wooden prod. The automobile goes backward. Fast. Just shoots backward. Strikes the child. She goes down hard. Goes down with one short scream. A tire thumps across her fragile skull. Her head bursts like a blood-filled balloon. And when the men in the ambulance arrive, they find the mother sitting on the lawn, legs akimbo, face blank, saying the same thing over and over again. ''It just popped. Just popped open. Just like that. Her little head. It just popped.''

Popped.

Popper.

Colin switched off the machine.

He wished he could switch off his mind.

THIRTY-ONE

◆

He got home a few minutes before five o'clock.

Weezy walked in one minute later.

''Hello, Skipper.''

''Hi.''

''Have a good day?''

''It was okay.''

''What'd you do?''

''Not much.''

''I'd like to hear about it.''

He sat down on the sofa.

''I went to the library,'' he said.

''What time was that?''

''Nine this morning.''

''You were gone when I got up.''

"I went straight to the library."

"And after that?"

"Nowhere."

"When did you come home?"

"Just now."

She frowned.

"You were at the library all day?"

"Yeah."

"Come on now."

"I was."

She paced the middle of the living room.

He stretched out on his back, on the sofa.

"You're making me angry, Colin."

"It's true. I like the library."

"I'll restrict you to the house again."

"Because I went to the library?"

"Don't get smart with me."

He closed his eyes.

"Where else did you go?"

He sighed.

"I guess you want a juicy story," he said.

"I want to know everywhere you went today."

"Well," he said, "I went down to the beach."

"Did you stay away from those kids, like I told you to?"

"I had to meet someone at the beach."

"Who?"

"A dope pusher I know."

"What?"

"He deals out of his van at the beach."

"What are you saying?"

"I bought a mayonnaise jar full of pills."

"Oh my God."

"Then I brought the pills back here."

"Here? Where? Where are they?"

"I split them up into cellophane ten-packs."

"Where have you hidden them?"

"I took them into town and sold them retail."

"Oh Jesus. Oh my God. What have you gotten into? What's *wrong* with you?"

"I paid five thousand bucks for the dope and sold it for fifteen thousand."

"Huh?"

"That's ten thousand clear. Now, if I can make that much profit every day for one month, I can get enough money together to buy a clipper ship and smuggle tons of opium from the Orient."

He opened his eyes.

She was red-faced.

"What the *hell* has gotten into you?" she demanded.

"Call Mrs. Larkin," he said. "She'll probably still be there."

"Who is Mrs. Larkin?"

"The librarian. She'll tell you where I was all day."

Weezy stared at him for a moment, then went into the kitchen to use the telephone. He couldn't believe it. She actually called the library. He was humiliated.

When she came back to the living room, she said, "You *were* at the library all day."

"Yeah."

"Why'd you do that?"

"'Cause I like the library."

"I mean, why'd you make up that story about buying pills down at the beach?"

"I thought that's what you wanted to hear."

"I suppose you think it's funny."

"Kind of funny."

"Well, it's not."

She sat down in an armchair.

"All the conversations I've had with you during the past week—haven't any of them sunk in?"

"Every word," he said.

"I've told you that if you want to be trusted, you've got to earn that trust. If you want to be treated like an adult, you've got to behave like one. You seem to listen, and I let myself hope we're getting somewhere, and then you pull a silly stunt like this. Do you understand what that does to me?"

"I think I do."

"This childish thing you did, making up this story about buying pills down at the beach . . . it just makes me distrust you all the more."

For a while neither of them spoke.

At last Colin broke the silence. "Are you eating at home tonight?"

"I can't, Skipper. I've got—"

"—a business engagement."

"That's right. But I'll make your supper before I go."

"Don't bother."

"I don't want you eating junk."

"I'll make a cheese sandwich," he said. "That's as good as anything."

"Have a glass of milk with it."

"Okay."

"What are your plans for the evening?"

"Oh, I guess maybe I'll go to the movies," he said, purposefully failing to mention Heather.

"Which theater?"

"The Baronet."

"What's playing?"

"A horror flick."

"I wish you'd outgrow that sort of trash."

He said nothing.

She said, "You'd better not forget your curfew."

"I'm going to the early show," Colin said. "It lets out by eight o'clock, so I'll be home before dark."

"I'll check on you."

"I know."

She sighed and stood up. "I'd better shower and change." She walked to the hallway, then turned and looked at him again. "If you'd behaved differently a little while ago, maybe I wouldn't find it necessary to check on you."

"Sorry," he said. And when he was alone, he said, "Bullshit."

THIRTY-TWO

◆

Colin's first date with Heather was wonderful. Although the horror movie was not as good as he had hoped it would be, the last half hour was very scary; Heather was more frightened than he was, and she leaned toward him, held his hand in the dark, seeking reassurance and security. Colin felt uncharacteristically strong and brave. Sitting in the cool theater, in the velveteen shadows, in the pale, flickering light cast back by the screen, holding his girl's hand, he thought he knew what heaven must be like.

After the movie, as the sun settled toward the Pacific, Colin walked her home. The air from the ocean was sweet. Overhead, the palms swayed and whispered.

Two blocks from the theater, Heather tripped on a hoved-up piece of the side-walk. She didn't fall or even come close to losing her balance, but she said, "Damnit!" She blushed. "I'm so damned clumsy."

"They shouldn't let the sidewalk deteriorate like that," Colin said. "Someone could get hurt."

"Even if they made it perfectly straight and smooth, I'd probably trip on it."

"Why do you say that?"

"I'm such a klutz."

"No, you aren't," he said.

"Yes, I am." They started to walk again, and she said, "I'd give anything to be just half as graceful as my mother."

"You are graceful."

"I'm a klutz. You should see my mother. She doesn't walk—she *glides*. If you saw her in a long dress, something long enough to cover her feet, you'd think she wasn't really walking at all. You'd think she was just floating along on a cushion of air."

For a minute they walked in silence.

Then Heather sighed and said, "I'm a disappointment to her."

"Who?"

"My mother."

"Why?"

"I don't measure up."

"Up to what?"

"To her," Heather said. "Did you know that my mother was Miss California?"

"You mean like in a beauty contest?"

"Yeah. She won. She won a lot of other contests, too."

"When was this?"

"She was Miss California seventeen years ago, when she was nineteen."

"Wow!" Colin said. "That's really something."

"When I was a little girl, she entered me in a lot of beauty pageants for children."

"Yeah? What titles did you win?"

"None," Heather said.

"I find that hard to believe."

"It's true."

"What were the judges—blind? Come on, Heather. You must have won something."

"No, really. I never placed better than second. And I was usually just third."

"Usually? You mean most of the time you won either second or third place?"

"I placed second four times. I got third place ten times. And five times I didn't place at all."

"But that's fantastic!" Colin said. "You made it to the top three spots in fourteen out of nineteen tries!"

"In a beauty contest," Heather said, "the only thing that counts is being No. 1, winning the title. In children's contests, nearly everyone gets to be No. 2 or No. 3 every once in a while."

"Your mother must have been proud of you," Colin insisted.

"She always said she was, every time that I came in second or third. But I always got the impression she was really very disappointed. When I hadn't won a first place by the time I was ten, she stopped entering me in the contests. I guess she figured I was a hopeless case."

"But you did great!"

"You forget that she was No. 1," Heather said. "She was Miss California. Not No. 3 or No. 2. No. 1."

He marveled at this lovely girl who didn't seem to know how truly lovely she was. Her mouth was sensuous; she thought it was merely too wide. Her teeth were straighter and whiter than most kids' teeth; she thought they were a bit crooked. Her hair was thick and shiny; she thought it was lank and dull. Graceful as a cat, she called herself a klutz. She was a girl who ought to be brimming with self-assurance; instead, she was plagued by self-doubt. Beneath her sparkling surface she was just as uncertain and worried about life as Colin was; and suddenly he felt very protective toward her.

"If I'd been one of the judges," he said, "you'd have won all of those contests."

She blushed again and smiled at him. "You're sweet."

A moment later they reached her house and stopped at the end of the front walkway.

"You know what I like about you?" she asked.

"I've been wracking my brain, trying to figure out what it could possibly be," he said.

"Well, for one thing, you don't talk about the same stuff that all the other boys talk about. They all seem to think that guys aren't supposed to be interested in anything but football and baseball and cars. All of that stuff bores me. And besides, you don't just talk—you *listen*. Almost no one else listens."

"Well," he said, "one of the things I like about you is that you don't care that I'm not much like other boys."

They stared self-consciously at each other for a moment, and then she said, "Call me tomorrow, okay?"

"I will."

"You better be getting home. You don't want to make your mother angry."

She planted a shy little kiss on the corner of his mouth, turned away, and hurried into the house.

For a few blocks Colin drifted like a sleepwalker, meandering toward home in a pleasant daze. But suddenly he became aware of the darkening sky, the spreading pools of shadow, and the creeping night chill. He was not afraid of violating the curfew, not afraid of his mother. But he was afraid of encountering Roy after dark. He ran the rest of the way home.

THIRTY-THREE

◆

Thursday morning, Colin returned to the library and continued his search through the microfilm files of the local newspaper. He studied only two parts of each edition: the front page and the list of hospital admissions and discharges. Nevertheless, he needed more than six hours to find what he was looking for.

One year to the day after his baby sister's death, Roy Borden was admitted to the Santa Leona General Hospital. The one-line notice in the May 1 edition of the *News Register* didn't mention the nature of his illness; however, Colin was certain that it had to do with the strange accident that Roy had refused to discuss, the injury that had left such a great deal of terrible scar tissue on his back.

The name immediately below Roy's on the admissions roster was Helen Borden. His mother. Colin stared at that line for a long time, wondering. Because of the scars he had seen, he had expected to find Roy's name sooner or later, but the mother's appearance surprised him. Had she and her son been hurt in the same mishap?

Colin rolled the film back and carefully scanned every page of the April 30 and May 1 editions of the newspaper. He was looking for a story about an automobile wreck, or an explosion, or a fire, some sort of accident in which the Bordens had been involved. He found nothing.

He wound the film forward again, finished that spool and a few more, but uncovered only two additional bits of useful information, the first of which was rather puzzling. Two days after being admitted to Santa Leona General, Mrs. Borden was transferred to a larger hospital, St. Joseph's, over at the county seat. Colin wondered why she had been moved, and he could think of only one reason. She must have been so badly injured that she required very special care, something exotic that the smaller Santa Leona General could not provide.

He didn't discover anything more about Mrs. Borden, but he did learn that Roy had spent exactly three weeks in the local hospital. Whatever the source of the wounds on his back, they clearly had been quite serious.

At a quarter till five, Colin finished with the microfilm and went to Mrs. Larkin's desk.

"That new Arthur C. Clarke novel was just returned," she said before Colin could speak. "I've already checked it out for you."

He didn't really want the novel right now, but he didn't want to appear ungrateful. He took it, looked at the jacket, front and back. "Thanks a lot, Mrs. Larkin."

"Let me know what you think of it."

"I was wondering if you could help me find a couple of books on psychology."

"What kind of psychology?"

He blinked. "There's more than one kind?"

"Well," she said, "under the general topic, we've got books on animal psychology, educational psychology, popular psychology, industrial psychology, political psychology, the psychology of the aged, of the young, Freudian psychology, Jungian psychology, general psychology, abnormal psychology—"

"Abnormal psychology," Colin said. "Yeah. That's what I've got to learn all about. But I also want a couple of general books that tell me how the mind works. I mean, I want to know why people do the things they do. I want something that covers the basics. Something easy, for beginners."

"I think we can find what you need," she said.

"I'd really appreciate it."

As he followed her toward the stacks at the far end of the room, she said, "Is this another idea for school?"

"Yeah."

"Isn't abnormal psychology a rather heavy subject for a tenth-grade project?"

"It sure is," he said.

THIRTY-FOUR

◆

Colin ate supper alone, in his room.

He called Heather, and they made a date to go to the beach on Saturday. He wanted to tell her about Roy's madness, but he was afraid she wouldn't believe him. Besides, he still didn't feel confident enough about their relationship to tell her that he and Roy were now enemies. Initially, she had seemed attracted to him because he and Roy were friends. Would she lose interest when she discovered he was no longer Roy's buddy? He wasn't sure, and he didn't want to risk losing her.

Later, he read the psychology books that Mrs. Larkin had chosen for him. He finished both volumes by two in the morning. For a while he sat in bed, staring and thinking. Then, mentally exhausted, he slept without nightmares—and without a single thought for the monsters in the attic.

Friday morning, before Weezy woke, he went to the library, returned the psychology books, and checked out three more.

"Is the science fiction novel good?" Mrs. Larkin asked.

"Haven't started it yet," Colin said. "Maybe tonight."

From the library he went down to the harbor. He didn't want to go home while Weezy was still there; he wasn't ready to endure another interrogation. He ate breakfast at the counter in a waterfront coffee shop. Later, he strolled to the southern end of the boardwalk, leaned against the railing, and watched the dozens of crabs that were sunning on the rocks a few feet below.

At eleven o'clock he went home. He let himself into the house with the spare key that was kept in the redwood planter near the front door. Weezy was long gone; the coffee in the pot was cold.

He got a Pepsi from the refrigerator and went upstairs with the three psychology books. In his room, sitting on the bed, he took only one swallow of the soda and read only one paragraph of the first book before he sensed that he was not alone.

He heard a muffled, scraping sound.

Something was in the closet.

—Ridiculous.

I heard it.

—You imagined it.

He had read two books on psychology, and he knew that he was probably guilty of transference. That's what the psychologists called it: transference. He couldn't face up to the people and things he was *really* afraid of, couldn't admit those fears to himself, so he transferred the anxiety to other things, to simple things—even simple-minded things—like werewolves and vampires and imaginary monsters that hid in the closet. That's what he had been doing all of his life.

Yeah, maybe that's true, he thought. But I'm *sure* I heard something move in the closet.

He leaned away from the headboard. He held his breath and listened intently. Nothing. Silence.

The closet door was shut tight. He couldn't remember if he had left it that way.

There! Again. A soft, scraping sound.

He slid silently off the bed and took a few steps toward the hall door, away from the closet.

The closet doorknob began to turn. The door eased open an inch.

Colin stopped. He desperately wanted to keep moving, but he was frozen in place as if a spell had been cast upon him. He felt as if he had been transformed into a specimen fly trapped in air that, through sorcery, had been turned to solid amber. From within that magic prison, he was watching a nightmare come to life; he stared at the closet, transfixed.

The door suddenly opened wide. There was no monster hiding among the clothes, no werewolf, no vampire, no hideous beast-god out of H. P. Lovecraft. Just Roy.

Roy looked surprised. He had started toward the bed, thinking his prey was there. Now he saw that Colin had anticipated him and was only a few steps from the open door that led to the second-floor hall. Roy stopped, and for an instant they stared at each other.

Then Roy grinned and raised his hands so that Colin could see what he held.

"No," Colin said softly.

In Roy's right hand: a cigarette lighter.

"No."

In his left hand: a can of lighter fluid.

"No, no, no! Get out of here!"

Roy took a step toward him. Then another.

"No," Colin said. But he couldn't move.

Roy pointed the squeeze can and pressed on it. A jet of clear liquid arced through the air.

Colin ducked to the left, and the lighter fluid missed him, and he ran.

"Bastard!" Roy said.

Colin dashed through the open door and slammed it.

Even as the door was being drawn shut, Roy crashed into the other side.

Colin sprinted for the stairs.

Roy jerked open the door and rushed out of the bedroom. "Hey!"

Colin descended two steps at a time, but he had gone only halfway when he heard Roy thundering down after him. He plunged on. He jumped the last four steps, into the first-floor hall, and ran to the front door.

"Got ya!" Roy shouted triumphantly behind him. "Got ya, damnit!"

Before Colin could throw off the two locks on the door, he felt something cold and wet pouring down his back. He gasped in surprise and turned to Roy.

Lighter fluid!

Roy squirted him again, drenched the front of his thin cotton shirt.

Colin shielded his eyes with his hands. He was just in time.

Flammable liquid splashed over his forehead, over his fingers, nose, and chin. Roy laughed.

Colin couldn't breathe. The fumes choked him.

"What a popper!"

Finally the can of lighter fluid was empty. Roy threw it aside, and it clattered along the hardwood floor of the hallway.

Coughing, wheezing, Colin took his hands from his face and tried to see what was happening. The fumes stung his eyes; he closed them again. Tears oozed from beneath his eyelids. Though darkness had always terrified him, it had never been so awful as it was now.

"You stinking bastard," Roy said. "Now you'll pay for turning on me. Now you'll pay. You're gonna burn."

Gasping for breath, barely able to get any air at all, temporarily blinded, hysterical, Colin threw himself toward the sound of the other boy's voice. He collided with Roy, clutched him, and held on.

Roy staggered backward and tried to shake loose, as if he were a cornered fox wrestling free of a determined terrier. He put his hands against Colin's chin, tried to force his head up and back, then grabbed him by the throat and attempted to strangle him. But they were face to face, and much too close for Roy to get sufficient leverage to be effective.

"Do it now," Colin wheezed through the acrid fumes that filled his nose and mouth and lungs. "Do it . . . and we'll . . . burn together."

Roy tried again to throw him off. In the process, he stumbled and fell.

Colin went down with him. He held tightly to Roy; his life depended on it.

Cursing, Roy punched him, pummeled his back, slapped him alongside the head, pulled his hair. He even twisted Colin's ears until it seemed that they would come out by the roots.

Colin howled in pain and tried to fight back. But the moment he let go of Roy in order to hit him, Roy rolled away. Colin grabbed for him and missed.

Roy scrambled to his feet. He backed up against the wall.

Even through the veil of stinging tears brought on by the fumes, Colin could see that the lighter was still in Roy's right hand.

Roy snapped the flint wheel with his thumb. It didn't spark, but it surely would the next time or the time after that.

Frantic, Colin launched himself at the other boy, slammed into him, and knocked the lighter out of his hand. It flew through the open archway, into the living room, where it banged against a piece of furniture.

"You *creep!*" Roy shoved him out of the way and ran after the lighter.

Having imbibed nothing more than the reeky air around him, Colin staggered drunkenly to the front door. He threw off the deadbolt lock with no difficulty, but then he fumbled with the stubborn security chain for what seemed like hours. Seemed. But of course couldn't be. Probably only a few seconds. Or maybe even just fractions of a single second. He had no real sense of time. He was spinning. Floating. High on the fumes. He was getting just enough air to keep from passing out but not one whiff more. That's why he was having so much trouble with the security chain. He was dizzy. The security chain seemed to be evaporating in his fingers, just as the lighter fluid was evaporating from his clothes and hands and face. His ears were ringing. The security chain. Concentrate on the security chain. Second by second, his coordination was deteriorating. Getting sloppy. The damned security chain. Sloppier and sloppier. Sick and burning. Going to burn. Like a torch. *The goddamned, fucking security chain!* At last, in a burst of concentrated effort, he tore the chain out of its slot and opened the door wide. Expecting flames to explode along his back at any second, he ran from the house, down the walk, across the street, and stopped at the edge of the small park. A wonderfully sweet wind washed over him and began to scour the fumes away. He drew several deep breaths, trying to regain a measure of sobriety.

On the far side of the street, Roy Borden came out of the house. He spotted his prey at once and loped to the end of the walk, but he didn't cross the roadway. He stood over there, hands on his hips, staring at Colin.

Colin stared back at him. He was still dizzy. He still had difficulty drawing his breath. But he was ready to scream for help and run like hell the instant that Roy stepped off the curb.

Realizing that the game was lost, Roy walked away. In the first block, he looked back half a dozen times. In the second block, he glanced over his shoulder only twice. In the third block, he didn't look back at all, and then he turned the corner and was gone.

On the way into the house, angry with himself, Colin stopped at the redwood planter and took the key from its place under the ivy. He was amazed that he had been so unthinking, so stupid. He had brought Roy to the house half a dozen times during the past month. Roy had known where the spare key was kept, and Colin had been careless enough to leave it there. From now on, he would carry it with him; and hereafter, he would maintain his defenses with considerably more diligence than he had shown to date.

He was at war.

Nothing less.

He went inside and locked the door.

In the powder room at the end of the hall, he stripped out of his saturated shirt and threw it on the floor. He scrubbed his hands vigorously, using lots of perfumed soap and hot water. Then he washed his face several times. Although he could still detect the fumes, the worst of the stench was gone. His eyes stopped tearing, and he was able to breathe normally once again.

In the kitchen he went directly to the telephone, but he hesitated with his hand on the receiver. He couldn't call Weezy. The only proof he had that Roy attacked him was the soaked shirt, and that was really no proof at all. Besides, by the time she got home, most of the lighter fluid would have evaporated, leaving no stains. The empty can was on the floor in the hallway, and Roy's fingerprints probably were all over it. But, of course, only the police had the equipment and expertise to test for prints and to prove whose they were, and the police would never take his story seriously. Weezy would think he had popped pills and hallucinated the whole thing, and he would be in trouble again.

If he explained the situation to his father and asked for help, the old man would call Weezy and demand to know what was happening. Pressed for an explanation, she would tell him a lot of silly stories about pills and pot and all-night drug parties. In spite of the fact that everything she would have to say would be clearly absurd, she would convince Frank because that was the kind of thing he would want to hear. The old man would accuse her of neglecting her duties as a parent. He'd be very self-righteous. He'd use her failure as an excuse to bring in his pack of hungry attorneys. A telephone call to Frank Jacobs would lead inevitably to another custody battle, and that was the last thing Colin wanted.

The only other people to whom he could turn were his grandparents. All four of them were alive. His mother's folks lived in Sarasota, Florida, in a big white stucco place with lots of windows and shiny terrazzo floors. His father's people had a small farm in Vermont. Colin hadn't seen his grandparents in three years, and he'd never been close to any of them. If he called them, they would call Weezy. His relationships with them were not such that they would keep a secret for him. And they certainly wouldn't come across country to take his side in this little war, not in a million years; that was a pipe dream.

Heather? Perhaps it was time to tell her, to ask for her help and suggestions. He could not hide his separation from Roy forever. But what could she do? She was a slender, rather timid girl, very pretty and nice and smart, but not much good in a fight like this.

He sighed.

"Jeez."

He took his hand off the telephone.

There was no one on earth from whom he could hope to get help. No one.

He was as alone as if he had been standing at the North Pole. Utterly, perfectly, unrelievedly alone. But he was accustomed to that.

When had it ever been different?

He went upstairs.

In the past, whenever the world seemed too harsh and difficult to handle, he simply retreated from it. He had squirreled away with his monster models, his comic-book collection, and his shelves of science fiction and horror novels. His room had been a sanctuary, the eye of the hurricane, where the storm could not touch him, where it could even be forgotten for a while. His room had always done for him what a hospital did for a sick man and what a monastery did for a monk: It healed him and it made him feel that in some mystical way he was part of something far, far more important and *better* than everyday life. His room had been filled with magic. It had been his refuge and his stage, where he could either hide from the world and from himself, too—or act out his fantasies for an audience of one. His room had been his place to weep and his playground, his church and his laboratory, the repository of his dreams.

Now it was just a room like any other. A ceiling. Four walls. A floor. A window. A door. Nothing more than that. Just one more place to be.

When Roy had come in here alone, uninvited, unwanted, he had broken the delicate spell that made this place unique. He had surely snooped through all the drawers and books and monster model kits, and in doing that he had also pawed through Colin's soul without ever realizing it. With his crude touch he had drained the magic out of everything in the room, just as a lightning rod draws magnificent bolts of energy from the sky and disperses them so widely in the earth that they cease to exist at all. Nothing here was special any longer, and none of it would ever be special again. Colin felt violated, raped; he felt used and discarded. But Roy Borden had stolen a great deal more than privacy and pride; he had also made off with what remained of Colin's shaky sense of security. And even more than that, much worse than that, he was a thief of illusions; he had taken all of those false but wonderfully comforting beliefs that Colin had long cherished.

Colin was depressed, yet he was also aware of a strange new power that was beginning to shine within him. Although he nearly had been killed just minutes ago, he was less afraid at this moment than at any time in memory. For the first time in his life, he did not feel weak or inferior. He was still the same second-rate physical specimen that he had always been—skinny, myopic, poorly coordinated—but inside he felt all new, fresh, and capable of anything.

He did not cry, and he was proud of that.

At the moment there was no room in him for tears; he was filled with a need for revenge.

PART THREE

◆ ◆ ◆

THIRTY-FIVE

◆

Colin spent the rest of Friday in his room. He read parts of the three psychology books that he'd brought home from the library, and he reread some pages as often as half a dozen times. When he wasn't studying, he stared at the wall, sometimes for as long as an hour, just thinking. And planning.

When he left the house early the next morning, the sky was high and bright and cloudless. He intended to meet Heather at twelve o'clock, spend the afternoon at the beach, and be home by nightfall; nevertheless, he took a flashlight with him.

He rode his bicycle down to the beach, then to the harbor, even though he didn't have any immediate business in either of those places. He was taking a roundabout route to his real destination in order to make certain that he wasn't followed. He could see that Roy wasn't close behind him, but perhaps the boy was watching from a distance through the same pair of high-power binoculars they had used when they were spying on Sarah Callahan. From the harbor, Colin cycled to the tourist information center at the north end of town. Satisfied that he had no tail, he finally struck out directly for Hawk Drive and the Kingman place.

Even in bright daylight, the abandoned house loomed threateningly at the top of the hill. Colin approached it with uneasiness that changed to quiet fear by the time he entered the gate and started up the broken flagstone walk. If he had been the state official in charge of the property, or the mayor of Santa Leona, he would have called for the complete and immediate destruction of the place for the good of the community. He still thought the house exuded a tangible evil, a menace that could be felt and seen as clearly as the California sunshine that now dazzled his eyes and warmed his face. Three large, black birds circled over the roof and finally perched on a chimney. The house seemed to be aware, watchful, infused with a malignant life force. The weathered gray walls looked scabrous, diseased, cancerous. Rusting nails resembled old wounds: stigmata. Sunlight seemed unable to penetrate the mysterious spaces beyond the missing windowpanes, and from outside, at least, the inside of the mansion appeared to be as dark now as it would be at midnight.

Colin put his bicycle down in the grass, climbed the sagging porch steps, and looked through the shattered window where he and Roy had stood one night not long ago. On closer inspection, Colin saw that some light did reach into the house. The drawing room was visible in every detail. At one time it must have served as a clubhouse for a group of boys—for candy wrappers, empty soda cans, and cigarette butts were strewn across the bare, scarred floor. A faded and tattered *Playboy* centerfold was fixed above the fireplace, over the same mantel on which Mr. Kingman had lined up the blood-splashed heads of his slaughtered family.

The kids who had been using the house as a hangout had not been around for many months—a thick, undisturbed layer of dust covered everything.

The front entrance was unlocked, but the corroded hinges squealed as Colin pushed on the warped door. The wind rushed in around him and stirred up a small cloud of dust in the foyer. Inside, the air was heavily tainted with the odors of mildew and dry rot.

As Colin prowled from room to room, he saw that vandals had been at work in every corner of the huge house. Boys' names, obscene words, dirty limericks, and crude drawings of male and female genitalia were scrawled wherever there was bare plaster or fairly plain wallpaper. Ragged holes—some only as large as a hand, others nearly as big as a door—had been knocked in the walls. Piles of plaster and splintered laths littered the place.

When Colin stood perfectly still, the old house was ethereally quiet. But when he moved, the arthritic structure responded to each step he took; its joints groaned on all sides of him.

Several times he thought he heard something creeping up behind him, but when he looked he was always alone. For the most part, he moved through the ruins without a thought for ghosts and monsters. He was surprised and pleased by his newly acquired bravery—and just a bit uncomfortable with it. Only a few weeks ago, he would have refused to cross the Kingman threshold by himself, even if there had been a million-dollar prize at stake.

He was in the mansion more than two hours. He did not overlook a room or even a closet. In those chambers where all the windows were boarded shut, he used the flashlight that he had brought along. He spent most of the time on the second floor, exploring every nook—and planning a surprise or two for Roy Borden.

THIRTY-SIX

◆

There was, after all, something that Heather could do to help him. In fact, she was perhaps the most essential part of the revenge plot that he concocted. Without her cooperation, he would have to find another way to get Roy. Colin didn't intend that she fight at his side. He wasn't relying on her strength or agility. He wanted to use her as bait.

If she agreed to help him, she would be in some danger. But he was certain that he could protect her. He was not the same weak and ineffectual Colin Jacobs who had moved to Santa Leona at the beginning of the summer, and his new aggressiveness would come as a surprise to Roy. A nasty surprise. And surprise was very definitely to his advantage.

Heather was waiting at the beach, in the shadow of the pier. She was wearing a one-piece blue swimsuit. She didn't like two-piece suits or bikinis or anything like that because she didn't think she looked good enough in them. Colin thought she would have looked as appealing as any other teen-age girl on the beach, better than many of them, and he told her that. He could see that the compliment pleased her, but it was equally obvious that she did not really believe it.

They chose a spot on the hot sand to spread their beach towels. For a while they lay on their backs, in companionable silence, basking in the sun.

At last Colin turned on his side and rose up slightly, supporting himself on one bent elbow, and said, "How much does it matter to you that I'm Roy Borden's friend?"

She frowned, but she didn't open her eyes or turn away from the sun. "What do you mean?"

"How much does it matter?" he persisted, his heart beginning to pound.

"Why should it matter to me?" she asked. "I don't understand."

Colin took a deep breath and plunged ahead. "Would you still like me if I wasn't Roy's friend?"

Now she turned her head toward him and opened her eyes. "Are you serious?"

"Yeah."

She rolled onto her side and rose on one elbow to face him. The wind stirred her hair. "You mean you think maybe I'm interested in you only because you're the best friend of the school big shot?"

Colin blushed. "Well. . ."

"That's a terrible thing to think," she said, but she didn't sound angry.

He shrugged, embarrassed but still anxious to hear her answer.

"And it's insulting," she said.

"I'm sorry," he said quickly, placatingly. "I didn't mean it that way. It's just . . . I had to ask. It's important to know if you—"

"I like you because you're you," Heather said. "I'm here right now because you're fun to be with. Roy Borden doesn't have anything to do with it. Actually, I'm here in spite of the fact that you're his buddy."

"Huh?"

"I'm one of the few people at school who doesn't really care what Roy does or says or thinks. Most everyone wants to be his friend, but I don't particularly care if he even knows I exist."

Colin blinked, surprised. "You don't like Roy?"

She hesitated, then said, "He's your friend. I don't want to talk against him."

"But that's just it," Colin said excitedly. "He isn't my friend any more. He hates me."

"What? What happened?"

"I'll tell you in a minute. Don't worry about that. I've been just about bursting to tell someone." Colin sat up on his beach towel. "But first I've got to know what you think of him. I thought you liked him. One of the first things you said to me was that you'd seen me with Roy. So I figured—"

"I was just curious about you and him," she said. "You didn't seem like the kind of guy who usually hangs around with him. And the better I've gotten to know you, the stranger it seems."

"Tell me why you don't like him."

She sat up, too.

The ocean wind was warm and salt-scented.

"Well," she said, "I don't exactly dislike him. Not a lot. I mean, not actively or passionately or anything. I don't really know him well enough for that. But I do know him well enough to know I could never be a fan of his. There's something sleazy about him."

"Sleazy?"

"It's hard to put into words," Heather said. "But I always get the feeling that Roy's never . . . sincere. Not ever. Not about anything. Most of the time he seems to be putting on an act. Apparently, no one else ever notices it. But I get the feeling he's always manipulating people, using them one way or another, and then laughing about it inside."

"Yeah!" Colin said. "Oh yeah! Exactly. That's exactly what he's doing. And he's good at it. Not just with other kids. He can manipulate adults, too."

"My mother met him once," Heather said. "I didn't think she was ever going to stop talking about him. She thought he was so charming, so polite."

"My mother, too," Colin said. "She'd rather have him for a son than me."

"So what happened?" Heather asked. "Why aren't you and Roy friends any more?"

He told her everything, beginning with the day he had first met Roy. He told her about the cat in the birdcage. The games with the electric trains. Roy's story about killing two other boys just for kicks. Roy's desire to rape and kill Sarah Callahan, his neighbor. The nightmare at Hermit Hobson's automobile graveyard. The lighter-fluid attack. He told her everything that he'd learned in the library, the entire story of Belinda Jane Borden's hideous accidental death—and the eventual hospitalization of both Roy and Mrs. Borden.

Heather listened in stunned silence. Initially, her face registered doubt, but the skepticism gradually faded and was replaced by a look of growing if reluctant belief. She was horrified, and when Colin finally finished, she said, "You've got to tell the police."

He looked out at the rolling sea and the sky with its swooping gulls. "No," he said. "They won't believe me."

"Sure they will. You convinced *me*."

"That's different. You're a kid, like me. They're adults. Besides, when they call my mother to ask her if she knows anything about it, she'll tell them I'm lying and that I've got a drug problem. God knows what they'll do to me then."

"We'll tell my folks," Heather said. "They're not really all that bad. Better than yours, I guess. They actually listen now and then. We can convince them. I know we can."

He shook his head. "No. Roy charmed your mother before. Remember? He'll charm her all over again if he has to. She'll believe him, not us. And if your folks call Weezy to discuss it with her, she'll convince them I'm a crazed doper. They'll split us up. You won't be allowed to come near me. Then if Roy knows you believe me, he'll try to kill *both* of us."

She was silent for a while. Then she shuddered and said, "You're right."

"Yeah," he said miserably.

"What are we going to do?"

He looked at her. "Did you say 'we'?"

"Well, of course I said 'we.' What do you think—That I'd turn my back on you at a time like this? You can't handle it alone. No one could."

Relieved, he said, "I was hoping you'd say that."

She reached out, took hold of his hand.

"I've got a plan," he said.

"A plan for what?"

"For trapping Roy. There's a part in it for you."

"What do I have to do?"

"You're the bait," Colin said. He told her about his scheme.

When he was finished, she said, "It's clever."

"It'll work."

"I'm not sure."

"Why not?"

"Because I don't make very good bait," she said. "You need to use a girl that Roy would find . . . desirable . . . sexy. A girl he'd want real bad." Her face colored. "I'm just not . . . enough."

"You're wrong about that," Colin said. "You're enough. You're more than enough. You're plenty."

She looked away from him, looked down at her knees.

"Pretty knees," Colin said.

"Knobby."

"No."

"Knobby and red."

"No."

Sensing that it was what she wanted him to do, he put a hand on her knee, moved it up her thigh a few inches, then down again, stroking softly.

She closed her eyes, trembled slightly.

He felt his own body responding.

"It would be dangerous," she said.

He couldn't lie to her. He couldn't minimize the risk just to secure her cooperation. "Yes," he said. "It would be very, very dangerous."

She picked up a handful of sand and let it trickle slowly through her fingers.

He gently stroked her knee, her thigh. He couldn't believe he was touching her like that. He stared at his bold hand with excitement and amazement, as if it had acquired a will of its own.

"On the other hand," she said, "we'd have the advantage of planning."

"And surprise."

"And the gun," she said.

"Yes. And the gun."

"You're sure you can get the gun?"

"Positive."

"Okay," she said. "I'll do it. We'll trap him. Together."

Colin's stomach rolled unpleasantly, powered by a strange mixture of energies: desire and fear in equal measure.

"Colin?"

"What?"

"Do you really think I'm . . . enough?"

"Yes."

"Pretty?"

"Yes."

She looked deep into his eyes, and then she smiled and turned away, stared out to sea.

He thought he saw tears in her eyes.

"You'd better go now," she said.

"Why?"

"It'll work better if Roy doesn't realize you and I know each other. If he happens to see us here, together, he might not fall for the trick later."

She was right. Besides, he had things to do, preparations to make. He got up and folded his beach towel.

"Call me tonight," she said.

"I will."

"And be careful."

"You too."

"And Colin?"

"Yeah?"

"I think you're enough, too. You're plenty."

He grinned and tried to think of something to say and couldn't think of anything and turned and raced off, toward the bicycle lockup in the parking lot.

THIRTY-SEVEN

◆

The plan required one piece of expensive equipment, and Colin had to raise a considerable sum of money.

He went home from the beach, went up to his room, and opened the big metal bank that was shaped like a flying saucer. He shook it; a few tightly folded bills and a great many coins spilled onto the bedspread. He tallied the lot and found that he had exactly seventy-one dollars—which was approximately one third of what he needed.

He sat on the bed for a few minutes, staring at the money. He considered his options.

Finally he went to the closet and hauled out several large boxes that were filled with comic books, each in a sealed Ziploc plastic bag, preserved in mint condition. He sorted through them and pulled out some of the most valuable editions.

At one-thirty, he took sixty comic books down to Nostalgia House on Broadway. The store catered to collectors of science fiction, first-edition mysteries, comic books, and tapes of old radio shows.

Mr. Plevich, the proprietor, was a tall, white-haired man with a bushy mustache. He stood with his big belly pressed against the counter while he looked through Colin's offering.

"S-s-some really n-nice items," Mr. Plevich said.

"What can you give me for them?"

"I c-c-can't give you w-what they're worth," Mr. Plevich said. "I've g-got to leave room for my p-p-profit."

"I understand," Colin said.

"Actually, I'd advise against s-s-selling these now. They're all mint c-condition f-f-first issues."

"I know."

"They're already w-worth a good d-d-deal more than you p-paid for them at the newsstand. If you hold on to them for t-t-t-two years or so, they'll probably t-triple in value."

"Yeah. But I need the money now. I need it right away."

Mr. Plevich winked at him. "You have a g-g-girlfriend?"

"Yeah. And her birthday's coming up," Colin lied.

"You'll b-b-be sorry. A g-g-girlfriend will w-walk away sooner or later, but a g-good comic b-b-b-book c-can be enjoyed over and over again."

"How much?"

"I was thinking one hundred d-d-dollars."

"Two hundred."

"Much t-too much. She d-doesn't n-n-need such an expensive g-g-g-gift. How about one hundred and t-twenty?"

"No."

Mr. Plevich looked through the batch of comics two more times, and they finally settled on one hundred and forty dollars, cash.

California Federal Trust stood on the corner, half a block from Nostalgia House. Colin gave one of the tellers the coins that had been in his flying-saucer bank, and she gave him some folding money.

With $211 stuffed in his pockets, he went to Radio Shack on Broadway and bought the best compact tape recorder he could afford. He already owned a cassette recorder, but it was bulky; and besides, the microphone didn't pick up anything farther away than three or four feet. The one he bought for $189.95, on sale, $30 off the regular price, picked up and clearly recorded voices as far away as thirty feet; at least that's what the salesman said. Furthermore, it was only nine inches long, five inches wide, and just three inches thick; it could be hidden easily.

A few minutes after he got home and stashed the recorder in his room, his mother stopped by long enough to change clothes for a dinner date. She gave him money to eat at Charlie's Cafe. When she was gone, he made a cheese sandwich and washed it down with chocolate milk.

After supper he went up to his room and experimented with the new tape recorder for a while. It was a fine machine. In spite of its compact size, it provided a clear and remarkably lifelike reproduction of his voice. It was capable of picking up voices from as much as thirty feet away, as promised, but at its maximum range the fidelity was not adequate for Colin's purposes. He tested the machine again and again and determined that it could record a conversational tone of voice only up to twenty-five feet. That was good enough.

He went into his mother's bedroom and looked in the nightstands, then the dresser. The gun was in a dresser drawer. It was a pistol. There were two safety catches, and when you switched them off, a pair of red warning dots shone on the blue-black gun metal. When he had told Roy about the pistol, he had said that it probably wasn't even loaded. But it was. He put the safeties on again and replaced the weapon; it rested on a pile of his mother's silky panties.

He called Heather, and they discussed the plan again, searching for potential problems that they had overlooked before. The scheme still appeared to be workable.

"Tomorrow, I'll talk to Mrs. Borden," Colin said.

"Do you think it's really necessary?"

"Yes," he said. "If I can get her to open up even a little bit and get it on tape, it'll help support our story."

"But if Roy knows you've been talking to her, he might get suspicious. He might realize something's up, and we'll lose the advantage of surprise."

"They don't communicate well in that family," Colin said. "Maybe she won't even tell Roy she talked to me."

"And maybe she will."

"We have to risk it. If she tells us something that helps explain Roy, something that explains his motivation, then we'll have an easier time getting the police to believe us."

"Well . . . okay," Heather said. "But call me after you've talked to her. I want to hear all about it."

"I will. And then tomorrow night we'll set the trap for Roy."

She was silent a moment. Then she said, "So soon?"

"There's no reason to wait any longer."

"It wouldn't hurt to take an extra day or two to think about it. The plan, I mean. Maybe there's a hole in it. Maybe we're overlooking something."

"We aren't," he said. "We've talked about it and thought about it enough. It'll work."

"Well . . . all right."

"You can always back out," he said.

"No."

"I won't hold it against you."

"No," she said. "I'm going to help you. You need me. We'll do it tomorrow night."

Several hours later, Colin woke from a nightmare, sweating and shaking. He couldn't remember exactly what the dream had been about. The only thing he could recall was that Heather had been in it; her screams had awakened him.

THIRTY-EIGHT

◆

At eleven-thirty Sunday morning, Colin went down to the harbor and sat on a bench on the boardwalk, where he could see every approach to a store called Treasured Things. It was a gift shop that survived off the tourists. In Treasured Things you could buy postcards, lamps made out of seashells, belts made out of seashells, paperweights made out of seashells, seashells made out of chocolate, T-shirts bearing supposedly funny slogans, books about Santa Leona, candles shaped like the famous bell tower of Santa Leona Mission, china plates painted with scenes of Santa Leona, and a wide variety of other useless junk. Roy Borden's mother worked in the shop five afternoons a week, including Sundays.

Colin was carrying a folded nylon windbreaker. The new tape recorder was concealed in it. Even with the stiff breeze coming in off the ocean, the day was much too warm for a jacket, but Colin didn't think Mrs. Borden would notice it. After all, there was no reason for her to be suspicious of him.

A lot of people were strolling along the boardwalk, talking and laughing and window-shopping and eating chocolate-covered bananas; and a number of them were good-looking, leggy young girls in shorts and bikinis. Colin forced himself not to stare at them. He didn't want to be distracted, to miss Helen Borden, and then have to approach her in the busy gift shop.

He spotted her at ten minutes of twelve. She was a thin, birdlike woman. She walked briskly, head up, shoulders back, very businesslike.

He reached into the folded windbreaker and switched on the recorder, then got up and hurried across the wide boardwalk. He intercepted her before she reached Treasured Things.

"Mrs. Borden?"

She stopped abruptly at the sound of her name and turned to him. She was clearly perplexed. She didn't recognize him.

"We've met twice," he said, "but only for a minute or two each time. I'm Colin Jacobs. Roy's friend."

"Oh. Oh yes."

"I have to talk to you."

"I'm on my way to work."

"It's important."

She looked at her watch.

"Very, very important," he said.

She hesitated, glanced at the gift shop.

"It's about your daughter," he said.

Her head snapped around.

"It's about Belinda Jane," he said.

Helen Borden's face was well tanned. At the mention of her dead daughter's name, the tan remained but the blood drained out of the skin beneath it. She looked suddenly old and sick.

"I know how she died," Colin said.

Mrs. Borden said nothing.

"Roy told me about it," he lied.

The woman appeared to be frozen. Her eyes were cold.

"We talked for hours about Belinda," Colin said.

When she spoke her thin lips barely moved. "This is none of your business."

"Roy made it my business," Colin said. "I didn't want to hear about it. But he told me secrets."

She glared at him.

"Awful secrets," he said. "About how Belinda died."

"That's no secret. I know how she died. I *saw*. It was . . . an accident. A horrible accident."

"Was it? Are you absolutely sure?"

"What are you saying?"

"He told me these secrets, made me swear never to tell anyone. But I can't keep it in. It's too awful."

"What did he tell you?"

"Why he killed her."

"It was an accident."

"He'd been planning it for months," Colin lied.

She suddenly took him by one arm and led him across the boardwalk to an isolated bench by the railing. He was holding the windbreaker in that same arm, and he was afraid that she would discover the tape recorder. She didn't. They sat side by side with the sea at their backs.

"He told you he murdered her?"

"Yeah."

She shook her head. "No. It had to be an accident. It had to be. He was only eight years old."

"I think maybe some kids are born bad," Colin said. "I mean, you know, not many. Just a few. But every once in a while, you know, you read about it in the papers, about how some young kid committed cold-blooded murder. I think maybe, you know, like one in a hundred thousand is born twisted. You know? *Born* evil. And whatever a kid like that does, you can't blame it on the way he was raised or the things he was taught because, you know, he was born to be the way he is.''

She stared intently at him as he rambled on, but he wasn't sure that she heard a word he said. When he finally stopped, she was silent for a while, and then she said, ''What does he want from me?''

Colin blinked. ''Who?''

''Roy. Why did he put you up to this?''

''He didn't,'' Colin protested. ''Please, don't tell him I talked to you. Please, Mrs. Borden. If he knew I was here, telling you this, he'd kill me.''

''Belinda's death was an accident,'' she said. But she didn't sound convinced of that.

''You didn't always think it was accidental,'' he said.

''How do you know?''

''That's why you beat Roy.''

''I didn't.''

''He told me.''

''He lied.''

''That's where he got the scars.''

She was nervous, fidgety.

''It was one year after Belinda died.''

''What did he tell you?'' she asked.

''That you beat him because you knew he killed her on purpose.''

''He said that?''

''Yeah.''

She turned slightly on the bench so that she could look out to sea. ''I'd just finished cleaning and waxing the kitchen floor. It was clean as a whistle. Perfect. Absolutely spotless. You could have eaten off that floor. Then he came in with muddy shoes. He was mocking me. He didn't say a word, but when I saw him walking across that floor in his muddy shoes, I knew he was mocking me. He had killed Belinda, and now he was mocking me, and in some way one thing seemed as bad as the other. I wanted to kill him.''

Colin almost sighed with relief. He hadn't been sure that Mrs. Borden had put the scars on her son's back. He had been operating on a hunch, and now that it had proved true, he felt more secure about the rest of his theory.

''I knew he'd killed her on purpose. But they wouldn't believe me,'' she said.

''I know.''

''I always knew it. There was never a time I didn't know it. He killed his baby sister.'' She was talking to herself now, looking out to sea and into the past as well. ''When I hit him, I was just trying to make him admit the truth. She deserved that much, didn't she? She was dead, and she deserved to have her killer punished. But they didn't believe me.''

Her voice trailed away, and she was silent for so long that Colin finally tried to get her talking again. ''Roy laughed about that. He thought it was funny that no one took you seriously.''

She didn't need much coaxing. ''They said I had a nervous breakdown. Sent me away to the county hospital. I had therapy. They called it that. Therapy. As if I was the crazy one. An expensive psychiatrist. He treated me as if I were a child. A foolish man. I was there a long time—until I realized that all I had to do was pretend that I'd been wrong about Roy.''

''You never were wrong.''

She looked at him. ''He told you why he killed Belinda?''

''Yeah.''

"What reason did he give?"

Colin shifted uneasily on the bench because he didn't have an answer to her question, and he didn't want her to realize that he had engaged her attention with a string of lies. He had been leading her on, trying to get her to say certain things that he wanted to have on the tape. She said some of them, but not all of them. He hoped to keep her confidence until he had everything he needed.

Fortunately, when he hesitated, Mrs. Borden answered the question for him. "It was jealousy, wasn't it? He was jealous of my little girl because after she was born he knew he'd never really be one of us."

"Yeah. That's what he told me," Colin said, though he wasn't sure what she meant.

"It was a mistake," she said. "We never should have adopted him."

"Adopted?"

"He didn't tell you that?"

"Well . . . no."

He'd blown it. She would wonder why Roy had revealed everything else, every ugly secret, but not this. Then she'd realize that Roy hadn't told him anything about Belinda Jane, that he was lying, that he was playing a bizarre game with her.

But she surprised him. She was so deeply involved in her memories, and so focused on the fact that her son had admitted to premeditated sororicide, that she didn't have the presence of mind to consider the curious gaps in Colin's knowledge.

"We wanted a child more than anything in the world," she said, looking out to sea once more. "A child of our own. But the doctors said we never could. My fault. There were . . . things wrong with me. Alex, my husband, was terribly upset. Terribly. He had counted so much on a child of his own. But the doctors said it just wasn't possible. We went to half a dozen doctors, and they all said the same thing. Not remotely possible. Because of me. So I talked him into adoption. My fault again. Entirely my fault. It was the wrong thing to do. We don't even know who Roy's real parents were—or *what* they were. That bothers Alex. What kind of people did Roy come from? What was wrong with them? What flaws and sickness did they pass on to him? It was an awful mistake to take him in. By the time we'd had him a few months, I knew he was wrong for us. He was a good baby, but Alex didn't take to him. I'd wanted so much for Alex to have his child, but what *he* wanted was a child with his own blood in its veins. That was quite important to Alex. You can't imagine *how* important. An adopted child is different from your flesh, Alex says. He says you can't ever feel as close to it as you can to your own blood. He says it's like training a dangerous wild animal from the time it's a cub and keeping it as a pet; you just never know when it might turn on you because deep down it isn't at all like what you've tried to make it. And so that was another thing I'd done wrong: bringing someone else's child into our home. A stranger. And he turned on us. I'm always doing something wrong. I've failed Alex. All he ever wanted was a child of his own."

When Colin had been sitting on the bench, waiting for her to show up, he had expected to have trouble getting her to talk. But he had pushed the right button. She wouldn't shut up. She droned on and on, as if she were an Ancient Mariner robot, a machine with a tale to tell. And it looked to him as if she were also a machine with very little time left; beneath the cool veneer of businesslike efficiency, serious instabilities were generating a lot of inner heat. As he listened to what she said, he also listened for the sound of gears stripping and mainsprings breaking and vacuum tubes popping.

"We'd had Roy two and a half years," she said, "when I discovered that I was going to have a baby. The doctors were wrong about me. I almost died in labor, and there was no doubt afterward that she would be my first and last, but I *did* have her. They were wrong. In spite of all their complicated tests and consultations and sky-high fees, every one of them was wrong. She was a miracle child. God meant all along for us to have the impossible, the miracle child, that special blessing, and I was too impatient to wait. I didn't have faith enough. Not nearly enough. I hate myself for that. I talked Alex into the adoption. Then along came Belinda, the one we were *meant* to have. I had no faith. So after just five years, she was taken away from us. Roy took her away from us. The child we were never meant to have took away the one that God sent us. You see?"

Colin's fascination was changing to embarrassment. He didn't need or want to hear every sordid detail. He looked around self-consciously to see if anyone could overhear, but there was no one near the bench.

She turned away from the sea and stared into his eyes. "Why did you come here, young man? Why did you tell me Roy's secret?"

He shrugged. "I thought you ought to know."

"Did you expect me to do something to him?"

"Aren't you going to?"

"I wish I could," she said with genuine malice. "But I can't. If I start telling them that he killed my little girl, it'll be like before. They'll send me away to the county hospital again."

"Oh." That was what he had figured even before he spoke to her.

"Nobody will ever believe me when it comes to Roy," she said. "And who's going to believe you? I understand from your mother that there's some problem with drugs."

"No. That's not true."

"Who's going to believe either of us?"

"No one," he said.

"What we need is proof."

"Yeah."

"Irrefutable proof."

"Right."

"Something tangible," she said. "Maybe . . . if you could get him to tell you all about it again . . . about how he killed her on purpose . . . and maybe have a tape recorder hidden someplace. . . ."

Colin winced at the mention of a recorder. "That's a thought."

"There must be a way," she said.

"Yeah."

"We'll both think about it."

"All right."

"Think about a way to trap him."

"Okay."

"And we'll meet again."

"We will?"

"Here," she said. "Tomorrow."

"But—"

"It's always been just me against him," she said, leaning close to Colin. He could feel her breath against his face. And he could smell it, too: spearmint. "But now there's you," she said. "Two people know about him now. Together we ought to be able to think of a way to get him. I want to get him. I want everyone to know how he *planned* to kill my little girl. When they know the truth, how can they expect me to keep him in my house? We'll send him back where he came from. The neighbors won't talk. How can they, after they know what he did? I'll be free of him. I want that more than anything." Her voice fell to a conspiratorial whisper. "You'll be my ally, won't you?"

He had the insane thought that she was going to go through the blood-brother ritual with him.

"Won't you?" she asked.

"Okay." But he didn't intend to meet with her again; she was almost as scary as Roy.

She put her hand on his cheek, and he started to pull away before he realized that she was only being affectionate. Her fingers were cold.

"You're a good boy," she said. "You did a good thing—coming to me like this."

He wished she would take her hand away.

"I've always known the truth," she said, "but what a relief it is to have someone else who knows. You be here tomorrow. Same time."

Just to get rid of her, he said, "Sure."

She got up abruptly and walked away, toward Treasured Things.

As Colin watched her go, he thought that she was far more terrifying than any of the monsters he'd feared throughout his childhood and adolescence. Christopher Lee, Peter Cushing, Boris Karloff, Bela Lugosi—none of them had ever portrayed a character quite as chilling as Helen Borden. She was worse than a ghoul or a vampire, doubly dangerous because she was so well disguised. She looked rather ordinary, even drab, unremarkable in every respect, but inside she was an awful creature. He could still feel where her icy fingers had pressed against his face.

He took the recorder out of the windbreaker and switched it off.

Incredibly, he was ashamed of himself for some of the things he had said about Roy, and for the way he had so eagerly played to her hatred of her son. It was true that Roy was sick; it was also true that he was a killer; but it was not true that he had always been that way. He wasn't, as Colin had said, "born evil." Fundamentally, he was not less of a human being than anyone else. He had not murdered his sister in cold blood. Judging from all the evidence that Colin had seen, Belinda Jane's death had been an accident. Roy's sickness had developed in the aftermath of that tragedy.

Depressed, Colin got off the bench and went out to the parking lot. He unchained his bike from the security rack.

He no longer wanted revenge against Roy. He just wanted to put a stop to the violence. He wanted to get the evidence so the proper authorities would believe and act. He was weary.

Although it was pointless to tell them, although they would never understand, Mr. and Mrs. Borden were killers, too. They had turned Roy into one of the living dead.

THIRTY-NINE

◆

Colin called Heather.

"Did you talk to Roy's mother?" she asked.

"Yeah. And I got more than I bargained for."

"Tell me."

"It's too complicated over the phone. You've got to hear the tape."

"Why don't you bring it here? My parents are gone for the day."

"I'll be there in fifteen minutes."

"Don't come by the front way," she said. "Roy just might happen to be at the cemetery across the street; you never can tell. Take the alley and come through the backyard."

He made certain he wasn't followed, and she was waiting for him on the patio behind the house. They went into the cheery yellow-and-white kitchen, sat at the table, and listened to the taped conversation between him and Mrs. Borden.

When Colin finally switched off the machine, Heather said, "It's awful."

"I know."

"Poor Roy."

"I know what you mean," Colin said morosely.

"I'm kind of sorry I said those mean things about him. He can't help what he is, can he?"

"It affected me the same way. But we can't let ourselves feel too sorry for him. Not yet. We don't dare. We've got to remember that he's dangerous. We've got to keep in mind that he'd happily kill me—and rape and kill you—if he thought he could get away with it."

The kitchen clock ticked hollowly.

Heather said, "If we played this tape for the police, it might convince them."

"Of what? That Roy was an abused child? That he was maybe abused enough to grow up twisted? Yeah. Maybe it would convince them of that, all right. But it wouldn't prove a thing. It wouldn't prove that Roy killed those two boys or that he tried to wreck a train the other night or that he's trying to kill me. We need more than this. We have to go through with the rest of the plan."

"Tonight," she said.

"Yeah."

FORTY

♦

Weezy came home at five-thirty, and they had an early supper together. She brought stuff from the deli: sliced ham, sliced turkey breast, sliced cheese, macaroni salad, potato salad, big dill pickles, and wedges of cheesecake. There was a lot of food, but neither of them ate much; she was always watching her figure, conscious of every extra ounce, and Colin was simply too worried about the coming night to have much of an appetite.

"You going back to the gallery?" he asked.

"In about an hour."

"Be home at nine?"

"'Fraid not. We close at nine, sweep the floor, dust the furniture, and open again at ten."

"What for?"

"We've having a private, invitation-only showing of a new artist."

"At ten o'clock at night?"

"It's supposed to be an elegant after-dinner affair. Guests will have their choice of brandy or champagne. Sound swell to you?"

"I guess."

She put a daub of mustard on her plate, rolled up a slice of ham, dipped the ham in the mustard, and nibbled daintily. "All of our best local customers are coming."

"How late will it last?"

"Midnight or thereabouts."

"Will you come home after that?"

"I expect so."

He tasted the cheesecake.

"Don't forget your curfew," she said.

"I won't."

"You be home before dark."

"You can trust me."

"I hope so. For your sake, I hope so."

"Call and check if you want."

"I probably will."

"I'll be here," he lied.

After she had showered and changed and left for the evening, he went into her room and took the pistol from the dresser drawer. He put it in a small cardboard box. He also put the tape recorder, two flashlights, and a squeeze bottle of ketchup in the box. He took a dish towel out of the linen closet and cut it in half, the long way. He put the two strips of cloth with the other things. He went out to the garage and fetched a coil of rope from the wall, where it had been hanging ever since they moved into the house, and he added that to the bundle.

He had some time to kill before he could set out for the Kingman house. He went to his room and tried to work on one of his monster models. He couldn't do it. His hands wouldn't stop shaking.

An hour before nightfall, he picked up the box that contained the pistol, the tape recorder, and the other items. He left the house and strapped the package to the carrier on his bicycle. He followed an indirect route to the abandoned Kingman house at the top of Hawk Drive, and he was certain he was not followed.

Heather was waiting just inside the front door of the ruined mansion. She stepped out of the shadows when Colin arrived. She was wearing short blue shorts and a long-sleeved white blouse, and she was beautiful.

He put the bicycle on its side, out of sight in the tall dry grass, and he carried the cardboard box inside.

The house was always a strange place, but perhaps even stranger than usual at twilight. The slanting copper sunlight streamed through a few broken, shutterless windows and gave the place a somewhat bloody look. Motes of dust spun lazily in the fading beams. In one corner a huge spider web gleamed like crystal. The shadows crept as if they were living things.

"I look terrible," Heather said as soon as he joined her in the house.

"You look great. Terrific."

"My shampoo didn't work," she said. "My hair came out all stringy."

"Your hair is nice. Very nice. You couldn't ask for prettier hair."

"He's not going to be interested in me," she said, quite sure of that. "As soon as he sees that it's me you've got here, he'll just turn and walk out."

"Don't be silly. You're perfect. Absolutely perfect."

"Do you really think so?"

"I really do." He gave her a warm, tender, lingering kiss. Her lips were soft, tremulous. "Come on," he said gently. "We have to get the trap set." He was involving her in an extremely dangerous situation, using her, manipulating her, not unlike Roy had manipulated him, and he hated himself for it. But he didn't call it off while there was still time.

She followed him, and as he started up the stairs toward the second floor, she said, "Why not down here?"

He stopped, turned, looked down at her. "The shutters have fallen or been torn off almost all the windows on the first floor. If we staged it down there, the lights would be visible outside the house. We might attract someone. Other kids. They might interrupt us before we've gotten what we want out of Roy. Some of the rooms on the second floor still have all their shutters."

"If something goes wrong," she said, "it would be easier to get away from him if we were on the first floor."

"Nothing's going to go wrong," he said. "Besides, we've got the gun. Remember?" He patted the box that he was carrying under his right arm.

He started up the steps again and was relieved to hear her following him.

The second-floor hall was gloomy, and the room he was interested in was dark except for threads of late-afternoon sun around the edges of the bolted shutters. He switched on one of the flashlights.

He had chosen a large bedroom just to the left of the head of the stairs. Ancient, yellowed wallpaper was peeling off the walls and hanging in long loops across the ceiling, like old bunting left over from a festive occasion a hundred years ago. The room was dusty and smelled vaguely of mildew, but it wasn't littered with rubble as many of the other chambers were; there were only scattered pieces of lath and a few chunks of plaster and a couple of ribbons of wallpaper on the floor along the far wall.

He handed Heather the flashlight and put down the box. He picked up the second light, turned it on, and propped it against the wall so that the beam shone up at the ceiling and was reflected back down.

"It's a spooky place," Heather said.

"There's nothing to be scared of," Colin said.

He took the tape recorder out of the box and placed it on the floor, near the wall that was opposite the door. He gathered up some of the rubble and carefully arranged it over the small machine, letting only the head of the microphone in the open, and concealing even that in a shadowy little pocket of tangled wallpaper.

"Does it look natural?" he asked.

"I guess so."

"Look at it closely."

She did. "It's okay. It doesn't look arranged."

"You can't see the recorder at all?"

"No."

He retrieved the second flashlight and shone it on the pile of trash, looking closely for a glint of metal or plastic, a reflection that would betray the trick.

"Okay," he said at last, satisfied with his work. "I think it'll fool him. He probably won't even give it a second look."

"Now what?" she asked.

"We've got to make you look like you've been roughed up a bit," Colin said. "Roy won't believe a word of it unless you look like you put up a struggle." He took the squeeze bottle of ketchup out of the box.

"What's that for?"

"Blood."

"Are you serious?"

"I'll admit it's trite," Colin said. "But it ought to be effective."

He squeezed some of the ketchup onto his fingers, then artfully smeared it along her left temple, matting her golden hair with it.

She winced. "Yuck."

Colin stepped back a couple of feet and studied her. "Good," he said. "It's a little too bright right now. Too red. But when it dries a bit, it ought to look just about like the real thing."

"If we'd really struggled, like you're going to tell him we did, then I'd be rumpled and dirty," she said.

"Right."

She pulled her blouse half out of her shorts. She stooped, wiped her hands over the dust-covered floor, and made long sooty marks on her shorts and blouse.

When she stood up, Colin regarded her critically, looking for the false note, trying to see her as Roy would see her. "Yeah. That's better. But maybe one more thing might help."

"What's that?"

"If the sleeve of your blouse was torn."

She frowned. "It's one of my better blouses."

"I'll pay for it."

She shook her head. "No. I said I'd help. I'm in this all the way. Go ahead. Tear it."

He jerked on the material on both sides of her left shoulder seam, jerked once, twice, three times. The stitching finally parted with a nasty sound, and the sleeve sagged on her arm, torn half away.

"Yeah," he said. "That sure does it. You're very, very convincing."

"But now that I'm such a mess, will he want anything to do with me?"

"It's funny. . . ." Colin stared at her thoughtfully. "In a strange way, you're even more appealing than you were before."

"Are you sure? I mean, I'm all dirty. And I wasn't all that fabulous when I was clean."

"You look great," he assured her. "Just right."

"But if this is going to work, he really has to want to . . . well . . . he has to want to rape me. I mean, he'll never get the chance. But he has to *want* to."

Again, Colin was acutely aware of the danger into which he was putting her, and he didn't like himself very much.

"There's just one more thing I can do that might help," she said.

Before he realized what she intended, she grasped the front of her blouse and tugged hard on it. Buttons popped; one of them struck Colin's chin. She tore the blouse open all the way, and for an instant he saw one small, beautiful, quivering breast and a dark nipple, but then the halves of the blouse fell part of the way together again, and he could see nothing more than the soft, sweet swell of flesh that marked the beginning of her breasts.

He looked up, met her eyes.

She was blushing fiercely.

For a long moment neither of them spoke.

He licked his lips. His throat was suddenly parched.

At last, trembling, she said, "I don't know. Maybe it doesn't help much to have my blouse open a little. I mean, I don't have much to show."

"Perfect," he said weakly. "It's the perfect touch." He looked away from her, went to the cardboard box, and picked up the coil of rope.

"I wish I didn't have to be tied up," she said.

"There's no other way," he said. "But you won't really be tied. Not tightly. The rope will just be wrapped around your wrists a few times; it won't be knotted there. You'll be able to get your hands free in a flash. And where there are knots, they'll be the kind that slip open easily. I'll show you how. You'll be able to get out of the ropes in a couple of seconds if you have to. But you *won't* have to. He won't get anywhere near you. He won't get his hands on you. Nothing will go wrong. I have the gun."

She sat down on the floor, with her back against the wall. "Let's get it over with."

By the time he finished tying her, night had fallen outside, and there were not even threads of light at the unraveling edges of the aging, splintered shutters.

"It's time to make the phone call," Colin said.

"I'm going to hate being alone in this place."

"It'll only be for a few minutes."

"Can you leave both flashlights?" she asked.

He was moved by her fear; he knew what it was like. But he said, "Can't. I'll need one to get in and out of the house without breaking my neck in the dark."

"I wish you'd brought three."

"You'll have enough light with one," he said, knowing that it would be pathetically little comfort in this creepy place.

"Hurry back," she said.

"I will."

He stood up and walked away from her. At the doorway he turned and looked back. She was so vulnerable that he could hardly stand it. He knew he should return and take the ropes off her and send her home. But he had to trap Roy, get the truth on tape, and this was the easiest way to accomplish that.

He left the room and went down the stairs to the first floor, then out of the mansion by way of the front door.

The plan would work.

It *had* to work.

If something went wrong, his and Heather's bloody heads might wind up on the mantel in the Kingman house.

FORTY-ONE

◆

Colin stepped into a telephone booth at a service station, four blocks from the Kingman mansion. He dialed the Borden number.

Roy answered. "Hello?"

"Is that you, blood brother?"

Roy didn't respond.

"I was wrong," Colin said.

Roy was silent.

"I called to say I was wrong."

"Wrong about what?"

"Everything. About breaking our blood-brother oath."

"What're you after?" Roy asked.

"I want to be friends again."

"You're an asshole."

"I mean it. I really want to be friends again, Roy."

"It isn't possible."

"You're smarter than all of them," Colin said. "You're smarter and tougher. You're right; they're all a bunch of jerks. The grown-ups, too. It's easy to manipulate them. I see that now. I'm not one of them. I never was. I'm like you. I want to be on your side."

Roy was silent again.

"I'll prove I'm on your side," Colin said. "I'll do what you wanted to do. I'll help you kill someone."

"Kill someone? Colin, have you been popping pills again? You aren't making sense."

"You think I've got someone listening in on this," Colin said. "Well, I don't. But if you're worried about talking on the phone, then let's talk face to face."

"When?"

"Now."

"Where?"

"The Kingman house," Colin said.

"Why there?"

"It's the best place."

"I can think of better."

"Not for what we're going to do. It's private, and that's what we need."

"For what? What are you talking about?"

"We're going to screw her and then kill her," Colin said.

"Are you crazy? What kind of talk is that?"

"There's no one listening in, Roy."

"You're a lunatic."

"You'll like her," Colin said.

"You must be full of dope."

"She's foxy."

"Who?"

"The girl I've got for us."

"*You* lined up a girl?"

"She doesn't know what's going to happen."

"Who is she?"

"She's my peace offering to you," Colin said.

"What girl? What's her name?"

"Come and see."

Roy didn't respond.

"Are you scared of me?" Colin asked.

"Hell, no."

"Then give me a chance. Let's meet at the Kingman house."

"You and your doper buddies are probably laying for me," Roy said. "You planning to gang up on me?"

Colin laughed sourly. "You're good, Roy. You're real good. That's why I want to be on your side. Nobody's smarter than you are."

"You've got to stop gobbling pills," Roy said. "Colin, dope kills. You're going to ruin yourself."

"So come talk to me about it. Convince me to go straight."

"I've got something to do for my father. I can't get out of it. I won't be able to get away from here for at least an hour."

"Okay," Colin said. "It's almost a quarter past nine. We'll meet at the Kingman place at ten-thirty."

Colin hung up, opened the telephone-booth door, and ran like hell. He went back up the steep hill, fast as he could, arms tucked close to his sides.

He reached the Kingman house, went through the gate, up the walk. Inside, he climbed the creaking stairs and heard Heather hesitantly calling his name before he reached the second floor.

She was still in the first bedroom on the left, sitting as he had left her, roped, ravishing.

"I was afraid it was someone else," she said.

"You okay?"

"One flashlight wasn't enough," she said. "It was too dark in here."

"Sorry."

"And I think this place has rats. I heard scratching noises in the walls."

"We won't have to stay here much longer," he said. He bent over the cardboard box and snatched out the two long strips of dish towel that he had brought from home. "Things are moving fast now."

"Did you talk to Roy?"

"Yeah."

"He's coming?"

"He says he's got things to do for his father and can't get out of the house right away. He says he can't make it before ten-thirty."

"Then it wasn't necessary to tie me up before you made the call," she said.

"Yes, it was," he said. "Don't pull the ropes apart. He's on his way now."

"I thought you said ten-thirty."

"He was lying."

"How do you know?"

"I just *know*. He's trying to get here ahead of me and set a trap. He thinks I'm as naïve as I used to be."

"Colin . . . I'm scared."

"It'll be all right."

"Will it?"

"I have the gun."

"What if you have to use it?"

"I won't have to."

"He might force you to."

"Then I will. I'll use it if he forces me."

"But then you'd be guilty—"

"Of self-defense," Colin said.

"*Can* you use it?"

"In self-defense. Sure. Of course."

"You aren't a killer."

"I'll just wound him if I have to," he said. "Now we've got to hurry. I've got to put the gag on you. It has to be tight if it's going to look convincing, but tell me if I make it too tight for comfort." He fashioned a gag from the two pieces of the dish towel, then said, "Okay?"

She made an unintelligible sound.

"Shake your head—yes or no. Is it too tight?"

She shook her head: no.

He could see that her doubts were growing by the second; she wished she'd never gotten into this. Genuine fear sparked in her eyes, but that was good; it made her look as if she really were the helpless victim that she was pretending to be. Roy, possessed of the instincts of a cunning, vicious animal, would instantly recognize her terror and would be convinced by it.

Colin went to the tape recorder, lifted a piece of trash that was covering it, switched it on, carefully replaced the camouflage, and looked at Heather again. "I'm going out to the head of the stairs to wait for him. Don't worry."

He left the room, taking the pistol, one flashlight, and the cardboard box that now contained only the squeeze bottle of ketchup. He put the ketchup and the box in another room, then went to the head of the stairs and switched off his light.

The house was very dark.

He tucked the pistol under his belt, against the small of his back, where Roy couldn't see it. He wanted to appear unarmed, defenseless, in order to sucker Roy upstairs.

Colin was breathing noisily, virtually gasping, not because he was physically exhausted, but because he was afraid. He concentrated on breathing quietly, but it wasn't easy.

Something crashed downstairs.

He held his breath, listened.

Another noise.

Roy had arrived.

Colin looked at his read-out watch. Exactly fifteen minutes had passed since he'd left the telephone booth.

It was exactly as Colin had told Heather: Roy had lied about not being able to make it until ten-thirty. He had just wanted to be sure he was the first person in the house. If a trap was going to be laid for him, he intended to be there in the shadows to watch it being set.

Colin had anticipated this development, and he felt good about that. Standing in the dark hall, he smiled.

Something moved in the wall beside him, and he jumped. A mouse. Nothing more than that. It wasn't Roy. He could still hear Roy downstairs. Just a mouse. Maybe a rat. At worst, a couple of rats. Nothing to worry about. But he knew he had better guard against overconfidence, because if he didn't he would be nothing but food for those rats before the night was out.

Footsteps.

A flashlight, hooded by a hand.

The light moved to the foot of the stairs.

Roy was coming up.

Suddenly, Colin felt that the plan was childish, stupid, naïve. It would never work. Not in a million years. He and Heather were going to die.

He swallowed hard and switched on his own light, shone it down the steps. "Hello, Roy."

FORTY-TWO

◆

Roy stopped, pointed his flashlight at Colin.

For several seconds they stared at each other. Colin could see the hatred in Roy's eyes and he wondered if his own fear was equally visible.

"You're here already," Roy said.

"The girl's up here."

"There isn't any girl."

"Come see."

"Who is she?"

"Come see," Colin said.

"What's the trick?"

"There isn't one. I told you on the phone. I want to be on your side. I've tried being on *their* side. It didn't work. They don't believe me. They don't care about me. None of them. I hate them. All of them. My mother, too. You were right about her. She's a fucking bitch. You were right about all of them. They'll never help me. Never. They're no good to me at all. And I don't want to have to run from you forever. I don't want to have to be looking over my shoulder for the rest of my life. You can't be beat. You'll get me sooner or later. You're a winner.

You win at everything eventually. I see that now. I'm tired of being a loser. That's why I want to be on your side. I want to win. I want to get even with them, all of them. I'll do anything you want to do, Roy. Anything.''

"So you got a girl for us."

"Yeah."

"How'd you get her up there?"

"I saw her yesterday," Colin said, trying to sound excited, as if he hadn't carefully worked out every word of what he was about to say. "I was riding my bike, just cruising, thinking, trying to think of some way to make up with you. I passed here, and I saw her sitting on the front walk. She had a drawing tablet. She's interested in art. She was sketching the mansion. I stopped and talked to her, and I found out she'd been working on sketches of the place for a few days. She said she was coming back this evening, so she could draw the place with late-afternoon shadows. I knew right away she was what I was looking for. I knew if I gave her to you that we'd be friends again. She's foxy as hell, Roy. She's really something. I set up a trap for her. Now she's up here, in one of the bedrooms, tied and gagged."

"Just like that?" Roy asked.

"Huh?"

"You just set a trap and single-handedly tied and gagged her. It was that easy?"

"Hell, no!" Colin said. "It wasn't easy at all. I had to hit her. Knocked her out. Bloodied her up a little. But I got her. You'll see."

Roy stared up at him, thinking about it, making up his mind to either stay or leave. His icy eyes gleamed in the thin, cold light.

"Are you coming?" Colin asked. "Or are you afraid to really do it to her?"

Roy slowly climbed the steps.

Colin backed away from the head of the stairs to the open door of the room where Heather waited.

Roy stepped into the second-floor hallway.

The two boys were no more than fifteen feet apart.

"In here," Colin said.

But Roy stayed against the far wall and moved toward the door of the room opposite the one where Colin wanted him to go.

"What are you doing?" Colin asked.

"I want to see who else is here," Roy said.

"No one. I told you."

"I want to see for myself."

Keeping one eye on Colin, Roy shone his light into the room across the hall. Colin thought of the cardboard box he had left in there, and his heart began to pound furiously. He knew the trick would be exposed and the plan ruined if Roy saw the bottle of ketchup. But the box must not have looked out of place among the other trash that littered the floors of the rotting mansion, for Roy didn't go into the room to investigate it. He moved on down the hall to see whether the rest of the second floor was deserted.

Colin waited in the doorway until Roy had looked in all the other rooms.

"No one," Roy said.

"I'm being straight with you."

Roy started toward him.

Colin backed into the bedroom and went quickly to Heather. He stood beside her.

She looked as if she might scream in spite of the gag in her mouth. Colin wanted to smile and reassure her, but he didn't dare; Roy might step inside and see the exchange, and then he would realize they were in collusion.

Roy entered cautiously. Shadows danced out from his moving flashlight beam. When he saw the girl, he stopped, surprised. He was only fifteen feet away, and he was blocking the only exit; this was the moment of truth. "Is that . . . ?"

"Yeah," Colin said thickly. "You know her? Isn't she something?"

Roy looked her over with growing interest. Colin saw the boy's eyes lingering on the curve of her smooth, sleek calves, then her knees, then her taut thighs. For a minute Roy didn't seem capable of lifting his gaze from those slender, shapely legs. Then he finally looked up at her ruined blouse, at the swell of breasts that were partly visible through the torn material. He looked at the ropes, at the gag in her mouth, and at her wide, frightened eyes. He saw that she was genuinely afraid, and her fear pleased him. He smiled and turned to Colin. "You did it."

Colin knew the trick had worked. Roy couldn't conceive of Colin and Heather setting a trap all by themselves, without adults to back them up. As soon as Roy had seen that they were alone in the mansion, that there were no reinforcements waiting in another room, he had been convinced. The Colin he knew was too much of a coward to try anything like that. But the Colin he knew no longer existed. The new Colin was a stranger to him.

"You really, really did it," Roy said.

"Didn't I tell you?"

"Is that blood on her head?"

"I had to hit her pretty hard. She was unconscious for a while," Colin said.

"Jesus."

"Now do you believe me?"

"You really want to fuck her?" Roy asked.

"Yeah."

"Then kill her?"

"Yeah."

Heather protested through her gag, but her voice was weak and unintelligible.

"How will we kill her?" Roy asked.

"You have your penknife with you?"

"Yeah."

"Well," Colin said, "I've got mine, too."

"You mean—stab her?"

"Just like you did the cat."

"With penknives, it'll take a long time."

"The longer the better—right?"

Roy grinned. "Right."

"So are we friends again?"

"I guess we are."

"Blood brothers?"

"Well . . . all right. Sure. You've made up for what you did."

"You'll stop trying to kill me?"

"I'd never hurt a blood brother."

"You tried to hurt me before."

"Because you stopped acting like a blood brother."

"You won't throw me off a cliff like you did Steve Rose?"

"He wasn't my blood brother," Roy said.

"You won't squirt lighter fluid on me and set me on fire like you did Phil Pacino?"

"He wasn't my blood brother either," Roy said impatiently.

"You tried to set me on fire."

"Only when I thought you betrayed our oath. You didn't want to be my blood brother any more, so you were fair game. But now you want to uphold the oath, so you're safe. I won't hurt you now. Not ever. In fact, it's just the opposite. Don't you see? You're my blood brother. I'd die for you if I had to."

"Okay," Colin said.

"But don't ever turn against me again like you did before," Roy said. "I guess a blood brother ought to be given a second chance. But not a third."

"Don't worry," Colin said. "We're together from here on out. Just the two of us."

Roy looked down at Heather again and licked his lips. He put one hand on his crotch and rubbed himself through his jeans. "We're going to have fun," Roy said, "and this little bitch is just the start of it. You'll see, Colin. You understand now. You understand how it's us against them. We're going to have a barrel of laughs. It'll be a real popper."

Conscious of the tape recorder, his heart exploding as Roy took a step toward Heather, Colin said, "If you want, some night we'll go back out to the junkyard and push that old truck down on the tracks, in front of a train."

"Nah," Roy said. "We can't do that any more. Not now that you've told your old lady about it. We'll figure something else." He took another step toward Heather. "Come on. Let's get that gag out of her mouth. I have something else I'm aching to put between her pretty lips."

Colin reached behind his back and pulled the pistol from his belt. "Don't touch her."

Roy didn't even look at him. He moved toward Heather.

Colin shouted: "I'll blow your head off, you son-of-a-bitch!"

Roy was stunned. At first he didn't comprehend, but then he saw Heather shrugging off the ropes that bound her wrists, and he realized that he had been tricked after all. The blood left his face, and he was white with rage.

"All of this was recorded," Colin said. "I've got it on tape. Now I'll be able to make someone believe me."

Roy started toward him.

"Don't move!" Colin said, jabbing the pistol at him.

Roy stopped.

Heather removed her gag.

"You all right?" Colin asked her.

"I'll be better when we're out of here," she said.

To Colin, Roy said, "You creepy little bastard. You don't have the guts to shoot anyone."

Brandishing the pistol, Colin said, "Take one more step, and you'll find out you're wrong."

Heather had frozen in the act of disentangling her legs from the ropes.

Everyone was perfectly silent for a moment.

Then Roy took the step.

Colin pointed the gun at Roy's feet and squeezed off a warning shot.

Except the gun didn't fire.

He tried again.

Nothing.

"You told me your mother's gun wasn't loaded," Roy said. "Remember?" His face was split by a rictuslike grin of fury.

Frantically, desperately, Colin squeezed the trigger again. Again. *Again!*

Still nothing.

He *knew* it was loaded. He had checked. Damnit, he had seen the bullets! Then he remembered the safeties. He'd forgotten to switch them off.

Roy rushed him, and Heather screamed.

Before he could flip the two small switches on the gun, Colin went down under the bigger boy, and they rolled over and over again on the thick carpet of dust, and Colin's head banged hard against the floor, and Roy backhanded him across the face, swung once, twice, three times with fists like blocks of marble, hitting Colin in the ribs and then in the stomach, knocking the wind out of him, and Colin tried to use the gun as a club, but Roy seized his wrist and wrenched the weapon out of his hand, used it as Colin had tried to use it, swung it, struck Colin alongside the head, twice, and blackness welled up, a welcoming, warm, velvety, immensely appealing blackness.

Colin realized that one or two more blows would either render him unconscious or kill him, and then he would be no help whatsoever to Heather. There was only one thing he could do; he went limp and played dead. Roy stopped beating him and sat on him, gasping. Then, just for good measure, he slammed the gun into Colin's skull once more.

Pain exploded from Colin's left ear, through his cheek, into the bridge of his nose, as if dozens of sharp needles had been pounded through his face. He passed out.

FORTY-THREE

◆

He was not unconscious a long time. Only a few seconds. A vision of Heather, obscenely pinned under Roy, flashed through the blackness in which Colin drifted, and that terrible image propelled him out of the darkness.

Heather screamed, but her scream was cut short by the sound of a hand striking her face.

Colin's glasses were gone. Everything was blurred. He sat up, expecting Roy to leap on him, and felt the floor around him. He found his specs. The frames were twisted, but both lenses were intact. He put them on, bending them to make them fit.

Heather was on the floor on the other side of the room, flat on her back, and Roy was straddling her, facing away from Colin. Her blouse was open, and her breasts were bare. Roy was trying to pull off her shorts. She struggled, and he hit her again. She began to weep.

Groggy, hurting badly, but given strength by his own anger, Colin flung himself across the room, grabbed Roy by the hair, and pulled him off the girl. They staggered backward, then toppled sideways and rolled apart.

Roy scrambled to his feet and seized Heather as she ran for the door. He turned her away from the exit and shoved her toward the wall. She tripped and fell on the hidden tape recorder.

Colin was lying on something hard and sharp-edged, and, as dizzy as he was, he needed a moment to realize that it was the pistol beneath him. He pulled it from under him and rose to his knees and fumbled with the safeties as Roy started toward him again and as sparks of pain flashed behind his eyes.

Roy laughed with vicious delight. "You think I'm scared of an unloaded gun? Jesus, you're a wimp! I'm going to kick your head apart, you stupid little creep. Then I'm going to fuck your stupid girlfriend till she bleeds."

"You're a filthy, rotten bastard!" Colin said, burning with rage, more furious than he'd ever imagined he could be. He staggered to his feet. "You stop. Stop right where you are. The safety catches were on. Now they're off. You hear me? The gun's loaded. And I'll use it. I swear to God, I'll blow your guts all over the wall!"

Roy laughed again. "Colin Jacobs, the big tough killer." He kept coming, grinning, confident.

Colin cursed him and pulled the trigger. The shot was deafening in the shuttered room.

Roy stumbled backward, but not because he had been hit. He was only surprised. The bullet had missed him.

Colin pulled the trigger again.

The second shot missed too, but Roy cried out and threw up his hands placatingly. "No! Wait! Wait a minute! Don't!" Colin advanced on him, and Roy backed into the wall and Colin pulled the trigger again. He couldn't stop himself. He was hot, white hot, burning with anger, seething, boiling, so hot with rage that he felt as if he would start melting, flowing like lava, his heart thumping so hard that each beat was like the explosion of a volcano. He was not human any more, just animal, savage, barbarian, fighting a brutal territorial battle with another male, driven to attack until he drew blood, powered by a terrifying but irresistible primitive lust to dominate, to conquer, to destroy.

The third shot grazed Roy's right arm, and the fourth bullet took him squarely in the right leg. He collapsed as dark blood suddenly stained his sleeve and soaked through one leg of his jeans. And for the first time since Colin had known him, Roy looked—in the face, at least—like a child, like the child he actually was. His face was contorted by a look of helplessness, an expression of stark terror.

Colin towered over him and lined the sight up with the bridge of Roy's nose. He almost pulled the trigger one last time. But before he could take that final step into total savagery, he became aware that there was more than fear in Roy's eyes. He saw despair, too. And a pitiful, lost look, a deep and abiding loneliness. Worst of all, he saw that part of Roy was beseeching him to squeeze off one more shot; a part of the poor bastard was begging to be killed.

Slowly, Colin lowered the gun. "I'll get help for you, Roy. They'll fix the leg. And the other things, too. They'll help you with the other things. Psychiatrists. Good doctors, Roy. They'll help you get well. Belinda wasn't your fault. It was an accident. They'll help you understand that."

Roy began to cry. He gripped his shattered leg with both hands and wept uncontrollably, moaned, wailed, rocked back and forth—either because the shock had worn off and his wound was hurting him . . . or because Colin had not put him out of his misery.

Colin was unable to hold back his own tears. "Oh God, Roy, what they did to you. What they did to me. What all of us do to each other every day, all the time. It's terrible. Why? For God's sake, why?" He threw the gun across the room; it hit the wall with a crash, clattered to the floor. "Look, Roy, I'll come visit you," he said, through tears that wouldn't stop. "In the hospital. Then wherever they take you. I'll always come. I won't forget, Roy. Not ever. I promise. I won't forget that we're blood brothers.''

Roy didn't seem to hear. He was lost in his own pain and anguish.

Heather came to Colin and tentatively put one hand against his battered face. He saw that she was limping. "Are you hurt?"

"It's nothing serious," she said. "I twisted my ankle when I fell. What about you?"

"I'll live."

"Your face looks awful. It's swollen where he hit you with the gun, and it's turning all dark."

"It hurts," he admitted. "But right now we've got to get an ambulance for Roy. We don't want him to bleed to death." He reached into a pocket of his jeans and took out some coins. "Here. Take this. There's a pay phone at the service station at the bottom of the hill. Call the hospital and the police."

"You better go," she said. "I'll take forever with this bad ankle."

"You don't mind staying here with him?" Colin asked.

"He's harmless now," she said.

"Well . . . okay."

"Just hurry back."

"I will. And Heather . . . I'm sorry."

"For what?"

"I said he'd never get his hands on you. I failed you."

"He didn't do anything to me," she said. "You protected me. You did very well."

Tears shimmered in her eyes. They held each other for a moment.

"You're so pretty," he said.

"Am I?"

"Don't ever tell yourself you aren't. Don't ever again think you're ugly in any way. Not ever. Tell them all to go to hell. You're pretty. Remember that. Promise me you'll remember that."

"Okay."

"Promise me."

"I promise."

He went to call the ambulance.

Outside, the night was very dark.

As he walked down the long hill, heading for the phone at the service station, he realized he could no longer hear the voice of the night. There were toads and crickets and the distant rumble of a train. But that low, sinister murmuring that he had always thought was there, that sound of supernatural machinery laboring at evil tasks, was gone. A few steps farther on, he realized that the voice of the night was now within him, and that, in fact, it always had been. It was within everyone, whispering maliciously, twenty-four hours a day, and the most important task in life was to ignore it, shut it out, refuse to listen.

He called the ambulance, then the police.

THE MASK

◆ ◆ ◆

This book is dedicated to
Willo and Dave Roberts
and to
Carol and Don McQuinn
who have no faults—
except that they live
too far away from us.

*A dirge for her, the doubly dead, in that
she died so young.*
　　—EDGAR ALLAN POE, "Lenore"

*And much of Madness, and more of Sin,
And Horror the soul of the plot.*
　　　　—EDGAR ALLAN POE,
　　　"The Conqueror Worm"

　*Extreme terror gives us back
　the
　gestures of our childhood.*
　　　　—CHAZAL

PROLOGUE

◆

Laura was in the cellar, doing some spring cleaning and hating every minute of it. She didn't dislike the work itself; she was by nature an industrious girl who was happiest when she had chores to do. But she was afraid of the cellar.

For one thing, the place was gloomy. The four narrow windows, set high in the walls, were hardly larger than embrasures, and the dust-filmed panes of glass permitted only weak, chalky light to enter. Even brightened by a pair of lamps, the big room held on tenaciously to its shadows, unwilling to be completely disrobed. The flickering amber light from the lamps revealed damp stone walls and a hulking, coal-fired furnace that was cold and unused on this fine, warm May afternoon. On a series of long shelves, row upon row of quart jars reflected splinters of light, but their contents—home-canned fruit and vegetables that had been stored here for the past nine months—remained unilluminated. The corners of the room were all dark, and the low, open-beamed ceiling was hung with shadows like long banners of funeral crepe.

The cellar always had a mildly unpleasant odor, too. It was musty, rather like a limestone cave. In the spring and summer, when the humidity was high, a mottled gray-green fungus sometimes sprang up in the corners, a disgusting scab-like growth, fringed with hundreds of tiny white spores that resembled insect eggs; that grotesquery added its own thin but nonetheless displeasing fragrance to the cellar air.

However, neither the gloom nor the offending odors nor the fungus gave rise to Laura's fears; it was the spiders that frightened her. Spiders ruled the cellar. Some of them were small, brown, and quick; others were charcoal gray, a bit bigger than the brown ones, but just as fast-moving as their smaller cousins. There were even a few blue-black giants as large as Laura's thumb.

As she wiped dust and a few cobwebs from the jars of home-canned food, always alert for the scuttling movement of spiders, Laura grew increasingly angry with her mother. Mama could have let her clean some of the upstairs rooms instead of the cellar; Aunt Rachael or Mama herself could have cleaned down here because neither of them worried about spiders. But Mama knew that Laura was afraid of the cellar, and Mama was in the mood to punish her. It was a terrible mood, black as thunderclouds. Laura had seen it before. Too often. It descended over Mama more frequently with every passing year, and when she was in its thrall, she was a different person from the smiling, always singing woman that she was at other times. Although Laura loved her mother, she did not love the short-tempered, mean-spirited woman that her mother sometimes became. She did not love the hateful woman who had sent her down into the cellar with the spiders.

Dusting the jars of peaches, pears, tomatoes, beets, beans, and pickled squash, nervously awaiting the inevitable appearance of a spider, wishing she were grown up and married and on her own, Laura was startled by a sudden, sharp sound that pierced the dank basement air. At first it was like the distant, forlorn wail of an exotic bird, but it quickly became louder and more urgent. She stopped dusting, looked up at the dark ceiling, and listened closely to the eerie ululation that came from overhead. After a moment she realized that it was her Aunt Rachael's voice and that it was a cry of alarm.

Upstairs, something fell over with a crash. It sounded like shattering porcelain. It must have been Mama's peacock vase. If it was the vase, Mama would be in an *extremely* foul mood for the rest of the week.

Laura stepped away from the shelves of canned goods and started toward the cellar stairs, but she stopped abruptly when she heard Mama scream. It wasn't a scream of rage over the loss of the vase; there was a note of terror in it.

Footsteps thumped across the living room floor, toward the front door of the house. The screen door opened with the familiar singing of its long spring, then banged shut. Rachael was outside now, shouting, her words unintelligible but still conveying her fear.

Laura smelled smoke.

She hurried to the stairs and saw pale tongues of fire at the top. The smoke wasn't heavy, but it had an acrid stench.

Heart pounding, Laura climbed to the uppermost step. Waves of heat forced her to squint, but she could see into the kitchen. The wall of fire wasn't solid. There was a narrow route of escape, a corridor of cool safety; the door to the back porch was at the far end.

She lifted her long skirt and pulled it tight across her hips and thighs, bunching it in both hands to prevent it from trailing in the flames. She moved gingerly onto the fire-ringed landing, which creaked under her, but before she reached the open door, the kitchen exploded in yellow-blue flames that quickly turned orange. From wall to wall, floor to ceiling, the room was an inferno; there was no longer a path through the blaze. Crazily, the fire-choked doorway brought to Laura's mind the image of a glittering eye in a jack-o'-lantern.

In the kitchen, windows exploded, and the fire eddied in the sudden change of drafts, pushing through the cellar door, lashing at Laura. Startled, she stumbled backwards, off the landing. She fell. Turning, she grabbed at the railing, missed it, and stumbled down the short flight, cracking her head against the stone floor at the bottom.

She held on to consciousness as if it were a raft and she a drowning swimmer. When she was certain she wouldn't faint, she got to her feet. Pain coruscated across the top of her head. She raised one hand to her brow and found a trickle of blood, a small abrasion. She was dizzy and confused.

During the minute or less that she had been incapacitated, fire had spread across the entire landing at the head of the stairs. It was moving down onto the first step.

She couldn't keep her eyes focused. The rising stairs and the descending fire repeatedly blurred together in an orange haze.

Ghosts of smoke drifted down the stairwell. They reached out with long, insubstantial arms, as if to embrace Laura.

She cupped her hands around her mouth. "Help!"

No one answered.

"Somebody help me! I'm in the cellar!"

Silence.

"Aunt Rachael! Mama! For God's sake, somebody help me!"

The only response was the steadily increasing roar of the fire.

Laura had never felt so alone before. In spite of the tides of heat washing over her, she felt cold inside. She shivered.

Although her head throbbed worse than ever, and although the abrasion above her right eye continued to weep blood, at least she was having less trouble keeping her eyes focused. The problem was that she didn't like what she saw.

She stood statue-still, transfixed by the deadly spectacle of the flames. Fire crawled lizardlike down the steps, one by one, and it slithered up the rail posts, then crept down the rail with a crisp, chuckling sound.

The smoke reached the bottom of the steps and enfolded her. She coughed, and the coughing aggravated the pain in her head, making her dizzy again. She put one hand against the wall to steady herself.

Everything was happening too fast. The house was going up like a pile of well-seasoned tinder.

I'm going to die here.

That thought jolted her out of her trance. She wasn't ready to die. She was far too young. There was so much of life ahead of her, so many wonderful things to do, things she had long dreamed about doing. It wasn't fair. She *refused* to die.

She gagged on the smoke. Turning away from the burning stairs, she put a hand over her nose and mouth, but that didn't help much.

She saw flames at the far end of the cellar, and for an instant she thought she was already encircled and that all hope of rescue was gone. She cried out in despair, but then she realized the blaze hadn't found its way into the other end of the room after all. The two points of fire that she was seeing were only the twin oil lamps that had provided her with light. The flames in the lamps were harmless, safely ensconced in tall glass chimneys.

She coughed violently again, and the pain in her head settled down behind her eyes. She found it difficult to concentrate. Her thoughts were like droplets of quicksilver, sliding over one another and changing shape so often and so fast that she couldn't make sense of some of them.

She prayed silently and fervently.

Directly overhead, the ceiling groaned and appeared to *shift*. For a few seconds she held her breath, clenched her teeth, and stood with her hands fisted at her sides, waiting to be buried in rubble. But then she saw that the ceiling wasn't going to collapse—not yet.

Trembling, whimpering softly, she scurried to the nearest of the four high-set windows. It was rectangular, approximately eight inches from sill to top and eighteen inches from sash to sash, much too small to provide her with a means of escape. The other three windows were identical to the first; there was no use even taking a closer look at them.

The air was becoming less breathable by the second. Laura's sinuses ached and burned. Her mouth was filled with the revulsive, bitter taste of the smoke.

For too long she stood beneath the window, staring up in frustration and confusion at the meager, milky light that came through the dirty pane and through the haze of smoke that pressed tightly against the glass. She had the feeling she was overlooking an obvious and convenient escape hatch; in fact she was sure of it. There *was* a way out, and it had nothing to do with the windows, but she couldn't get her mind *off* the windows; she was fixated on them, just as she had been fixated on the sight of the advancing flames a couple of minutes ago. The pain in her head and behind her eyes throbbed more powerfully than ever, and with each agonizing pulsation, her thoughts became more muddled.

I'm going to die here.

A frightening vision flashed through her mind. She saw herself afire, her dark hair turned blond by the flames that consumed it and standing straight up on her head as if it were not hair but the wick of a candle. In the vision, she saw her face melting like wax, bubbling and steaming and liquefying, the features flowing together until her face no longer resembled that of a human being, until it was the hideously twisted countenance of a leering demon with empty eye sockets.

No!

She shook her head, dispelling the vision.

She was dizzy and getting dizzier. She needed a draught of clean air to rinse out her polluted lungs, but with each breath she drew more smoke than she had drawn last time. Her chest ached.

Nearby, a rhythmic pounding began; the noise was even louder than her heartbeat, which drummed thunderously in her ears.

She turned in a circle, gagging and coughing, searching for the source of the hammering sound, striving to regain control of herself, struggling hard to *think*.

The hammering stopped.

"Laura . . . "

Above the incessant roar of the fire, she heard someone calling her name.

"Laura . . . "

"I'm down here . . . in the cellar!" she shouted. But the shout came out as nothing more than a whispered croak. Her throat was constricted and already raw from the harsh smoke and the fiercely hot air.

The effort required to stay on her feet became too great for her. She sank to her knees on the stone floor, slumped against the wall, and slid down until she was lying on her side.

"Laura . . . "

The pounding began again. A fist beating on a door.

Laura discovered that the air at floor level was cleaner than that which she had been breathing. She gasped frantically, grateful for this reprieve from suffocation.

For a few seconds the throbbing pain behind her eyes abated, and her thoughts cleared, and she remembered the outside entrance to the cellar, a pair of doors slant-set against the north wall of the house. They were locked from the inside, so that no one could get in to rescue her; in the panic and confusion she had forgotten about those doors. But now, if she kept her wits about her, she would be able to save herself.

"Laura!" It was Aunt Rachael's voice.

Laura crawled to the northwest corner of the room, where the doors sloped down at the top of a short flight of steps. She kept her head low, breathing the tainted but adequate air near the floor. The edges of the mortared stones tore her dress and scraped skin off her knees.

To her left, the entire stairwell was burning now, and flames were spreading across the wooden ceiling. Refracted and diffused by the smoky air, the firelight glowed on all sides of Laura, creating the illusion that she was crawling through a narrow tunnel of flames. At the rate the blaze was spreading, the illusion would soon be fact.

Her eyes were swollen and watery, and she wiped at them as she inched toward escape. She couldn't see very much. She used Aunt Rachael's voice as a beacon and otherwise relied on instinct.

"Laura!" The voice was near. Right above her.

She felt along the wall until she located the setback in the stone. She moved into that recess, onto the first step, lifted her head, but could see nothing: the darkness here was seamless.

"Laura, answer me. Baby, are you in there?"

Rachael was hysterical, screaming so loudly and pounding on the outside doors with such persistence that she wouldn't have heard a response even if Laura had been capable of making one.

Where was Mama? Why wasn't Mama pounding on the door, too? Didn't Mama care?

Crouching in that cramped, hot, lightless space, Laura reached up and put her hand against one of the two slant-set doors above her head. The sturdy barrier quivered and rattled under the impact of Rachael's small fists. Laura groped blindly for the latch. She put her hand over the warm metal fixture—and squarely over something else, too. Something strange and unexpected. Something that squirmed and was alive. Small but *alive*. She jerked convulsively and pulled her hand away. But the thing she touched had shifted its grip from the latch to her flesh, and it came away from the door when she withdrew her hand. It skittered out of her palm and over her thumb and across the back of her hand and along her wrist and under the sleeve of her dress before she could brush it away.

A spider.

She couldn't see it, but she knew what it was. A spider. One of the really big ones, as large as her thumb, a plump black body that glistened like a fat drop of oil, inky black and ugly. For a moment she froze, unable even to draw a breath.

She felt the spider moving up her arm, and its bold advance snapped her into action. She slapped at it through the sleeve of her dress, but she missed. The spider bit her above the crook of her arm, and she winced at the tiny nip of pain, and the disgusting creature scurried into her armpit. It bit her there, too, and suddenly she felt as though she was living through her worst nightmare, for she feared spiders more than she feared anything else on earth—certainly more than she feared fire, for in her desperate attempt to kill the spider, she had forgotten all about the burning house that was dissolving into ruin above her—and she flailed in panic, lost her balance, rolled backwards off the steps, into the main room of the cellar, cracking one hip on the stone floor. The spider tickled its way along the inside of her bodice until it was between her breasts. She screamed but could make no sound whatsoever. She put a hand to her bosom and pressed hard, and even through the fabric she could feel the spider squirming angrily against the palm of her hand, and she could feel its frenzied struggle even more directly on her bare breast, to which it was pressed, but she persisted until at last she crushed it, and she gagged again, but this time not merely because of the smoke.

For several seconds after killing the spider, she lay on the floor in a tight fetal position, shuddering violently and uncontrollably. The repulsive, wet mass of the smashed spider slid very slowly down the curve of her breast. She wanted to reach inside her bodice and pluck the foul wad from herself, but she hesitated because, irrationally, she was afraid it would somehow come to life again and sting her fingers.

She tasted blood. She had bitten her lip.

Mama . . .

Mama had done this to her. Mama had sent her down here, knowing there were spiders. Why was Mama always so quick to deal out punishment, so eager to assign penance?

Overhead, a beam creaked, sagged. The kitchen floor cracked open. She felt as though she were staring up into Hell. Sparks showered down. Her dress caught fire, and she scorched her hands putting it out.

Mama did this to me.

Because her palms and fingers were blistered and peeling, she couldn't crawl on her hands and knees any longer, so she got to her feet, although standing up required more strength and determination than she had thought she possessed. She swayed, dizzy and weak.

Mama sent me down here.

Laura could see only pulsing, all-encompassing orange luminescence, through which amorphous smoke ghosts glided and whirled. She shuffled toward the short flight of steps that led to the outside cellar doors, but after she had gone only two yards, she realized she was headed in the wrong direction. She turned back the way she had come—or back the way she *thought* she had come—but after a few steps she bumped into the furnace, which was nowhere near the outside doors. She was completely disoriented.

Mama did this to me.

Laura squeezed her ruined hands into raw, bloody fists. In a rage she pounded on the furnace, and with each blow she fervently wished that she were beating her mother.

The upper reaches of the burning house twisted and rumbled. In the distance, beyond an eternity of smoke, Aunt Rachael's voice echoed hauntingly: ''Laura . . . Laura . . . ''

Why wasn't Mama out there helping Rachael break down the cellar doors? Where in God's name *was* she? Throwing coal and lamp oil on the fire?

Wheezing, gasping, Laura pushed away from the furnace and tried to follow Rachael's voice to safety.

A beam tore loose of its moorings, slammed into her back, and catapulted her into the shelves of home-canned food. Jars fell, shattered. Laura went down in a rain of glass. She could smell pickles, peaches.

Before she could determine if any bones were broken, before she could even lift her face out of the spilled food, another beam crashed down, pinning her legs.

There was so much pain that her mind simply blanked it out altogether. She was not even sixteen years old, and there was only so much she could bear. She sealed the pain in a dark corner of her mind; instead of succumbing to it, she twisted and thrashed hysterically, raged at her fate, and cursed her mother.

Her hatred for her mother wasn't rational, but it was so passionately felt that it took the place of the pain she could not allow herself to feel. Hate flooded through her, filled her with so much demonic energy that she was nearly able to toss the heavy beam off her legs.

Damn you to Hell, Mama.

The top floor of the house caved in upon the ground floor with a sound like cannons blasting.

Damn you, Mama! Damn you!

The first two floors of flaming rubble broke through the already weakened cellar ceiling.

Mama—

PART ONE

◆ ◆ ◆

SOMETHING
WICKED
THIS WAY COMES...

By the pricking of my thumbs,
Something wicked this way comes.
Open, locks,
whoever knocks!
       —SHAKESPEARE, *Macbeth*

ONE

◆

Across the somber gray clouds, lightning followed a jagged course like cracks in a china plate. In the unsheltered courtyard outside Alfred O'Brian's office, the parked cars glimmered briefly with hard-edged reflections of the storm light. The wind gusted, whipping the trees. Rain beat with sudden fury against the three tall office windows, then streamed down the glass, blurring the view beyond.

O'Brian sat with his back to the windows. While thunder reverberated through the low sky and seemed to hammer on the roof of the building, he read the application that Paul and Carol Tracy had just submitted to him.

He's such a neat little man, Carol thought as she watched O'Brian. When he sits very still like that, you'd almost think he was a mannequin.

He was exceedingly well groomed. His carefully combed hair looked as if it had received the attention of a good barber less than an hour ago. His mustache was so expertly trimmed that the halves of it appeared to be perfectly symmetrical. He was wearing a gray suit with trouser creases as tight and straight as blades, and his black shoes gleamed. His fingernails were manicured, and his pink, well-scrubbed hands looked sterile.

When Carol had been introduced to O'Brian less than a week ago, she had thought he was prim, even prissy, and she had been prepared to dislike him. She was quickly won over by his smile, by his gracious manner, and by his sincere desire to help her and Paul.

She glanced at Paul, who was sitting in the chair next to hers, his own tensions betrayed by the angular position of his lean, usually graceful body. He was watching O'Brian intently, but when he sensed that Carol was looking at him, he turned and smiled. His smile was even nicer than O'Brian's, and as usual, Carol's spirits were lifted by the sight of it. He was neither handsome nor ugly, this man she loved; you might even say he was plain, yet his face was enormously appealing because the pleasing, open composition of it contained ample evidence of his gentleness and sensitivity. His hazel eyes were capable of conveying amazingly subtle degrees and mixtures of emotions. Six years ago, at a university symposium entitled ''Abnormal Psychology and Modern American Fiction,'' where Carol had met Paul, the first thing that had drawn her to him had been those warm, expressive eyes, and in the intervening years they had never ceased to intrigue her. Now he winked, and with that wink he seemed to be saying: *Don't worry; O'Brian is on our side; the application will be accepted; everything will turn out all right; I love you.*

She winked back at him and pretended to be confident, even though she was sure he could see through her brave front.

She wished that she could be certain of winning Mr. O'Brian's approval. She knew she ought to be overflowing with confidence, for there really was no reason why O'Brian would reject them. They were healthy and young. Paul was thirty-five, and she was thirty-one, and those were excellent ages at which to set out upon the adventure they were contemplating. Both of them were successful in their work. They were financially solvent, even prosperous. They were respected in their community. Their marriage was happy and trouble-free, stronger now than at any time in the four years since their wedding. In short, their qualifications for adopting a child were pretty much impeccable, but she worried nonetheless.

She loved children, and she was looking forward to raising one or two of her own. During the past fourteen years—in which she had earned three degrees at three universities and had established herself in her profession—she had postponed many simple pleasures and had skipped others altogether. Getting an education and launching her career had always come first. She had missed too many good parties and had forgone an unremembered number of vacations and getaway weekends. Adopting a child was one pleasure she did not want to postpone any longer.

She had a strong psychological need—almost a *physical* need—to be a mother, to guide and shape children, to give them love and understanding. She was intelligent enough and sufficiently self-aware to realize that this deep-seated need arose, at least in part, from her inability to conceive a child of her own flesh and blood.

The thing we want most, she thought, is always the thing we cannot have.

She was to blame for her sterility, which was the result of an unforgivable act of stupidity committed a long time ago; and of course her culpability made her condition harder to bear than it would have been if nature—rather than her own foolishness—had cursed her with a barren womb. She had been a severely troubled child, for she had been raised by violent, alcoholic parents who had frequently beaten her and who had dealt out large doses of psychological torture. By the time she was fifteen, she was a hellion, engaged in an angry rebellion against her parents and against the world at large. She hated everyone in those days, especially herself. In the blackest hours of her confused and tormented adolescence, she had gotten pregnant. Frightened, panicky, with no one to turn to, she tried to conceal her condition by wearing girdles, by binding herself with elastic cloth and tape, and by eating as lightly as possible to keep her weight down. Eventually, however, complications arose because of her attempts to hide her pregnancy, and she nearly died. The baby was born prematurely, but it was healthy. She had put it up for adoption and hadn't given it much thought for a couple of years, though these days she often wondered about the child and wished she could have kept it somehow. At the time, the fact that her ordeal had left her sterile did not depress her, for she didn't think she would ever want to be pregnant again. But with a lot of help and love from a child psychologist named Grace Mitowski, who did charity work among juvenile wards of the court, Carol had turned her life completely around. She had learned to like herself and, years later, had come to regret the thoughtless actions that had left her barren.

Fortunately, she regarded adoption as a more-than-adequate solution to her problem. She was capable of giving as much love to an adopted child as she would have given to her own offspring. She knew she would be a good and caring mother, and she longed to prove it—not to the world but to herself; she never needed to prove anything to anyone but herself, for she was always her own toughest critic.

Mr. O'Brian looked up from the application and smiled. His teeth were exceedingly white. ''This looks really fine,'' he said, indicating the form he had just finished reading. ''In fact, it's splendid. Not everyone that applies to us has credentials like these.''

"It's kind of you to say so," Paul told him.

O'Brian shook his head. "Not at all. It's simply the truth. Very impressive."

Carol said, "Thank you."

Leaning back in his chair, folding his hands on his stomach, O'Brian said, "I *do* have a couple of questions. I'm sure they're the same ones the recommendations committee will ask me, so I might as well get your responses now and save a lot of back-and-forth later on."

Carol stiffened again.

O'Brian apparently noticed her reaction, for he quickly said, "Oh, it's nothing terribly serious. Really, it isn't. Believe me—I won't be asking you half as many questions as I ask most couples who come to see us."

In spite of O'Brian's assurances, Carol remained tense.

Outside, the storm-dark afternoon sky grew steadily darker as the thunderheads changed color from gray to blue black, thickened, and pressed closer to the earth.

O'Brian swiveled in his chair to face Paul. "Dr. Tracy, would you say you're an overachiever?"

Paul seemed surprised by the question. He blinked and said, "I'm not sure what you mean."

"You *are* the chairman of the department of English at the college, aren't you?"

"Yes. I'm on sabbatical this semester, and the vice-chairman is handling most things for the time being. Otherwise, I've been in charge of the department for the past year and a half."

"Aren't you rather young to hold such a post?"

"Somewhat young," Paul admitted. "But that's no credit to me. You see, it's a thankless position, all work and no glory. My senior colleagues in the department craftily maneuvered me into it so that none of them would be stuck with the job."

"You're being modest."

"No, I'm really not," Paul said. "It's nothing much."

Carol knew that he *was* being modest. The departmental chairmanship was a prized position, an honor. But she understood why Paul was playing it down; he had been unsettled by O'Brian's use of the word *overachiever*. She had been unsettled by it, too. Until this moment she had never thought that an unusually long list of achievements might count *against* them.

Beyond the tall windows, lightning zigzagged down the sky. The day flickered and, just for a second or two, so did the electric lights in O'Brian's office.

Still addressing Paul, O'Brian said, "You're also an author."

"Yes."

"You've written a very successful textbook for use in American literature courses. You've turned out a dozen monographs on a variety of subjects, and you've done a local history of the county. *And* two children's books, *and* a novel. . . ."

"The novel was about as successful as a horse trying to walk a tightrope," Paul said. "The *New York Times* critic said it was 'a perfect example of academic posturing, stuffed full of themes and symbols, utterly lacking in substance and narrative drive, infused with ivory-tower naivete.'"

O'Brian smiled. "Does every writer memorize his bad reviews?"

"I suppose not. But I have that one engraved on my cerebral cortex because there's an uncomfortable amount of truth in it."

"Are you writing another novel? Is that why you've taken a sabbatical?"

Paul was not surprised by the question. Clearly he now understood what

O'Brian was digging for. "Yes, in fact I *am* writing a new novel. This one actually has a plot." He laughed with easy self-deprecation.

"You're also involved in charity work."

"Not much."

"Quite a lot," O'Brian disagreed. "The Children's Hospital Fund, the Community Chest, the student scholarship program at the college—all of that in addition to your regular job and your writing. Yet you don't think you're an overachiever?"

"No, I really don't think I am. The charity work amounts to just a couple of meetings a month. It's no big thing. It's the least I can do, considering my own good fortune." Paul edged forward on his chair. "Maybe you're worried that I won't have time to give to a child, but if that's what's troubling you, then you can put your mind at rest. I'll *make* the time. This adoption is extremely important to us, Mr. O'Brian. We both want a child very badly, and if we are lucky enough to get one, we certainly won't ever neglect it."

"Oh, I'm sure you won't," O'Brian said quickly, raising his hands placatingly. "That isn't at all what I meant to imply. Oh, certainly not. I'm on *your* side in this matter. I mean that very sincerely." He swiveled to face Carol. "Dr. Tracy—the *other* Dr. Tracy—what about you? Do you consider yourself an overachiever?"

Lightning slashed through the panoply of clouds again, nearer this time than before; it seemed to strike the ground no more than two blocks away. The ensuing crash of thunder rattled the tall windows.

Carol used the interruption provided by the thunderclap to consider her response, and she decided that O'Brian would appreciate forthrightness more than modesty. "Yes. I'd say I'm an overachiever. I'm involved in two of the three charities that Paul has his hand in. And I know I'm a bit young to have established a psychiatric practice as successful as mine is. I'm also a guest lecturer at the college on a fairly regular basis. And I'm doing post-doctoral research on autistic children. During the summer I manage to keep a little vegetable garden going, and I do some needlepoint in the winter months, and I even brush my teeth *three* times a day, every day, without fail."

O'Brian laughed. "Three times a day, huh? Oh, you're most *definitely* an overachiever."

The warmth of his laughter reassured Carol, and with renewed confidence she said, "I believe I understand what you're concerned about. You're wondering if Paul and I might expect too much of our child."

"Exactly," O'Brian said. He noticed a speck of lint on his coat sleeve and plucked it off. "Parents who are overachievers tend to push their kids too hard, too fast, too soon."

Paul said, "That's a problem that arises only when parents are unaware of the danger. Even if Carol and I are overachievers—which *I'm* not prepared to admit just yet—we wouldn't pressure our kids to do more than they were capable of doing. Each of us has to find his own pace in life. Carol and I realize that a child should be guided, not hammered into a mold."

"Of course," Carol said.

O'Brian appeared to be pleased. "I knew you'd say that—or something very like it."

Lightning flashed again. This time it seemed to strike even closer than before, only a block away. Thunder cracked, then cracked again. The overhead lights dimmed, fluttered, reluctantly came back to full power.

"In my psychiatric practice, I deal with a wide variety of patients who have all kinds of problems," Carol told O'Brian, "but I specialize in the mental disorders and emotional disturbances of children and adolescents. Sixty or seventy percent of my patients are seventeen or younger. I've treated several kids who've suffered serious psychological damage at the hands of parents who were too demanding, who pushed them too hard in their schoolwork, in every aspect of their intellectual and personal development. I've seen the wounded ones, Mr. O'Brian, and I've nursed them as best I could, and because of those experiences, I couldn't possibly turn around and do to my children what I've seen some parents do to theirs. Not that I won't make mistakes. I'm sure I will. My full share of them. But the one that you mentioned won't be among them.''

"That's valid,'' O'Brian said, nodding. "Valid and very well put. I'm sure that when I tell the recommendations committee what you've just said, they'll be quite satisfied on this point.'' He spotted another tiny speck on his sleeve and removed it, frowning as if it were not merely lint, but offal. "Another question they're bound to ask: Suppose the child you adopt turns out to be not only an underachiever but . . . well . . . basically less intelligent than either of you. For parents as oriented toward an intellectual life as you are, wouldn't you be some-what frustrated with a child of just average—or possibly slightly below average—intelligence?''

"Well, even if we were capable of having a child of our own,'' Paul said, "there wouldn't be any guarantee that he'd be a prodigy or anything of that sort. But if he was . . . slow . . . we'd still love him. Of course we would. And the same goes for any child we might adopt.''

To O'Brian, Carol said, "I think you've got too high an opinion of us. Neither of us is a *genius,* for heaven's sake! We've gotten as far as we have primarily through hard work and perseverence, not because we were exceptionally bright. I wish it *had* come that easy, but it didn't.''

"Besides,'' Paul said, "you don't love a person merely because he's intelligent. It's his entire personality that counts, the whole package, and a lot of factors contribute to that package, a great many things other than just intellect.''

"Good,'' O'Brian said. "I'm glad to hear you feel that way. The committee will respond well to that answer, too.''

For the past few seconds, Carol had been aware of the distant wail of sirens. Fire engines. Now they were not as distant as they had been; they were rapidly growing nearer, louder.

"I think maybe one of those last two bolts of lightning caused some real damage when it touched down,'' Paul said.

O'Brian swung his chair around toward the center window, which was directly behind his desk. "It *did* sound as if it struck nearby.''

Carol looked at each of the three windows, but she couldn't see any smoke rising from behind the nearest rooftops. Then again, the view was blurred and visibility was reduced by the water-spotted panes of glass and by the curtains of mist and gray rain that wavered and whipped and billowed beyond the glass.

The sirens swelled.

"More than one truck,'' O'Brian said.

The fire engines were right outside the office for a moment—at least two trucks, perhaps three—and then they passed, heading into the next block.

O'Brian pushed up from his chair and stepped to the window.

As the first sirens dwindled just a little, new ones shrieked in the street behind them.

"Must be serious,'' Paul said. "Sounds as if at least two engine companies are responding.''

"I see smoke,'' O'Brian said.

Paul rose from his chair and moved toward the windows to get a better look. *Something's wrong here.*

That thought snapped into Carol's mind, startling her as if a whip had cracked in front of her face. A powerful, inexplicable current of panic surged through her, electrified her. She gripped the arms of her chair so tightly that one of her fingernails broke.

Something . . . is . . . wrong . . . very wrong . . .

Suddenly the air was oppressively heavy—hot, *thick,* as if it were not air at all but a bitter and poisonous gas of some kind. She tried to breathe, couldn't. There was an invisible, crushing weight on her chest.

Get away from the windows!

She tried to shout that warning, but panic had short-circuited her voice. Paul and O'Brian were at different windows, but they both had their backs to her, so that neither of them could see she had been gripped by sudden, immobilizing fear.

Fear of what? she demanded of herself. What in the name of God am I so scared of?

She struggled against the unreasonable terror that had locked her muscles and joints. She started to get up from the chair, and that was when it happened.

A murderous barrage of lightning crashed like a volley of mortar fire, seven or eight tremendous bolts, perhaps more than that—she didn't count them, couldn't count them—one right after the other, without a significant pause between them, each fierce boom overlapping the ones before and after it, yet each clearly louder than its predecessors, so loud that they made her teeth and bones vibrate, each bolt smashing down discernibly closer to the building than had the bolt before it, closer to the seven-foot-high windows—the gleaming, flashing, rattling, now-black, now-milky, now-shining, now-blank, now-silvery, now-coppery windows. . . .

The sharp bursts of purple-white light produced a series of jerky, stroboscopic images that were burned forever into Carol's memory: Paul and O'Brian standing there, silhouetted against the natural fireworks, looking small and vulnerable; outside, the rain descending in an illusion of hesitation; wind-lashed trees heaving in a strobe-choppy rage; lightning blasting into one of those trees, a big maple, and then an ominous dark shape rising from the midst of the explosion, a torpedolike thing, spinning straight toward the center window (all of this transpiring in only a second or two, but given a queer, slow-motion quality by the flickering lightning and, after a moment, by the overhead electric light as well, which began to flicker, too); O'Brian throwing one arm up in front of his face in what appeared to be half a dozen disconnected movements; Paul turning toward O'Brian and reaching for him, both men like figures on a motion picture screen when the film slips and stutters in the projector; O'Brian lurching sideways; Paul seizing him by a coat sleeve, pulling him back and down toward safety (only a fraction of a second after the lightning splintered the maple); a huge tree limb bursting through the center window even as Paul was pulling O'Brian out of the way; one leafy branch sweeping across O'Brian's head, ripping his glasses loose, tossing them into the air—his face, Carol thought, his *eyes!*—and then Paul and O'Brian falling to the floor, out of sight; the enormous limb of the shattered maple slamming down on top of O'Brian's desk in a spray of water, glass, broken mullions, and smoking chips of bark; the legs of the desk cracking and collapsing under the brutal impact of the ruined tree.

Carol found herself on the floor, beside her overturned chair. She couldn't remember falling.

The fluorescent tubes blinked off, stayed off.

She was lying on her stomach, one cheek pressed to the floor, staring in shock at the shards of glass and the torn maple leaves that littered the carpet. As lightning continued to stab down from the turbulent sky, wind roared through the missing window and stirred some of the loose leaves into a frantic, dervishlike dance; accompanied by the cacophonous music of the storm, they whirled and capered across the office, toward a row of green filing cabinets. A calendar flapped off the wall and swooped around on wings of January and December, darting and soaring and kiting as if it were a bat. Two paintings rattled on their wire hangers, trying to tear themselves free. Papers were everywhere—stationery, forms, small sheets from a note pad, bulletins, a newspaper—all rustling and skipping this way and that, floating up, diving down, bunching together and slithering along the floor with a snakelike hiss.

Carol had the eerie feeling that all of the movement in the room was not solely the result of the wind, that some of it was caused by a . . . *presence*. Something threatening. A bad poltergeist. Demonic spirits seemed to be at work in the office, flexing their occult muscles, knocking things off the walls, briefly taking up residence in a body composed only of leaves and rumpled sheets of newsprint.

That was a crazy idea, not at all the sort of thing she would ordinarily think of. She was surprised and disconcerted by a thrill of superstitious fear that coursed through her.

Lightning flared again. And again.

Wincing at the painfully sharp sound, wondering if lightning could get into a room through an open window, she put her arms over her head, for what little protection they provided.

Her heart was pounding, and her mouth was dry.

She thought about Paul, and her heartbeat grew even more frantic. He was over by the windows, on the far side of the desk, out of sight, under some of the maple tree's branches. She didn't think he was dead. He hadn't been directly in the path of the tree. O'Brian might be dead, yes, depending on how that small branch had struck his head, depending on whether he had been lucky or not, because maybe a pointed twig had been driven deep into his eye and his brain when his glasses had been knocked off, but Paul was surely alive. Surely. Nevertheless, he could be seriously injured, bleeding. . . .

Carol started to push herself up onto her hands and knees, anxious to find Paul and give him any first aid he might need. But another bolt of blinding, ear-shattering lightning spent itself just outside the building, and fear turned her muscles into wet rags. She didn't even have the strength to crawl, and she was infuriated by her weakness, for she had always been proud of her strength, determination, and unflagging willpower. Cursing herself, she slumped back to the floor.

Something's trying to stop us from adopting a baby.

That incredible thought struck her with the same cold, hard force as had the forewarning of the window's implosion, which had come to her an instant before the impossible barrage of lightning had blasted into the courtyard.

Something's trying to stop us from adopting a baby.

No. That was ridiculous. The storm, the lightning—they were nothing more than acts of nature. They hadn't been directed against Mr. O'Brian just because he was going to help them adopt a child. Absurd.

Oh, yeah? she thought as the deafening thunder and the unholy light of the storm filled the room. Acts of nature, huh? When have you ever seen lightning like *this* before?

She hugged the floor, shaking, cold, more afraid than she had been since she was a little girl. She tried to tell herself that it was only the lightning that she was afraid of, for that was very much a legitimate, rational fear, but she knew she was lying. It was *not* just the lightning that terrified her. In fact, that was the least of it. There was something else, something she couldn't identify, something formless and nameless in the room, and the very presence of it, whatever the hell it was, pushed a panic button deep inside her, on a sub-subconscious, primitive level; this fear was gut-deep, instinctive.

A dervish of windblown leaves and papers whirled across the floor, directly toward her. It was a big one: a column about two feet in diameter, five or six feet high, composed of a hundred or more pieces of this and that. It stopped very near her, writhing, churning, hissing, changing shape, glimmering silver-dark in the flashing storm light, and she felt threatened by it. As she stared up at the whirlwind, she had the mad notion that it was staring down at her. After a moment it moved off to the left a few feet, then returned, paused in front of her again, hesitated, then scurried busily to the right, but came back once more, looming above her as if it were trying to make up its mind whether or not to pounce and tear her to shreds and sweep her up along with the leaves, newspaper pages, envelopes, and other flotsam by which it defined itself.

It's nothing more than a whirlwind of lifeless junk! she told herself angrily.

The wind-shaped phantom moved away from her.

See? she told herself scornfully. Just lifeless junk. What's wrong with me? Am I losing my mind?

She recalled the old axiom that was supposed to provide comfort in moments like these: If you think you're going mad, then you must be completely sane, for a lunatic never has doubts about his sanity. As a psychiatrist, she knew that hoary bit of wisdom was an oversimplification of complex psychological principles, but in essence it was true. So she must be sane.

Nevertheless, that frightening, irrational thought came to her again, unbidden, unwanted: *Something's trying to stop us from adopting a baby.*

If the maelstrom in which she lay was not an act of nature, then what *was* it? Was she to believe that the lightning had been sent with the conscious intent of transforming Mr. O'Brian into a smoking heap of charred flesh? That was a fruitcake notion, for sure. Who could use lightning as if it were a pistol? God? God wasn't sitting up in Heaven, aiming at Mr. O'Brian, popping away at him with lightning bolts, just to screw up the adoption process for Carol and Paul Tracy. The Devil? Blasting away at poor Mr. O'Brian from the depths of Hell? That *was* a looney idea. *Jesus!*

She wasn't even sure she believed in God, but she knew she definitely did not believe in the Devil.

Another window imploded, showering glass over her.

Then the lightning stopped.

The thunder decreased from a roar to a rumble, fading like the noise of a passing freight train.

There was a stench of ozone.

The wind was still pouring in through the broken windows, but apparently with less force than it had exerted a moment ago, for the whirling columns of leaves and papers subsided to the floor, where they lay in piles, fluttering and quivering as if exhausted.

Something . . .

Something . . .

Something's trying to stop us from—

She clamped off that unwanted thought as though it were a spurting artery. She was an educated woman, dammit. She prided herself on her levelheadedness and common sense. She couldn't permit herself to succumb to these disturbing, uncharacteristic, utterly superstitious fears.

Freaky weather—that was the explanation for the lightning. Freaky weather.

You read about such things in the newspapers every once in a while. A half an inch of snow in Beverly Hills. An eighty-degree day in the middle of an otherwise frigid Minnesota winter. Rain falling briefly from an apparently cloudless blue sky. Although a lightning strike of this magnitude and intensity was undoubtedly a rare occurrence, it probably had happened before, sometime, somewhere, probably more than once. Of course it had. Of course. In fact, if you picked up one of those popular books in which the authors compiled all kinds of world records, and if you turned to the chapter on weather, and if you looked for a subsection entitled "Lightning," you would most likely find an impressive list of other serial lightning strikes that would put this one to shame. Freaky weather. That's what it was. That's *all* it was. Nothing stranger than that, nothing worse.

For the time being, at least, Carol managed to put aside all thoughts of demons and ghosts and malign poltergeists and other such claptrap.

In the relative quiet that followed in the wake of the fast-diminishing thunder, she felt her strength returning. She pushed up from the floor, onto her knees. With the clinking sound of mildly disturbed wind chimes, pieces of glass fell from her gray skirt and green blouse; she wasn't cut or even scratched. She was a bit dazed, however, and for a moment the floor appeared to roll sickeningly from side to side, as if this were a stateroom aboard a ship.

In the office next door, a woman began to cry hysterically. There were shouts of alarm, and someone began calling for Mr. O'Brian. No one had yet burst into the office to see what had happened, which meant that only a second or two had elapsed since the lightning had stopped, although it seemed to Carol as if a minute or two had passed.

Over by the windows, someone groaned softly.

"Paul?" she said.

If there was an answer, it was drowned out by a sudden gust of wind that briefly stirred the papers and leaves again.

She recalled the way that branch had whipped across O'Brian's head, and she shuddered. But Paul hadn't been touched. The tree had missed him. Hadn't it?

"Paul!"

With renewed fear, she got to her feet and moved quickly around the desk, stepping over splintered maple branches and an overturned wastebasket.

TWO

◆

That Wednesday afternoon, following a lunch of Campbell's vegetable soup and a grilled cheese sandwich, Grace Mitowski went into her study and curled up on the sofa to sleep for an hour or so. She never napped in the bedroom because that formalized it somehow, and though she had been taking naps three or four days a week for the past year, she still had not reconciled herself to the fact that she needed a midday rest. To her way of thinking, naps were for children and for old, used-up, burnt-out people. She wasn't in her childhood any more—neither the first nor the second, thank you—and although she *was* old, she certainly wasn't used up or burnt out. Being in bed in the middle of the day made her feel lazy, and she couldn't abide laziness in anyone, especially not in herself. Therefore, she took naps on the study sofa, with her back to the shuttered windows, lulled by the monotonous ticking of the mantel clock.

At seventy, Grace was still as *mentally* agile and energetic as she had ever been. Her gray matter hadn't begun to deteriorate at all; it was only her treacherous body that caused her grief and frustration. She had a touch of arthritis in her hands, and when the humidity was high—as it was today—she also suffered from a dull but unrelenting ache of bursitis in her shoulders. Although she did all of the exercises that her doctor recommended, and although she walked two miles every morning, she found it increasingly difficult to maintain her muscle tone. From the time she was a young girl, throughout most of her life, she had been in love with books, and she had been able to read all morning, all afternoon, and most of the evening without eyestrain; nowadays, usually after only a couple of hours of reading, her eyes felt grainy and hot. She regarded each of her infirmities with extreme indignation, and she struggled against them, even though she knew this was a war she was destined to lose.

That Wednesday afternoon she took a break from the battle, a brief period of R and R. Two minutes after she stretched out on the sofa, she was asleep.

Grace did not dream often, and she was even less often plagued by *bad* dreams. But Wednesday afternoon, in the book-lined study, her sleep was continuously disturbed by nightmares. Several times she stirred, came half awake, and heard herself gasping in panic. Once, drifting up from some hideous and threatening vision, she heard her own voice crying out wordlessly in terror, and she realized she was thrashing on the couch, twisting and torturing her aching shoulders. She tried to come fully awake, but she could not; something in the dream, something dark and menacing, reached up with icy, clammy hands and pulled her down into deep sleep again, down and down, all the way down into a lightless place where an unnameable creature gibbered and muttered and chuckled in a mucous-wet voice.

An hour later, when she finally woke up and managed to cast off the clutching dream, she was standing in the middle of the shadow-shrouded room, several steps away from the sofa, but she had no memory of getting to her feet. She was shaking, sheathed in sweat.

—*I've got to tell Carol Tracy.*

—*Tell her what?*

—*Warn her.*

—*Warn her about what?*

—*It's coming. Oh, God . . .*

—*What's coming?*

—*Just like in the dream.*

—*What about the dream?*

Already her memory of the nightmare had begun to dissolve; only fragments of it remained with her, and each of those disassociated images was evaporating as if it were a splinter of dry ice. All she could remember was that Carol had been a part of it, and had been in awful danger. And somehow she knew that the dream had been more than just an ordinary dream. . . .

As the nightmare receded, Grace became uncomfortably aware of how gloomy the study was. Before taking her nap, she had switched off the lamps. The shutters were all closed, and only thin blades of light were visible between the wooden slats. She had the irrational but unshakable feeling that something had followed her up from the dream, something vicious and evil that had undergone a magical metamorphosis from a creature of the imagination into one composed of solid flesh, something that was now crouched in a corner, watching, waiting.

—*Stop it!*

—*But the dream was . . .*

—*Only a dream.*

Along the edges of the shutters, the taut threads of light abruptly brightened, then dimmed, then grew bright again as lightning flashed outside. A roof-rattling crash of thunder quickly followed, and more lightning, too, an unbelievable amount of it, one blue-white explosion after another, so that for at least half a minute the cracks in the shutters looked like sputtering electrical wires, white-hot with sparking current.

Still drugged with sleep and slightly confused, Grace stood in the middle of the unlighted room, rocking from side to side, listening to the thunder and the wind, watching the intense pulse of lightning. The extreme violence of the storm seemed unreal, and she concluded that she was still under the influence of the dream, misinterpreting what she was seeing. It couldn't possibly be as savage outside as it appeared to be.

"Grace . . ."

She thought she heard something call to her from over by the tallest set of bookshelves, directly behind her. Judging from its slurred, distorted pronunciation of her name, its mouth was severely malformed.

There's nothing behind me! Nothing.

Nevertheless, she did not turn around.

When the lightning finally stopped and the long-sustained crescendo of thunder subsided, the air seemed thicker than it had been a minute ago. She had difficulty breathing. The room was darker, too.

"Grace . . ."

A confining mantle of claustrophobia settled over her. The dimly visible walls appeared to ripple and move closer, as if the chamber might shrink around her until it was precisely the size and shape of a coffin.

"Grace . . ."

She stumbled to the nearest window, banging her hip against the desk, nearly tripping over a lamp cord. She fumbled with the lever on the shutters, her fingers stiff and unresponsive. At last the slats opened wide; gray but welcome light poured into the study, forcing her to squint but gladdening her as well. She leaned against the shutters and stared out at the cloud-plated sky, resisting the insane urge to look over her shoulder to see if there really was something monstrous lurking there with a hungry grin on its face. She drew deep, gasping breaths, as if the daylight itself—rather than the air—sustained her.

Grace's house was atop a small knoll, at the end of a quiet street, sheltered by several large pine trees and by one enormous weeping willow; from her study window she could see the rain-swollen Susquehanna a couple of miles away. Harrisburg, the state capital, huddled solemnly, drearily along the river's banks. The clouds hung low over the city, trailing bedraggled beards of mist that obscured the upper floors of the tallest buildings.

When she'd blinked the last grains of sleep out of her eyes, when her nerves had stopped jangling, she turned around and surveyed the room. A quiver of relief swept through her, unknotting her muscles.

She was alone.

With the storm temporarily quiet, she could hear the mantel clock again. It was the only sound.

Hell, yes, you're alone, she told herself scornfully. What did you expect? A green goblin with three eyes and a mouthful of sharp teeth? You better watch yourself, Grace Louise Mitowski, or you'll wind up in a rest home, sitting all day in a rocking chair, happily chatting with ghosts, while smiling nurses wipe drool off your chin.

Having led an active life of the mind for so many years, she worried more about creeping senility than about anything else. She knew she was as sharp and alert as she had ever been. But what about tomorrow and the day after? Because of her medical training, and because she had kept up with her professional reading even after closing down her psychiatric practice, she was up to date on all the latest findings about senility, and she knew that only fifteen percent of all elderly people suffered from it. She also knew that more than half of those cases were treatable with proper nutrition and exercise. She knew her chances of becoming mentally incapacitated were small, only about one in eighteen. Nevertheless, although she was conscious of her excessive sensitivity regarding the subject, she still worried. Consequently, she was understandably disturbed by this uncharacteristic notion that something had been in the study with her a few moments ago, something hostile and . . . supernatural. As a lifelong skeptic with little or no patience for astrologers and psychics and their ilk, she could not justify even a fleeting belief in such superstitious nonsense; to her way of thinking, beliefs of that nature were . . . well . . . feebleminded.

But good, sweet God, what a nightmare that had been!

She had never before experienced a dream even one-tenth as bad as that one. Although the grisly details had completely faded away, she could still clearly remember the mood of it—the terror, the gut-wrenching horror that had permeated every nasty image, every ticking sound.

She shivered.

The sweat that the dream had squeezed out of her was beginning to feel like a thin glaze of ice on her skin.

The only other thing she remembered from the nightmare was Carol. Screaming. Crying for help.

Until now, none of Grace's infrequent dreams had included Carol, and there was a temptation to view her appearance in this one with alarm, to see it as an omen. But of course it wasn't surprising that Carol should eventually have a role in one of Grace's dreams, for the loved-one-in-danger theme was common in nightmares. Any psychologist would attest to that, and Grace was a psychologist, a good one, although she was entering her third year of retirement. She cared deeply about Carol. If she'd had a child of her own, she couldn't have loved it any more than she loved Carol.

She had first met the girl sixteen years ago, when Carol had been an angry, obstinate, obstreperous fifteen-year-old delinquent who had recently given birth to a baby that had nearly killed her, and who, subsequent to that traumatic episode, had been remanded to a juvenile detention facility for possession of marijuana and for a host of other offenses. In those days, in addition to a private psychiatric practice, Grace had performed eight hours a week of free service to assist the overworked counseling staff at the reform school in which Carol was held. Carol was incorrigible, determined to kick you in the teeth if you smiled at her, but even then her intelligence and innate goodness were there, to be seen by anyone who looked closely enough, beneath the rough exterior. Grace had taken a very close look indeed, and had been intrigued, impressed. The girl's obsessively foul language, her vicious temper, and her amoral pose had been nothing more than defense mechanisms, shields with which she protected herself from the physical and psychological abuse dished out by her parents.

As Grace gradually unearthed the horrendous story of Carol's monstrous home life, she became convinced that reform school was the wrong place for the girl. She used her influence with the court to get Carol permanently removed from the custody of her parents. Later, she arranged to serve as Carol's foster parent. She had watched the girl respond to love and guidance, had watched her grow from a brooding, self-centered, self-destructive teenager into a warm, self-assured, admirable young woman with hopes and dreams, a woman of character, a sensitive woman. Playing a part in that exciting transformation had been perhaps the most satisfying thing that Grace had ever done.

The only regret she had about her relationship with Carol was the role she had played in putting the baby up for adoption. But there had been no reasonable alternative. Carol simply hadn't been financially or emotionally or mentally capable of providing for the infant. With that responsibility to attend to, she would never have had an opportunity to grow and change. She would have been miserable all her life, and she would have made her child miserable, too. Unfortunately, even now, sixteen years later, Carol felt guilty about giving her baby away. Her guilt became overpowering on each anniversary of the child's birth. On that black day, Carol sank into a deep depression and became uncharacteristically uncommunicative. The excessive anguish that she suffered on that one day was evidence of the deep-seated, abiding guilt that she carried with her, to a lesser degree, during the rest of the year. Grace wished she had foreseen this reaction, wished she had done more to assuage Carol's guilt.

I'm a psychologist, after all, she thought. I should have anticipated it.

Perhaps when Carol and Paul adopted someone else's child, Carol would feel that the scales had at last been balanced. The adoption might relieve some of her guilt, in time.

Grace hoped it would. She loved Carol like a daughter and wanted only the best for her.

And of course she couldn't bear the thought of losing Carol. Therefore, Carol's appearance in a nightmare wasn't the least bit mysterious. It was certainly *not* an omen.

Clammy with stale sweat, Grace turned to the study window again, seeking warmth and light, but the day was ashen, chilly, forbidding. Wind pressed on the glass, soughed softly under the eaves one floor above.

In the city, near the river, a roiling column of smoke rose into the rain and mist. She had not noticed it a minute ago, but it must have been there; it was too much smoke to have appeared in only a few seconds. Even from this distance, she could see a glint of fire at the base of the dark column.

She wondered if lightning had done the dirty work. She recalled the storm flashing and roaring with extraordinary power in those first seconds after she had awakened. At the time, groggy and bleary-eyed, she had thought her sleep-dulled senses were misleading her and that the extreme violence of the lightning was largely illusory or even imaginary. Could that incredible, destructive barrage have been real after all?

She glanced at her wristwatch.

Her favorite radio station would carry its hourly newscast in less than ten minutes. Maybe there would be a story about the fire and the lightning.

After she'd straightened the throw pillows on the sofa, she stepped out of the study and spotted Aristophanes at the far end of the downstairs hall, near the front door. He was sitting up straight and tall, his tail curled forward and across his front paws, his head held high, as if he were saying, ''A Siamese cat is the very best thing on earth, and I am an exceedingly handsome example of the species, and don't you dare forget it.''

Grace held one hand toward him, rapidly rubbing her thumb against her forefinger. ''Kitty-kitty-kitty.''

Aristophanes didn't move.

''Kitty-kitty-kitty. Come here, Ari. Come on, baby.''

Aristophanes got up and went through the archway on his left, into the dark living room.

''Stubborn damn cat,'' she said affectionately.

She went into the downstairs bathroom and washed her face and combed her hair. The mundane task of grooming herself took her mind off the nightmare. Gradually, she began to relax. Her eyes were watery and bloodshot. She rinsed them out with a few drops of Murine.

When she came out of the bathroom, Aristophanes was sitting in the hallway again, watching her.

''Kitty-kitty-kitty,'' she coaxed.

He stared unblinkingly.

''Kitty-kitty-kitty.''

Aristophanes rose to his feet, cocked his head, and examined her with curious, shining eyes. When she took a step toward him, he turned and quickly slunk away, casting one backward glance, then disappearing into the living room again.

''Okay,'' Grace said. ''Okay, buster. Have it your way. Snub me if you want. But just see if there's any Meow Mix in *your* bowl tonight.''

In the kitchen she snapped on the lights, then the radio. The station came in clearly enough, though there was a continuous crackle of storm-generated static.

While she listened to tales of economic crises and breathless accounts of airplane hijackings and rumors of war, Grace put a clean paper filter in the coffee machine, filled the brewing basket with drip-ground Colombian, and added half a spoonful of chicory. The story of the fire came at the end of the newscast, and it was only a sketchy bulletin. The reporter knew nothing more than that lightning had struck a couple of buildings in the heart of the city and that one of them, a church, was afire. He promised more details on the half hour.

When the coffee was ready, Grace poured some for herself. She took her mug to the small table by the kitchen's only window, pulled out a chair, and sat down.

In the backyard, the myriad roses—red, pink, orange, white, yellow—looked preternaturally bright, almost phosphorescent, against the cinereous backdrop of the rain.

Two psychology journals had arrived in the morning mail. Grace opened one of them with pleasant anticipation.

Halfway through an article about new findings in criminal psychology, as she finished her first mug of coffee, there was a pause between songs on the radio, a few seconds of dead air, and in that brief quietude, she heard furtive movement behind her. She turned in her chair and saw Aristophanes.

''Come to apologize?'' she asked.

Then she realized that he appeared to have been sneaking up on her, and that now, confronted, he was frozen; every lithe muscle in his small body was spring-taut, and the fur bristled along his arched back.

''Ari? What's wrong, you silly cat?''

He whirled and ran out of the kitchen.

THREE

◆

Carol sat in a chrome chair with shiny black vinyl cushions, and she slowly sipped whiskey from a paper cup.

Paul slumped in the chair next to hers. He didn't sip his whiskey; he gulped the stuff. It was an excellent bourbon, Jack Daniel's Black Label, thoughtfully provided by an attorney named Marvin Kwicker, who had offices down the hall from Alfred O'Brian and who realized that a restorative was urgently needed. Pouring bourbon for Carol, Marvin had said, "Kwicker with liquor," which he had probably said ten thousand times before, but he still enjoyed his own joke. "Kwicker with liquor," he repeated when dispensing a double shot to Paul. Although Paul wasn't much of a drinker, he needed every drop that the attorney gave him. His hands were still shaking.

The reception lounge that served O'Brian's office was not large, but most of the people who worked on the same floor had congregated here to talk about the lightning that had shaken the building, to marvel that the place hadn't caught fire, to express surprise that the electric power had been restored so quickly, and to wait their turns for a peek at the rubble and ruin in O'Brian's inner sanctum. The resultant roar of conversation did nothing to soothe Paul's nerves.

Every thirty seconds or so, a bleached blonde with a shrill voice repeated the same words of amazement: "I can't believe nobody got killed in all that! I can't believe *nobody* got killed." Each time she spoke, regardless of where she was in the room, her voice carried over the din and made Paul wince. "I can't believe *nobody* got killed." She sounded somewhat disappointed.

Alfred O'Brian was sitting at the reception desk. His secretary, a prim-looking woman whose hair was drawn back in a tight bun, was trying to apply Merthiolate to half a dozen scratches on her boss's face, but O'Brian seemed more concerned about the condition of his suit than he was about himself. He plucked and brushed at the dirt, lint, and small fragments of tree bark that clung to his jacket.

Paul finished his whiskey and looked at Carol. She was still badly shaken. Contrasted with her glossy dark hair, her face was very pale.

Apparently, she saw the concern in his eyes, for she took his hand, squeezed it, and smiled reassuringly. However, the smile didn't set well on her lips; it was tremulous.

He leaned close to her, so that she could hear him above the excited chatter of the others. "Ready to get out of here?"

She nodded.

Over by the window, a young executive type raised his voice. "Hey! Hey, everybody! Better look sharp. The TV news people just drove up to the front door."

"If we get trapped by reporters," Carol said, "we'll be here an hour or more."

They left without saying goodbye to O'Brian. In the hall, as they headed toward a side entrance, they slipped into their raincoats. Outside, Paul opened his umbrella and put one arm around Carol's waist. They hurried across the slippery macadam parking lot, stepping gingerly around huge puddles. The gusting wind was chilly for early September, and it kept changing direction until it finally got under the umbrella and turned it inside out. The cold, wind-driven rain was falling so hard that it stung Paul's face. By the time they reached the car, their hair was plastered to their heads, and a lot of water had found its way down the backs of their necks, under the collars of their coats.

Paul half expected the Pontiac to be lightning-damaged, but it was just as they had left it. The engine turned over without protest.

Leaving the parking lot, he started to turn left but put his foot on the brake pedal when he saw that the street was sealed off by police cars and fire trucks just half a block away. The church was still ablaze, in spite of the pouring rain and in defiance of the big streams of water that the firemen directed onto it. Black smoke billowed into the gray day, and behind the blasted windows, flames spurted and churned. Clearly, the church was going to be a total loss.

He turned right, instead, and drove home through rain-choked streets, where the gutters overflowed and where every depression in the pavement had been transformed into a treacherous lake that had to be negotiated with utmost caution to avoid drowning the engine and stalling out.

Carol slouched in her seat and huddled against the passenger-side door, hugging herself. Although the heater was on, she was obviously cold.

Paul realized his teeth were chattering.

The trip home took ten minutes, and during that time neither of them said a word. The only sounds were the whispery hiss of the tires on the wet pavement and the metronomic thump of the windshield wipers. The silence was not uncomfortable or strained, but there was a peculiar intensity about it, an aura of tremendous, pent-up energy. Paul had the feeling that if he *did* speak, the surprise would send Carol straight through the roof of the car.

They lived in a Tudor-style house, which they had painstakingly restored, and as always, the sight of it—the stone walk, the big oak doors framed by carriage lamps, the leaded-glass windows, the gabled roofline—pleased Paul and gave him the warm feeling that this was where he belonged. The automatic garage door rolled up, and he pulled the Pontiac inside, next to Carol's red Volkswagen Rabbit.

In the house, they maintained their silence.

Paul's hair was wet, and the legs of his trousers clung damply to him, and the back of his shirt was still soaked. He figured he was going to come down with a nasty cold if he didn't get into some dry clothes right away. Apparently, Carol had the same thought, and they went straight upstairs to the master bedroom. She opened the closet doors, and he switched on a bedside lamp. Shivering, they stripped out of their wet clothes.

When they were nearly undressed, they glanced at each other. Their eyes locked.

Still, they didn't speak. They didn't need to.

He took her in his arms, and they kissed lightly at first, tenderly. Her mouth was warm and soft and vaguely flavored with whiskey.

She clutched him, pulled him closer, her fingertips digging into the muscles of his back. She pushed her mouth hard against his, scraped his lip with her teeth, thrust her tongue deep, and abruptly their kisses grew hot, demanding.

Something seemed to snap in him, and in her, too, for their desire was suddenly marked by animal urgency. They responded to each other in a hungry, almost frenzied fashion, hastily casting off the last of their clothes, pawing at each other, squeezing, stroking. She nipped his shoulder with her teeth. He gripped her buttocks and kneaded them with uncharacteristic crudity, but she didn't wince or try to pull away; indeed, she pressed even more insistently against him, rubbing her breasts over his chest and grinding her hips against his. The soft whimpers that escaped from her were not sounds of pain; they clearly expressed her eagerness and need. In bed, his energy was manic, and his staying power amazed him. He was insatiable, and so was she. They thrust and thrashed and flexed and tensed in perfect harmony, as if they were not only joined but *fused,* as if they were a single organism, shaken by only one set of stimuli instead of two. Every vestige of civilization slipped from them, and for a long while the only noises they made were animal sounds: panting; groaning; throaty grunts of pleasure; short, sharp cries of excitement. At last Carol uttered the first word to pass between them since they had left O'Brian's office: "Yes." And again, arching her slender, graceful body, tossing her head from side to side on the pillow: "Yes, yes!" It was not merely an orgasm to which she was saying yes, for she'd already had a couple of those and had announced them with only ragged breathing and soft mewling. She was saying yes to life, yes to the fact that she still existed and was not just a charred and oozing lump of unanimated flesh, yes to the miraculous fact that they had both survived the lightning and the deadly, splintered branches of the toppling maple tree. Their unrestrained, fiercely passionate coupling was a slap in Death's face, a not wholly rational but nevertheless satisfying denial of the grim specter's very existence. Paul repeated the word as if chanting an incantation—"Yes, yes, yes!"—as he emptied himself into her a second time, and it seemed as though his fear of death spurted out of him along with his seed.

Spent, they stretched out on their backs, side by side on the disheveled bed. For a long time they listened to the rain on the roof and to the persistent thunder, which was no longer loud enough to rattle the windows.

Carol lay with her eyes closed, her face completely relaxed. Paul studied her, and, as he had done on countless other occasions during the past four years, he wondered why she had ever consented to marry him. She was beautiful. He was not. Anyone putting together a dictionary could do worse than to use a picture of his face as the sole definition of the word *plain.* He had once jokingly expressed a similar opinion of his physical appearance, and Carol had been angry with him for talking about himself that way. But it was true, and it didn't really matter to him that he was not Burt Reynolds, just so long as Carol didn't notice the difference. It was not only his plainness of which she seemed unaware; she could not comprehend her own beauty, and she insisted *she* was actually rather plain, or at least no more than "a little bit pretty, no, not even pretty, just sort of cute, but kind of funny-looking cute." Her dark hair—even now, when it was matted and curled by rain and sweat—was thick, glossy, lovely. Her skin was flawless, and her cheekbones were so well sculpted that it was difficult to believe the clumsy hand of nature could have done the job. Carol was the kind of woman you saw on the arm of a tall, bronzed Adonis, not with the likes of Paul Tracy. Yet here she was, and he was grateful to have her beside him. He never ceased to be surprised that they were compatible in every respect—mentally, emotionally, physically.

Now, as rain began to beat on the roof and windows with renewed force, Carol sensed that he was staring at her, and she opened her eyes. They were so brown that, from a distance of more than a few inches, they looked black. She smiled. "I love you."

"I love you," he said.

"I thought you were dead."

"Wasn't."

"After the lightning stopped, I called you, but you didn't answer for the longest time."

"I was busy with a call to Chicago," he said, grinning.

"Seriously."

"Okay. It was San Francisco."

"I was scared."

"I *couldn't* answer you right away," he said soothingly. "In case you've forgotten, O'Brian fell on top of me, knocked the wind right out. He doesn't look so big, but he's as solid as a rock. I guess he builds a lot of muscles by picking lint off his suits and shining his shoes nine hours a day."

"That was a pretty brave thing you did."

"Making love to you? Think nothing of it."

Playfully, she slapped his face. "You know what I mean. You saved O'Brian's life."

"Nope."

"Yes, you did. He thought so, too."

"For God's sake, I didn't step in front of him and shield him from the tree with mine own precious bod! I just pulled him out of the way. Anyone would have done the same."

She shook her head. "Wrong. Not everyone thinks as fast as you do."

"A fast thinker, huh? Yeah. That's something I'll admit to being. I'm a fast thinker, but I'm sure no hero. I won't let you pin *that* label on me because then you'll expect me to live up to it. Can you just imagine what a hell on earth Superman's life would be if he ever married Lois Lane? Her expectations would be so high!"

"Anyway," Carol said, "even if you won't admit it, O'Brian knows you saved his life, and that's the important thing."

"It is?"

"Well, I was pretty sure the adoption agency would approve us. But now there's not the slightest doubt about it."

"There's always a slim chance—"

"No," she said, interrupting him. "O'Brian's not going to fail you after you saved his life. Not a chance. He's going to wrap the recommendations committee around his finger."

Paul blinked, then slowly broke into a smile. "I'll be damned. I didn't think of that."

"So you're a hero, Papa."

"Well . . . maybe I am, Mama."

"I think I prefer 'Mom.' "

"And I prefer 'Dad.' "

"What about 'Pop'?"

"Pop isn't a name. It's a sound a champagne cork makes."

"Are you suggesting a celebration?" she asked.

"I thought we'd put on our robes, mosey down to the kitchen, and whip up an early dinner. If you're hungry, that is."

"Famished."

"You can make a mushroom salad," he said. "I'll whip up my famous fettuccine Alfredo. We've got a bottle or two of Mumm's Extra Dry we've been saving for a special occasion. We'll open that, pile our plates high with fettuccine Alfredo and mushrooms, come back up here, and have dinner in bed."

"And watch the TV news while we eat."

"Then pass the evening reading thrillers and sipping champagne until we can't keep our eyes open."

"Sounds wonderfully, sinfully lazy," she said.

More evenings than not, he spent two hours proofreading and polishing his novel. And it was an unusual night when Carol didn't have some paperwork to catch up on.

As they dressed in robes and bedroom slippers, Paul said, "We've got to learn to take *most* evenings off. We'll have to spend plenty of time with the kid. We'll owe it to him."

"Or her."

"Or them," he said.

Her eyes shone. "You think they'll let us adopt more than one?"

"Of course they will—once we've proven we can handle the first. After all," he said self-mockingly, "am I not the hero who saved good old Al O'Brian's life?"

On their way to the kitchen, halfway down the stairs, she stopped and turned and hugged him. "We're really going to have a family."

"So it seems."

"Oh, Paul, I don't remember when I've ever been so happy. Tell me this feeling's going to last forever."

He held her, and it was very fine to have her in his arms. When you got right down to it, affection was even better than sex; being needed and loved was better than making love.

"Tell me nothing can go wrong," she said.

"Nothing can go wrong, and that feeling you have will last forever, and I'm glad you're so happy. There. How's that?"

She kissed his chin and the corners of his mouth, and he kissed her nose.

"Now," he said, "can we please get some fettuccine before I start chewing my tongue?"

"Such a romantic."

"Even romantics get hungry."

As they reached the bottom of the steps, they were startled by a sudden, loud hammering sound. It was steady but arhythmic: *Thunk, thunk, thunk-thunk-thunk, thunk-thunk* . . .

Carol said, "What the devil's that?"

"It's coming from outside . . . and above us."

They stood on the last step, looking up and back toward the second floor.

Thunk, thunk-thunk, thunk, thunk . . .

"Damn," Paul said. "I'll bet one of the shutters came loose in the wind." They listened for a moment, and then he sighed. "I'll have to go out and fix it."

"Now? In the rain?"

"If I don't do anything, the wind might tear it clean off the house. Worse yet, it might just hang there and clatter all night. We won't get any sleep, and neither will half the neighborhood."

She frowned. "But the lightning . . . Paul, after everything that's happened, I don't think you should risk climbing around on a ladder in the middle of a storm."

He didn't like the idea, either. The thought of being high on a ladder in the middle of a thunderstorm made his scalp prickle.

She said, "I don't want you to go out there if—"

The hammering stopped.

They waited.

Wind. The patter of rain. The branches of a tree scraping lightly against an outside wall.

At last, Paul said, "Too late. If it was a shutter, it's been torn off."

"I didn't hear it fall."

"It wouldn't make much noise if it dropped in the grass or the shrubbery."

"So you don't have to go out in the rain," she said, crossing the foyer toward the short hall that led to the kitchen.

He followed her. "Yeah, but now it's a bigger repair job."

As they entered the kitchen, their footsteps echoing hollowly off the quarry-tile floor, she said, "You don't have to worry about it until tomorrow or the day after. Right now, all you've got to worry about is the sauce for the fettuccine. Don't let it curdle."

Taking a copper saucepan from a rack of gleaming utensils that hung over the center utility island, he pretended to be insulted by her remark. "Have I *ever* curdled the sauce for the fettuccine?"

"Seems to me the last time you made it, the stuff was—"

"Never!"

"Yes," she said teasingly. "Yes, it definitely wasn't up to par the last time." She took a plastic bag of mushrooms from the big, stainless-steel refrigerator. "Although it breaks my heart to tell you this, the last time you made fettuccine Alfredo, the sauce was as lumpy as the mattress in a ten-dollar-a-night motel."

"What a vile accusation! Besides, what makes you such an expert on ten-dollar-a-night motels? Are you leading a secret life I ought to know about?"

Together, they prepared dinner, chatting about this and that, bantering a lot, trying to amuse each other and to elicit a laugh now and then. For Paul, the world dwindled until they were the only two people in it. The universe was no larger than the warm, familiar kitchen.

Then lightning flickered, and the cozy mood was broken. It was soft lightning, nothing as dazzling and destructive as the bolts that had struck outside of O'Brian's office a few hours ago. Nevertheless, Paul stopped talking in midsentence, his attention captured by the flash, his eyes drawn to the long, many-paned window behind the sink. On the rear lawn, the trees appeared to writhe and shimmer and ripple in the fluttering storm light, so that it seemed he was looking not at the trees themselves but at their reflections in the surface of a lake.

Suddenly, another movement caught his eye, though he wasn't sure what he was seeing. The afternoon, which had been gray and dark to begin with, was now gradually giving away to an early night, and thin fog was drifting in. Shadows lay everywhere. The meager daylight was deceptive, muddy; it distorted rather than illuminated those things it touched. In that penumbral landscape, something abruptly darted out from behind the thick trunk of an oak tree, crossed a stretch of open grass, and quickly disappeared behind a lilac bush.

Carol said, "Paul? What's wrong?"

"Someone's out on the lawn."

"In this rain? Who?"

"I don't know."

She joined him by the window. "I don't see anybody."

"Someone ran from the oak to the lilac bush. He was hunched over and moving pretty fast."

"What's he look like?"

"I can't say. I'm not even sure it was a man. Might have been a woman."

"Maybe it was just a dog."

"Too big."

"Could've been Jasper."

Jasper was the Great Dane that belonged to the Hanrahan family, three doors down the street. He was a large, piercing-eyed, friendly animal with an amazing tolerence for small children and a liking for Oreo cookies.

"They wouldn't let Jasper out in weather like this," Paul said. "They pamper that mutt."

Lightning pulsed softly again, and a violent gust of wind whipped the trees back and forth, and rain began to fall harder than before—and in the middle of that maelstrom, something rushed out from the lilac bush.

"There!" Paul said.

The intruder crouched low, obscured by the rain and the mist, a shadow among shadows. It was illuminated so briefly and strangely by the lightning that its true appearance remained tantalizingly at the edge of perception. It loped toward the brick wall that marked the perimeter of the property, vanished for a moment in an especially dense patch of fog, reappeared as an amorphous black shape, then changed direction, paralleling the wall now, heading toward the gate at the northwest corner of the rear lawn. As the darkening sky throbbed with lightning once more, the intruder fled through electric-blue flashes, through the open gate, into the street, and away.

"Just the dog," Carol said.

Paul frowned. "I thought I saw . . . "

"What?"

"A face. A woman looking back . . . just for a second, just as she went through the gate."

"No," Carol said. "It was Jasper."

"You saw him?"

"Yes."

"Clearly?"

"Well, no, not clearly. But I could see enough to tell that it was a dog the size of a small pony, and Jasper's the only pooch around who fits that description."

"I guess Jasper's a lot smarter than he used to be."

Carol blinked. "What do you mean?"

"Well, he had to unlatch the gate to get into the yard. He never used to be able to do that trick."

"Oh, of course he didn't. We must have left the gate open."

Paul shook his head. "I'm sure it was closed when we drove up a while ago."

"Closed, maybe—but not latched. The wind pushed it open, and Jasper wandered in."

Paul stared out at the rain-slashed fog, which glowed dully with the last somber rays of the fading twilight. "I guess you're right," he said, though he was not entirely convinced. "I better go latch the gate."

"No, no," Carol said quickly. "Not while the storm's on."

"Now look here, sugarface, I'm not going to jump into bed and pull the blankets over my head every time there's a little thunder—just because of what happened this afternoon."

"I don't expect you to," she said. "But before you start dancing in the rain like Gene Kelly, you've got to let *me* get over what happened today. It's still too fresh in my mind for me to stand here watching you while you cavort across the lawn in the lightning."

"It'll only take a moment and—"

"Say, are you trying to get out of making that fettuccine?" she asked, cocking her head and looking at him suspiciously.

"Certainly not. I'll finish making it as soon as I've gone and closed the gate."

"I know what you're up to, mister," she said smugly. "You're hoping you *will* be struck by lightning because you *know* your sauce is going to turn out lumpy, and you simply can't take the humiliation."

"That's a base canard," he said, falling easily into their game again. "I make the silkiest fettuccine Alfredo this side of Rome. Silkier than Sophia Loren's thighs."

"All I know is, the last time you made it, the stuff was as lumpy as a bowl of oatmeal."

"I thought you said it was as lumpy as a mattress in a ten-dollar-a-night motel."

She lifted her head proudly. "I'm not just a one-simile woman, you know."

"How *well* I know."

"So are you going to make fettuccine—or will you take the coward's way out and get killed by lightning?"

"I'll make you eat your words," he said.

Grinning, she said, "That's easier than eating your lumpy fettuccine."

He laughed. "All right, all right. You win. I can latch the gate in the morning."

He returned to the stove, and she went back to the cutting board where she was mincing parsley and scallions for the salad dressing.

He knew she was probably right about the intruder. Most likely, it had been Jasper, chasing a cat or looking for an Oreo handout. The thing he'd thought he had seen—the slightly twisted, moon-white face of a woman, lightning reflected in her eyes, her mouth curled into a snarl of hatred or rage—had surely been a trick of light and shadow. Still, the incident left him uneasy. He could not entirely regain the warm, cozy feeling he'd had just before he'd looked out the window.

Grace Mitowski filled the yellow plastic bowl with Meow Mix and put it in the corner by the kitchen door.

"Kitty-kitty-kitty."

Aristophanes didn't respond.

The kitchen wasn't Ari's favorite place in the house, for it was the only room in which he was not permitted to climb wherever he wished. He wasn't actually much of a climber anyway. He lacked the spirit of adventure that many cats had, and he usually stayed on the floor. However, even though he had no burning desire to scamper up on the kitchen counters, he didn't want anyone telling him he *couldn't* do it. Like most cats, he resisted discipline and despised all rules. Nevertheless, as little as he liked the kitchen, he never failed to put in an appearance at mealtime. In fact, he was often waiting impatiently by his bowl when Grace came to fill it.

She raised her voice. "Kitty-kitty-kitty."

There was no answering meow. Aristophanes did not, as expected, come running, his tail curled up slightly, eager for his dinner.

"Ari-Ari-Ari! Soup's on, you silly cat."

She put away the box of cat food and washed her hands at the sink.

Thunk, thunk-thunk!

The hammering sound—one hard blow followed by two equally hard blows struck close together—was so sudden and loud that Grace jerked in surprise and almost dropped the small towel on which she was drying her hands. The noise had come from the front of the house. She waited a moment, and there was only the sound of the wind and falling rain, and then—

Thunk! Thunk!

She hung the towel on the rack and stepped into the downstairs hallway.

Thunk-thunk-thunk!

She walked hesitantly down the hall to the front door and snapped on the porch light. The door had a peephole, and the fish-eye lens provided a wide view. She couldn't see anyone; the porch appeared to be deserted.

THUNK!

That blow was delivered with such force that Grace thought the door had been torn from its hinges. There was a splintering sound as she jumped back, and she expected to see chunks of wood exploding into the hall. But the door still hung firmly in place, though it vibrated noisily in its frame; the deadbolt rattled against the lock plate.

THUNK! THUNK! THUNK!

''Stop that!'' she shouted. ''Who are you? Who's there?''

The pounding stopped, and she thought she heard adolescent laughter.

She had been on the verge of either calling the police or going for the pistol she kept in her nightstand, but when she heard the laughter, she changed her mind. She could certainly handle a few kids without help. She wasn't so old and weak and fragile that she needed to call the cops to deal with a bunch of ornery little pranksters.

Cautiously, she drew aside the curtain on the long, narrow window beside the door. Tense, ready to step away quickly if someone made a threatening move toward the glass, she looked out. There was no one on the porch.

She heard the laughter again. It was high-pitched, musical, girlish.

Letting the curtain fall back into place, she turned to the door, unlocked it, and stepped onto the threshold.

The night wind was raw and wet. Rain drizzled off the scalloped eaves of the porch.

The immediate area in front of the house offered at least a hundred hiding places for the hoaxers. Bristling shrubbery rustled in the wind, just the other side of the railing, and the yellowish glow from the insect-repelling bulb in the porch ceiling illuminated little more than the center of the porch. The walkway that led from the bottom of the porch steps to the street was flanked by hedges that looked blue black in the darkness. Among the many shades of night, none of the pranksters was visible.

Grace waited, listened.

Thunder rumbled in the distance, but there was no laughter, no giggling in the darkness.

—Maybe it wasn't kids.

—Who else?

—You see them on TV news all the time. The iron-eyed ones who shoot and stab and strangle people for the fun of it. They seem to be everywhere these days, the misfits, the psychopaths.

—That was not adult laughter. This is kids' work.

—Still, maybe I better get inside and lock the door.

—Stop thinking like a frightened old lady, dammit!

It *was* odd that any of the neighborhood children would harass her, for she was on excellent terms with all of them. Of course, maybe these weren't kids from the immediate neighborhood. Just a couple of streets away, everyone was a stranger to her.

She turned and examined the outer face of the front door. She could find no indication that it had been struck repeatedly and violently only moments ago. The wood was not chipped or cracked; it wasn't even slightly marred.

She was amazed because she was certain she had heard the wood splintering. What would kids use that would make a lot of noise while leaving absolutely no marks on the door? Bean bags or something of that nature? No. A bean bag wouldn't have made such a horrendous racket; the impact of the bag against the door might have been loud, yes, very loud indeed, if it had been swung with sufficient force, but the sound wouldn't have been so hard, so sharp.

Again, she slowly scanned the yard. Nothing moved out there except the wind-stirred foliage.

For nearly a minute she watched and listened. She would have waited longer, if only to prove to any mischievous young observers that she was not a frightened old lady who could be easily intimidated; but the air was damp and chilly, and she began to worry about catching a cold.

She went inside and closed the door.

She waited with her hand on the knob, expecting the kids to return shortly. The first time they hit the door, she would jerk it open and catch them red-handed, before they could dart off the porch and hide.

Two minutes passed. Three minutes. Five.

No one hammered on the door, which was distinctly strange. To pranksters, the fun wasn't in the first assault so much as in the second and third and fourth; their intent was not to startle but to torment.

Apparently, the defiant stance she had taken in the doorway had discouraged them. Very likely, they were on their way to another house, seeking a more excitable victim.

She snapped the lock into place.

What kind of parents would allow their children to be out playing in an electrical storm like this?

Shaking her head in dismay at the irresponsibility of some parents, Grace headed back the hall, and with each step she half expected the hammering to start again. But it didn't.

She had planned to have a light, nutritious dinner of steamed vegetables covered with Cheddar cheese, accompanied by a slice or two of home-baked cornbread, but she wasn't hungry yet. She decided to watch the ABC evening news before preparing dinner—although she knew that, with the world in the state it was, the news might put her off her dinner altogether.

In the study, before she had a chance to turn on the television set and hear the latest atrocity stories, she found a mess on the seat of her big armchair. For a moment she could do nothing but stare at the ruin in disbelief: hundreds of feathers; shreds of cloth; colorful, unraveled threads that had once constituted a needlework pattern, but which now lay in a bright, meaningless tangle amidst drifts of goosedown. A couple of years ago, Carol Tracy had given her a set of three small, exceedingly lovely, handmade needlework throw pillows. It was one of those gifts that had been clawed to pieces and left on the armchair.

Aristophanes.

Ari hadn't ripped up anything important since he was a kitten. An act as destructive as this was quite out of character for him, but he was surely the culprit. There was not really another suspect to be seriously considered.

"Ari! Where are you hiding, you sneaky Siamese?"

She went to the kitchen.

Aristophanes was standing at the yellow bowl, eating his Meow Mix. He glanced up as she entered the room.

"You fur-footed menace," she said. "What in the world has gotten into you today?"

Aristophanes blinked, sneezed, rubbed his muzzle with one paw, and returned to his dinner with lofty, catlike indifference to her exasperation and puzzlement.

Later that night, in her darkened bedroom, Carol Tracy stared at the adumbral ceiling and listened to her husband's soft, steady breathing. He had been asleep for only a few minutes.

The night was quiet. The rain had stopped, and the sky was no longer shaken by thunder. Occasionally, wind brushed across the shingled roof and sighed wearily at the windows, but the fury had gone out of it.

Carol teetered pleasantly on the edge of sleep. She was a bit lightheaded from the champagne she had been slowly sipping throughout the evening, and she felt as if she were floating in warm water, with gentle waves lapping at her sides.

She thought dreamily about the child they would adopt, tried to envision its appearance. A gallery of sweet young faces filled her imagination. If it was an infant, rather than a three- or four-year-old, they would name it themselves: Jason, if a boy; Julia, if a girl. Carol rocked herself on the thin line between wakefulness and dreams by rolling those two names back and forth in her mind: *Jason, Julia, Jason, Julia, Jason . . .*

Falling off the edge, dropping into a well of sleep, she had the ugly, unwelcome thought she had resisted so strenuously earlier in the day: *Something's trying to stop us from adopting a baby.*

Then she was in a strange place where there was not much light, where something hissed and murmured sullenly just out of sight, where the purple-amber shadows had substance and crowded close with menacing intent. In that unknown place, the nightmare unrolled with the frantic, nerve-jarring rhythm of player-piano music.

At first she was running in utter lightlessness, and then she was suddenly running from one room to another in a large house, weaving through a forest of furniture, knocking over a floor lamp, banging one hip against the sharp corner of a credenza, stumbling and nearly falling over the loose edge of an oriental carpet. She plunged through an archway, into a long hall, and turned and looked back into the room from which she had come, but the room wasn't there any longer. The house existed only in front of her; behind, there was perfect, featureless blackness. Blackness . . . and then a glimmer of something. A glint. A splinter of light. A silvery, moving object. The thing swung from side to side, vanishing into darkness, reappearing with a gleam a second later, vanishing again, back and forth, back and forth, rather like a pendulum, never visible long enough to be identified. Although she couldn't quite see what the silvery thing was, she could tell that it was moving toward her, and she knew she must get away from it or die. She ran along the hall to the foot of the stairs, climbed quickly to the second floor. She glanced back and down, but the stairs were not there any more. Just an inky pit. And then the brief flash of something swinging back and forth in that pit . . . again . . . again . . . like a ticking metronome. She rushed into the bedroom, slammed the door, grabbed a chair with the intention of bracing it under the knob—and discovered that, while her back was turned, the door had disappeared, as had the wall in which it had been set. Where the wall had been, there was subterranean gloom. And a silvery flicker. Very close now. Closer still. She screamed but made no sound, and the mysteriously gleaming object arched over her head and—

(Thunk!)

—This is more than just a dream, she thought desperately. Much more than that. This is a memory, a prophecy, a warning. This is a—

(Thunk!)

—She was running in another house that was altogether different from the first. This place was smaller, the furnishings less grand. She did not know where she was, yet she knew she had been here before. The house was familiar, just as the first place had been. She hurried through a doorway, into a kitchen. Two bloody, severed heads were on the kitchen table. One of them was a man's head, and the other was a woman's. She recognized them, felt that she knew them well, but was unable to think of their names. The four dead eyes were wide but sightless; the two mouths gaped, the swollen tongues protruding over the purple lips. As Carol stood transfixed by that grisly sight, the dead eyes rolled in their sockets and focused on her. The cold lips twisted into icy smiles. Carol turned, intending to flee, but there was only a void behind her and a glint of light off the hard surface of something silvery and then—

(Thunk!)

—She was running through a mountain meadow in reddish, late-afternoon light. The grass was knee-high, and the trees loomed ahead of her. When she looked over her shoulder, the meadow was no longer back there. Only blackness, as before. And the rhythmically swinging, shimmering, steadily approaching *thing* to which she was unable to fix a name. Gasping, her heart racing, she ran faster, reached the trees, glanced back once more, saw that she had not run nearly fast enough to escape, cried out and—

(Thunk!)

For a long time the nightmare shifted from one of those three dreamscapes to the other—from the first house to the meadow to the second house to the meadow to the first house again—until at last she woke with an unvoiced scream caught in her throat. She sat straight up, shuddering. She was cold and yet slick with sweat; she slept in just a T-shirt and panties, and both garments clung to her skin, unpleasantly sticky. The frightening sound from the nightmare continued to echo in her mind—*thunk, thunk, thunk-thunk, thunk*—and she realized that her subconscious had borrowed that noise from reality, from the wind-loosened shutter that had startled her and Paul earlier. Gradually, the pounding noise faded and blended with the thumping of her heart.

She drew back the covers and swung her bare legs out of bed. She sat on the edge of the mattress, hugging herself.

Dawn had come. Gray light seeped in around the drapes; it was too dim to reveal the details of the furniture, but it was just bright enough to deepen the shadows and distort the shapes of everything, so that the room seemed like an alien place.

The rain had stopped a couple of hours before she'd gone to bed, but the storm had returned while she'd been sleeping. Rain pattered on the roof and gurgled through the gutters and the downspouts. Low thunder rumbled like a distant cannonade.

Paul was still asleep, snoring softly.

Carol knew she wouldn't be able to get back to sleep. Like it or not, rested or not, she was up for the day.

Without turning on a light, she went into the master bathroom. In the weak glow of dawn, she stripped out of her damp T-shirt and panties. While soaping herself in the shower, she thought about the nightmare, which had been considerably more vivid than any dream she'd ever had before.

That strange, jarring sound—*thunk, thunk*—had been the most frightening thing in the dream, and the memory of it still nagged her. It wasn't just an ordinary hammering noise; there was an odd echo to it, a hardness and sharpness she

THE MASK ◆ 649

couldn't quite define. She decided it was not *only* a case of her subconscious mind borrowing the noise the shutter had made earlier. The terrifying sound in the dream was caused by something considerably more disturbing than the mere banging of an unmoored shutter. Furthermore, she was sure she had heard *precisely* that sound on another occasion, too. Not in the nightmare. In real life. In another place . . . a long time ago . . .

As she let the hot water stream over her, sluicing away the soap, she tried to recall where and when she had heard exactly that same unsettling sound, for it suddenly seemed important for her to identify it. Without understanding why, she felt vaguely threatened as long as she could not recall the source of the sound. But remembrance hung tantalizingly beyond the limits of her reach, like the title of a hauntingly familiar but unnameable piece of music.

FOUR

◆

At 8:45, after breakfast, Carol left for work, and Paul went upstairs to the rear bedroom that he had converted into an office. He had created a Spartan atmosphere in which to write without distraction. The off-white walls were bare, unadorned by even a single painting. The room contained only an inexpensive desk, a typist's chair, an electric typewriter, a jar bristling with pens and pencils, a deep letter tray that now contained nearly two hundred manuscript pages of the novel he had started at the beginning of his sabbatical, a telephone, a three-shelf bookcase filled with reference works, a bottled-water dispenser in one corner, and a small table upon which stood a Mr. Coffee machine.

This morning, as usual, he prepared a pot of coffee first thing. Just as he pressed the switch labeled BREWER and poured water into the top of the Mr. Coffee, the telephone rang. He sat on the edge of the desk, picked up the receiver. "Hello."

"Paul? Grace Mitowski."

"Good morning, love. How are you?"

"Well, these old bones don't like rainy weather, but otherwise I'm coping."

Paul smiled. "Listen, I know you can still run circles around me any time."

"Nonsense. You're a compulsive worker with a guilt complex about leisure. Not even a nuclear reactor has your energy."

He laughed. "Don't psychoanalyze me, Grace. I get enough of that from my wife."

"Speaking of whom . . . "

"Sorry, but you just missed her. You ought to be able to catch her at the office in half an hour."

Grace hesitated.

Hot coffee began to drizzle into the Pyrex pot, and the aroma of it swiftly filled the room.

Sensing tension in Grace's hesitation, Paul said, "What's wrong?"

"Well . . . " She cleared her throat nervously. "Paul, how *is* she? She's not ill or anything?"

"Carol? Oh, no. Of course not."

"You're sure? I mean, you know that girl's like a daughter to me. If anything was wrong, I'd want to know."

"She's fine. Really. In fact she had a physical exam last week. The adoption agency required it. Both of us passed with flying colors."

Grace was silent again.

Frowning, Paul said, "Why are you worried all of a sudden?"

"Well . . . you'll think old Gracie is losing her marbles, but I've had two disturbing dreams, one during a nap yesterday, the other last night, and Carol was in both. I seldom dream, so when I have *two* nightmares and wake up both times feeling I've got to warn Carol . . . "

"Warn her about what?"

"I don't know. All I remember about the dreams is that Carol was in them. I woke up thinking: *It's coming. I've got to warn Carol that it's coming.* I know that sounds silly. And don't ask me what 'it' might be. I can't remember. But I feel Carol's in danger. Now Lord knows, I don't believe in dream prophecies and garbage like that. I *think* I don't believe in them—yet here I am calling you about this."

The coffee was ready. Paul leaned over, turned off the brewer. "The strange thing is—Carol and I were nearly hurt in a freak accident yesterday." He told her about the damage at O'Brian's office.

"Good God," she said, "I saw that lightning when I woke up from my nap, but it never occurred to me that you and Carol . . . that the lightning might be the very thing I was . . . the very thing my *dream* oh, hell! I'm afraid to say it because I might sound like a superstitious old fool, but here goes anyway: *Was* there actually something prophetic about that dream? Did I foresee the lightning strike a few minutes before it happened?"

"If nothing else," Paul said uneasily, "it's at least a remarkable coincidence."

They were silent for a moment, wondering, and then she said, "Listen, Paul, I don't recall that we've ever discussed this subject much before, but tell me— do *you* believe in dream prophecies, clairvoyance, things of that nature?"

"I don't believe, and I don't disbelieve. I've never really made up my mind."

"I've always been so smug about it. Always considered it a pack of lies, delusions, or just plain nonsense. But after this—"

"You're reconsidering."

"Let's just say a tiny doubt has cropped up. And now I'm more worried about Carol than I was when I called you."

"Why? I told you she wasn't even scratched."

"She escaped once," Grace said, "but I had *two* dreams, and one of them came to me hours after the lightning. So maybe the 'it' is something else. I mean, if the first dream had some truth in it, then maybe the second does, too. God, isn't this crazy? If you start believing in just a little bit of this nonsense, you get carried away with it real fast. But I can't help it. I'm still concerned about her."

"Even if your first dream was prophetic," Paul said, "the second one was probably just a repeat of it, an echo, not a whole new dream."

"You think so?"

"Sure. This never happened to you before, so why should it happen again? Most likely, it was just a freak thing . . . like the lightning yesterday."

"Yeah, I guess you're probably right," she said, sounding somewhat relieved. "Maybe it could happen once. Maybe I can accept that. But I'm not Edgar Cayce or Nostradamus. And I can guarantee you I'm never going to be writing a weekly column of predictions for the *National Enquirer*.''

Paul laughed.

''Still,'' she said, ''I wish I could remember exactly what happened in *both* those nightmares.''

They talked a while longer, and when Paul finally hung up, he stared at the receiver for a moment, frowning. Although he was pretty much convinced that the timing of Grace's dream had been merely a strange coincidence, he was nonetheless affected by it, more profoundly affected than seemed reasonable.

It's coming.

The moment Grace had voiced those two words, Paul had felt a gut-deep, bone-deep chill.

It's coming.

Coincidence, he told himself. Sheer coincidence and nonsense. Forget about it.

Gradually he became aware, once again, of the rich aroma of hot coffee. He rose from the edge of the desk and filled a mug with the steaming brew.

For a minute or two he stood at the window behind the desk, sipping coffee, staring out at the dirty, scudding clouds and at the incessant rain. Eventually he lowered his gaze and looked down into the rear yard, instantly recalling the intruder he had seen last evening while he and Carol had been making dinner: that briefly glimpsed, pale, distorted, lightning-illuminated face; a woman's face; shining eyes; mouth twisted into a snarl of rage or hatred. Or perhaps it had just been Jasper, the Great Dane, and a trick of light.

THUNK!

The sound was so loud and unexpected that Paul jumped in surprise. If his mug hadn't been half empty, he would have spilled coffee all over the carpet.

THUNK! THUNK!

It couldn't be the same shutter they'd heard last evening, for it would have continued banging all night. Which meant there were now two of them to repair.

Jeez, he thought, the old homestead is falling down around my ears.

THUNK!

The source of the sound was nearby; in fact it was so close that it seemed to originate within the room.

Paul pressed his forehead against the cool window glass, peered out to the left, then to the right, trying to see if that pair of shutters was in place. As far as he could see, they were both properly anchored.

Thunk, thunk-thunk, thunk, thunk . . .

The noise grew softer but settled into a steady, arhythmical beat that was more irritating than the louder blows had been. And now it seemed to be coming from another part of the house.

Although he didn't want to get up on a ladder and fix a shutter in the rain, that was exactly what had to be done, for he couldn't get any writing accomplished with that constant clattering to distract him. At least there hadn't been any lightning this morning.

He put his mug on the desk and started out of the room. Before he reached the door, the telephone rang.

So it's going to be one of *those* days, he thought wearily.

Then he realized that the shutter had stopped banging the moment the phone had rung. Maybe the wind had wrenched it loose of the house, in which case repairs could wait until the weather improved.

He returned to his desk and answered the telephone. It was Alfred O'Brian, from the adoption agency. Initially, the conversation was awkward, and Paul was embarrassed by it. O'Brian insisted on expressing his gratitude: "You saved my life; you really did!" He was equally insistent about repeatedly and quite unnecessarily apologizing for his failure to express that gratitude yesterday, immediately following the incident in his office: "But I was so shaken, stunned, I just wasn't thinking clearly enough to thank you, which was unforgivable of me." Each time Paul protested at the mention of words like "heroic," and "brave," O'Brian became even more vociferous than before. At last, Paul stifled his objections and allowed the man to get it out of his system; O'Brian was determined to cleanse his conscience in much the same way that he fussed with the minute specks of lint on his suit jacket. Finally, however, he seemed to feel he had atoned for his (largely imaginary) thoughtlessness, and Paul was relieved when the conversation changed directions.

O'Brian had a second reason for calling, and he got straight to it now, as if he, too, was suddenly embarrassed. He could not (he explained with more apologies) locate the application form that the Tracys had brought to his office the previous day. "Of course, when that tree crashed through the window, it scattered a lot of papers all over the floor. A terrible mess. Some of them were rumpled and dirty when we gathered them up, and a great many of them were damp from the rain. In spite of that, Margie, my secretary, was able to put them in order—except, of course, for your application. We can't find it anywhere. I suppose it might have blown out through one of the broken windows. I don't know why your papers should be the only ones we've lost, and of course we must have a completed, signed application before we can present your names to the recommendations committee. I'm extremely sorry about this inconvenience, Mr. Tracy, I truly am."

"It wasn't your fault," Paul said. "I'll just stop in later today and pick up another form. Carol and I can fill it out and sign it tonight."

"Good," O'Brian said. "I'm glad to hear that. It has to be back in my hands early tomorrow morning if we're going to make the next meeting of the committee. Margie needs three full business days to run the required verifications on the information in your application, and that's just about how much time we have before next Wednesday's committee meeting. If we miss that session, there's not another one for two weeks."

"I'll be in to pick up the form before noon," Paul assured him. "And I'll have it back to you first thing Friday morning."

They exchanged goodbyes, and Paul put down the phone.

THUNK!

When he heard that sound, he sagged, dispirited. He was going to have to fix a shutter after all. And then drive into the city to pick up the new application. And then drive home. And by the time he did all of that, half the day would be shot, and he wouldn't have written a single word.

THUNK! THUNK!

"Dammit," he said.

Thunk, thunk-thunk, thunk-thunk . . .

It definitely was going to be one of *those* days.

He went downstairs to the hall closet where he kept his raincoat and galoshes.

The windshield wipers flogged back and forth, back and forth, with a short, shrill squeak that made Carol grit her teeth. She hunched forward a bit, over the steering wheel, squinting through the streaming rain.

The streets glistened; the macadam was slick, greasy looking. Dirty water raced along the gutters and formed filthy pools around clogged drainage grids.

At ten minutes past nine, the morning rush hour was just over. Although the streets were still moderately busy, traffic was moving smoothly and swiftly. In fact everyone was driving too fast to suit Carol, and she hung back a little, watchful and cautious.

Two blocks from her office, her caution proved justified, but it still wasn't enough to avert disaster altogether. Without bothering to look for oncoming traffic, a young blond woman stepped out from between two vans, directly into the path of the VW Rabbit.

"Christ!" Carol said, ramming her foot down on the brake pedal so hard that she lifted herself up off the seat.

The blonde glanced up and froze, wide-eyed.

Although the VW was moving at only twenty miles an hour, there was no hope of stopping it in time. The brakes shrieked. The tires bit—but also skidded—on the wet pavement.

God, no! Carol thought with a sick, sinking feeling.

The car hit the blonde and lifted her off the ground, tossed her backwards onto the hood, and then the rear end of the VW began to slide around to the left, into the path of an oncoming Cadillac, and the Caddy swerved, brakes squealing, and the other driver hit his horn as if he thought a sufficient volume of sound might magically push Carol safely out of his way, and for an instant she was certain they would collide, but the Caddy slid past without scraping, missing her by only an inch or two—all of this in two or three or four seconds—and at the same time the blonde rolled off the hood, toward the right side, the curb side, and the VW came to a full stop, sitting aslant the street, rocking on its springs as if it were a child's hobby horse.

None of the shutters was missing. Not one. None of them was loose and flapping in the wind, as Paul had thought.

Wearing galoshes and a raincoat with a hood, he walked all the way around the house, studying each set of shutters on the first and second floors, but he couldn't see anything amiss. The place showed no sign of storm damage.

Perplexed, he circled the house again, each step resulting in a squishing noise as the rain-saturated lawn gave like a sodden sponge beneath him. This time around, he looked for broken tree limbs that might be swinging against the walls when the wind gusted. The trees were all intact.

Shivering in the unseasonably chilly autumn air, he just stood on the lawn for a minute or two, cocking his head to the right and then to the left, listening for the pounding that had filled the house moments ago. He couldn't hear it now. The only sounds were the soughing wind, the rustling trees, and the rain driving into the grass with a soft, steady hiss.

At last, his face numbed by the cold wind and by the heat-leaching rain, he decided to halt his search until the pounding started again and gave him something to get a fix on. Meanwhile, he could drive downtown and pick up the application form at the adoption agency. He put one hand to his face, felt his beard stubble, remembered Alfred O'Brian's compulsive neatness, and figured he ought to shave before he went.

He reentered the house by way of the screened-in rear porch, leaving his dripping coat on a vinyl-upholstered glider and shedding his galoshes before going into the kitchen. Inside, he closed the door behind him and basked for a moment in the warm air.

THUNK! THUNK! THUNK!

The house shuddered as if it had received three extremely hard, rapid blows from the enormous fist of a giant. Above the kitchen's central utility island, where a utensil rack was suspended from the ceiling, copper pots and pans swung on their hooks and clattered against one another.

THUNK!

The wall clock rattled on its hook; if it had been any less firmly attached than it was, it would have flung itself off the wall, onto the floor.

Paul moved toward the middle of the room, trying to ascertain the direction from which the pounding was coming.

THUNK! THUNK!

The oven door fell open.

The two dozen small jars nestled in the spice rack began to clink against one another.

What the hell is happening here? he wondered uneasily.

THUNK!

He turned slowly, listening, seeking.

The pots and pans clattered again, and a large ladle slipped from its hook and fell with a clang to the butcher-block work surface that lay under it.

Paul looked up at the ceiling, tracking the sound.

THUNK!

He expected to see the plaster crack, but it didn't. Nevertheless, the source of the sound was definitely overhead.

Thunk, thunk-thunk, thunk . . .

The pounding suddenly grew quieter than it had been, but it didn't fade away altogether. At least the house stopped quivering, and the cooking utensils stopped banging together.

Paul headed for the stairs, determined to track down the cause of the disturbance.

The blonde was in the gutter, flat on her back, one arm out at her side with the palm up and the hand slack, the other arm draped across her belly. Her golden hair was muddy. A three-inch-deep stream of water surged around her, carrying leaves and grit and scraps of paper litter toward the nearest storm drain, and her long hair fanned out around her head and rippled silkily in those filthy currents.

Carol knelt beside the woman and was shocked to see that the victim wasn't actually a woman at all. She was a girl, no older than fourteen or fifteen. She was exceptionally pretty, with delicate features, and at the moment she was frighteningly pale.

She was also inadequately dressed for inclement weather. She wore white tennis shoes, jeans, and a blue and white checkered blouse. She had neither a raincoat nor an umbrella.

With trembling hands, Carol lifted the girl's right arm and felt the wrist for a pulse. She found the beat at once; it was strong and steady.

"Thank God," Carol said shakily. "Thank God, thank God."

She began to examine the girl for bleeding. There did not seem to be any serious injuries, no major blood loss, just a few shallow cuts and abrasions. Unless, of course, the bleeding was internal.

The driver of the Cadillac, a tall man with a goatee, stepped around the end of the VW Rabbit and looked down at the injured girl. "Is she dead?"

"No," Carol said. She gently thumbed back one of the girl's eyelids, then the other. "Just unconscious. Probably a mild concussion. Is anyone calling an ambulance?"

"I don't know," he said.

"Then you call one. Quickly."

He hurried away, splashing through a puddle that was deeper than the tops of his shoes.

Carol pressed down on the girl's chin; the jaw was slack, and the mouth fell open easily. There was no visible obstruction, no blood, nothing that might choke her, and her tongue was in a safe position.

A gray-haired woman in a transparent plastic raincoat, carrying a red and orange umbrella, appeared out of the rain. "It wasn't your fault," she told Carol. "I saw it happen. I saw it all. The child darted out in front of you without looking. There wasn't a thing you could have done to prevent it."

"I saw it, too," said a portly man who didn't quite fit under his black umbrella. "I saw the kid walking down the street like she was in a trance or something. No coat, no umbrella. Eyes kind of blank. She stepped off the curb, between those two vans, and just stood there for a few seconds, like she was just waiting for someone to come along so she could step out and get herself killed. And by God, that's what happened."

"She's not dead," Carol said, unable to keep a tremor out of her voice. "There's a first-aid kit on the back seat of my car. Will one of you get it for me?"

"Sure," the portly man said, turning toward the VW.

The first-aid kit contained, among other things, a packet of tongue depressors, and Carol wanted to have those handy. Although the unconscious girl didn't appear to be headed for imminent convulsions, Carol intended to be prepared for the worst.

A crowd had begun to gather.

A siren sounded a couple of blocks away, approaching fast. It was probably the police; the ambulance couldn't have made it so fast.

"Such a pretty child," the gray-haired woman said, staring down at the stricken girl.

Other onlookers murmured in agreement.

Carol stood up and stripped out of her raincoat. There was no point in covering the girl, for she was already as wet as she could get. Instead, Carol folded the coat, knelt down again, and carefully slipped the makeshift pillow under the victim, elevating her head just a bit above the gushing water.

The girl didn't open her eyes or stir in any way whatsoever. A tangled strand of golden hair had fallen across her face, and Carol carefully pushed it aside for her. The girl's skin was hot to the touch, fevered, in spite of the cold rain that bathed it.

Suddenly, while her fingers were still touching the girl's cheek, Carol felt dizzy and was unable to get her breath. For a moment she thought she was going to pass out and collapse on top of the unconscious teenager. A black wave rose behind her eyes, and then in that darkness there was a brief flash of silver, a glint of light off a moving object, the mysterious thing from her nightmare.

She gritted her teeth, shook her head, and refused to be swept away in that dark wave. She pulled her hand away from the girl's cheek, put it to her own face; the dizzy spell passed as abruptly as it had come. Until the ambulance arrived, she was responsible for the injured girl, and she was determined not to fail in that responsibility.

Huffing slightly, the portly man hurried back with the first-aid kit. Carol took one of the tongue depressors out of its crisp cellophane wrapper—just in case.

A police car rounded the corner and stopped behind the Volkswagen. Its revolving emergency beacons splashed red light across the wet pavement and appeared to transform the puddles of rainwater into pools of blood.

As the squad car's siren died with a growl, another, more distant siren became audible. To Carol, that warbling, high-pitched wail was the sweetest sound in the world.

The horror is almost over, she thought.

But then she looked at the girl's chalk-white face, and her relief was clouded with doubt. Perhaps the horror wasn't over after all; perhaps it had only just begun.

Upstairs, Paul walked slowly from room to room, listening to the hammering sound.

Thunk . . . thunk . . .

The source was still overhead. In the attic. Or on the roof.

The attic stairs were behind a paneled door at the end of the second-floor hallway. They were narrow, unpainted, and they creaked as Paul climbed them.

Although the attic had full flooring, it was not otherwise a finished room. The construction of the walls was open for inspection; the pink fiber glass insulation, which somewhat resembled raw meat, and the regularly spaced supporting studs, like ribs of bone, were visible. Two naked, hundred-watt bulbs furnished light, and shadows coiled everywhere, especially toward the eaves. For all of its length and for half of its width, the attic was high enough to allow Paul to walk through it without stooping.

The pattern of rain on the roof was more than just a pattern up here. It was a steady hissing, a soft, all-encompassing roar.

Nevertheless, the other sound was audible above the drumming of the rain:

Thunk . . . thunk-thunk . . .

Paul moved slowly past stacks of cardboard cartons and other items that had been consigned to storage: a pair of large touring trunks; an old six-pronged coat rack; a tarnished brass floor lamp; two busted-out, cane-bottomed chairs that he intended to restore some day. A thin film of whitish dust draped shroudlike over all the contents of the room.

Thunk . . . thunk . . .

He walked the length of the attic, then slowly returned to the center of it and stopped. The source of the sound seemed to be directly in front of his face, only inches away. But there was nothing here that could possibly be the cause of the disturbance; nothing moved.

Thunk . . . thunk . . . thunk . . . thunk . . .

Although the hammering was softer now than it had been a few minutes ago, it was still solid and forceful; it reverberated through the frame of the house. The pounding had acquired a monotonously simple rhythm, too; each blow was separated from the ones before and after it by equal measures of time, resulting in a pattern not unlike the beating of a heart.

Paul stood in the attic, in the dust, smelling the musty odor common to all unused places, trying to get a fix on the sound, trying to understand how it could be coming out of thin air, and gradually his attitude toward the disturbance changed. He had been thinking of it as nothing more than the audible evidence of storm damage to the house, as nothing more than tedious and perhaps expensive repairs that might have to be made, an interruption in his writing schedule, an inconvenience, nothing more. But as he turned his head from side to side and squinted into every shadow, as he listened to the relentless thudding, he suddenly perceived that there was something ominous about the sound.

Thunk . . . thunk . . . thunk . . .

For reasons he could not define, the noise now seemed threatening, malevolent. He felt colder in this sheltered place than he had felt outside in the wind and rain.

* * *

Carol wanted to ride to the hospital in the ambulance with the injured girl, but she knew she would only be in the way. Besides, the first police officer on the scene, a curly-headed young man named Tom Weatherby, needed to get a statement from her.

They sat in the front seat of the patrol car, which smelled like the peppermint lozenges on which Weatherby was sucking. The windows were made opaque by shimmering streams of rain. The police radio sputtered and crackled.

Weatherby frowned. "You're soaked to the skin. I've got a blanket in the trunk. I'll get it for you."

"No, no," she said. "I'll be fine." Her green knit suit had become saturated. Her rain-drenched hair was pasted to her head and hung slackly to her shoulders. At the moment, however, she didn't care about her appearance or about the goosebumps that prickled her skin. "Let's just get this over with."

"Well . . . if you're sure you're okay."

"I'm sure."

As he turned up the thermostat on the car heater, Weatherby said, "By any chance, do you know the kid who stepped in front of your car?"

"Know her? No. Of course not."

"She didn't have any ID on her. Did you notice if she was carrying a purse when she walked into the street?"

"I can't say for sure."

"Try to remember."

"I don't think she was."

"Probably not," he said. "After all, if she goes walking in a storm like this without a raincoat or an umbrella, why would she bother to take a purse? We'll search the street anyway. Maybe she dropped it somewhere."

"What happens if you can't find out who she is? How will you get in touch with her parents? I mean, she shouldn't be alone at a time like this."

"No problem," Weatherby said. "She'll tell us her name when she regains consciousness."

"*If* she does."

"Hey, she will. There's no need to be concerned about that. She didn't seem seriously injured."

Carol worried about it nonetheless.

For the next ten minutes, Weatherby asked questions, and she answered them. When he finished filling out the accident report, she quickly read over it, then signed at the bottom.

"You're in the clear," Weatherby said. "You were driving under the speed limit, and three witnesses say the girl stepped out of a blind spot right in front of you, without bothering to look for traffic. It wasn't your fault."

"I should have been more careful."

"I don't see what else you could have done."

"Something. Surely I could have done something," she said miserably.

He shook his head. "No. Listen, Dr. Tracy, I've seen this sort of thing happen before. There's an accident, and somebody's hurt, and nobody's really to blame— yet one of the people involved has a misplaced sense of responsibility and insists on feeling guilty. And in this case, if there *is* anybody to blame, it's the kid herself, not you. According to the witnesses, she was behaving strangely just before you turned the corner, almost as if she *intended* to get herself run down."

"But why would such a pretty girl want to throw herself in front of a car?"

Weatherby shrugged. "You told me you were a psychiatrist. You specialize in children and teenagers, right?"

"Yes."

"So you must know all the answers better than I do. Why would she want to kill herself? Could be trouble at home—a father who drinks too much and makes heavy passes at his own little girl, a mother who doesn't want to hear about it. Or maybe the kid was just jilted by her boyfriend and thinks the world is coming to an end. Or just discovered she was pregnant and decided she couldn't face her folks with the news. There must be hundreds of reasons, and I'm sure you've heard most of them in your line of work."

What he said was true, but it didn't make Carol feel better.

If only I'd been driving slower, she thought. If only I'd been quicker to react, maybe that poor girl wouldn't be in the hospital now.

"She might have been on drugs, too," Weatherby said. "Too damned many kids fool around with dope these days. I swear, some of them'll swallow any pill they're given. If it isn't something that can be swallowed, they'll sniff it or stick it in a vein. This kid you hit might have been so high she didn't even know where she was when she stepped in front of your car. Now, if that's the case, are you going to tell me it's *still* somehow your fault?"

Carol leaned back in the seat, closed her eyes, and let her breath out with a shudder. "God, I don't know *what* to tell you. All I know is . . . I feel wrung out."

"That's perfectly natural, after what you've just been through. But it isn't natural to feel guilty about this. It wasn't your fault, so don't dwell on it. Put it behind you and get on with your life."

She opened her eyes, looked at him, and smiled. "You know, Officer Weatherby, I have a hunch you'd make a pretty good psychotherapist."

He grinned. "Or a terrific bartender."

Carol laughed.

"Feeling better?" he asked.

"A little bit."

"Promise me you won't lose any sleep over this."

"I'll try not to," she said. "But I'm still concerned about the girl. Do you know which hospital they've taken her to?"

"I can find out," he said.

"Would you do that for me? I'd like to go talk to the doctor who's handling her case. If he tells me she's going to be all right, I'll find it a whole lot easier to take your advice about getting on with my life."

Weatherby picked up the microphone and asked the police dispatcher to find out where the injured girl had been taken.

The television antenna!

Standing in the attic, staring up at the roof above his head, Paul laughed out loud when he realized what was causing the pounding noise. The sound wasn't coming out of the empty air in front of his face, which was what he had thought for one unsettling moment. It was coming from the roof, where the television antenna was anchored. They had subscribed to cable TV a year ago, but they hadn't removed the old antenna. It was a large, directional, remote-control model affixed to a heavy brace-plate; the plate was bolted through the shingles and attached directly to a roof beam. Apparently, a nut or some other fastener had loosened slightly, and the wind was tugging at the antenna, rocking the brace-plate up and down on one of its bolts, slamming it repeatedly against the roof. The solution to the big mystery was amusingly mundane.

Or was it?

Thunk . . . thunk . . . thunk . . .

The sound was softer now than ever before, barely audible above the roar of the rain on the roof, and it was easy to believe that the antenna could be the cause of it. Gradually, however, as Paul considered this answer to the puzzle, he began to doubt if it was the *correct* answer. He thought about how loud and violent the pounding had been a few minutes ago when he had been in the kitchen: the entire house quivering, the oven door falling open, bottles rattling in the spice rack. Could a loose antenna really generate so much noise and vibration?

Thunk . . . thunk . . .

As he stared up at the ceiling, he tried to make himself believe unequivocally in the antenna theory. If it was striking a roof beam in precisely the right way, at a very special angle, so that the impact was transmitted through the entire frame of the house, perhaps a loose antenna *could* cause the pots and pans to clatter against one another in the kitchen and could make it seem as if the ceilings were about to crack. After all, if you set up exactly the right vibrations in a steel suspension bridge, you could bring it to ruin in less than a minute, regardless of the number of bolts and welds and cables holding it together. And although Paul didn't believe there was even a remote danger of a loose antenna causing that kind of apocalyptic destruction to a wood-frame house, he knew that moderate force, applied with calculation and pinpoint accuracy, could have an effect quite out of proportion to the amount of energy expended. Besides, the TV antenna *had* to be the root of the disturbance, for it was the only explanation he had left.

The hammering noise became even softer and then faded altogether. He waited for a minute or two, but the only sound was the rain on the shingles overhead.

The wind must have changed direction. In time it would change back again, and the antenna would begin to rock on its brace-plate, and the pounding would start once more.

As soon as the storm was over, he would have to get the extension ladder out of the garage, go up onto the roof, and dismantle the antenna. He should have taken care of that chore shortly after they had subscribed to the cable television service. Now, because he had delayed, he was going to lose precious writing time—and at one of the most difficult and crucial points in his manuscript. That prospect frustrated him and made him nervous.

He decided to shave, drive downtown, and pick up the new set of application papers at the adoption agency. The storm might pass by the time he got home again. If it did, if he could be on the roof by eleven-thirty, he ought to be able to tear down the antenna, then have a bite of lunch, and work on his book all afternoon, barring further interruptions. But he suspected there *would* be further interruptions. He had already resigned himself to the fact that it was one of those days.

As he left the attic and turned out the lights, the house quivered under another blow.

THUNK!

Just one this time.

Then all was quiet again.

The visitors' lounge at the hospital looked like an explosion in a clown's wardrobe. The walls were canary yellow; the chairs were bright red; the carpet was orange; the magazine racks and end tables were made of heavy purple plastic; and the two large abstract paintings were done primarily in shades of blue and green.

The lounge—obviously the work of a designer who had read too much about the various psychological mood theories of color—was supposed to be positive, life-affirming. It was supposed to lift the spirits of visitors and take their minds off sick friends and dying relatives. In Carol, however, the determinedly cheery decor elicited the opposite reaction from that which the designer had intended. It was a frenetic room; it abraded the nerves as effectively as coarse sandpaper would abrade a stick of butter.

She sat on one of the red chairs, waiting for the doctor who had treated the injured girl. When he came, his stark white lab coat contrasted so boldly with the flashy decor that he appeared to radiate a saintlike aura.

Carol rose to meet him, and he asked if she was Mrs. Tracy, and he said his name was Sam Hannaport. He was tall, very husky, square-faced, florid, in his early fifties. He looked as if he would be loud and gruff, perhaps even obnoxious, but in fact he was soft-spoken and seemed genuinely concerned about how the accident had affected Carol both physically and emotionally. It took her a couple of minutes to assure him that she was all right on both counts, and then they sat down on facing red chairs.

Hannaport raised his bushy eyebrows and said, "You look as if you could use a hot bath and a big glassful of warm brandy."

"I was soaked to the skin," she said, "but I'm pretty well dried out now. What about the girl?"

"Cuts, contusions, abrasions," he said.

"Internal bleeding?"

"Nothing showed up on the tests."

"Fractures?"

"Not a broken bone in her body. She came through it amazingly well. You couldn't have been driving very fast when you hit her."

"I wasn't. But considering the way she slipped up onto the hood and then rolled off into the gutter, I thought maybe . . . " Carol shuddered, unwilling to put words to what she had thought.

"Well, the kid's in good condition now. She regained consciousness in the ambulance, and she was alert by the time I saw her."

"Thank God."

"There's no indication that she's even mildly concussed. I don't foresee any lasting effects."

Relieved, Carol sagged back in the red chair. "I'd like to see her, talk to her."

"She's resting now," Dr. Hannaport said. "I don't want her disturbed at the moment. But if you'd like to come back this evening, during visiting hours, she'll be able to see you then."

"I'll do that. I'll definitely do that." She blinked. "Good heavens, I haven't even asked you what her name is."

His bushy eyebrows rose again. "Well, we've got a small problem about that."

"Problem?" Carol tensed up again. "What do you mean? Can't she remember her name?"

"She hasn't remembered it yet, but—"

"Oh, God."

"—she will."

"You said no concussion—"

"I swear to you, it *isn't* serious," Hannaport said. He took her left hand in his big hard hands and held it as if it might crack and crumble at any moment. "Please don't excite yourself about this. The girl is going to be fine. Her inability to remember her name isn't a symptom of severe concussion or any serious brain injury; not in her case, anyway. She isn't confused or disoriented. Her field of vision is normal, and she has excellent depth perception. We tested her thought processes with some math problems—addition, subtraction, multiplication—and she got them all correct. She can spell any word you throw at her; she's a damn good speller, that one. So she's not severely concussed. She's simply suffering from mild amnesia. It's selective amnesia, you understand, just a loss of personal memories, not a loss of skills and education and whole blocks of social concepts. She hasn't forgotten how to read and write, thank God; she's only forgotten who she is, where she came from, and how she got to this place. Which sounds more serious than it really is. Of course, she's disconcerted and apprehensive. But selective amnesia is the easiest kind to recover from.''

''I know,'' Carol said. ''But somehow that doesn't make me feel a whole hell of a lot better.''

Hannaport squeezed her hand firmly and gently. ''This kind of amnesia is only very, very rarely permanent or even long-lasting. She'll most likely remember who she is before dinnertime.''

''If she doesn't?''

''Then the police will find out who she is, and the minute she hears her name, the mists will clear.''

''She wasn't carrying any ID.''

''I know,'' he said. ''I've talked to the police.''

''So what happens if they can't find out who she is?''

''They will.'' He patted her hand one last time, then let go.

''I don't see how you can be so sure.''

''Her parents will file a missing-persons report. They'll have a photograph of her. When the police see the photograph, they'll make a connection. It'll be as simple as that.''

She frowned. ''What if her parents *don't* report her missing?''

''Why wouldn't they?''

''Well, what if she's a runaway from out of state? Even if her folks did file a missing-persons report back in her hometown, the police here wouldn't necessarily be aware of it.''

''The last time I looked, runaway kids favored New York City, California, Florida—just about any place besides Harrisburg, Pennsylvania.''

''There's always an exception to any rule.''

Hannaport laughed softly and shook his head. ''If pessimism were a competitive sport, you'd win the world series.''

She blinked in surprise, then smiled. ''I'm sorry. I guess I am being excessively gloomy.''

Glancing at his watch, getting up from his chair, he said, ''Yes, I think you are. Especially considering how well the girl came through it all. It could have been a lot worse.''

Carol got to her feet, too. In a rush, the words falling over one another, she said, ''I guess maybe the reason it bothers me so much is because I deal with disturbed children every day, and it's my job to help them get well again, and that's all I ever wanted to do since I was in high school—work with sick kids, be a healer—but now I'm responsible for all the pain this poor girl is going through.''

''You mustn't feel that way. You didn't *intend* to harm her.''

Carol nodded. ''I know I'm not being entirely rational about the situation, but I can't help feeling the way I feel.''

''I have some patients to see,'' Hannaport said, glancing at his watch again. ''But let me leave you with one thought that might help you handle this.''

''I'd like to hear it.''

''The girl suffered only minor physical injuries. I won't say they were negligible injuries, but they were damned close to it. So you've got nothing to feel guilty about on that score. As for her amnesia . . . well, maybe the accident had nothing to do with it.''

''Nothing to do with it? But I assumed that when she hit her head on the car or on the pavement—''

''I'm sure you know a blow on the head isn't the only cause of amnesia,'' Dr. Hannaport said. ''It's not even the most common factor in such cases. Stress, emotional shock—they can result in loss of memory. In fact we don't yet understand the human mind well enough to say for sure exactly what causes most cases of amnesia. As far as this girl is concerned, everything points to the conclusion that she was in her current state even before she stepped in front of your car.'' He emphasized each argument in favor of his theory by raising fingers on his right hand. ''One: She wasn't carrying any ID. Two: She was wandering around in the pouring rain without a coat or an umbrella, as if she was in a daze. Three: From what I understand, the witnesses say she was acting very strange before you ever came on the scene.'' He waggled his three raised fingers. ''Three very good reasons why you shouldn't be so eager to blame yourself for the kid's condition.''

''Maybe you're right, but I still—''

''I *am* right,'' he said. ''There's no maybe about it. Give yourself a break, Dr. Tracy.''

A woman with a sharp, nasal voice paged Dr. Hannaport on the hospital's tinny public address system.

''Thank you for your time,'' Carol said. ''You've been more than kind.''

''Come back this evening and talk to the girl if you want. I'm sure you'll find she doesn't blame you one bit.''

He turned and hurried across the gaudy lounge, in answer to the page's call; the tails of his white lab coat fluttered behind him.

Carol went to the pay phones and called her office. She explained the situation to her secretary, Thelma, and arranged for the rescheduling of the patients she had intended to see today. Then she dialed home, and Paul answered on the third ring.

''You just caught me as I was going out the door,'' he said. ''I've got to drive down to O'Brian's office and pick up a new set of application papers. Ours were lost in the mess yesterday. So far, this has been a day I should have slept through.''

''Ditto on this end,'' she said.

''What's wrong?''

She told him about the accident and briefly summarized her conversation with Dr. Hannaport.

''It could have been worse,'' Paul said. ''At least we can be thankful no one was killed or crippled.''

''That's what everyone keeps telling me: 'It could have been worse, Carol.' But it seems plenty bad enough to me.''

''Are you all right?''

''Yeah. I told you. I wasn't even scratched.''

''I don't mean physically. I mean, are you together emotionally? You sound shaky.''

''I am. Just a little.''

''I'll come to the hospital,'' he said.

''No, no. That's not necessary.''

''Are you sure you should drive?''

''I drove here after the accident without trouble, and I'm feeling better now than I did then. I'll be okay. What I'm going to do is, I'm going over to Grace's house. She's only a mile from here; it's easier than going home. I have to sponge off my clothes, dry them out, and press them. I need a shower, too. I'll probably have an early dinner with Grace, if that's all right by her, and then I'll come back here during visiting hours this evening.''

"When will you be home?''

"Probably not until eight or eight-thirty.''

"I'll miss you.''

"Miss you, too.''

"Give my best to Grace,'' he said. "And tell her I think she *is* the next Nostradamus.''

"What's that supposed to mean?''

"Grace called a while ago. Said she had two nightmares recently, and you figured in both. She was afraid something was going to happen to you.''

"Seriously?''

"Yeah. She was embarrassed about it. Afraid I'd think she was getting senile or something.''

"You told her about the lightning yesterday?''

"Yeah. But she felt something else would happen, something bad.''

"And it did.''

"Creepy, huh?''

"Decidedly,'' Carol said. She remembered her own nightmare: the black void; the flashing, silvery object drawing nearer, nearer.

"I'm sure Grace'll tell you all about it,'' Paul said. "And I'll see you this evening.''

"I love you,'' Carol said.

"Love you, too.''

She put down the phone and went outside to the parking lot.

Gray-black thunderheads churned across the sky, but only a thin rain was falling now. The wind was still cold and sharp; it sang in the power lines overhead, sounding like a swarm of angry wasps.

The semiprivate room had two beds, but the second one was not currently in use. At the moment, no nurse was present either. The girl was alone.

She lay under a crisp white sheet and a cream-colored blanket, staring at the acoustic-tile ceiling. She had a headache, and she could feel each dully throbbing, burning cut and abrasion on her battered body, but she knew she was not seriously hurt.

Fear, not pain, was her worst enemy. She was frightened by her inability to remember who she was. On the other hand, she was plagued by the inexplicable yet unshakable feeling that it would be foolish and exceedingly dangerous to remember her past. Without knowing why, she suspected that full remembrance would be the death of her—an odd notion that she found more frightening than anything else.

She knew her amnesia wasn't the result of the accident. She had a misty recollection of walking along the street in the rain a minute or two before she had blundered in front of the Volkswagen. Even then, she had been disoriented, afraid, unable to remember her name, utterly unfamiliar with the strange city in which she found herself and unable to recall how she had gotten there. The thread of her memory definitely had begun unraveling prior to the accident.

She wondered if it was possible that her amnesia was like a shield, protecting her from something horrible in the past. Did forgetfulness somehow equal safety?

Why? Safety from what?

What could I be running from? she asked herself.

She sensed that recovery of her identity was possible. In fact her memories seemed almost within her grasp. She felt as though the past lay at the bottom of a dark hole, close enough to touch; all she had to do was summon sufficient strength and courage to poke her hand into that lightless place and grope for the truth, without fear of what might bite her.

However, when she tried hard to remember, when she probed into that hole, her fear grew and grew until it was no longer just ordinary fear; it became incapacitating terror. Her stomach knotted, and her throat swelled tight, and she broke out in a greasy sweat, and she became so dizzy that she nearly fainted.

On the edge of unconsciousness, she saw and heard something disturbing, alarming—a fuzzy fragment of a dream, a vision—which she couldn't quite identify but which frightened her nonetheless. The vision was composed of a single sound and a single, mysterious image. The image was hypnotic but simple: a quick flash of light, a silvery glimmer from a not-quite-visible object that was swinging back and forth in deep shadows; a gleaming pendulum, perhaps. The sound was hard-edged and threatening but not identifiable, a loud hammering noise, yet more than that.

Thunk! Thunk! Thunk!

She jerked, quivered, as if something had struck her.

Thunk!

She wanted to scream, couldn't.

She realized that her hands were fisted and that they were full of twisted, sweat-soaked sheets.

Thunk!

She stopped trying to remember who she was.

Maybe it's better that I don't know, she thought.

Her heartbeat gradually slowed to normal, and she was able to draw her breath without wheezing. Her stomach unknotted.

The hammering sound faded.

After a while she looked at the window. A flock of large, black birds reeled across the turbulent sky.

What's going to happen to me? she wondered.

Even when the nurse came in to see how she was doing, and even when the doctor joined the nurse a moment later, the girl felt utterly, dishearteningly alone.

FIVE

◆

Grace's kitchen smelled of coffee and warm spice cake. Rain washed down the window, obscuring the view of the rose garden that lay behind the house.

"I've never believed in clairvoyance or premonitions."

"Neither have I," Grace said. "But now I wonder. After all, I have two nightmares about you getting hurt, and the next thing I hear is that you've had two close calls, just as if you were acting out a script or something.''

They sat at the small table by the kitchen window. Carol was wearing one of Grace's robes and a pair of Grace's slippers while her own clothes finished drying out.

"Only *one* close call," she told Grace. "The lightning. That was a gut-wrencher, all right. But I wasn't really in any danger this morning. That poor girl was the one who nearly got killed."

Grace shook her head. "No. It was a close call for you, too. Didn't you tell me you slid toward the oncoming traffic when you braked to avoid the girl? And didn't you say the Cadillac missed you by an inch or less? Well, what if it *hadn't* missed? If that Caddy had rammed your little VW, you certainly wouldn't have walked away without a scratch."

Frowning, Carol said, "I hadn't looked at it that way."

"You've been so busy worrying about the girl that you haven't had a chance to think about yourself."

Carol ate a bite of spice cake and washed it down with coffee. "You're not the only one having nightmares." She summarized her own dream: the severed heads, the houses that dissolved behind her as she passed through them, the flickering, silvery object.

Grace clasped her hands around her coffee cup and hunched over the table. There was worry in her blue eyes. "That's one nasty dream. What do you make of it?"

"Oh, I don't think it's prophetic."

"Why couldn't it be? Mine appear to have been."

"Yes, but it doesn't follow that both of us are turning into soothsayers. Besides, my dream didn't make a whole lot of sense. It was just too wild to be taken seriously. I mean, severed heads that suddenly come to life—that sort of thing isn't really going to happen."

"It could be prophetic without being *literally* prophetic. I mean, it might be a symbolic warning."

"Of what?"

"I don't see any easy interpretation of it. But I really think you ought to be extra careful for a while. God, I know I'm starting to sound like a phony gypsy fortune-teller, like Maria Ouspenskya in all those old monster movies from the thirties, but I still don't think you should dismiss it as just an ordinary dream. Especially not after what's already happened."

Later, after lunch, as Grace squirted some liquid soap into the sinkful of dirty dishes, she said, "How's the situation with the adoption agency? Does it look like they'll give you and Paul a child soon?"

Carol hesitated.

Grace glanced at her. "Something wrong?"

Taking the dish towel from the rack and unfolding it, Carol said, "No. Not really. O'Brian says we'll be approved. It's a sure thing, he says."

"But you're still worried about it."

"A little," Carol admitted.

"Why?"

"I'm not sure. It's just that . . . I've had this feeling. . . . "

"What feeling?"

"That it won't work out."

"Why shouldn't it?"

"I can't shake the idea that somebody's trying to stop us from adopting."

"Who?"

Carol shrugged.

"O'Brian?" Grace asked.

"No, no. He's on our side."

"Someone on the recommendations committee?"

"I don't know. I don't actually have any evidence of ill will toward Paul and me. I can't point my finger at anyone."

Grace washed some silverware, put it in the drainage rack, and said, "You've wanted to adopt for so long that you can't believe it's finally happening, so you're looking for boogeymen where there aren't any."

"Maybe."

"You're just spooked because of the lightning yesterday and the accident this morning."

"Maybe."

"That's understandable. It spooks me, too. But the adoption will go through as smooth as can be."

"I hope so," Carol said. But she thought about the lost set of application forms, and she wondered.

By the time Paul got back from the adoption agency, the rain had stopped, though the wind was still cold and damp.

He got the ladder out of the garage and climbed onto the least slanted portion of the many-angled roof. The wet shingles squeaked under his feet as he moved cautiously across the slope toward the television antenna, which was anchored near a brick chimney.

His legs were rubbery. He suffered from a mild case of acrophobia, a fear that had never become incapacitating because he occasionally forced himself to challenge and overcome it, as he was doing now.

When he reached the chimney, he put a hand against it for support and looked out across the roofs of the neighboring homes. The storm-dark September sky had settled lower, lower, until it appeared to be only six or eight feet above the tallest houses. He felt as if he could raise his arm and rap his knuckles on the bellies of the clouds, eliciting a hard, ironlike *clank*.

He crouched with his back to the chimney and inspected the TV antenna. The brace-plate was held down by four bolts that went through the shingles, either directly into a roof beam or into a stud linking two beams. None of the bolts was missing. None of them was loose. The plate was firmly attached to the house, and the antenna was anchored securely to the plate. The antenna could not possibly have been responsible for the hammering sound that had shaken the house.

After washing the dishes, Grace and Carol went into the study. The room reeked of cat urine and feces. Aristophanes had made his toilet on the seat of the big easy chair.

Stunned, Grace said, "I don't believe it. Ari *always* uses the litter box like he's supposed to do. He's never done anything like this before."

"He's always been a fussy cat, hasn't he? Fastidious."

"Exactly. But now look what he's done. That chair'll have to be reupholstered. I guess I'd better find the silly beast, put his nose to this mess, and give him a good scolding. I don't want this to become a habit, for God's sake."

They looked in every room, but they couldn't find Aristophanes. Apparently, he had slipped out of the house by way of the pet door in the kitchen.

Returning to the study with Grace, Carol said, "Earlier, you mentioned something about Ari tearing up a few things."

Grace winced. "Yes. I didn't want to have to tell you—but he shredded two of those lovely little needlepoint pillows you made for me. I was sick about it. After all the work you put into those, and then he just—"

"Don't worry about it," Carol said. "I'll make you a couple of new pillows. I enjoy doing it. Needlepoint relaxes me. I only asked because I thought maybe, if Ari's been doing a lot of things that're out of character, it might be a sign that he isn't well."

Grace frowned. "He *looks* healthy. His coat's glossy, and he's certainly as spry as ever."

"Animals are like people in some ways. And when a person suddenly starts behaving strangely, that *can* be an indication of a physical malady, anything from a brain tumor to an imbalanced diet."

"I suppose I ought to take him to the vet."

Carol said, "While there's a break in the rain, why don't we go outside and see if we can find him?"

"Wasted effort. When a cat doesn't want to be found, it *won't* be found. Besides, he'll come back by dinnertime. I'll keep him in all night, and take him to the vet's in the morning." Grace looked at the mess on the easy chair, grimaced, and shook her head. "This isn't like my Ari," she said worriedly. "It's just not like him at all."

The number on the open door was 316.

Hesitantly, Carol stepped into the white and blue hospital room and stopped just past the threshold. The place smelled vaguely of Lysol.

The girl was sitting up in the bed nearest the window, her face averted from the door, staring out at the twilight-shrouded hospital grounds. She turned her head when she realized she was no longer alone, and when she looked at Carol there was no recognition in her blue-gray eyes.

"May I come in?" Carol asked.

"Sure."

Carol went to the foot of the bed. "How are you feeling?"

"Okay."

"With all the scrapes and cuts and bruises, it must be hard to get comfortable."

"Gee, I'm not banged up all that bad. I'm just a little sore. It's nothing that's going to kill me. Everyone's so nice; you're all making too much of a fuss about me."

"How's your head feel?"

"I had a headache when I first came to, but it's been gone for hours."

"Double vision?"

"Nothing like that," the girl said. A strand of golden hair slipped from behind her ear and fell across her cheek; she tucked it back in place. "Are you a doctor?"

"Yes," Carol said. "My name's Carol Tracy."

"You can call me Jane. That's the name on my chart. Jane Doe. I guess it's as good as any. It might even turn out to be a lot nicer than my real name. Maybe I'm actually Zelda or Myrtle or something like that." She had a lovely smile. "You're the umpteenth doctor who's been in to see me. How many do I have, anyway?"

"I'm not one of yours," Carol said. "I'm here because . . . well . . . it was my car you stepped in front of."

"Oh. Hey, gee, I'm awfully sorry. I hope there wasn't a lot of damage."

Surprised by the girl's statement and by the genuine look of concern on her face, Carol laughed. "For heaven's sake, honey, don't worry about my car. It's your health that's important, not the VW. And *I'm* the one who should be apologizing. I feel terrible about this."

"You shouldn't," the girl said. "I still have all my teeth, and none of my bones are broken, and Dr. Hannaport says the boys will still be interested in me." She grinned self-consciously.

"He's certainly right about the boys," Carol said. "You're a very pretty girl."

The grin became a shy smile, and the girl looked down at the covers on her lap, blushing.

Carol said, "I was hoping I'd find you here with your folks."

The girl tried to maintain a cheerful facade, but when she looked up, fear and doubt showed through the mask. "I guess they haven't filed a missing-persons report yet. But it's only a matter of time."

"Have you remembered anything at all about your past?"

"Not yet. But I will." She straightened the collar of her hospital gown and smoothed the covers over her lap as she talked. "Dr. Hannaport says everything'll probably come back to me if I just don't push too hard at remembering. He says I'm lucky I don't have global amnesia. That's when you even forget how to read and write. I'm not *that* bad off! Heck, no. Boy, wouldn't that be something? What if I had to learn to read, write, add, subtract, multiply, divide, and spell all over again? What a bore!" She finished smoothing her covers and looked up again. "Anyway, I'll most likely have my memory back in a day or two."

"I'm sure you will," Carol said, though she wasn't sure at all. "Is there anything you need?"

"No. They supply everything. Even tiny tubes of toothpaste."

"What about books, magazines?"

The girl sighed. "I was bored out of my skull this afternoon. You think they might keep a pile of old magazines for the patients?"

"Probably. What do you like to read?"

"Everything. I *love* to read; I remember that much. But I can't remember the titles of any books or magazines. This amnesia sure is funny, isn't it?"

"Hilarious," Carol said. "Sit tight. I'll be right back."

At the nurses' station at the end of the hall, she explained who she was and arranged to rent a small television set for Jane Doe's room. An orderly promised to hook it up right away.

The chief RN on duty—a stocky, gray-haired woman who wore her glasses on a chain around her neck—said, "She's such a sweet girl. She's charmed everyone. Hasn't complained or uttered a cross word to a soul. There aren't many teenagers with her composure."

Carol took the elevator down to the ground-floor lobby and went to the newsstand. She bought a Hershey bar, an Almond Joy, and six magazines that looked as if they would appeal to a young girl. By the time she got back to room 316, the orderly had just finished installing the TV.

"You shouldn't have done all this," the girl said. "When my parents show up, I'll make sure they pay you back."

"I won't accept a dime," Carol said.

"But—"

"No buts."

"I don't need to be pampered. I'm fine. Really. If you—"

"I'm not pampering you, honey. Just think of the magazines and the television as forms of therapy. In fact, they might be precisely the tools you need to break through this amnesia."

"What do you mean?"

"Well, if you watch enough television, you might see a show you remember seeing before. That might spark a sort of chain reaction of memories."

"You think so?"

"It's better than just sitting and staring at the walls or out the window. Nothing in this place is going to spark a memory because none of it is related to your past. But there's a chance the TV will do the trick."

The girl picked up the remote-control device that the orderly had given her, and she switched on the television set. A popular situation comedy was on.

"Familiar?" Carol asked.

The girl shook her head: no. Tears glistened in the corners of her eyes.

"Hey, don't get upset," Carol said. "It would be amazing if you remembered the first thing you saw. It's bound to take time."

She nodded and bit her lip, trying not to cry.

Carol moved close, took the girl's hand; it was cool.

"Will you come back tomorrow?" Jane asked shakily.

"Of course I will."

"I mean, if it's not out of your way."

"It's no trouble at all."

"Sometimes . . . "

"What?"

The girl shuddered. "Sometimes I'm so afraid."

"Don't be afraid, honey. Please don't. It'll all work out. You'll see. You're going to be back on the track in no time," Carol said, wishing she could think of something more reassuring than those few hollow platitudes. But she knew her inadequate response was occasioned by her own nagging doubts.

The girl pulled a tissue out of the Kleenex dispenser that was built into the side of the tall metal nightstand. She blew her nose, used another tissue to daub at her eyes. She had slumped down in the bed; now she sat up straight, lifted her chin, squared her slender shoulders, and readjusted her covers. When she looked up at Carol, she was smiling again. "Sorry," she said. "I don't know what got into me. Being a crybaby isn't going to solve anything. Anyway, you're right. My folks will probably show up tomorrow, and everything'll work out for the best. Look, Dr. Tracy, if you come to see me tomorrow—"

"I will."

"If you do, promise not to bring me any more candy or magazines or anything. Okay? There's no reason for you to spend your money like that. You've already done too much for me. Besides, the best thing you could do is just come. I mean, it's nice to know someone outside the hospital cares about me. It's nice to know I haven't been lost or forgotten in here. Oh, sure, the nurses and the doctors are swell. They really are, and I'm grateful. They care about me, but it's sort of their job to care. You know? So that's not exactly the same thing, is it?" She laughed nervously. "Am I making sense?"

"I know exactly what you're feeling," Carol assured her. She was achingly aware of the girl's profound loneliness, for she had been lonely and frightened when she was the same age, before Grace Mitowski had taken custody of her and had given her large measures of guidance and love.

She stayed with Jane until visiting hours were over. Before she left, she planted a motherly kiss on the girl's forehead, and it seemed like a perfectly natural thing to do. A bond had formed between them in a surprisingly short time.

Outside, in the hospital parking lot, the sodium-vapor lights leached the true colors from the cars and made them all look yellowish.

The night was chilly. No rain had fallen during the afternoon or evening, but the air was heavy, damp. Thunder rumbled in the distance, and a new storm appeared to be on the way.

She sat for a moment behind the wheel of the VW, staring up at the third-floor window of the girl's room.

"What a terrific kid," she said aloud.

She felt that someone quite special had come unexpectedly into her life.

Near midnight, a river-cold wind came out of the west and made the trees dance. The starless, moonless, utterly lightless night pressed close around the house and seemed to Grace to be a living thing; it snuffled at the doors and windows.

Rain began to fall.

She went to bed as the hall clock was striking twelve, and twenty minutes later she began to drift over the edge of sleep as if she were a leaf borne by cool currents toward a great waterfall. On the brink, with only darkness churning under her, she heard movement in the bedroom and instantly came awake again.

A series of stealthy sounds. A soft scrape. A rattle that died even as it began. A silken rustle.

She sat up, heart quickening, and opened the nightstand drawer. With one hand she felt blindly for the .22 pistol she kept in the drawer, and with the other hand she groped silently for the lamp switch. She touched the gun and lamp at the same moment.

With light, the source of the noise was clearly visible. Ari was crouched atop the highboy, staring down at her, as if he had been about to spring onto the bed.

"What are you doing in here? You know the rules."

He blinked but didn't move. His muscles were bunched and taut; his fur was standing up on the back of his neck.

For sanitary reasons, she would allow him to climb neither onto the kitchen counters nor into her bed; generally, she kept the master bedroom door firmly shut, day and night, rather than tempt him. Already, housecleaning required extra hours each week because of him, for she was determined that the air should not contain even the slightest trace of cat odor; likewise, she was not about to subject her visitors to furniture covered with loose animal hairs. She loved Ari, and she thought him fine company, and for the most part she gave him the run of the house in spite of the extra work he caused her. But she was not prepared to live with cat hairs in her food or in her sheets.

She got out of bed, stepped into her slippers.

Ari watched.

"Come down from there this instant," Grace said, looking up at him with her sternest expression.

His shining eyes were gas-flame blue.

Grace went to the bedroom door, opened it, stepped out of the way, and said, "Shoo."

The cat's muscles relaxed. He slumped in a furry puddle atop the highboy, as if his bones had melted. He yawned and began to lick one of his black paws.

"Hey!" she said.

Aristophanes raised his head languidly, peered down at her.

"Out," she said gruffly. "Now."

When he still didn't move, she started toward the highboy, and he was at last encouraged to obey. He jumped down and darted past her so fast she didn't have time to swat him. He went into the hall, and she closed the door.

In bed again, with the lights out, she remembered the way he had looked as he perched atop the highboy: facing her, *aimed* at her, shoulders drawn up, head held low, haunches tense, his fur electrified, his eyes bright and slightly demented. He had intended to jump onto the bed and scare the bejesus out of her; there was no doubt about that. But such schemes were a kitten's games; Ari had not been playful in that fashion for the past three or four years, ever since he had attained a rather indolent maturity. What on earth had gotten into him?

That settles it, she told herself. We'll pay a visit to the veterinarian first thing in the morning. Good Lord, I might have a schizophrenic cat on my hands!

Seeking rest, she let the night embrace her again. She allowed herself to be carried along by the riverlike sound of the soughing wind. Within a few minutes she was once more being borne toward the waterfall of sleep. She trembled on the edge of it, and a quiver of uneasiness passed through her, a chill that nearly broke the spell, but then she dropped down into darkness.

She dreamed that she was trekking across a vast underwater landscape of brilliantly colored coral and seaweed and strange, undulating plants. A cat lurked among the plants, a big one, much bigger than a tiger, but with the coloring of a Siamese. It was stalking her. She could see its saucer eyes peering at her through the murky sea, from among wavering stalks of marine vegetation. She could hear and feel its low purr transmitted by the water. She paused repeatedly during her suboceanic trek so that she could fill a series of yellow bowls with generous portions of Meow Mix in the hope of pacifying the cat, but she knew in her heart that the beast would not be content until it had sunk its claws into her. She moved steadily past towers of coral, past grottoes, across wide aquatic plains of shifting sand, waiting for the cat to snarl and lunge from concealment, waiting for it to rip open her face and gouge out her eyes. . . .

Once, she woke and thought she heard Aristophanes scratching insistently on the other side of the closed bedroom door. But she was groggy and couldn't trust her senses; she wasn't able to wrench herself fully awake, and in a few seconds she sank down into the dream once more.

At one o'clock in the morning, the third floor of the hospital was so quiet that Harriet Gilbey, the head nurse on the graveyard shift, felt as though she was deep underground, in some kind of military complex, tucked into the stony roots of a mountain, far from the real world and the background noises of real life. The only sounds were the whisper of the heating system and the occasional squeak of the nurses' rubber-soled shoes on the highly polished tile floors.

Harriet—a small, pretty, neatly uniformed black woman—was at the nurses' station, around the corner from the bank of elevators, entering data on patients' charts, when the tranquility of the third floor was abruptly shattered by a piercing scream. She moved out from behind the reception desk and hurried along the hall, following the shrill cry. It came from room 316. When Harriet pushed open the door, stepped into the room, and snapped on the overhead lights, the screaming stopped as suddenly as it had begun.

The girl they called Jane Doe was in bed, flat on her back, one arm raised and angled across her face as if she were warding off a blow, the other hand hooked on to one of the safety rails. She had kicked the sheets and the blanket into a tangled wad at the foot of the bed, and her hospital gown was rucked up over her hips. She tossed her head violently from side to side, gasping, pleading with an imaginary assailant: "No . . . no . . . no. Don't! Please don't kill me! *No!*"

With gentle hands, a gentle voice, and patient insistence, Harriet tried to quiet the girl. At first Jane resisted all ministrations. She had been given a sedative earlier. Now she was having trouble waking up. Gradually, however, she shook off the nightmare and calmed down.

Another nurse, Kay Hamilton, appeared at Harriet's side. "What happened? Must've woke up half the floor."

"Just a bad dream," Harriet said.

Jane blinked sleepily at them. "She was trying to kill me."

"Hush now," Harriet said. "It was only a dream. No one here will hurt you."

"A dream?" Jane asked, her voice slurred. "Oh. Yeah. Just a dream. Whew! What a dream."

The girl's thin white gown and the tangled sheets were damp with perspiration. Harriet and Kay replaced them with fresh linens.

As soon as the bed had been changed, Jane succumbed to the lingering tug of the sedative. She turned onto her side and murmured happily in her sleep; she even smiled.

"Looks like she switched to a better channel," Harriet said.

"Poor kid. After what she's been through, the least she deserves is a good night's sleep."

They watched her for a minute, then left the room, turning off the lights and closing the door.

Alone, deep in sleep, transported into a different dream from the one that had elicited her screams, Jane sighed, smiled, giggled quietly.

"The ax," she whispered in her sleep. "The ax. Oh, the ax. Yes. Yes."

Her hands curled slightly, as if she were clutching a solid but invisible object.

"The ax," she whispered, and the second of those two words reverberated softly through the dark room.

Thunk!

Carol ran through the huge living room, across the oriental carpet, banging her hip against the edge of the credenza.

Thunk! Thunk!

She dashed through the archway, into a long hall, headed toward the stairs that led to the second floor. When she glanced behind her, she saw that the house had vanished in her wake and had been replaced by a pitch-black void in which something silvery flickered back and forth, back and forth. . . .

Thunk!

Understanding came with a flash; she knew what the glimmering object was. An ax. The blade of an ax. Glinting as it swung from side to side.

Thunk . . . thunk-thunk . . .

Whimpering, she climbed the stairs toward the second floor.

Thunk . . . thunk . . .

At times the blade seemed to be biting into wood; the sound of it was dry, splintery. But at other times the sound had a subtly different quality, as if the blade were slicing brutally into a substance much softer than wood, into something wet and tender.

Into flesh?

Thunk!

Carol groaned in her sleep, turned restlessly, flinging off the sheets.

Then she was running across the high meadow. The trees ahead. The void behind. And the ax. The ax.

SIX

◆

Friday morning, there was another break in the rain, but the day was dressed in fog. The light coming through the hospital window was wintry, bleak.

Jane had only a hazy recollection of the nurses changing her sheets and her sweat-soaked bed gown during the night. She vaguely recalled having a frightening dream, too, but she couldn't bring to mind a single detail of it.

She was still unable to remember her name or anything else about herself. She could cast her mind back as far as the accident yesterday morning, perhaps even to a point a minute or so on the other side of the accident, but beyond that there was only a blank wall where her past should have been.

During breakfast, she read an article in one of the magazines that Carol Tracy had bought for her. Although there were no visiting hours until this afternoon, Jane was already looking forward to seeing the woman again. Dr. Hannaport and the nurses were nice, every one of them, but none of them affected her as positively as Carol Tracy did. For reasons she could not understand, she felt more secure, more at ease, less frightened by her amnesia when she was with Dr. Tracy than when she was with the others. Maybe that was what people meant when they said a doctor had a good bedside manner.

Shortly after nine o'clock, when Paul was on the freeway, headed downtown to deliver the new set of application papers to Alfred O'Brian's office, the Pontiac's engine cut out. It didn't sputter or cough; the pistons simply stopped firing while the car was hurtling along at nearly fifty miles an hour. As the Pontiac's speed plummeted, its power steering began to freeze up. Traffic whizzed past on both sides at sixty and sixty-five, faster than the speed limit, too fast for the misty weather. Paul maneuvered the car across two lanes, toward the right-hand shoulder of the road. Second by second, he expected to hear a short squeal of brakes and feel the sickening impact of another car against his, but amazingly, he was able to avoid a collision. Wrestling with the stiffening steering wheel, he brought the Pontiac to a full stop on the berm.

He leaned back in his seat and closed his eyes until he had regained his composure. When at last he leaned forward and twisted the key in the ignition, the starter didn't make the slightest response; the battery had no juice to offer. He tried a few more times, then gave up.

A freeway exit was just ahead, and there was a service station less than a block from the off-ramp. Paul walked to it in ten minutes.

The station was busy, and the owner couldn't spare his young assistant—a big, redheaded, open-faced kid named Corky—until the stream of customers subsided to a trickle shortly before ten o'clock. Then Paul and Corky rode back to the crippled Pontiac in a tow truck.

They tried jump-starting the car, but the battery wouldn't hold a charge. The Pontiac had to be towed back to the station.

Corky intended to replace the battery and have the car running in half an hour. But it wasn't the battery after all, and the estimated time for completion of the repairs was extended again and again. Finally, Corky found a problem with the electrical system and fixed it.

Paul was stranded for three hours, always sure he would be on his way in just another twenty or thirty minutes. But it was one-thirty when he finally parked the revitalized Pontiac in front of the adoption agency's offices.

Alfred O'Brian came out to the reception lounge to greet Paul. He was wearing a well-tailored brown suit, a neatly pressed, cream-colored shirt, a neatly arranged, beige display handkerchief in the breast pocket of his suit jacket, and a pair of neatly shined, brown wing-tip shoes. He accepted the application, but he wasn't optimistic about the possibility of making all the required verifications prior to the recommendations committee's meeting next Wednesday morning.

"We'll try to do a rush job on your papers," he told Paul. "I owe you that much at least! But in getting these verifications, we have to deal with people outside this office, and some of them won't get back to us right away or won't like being hurried. It always takes a minimum of three full business days to run a complete verification, sometimes four or five days, sometimes even longer, so I very much doubt that we'll be ready for this session of the recommendations committee, even though I want to be. We'll probably have to submit your application at the second September meeting, at the end of the month. I feel terrible about that, Mr. Tracy. I'm more sorry than I can say. I truly am. If we hadn't lost those papers in the turmoil yesterday—"

"Don't worry about it," Paul said. "The lightning wasn't your doing, and neither was the problem with my car. Carol and I have waited a long, long time to adopt a child. Another two weeks isn't much in the scheme of things."

"When your papers *are* presented to the committee, you'll be approved quickly," O'Brian said. "I've never been more sure about a couple than I am about you. That's what I'm going to tell them."

"I appreciate that," Paul said.

"If we can't make Wednesday's meeting—and I assure you we'll try our best—then it's only a minor, temporary setback. Nothing to be concerned about. Just a bit of bad luck."

Dr. Brad Templeton was a fine veterinarian. However, to Grace, he always looked out of place when he was ministering to a cat or dog. He was a big man who would have looked more at home treating horses and farm animals in a country practice, where his massive shoulders and muscular arms would be of more use. He stood six-five, weighed about two hundred and twenty pounds, and had a ruddy, rugged, but pleasing face. When he plucked Aristophanes out of the padded travel basket, the cat looked like a toy in his enormous hands.

"He looks fit," Brad said, putting Ari on the stainless-steel table that stood in the middle of the sparkling clean surgery.

"He's never been one to tear up the furniture, not since he was just a kitten," Grace said. "He's never been a climber, either. But now, every time I turn around, he's perched on top of something, peering down at me."

Brad examined Ari, feeling for swollen glands and enlarged joints. The cat cooperated docilely, even when Brad used a rectal thermometer on him. "Temperature's normal."

"*Something's* wrong," Grace insisted.

Aristophanes purred, rolled onto his back, asking for his belly to be rubbed.

Brad rubbed him and was rewarded with an even louder purr. "Is he off his food?"

"No," Grace said. "He still eats well."

"Vomiting?"

"No."

"Diarrhea?"

"No. He hasn't shown any symptoms like those. It's just that he's . . . different. He's not at all like he was. Every symptom I can point to is a symptom of a *personality* change, not an indication of physical deterioration. Like destroying the pillows. Leaving the mess on the armchair. The sudden interest he's taken in climbing. And he's gotten very sneaky lately, always creeping around, hiding from me, watching me when he thinks I don't see him."

"All cats are a bit sneaky," Brad said, frowning. "That's the nature of the beast."

"Ari didn't used to sneak," Grace said. "Not like he's been doing the last couple of days. And he's not as friendly as he used to be. The last two days, he hasn't wanted to be petted or cuddled."

Still frowning, Brad lifted his gaze from the cat and met Grace's eyes. "But dear, look at him."

Ari was still on his back, getting his belly rubbed, and clearly relishing all the attention being directed at him. His tail swished back and forth across the steel table. He raised one paw and batted playfully at the doctor's large, leathery hand.

Sighing, Grace said, "I know what you're thinking. I'm an old woman. Old women get funny ideas."

"No, no, no. I wasn't thinking any such thing."

"Old women become obsessively attached to their pets because sometimes their pets are the only company they have, their only real friends."

"I am perfectly aware that doesn't apply to you, Grace. Not with all the friends you've got in this town. I merely—"

She smiled and patted his cheek. "Don't protest too strongly, Brad. I know what's going through your mind. Some old women are so afraid of losing their pets that they think they see signs of illness where there are none. Your reaction is understandable. It doesn't offend me. It *does* frustrate me because I know something *is* wrong with Ari."

Brad looked down at the cat again, continued stroking its belly, and said, "Have you changed his diet in any way?"

"No. He gets the same brand of cat food, at the same times of day, in the same quantities he's always gotten it."

"Has the company changed the product recently?"

"How do you mean?"

"Well, does the package say 'new, improved,' or 'richer flavor,' or anything like that?"

She thought about it for a moment, then shook her head. "I don't think so."

"Sometimes, when they change a formula, they add a new preservative or a new artificial flavoring or coloring agent, and some pets have an allergic reaction to it."

"But wouldn't that be a physical reaction? Like I said, this seems to be strictly a personality change."

Brad nodded. "I'm sure you know food additives can cause behavioral problems in some children. A lot of hyperactive kids calm down when they're put on a diet free of the major additives. Animals can be affected by these things, too. From what you've told me, it sounds like Aristophanes is intermittently hyperactive and may be responding to a subtle change in the formulation of his cat food. Switch him to another brand, wait a week for his system to purge itself of whatever additives have offended it, and he'll probably be the old Ari again."

"If he isn't?"

"Then bring him in, leave him with me for a couple of days, and I'll give him a really thorough going over. But I strongly recommend that we try changing his diet first, before we go to all that trouble and expense."

You *are* humoring me, Grace thought. Just coddling an old lady.

"Very well," she said. "I'll try changing his food. But if he's still not himself a week from now, I'll want you to give him a complete battery of tests."

"Of course."

"I'll want an answer."

On the stainless-steel table, Aristophanes purred, happily twitched his long tail, and looked infuriatingly *normal*.

Later, at home, just inside the front door, when Grace slipped the latch on the padded travel basket and opened the lid, Aristophanes exploded out of confinement with a hiss and a snarl, his fur bristling, his ears laid back against his head, eyes wild. He clawed her hand and squealed as she thrust him away from her. He sprinted down the hall, disappeared into the kitchen, where the pet door gave him access to the rear yard.

Shocked, Grace stared at her hand. Ari's claws had made three short furrows in the meaty edge of her palm. Blood welled up and began to trickle down her wrist.

Carol's last appointment on Friday was at one o'clock: a fifty-minute session with Kathy Lombino, a fifteen-year-old girl who was gradually recovering from anorexia nervosa. Five months ago, when she had first been brought to Carol, Kathy had weighed only seventy-five pounds, at least thirty pounds below her ideal weight. She had been teetering on the edge of starvation, repelled by the sight and even the thought of food, stubbornly refusing to eat more than an occasional soda cracker or slice of bread, often gagging on even those bland morsels. When she was put in front of a mirror and forced to confront the pathetic sight of her emaciated body, she still berated herself for being fat and could not be convinced that she was, in fact, frighteningly thin. Her prospects for survival had seemed slight. Now she weighed ninety pounds, up fifteen, still well below a healthy weight for a girl of her height and bone structure, but at least she was no longer in danger of dying. A loss of self-respect and self-confidence was nearly always the seed from which anorexia nervosa grew, and Kathy was beginning to like herself again, a sure sign that she was on her way back from the brink. She hadn't yet regained a normal appetite; she still experienced mild revulsion at the sight and taste of food; but her attitude was far better than it had been, for now she recognized the *need* for food, even though she didn't have any desire for it. The girl had a long way to go before she would be fully recovered, but the worst was past for her; in time she would learn to enjoy food again, and she would gain weight more rapidly than she had done thus far, stabilizing around a hundred and five or a hundred and ten pounds. Kathy's progress had been immensely satisfying to Carol, and today's session only added to that satisfaction. As had become customary, she and the girl hugged each other at the end of the session, and Kathy held on tighter and longer than usual. When the girl left the office, she was smiling.

A few minutes later, at two o'clock, Carol went to the hospital. In the gift shop off the lobby, she bought a deck of playing cards and a miniature checkerboard with nickle-sized checkers that all fit neatly into a vinyl carrying case.

Upstairs, in 316, the television was on, and Jane was reading a magazine. She looked up when Carol entered, and she said, "You really came."

"Said I would, didn't I?"

"What've you got?"

"Cards, checkers. I thought maybe they'd help you pass the time."

"You promised you wouldn't buy me anything else."

"Hey, did I say I was *giving* these to you? No way. You think I'm a soft touch or something? I'm *lending* them, kid. I expect them back. And whenever you return them, they'd better be in as good condition as they are now, or I'll take you all the way to the Supreme Court to get compensated for the damage."

Jane grinned. "Boy, you're tough."

"I eat nails for breakfast."

"Don't they get stuck in your teeth?"

"I pluck 'em out with pliers."

"Ever eat barbed wire?"

"Never for breakfast. I have it for lunch now and then."

They both laughed, and Carol said, "So do you play checkers?"

"I don't know. I don't remember."

"Cards?"

The girl shrugged.

"Nothing's come back yet?" Carol asked.

"Not a thing."

"Don't worry. It will."

"My folks haven't shown up, either."

"Well, you've only been missing for one day. Give them time to find you. It's too soon to start worrying about that."

They played three games of checkers. Jane remembered all of the rules, but she couldn't recall where or with whom she had played before.

The afternoon passed quickly, and Carol enjoyed every minute of it. Jane was charming, bright, and blessed with a good sense of humor. Whether the game was checkers, hearts, or five-hundred rummy, she played to win, but she never pouted when she lost. She was very good company.

The girl's charm and pleasing personality made it highly unlikely that she would go unclaimed for long. Some teenagers are so self-centered, spaced out on drugs, bullheaded, and destructive that when one of them decides to run away from home, his decision often elicits only a sigh of relief from his mother and father. But when a good kid like Jane Doe disappears, a lot of people start sounding alarms.

There must be a family that loves her, Carol thought. They're probably crazy with worry right now. Sooner or later they'll turn up, crying and laughing with relief that their girl has been found alive. So why not sooner? Where *are* they?

* * *

The doorbell rang at precisely three-thirty. Paul answered it and found a pallid, gray-eyed man of about fifty. He wore gray slacks, a pale gray shirt, and a dark gray sweater.

"Mr. Tracy?"

"Yes. Are you from Safe Homes?"

"That's right," the gray man said. "Name's Bill Alsgood. I *am* Safe Homes. Started the company two years ago."

They shook hands, and Alsgood entered the foyer, looking with interest at the interior of the house. "Lovely place. You're lucky to get same-day service. Usually, I'm scheduled three days in advance. But when you called this morning and said it was an emergency, I'd just had a cancellation."

"You're a building inspector?" Paul asked, closing the door.

"Structural engineer, to be precise. What our company does is inspect the house before it's sold, usually on behalf of the buyer, at his expense. We tell him if he's buying into a heartache of any sort—a leaky roof, a cellar that floods, a crumbling foundation, faulty wiring, bad plumbing, that kind of thing. We're fully bonded, so even if we overlook something, our client is protected. Are you the buyer or the seller?"

"Neither," Paul said. "My wife and I own the place, but we aren't ready to sell it. We're having a problem with the house, and I can't pinpoint the cause of it. I thought you might be able to help."

Alsgood raised one gray eyebrow. "May I suggest that what you need is a good handyman. He'd be considerably cheaper, and once he'd found the trouble, he could fix it, too. We don't do any repair work, you know. We only inspect."

"I'm aware of that. I'm pretty handy myself, but I haven't figured out what's wrong or how to fix it. I think I need the kind of expert advice that no handyman can give me."

"You *do* know we charge two hundred and fifty dollars for an inspection?"

"I know," Paul said. "But this is an extremely annoying problem, and it might be causing serious structural damage."

"What is it?"

Paul told him about the hammering sounds that occasionally shook the house.

"That's peculiar as hell," Alsgood said. "I've never heard a complaint like it before." He thought for a moment, then said, "Where's your furnace?"

"In the cellar."

"Maybe it's a heating duct problem. Unlikely. But we can start down there and work our way up to the roof until we've found the cause."

For the next two hours, Alsgood looked into every cranny of the house, poked and probed and rapped and visually inspected every inch of the interior, then every inch of the roof, while Paul tagged along, assisting wherever he could. A light rain began to fall when they were still on the roof, and they were both soaked by the time they finished the job and climbed down. Alsgood's left foot slipped off the last rung of the ladder, just as he was about to step onto the water-logged lawn, and he twisted his ankle painfully. All that risk and inconvenience was for nothing because Alsgood didn't find anything out of the ordinary.

At five-thirty, in the kitchen, they warmed up with coffee while Alsgood filled out his report. Wet and bedraggled, he looked even more pallid than when Paul had first seen him. The rain had transformed his gray clothes—once a variety of shades—into a single, dull hue, so that he appeared to be wearing a drab uniform. "It's basically a solid house, Mr. Tracy. The condition is really topnotch."

"Then where the devil did that sound come from? And why was the whole house shaken by it?"

"I wish I'd heard it."

"I was sure it'd start up at least once while you were here."

Alsgood sipped his coffee, but the warm brew added no color to his cheeks. "Structurally, there's not a thing wrong with this house. That's what my report will say, and I'd stake my reputation on it."

"Which puts me right back at square one," Paul said, folding his hands around his coffee cup.

"I'm sorry you spent all this money without getting an answer," Alsgood said. "I really feel bad about that."

"It isn't your fault. I'm convinced you did a thorough job. In fact, if I ever buy another house, I'll definitely want you to inspect it first. At least I now know the trouble isn't structural, which rules out possibilities and narrows the field of inquiry."

"Maybe you won't even hear it again. It might stop just as suddenly as it started."

"Somehow, I suspect you're wrong about that," Paul said.

Later, at the front door, as Alsgood was leaving, he said, "One thought has occurred to me, but I hesitate to mention it."

"Why?"

"You might think it's off the wall."

"Mr. Alsgood, I'm a desperate man. I'm willing to consider anything, no matter how farfetched it might be."

Alsgood looked at the ceiling, then at the floor, then back along the hall that lay behind Paul, then down at his own feet. "A ghost," he said quietly.

Paul stared at him, surprised.

Alsgood cleared his throat nervously, shifted his eyes to the floor again, then finally raised them and met Paul's gaze. "Maybe you don't believe in ghosts."

"Do you?" Paul asked.

"Yes. I've been interested in the subject most of my life. I have a large collection of publications dealing with spiritualism of all sorts. I've had some personal experiences in haunted houses, too."

"You've seen a ghost?"

"I believe I have, yes, on four occasions. Ectoplasmic apparitions. Insubstantial, manlike shapes drifting in the air. I've also twice witnessed poltergeist phenomena. As far as this house is concerned . . . " His voice trailed away, and he licked his lips nervously. "If you find this boring or preposterous, I don't want to waste your time."

"Quite frankly," Paul said, "I can't picture myself calling an exorcist in to deal with this. But I'm not entirely close-minded where ghosts are concerned. I find it hard to accept, but I'm certainly willing to listen."

"Reasonable enough," Alsgood said. For the first time since he had rung the doorbell more than two hours ago, color rose into his milky complexion, and his watery eyes brightened with a spark of enthusiasm. "All right. Here's something to consider. From what you've told me, I'd say there might be a poltergeist at work here. Of course, no objects have been hurled around by an unseen presence; there's been no breakage, and poltergeists dearly love to break things. But the shaking of the house, the clattering pots and pans, the little bottles clinking against one another in the spice rack—those are all indications of a poltergeist at work, one that's just beginning to test its powers. If it *is* a poltergeist, then you can expect worse to come. Oh, yes. Definitely. Furniture moving across the floor all by itself. Pictures flung off the walls, lamps knocked down and broken. Dishes flying around the room as if they were birds." His wan countenance flushed with excitement as he considered the supernatural destruction. "Levitations of heavy objects like sofas and beds and refrigerators. Now mind you, there *are* some recorded cases of people being plagued by *benign* poltergeists that don't break much of anything, but the overwhelming number of them are malign, and that's what you'll most likely have to deal with—if indeed you've got one here at all." Having warmed to his subject, he finished in an almost breathless rush of words: "In its most active form, even a benign poltergeist can completely disrupt a household, interfere with your sleep, and keep you so on edge that you don't know whether you're coming or going."

Startled by Alsgood's passionately delivered speech and by the odd new light in the man's eyes, Paul said, "Well . . . uh . . . it's really not that bad. Not nearly that bad. Just a hammering sound and—"

"It's not that bad *yet*," Alsgood said somberly. "But if you have a poltergeist here, the situation could deteriorate rapidly. If you've never seen one in action, Mr. Tracy, you simply can't understand what it's like."

Paul was disconcerted by the change in the man. He felt as if he had opened the door to one of those wholesome-looking types who turned out to be pushing crackpot religious pamphlets and who proclaimed the imminence of Judgment Day in the same bubbly, upbeat tone of voice that Donny Osmond might use to introduce his cute little sister, Marie, to a panting audience of Osmond fans. There was a disquieting zeal in Alsgood's manner.

"If it *does* turn out to be a poltergeist," Alsgood said, "if things *do* get a lot worse, will you call me right away? I've been fortunate enough to observe two poltergeists, as I said. I'd like nothing better than to see a third going through its tricks. The opportunity doesn't arise very often."

"I guess not," Paul said.

"So you'll call me?"

"I very much doubt there's a poltergeist involved here, Mr. Alsgood. If I keep looking long enough and hard enough, I'll find a perfectly logical explanation for what's been happening. But on the off-chance that it *is* a malign spirit, rest assured I'll give you a call the moment the first refrigerator or chiffonier levitates."

Alsgood wasn't able to see anything amusing about their conversation. He frowned when he detected levity in Paul's voice, and he said, "I didn't really expect you to take me seriously."

"Oh, please don't think I'm not grateful for—"

"No, no," Alsgood said, waving him to silence. "I understand. No offense taken." The excitement had gone out of his watery eyes. "You've been raised to believe strictly in science. You've been taught to put your faith only in things that can be seen and touched and measured. That's the modern way." His shoulders slumped. The color in his face faded, and his skin became pale, grayish, and slack, as it had been a few minutes ago. "Asking you to be open-minded about ghosts is as pointless as trying to convince a deep-sea creature that there are such things as birds. It's sad but true, and I have no reason to be angry about it." He opened the front door, and the sound of the rain grew louder. "Anyway, for your sake, I hope it isn't a poltergeist you've got here. I hope you find that logical explanation you're looking for. I really do, Mr. Tracy."

Before Paul could respond, Alsgood turned and walked out into the rain. He no longer seemed like a zealot; there was no trace of passion in him. He was just a thin, gray man, shuffling through the gray mist, head slightly bowed against the gray rain, illuminated by the gray light of the storm; he almost seemed like a ghost himself.

Paul closed the door, put his back against it, and looked around the hall, through the nearest archway, which opened onto the living room. Poltergeist? Not very damned likely.

He preferred Alsgood's other suggestion: that the hammering might simply stop as suddenly and inexplicably as it had started, without the cause ever being known.

He glanced at his watch. 6:06.

Carol had said she would remain at the hospital until eight o'clock and would then come home for a late meal. That gave him an hour or so to work on his novel before he had to start cooking dinner—broiled chicken breasts, steamed vegetables, and rice with bits of green pepper.

He went upstairs to his office and sat down at the typewriter. He picked up the last page he had written, intending to reread it a few times and get back into the mood and tone of the story he was telling.

THUNK! THUNK!

The house shook. The windows rattled.

He bolted up from his chair.

THUNK!

On his desk, the jar full of pens and pencils toppled over, cracked into several pieces, and spilled its contents onto the floor.

Silence.

He waited. One minute. Two minutes.

Nothing.

There was no sound except the snapping of the rain against the windows and the drumming of it on the roof.

Only three hammer blows this time. Harder than any that had come before. But only three. Almost as if someone were playing games with him, taunting him.

Shortly before midnight, in room 316, the girl laughed softly in her sleep.

Outside her window, lightning pulsed, and the night flickered, and the darkness seemed to gallop for a moment, as if it were a huge and eager beast.

The girl turned onto her stomach without waking, murmured into her pillows. "The ax," she said with a wistful sigh. "The ax . . . "

On the stroke of midnight, just forty minutes after she had fallen asleep, Carol bolted up from her pillows, trembling violently. As she struggled out of the grip of her nightmare, she heard someone say, "It's coming! It's coming!" She stared wildly, blindly into the lightless room until she realized the panic-stricken voice had been her own.

Suddenly she could not tolerate the darkness one second longer. She fumbled desperately for the switch on the bedside lamp, found it, and sagged with relief.

The light didn't disturb Paul. He mumbled in his sleep but didn't wake.

Carol leaned back against the headboard and listened to her racing heart as it gradually slowed to a normal beat.

Her hands were icy. She put them under the covers and curled them into warming fists.

The nightmares have got to stop, she told herself. I can't go through this every night. I need my sleep.

Perhaps a vacation was called for. She had been working too hard for too long. The accumulated weariness was probably partly to blame for her bad dreams. She had also been under a great deal of unusual stress lately: the pending adoption, the near-tragic events in O'Brian's office on Wednesday, the accident just yesterday morning, the girl's amnesia for which she felt responsible. . . . Living with too much tension could cause exceptionally vivid nightmares of the sort she was experiencing. A week in the mountains, away from everyday problems, seemed like the perfect medicine.

In addition to all the other sources of stress, *that* day was approaching, the birthday of the child she had put up for adoption. A week from tomorrow, the Saturday after next, would mark sixteen years since she had relinquished the baby. Already, eight days in advance of that anniversary, she was burdened by a heavy mantle of guilt. By the time next Saturday rolled around, she would most likely be thoroughly depressed, as usual. A week in the mountains, away from everyday problems, might be the perfect medicine for *that* ailment, too.

Last year, she and Paul had purchased a vacation cabin on an acre of timbered land in the mountains. It was a cozy place—two bedrooms, one bath, a living room with a big stone fireplace, and a complete kitchen—a retreat that combined all the comforts of civilization with the clean air, marvelous scenery, and tranquility that could not be found in the city.

They had planned to get away to the cabin at least two weekends every month during the summer, but they had made the trip only three times in the past four months, less than half as often as they had hoped. Paul had labored hard to meet a series of self-imposed deadlines on his novel, and she had taken on more patients—a couple of really troubled kids who simply could not be turned away— and for both herself and Paul, work had expanded to fill every spare moment. Perhaps they were the overachievers that Alfred O'Brian had thought they might be.

But we'll change when we have a child, Carol told herself. We'll make lots of time for leisure and for family outings because creating the best environment for our child is the job we're looking forward to more than any other.

Now, sitting up in bed, the grisly nightmare still chillingly fresh in her mind, she decided to start changing her life from this moment on. They *would* take off a few days, maybe a whole week, and go to the mountains before the recommendations committee's meeting at the end of the month, so they would be rested and composed when at last they met the child who would be theirs. They couldn't take off this coming week, of course. She would need time to reschedule her appointments. Besides, she didn't want to leave town until Jane Doe's parents showed up and properly identified the girl; that might take a few more days. But they ought to be able to carve a large chunk of time out of the week after next, and she made up her mind to start nudging Paul about it first thing in the morning.

Having reached that decision, she felt better. The mere prospect of a vacation, even a brief one, relieved much of her tension.

She looked at Paul and said, "I love you."

He continued to snore softly.

Smiling, she clicked off the light and settled under the covers again. For a couple of minutes she listened to the rain and to her husband's rhythmic breathing; then she drifted into a sound, satisfying sleep.

Rain fell throughout Saturday, rounding out a monotonously watery, sunless week. The day was cool, too, and the wind had teeth.

Carol visited Jane in the hospital on Saturday afternoon. They played cards and talked about some of the articles the girl had read in the magazines Carol had bought for her. Through every conversation, regardless of the subject, Carol probed continuously but subtly at the girl's amnesia, prodded her memory without letting her see that she was being prodded. But it was all wasted effort, for Jane's past remained beyond her grasp.

At the end of the afternoon visiting hours, as Carol was heading toward the elevators on the third floor, she encountered Dr. Sam Hannaport in the corridor.

"Haven't the police come up with any leads at all?" she asked.

He shrugged his burly shoulders. "Not yet."

"It's been over two days since the accident."

"Which isn't all that long."

"It seems like an eternity to that poor kid in there," Carol said, gesturing toward the door of 316.

"I know," Hannaport said. "And I feel just as bad about it as you do. But it's still too soon to be pessimistic."

"If *I* had a girl like her, and if *my* kid turned up missing for even one day, I'd be pushing the police hard, and I'd make damned sure the story was in all the papers, and I'd be pounding on doors and making a nuisance of myself all over the city."

Hannaport nodded. "I know you would. I've seen how you operate, and I admire your style. And listen, I think your visits with the girl have an awful lot to do with keeping her spirits up. It's good of you to take all this time with her."

"Well, I'm not angling for a testimonial dinner," Carol said. "I don't think I'm doing any more than I have to do. I mean, I've got a responsibility here."

A nurse came along, pushing a patient in a wheelchair. Carol and Hannaport stepped out of the way.

"At least Jane seems to be in good physical shape," Carol said.

"Like I told you on Wednesday—there were no serious injuries. In fact, because she *is* in such good condition, she presents us with a problem. She doesn't really belong in a hospital. I just hope her parents show up before I'm forced to discharge her."

"Discharge her? But you can't do that if she has nowhere to go. She can't cope outside. For God's sake, she doesn't even know who she is!"

"Naturally, I'll keep her here as long as I possibly can. But by late tonight or tomorrow morning, all of our beds are probably going to be full. Then, if the number of emergency admissions is greater than the number of discharges already scheduled, we'll have to look around for a few other patients who can be safely released. Jane's bound to be one of them. If some guy's brought in here with a cracked skull from an auto accident, or if an ambulance delivers a woman who's been stabbed by a jealous boyfriend, I can't justify turning away seriously injured people while I'm keeping a perfectly healthy girl whose worst physical problem is a contusion on her left shoulder."

"But her amnesia—"

"Is something we can't treat anyway."

"But she has nowhere to go," Carol said. "What would happen to her?"

In his calm, soft, reassuring voice, Hannaport said, "She'll be okay. Really. We're not going to just abandon her. We'll petition to have her declared a ward of the court until her parents show up. In the meantime, she'll do just as well at some minimal-care facility as she would do here."

"What facility are you talking about?"

"Just three blocks from here, there's a home for runaway and pregnant teenage girls, and it's far cleaner and better managed than the average state institution."

"The Polmar Home," Carol said. "I know it."

"Then you know it's not a dungeon or a dump."

"I still don't like moving her out of here," Carol said. "She's going to feel as if she's being shunted aside, forgotten, and left to rot. She's on very shaky ground already. This'll scare her half to death."

Frowning, Hannaport said, "I don't like it much myself, but I truly don't have an option. If we're short on bed space, the law says we've got to consider degrees of need and take in those patients who have the most to lose by being denied care or by having treatment delayed. I'm in a bind."

"I understand. I'm not blaming you. Dammit, if someone would just come forward to claim her!"

"Someone might, any minute."

Carol shook her head. "No. I've got a feeling it's not going to be that easy. Have you told Jane yet?"

"No. We won't make the petition to the court sooner than Monday morning, so I might as well wait until tomorrow to explain it to her. Maybe something'll happen between now and then to make it unnecessary. No use worrying her until we have to."

Carol was depressed, remembering her own days in a state-run institution, before Grace had come along to rescue her. She had been a tough kid, street-smart, but the experience had nevertheless scarred her. Jane was bright and spunky and strong and sweet, but she wasn't *tough,* not like Carol had been at her age. What would institutional living do to her if she had to endure it for more than a day or two? If she was simply dropped in among kids who *were* street-smart, among kids who had drug and behavioral problems, she would most likely be victimized, perhaps even violently. What she needed was a real home, love, guidance—

"Of course!" Carol said. She grinned.

Hannaport looked at her questioningly.

"Why can't she come with *me?*" Carol asked.

"What?"

"Look, Dr. Hannaport, if it's all right with Paul, my husband, why couldn't you recommend to the court that I be awarded temporary custody of Jane until someone shows up who can identify her?"

"You really better think twice about that," Hannaport said. "Taking her in, disrupting your lives—"

"It won't be a disruption," Carol said. "It'll be a pleasure. She's a delightful kid."

Hannaport stared at her a long moment, searching her face and her eyes.

"After all," Carol argued as persuasively as she could, "the only kind of doctor who might be able to cure Jane's amnesia is a psychiatrist. And in case you've forgotten, that's what I am. I'd not only be able to provide a decent home for her; I'd also be able to treat her rather intensively."

Finally, Hannaport smiled. "I think it's a grand and generous offer, Dr. Tracy."

"Then you'll make the recommendation to the court?"

"Yes. Of course, you never can be sure what a judge will do. But I think there's a pretty good chance he'll see where the best interests of the girl lie."

A few minutes later, in the hospital lobby, Carol used a pay phone to call Paul. She recounted the conversation she'd had with Dr. Hannaport, but before she got to the big question, Paul interrupted her. "You want to make a place for Jane," he said.

Surprised, Carol said, "How'd you guess?"

He laughed. "I know you, sugarface. When it comes to kids, you've got a heart the consistency of vanilla pudding."

"She won't be in your way," Carol said quickly. "She won't distract you from your writing. And now that O'Brian won't be able to present our application for the adoption until the end of the month, there's no chance we'll have *two* kids to take care of. In fact maybe the delay at the agency was meant to be—so we'd have a place for Jane until her folks show up. It's only temporary, Paul. Really. And we—"

"Okay, okay," he said. "You don't have to sell me on it. I approve of the plan."

"If you'd like to come here and meet Jane first, that's—"

"No, no. I'm sure she's everything you've said she is. Don't forget, though, you were planning to go to the mountains in a week or so."

"We might not even have Jane that long. And if we do, we can probably take her with us, so long as we let the court know where we're going."

"When do we have to appear in court?"

"I don't know. Probably Monday or Tuesday."

"I'll be on my best behavior," Paul said.

"Scrub behind your ears?"

"Okay. And I'll also wear shoes."

Grinning, Carol said, "Don't pick your nose in front of the judge."

"Not unless he picks his first."

She said, "I love you, Dr. Tracy."

"I love *you*, Dr. Tracy."

When she put down the receiver and turned away from the pay phone, she felt wonderful. Not even the gaudy decor of the visitors' lounge could get on her nerves now.

That night, there was no hammering sound in the Tracy house, no evidence of the poltergeist that Mr. Alsgood had warned Paul about. There was no disturbance the following day, either, and none the day after that. The strange noise and the vibrations had ceased as inexplicably as they had begun.

Carol stopped having nightmares, too. She slept deeply, peacefully, without interruption. She quickly forgot about the flickering, silvery blade of the ax swinging back and forth in the strange void.

The weather improved, too. The clouds dissipated on Sunday. Monday was summery, blue.

Tuesday afternoon, while Paul and Carol were in court trying to obtain temporary custody of Jane Doe, Grace Mitowski was cleaning her kitchen. She had just finished dusting the top of the refrigerator when the telephone rang.

"Hello."

No one answered her.

"Hello," she said again.

A thin, whispery, male voice said, "Grace . . . "

"Yes?"

His words were muffled, and there was an echo on the line, as if he were talking into a tin can.

"I can't understand you," she said. "Can you speak up?"

He tried, but again the words were lost. They seemed to be coming from an enormous distance, across an unimaginably vast chasm.

"We have a terrible connection," she said. "You'll have to speak up."

"Grace," he said, his voice only slightly louder. "Gracie . . . it's almost too late. You've got to . . . move fast. You've got to stop it . . . from happening . . . again." It was a dry, brittle voice; it cracked repeatedly, with a sound like dead autumn leaves underfoot. "It's almost . . . too late . . . too late. . . ."

She recognized the voice, and she froze. Her hand tightened on the receiver, and she couldn't get her breath.

"Gracie . . . it can't go on forever. You've got . . . to put an end to it. Protect her, Gracie. Protect her. . . . "

The voice faded away.

There was only silence. But not the silence of an open phone line. There was no hissing. No electronic beeping in the background. This was perfect silence, utterly unmarred by even the slightest click or whistle of electronic circuitry. Vast silence. Endless.

She put the phone down.

She started to shake.

She went to the cupboard and got down the bottle of Scotch she kept for visitors. She poured herself a double shot and sat down at the kitchen table.

The liquor didn't warm her. Chills still shook her.

The voice on the phone had belonged to Leonard. Her husband. He had been dead for eighteen years.

PART TWO

◆ ◆ ◆

EVIL WALKS
AMONG US . . .

Evil is no faceless stranger,
living in a distant neighborhood.
Evil has a wholesome, hometown face,
with merry eyes and an open smile.
Evil walks among us, wearing a mask
which looks like all our faces.
—THE BOOK OF COUNTED SORROWS

SEVEN

◆

Tuesday, after winning temporary custody of Jane Doe, Paul went home to work on his novel, and Carol took the girl shopping. Because Jane had no clothes except those she'd been wearing when she'd stepped in front of the Volkswagen last Thursday morning, she needed a lot of things, even for just a few days. She was embarrassed about spending Carol's money, and at first she was reluctant to admit that she liked anything she saw or that anything fit her well enough to buy it.

At last Carol said, "Honey, you *need* this stuff, so please just relax and let me buy it for you. Okay? In the long run, it won't be coming out of my pocket anyway. I'll most likely be reimbursed either by your parents, by the foster children program, or by some other county agency."

That argument worked. They quickly purchased a couple of pairs of jeans, a few blouses, underwear, a good pair of sneakers, socks, a sweater, and a windbreaker.

When they got home, Jane was impressed by the Tudor house with its leaded-glass windows, gabled roof, and stonework. She fell in love with the guest room in which she was to stay. It had a cove ceiling, a long window seat inset in a bay window, and a wall of mirrored closet doors. It was done in deep blue and pale beige, with Queen Anne furniture of lustrous cherrywood. "It's really just a guest room?" Jane asked, incredulous. "You don't use it regularly? Boy, if this were my house, I'd come in here all the time! I'd just sit and read for a little while every day—read and sit there in the window and soak up the atmosphere."

Carol had always liked the room, but through Jane's eyes she achieved a new perception and appreciation of it. As she watched the girl inspecting things—sliding open the closet doors, checking the view from each angle of the bay window, testing the firmness of the mattress on the queen-sized bed—Carol realized that one advantage of having children was that their innocent, fresh reactions to everything could keep their parents young and open-minded, too.

That evening, Carol, Paul, and Jane prepared dinner together. The girl fit in comfortably and immediately, in spite of the fact that she was somewhat shy. There was a lot of laughter in the kitchen and at the dinner table.

After dinner, Jane started washing dishes while Carol and Paul cleared the table. When they were separated from the girl for a moment, alone in the dining room, Paul said quietly, "She's a terrific kid."

"Didn't I tell you so?"

"Funny thing, though."

"What?"

"Ever since I saw her this afternoon, outside the courtroom," Paul said, "I've had the feeling that I've seen her somewhere before."

"Where?"

He shook his head. "I'll be damned if I know. But there's something familiar about her face."

Throughout Tuesday afternoon, Grace expected the phone to ring again.

She dreaded having to answer it.

She tried to work off her nervous energy by cleaning the house. She scrubbed the kitchen floor, dusted the furniture in every room, and swept all the carpets.

But she couldn't stop thinking about the call: the paper-dry, echo-distorted voice that had sounded like Leonard; the odd things he had said; the eerie silence when he had finished speaking; the disquieting sense of vast distances, an unimaginable gulf of space and time. . . .

It had to be a hoax. But who could be responsible for it? And why torment her with an imitation of Leonard's voice, eighteen years after the man had died? What was the point of playing games like this *now*, after so much time had passed?

She tried to get her mind off the call by baking apple dumplings. Thick, crusty dumplings—served with cinnamon, milk, and just a bit of sugar—were a suppertime favorite of hers, for she had been born and raised in Lancaster, the heart of the Pennsylvania Dutch country, where that dish was considered a meal in itself. But Tuesday evening, she had no appetite, not even for dumplings. She ate a few bites, but she couldn't even finish half of one dumpling, though she usually ate two whole ones in a single meal.

She was still picking disinterestedly at her food when the telephone rang.

Her head jerked up. She stared at the wall phone that was above the small, built-in desk beside the refrigerator.

It rang again. And again.

Trembling, she got up, went to the phone, and lifted the receiver.

"Gracie . . . "

The voice was faint but intelligible.

"Gracie . . . it's almost too late."

It was him. Leonard. Or someone who sounded exactly like Leonard had sounded.

She couldn't respond to him. Her throat clutched tight.

"Gracie . . . "

Her legs seemed to be melting under her. She pulled out the chair that was tucked into the kneehole of the desk, and she sat down quickly.

"Gracie . . . stop it from happening again. It mustn't . . . go on forever . . . time after time . . . the blood . . . the murder. . . . "

She closed her eyes, forced herself to speak. Her voice was weak, quavery. She didn't even recognize it as her own. It was the voice of a stranger—a weary, frightened, frail old woman. "Who is this?"

The whispery, vibrative voice on the telephone said, "Protect her, Gracie."

"What do you want from me?"

"Protect her."

"Why are you doing this?"

"Protect her."

"Protect who?" she demanded.

"Willa. Protect Willa."

She was still frightened and confused, but she was beginning to be angry, too. "I don't *know* anyone named Willa, dammit! Who is this?"

"Leonard."

"No! Do you think I'm a doddering, senile old fool? Leonard's dead. Eighteen years! You're not Leonard. What kind of game are you playing?"

She wanted to hang up on him, and she knew that was the best thing to do with a crank like this, but she couldn't make herself put down the receiver. He sounded so much like Leonard that she was mesmerized by his voice.

He spoke again, much softer than before, but she could still hear him. "Protect Willa."

"I tell you, I don't know her. And if you keep calling me with this nonsense, I'm going to tell the police that some sick practical joker is—"

"Carol . . . Carol," the man said, his voice fading syllable by syllable. "Willa . . . but you call her . . . Carol."

"What the hell is going on here?"

"Beware . . . the . . . cat."

"What?"

The voice was so distant now that she had to strain to hear it. "The . . . cat . . . "

"Aristophanes? What about him? Have you done something to him? Have you poisoned him? Is that what's been wrong with him lately?"

No response.

"Are you there?"

Nothing.

"What about the cat?" she demanded.

No answer.

She listened to the pure, pure silence, and she began to tremble so violently that she had trouble holding the phone. "Who are you? Why do you want to torment me like this? Why do you want to hurt Aristophanes?"

Far, far away, the achingly familiar voice of her long-dead husband uttered a few final, barely audible words. "Wish . . . I was there . . . for the . . . apple dumplings."

They had forgotten to buy pajamas for Jane. She went to bed in knee socks, panties, and one of Carol's T-shirts, which was a bit large for her.

"What happens tomorrow?" she asked when she was tucked in, her head raised on a plump pillow.

Carol sat on the edge of the bed. "I thought we might start a program of treatment designed to pry open your memory."

"What kind of treatment?"

"Do you know what hypnotic regression therapy is?"

Jane was suddenly frightened. Several times since the accident, she had made a conscious, concerted effort to remember who she was, but on each occasion, as she felt herself coming close to a disturbing revelation, she had become dizzy, disoriented, and panicky. When she pressed her mind back, back, back toward the truth, a psychological defense mechanism cut off her curiosity as abruptly as a strangler's garrotte might have cut off her air supply. And every time, on the edge of unconsciousness, she saw a strange, silvery object swinging back and forth through blackness, an utterly indecipherable yet blood-chilling vision. She sensed there was something hideous in her past, something so terrible that she would be better off *not* remembering. She had just about made up her mind not to seek what had been lost, to accept her new life as a nameless orphan, even though it might be filled with hardships. But through hypnotic regression therapy, she could be forced to confront the specter in her past, whether she wanted to or not. That prospect filled her with dread.

"Are you all right?" Carol asked.

The girl blinked, licked her lips. "Yeah. I was just thinking about what you said. Hypnotic regression. Does that mean you're going to put me in a trance and make me remember everything?''

"Well, it isn't that easy, honey. There's no guarantee it'll work. I'll hypnotize you and ask you to think back to the accident on Thursday morning; then I'll nudge you further and further into the past. If you're a good subject, you might remember who you are and where you come from. Hypnotic regression is a tool that comes in handy sometimes when I'm trying to get a patient to relive a deeply hidden, severely regressed trauma. I've never used the technique on an amnesia victim, but I know it's applicable to a case like yours. Of course, it only works about half the time. And when it does work, it takes more than one or two sessions. It can be a tedious, frustrating process. We're not going to get much of anywhere tomorrow, and in fact your parents will probably show up before I've been able to help you remember. But we might as well make a start. That is, if it's all right with you.''

She didn't want Carol to know that she was afraid to remember, so she said, "Oh, sure! It sounds fascinating.''

"I've got four patients scheduled for tomorrow, but I can work you in at eleven o'clock. You'll have to spend a lot of time in the waiting room, before and after your session, so first thing in the morning, we'll find a book for you to take along. Do you like to read mystery stories?''

"I guess so.''

"Agatha Christie?''

"The name's familiar, but I don't know whether I've ever read any of her books.''

"You can try one tomorrow. If you were a big fan of mysteries, maybe Agatha Christie will open your memory for you. Any stimulus, any connection whatsoever with your past can act like a doorway.'' She leaned down, kissed Jane's forehead. "But don't worry about it now. Just get a good night's sleep, kiddo.''

After Carol left the room, closing the door behind her, Jane didn't immediately switch off the light. She let her gaze travel slowly around the room and then slowly back again, her eyes resting on each point of beauty.

Please, God, she thought, let me stay here. Somehow, some way, let me stay in this house forever and ever. Don't make me go back where I came from, wherever that might be. This is where I want to live. This is where I want to *die,* it's so pretty.

Finally, she reached out and snapped off the bedside lamp.

Darkness folded in like bat wings.

Using a piece of Masonite and four nails, Grace Mitowski fixed a temporary seal over the inside of the pet door.

Aristophanes stood in the center of the kitchen, his head cocked to one side, watching her with bright-eyed interest. Every few seconds, he meowed in what seemed to be an inquisitive tone.

When the last nail was in place, Grace said, "Okay, cat. For the time being, your license to roam has been suspended. There might be a man out there who's been feeding you small amounts of drugs or poison of some sort, and maybe that's been the cause of your bad behavior. We'll just have to wait and see if you improve. Have you been flying high on drugs, you silly cat?''

Aristophanes meowed questioningly.

"Yes," Grace said. "I know it sounds bizarre. But if it's not some kook I've got to deal with, then it really must've been Leonard on the phone. And that's even *more* bizarre, don't you think?''

The cat turned his head from one side to the other, as if he really were trying to make sense of what she was saying.

Grace stopped, held out her hand, and rubbed her thumb and forefinger together. "Here, kitty. Here, kitty-kitty-kitty."

Aristophanes hissed, spat, turned, and ran.

For a change, they made love with the lights off. Carol's breath was hot against his neck. She pressed close, rocked and tensed and twisted and flexed in perfect harmony with him; her exquisite, pneumatic movements were as fluid as currents in a warm river. She arched her elegant back, lifted and subsided in tempo with his measured strokes. She was as pliant, as silken, and eventually as all-encompassing as the darkness.

Afterwards, they held hands and talked about inconsequential things, steadily growing drowsy. Carol fell asleep while Paul was talking. When she failed to respond to one of his questions, he gently disentangled his hand from hers.

He was tired, but he couldn't find sleep as quickly as she had found it. He kept thinking about the girl. He was certain he had seen her prior to their meeting outside the courtroom this morning. During dinner, her face had grown more and more familiar. It continued to haunt him. But no matter how hard he tried, he couldn't recall where else he had seen her.

As he lay in the dark bedroom, paging through his memory, he gradually became uneasy. He began to feel—utterly without reason—that his previous encounter with Jane had been strange, perhaps even unpleasant. Then he wondered if the girl might actually pose some sort of threat to Carol and himself.

But that's absurd, he thought. Doesn't make any sense at all. I must be even more tired than I thought. Logic seems to be slipping out of my grasp. What possible threat could Jane pose? She's such a nice kid. An exceptionally nice kid.

He sighed, rolled over, and thought about the plot of his first novel (the failed one), and that quickly put him to sleep.

At one o'clock in the morning, Grace Mitowski was sitting up in bed, watching a late movie on the Sony portable. She was vaguely aware that Humphrey Bogart and Lauren Bacall were engaged in witty repartee, but she didn't really hear anything they said. She had lost track of the film's plot only minutes after she had turned it on.

She was thinking about Leonard, the husband she had lost to cancer eighteen years ago. He had been a good man, hard-working, generous, loving, a grand conversationalist. She had loved him very much.

But not *everyone* had loved Leonard. He had had his faults, of course. The worst thing about him had been his impatience—and the sharp tongue that his impatience had encouraged. He couldn't tolerate people who were lazy or apathetic or ignorant or foolish. "Which includes two-thirds of the human race," he had often said when he was feeling especially curmudgeonly. Because he was an honest man with precious little diplomacy in his bones, he had told people exactly what he thought of them. As a result, he had led a life remarkably free of deception but rich in enemies.

She wondered if it had been one of those enemies who had called her, pretending to be Leonard. A sick man might get as much pleasure from tormenting Leonard's widow as he would have gotten from tormenting Leonard himself. He might get a thrill from poisoning her cat and from harassing her with weird phone calls.

But after *eighteen years?* Who would have remembered Leonard's voice so well as to be able to imitate it perfectly such a long time later? Surely she was the only person in the world who could still recognize that voice upon hearing it speak only a word or two. And why bring Carol into it? Leonard had died three years before Carol had entered Grace's life; he had never known the girl. His enemies couldn't possibly have anything against Carol. What had the caller meant when he'd referred to Carol as "Willa"? And, most disturbing of all, how did the caller know she had just made apple dumplings?

There *was* another explanation, though she was loath to consider it. Perhaps the caller hadn't been an old enemy of Leonard's. Maybe the call actually had come from Leonard himself. From a dead man.

—*No. Impossible.*

—*A lot of people believe in ghosts.*

—*Not me.*

She thought about the strange dreams she'd had last week. She hadn't believed in dream prophecies then. Now she did. So why not ghosts, too?

No. She was a level-headed woman who had lived a stable, rational life, who had been trained in the sciences, who had always believed that science held all the answers. Now, at seventy years of age, if she made room for the existence of ghosts within her otherwise rational philosophy, she might be opening the floodgates on madness. If you truly believed in ghosts, what came next? Vampires? Did you have to start carrying a sharp wooden stake and a crucifix everywhere you went? Werewolves? Better buy a box of silver bullets! Evil elves who lived in the center of the earth and caused quakes and volcanoes? Sure! Why not?

Grace laughed bitterly.

She couldn't suddenly become a believer in ghosts, because acceptance of that superstition might require the acceptance of countless others. She was too old, too comfortable with herself, too accustomed to her familiar ways to reconsider her entire view of life. And she certainly wasn't going to contemplate such a sweeping reevaluation merely because she had received two bizarre phone calls.

That left only one thing to be decided: whether or not she should tell Carol that someone was harassing her and had used Carol's name. She tried to hear how she would sound when she explained the telephone calls and when she outlined her theory about Aristophanes being drugged or poisoned. She couldn't hope to sound like the Grace Mitowski that everyone knew. She'd come off like an hysterical old woman who was seeing nonexistent conspirators behind every door and under every bed.

They might even think she was going senile.

Am I? she wondered. Did I imagine the telephone calls? No. Surely not.

She wasn't imagining Aristophanes's changed personality, either. She looked at the claw marks on the palm of her hand; although they were healing, they were still red and puffy. Proof. Those marks were proof that *something* was wrong.

I'm not senile, she told herself. Not even a little bit. But I sure don't want to have to convince Carol or Paul that I've got all my marbles, once I've told them that I'm getting phone calls from Leonard. Better go easy for the time being. Wait. See what happens next. Anyway, I can figure this out on my own. I can handle it.

On the Sony, Bogart and Bacall grinned at each other.

When Jane woke up in the middle of the night, she discovered she had been sleepwalking. She was in the kitchen, but she couldn't recall getting out of bed and coming downstairs.

The kitchen was silent. The only sound was from the softly purring refrigerator. The only light was from the moon, but because the moon was full and because the kitchen had quite a few windows, there was enough light to see by.

Jane was standing at a counter near the sink. She had opened one of the drawers and had taken a butcher knife out of it.

She stared down at the knife, startled to find it in her hand.

Pale moonlight glinted on the cold blade.

She returned the knife to the drawer.

Closed the drawer.

She had been gripping the knife so tightly that her hand ached.

Why did I want a knife?

A chill skittered like a centipede along her spine.

Her bare arms and legs broke out in gooseflesh, and she was suddenly very aware that she was wearing only a T-shirt, panties, and knee socks.

The refrigerator motor shut off with a dry rattle that made her jump and turn.

Now the house was preternaturally silent. She could almost believe that she had gone deaf.

What was I doing with the knife?

She hugged herself to ward off the chills that kept wriggling through her.

Maybe she had dreamed about food and had come down here in her sleep to make a sandwich. Yes. That was probably what had happened. In fact she *was* a bit hungry. So she had gotten the knife out of the drawer in order to slice some roast beef for a sandwich. There was a butt end of a roast in the refrigerator. She had seen it earlier, when she had been helping Carol and Paul make dinner.

But now she didn't think she could eat a sandwich or anything else. Her bare legs were getting colder by the moment, and she felt immodestly exposed in just flimsy panties and a thin T-shirt. All she wanted now was to get back to bed, under the covers.

Climbing the steps in the darkness, she stayed close to the wall, where the treads were less likely to creak. She returned to her room without waking anyone.

Outside, a dog howled in the distance.

Jane burrowed deeper in her blankets.

For a while she had trouble getting to sleep because she felt guilty about prowling through the house while the Tracys slept. She felt sneaky. She felt as if she had been taking advantage of their hospitality.

Of course, that was silly. She hadn't been nosing around on purpose. She had been sleepwalking, and there was no way a person could control something like that.

Just sleepwalking.

EIGHT

◆

The focal point of Carol Tracy's office was Mickey Mouse. One long wall of the room was fitted with shelves on which were displayed Mickey Mouse memorabilia. There were Mickey Mouse buttons, Mickey Mouse pins, a wristwatch, belt buckles, a Mickey Mouse phone, drinking glasses bearing the famous mouse's countenance, a beer mug on which there was a likeness of Mickey dressed in lederhosen and a Ty-

rolean hat. But mostly there were statuettes of the cartoon star: Mickey standing beside a little red car; Mickey curled up in striped pajamas, sleeping; Mickey dancing
a jig; Mickey with Minnie; Mickey with Goofy; Mickey holding barbells; Mickey
with Pluto; Mickey and Donald Duck with their arms around each other's shoulders, looking like the best of friends; Mickey riding a horse, with a cowboy hat
raised in one white-gloved, four-fingered hand; Mickey dressed like a soldier, a
sailor, a doctor; Mickey in swimming trunks, clutching a surfboard. There were
wooden, metal, chalk, porcelain, plastic, glass, and clay statuettes of Mickey; some
of them were a foot high, and some were no more than one inch tall, though most
were in between. The only thing those hundreds of Mickeys had in common was the
fact that every one of them was smiling broadly.

The collection was an icebreaker with patients of all ages. No one could resist
Mickey Mouse.

Jane responded as scores of patients had done before her. She said ''oooh''
and ''aaah'' a lot, and she laughed happily. By the time she had finished admiring
the collection and had sat down in one of the big leather armchairs, she was ready
for the therapy session; her tension and apprehension had disappeared. Mickey
had worked his usual magic.

Carol didn't have an analyst's couch in her office. She preferred to conduct
sessions from a large wing chair, with the patient seated in an identical chair on
the other side of the octagonal coffee table. The drapes were always kept tightly
shut; soft, golden light was provided by shaded floor lamps. Except for the wall
of Mickey Mouse images, the room had a nineteenth-century air.

They chatted about the collection for a couple of minutes, and then Carol said,
''Okay, honey. I think we ought to begin.''

Worry lines appeared on the girl's forehead. ''You really think this hypnosis
is a good idea?''

''Yes. I think it's the best tool we have for restoring your memory. Don't
worry. It's a simple process. Just relax and flow with it. Okay?''

''Well . . . okay.''

Carol got up and stepped around the coffee table, and Jane started to get up,
too. ''No, you stay there,'' Carol said. She moved behind the wing chair and put
her fingertips against the girl's temples. ''Relax, honey. Lean back. Hands in your
lap. Palms up, fingers slack. That's fine. Now close your eyes. Are they closed?''

''Yes.''

''Good. Very good. Now I want you to think of a kite. A large, diamond-
shaped kite. Picture it in your mind. It's an enormous, blue kite sailing high in
the blue sky. Can you see it?''

After a brief hesitation, the girl said, ''Yes.''

''Watch the kite, honey. See how gently it rises and falls on the currents of
air. Rises, falls, up and down, up and down, side to side, sailing so gracefully,
far above the earth, halfway between the earth and the clouds, far above your
head,'' Carol said in a mellow, soothing, rhythmic voice as she stared down at
the girl's thick blond hair. ''While you're watching the kite, you'll gradually
become as light and as free as it is. You'll learn to soar up and up into the blue
sky, just like the kite.'' With her fingertips, she lightly traced circles on the girl's
temples. ''All the tension is leaving you, all the worries and cares are floating
away, away, until the only thought in your head is the kite, the sailing kite in the
blue sky. A great weight has been removed from your skull, from your forehead
and your temples. Already, you feel much lighter.'' She moved her hands down
to the girl's neck. ''The muscles in your neck are relaxing. Tension is dropping
away. A great weight is dropping away. You are so much lighter now that you

can almost feel yourself rising up toward the kite ... almost ... almost ... '' She moved her hands down, touched the girl's shoulders. ''Relax. Let the tension fall away. Like blocks of concrete. Making you lighter, lighter. A weight is falling off your chest, too. And now you're floating. Just a few inches off the ground, but you *are* floating.''

''Yes ... floating ... '' she said, her voice thick.

''The kite is gliding far above, but you are slowly, slowly moving up to join it. ... ''

She went on like that for a minute, then returned to her own chair and sat down.

Jane was slumped in the other wing chair, head tilted to one side, eyes closed, face soft and slack, breathing softly.

''You are in a very deep sleep,'' Carol told her. ''A very relaxed, very deep, deep sleep. Do you understand?''

''Yes,'' the girl murmured.

''You will answer a few questions for me.''

''Okay.''

''You will remain in your deep sleep, and you will answer my questions until I tell you it's time to wake up. Understood?''

''Yes.''

''Good. Very good. Now tell me—what is your name?''

The girl was silent.

''What is your name, honey?''

''Jane.''

''Is that your real name?''

''No.''

''What is your real name?''

Jane frowned. ''I ... don't remember.''

''Where did you come from?''

''The hospital.''

''Before that?''

''Nowhere.''

A bead of saliva glistened at the corner of the girl's mouth. Languorously, she licked it away before it could drool down her chin.

Carol said, ''Honey, do you remember the Mickey Mouse watch you saw a few minutes ago?''

''Yes.''

''Well, I've taken that watch from the shelf,'' Carol said, though she hadn't moved from her chair. ''And now I'm turning the hands on it backwards, around and around the dial, always backwards. Can you see the hands moving backwards on that Mickey Mouse watch?''

''Yes.''

''Now something amazing is happening. As I turn those hands backwards and backwards, time itself begins to flow in reverse. It isn't a quarter past eleven any more. It's now eleven o'clock. This is a magic watch. It governs the flow of time. And now it's ten o'clock in the morning ... nine o'clock ... eight o'clock. ... Look around you. Where are you now?''

The girl opened her eyes. They were fixed on a distant point. She said, ''Ummm ... the kitchen. Yeah. The breakfast nook. Boy, the bacon's nice and crisp.''

Gradually, Carol moved her back in time, back through the days she had spent in the hospital, finally regressing to the accident last Thursday morning. The girl winced as she relived the moment of impact, and cried out, and Carol soothed her, and then they went back a few minutes further.

"You're standing on the sidewalk," Carol said. "You're dressed only in a blouse and jeans. It's raining. Chilly."

The girl closed her eyes again. She shivered.

"What's your name?" Carol asked.

Silence.

"What's your name, honey?"

"I don't know."

"Where have you just come from?"

"Nowhere."

"You mean you have amnesia?"

"Yes."

"Even before the accident?"

"Yes."

Although she was still very concerned about the girl, Carol was relieved to hear that she wasn't responsible for Jane's condition. For a moment she felt like that blue kite, capable of soaring up and away. Then she said, "Okay. You're about to step into the street. Do you just want to cross it, or do you intend to walk in front of a car?"

"I . . . don't . . . know."

"How do you feel? Happy? Depressed? Indifferent?"

"Scared," the girl said in a small, shaky voice.

"What are you scared of?"

Silence.

"What are you scared of?"

"It's coming."

"What's coming?"

"Behind me!"

"What's behind you?"

The girl opened her eyes again. She was still staring at a distant point, but now there was stark terror in her eyes.

"What's behind you?" Carol asked again.

"Oh God," the girl said miserably.

"What is it?"

"No, no." She shook her head. Her face was bloodless.

Carol leaned forward in her chair. "Relax, honey. You will relax and be calm. Close your eyes. Calm . . . like the kite . . . far above everything . . . floating . . . warm."

The tension went out of Jane's face.

"All right," Carol said. "Staying calm, always relaxed and calm, you will tell me what you're afraid of."

The girl said nothing.

"Honey, what are you scared of? What's behind you?"

"Something . . . "

"What?"

"Something . . . "

Patiently, Carol said, "Be specific."

"I . . . don't know what it is . . . but it's coming . . . and it scares me."

"Okay. Let's go back a bit further." Using the image of the backwards-moving hands on the Mickey Mouse wristwatch, she regressed the girl another full day into the past. "Now look around. Where are you?"

"Nowhere."

"What do you see?"

"Nothing."

"You must see something, honey."

"Darkness."

"Are you in a dark room?"

"No."

"Are there walls in the darkness?"

"No."

"Are you outdoors at night?"

"No."

She regressed the girl another day. "Now what do you see?"

"Just the darkness."

"There must be something else."

"No."

"Open your eyes, honey."

The girl obeyed. Her blue eyes were vacant, glassy. "Nothing."

Carol frowned. "Are you sitting or standing in that dark place?"

"I don't know."

"What do you feel under you? A chair? A floor? A bed?"

"Nothing."

"Reach down. Touch the floor."

"There isn't a floor."

Uneasy about the direction the session was taking, Carol shifted in her chair and stared at the girl for a while, wondering what to try next.

After a few seconds, Jane's eyes fluttered and went shut.

Finally, Carol said, "All right. I'm turning the hands of the watch counterclockwise again. Time is flowing in reverse. It will continue to flow backwards, hour by hour, day by day, faster and faster, until you stop me. I want you to stop me only when you come out of the darkness and can tell me where you are. I'm turning the hands now. Backwards . . . backwards . . . "

Ten seconds passed in silence. Twenty. Thirty.

After a full minute, Carol said, "Where are you?"

"Nowhere yet."

"Keep going. Backwards . . . back in time . . . "

After another minute, Carol began to think something was wrong. She had the disquieting feeling that she was losing control of the situation and placing her patient in some kind of danger that could not be foreseen. But as she was about to call a halt to the regression and bring the girl forward again, Jane spoke at last.

The girl shot up out of the chair, onto her feet, flailing and screaming. "Somebody help me! Mama! Aunt Rachael! For God's sake, help me!"

The voice wasn't Jane's. It came from her mouth, through her tongue and lips, but it didn't sound at all like her. It wasn't merely distorted by panic. It was an entirely different voice from Jane's. It had its own character, its own accent and tone.

"I'm going to die here! Help! *Get me out of here!*"

Carol was on her feet, too. "Honey, stop it. Calm down."

"I'm on fire! I'm on fire!" the girl screamed, and she slapped at her clothes as if trying to put out the flames.

"No!" Carol said sharply. She stepped around the coffee table and managed to seize the girl's arm, taking several glancing blows in the process.

Jane thrashed, tried to break loose.

Carol held on and began to talk softly but insistently to her, calming her down.

Jane stopped struggling, but she began to gasp and wheeze. "Smoke," she said, gagging. "So much smoke."

Carol talked her out of that, too, and gradually brought her down from the peak of hysteria.

At last Jane sank back into the wing chair. She was wan, and her forehead was strung with beads of sweat. Her blue eyes, staring into a distant place and time, looked haunted.

Carol knelt beside the chair and held the girl's hand. "Honey, can you hear me?"

"Yes."

"Are you okay?"

"I'm afraid . . . "

"There is no fire."

"There was. Everywhere," the girl said, still speaking with the unfamiliar voice.

"There isn't any more. No fire anywhere."

"If you say so."

"I do. I say so. Now tell me your name."

"Laura."

"Do you remember your last name?"

"Laura Havenswood."

Carol flushed with triumph. "Very good. That's just fine. Where's your home, Laura?"

"Shippensburg."

Shippensburg was a small town less than an hour from Harrisburg. It was a quiet, pleasant place that existed to serve a flourishing state college and a large number of surrounding farms.

"Do you know the address where you live in Shippensburg?" Carol asked.

"There's no street name. It's a farm. Just outside of town, off Walnut Bottom Road."

"So you could take me there if you had to?"

"Oh, yes. It's a pretty place. There are a pair of stone gateposts by the verge of the county lane; they mark the entrance to our land. And there's a long drive flanked by maples, and there are big oaks around the house. It's cool and breezy in the summer with all those shade trees."

"What's your father's first name?"

"Nicholas."

"And his phone number?"

The girl frowned. "His what?"

"What's the telephone number at your house?"

The girl shook her head. "I don't know what you mean."

"Don't you have a telephone?"

"What *is* a telephone?" the girl asked.

Carol stared at her, puzzled. It wasn't possible for a person under hypnosis to be coy or to make jokes of this sort. As she considered her next move, she saw that Laura was becoming agitated again. The girl's brow furrowed, and her eyes widened. She started breathing hard again.

"Laura, listen to me. You will be calm. You will relax and—"

The girl writhed uncontrollably in her chair. Squealing and gasping, she slid off the chair, rolled onto the floor, bumping the coffee table and pushing it aside. She twisted and shuddered and wriggled as if she were having a severe epileptic fit, though she was not; she brushed frantically at herself, for again she seemed to believe she was on fire. She called for someone named Rachael and choked on nonexistent smoke.

Carol required almost a minute to talk her down, which was a serious loss of control; a hypnotist could usually calm a subject in only seconds. Apparently, Laura had lived through an extremely traumatic fire or had lost a loved one in a blaze. Carol wanted to pursue the matter and learn what was at the root of it, but this wasn't the right time. After taking so long to quiet her patient, she knew the session should be ended quickly.

When Laura was seated in the wing chair again, Carol crouched beside her and instructed her to remember everything that had happened and everything that had been said during the session. Then she led the girl forward through time to the present and brought her out of the trance.

The girl wiped at the moist corner of one eye, shook her head, cleared her throat. She looked at Carol and said, "I guess it didn't work, huh?" She sounded like Jane again; the Laura voice was gone.

But why the hell had her voice changed in the first place? Carol wondered.

"You don't remember what happened?" Carol asked.

"What's to remember? All that talk about a blue kite? I could see what you were trying to do, how you were trying to lull me into a trance, so I guess that's why it didn't work."

"But it *did* work," Carol assured her. "And you should be able to recall all of it."

The girl looked skeptical. "All of what? What happened? What did you find out?"

Carol stared at her. "Laura."

The girl didn't even blink. She merely looked perplexed.

"Your name is Laura."

"Who said?"

"You did."

"Laura? No. I don't think so."

"Laura Havenswood," Carol said.

The girl frowned. "It doesn't ring any bells at all."

Surprised, Carol said, "You told me you live in Shippensburg."

"Where's that?"

"About an hour from here."

"I never heard of it."

"You live on a farm. There are stone gateposts to mark the entrance to your father's property, and there's a long driveway flanked by maple trees. That's what you told me, and I'm sure it'll turn out to be just like you said. It's virtually impossible to answer questions incorrectly or deceptively while you're hypnotized. Besides, you don't have any reason to deceive me. You have nothing to lose and everything to gain if we break through this memory block."

"Maybe I *am* Laura Havenswood," the girl said. "Maybe what I told you in the trance was true. But I can't remember it, and when you tell me who I am, it doesn't mean a thing to me. Boy, I thought if I could just remember my name, then everything would fall into place. But it's still a blank. Laura, Shippensburg, a farm—I can't *connect* with any of it."

Carol was still crouched beside the girl's chair. She rose and flexed her stiff legs. "I've never encountered anything quite like this. And so far as I know, a reaction like yours hasn't ever been reported in any of the psychology journals. Whenever a patient *is* susceptible to hypnosis, and whenever a patient *can* be regressed to a moment of trauma, there's always a profound effect. Yet you weren't touched at all by it. Very odd. If you remembered while you were under hypnosis, you ought to be able to remember now. And just hearing your name ought to open doors for you.''

''But it doesn't.''

''Strange . . . ''

The girl looked up from the wing chair. ''What now?''

Carol thought for a moment, then said, ''I suppose we ought to have the authorities check out the Havenswood identity.''

She went to her desk, picked up the phone, and called the Harrisburg police.

The police operator referred her to a detective named Lincoln Werth, who was in charge of a number of conventional missing-persons files as well as the Jane Doe case. He listened to Carol's story with interest, promised to check it out right away, and said he would call her back the instant he obtained confirmation of the Havenswood identity.

Four hours later, at 3:55, after Carol's last appointment for the day, as she and the girl were about to leave the office and go home, Lincoln Werth rang back as promised. Carol took the call at her desk, and the girl perched on the edge of the desk, watching, clearly a bit tense.

''Dr. Tracy,'' Werth said, ''I've been back and forth on the phone all afternoon with the police in Shippensburg and with the county sheriff's office up there. I'm afraid I have to report it's all been a wild-goose chase.''

''There must be some mistake.''

''Nope. We can't find anyone in Shippensburg or the surrounding county with the name Havenswood. There's no telephone listed for anyone of that name, and—''

''Maybe they just don't have a phone.''

''Of course, we considered that possibility,'' Werth said. ''We didn't jump to conclusions, believe me. For instance, when we checked with the power company, we discovered they don't have a customer named Havenswood anywhere in Cumberland County, but that didn't discourage us either. We figured these people we're looking for might be Amish. Lots of Amish in that neck of the woods. If they were Amish, of course, they wouldn't have electricity in their house. So next we went to the property-tax rolls at the county offices up there. What we found was that nobody named Havenswood owns a house, let alone a farm, in that whole area.''

''They could be tenants,'' Carol said.

''Could be. But what I really think they are is nonexistent. The girl must've been lying.''

''Why would she?''

''I don't know. Maybe the whole amnesia thing is a hoax. Maybe she's just an ordinary runaway.''

''No. Definitely not.'' Carol looked up at Laura—no, her name was still Jane— looked into those clear, bottomless blue eyes. To Werth, she said, ''Besides, it just isn't possible to lie that well or that blatantly when you're hypnotized.''

Although Jane could hear only half of the conversation, she had begun to perceive that the Havenswood name wasn't going to check out. Her face clouded. She got up and went to the display shelves to study the statuettes of Mickey Mouse.

''There *is* something damned odd about the whole thing,'' Lincoln Werth said.

''Odd?'' Carol asked.

''Well, when I passed along the description of the farm that the girl gave— those stone gateposts, the long driveway with the maples—and when I said it was off Walnut Bottom Road, the Cumberland County sheriff and the various

Shippensburg policemen I talked to all recognized the place right off the bat. It actually does exist.''

"Well, then—"

"But nobody named Havenswood lives there," Detective Werth said. "The Ohlmeyer family owns that spread. Really well known around those parts. Highly thought of, too. Oren Ohlmeyer, his wife, and their two sons. Never had a daughter, so I'm told. Before Oren owned the farm, it belonged to his daddy, who bought it seventy years ago. One of the sheriff's men went out there and asked the Ohlmeyers if they'd ever heard of a girl named Laura Havenswood or anything even similar to that. They hadn't. Didn't know anyone fitting our Jane Doe's description, either.''

"Yet the farm *is* there, just like she told us it was.''

"Yeah," Werth said. "Funny, isn't it?''

In the Volkswagen, on the way home from the office, as they drove along the sun-splashed autumn streets, the girl said, "Do you think I was faking the trance?''

"Heavens, no! You were *very* deeply under. And I'm quite sure you aren't a good enough actress to fake that business about the fire.''

"Fire?''

"I guess you don't remember that, either." Carol told her about Laura's screaming fit, the desperate cries for help. "Your terror was genuine. It came from experience. I'd bet anything on that.''

"I don't remember any of it. You mean I really was in a fire once?''

"Could be." Ahead, a traffic light turned red. Carol stopped the car and looked at Jane. "You don't have any physical scars, so if you were in a fire, you escaped unharmed. Of course, it might be that you *lost* someone in a fire, someone you loved very much, and maybe you weren't actually in a fire yourself. If that's the case, then when you were hypnotized, you might have confused your fear for that person with fear for your own life. Am I making myself clear?''

"I think I get what you mean. So maybe the fire—the *shock* of it—is responsible for my amnesia. And maybe my parents haven't shown up to claim me because . . . they're dead, burned to death.''

Carol took the girl's hand. "Don't worry about it now, honey. I may be all wrong. I probably am. But I think it's a possibility you ought to be prepared for.''

The girl bit her lip, nodded. "The idea scares me a little. But I don't exactly feel sad. I mean, I don't remember my folks at all, so losing them would almost be like losing strangers.''

Behind them, the driver of a green Datsun blew his horn.

The light had changed. Carol let go of the girl's hand and touched the accelerator. "We'll probe into the fire during tomorrow's session.''

"You still think I *am* Laura Havenswood?''

"Well, for the time being, we'll keep calling you Jane. But I don't see why you'd come up with the name Laura if it wasn't yours.''

"The identity didn't check out," the girl reminded her.

Carol shook her head. "That's not exactly true. We haven't proved or disproved the Havenswood identity. All we know for sure is that you never lived in Shippensburg. But you must have been there at least once because the farm exists; you've seen it, if only in passing. Apparently, even under hypnosis, even regressed beyond the onset of your amnesia, your memories are tangled. I don't know how that's possible or why. I've never encountered anything quite like it.

But we'll work hard at untangling them for you. The problem might lie in the questions I asked and the way I asked them. We'll just have to wait and see.''

They rode in silence for a moment, and then the girl said, ''I half hope we don't get things untangled too quickly. Ever since you told me about your cabin in the mountains, I've really been looking forward to going up there.''

''Oh, you'll get to go. Don't worry about that. We're leaving on Friday, and even if tomorrow's session goes well, we won't be able to untangle this Laura Havenswood thing *that* fast. I warned you, this could be a slow, complicated, frustrating process. I'm surprised we made any progress at all today, and I'll be twice as surprised if we make even half as much headway tomorrow.''

''I guess you'll be stuck with me for a while.''

Carol sighed and pretended weariness. ''Looks that way. Oh, you're such a terrible, terrible, terrible burden. You're just too much to bear.'' She took one hand off the steering wheel long enough to clutch her heart in a melodramatic gesture that made Jane giggle. ''Too much! Oh, oh!''

''You know what?'' the girl asked.

''What?''

''I like you, too.''

They looked at each other and grinned.

At the next red light, Jane said, ''I've got a feeling about the mountains.''

''What's that?''

''I have this strong feeling that it's going to be a lot of fun up there. Really exciting. Something special. A real adventure.'' Her blue eyes were even brighter than usual.

After dinner, Paul suggested they play Scrabble. He set up the board on the game table in the family room, while Carol explained the rules to Jane, who couldn't remember whether or not she had ever played it before.

After winning the starting lottery, Jane went first with a twenty-two-point word that took advantage of a double-count square and the automatic double score for the first word of the game.

BLADE

''Not a bad start,'' Paul said. He hoped the girl would win, because she got such a kick out of little things like that. The smallest compliment, the most modest triumph delighted her. But he wasn't going to throw the game just to please her; she would have to earn it, by God. He was incapable of giving the match away to anyone; regardless of the kind of game he was playing, he always put as much effort and commitment into it as he put into his work. He didn't *indulge* in leisure activities; he *attacked* them. To Jane, he said, ''I have a hunch you're the kind of kid who says she's never played poker before—and quickly proceeds to win every pot in the game.''

''Can you bet on Scrabble?'' Jane asked.

''You can, but we won't,'' Paul said.

''Scared?''

''Terrified. You'd wind up with the house.''

''I'd let you stay.''

''How decent of you.''

''For very low rent.''

''Ah, this child truly has a heart of gold!''

While he bantered with Jane, Carol studied her own group of letters. ''Hey,'' she said, "I've got a word that ties right in with Jane's." She added LOOD to the B in BLADE, forming BLOOD.

"Judging from your words," Paul said, "I guess you two intend to play a cutthroat game."

Carol and Jane groaned dutifully at his bad joke and refilled their letter trays from the stock in the lid of the game box.

To Paul's surprise, when he looked at his own seven letters, he saw that he had a word with which to continue the morbid theme that had been established. He added EATH to the D at the end of BLOOD, creating DEATH.

"Weird," Carol said.

"Here's something weirder still," Jane said, taking her second turn by adding OMB to the T in DEATH.

```
B L A D E
L
O
O
D E A T H
        O
        M
        B
```

Paul stared at the board. He was suddenly uneasy. What were the odds that the first four words in a game would be so closely related in theme? Ten thousand to one? No. It had to be much higher than that. A hundred thousand to one? A million to one?

Carol looked up from her unusual letters. "You aren't going to *believe* this." She added three letters to the board.

```
    B L A D E
K I L L
    O
    O
D E A T H
        O
        M
        B
```

" 'Kill'?" Paul said. "Oh, come on. Enough's enough. Take it away and make another word."

"I can't," Carol said. "That's all I have. The rest of my letters are useless."

"But you could have put 'lik' above the 'e' in 'blade,' " Paul said. "You could have spelled 'like' instead of 'kill.' "

"Sure, I could have done that, but I'd have gotten fewer points if I had. You see? There's no square with a double-letter score up there."

As he listened to Carol's explanation, Paul felt strange. Bitterly cold inside. Hollow. As if he were balancing on a tightrope and knew he was going to fall and fall and fall . . .

He was gripped by déjà vu, by such a strikingly powerful awareness of having lived through this scene before that, for a moment, his heart seemed to stop beating. Yet nothing like this had ever happened in any other Scrabble game he'd ever played. So why was he so certain he had witnessed this very thing on a previous occasion? Even as he asked himself that question, he realized what the answer was. The seizure of déjà vu wasn't in reference to the words on the Scrabble board; not directly anyway. The thing that was so frighteningly familiar to him was the unusual, soul-shaking *feeling* that the coincidental appearance of those words aroused in him; the iciness that came from within rather than from without; the awful hollowness deep in his guts; the sickening sensation of teetering on a high wire, with only infinite darkness below. He had felt exactly the same way in the attic last week, when the mysterious hammering sound had seemed to issue out of the thin air in front of his face, when each *thunk!* had sounded as if it were coming from a sledge and anvil in another dimension of time and space. That was how he felt now, at the Scrabble board: as if he were confronted with something extraordinary, unnatural, perhaps even supernatural.

To Carol, he said, "Listen, why don't you just take those last three letters off the board, put them back in the box, choose three brand-new letters, and make some other word besides 'kill.' "

He could see that his suggestion startled her.

She said, "Why should I do that?"

Paul frowned. "Blade, blood, death, tomb, kill—what kind of words are they for a nice, friendly, peaceable game of Scrabble?"

She stared at him for a moment, and her piercing eyes made him a bit uncomfortable. "It's only coincidence," she said, clearly puzzled by his tenseness.

"I *know* it's only coincidence," he said, though he didn't know anything of the sort. He was simply unable to explain rationally the eerie feeling that the words on the board were the work of some force far stronger than mere coincidence, something worse. "It still gives me the creeps," he said lamely. He turned to Jane, seeking an ally. "Doesn't it give you the creeps?"

"Yeah. It does. A little," the girl agreed. "But it's also kind of fascinating. I wonder how long we can keep going with words that fit this pattern."

"I wonder, too," Carol said. Playfully, she slapped Paul's shoulder. "You know what your trouble is, babe? You don't have any scientific curiosity. Now come on. It's your turn."

After putting DEATH on the board, he hadn't replenished his supply of letter tiles. He drew four of the small wooden squares from the lid of the game box, put them on the rack in front of him.

And froze.

Oh God.

He was on that tightrope again, teetering over a great abyss.

"Well?" Carol asked.

Coincidence. It *had* to be just coincidence.

"Well?"

He looked up at her.

"What have you got?" she asked.

Numb, he shifted his eyes to the girl.

She was hunched over the table, as eager as Carol to hear his response, anxious to see if the macabre pattern would continue.

Paul lowered his eyes to the row of letters on the wooden rack. The word was still there. Impossible. But it was there anyway, possible or not.

"Paul?"

He moved so quickly and unexpectedly that Carol and Jane jumped. He scooped up the letters on his rack and nearly flung them back into the lid of the box. He swept the five offensive words off the board before anyone could protest, and he returned those nineteen tiles to the box with all the others.

"Paul, for heaven's sake!"

"We'll start a new game," he said. "Maybe those words didn't bother you, but they bothered me. I'm here to relax. If I want to hear about blood and death and killing, I can switch on the news."

Carol said, "What word did you have?"

"I don't know," he lied. "I didn't work with the letters to see. Come on. Let's start all over."

"You *did* have a word," she said.

"No."

"It looked to me like you did," Jane said.

"Open up," Carol said.

"All right, all right. I had a word. It was obscene. Not something a gentleman like me would use in a refined game of Scrabble, with ladies present."

Jane's eyes sparkled mischievously. "Really? Tell us. Don't be stuffy."

"Stuffy? Have you no manners, young lady?"

"None!"

"Have you no modesty?"

"Nope."

"Are you just a common *broad?*"

"Common," she said, nodding rapidly. "Common to the core. So tell us what word you had."

"Shame, shame, shame," he said. Gradually, he cajoled them into dropping their inquiry. They started a new game. This time all the words were ordinary, and they did not come in any unsettling, related order.

Later, in bed, he made love to Carol. He wasn't particularly horny. He just wanted to be as close to her as he could get.

Afterwards, when the murmured love talk finally faded into a companionable silence, she said, "What *was* your word?"

"Hmmmm?" he said, pretending not to know what she meant.

"Your obscene word in the Scrabble game. Don't try to tell me you've forgotten what it was."

"Nothing important."

She laughed. "After everything we just did in this bed, surely you don't think I need to be sheltered!"

"I didn't have an obscene word." Which was the truth. "I didn't really have any word at all." Which was a lie. "It's just that . . . I thought those first five words on the board were bad for Jane."

"Bad for her?"

"Yes. I mean, you told me it's quite possible she lost one or both of her parents in a fire. She might be on the brink of learning about or remembering a terrible tragedy in her recent past. Tonight she just needed to relax, to laugh a bit. How could the game have been fun for her if the words on the board started to remind her that her parents might be dead?''

Carol turned on her side, raised herself up a bit, leaned over him, her bare breasts grazing his chest, and stared into his eyes. ''Is that really the only reason you were so upset?''

''Don't you think I was right? Did I overreact?''

''Maybe you did. Maybe you didn't. It *was* creepy.'' She kissed his nose. ''You know why I love you so much?''

''Because I'm such a great lover?''

''You are, but that's not why I love you.''

''Because I have tight buns?''

''Not that.''

''Because I keep my fingernails so neat and clean?''

''Not that.''

''I give up.''

''You're so damned sensitive, so caring about other people. How typical of my Paul to worry about the Scrabble game being fun for Jane. *That's* why I love you.''

''I thought it was my hazel eyes.''

''Nah.''

''My classic profile.''

''Are you kidding?''

''Or the way my third toe on my left foot lays half under the second toe.''

''Oh, I'd forgotten about that. Hmmmmm. You're right. *That's* why I love you. Not because you're sensitive. It's your *toes* that drive me wild.''

Their teasing led to cuddling, and the cuddling led to kissing, and the kissing led to passion again. She reached her peak only a few seconds before he spurted deep within her, and when they finally parted for the night, he felt pleasantly wrung out.

Nevertheless, she was asleep before he was. He stared at the dark ceiling of the dark bedroom and thought about the Scrabble game.

BLADE, BLOOD, DEATH, TOMB, KILL . . .

He thought about the word he had hidden from Carol and Jane, the word that had compelled him to end the game and start another. After adding EATH to the D in BLOOD, he'd been left with just three letter tiles on his rack: X, U, and C. The X and the U had played no part in what was to follow. But when he had drawn four new letters, they had gone disconcertingly well with the C. First he'd picked up an A, then an R. And he had known what was going to happen. He hadn't wanted to continue; he'd considered throwing all the tiles back into the box at that moment, for he dreaded seeing the word that he knew the last two letters would spell. But he hadn't ended it there. He had been too curious to stop when he should have stopped. He had drawn a third tile, which had been an O, and then a fourth, L.

C . . . A . . . R . . . O . . . L . . .

BLADE, BLOOD, DEATH, TOMB, KILL, CAROL.

Of course, even if he was able to fit it in, he couldn't put CAROL on the board, for it was a proper name, and the rules didn't allow the use of proper names. But that was a moot point. The important thing was that her name had been spelled out so neatly, so boldly on his rack of letters that it was uncanny. He had drawn the letters in their proper order, for God's sake! What were the odds against *that*?

It seemed to be an omen. A warning that something was going to happen to Carol. Just as Grace Mitowski's two nightmares had turned out to be prophetic.

He thought about the other strange events that had transpired recently: the unnaturally violent lightning strikes at Alfred O'Brian's office; the hammering sound that had shaken the house; the intruder on the rear lawn during the thunderstorm. He sensed that all of it was tied together. But for Christ's sake, *how?*

BLADE, BLOOD.

DEATH, TOMB.

KILL, CAROL.

If the series of words on the Scrabble tiles had constituted a prophetic warning, what was he supposed to do about it? The omen, if it *was* an omen, was too vague to have any value. There was nothing specific to guard against. He couldn't protect Carol until he knew from which direction the danger was coming. A car wreck? A plane crash. A mugger? Cancer? It could be anything. He could see nothing to be gained by telling Carol that her name had turned up on his rack of Scrabble tiles; there was nothing she could do, either, nothing except worry about it.

He didn't want to worry her.

Instead, lying in the darkness, feeling icy even under the covers, he worried *for* her.

At two o'clock in the morning, Grace was still reading in the study. There wasn't any point in going to bed for at least another hour or two. The events of the last week had turned her into an insomniac.

The day just past had been relatively uneventful. Aristophanes was still behaving oddly—hiding from her, sneaking about, watching her when he thought she didn't know he was there—but he hadn't torn up any more pillows or furniture, and he had used his litter box as he was supposed to do, which were encouraging signs. She hadn't received any more telephone calls from the man who had pretended to be Leonard, and for that she was grateful. Yes, it had been pretty much an ordinary day.

And yet . . .

She was still tense and unable to sleep because she sensed that she was in the eye of the hurricane. She sensed that the peace and quiet in her house were deceptive, that thunder and lightning raged on all sides of her, just beyond the range of her hearing and just out of sight. She expected to be plunged back into the storm at any moment, and that expectation made it impossible for her to relax.

She heard a furtive sound and glanced up from the novel she was reading.

Aristophanes appeared at the open study door, peering in from the hallway. Only his elegant Siamese head was visible as he craned it cautiously around the doorframe.

Their eyes met.

For an instant, Grace felt that she was not looking into the eyes of a dumb animal. They seemed to contain intelligence. Wisdom. Experience. More than mere animal intent and purpose.

Aristophanes hissed.

His eyes were cold. Twin balls of crystal-clear, blue-green ice.

"What do you want, cat?"

He broke the staring contest. He turned away from her with haughty indifference, padded past the doorway, and went softly down the hall, pretending that he hadn't been spying on her, even though they both knew he had been doing exactly that.

Spying? she thought. Am I crazy? Who would a cat be spying for? Catsylvania? Great Kitten? Purrsia?

She could think of other puns, but none of them brought a smile to her lips.

Instead, she sat with the book on her lap, wondering about her sanity.

NINE

◆

Thursday afternoon.

The office drapes were tightly closed as usual. The light from the two floor lamps was golden, diffuse. Mickey Mouse was still smiling broadly in all his many incarnations.

Carol and Jane sat in the wing chairs.

The girl slipped into a trance with only a little assistance from Carol. Most patients were more susceptible to hypnosis the second time than they had been the first, and Jane was no exception.

Again using the imaginary wristwatch, Carol turned the hands of time backwards and regressed Jane into the past. This time the girl didn't need two minutes to get beyond her amnesia. In only twenty or thirty seconds, she reached a point at which memories existed for her.

She twitched and suddenly sat up ramrod-straight in her chair. Her eyes popped open like the eyes on a doll; she was looking *through* Carol. Her face was twisted with terror.

"Laura?" Carol asked.

Both of the girl's hands flew up to her throat. She clutched herself, gasping, gagging, grimacing in pain. She appeared to be reliving the same traumatic experience that had panicked her during yesterday's sessions, but today she did not scream.

"You can't feel the fire," Carol told her. "There is no pain, honey. Relax. Be calm. You can't smell the smoke, either. It doesn't bother you at all. Breathe easily, normally. Be calm and relax."

The girl didn't obey. She quivered and broke out in a sweat. She retched repeatedly, dryly, violently, yet almost silently.

Afraid that she had lost control again, Carol redoubled her efforts to soothe her patient, without success.

Jane began to gesture wildly, her hands cutting and stabbing and tugging and hammering at the air.

Abruptly, Carol realized the girl was trying to talk, but for some reason had lost her voice.

Tears welled up and slid down Jane's face. She was moving her mouth without the slightest result, desperately trying to force out words that refused to come. In addition to the terror in her eyes, there was now frustration.

Carol quickly fetched a notebook and a felt-tipped pen from her desk. She put the notebook on Jane's lap and pressed the pen into her hand.

"Write it for me, honey."

The girl squeezed the pen so hard that her knuckles were white and nearly as sharp as the knuckles on a skeleton's fleshless hand. She looked down at the notebook. She stopped retching, but she continued to quiver.

Carol crouched beside the wing chair, where she could see the notebook. "What is it you want to say?"

Her hand shaking like that of a palsied old woman, Jane hurriedly scrawled two words that were barely legible: *Help me.*

"Why do you need help?"

Again: *Help me.*

"Why can't you speak?"

Head.

"Be more specific."

My head.

"What about your head?"

The girl's hand began to form a letter, then jumped down one line and made another false start, jumped to a third line—as if she couldn't figure out how to express what she wanted to say. At last, in a frenzy, she started slashing at the paper with the felt-tipped pen, making a meaningless crosshatching of black lines.

"Stop it!" Carol said. "You *will* relax, dammit. Be calm."

Jane stopped slashing at the paper. She was silent, staring down at the notebook on her lap.

Carol tore off the smeared page and threw it on the floor. "Okay. Now you're going to answer my questions calmly and as fully as you can. What is your name?"

Millie.

Carol stared at the handwritten name, wondering what had happened to Laura Havenswood. "Millie? Are you sure that's your name?"

Millicent Parker.

"Where is Laura?"

Who's Laura?

Carol stared at the girl's drawn face. The perspiration was beginning to dry on her porcelain-smooth skin. Her blue eyes were blank, unfocused. Her mouth was slack.

Carol abruptly flashed a hand past the girl's face. Jane didn't flinch. She wasn't faking the trance.

"Where do you live, Millicent?"

Harrisburg.

"Right here in town. What's your address?"

Front Street.

"Along the river? Do you know the number?"

The girl wrote it down.

"What's your father's name?"

Randolph Parker.

"What's your mother's name?"

The pen made a meaningless squiggle on the notebook page.

"What's your mother's name?" Carol repeated.

The girl surrendered to a new series of spasmic tremors. She retched soundlessly and put her hands to her throat once more. The felt-tipped pen made a black mark on the underside of her chin.

Apparently, the mere mention of her mother frightened her. That was territory that would have to be explored, though not right now.

Carol talked her down, calmed her, and asked a new question. "How old are you, Millie?"

Tomorrow's my birthday.

"Is it really? How old will you be?"

I won't make it.

"What won't you make?"

Sixteen.

"Are you fifteen now?"

Yes.

"And you think you won't live to be sixteen? Is that it?"

Won't live.

"Why not?"

The sheen of sweat had nearly evaporated from the girl's face, but again perspiration popped out along her hairline.

"Why won't you live to see your birthday?" Carol persisted.

As before, the girl used the felt-tipped pen to slash angrily at the notebook.

"Stop that," Carol said firmly. "Relax and be calm and answer my question." She tore the ruined page out of the book and tossed it aside, then said, "Why won't you live to see your sixteenth birthday, Millie?"

Head.

So we're back to this, Carol thought. She said, "What about your head? What's wrong with it?"

Cut off.

Carol stared at those two words for a moment, then looked up at the girl's face.

Millie-Jane was struggling to remain calm, as Carol had told her she must. But her eyes jiggled nervously, and there was horror in them. Her lips were utterly colorless, tremulous. Beneath the rivulets of sweat that coursed down her forehead, her skin was waxy and mealy white.

She continued to scribble frantically in the notebook, but all she wrote was the same thing over and over again: *Cut off, cut off, cut off, cut off . . .* She was bearing down on the page with such great pressure that the head of the felt-tipped pen was squashed into shapeless mush.

My God, Carol thought, this is like a live report from the bottom of Hell.

Laura Havenswood. Millicent Parker. One girl screaming in pain as fire consumed her, the other a victim of decapitation. What did either of those girls have to do with Jane Doe? She couldn't be *both* of them. Perhaps she wasn't either of them. Were they people she had known? Or were they only figments of her imagination?

What in Christ's name is happening here? Carol wondered.

She put her own hand over the girl's writing hand and stilled the squeaking pen. Speaking gently, rhythmically, she told Millie-Jane that everything was all right, that she was perfectly safe, and that she must relax.

The girl's eyes stopped jiggling. She sagged back in her chair.

"All right," Carol said. "I think that's enough for today, honey."

Employing the imaginary wristwatch, she brought the girl forward in time.

For a few seconds everything went well, but then, without warning, the girl erupted from her chair, knocking the notebook off her lap and flinging the pen across the room. Her pale face flushed red, and her placid expression gave way to a look of pure rage.

Carol rose from beside the girl's chair and stepped in front of her. "Honey, what's wrong?"

The girl's eyes were wild. She began to shout with such force that she sprayed Carol with spittle. "Shit! The bitch did it! The rotten, goddamn bitch!"

The voice wasn't Jane's.

It wasn't Laura's either.

It was a new voice, a third one, with its own special character, and Carol had a hunch it didn't belong to Millicent Parker, the mute. She suspected that an entirely new identity had surfaced.

The girl stood very stiff and straight, her hands fisted at her sides, staring off into infinity. Her face was distorted by anger. "The stinking bitch did it! She did it to me *again!*"

The girl continued to shout at the top of her voice, and half of the words she blurted out were obscene. Carol tried to soothe her, but this time it wasn't easy. For at least a minute the girl continued to wail and curse. At last, however, at Carol's urging, she got control of herself. She stopped shouting, but there was still anger in her face.

Holding the girl by the shoulders, face to face with her, Carol said, "What's your name?"

"Linda."

"What's your last name?"

"Bektermann."

It was yet another identity, as Carol had thought. She had the girl spell the name.

Then: "Where do you live, Linda?"

"Second Street."

"In Harrisburg?"

"Yes."

Carol asked for the exact address, and the girl responded. It was only a few blocks from the Front Street address that Millicent Parker had provided.

"What's your father's name, Linda?"

"Herbert Bektermann."

"What's your mother's name?"

That question had the same effect on Linda as it had had on Millie. She rapidly became agitated and began to shout again. "The bitch! Oh, God, what she *did* to me. The slimy, rotten bitch! I hate her. I hate her!"

Chilled by the combination of fury and agony in the girl's tortured voice, Carol quickly quieted her.

Then: "How old are you, Linda?"

"Tomorrow's my birthday."

Carol frowned. "Am I talking to Millicent now?"

"Who's Millicent?"

"Is this still Linda I'm talking to?"

"Yes."

"And your birthday is tomorrow?"

"Yes."

"How old will you be?"

"I won't make it."

Carol blinked. "You mean you won't live to see your birthday?"

"That's right."

"Is it your sixteenth birthday?"

"Yes."

"You're fifteen now?"

"Yes."

"Why are you worried about dying?"

"Because I know I will."

"How do you know?"

"Because I already am."

"You're already dying?"

"Dead."

"You're already dead?"

"I will be."

"Please be specific. Are you telling me that you're already dead? Or are you saying that you're merely afraid you're *going* to die sometime soon?"

"Yes."

"Which is it?"

"Both."

Carol felt as if she were in the middle of a tea party at the Mad Hatter's house. "How do you think you're going to die, Linda?"

"She'll kill me."

"Who?"

"The bitch."

"Your mother?"

The girl doubled over and clutched at her side, as if she had been struck. She screamed, turned, staggered two steps, and fell with a crash. On the floor she still clutched her side, and she kicked her legs, writhed. She was obviously in unendurable pain. It was only imaginary pain, of course, but to the girl it was indistinguishable from the real thing.

Frightened, Carol knelt beside her, held her hand, and urged her to be calm. When the girl eventually relaxed, Carol quickly brought her all the way back to the present and out of the trance.

Jane blinked, stared up at Carol, and put one hand on the floor beside her, as if testing the truth of what her eyes told her. "Wow, what am I doing down here?"

Carol helped her to her feet. "I suppose you don't remember?"

"No. Did I tell you anything more about myself?"

"No. I don't think so. You told me you were a girl named Millicent Parker, and then you told me you were a girl named Linda Bektermann, but obviously you can't be *both* of them *and* Laura, too. So I suspect that you aren't any of them."

"I don't think so, either," Jane said. "Those two new names don't mean anything more to me than Laura Havenswood did. But who *are* those people? Where did I get their names, and why did I tell you I was any of them?"

"I'll be damned if I know," Carol said. "But sooner or later, we'll figure it out. We'll get to the bottom of all this, kiddo. I promise you that."

But what in God's name will we find at the bottom, down there in the dark? Carol wondered. Will it be something we'll wish we'd left buried forever?

Thursday afternoon, Grace Mitowski worked in the rose garden behind her house. The day was warm and clear, and she felt the need for some exercise. Besides, in the garden she wouldn't be able to hear the telephone ringing and wouldn't be tempted to answer it. Which was fine, because she wasn't psychologically prepared to answer the phone just yet; she hadn't decided how to deal with the hoaxer the next time he called and pretended that he was her long-dead husband.

Because of last week's torrential rains, the roses were past their prime. The last flowers of the season should have been at the peak of their beauty right now, but many of the big blooms had lost a fifth or even a fourth of their petals under the lashing of the wind-whipped rain. Nevertheless, the garden was still a colorful, cheery sight.

She had let Aristophanes out for some exercise. She kept an eye on him, intending to call him back the moment he headed off the property. She was determined to keep him away from whoever had poisoned or drugged him. But he didn't seem to be in a rambling mood; he stayed nearby, creeping among the roses, stirring up a moth or two and chasing them with catlike singlemindedness.

Grace was on her hands and knees in front of a row of intermingled yellow and crimson and orange flowers, hand-spading the earth with a trowel, when someone said, "You have a magnificent garden."

Startled, she looked up and saw a thin, jaundice-skinned man in a rumpled blue suit that hadn't been in fashion for many years. His shirt and tie were hopelessly out of style, too. He looked as if he had stepped out of a photograph taken in the 1940s. He had thinning hair the color of summer dust, and his eyes were an unusual shade of soft brown, almost beige. His face was composed entirely of narrow features and sharp angles that gave him a look halfway between that of a hawk and that of a parsimonious moneylender in a Charles Dickens novel. He appeared to be in his early or middle fifties.

Grace glanced at the gate in the white board fence that separated her property from the street. The gate was standing wide open. Evidently, the man had been strolling by, had seen the roses through a gap in the poplar-tree hedge that stood on the outside of the fence, and had decided to come in and have a closer look.

His smile was warm, and there was kindness in his eyes, and he seemed not to be intruding, even though he was. "You must have two dozen varieties of roses here."

"Three dozen," she said.

"Truly magnificent," he said, nodding approval. His voice wasn't thin and sharp like the rest of him. It was deep, mellow, friendly, and would have seemed more fitting if it had issued from a brawny, hearty fellow half again this man's size. "You take care of the entire garden yourself?"

Grace sat back on her heels, still holding the trowel in one gloved hand. "Sure. I enjoy it. And somehow . . . it just wouldn't be *my* garden if I hired someone to help me with it."

"Exactly!" the stranger said. "Yes, I can understand how you feel."

"Are you new in the neighborhood?" Grace asked.

"No, no. Used to live just a block from here, but that was a long, long time ago." He took a deep breath and smiled again. "Ah, the wonderful aroma of roses! Nothing else smells half so pretty. Yes, you've got a superb garden. Really superb."

"Thank you."

He snapped his fingers as a thought occurred to him. "I ought to write something about this. It might make a first-rate human-interest piece. This fantasyland tucked away in an ordinary backyard. Yes, I'm sure it would be just the thing. A nice change of pace for me."

"Are you a writer?"

"Reporter," he said, still taking deep breaths and savoring the aroma of the blooms.

"Are you with a local paper?"

"The *Morning News*. Name's Palmer Wainwright."

"Grace Mitowski."

"I hoped you might recognize my byline," Wainwright said, grinning.

"Sorry. I don't read the *Morning News*. I take the *Patriot-News* from the delivery boy every morning."

"Ah, well," he said, shrugging, "that's a good paper, too. But of course, if you don't read the *Morning News,* you never saw my story about the Bektermann case."

As Grace realized that Wainwright intended to hang around awhile, she got off her haunches, stood up, and flexed her rapidly stiffening legs. "The Bektermann case? That sounds familiar."

"All the papers reported it, of course. But I did a five-part series. Good stuff, even if I do say so myself. I got a Pulitzer nomination for it. Did you know that? An honest-to-God Pulitzer nomination."

"Really? Why, that's something," Grace said, not sure if she should take him seriously but not wanting to offend him. "That is *really* something. Imagine. A Pulitzer nomination."

It seemed to her that the conversation had suddenly taken an odd turn. It wasn't casual any longer. She sensed that Wainwright had come into the yard not to admire her roses and not to have a friendly chat, but to tell her, a complete stranger, about his Pulitzer nomination.

"Didn't win," Wainwright said. "But the way I look at it, a nomination is almost as good as the prize itself. I mean, out of the tens of thousands of newspaper articles that're published in a year, only a handful are up for the prize."

"Refresh my memory, if you will," Grace said. "What was the Bektermann case about?"

He laughed good-naturedly and shook his head. "Wasn't about what I *thought* it was about. That's for damned sure. I wrote it up as a tangled, Freudian puzzle. You know—the iron-willed father, with perhaps an unnatural attraction for his own daughter, the mother with a drinking problem, the poor girl caught in the middle. The victimized young girl subjected to hideous psychological pressures beyond her understanding, beyond her tolerance, until at last she simply— *snapped.* That's how I saw it. That's how I wrote it up. I thought I was a brilliant detective, digging to the deepest roots of the Bektermann tragedy. But all I ever saw was the window-dressing. The real story was far stranger than anything I ever imagined. Hell, it was too strange for any serious reporter to risk handling it. No reputable paper would have printed it as news. If I *had* known the truth, and if I *had* somehow gotten it published, I'd have destroyed my career."

What the devil's going on? Grace wondered. He seems obsessed with telling me about this in detail, *compelled* to tell me, even though he's never even seen me before. Is this life imitating art—Coleridge's poem reset in a rose garden? Am I the partygoer and Wainwright the Ancient Mariner?

As she looked into Wainwright's beige eyes, she suddenly realized how alone she was, even here in the yard. Her property was ringed by trees, sheltered, private.

"Was it a murder case?" she asked.

"Was and is," Wainwright said. "It didn't end with the Bektermanns. It's still going on. This damned, endless pursuit. It's still going on, and it's got to be stopped this time around. That's why I'm here. I've come to tell you that your Carol is in the middle of it. Caught in the middle. You've got to help her. Get her out of the girl's way."

Grace gaped at him, reluctant to believe that she had heard what she knew she had heard.

"There are certain forces, dark and powerful forces," Wainwright said calmly, "that want to see—"

Shrieking angrily, Aristophanes sprang at Wainwright with berserk passion. He landed on the man's chest and scrambled onto his face.

Grace screamed and jumped back in fright.

Wainwright staggered to one side, grabbed the cat with both hands, and tried unsuccessfully to wrench it off his face.

"Ari!" Grace cried. "Stop it!"

Aristophanes had his claws in the man's neck and was biting his cheek.

Wainwright wasn't screaming as he ought to have been. He was eerily silent as he wrestled with the cat, even though the creature seemed determined to tear off his face.

Grace moved toward Wainwright, wanting to help, not knowing what to do.

The cat was squealing. It bit off a gobbet of flesh from Wainwright's cheek.

Oh Jesus, no!

Grace moved in quickly, raising the trowel, but hesitated. She was afraid of hitting the man instead of the cat.

Wainwright suddenly turned away from her and stumbled through the rose bushes, past white and yellow blooms, the cat still clinging to him. He walked into a waist-high hedge, fell through it, onto the lawn on the other side, out of sight.

Grace hurried to the end of the hedgerow, stepped around it, heart hammering, and discovered that Wainwright had vanished. Only the cat was there, and it bolted past her, sprinted across the garden, up the back porch steps, and into the house through the half-open rear door.

Where was Wainwright? Had he crawled away, dazed, wounded? Had he passed out in some sheltered corner of the garden, bleeding to death?

The yard contained half a dozen shrubs large and dense enough to conceal the body of a man Wainwright's size. She looked around all of them, but she could find no trace of the reporter.

She looked toward the garden gate that led to the street. No. He couldn't have gone that far without drawing her attention.

Frightened, confused, Grace blinked at the sun-dappled garden, trying to understand.

The Harrisburg telephone book contained neither a listing for Mr. Randolph Parker nor one for Herbert Bektermann. Carol was perplexed but not surprised.

After she saw her final patient of the day, she and Jane drove to the address on Front Street where Millicent Parker had claimed to live. It was a huge, impressive Victorian mansion, but it hadn't been anyone's home for a long time. The front lawn had been paved over for a parking lot. There was a small, tasteful sign by the entrance drive:

MAUGHAM & CRICHTON, INC.

A MEDICAL CORPORATION

Many years ago, this portion of Front Street had been one of the most elegant neighborhoods in Pennsylvania's capital city. During the past couple of decades, however, many of the riverfront boulevard's grand old houses had been razed to make room for sterile, modern office buildings. A few of the rambling houses had been preserved, at least after a fashion—the exteriors beautifully restored, the interiors gutted and converted to various commercial uses. Farther north, there was still a section of Front Street that was a desirable residential area, but not here, not where Millicent Parker had sent them.

Maugham & Crichton was a group medical practice that included seven physicians: two general internists and five specialists. Carol had a chat with the receptionist, a henna-haired woman named Polly, who told her that none of the doctors was named Parker. Likewise, no one of that name was employed as a nurse or as a member of the clerical staff. Furthermore, Maugham & Crichton had been at their current address for nearly seventeen years.

It had occurred to Carol that Jane might once have been a patient of one of Maugham & Crichton's physicians, and that her subconscious mind had made use of the firm's address to flesh out the Millicent Parker identity. But Polly, who had worked for Maugham & Crichton ever since they'd opened their doors, was sure she had never seen the girl. However, intrigued by Jane's amnesia and sympathetic by nature, Polly agreed to check the files to see if Maugham & Crichton had ever treated anyone named Laura Havenswood, Millicent Parker, or Linda Bektermann. It was a fruitless search; none of those names appeared in the patient records.

Grace stepped through the gate, into the street, and looked both ways. There was no sign of Palmer Wainwright.

She returned to her own backyard, closed and latched the gate, and walked toward the house.

Wainwright was sitting on the porch steps, waiting for her.

She stopped fifteen feet from him, amazed, confused.

He got up from the steps.

"Your face," she said numbly.

His face was unscarred.

He smiled as if nothing had happened and took two steps toward her. "Grace—"

"The cat," she said. "I saw your cheek . . . your neck . . . it's claws tore out. . ."

"Listen," he said, taking another step toward her, "there are certain forces, dark and powerful forces, that want to see this played out the wrong way. Dark forces that thrive on tragedy. They want to see it end in senseless violence and blood. That mustn't be allowed to happen, Grace. Not again. You've got to keep Carol out of the girl's way, for her sake and for the sake of the girl, too."

Grace gaped at him. "Who the hell are you?"

"Who are *you?*" Wainwright asked, raising one eyebrow quizzically. "*That* is the important question right now. You aren't only who you think you are. You aren't only Grace Mitowski."

He's mad, she thought. Or I'm mad. Or we both are. Stark, raving mad.

She said, "You're the one on the phone. You're the creep who imitates Leonard's voice."

"No," he said. "I am—"

"No wonder Ari attacked you. You're the one who's been giving him drugs or poison or something like that. You're the one, and he *knew*."

But what about the facial wounds, the gouged neck? she asked herself. How in the name of God did those injuries heal so quickly?

How?

She pushed those thoughts out of her mind, refused to think about such things. She must have been mistaken. She must have imagined that Ari had actually hurt the man.

"Yeah," she said, "you're the one who's behind all of these weird things that've been happening. Get off my property, you son of a bitch."

"Grace, there are forces aligned . . . " He looked no different now from the way he had looked when he'd first spoken to her, several minutes ago. He hadn't looked crazed then; he didn't look crazed now. He didn't look dangerous, and yet he continued to babble about dark forces. " . . . good and evil, right and wrong. You're on the right side, Grace. But the cat—ah, the cat's a different story. At all times, you must be wary of the cat."

"Get out of my way," she said.

He took a step toward her.

She slashed at him with the gardening trowel, missing his face by just an inch or two. She slashed again and again and again, cutting only empty air, not really wanting to cut anything else unless she had no choice, just hoping to keep him at bay until she could slip around him, for he was between her and the house. And then she *was* around him; she turned and ran for the kitchen door, painfully aware that her legs were old and arthritic. She went only a few steps before she realized she shouldn't have turned her back on the lunatic, and she wheeled to confront him, gasping, certain that he was leaping toward her, perhaps with a knife in his hand—

But he was gone.

Vanished. Again.

He hadn't had time to reach any of the shrubs that were large enough to conceal a man, not during the split second her back had been turned. Even if he had been a much younger man than he was, in the very best condition, a trained runner—even then he couldn't have gone more than halfway to the gate in such a short time.

So where was he?

Where was he?

From the offices of Maugham & Crichton on Front Street, Carol and Jane drove a few blocks to the Second Street address that was supposed to be the home of Linda Bektermann. It was in a good neighborhood; a lovely French country house, at least fifty years old, in fine condition. No one was at home, but the name on the mailbox was Nicholson, not Bektermann.

They rang the bell at the house next door and talked to a neighbor, Jean Gunther, who confirmed that the French country place was owned and occupied by the Nicholson family.

"My husband and I have lived here for six years," Mrs. Gunther said, "and the Nicholsons were next door when we moved in. I think I once heard them say they'd lived in that house since 1965."

The name Bektermann meant nothing to Jean Gunther.

In the car again, on the way home, Jane said, "I'm really a lot of trouble for you."

"Nonsense," Carol said. "I kind of enjoy playing detective. Besides, if I can help you break through your memory block, if I can uncover the truth behind all the sleight-of-hand tricks that your subconscious is playing, then I'll be able to write about this case for any psychology journal I choose. It'll definitely make my name in the profession. I might even wind up with a book out of it. So you see, because of you, kiddo, I could become rich and famous some day."

"When you're rich and famous, will you still talk to me?" the girl teased.

"Certainly. Of course, you'll have to make an appointment a week in advance."

They grinned at each other.

Using the kitchen phone, Grace called the offices of the *Morning News.*

The switchboard operator at the newspaper didn't have an extension number listed for Palmer Wainwright. She said, "So far as I know, he don't even work here. And I'm sure he's no reporter. Maybe one of the new copy editors or somebody like that."

"Could you connect me with the managing editor's office?" Grace asked.

"That would be Mr. Quincy," the operator said. She buzzed the proper extension.

Quincy wasn't in his office, and his secretary didn't know whether or not the paper employed a man named Palmer Wainwright. "I'm new here," she said apologetically. "I've only been Mr. Quincy's secretary since Monday, so I don't know everybody yet. If you'll leave your name and number, I'll have Mr. Quincy return your call."

Grace gave her the number and said, "Tell him Dr. Grace Mitowski wishes to speak with him and that I'll only need a few minutes of his time." She seldom used the honorific in front of her name, but it came in handy in cases like this, for a doctor's phone calls were *always* returned.

"Is this an emergency, Dr. Mitowski? I don't think that Mr. Quincy's going to be back until tomorrow morning."

"That'll be good enough," she said. "Have him call me first thing, no matter how early he gets in."

After she hung up, she went to the kitchen and stared out at the rose garden. How could Wainwright vanish like that?

For the third evening in a row, Paul and Carol and Jane prepared dinner together. The girl was fitting in better day by day.

If she stays with us just another week, Paul thought, it'll seem like she's *always* been here.

The salad consisted of hearts of palm and iceberg lettuce. That was followed by eggplant Parmigiana with spaghetti on the side.

As they were starting dessert—small dishes of richly flavored spumoni—Paul said, "Any chance we could postpone the trip to the mountains for two days?"

"Why?" Carol asked.

"I'm a bit behind in my writing schedule, and I'm at a very critical point in the book," he said. "I've written two-thirds of the toughest scene in the story, and I hate to leave it unfinished just to go on vacation. I won't enjoy myself. If we left Sunday instead of tomorrow, that would give me time to polish off the end of the chapter. And we'd still have eight days at the cabin."

"Don't look at me," Jane said. "I'm just excess baggage. I'll go wherever you take me, whenever you take me."

Carol shook her head. "Just last week, when Mr. O'Brian said we were compulsive overachievers, we made up our minds to change our ways, didn't we? We've *got* to learn to make time for leisure and not let our work encroach on that."

"You're right," Paul said. "But just this once—" He broke off in midsentence because he saw that Carol was determined. She was rarely intractable, but when she *did* decide not to compromise on an issue, she was about as movable as Gibraltar. He sighed. "Okay. You win. We'll leave tomorrow morning. I'll just bring along the typewriter and the manuscript. I can finish the scene up at the cabin and—"

"Nothing doing," Carol said, emphasizing each word by tapping her spoon against her ice cream dish. "If you bring it along, you won't stop when you've reached the end of the scene you're working on. You'll keep going. You *know* you will. Having the typewriter within easy reach will just be too much of a temptation. You won't be able to resist it. The whole vacation will go down the drain."

"But I just *can't* put that scene on hold for ten days," he said pleadingly. "By the time I get back to it, the tone and the spontanaeity will be lost."

Carol ate a spoonful of spumoni and said, "All right. Here's what we'll do. Jane and I will leave for the mountains first thing in the morning, just as we planned. You stay here, finish your scene, and then drive up to join us whenever you're ready."

He frowned. "I'm not sure that's a good idea."

"Why not?"

"Well, is it really wise for the two of you to go up there alone? I mean, the summer season is over. There aren't going to be many campers in the woods now, and most of the other cabins will be deserted."

"For heaven's sake," Carol said, "there's no Abominable Snowman lurking around in *those* mountains, Paul. We're in Pennsylvania, not Tibet." She smiled.

"It's nice to know you're so concerned about us, darling. But we'll be perfectly safe."

Later, after Jane had gone to bed, Paul made one last attempt to change Carol's mind, although he knew the effort would be wasted.

He leaned against the frame of the closet door and watched as Carol selected clothes for the suitcases. "Listen, be straight with me, okay?"

"Aren't I always? Straight about what?"

"The girl. Is there any chance she's dangerous?"

Carol turned from the clothes rack and stared at him, obviously surprised by his question. "Jane? Dangerous? Well, a girl as pretty as she is will probably break a lot of hearts over the years. And if cuteness could kill, she'd leave the streets littered with bodies behind her."

He refused to be amused. "I don't want you to be flippant about this. I think it's important. I want you to give it careful thought."

"I don't *need* to give it a lot of thought, Paul. She's lost her memory, sure. But she's a stable, mentally healthy kid. In fact, it takes an *amazingly* stable personality to handle amnesia the way she's handled it. I don't know that I'd do half as well if I were in her shoes right now. I'd either be a nervous wreck or sunk neck-deep in depression. She's resilient, flexible. Resilient and flexible people aren't dangerous."

"Never?"

"Hardly ever. It's the rigid ones who crack."

"But after what's happened in your therapy sessions with her, isn't it reasonable to wonder about what she might be capable of doing?" he asked.

"She's a tortured girl. I believe she's been through a truly terrifying experience, something so awful that she refuses to relive it, even under hypnosis. She obfuscates, misdirects, and holds back vital information, but that doesn't mean she's the least bit dangerous. Just scared. It seems evident to me that she was the victim of either physical or psychological violence at some time in her life. The *victim,* Paul, not the perpetrator."

She carried a few pairs of jeans to the suitcases that were open on the bed.

Paul followed her. "Are you going to continue her therapy while you're at the cabin?"

"Yes. I think it's best to keep chipping away at the wall of confusion she's thrown up."

"No fair."

"Huh?"

"That's work," he said. "I'm not allowed to take *my* work up to the cabin, but *you're* going to work. That's a double standard, Dr. Tracy."

"Double standard, my ass, Dr. Tracy. I'll need only half an hour a day for Jane's therapy. That's a lot different than lugging an IBM Selectric into the piney woods and pounding on the keys ten hours a day. Don't you realize that all the squirrels and deer and bunny rabbits would complain about the noise?"

Later still, when they were in bed and the lights were out, he said, "Hell, I'm letting this book take possession of me. Why *can't* I let the scene lie unfinished for ten days? I might even do a better job with it if I take the time to think about it. I'll come along with you and Jane tomorrow, and I won't bring the typewriter. Okay? I won't even bring a pencil."

"No," Carol said.

"No?"

"When you *do* get to the mountains, I want you to be able to put the book completely out of your mind. I want us to take long walks in the forest. I want us to go boating on the lake and do some fishing and read a couple of books and act like bums who never even heard the word 'work.' If you don't finish that scene before you go, you'll just brood about it during the entire vacation. You won't have a moment's real peace, which means *I* won't have a moment's peace, either. And don't tell me I'm wrong. I know you better than I know myself, buster. You stay here, write the end of that scene, and then join us on Sunday."

She kissed him goodnight, fluffed her pillows, and settled down to sleep.

He lay in the dark, thinking about the words in yesterday's Scrabble game.

```
                    B L A D E
          K I L L
                O
                O
          D E A T H
                O
                M
                B
```

And the one word he had refused to reveal: CAROL . . .

He still didn't think anything would be gained by telling her what the last of those six words had been. What could she do about it other than worry? Nothing. She could do nothing, and he could do nothing. Except wait and see. A threat— if one actually arose—could come from any of ten thousand or a hundred thousand sources. It could come anytime, anywhere. At home or in the mountains. One place was as safe—or as dangerous—as the other.

Anyway, maybe the appearance of those six words *had* been merely coincidence. An incredible but meaningless coincidence.

He stared into the darkness, trying hard to convince himself that there were no such things as spirit messages, omens, and clairvoyant prophecies. Only a week ago, he wouldn't have *needed* convincing.

Blood.

Get it off, scrub it off, every sticky drop of it, wash it off, quickly, quickly, down the drain, every incriminating drop of it, off, before someone finds out, before someone sees and knows what's been done, wash it off, off. . . .

The girl woke in the bathroom, in a fluorescent glare. She had been sleep-walking again.

She was surprised to find that she was nude. Her knee socks, panties, and T-shirt were scattered on the floor around her.

She was standing in front of the sink, scrubbing herself with a wet washcloth. When she looked at her reflection in the mirror, she was briefly paralyzed by what she saw.

Her face was smeared with blood.

Her arms were spattered with blood.

Her sweetly uptilted, bare breasts glistened with blood.

And she knew instantly that it wasn't her own. She had not been slashed or stabbed. *She* was the one who had done the slashing, the stabbing.

Oh God.

She stared at her gruesome reflection, morbidly fascinated by the sight of her blood-moistened lips.

What have I done?

She slowly lowered her gaze along her crimsoned neck, looked down at the reflection of her right nipple, on which hung a very fat, carmine droplet of gore. The gleaming pearl of blood quivered for an instant on the tip of her erect nipple; then it succumbed to gravity and fell away from her.

She pulled her gaze from the mirror, lowered her head to see where the droplet had struck the floor.

There was no blood.

When she looked directly at herself, rather than at her reflection, she discovered that her body was not covered with blood after all. She touched her bare breasts. They were damp because she had been scrubbing them with the washcloth, but the dampness was nothing more than water. Her arms weren't spattered with blood, either.

She squeezed the washcloth. Clear water dripped from it; the cloth bore no grisly stains.

Confused, she raised her eyes to the mirror once more and saw the blood, as before.

She held out her hand. In reality it was not bloody, but in the mirror it was sheathed in a glove of gore.

A vision, she thought. A weird illusion. That's all. I didn't hurt anyone. I didn't spill anyone's blood.

As she struggled to understand what was happening, her mirror image faded, and the glass in front of her turned black. It seemed to have been transformed into a window that looked out onto another dimension, for it reflected nothing that was in the bathroom.

This is a dream, she thought. I'm really snug in bed, where I belong. I'm only dreaming that I'm in the bathroom. I can put a stop to this just by waking up.

On the other hand, if it was a dream, would she be able to feel the cold ceramic floor beneath her bare feet as vividly as she could feel it now? If it was really only a dream, would she be aware of the cold water on her bare breasts?

She shivered.

In the lightless void on the other side of the mirror, something flickered far off in the darkness.

Wake up!

Something silvery. It flashed again and again, back and forth, the image growing steadily larger.

For God's sake, wake up!

She wanted to run. Couldn't.

She wanted to scream. Didn't.

In seconds the flickering object filled the mirror, pushing back the darkness out of which it had come, and then somehow it burst out of the mirror without shattering the glass, exploded out of the void and into the bathroom with one final, murderous swing, and she saw that it was an ax, bearing down on her face, the steel blade gleaming like the finest silver under the fluorescent lights. As the wickedly sharp edge of the ax swept inexorably toward her head, her knees buckled, and she fainted.

* * *

Near dawn, Jane woke again.

She was in bed. She was nude.

She threw the covers back, sat up, and saw her T-shirt, panties, and knee socks on the floor beside the bed. She dressed quickly.

The house was silent. The Tracys weren't up yet.

Jane hurried quietly down the hallway to the guest bathroom, hesitated on the threshold, then stepped inside and snapped on the lights.

There was no blood, and the mirror above the sink was only an ordinary mirror, reflecting her worried face but contributing no bizarre images of its own.

Okay, she thought, maybe I *was* sleepwalking. And maybe I *was* actually here without any clothes on, trying to scrub nonexistent blood off my body. But the rest of it was just part of the nightmare. It didn't happen. It couldn't. Impossible. The mirror couldn't really *change* like that.

She stared into her own blue eyes. She wasn't sure what she saw in them.

"Who *am* I?" she asked softly.

All week, Grace's sleep—what little she had managed to get between bouts of insomnia—had been dreamless. But tonight she thrashed for hours in the sheets, trying to fight her way out of a nightmare that seemed to last an eternity.

In the dream, a house was on fire. A big, beautifully ornamented Victorian house. She was standing outside the blazing structure, pounding on a pair of slant-set cellar doors and calling a name over and over again. "Laura! Laura!" She knew that Laura was trapped in the cellar of the burning house and that these doors were the only way out, but the doors were latched on the inside. She hammered on the wood with her bare hands until each blow sent a cruel bolt of pain the length of her arms, through her shoulders, and up the back of her neck. She wished desperately that she had an ax or a pry-bar or some other tool with which she could smash through the cellar doors, but she had nothing other than her fists, so she pounded and pounded until her flesh bruised and split and bled, and she kept on pounding even then, all the while screaming for Laura. Windows exploded on the second floor, showering glass down over her, but she didn't turn away from the slant-set cellar doors; she didn't run. She continued to slam her bloodied fists into the wood, praying that the girl would answer at any moment. She ignored the sparks that showered down on her and threatened to set her gingham dress afire. She wept, and she coughed when the wind blew the acrid smoke in her direction, and she cursed the wood that so easily resisted her fierce but ineffectual attack.

The nightmare had no climax, no peak of terror. It simply went on all night long at a continuously breathless pace until, a few minutes after dawn, Grace finally wrenched herself out of the hot, clutching arms of sleep and woke with a wordless cry, flailing at the mattress.

She sat up on the edge of the bed and held her throbbing head in her hands.

Her mouth was filled with the taste of ashes and bile.

The dream had been so vivid that she had even felt the high-necked, long-sleeved, blue and white gingham dress binding at her shoulders and across her bust as she had hammered on the cellar doors. Now, wide awake, she could *still* feel the dress binding her, even though she was wearing a loose nightgown, and even though she had never worn such a dress in her entire life.

Worse, she could smell the house burning.

The smoke odor lingered so long after she had awakened that she became convinced that her own house was ablaze. Quickly, she pulled on a robe, stepped into her slippers, and went from one room to another, searching for the fire.

There was no fire.

Yet for almost an hour, the stench of burning wood and tar stayed with her.

TEN

◆

Friday morning at nine o'clock, Paul sat down at his writing desk, picked up the phone, and called Lincoln Werth, the police detective in charge of the Jane Doe case. He told Werth that Carol was taking the girl out of town for a few days of rest and recreation.

"Might as well," Werth said. "We don't have any leads, and I sure don't think this is going to break wide open anytime soon. We keep expanding the search area, of course. At first we just put the kid's photo and description out to authorities in the surrounding counties. When that didn't do us any good, we put it on the wire to police agencies all over the state. Yesterday morning we took another step and wired the same data to seven neighboring states. But I'll tell you something, just between you and me. Even if we expand the search area all the way to Hong Kong, I got a feeling we ain't never going to find anyone who knows the kid. I just have a hunch. We're going to keep coming up empty-handed."

After talking to Werth, Paul went down to the garage, where Carol and Jane were putting their gear in the trunk of the Volkswagen. To spare the girl grief, Paul didn't pass along Werth's pessimistic assessment of the situation. "He said it's all right to leave town for a few days. The court didn't restrict you to Harrisburg. I told him where the cabin is, so if anyone turns up to claim our girl here, the Harrisburg police will contact the county sheriff out that way, and he or one of his deputies will drop by the cabin and let you know you've got to come back."

Carol kissed him goodbye. Jane kissed him, too; hers was a shy, chaste kiss, lightly planted on his cheek, and when she got into the car, she was blushing brightly.

He stood in front of the house and watched them drive away until the red Volkswagen Rabbit was out of sight.

After almost a week of blue skies, clouds had drifted in again. They were flat, slate gray. They matched Paul's mood.

When the kitchen phone rang, Grace steeled herself for the sound of Leonard's voice. She sat down in the chair at the small built-in desk, reached up, put her hand on the receiver that hung on the wall, let it ring once more, then picked it up. To her relief, it was Ross Quincy, the managing editor of the *Morning News,* returning the call she'd made late yesterday afternoon.

"You were inquiring about one of our reporters, Dr. Mitowski?"

"Yes. Palmer Wainwright."

Quincy was silent.

"He does work for you, doesn't he?" Grace asked.

"Uh . . . Palmer Wainwright has been an employee of the *Morning News,* yes."

"I believe he nearly won a Pulitzer Prize."

"Yes. But of course . . . that was quite a while back."

"Oh?"

"Well, if you know about the Pulitzer nomination, you must know it was for the series he did on the Bektermann murders."

"Yes."

"Which was back in 1943."

"That long ago?"

"Uh . . . Dr. Mitowski, exactly what is it you wanted to know about Palmer Wainwright?"

"I'd like to talk with him," she said. "We've met, and we have some unfinished business that I'm rather anxious to take care of. It's a . . . personal matter."

Quincy hesitated. Then: "Are you a long-lost relative?"

"Of Mr. Wainwright's? Oh, no."

"A long-lost friend?"

"No. Not that either."

"Well, then, I guess I don't have to be delicate about this. Dr. Mitowski, I'm afraid that Palmer Wainwright is dead."

"Dead!" she said, astounded.

"Well, surely you realized there was that possibility. He was never a well man, downright sickly. And you've obviously been out of touch with him for a long time."

"Not all that long," she said.

"Must be at least thirty-five years," Quincy said. "He died back in 1946."

The air at Grace's back seemed suddenly colder than it had been an instant ago, as if a dead man had expelled his icy breath against the nape of her neck.

"Thirty-one years," she said numbly. "You must be wrong."

"Not a chance. I was just a green kid back then, a copyboy. Palmer Wainwright was one of my heroes. I took it pretty hard when he went."

"Are we talking about the same man?" Grace asked. "He was quite thin, with sharp features, pale brown eyes, and a rather sallow complexion. His voice was several notes deeper than you'd expect from just looking at him."

"That was Palmer, all right."

"About fifty-five?"

"He was thirty-six when he died, but he did *look* twenty years older," Quincy said. "It was that string of illnesses, one thing right after another, with cancer at the end. It just wore him down, aged him fast. He was a fighter, but he just couldn't hold on any longer."

Thirty-one years in the grave? she thought. But I saw him yesterday. We had a strange conversation in the rose garden. What do you say to that, Mr. Quincy?

"Dr. Mitowski? Are you still there?"

"Yes. Sorry. Listen, Mr. Quincy, I hate to take your valuable time, but this is really important. I believe the Bektermann case had a lot to do with the personal business I wanted to discuss with Mr. Wainwright. But I don't really know anything about those murders. Would you mind telling me what it was all about?"

"Family tragedy," Quincy said. "The Bektermanns' daughter went berserk the day before her sixteenth birthday. Her mind just snapped. Apparently, she got it in her head that her mother intended to kill her before she turned sixteen, which was not true, of course. But she *thought* it was true, and she went after her mother with an ax. Her father and a visiting cousin got in the way, and she killed them. Her mother actually managed to wrench the ax out of the girl's hands. But that didn't stop the kid. She just picked up a fireplace poker and kept coming. When the mother, Mrs. Bektermann, was backed into a corner and was about to have her skull cracked open with the poker, she didn't have any choice but to swing the ax at her daughter. She hit the girl once, in the side. A pretty deep cut. The kid died in the hospital the next day. Mrs. Bektermann only killed in self-defense, and no charges were brought against her, but she felt so guilty about killing her own child that she had a complete breakdown and eventually wound up in an institution.''

''And that's the story that won Mr. Wainwright his Pulitzer nomination?''

''Yeah. In the hands of a lot of reporters, the piece would have been nothing but sensationalistic garbage. But Palmer was good. He wrote a sensitive, well-researched study of a family with serious emotional, interpersonal problems. The father was a domineering man who set extremely high standards for his daughter and very likely had an unnatural attraction to her. The mother was always competing with the father for the girl's heart, mind, and loyalty, and when she saw she was losing that battle, she turned to drink. There were extraordinary psychological pressures brought to bear on the daughter, and Palmer made the reader feel and understand those pressures.''

She thanked Ross Quincy for his time and consideration. She hung up the phone.

For a while she just sat there, staring at the softly humming refrigerator, trying to make sense of what she had been told. If Wainwright had died in 1946, whom had she talked to in the garden yesterday?

And what did the Bektermann murders have to do with her? With Carol?

She thought of what Wainwright had told her: *This damned, endless pursuit. It's still going on, and it's got to be stopped this time around. . . . I've come to tell you that your Carol is in the middle of it. . . . You've got to help her. Get her out of the girl's way.*

She felt she was on the verge of understanding what he had meant. And she was scared.

Even though a number of impossible things had transpired within the past twenty-four hours, she no longer questioned either her sanity or her perceptions. She was sane, perfectly sane, and in command of all her faculties. Senility was not even a remote possibility any longer. She sensed that the explanation for these events was far more frightening, more soul-shattering even than the prospect of senility, which had once terrified her.

She recalled something else that Palmer Wainwright had said yesterday in the garden: *You aren't only who you think you are. You aren't only Grace Mitowski.*

She knew the solution to the puzzle was within her grasp. She sensed a dark knowledge within her, long-forgotten memories waiting to be tapped. She was afraid to tap them, but she knew she must do precisely that, for Carol's sake, and perhaps for her own sake as well.

Suddenly, the air in the kitchen, though still quite clear, reeked of wood and tar smoke. Grace could hear the crackle of fire, although there were no flames here, now, in this place and time.

Her heart pounded frantically, and her mouth turned dry and sour.

She closed her eyes and could see the burning house as vividly as she had seen it in the dream. She could see the cellar doors, and she could hear herself screaming, calling Laura.

She knew it hadn't been only a dream. It had been a memory, lost for ages, surfacing now, reminding her that, indeed, she was not only Grace Mitowski.

She opened her eyes.

The kitchen was hot, stifling.

She felt herself being pulled along by forces she could not comprehend, and she thought: Is this what I want? Do I really want to flow with this and discover the truth and turn my little world upside down? Can I handle it?

The stench of nonexistent smoke grew stronger.

The roar of nonexistent flames grew louder.

I guess there's no turning back now, she thought.

She held her hands up in front of her face and stared at them, amazed. Her flesh had been miraculously disfigured by stigmata. Her hands were bruised, abraded, bloody. There were splinters of wood embedded in her palms, splinters from the cellar doors on which she had pounded such a long, long time ago.

At ten o'clock, when the phone rang, Paul had been at his desk, writing, for almost an hour. The work had just begun to flow smoothly. He snatched up the receiver and said, a bit impatiently, "Yes?"

An unfamiliar female voice said, "Could I speak to Dr. Tracy, please?"

"Speaking."

"Oh. Uh . . . no . . . the Dr. Tracy I'm looking for is a woman."

"It's my wife you want," he said. "She's out of town for a few days. Can I take a message?"

"Yes, please. Would you tell her that Polly called from Maugham & Crichton?"

He jotted the name down on a notepad. "And what's this in reference to?"

"Dr. Tracy was here yesterday afternoon with a young girl who's suffering from amnesia. . . . "

"Yes," Paul said, suddenly more interested than he had been. "I know the case."

"Dr. Tracy was asking if we'd ever heard of anyone named Millicent Parker."

"That's right. She told me about it last evening. It was another dead end, I gather."

"It seemed to be a dead end yesterday," Polly said, "but now it turns out that one of our doctors is familiar with the name. Dr. Maugham himself, in fact."

"Listen, rather than waiting for my wife to call you back, why don't you just tell *me* what you've come up with, and I can pass the information along to her."

"Well, sure, why not? See, Dr. Maugham is the senior partner in the practice. He bought this property eighteen years ago and personally oversaw the restoration of the outside and the renovation of the interior. He's a history bug, so it was natural for him to want to know the history of the building he purchased. He says this place was built in 1902 by a man named Randolph Parker. Parker had a daughter named Millicent."

"1902?"

"That's right."

"Interesting."

"You haven't heard the best part," Polly said, the eagerness of a gossip-monger in her voice. "Seems that back in 1905, the night before Millie's sixteenth birthday party, Mrs. Parker was in the kitchen, decorating a big cake for the girl. Millie snuck in behind her and stabbed her in the back four times."

Unthinking, Paul snapped the pencil he'd been holding ever since he'd written Polly's name on the notepad. One broken piece popped out of his hand, spun across the top of the desk, and fell to the floor.

"She stabbed her own mother?" he asked, hoping that he had not heard correctly.

"Isn't that something?"

"Kill her?" he asked numbly.

"No. Dr. Maugham says that according to the newspaper accounts at that time, the girl used a short-bladed knife. It didn't sink in far enough to do really major damage. No vital organs or blood vessels were affected. Louise Parker—that was the mother's name—managed to grab a meat cleaver from a kitchen rack. She tried to hold the girl off with that. But I guess Millie must have been completely off her rocker, 'cause she charged straight at Mrs. Parker again, and Mrs. Parker had to use that cleaver."

"Jesus."

"Yeah," Polly said, obviously enjoying his shocked reaction. "Dr. Maugham says she put that cleaver right into her daughter's throat. Pretty much cut the girl's head clear off. Isn't that a terrible thing? But what else could she do? Just let the kid go on jabbing that knife into her?"

Stunned, Paul thought about yesterday's hypnotic regression therapy session, which Carol had recounted for him in some detail. He remembered the part about how Jane had claimed to be Millicent Parker and had insisted on writing out her answers to questions and had written that she was unable to talk because her head had been cut off.

"Are you still there?" Polly asked.

"Oh. Uh . . . sorry. Is there more to the story?"

"More?" Polly asked. "Wasn't that *enough?*"

"Yes," he said. "You're absolutely right. That was enough. More than enough."

"I don't know if this information is of any help to Dr. Tracy."

"I'm sure it will be."

"I don't see how it could have anything to do with the girl she brought in here with her yesterday."

"Neither do I," Paul said.

"I mean, that girl can't be Millicent Parker. Millicent Parker has been dead for seventy-six years."

In the study, Grace stood at her desk, looking down at the open dictionary.

> **Reincarnation** (rē'-in-kär-nā'-shen),
> *n.* 1. the doctrine that the soul,
> upon death of the body, comes back
> to earth in another body or form.
> 2. rebirth of the soul in a new body.
> 3. a new incarnation or embodiment,
> as of a person.

Bunk? Nonsense? Superstition? Bullshit?

At one time, not long ago, those were all the words she would have used to write her own irreverent definition of reincarnation. But not now. Not any longer.

She closed her eyes, and with only the slightest effort, she was able to bring back the image of the burning house. She wasn't just envisioning it; she was *there,* hammering with her fists on the cellar door. She was not Grace Mitowski now; she was Rachael Adams, Laura's aunt.

The fire scene was not the only part of Rachel's life that she could recall with perfect clarity. She knew the woman's most intimate thoughts, her hopes and dreams and hates and fears, shared her most closely held secrets, for those thoughts and hopes and dreams and fears and secrets had been her own.

She opened her eyes and needed a moment to refocus them on the present-day world.

REINCARNATION

She closed the dictionary.

God help me, she thought, do I really believe it? Can it be true that I've lived before? And that Carol's lived before? And the girl they're calling Jane Doe?

If it *was* true—if she had been permitted to recall her previous existence as Rachael Adams in order to save Carol's life in this incarnation—then she was wasting valuable time.

She picked up the phone to call the Tracys, wondering how in God's name she was going to make them believe her.

There was no dial tone.

She jiggled the receiver-cradle buttons.

Nothing.

She put the receiver down and followed the cord around the side of the desk to the wall, to see if it had come unplugged. It wasn't unplugged; it was *chewed*. Bitten in two.

Aristophanes.

She remembered other things that Palmer Wainwright had said in the garden: *There are certain forces, dark and powerful forces, that want to see this played out the wrong way. Dark forces that thrive on tragedy. They want to see it end in senseless violence and blood . . . There are forces aligned . . . good and evil, right and wrong. You're on the right side, Grace. But the cat—ah, the cat's a different story. At all times, you must be wary of the cat.*

She also remembered when the series of paranormal events had begun, and she realized that the cat had been an integral part of it all, from the very start. Wednesday of last week. When she had suddenly awakened from her afternoon nap that day—catapulted out of a nightmare about Carol—there had been an incredibly brilliant and violent barrage of lightning beyond the study windows. She had staggered to the nearest window, and while she had stood there on unsteady, arthritic legs, half-awake and half-asleep, she'd had the eerie feeling that something monstrous had followed her up from the world of her nightmare, something demonic with a hungry grin on its face. For a few seconds that feeling had been so strong, so real, that she had been afraid to turn around and look into the shadowy room behind her. But then she had dismissed that weird thought as nothing more than the cold residue of the nightmare. Now, of course, she knew she shouldn't have dismissed it so quickly. Something strange *had* been in the room with her—a spirit; a presence; call it what you will. It had been there. And now it was in the cat.

She left the study and hurried down the hall.

In the kitchen, she found that phone cord also chewed apart.

There was no sign of Aristophanes.

Nevertheless, Grace knew he was nearby, perhaps even close enough to be watching her. She sensed his—or *its*—presence.

She listened. The house was too silent.

She wanted to cross the few feet of open floor to the kitchen door, open it boldly, and walk away from the house. But she strongly suspected that any attempt to leave would trigger an immediate and vicious attack.

She thought about the cat's claws, teeth, fangs. It wasn't merely a house pet, not just an amusing Siamese with a cute, furry face. It was actually a tough little killing machine, too; its feral impulses lay beneath a thin veneer of domestication. It was both respected and dreaded by mice and birds and squirrels. But could it kill a grown woman?

Yes, she thought uneasily. Yes, Aristophanes could kill me if he caught me by surprise and if he went for either my throat or my eyes.

The best thing she could do was stay within the house and not antagonize the cat until she had armed herself and could feel confident of winning any battle.

The only other telephone was in the second-floor bedroom. Wary, she went upstairs, even though she knew the third extension would be out of order, too.

It was.

But there was something in the bedroom that made the journey up the stairs worthwhile. The gun. She pulled open the top drawer of her nightstand and took out the loaded pistol she kept there. She had a hunch she would need it.

A hiss. A rustle.

Behind her.

Before she could swing around and confront her adversary, he was on her. He vaulted from the floor to the bed, sprang from the bed to her back, landing with nearly enough force to knock her off balance. She tottered for a moment and almost fell forward into the bedside lamp.

Aristophanes hissed and spat and scrambled for purchase on her back.

Fortunately, she kept her feet under her. She spun around and shook herself, frantically attempting to throw him off before he could do any damage.

His claws were hooked in her clothes. Although she was wearing both a blouse and a sweater, she felt a couple of his razor-tipped nails puncturing her skin— hot little points of pain. He wouldn't let go.

She drew her shoulders up and tucked her head down, pulling her chin in tight against her chest, protecting her neck as best she could. She swung one fist up behind her back, struck only air, tried again, and hit the cat with a blow that was too weak to have done any harm.

Nevertheless, Aristophanes squealed with rage and snapped at her neck. He was foiled by her hunched shoulders and by her thick hair, which got in his mouth and gagged him.

She had never wanted anything half so much as she wanted to kill the little bastard. He was no longer the familiar pet she had loved; he was a strange and hateful beast, and she harbored no ghost of affection for him.

She wished she could use the gun she was clutching in her right hand, but there was no way she could shoot him without shooting herself, too.

She struck at him repeatedly with her left hand, her arthritic shoulder protesting sharply, painfully when she twisted her arm up and backwards at such an unnatural angle.

At least for a moment, the cat abandoned its relentless but thus far ineffective attack on her neck. It slashed its claws across her flailing fist, slicing open the skin on her knuckles.

Her fingers were instantly slick with blood. They stung so badly that her eyes started to water.

Either the sight or the odor of the blood encouraged the cat. It shrieked with savage glee.

Grace began to think the unthinkable—that she was going to lose this fight.

No!

She struggled against the grip of fear that threatened to incapacitate her, tried to clear her panic-befuddled mind, and suddenly had an idea that she thought might save her life. She stumbled toward the nearest stretch of open wall, to the left of the dresser.

The cat clung tenaciously to her back, insistently pressing its snout against the base of her skull, hissing and snarling. It was determined to force its way to her sheltered neck and rip open her jugular vein.

When Grace reached the wall, she turned her back to it, then fell against it with all her weight, slamming the cat into the plaster behind her, pinning it hard between her body and the wall, hoping to break its spine. The jolt brought a flash of pain through her shoulders and drove the animal's claws deeper into her back muscles. The cat's scream was nearly shrill enough to shatter fine crystal, and it sounded almost like the wail of a human infant. But its grip on her didn't weaken. Grace pushed away from the wall, then slammed into it a second time, and the cat wailed as before, but still held fast. She thrust herself off the wall, intending to make a third attempt to crush her adversary, but before she could fall back on him, the cat let go of her. He dropped to the floor, rolled, sprang to his feet, and scurried away from her, favoring his right foreleg.

Good. She had hurt him.

She sagged against the wall, raised the .22 pistol that was still in her right hand, and squeezed the trigger.

Nothing.

She had forgotten to switch off the safeties.

The cat hurried through the open door and disappeared into the upstairs hall.

Grace went to the door, closed it, leaned wearily against it. Gasping.

Her left hand was scratched and bleeding, and her back bore half a dozen claw punctures, but she had won the first round. The cat was limping; he was injured, perhaps as badly as she was, and *he* was the one who had retreated.

No celebration, though. Not yet.

Not until she had gotten out of the house alive. And not until she was certain that Carol was safe, too.

After the unsettling telephone conversation he'd had with the receptionist at Maugham & Crichton, Paul didn't know what the hell to do.

He couldn't write. That was for sure. He couldn't get his mind off Carol long enough to advance the plot of his novel by so much as even one sentence.

He wanted to call Lincoln Werth, at police headquarters, and arrange to have a sheriff's deputy waiting at the cabin when Carol and Jane arrived up there. He wanted them brought home. But he could imagine the conversation he would have with Detective Werth, and the thought of it daunted him:

"You want a deputy to meet them at the cabin?"

"That's right."

"Why?"

"I think my wife's in danger."

"What kind of danger?"

"I think the girl, Jane Doe, might be violent. Maybe even homicidal."

"Why do you think that?"

"Because under hypnosis she claimed to be Millie Parker."

"Who's that?"

"Millie Parker once tried to kill her mother."

"She did? When was that?"

"Back in 1905."

"Then she'd be a little old lady today, for Christ's sake. The kid's only fourteen or fifteen."

"You don't understand. Millie Parker's been dead for about seventy-six years and—"

"Wait a minute, wait a minute! What the hell are you saying? That your wife might be murdered by some kid who's been dead for most of the century?"

"No. Of course not."

"Then what do you mean?"

"I . . . don't know."

Werth would think that he had been out boozing all night, or that he had started the morning with a couple of joints of good grass.

Besides, it wasn't fair to Jane to accuse her publicly of being a potential killer. Perhaps Carol was right. Maybe the kid was just a victim. Except for what she said under hypnosis, she certainly *seemed* to be incapable of violence.

On the other hand, of all the people she could have claimed to be, why had she said that she was Millicent Parker, the would-be murderess? Where had she heard that name before. Didn't the use of it indicate latent hostility?

Paul swiveled his typing chair away from the desk and stared out the window at the gray sky. The wind was picking up by the minute. The clouds were racing westward across the sky, as if they were enormous, swift, dark ships with billowing sails the color of thunderstorms.

BLADE, BLOOD, DEATH, TOMB, KILL, CAROL.

I've got to go to the cabin, he thought with sudden decisiveness, and he got to his feet.

Maybe he was overreacting to this Millicent Parker business, but he couldn't just sit here, wondering. . . .

He went into the master bedroom to throw some things into a suitcase. After only a brief hesitation, he decided to pack his .38 revolver.

The girl said, "How much farther to the cabin?"

"Another twenty minutes," Carol said. "The whole drive usually takes just about two hours and fifteen minutes, and we're pretty much on schedule."

The mountains were cool and green. Some trees had already been touched by the artful hand of autumn, and most—all but the evergreens—would change the color of their leaves during the next few weeks. Today, however, the predominant shade was still green, with a smattering of gold here and there, an occasional touch of red. The edge of the forest—wherever the meadow or the roadway met the trees—was decorated with a few end-of-the-season wildflowers, blue and white and purple.

"It's beautiful up here," Jane said as they followed the two-lane county road around a curve. The right-hand bank, which sloped down to the macadam, was covered with vividly green clusters of rhododendron shrubs.

"I love the Pennsylvania mountains," Carol said. She felt more relaxed now than she had in weeks. "It's so peaceful here. Wait till you've been at the cabin a day or two. You'll forget the rest of the world exists."

They came out of the curve onto an ascending straightaway, where the interlocking branches of the trees formed a tunnel over portions of the lane. At those points where the trees parted sufficiently to provide a glimpse of the sky, there was nothing to be seen but massive, gray-black clouds clotted together in surging, ugly, threatening formations.

"I sure hope it doesn't rain and spoil our first day here," Jane said.

"Rain won't spoil anything," Carol assured her. "If we're forced to stay inside, we'll just throw a whole bunch of logs in the big stone fireplace and roast some hot dogs *in*doors. And we have a closetful of games to help us pass rainy days. Monopoly, Scrabble, Clue, Risk, Battleship, and at least a dozen others. I think we'll be able to avoid cabin fever."

"It's going to be *fun*," Jane said enthusiastically.

The canopy of trees parted overhead, and the September sky churned darkly.

ELEVEN

◆

Grace sat on the edge of the bed, holding the .22 pistol, considering her options. She didn't have many.

In fact, the more she thought about it, the more it seemed to her that the cat had a better chance of winning this duel than she did.

If she attempted to leave the house by way of the bedroom window, she would surely break a leg and probably her neck as well. If she had been only twenty years younger, she might have tried it. But at seventy, with her swollen joints and brittle bones, jumping from a second-floor window onto a concrete patio could only end in misery. Anyway, the point wasn't just to get out of the house, but to get out in one piece, so she could make it across town to Carol's and Paul's place.

She could open the window and start screaming for help. But she was afraid that Aristophanes—or the thing using Aristophanes's body—would attack anyone who showed up and tried to assist her, and she didn't want a neighbor's death on her conscience.

This was her battle. No one else's. She would have to fight it alone.

She considered all the routes by which she might possibly leave the house once she had reached the bottom floor—if she reached the bottom floor—but no particular route seemed less dangerous than any other. The cat could be anywhere. Everywhere. The bedroom was the only safe place in the house. If she ventured out of this sanctuary, the cat would be waiting for her and would attack her, regardless of whether she tried to exit the house by the front door, the kitchen door, or one of the ground-floor windows. It would be crouched in one shadow or another, perhaps perched atop a bookcase or cupboard or hutch, tensed and ready to launch itself down onto her startled, upturned face.

She had the gun, of course. But the cat, stealthy by nature, would always have the advantage of surprise. If it got just a two- or three-second lead on her, if she was only that little bit slower to react than was the cat, it would have ample time to fasten onto her face, tear open her throat, or gouge her eyes out with its quick, stiletto claws.

Strangely, though she had accepted the doctrine of reincarnation, though she now knew beyond doubt that there was some kind of life after death, she nevertheless feared dying. The certainty of eternal life in no way diminished the value of *this* life. Indeed, now that she could discern godlike machinery just below the visible surface of the world, her life seemed to have more meaning and purpose than ever before.

She didn't want to die.

However, although the odds of her leaving the house alive were, at best, only fifty-fifty, she couldn't stay in the bedroom indefinitely. She had no water, no food. Besides, if she didn't get out of here in the next few minutes, she might be too late to be of any help to Carol.

If Carol is killed simply because I lack the courage to face that damned cat, she thought, then I might as well be dead anyway.

She switched off the two safeties on the pistol.

She got up and went to the door.

For nearly a minute she stood with one ear pressed to the door, listening for scratching noises or other indications that Aristophanes was nearby. She heard nothing.

Holding the pistol in her right hand, she used her bloody, claw-torn left hand to turn the knob. She opened the door with the utmost caution, half an inch at a time, expecting the cat to dart through the opening the instant it was wide enough to admit him. But he didn't.

Finally, reluctantly, she poked her head out into the hall. Looked left. Right.

The cat wasn't anywhere in sight.

She stepped into the hall and paused, afraid to move away from the bedroom door.

Go! she told herself angrily. Move your ass, Gracie!

She took a step toward the head of the stairs. Then another step. Trying to be quiet.

The stairs appeared to be a mile away.

She looked behind her.

Still no Aristophanes.

Another step.

This was going to be the longest walk she had ever taken.

Paul latched his suitcase, picked it up, turned away from the bed—and jumped, startled, when the entire house shook as if a wrecker's ball had struck the side of it.

THUNK!

He looked up at the ceiling.

THUNK! THUNK! THUNK!

During the past five days there had been no hammering to disturb the peace. He hadn't entirely forgotten about it, of course; he still occasionally wondered where that mysterious sound had come from. For the most part, however, he had put it out of his mind; there had been other things to worry about. But now—

THUNK! THUNK! THUNK!

The nerve-fraying noise reverberated in the windows and bounced off the walls. It seemed to vibrate in Paul's teeth and bones, too.

THUNK!

After spending days trying to identify the source of that sound, understanding came to him unexpectedly, in a flash. *It was an ax.* It was not a hammering, which was how he had been thinking of it. No. There was a sharp edge to it, a brittle, cracking quality at the end of each blow. It was a *chopping* sound.

THUNK!

Being able to identify the noise did absolutely nothing to help him understand where it was coming from. So it was an ax instead of a hammer. So what? He still couldn't make sense of it. Why were the blows shaking the entire house? It would have to be the mythical Paul Bunyan's ax to have such a tremendous impact. And regardless of whether it was a hammer or an ax or even, for Christ's sake, a *salami,* how could the sound of it issue from thin air?

Suddenly, inexplicably, he thought of the meat cleaver that Louise Parker had buried in the throat of her maniacal daughter back in 1905. He thought about the freakish lightning strikes at Alfred O'Brian's office; the strange intruder he had seen on the rear lawn during the thunderstorm that evening; the Scrabble game two nights ago (BLADE, BLOOD, DEATH, TOMB, KILL, CAROL); Grace's two prophetic dreams. And he knew beyond doubt—without understanding *how* he knew—that the sound of the ax was the thread that sewed together all these recent extraordinary events. Intuitively, he knew that an ax would be the instrument by which Carol's life would be endangered. He didn't know how. He didn't know why. But he *knew*.

THUNK! THUNK!

A painting popped off its wall hook and clattered to the floor.

The river of blood in Paul's veins turned winter-cold.

He had to get to the cabin. Fast.

He started toward the bedroom door, and it slammed shut in front of him. No one had touched it. There had been no sudden draft that might have moved it. One moment the door was standing wide open, and the next instant it was flung shut as if it had been shoved hard by an invisible hand.

Out of the corner of his eye, Paul saw something move. Heart banging, breath trapped in his constricted throat, he twisted around toward the movement and instinctively raised his suitcase to partially shield himself.

One of the two heavy, mirrored closet doors was sliding open. He expected someone to step out of the closet, but when the door was all the way open, he could see nothing in there except clothes on hangers. Then it slid shut, and the other door slid open. Then both of them started sliding at the same time, one crossing behind the other, back and forth, back and forth on their silent plastic wheels.

THUNK! THUNK!

A lamp crashed over on one of the nightstands.

Another painting fell off the wall.

THUNK!

On the dresser, two porcelain figurines—a ballerina and her male dancing partner—began to circle one another, almost as if they had come to life and were performing for Paul. They moved slowly at first, then faster, faster, until they were swept into the air and tossed halfway across the room and dashed to the floor.

The cabin was constructed of logs and was nestled in the cool shadows beneath the trees. It had a long, covered, screened porch out front and an excellent view of the lake.

It was one of ninety vacation cabins tucked into the scenic mountain valley, each on an acre or half-acre of its own. They were all built along the south shore of the lake and were reachable only by way of a private, gated, gravel-surfaced road that curved around the water. Some of the cabins were made of logs, like the one Paul and Carol had bought, but there were also white clapboard New England models, modern A-frames, and a few that resembled small Swiss chalets.

At the end of her own graveled drive, which branched off the community road, Carol parked the car near the front door of the cabin. She and Jane got out and stood for a moment in companionable silence, listening to the stillness, breathing the wonderfully fresh air.

"It's lovely," Jane said at last.

"Isn't it, though?"

"So quiet."

"It isn't always. Not when most of the cabins are in use. But right now there's probably no one here except Peg and Vince Gervis."

"Who're they?" Jane asked.

"The caretakers. The homeowner's association pays their salaries. They live year-round in the last cabin, out at the end of the lake. In the off season, they run a couple of inspection tours every day, just keeping a lookout for fire and vandals and whatnot. Nice people."

Above the distant north shore of the lake, lightning blazed across the malevolent sky. A clap of thunder fell from the clouds and rolled across the water.

"We better get the suitcases and the food out of the car before we have to unload everything in the rain," Carol said.

Grace expected to be attacked on the stairs, for that was where she would find it most difficult to defend herself. If the cat frightened her and caused her to lose her balance, she might fall. If she fell, she would probably break a leg or a hip, and while she was temporarily stunned by the shock and pain of the fall, the cat would be all over her, tearing, biting. Therefore, she descended the stairs sideways, with her back against the wall, so she could look both ahead and behind.

But Aristophanes did not show up. Grace reached the downstairs hall without incident.

She looked both ways along the hall.

To reach the front door, she had to pass the open door of the study and the archway that led to the living room. The cat could bolt out of either place as she was passing by and could leap for her face before she would have time to spot him, aim the pistol, and pull the trigger.

To reach the other door, the one at the back of the house, she had to go right, along the hallway, past the open dining room door, into the kitchen. That route didn't look any less dangerous.

The rock and the hard place, she thought unhappily. The devil and the deep blue sea.

Then she remembered that her car keys were in the kitchen, hanging on the pegboard beside the back door, and that settled it. She would have to leave through the kitchen.

She moved cautiously along the hall until she came to a wall mirror, beneath which stood a narrow, decorative table. There were two tall vases on the table, bracketing the mirror. She picked up one of them in her injured left hand and sidled toward the open dining room door.

She paused before reaching the doorway, listened.

Silence.

She leaned forward and risked her eyes by peering into the dining room. She could not see any sign of the cat. That didn't mean it wasn't in there. The drapes were half drawn, and the day was gloomy; there were lots of shadows, many places where a cat could hide.

For the purpose of creating a diversion in the event that Aristophanes *was* in one of those shadows, Grace pitched the vase inside. As it landed with a loud crash, she stepped across the threshold just far enough to grasp the doorknob, then pulled the door shut as she backed quickly into the hallway again. Now, if the cat was in there, it would bloody well have to *stay* in there.

She heard no noise from the dining room, which probably meant she hadn't managed to trap the elusive beast. If he'd been in there, he would have been squealing with rage and scratching at the inside of the closed door by now. Most likely, she had only wasted time and energy with her little trick. But at least there was now one downstairs room to which she could turn her back with impunity.

Repeatedly glancing left and right, forward and back, she crept to the kitchen door, hesitated, then stepped through it, the gun thrust out in front of her. She looked the room over slowly, thoroughly, before venturing farther. The small table and chairs. The humming refrigerator. The dangling, cat-chewed phone cord. The gleaming chrome fixtures on the oven. The double sinks. The white countertops. The small countertop wine rack. The cookie jar and the breadbox lined up beside the wine.

Nothing moved.

The refrigerator motor shut off, and the subsequent quiet was deep, unbroken.

Okay, she thought. Grit your teeth and move, Gracie.

She walked silently across the room, her eyes sweeping every niche, every nook: the opening under the built-in writing desk, the narrow space beside the refrigerator, the blind spot beyond the end of one row of cabinets. No cat.

Maybe I hurt him worse than I thought I did, she told herself hopefully. Maybe I didn't just lame the bastard. Maybe he crawled away and died.

She reached the back door.

She didn't dare breathe for fear her own breathing would mask whatever furtive sounds the cat might make.

A ring of keys, including those for the car, hung on a small oval pegboard beside the door. She slipped it off the hook.

She reached for the doorknob.

The cat hissed.

Grace cried out involuntarily and swung her head to the right, in the direction of the sound.

She was standing at one end of the long row of cabinets. At the far end, the wine rack and the breadbox and the cookie jar were lined up side by side; she had seen them from a front-on angle when she had first come into the room. Now she had a side view. From this angle she saw something she couldn't have seen from in front: The cookie jar and breadbox, which usually rested snug against the wall behind the counter, had been moved out a few inches. The cat had squeezed in behind those two objects, muscling them slowly out of its way. It had crouched in that hiding place, its butt against the wine rack, facing out toward the kitchen door. It was approximately twelve feet from her, and then it wasn't even that far away because it launched itself across the counter, hissing.

The confrontation was over in a few seconds, but during those seconds, time seemed to slow to a crawl, and Grace felt as if she were trapped in a slow-motion film. She stumbled backwards, away from the counter and the cat, but she didn't get far before she collided with a wall; as she moved, she raised the gun and fired two rounds in quick succession. The cookie jar exploded, and wood chips flew off one of the cabinet doors. But the cat kept coming, coming, in slow-motion strides across the slippery tile countertop, its mouth gaping and its fangs bared. She realized that hitting such a small, quick target was not easy, even at such short range as this. She fired again, but she knew the gun was wavering in her hand, and she wasn't surprised when she heard the bullet ricochet—making a high, piercing *eeeee*—off something wide of the mark. To her terror-heightened perceptions, the echoes of the ricochet continued to infinity: *eeeee, eeeee, eeeee, eeeee, eeeee. . . .* Then the cat reached the end of the counter and leapt into the air, and Grace fired again. This time she hit the mark. The cat yelped. The bullet had sufficient impact to deflect the animal only an instant before it would have landed, scratching and biting, on her face. It was pitched back and to the left as if it were a bundle of rags. It slammed into the kitchen door and dropped stonelike to the floor, where it lay silent and motionless.

Paul couldn't decide what the poltergeist intended to accomplish by its impressive displays of power. He didn't know whether or not he had anything to fear from it. Was it trying to delay him, trying to keep him here until it was too late for him to help Carol? Or perhaps it was urging him on, trying its best to convince him that he must go to the cabin immediately.

Still holding the suitcase in one hand, he approached the bedroom door that had been flung shut by the unseen presence. As he reached for the knob, the door began to rattle in its frame—gently at first, then fiercely.

Thunk . . . thunk . . . thunk . . . THUNK!

He jerked his hand back, unsure what he ought to do.

THUNK!

The sound of the ax was coming from the door now, not from overhead, as it had been. Although the solid-core, raised-panel, fir door was a formidable barrier rather than just a flimsy Masonite model, it shook violently and then cracked down the middle as if it were constructed of balsa wood.

Paul backed away from it.

Another crack appeared, parallel to the first, and chips of wood flew into the room.

Sliding closet doors and flying porcelain figurines might be the work of a poltergeist, but this was something else again. Surely no spirit could chop apart a heavy door like this. There *had* to be someone swinging a very real ax against the other side.

Paul felt defenseless. He scanned the room for makeshift weapons, but he saw nothing useful.

The .38 revolver was in the suitcase. He wouldn't be able to get to it in time to defend himself with it, and he wished fervently that he had kept the gun in his hand.

THUNKTHUNKTHUNKTHUNK!

The bedroom door exploded inward in half a dozen large pieces and countless smaller chunks and scraps.

He threw one arm over his face to protect his eyes. Wood rained down on all sides of him.

When he lowered his arm, he saw there was no one standing beyond the doorway, no man with an ax. The chopper-of-doors was, after all, the unseen presence.

THUNK!

Paul stepped over a shattered section of the door and went out into the hallway

The fuse box was in the kitchen pantry. Carol engaged all the breaker switches, and the lights came on.

There was no telephone. That was virtually the only modern convenience the cabin lacked.

"Do you think it's chilly in here?" Carol asked.

"A little."

"We have a bottled-gas furnace, but unless it's *really* cold, the fireplace is nicer. Let's bring in some firewood."

"You mean we've got to cut down a tree?"

Carol laughed. "That won't be necessary. Come see."

She led the girl outside, to the rear of the cabin, where an open porch ended in steps leading down to a short rear yard. The yard met the edge of a small meadow where the grass was knee-deep, and the meadow climbed up toward a wall of trees fifty yards away.

When Carol saw that familiar landscape, she stopped, surprised, remembering the dream that had spoiled her sleep several nights last week. In the nightmare, she had been running through one house, then through another house, then across a mountain meadow, while something silvery flickered in the darkness behind her. At the time, she had not realized that the meadow in the dream was *this* meadow.

"Something wrong?" Jane asked.

"Huh? Oh. No. Let's get that firewood."

She led the girl down the porch steps and to the left, to where a woodshed was attached to the southwest corner of the cabin.

Thunder rumbled in the distance. The rain hadn't begun to fall yet.

Carol keyed open the heavy-duty padlock on the woodshed, took it off the hasp, and slipped it in her jacket pocket. There would be no need to replace it until they were ready to return to Harrisburg, nine or ten days from now.

The woodshed door creaked open on unoiled hinges. Inside, Carol tugged on the chain-pull light, and a bare hundred-watt bulb revealed stacks of dry cordwood being protected from inclement weather.

A scuttle for carrying firewood hung from a ceiling hook. Carol got it down and handed it to the girl. "If you fill it up four or five times, we'll have more than enough wood to last us until tomorrow morning."

By the time Jane returned from taking the first scuttle-load into the cabin, Carol was at the chopping block, using an ax to split a short log into four sticks.

"What're you doing?" the girl asked, stopping well out of the way and staring warily at the ax.

"When I build a fire," Carol said, "I put kindling on the bottom, a layer of these splits on top of that, and then the full logs to crown it off. It never fails to burn well that way. See? I'm a regular Daniel Boone."

The girl scowled. "That ax looks awful sharp."

"Has to be."

"Are you sure it's safe?"

"I've done it lots of times before, here and at home," Carol said. "I'm an expert. Don't worry, honey. I'm not going to accidentally amputate my toes."

She picked up another short log and started to split it into quarters.

Jane went to the woodshed, giving the chopping block a wide berth. When she returned, carrying her second scuttle-load to the house, she repeatedly glanced over her shoulder, frowning.

Carol began quartering another log.

THUNK!

Carrying his suitcase, Paul walked down the second-floor hall to the stairway, and the poltergeist went with him. On both sides, doors opened and slammed shut, opened and slammed shut, again and again, all by themselves and with such tremendous force that it sounded as if he were walking through a murderous barrage of cannon fire.

As he descended the stairs, the chandelier at the top of the well began describing wide circles on the end of its chain, stirred by a breeze that Paul could not feel or moved by a hand that had no substance.

On the first floor, paintings were flung off walls as he passed by. Chairs toppled over. The living room sofa rocked wildly on its four graceful wooden legs. In the kitchen, the overhead utensil rack shook; pots and pans and ladles banged against one another.

By the time he reached the Pontiac in the garage, he knew he didn't have to bother taking the entire suitcase to the mountains. He hadn't wanted to go charging into the cabin with just a gun and the clothes on his back, for if nothing had been wrong, he would have looked like an idiot, and he would have done Jane a grave injustice. But now, because of the call from Polly at Maugham & Crichton, and because of the astounding display put on by the poltergeist, he knew that *everything* was wrong; there was no chance whatsoever that he would reach the cabin only to discover that all was peaceful. He would be walking into a nightmare of one kind or another. No doubt about it. So he opened the suitcase on the garage floor beside the car, took out the loaded revolver, and left the rest of his stuff behind.

As he was backing out of the driveway, he saw Grace Mitowski's blue Ford turn the corner, too fast. It angled toward the curb in front of the house, scraping its sidewalls so badly that blue-white smoke rose from them.

Grace was out of the car the instant it stopped. She rushed to the Pontiac, moving faster than Paul had seen her move in years. She pulled open the front, passenger-side door and leaned in. Her hair was in complete disarray. Her face was eggshell white and spattered with blood.

"Good God, Grace, what's happened to you?"

"Where's Carol?"

"She went to the cabin."

"Already?"

"This morning."

"Damn? Exactly when?"

"Three hours ago."

Grace's eyes contained a haunted expression. "The girl went with her?"

"Yes."

She closed her eyes, and Paul could see she was on the edge of panic, trying to deal with it and calm herself. She opened her eyes and said, "We've got to go after them."

"That's where I'm headed."

He saw her eyes widen as she noticed the revolver lying on the car seat beside him, the muzzle pointed forward, toward the dashboard.

She raised her eyes from the gun to his face. "You know what's happening?" she asked, surprised.

"Not really," he said, putting the gun in the glove compartment. "All I know for sure is that Carol's in trouble. Damned serious trouble."

"It's not just Carol we've got to worry about," Grace said. "It's both of them."

"Both? The girl, you mean? But I think the girl's the one who's going to—"

"Yes," Grace said. "She's going to try to kill Carol. But she might be the one who ends up dead. Like before."

She got in the car and pulled the door shut.

"Like before?" Paul said. "I don't—" He saw her blood-crusted hand. "That needs medical attention."

"There's no time."

"What the hell's happening?" he demanded, his fear for Carol briefly giving way to frustration. "I know something strange is going on, but I don't know what in Christ's name it is."

"I do," she said. "I know. In fact I know a lot more than maybe I want to know."

"If you've got anything that makes sense, anything concrete," he said, "we should call the cops. They can put in a call to the sheriff's department up there and get help sent out to the cabin real fast, faster than we can get there."

"What I've got, my information, is harder than concrete, so far as I'm concerned," Grace said. "But the police wouldn't see it the same way I do. They'd say I was just a senile old fool. They'd want to lock me up in a nice safe place for my own good. At best, they'd laugh at me."

He thought about the poltergeist—the sound of the ax, the splintering door, the airborne ceramic figurines, the toppling chairs—and he said, "Yeah. I know exactly what you mean."

"We'll have to handle this ourselves," Grace said. "Let's get rolling. I can tell you everything I know on the way. Each minute we waste, I just get sicker and sicker, thinking about what might be happening in the mountains."

Paul backed the car into the street and drove away from the house, heading for the nearest freeway entrance. When he was on the open highway, he floored the accelerator, and the car rocketed ahead.

"How long does it usually take to get there?" Grace asked.

"About two hours and fifteen minutes."

"Too long."

"We'll do better than that."

The speedometer needle touched eighty.

TWELVE

◆

They had brought a lot of food in cardboard cartons and ice chests. They transferred all of those items to the cupboards and refrigerator, agreeing to forgo lunch altogether in order to indulge themselves guiltlessly in a glutton's dinner.

"All right," Carol said, producing a list from one of the kitchen drawers, "here's what we need to do to make this place livable." She read from the list: "Remove plastic dropcloths from furniture; dust everything; scrub the kitchen sink; clean the bathroom; and put sheets and blankets on the beds."

"You call this a *vacation?*" Jane asked.

"What's wrong? Doesn't that sound like a fun agenda to you?"

"Thrilling."

"Well, the cabin's not enormous. The two of us will go through the list of chores in an hour or an hour and a half."

They had barely started when they were interrupted by a knock at the door. It was Vince Gervis, the colony's caretaker. He was a big, barrel-chested man with enormous shoulders, enormous biceps, enormous hands, and a smile to match the rest of him.

"Just makin' my rounds," he said. "Saw your car. Thought I'd say hello." Carol introduced him to Jane and said she was a niece (a convenient white lie), and there was some polite chitchat, and then Gervis said, "Dr. Tracy, where's the *other* Dr. Tracy? I'd like to give him my best, too."

"Oh, he isn't with us right now," Carol said. "He's coming up on Sunday, after he finishes some important work he couldn't just put aside."

Gervis frowned.

Carol said, "Is something wrong?"

"Well . . . me and the missus was plannin' to go into town to do some shoppin', maybe see a movie, eat a restaurant meal. It's what we generally do on Friday afternoons, you see. But there isn't another soul up here besides you and Jane. Will be tomorrow, bein' as it's a Saturday, and seein' as if the weather don't get too bad so that everybody stays to home. But there's no one else so far today except you."

"Don't worry about us," Carol said. "We'll be fine. You and Peg go on into town like you planned."

"Well . . . I'm not sure I like the idea of you two ladies out here all by your lonesome, twenty miles from other folks. No sir, I don't like it much."

"Nobody's going to bother us, Vince. The road's gated; you can't even get in without a key card."

"Anybody can *walk* in if he's willin' to go overland just a little ways."

Carol required several minutes and a lot of words to reassure him, but at last he decided that he and his wife would keep to their usual Friday schedule.

Shortly after Vince left, the rains came. The soft roar of a hundred million droplets striking a hundred million rustling leaves was soothing to Carol.

But Jane found the noise somewhat unpleasant. "I don't know why," she said, "but the sound makes me think of fire. Hissing . . . just like a lot of flames eating up everything in sight. Sizzle, sizzle, sizzle . . . "

The rain forced Paul to slow down to sixty, which was still too fast for highway conditions, but the situation called for the taking of some risks.

The windshield wipers thumped metronomically, and the tires sang softly on the wet macadam.

The day was dark and growing darker. It looked more like twilight than like midday. The wind blew obscuring curtains of rain across the treacherously wet pavement, and the gray-brown road spray flung up by other traffic hung in the air, a thick and dirty mist.

It seemed almost as if the Pontiac were a tiny vessel sailing through the deep currents of a vast, cold sea, the only pocket of warmth and light within a million miles.

Grace said, "You probably won't believe what I've got to tell you, and that would be understandable."

"After what's happened to me today," Paul said, "I'm ready to believe anything."

And maybe *that's* what the poltergeist meant to do, he thought. Maybe it meant to prepare me for whatever story Grace has to tell. In fact, if I hadn't been delayed by the poltergeist, I would have left the house before Grace arrived.

"I'll keep it as simple and straightforward as I can," Grace said. "But it's not a simple and straightforward matter." She cradled her torn left hand in her right hand; the bleeding had stopped, and the cuts were all crusty, clotted. "It starts in 1865, in Shippensburg. The family was named Havenswood."

Paul glanced at her, startled by the name.

She looked straight ahead, at the rain-sodden land through which they were rushing. "The mother was Willa Havenswood, and the daughter's name was Laura. Those two didn't get along well. Not well at all. The fault was on both sides, and the reasons for their constant bickering aren't really important here. What's important is that one day in the spring of 1865, Willa sent Laura into the cellar to do some spring cleaning, even though she knew perfectly well that the girl was deathly afraid of the cellar. It was punishment, you see. And while Laura was down there in the cellar, a fire broke out upstairs. She was trapped and burned to death. She must have died blaming her mother for putting her in that trap in the first place. Maybe she even blamed Willa for starting the fire—which she didn't. It was accidentally started by Rachael Adams, Laura's aunt. It's even possible that Laura wondered if her mother had started the fire *on purpose,* just to get rid of her. The child had emotional problems; she was capable of melodramatic notions of that sort. The mother had emotional problems, too; she was capable of *inspiring* paranoia, for sure. Anyway, Laura died a gruesome death, and we can be pretty certain that her last thought was an ardent wish for revenge. There was no way she could have known that *her mother perished in that fire, too!*"

So that's why the Havenswood identity didn't check out when Carol put the police on to it, Paul thought. They'd have had to go all the way back to the 1800s in order to find the Havenswood family. County records for that period probably don't even exist any more.

A slow-moving truck appeared out of the mists ahead, and Paul passed it. For a moment the filthy spray from the truck's big tires drummed on the side of the Pontiac, and the noise was too loud for Grace to speak above it.

When they had passed the truck, she said, "Since 1865, Laura has been pursuing revenge through at least two and probably three other lives. Reincarnation, Paul. Can you believe in that? Can you believe that in 1943, Laura Havenswood was a fifteen-year-old girl named Linda Bektermannn and that the night before her sixteenth birthday she tried to kill her mother, who was Willa Havenswood reincarnated? It's a true case. Linda Bektermann went berserk and tried to ax her mother to death, but her mother turned the tables and killed the girl instead. *Laura didn't get her revenge.* And can you believe that Willa is now alive again and that she's our Carol this time? And that Laura is alive again, too?"

"Jane?"

"Yes."

Together, Carol and Jane cleaned the cabin in an hour and fifteen minutes. Carol was delighted to see that the girl was an industrious worker who took great pleasure in doing even a menial job well.

When they were finished, they poured two glasses of Pepsi to reward themselves, and they sat in the two big easy chairs that faced the mammoth fireplace.

"It's too early to start cooking dinner," Jane said. "And it's too wet out there to go for a walk, so what game do you want to play?"

"Anything that looks good to you is fine with me. You can look over all the stuff in our game closet and take your pick. But first, I think we really should get the therapy session out of the way."

"Are we going to keep that up even on vacation?" the girl asked. She was clearly uneasy about it, though she had not been noticeably uneasy before, even on the occasion of the first session, the day before yesterday.

"Of course we've got to keep on with it," Carol said. "Now that we've made a start, it's best to continue working at it, pushing and probing a little bit every day."

"Well . . . all right."

"Good. Let's turn these chairs around to face each other."

The fire flickered off to one side, creating dancing shadows on the hearth.

Outside, the rain rattled ceaselessly through the trees and pattered on the roof, and Carol realized that it *did* sound like even more fire, as Jane had said, so that they seemed to be totally surrounded by the hiss and crackle of flames.

She needed only a few seconds to put Jane into a trance this time. But as had happened during the first session, the girl needed almost two minutes to regress to a period at which memories existed for her. This time the long silence didn't disturb Carol as it had done before.

When the girl spoke at last, she used the Laura voice. "Mama? Is that you? Is that you, Mama?"

"Laura?"

The girl's eyes were squeezed shut. Her voice was tight, tense. "Is that you? Is it you, Mama? Is it?"

"Relax," Carol said.

Instead of relaxing, the girl became visibly more tense. She hunched her shoulders, fisted her hands in her lap. Lines of strain appeared in her forehead and at the corners of her mouth. She leaned away from the back of her chair, toward Carol.

"I want you to answer some questions," Carol said. "But you must be calm and relaxed first. Now, you will do exactly as I say. You will unclench your fists. You will—"

"I won't!"

The girl's eyes popped open. She leapt up out of her chair and stood before Carol, quivering.

"Sit down, honey."

"I won't do what you say! I'm sick of doing what you tell me to do, sick of your punishments."

"Sit down," Carol said softly but forcefully.

The girl glared at her. "You did it to me," she said in the Laura voice. "You put me down there in that awful place."

Carol hesitated, then decided to flow with it. "What place do you mean?"

"You *know*," the girl said accusingly. "I *hate* you."

"Where is this awful place you spoke of?" Carol persisted.

"The cellar."

"What's so awful about the cellar?"

Hatred seethed in the girl's eyes. Her lips were peeled back from her teeth in a feral snarl.

"Laura? Answer me. What's so awful about the cellar?"

The girl slapped her across the face.

The blow stunned Carol. It was sharp, painful, unexpected. For an instant she simply couldn't believe that she actually had been hit.

Then the girl hit her again. Backhanded.

And again. Harder than before.

Carol grabbed her adversary's slender wrists, but the girl wrenched loose. She kicked Carol in the shins, and when Carol cried out and sagged for an instant, the girl went for her throat. Carol fended her off, though not easily, and attempted to get up from the armchair. Jane pushed her down and fell on top of her. She felt the girl bite her shoulder, and suddenly her shock and confusion turned to fear. The chair tipped over, and they both rolled onto the floor, flailing.

The flat land through which they had been driving began to rise and form itself into gently rolling hills, but the mountains were still a long way off.

If there had been any change in the weather during the last half hour, it had been for the worse. Rain was falling harder than ever; the hard, fat pellets of water shattered like glass on the roadway, and the amorphous fragments bounced high. Paul kept the speedometer needle at eighty.

"Reincarnation," he said thoughtfully. "Just a few minutes ago, I told you that I could believe anything today, but that's wild. Reincarnation? Where in the devil did you come by this theory?"

As the windshield wipers continued to thump, and as the tires sang a shrill dirge on the rain-puddled pavement, Grace told him about the telephone calls from Leonard, the visit from the long-dead reporter, the prophetic dreams; she told him about the grim battle with Aristophanes. "I am Rachael Adams, Paul. That other life had been revealed to me so that I can stop this murderous cycle. Willa did not start the fire. *I* started it accidentally. There is no reason for the girl to seek revenge. It's all a mistake, a dark misunderstanding. If I can talk to the girl, Jane, while she's regressed to her Laura phase, I can persuade her of the truth. I know I can. I can stop all of this here, now, once and forever. Do you think I'm babbling? Senile? I don't believe I am. In fact, I *know* I'm not. And I suspect you've had some strange experiences recently that confirm what I'm telling you."

"You hit that one on the head, all right," he told her.

Nevertheless, reincarnation—being born again in a new body—it was a stunning, soul-shaking thing to accept. *There is no lasting death.* Yes, that was much harder to accept than the existence of poltergeists.

"Do you know about Millicent Parker?" he asked her.

"Never heard the name," Grace said.

The rain started falling even harder. He turned the windshield wipers up to their highest speed.

"In 1905," he told Grace, "Millie Parker attempted to kill her mother—on the night before her sixteenth birthday. Like the Linda Bektermann case, the mother ended up killing Millie, instead of the other way around. Purely self-defense. And here's what you might not realize: Under hypnosis, Jane claimed to be Laura, Millie, and then Linda Bektermann. But the names meant nothing to us."

"And again, in the Millicent Parker case," Grace said, "the girl's desire for revenge was frustrated. Yes. I knew there must be another life between Laura and Linda."

"But why this night-before-the-birthday thing that keeps cropping up?"

"Laura was looking forward to *her* sixteenth birthday with great eagerness," Grace-Rachael said. "It was going to be the best day of her life, she said. She had all sorts of plans for it—and for how her life would be changed after she attained that magical age. I think, somehow, she felt her mother's treatment of her would change once she was 'grown up.' But she died in the fire before her birthday."

"And in life after life, as her sixteenth birthday approaches, the fear of her mother and the hatred of her mother wells up from her subconscious."

Grace nodded. "From the subconscious of the girl she was in 1865, the girl—the identity—who is buried down at the bottom of Jane's psyche."

They rode in silence for a minute or two.

Paul's hands were sweaty on the steering wheel.

His mind spun as he tried to absorb the story she had told, and he had that old feeling of balancing on a tightrope high above a deep, deep, dark chasm.

Then he said, "But Carol isn't Jane's mother."

"You've forgotten something," Grace said.

"What?"

"Carol had a child out of wedlock when she was a teenager. I know she told you all about it. I'm giving away no secrets."

Paul's stomach quivered. He was cold all the way into the marrow of his bones. "My God. You mean . . . Jane is the child that Carol put up for adoption."

"I have no proof of it," Grace said. "But I bet that when the police spread their search nets wide enough, when they finally locate the girl's parents in some other state, we'll learn that she's adopted. And that Carol is her natural mother."

For what seemed like an eternity, they struggled on the floor by the hearth, grunting, twisting, the girl throwing punches, Carol trying to resist without hurting her. At last, when it became clear that Carol was unquestionably the stronger of the two and would eventually gain control of the situation, the girl shoved away from her, scrambled up, kicked her in the thigh, and ran out of the room, into the kitchen.

Carol was shocked and dazed both by the girl's unexpected violence and by the maniacal power of the blows. Her face stung, and she knew her cheeks were going to bruise. Her bitten shoulder was bleeding; a large, damp, red stain was spreading slowly down the front of her blouse.

She got up, swayed unsteadily for a moment. Then she went after the girl. "Honey, wait!"

In the distance, outside the house, Laura's voice rose in a sharp, shrill scream: "I *haaaaaate* you!"

Carol reached the kitchen, leaned against the refrigerator. The girl was gone. The back door was open.

The sound of the rain was very loud.

She hurried to the door and looked out at the rear lawn, at the small meadow, at the forest that crowded in at the edge of the meadow. The girl had disappeared.

"Jane! Laura!"

Millicent? She wondered. Linda? What on earth *should* I call her?

She crossed the porch and went down the steps into the yard, into the pelting, cold rain. She turned right, then left, not sure where to look first.

Then Jane appeared. The girl came out of the woodshed at the southwest corner of the cabin. She was carrying an ax.

" . . . *and Carol is her natural mother.*"

Grace's words echoed and reechoed in Paul's head.

For a moment he was incapable of speech.

He stared ahead, shocked, not really seeing the road, and he nearly ran up the back end of a sluggishly moving Buick. He jammed on his brakes. He and Grace were thrown forward, testing their seat belts. He slowed down until he could regain control of himself.

Finally, the words burst out of him like machine-gun fire: "But how in the hell did the kid find out who her real mother was, they don't give out that kind of information to children her age, how did she get here from whatever state she was living in, how did she track us down and make it all happen like this? Good Christ, she *did* step in front of Carol's car on purpose. It was a setup. The whole damned thing was a setup!"

"I don't know how she found her way to Carol," Grace said. "Maybe her parents knew who the child's natural mother was, and kept the name around in the family records, in case the girl ever wanted to know it when she grew up. Perhaps not. Perhaps anything. Maybe she was simply drawn to Carol by the same forces that tried to get to me through Aristophanes. That might explain why she appeared to be in a daze before she stepped in front of the car. But I don't really know. Maybe we'll *never* know.''

"Oh, shit,'' Paul said, and his voice wavered. "Oh, no, no. Goddamn!''

"What?''

"You know how Carol is on *that* day,'' he said shakily. "The day her baby was born, the baby she gave up. She's different from the way she is every other day of the year. Depressed, withdrawn. It's always such a bad day for her that the date's engraved on my memory.''

"On mine, too,'' Grace said.

"It's tomorrow,'' he said. "If Jane *is* Carol's child, she'll be sixteen tomorrow.''

"Yes.''

"And she'll try to kill Carol today.''

Sheets of dark rain rippled and flapped like wind-whipped canvas tents.

Carol stood on the soggy lawn, unable to move, numbed by fear, frozen by the cold rain.

Twenty feet away, the girl stood with the ax, gripping it in both hands. Her drenched hair hung straight to her shoulders, and her clothes were pasted to her. She appeared to be oblivious to the storm and the chilly air. Her eyes were owlish, as if she were high on amphetamine, and her face was distorted by rage.

"Laura?'' Carol said at last. "Listen to me. You will listen to me. You will drop the ax.''

"You stinking, rotten bitch,'' the girl said through tightly clenched teeth.

Lightning cracked open the sky, and the falling rain glittered for a moment in the stroboscopic flashes that came through from the other side of the heavens.

When the subsequent thunder rolled away and Carol could be heard, she said, "Laura, I want you to—''

"I hate you!'' the girl said. She took one step toward Carol.

"Stop this right now,'' Carol said, refusing to retreat. "You will be calm. You will relax.''

The girl took another step.

"*Drop the ax,*'' Carol insisted. "Honey, listen to me. You *will* listen to me. You are only in a trance. You are—''

"I'm going to get you this time, Mama. This time I'm not going to lose.''

"I'm not your mother,'' Carol said. "Laura, you are—''

"I'm going to cut your goddamn head off this time, you bitch!''

The voice had changed.

It wasn't Laura's now.

It belonged to Linda Bektermann, the third identity.

"I'm going to cut your goddamn head off and put it on the kitchen table with Daddy's.''

With a jolt, Carol recalled last week's nightmare. There had been a moment in the dream when she had stepped into the kitchen and had encountered two severed heads on the table, a man's and a woman's. But how could Jane know what had been in that nightmare?

Carol finally took a step backwards, then another. Although the rain was cold, she began to sweat.

"I'm only going to tell you one more time, Linda. You must put the ax down and—''

"I'm going to cut your head off and chop you into a thousand little pieces,'' the girl said.

And the voice now belonged to Jane.

It wasn't the voice of an identity heretofore only evident in a trance. This was *Jane's* voice. She had come out of the trance on her own power. She knew who she was. She knew who Carol was. And she *still* wanted to use the ax.

Carol edged toward the back porch steps.

The girl quickly circled in that direction, blocking access to the cabin. Then she started toward Carol, moving fast, grinning.

Carol turned and ran toward the meadow.

In spite of the pounding rain, which snapped with bulletlike power into the windshield, in spite of the dirty mist that hung over the road, in spite of the treacherously greasy pavement, Paul slowly pressed the accelerator all the way to the floor and swung the Pontiac into the passing lane.

"It's a mask," he said.

Grace said, "What do you mean?"

"The Jane Doe identity, the Linda Bektermann and Millie Parker identities—each of them was just a mask. A very real, very convincing mask. But a mask nonetheless. Behind the mask there was always the same face, the same person. Laura."

"And we've got to put an end to the masquerade once and for all," Grace said. "If I can just talk to her as her Aunt Rachael, I'll be able to stop this madness. I'm sure I will. She'll listen to me . . . to Rachael. That's who she was closest to. Closer than she was to her mother. I can make her understand that her mother, Willa, didn't intentionally or even accidentally start that fire back in 1865. At last she'll understand. She'll see that there's no justification for revenge. The cycle will come to an end."

"If we're in time," Paul said.

"If," Grace said.

Carol ran through the stinging rain and through the knee-high grass. She ran up the sloping meadow, her arms tucked in close to her side, legs pumping high, gasping for breath, each stride jarring her to the bones.

Ahead lay the forest, which seemed to be her only salvation. There were thousand of places to hide in the wilderness, countless trails on which she could lose the girl. After all, she was somewhat familiar with the land, but to the girl it was a strange place.

Halfway across the meadow, she risked a glance behind her. The girl was only fifteen feet away.

Lightning slashed through the bellies of the clouds, and the blade of the ax flashed once, twice, with a brilliant reflection of that icy electric glow.

Carol looked straight ahead once more and redoubled her efforts to reach the trees. The meadow was wet, spongy, and in some places slippery. She expected to fall or at least twist an ankle, but she reached the perimeter of the forest without trouble. She plunged in among the trees, among the purple and brown and black shadows, into the lush undergrowth, and she began to think there was a chance— maybe only a very small chance, but a chance nonetheless—that she would come out of this alive.

Hunching over the steering wheel, squinting at the rain-swept highway, Paul said, "I want one thing perfectly clear between us."

Grace said, "What's that?"

"Carol's my first concern."

"Of course."

"If we walk into the middle of a nasty situation at the cabin, I'll do whatever's necessary to protect Carol."

Grace glanced at the glove compartment. "You mean . . . the gun."

"Yes. If I have to, if there's no other way, I'll use it, Grace. I'll shoot the girl if there's no other choice."

"It's unlikely that we'll walk into the middle of a confrontation," Grace said. "Either it won't have begun yet—or it'll all be over with by the time we get there."

"I won't let her hurt Carol," he said grimly. "And if worse comes to worst, I don't want you trying to stop me."

"There are some things you should consider," Grace said.

"What?"

"First of all, it'll be just as tragic if Carol kills the girl. And that's the pattern, after all. Both Millie and Linda attacked their mothers, but *they* were the ones killed. What if that happens this time? What if Carol is forced to kill the girl in self-defense? You know she's never stopped feeling guilty about putting the baby up for adoption. She carries that on her shoulders sixteen years after the fact. So what will happen when she discovers she's killed her own daughter?"

"It'll destroy her," he said without hesitation.

"I think it very well might. And what'll it do to your relationship with Carol if *you* kill her daughter, even if you do it to save Carol's life?"

He thought about that for a moment. Then he said, "It might destroy *us,* and he shuddered.

For a while, no matter how tortuous the path she followed through the woods, Carol could not lose the girl. She switched from one natural trail to another, crossed a small stream, doubled back the way she had come. She moved in a crouch at all times, staying out of sight below the brush line. She made no sound that could be heard above the constant hissing of the rain. Most of the time she carefully stepped on old leaves or made her way from stone to stone, from log to log, leaving no footprints, in the damp, bare earth. Yet Jane pursued her with uncanny confidence, without hesitation, as if she were part bloodhound.

At last, however, Carol was certain she had lost the girl. She squatted under a huge pine, leaned back against the damp bark, and breathed deeply, rapidly, raggedly, while waiting for her heart to stop racing.

A minute passed. Two. Five.

The only sound was the rain drizzling down through the leaves and through the interlaced pine needles.

She became aware of the dank odor of heavy vegetation—moss and fungus and forest grass and more.

Nothing moved.

She was safe, at least for now.

But she couldn't just sit beneath the tall pine, waiting for help to arrive. Eventually, Jane would stop searching for her and would try to find a way back to the cabin. If the girl didn't get lost—which she most likely would do—if she somehow managed to return to the cabin, and if she was still in a psychotic fugue when she got there, she might murder the first person she encountered. If she took Vince Gervis by surprise, even his great size and impressive muscles would be of no use against the blade of an ax.

Carol stood up, moved away from the tree, and began to circle back toward the cabin. The keys to the Volkswagen were in her purse, and her purse was in one of the bedrooms. She had to get the keys, drive into town, and ask the county sheriff for assistance.

What went wrong? she wondered. The girl shouldn't have become violent. There was no indication that she was capable of such a thing. The potential to kill simply was not a part of her psychological profile. Paul was right to be worried. But *why?*

Proceeding with utmost caution, expecting the girl to leap at her from behind every tree and bush, Carol needed fifteen minutes to reach the edge of the forest at a point not far from the place at which she had entered the trees with the girl in hot pursuit. The meadow was deserted. At the bottom of the slope, the cabin huddled in the pouring rain.

The kid's lost, Carol thought. All of that twisting and turning and doubling back through unfamiliar territory was too much for her. She'll never find the way home by herself.

The sheriff's men weren't going to like this one: a search in the rain, in the forest, for a violent girl who was armed with an ax. No, they weren't going to like this one at all.

Carol navigated the meadow at a run.

The rear door of the cabin was standing open, just as she had left it.

She hurried inside, slammed the door, and threw the bolt. Relief swept through her.

She swallowed a couple of times, caught her breath, and crossed the kitchen to the door that led into the living room. She was about to step across that threshold when she was stopped by a sudden, terrible certainty that she was not alone.

She jumped back, spurred by intuition more than anything else, and even as she moved, the ax swung in from the left, through the doorway. It sliced the air where she had been. If she hadn't moved, she would have been cut in half.

The girl stepped into the room, brandishing the ax. "Bitch."

Carol backed to the door that she had just latched. She fumbled behind her for the bolt. Couldn't find it.

The girl closed in.

Whimpering, Carol turned to the door, seized the latch. She sensed the ax rising into the air behind her and knew she wouldn't have time to open the door, and she jerked to one side, and the blade bit into the door just where her head would have been.

With superhuman strength, the girl wrenched the ax out of the wood.

Gasping, Carol ducked past her and ran into the living room. She looked for something with which to defend herself. The only thing available was a poker in the rack of fireplace tools. She grabbed it.

Behind her, Jane said, "I hate you!"

Carol whirled.

The girl swung the ax.

Carol brought the poker up without any time to spare, and it rang against the gleaming, viciously sharp blade, deflecting the blow.

The impact rang back the length of the poker, into Carol's hands, numbing them. She couldn't maintain her grip on the iron rod; it fell from her tingling hands.

The impact did not ring back along the wooden handle of the ax, and Jane still held that weapon with firm determination.

Carol backed up onto the wide hearth of the stone fireplace. She could feel the heat against her legs.

She had nowhere else to run.

"Now," Jane said. "Now. At last."

She lifted the ax high, and Carol cried out in anticipation of the pain, and the front door was flung open. It crashed against the wall. Paul was there. And Grace.

The girl glanced at them but was not going to be distracted; she brought the ax down toward Carol's face.

Carol collapsed onto the hearth.

The ax struck the stone mantel over her head; sparks flew.

Paul rushed at the girl, but she sensed him coming. She turned toward him, slashed with the ax, and drove him back.

Then turned on Carol again.

"Cornered rat," she said, grinning.

The ax came up.

This time it won't miss, Carol thought.

Someone said, "Spiders!"

The girl froze.

The ax was suspended in midair.

"Spiders!" It was Grace. "There are spiders on your back, Laura. Oh God, they're all over your back. Spiders! Laura, look out for the spiders!"

Carol watched, bewildered, as a look of stark terror took possession of the girl's face.

"Spiders!" Grace shouted again. "Big, black, hairy spiders, Laura. Get them off! Get them off your back. Quick!"

The girl screamed and dropped the ax, which clattered against the stone hearth. She brushed frantically at her back, twisting her arms up behind her. She was snuffling and squealing like a very small child. "Help me!"

"Spiders," Grace said again, as Paul picked up the ax and put it out of the way.

The girl tried to tear off her blouse. She dropped to her knees, then fell onto her side, gibbering in terror. She writhed on the floor, brushing imaginary spiders off her body. Within a minute she seemed to be in a state of shock; she lay shuddering, weeping.

"She was always afraid of spiders," Grace said. "That was why she hated the cellar."

"The cellar?" Carol asked.

"Where she died," Grace said.

Carol didn't understand. But at the moment she didn't care. She watched the girl writhing on the floor, and she suddenly felt overwhelming pity for her. She knelt beside Jane, lifted her up, hugged her.

"You okay?" Paul asked her.

She nodded.

"Spiders," the girl said, quivering uncontrollably.

"No, honey," Carol said. "No spiders. There aren't any spiders on you. Not now. Not any more." And she looked at Grace, wondering.